STAGE BY STAGE
ORIENTAL THEATRE

BY THE SAME AUTHOR

Novels
The Volcano God
The Zoltans: A Trilogy
The Dark Shore
The Evening Heron
Dreams of Youth
Easter Island
Searching

Short Stories
The Devious Ways
The Beholder
The Snow
Three Exotic Tales
A Man of Taste
The Young Greek and the Creole
The Spymaster
The Young Artists

Fantasy
The Merry Communist

Plays
Prince Hamlet
Mario's Well
Black Velvet
Simon Simon
Three Off-Broadway Plays
More Off-Broadway Plays
Three Poetic Plays

Criticism
Myths of Creation
The Art of Reading the Novel
Preface to Otto Rank's *The Myth of the Birth of the Hero and Other Essays*
Preface to Kimi Gengo's *To One Who Mourns at the Death of the Emperor*
Some Notes on Tragedy
Preface to Joseph Conrad's *Lord Jim*
Stage by Stage: The Birth of Theatre

Poetry
Private Speech

Philip Freund

STAGE BY STAGE

ORIENTAL THEATRE

Drama, Opera, Dance and Puppetry in the Far East

PETER OWEN
London and Chester Springs

PETER OWEN PUBLISHERS
73 Kenway Road, London SW5 0RE

Peter Owen books are distributed in the USA by
Dufour Editions Inc., Chester Springs, PA 19425-0007

First published in Great Britain 2005 by
Peter Owen Publishers

ISBN 0 7206 1208 X

A catalogue record for this book is available from the British Library

Printed and bound in Spain by
Gráficas Diaz Tuduri S.L.

For Robert H. Heiser
– a friend indeed

CONTENTS

ILLUSTRATIONS

Between pages 304 and 305

The Little Clay Cart (*Mrichakatika*) by Shadraka, in a version by Jatinder Verma and directed by Jatinder Verma for Tara Arts, London, 1986 (photographs courtesy of Jatinder Verma)

Scene from *Shakuntala* by Kalidasa; miniature from a Hindi manuscript, 1789 (© National Museum of India, New Delhi)

A Sri Lankan magic mask worn by devil dancers to cure people of catarrh (© Bridgeman Art Library)

Sri Lankan dancers from Kandy (© Keith Bernstein/Impact Photos)

Coloured engravings by George Newenham Wright (1790–1877) after paintings by Allom Thomas (1804–1872) from *China in a Series of Views*, 1843; theatre at Tien Sing and a scene from the spectacle *The Sun and Moon* (© Bridgeman Art Library)

Kuan Yu – a General, a leading character in the 'Huarong Path' incident in *The Battle of Red Cliff* (© Pat Blehnke/Alamy Images)

A scene from *Peony Pavilion* by Tang Xianzu (1550–1617), Lincoln Center, New York, 1998 (© Stephanie Berger 2003)

Actor Mei Langfang (1894–1961), famous for his interpretation of female roles in the Chinese opera (© Chinastock 2003)

Tang Seng – the master of Sun Wu in *Journey to the West* (© Pat Blehnke/Alamy Images)

A performance of the Peking opera *The Legend of the White Snake* (© Information Division, Taipei Representative Office, London)

Chinese shadow puppets (© Information Division, Taipei Representative Office, London)

Scene from a revolutionary ballet, *The White-Haired Girl*, 1966 (© Vanya Edwards, Sovfoto/Eastfoto)

Chinese State Circus acrobat (© Linda Rich, Dance Picture Library)

The new opera house in Shanghai (© Jon Arnold Images/Alamy Images)

A Taiwanese opera troupe performing on a traditional teahouse-style opera stage (© Information Division, Taipei Representative Office, London)

A Taiwanese marionette theatre with puppets based on Chinese opera characters (© Information Division, Taipei Representative Office, London)

A Korean fan dance at the Korea House Theatre, Seoul (© Alain Evrard/Impact Photos)

Korean Andong mask festival; Eunyul mask dance (© David Sanger Photography/Alamy Images)

Bugaku dancer, Itsukushima Shrine, Miyajima, Japan (© Nancy Warner)

Four Nōh masks (© Dr Margaret Coldiron)

The Kanze Nōh Theatre, Tokyo (© Japan National Tourist Organization, London)

Scenes from a Bunraku Japanese puppet play (© Japan National Tourist Organization, London)

Interior of a Kabuki theatre at Edo, *c.* 1745, showing an actor in the play *Shibaraku* (print based on an original by Masanobu Okumura (1688–1764) (© Bridgeman Art Library)

Scenes from Kabuki plays (© Japan National Tourist Organization, London)

Butoh dancers from the Sankai Juku Dance Company in *Jōmon Shō*, 1982 (© Linda Rich, Dance Picture Library)

The Japanese writer and dramatist Yukio Mishima

Ram Leela, Dashera Festival, Azad Maidan, Bombay (© Dinodia Picture Agency)

Hand gestures or mudras used in Indian acting and dancing

Indian Kathak dancers (© Dinodia Picture Agency)

Between pages 560 and 561

Kathakali dancer from Kerala, India (© Dinodia Picture Agency)

Uday Shankar and company (© Victoria and Albert Museum, London)

The Indian writer Rabindrinath Tagore (© Dinodia Picture Agency)

Shantiniken (the Abode of Peace), Bolpur, West Bengal; the theatre is part of the Tagore estate (© Dinodia Picture Agency)

A dance-drama in the classical Manipuri style of Tagore (© Dinodia Picture Agency)

The Royal Cambodian Dance Troupe (© Kayte Deioma, 2003)

Asparas or dancing nymphs carved during the twelfth century at Angkor Wat in Cambodia

The Royal Thai Dance Company (© Linda Rich, Dance Picture Library)

Classical Thai dancer (© John Grover Nash)

Leking dance, Bali, Indonesia (© Dr Margaret Coldiron)

Trance dance, Bali (© Rob Walls)

Kecak or monkey dance, Bali (© Image State/Alamy Images)

Temple dancer, Gulah, Bali (© Dr Margaret Coldiron)

Shadow puppets, Wayang Kulit, Bali (© SC Photos/Alamy Images)

Barong, the mythical monster who chases the dancers during the trance dance, Bali (© Dr Margaret Coldiron)

Shadow puppets, Wayang Kulit, Java, Indonesia (© Petr Svarc)

Shadow puppets, Wayang Kulit, Bali (© Michael Burr)

Wooden puppets, Wayang Golek, Java (© Tom Cochrem)

Barong mask, Bali (Deutsches Ledermuseum, Offenbach am Main)

Clay figure of a Cham dancer, Hoshang, a comic figure in Tibetan dance-drama (Museum für Vöslkerkunde, Vienna)

Audiences watching Cham dancers at Tashikhyil Monastery in eastern Tibet (© Ian Cumming, Tibet Images)

A procession of Cham dancers, Tibet (© Diego Alonso, Tibet Images)

Monks performing a Cham dance, Tibet (© Diego Alonso, Tibet Images)

Monks performing a skeleton dance, Tibet (© Ian Cumming, Tibet Images)

Tschechu dance, Bhutan (© Tewfic El-Sawy, 2003)

Dancers, Thimpu Festival, Bhutan (© Tewfic El-Sawy, 2003)

Philippine stick dance (PerfectPhoto CA/© Rob van Nostrand)

Philippine passion play showing Christ figure carrying the Cross at the annual Moriones festival (© Alain Evrard/Impact Photos)

FOREWORD

The vast width of the Pacific Ocean is not the only barrier to a firm and satisfactory bridge between the somewhat incompatible civilizations of the Occident and Orient; religious and racial differences and the off-putting, tongue-twisting languages spoken in what we call the Far East also intervene to baffle at times even the most earnest and learned, particularly when it comes to reaching a full understanding of the arts fostered in each of our two separate worlds. This is especially true of the theatre that has evolved at odds in our long-divided realms. In the Orient, theatre has flourished in its own way for over 2,000 years – indeed, since time immemorial – created by inspired priests and artists for the moral instruction and entertainment of the hundreds of millions of believers living there.

The plays, operas and dances have an extensive variety, a richness and exotic colour, an abundance of wisdom and delicate fantasy, a universality, a depth of myth-making that offer infinite rewards. Yet very little about all that is known to us. My hope is to give some insight into what happens on the traditional and current stages of India and China, Japan and Korea, and the many independent lands surrounding them – Sri Lanka, Nepal, Bhutan, Thailand, Cambodia and Myanmar, among others – that have fascinating histories and are now encountering many changes as they enter a new millennium. Today, East is clashing with West as never before, and significant challenges are being met – I have tried to depict them. It also seems to me that not to know what half or more of the world's population looks for and finds in its theatres is to miss much, is indeed for an educated playgoer a kind of personal cultural impoverishment.

Yes, there are a great many marked cultural differences. At the same time, what continuously astonished me, despite them, is how some aspects of human nature are constants, how people in twelfth-century China and seventeenth-century Japan bare the same motives and desires and traits of behaviour as do ancient Greeks, and as I share with my friends even now, and how strong and compelling in all centuries and in all areas of the globe has always been the impulse to dramatize our experiences and to externalize and act out our fancies, tapping our dream-life and borrowing frightening, tragic and comic themes from everyday incidents. This has confirmed again my assumption that theatre is not mere superficial entertainment – though, thankfully, it is often that and thus at times of stress a benediction – but also an impulse, a demand, that arises from somewhere deep in our psyche. It meets many emotional and intellectual needs, and serves as a communal binder, as I trust this book will illustrate. But in the West, as I have said, we know only half the story. Here is an attempt to present the other half.

Is our lack of knowledge of Far Eastern stagecraft and drama actually so scanty? True, each year swarms of travellers breach the Orient, most of them well educated and sophisticated. But they are on holiday; their time is limited. Guided, they are apt to see just one unintelligible opera in Beijing, or a circus in Shanghai, or excerpts from a Kabuki play in Tokyo, or a dance recital with intricate and bewildering finger-work conveying subtle ideas in Bali or Madras – certainly never a modern play any-where, if only because of the language impediment.

At intervals, outstanding works are sent on tours by their governments or are brought to the West by museums and groups such as the Asia Society or Japan Society. We must be grateful for them; they import delight and information. But they tend to have only two or three showings, or often only one, and draw small audiences, constituted mostly of those holding membership in the sponsoring institution. The broad gap is not filled.

In writing this book I have learned for myself as never before the problem of language. The people of India cope with a maze of tongues from state to state; for a resident of one to converse across a border may require an interpreter. Besides this, there are scores of local dialects. If a play is a success and tours even to an adjacent territory, the author's name may be spelled differently and the work's title changed. This happens from region to region everywhere on the subcontinent.

In China, too, confusing verbal obstacles are profuse; many dialects are spoken, varying from province to province. Helpfully, the majority of Chinese use either Cantonese – in Hong Kong and the south – or Mandarin – elsewhere. Even so, this results in the name of a playwright and the title of the script also undergoing change. Wherever I know this to have happened, I have given one and noted the other parenthetically alongside it.

In Japan a patronymic – surname – is put down first; for instance, in the *Japanese Encyclopedia* Tsubouchi Shōyō is listed that way, indicating that his last name is Tsubouchi. Yet in the article that follows he is referred to throughout as Shōyō. It is not always easy to recognize what is a given name and a family name. In addressing an elder statesman by his first name is one being too familiar or is one behaving properly? Apparently the custom is flexible, as if one might say either James Smith or

Smith James, which is somewhat like the Russian habit of referring to people by their first two names rather than by the third and last. I am not sure about this but I have chosen the English style, first name, second name.

Beside the complexities abounding in the discourse of these countries, what about all the esoteric languages of the inhabitants of Sri Lanka, Thailand, Malaysia, the Philippines, of which I confess there could never have been time enough for me to master? Needless to say I have been very dependent on translations, where they exist, and secondary sources.

Another vexation: the British and Americans often spell (and pronounce) the same words differently: "favour", "favor"; "harbour", "harbor"; "judgement", "judgment"; "artefact", "artifact". Some British writers look on the American versions as barbaric, and some of my fellow countrymen think British accents and spellings are signs of affectation, if only because the words are often elided – "sec-re-tree" rather than "sec-re-tary", and do not sound the way they look. I am sympathetic to both sides of this dispute and decided that if I quoted a British critic I would keep his or her spelling, and extend the same courtesy to American sources; otherwise I adhere to the British conventions in this book.

Going back to China: the reader should appreciate the distinction between Peking Opera – a capital "O" – and Peking opera – small "o". The capital "O" designates the celebrated theatre in Beijing, the latter a genre of musical drama distinct from competing forms such as Cantonese opera, Shanghai opera or Kunqu favoured outside the capital.

In discussing dance I am greatly beholden to the *New York Times* which has a staff of three very knowledgeable critics – Anna Kisselgoff, Jennifer Dunning and Jack Anderson – who are truly attentive. They seem to cover every recital and to be well informed about every genre. No other newspaper is as thorough. In addition, the *New York Times* is delivered to my door every morning, which has become an advantage since I am now in my ninth decade and largely unable to walk. This does not mean that I have not had a good many other sources, and that I have not myself observed most types of dance at first hand. I have visited all the countries studied here, save for North Korea.

As I explained in a previous book, I have eschewed footnotes – they are too costly and, in my opinion, deface a page. At the back of the book they are a nuisance. Acknowledgements of my sources are inserted parenthetically in the text of each chapter; I am meticulous about paying my debts. From concern about length and cost, too, I have not appended a bibliography. My book is intended for the general reader, not for a handful of experts in this field who probably have no need of it. Seeking guidance to the applicable literature, one has only to consult an index card file in any large library, as

I often did. Once there, I was usually reluctant to leave. In fact, I have never made use of a bibliography except possibly to check the spelling of an author's name.

As I proceeded with this work, I worried that it was becoming too long. It would be quite expensive to print. But I decided that rather than write a short book – sketchy – I would try for a good one, truly comprehensive. It is not meant to be read at one sitting, but to be dipped into at intervals and to be accessible if one is going to observe performers brought from the Orient, to help understanding and to increase pleasure on such occasions. I also have in mind alert workers in the theatre; it might sharpen their perspective and broaden their resources.

Antonia Owen, James Robert Carson, Dr Zenaida Patricio Asiain and the erudite James Ryan have made estimable contributions to this book.

P. F.

INDIA: SACRED PAVILION AND FLAGSTAFF

A plausible assumption is that Far Eastern theatre is quite as ancient as Western, having arisen in much the same way from early magical beliefs and ever more elaborate proprietary rituals. But though drama advanced in both cultures for a while along closely parallel courses, somehow it split and evolved into forms that became very different. Today it is often difficult for a Westerner to grasp the basic premise of Eastern theatre art: it offers a quite opposed kind of aesthetic experience and yields an entirely other kind of enjoyment. Paradoxically, Eastern theatre art is at the same time both more sophisticated and more naïve, more sensuous and more abstract, the latter because it is largely expressed in symbolic gestures and dramatic canons that are specific and traditional but also far from realistically graphic or logically organized. Classic Oriental artworks are pervaded with mysticism, with philosophical and religious intention; they are replete with spirituality, yet lack heights and depths of emotion – exaltation, katharsis – that characterize Western tragedy. Oriental comedy is similarly more limited in scope. Into this strange – to Occidentals – world of theatre one ventures with frequent bafflement, yet the exploration richly repays foreign theatre-lovers. Oriental drama, which includes both music and dance, as well as poetry and dilute theology, is brilliantly colourful, extravagantly imaginative, often exquisite, always precisely disciplined. It opens another dimension of stagecraft that even at first glance is quite dazzling.

India is not the source of all Far Eastern theatre art forms. Those of China and Japan took their special shapes independently. Yet Indian influence subtly touched and infused them, while for many of the stages of the Far East – Burma, Ceylon, Cambodia, Thailand, Indonesia – India's example has been strongly dominant. For centuries, bold turbaned traders, marauders wielding scimitars, Tamil warriors bent on conquest, along with mild Buddhist missionaries, carried with them to these other areas of the Asian world the unique artefacts, predilections, dogmas and practices with which the arts of India were filled. The invaders gradually brought with them the musical instruments, melodies, sculptural dances and ornate costumes used by their performers at home. Oddly, it is in the Indonesian archipelago – notably Java and Bali – that Indian art survives today in its purest state: long since, with the Islamic takeover of India itself, its traditional arts withered and largely disappeared from their birthplace. In India now, performances of classic dance and drama are comparative rarities, revived only on occasion as though they are museum-pieces. In Java and Bali, and elsewhere in the Far East, they are still living art-forms, only slightly modified by local tastes and conditions.

Legend and fact are mingled so hazily about the origin of drama in India that no positive date can be set for it, and no one named as particularly responsible for it. No Thespis, no Aeschylus. Indeed, a myth has it that in the Golden Age there were no plays, for that was a happy time of no cosmic conflict. The gods ruled and dwelled serenely in their heavenly realm. But in the Silver Age which followed, warfare between the forces of Good and Evil broke out and went through many complex phases, with dominance shifting between the many benign gods and a host of attacking demons, ending with victory for the Good. To celebrate, Brahma, the supreme deity, asked that the battle be re-enacted in heaven, but only for the amusement of Indra, the storm god with a thousand eyes. Instead, the celestial struggle was resumed in dead earnest: the good gods triumphed once more, using as one of their most lethal weapons a flagstaff that chanced to be nearby. Brahma explained that the wild "combat" had only been meant as an entertainment; the demons, mollified, promised to regard it in that lighter spirit. But it was decided that in the future "in order to protect the theatre a sacred pavilion would be provided to shelter the players, and the area would be marked and made sacred by a flagstaff". This has, in some measure, persisted in villages in many parts of Asia: the stage is covered; a tall bamboo pole with a banner designates the area of the performance; the audience squats on the warm, grassy ground in the open air. The cherished legend says further that after the world was created Brahma confided all the secrets of dramaturgy to the fabled sage Bharata, possibly in some respects an actual person, long ago embellished with mythical qualities, whose period is loosely placed some time between 200 BC and AD 200. From the first four *Vedas*, sacred books, Brahma culled and combined precepts for the arts of recitation, song, mime and feeling ("sentiment") to embody a single form. Brahma also instructed the sage in how to construct a proper stage and playhouse with guidance from a heavenly designated architect. The other gods contributed rules for added elements of drama. In the lead was Shiva, exemplifier of the creative potency of dance – he is the deity whose magical stamping feet dance the world into being at each dawn, only to destroy it ambivalently by his more savage stamping at the moment of sunset above the lofty, snowy Himalayas. Observing an early theatrical performance from which dance was missing, Shiva commanded that henceforth the angels include it as an ingredient and always stress its vital importance. After this, in India, the words for "drama" and "dance" have been virtually synonymous.

Thus divinely inspired, Bharata compiled his knowledge of theatre in the *Bharata Natya Sastra (Canons of Dance and Drama)*, an incredibly thorough and detailed handbook and bible for playwrights, producers and actors. In the realm of Oriental stagecraft, this work is the equivalent of the *Poetics*, Aristotle's magisterial essay on tragedy. At first passed along orally, it was finally gathered in written form, and remains the authoritative text on every aspect of classical tradition, even including rules for the performer's make-up, appropriate costumes, significant gestures, acrobatic stance and rhythm. Everything is meticulously, rigidly ordained; nothing is omitted. Proper movements of the eyeballs and the hands, as well as acceptable plot situations and lists of taboos, are described. The treatise is far broader in scope than anything Aristotle attempted on this subject. Today, the very term "Bharata" has come to denote "actor".

No scholar has determined with certainty when, where or how this remarkable compendium of stage techniques was composed, or even whether an all-knowing, divinely instructed Bharata ever existed. He is a figure as problematical and elusive as the Greek bard Homer. What is widely conjectured, however, is that ancient Sanskrit drama sprang from recitations and partial enactments in temples presided over by priests, their source-material simply passages from the sacred books, the epics – or sacred anthologies – familiarly known as the *Ramayana* and the *Mahābhārata*. These enormously long poems, transmitted in writing, with some episodes providing active dialogue, are thought to be about 1,500 years old, though in oral form they might go back another 1,000 years. Like the *Iliad* and the *Odyssey*, and the Christian Scriptures, they contain countless anecdotes and vignettes drawn from early myth and history: tales of gods, demigods, demons, angels, kings and queens, love-sick princes and maidens, together with *fabliaux* – stories of animals – and moral allegories, along with maxims and lyric poetry. They might best be summed up as immeasurably rich anthologies, as are the Biblical Testaments. From them in abundance have come most of the plots and themes of Asian folk-drama, not only in India, but elsewhere throughout the East. As has been said, the generative impulse for both the myths in these epics and the dance and pantomime illustrating them arose from rites of sowing, harvest festivals and other primitive observances prompted by mankind's urgent wish to interpret and control the daunting natural world.

In time, a great many of these colourful but crude tales were spiritualized, or secularized, to suit an ever more sophisticated audience. The initial meaning of the stories was altered. By the first century AD the oldest preserved forms of Sanskrit drama had appeared. From that period, or a slightly later date, fragments of several plays by Ashvaghosha (*c.* AD 120), a religious teacher at the court of the great King Kanishka, were found on palm-leaf manuscripts in what is now Chinese Turkestan. One of them describes the conversion of "unbelievers" to Buddhism, a creed to which Ashvaghosha was an adherent; another is a didactic allegory populated with abstract characters named Glory, Wisdom and Firmness; and the third depicts the worldly misfortunes of a courtesan, but at the same time appeals to common risibilities by inserting touches of low comedy. The fragments suggest that the theatrical form was already well established; it was certainly not Ashvaghosha's invention. It should also be recalled that Alexander's invasion of India (327 BC) had brought with it a degree of lingering Greek influence, which – coupled with the steady rise of Buddhism, its followers' missionary zeal a prompting factor – did much to stimulate the development of a more structured drama.

(Much that is imparted here is taken from chapters in Will Durant's *Our Oriental Heritage*, Faubion Bowers's *Theatre in the Far East*, and the broader surveys of theatre history by Allardyce Nicoll, John Gassner, George Freedley, Vera Moury Roberts, Margot Berthold and Oscar G. Brockett.)

The principal theatrical form was still a dance-drama, as prescribed by Bharata. Though such plays were performed at court and in the lavish palaces of nobles, the overwhelming majority continued to be seen in temples, where priests kept watch over them, monitoring their content, firmly disciplining the dancers. Temples abound throughout India, and, further attesting to the influence of the *Natya Sastra*'s emphasis on the ceremonial inclusion of dance, the weathered, pitted stone walls are often decorated with hundreds of sculptured images of dancing girls, swaying, animated, sinuous, exaggeratedly curvilinear, with averted yet inviting eyes, erotic and seductive smiles.

Line sketches in Berthold's *A History of World Theatre* show ten of the dancer's codified twenty-four finger-signs and what each symbolically conveys. In addition, there are thirteen variant head movements, seven of the eyebrows, six of the delicate, quivering nose, six of the cheeks, nine of the flexible neck, seven of the chin, five of the chest and thirty-six of the darting eyes, all calling for the utmost physical dexterity. The actor's feet may assume any of sixteen positions when he or she stands, sixteen in the air when aloft, and a long range of ways of walking, to suggest a character: "striding, mincing, limping, shuffling. A courtesan moves with a swaying gait, a court lady with mincing steps, a fool walks with his toes pointed upward, a courtier with solemn steps, and a beggar with a shuffle." If a play is addressed to an educated audience, Sanskrit is to be spoken; if to the unlearned, Prakrit, a dialect.

The exact plan of the temporary pavilion is also spelled out in the *Natya Sastra*: "A rectangular site is to be divided into two squares: an auditorium and a stage. Four columns are to hold up the roof beams. The color scheme must strictly follow traditional symbolism: red for the king and the nobility; yellow for the citizenry; blue-black for the cast of artisans, thieves and day laborers. (And all these are the colors of Indra's staff.)"

Berthold offers further details: "At the eastern end of the terraced auditorium the king sits on his throne, surrounded by ministers, poets, and sages, with the ladies of the court to his left. The stage, as too the entire building, is richly decorated with wood carvings and pottery reliefs. It is divided by a curtain into a fore and a backstage. The actors and dancers appear on the forestage, while their dressing rooms are backstage, hidden by the dividing curtain. The sources of acoustic effects, representing divine voices, the noise of crowds and battle, are also kept backstage and invisible to the public." The curtain is called *vavanika*, a word that hints of a Greek origin.

The Golden Age of Indian art spans 500 years from the fourth to the ninth centuries AD. Four names of classical dramatists are pre-eminent: Bhasa, Shudraka, Kalidasa and Bharabhuti. Bhasa (*c.* AD 350, though some place him considerably earlier) was a mere historical footnote, as was the Greek Menander, until as recently as 1910 when thirteen scripts assumed to be his were found in Travancore, in India's south west. As with Menander, subsequent playwrights – notably King Shudraka and Kalidasa – drew upon his works for plots and poetic inspiration. This long-held suggestion is easy to credit, for the newly discovered manuscripts are of high quality. One of the most acclaimed is *Svapnavasa-vadatta*, the account of a fond queen who sacrifices herself to allow her husband to make a second and more advantageous marriage to the daughter of a minister of state. Her royal husband is adamantly faithful to her; whereupon she feigns her death in a fire, while actually withdrawing to a hermitage. When she comes forth later to serve the new queen, her husband loyally and gratefully reclaims her. Another effective piece by Bhasa is *The Poor Charudatta*, about a pious Brahmin merchant of that name who becomes impoverished by being overly generous to others and by losing his bearings because of his infatuation for Vasantasena, a high-minded courtesan, though he has a dutiful wife. These characters and a similar theme reappear in the far better-known *Little Clay Cart* (*Mrichakatika*), also among the scripts found in Travancore. It has long been attributed to King Shudraka. In ten acts, this romantic drama relates how the beauteous and pure-spirited courtesan Vasantasena takes refuge in Charudatta's dwelling to evade the amorous pursuit of Prince Samsthanaka, brother-in-law of the treacherous King Palaka. Charudatta's wife does not seem to mind the affair that flares up between her husband and Vasantasena. At dusk, Vasantasena entrusts her jewels to Charudatta's care, but they are stolen. To replace them, at his wife's insistence, the virtuous Charudatta gives his wife's necklace to the courtesan. Subsequently the lost gems are restored by Vasantasena's maidservant, whose lover has been the thief. In another phase of the complex plot-line, the courtesan befriends a cowherd, Aryaka, who in fact is the rightful pretender to the throne. She helps Aryaka escape from imprisonment at the hands of her unwelcome suitor Samsthanaka. The courtesan impulsively rewards Charudatta by giving his little boy a heap of diamonds with which to purchase a golden cart, because the child tearfully complains that his toy cart is only of clay. Pleased with herself for her generous deed, she makes a seemingly fatal mistake as she leaves, stepping in the bullock-drawn, curtained wagon of the hated Samsthanaka, instead of Charudatta's carriage. She is kidnapped. When she repulses the importunities of her sinister persecutor, he strangles her in a fit of fury. Samsthanaka charges Charudatta with having committed the murder to seize the jewels, and though the judge suspects the powerful Prince Samsthanaka of being the true culprit, he fears to affront him. Sentenced to die, Charudatta is about to be decapitated when the driver of the wagon accuses the prince of having testified falsely. At this juncture Vasantasena, who is not really dead, appears and identifies her actual assailant. (She has been buried but exhumed in time and revived by the thief, Sharvilaka, who now bears witness against Samsthanaka.) The kind-hearted Charudatta intervenes on behalf of the prince, who is also released. To provide an even happier climax, the "cowherd" overthrows King Palaka and mounts the throne in his place. He appoints the saintly Charudatta to the headship of a province, and lifts Vasantasena from her status as a courtesan, which permits her to marry Charudatta, albeit polygamously.

The plot of this lengthy work is difficult for modern Westerners to follow, but many of its incidents, though digressive or largely irrelevant, are charming and provide glimpses of ancient social life and customs. The characters are remarkably vivid. Charudatta, the overly benign merchant, is a model of goodness and propriety. His wife is similarly warm-hearted, as is the wealthy, noble courtesan. A fine comic figure is Maitreya, the merchant's servant, and a very funny interlude is furnished by the thief who cites various authorities on the fine art of robbery, as he goes about his task. When the maid-servant, whose hand he seeks, rejects his gift of the stolen jewels and chides him for his misdeeds, he defends himself in these cynical terms (quoted by Durant, crediting no translator):

> A woman will for money smile or weep
> According to your will; she makes a man
> Put trust in her, but trusts him not herself.
> Women are as inconstant as the waves
> Of ocean, their affection is as fugitive
> As streaks of sunset glow upon a cloud.
> They cling with eager fondness to the man
> Who yields them wealth, which they squeeze out like sap
> Out of a juicy plant, and then they leave him.

But with Vasantasena's approval, the maidservant and her dishonest lover do marry, despite his complaint of womankind's essential greediness.

Though the style is simple, there are lyric passages of great beauty, and in the tale no little social criticism of the corruption at the courts of rulers. Indeed, the play even dares to justify a political revolt, the overthrow of an equivocating tyrant. Whether the author, Shudraka, was really a king, and how much of the plot is owed to Bhasa's earlier play, of which only four acts are extant, are questions not yet answered by Sanskrit scholars. It is possible that the melodrama was composed by a court poet and dedicated to the king. Whimsically, the playwright describes himself in one passage as gifted with many talents: he was an amorist of surpassing ardour, a keen mathematician, an expert on the proper care of elephants. His dates are somewhat uncertain: the play is placed somewhere in the third or fourth century AD.

The Little Clay Cart, though highly cherished, does not belong in the mainstream of classic Sanskrit drama, but is *sui generis*, especially since it deals with people from ordinary life. It is lively, inventive, and moves at a faster pace than most works of this remote period; at moments, too, it attains to pathos. Often revived, it has enjoyed successful off-Broadway productions in New York City, among them a skilfully shortened version at the Neighborhood Playhouse in the early 1920s.

An even greater name in Sanskrit drama is that of Kalidasa. His dates are variously placed in one decade or another of the first century AD, or later when he is said to have graced the court of King Vidramaditya, during the Gupta dynasty in Ujjain; in fact he probably belongs to the fourth, fifth or sixth century AD – such vagueness is bafflingly characteristic of the history of ancient Indian drama. Considered the finest of Sanskrit poets, Kalidasa is a figure almost lost in legend; but again biographical data about the great playwrights can hardly be had. He is believed to have been of humble origin, left an orphan at six months, to have become an uneducated ox-driver in his youth. Lithe and handsome, he caught the eye and won the affections of a studious Benares princess, who wed him, thinking him a learned young man. When she discovered through the contrivance of a rejected suitor that she had been tricked, she advised her bridegroom to pray to the goddess Kali for wisdom, and the goddess responded by bestowing a great many extra talents on the youth. To express his gratitude, he assumed the name "Kalidasa", meaning "servant of Kali". Much later he took a mistress, who murdered him in a fit of jealousy . . . or perhaps to win a reward that she coveted.

Such fanciful tales lend colour to his legend, however dubious they may be. But it is certain that he is the most admired of all Sanskrit poets. His extant works include two poems of epic length, outstanding for their lyrical descriptions, *The Seasons*, an elegy, and *The Cloud-Messenger*; and three plays.

From hints in his text, he seems to have travelled to many parts of India, for he offers splendid pictures of its various regions, especially the Himalayas. He appears also to have studied dramatic theory, philosophy, astronomy and law; he displays considerable learning, even if he was not a profound scholar. He is religious, but not fanatically so – he shows a preference for no one sect. In his writing he presents a well-balanced, attractive personality.

His earliest drama, *Malavika and Agnimitra*, revolves around a king, Agnimitra, who grows enamoured of the picture of a poor maiden, once in the queen's retinue, now in exile. His comic servant helpfully contrives to have Agnimitra obtain a glimpse of the young woman, now being trained as a dancer. Her master, a famed teacher, is ordered to stage a dance contest at the king's court, and to bring with him the girl, Malavika. Queen Dharini, observing her mate's obsessive interest in the young dancer, has her cast into a dark, dank dungeon. From this the girl is finally rescued by the resourceful comic servant; whereupon she is able to prove herself to be of royal blood and eligible to become another of the rajah's wives (he already has two, the second the jealous Iravati, who is exceptionally well characterized). All this is treated with wry humour, as a light comedy enhanced by lovely poetry. The overall quality of Kalidasa's dramatic work is adult charm, with an ineluctable tincture of polite irony.

His second play, *Shakuntala*, is far and away the most famous of all Indian stage- works; it is the chief reason Kalidasa is the most widely read of Sanskrit writers by Westerners. Amusing, whimsical, it is infused with unfailingly delicate poetry, evocative of the beauty of the natural world – Kalidasa is particularly esteemed for his acute observation of trees, flowers and streams, all of which he summons to the listener's imagination enchantingly in word-pictures of the idyllic sylvan setting of his tale. (His plays are partly in prose, with alternating passages in verse.)

Rajah Dushyanta, while in the forest on a deer-hunt with his charioteer, approaches the leafy abode of a hermit saint. In this secluded spot Dushyanta is about to draw tight the string and loose his arrow when he is stopped by warning voices, lest he profane a sanctuary, a holy retreat. Shortly he beholds the old man's ward, Shakuntala, a virgin of rare grace and beauty. He saves her from a bee-sting. Deserted by her female companions, she finds an excuse to linger, pretending lameness. As the bewitched rajah himself describes it:

> When I was near, she could not look at me;
>> She smiled – but not to me – and half denied it;
> She would not show her love for modesty,
>> Yet did not try very hard to hide it.

Further:

> When she had hardly left my side,
>> "I cannot walk," the maiden cried,
> And turned her face, and feigned to free
>> The dress not caught upon the tree.
>>> [Translation: Arthur W. Ryder]

The rajah abruptly falls in love with her. He does not reveal to her his royal status, but offers to serve her. Before long he learns that she is partly of divine origin, the daughter of a nymph and a devout king, and for safekeeping was entrusted to the pious hermit, Kanva. In delightful and witty scenes of tender dalliance, Dushyanta woos the shy girl:

> . . . A king, and a girl of the calm hermit-grove,
> Bred with the fawns, and a stranger to love!

He searches for her in the woods, where he finds traces of her recent passing:

> The stems from which she gathered flowers
>> Are still unhealed;
> And sap where twigs were broken off
>> Is uncongealed.

Concerning himself, the lovelorn king confesses:

> The hot tears, flowing down my cheek
>> All night on my supporting arm
> And on the golden bracelet, seek
>> To stain the gems and do them harm.

He swears eternal devotion:

> When evening comes, the shadow of the tree

> Is cast far forward, yet does not depart;
>
> Even so, beloved, whereso'er you be,
>
> The thought of you can never leave my heart.

Dushyanta weds her. In response to an urgent summons, he departs for his court, promising to receive her there; but first he gives her a signet ring, which attests to the marriage.

Shakuntala loses the precious ring while bathing in a river. She is about to bear his child, and sets out to the palace to claim Dushyanta's protection. In a poignant passage, she bids farewell to Kanva, who blesses her, and to her forest friends, the deer and other wild, shy creatures of the sacred grove.

Unfortunately, an offended sage with supernatural powers, taking umbrage at her carelessness in losing the ring, which he has warned she must never do, has erased her image from Dushyanta's memory. When she reaches her husband's court he has no recollection of her and is astonished by her assertion. He is once again quickly attracted to her, but refuses to acknowledge that he has been an adulterer (for he has other wives, to whom the poet alludes, though tactfully he never has them appear).

In this exchange, Shakuntala seeks to evoke the scenes of their meetings and trysts:

> Do you not remember in the jasmine-bower,
>
> One day, how you had poured the rain-water
>
> That a lotus had collected in its cup
>
> Into the hollow of your hand?

The rajah:

> Tell on,
>
> I am listening.

She:

> Just then my adopted child,
>
> The little fawn, ran up with long, soft eyes,
>
> And you, before you quenched your own thirst, gave
>
> To the little creature, saying, "Drink you first,

Gentle fawn!" But she would not from strange hands.

And yet, immediately after, when

I took some water in my hand, she drank,

Absolute in her trust. Then, with a smile,

You said: "Each creature has faith in its own kind.

You are children both of the same wild wood, and each

Confides in the other, knowing where its trust is."

He:

Sweet, fair and false! Such women entice fools . . .

The female gift of cunning may be marked

In creatures of all kinds; in women most.

The cuckoo leaves her eggs for dupes to hatch,

Then flies away secure and triumphing.

[Translation: Monier-Williams]

Without the token ring, Shakuntala has no proof of her bond to him. Rebuffed and miserable, she leaves his presence, but is suddenly snatched away and miraculously borne to the mountain-top hermitage of the divine patriarch, Kashyapa. There she bears a son, Bharata, destined to sire many heroic battlers whose feats are recounted in the *Mahābhārata*.

A fisherman brings to court a handsome ring engraved with the king's initials. He is arrested, charged with theft; he explains that he found it in the maw of a carp caught by him at the same spot in the holy Ganges where Shakuntala had earlier bathed. By royal command he is freed and given a large reward. The ring has restored Dushyanta's memory (as the offended sage, relenting, has ordained). The rajah mourns for his lost love, reproaching himself for his inexplicable forgetfulness.

It is the time of the spring festival, when the mango blooms, but the remorseful Dushyanta forbids any celebration of the season. He spends his time painting Shakuntala's picture and talking to it. A nymph, sent to reconnoitre, learns of his despair and self-blame and brings word of it to Shakuntala, who promptly forgives him. A celestial chariot is dispatched to bear the king to his beloved; the pair are joyously reunited, together with their splendid little son, the future "All-Tamer", Bharata, chosen to be a more than worthy successor to his brave, virtuous father.

In this fairy-tale are displayed many characteristics of classic Sanskrit drama. It opens with offering a blessing extended to the audience. Violent occurrences take place only offstage. The writing is marked by delicate eroticism and a pantheistic love of nature and superb imagery drawn from the flowering landscape. There is deft wit and a flow of comedy supplied by a clown servant. A plenitude of fantasy is provided by events of a supernatural kind. The love-making is presented in sensual metaphors, the lovers scarcely touching each other on stage. Physical action tends to be kept to a minimum. The emphasis is on evoking from the audience what is called *rasa* – a very special emotional response. In the *Natya Sastra* eight such dominant emotions are listed, among them: "love, mirth, energy (the heroic feeling), terror, disgust, and astonishment". A play is designed to arouse in the spectator a single, prevailing emotion, though there should also be variety within unity – for instance, the distinctive *rasa* of *Shakuntala* is erotic, but each of its scenes calls forth yet another feeling that is never allowed to detract from the *rasa* that colours the whole. All kinds of love are exemplified in *Shakuntala*, from the physical to the spiritual, from the love of a man for a maid to the love of a father for his son, along with protective love of the old – Kanva – for the young Shakuntala, and the self-denying and mystical love of the ascetic hermit for the truth, right living, and for the godly forces that rule the universe, a feeling expressed as well in a mystical love of nature: wild creatures, flowers, trees, waters, clouds, mountains. Plot is secondary to *rasa*; it contributes to interest but must not swerve attention from the emotional tone of the work.

Shakuntala is based on a tale in the *Mahābhārata*, one of the holy books, as are most classic Indian plays. (An exception is Bhasa's *Dream of Vasavadatta*, the plot of which is believed to be entirely original, though it resembles certain topical events of his day. Nor is *The Little Clay Cart* drawn from the epics, but from a popular tale.) In the instance of *Shakuntala*, Kalidasa has developed the story most resourcefully; he has transformed it from a small, inconsequential anecdote – his source – into a work of many virtues: dramatic suspense, poetic atmosphere, subtly and convincingly motivated characters, who in themselves are most appealing, as they elicit the respect and affection of the spectator. Much of the humour is sly or rollicking, amid episodes of pathos, and finally the closing scenes add elements of grandeur and the awesome.

In translation it has been widely studied in the West, more so than any other Indian drama. The first English version was published by Sir William Jones (1746–94); many others have followed. Goethe hailed it with delight and wrote an extravagant tribute to it. More than that, it influenced his own masterwork, *Faust*, particularly in having him compose a prologue like that in which Kalidasa has the play's director introduce the leading actress and briefly and somewhat whimsically discuss the forthcoming work with her. He suggests on impulse that she begin the performance by singing a pleasant tune, and when it is finished remarks: "Well done! The whole theatre is captivated by your song, and sits as if painted. What play shall we give them to keep their good will?" He has already forgotten that *Shakuntala* is intended, and she laughingly reminds him of it. It is a passage that illustrates Kalidasa's suave wit. In *Shakuntala*, Goethe declares, we are offered "the young year's blossoms, and the fruits of its decline", together with "all by which the soul is charmed, enraptured, fed", so that:

> Wouldst thou the earth and heaven itself in one name combine?
> I name thee, O Shakuntala!, and all at once is said.

(The eminent twentieth-century dancer and choreographer, Uday Shankar, transferred *Shakuntala* to film, capturing its enchantment. It has had fugitive stage productions in Paris, Berlin and New York.)

Some commentators see a decline of accomplishment in Kalidasa's third play, *The Tale of Urvashi Won by Valour*, which is conjectured to be his last work, and perhaps not staged in his lifetime. Gassner, however, finds it rich in poetic beauty and truly fanciful. Once again, it derives from a sacred book, the *Rigveda*, but instead of enhancing the original story, as he did with *Shakuntala*, Kalidasa reduces its cosmic stature by his conventional handling of it, especially by his prettifying it. It also repeats many of the devices used in the earlier script. King Pururavas, a mortal, loves the heavenly nymph Urvashi, whom he rescues from the clutches of a demon, but their affair is a troubled one, since she is invisible a fair share of the time; besides, she falls under a curse and is banished from the celestial realm for missing a cue and inadvertently pronouncing his name while performing in a play given for the gods. Unable to resist his ardour, she reciprocates his passion, even writing of it on a birch-leaf which flutters from a tree and falls to his feet. Embarrassingly, the wind lifts it and blows it away, so that it comes to the eyes of his jealous queen. He desires a son by Urvashi and is unaware that he has already fathered one by her, a fact which she dare not reveal, lest she violate the gods' edict. At last the secret comes out, the harsh gods relent, and the happy pair are allowed to live together, with his queen granting Pururavas permission to take another wife. Urvashi is to be a mortal until her lover's life ends.

In addition to some passages of beautiful poetry, the play contains exceedingly fantastic episodes: at times, having by error intruded on a sacred grove, Urvashi is metamorphosed into a vine. Disconsolately seeking her, Pururavas asks help from a peacock, a cuckoo, a swan, a paddling goose, a bee, an elephant, a hill-echo, a river and an antelope. Some morsels of humour are contributed by the king's friend, the inevitable clown-servant. With its overall fairy-tale quality, again, the play has been appropriately compared to *A Midsummer Night's Dream*.

But where the *Rigveda* tale is meant to show that any love between mortal and immortal is doomed to transience, here Kalidasa gives a patly contrived happy ending. This accords, however, with the firm tradition that dramas of this epoch always conclude joyfully; there are no Sanskrit tragedies, only comedies and tragicomedies, the latter being the genre to which *Shakuntala* belongs. It should be remembered, too, that this work – like the others – was intended to be an opera, and was to be seen on stage as a bright spectacle, with sinuous dance and twanging music.

As with earlier Sanskrit works, these plays were probably not given in theatres, but privately at the courts of rajahs and princes, as well as in temples, if the subject-matter was deemed suitable. In secular settings the stagings are believed to have had no scenery other than a few curtains and the rich décor of the palace throne-room or sunny open garden. The king sat on his cushioned dais or in a royal box, surrounded by courtiers and guests. So far as is known, there were no playhouses. In some places, as at Trichur in Cochin State, Kerala, in the southern region, some theatres were included in temple structures, testifying to the intimate connection between the drama and religion. But whether in palace, garden or temple, the elaborate environment would have added to the colour and beauty of the presentation. The enclosing walls would be of ornately carved woodwork, or granite, and lined with relief-incised pillars, some of which would be inlaid with ivory, sandalwood and even semi-precious stones. On the walls, too, were handsome paintings, with tradition prescribing that they be "pictures of pleasure", nothing else. At first the theatre was triangular in shape; but later a square was preferred, and finally a rectangle. (Circular playhouses are also mentioned.) Such theatres were of three sizes: the smallest for recitations, perhaps monologues; the next for ordinary presentations; and the largest for spectacles. About half the area was allotted to players, the remainder to spectators. Sometimes the stage was partly elevated, divided in two, front and back, the rear section marked off by screens letting the actors retire. From there emanated the offstage noises or voices often called for in the text. The spectators might sit on benches of stone or wood, some rows accommodatingly higher than others, and the graven pillars would help to separate the four castes. (Very specific details are set forth by Vera Roberts in her *On Stage*.)

The performances were lengthy, lasting twice as many hours as modern dramas – *Shakuntala* has seven acts. The actors – women took female roles – were professionals, long trained. Every gesture was stylized and symbolic, borrowed from the dance, these formalized pantomimes being known as *mudras*. The actors constituted a caste of their own, one that was not highly ranked, though an occasional "star" proved the exception. The leader, known as the *Sutradhara*, or "Stringholder", reminiscent of the term applied to puppeteers, was usually married to the leading lady of the troupe, who assisted him in the staging. He was the principal actor, but also the director and producer. In

INDIA: SACRED PAVILION AND FLAGSTAFF | 33

Shakuntala, as has been noted, he speaks directly to the audience, introducing the play to them, as well as presenting his wife. Apparently, this was customary. He was also apt to pay verbal tribute to the author, and to commend the spectators – in advance – on their good taste and sophistication. The troupe might consist of a dozen players, and they might take their repertoire from city to city, seeking engagements from the local rulers, or sometimes performing in makeshift structures in the market-place.

Though the actors had little or no scenery, they did make profuse use of properties: weapons and other accessories might be of wood, burnished metal, starched cloth, wax or dried clay (as in the instance of the little cart in Shudraka's masterpiece). An artificial elephant is said to have been employed for one work. There are references to live animals participating, too; for example, on some occasions, a deer. Generally, however, symbolic gestures sufficed: an actor might simulate that he was riding astride a horse. The texts are highly descriptive, telling not only what the characters are think-ing but also what they are *doing*. The audience is asked to imagine what is being talked about. But more than expert symbolic pantomime was required: the actors also needed very expressive voices, to suggest the whole story. The "Stringholder" helped to tie plot threads together, addressing the audi-ence, commenting on the action and probing for the characters' actual motivations. A reading of the plays reveals that the minor figures – the clown-servants, the devoted friends and faithful hand-maidens – also describe the compelling aims of the principals. Often this is done ironically, or jocularly, or sympathetically, but in whatever mode it is a device by which the author makes clear exactly what is happening.

Costuming was realistic, appropriate to the role, even if this meant donning rags or bark. Make-up denoted the region in India from which the characters came: a dark-brown tint for persons from the slopes of the Ganges; reddish-yellow for Brahmins and kings, and for folk from the north and west; black for those from the south and for primitive tribesmen. (These details from Roberts.)

The actors were typecast: the handsome, noble hero; the ingenious villain; the clown-servant, immemorially identified as Vidushaka, the bald, big-bellied jester; the dignified counsellor; the lovely heroine; and her close friend and confidante, perhaps her handmaiden; these forming an ensemble like that brought together in a later standard European theatre group. Each member of the company was likely to be a specialist in a stock role. The clown and other lower-caste and female figures spoke not Sanskrit, which even in Kalidasa's time was a literary language not widely understood, but Prakrit or another local dialect. The minor persons, by largely repeating everything said by their superiors, in effect "translated" the dialogue into the vernacular, more readily grasped by the largest segment of the audience, establishing a pattern broadly copied by theatres in other parts of the Orient. Essentially,

Sanskrit drama was for an élite group of nobles and intelligentsia, able to appreciate allusions to mythology, to the *Vedas*, much as had limited circles of Athenian patricians been able to recognize and relish elements from Homer and Greek history.

The Sanskrit plays are didactic, and forever preach high-mindedness along with the exemplary purity of hermits, such as Kanva in *Shakuntala*. Later plays are more hedonistic, worldly, filled with facetious humour and whimsy, opulently set at court, though they might alternate such scenes with idyllic representations of the simple life, again as in Kanva's peaceful forest hermitage.

Traditionally a play belonged to one of twenty-eight categories, the principal determinants being the subject-matter, the rank and caste of the leading characters, the degree to which the supernatural was involved, the *rasa* to be evoked, the source of the plot – from myth, history or a current event – and so on. Ten genres of drama were "higher", eighteen "lower". The most sublime was one in which a legend provided the story, the hero was divine or regal, and the *rasa* was noble or erotic.

After Kalidasa, several more dramatists of consequence appeared, but they lived in more disturbed times, with dynastic struggles as their background, and their output, though filled with merits, is less esteemed than his. Altogether about twenty-five scripts of all eras have survived. King Harsa, who reigned in northern India from AD 607 to 647, is the author of three works that were frequently revived. They are love triangles, mostly. In *The Pearl Necklace*, the heroine's declaration of love for a prince is repeated and conveyed by a parrot, an ingenious touch. In *Privadarshnika* the now familiar device of a play within a play is introduced, the royal dramatist anticipating *Hamlet* by 1,000 years. The story is of the misfortunes of a lovelorn princess. *Nagamanda*, the third work, depicts the self-sacrifice of a Buddhist saint. To save the Naga people, he permits himself to be swallowed by a monster. At the conclusion, the greedy creature has a change of heart: the hero is returned to existence together with all other Naga victims similarly devoured. A Buddhist teaching, that life is sacred and that men should treat one another kindly, is this play's *rasa*. The style is simple yet evocative.

More notable, early in the eighth century, is Bhavabhuti, a Brahman of Berar, who deals with couples who are invariably star-crossed in love. His is the most illustrious name after Kalidasa. His temperament is very different, however; though poetic, his work is melancholy. He is more realistic, less romantic than his predecessors, and his tone is strongly emotional. The clown-servant is omitted from his scripts, one reason for their not having much leaven of humour. His fame, too, is kept alive by three extant works. Indeed, he wrote so slowly and scrupulously that these are believed to be his whole output. His chief piece, *The Stolen Marriage*, relates the vicissitudes of a young man and a girl who meet with a nun as intermediary; they rapidly fall in love. A high-born claimant asks for the girl's hand, and her father lacks courage to refuse the bid, for the man is a confidant of the king. With the nun's aid the brave, if rash, young people elope. A veiled friend of the girl substitutes for her at a mock marriage to the courtier, which provides a scene more amusing than most by this solemn poet. The play is also populated by ghosts, and features incidents of demon-worship, which envelopes it with a special atmosphere not without thrills, a partial compensation for its lack of lyric delicacy. It has been called the Hindu *Romeo and Juliet*. Bhavabhuti's writing has virile strength, is imaginative, and at moments attains grandeur, nor does he shun violence. Kalidasa is known as the "bridegroom of poetry", and Bhavabhuti bears the title of the "master of eloquence". He won recognition belatedly and claimed to be scornful of popular success: when his style was criticized as over-elaborate and unclear, he replied loftily: "How little they know who speak of us with censure. The entertainment is not for them." He sought only an informed audience, he avowed, as poets so greeted often tend to do. "Possibly someone exists or will exist, of similar tastes with myself; for time is boundless, and the world is wide." In this is more than a tinge of Oriental fatalism. In his writing, however, there is a forecast of the artificiality and grandiosity that would mark the decline of Sanskrit drama, to which the inferiority of the poets who followed him also contributed. His other two plays, though they contain poetic rewards, are not the equals of *The Stolen Marriage*.

Among his successors is Visakhadatta, whose *Signet of Bakshasa* exposes political infighting among leaders. Bhatta Narayana is known for his *Binding of the Braid of Hair*, much esteemed for its fine craftsmanship; and Rajasekhara, for his *The Camphor Cluster*, which is wholly in Prakrit, a signal literary deviation. Also in the eleventh century, before the Moslem invasion and conquest, Krishna Mishra brought forth *The Rise of the Moon of Knowledge*, a moral allegory with figures such as King Error and King Reason in conflict to govern a man's mind and soul, a genre of drama resembling that then prevalent in Western Europe. After India's subjection by the invaders, the Sanskrit stage lost whatever was left of its appeal and residual force and the ever more élite language itself all but ceased to be used. Gassner, dipping into works by later playwrights, confesses that he was defeated by their "formidable length and dullness". Durant offers this objective critical summary:

We cannot rank the dramatic literature of India on a plane with that of Greece or Elizabethan England; but it compares favorably with the theater of China or Japan. Nor need we look to India for the sophistication that marks the modern stage; that is an accident of time rather than an eternal verity, and may pass away – even into its opposite. The supernatural agencies of Indian drama are as alien to our taste as the *deus ex machina* of the enlightened Euripides; but this, too, is a fashion of history. The weaknesses of Hindu drama (if they may be listed diffidently by an alien) are artificial diction disfigured by alliteration and verbal conceits, monochromatic characterization in which each person is thoroughly good or thoroughly bad, improbable plots turning upon unbelievable coincidences, and an excess of description and discourse over that action which is, almost by definition, the specific medium by which drama conveys significance. Its virtues are its creative fancy, its tender sentiment, its sensitive poetry, and its sympathetic evocation of nature's beauty and terror. About national types there can be no disputation; we can judge them only from the provincial standpoint of our own, and mostly through the prism of translation.

CHINA: THE PEAR ORCHARD

If anything, the origin of Chinese theatre is even hazier than that of India's stage, though great libraries are filled with commentaries seeking to trace it. A pretty tale is told about a journey to the moon accomplished by the Emperor Ming Huang ("the Brilliant Emperor"). He saw dramatic presentations there, and on his return ordered that a similar stage and a troupe of young men and women be set up in his pear orchard. Consequently, actors today are still referred to as "Youths [or Members] of the Pear Orchard", and before each performance incense is burned in honour of the Emperor, the Founder, whose image is erected in every theatre.

Alas, this account cannot be wholly credited, if only because Emperor Ming Huang reigned in the eighth century AD, and it is known that some forms of pantomime and dance were performed at festivals in the kingdom close to three millennia earlier in the fabled Golden Age, or Second Dynasty, dating from 2205 to 1766 BC. As elsewhere, such dances most likely had their roots in religious and martial ritual. During the ancient Zhou (or Chou) dynasty (1122–255 BC) a dance with wands was a feature at rites, but this kinetic observance was later suppressed because it became too indecent, a primary token of the secularization of such ceremonies. William Dolby, from whose *A History of Chinese Drama* much has been taken, relates:

> Religious ritual and dancing occurred in the shamanistic and court dances of the Zhou dynasty. . . . The shamans or sorcerers invoked gods by means of highly erotic wooing songs. They undoubtedly acted, sang and danced, and may well have worn costume and make-up. The court dances, which were refined versions of orgiastic and other religious and quasi-religious dances from furthest antiquity, had set movements that were sometimes almost equivalent to the enacting of a drama-like story and involved acting, singing, dancing, dressing up and other features reminiscent of drama.

Very early, Chinese theatre took on its dominant symbolic aspect: prescriptions were established even for the proper shape and decoration of shields (vermilion) and battle-axes (jade-embossed) used to celebrate battle triumphs. The jade indicated that "virtue" had won, and vermilion suggested that kindness should be shown to the conquered foe.

Late in the Zhou dynasty the power to rule was dispersed among feudal lords in scattered regions, each of whom cultivated his own court ritual and music. They had their own dancers and jesters, the role of the latter frequently not only to amuse but also to criticize and subtly advise, cloaking their objective counsel with humour, sometimes audacious, at other times disarmingly witty. On occasion this led them to song, bizarre costumes, elementary acting, in satirical skits; an approach to drama.

The Han dynasty (206 BC–AD 220) saw a proliferation of dance forms and an enlargement of the jesters' antics. An element of "story" is included in the skits, an example being *Mr Huang of the Eastern Ocean*, which gained wide and lasting popularity. In the Eastern Ocean (that is, Japan or Korea?) was a young magician, Mr Huang, who by his art could subdue tigers and snakes. But aged and after years of imbibing too much wine, his art failed him. A ferocious tiger began to haunt the area, and Mr Huang was urged to respond to the peril. He wrapped a red turban about his head, took up a gold sword and confronted the beast, but his magic no longer prevailed and the tiger duly feasted on him. This tale pleased the Han emperor, who had it adapted into a game played at court. Dolby hazards that it employed two actors, one as the magician, the other as the predatory tiger, and that it might have incorporated a wrestling match between the pair. Dolby also sees the possibility that the sketch was a satire directed against the sorcerers and magicians who had surrounded and misled the Martial Emperor Wu Di (r. 141–87 BC).

Another popular entertainment was the circus-like Hundred Games, spectacular fairs for the diversion of the general populace that were also staged by order of the Han imperial court. Here would be pole-climbing, tight-rope walking, equestrian acts, weight-lifting, conjuring tricks, juggling of many sorts – balls, knives, swords – tumbling and balancing acts, fire-eating, sword-swallowing, acrobatics, leaps through fiery hoops, somersaulting, dancing in ghost and animal disguises, hand-to-hand combat. Some elements of such displays of physical skill were to become constants in Chinese drama throughout its history. The old words for "game" and "play" are synonymous.

Several centuries that followed witnessed turmoil and disunity in China, abetted by invading foreign armies, who also brought alien ideas and influences. In this period, too, Buddhism was introduced, borne by Indian missionaries. By the sixth century AD it claimed millions of adherents, becoming China's major faith. In the twentieth century an ancient, partial manuscript of *Shakuntala*, the Sanskrit drama, was discovered in the precincts of a temple close by Wenzhou in Chekiang province. In the early seventh century AD a revered Buddhist pilgrim to India, Xuanzang, visited the city of Kanchipuram, capital of Pallava, ruled by Mahendra Varman, a famous Sanskrit dramatist. These facts prompted speculation that to some degree Chinese poet-playwrights of those remote days had knowledge of Indian theatre and sought to emulate it. Wenzhou is where an aspect of

Chinese theatre developed. Buddhist priests, when preaching, often heightened the effect of their sermons by dramatizing the stories of saints and other holy exemplars, inserting "vivid dialogue" into their accounts. Indian influence was not dominant in Chinese theatre, but these traits of it are discernible.

During those years, too, the popular art of puppetry began to flourish, especially in the Sui dynasty (AD 589–618), following an earlier appearance in the Han dynasty. Wooden models, cleverly manipulated, were held aloft at funerals, or sang and danced to amuse guests at wedding feasts and other banquets. As yet the figurines did not enact stories, but were merely regarded as intricate toys, "mechanically or water-operated", and remarkably flexible – they could bow, prostrate themselves, climb ropes, perform handstands.

Acting *per se* was still far from a full-blown profession, and Dolby observes that the employment of jesters and other court hirelings tended to be most favoured by decadent rulers for crazed purposes. An instance is Cao Huan (*c.* 260–65), who each day ordered two of his retainers to sport naked in front of his palace. "He would also take up a position at some high vantage-point and have his entertainers do the *Witch of Liaodong*. It may well have been an acted sketch, but equally well may have been a dance or some other kind of performance."

In Chinese history few periods are more glorious than the Tang dynasty (618–907), when the nation's culture reached new peaks, enabled by spans of relative peace and strong, stable government. This is reflected in dances such as the *Melody of the Prince of Orchid Mound's Going Into Battle* (*c.* 550–77), in which before entering into combat the hero dons a mask to hide his effeminate, delicate features. The libretto apparently called for the participants to assemble in martial array and to mime an advance against the foe, wielding maces and whips. To this era, too, belongs the *Botou* dance, portraying a hapless non-Chinese digested by a tiger; in turn, the beast is killed by the man's vengeful son. This work is thought to be non-Chinese in origin, perhaps from India or Central Asia. The performers, hair loose, were dressed in white mourning robes and shrilly wailed their grief.

Another much-liked work was *Stepping and Singing Woman*, attributed to the sixth century. It depicted an alcoholic, ugly scholar, red-nosed from his drinking and defeated in his career, who likes to dress as a Government Secretary, a rank that he has never attained. Habitually returning home drunk, he abuses his wife, who, mistreated, complains to the neighbours. She does this in songs of her own composition, filled with poignance and beauty.

A strapping man would dance or "step" slowly on stage or into the area of performance, singing the wife's songs as he went. The songs were accompanied by string and wooden instruments. At the end of every stanza bystanders, presumably the players but quite possibly the audience, would chime in with the chorus. "Stepping and singing come with us,/Poor suffering stepping and singing woman, come with us." When the person playing the husband arrived and the couple had a fight, it was an occasion for great merriment among the audience.

Later the wife's part was assumed by a woman, the husband no longer pretended to be a Government Secretary and was simply called Uncle A, and other characters were added, altering the form and substance of the skit. Uncle A now wears a hot, red suit and has a crimson face to signify his over-exercise with a wine-flask; or else he puts on a mask. The title was changed to *Tân Comely Maiden*. Dolby remarks: "The red nose or red face are regular universal stocks-in-trade of coarse farce, and the skit must have been akin to a very simple stage play, although the plot seems gossamer-thin. . . . In all three dance-sketches we note an element of conflict or combat." These are proto-plays, hardly more than enacted anecdotes.

Another genre of theatre that arose in the Tang era is the *canjunxi*, or Adjutant Play. There are three explanations for the name. One is that Shi Dan, a magistrate in Guantao (89–105), was trapped in the act of taking bribes. Even so, he was pardoned by the Emperor, who thought highly of his services; however, for many years thereafter the guilty official had to put on a white smock whenever he attended a feast and while there was subjected to humiliating mockery by the court players. The second story has it that the dishonest magistrate was one Zhou Yan or Zhou Ya, thriving somewhere in the period 319–33, who also bore the rank of *canjun*, or Adjutant. He was accused of helping himself to several thousand bolts of precious silk belonging to the government, and as punishment had to appear at every important banquet among the comedians, wearing "an official's hat and an unlined yellow silk robe". He would be asked by a jester: "'What sort of an official are you, roughing it with the likes of us?'" His reply: "'I used to be the magistrate of Guantao'"; whereupon he would unfold his robe and confess: "'I was had up for pinching this. That's why I've joined you lot.' This drew forth great guffaws." The third account of how the name came about is that a celebrated actor, Li Xianhe (Li Immortal Crane) portrayed the role of the embarrassed magistrate with such panache that the Emperor bestowed on him the rank of Adjutant, a lucrative sinecure.

Though slight of content, the Adjutant Play was widely performed throughout the imperial realm for at least two centuries. It called for a cast of two or three, required to act, sing, speak, put on make-up and wear special costumes, and some variations of it evolved, one in particular known as the Adjutant Lu (Lu Canjun). On occasion an actress might take the leading part. Several poets of the period allude to them. It is also reported that after a Tatar general was put to death, his wife was placed among the ladies of the court. Displaying talent as an actress, she was ordered to join the band of musicians at a banquet and greatly pleased the Emperor with her interpretation of the false Adjutant (755). It is apparent that by this time, from gradual experience, certain players were chosen for parts for which they were physically most suitable and were trained along appropriate lines, setting a tradition followed long after. This was definitely so with those assigned to be the Adjutant and with his principal antagonist, eventually designated the Grey Hawk (Canggu), who had hemp-strewn hair and wore dishevelled, ragged and patched clothes and probably wielded a soft cudgel with which to strike comic blows – an immemorial form of "slapstick". Why "hawk"? Because he was the one who attacked.

The Adjutant Play outlasted the Tang epoch, extending well into the tenth century. Such performances are still reported in the Sông dynasty (960–1224).

In the new age, the imperial palace welcomed a different kind of play, one with more content, such as *Fan Kuai Rescues His Monarch from Distress* or *Fan Kuai Pushes Open the Palace Door* (901), the product of an emperor's brush. It celebrates the putting down of a rebellion and honours the general who led the loyal forces. It hearkens back to a historical incident during the reign of the first Han ruler (206 BC), who was saved from assassination by the intervention of a loyal subject, Fan Juai, formerly a dog-butcher. But details of the story and how it was presented are lacking.

A vogue for puppetry broadened throughout the years of the Sông dynasty, the shows exhibited in both the palace and thronging marketplace. A favourite figure was Mr Guo or Baldy Guo, a plump, jolly prankster. He became so firmly identified that any kind of puppet entertainment came to be known as a "Baldy Guo", much as in later times a Western marionette show would be referred to as a "Punch and Judy" performance, a reference to its raucous, quarrelsome leading characters. Songs, jerky dancing and jests made up the offering. A high official, Du You (735–812), took pleasure in watching another kind of puppetry, Plate Bell; he declared that he enjoyed nothing more than a tour of the markets of Yangzhou where he might watch the antic figurines. The exact nature of Plate Bell puppets is not clear; the name might be derived from cymbals used by the non-Chinese people of Central Asia or by the inhabitants of India. The clashing of these instruments could have accompanied the puppet dances.

Another admirer of puppetry was the Emperor Xuanzong (*c.* 712–56), in whose inner palace was established the Imperial Academy of Music (714). In his later years, rueful after having been compelled to abdicate, he wrote a melancholy quatrain about them:

> They've made an old man, wood-carved, string-pulled,
> Chicken-skinned, crane haired, like the genuine thing,

The show over in a flash, lonely, loose-ended,

Once more I am back in this dreamlike human life.

[Quoted by Dolby]

Bitterly, as he languishes in exile, he identifies himself with the volition-less puppets.

A governor of Szechwan Province, Cui Anquin, entertained his soldiers and won the applause of his people by offering free puppet shows in front of his official residence, this done to maintain his subjects' loyalty (878–80). Quite Machiavellian was a rebel general who, whenever he seized a new district, ordered a public marionette show to help him sense the attitude of the local citizenry.

At the funeral of Imperial Commissioner Xin Yunjing (768) the mourners were consoled by beholding a puppet depiction of a heroic dual between a Turkic and a Chinese general, as well as a reproduction of the famous battle that had inspired *Fan Kuai Rescues His Monarch from Distress*, the remarkable exploit of the ex-dog-butcher who saved his king.

Originally the Pear Orchard Academy, founded by Emperor Ming Huang in the Tang capital, Changan, was dedicated to training musicians; but since music was so integral to all forms of staged presentation the Academy indirectly encouraged the advancement of acting and linked theatrical skills. The same is true of the development of dance learned as a separate art: it involved mime, ingenuity in costuming and make-up, which also contributed to heightening the closely associated art of play-acting. Dolby relates how for the funeral of a princess, Li Keji (c. 860–74), an imperial actor–jester–musician prepared an opulent ballet. "He composed a lament or dirge, which brought tears to the eyes of all who heard it, taking jewels and especially pearls from the imperial treasuries to fashion into adornments for their hair and painting eight hundred bolts of government silk with patterns of fish, dragons and waves to serve as a carpet for them to dance upon. As they danced, the whole floor would be covered with precious stones. Elaborate spectacles such as this may well have encouraged a taste for novel visual entertainment."

All this while, the narrative arts were burgeoning, especially during the long Tang reign. *Chuanqui*, "short stories", or "marvel tales" as they were dubbed, often achieved a high level of literary accomplishment. In subsequent centuries, too, many would be adapted for the stage, proving to be a valuable source of situations and plots, to be liberally borrowed. In them were likely to be examples of deftly written dialogue and devices for sustaining interest and inculcating taut suspense, the tricks of the trade that any playwright would have to acquire. The eloquent sermons of Buddhist priests, who fervently sought to dramatize moral points, also served as models of how to make emphatic their dire warning and paradisiacal promises by resorting to means that were ever more secular. Drawing on fables in the *sutras*, now accessible in Chinese, they drew crowds that came as much to be shocked and titillated as edified. This, too, was an aspect of theatre that was to be influential. The term for these works was *biawen*, "Mandala texts". Such a one is the great *Maudgalyana Saves His Mother in the Underworld* (*c.* 806–20), which survives in several versions, including a copy of one dated 921 preserved in the British Museum. Because she has been incessantly deceitful, Maudgalyana's mother dies and is condemned to Hell, where she is transformed into a starving demon. She wastes to shrivelled skin and bones. Aided by the merciful Buddha, her son undergoes appalling hardships to rescue her, along with a flock of equally hungry ghosts also confined in the infernal regions. This story is repeated in innumerable popular tales and ballads and is dramatized almost as frequently. The *biawen* combine prose – literary and vernacular – song, poetry, and insertions of rhymed proverbs and common sayings, much as do plays in succeeding periods, and Dolby guesses that they "set minds thinking along the path to drama".

What is known of this early era is mostly of activities at the palace, of which descriptions were kept, even the expense lists. It is likely that many forms of entertainment existed at village festivals, of which there were a great many, and in the streets and markets of the teeming cities. But of these, present knowledge is unluckily scant.

The Sông dynasty, lasting from the middle of the tenth century to half-way through the thirteenth, is divided into two periods, the Northern Sông (960–1126) and the Southern (1127–1279): a competing rule, the Jin, was established in the North, when the non-Chinese Jurched, progenitors of the Manchus, over-ran that region and chose Peking as one of its several capitals (1115–1234). During this time theatre took a forward leap, with presentations of *zaju* becoming profuse. The term refers to "variety" or miscellany, offerings made up of sketches "big" or "little", some comic, some featuring only song and dance, or possibly just puppet plays. Also there were "dumb *zaju*", performed only in pantomime. Dolby:

> On one occasion a dumb play involved two or three emaciated players powdered all over and made up with "golden eyes" and white faces to make them look like skeletons. They wore brocade and embroidered stomachers, held "soft staffs" in their hands and, making comic gestures and rushing around, comported themselves as if acting a play. In this instance the dumb play came during a Hundred Games show and was sandwiched between a dance duo, one of the dancers being masked and dressed in the part of Zhong Kui, the fearsome ghost-catcher, and a gruesome sword-fighting act of seven people in costume lunging realistically at one another with real swords. Each item was preceded by fireworks. Other shows were called "supernatural *zaju*" and "rake *zaju*" the former no

doubt concerned with ghosts, demons and divine beings, and the latter perhaps with romance and naughty sex.

The *zaju* were most often included in the ever more elaborate Hundred Games shows, or at the imperial palace as adjunct to huge banquets where dishes were heaped high with rich food downed with wine. A Hundred Games programme lists "*zaju* immediately after cock-fighting and along with horn butting, football, juggling and other games". Or else the sketch might occur between concerts of singing and instrumental music. *Zaju*, more or less of the same kind, continued to be offered throughout the Sông and Jin dynasties.

In the Jin years another kind of entertainment, the *yuanben*, is credited with foreshadowing the appearance of drama. The exact meaning of "*yuanben*" is unclear but it seems to denote "entertainers' quarters" or "brothel texts", since the women who took part in them might be "singing girls" or "tarts". Yet, though designated as a separate genre, these seem to have been much like the *zaju* in style and content.

By now, "writing societies", or *shuhi*, had come into being. They were amateur groups that provided the texts of the *yuanben* and *zaju*, while others were improvised by the largely uneducated players. Troupes of actors were maintained at court, and also in the households of high officials, or else there were independent ensembles that were engaged to perform on festive occasions. Of interest, an emperor, Zhenzong (*c.* 988–1022), composed the lyrics of a *zaju*, but chose to have his effort remain anonymous.

In the now booming cities, Hangzhou, Bianliang and Jin Zhongdu (afterwards Peking), amusement sections sprang up, much like permanent fairgrounds filled with booths and arcades dispensing a vast array of entertainment, among the choices being strings of theatres now called "*peng*, 'awnings', *kanpeng*, 'watching awnings', *gousi*, 'hook booths', or *goulan*, 'hook balustrades' ". Dolby: "Most probably these were fairly solid enclosures with a raised stage open on three sides and hemmed in by a low railing or balustrade. There were as many as fifty or more such theatres in two of the Bianliang *wazi* (amusement quarters), and the bigger ones, called Lotus Flower Awning, Peony Awning, Yaksha Awning and Elephant Awning, were capable of holding several thousand spectators."

The Sông court shifted to the south from Bianliang and set up afresh at Hangzhou, followed by a large share of the popular entertainers: theatres in the *wazi*, which had been comparatively few, rapidly increased in number to as many as twenty-three. Apparently some of them were quite large, multi-storeyed. The streets of the sector thronged with all kinds of performers, proffering circus and carnival acts as well as skits and more serious musical presentations. Temporary stages were also put up outdoors to accommodate itinerant players and then razed as the troupes wandered on. As dramatic fare, however, their offerings seem to have been skimpy. Some were apparently no more than comic monologues or jocular exchanges between two persons. Or they might employ three or four. Again, these were "turns", only part of a fuller programme, inserted between juggling, dancing, acrobatics. By now, the *zaju* even more often had a moral point or contained a satirical innuendo aimed at a tolerant ruler.

The *zajus* were categorized into more and more sub-types, the distinctions between them often slight or subtle: the *zaban*, the *qupo*, the *zhuanta*, the *sanyue*, to cite a few. These, too, were filled with elementary plots that were subsequently to be enlarged into more complex dramatic structures. The various sorts of skit might also be mixed, as was *Eye-medicine Suan*, which combined the characteristics of a Sông *zaju* and a Jin *yuanben* in dealing with a slapstick encounter between an eye-doctor and a clown, a topic that has a rather modern ring. But, alas, no text remains, only a depiction of the scene on a coloured tile – hints of what the *zaju* were like have survived in this way, illustrated tiles more durable than scrolls.

The best insight into the nature of these sketches is to be found in several narrative poems that are unfortunately rather belated, dating from almost the very end of the Sông era. One is *Farmer's First Visit to the Theatre*, by Du Renjie (*c.* 1190–*c.* 1270). Prosperous from a good harvest, the farmer ventures into the city. In a *wazi*, he is drawn by a crowd around a poster and by the promises of a barker outside a gaudily decorated playhouse; curious, he buys his way in. Spectators are ranged on tiered benches or else standing in the pit about a raised stage. The initial offering is musical, a group of women rhythmically striking drums and an array of small gongs. Then comes a *yuanben* entitled *Fixing the Romance*. A rich man, entering a restaurant, espies a pretty girl; he asks a waiter to convey seductive marriage offers to her. She spurns his avowals until, frustrated, the suitor vents his anger on the go-between, the hapless waiter, belabouring him with a leather baton which splits in two. At this tantalizing juncture, as Du Renjie's poem has it, the farmer's excessive laughter induces a wrenching stomach cramp; he has to depart urgently, much to his regret, for he misses the outcome of the sketch along with any glimpse at the other items on the programme, to which the *yuanben* has been merely a precursor.

Elsewhere, a poem by Gao Andao, dating from the thirteenth or early fourteenth century, pictures another theatre visit, but an unpleasant one. The doorkeeper is a roughneck, the audience unruly, the musicians – a drummer, a flute-player – inept, as are the women who comprise the other players on the "music bench"; to make matters worse, they are "ugly and sluttish". All that follows is disappointing; the dancers are awkward, the acrobats become dangerously entangled in "flags and streamers"; the stilt-walkers, losing their balance, almost fall; a tumbler strains his back and stumbles. A "demon act" fails to elicit chills or horror. The actors in a *yuanben* are nervously inadequate. The poet's intent seems to be satirical.

The scholar Tao Zongyi, in the mid-fourteenth century, lists the titles of more than 700 *yuanben*, appending comments on some of them, but further details are lacking. Most likely some were curtain-raisers, others mere comic duos, engaged in clever repartee and perhaps bawdy, or they were dances, or highlighted acrobatics. *Zaju* of this sort were given as late as the Liao dynasty (947–1125), and *yuanben* well into the Ming dynasty (1368–1644).

From the Ming period there is the text of one, *Meeting of Immortals*, by a princely hand, that of Zhu Youdun (1379–1439). It is a celebratory piece, rather dull, about the Angel of the Peaches of Immortality. Having frequently deviated from the strict virtues expected of her, she is exiled to Earth to be a courtesan, becoming acquainted with the cardinal vices of ordinary folk, "wine-drinking, sex, greed for money, and wrath". Inevitably the enjoyment they yield her grows stale. Her habits changed, she gives a birthday party for her human lover, the scholar Shuang. Several gods, in disguise, are sent to help her, without ever revealing their supernatural identity. They pretend to be entertainers hired to enliven the feast. They assume the roles of the Star Gods of Longevity, *fumo, jing, moni, jieji*, and bear choice gifts along with wishes for happiness, good health and long life. Accordingly there is a "play within a play", the quality uneven. The dialogue is mostly in rhymed verse; the attempts at humour somewhat clumsy. The action and poetry are supported by "dulcet music": plucked mandolins, castanets, piccolos, songs, and there are dances. On the surface this is a decorous work, yet there are many hints of half-hidden coarseness and sexual innuendo, and at times the classical Chinese is replaced by colloquialisms, especially in songs allotted to the clown (*jing*). The rhyme scheme is remarkably complex. At the end, Scholar Shuang voices his gratitude: "I thank you, sir actors, for your impromptu play. Indeed it was a splendid saucy piece, rendered most eloquently."

What is to be noticed here is a likeness to the Moralities, the semi-abstract allegories that served religion and the Church in medieval Europe at about this time. They are dramatized homilies.

The Ming dynasty brought forth other kinds of *yuanben*, good-humoured short plays, in some aspects very different from the earlier species. An instance of one such is *Wolf of Mount Zhong* by Wang Jiusi (1468–1551). Space is lacking here for due specificity about these many ephemeral forms, geography being a factor. Also close akin were the *goujin*, "intermezzo brocade", robust farces favoured at the imperial palace on festive days. They combined elements of refinement and vulgarity, but again with emphasis on comedy, enacted by the clown with painted face, and his partner, who cudgelled him, while their banter provided a moral comment or two on a topical custom or event. A few other players might participate in the action, but the troupe was always small. The *kegua*, the oft-wielded cudgel, was of wood padded with felt and wrapped in strips of tender leather. The other characters might be a *zhuanggu* – a dignified government official or wealthy gentleman – and a man impersonating a woman, designated a *shuangdan*, but this could vary. There might be a young scholar, solemn and "intellectual-looking"; a bawd or whore, somewhat the worse for wear; and other familiar types.

The scholar, faithless to his wife, was a leading role in the Wenzhou *zaju*, an emergent genre which had its origin during the Northern Sông (960–1127) in a region of Chekiang Province . Betraying his virtuous spouse, the learned adulterer is eventually destroyed by thunder and lightning – as in *Zhao Chaste Maid* – or by some other heavenly retribution, a frightful, ghostly intervention – as in *Wang Kui* (c. 1190–94). *Zhao Chaste Maid* gave offence and was banned along with several others on similar subjects, perhaps because the hierarchy of ministers was populated by now with powerful, unsmiling scholars. A play that somehow evaded the ban is *Top Graduate Zhang Xie* (author unknown, mid or late thirteenth century) in which the scholar–protagonist betrays and mistreats his wife, even angrily slashing her with a sword; at the conclusion, however, the pair are happily reconciled, signifying the scholar's moral redemption. This work is the product of a writing society or of a singularly gifted member, and is one of the few scripts of its type and period that is still accessible. It possesses remarkable strength and richness, its tone often "tongue-in-cheek", which may be why it chanced to be exempt from official interdiction. Dolby has translated the prologue, of which this is an excerpt:

Time hurries our hair white, and years change our ruddy cheeks. Life in this drifting, shifting world wholly resembles stems of duckweed driven hither and thither. Along the path the scarlets and purples vie in splendor. Outside the window, orioles trill and swallows chatter. And when the flowers fall, the whole garden is empty. Such is the way of the world, and let it be. For what use is toil and fret!

But amongst us here, though scions of patrician families we be, everyone is versed in the strumming of strings and the blowing of woodwind; not only do we spill song and poesy of gay romance, not only are we thoroughly accomplished in miming, gestures, and quick repartee, but neither do we stint the painted clownery and farce by which we fill the hall with song and laughter. Yes, just like the Yangtse with its thousand-foot waves, we are a very different, quite a special "stream" of tradition!

Cease now your hubbub, pause a little in your merry conversation, and let us take a look at another, unique line of entertainment. In the manner and style of the Music Academy, and worthy of mention in the same breath as the Crimson and the Green, we entertain you with our endless flow of lyric charm, our banter and joking repartee, and when you hear our disquisition all present will be filled with wonder. . . . Previous performances have enacted the story of Top Graduate Zhang Xie for you, but now this writing society wishes to bear the palm, and to reign supreme for prolific achievements in all Eastern Ou, we shall sing forth the motive of our play. . . . So, noble sirs, I bid you pray be silent, and we shall let you hear our minute exposition.

("Eastern Ou" was a prefecture in Chekiang Province. "Crimson and Green" was a rival writing society.)

What follows recounts in detail the scholar's departure from home and parents as he leaves for the city to take his examinations and form his career, and then the hazards of his journey and those he meets on the road, including a brigand who beats and robs him; the beauty of the mountainous country through which he passes; and so on.

Puppeteers continued to practise their enchanting art more prominently than ever, in the palace – where they might be retained to divert the Emperor and take part in the formal greeting of foreign ambassadors – and in the *wazis* and elsewhere outdoors in the streets. They were of several kinds of puppet: rod puppets, marionettes and flickering shadow figures. "There were guilds of societies of puppeteers in Bianliang, and in a certain two lanes there were simultaneously twenty-four puppet shows, with puppets dressed in bright, gay clothes. The fine lady puppets wore flowers, embroidered cloaks and bejeweled and emerald-clustered headdresses, and, with their slim, willowy waists, were as lithely graceful as real women." Their offerings comprised legends told in ballads, along with memoirs of historical events, and dramatizations of popular stories. In the Southern Sông one form of shadow play was enacted not by paper or leather cut-outs but by live actors whose shapes were projected onto the screen. The puppeteers were organized into guilds or societies, some of whose members were highly acclaimed.

Story-tellers and ballad singers abounded in the marketplace, keeping alive melodramatic tales and catchy music that would be appreciated by future playwrights.

Invading the northern regions of China, after raids and battles that had been carried on for decades, the Mongols enjoyed a culminating success in 1234 and permanently occupied those colder provinces. The Jin dynasty ended. The dreaded Genghis Khan, conqueror of much of Europe as well as broad Asian realms, died seven years before this final victory; in his stead, Kublai Khan ascended the throne of the Celestial Empire and ruled it quite wisely, bringing a much-needed stability. His arrival profoundly changed the local culture. The long-enduring image of the Mongols as a barbarous, marauding horde is now seen to have been a gross misconception. They brought special talents that blended with Chinese traits, strengthening both. At first, however, the mutual adaptation was difficult. Widely, Confucianism gave way to rival faiths, propagated by the Muslims, who, together with the

Buddhists, now largely staffed much of the governing bureaucracy, displeasing a host of Confucian scholars. That erudite class, suddenly outcast, was dispossessed and dispersed. Their plight was not easy; their high status and rich privileges were lost. Some bureaucrats were slain during the prolonged wars, or were punished for their stubborn loyalty to the Jin regime or were beggared by its collapse; a few were enslaved. A good number, now reclusive, withdrew from the troubled world to become hermits, bent on painting serene natural scenes, meditating, philosophizing. Other survivors gradually reconstituted themselves as literati, composing novels, songs, lyric poetry and plays. The result was an explosive flowering of the arts, which also received a stimulus from new forms created by the invaders, who for a time ruled but did not even speak Chinese.

The Chinese classical theatre owes much to the Mongols, for it appeared "full grown" shortly after their victorious incursion. Just how the transformation came about is unclear, but an altered stage, more professional and mature in contrast to all that preceded it, was established by the start of the Yuan dynasty (1279–1368), a bare fifty years after Kublai Khan's arrival. This was a golden age for Chinese literature, including the theatre.

The Mongols had plays that apparently were like the *yuanben*. As early as 1031 a Chinese ambassador, K'ung Tao-fu, who claimed descent from Confucius, had been despatched to the Mongol court where, as part of ceremonious greeting, a play was presented by Khitan Mongols. (The Khitai were Chinese whose leaders were among the very first to yield to the foreign armies and shortly collaborated with them.) Tactlessly, Confucius was represented in the farce by a clown; affronted by this portrayal of his revered ancestor, the envoy stalked out. But in their report, he and others in his delegation observed that, apart from it having been offensive, the offering was in most aspects far superior to anything ever shown at home. In fact, it was "wondrous".

(For a great deal of the historical detail here, I am beholden not only to Dolby and the half-dozen authors of general chronicles I have previously acknowledged, but also to J.I. Crump's lively, well-documented *Chinese Theatre in the Days of Kublai Khan*.)

The Mongol invaders were merciless when resisted by the inhabitants of cities to which they laid siege and, entering them, slaughtered all males old enough to bear arms; they spared everyone in places that did not fight but promptly surrendered. One explanation put forth for the sudden efflorescence of Chinese theatre in the Mongol and Yuan eras is that it is the output of playwrights who lived in just such prudent, safe enclaves. But a study of where the outstanding stage-writers of this period dwelled reveals that about as many lived in cities over-run and laid waste as in those that proved to be comparative havens.

The dramatic activity that now flourished had as its centre Khanbalik, as the Mongols called their throne-city (to the Chinese, Dadu, "the Great Capital", later Peking), so that playwrights were attracted there from elsewhere. Their scripts are a blend of Chinese and Mongol styles, the latter exhibiting a readier acceptance of discipline and firmer organization, a reflection of what was happening in the society by assimilation as the racial strains intermingled. The Yuan plays, as they are called, retain many elements of the *zaju* and *yuanben* but show a clearer structure, and are more substantial, though hardly ever weighty.

At first the Mongols, led by the astute Kublai Khan, displayed a marked tolerance for entertainers, exempting them from edicts against a wide variety of professions and enterprises. Before long, however, this changed: the lower class of performers – "animal trainers, snake charmers, puppeteers, performers of sleight-of-hand, players of cymbals and Taoist drums, and those who deceive men and gather crowds for the purpose of practising quacksalving" – were ordered to quit their pernicious trades on pain of "severe punishment" (translation: J.I. Crump). Censorship took an early hold.

Some historians trace another influence on the new drama to the Chin (or Jurched people), a barbaric tribe on the border who had invaded northern China (1151) before the Mongols' success and then established a short-lived dynasty (1154–1234), ruling in Peking. The Chin were respected for their music, later described by the critic–dramatist Hsu Wei (1521–93) as "vigorous, powerful and very savage – the songs of warriors on horseback". This music, far more modal, infiltrated Chinese compositions and also, though somewhat tamed, infused Chinese folk songs, eventually replacing earlier, prevalent musical forms almost completely. It became the core around which musical plays, in time to be classical operas, were constructed. In some minds, to write plays one also had to be a composer; the score was the *raison d'être* for the stage-work. Such plays have been likened in many respects to English ballad operas.

In the opening years of the Yuan era three prominent members of the Academy of Music undertook to revise and update the traditional form of the *yuanben*; it is not known with much exactitude of what their alterations consisted. It is probably significant, however, that some of the first Yuan playwrights were sons-in-law of a celebrated actor who was associated with the Academy. By now, too, as noted, there was a considerable if scattered circle of well-educated, literary persons, displaced by the Mongol usurpation, who had turned to writing and on whose talents the nascent theatre could draw.

Scholars seeking data about Yuan drama turn to Zhong Sicheng's *Register of Ghosts* (*Lu-kuei Pu*), published in the 1330s, more or less sixty years after the Academy's inception. A native of Pien-lieng, in North China, Zhong Sicheng passed most of his maturity in Hanchow. The little book's subtitle is *Fifty-six Talents of an Earlier Generation Whose Dramas Are Still with Us*. He claims to have known some of these playwrights, though others he has only heard of; those with whom he has had personal acquaintance are northerners, those about whom he has information at second hand are southerners. He groups them by their dates, listing first those who have "departed" – hence the title's allusion to ghosts – and then those still alive. For each of his fifty-six dramatists he cites a birthplace, and next lists the titles of his plays, varying from a single script to as many as thirty-two and fifty-eight. The dramatists' workplaces are many, but chiefly the fifty-six seem to have dwelled in the cities of Tatu (the Mongolian name for Peking), Chen-ting and P'ing-yang, where it must be supposed the impulse to write for the stage received a special push, obviously from local acting troupes. Concerning three of the fifty-six script-writers, he appends a few biographical facts, but otherwise tells little more than each man's occupation apart from literature, or not even that. So the yield is sparse.

The titles in the *Register* add up to 320 Yuan plays deemed by Zhong Sicheng to possess a degree of lasting merit. Nothing is said of their contents. During the ensuing Ming period, however, two large anthologies were brought out (1615), compilations preserving 162 works. Not all the scripts listed in the *Register* are to be found in the collections, which frustrates scholars. Yet there is copious treasure.

It is argued that an outburst of distinguished art-work in a nation's history – its "Golden Age" – is owing to the existence of an extraordinarily gifted individual, such as an Aeschylus, a Marlowe or Shakespeare, a Goethe, a creative spirit far more than talented, a rarely matched genius, who sets an example of high achievement and inspires others to emulate him, hoping to equal and rival him. In the annals of Chinese theatre Guan Hanqing (*c.* 1220–1300; also known as Kuan Han Ch'ing), though hardly a Shakespeare, is felt to fill an equivalent role.

Biographical facts about him are almost as elusive as those about Shakespeare. He is said to have failed his examinations and, in consequence, was forced to accept a humble clerical post in a medical bureau; but this permanent setback may have been due to his having remained loyal to the Jin dynasty after the Mongol takeover, a steadfastness for which he was punished. He enjoyed the company and liking of a celebrated courtesan, Pearl Curtain Beauty, herself an accomplished poet and the intimate of many eminent persons. He was also a close friend of a famed wit, Wang Hequin, a master of deft ripostes, with whom for decades he fondly exchanged sharp, humorous banter. His plays, mostly comedies, won applause and popularity, as they have continued to do ever since. He wrote poems and songs, many tinged with eroticism, especially alluding to illicit liaisons. It is he whom Zhong Sicheng's *Register* credits with having written fifty-eight plays, attesting that he was remarkably prolific, a characteristic of genius. Eight are extant, but some are deemed so inferior that, again as with Shakespeare, scholars prefer to believe that they are from another hand.

One script that is still a favourite, *Slicing Fish*, tells of a resourceful young woman full of guile, whose husband is condemned to die; she helps him avoid execution by seducing the evil lord who has concocted the charge for which her luckless mate has been sentenced to lose his life. The plot is exceedingly well devised, the dialogue rippling with wit, the heroine engagingly realized, boldly sensual.

Moon Prayer Pavilion looks back to the fall of the Jin capital, Zhongdu; among those taking flight are a mother and daughter who become separated from each other; the year is 1213. Also refugees are a young man and his sister who are similarly parted in the general fright and confusion. The girl and the young man join forces as they search and journey onward; of course, their improvised partnership develops into a mutual love. At an inn the young man is overtaken by illness. The girl's father, holder of a high ministerial post, finds the pair there and, infuriated, carries her off. Meanwhile, the young man's sister has met the mother who has lost her daughter; the older woman takes this distraught girl into her care, treating her like one of her own family. As domestic conditions return to a semblance of peace, the young man resumes his studies, passing his civil service examinations at the very top of his class. He is truly the kind of son-in-law the minister is seeking; a match is arranged, and wholly by chance the young man is reunited with the girl he loves and who has steadfastly loved him. A happy marriage is set for the sister, for whom a competent military graduate is chosen, a young man who has become the brother's best friend, also a neat pairing.

Though Guan Hanqing's plays are mostly about the emotion of love, as experienced by virgins, married ladies, courtesans and prostitutes, his range is broad and includes an extensive scale of moods and themes. As a rule, bright flashes of humour enlighten them. Very exciting is *Single Sword Meeting*, which is about the warrior lord Kuan Wu. Lu Su, the sinister and devious minister of a hostile, rival state, invites the hero to a banquet and plans to have him ambushed. Kuan Wu, with outstanding poise and courage, outwits his treacherous host, who finds that he personally has to extricate his guest from the ambush and be his escort in their escape. A *coup de théâtre* is Kuan Wu's late entrance on stage, at mid-point in the play, a ploy that builds up growing expectancy in spectators while he is glowingly described but not yet seen. This places an extra burden on the playwright and actor, who must prove themselves equal to justifying the lengthy preparation for the invincible hero's arrival. Will he prove to be all that he is said to be?

A darker mood infuses *Dream of Two on a Journey*, a sense of foreboding, otherworldly doom. Emperor Liu Bei of Shu yearns for his "sworn brothers", his loyal generals Zhang Fei and Kuan Yu, stationed at vital outposts. He orders their return to court, but word comes that both have been treacherously slain. A minister, Zhuge Liang, keeps this dire news from the Emperor, lest his likely wild grief add to the national calamity. But the ghosts of the murdered men travel back to the capital; *en route*, the two meet and recognize each other. Grasping how great has been the blow to their cause, their dismay is heightened. Reaching the palace, they enter and survey with bitter rue the richness and splendour in which they once moved. Liu Bei, solitary in his bedchamber, beholds them; at first he does not realize that they are spectres and hails them joyfully, but gradually he sees that they are sorrowing ghosts. His despair is intense. They vanish at dawn, first bidding him to avenge their deaths. (Actual historical persons, the two generals died years apart. Guan Hanqing alters the factual details, creating a more compact tale, one with sharper impact.)

Familiarly referred to as the "Old Man of Yi-chai", as well as the "father of Yuan *zaju*, and its first creator", Guan Hanqing was accorded special honours and acclaimed as "a people's writer" on the occasion (somewhat hypothetical) of his 700th birthday in 1958. Throughout Communist-ruled China new and variorum editions of his works were issued. His scripts were more widely produced than was usual, and a biographical play was staged, one that was about as faithful to facts about him as those purporting to depict episodes in William Shakespeare's love-life. Also distributed were drawings and ink sketches supposedly portraying him, though no true likeness of him is known. Such are the rewards of fame and immortality.

Guan Hanqing is one of the so-called "Four Great Men of Yuan *zaju* drama". Another is his contemporary, Bai Pu (1226–post-1306), who differs markedly from him in background and temperament. He, too, suffered under the Mongol regime. His father, a high Jin official, lost his post; this led to the break-up of the family. The son came under the tutelage of Yuan Haowen (1190–1257), a highly respected literary figure of conservative bent, who remained a family friend, and who treated the boy with remarkable kindness and presided over his education, which was unusually thorough for the times. Even so, the boy never fully recovered from the pain of having been torn from his fond parents; a strain of melancholy runs through all his work. Sharing his father's loyalty to the Jin dynasty, he refused offers to serve the Mongol rulers; he seemed disdainful of achieving high rank and fortune. Instead, he adopted a hedonistic way of life, given to carousing and wild adventures. (He was to beget a son who, after his father's death, rose to an illustrious post and may have been responsible for the award of posthumous honours and titles to his sire.) Some time after 1280 Bai Pu went to live in the South, in Kiangsu Province, where he settled for his remaining days.

The poignant and tragically moving *Rain on the Paulownia Tree* is Bai Pu's most applauded work; it celebrates the love story of Tang Emperor Minghuang and Lady Yang. Growing fond of a somewhat rough-mannered and aggressive young general, the Emperor chooses him to be Lady Yang's adopted son. Her brother, an influential minister, has the general transferred to a frontier post. At night in a garden, Emperor Minghuang and Lady Yang pledge lasting love under the boughs of a paulownia tree. The next day word is brought that the general, angered by his demotion, is leading a rebellion and advancing towards the capital. The Emperor, unprepared to resist the uprising, takes flight to Szech-wan; on the journey his guards threaten to desert him; they blame Lady Yang for his troubles. He is forced to accept her offer of suicide. In time the rebellion is put down, though the Emperor has to yield the throne to his natural son. Returned to the capital, he is forlorn, desperately unhappy at hav-ing lost Lady Yang. In a dream, she reappears and bids him to go with her to a lovers' gathering. He is awakened by the plangent sound of rain spattering on the paulownia leaves outside. Weighed down by mournful memories, he weeps. This play is one of the very few early Chinese dramas ever to approach tragedy. Some resonate with sad or nostalgic notes, but almost inevitably they end happily.

Ma Zhiyuan (*fl. c.* 1280), a native of Dadu, apparently retired from a minor post in the Southern region – perhaps as a tax collector – and thereafter led a reclusive, bucolic life, during which he wrote songs and poems in praise of the contemplation of nature and a rustic existence such as his. Many of the songs have survived and excel in wit and fancy, and show his skill at evoking a scene in just a few words. He is also considered one of the "four Great Men of Yuan *zaju*" for his *Autumn in the Han Palace*, another account of an emperor seeking love. Wishing to find a wife, the Emperor designates a minister, the deceitful Mao Yanshow, to select a covey of beautiful maidens for the imperial harem; the Emperor will make his final choice after examining their portraits. The most lovely candidate is Wang Lady Splendour, but her father neglects to bribe Mao Yanshow, who retaliates by substituting an ugly picture of the daughter. The Emperor, discovering the truth, is instantly infatuated with the ravishing girl. Alas, fearing exposure Mao has escaped and carried the proper image of Wang Lady Splendour to the court of the Hunnish Khan, who is also smitten by what he beholds. He threatens war unless Lady Splendour is delivered to him to be his wife. The grieving Emperor is forced to submit to this demand; he and Lady Splendour bid each other a sorrowful farewell. In her new home, miserable, she drowns herself in the River Amur.

The desolate Emperor dreams of his lost love, but even then she is snatched away from him. Awakened by the honks of migrating wild geese, he is made further aware of how distant from him is the person he loves. A messenger arrives with news of her deed, accompanied by the traitorous Mao Yanshow, sent back in chains, to be put to death at the order of the Khan, who also is in the throes of grief.

Ma Zhiyuan collaborated on the classic Yuan drama *Yellow Millet Dream*, providing the first act, the remaining three coming from other brushes, among them those of a pair of actor-playwrights. Such teamwork was frequent, much as it was later in the Elizabethan theatre. It is evidence of how closely and fraternally actors and dramatists pragmatically mingled their talents to achieve a success.

The fourth of the "Great Men" of Yuan *zaju*, Zheng Guanzu (*c.* 1280–*c.* 1330?), is thought to have lived in a somewhat later period; he is not in the *Register of Ghosts*. He was born in Shansi Province; well trained in Confucian precepts, he won a minor post as a regional bureaucrat in Hangzhou. His was a cautious, meticulous temperament; he did not make friends hastily, with the result that he was late in establishing himself in literary circles; this delayed his achieving the reputation he merited. Yet he was dogged and gifted. He was especially well liked by actors, by whom he came to be called the "Venerable Mr Zheng".

Many of his scripts are available in whole or in part, such as *Wang Can Ascends the Tower*, *Qiannu's Soul Goes Wandering* and *Romance of the Hanlin Academician*. All show him to be exceedingly shrewd at dramatic construction. *Regency of the Duke of Zhou* delves into history to portray the much-admired Ji Dan, who, after joining with the Warrior King to expel the Shang dynasty and put the Zhou dynasty firmly in power, seeks to withdraw from palace life to dwell in rustic surroundings and engage in contemplation. He is persuaded to remain at court, where he is still truly needed. A decade and a half elapse, and now the Emperor is deathly ill. Duke Ji Dan offers prayers to the Zhou ancestral gods, proposing to sacrifice his own life in exchange for the Emperor's recovery. By error, a parchment on which is inscribed his remarkably altruistic prayer is enclosed in a gold-enchased casket that also contains sacred divinations. The Emperor dies, leaving a successor who is a minor. Duke Ji Dan serves as the regent, earning praise for invariably dispensing justice in a fair and kindly manner. In an uprising, rebels wrongly accuse him of plotting to supplant the child heir to the throne. Once again, Ji Dan is ready to give up his life, even willing to let himself be physically dismembered to prove his loyalty. His gesture is not accepted; instead, he is asked to lead an army against the dissidents. On his return, after a decisive victory, a tempest that hurls and whirls dirt and stones suddenly arises, obscuring the sun. Seeking an explanation of this ominous natural warning, an aged minister opens the gold casket and comes upon the parchment on which Ji Dan, two decades earlier, had set down his prayer; it is further testimony of the Duke's life-long, selfless fidelity to the Zhou dynasty. In another demonstration of his lack of personal ambition, he relinquishes his posts at court, giving the reins to the young monarch. A play like this, preaching loyalty to the regime, might partly account for the esteem in which Zheng Guanzu was held in the imperial precincts.

Too little has been learned about Wang Shifu (*fl.* late thirteenth century), whom the *Register* cites as a resident of Tatu (Peking) and the author of fourteen scripts. One of these, *West Wing* (the title used by Dolby, though Brockett identifies the play as *Romance of the Western Chamber* and Gassner as *Romance of the Western Pavilion*), has been the most famous of all Chinese plays throughout the centuries. Of great length, having five times as much text as the usual Yuan *zaju*, it owes part of its theme and language to a ballad – one of the few wholly preserved – by Dong Jie-yuan (composed some time between 1190 and 1208), which in turn is derived from a novella by a Tang poet, Yuan Zhen (779–831). Thus it obliquely profits by incorporating the material of a familiar friend.

On a journey, the brash young scholar Zhang Junrui takes up lodging in a Buddhist monastery. Other guests there are Madame Cui, widow of a Prime Minister and a lady of rigid propriety, and her beautiful daughter, Little Oriole. The "west wing" indicated in the title is where the mother and daughter are staying and where the impetuous Zhang asks the Abbot to let him have a room, so as to be near them. The young man instantly and aggressively lays suit to the girl, without letting the mother be aware of it. The two women are at the monastery to have a requiem performed for the late Prime Minister.

Word of the girl's infinite charm spreads throughout the countryside and reaches a brigand chief. He brazenly attacks the monastery to abduct her. Sending a message to a friend, a general posted near by, Zhang brings about the rescue of the party besieged by the brigand's men.

Madame Cui, having agreed to reward the scholar with her daughter's hand, now breaks her promise, revealing that Little Oriole is already plighted to another suitor. Red Maid, Little Oriole's keen-witted servant, serves as go-between for the lovers; they meet in secret, giving lyrical voice to their pent-up feelings.

Finally, Madame Cui grants her consent, but on condition that Zhang does well in the imperial examinations he is about to take. Of course he is successful, but only to find that Little Oriole's earlier intended has arrived at the monastery and has convinced Madame Cui that he is a better choice for her daughter. He does this by egregiously slandering his rival.

Countering the untrue accusations, Zhang is once again assisted by his friend, the general. The rival, his mean falsehoods exposed, kills himself; and at last the resourceful young scholar is happily wedded to Little Oriole.

The play is a feast of "roguish humour", "titillating suspense", "plentiful spice", "delicate emotion", "vigorous action". The characters have more than adequate complexity.

This is how the young man sings of his beloved after an initial glimpse of her:

> Paradise on earth,
> a look at Little Oriole
> is more blessing than any requiem brings.
> She is supple jade,
> she is warming perfume
> And – even not to hold her close –

if one could manage one small touch,

it would absolve one from all sinful karma,

all still-to-come calamity.

[Translation: William Dolby]

A twentieth-century adaptation of *West Wing* was prepared for a London stage production by S.I. Hsiung.

After a surprisingly short interval, the Mongol regime decayed and fell apart, that fiery alien race gradually absorbed into the Chinese mass, as happened to so many other invaders. Throughout the Yuan dynasty that succeeded it, plays poured forth in full measure and, as has been said, many are to be found almost intact in the two anthologies, along with the titles of hundreds now lost. Mostly these originated in the South, progressively the dominant region; the scripts delved into almost every conceivable subject: the frustrations and rewards of love; the intricate workings of political intrigue; the heroic exploits of warriors; the intrusion of ghosts, demons and gods; the adventures of bandits; the misconduct of monks and priests; the tense and jealous opposition of wives and concubines . . . the stories variously populated with delicate, high-born virgins, rapacious courtesans, ever-wily servants, resolute young scholars, devout hermits, hypocritical and smooth-talking religious orators, firm-handed rulers, all this presenting an animated panorama of the age, like an illustrated scroll on which figures miraculously come to life.

Considerable editing of the plays took place during the Ming period, before their inclusion in the anthologies. One group of scripts exists only in skeleton form, retaining barely more than the words of the songs, the dialogue most likely left to be improvised by the performers. This omission might also have been a dodge, the authors protecting themselves from censorship: there is no *written* proof of an offence. Anyhow, the songs are usually the principal substance of all Yuan *zajus*: they convey the playwright's "poetic, spiritual and philosophical" intention. The scripts are not designed to be plotless; if anything, they tend to have strong dramatic premises handled so as to project the utmost sensational effect. But the music carries the weightier burden of propelling the action and defining the characters.

Most of the Yuan *zaju* are in four main acts, with perhaps the insertion of two brief interludes or "wedge acts" consisting of a single tune, at convenient breaks. *West Wing*, which is exceptionally long, is seen by some as really five works linked together by having the same leading characters and ongoing subject.

These plays of the second "Golden Age" are still read today by the highly educated but not often heard; they are in an antique Chinese that very few modern spectators can comprehend, a case paralleling that of today's Athenians listening to ancient Greek. It is true, too, that the best poets of that era did not write for the stage but looked down upon the theatre as not a truly artistic literary medium; most of the poetry for the theatre is of less than high quality, and a further diminishment occurs when the comic characters use colloquial prose or street argot. The humour is likely to be coarse or worse, as befitted the times.

All the music, essential and abundant throughout the Yuan *zaju*, is lost; the most frequently used type of song, called *qu*, has been distinguished from two other earlier kinds, the Tang *shi* and the Sông *ci*. As in English ballad operas, as already observed, new words were set to already popular tunes; the same melodies were utilized over and over again to convey different messages in new story contexts, by simply revising the lyrics to have them freshly appropriate. By this time, the mid and late thirteenth century, a great body of such tunes was available. Many were non-Chinese, borrowed from the folk songs of neighbouring Asian peoples. As many as 335 of them appear on one scholar's list.

A mixture of light and serious moods, the plays generally fell into one of two classes, the military ("*Wu*"), treating with historical or pseudo-historical events, with many focusing on dynastic struggles; and those looking at domestic affairs ("*Wen*"), husband and long-suffering wife, parents and disobedient children; but not a few are given over to fantasy, the supernatural enveloping the harried characters, or helping them. The tone is often didactic, the characters confronting ethical dilemmas, parlous social questions. At the conclusion, virtue triumphs: the hero rises to high office after many ordeals, or the loyalty of the faithful wife or concubine is fully requited, and the scheming rival or evil minister is routed and perhaps utterly destroyed. Sometimes much contrivance may be needed to achieve these endings and the spirits of the dead emanate to assure the attainment of moral justice.

Singing roles were restricted to the male (*tan*) and female (*mo*) leads, frequently in alternate scenes, the male given all the vocalizing in one act, the female in the next – perhaps allowing each an interval of rest; but this was hardly a fixed pattern, since the assignment and order of solos could vary. Furthermore, the players, on demand, could exchange genders, the man appearing as an enticing girl, the woman in the bravura roles of virile warrior or defiant brigand.

Seemingly, actresses were more prominent during the Yuan period: they proved to be glamorous and multi-talented. Some, like Pearl Curtain Beauty, wrote poetry; others excelled at calligraphy or attempted novels and plays; some were outstanding at instrumental musical performances and compositions; a few were even accomplished at acrobatics; one was praised for her landscape paintings; and many were noted for their good looks, charm, bright conversation and wit. Besides appearing regularly at the imperial palace and city theatres, they entertained at private feasts given at the well-furnished dwellings of the rich. They were assiduously courted by ministers, generals, lesser members of the aristocracy and the intelligentsia, consorting with them and pursuing intimate affairs.

Not much is recorded about the distinguished men seen on stage, but in 1354 Xia Tingzhi (1310–68) published his *Green Bower Collection*, a file of biographical sketches of the most celebrated singing girls and actresses of the preceding twelfth century and his own thirteenth. Most of the ladies on his roster have poetic names, given at birth or acquired at a later date, such as Any Time Beauty, Vying Heaven Perfume, Beautiful Yang Bought Slave, Jade Lotus, Cinnabar Steps Beauty, Dragon Tower Scene, Pingyang Slave. They often had quite unique quirks. Vying Heaven Perfume, wed to Li Fish Head, had what would today be dubbed a "detergent complex", incessantly dousing herself with fragrances, highly attractive to would-be suitors. Yang Bought Slave, ravishing to behold, was unfortunately addicted to tippling. Pingyang Slave had only one eye and a body that was entirely tattooed. The special gift of Jade Lotus was her skill in martial arts, an agility at handling weaponry.

In most instances the ladies were given roles to which they had proved themselves best adapted: the shy heroine; the noble, patient wife; the clever maidservant; the pert or unscrupulous concubine. Their backgrounds differed greatly: some were of respectable families that had become impoverished, or they had risen from the lower classes; others were non-Chinese. Eventually many married high-ranking court officials or generals, artists, illustrious poets and playwrights, but even more were chosen to be wives by fellow professionals with whom they shared careers. Surprisingly, after the close of their gaudy lives on stage, a number of them became Buddhist nuns or Taoist priestesses. One such retired actress, turning pious after the death of her husband, her chastity threatened by disrespectful and persistent wooers, mutilated her lovely face and was better able to stay faithful to the dead man's memory and her ascetic vows.

Intermarriage in a troupe led to the establishment of "theatre families", children beginning early to appear on stage and speak lines and to learn the conventions and tricks of the trade, which they perpetuated and might improve. Such early training was required for the mastery of pantomime and especially for adeptness at tumbling and other acrobatics which became, as has been said, a facet of the pantomime. The somersaults and other physical feats were often another means of expressing the character's tacit emotions, an added emphasis, a gestural device found only in the Chinese theatre. The young aspirants also had to be supple dancers and exhibit trained voices. The physical action was stylized and prescribed, so here, too, were traditions for performers to absorb. The preserved Yuan scripts contain scarcely any adequate stage-instructions. What is happening, what the actors are doing, is best reconstructed from the content of their songs and speeches. It is likely that even most exits and entrances were choreographed, though some – for contrast – were "realistic". "Theatre families", continuing for generations, have apparently held fast to these long-lived conventions. Indeed,

Crump speculates that in many aspects Chinese acting in classic works was not much different in the thirteenth century from what it is today.

Make-up has also been guided by tradition. In the Yuan age its application was comparatively restrained, unlike in the subsequent Ming period, an impression given by a temple wall-painting showing a pair of performers, male and female, all in stage attire. It is believed that masks were still worn by players filling the roles of gods. The clown or villain (apt to be represented on different occasions by the same actor) would exaggerate and comically or sinisterly distort his features with lines of lamp-black and white chalk, and a dignified gentlemen would sport a false goatee or beard. Other materials employed for effects were ink, soot, cinnabar and perhaps white lead, each mixed in some sort of grease or other emollient salve.

Costuming might require that a distinction be made between ancient dress and what was then contemporary garb. Professions or humbler occupations, as well as social status, were established by appropriate garments: a beggar or lowly fisherman would have a ragged, patched tunic or thatched cloak; a pampered concubine, an ornate silk robe; but there was not much of the daz-zlingly elaborate attire that is later to be a feature of Peking Opera; indeed, the stage clothes might be rather simple, depending on the financial condition of the troupe, many having modest resources.

Scenic investiture consisted mostly of a plain backdrop, though a few of them may have displayed some paintings, and there was no front curtain. In addition, there might be hangings or curtains dividing the stage into sections, if several actions were ongoing at the same time at separate locations. Though the stage was almost bare, the actors made full and dexterous use of props, wielding bright swords, handling fragile tea cups, swatting viciously with fly-whisks, poring over parchment documents and crinkly maps, and mounting hobby-horses to gallop off to battle, while snapping whips.

Further limiting any approximation of realism – visually – was the intrusive presence of the "music bench" at one side of the stage where the orchestra was seated, possibly an ensemble of drums, gongs, clappers and the shrill, ubiquitous flute; or the instrumentalists might occupy space at the rear.

Despite the absence of scenery, there could be spectacular effects, as in a military play, with a vic-torious army returning from the field, flags flying, shields flashing, helmets be-plumed, appealing to the Chinese deep love of pageantry. Or it might be a dance of demons in a drama treating of Taoist redemption, a favourite subject. In one military play as many as twenty-seven generals and their atten-dants were on stage at one time, a costly sight subsidized by the emperor's court at which the drama was presented to mark a festival. Such martial display was also a likely setting and logical pretext for mock-combats, soldiers boldly confronting one another and fencing with lethal quarterstaffs. By themselves, too, court scenes could be impressive, boasting the ceremonial etiquette of envoys and other onlookers, among them eunuchs and jesters, the richly gowned wives and harem girls, the bowing-and-scraping ministers of state, the expectant princes and princesses clustered about the paternal throne. Or the occasion for the spectacle might be an on-stage banquet, tables opulently adorned with glistening wine-cups and vessels, and rare bowls and dishes heaped to the rim.

Much commented upon is the "empty exit" ((*hsu-hsia*), a bit of stage business peculiar to this theatre. The actor did not have to leave a scene but had only to imply that he had done so by remaining on stage and turning his back on what was occurring behind him. As simply as that, he is no longer there. Many Yuan scripts give this instruction.

A remarkable fount of information is a play, *Lan Caihe* (late Yuan or early Ming), author anonymous, which is about a theatre company putting on a work, a "play within a play". Many of the actors' preparatory steps are detailed in it. The hero, Xu Jian, is the director and plans to carry the lead singing part; in that role his "music name" will be Lan Caih (or Lan S'ai-ho, the spellings vary), echoing the title of the drama about to be put on. The playhouse used by the troupe is called Liang Park Awning; a verbal picture of it is offered in the script. Dolby:

[It] is a permanent structure with a lockable door, probably open to the sky. There are loges situated high up and known as "bowers of the gods" and more general seating known as "waist awnings," presumably benches. On the stage is a *yuechuang* reserved for the female musicians. Colored posters and backcloths and other drapes and advertisements are hung up before the performance, very similar in wording to the announcement on the Yuan mural. Both *yuanben* and *zaju* are performed by this troupe, having been written by "kind gentlemen of the *shuhui.*" Sometimes the same play is showing elsewhere, promoting sharp competition between troupes. The audiences for this theater would seem to be rather exclusive, since the hero at one point declares that "only officials, solid citizens and moneyed gentlemen are allowed to divert themselves in the theaters," but that is unlikely to have always been the case, and it is probably not meant too literally even in this instance. Spectators are known as *kanguan*, "looking officials," and it is the custom to allow them to choose what plays they wish to see performed.

Crump provides excerpts from the first and last acts of *Lan Caihe*. The initial lines, a quatrain spoken by the secondary lead, Chung-li Ch'uan are almost an invocation:

> Birth is my door as death is my gate;
>
> Those who comprehend this, those I liberate.
>
> To all at night comes doubt's small voice:
>
> Salvation is his who dares to make the choice.

The speaker identifies the theatre and the city, Loyang, in which it is located. He alludes to Xu Jian, the lead actor "whose destiny has already brought him halfway down the road to immortality". (It is not clear whether this reference is to Xu Jian's age or to his climb to fame in his profession.) The next to enter are two women and two younger persons, all of whom are to have roles in the play: they are Xu Jian's wife (the first female lead) and his daughter-in-law (the secondary female lead) and Wang Pa-se and Li Pao-t'ou, his younger siblings (the *chings*) – this troupe is largely a family affair. Supervised by Chung-li, all set about sweeping and cleaning the empty Liang Park Awning. On stage, Chung-li adjusts the curtains and drapes, which can be hung in various configurations to meet the demands of the play's action.

Suddenly onto the stage comes a stranger, hereafter addressed as Master Taoist, who announces that he has come all the way from the "cloud tops" – it is actually Chung-li in a new guise, the character he will assume in the forthcoming play. Without ado, he seats himself in the "music crib". When asked to move elsewhere, perhaps to the "gods' tower", since he is occupying the place reserved for the orchestra, he adamantly refuses. Asking to see Xu Jian, he is told he must wait. Questioned by Wang, he will not reveal the purpose of his visit. When Xu Jian does arrive, he promptly identifies himself to the audience and explains the relationship of all on the scene, though somewhat confusingly designating Wang and Li at one moment as his brothers and at the next as his cousins. He lays out the programme of the troupe:

> We take what is written in Ancient Works
>
> And bend it to the street players' ways.
>
> I've grown practised in the theatre's styles
>
> Of bawdy farce and Buddhist chant,
>
> And exhausted all my meagre skill
>
> To learn where the reefs and shallows lie.

The company tours but has returned to the Liang Park Awning for a season's run at least once every twenty years.

. . . called back

No doubt because we pleased them and

Because we treat our patrons well.

We do a new *yuan-ben* of love and hate

That urges piety and good,

And earns my feed-the-family-

Clothe-the-children wage.

We are better off here than anywhere.

Here, these few gifts of mine

Yield us more than would a valley full of fertile land.

Informed by Wang of the Stranger's obdurate refusal to shift to another place, Xu Jian approaches him. He is anxious not to affront a paying spectator, who abruptly asks him what play is scheduled for that day's performance. "What would you like, Master?" The reply: "That's for *you* to tell *me*; let me hear what dramas you can do." After further colloquy, Xu Jian offers in song the titles of new works in his repertory: two are Yü Yu-chih's *T'i Hung-yuan at Chin Stream* and Chang Chung-tse's *Jade Lady's Sad Lute Song*. But these are not to the Master's taste. "Can you do 'strip and fight' plays?" Indeed, Xu Jian is capable of doing such thrillers. He lifts his voice in song:

I will play you *Lao Ling-kung Sword against Sword*

Or sing *Hsiao Yü-ch'ih Mace against Mace*;

Perhaps *Three Princes at Tiger Palace*?

To the Master's, "I don't want them – name another," the resourceful actor–manager adds:

Ah, none is the equal of *Black Whirlwind at Li-ch'un Garden*.

Even this does not please. "No, another." Xu Jian ventures:

Perhaps I should do *Snow Closes Blue Pass*?

Still a rebuff. "A different one." But the actor has reached his limit.

> Have pity, my lord, my talents are not that great.

He abandons trying to satisfy the Stranger and turns to having his associates make the final preparations for the performance: Are the backdrops in place? And the banners proclaiming that he will appear in *Lan Caihe*?

> That my name is on every tongue in the Empire.

Now, as had Wang, he hopes to persuade the Master Taoist to take a seat elsewhere but meets with the same opposition. Angered, he orders the Stranger to depart, for he has disrupted the rehearsal. "I don't want to go, I'm going to see the play." Even more irate, Xu Jian shouts for Wang to lock the door to the theatre, threatening the Intruder that it will be kept locked for a week "and starve you to death!" Here ends the first episode.

The last act occurs after a good lapse of time. Xu Jian has been away and returns to the playhouse to find his former fellow-players have aged greatly, while he still looks to be only in his middle years. Wang asks him to rejoin the company. Xu Jian recalls:

> Ah, in gestures I knew no match . . .
> And I knew the pace and timing for the play.

Wang tells him: "All the costumes you wore for the plays are still kept unharmed. Here, pull back the hangings and look at them." Touched by this, Xu Jian does so, but behind the curtain he discovers the mysterious Chung Li – the Master Taoist – and a companion.

> Xu Jian, you haven't lost all thought of the world of dust . . .

Another revelation to him is that some of the members of the troupe are no longer on stage as actors but have become musicians whose new task it is to accompany fresh younger players. One reason Xu Jian has lost awareness of how much time has passed is because he has been undergoing enlightenment about his destiny under the tutelage of Taoist masters; for him, time no longer has a fixed rhythm and pace. This is a surprisingly complex play, and one might wonder if Pirandello was familiar with it when he wrote *Six Characters* and *Tonight We Improvise*.

Many of the details of stage-life fortuitously revealed in *Lan Caihe* accord with those in Du

Renjie's *Farmer's First Visit to the Theatre*, as well as in a set of songs by the dramatist and poet Tang Shi, of the late Yuan and early Ming era, works composed between 1368 and 1398; though dating from a subsequent era, this suite presents an image more or less similar.

Requested by the Academy of Music, the group of songs was intended for a dedication ceremony at the inauguration of a new playhouse in Nanking, capital of the Ming dynasty. This structure paid homage to the emperor for his many accomplishments. An account of the building is rhapsodic: its foundations were "massive", its plan and proportions "magnificent", the materials used in its construction sturdy and superior and certain "to last forever", consisting of "iron-trunked, frost-barked timber of specially selected trees from the Southern mountains". The wave-marked rock bases of the giant pillars had been "fished up from all over the Eastern ocean". Further, Dolby quotes and paraphrases: "The curving roof-tiles soar into the sky over a splendid, powerful edifice. High up, there are intricately carved and latticed windows and below, possibly leading to them, are steep steps 'a hundred feet high.' Leaning over the balustrade one has a view over vast stretches of the River Yangtse. There are fine tapering tiles stretching aloft in the form of wings of colorfully patterned mandarin ducks and projecting from the 'wind-barring eaves,' while from the corners of the eaves the 'cloud-flying' ridge-beams with grim monster tails stick boldly forth." To this, Dolby adds his own poetic word-painting of the landscape surrounding the theatre, the fabled terraces, the infinite vistas "of the kingfisher-blue slopes of the Bell mountains peeping through white clouds".

Alongside the theatre were noisy wine houses, resounding with the shouts and singing of carousers; and bath-houses from which drifted "the titillating perfumes of orchid and musk". And near by was the emperor's grand residence, whence could be heard "the roll of drums, the rattle of clappers and the sounds of all kinds of other instruments as some lofty procession enters the palace".

The poet Tang Shi likens this theatre to paradise, one that was filled with gaiety and romance, in an interior setting that was spacious and splendid. He also has praise for the company that performed in it, apparently most of its members female. The leading lady had a dancing posture "as supply wafting as the willows where sleep the sloughing silkworms", while the male lead had a singing voice that "strews one continuous string of pearls"; the energetic clown had "a flustered doggy face and weird features, body and bones all at odds with the norms of this world"; and the person, male or female, playing the overbearing official or warrior was "mighty and imposing of mien, cock-bold and martial in his bearing".

Among the spectators were young lords anxious to buy the favours of the actresses; other young blades – scholars, eager merchants – bearing gifts for them; and wealthy older men with avid eyes; all this creating an electric aura of pleasure and excitement, like the bustle of a temple fair. The poet insists that this was the most famous theatre in the world, even "supreme in the universe".

During the waning years of the Yuan reign, government officials took a harder stance towards the stage, fearing its influence, perceiving it as an incessant seedbed of sedition and immorality. Though plays were granted considerable leeway, a number of interdictions were directed against the contents of satiric and obscene ballads; and there were prohibitions against lewd or subversive puppet shows, and wandering street entertainers, who beat fish-drums to draw unruly crowds and hawk worthless nostrums; the punishment could be flogging with rods – anywhere from twenty-seven to forty-seven strokes, to be determined by the local mayor – or, in some instances, as severe as deportation or even death. One charge, lodged against nomadic storytellers, was for impeding traffic in the marketplace.

Actors, in general, were the victims of an increasing prejudice; after 1313 they were not allowed to take the all-important imperial civil service examinations, an entry to better careers; the change reduced their legal status to that of convicted felons. To protect the dignity and respect due to religious icons, a ban had been issued (1281) against representing Buddhist deities, donning skull masks and enacting the roles of demon kings in *zaju*. In some places the performance of all masked plays was suppressed. Village festivals were viewed with growing disapproval, the government wishing that, instead, the peasants should be kept busy sowing, weeding and harvesting, not wasting time at idle gatherings and costly frivolity (1317). Since many of these rules were hard to enforce *en masse* in the far-flung domain, a fine might be imposed on local magistrates or other officials for failing to implement them. Taxed by these restrictions, Yuan drama began to lose much of its exuberance, strength and originality.

Contemporaneous with the development of Yuan *zaju* in the North, the *nanxi*, another genre, was flourishing on stages in the richer and more populous South; but so few examples of this type of play have survived that historians have largely neglected it; they can be certain of hardly anything about it, so the *nanxi* has not been a promising subject for research and dissertations. Guesswork has been the major approach. Mostly what remain are fragments of songs and a haphazard, inadequately analysed collection of 107 titles of pieces from the Southern Sông to the early Ming; scarcely any names of the authors are known.

Apparently a chief difference is that the Yuan *zaju*, siphoning its tunes from Jurched folk songs, relied on the *qu*, a vigorous music, admixed with the *ci*, which was "soft and beguiling"; while the *nanxi* depended less on the *qu* and more on the *ci*, a blend more characteristically Chinese. After all, the South had successfully resisted the Mongols, so its culture was purer, its traditions largely undiluted. In the *nanxi*, in contrast to the *zaju*, the singing was not limited to solos; instead, the Southern scripts called for duets and sometimes trios, in which the three performers might be heard separately, or two were paired, or all three sang together. With the *zaju*, spoken lines usually came before a song, leading into it; with the *nanxi*, the routine was the opposite, speech was more likely to follow a musical introduction. The Southern rules for rhyming were less fixed. The *nanxi* seems also to have been more loosely organized, quite flexible, yet not lacking in power – indeed, from the handful of texts left, the plays tend to be stronger than the Yuan *zaju*. Then, too, pronunciations were at odds, the same words sounding at some variance in North and South. It should be added, however, that the *nanxi* were also presented in the North, frequently by the same companies, and Yuan *zaju* were included in the programmes of Southern troupes, eventually becoming the dominant form; that happened as the result of the long intermingling of the two peoples, notably after the Mongols were replaced and China, having been split in two, was finally reunited.

In 1920 a volume containing three complete *nanxi* scripts was found by Ye Gong-chuo (1881–?), a railway administrator, on a London bookstall among a well-picked-over collection of Ming relics. One of the plays was *Top Graduate Zhang Xie*, the story of which has already been synopsized in the discussion of Sông dramas; it probably dates from the mid or late thirteenth century, and its form is that of the *nanxi* rather than the *zaju* – the reader will recall that it concerns a surly, faithless young scholar who in a rage slashes his wife with a sword but is later forgiven, so that the couple are happily brought together again. The author, anonymous, belonged to a writing society. But could it not also be considered a *zaju*? Some scholars argue that the two forms are very much alike and should not be looked upon as truly independent genres. But haughty North Yuan literati disparaged the Southern plays, perhaps because their authors were reputedly less educated; though in fact the scripts are apt to contain more verse, "sometimes more ornate and intricate", than do most Northern ones, and spoken passages prove to be more deftly handled, the lines pointed and coherent, the humour nimble. Another objection to them was that the subjects and the treatments might be unabashedly vulgar, using slang, offensive to the Northern élite, especially the later Ming commentators. To a few critics, however, this lent the works strength; they were "natural", not affected or pretentious, the authors avoiding the sin of putting on literary airs. On occasion, the *nanxi* playwrights chose the same themes as had the Yuan *zaju* writers, even giving their works the same titles, but to a degree fashioning them in their own way, so that they ranged from being obvious plagiarisms to almost entirely new.

At the start, the *nanxi* dramatists were at work in and around the city of Hangzou, before its conquest by the Mongols. As early as 1190–94 plays such as *Zhao Chaste Maid* and *Wang Kui* won popularity; even greater success met the factually based *Wang Huan* (1268–9), relating the evil acts of an influential Buddhist priest who has been carrying on a liaison with an attractive concubine. Having impregnated her, he forces the son of one of his more humble devotees to marry the girl so as to avoid an open scandal, but afterwards resumes the illicit affair. Whispers about this spread, prompting the humiliated young husband to take his new bride and flee. To recapture her, the priest concocts charges against the pair's family, who are subjected to beatings by a court order, the unscrupulous judges having been lavishly bribed. An appeal to higher officials fails due to more bribery, and the desperate family members have even more severe punishment meted out to them. This leads the priest's innocent victims to seek justice from the far-off capital, but before a new hearing is granted, thugs hired by the ruthless and relentless priest kidnap them, carry them to a desolate place and drown them, forever silencing their anguished pleas and complaints. Word of their violent deaths outrages the public and demands are widely heard that the corrupt priest pay for his hideous crimes. Even now, the regional authorities, having also been well bribed, delay in carrying out his sentence, stalling for time until an expensive pardon comes from the capital. But the play so aroused public anger and pressure that the actual priest, Zhu Jie, the inspiration for the work, was killed in prison at the instigation of frightened local officials a bare five days before the expected order for his release reached the city.

Among the *nanxi* fragments of scripts that have been discovered are *Little Butcher Sun* and *In the Wrong Career*; their texts, brief, are incomplete; also *Killing a Dog*, attributed to the little-known Xu Zhen, and then *White Rabbit, Moon Prayer*, credited to Shi Hui, and *Thorn Hairpin*, from the pen of either Ke Danquiu or a Top Graduate Wang. What remains of them is notable for their vigour, their abundant use of current slang and lusty argot, and, in the particular instance of *Killing a Dog*, a pervasive coarseness. In *White Rabbit, Moon Prayer*, Shi Hui has not hesitated to appropriate his plot from the celebrated Guan Hanqing's *Moon Prayer Pavilion*, a drama described a few pages earlier. In places the liftings are word for word.

Though the full text of *Little Butcher Sun* is lost, its prologue escaped that fate and contains a partial summary of the ensuing action. The same is true of *In the Wrong Career*, though its introductory verses are extraordinarily succinct. The first of these two has to do with the high-spirited, simple Bida Sun who one bright, breezy spring day meets a certain Jewel Plum Blossom, of the Li family, who is selling wine in her pavilion. Quickly they fall in love and are betrothed. Bida's wiser brother, Bigui, warns him of trouble to come, but is not heeded. Jewel Plum Blossom's emotions are fickle, and not long after the wedding she returns to an affair with a former lover; the adulterous couple plot to get rid of Bida. They murder a maidservant, cut off her head, and arrange to have the husband blamed for the deed. His brother, the butcher, accepts responsibility to spare Bida, and is hanged as the culprit. By heavenly intervention, Bigui is brought back to the world of the living; he encounters Jewel Plum Blossom and extorts the truth from her. Three ghosts, among them that of the decapitated maidservant, effect an arrest, and the guilty pair are judged at Kaifeng.

In the Wrong Career tells of a young lord, Wanyan Shouma, who becomes infatuated with an actress, Wang Golden Notice. His father, an eminent official, discovers this; to escape the paternal ire, the son forthwith takes to his heels. Soon penniless, he joins the travelling vaudeville troupe staffed by his beloved's family. But is this not the wrong choice of a career? The father, sent by the government on an inspection tour, reaches a town where the company is performing. Weary, he summons the troupe to entertain him and is astonished to behold his son and the actress among the talented players. Happy to find the young man, he generously acquiesces to a wedding.

One of the most important scripts of the period is *The Lute* (1367; or *The Romance of the Lute* or *The Lute Song*) by Kao Ming (*c.* 1301–*c.* 1370), from Yongia in the Wenzhou region. It is credited with having revived and elevated the *nanxi* form by virtue of its "lofty, exquisite poetry", a text free of the vulgarities that besotted too many earlier examples. Yet it contrives to sound utterly "natural" as well. The author, a government official of superior learning, had withdrawn to a quiet retreat from the military clashes and chaos around him. Legend asserts that he dwelled in a small tower for three years while he composed the play; further, it is said that he habitually tapped out the rhythm of his verses and songs with his sandaled feet, resulting in a hole in the floorboards from the light but overly persistent pounding.

Kao Ming was annoyed by the treatment accorded the scholar protagonist in *Zhao Chaste Maid*, who to his mind was unfairly portrayed, and whose ultimate fate – his cries muted by thunder, his life ended by a lightning bolt – was not truly earned. To prove this, he set himself to write a script on a like subject, one that would justify the young man's seemingly immoral behaviour, showing that he was not wholly at fault.

The gifted young scholar, Cai Boxie, has to go to the capital to take the imperial examinations; reluctantly he parts from his home, parents, and Zhao Fifth Maiden, his cherished wife of two months. He does so well at the tests, singled out as Top Graduate, that his brilliance brings him to the notice of the Prime Minister, who chooses the unwilling Cai Boxie to become his son-in-law. Unable to withstand the Prime Minister's imperious command, the ambitious young man is wed to the daughter, Miss Nui. Now he has two wives, as well as duties which absolutely prevent his leaving the capital.

Back home, famine sweeps the region. Zhao Fifth Maiden tends to her absent husband's parents with love and incessant care. She pawns all her possessions to help them, and cuts off her hair to sell; even so, both elders die of starvation. Far away, Cai Boxie, greatly concerned, has been writing letters to them and enclosing money, but a dishonest messenger habitually steals the contents. At last, in desperation, the young woman leaves to find her husband. She plays the lute and begs, to pay her way. Meanwhile, Miss Nui, the second wife, grows aware of Cai Boxie's unhappiness. She intervenes with her father to send Li Wang, one of his retainers, to fetch Cai Boxie's parents and his first wife. Of course, Li Wang arrives too late. He is a comic figure, but one of the best-written scenes in the script is his sober encounter in a cemetery with Zhang Gaungcai, a kindly neighbour, in whose hands the absent Zhao Fifth Maiden has entrusted watch of the family farmstead and the parents' graves. In the end, all is set to rights: Cai Boxie, noble at heart, is reunited with his sweet, faithful Zhao Fifth Maiden, and promoted to a higher and even more illustrious title.

Throughout, the dialogue is nicely interlinked, the sentiment falls short of banal pathos, the humour is subtle and muted yet pleasing. These qualities and its lyricism account for much of the high regard in which the play has been held, an admiration outlasting many centuries.

Berthold remarks that much of Chinese drama has moral depth because of the pervasiveness and continued influence of Confucius's teachings. Said the Sage: "Whoever understands the meaning of the great sacrifices understands the world order as though he were holding it in the palm of his hand." The presence of this moral depth in Chinese plays is unappreciated by most Western spectators. But it may be another explanation for *The Lute*'s apparently undying appeal. Very simply, as Berthold puts it, "The consequence of this world order is that virtue is rewarded and evil punished. . . . Heroism is the highest perfection of human life, and on the stage it celebrated its most striking triumphs either in the form of mighty valor or in that of humble endurance." Here the characters are endearingly good or treacherously bad.

Zhu Yanzhang, bold leader of the successful military thrusts against the Mongols, saw *The Lute* and thoroughly enjoyed it. Not long after his final victory over the occupiers and his own accession to the throne of China (1368), he moved to draw Kao Ming into his government; the playwright evaded service to the new emperor by pretending to be mentally ill. However, given an elaborate written copy of *The Lute*, Zhu Yanzhang smiled and stated: "*The Five Classics* and *Four Books* are cloth, silk, pulse and millet – something that every household has. Kao Ming's *Lute* is like some splendid delicious delicacy, and no noble household should be without it." He ordered the court players to stage it daily. After a time, unhappy with its lack of accompaniment by stringed instruments, he commanded officials of the Academy of Music to create a somewhat different score for it, replacing Southern tunes with Northern ones, so that the orchestra would include his favourite *pipa* (lute) and *zheng* (zither). Even with this alteration, the singing had none of the stridency and harshness of most Northern music, but remained insinuatingly soft and mellifluous, a freely wandering and random sound.

The permanence of *The Lute* as a Chinese classic has continued unchallenged; it is revived there without lapse. A number of productions of it have taken place on college campuses in the United States, especially one by Chinese–American students at the University of Hawaii, which had added to its faculty a director from China. As a consequence of these, Michael Meyerberg, a Broadway producer of refined and esoteric tastes – somewhat of an anomaly – was persuaded that it would be a suitable Broadway vehicle for the young singing actress Mary Martin, then rising to become very much a star, possessed vocally of a sweet, delicate coloratura. Will Irwin completed the English adaptation; Sidney Howard had worked on it before his untimely death (1939), so the two were listed as collaborators. Some pleasing, vaguely Oriental music by Raymond Scott, with lyrics by Bernard Hanighen, was added to the score. A group of distinguished craftsmen were engaged by Meyerberg: the pseudo-Chinese décor was by Robert Edmond Jones, the direction by John Houseman, and the effect was not without an attenuated charm. Opening at the Plymouth Theater (1946), the play's critical reception was more than good enough. Even so, it had only a modest run, mostly sustained by Mary Martin's presence in the cast as the fragile, self-sacrificing wife, opposite Yul Brynner, also on his way to stardom. One song, *Mountain High, Valley Low*, has had a lasting life, if a somewhat narrow one.

Founder of the Ming dynasty, which was to hold power for well over 250 years (1368–1644), Zhu Yanzhang was not of regal blood but, instead, of plain stock, the last of a chain of hard-working farmers, gold-nugget panners and patient, watchful silkworm breeders. Even odder, in his earlier years he had been a Buddhist priest and gone about with a bowl humbly seeking alms. Becoming a rebel leader, strong-willed and given to fierce action, he had united diverse armies under his command, driven the Mongols from their capital, and then seized the throne. Established as a firm-handed ruler, he soon revealed a lighter side: he was heartily fond of theatre, as were to be other rulers among his many Ming successors. Most in the imperial line after him kept a troupe or two of entertainers at court; intermittently, huge companies lived and thronged in the palace halls, where were elegantly constructed private stages, with *zaju* and *nanxi* music resounding for hours on end.

The Ming sovereigns collected small, richly bound books containing playscripts and formed large libraries of them – as will be explained in the paragraph below, it was perilous to produce the plays and far simpler to pass the scripts from hand to hand for each individual's thoughtful perusal, which became the custom among the literati.

Zhu Yanzhang required the various princes of his expanded realm to find and send him all available volumes of songs – many of the songs inserted in playscripts – and gathered, in sum, at least 1,700 of them. Of the imperial Ming passion for music and drama there is other ample evidence: Emperor Chengzu (r. 1402–24) had an enormous anthology of stories and drama compiled, in which – along with many tales – are over a hundred Yuan and Ming *zaju* and thirty-four *nanxi*. Emperor Xianzong's (r. 1464–87) addiction to songs and playscripts was so compulsive that he "almost exhausted the world of their editions". Emperor Wuzong (r. 1506–21), harbouring much the same passion, unstintingly rewarded anyone who presented him with such esteemed gifts; on one striking occasion three gentlemen handed over several thousand volumes for his delectation. Some emperors yielded to the temptation to write their own plays, and Emperor Xizong (r. 1621–7) even took a role in one, assuming a character that he could interpret quite convincingly, that of an emperor, a person not unlike himself.

But though Zhu Yanzhang applauded *The Lute Song* and its ilk, he was wary of the stage's influence on the illiterate populace. Many of the plays were filled with implied or obliquely voiced protests at social inequality and official corruption, the gap between the privileged and the deprived, the very rich and the very poor, the well-fed and the hungry, depicted even in *The Lute Song*; such dramas endangered political stability. In 1369, a bare year after he occupied the throne, the new emperor issued a series of edicts restricting public performances. The rule against actors and their families undertaking the imperial examinations was strengthened and applied to dramatists. A more severe ban followed in 1389, when officers and soldiers posted in the capital who studied the art of singing risked having their tongues severed. The only plays that could be given were those dealing with saintly figures such as Confucius and other sages, thoroughly virtuous women, truly good sons and respectful grandsons, and other proper subjects contributing to and firmly supporting public order, civility and morality.

Actors participating in offensive works could be flogged, hit with a sharp rod up to a hundred blows. Plays that defamed the imperial court, so-called "throne plays", could bring even more atrocious punishment. Printing, selling or merely possessing seditious plays could lead to arrest and other harsh reprisals. After the edict was announced, those who owned forbidden books had five days' grace in which to burn or otherwise destroy them.

Ming drama was now largely shaped by this climate of repression. For decades the theatre had been designed largely for the imperial court, as well as for a small circle of nobles and intelligentsia. The *zaju* and *nanxi* did not immediately disappear, but the Northern plays were ever more about well-born scholars and imperilled, chaste maidens of good lineage. The earthier, everyday characters who populated the Southern *nanxi* were henceforth less frequently seen. The *nanxi* steadily lost a following among the élite, who at least glimpsed in the *zaju* dealing with the sophisticated upper class a partial refection of their own lives and more civilized and erudite interests. Most of the authors of the Northern *zaju* had been born and started their careers during Mongol and Yuan days, and now had to adapt and carry on in altered circumstances. Many of these writers were also in the professions and had other non-literary concerns; substantial numbers of them were physicians or government bureaucrats. They did not need to compose plays.

Called to the Ming court as an adviser (*c.* 1403) was a Yuan Mongol, Yang Ne. He was a skilled *pipa*-lutanist, an admired wit and clever concocter of riddles, yet was also able to turn out eighteen *zaju*, one of which, *Pilgrim to the West*, consists of twenty-four acts. It follows the journey of the pious Xuanzang and his disciples, Buddhists all, whose goal is to recover certain sacred scriptures and thereby attain personal immortality. In this dedicated quest they are confronted by a host of hostile demons and otherworldly monsters. The script rings with the noise of combat and is filled with a plethora of fabulous events.

Emperor Chengzu's court was graced by Jia Zhongming (1343–post-1422), an acquaintance or friend of most of the better playwrights and literary figures of his day, and whose own writings are a fecund source of information about his contemporaries in the Ming world of letters and theatre; it is not quite clear whether a laudatory biography of him is not in fact a pseudonymous self-congratulatory autobiography. His friendship with the ruler was formed before 1402 while Chengzu was still a prince. Jia Zhongming was reputedly of noble bearing, handsome, always richly attired, and prized for his kind, generous temperament – according to what might be his self-description. At court, Emperor Chengzu commissioned him to write a song or play on every festive occasion and always strongly commended his poetry. In all, Jia wrote about fourteen plays and many songs and essays, winning unfailing praise from his peers. His works display his considerable knowledge of the Yuan *zaju* form and his respect for its conventions; he was probably helped by having the emperor's vast library of *zaju* freely open to him. At the same time, some of his plays show a tendency to bold novelty. His *Dream of Immortality*, for one, departs from the conventional by not only making use of both Northern and Southern songs, and by not having the male leads and female leads alternate musically, but also by giving the virile Northern songs to the man and having the lady responsible for the more dulcet Southern ones.

Among Jia Zhongming's good friends at court was Tang Shi, who had risen from a lowly post in a local government department. After a lengthy spell there, frustrated by his lack of advancement, he had gradually joined the ranks of wandering entertainers. About 1380 he, too, came to the notice of the prince, the future Emperor Chengzu, who subsequently enlisted his service at the palace and granted him many royal bounties. Two of his plays earned much applause, and he composed a vast list of songs – *qu* – an impressive number of which remain popular. It is known that he lived after 1422.

Of princely aspirants to literary fame, few if any outshone Zhu Quan (d. 1448), sixteenth son of the fertile founder of the Ming dynasty. With a passion for knowledge, he occupied himself by writing discourses on disparate topics such as the intricacies of chess, the secrets of divination, the delicate technique of performing on the *qin* (dulcimer), the mystical aspects of Taoist yoga. He was especially apt at composing songs for plays, authored a dozen meritorious *zaju*, as well as the earliest serious disquisitions on the prosody of the Yuan *qu*, and two volumes, one entitled *Jewelled Grove Refined Rhymes* (1398) and the other, in the same year, *Great Peace Tablets for Correcting Sounds*. He participated with equal zest in the political and military affairs of his day.

Of like stature and fully as prolific was Zhu Youdun (1379–1439), a grandson of the Ming regime's founder – he was the eldest scion of Zhu Yanzhang's fifth son – who contributed thirty-one *zaju*, none of which is lost. His literary career began somewhat late, after 1425, when he reached about forty-six and became Prince of Zhu. Like his uncle, Zhu Quan, he was fascinated by learning, choosing to probe historical subjects, making himself an authority on music and calligraphy. Many of his songs stayed current and were widely heard centuries after he wrote them.

His plays revolve about sympathetically portrayed female characters, a surprising range of them, including lady saints, artful whores, concubines and troubled singing-girls. But he also depicts vigorous bandits and warriors, building up great excitement. His *Peach Spring Scenes* introduces several Mongol characters, who use their native language and songs, a rarity. His technical experiments go beyond Jia Zhongming's: he distributes the singing to more than the two leads and does not hesitate to use choral song. Deliberately he borrowed aspects of the *nanxi* and Southern music, while forfeiting the intrinsic and extrinsic strengths of Northern *zaju* drama.

The playwrights of the late fifteenth century seem to have been less gifted and productive. The supremacy of the Northern *zaju* slowly faded. A new style of script superseded it, appearing first in the South and called the *chuanqui*; it carried to an extreme a potentially distracting tendency which is to be noted in *The Lute*, a fondness for engaging in overly fine writing, flaunting elegant phrases and elaborate images for their own sake, having them conspicuously adorn the soliloquies and formerly succinct dialogue. The vogue is equivalent to that encouraged in sixteenth-century England by Lyly's *Euphues* and in seventeenth-century Spain by the affectations of Gongora y Argote, now called Gongorisms; but Ming dramatists seem to have developed this form of excess well ahead of those precious Europeans. One of the founders of *chuanqui* is Shao Can, a prominent scholar of ultra-orthodox leanings, who engaged not only in overly literary flights of speech and inflated emotions, but also supported very strict morality and had conservative political loyalties. His *Perfume Sachet* has characters who express themselves in quite inappropriate, high-flown prose and verse, and frequently quote from ancient sources – the *Book of Odes* and the Tang poet Du Fu – in a mere display of pedantry.

Shao Can, in turn, was inspired to some extent by Qiu Jun (1421–95). A good many of this school of Chinese euphuists were natives of Kiangsu or Chekiang, but Qiu Jun was from the deep South, a Cantonese. Like the others, he was scholarly and attained high government positions, as Grand Academician and Grand Protector of the Crown Prince, to cite a couple; he was expert in many phases of

Confucian philosophy, on which he wrote with profound insight, coupling that with a broad knowledge of Taoism, Buddhism and medical lore, combined with a talent for poetry. In his youth, legend has it, he authored a novel, *Beautiful Loves*, describing illicit liaisons based on his personal experiences. This did dire harm to his reputation, and in an attempt at extenuation he composed a play, *Five Moral Relationships*, calculated to portray him in a better light. His ploy was not fully successful, some Ming critics faulting him for "showing off his learning and writing stinking rotten pedantry".

The precedents set by Shao Can and Qiu Jun were followed by a covey of other dramatists, some of whose works were less literary in tone and hence a bit more adaptable to staging. One who did not conform to the "Mandarin" mode is Shen Shouxian (*fl.* 1475), whose *Three Origins* echoes market slang, a refreshing exception; though any such excursion into vulgarity invited risk. On the other hand, the unquestioned respect in which these politically orthodox scholar–dramatists were held served to protect the theatre from outright official and public hostility, at a time when it was otherwise regarded as suspect. As notables like Qiu Jun and Shao Can dipped their brushes in ink to write plays, the enterprise could not wholly be outcast or condemned.

Moving on rapidly to the next century, one encounters Kang Hai (1475–1540) and Wang Jiusi (1468–1551), each of whom wrote a play on the same subject and with an identical title: *Wolf of Mount Zhong*; both scripts are derived from a legend told by people of many races in many distant and diverse regions world-wide, a truly universal motif. A philosopher, having saved a wolf from hunters, is disconcerted to realize that the ungrateful beast intends to devour him. He demands that three arbitrators decide whether his fate is a just one. Actually, both plays are satiric, their animus aimed at a particularly disliked government official.

Kang's script is in four acts, the traditional *zaju* form and length; that by Wang (*c.* 1510) is one act – such shorter works were becoming commonplace, as were some that stretched to five, six or as many as seven acts. The rules for the typical *zaju* were dissolving. This applied to the admixture of music, too, with Southern songs heard far more often, the Northern dying out. The scarcity of the vanishing Northern tunes began to interest scholars with a historical bent. Li Kaixian (1501–68) was such a one. Coming from the region of Shantun, he rose through the bureaucracy to hold at thirty-nine what was a major government post, whereupon he withdrew from public life to his native village. In retirement he devoted his varied talents to composing, singing and playing stringed instruments. To abet his zealous collecting of folk songs and popular ditties, he gathered around him a broad cross-section of musicians and entertainers; he also compiled a library of writings about music that was by far the largest in the Shantun area. His own compositions were unconventional, and he had a rare facility with prose and verse. He is the author of six *zaju*, probably akin to Jin and Yuan *yuanben*, as well as three *chuanqui* offerings. Best known of the latter is his *Precious Sword* (printed 1549), another political satire, denigrating the malign, hated Prime Minister Yan Song. Among its characters are adventurous bandits, types not usually found in a *chuanqui* play. Some of the writing is euphuistic, but for the most part the style has considerable force.

Increasingly in the Ming period, music became the dominant element of a theatrical work, whether *zaju*, *nanxi* or *chuanqui*. Among the populace, newer kinds of songs and instrumental pieces gained overwhelming if transient favour, while the older forms, the *qu* and the *ci*, were subtly altered to cope with each usurping fad. To trace the regional and ethnic origins and distinctions between the various new musical idioms is far beyond the scope of this book, quite apart from all manner of Chinese music being inherently alien and baffling to Western ears. In the last decades of the sixteenth century, however, a fresh sort of music, Kunshan-*qiang*, was created as one among many and finally took over, being heard in the theatre as well as widely among the novelty-loving public. This new type of composition was introduced by the singer Wei Lianfu (who lived some time after 1522) and by two old music masters fancifully named Yuan the Beard and You the Camel-hump – doubtless inspired by their physical lineaments – later assisted by the admired songster Zhang Yetang and others emulating him. It blended tunes and keys of *qu* and *ci* in an unusual fashion, often radically, so that old songs, after such transpositions, could no longer be recognized. As Dolby describes it, "Essentially Southern in character, but utilizing both Southern and Northern *qu* tunes for its basis, it was accompanied by strings and various pipes and flutes. The cool, plaintive note of the bamboo flute became the most characteristic accompaniment of Kunshan-*quiang* singing." It was also called Shuimodiao music, that is, "water-polished music", because of the patient craftsmanship required to fashion it.

Its popularity waxing at a rapid pace, Kunshan-*qiang* was borrowed by Liang Chenyu (1520–80, or later) and inserted into his *chuanqui*, *Washing Silk* (1579); the play brought him almost unprecedentedly loud applause and celebrity. The story is about the intrigues of Fan-Li, a merchant turned politician, and his beloved, the irresistibly beautiful Xishi, who helps the King of Yue take vengeance on a foe, the King of Wu; after which the enamoured pair wisely flee together into the wilds. In style it echoes to some degree the refined prose and verse of ever-influential *The Lute*, if a touch more "prettified" and "elegant". A growing school of playwrights quickly chose it as a model. Scripts using this precious language and Kunshan-*qiang* music came to be known as Kunqu (wrought from "Kun *qu*"), soon destined in large measure to supplant the Yuan *zaju* and Southern *nanxi*, as well as the bombastic *chuanqui*, too.

To meet this change in taste, plays written earlier and abounding in Northern *qu* and Southern *ci* were, for pragmatic reasons, promptly adapted to incorporate the melismatic Kunshan-*qiang* music in their stead, which also called for providing new instrumental accompaniments. Oddly, before much passage of time, Kunshan-*qiang* had less popular appeal but was ever more the preferred music of the court and intellectual élite, one explanation for this being that the plays retained their elevated language. Theatres were now places of entertainment mostly designed for the aristocracy and educated upper class. The effect of this shift in musical likings was that a considerable number of ancient and classic plays were transformed from what they had originally been.

Two exponents of Kunshan-*qiang* are Tang Xianzu (1550–1617) and Shen Jing (1553–1610). Independent, outspoken, though also endowed with benevolent traits, Tang Xianzu's candid fault-finding of incompetent fellow-bureaucrats ruined his civil service career. Transferred to distant Kwantung province (1590), he continued to voice criticism of the government. His transgression brought about the final loss of his post as county magistrate, a consequence which he had perhaps deliberately sought (1598). In retirement he had time in which to express himself in print, a task for which he was well equipped. He poured out reams of prose and poetry, including four *chuanqui* that accrued much praise. They embody aspects of his philosophy and bright bits of practical wisdom gathered from his experiences as a judge. His style is far from simple – it is intricate and even convoluted, which is why his plays qualify as *chuanqui* – but this results not from a desire to parade his learning but from his respect for nuance and minute detail. In the view of some critics, however, he lacked a sharp ear for matching verse to music, an ability to select the best measures and accents, though more kindly commentators say that these failings might have been owing to a wish to experiment.

His most cherished play is *Peony Pavilion*. Dreaming too ardently of a perfect lover, an impossible ideal, Du Fair Maiden pines to an early death. While staying in the home where she dwelled, Liu Mengmei, a young student, is entranced by her portrait; also dreaming, he converses with her. Miraculously, she returns from the grave and joins him. Liu Mengmei journeys to the capital to undertake the imperial examinations; by chance he meets Du Fair Maiden's father, a high-ranking official, who furiously refuses to believe the young scholar's story. Threatened with dire punishment, Liu Mengmei is reprieved by word of his success in the examinations and Du Fair Maiden's intervention, which leads all three to a joyful union.

In his poetic vein, Tang Xianzu depicts the fifteen-year-old Du Fair Maiden as so shy, yet coy, that she only glances sideways in a mirror, lest her fully reflected image flatter her too much; but deplorably a mere profile robs her of half her seductive features – she is not beset by false modesty. Too many of the flowery similes and metaphors are hyperbolic, though a good number of them are quoted from other bards – a practice of *chuanqui* writers. The shifting moods of the action, from waking reality to rapturous dream and back to disappointing reality, are handled quite smoothly. Later European dramatists, among them Calderón, Strindberg and Hauptmann, are not more accomplished at doing this.

(Four hundred years later, at the close of the twentieth century, a revival of *Peony Pavilion* by a touring Chinese company was to cause a sharp international controversy.)

Like Tang Xianzu, several other Ming dramatists came from Linchuan in Kiangsi Province. Embracing his literary style, they are known as the Linchuan School, a group made up of Wu Bing (d. 1650), Meng Chengshun (*fl. c.* 1644) and Ruan Dacheng (*c.* 1587–1646). Of these three, two had unfortunate ends: Wu Bing, captured by Qing forces, refused to take nourishment and died of self-starvation, and Ruan Dacheng, after a tumultuous life, perished in a battle against a last segment of Ming loyalists.

Tang Xianzu's contemporary, Shen Jing, was from Wujiang in Kiangsu Province; a rival, he expressed scorn at Tang Xianzu's ineptitude in setting words to music and even composed a satiric *qu* song-set about it. He wrote with authority on dramatic and musical theories. Very handsome from childhood, and a prodigy, he entered government service in his early adulthood and ascended high, but dogged by ill-health was forced to retire in his thirty-fifth year (1588). He turned to literature, composing plays and *qu* poetry. With great self-confidence he revised *The Lute* and even several of Tang Xianzu's scripts, adapting the Northern tunes in them to the now more acceptable Southern type. He published further comprehensive treatises on poetic and musical forms. To him are attributed two collections of *zaju*. In contrast to those by Tang Xianzu, his *chuanqui* nicely fit together words and melody, though he chided himself for perhaps being over-fussy and precise in this respect. His language is "natural, easy", quite effective.

Shen Jing had many disciples; they formed the Wujiang School of dramatists. Among them was his nephew, Shen Wujiang (*fl. c.* 1628), who like him turned out poetry and scholarly essays on music. Wang Jide (d. 1623/4) boasted a collection of several hundred Yuan *zaju*.

The free-spirited Yuan Yuling (1600–74) is recalled as a "wag" and a "rogue" who twice succeeded in demolishing what might have been a rewarding career, first by a scandalous liaison with a whore, and again by heedlessly giving vent to his acid wit on what he should have realized to be prohibited subjects.

Finally, the school included Feng Menlong (1574–1646), one of China's most revered, indefatigable, versatile men of letters, an eminent novelist and poet who also revised the scripts of other playwrights, wrote perceptive studies of the classics, and compiled heaps of off-colour folk songs, raunchy jokes and fabulous tales.

Somewhere between these two schools, Linchuan and Wujiang, is placed Ye Xianzu (1566–1641), who kept somewhat distant from them. The period also boasts few more colourful and idiosyncratic figures than Xu Wei (1521–93); unlike his peers, who composed both *zaju* and *chuanqui*, he was dedicated to *zaju* only. Nervous and quite lacking in self-control, often given to frenzies, he nearly lost his mind from worry when a patron of his was ordered to prison, a turn of events that led Xu Wei to repeated attempts to kill himself. Then he himself was sentenced to several years in gaol, until a friend's influence freed him. He took refuge in his country home, where he devoted himself to painting – he excelled at calligraphy – and poetry, his lyrics celebrating the glories of Nature and the encompassing world created by man. His five published *zaju* were widely read, four of them going through many editions; he contributed a definitive treatise on *nanxi*, offering interesting theories about music and precepts for dramaturgy. Thoroughly eccentric, he broke many conventions, the structure of his plays irregular in the number of acts, while their musical scores mixed various idioms in bold, helter-skelter fashion. Dolby remarks: "Others tried to imitate him, but he stood alone in his ebullient genius, rhyming and versifying in the spirit of the Yuan, akin in versatility and vigor to the best playwrights of the classical period."

In the closing phase of the Ming dynasty the accumulated stock of plays – ancient, more recent, contemporary – was abundant; actors had less need for new scripts, and the prestige accorded playwrights was diminished. As has been mentioned, a great many plays were only printed, passed around to be read, never acted. What kept writers busy was adaptations, revising old scripts, updating them, sometimes improving them, sometimes not, adjusting them to new music. (One notes that in roughly the same era in Elizabethan and Jacobean England, journeymen dramatists were occupied at much the same task to earn a meagre sustenance. Even masters such as Shakespeare and Webster did such work.) In this late Ming period, therefore, the poets are less prominent and players and theatrical companies come to the fore.

The court, the aristocracy, the highest-ranking officials – Prime Minister Shen Shixing (1535–1614), for one – and even wealthy merchants still kept private troupes; in the instance of the merchants, the performers often doubled as household servants. On occasion the prince, lord or prudent merchant might rent out his band of players to mitigate the expense. A few authors of ample means had their own companies. One was the politician Ruan Dacheng who retained a group that he meticulously trained to act in his plays, which they toured. Another as fortunate was the playwright and rich landowner Zhang Dai (1597–1689?), born into a family in Chekiang that maintained not one but several bands of comely actresses.

Despite the government's frowns, independent companies persisted, some as resident repertory troupes in small or large towns, others confining their activities to a single region; and, as always, some footloose, wandering ragtag from village to village, as hungry and besotted actors have done immemorially.

Some changes from tradition had gradually come about. As the number of characters in a script multiplied, so did the size of the companies obliged to cast them. Where formerly the roster included just one player specializing in a certain kind of role – the bumptious clown, the dauntless warrior, the heavy-browed villain – now there might be at least two performers belonging to the same category, one ranked as the "first" and his colleague as the "secondary" in a standard part.

Costumes were ever more costly and elaborate, as were carry-on properties – the Chinese concentrated on these, rather than on the *mise en scène*, which generally continued to be sparse. This was to the advantage of the many troupes that were financially straitened; since they could afford little more than the barest essentials, they relied on their ingenuity to make up their wants, with the audience's imagination adding whatever else was lacking.

But some companies were prosperous, endowed by a royal patron or spendthrift lord. An inventory of fifteen Yuan *zaju* in one repertory reveals that the following garments and accessories were required: forty-six varieties of hats – for a rich student, a minister and so forth; forty-seven kinds of brocaded robes and silken gowns – male or female; five sorts of shoes, sandals, embroidered slippers and many-coloured stockings; six different enchased belts and gilded girdles – with the male attire slightly more resplendent than that of the female. One listing was of a "smock sprinkled with gold". There were a few stabs at realism and historical accuracy: a mendicant might appear in rags; a poor woman in a patchwork, quilted jacket; a soldier in garb appropriate to his rank and race – Mongols wore "Uighur hats", Chinese recruits had distinctive "red-bowl" helmets and were sheathed in "black-cloth nail armour"; and a high-ranking commander was instantly recognized by his bright, loose "full-length battle robe".

Sound-effects from backstage had become even more emphatic: barking dogs; cock-crows, to mark the time of day; honking geese, to denote the migrating season; shrieking parrots; drums and other deafening battle noises; thunder-claps; and all kinds of strong action were punctuated by clashing gongs.

Temple stages were still available, as well as open city squares and private gardens; large guild halls could be borrowed, or a wealthy family's courtyard; or platforms could be set here and there, by a river-bank, in a grain-drying yard or on a hillside. Finding places to perform, travelling companies had to be endlessly resourceful. If a formal stage or raised platform was not to be had, a red carpet would be spread outdoors on the ground or on cobblestones in a hospitable courtyard, or within a hall of a manor house. The orchestra would be seated on the back edge of the carpet. Actors made their entrances from the left of the spectators, and departures in the opposite direction. Because of its intimate nature, Kunqu drama was well adapted to simple, improvised settings: it usually called for delicate singing, to a soft musical accompaniment – no big drums or loud gongs – and more finesse in physical movements. The phrase "on the red carpet" became synonymous with "on stage", even in more commodious great houses and palaces. In time, the now traditional red carpet was placed on stage to indicate the actors' special area.

For outdoor performances, watched by restless crowds and surrounded by the echoing din of the marketplace, with its food-stalls and shouting vendors, other kinds of music, stronger, more strident than Kunshan-*qiang* were preferred, such as Yiyang-*qiang*, with heavier percussion and more sturdy singing. Also, action-filled plays were a better choice here, in place of the refined Kunqu. Indeed, the selection of a play was a clear sign of how a host regarded a guest, the degree of his taste and sophistication. If a rough-and-tumble piece was offered, it might be seen as an insult by a person of cultivation.

One reason the companies had grown larger was the multiplication of stock characters, the conventional four main categories having gradually been subdivided into as many as twenty-five, each externalized by fine distinctions in make-up, costume and gesture. There was no longer just one type of "beard" role, or of penniless young scholar, or ardent lover; the warrior who formerly had simply been called the "painted face" might now be joined or supplanted by the "big face" or "second face"; or, among comedians, the traditional *chou* might be abetted in his mischief by a "little face". These subsidiary figures were visually identified by strong black lines and glaring colours of chalked whiting applied to the actor's features, together with a reliance on dress, voice and formal posture. In his memoirs a renowned *chou* tells of his having to master no fewer than twenty-seven important, clearly specified steps and stances, together with a vocabulary of thirty-seven finger, hand and sleeve manipulations, and a great many other imposed techniques.

Though the government kept up a close watch on these semi-illicit entertainments, huge audiences flocked to them, especially at times of festivals and at country fairs. The stage also won the disapprobation of puritans, official and non-official, who busied themselves seeking to sustain decorum and a proper moral climate. Such concerns were well founded. Expenditures for the bejewelled headdresses, silken costumes and ostentatious properties – decorative swords, intricately braided whips, daintily painted fans, glittering fly-whisks – might be denounced as unseemly, since these years were often marked by famine and consuming plagues elsewhere in the country. In 1592 a firm ban on plays was issued by one provincial governor.

Objections were voiced to the presence of women who took roles in "lewd" dramas, their seductive gestures and glances evoking unsanctioned desires in male spectators. But the aristocracy paid no heed to these dour complaints, which were broadened to include shocked protests against "useless diversions" such as hunting, polo, horse-racing, hawking, gambling, chess and other trivial pursuits. Another charge was that plays not only stirred wanton feelings but also the debilitating emotion of melancholy when audiences were moved to tears by over-sentimental stories. To be deplored, too, was that some young men of estimable families sought to participate in stage performances, fancying themselves possessed of acting talent; hardly a path to a virtuous life. Warnings against this became shrill and were raised in chorus, ensuring that they were clearly heard. One gentleman, Tao Shiling (d. 1640), listed all plays, ancient and modern, in one of four categories, designating which of them were suitable for weddings and other sober family celebrations, or only for banquets, or else for private stagings. He singled out those that he deemed "loathsome", "disgusting", "lamentable", certainly not to be viewed by men – fathers, sons, brothers – and their women-folk, while together in the same room. Even the cherished classics, *West Wing* and *Thorn Hairpin,* ought to be shunned, because they were salacious. The books containing them should not be sold, nor actors allowed to memorize and recite lines from them. Other commentators were simply against plays of any kind. But Tao Shiling – as did Wang Yangming (1472–1528) – suggested that some dramas could be used to proselytize and, by providing good examples, sharpen consciences and encourage general reform.

The trend was against mixing the sexes in troupes; there were growing numbers of segregated all-male and all-female ensembles, with the men artfully impersonating women, and the women shouting, feinting and striding as male characters. The male companies were increasingly preferred, their leads winning larger public followings. The women more often accrued notice and praise for ballad singing rather than for acting, though sometimes unjustly. At the very least, all needed pleasing voices.

Among the most renowned during the Ming years was Zhou Tiedun, envied for his "verve and agility", which was likened to that of a falcon or hawk aloft in flight and abruptly swooping at its prey. Also prized was Yan Rong, given the honorific name Keguan ("Worth Seeing" or "Admirable"), handsome of aspect, with a strong voice and a mobile, expressive face, envied by his rivals for his mastery of gesture and posture. Once, during a poignant scene, he failed to rouse the audience. At home, in a mood of self-flagellation, he studied himself in a mirror, sharply slapped himself, yanked his beard until faint from pain. For hours, clasping a wooden doll – the role had called for him, as an aged former minister, to protect an orphan baby – he continued to stand before the glass, going over the part without cease, singing and reciting the poet's emotional lines. On stage, at the next performance, his portrayal was so stirring that thousands of tearful spectators wept loudly and wailed hoarsely until utterly exhausted by grief. At home once more, he took a pose before the mirror, bowed to his proud reflection in it, joyfully exclaimed: "You really *are* 'Worth Seeing' now!"

Even more zealous devotion to his craft and concern with professional status was exhibited by Mah Jin, of Islamic extraction and popularly known as Mohammedan Ma. Dolby recounts that, by chance, two presentations of a play were competing in Nanking. Mah Jin, to his humiliation, heard that he was outshone by the actor in the other company taking the same *jing* role, that of the actual stern former Ming Prime Minister Yan Song. In response, he quit Nanking and hastened to Peking, where – in disguise – he took employment as a footman in the lavish dwelling of a very important minister, a humble post he held for three years, never exposing his true identity, all the while studying with unswerving closeness the style and speech mannerisms of his haughty master. At last he went back to Nanking to resume the role earlier abandoned, and now performed it with a fidelity that forced even his rival to recognize the superiority of his interpretation.

As ever, novices who aspired to lead singing roles had to undergo long, unremitting preparation. One Ming teacher conducted his classes in a sweet-scented, darkened room, as he faced his students, who caught the exact beat of the music by watching his moving, fuming "baton", a glowing incense-stick.

Among the limber, hurtling acrobats, the best-trained came from the province of Anhwei, far-famed for its youths' superb physicality. They performed the frequent battle scenes, their tumbles, leaps and twirlings not meant to be a realistic image but a breathless projection of headlong attack and counterattack, merely suggesting the confusion and dismaying celerity of combat, shrewdly choreographed. The "fighting men" bore no weapons, as they had to be unimpeded while engaged in their nimble feats; but in one memorable instance, a bout staged by the private troupe of Mi Wanzhong (d. 1628), the fearless actor–athletes wielded lethal swords and flung sharp-pointed spears, displaying sure control, along with a confidence mutually shared. (A model Chinese patron of the arts in the enriched Ming era, Mi Wanzhong held political office and was equally noted as a "painter, calligrapher, seal-carver, landscape gardener and collector of ornamental rocks".)

An exception to the spare scenery was an experiment by actress Liu Sunlight Fortune. In her late Ming staging of *The Resplendent Emperor of Tang Travels to the Moon*, the platform was bare save for a black curtain at the back. A Taoist magician, charged with readying the impending space journey, swung his sword and, to the accompaniment of loud percussion, the black curtain drew apart to expose a full moon encircled by fluffy clouds – a painted cut-out – whereon was enthroned the Moon

Fairy. Other mythical inhabitants of the lunar orb surrounded her: Wu Gang, eternally doomed to chop at a cassia tree; and the White Rabbit, pounding his necromantic nostrums in a mortar. They were partly concealed by a diaphanous silk veil, with lamps behind it, creating a hazy moonlit effect, of a slightly green hue like that of fresh dawn. A length of cloth was laid to bridge the otherwise airy path upward; on this the Magician slowly preceded the Emperor on their approach to a luminous destination.

By the close of the Ming era, in spite of the government's suspicions and frequent harassment, the theatre was well entrenched, still fostered generously by the élite, and attended regularly by common people. Besides a host of playwrights, of varied talents, a captious tribe of critics flourished. From the intelligentsia came learned essays on dramaturgy and the technique of musical compositions. The issuance of anthologies of plays, especially of Yuan *zaju*, helped to save outstanding examples of them for posterity and was carried on by a worthy roster of busy scholars.

Tang Xianzu and Shen Jin had major libraries of Yuan *zaju* that are a significant source of knowledge about those works. Another important contribution by a collector and anthologist is that of Zang Maoxun (d. 1621), though unfortunately he chose to edit the plays at will, cutting and adding lines, changing bits of action, which befogs later estimates of them. Meng Chengsun's two anthologies (1633) duplicate earlier selections of Yuan and Ming *zaju* on a large scale, but are an enriching legacy none the less. Many of the collections are strikingly illustrated by woodcut artists, giving fascinatingly detailed pictures of a colourful age.

The fateful year 1644 saw the end of the two-and-a-half-century Ming ("Brilliant") reign, swept away by the Manchus, a Tungusic people from what is now called Manchukuo, in north-east China, who some ethnologists believe to have been related to the Jurcheds, the much earlier northern invaders. Taking advantage of disunity and chaos during an ongoing Chinese rebellion, they breached the Great Wall. Marching against Peking, they were assisted by disaffected generals, officials and even some literati. At the approach of the foe the last Ming emperor ordered his wife to commit suicide, then knotted the girdle of his robe about his neck and hanged himself. A farewell note was pinned on the lapel of his robe: "We, poor in virtue and of contemptible personality, have incurred the wrath of God on high. Therefore I myself take off my crown, and with my hair covering my face await dismemberment at the hands of rebels. Do not hurt a single one of my people." (Quoted by Durant) The conquerors entombed him with due honours.

The Manchus established their Qing (or Ch'ing, "Unsullied") dynasty, fated to last 267 years, into the twentieth century (1644–1912). More sensible than their predecessors, they embraced and deftly encouraged many positive aspects of Ming culture, successfully wooing the loyalty of a large segment of their new subjects. The Chinese now enjoyed a prolonged spell of peace and expansion that allowed the nation's varied arts to prosper, though the years brought occasional disturbances.

During a span of four decades, in particular, two emperors – K'ang-hsi (1661–1722) and Ch'ien Lung (or Gaozong, 1711–99) – were refreshingly enlightened, in some respects surprisingly tolerant. Truly appreciative of literary accomplishments, each of the two rulers had a fondness for the paintings and precious porcelains for which China is celebrated. The studious Ch'ien Lung, who was exceedingly well read, wrote 34,000 poems, one of which – the subject "Tea" – came to the eyes of the French iconoclastic philosopher Voltaire, who expressed his pleasure at it by sending "his compliments to the charming King of China". Everywhere, the erudite Ch'ien Lung was hailed as "the most lettered man in his empire".

In the early Qing, the drama differed little from what it had been, though change did slowly occur. A minority of playwrights had belonged to the Ming faction and were still angered at the new regime. They shunned posts in its bureaucracy and engaged in more creative pursuits. Peking, formerly the Ming capital, was now the seat of governance for all China and the centre of theatrical activity, attracting dramatists to it. Kunshan-*qiang* was still very much in vogue, and many Kunqu composers were drawn from Kiangsu Province, where that music had originated. Also contributing writers was Suzhou, the first home of Li Yù (c. 1590–c. 1660; here, the name "Yù" implies "Jade"), to whom are attributed no fewer than thirty-one scripts, along with two that were written with collaborators.

Much of Li Yù's early career was passed in service of an unspecified nature in the household of Prime Minister Shen Shixing. To Li Yù these were years of frustration; he was convinced that his employer's son was placing obstacles to his advancement. His resentment found voice in four of his most widely liked plays. After the Manchu conquest he turned his back on employment as an administrator. Some of his later plays deal with very recent, almost contemporary historical and social events. In one, the populace rises up against unjust officials in an attempt to free a virtuous man who has been wrongly accused; in another, Li Yù depicts a strike organized as a protest by rebellious weavers. Besides these, a large group of his scripts have romantic themes, touching love stories.

Equally prolific was Zhu Zuochao (*fl. c.* 1644), author of thirty or more plays, one of them jointly with several other dramatists. Among them was Zhu Hao (or Zhu Que, or even more widely known as Zhu Suchen, *fl. c.* 1644), who on his own composed *Fifteen Strings of Cash*, a work of enduring popularity, so appealing that it stays alive in endless, well-presented stage and screen adaptations even now.

Another early Qing playwright, Ye Zhifei (*fl. c.* 1644), from Suzhou and credited with eight plays, engendered serious trouble for himself when one of his scripts portrayed a pirate in a too kindly light.

This was considered subversive; the author was thrown into prison, where he almost lost his life. As has been seen, over and over, playwrighting in China was hazardous.

From Suzhou, too, came Quiu Yuan (*fl. c.* 1644), a raucous, bohemian poet, fond of tippling, adept at painting snowy landscapes. To him are attributed eight plays. Quite a different sort of person was Zhang Dafu (*fl. c.* 1644), a simple austere soul, indifferent to worldly possessions, exceedingly well learned in Buddhist scriptures. His asceticism did not prevent him from composing twenty-three dramas before he chose to retire to a Buddhist monastery. At times the "Suzhou playwrights" tended to sound pedantic, but their output proved to be stageworthy, with dialogue that is plain and effective. They have earned a great many revivals.

In referring to one of China's major playwrights, Li Yú (1611–85), a problem arises: his name is almost identical, at least to Western eyes, to that of his contemporary, Li Yù, alluded to a few paragraphs above. But the reversal of the accent over the "u" alters the character meaning "Jade" to one that identifies a "fisherman". However, Li Yú is also known as Li Liweng, or "Old man with a bamboo rain-hat", which is what he will be called here. His personal history is most remarkable, as are his multiple accomplishments. During the Ming reign he aspired to an official post and took the examinations repeatedly, only to fail again and again. With the accession of the Manchus he relinquished his early goal, but found himself desperately needing to support his forty wives, concubines and legion of offspring. To ease his heavy burden, he elected a turn to the theatre, organizing a troupe of singing-girl actresses, with whom he toured arduously in every region and nook of China for a decade and a half, performing scripts of his own. Mostly they were put on in the residences of ministers and other patrons, where he was often welcomed as not an employee but a guest. Highly gifted, he mingled with eminent men, yet his expenses continued to be so harsh that he was frequently out of pocket, totally impoverished. Several times he had to resort to the sale of whatever home he happened to be occupying, in each instance along with its remarkable garden – added to his other talents, he was an outstanding horticulturist. Further, he ran a bookshop, the Mustard Seed Garden, a name borrowed from a landscaped retreat once his in Nanking. His literary labours extended far beyond those for the stage; he is a cornucopia of poems, novels, discourses on gardening, architecture, travel, hygiene, nutrition, home furnishings and sexual practices, together with helpful advice on the cultivation of womanly charms and wiles.

He had interesting ideas about what is required of dramatists, set forth in his *Random Expression of Idle Feelings,* a volume of essays by no means casual but thorough and insightful. He advocated the use of simple dialogue and verse, plain enough to be readily comprehended by the ordinary man, even by the uneducated and by mere children. He ranked passages in prose on a level with those in verse and song. He stressed the great need for empathy on the part of the author, who must put himself simultaneously in the hearts and minds of both actor and spectator. Of himself, while composing a play, he revealed that "his hand grasped the writing-brush but his mouth mounted the stage". Again: "The flourishing of the spoken parts in plays really began with me. Half the world applauds me for it, while half condemns me for it. My admirers say: 'Until now, dramatic speech was always regarded as just talking, something to be uttered just as the mood takes one at a time. But Liweng creates dramatic speech as literature, making a real effort, and weighing the pros and cons of every single word. . . .' My critics say: 'the songs should be the main thing. . . . What is the point of making the tree bigger than the roots?'" He recognized that actors who only speak cope with more difficulties than those who only sing. "There must be two or three in every ten actors who excel in singing, but, as for those skilled in spoken delivery, there can be only one or two in every hundred." (Translation: Dolby)

As he stated, he was regarded with contempt by élitists for his cavalier attitude towards long-held conventions, but his reputation and popularity spread as far as Japan, where his amazing versatility inspired emulation. One Japanese author wrote a book and unscrupulously put Li Liweng's name on it, to abet its distribution. His plays are mostly about love and its intrigues; they illustrate his theories, the characters expressing themselves colloquially, capturing the flavour and muscular strength of natural speech. (*The Mustard Seed Garden* was later adopted as a title by one of Li Liweng's sons-in-law who collaborated with others on what up to their day was a definitive history of Chinese paintings, a work still deemed invaluable.)

A quite different sort of artist was You Tong (1618–1704), proudly displaying his erudition and mastery of elegant prose and verse. Though renowned for his eclectic knowledge, he, too, met with frustrations in his career, which he began as a police magistrate (1652–6). The times were disturbed by the exposure of corruption in the imperial examinations that involved a wide circle of well-connected persons. While on a journey, You Tong was delayed at an inn and decided to make use of his unwelcome idleness by writing a satirical play about the scandal. It was produced in Suzhou, but on the first night the actors were seized by the police and mercilessly flogged for a rash affront to authority. A demand was made for the names of the author and producer of the offensive script. You Tong, by now safe in Peking, was able to temper the official wrath through intermediaries, and the affair was quietly dropped. Chastened, he himself took further examinations, which led to his appointment to the Hamlin Academy (1679). There he participated in the compilation of an authorized history of the Ming dynasty, as well as a huge bibliography of all paintings of the now vanishing Ming era.

In a like approved "literary" style are the twenty-two or more scripts of Wan Shu (*fl. c.* 1692), also an author of a study of prosody and music. He himself excelled at neatly fitting words to music. Of him it was said that "he slept and ate the Yuan playwrights", and some critics agreed with Wu Xuefang who rated him "the best of those sixty years", specifying the span from late Ming to early Qing. For Wan Shu, playwriting was an avocation; full-time, he was an aide to the Governor General of Kwangtung Province and wrote only when free from his demanding duties. His efforts were greatly appreciated, at least locally. As soon as Wan Shu completed a script, the admiring Governor General commanded its performance by his private troupe. This did not wholly satisfy the poet, who was inclined to depression and died feeling that his gifts had never won the broader recognition they deserved.

For a time, most of the new playwrights came in a stream from the South, but not so Pu Songling (1640–1715), who originated in Shantung Province. His forefathers, either Mongol or Turkic, had held high posts during the Yuan dynasty; from them, he apparently inherited a strong sense of fantasy, which led him to collecting 430 short tales dealing with the supernatural: ghosts, sprites, odd creatures and emanations of every conceivable kind. (He kept a cup and teapot on a small stand before the gate to his house; passers-by were invited to partake of the tea, but only if they shared strange tales with him. He maintained this unusual, successful device for two decades.) He wrote poems, many ballads, a lengthy novel and three plays, these last unfortunately lost. Some of the ballads, however, suggest what his stage-works might have been like, especially one, *Spell to Tame the Shrew*, consisting of thirty-three sections resembling brief episodes or acts in a play. In Shanghai dialect, very colloquial, a bit raunchy, the verses are set to Northern folk-tunes, using not the soft Kunshan-*qiang* music but the rougher Yiyang-*qiang*, which by now was everywhere, overtaking the hitherto prevalent Southern mode.

Indeed, Yiyang-*qiang*, too, was splintering, elements of it being adapted to a scattering of ever more novel musical forms that steadily encroached upon it and Kunshan-*qiang*. For a while it seemed that Kunshan-*qiang*, long the most esteemed theatre music, was destined soon to be prized only by the sophisticated, when suddenly two stage masterpieces appeared and for a short time re-established it.

From Chekiang Province, Hong Sheng (1645–1711) had the good fortune to be wed to the grand-daughter of a prime minister; in addition to boasting a noble strain, she was very knowledgeable about music and perhaps transferred some of her passion for it to him, or else reinforced a love for it that he already shared. A student of some of the most prominent scholars and poets of his day, Hong was a gifted versifier and held independent ideas about poetry that set him at odds with his teacher, the widely respected Wang Shizhen (1634–1711, not the sixteenth-century dramatist Wang Shizhen, 1526–90). In view of his mentor's reputation as a peerless *shi* poet, the young man's stance was quite reckless and hardly apt to help him advance in the academic realm. None the less, Hong pressed upwards, travelling to Peking and entering the National Academy (that is, the "National University").

He published several outstanding essays and composed ten or more plays, one of which, *The Palace of Eternal Life* was begun in Hangzhou (1679) and completed eight or nine years later (1687 or 1688). A stage production followed shortly and revived the fortunes of the troupe that presented it – the actors had been losing a following because they clung to now unfashionable Kunshan-*qiang* musical accompaniments. Joining in the excited acclaim, Emperor Shengzu enlarged on his praise by a grant of twenty silver taels to the members of this company.

The performers, delighted, invited the author to a special performance of excerpts from the play during the following summer of 1689. He brought along friends but failed to include a Mr Huang, who was deeply offended at not having been asked. Vengeful, Mr Huang took note that the nation was in mourning; there was a death in the royal family and entertainment of any sort was prohibited. He wrote to the authorities, urging stern punishment of the transgressors. The response was quick; all those who had participated in the showing, or were in the audience, were dismissed from their official posts, among them the jovial, quirky poet Zhao Zhixin (1662–1744), a close friend of Hong and newly in receipt of a hard-earned doctorate. Other accounts of the incident put the blame on the eccentric Zhao Zhixin for an affront to a vindictive, highly placed minister, a censor. Ringed by guards, Hong was banished from Peking. In exile he composed a mournful poem about his misfortune. Several years later, penniless and staggering drunk, he tripped into a river and ignominiously perished.

But *The Palace of Eternal Life*, true to its name, lived on, coming to be regarded a classic. Borrowing a Minghuang theme already much exploited, a romance between the Tang Emperor and his wife on whom he dotes, Lady Yang Yuhuan (Yang Gui-fei), Hong relates in fifty acts the progress of their love affair, her poignant early death and the lone, bereft Emperor's gripping sense of loss. Next comes her subsequent reappearance as a spirit, beholding what transpires after her earthly departure. Her scheming relatives are drastically punished. The Emperor orders a life-sized likeness of her carved in wood by his finest artists. A dissident, An Lushan, leads a rebellion in which an attempt to assassinate the Emperor fails, and An Lushan is killed by his adopted son. The uprising put down by loyal Tang armies, the triumphant Emperor returns to his capital. Passing the grave-site of Lady Yang, he commands her exhumation to accord her a more elaborate burial. The tomb is empty; only a hint of her perfume lingers in it. To assuage his shock, one of her maidservants brings him a pair of her stockings, but they merely exacerbate his pervasive grief. Once in his palace again, he summons a Taoist magician to put him in touch with his beloved's spirit. The master's necromancy and the intervention of the gods create a bridge that leads to the moon; ascending to it, Emperor Minghuang is finally reunited with Lady Yang. Themselves descended from the gods, they are again in the heavenly realm to which they belong, their deep, otherworldly love everlasting.

A lyrical paean to love and what amounts to an extra-terrestrial fidelity, the play is densely packed with incidents, highly imaginative, offering a parade of breathing, realistic characters and a plot that is well crafted throughout. Hong took his script through three painstaking revisions and also enlisted the help of a music expert to choose and fashion the songs, though he himself was unusually well informed on such matters. The happy ending, added because tradition insisted on one, has its illogic mitigated by the introduction of a supernatural agency. Despite this, the main content has loud echoes of personal loss and grief and also resonates harshly with tragedies brought on by festering political ambitions, treacheries and civil strife. Along with the erotic passages, too, there are suspenseful martial episodes that lend the story heightened theatricality.

A very brief excerpt, translated by Dolby, shows how evocative of time and place is the dialogue. In the absence of any solid or painted setting, an innkeeper, with only song and prose, describes his wine-shop, in which a bit of action is to occur:

> We're a very special public-house, with a high-class line of wine,
> I swore there'd be no booze on tick when I put up my sign,
> So if you have the money, you can drink and never stop,
> Without, you won't get water, not a single drip or drop!

I'm the taverner of this New Feng Restaurant and Grand Wine Emporium here in the center of Changan. This public-house of ours is situated between the eastern and western markets of the city, and there's always a mass of traffic here, crowds bustling to and fro. Without exception, all the lords, princes, government nobs, business people, and the ordinary soldiers and farmers from in and around the capital call here for a couple of pots in our establishment. Some come just for a drink, some have snacks with their wine, some buy liquor to carry out, and some make party bookings for drinking on the premises. It's one never-ending job serving them all. There, the words are hardly out of my mouth, and here comes another gent with a thirst!

Wealthy patrons laid out fortunes to have their private troupes do the utmost justice to the play, one salt merchant in Yangho expending 400,000 taels for opulent costumes and rich properties, perhaps quite needlessly. A high-ranking official, mesmerized by the episode in which the tearful Emperor Minghuang gazes at the figure of Lady Wang, laid out money to have her image carved in excessively costly, scented garu-wood.

Fame came as explosively to Hong Sheng's contemporary, Kong Shangren (or K'ung Shang-jen,

1648–1718), which led their admirers to exclaim of the two: "Hong in the South, and Kong in the North!" A native of Shantung, Kong claimed illustrious ancestry as a sixty-fourth descendent of Confucius. Inordinately proud to have such a forebear, he devoted much of his time to genealogy, tracing the many family branches and publishing a lengthy volume containing minute details of his findings. In addition to this pursuit, he was an authority on ritual and music. Emperor Shengzu, visiting Shantung, ordered Kong Shangren to discourse for him on those diverse subjects, and then requited the lecturer by naming him to the prestigious Imperial Academy. Later, he was appointed to major posts in the Yellow River Conservancy (Honan Province), as well as to the Peking Board of Revenue. Then he shared a fate somewhat like that of Hong Sheng: a reading of his play at the Manchu palace apparently led to his dismissal from all his posts, the work's sympathies being so obviously slanted towards the Ming dynasty's lost cause and blighted fortunes.

Besides his scholarly and administrative accomplishments, Kong Shangren was a shrewd collector of antique bronzes and scroll paintings, fine calligraphy and epigraphy (inscriptions). By chance, a *hulei* (mandolin), a small Tang instrument, came into his hands; this, along with other things, is said to have inspired his first effort as a dramatist, a collaboration with a friend (1694). But other scholarly sources suggest that his subsequent *chef-d'œuvre*, *The Peach Blossom Fan*, was already in his mind and under way five years earlier; it was only completed after a ten-year span, with much revision and polishing, in 1699. It had its première at the imperial palace in the autumn of that year and by the ensuing spring had already evoked a broad popular response elsewhere. During its prolonged composition he solicited the advice of Yang Shouxi, an expert on all matters musical, to assure himself about the best wording and settings of all the songs.

Though not as lengthy as Hong's *Palace of Eternal Life*, Kong's *The Peach Blossom Fan* unfolds through forty acts. Such plays are apt to seem even longer in performance because of the slow tempi of much of the singing and acting; most often they were not viewed by spectators at one sitting, but instead on four or five consecutive occasions. An opportune time for that might be the extended birthday celebration of a royal family member, or the protracted New Year's holiday or other lengthy festival. Since the legendary or historical material of many of the scripts was apt to be familiar to a well-read audience, it was hardly necessary to be present throughout; one could attend intermittently and still follow the story. Further, as the plays achieved the status of classics, the actors, to spare themselves, might offer only particular episodes, scenes of already proven attraction; or spectators might come for just their favourite episodes and leave at their discretion, some preferring lovers' interludes, some noisy battle scents, others – especially children – rough comedy, and still others the most captivating music.

The Peach Blossom Fan reflects what were comparatively recent historical events, the disorderly times following the collapse of the decadent Ming dynasty, which had occurred a bare fifty years earlier, so that there were still those in the audience who had personally experienced the suffering and chaos. Hong gathered his material by an assiduous canvass of his elder kinfolk who had harrowing stories to impart to him. At each performance, in the first years of the play's enactment, there would be spectators with tears welling forth because of their sharp, painful memories. Almost all the leading characters represent actual participants of that scarcely past, tumultuous era; they were easily recognized. Doubtless this topicality and immediacy accounted in part for the initial emotional impact of Hong's long, sweeping drama.

The play begins a few months after the suicides of the Ming emperor and his wife. Most of the North is occupied by the Manchu armies, but a defiant, last segment of loyalist forces is holding out in Nanking. Among those still faithful to the Ming cause and sworn to fight against the invaders is Hou Fang Yü, a heroic, idealistic scholar–politician, and his cherished Li Lady Perfume, a singing-girl. Much unscrupulous intrigue to wield control of this tottering remnant of Ming power is engaged in by Ma Shiying and his feral associate Ruan Dacheng. Seeking the support of Hou Fang Yü, Ruan Dacheng, not only an ambitious political schemer but also a playwright, is rebuffed; he vows to retaliate. He concocts false charges against Hou Fang Yü, who is seized but escapes. In her lover's absence, the influential Director of Military Supplies, Yang Wen-ts'ung, seeks to coerce Li Lady Perfume into marriage. Despite lavish inducements, she refuses him; he persists. In despair she dashes her pale brow against the rocky ground in an attempt to end her life; in her hand is a fan given to her by Hou Fang Yü as a token of their pledged love; by her act the fan's leaves are spattered with blood.

After a late-night abduction Li Lady Perfume is to be wed to the ruthless Yang Wen-ts'ung. To avert this, her place is secretly taken by her veiled foster-mother and singing teacher, Su K'un-sheng, and the outwitted minister goes off with the wrong bride.

Meanwhile the frightened, exhausted Li Lady Perfume sleeps. The stained fan is noted by Yang Wen-cong, the celebrated artist. Touched by the girl's plight, he quietly applies himself to restore the precious fan, using the juice of a verdant plant, transforming the blood spots into the image of a peach blossom.

Soon cast off by Yang Wen-ts'ung, whom she had deceived, Su K'un-sheng is married again, this time to a military officer about to join his army. Generously, she offers to bear a letter to Hou Fang Yü; Li Lady Perfume finds herself unable to express her feelings and decides to send her fan instead, its message implicit.

The fan is delivered to Hou Fang Yü, who is now in the ranks of forces opposing the Manchus. He returns to Nanking, only to find that Li Lady Perfume, obstinately refusing all suitors and other demands made on her, is now immured as a lowly entertainer in the palace, where he cannot reach her. Learning that Hou Fang Yü is in Nanking, his enemy Ruan Dacheng has him arrested and imprisoned. The ultimate victory of the Manchus brings freedom for Hou Fang Yü and others, while Li Lady Perfume flees from her indenture at the palace. Their reunion, with Hou Fang Yü still in possession of the fan, takes place in a temple, a palace retreat. But a Taoist priest rips apart the fan, shredding its decorated leaves; he persuades the couple to separate again and withdraw forever to monastic lives of meditation and Taoist quietism, emancipating themselves from physical desires and other worldly human attachments. This unhappy ending is most unusual in classic Chinese drama.

As has been mentioned, most of the characters are based on historical persons. Though the focus is on the frustrated love affair and the endless misadventures of Li Lady Perfume and Hou Fang Yü (both of whom are drawn from life), other story threads and subsidiary plots deal with rivalries and manoeuvrings by obsequious ministers and wily sycophants at the rump court in Nanking presided over by the effete and feckless Prince Fou, who has been proclaimed Emperor and for a few months is a claimant to the throne left empty by the suicides in Peking. Much time is taken up with debates over campaign strategies and political arguments among fervent loyalists and dissenters who are members of either the Revival Club or the Eastern Forest Party. For variety, there are episodes of amorous dalliance in a pavilion, an idyll by the banks of a stream; clashes on battlements; revelry, loud with music and dancing at the court; and a rehearsal of a play within the play in which the reluctant Li Lady Perfume is cast as the heroine at the would-be Emperor's behest after he first hears her sing. In a cavalcade of characters – more than thirty – are doughty, gallant military leaders, simple soldiers, boatmen, priests, booksellers, artists, minstrels and ordinary people, quite vitally depicted. All this is coupled with an almost self-conscious display of the poet's erudition, an array of countless allusions that only the most learned among the spectators could be expected to grasp and appreciate.

K'ung Shang-jen's style is less dense than that of Hong Sheng, as can be discerned by comparing the following excerpt to one just above from *The Palace of Eternal Life* – the translation here is by Sir Harold Actor and Chen Shih-hsiang, in collaboration with Cyril Birch:

> CH'EN [*sings*]: Hard by the examination halls
>> Is the Ch'in-huai pleasure-quarter.
>> Young candidates compete
>> At once for honours and for softer charms.
> WU [*sings*]: Double Fifth, the gay Summer Festival,

Is over in a twinkling.

The charms of Nature endure,

But local celebrities are soon forgotten.

CH'EN: Life at the inn has been so lonely that we came to the river to enjoy the festival.

So far we have seen none of our friends; I wonder why.

WU: I suppose they have all gone boating. Ting Chi-chih's water pavilion lies yonder;

let us go there. [*They enter with lanterns.*]

CH'EN[*calling*]: Is Old Master Ting at home?

This exchange sets the place and fixes the season, quite sufficient for the spectator to imagine the "where" and "when" of the action, but it hardly captures the animation conveyed by the tavern-keeper describing the location of his wine-shop and the busy city traffic hustling past it in two directions in Hong's play. Some will praise K'ung Shang-jen for fulfilling his task with a greater economy of means, however.

The dialogue in *The Peach Blossom Fan* is far more ornate and less natural than in Hong's play, as witness these speeches by Li Lady Perfume when she awakens from her faint and discovers that her foster-mother has been sent to deceive and wed the brutal Director of Military Supplies:

[*Speaks*]: The Prime Minister's hirelings would have forced me to marry, but how could I betray

my   lord?

[*Sings*]: They persecute me, feeble blossom afloat on the mist,

Helpless before the arrogance of these ministers.

But to preserve my purity, jade without flaw,

Gladly I wound the flower-like bloom of my cheeks.

[*Speaks*]: My poor mother is most to be pitied! Suddenly she left without a word, to take my place

on that disastrous night. Her bed remains, but when will she return?

[*Sings*]: Like a peach petal adrift in a snowstorm,

Like a willow catkin wafted by the wind,

Hiding her face behind her sleeve, she left at dead of night.

Now I am left alone.

No one to brush the dust from my coverlet,

Desolate,

A flower that opens for none to view.

[*Speaks*]: When I think of all this, I am heartbroken.

[*She weeps and sings*]: A broken heart,

> How many tears that fall!
>
> And never a companion's cheery call,
>
> Only the knocking of the curtain-hooks.

[*Speaks*]: I shall take out my precious fan again and read my beloved's poem. Ah me, it is stained
with blood. What shall I do?

[*Sings*]: The bloodstains spread in bright confusion,

> Some thick, some thin, some heavy and some light;
>
> Not the cuckoo's tears of blood,
>
> But raindrops reddened by the peachbloom of my cheeks
>
> Spattering this silken fan.

And so forth at length, with ever more elaborate and far-fetched similes and metaphors.

Much as patrons of private troupes laid out large sums to do justice to Hong's *Palace of Eternal
Life*, others now vied to stage *The Peach Blossom Fan* with all due éclat. A rich salt merchant, also from
Yangzhou, expended 160,000 taels on a production of the play. Today, however, full versions of it tend
to be more widely read than are ever acted.

The first two Manchu rulers, Emperor Shizu (1644–61) and his vigorous successor, Emperor Shengzu
(1662–1722), whose reigns together spanned seventy-eight years, took pleasure in the drama, among
the arts, and included plays in entertainments at the palace. At the order of Shizu, Wu Qi (1619–94)
wrote *Loyal Griefs* for enactment at the court and won a higher government post. Emperor Shizu was
also fond of alluding to passages from the classic *West Wing*, with which he was very familiar. Emperor
Shengzu had a private troupe at all times. Both of these rulers favoured Yiyang-*qiang* music over Kun-
shan-*qiang*, which continued to lose status after its brief re-efflorescence with *The Palace of Eternal Life*
and *The Peach Blossom Fan*. Puppetry also interested Shizu. Once, during a banquet at court honouring the Grand Lama and a group of Tartar princes, a puppet show so awed the visitors that they left
their food and wine untouched. Only the solemn Grand Lama, mindful of his dignity, lowered his eyes
and paid no heed to the antics of the flexible, manipulated figurines.

But these two Manchu rulers also moved to deny theatre to the always restless populace; not without reason, they feared that the drama was a dangerous instrument for subversion. Nor were the

theatres without faults: in their choice of material, some openly pandered to lewd appetites and tastes. Occasionally Emperor Shengzu relented; in 1683 he gave 1,000 taels of gold for the staging of a *Maudgalyayana* play, a work offering gruesome visions of Hell and its hosts of harassing demons, a drama that at least taught a moral lesson. In 1713, to mark his sixtieth birthday, the emperor mounted a city-wide pageant and gala fair that entailed a truly extravagant outlay; heading a progress from his palace in Peking to his second palace at a considerable distance outside the bedecked capital, he passed grandly decorated arches, booths and staged performances, the plays and actors assembled from every region of his now vast, solidly consolidated realm.

By some accounts, Shengzu was murdered by his son, Emperor Shizong (1723–36), who held on to the throne for a comparatively brief thirteen years. Inordinately suspicious of books and theatre, which he viewed as threatening tools for his overthrow, he promptly enlarged a system of spying throughout his domain. In particular, he found fault with those who shared his Manchu strain yet frequented playhouses; his officials and soldiers ought not to scant their duties in idle diversions but rather give their time to traditional, virile sports such as archery, equestrianism and the martial arts; to enforce this, theatre-going by most persons in the regime's employ was forbidden. He also objected to ministers and high administrators maintaining private troupes, a frivolous waste of money and an opening to moral corruption. To get around this fiat, one resourceful commander drafted his actors into military service, allowing them to live and eat at government expense. He and other offenders were investigated and subjected to harsh reprisals. Also prohibited were plays with religious overtones and supposedly performed in honour of the ruler by the citizens of Suzhou and Songjiang; Shizong pronounced those aspects of the scripts to be mere pretexts for evading the law. A similar ban was issued against putting on plays at funerals, as was a custom; and against staged portrayals of Guan Yu, the God of War (originally a hero-general, later enskyed).

Lengthier than any enjoyed by all his predecessors and successors was the ensuing reign of Emperor Ch'ien Lung (or variously Gaozong or Quianlong), from 1736 to 1799 – he abdicated in 1795, lest it seem that he had surpassed the remarkable longevity of his grandfather Shengzu's rule, but in fact he was in charge of the government for another four years, until finally deposed by death. This allowed him to dominate China for sixty-three years. His era was one of prosperity and expansion, achieved by his untiring energy and stable temperament. He was hailed as a paragon for his encouragement of the arts and what then passed as the sciences, an accolade that perhaps was not fully earned. True, he himself is credited with having composed 34,000 poems, among them the one on "Tea" that delighted Voltaire; but of what length and quality most of them were is not really known, and they are likely to have been "spontaneous", mere jottings. But the very throne he sat on was an artistic masterwork, as he demanded it must be. Like several of his Manchu ancestors, he was a gifted painter. He was fond of delicate porcelains; his was the period when *Famille Rose* attained its fullest perfection, boasting a brilliant glaze spread over reproductions of fragile flowers and ripe, many-hued fruits. As has been remarked, he was acclaimed for his vast learning. Under his aegis, clusters of industrious scholars gathered "facts" from all fields of existent knowledge, one collection said to fill 36,000 volumes. He was generous, even extravagant, in his personal support of the drama, in which he frequently took pleasure. On his aggrandizing travels and inspections through the Yangtze Valley, which he undertook on six tours in the years from 1771 to 1784, he was welcomed by ambitious stage performances in many cities and towns. He also chose to have plays put on at observances of his birthday, and when receiving foreign diplomats and other eminent guests from beyond the distant borders of his realm.

An account of such a festive event is contained in the diary of Lord George Macartney (who was later to be an earl), serving as British ambassador on a mission to the emperor in 1793. This diary, quoted by Dolby and others, provides a bright, interesting picture of Chinese drama at the end of the eighteenth century.

We went this morning to Court, in consequence of an invitation from the Emperor, to see the Chinese comedy and other diversions given on the occasion of his birthday. The comedy began at eight o'clock a.m., and lasted till noon. He was seated on a throne opposite the stage, which projects a good deal into the pit; the boxes are placed above, behind the lattices, so that they can enjoy the amusement of the theater without being observed. Soon after we came in the Emperor sent for me and Sir George Staunton to attend him, and told us, with great condescension of manner, that we should not be surprised to see a man of his age at the theater, for that he seldom came thither, except upon a very particular occasion like the present; for that, considering the extent of his dominions and the number of his subjects, he could spare but little time for such amusements. I endeavoured in the turn of my answer to lead him towards the subject of my Embassy, but he seemed not disposed to enter into it farther than by delivering me a little box of old japan . . . and a small book, written and painted by his own hand. . . .

The theatrical entertainments consisted of great variety, both tragical and comical; several distinct pieces were acted in succession, though without any apparent connection with one another. Some of them were historical, and others of pure fantasy, partly in recitative, partly in singing, and partly in plain speaking, without any accompaniment of instrumental music but abounding in love-scenes, battles, murders, and all the usual incidents of the drama.

Last of all was a grand pantomime, which, from the approbation it met with, is, I presume, considered as a first-rate effort of invention and ingenuity . . .

In the audience, besides the British envoys, were mostly Manchu officials, but also a number of "Mussulmen, chiefs of those hordes of Kalmucks". After an intermission, which lasted from one to four in the afternoon, the company reassembled for the rest of the programme, which took place on grass in front of "the great imperial tent". Here there were "wrestling, dancing, tumbling, acrobatics, balancing acts, 'posture-making' and juggling", which did not really hold Lord Macartney's attention, for he was of the opinion that such feats were far better performed at home in England at the Sadler's Wells. Even the equestrian acts did not impress him, "although I had always been told that the Tartars were remarkably skilful in the instruction and discipline of their horses".

The fireworks did win his applause. In addition:

However meanly we must think of the taste and delicacy of the Court of China, whose most refined amusements seem to be chiefly such as I have now described, together with the wretched dramas of the morning, yet it must be confessed there was something grand and imposing in the general effect that resulted from the whole spectacle, the Emperor himself being seated in front upon his throne, and all his great men and officers attending in their robes of ceremony, and stationed on each side of him, some standing, some sitting, some kneeling, and the guards and standard-bearers behind them in incalculable numbers. A dead silence was rigidly observed, not a syllable articulated nor even a laugh exploded during the whole performance.

(Thanks must go to J.L. Cranmer-Byng, who has edited Macartney's journal and saw it published in 1962.)

The British mission proceeded on to Kwangtun Province, where there were further exhibitions by a company of comedians dispatched from Nanking to keep the visitors occupied and always in good humour. Here posterity is afforded an invaluable glimpse of a typical presentation of that day:

The theatre, which is a very elegant building with the stage open to the garden, being just opposite my pavilion, I was surprised when I rose this morning to see the comedy already begun and the actors performing in full dress, for it seems this was not a rehearsal, but one of their regular formal pieces. I understand that whenever the Chinese mean to entertain their friends with particular distinction, an indispensable article is a comedy, or rather a string of comedies which are acted one after the other without intermission for several hours together. The actors now here have, I find, received directions to amuse us constantly in this way during our time of residence. But as soon as I see our conductors I shall endeavour to have them relieved, if I do it without giving offence to the taste of the nation or having my own called into question.

In case His Imperial Majesty Ch'ien Lung should send Ambassadors to the Court of Great Britain, there should be something comical, according to our manners, if my Lord Chamberlain Salisbury were to issue an order to Messrs Harris and Sheridan, the King's patentees, to exhibit Messrs Lewis and Kemble, Mrs Siddons, and Miss Farren during several days, or rather nights together, for the entertainment of their Chinese Excellencies. I am afraid they would at first feel the powers of the great buttresses of Drury Lane and Covent Garden as little affecting to them as the exertions of these capital actors from Nanking have been to us.

The names Sheridan, Kemble and Siddons will be familiar to those knowledgeable about the eighteenth-century English theatre. It is not clear how well equipped were Macartney and his party to comprehend Chinese, or how much they knew in advance about the unique conventions of this stage; a lack of understanding might account for the boredom they generally felt with it. On the other hand, Emperor Ch'ien Lung was very curious about European culture. He recruited two Jesuits to teach his musicians, who were instructed in how to put on *Cecchina*, a comic opera that was currently enjoying success in Rome. The emperor liked it so much that he commanded the formation of an orchestra of eighteen youthful instrumentalists, trained to play in Western fashion.

Some accounts have it that Empress Xiaoyi (1737–75), one of Ch'ien Lung's wives and the mother of his successor, Emperor Renzong, was an ex-actress from Suzhou.

But while Ch'ien Lung was ordering his scholars to compile tomes of "facts" from all fields of learning and fostering a range of plays in his palace, he was simultaneously ordering the destruction of thousands of other books and decreeing alterations and excisions in yet others, besides persecuting authors who were too outspoken – even their immediate families and descendants were at risk – and shutting theatres that attracted ordinary citizens. This policy was never carried out to full effect, because theatre was too prized by the masses. But the official opinion of it was none the less harshly pervasive. Though retaining and exploiting his reputation as a cultivated benefactor of the arts, the emperor issued a series of edicts hostile to them from 1774 to the end of his reign; they were to be enforced quietly and with specified "circumspection", restraining all forms of literature and setting severe punishments for those disregarding the sharp-edged guidelines. These grew progressively more restrictive. The chief "sins" were hints of antipathy to Manchu rule or nostalgic references to Ming days, along with any form of what was loosely defined as "immorality". Step by step came new prohibitions, some in Peking, others only in the provinces, where less outside notice would be accorded them. "Discretion" was stressed again and again in instructions distributed to regional governors. Night performances were banned, as were those enlisting the services of monks and nuns, such works purporting to be for charitable purposes. Officials were forbidden to have their own acting troupes, and especially those constituted of singing-boys, nor were young actresses to be lodged in the private homes of the very rich, though boys and girls were sometimes allowed to take stage roles at court. Scripts in the vernacular, whether enacted or merely printed, were outlawed as too "coarse"; hence Kunshan-*qiang* dramas were the most acceptable (besides, they were too literary and not widely read). In some parts of the empire, even *West Wing* was denied a licence.

This "inquisition", often subtle but all too successful, was directed against music, too. Certain groups of folk-singers, belonging to what was known as the *yangge*, were silenced, and Yiyang-*qiang* was looked on as suspect. In reports to Peking from officials in far-out regions are summaries of investigations into the origins of each of the musical genres and determinations of which were more frequently used in seditious works. Even costumes were subjected to surveillance: were they glorifying styles that were unsuitable because they were associated with pre-Manchu dynasties? Events occurring earlier than the Ming era, perhaps in the Southern Sông and Jin periods, might be proscribed as dramatic material. Even in the most remote "mountainous, out-of-the-way" regions, governors boasted of exercising a "constant look-out" for violations of Peking's strict dictates. Every visiting company was warned of the unyielding limits that must be observed in stage performances.

In 1777, or the next year, Ch'ien Lung set up a censorship bureau in Yangzho, which after four years of research published *Ocean of Plays*, classifying scripts as to their orthodoxy, thus equivalent to a Vatican *Index*. The watch kept on dramatists was unceasing, the details of their works minutely scrutinized.

Despite the emperor's assertion that under his benign rule no one was punished for reckless writings or careless spoken utterances, more than a few literary offenders paid with their lives. In one instance a scholar impulsively criticized a dictionary earlier sponsored by Emperor Shengzu; in the article he also thoughtlessly used the names of Confucius and the Qing emperors, a practice not countenanced. He was executed; twenty-one members of his family were taken into custody; a son and grandson were put to death, and other sons sent into exile and there enslaved. Three officials deemed to have mishandled the affair were deprived of their posts, as was a fourth who by error had composed a poem paying tribute to the dictionary.

A more frightful incident occurred in 1778 having to do with the dramatist Xu Shukui; he was already dead by the time the slow-moving censors scanned his work and judged it. His corpse and that of a son were exhumed and totally dismembered; a grandson was executed, a second son sentenced to slavery in a distant northern region populated by barbaric tribes; in addition, two of Xu Shukui's hapless students were meted death penalties. The Prefect of Yangzhou and a local magistrate endured a flogging before their banishment, and also condemned to perish were the Financial Commissioner of Kiangsu and a secretary. The Commissioner expired in prison before the date set for his dispatch. The Prefect and luckless magistrate were faulted for not having handled the case more expeditiously, allowing the offender to die of natural causes. All of Xu Shukui's work was expunged, only one play escaping the destruction.

The list of such repressions is long; writers, actors and theatre people in general lived in a constant state of anxiety. The government portrayed the stage and those who associated with it as a world of harlotry and moral decay, where were celebrated murder and other forms of violence, abductions and illicit love. The authorities even complained about the contents of puppet skits, and a rein was put on traditional religious dramas. Henceforth they could be enacted only at already well-established festivals, the number of which was gradually reduced. Certain rituals should no longer be staged as a kind of exorcism against locust plagues.

Sharper was the official hostility towards wandering troupes, because they brought strangers – vagabonds – into towns and villages; at night, when the men were no longer employed on stage, they were likely to scatter through dark lanes and alleys to commit thefts and other malefactions; besides, the women in such companies were too ready to beguile simple male citizens and sell themselves to any who would pay.

Wherever plays were put on in a town, permanently or in passing, crowds gathered; this inevitably led to pushing, quarrelling, rowdyism and criminal deeds by jostling pickpockets and deft cutpurses, glib fortune-tellers, devious gamblers with board games, all inimical to quiet and public order.

At Ch'ien Lung's court the staged entertainments were sumptuous, with actors robed in "costumes of Suzhou silk and pure gold". The emperor commissioned original works and adaptations from well-chosen writers, among whom was Zhang Zhao (1691–1745), an on-again, off-again royal favourite. A native of Kiangsu Province, who while young had sought a government career, he moved quickly and steadily upwards, by 1733 achieving a high if incongruous post (for a man of letters) – President of the Board of Punishments. A revolt by Miao tribesmen in Kweichow Province two years later seemed to offer him an opportunity for further advancement; incautiously, he volunteered to stamp out the uprising. For his subsequent failure he was sentenced to death and gained a pardon only because of his outstanding skill as a calligrapher, an art of abiding appeal to the capricious emperor. A fortunate detail was that Zhang Zhao's brushwork closely resembled Ch'ien Lung's own, so that it has since been suspected that many configurations purported to come from the imperial hand are in fact examples from the able brush of the playwright. By 1747 he was restored to his former lofty post, and had also been appointed head of the Office of State Music, his knowledge of that art being sure and capacious. Yet another of his talents was painting, in which he especially shone with his representations of dazzling plum blossoms.

Commissioned by the emperor, again looking upon him benignly, the versatile Zhang Zhao provided five works suitable for presentation at court. His contributions are works of extraordinary length, in what was to become a standard format: ten sections, each of twenty-four acts, adding up to a cycle of 240 acts; given in full, they would take ten days to unfold. Essentially these scripts are compilations of other, far earlier authors' novels, short stories and dramas, their ideas and characters borrowed, a few episodes lifted from here and there, disparate episodes and fragments pieced together into a changed, coherent whole. Cunningly combining the plots of several writers into a single new drama, now his own, his procedure was like that of a craftsman assembling a figurative mosaic of differently coloured stones. The tag affixed to such works is "bumper plays". Zhang Zhao's declared purpose was to "correct" the music and elevate the moral tone of the scripts that he raided: he removed any comments that might be offensive to his patron and inserted speeches that would inculcate strong feelings of loyalty to the emperor, or instil emotions of Buddhist piety and filial respect in the hearts and minds of spectators. In this worthy endeavour he was at times assisted by Yinlu, Prince Zhuang (1695–1767), Emperor Shengzu's sixteenth son, close to the throne but hardly a likely heir.

Golden Statutes for Promoting Virtue, derived from a Ming *Maudgalyayana* play, is typical. It retains only two or three tenths of the original script yet is now twice as long, with material from various stories and Yuan *zaju* added to it. *Precious Raft for a Pacific Era* is based on the sixteenth-century novel about the journey of Xuanzang, the revered Tang Buddhist pilgrim, to learn more in India about the tenets of his faith. The play is lengthened by extensive quotations from Buddhist scriptures. The Qing court was now Buddhist, and Zhang Zhao himself was a devout believer.

Possibly he was also chosen to edit plays by other living authors whose scripts were submitted for presentation at the palace. Death befell him while, a good son, he was *en route* to his father's funeral.

The "bumper plays" were usually given on the occasion of a festival, each work coming to be associated traditionally with a particular ceremonial event, such as the rites at year's end when demons were driven out. Some works were put on in full, but not infrequently only an excerpt, a segment of ten acts or two segments of twenty, would be offered.

At the imperial palaces the stages had been redesigned and much enlarged; three of them still exist. In height three storeys, they also have five sizeable "wells" beneath them, which means that they really consist of four levels. This allows a portrayal of various realms, from a top possibly representing Heaven, down to the lowest which could be Hell; above, Buddha might reign, while far below swarm demons and devils; the storeys between might be inhabited by lesser gods and mere mortals. These assignments of place were always flexible, depending on the demands of the play. Elaborate stage-machinery, winches attached to iron wheels, could raise a five-storey pagoda from the depths to the spectator's eye-level or higher; similarly, five large golden lotuses could be lifted to sight and then, as if by magic, open wide their petals to expose as many seated, contemplative Buddhas resting on them. To show two score of the Teacher's disciples crossing the sea, a huge whale was built with a hidden mechanical pump in its belly enabling it to spurt jets of water from its mouth, the liquid stored in a reservoir far below. Lord Macartney attests that several tons of water were expelled in this fashion from the huge simulated fish situated directly opposite the emperor's box. The British visitor was amazed by the ingenuity and invention displayed in the productions he viewed, some of which exhibited "dragons and elephants and tigers and eagles and ostriches; oaks and pines, and other trees of different kinds"; and not only was there a water-blowing whale but as well "ships, rocks, shells, sponges and corals, all performed by concealed actors who were quite perfect in their parts, and performed their characters to admiration".

The usually reserved Macartney was even more overwhelmed by a production of Zhang Zhao's *Precious Raft for a Pacific Era* at the Jehol palace:

The greatest number of actors was found in the palace troupe and their robes, official's writing tablets, armours, helmets, costumes and properties were the like of which the world has never seen. I once saw them at the Jehol Travel Palace . . . on a stage that was nine feast-mats wide, and altogether three storeys. Some of the sprites came down from above, while others would suddenly shoot up from below, the two wing buildings serving as the dwelling of Bodhisattvas, and the whole central area was filled with people astride camels and prancing horses. Sometimes all the deities and demons would assemble together, wearing hundreds of thousands of masks and not one the same as the other. . . . On the day when the bonze Xuanzang collected the sutras at Thunder Voice Monastery, the Buddha (Tat'agata) appeared in the temple, and the Kashyapas, the Arhats, the Pratyekas and the personal disciples were divided into nine tiers from top to bottom, several thousand of them in serried rows, and yet there was still plenty of space left on the stage.

[From the *Diary*, edited by Cranmer-Byng]

At court most of the actors and supernumeraries were eunuchs, who could number as many as 700, supplied after 1740 by a bureau called the Southern Treasury; others might be recruited from the troupes whose performances the emperor or his agents chanced to see, perhaps on his half-dozen tours. Those most frequently used on such occasions soon constituted a discrete group of "court-actors". The spectacular effects that characterized offerings at the imperial palaces gradually began to influence special productions elsewhere, as when officials and rich salt merchants staged fêtes to welcome Ch'ien Lung on his state travels (the government held a monopoly on salt, and those licensed to sell a prized commodity could grow immensely wealthy). Such beneficiaries of the emperor's bounty made certain that the entertainments greeting him were in scale, though they could hardly be expected to match the richness of those mounted under the auspices of imperious Ch'ien Lung himself.

Popular theatres were most active in the Yangzhou area. The emperor, sailing along the Cao River on his repeated visits there, could see plays in booths on both banks stretching a distance of several miles. Ten to twenty troupes would participate on the improvised stages, stationed at thirty designated intervals, each presenting a different drama with Kunshan-*qiang* or Yiyang-*qiang* music for his pleasure. Yangzhou had numerous permanent theatres, besides, offering "bumper plays" or best-liked excerpts from them. These companies were subsidized by the local salt-merchants, as were those maintained for the same purpose of welcoming Ch'ien Lung to Suzhou and Hangzhou by the affluent silk manufacturers located in these prosperous cities.

In a climate of oppression, the creation of great art is less likely. Writers of stature in these shadowed decades of the middle and late eighteenth century are rare, but a few playwrights were successful in walking the fine line, whether because their thoughts were innocuous – they were apolitical and embraced no bold, seditious causes – or they were pragmatists adhering to a course deliberately chosen to be as safe as possible. The least attempt to offer substantive literature was dangerous; a mere phrase or line of dialogue might unintentionally anger the authorities and provoke a dire reprisal. Many writers elected to remain anonymous, whether out of modesty or mature caution.

One who flourished in spite of these inhibitions was Shen Qifeng (1741–post-1784). His work was so highly appreciated in the Yangtze region that a constant, endless file of producers and actors approached his house to knock at the door and ask for his newest script; the number of persistent, eager supplicants was so great that, as put by an unattributed source, "the toes of the ones behind pressed on the heels of the ones in front". Shen Qifeng obliged his clients by handing over copies from his large output, amounting to between thirty and forty plays.

Charming anecdotes are told of Zhang Jian (1681–1771). In his boyhood he read *West Wing* and *Moon Prayer*, out of sight of his teacher, since those classic dramas were banned. At eighteen he wrote a play, but his intent was not serious; he deemed the piece worthless, let no one see it, and stowed it away at the proverbial bottom of a trunk. Ten years later he retrieved it, submitted it and had it accepted; it was a great success, which inspired a company of Nanking actors to buy his second attempt as soon as its first draft was ready. He wrote four plays in all.

One night in 1771, near his life's end, while staying in a tavern, he observed an elderly seamstress repairing clothes: she was following instructions from a notebook that also contained a handwritten copy of his first play, with marginal comments and emendations. Engaging the old woman in conversation, he discovered that the manuscript had belonged to her employer's daughter, a child who had a poetic gift and daily enjoyed reciting verses from his work. Dying of consumption at fifteen, the girl had bequeathed the manuscript to the kindly seamstress. The old woman would never tell him the girl's name, but was persuaded to sell him the text in return for a tael. Skimming through its pages, he came upon a poem by the girl in which she confessed her youthful love for him and deep awe for his genius.

Friends of Zhang Jian were Dong Rong (1711–60) and Tang Ying (pre-1713–post-1752) who won reputations for stageworthy works. Success for Dong Rong came with a drama (1751) about two women, untraditional historical figures, who were effective military leaders during the last years of the Ming dynasty. Tang Ying, besides fashioning thirteen plays, all before 1749, was acclaimed as a potter, his porcelains lastingly designated as Tang-*yao*; that is, from the Tang kiln. Much of the subject-matter of his plays, in the Kunqu genre, is apparently borrowed from folk-drama; however, he is best remembered for his writings about porcelain manufacture.

Like any other Chinese dramatist, Yang Chaoguan (1712–91) pursued a role in government and rose to be a prefect in Szechwan Province. He manifested his romantic and theatrical temperament by seeking out ruins on a site where a legendary heroine of a love affair had once dwelt; then he chose to build, on the very same spot, a manor house fancifully named Singing Wind Pavilion. To mark its completion, he wrote a sheaf of plays and hired actors to present them. From his active brush, too, flowed a collection of thirty-two one-act dramas, printed in 1774; they somewhat resemble episodes in the palace "bumper plays". *Stopping the Feast*, in the collection, had a strong emotional impact. Viewing it, Ruan Yuan, a high-ranking minister and himself a literary figure, identified with it so acutely that he wept uncontrollably: he was reminded of his mother; impoverished, she had sacrificed to have him educated but had died without seeing him attain a lofty position. Now, like the protagonist of the play, he resolved to change his way of life, to become an ascetic, forsaking his drunken feasting and other wild habits.

A poet and playwright with the highest profile in this period is Jiang Shiquan (1725–85). His was the physical advantage of being tall, with a noble mien and conspicuously dignified bearing, making him the very personification of a sage. In fact, he was of humble origin. Taught by his mother, he was able to read when only three. Her trick was to splinter dried bamboo shoots and arrange them to look like the basic elements of written characters, then give them to him to form into words. Later, he was respected not only for his great erudition but also for his unswervingly moral conduct. His temperament was patrician and conservative. All this, and especially his orthodoxy in most affairs, commended him to Ch'ien Lung, who frequently praised him as a human repository of vast learning. High government posts were bestowed on him; in turn, he was openly loyal to his patrons, the emperor and the Qing regime. By his peers, especially contemporary scholars, he was ranked as one of the empire's foremost poets. Between 1741 and 1780 he composed sixteen plays, four of them dedicated to the dowager empress when she celebrated her birthday (1751). Another was a portrait of the bold, intemperate seventeenth-century Tang Xianzu, author of the classic *Peony Pavilion*, but it did not show his defiant, bohemian side; instead, Tang was depicted as an upright government administrator, and hence theatrically rather less interesting.

Jiang Shiquan's stage-works were much admired by his fellow scholars. One critic wrote: "His plays are the best of modern times. With a deeply ingrained knowledge of the classics of poetry and history, he is able to pluck forth poesy at will. Always grateful and cultivated poetry. Not like Li Liweng and others, whose language is nothing but actors' wisecrack chatter." (Quoted by Dolby)

In spite of the high regard in which his printed plays were held by those of self-acknowledged superior taste, very few of them ever reached the stage, with only one of them having had much success. His were the usual themes: an intelligent concubine guides a rebel prince; another concubine suffers a tragic fate; a statesman displays fervent patriotism and bravery; an opportune letter spares the lives and fortunes of an official and his family.

Lacking exciting new plays during this era, the spectators' interest was inevitably diverted to the acting and a train of innovative techniques. The public also focused on the ever-changing genres of music, the continuing rivalry between Kunshan-*qiang* (disliked in Peking) and Yiyang-*qiang* (dissonant and less pleasing to Southern ears), and subsidiary forms into which both tended to evolve, such as Jing-*qiang*, not a recent variation but now a fad in the North. The actors who were linked to these different types rose and fell in popularity depending on the widening acceptance or diminishing vogue of the kind of music they chose.

Closely associated with Jing-*qiang*, which now unexpectedly won favour, were the Six Great Famous Troupes, constituted of performers with such vividly picturesque names as Baldy, Third Wang, Big-head Huan, Old Lu, Tiger-zhang, Six Huo, Ugly Chen and Continuous Delight. Equally prominent in the years 1778–9 was the Princely Palaces New Troupe. These groups were in great demand to entertain at banquets and other private and public festive affairs. Their cresting good fortune changed quite abruptly the very next year, 1779, however, upon the arrival in Peking of a competitor, Wei Changsheng (1744–1802), from Szechwan Province.

This was some months before Ch'ien's seventieth birthday (by the Chinese calendar), a truly major event, for which expensive preparations were already under way. From cities throughout his huge empire, troupes of excelling performers were being sent to Peking, along with costly gifts of every conceivable kind. Possibly Wei Changsheng headed a Szechwanese company that had been selected to participate; he was already an expert at *dan* (in his instance, female leading) roles.

A small turn of fortune brought him instant fame. A member of the Princely Palaces New Troupe arrived tardily at an important banquet; a censor, infuriated, rebuked the latecomer and struck him; for this lapse of self-control he was dismissed from his post, but public indignation was aroused on his behalf from a perception that the Princely Palaces New Troupe and the Six Great Famous Troupes were too indulgently treated by officials, and that both the authorities and singers abused their privileges and too often conducted themselves arrogantly. Jing-*qiang* music suffered in the general perception along with them.

Wei Changsheng, together with his Szechwanese colleagues, intervened on behalf of his disgraced rival, with a vow that he would restore their popularity in less than two months or accept a penalty. Overnight, with a single performance, he scored a hit that swept him to the very top rank, greeted by critics as unequalled. He loomed far above all others, including any in the unlucky Six Great Famous Troupes and Princely Palaces Troupe, whom he had boldly sought to help. He was offered incredible fees by rich mandarins, ministers and the most free-spending merchants to entertain at their homes. To claim his personal acquaintance was to borrow his lustre, and to have never been seen by his side most certainly detracted from one's social standing. Even the all-influential minister Heshen was delighted by him. For an appearance in a one-act play in a Yangzhou theatre, the triumphant Wei Changsheng was paid an unheard-of 1,000 taels.

He sang Qin-*qiang* music, which instantly achieved popularity along with him: it is a variant of Yiyang-*qiang*. He altered the way in which feminine *dan* roles were interpreted, heightening his impersonation by a better application of make-up, his coiffure enhanced by added hair-pieces; he also wore dainty clogs that made his feet look more tiny, abetting the sinuous, voluptuous sway of his walk. On stage he was captivating, acting with finesse, creating the illusion of utter femaleness, and he drew a special audience, men with bisexual desires; at this time homosexuality was overt among the literati and in the Qing government hierarchy, many of whom made no secret of deviant inclinations. In his stage characterizations he also projected an inherent personal charm, springing from a generous nature that had won him so many friends. His plays flourished, too, because they had erotic overtones; the dialogue was racily colloquial, an admixture of sexual innuendoes. Before long, he was attacked by moralists for portrayals that were "obscene and suggestive" with jocular *double-entendres*.

Prompted by his success, other Szechwan performers found theatre niches for themselves in Peking, and even members of the Six Great Famous Troupes felt it necessary to emulate his style, taking up Qin-*qiang* music and plays that featured it. This was the "rage" in Peking for a half-dozen years, with the actors increasingly stressing open sexual improprieties. One of Wei Changsheng's most prominent imitators, Chen Yinguan, even had nude mimes embracing and making love in a prologue to one of his works. Inevitably, this led to bans, the first in 1782 that prohibited Qin-*qiang* in Peking, an edict the well-entrenched Wei Changsheng was able to evade. Another order in 1785 was more effective, cutting short his career in the capital. Three years later (1788) he transferred his activities to Yangzhou, the other important nexus of theatre; he remained there until 1792, then went home to Szechwan. Desiring to recapture Peking, he returned to the capital in 1801 or 1802, but his comeback was sadly brief; in 1802, while on stage, he took ill, his death ensuing soon afterwards, his age believed to be about fifty-eight.

Meanwhile, the year 1790 had marked a signal occasion, the long-lived, long-reigning Ch'ien Lung's eightieth birthday, the well-planned, surpassing celebration once again bringing to Peking theatre groups from the many regions. Among them were the Anhwei Troupes, who for almost a decade (1790–98) supplanted in the city's favour Wei Changsheng's company and the other Szechwanese ensembles. They introduced Erhuang-*diao*, another kind of music, which quickly topped all others in acceptance in Peking, as it had earlier in Yangzhou; the Anhwei Troupes performed ably in Kunshan-*qiang* and Qin-*qiang*, too, as various types of script might require. Even more than they were admired for their versatility as singers, they extracted gasps of astonishment by stunning acrobatics, their leaps, boundings, tumbles; they set unprecedented standards, a challenge to the skills of stage-athletes ever since. Besides that, they outshone most others in the ostentation of their costuming and richly decorated props.

An opening having been made for them in Peking, other troupes from Anhwei invaded the capital. The force of the 1785 ban had waned. The *dan* of the first company to appear, Gao Langtin (?1774–?), replaced Wei Changsheng as foremost female impersonator, but he conveyed a very different impres-

sion; not his a flirtatious air, one of "romantic and naughty gaiety" that was Wei Changsheng's character, but instead, as a contemporary put it, an embodiment of "spiritual expressiveness and grace".

A light-hearted play of the middle and late eighteenth century that remains firmly in today's
repertory, and might have been an appropriate vehicle for such as Wei Changsheng, is *Longing for
Laity*. Of uncertain authorship, it could well have been adapted from one of the many episodes of
Golden Statutes for Promoting Virtue. A young nun is rebellious at being cooped up in a convent and
desperate to throw off her vow of chastity; she has been incarcerated by the wishes of her zealously
pious parents but long since much against her will. The script is almost a lengthy monologue in which
she laments her plight. These are her opening speech and song, after an evocation, as translated in
rhyme by Dolby:

> I shaved my hair and became a nun,
> poor me, it makes you weep,
> and one dhyana-lamp in my cell
> is my only bed-mate when I sleep.
> Time hurries you old, the years scurry by,
> I neglect my youth, fail to give it its due,
> while my beautiful springtide's green and new.

My name is Miss Zhao, and my dharma-name is Materiality Void. I entered the Doctrine of Vacuity,
became a Buddhist that is, when I was only a little girl, and years and years ago I wrapped the black
robes around myself and had my hair cut off, and was made a nun. Oh dear! I'm worshipping and
performing devotions day and night, chanting the name of Buddha, and reading the sutras – have I
got to carry on doing that for ever and ever! The convent cell's so bleak and lonely, you know, with no
man to share it with me. And the birds are calling and the blossoms falling, but no one knows or cares
about me. Oh, it makes me so utterly miserable!

> [*Sings*]: I'm a little nun, just sweet seventeen,
> in my tender prime, in life's morning fair,
> and along comes the abbess, snip snap snip,
> and shears off all my pretty hair.
> I light the incense and change the water
> in the Hall of Buddhas, day in day out,

and sometimes outside the convent portals

I spy young gentlemen larking about.

They eye me up, and eye me down,

and I eye them in return.

They for me, and me for them,

both sides we burn and yearn.

Here both the prose and verse are straightforward and plain, almost like everyday speech, without the hyperbolic metaphors and flowery similes of a Kunqu drama, and the little nun is poignantly real, not a creature of fantasy. The supernatural does enter when, to an accompanying din of gongs and drums, she is visited by Avalokhitesvara, the Goddess of Mercy, and her heavenly entourage, including a train of Arhats (demons) who display their amorous interest in the girl by their ogling and striking acrobatics. After their visit, and despite the implicit warning, she decides to throw off her black robes and escape.

The coronation of Ch'ien Lung's successor, Emperor Renzong (1796–1820), occurred just before the arrival of the nineteenth century. The new ruler confronted a morass of problems. The calm that the empire had long enjoyed was now disturbed, partly by the White Lotus Rebellion (1795–1804), which he had to quell, and by the previous several decades of maladministration during Ch'ien Lung's old age and weakened grasp of power. Seeking reforms, the new emperor had to curb financial irresponsibility, habitual corruption and long-tolerated administrative ineptitude. Of special concern, too, was the low Manchu military morale.

He was convinced that the theatre was a factor in this widespread malaise. This was certainly true at the palace, where the imperial acting troupe was under the sway of a eunuch who, due to his close link to Mianki, Prince Dun, the emperor's third son, was able to work around curbs imposed on him. For a time, even the dowager empress could not prevail against the two. Eventually, though, the prince's protection no longer prevailed, and the offending troupe was ordered home to Suzhou.

In 1798 a sterner edict was added to those already promulgated. It denounced "non-refined" species of music, among them Qin-*qiang* and the plays in which it was featured. Condemned, too, were scripts "of a nature which incites to lewd immorality", founded on "sordid, depraved, indecent and profane stories, or weird, monstrous, seditious and rebellious tales, which have a considerable effect on social customs and individual attitudes". The complaint was that the populace, bored and sated with Kunqu drama, was "infatuated with novelty". The only forms of music exempted from the ban were the long-established Kunshan-*qiang* and Yiyang-*qiang*. This prohibition was to apply with "all severity" to every area of Peking as well as to the provinces of Kiangsu, Anhwei and beyond. The bias in favour of Kunshan-*qiang* apparently bespoke the preference of the ever-influential élite, who intervened on its behalf because it was the most conservative genre, tending to be supportive of the political and social status quo – or, at least, not a threat to it – more likely to reflect a higher morality. It was also more elegant. To some degree, Kunshan-*qiang* did revive once again, as a number of troupes espousing it returned to Peking stages. But the Anhwei companies were able to survive, partly because the edict was maintained for less than ten years, and also because, showing their versatility, they resorted during the interim to doing Kunqu plays, after which they reverted to the forms they liked best and regained their stage-leadership in the capital.

With Kunqu having the assent of the authorities, a number of high-ranking officials held on to their own acting troupes, often kept at government expense, in effect with tax-money extorted from a resentful citizenry. Emperor Renzong frowned on this, citing the practice as one of the spurs of the White Lotus Rebellion. Accordingly, most of the private troupes were finally disbanded. Once again the emperor forbade the operation of theatres in the noisy, thronging Inner City, but with his recognition that the public wanted recreation, several playhouses in the Outer City were allowed to continue. He blamed the frivolous habit of theatre-going, as well as the popularity of gambling and wine-drinking, for the increasing decadence of his Manchu subjects, their neglect of the Manchu language and traditional military arts, their flaunting dandyism and fondness for "silk attire", their dissipation.

A result of his scoldings and reproaches was that some of his officials took to attending plays in semi-disguise, trying to pass as ordinary spectators. Worse was a scandal in 1806, when a censor charged six military Manchus of actually taking roles in plays, and they in turn accused him of frequently being in attendance at their performances, which was attested by an usher. Yet another "respectable" Manchu was exposed as the owner of a prosperous warehouse and shop that supplied rented ornate costumes and stage properties. Of even higher position, still another Manchu was sentenced to suffer forty strokes and to undergo hard labour for slipping incognito into theatres. And then, it was discovered that at Ili in Sinkiang, in a military camp where many exiles were sent to be reacquainted with pure, ascetic Manchu qualities, the inmates were acting in dramas, which occasioned another prohibition (1808).

Emperor Renzong found the proliferation of such derelictions greatly discouraging, and was annoyed at having to keep rejecting petitions from fellow Manchus to relax the restrictions on

Peking's Inner City playhouses (1811). He increased his efforts to dampen the public's eagerness to view immoral stage-works; in 1813 Qin-*qiang* music was again suppressed, as were dramas with too much violence – "fighting plays" – but in vain. Besides, the always anxious emperor was aware that many people earned their living in the acting profession, as did those who served in the adjacent wine-shops, tea houses and other vendors in the entertainment district. Shutting down all theatres would greatly enlarge the census of the impoverished and unemployed, which was politically danger-ous. Finally, he accepted the inevitable: if theatres did not provoke trouble, they would be allowed to function.

His heir, Emperor Xuanzong (r. 1821–50), presided over a China undergoing unhappy social instability coupled with military defeats. The new regime was weakened by financial drains resulting from the Opium War (1840–42) with the British, who extorted an indemnity and imposed trade in the noxious opiate. The serious-minded emperor urged his subjects to economize, himself setting an example by sometimes appearing in worn, patched attire. He sought to raise the morale of his dis-couraged Manchu armies and strengthen the ethical fibre of his administrators. At odds with his public show of austerity, he cherished the theatre, at times passionately. Yet he was convinced that it had a harmful effect on the morals of his too easy-going people. To rein in their appetite for such enter-tainment seemed impossible. Still more series of bans and other threats were announced during his years of rule, and drastic punishments openly meted out to violators, but the nobility – princes and dukes – and leading officials covertly defied the edicts, regardless of risk.

In 1824 Xuanzong forbade new theatres, permitting only the approximate ten already established and active. Next, in 1827, the palace troupe was further limited; it was stipulated that no outside actors were to be engaged on any occasion, and those permanently in residence should be more strictly dis-ciplined. In cities, certain types of plays and entertainers were now declared out of bounds.

A rash of thefts, kidnappings and horse-stealings led to an order (1835) expelling from Peking all vagabonds, quacks, cheats, peddlers and fortune-tellers, as well as "female acrobats, pole-climbers, tightrope dancers, and performers of the kind of play known as Gaoqiao, 'high stilts'". Another sort of drama much liked in Peking, Taipinggu, "great drums", was locally silenced. Such plays were put on by a horde of sheepskin-clad actors, perhaps 150 of them, who descended on the capital *en masse*, roaming about the night-darkened streets and making an excessively loud din with variously sized, long-handled tambourines. The popular suspicion was that, shielded by the deafening racket, they abducted, raped and covered the cries of any lone woman they happened to encounter. After the exe-cution of several ringleaders of these wild groups, the Taipinggu plays were extinct.

Emperor Xuanzong was followed by the nineteen-year-old Wenzong (r. 1851–61), who had a ten-year reign that had barely begun before he and his ministers had to cope with the Taiping Rebellion that almost dethroned him. The civil strife, lasting a half-decade, saw Nanking captured by the rebels, who were religious fanatics. The empire was almost torn asunder, and further disasters occurred when the flooding Yellow River shifted its course, ruining fields and despoiling cities, drowning many people. Next, from 1857 to 1860, the Second Opium War brought French and British invaders, the enemy forces reaching Peking, and even entering and pillaging the richly furnished Summer Palace. Another humiliating treaty, with draconian terms, was imposed on the empire.

During these devastating years Peking's theatrical fare and official opposition to it were little changed. As the authorities saw it, such indulgences in dire times were inappropriate. An 1852 measure, directed against playhouses, bore a rueful comment that in past decades their offerings had been superior, definitely more respectable. Since then the stage had degenerated; night-time performances were given, with women crowded among the spectators, the plays filled with too much fighting and lavishly overproduced, the music "mushy", the subjects hardly edifying but instead glorifying "heroic" bandits and traitors. Legal action was taken against some wandering actors, castigated as "rogues", who used a temple near Peking to put on ceremonial dramas coinciding with the summer and autumn festivals.

By 1860 European diplomats were taking up residence in Peking, "treaty ports" were opened, students were going abroad, and Western influences were becoming more evident, while the imperial government was even less in control of affairs. Emperor Wenzong's successor was five years old when he inherited the throne (1861); the rule was seized by his mother, his father's second wife, Yehonala (1835–1908), later familiarly "Cixi Taihou" or "Old Buddha". Every aspect of the regime, and especially the dynasty itself, was in an ever more rapid decline. Much of the last empress's time was absorbed by endless palace intrigues. On all sides were heard cries for political reform, the overthrow of the Manchus.

Extravagance at the palace was once more conspicuous, with the eunuchs who supervised court entertainment spending funds recklessly, one of them even rumoured to be raiding the imperial treasury for bolts of silk, which had been paid as tribute but were now being used illicitly for stage costumes. At the same time he was daily collecting grants of as much as 1,000 taels to mount his pageants and dramas. Yet the persecution of theatres did not let up; the Bannermen were still not allowed to attend plays, and a prefect here, a magistrate there, was castigated for having daringly observed a birthday or thankfully marked a recovery from illness by watching in private or public a farce or serious piece. Enforcement of the edicts was not rigorous, however, and tended to be aimed more at individual offenders rather than applied generally.

Once a beauty, the dowager empress was now famed and feared for her dynamic will. Shrewd and cynical, she could be ruthless. Her first son, the legitimate heir, died while still a minor; she placed her second son, Kuang Hsu, in immediate line of succession. He took the throne. During his brief rule he recognized the country's impending political and economic crises and surprised his mother and her advisers with a raft of decrees that set up a radically modern and comparatively democratic state, a list of shocking changes they could not countenance. She had him imprisoned in one of his palaces and annulled his edicts, then continued her strong grasp on power.

In Peking it was commonly known that the dowager empress was fascinated by theatrical presentations. In this she was under the sway of the wilful palace eunuchs, especially a handsome, persuasive actor, An Dehai (1844–69). He produced the opulent entertainments on which she doted insatiably. On occasions she participated in them. A photograph shows her attired as the Goddess of Mercy in one such play, posed alongside another of her wayward favourites, the eunuch Li Lianying, at that moment simulating a Bodhisattva. (He was often derisively referred to as "Cobbler's Wax Li", having in his youth been apprenticed to a shoemaker.) Though she pretended to concur with her censor's objections to the eunuchs' spendthrift ways, she habitually indulged their whims, particularly those of Li Lianying, who joined her in donning the rich attire of characters in historical dramas and making boating excursions on the private lake fronting the Summer Palace. Tea-house gossip pointed to him as the originator of less innocent, more scandalous goings-on within the precincts of the royal dwelling. The size of the palace troupe of actors was increased, with the eunuchs spinning out their ever more costly fantasies.

Among the aristocracy, too, theatre had regained a strong pull. One of those most defiant of the bans was Prince Zaicheng, a grandson of Emperor Xuanzong, who established a playhouse for the amusement of his mistress, whose favours he felt a perpetual need to woo. He did this during a period of mourning at the death of the dowager empress's co-regent, which meant that his indifference to the law was more flagrant. He also permitted a large number of women among the spectators, a precedent quickly followed by several other Inner City troupes. In disguise, he and his mistress went daily to take in the extravagantly furbished offerings. His father, warned that a higher-ranking prince was planning to lodge a complaint and have the heedless young man arrested, hastened to the censor and had the son's troupe instantly dismissed and the theatre razed, all in one day. Another playhouse, just opened in the Outer City by Prince Zaicheng, was also abruptly shut down.

Prince Pujun, chosen to be next in line to the throne, shared the dowager empress's intense fondness for theatre, but his boorish conduct at performances is described in a caustic report – "confidential" – found by Dolby in *China Under the Empress Dowager* by J.C.F. Bland and E. Backhouse. An excerpt:

The Heir Apparent is fifteen years of age; fat, coarse-featured, and of rude manners. He favours military habits of deportment and dress, and to see him when he goes to the play, wearing a felt cap with gold braid, a leather jacket and a red military overcoat, one would take him for a prize-fighter. He knows all the young actors and rowdies and associates generally with the very lowest classes. He is a good rider, however, and a fair musician. If, at the playhouses, the music goes wrong, he will frequently get up in his place and rebuke the performer, and at times he even jumps up on the stage, possesses himself of the instrument, and plays the piece himself. . . . On the 18th of the 10th Moon, accompanied by his brother and his uncle, the Boxer Duke Lan, and followed by a crowd of eunuchs, he got mixed up in a fight with some Kansu braves at a theatre in the temple of the City God. The eunuchs got the worst of it, and some minor officials who were in the audience were mauled by the crowd. The trouble arose, in the first instance, because of the eunuchs attempting to claim the best seats in the house. . . . The eunuchs were afraid to seek revenge on the Kansu troops directly, but they attained their end by denouncing the manager of the theatre to Governor Ts'en, and by inducing him to close every theatre in Hsi-an. Besides which, the theatre manager was put in a wooden collar, and thus ignominiously paraded through the streets of the city. The Governor was induced to take this action on the ground that Her Majesty, sore distressed at the famine in Shansi and the calamities which have overtaken China, was offended at these exhibitions of unseemly gaiety, and the proclamation which closed the playhouses ordered also that restaurants and other places of public entertainment should suspend business. Everybody in the city knew that this was the work of the eunuchs. Eventually, Chi Lu, Chamberlain of the Household, was able to induce the chief eunuch to ask the Old Bell to give orders that the theatres be reopened. This was accordingly done, but of course the real reason was not given, and the Proclamation stated that, since the recent fall of snow justified hopes of a prosperous year and good harvests, theatres would be reopened as usual, "but no more disturbances must occur".

The dowager empress's birthdays were occasions for ostentatious, bloated festivities; an example is her seventy-third – her last – in 1908, for which Peking's principal thoroughfares were richly if garishly adorned, while in the palace there were plays for five days running. In a masquerade, the "Old Buddha" was again garbed as the Goddess of Mercy. She not only chose the plays but also made suggestions to the actors as to how their characters should be interpreted, often as to very minor details.

Beyond Peking, the governors of some provinces zealously persecuted individual actors, troupes and writers who transgressed against the rule on entertainments. Among the penalties were confiscation of costumes and properties, along with the burning of printed scripts of banned dramatic works. An established Kiangsu custom was the hiring of priests to perform in plays at funerals, but this was no longer allowed. Songs, too, were scrutinized for offensive – "immoral" – phrases or thoughts. Ding Richang (1823–82), Governor of Kiangsu, bore a particular animus towards *West Wing* and *Fenlands* and was distressed that copies could be found in virtually every household and carried in the pockets of nearly everybody, or so he imagined. In Hunan a prefect was determined to stop women from seeing any temple plays. He ordered raids in which the women were seized; thereafter each monk present was forced to bear one of them on his back from the despoiled sacred precincts. This punitive approach was considered excessive; their husbands and kinfolk raised protests; the over-aggressive prefect lost his post. Another official was more successful when he led a raid on a city playhouse, rounded up the frightened young ladies there and had them held in detention until each pledged in writing never again to visit such off-limits, disreputable places.

As always, certain categories of plays were singled out for banning: those presenting bandits in a heroic light, various kinds of folk plays, dramas that were really little more than "stage harlotry", especially those that encouraged gambling – that is, supplied pretexts for gamblers to gather – *Fenlands* plays and *Maudgalyayana* plays abounding in violent scenes. Such works were likely to be done in villages that were somewhat remote, beyond likelihood of surveillance.

After the Four Great Anhwei Troupes had become dominant in the capital, been expelled and returned again – now in the early nineteenth century – each group was prized for a different speciality: one for its acrobatics; another for its incredible demonstration of martial arts; a third for its featuring of "boys", unusually young players who took male or female roles; and a fourth for putting on lengthy plays in their entirety, rather than the customary programme of short highlights from them, or a succession of one-act scripts. To show Gang Zhizhen's *Maudgalyayana* or a "bumper play" without excisions might require several days, unfolding through both afternoons and evenings. This practice earned applause for the Three Celebrations Troupe.

One explanation for the appeal of gymnastics and exceptional prowess in martial arts, emphasized by the Gentle Spring Troupe, is that rich spectators lived in fear due to ever-spreading lawlessness in the cities. Means of self-defence, together with the services of bodyguards, were at a premium; the alert guards were needed to accompany messengers with valuable loads and to stand watch in front of manor houses and upper-class residences. The stage acrobats provided models to guards of what could be accomplished by long training, the physical strength and agility they could acquire.

The boys in the Spring Stage Group ranged from twelve to thirteen years to sixteen or seventeen, at which point their careers usually ended. The children were indentured, or even as slaves purchased by older actors who instructed them in singing and dancing. A few, even younger – seven or eight – were "hired" from their parents. Any still on stage who had reached nineteen would be disparagingly dubbed a "granny"; he would no longer be in the Spring Stage Group, which was foremost in exploiting children. But few were truly talented enough to stay in the acting profession. Once schooled in performing, however, the youngsters could be profitable investments for their purchasers. With seductive make-up and glamorous dress, after being taught how to behave flirtatiously, they were sent to entertain at banquets and private feasts, where they were admired and petted. An element of pederasty was doubtless implicit in the enterprise. During their training period, which lasted about a year, they experienced harsh treatment and thereafter were underpaid, perhaps receiving only food and clothing; after six years, though, they were discharged, their servitude over. In some instances a boy's contract might be bought from his theatre-master by a rich host at a party where he had been seen, and, determined by his age, the price could be high.

The Four Delights Troupe still championed Kunqu, and won plaudits for an unabridged production of *Peach Blossom Fan*, but this genre was sporadically fading from view, its attraction diminishing; it would make a brief comeback, only to lose favour again. Even *Lute* had come to be considered old-fashioned. The vogue in Peking and even in Suzhou, the first home of Kunqu, was for more robust works, lavishly staged, perhaps with a good amount of rather unmusical din and flashy costumes; the actors were masked. A factor in its decline was the Taiping Rebellion, as disloyal troops seized and for nearly a decade occupied Suzhou and the surrounding region, cutting off a source of new Kunqu actors. Not long after the century's end, this Southern form of drama was virtually lost. In the 1920s, however, a clique of nostalgic patrons in Suzhou set up an Institute for the Teaching of Kunqu. A number of veteran players were brought back from retirement to pass on the conventions of the recently vanished art to new disciples; later, a Kunqu troupe was founded in Peking, too, to save Kunqu from total extinction.

Paradoxically, during this era of growing disorder and national decline, and of the intermittent repression of aspiring literary works and innovative musical compositions, an important new form of Chinese drama was gradually evolving. What is now known – and acclaimed worldwide – as Peking opera began with the conjoining of two types of music, Erhuang-*diao* and Xipi-*diao*. As observed above, the Anhwei Troupes had brought Erhuang-*diao* to the capital; its place of origin is disputed, some identifying Yihuang County in Kiangsi Province as its most likely birthplace; but only after it became a fad in Anhwei Province was it systematized and polished enough to be used in dramas. One of its early features was the prominence of the *di* (flute), to which was added in Peking the *huqin* (fiddle). Erhuang-*diao* was louder, faster than Kunshan-*qiang*, and often the words set to it were shockingly vulgar, which is why the authorities disapproved of it. Xipi-*diao* (or Xipi, for short) closely resembled Qin-*qiang*.

Between 1828 and 1838 singing actors from Hupeh Province reached Peking and introduced their own kind of music which soon had fervent devotees. Xipi was adopted by the city's theatre ensembles, but principally by the open-minded Anhwei Troupes; a single programme of theirs might offer both Erhuang-*diao* and Xipi; coexisting, the two types gradually mixed and blended. The result was a new musical genre called Pihuang; initially the voices were higher, the overall sound louder and somewhat monotonous – at least with scant variation – and the performances likely to lack finesse; until some decades of development went by, and Pihuang took on more cohesive and pleasing qualities.

Another factor in shaping Peking opera was the advent of three actors whose special talents brought about a shift in the leading role of a music drama from that of the *dan* (young male or female) to that of the *laosheng* (older male). One explanation for this is that the perilous times heightened the importance of the strong masculine traits that the often burly *laosheng* projected, in contrast to the effete appearance and concerns of the closeted scholar, merely worried about taking his examinations, or the fragile sensibilities of the delicate female impersonator, as both characters were portrayed by the hitherto more touted *dan*.

The first of these actors was Cheng Changgeng (1812–79/80), from Anhwei and a member of the Three Celebrations Troupe. At first he faced rejection because of his inadequate singing technique. To correct his faults he worked at them assiduously for three years; then one night, at a banquet honouring a clutch of high dignitaries, a call went up for excerpts from a play in which the song passages were exceedingly difficult to traverse. When none of his colleagues stepped forth to attempt the daunting test, Cheng Changgeng did so, to the chagrin of the others. "As they heard him, however, it was obvious that he was master of all the arts of singing, his voice 'like the wind in the heavens and billows of the ocean, golden carillons and mighty bells'. All present were utterly astonished, and the occasion gave a great boost to his reputation."

Principally he sang Erhuang-*diao*, but also Kunshan-*qiang* and other types, and not least Xipi-*diao*, in which his fully lifted voice would "soar through the clouds and split rocks, its reverberations trailing deliciously round the rafters, but amidst the superb, trailing clarity of it conveying another deeper and more powerful note". A Peking poet wrote in praise of him as a "Titan . . . flawless in his Kunqu, perfect in every word, so capturing those fine young peacock players that they all revere him as teacher and as lord". This oft-spoken appreciation of him by younger actors arose from his being the effective and generous leader of the Three Celebrations Troupe for a span of thirty-five years. He was outstanding in his loyalty to colleagues and spontaneous kindness to them, yet this was coupled with firmness in keeping discipline in the ensemble. When it had financial setbacks, he was able to pull the troupe through because of his fame and gifts as an actor. What is more, he never accepted invitations to appear alone for high fees at banquets but insisted that the entire company be included, so that his fellow-players shared in the large stipend. Subsequently he was looked upon as "the father of Peking opera"; even in the next century, the twentieth, people in the theatre world spoke of him with affection and awe, almost deifying him.

Yu Sansheng, who reigned on the Peking stage from 1821 to 1850, came to the capital from Hupeh Province. Expert in Xipi-*diao*, he had also fully mastered the techniques of Erhuang-*diao* and other musical forms, and was hailed for adeptness at mingling them for fresh and striking effects. He was also envied for his ability to improvise suavely, if a fellow-player missed a cue or entrance. He belonged to the Three Celebrations Troupe. On one memorable occasion he appeared jointly with Cheng Changgeng and Zhang Erkui but was given a minor role; he ingeniously overcame this by knowing so well the novel *The Three Kingdoms*, from which the script was adapted, that he was able, quite impromptu, to insert added lines without detracting from the story's progress, thereby enlarging his part. At the end, recognizing what he had done, the audience gave him an ovation.

Zhang Erkui (d. 1860?) is believed to have been a native of Peking, though some accounts have him from Anhwei or Chekiang. Physically he was well suited for *laosheng* roles, having an impressive, magisterial bearing; he was acclaimed for his portrayal of emperors and military leaders. His preference was for Xipi-*diao*; he is credited with being "clear and resounding of voice, not fond of decorative flourishes and turns to the melody" (in contrast, it seems, to Yu Sansheng), "but with every word firm and full, 'unbreakably strong and resilient' ".

Cheng Changgeng's success outlasted that of his two chief rivals. Dolby quotes a poem (1864):

> Now Erkui has sunk to perdition
> And Sansheng's fortunes wavered long,
> Who reigns in the world of song, you may ask,
> – Why, all yield place to Cheng Changgeng.

(The poet was Banhazhai.) The Peking public was inconstant.

Though the *laosheng* singers became more prominent, not all leading actors in the Anhwei troupes were limited to such roles, nor as yet were all productions in the novel, increasingly popular

Peking style. While Kunqu still lingered, a noted performer as a *chou* (clown) in plays in that gentler vein was Yang Mingyu, who established his Peking career during the 1850s and 1860s. Though handicapped by speaking only Suzhou dialect, he brought laughter and gasps from spectators by amazing tumbles, back-flips, somersaults, bends, splits and other physical feats with which he expressed agitation and panic, or joyous excitement, in each comic dilemma or discovery. He was most applauded as the villainous Rat Lou in Zhu Hao's (Zhu Suchen's) enduring seventeenth-century classic *Fifteen Strings of Cash*. (This comedy is preserved in a revised stage version prepared and then enacted in 1956 by the Chekiang Kunqu Opera Company, and even more recently in a highly esteemed colour film.)

A much appreciated *dan* of the day was Mei Qiaoling (1842–81) who when barely eight in Yangzhou was "adopted" by a man from Suzhou and next sold to a Peking troupe to serve in it as a youthful apprentice. He proved to be so talented that he rose to be manager of The Four Delights Troupe, where like Cheng Changgeng he won the loyalty of his fellow-actors by his instinctive generosity and amiability. Fated to be overweight, he was familiarly called "Chubby", but far from that shutting him out from *dan* roles he was enabled to impersonate with proper dignity a mature, easily identified, imposing empress. He founded a theatre dynasty. His two sons, Mei Zhufen and Mei Yutian, gained a similar stage celebrity, not only as singers but also as instrumentalists, both of them playing the *huqin* with remarkable virtuosity. Mei Yutian, who had an early death, was also a master of the *di*, could recite lines and sing the lyrics from 300 Kunqu, as well as undertake the percussion, drums, clappers and *suona* (clarion). (The family's most illustrious member was to be Mei Qiaoling's grandson, Mei Lanfang [1894–1961], of whom considerably more will be written later.)

For some decades after the two outrageous Opium Wars and the fourteen-year Taiping Rebellion (1850–64), China was permitted relative peace, under the guidance of the dowager empress and her clever advisers. During this time Peking opera continued to take form and flourish. Its growing popularity was chiefly due, once again, to its recruitment of a number of brilliant actors. The most prized of these was Tan Xinpei (1847–1917), who had earlier been a pupil of Cheng Changgeng. He was from Hupeh Province, as had been a long line of theatre entrants before him. His father, an actor, was familiarly known as Skylark, which led to the son being fondly nicknamed Little Skylark. His early training in the martial arts allowed him to earn a living for a while as a bodyguard. In Peking his first roles were as a *laosheng*. His rise in the theatre firmament was slow at the start; he obtained engagements with "porridge troupes", travelling companies that performed for a pittance in small towns and semi-primitive villages near Peking, but he profited from the basic experience.

After tutelage with Cheng Changgeng, he was admitted to the Three Celebrations Troupe (1875), in his twenty-fifth year. His mentor, perceiving his pupil's genius, predicted a great future for him, though the ageing Cheng hardly expected to live to witness it. Moving to Shanghai (1879), Tan Xinpei broadened his following, his reputation steadily spreading. Having hurt his voice, he fell back on taking *wusheng* (warrior) roles for which his previous training and competence with every sort of weapon had prepared him. By 1887 his voice fully restored, he attached himself to the Four Delights Troupe and assumed *laosheng* assignments again. With these, his fame truly soared.

He was versatile, playing scholars as well as emperors and warriors; his memory was superb, so that he was well acquainted with 300 or 400 scripts, including Kunqu. Reviving the classics, most of them almost forgotten, he enhanced them with fresh, illuminating insights and piquant bits of action, bringing to the ancient works a new vitality. His technique owed much to the devices of Cheng Changgeng and other outstanding predecessors, but he boasted a bagful of his own tricks, all these melded into a personal style, a quite individual one. His voice, preserved on old gramophone records, conveys – if imperfectly – an "airy deftness and vivacity, a natural ease of pitch", along with "an unpredictability and exciting wide range of possibilities". An awed contemporary likened him to "'a cloud-veiled moon', not very clear and ringing as he started to sing, but gradually becoming louder and more distinct". At times he was accompanied by Mei Yutian on the *huqin*.

Of his agility, it is told that he could kick off one of his shoes into the air and have it descend directly on to his bobbing head, a stunt he would resort to in a scene of riot and frenzy in one of his farces.

His popularity was so great, and his fans so worshipful, that during the anarchy of the Boxer Rebellion and the Western allies' invasion of Peking and Tientsin to rescue their expatriated nationals, a poet wrote, perhaps not wholly in praise but in ironic despair, "Who cares about the fate of the nation! The whole city competes to talk about Little Skylark." Earlier, the statesman Liang Qichao, gazing at a painting by this eminent actor, inscribed on its perimeter, "Unique in the universe, Tan Xinpei, whose fame these thirty years has shouted with the sound of thunder."

In 1917, well after the flight and death of the dowager empress and fall of the Manchu regime, Tan Xinpei was compelled to appear in plays hardly to his liking; deeply depressed, he died soon after. Like Mei Qiaoling, he left a dynasty of actors, composed of a son, a grandson and a great-grandson, all distinguished members of the profession.

Among Tan Xinpei's peers as a *laosheng* player in the same decades in Peking was Wang Guifen (1860–1908), irreverently known as Wang Big Head. He, too, was from Hupeh Province. From *dan* roles he graduated to heavier singing assignments. Suffering damage to his voice, which seems to have happened to many of these overly busy actors, he was perforce silent for a while, occupying himself

with playing the *huqin* for Cheng Changgeng. Perhaps from his close acquaintance with that master's style of performance, his similar manner when he returned to *laosheng* singing (1881) led to his being described as "a reincarnation of Cheng Changgeng", this meant as a compliment. Yet much about his stage persona was unique. His voice, exceptionally resonant, was distinctive, quite penetrating, a "back of the head sound", coming forth at full volume as soon as he began, "and still leaving lingering echoes in the head after he had stopped singing". Vocally, in this respect, he had no superior or equal, and defied imitation.

Wang Guifen died at forty-eight. The life-span of Sun Juxian (1841–1931) was almost twice as long, and his experiences more varied. Son of a Tientsin merchant, he was led to amateur acting by having a fine voice. His desire, however, was to take up a military career; accordingly, he enlisted in the army at twenty and quickly saw action, suffering wounds twice, in campaigns waged by the savage-tempered General Chen Gouri. In less than a decade a series of rapid promotions lifted him to the rank of Lieutenant-Major while he was stationed in Kwantung and Kiangsi Provinces. At twenty-nine he suddenly changed his goal and went to Shanghai, electing to be an actor. He joined some like-minded friends in setting up a combined tea-house and theatre that was soon shut down by a heavy burden of debts. Going to Peking, he was accepted by Four Delights Troupe and shortly made his mark in *laosheng* roles, though one would have expected that, with his army background, he would have been naturally suited for *wusheng* characterizations. His signal attribute was his voice, ample, indeed of immoderate size and easily projected, which allowed forthright singing, his technical control of it eclectic, with facets of it learned from all the three great *laoshengs* of the preceding generation. He avoided crowd-pleasing vocal pyrotechnics. His enunciation was strong and clear, curt and with a somewhat metallic timbre, likened to "chopped nails and sliced iron". He achieved an odd effect: "reaching the last line of a song, he would open his throat and let the sound pour out in an endless rumble like thunder going into the ground, which earned him the nickname Sun One Rumble". Living into his nineties, and during his later years seldom appearing on stage, he devoted himself to neighbourly charitable works, helping the hungry.

The *chou* (clown) roles also had notable exponents with hosts of admirers. One notorious *chou* was Liu Gansan, who so greatly amused the dowager empress that she had him perform regularly in the imperial precincts and bore tolerantly his bold, barefaced mockery. He put his neck at risk many times by daring, wry comments and egregious mimicry, often just skirting the very edge of safety. He was as much a comic figure outside the palace, riding through the streets of Peking astride a donkey, with jangling bells hanging from the beast's neck to announce his presence, thereby becoming very well known to a cross-section of the public. One of his stage devices was to be seated atop a table, while singing and playing the *huqin*, with cymbals attached to his knees, a drumstick clasped between his flexile toes, enabling him to strike a gong dangling from his left foot, a one-man band, accompanying himself with perfect timing and rhythm. On some occasions he would have his donkey appear on stage with him. In 1895, alas, he ventured beyond the limit, inserting satirical remarks into a play aimed at an official who was suffering disgrace for a military setback; the victim's well-connected brother-in-law was among the spectators and angrily complained to a very high-placed relative; Liu Gansan was taken into custody and brutally flogged, his trauma resulting in illness and death.

A typical Peking opera, much favoured by Yu Sansheng and Sun Juxian, is *The Capture and Release of Cao Cao.* (Dolby, who has translated and rhymed an excerpt from it, does not name the author.) A historical work, replete with violence, it is laid in the remote Three Kingdoms period and centres on Cao Cao, who is striking to gain and hold on to power in the last days of the Han dynasty. Legendary for his villainy, Cao Cao, a psychotic killer, has failed in an assassination attempt and taken flight. The Han ruler, Dong Zhuo, himself ruthless, has set a price on his murderous enemy's head. The fugitive takes shelter with an upright magistrate, Chen Gong, who, naïve and misguided, is persuaded to join Cao Cao's cause and travels onward with him. They spend a night with the elderly Lü Boshe, "sworn brother" to Cao Cao's father, but before they depart the paranoid Cao Cao, distrustful of everyone, slays Lü and his entire household. Hearing the cries, Chen Gong supposes a pig is being slaughtered for a feast. He learns the truth. As they ride on and stop at an inn, the appalled magistrate considers making his own escape.

INNKEEPER: What would you two gentlemen like me to bring you?

CHEN GONG: One bright lamp, and one bottle of the best wine!

INNKEEPER: Certainly, sir. One bright lamp and one bottle of the best wine. [*Fetches wine and lamp.*] Here's the lamp, and here's the wine.

CHEN GONG: We'll call you if we want you again.

INNKEEPER: Right. [*Exit.*]

CAO CAO: Couldn't swallow any? Come off it! It's quite obvious you're still peeved at seeing me kill those few members of the Lü family by mistake, eh?

CHEN GONG: Eh? You and I are planning great things together – where do words like "peeved" come into it! You're too suspicious.

CAO CAO: Yes, old Cao Cao's always been too suspicious all his life.

[*Sings*] Anyone I meet I tell but a third of what I think,

I'm used to pulling teeth from the tiger's jaw.

I'll drink a cup or two then go to sleep,

and in one brief dream return to my old home once more.

[Sound of the first watch. Chen Gong takes the lamp in his hand, and goes outside to patrol and check that all is well, after which he comes back into the room.]

CHEN GONG [*shouting to see if Cao Cao is still awake*]: Illustrious lord! illustrious lord! –

[*Sings*] The moon's bright wheel shines at the window,

and Chen Gong's mind is tangled as gale-blown straw.

How I repent that I conceived such wild ambitions,

that I followed him, that I darkened Lü Boshe's door.

Lü Boshe, there was a chivalrous man of honour,

– he slaughtered swine and purchased wine to entertain his brother's son.

But what happened? The wretch was over-suspicious,

drew his sword against Lü's family, and killed them every one.

A whole household was put to the sword, all slain,

its aged master lost his life and stained the yellow sand.

Wronged souls, victims of murder, bear me no grudge,

the truth only Heaven and the spirits may understand.

[Sound of second watch.]

Hear the watchtower drums die away as they beat the second watch.

the more I brood the more I'm sure I made a terrible mistake.

How I repent that I ever left my hearth and home,

and cast aside my black silk hat of office to follow in his wake.

I thought the rogue had princely schemes, was a man of magnanimity.

He's the very root of ruin, the house of Han's future calamity.

[Sound of third watch.]

[Takes sword..]

I draw a sword to lop a villain's head,

[Cao Cao turns over.]

And almost bungle things again instead!

[Puts sword away again.]

Yes, I really should dispatch him, with one blow of the sword, but I fear lest the world suspect that I and Dong Zhuo had some secret accord.

I must write a poem to shake the wretch from his complacency, yes, leave a verse upon the table, but what shall the topic be?

[Sound of fourth watch.]

Ah, yes . . . I'll take the fourth watch as my topic line . . .

The old magistrate writes his poem, leaves it on the table, goes out to his horse, mounts and gallops off. After the fifth watch Cao Cao awakes, recounts a dream of having returned to his home, finds Chen Gong's verse and, infuriated, vows not to spare him if they ever meet again.

The work is filled with dramatic tension; the language is natural and very direct; the illusion of time passing, of darkness settling and lifting, is created by the cries of the night-watch. Cao Cao's evil has complex depths, as indicated by his recurrent dream; he is an Iago far from one-dimensional.

From the capital, the new Peking opera spread to other cities, notably to Shanghai and Canton, where it was adapted to local tastes, so that independent variations came about, with actors migrating from one metropolis to another. In Shanghai, mountings and accessories were even more elaborate, the *mise en scène* showier. In turn, regional versions had an influence on productions in Peking.

The repertory of Peking opera is not wholly restricted to Pihuang but embraces Kunqu and other styles of singing and acting. Consequently, its library of scripts is vast, said to contain about 3,800 titles, of which about 1,400 are still thought to be feasible choices for staging.

The history of theatre buildings in China is somewhat vague; while the almost exact layout of those in Greece 2,000 years ago is familiar to experts today, as are the details of the wagon-shows of medieval Europe and the design of Shakespeare's Globe – contemporary with the late Ming period – much less is certain about Chinese playhouses and stages. What they were like away from the imperial palace in earlier eras, the Sung, Jin, Yuan, Ming, is indefinite. One reason for this is that to commentators in past days the subject was not deemed important.

Chinese architecture tends to be open and airy, and put up informally; no plans were filed or retained by authorities, so few records are available. The structures were of wood, for the most part, not long enduring and too often consumed by the fires that swept through close-packed, flimsily built cities of huts and small shops. What few theatres do survive date mostly from the late nineteenth century.

From what can be gathered, little changed over the centuries and decades, if only because the Chinese valued tradition so highly, and social and economic conditions were often static – the great mass of people engaged in their own architecture; the incentive for "progress" was uncommon and weak.

To the last days of the Manchus, up to the beginning of the twentieth century, plays were still given on red carpets in the ornate reception halls and banqueting rooms of private mansions occupied by the nobles and the very affluent, or outdoors in garden pavilions, though "red carpet" presentations were apparently becoming ever more rare. In temples and monasteries, enactments of hallowed religious dramas had, as always, an added ambiance of the "sacred" and "dedicated" in a hall smoky and incense-scented, before a gilded shrine.

In farming villages, too, the "stage" was as likely as ever to be roughly improvised, a hastily assembled platform of planks, mats, bamboo poles – these came to be known as "matshed" theatres. Some touring companies brought the necessary materials with them, by boat, cart, or possibly on their backs and under their arms; upon arrival at their destination they ably set up whatever was required for a performance. A shrewd manager would try to time each such venture to coincide with a regional fair or festival, when the crowds would be greatest, and, with luck, wealthy local sponsors or a single generous benefactor might be inclined to subsidize the entertainment. Some of the outdoor troupes did "pass the hat" or charged admission, the payer permitted to watch from up front, in a more advantageous spot.

In larger cities, as mentioned before, theatres that were more or less permanent were clustered in a sector dedicated to pleasure-seekers. They bid for notice in narrow lanes with bright posters and gaudy, fluttering banners. If temporary enterprises, they would be in large, square tents, supported by bamboo frames and roofed with matting, sited in an empty grain-yard or, in season, possibly in a conveniently close-by dry riverbed.

Several partly updated playhouses of the Qing era survive, but even better clues to what they were like are found in the reports of foreign envoys and other European visitors. One was Robert Fortune, on an expedition in 1848 to collect plant specimens in the region of Huizhou in Anhwei Province. Standing on a high bank, he looked down a drop of almost 200 feet to activities at a harvest festival:

One of the rivers was nearly dry, and its bed was now used for the purpose of giving a grand fête. . . . We had a capital view of what was going on below us.

The first and most prominent object which caught my eye was a fine seven-storeyed pagoda, forty or fifty feet high, standing on the dry bed of the river; near to it was a Summer-house upon a small scale, gaudily got up, and supposed to be in a beautiful garden. Artificial figures of men and women appeared to be sitting in the verandahs and balconies, dressed in the richest costumes. Singing birds, such as the favourite wame and canaries, were whistling about the windows. Artificial lakes were formed in the bed of the river, and the favoured Nelumbium appeared floating on the water. Everything denoted that the place belonged to a person of high rank and wealth.

At some little distance a theatre was erected, in front of which stood several thousands of the natives.

Eleven years later (1857), in a town in Chekiang Province, Fortune observed another stage performance, again located where a river had once flowed: "The Chinese have a curious fancy for erecting these temporary theatres on the dry beds of streams." What impressed him most was that there was no ticket sale, admission was as "free as their mountain air – each man, however poor, had as good a right to be there as his neighbour. And it is the same all over China – the actors are paid by the rich, and the poor are not excluded from participating in the enjoyments of the stage."

Here, too, watching the performance were "thousands of happy spectators". The sponsors, having subsidized the event, were on a raised platform about twenty yards from the stage. Though he was satisfied to stand in the pit among the huge crowd, Fortune was recognized as a foreign guest and invited by one of the sponsors to join them in their lofty boxes.

He led me up a narrow staircase and into a little room in which I found several of his friends amusing themselves by smoking, sipping tea, and eating seeds and fruits of various kinds. All made way for the stranger, and endeavoured to place me in the best position for getting a view of the stage. What a mass of bodies were below me! The place seemed full of heads, and one might suppose that the bodies were below, but it was impossible to see them, so densely were they packed together. Had it not been for the stage in the background with its actors dressed in the gay-coloured costumes of a former age, and the rude and noisy band, it would have reminded me more of the hustings at a contested election in England than any thing else.

That people were eating, talking and smoking while the play was going on would be true in a teahouse, too, and even in a more permanent theatre; that custom, which continues today, may partly account for the Chinese actor–singer's frequent reliance on the falsetto voice, striving to make himself heard over the clamour of gongs and percussive instruments, the clatter of teacups on saucers, the chatter of an audience only half attentive.

Some theatres in temples might be merely improvised or consist of platforms that were quickly assembled and only temporary, but by the time of the Qing era many were no longer in the sanctuary but outside and apart, solidly constructed, large and square-shaped, fronting on a courtyard. They were fixed adjuncts to the holy premises. This was true of a huge stage for actors, beginning in the eighteenth century, in the Chongning Monastery; and of two massive platforms similarly available in the City God Temples in Ningpo. A Mrs Gordon Cummings, in a travel book (1888), has bequeathed this description:

> The stage is always a separate building facing the temple – a sort of kiosque, open on three sides – its beautifully carved, curly roof being supported on carved pillars. The court is enclosed by open corridors with galleries, in which seats are provided by mandarins and principal citizens.
>
> In the lower corridors many barbers ply their trade diligently, for skull-scraping and hair plaiting is a business which must not be neglected, and which can be successfully combined with the enjoyment of the play. Vendors of refreshments find a good market for their wares. . . .
>
> The kindly priests put us into a good place just in front of the great altar, whence we had a perfect view, and a stranger scene I have never beheld – the temple, the theatre, and the side-courts one mass of richest carving in wood and stone, crimson and gold, with the grey, curiously carved roofs harmonizing with the brilliant blue sky. The pillars supporting both the theatre and temple are powerfully sculpted stone dragons.
>
> The vivid sunlight gave intensity to the dark shadows, and brilliancy to the gorgeous dresses of the actors.

Illustrations by Mrs Cummings – drawings helpfully reproduced in Dolby – bear out the opulence of the temple setting, as do later photographs by A.E. Moule (1891), which attest to the accuracy of her rendering of it.

A further comment by this English lady has to do with the audience as seen from her privileged perspective: "It is a strange sight to look down upon the densely packed yet ever-restless throng, almost all dressed in blue."

Cao Juren, a twentieth-century historian, remembers from childhood a theatre in the Lord Guan Temple:

> Opposite the image of Lord Guan was the stage, rectangular in shape, a pillar at all four corners, the southern side connecting with the backstage. On either side of the stage were the boxes from which the womenfolk watched the plays. Each and every one of them had to take her own stool along, and they would all squeeze together at the windows to try and watch the action, only able to see it sideways. In front of the stage was the throng of male spectators, but apart from Lord Guan himself none had a seat.

And although there were stone steps in front of the door to the god's throne room, they served only as tiers for a standing audience, affording no opportunity whatsoever for watching from a seated position.

Theatres for troupes seeking to profit in the large cities were usually specifically designed for that purpose. In some ways their architecture and interior décor indicated whether their owners hoped to attract élite or broadly popular audiences; during the middle and late Qing period there were over twenty of the latter kind in Peking alone, as well as a host of them scattered in cities elsewhere. Larger playhouses tended to be leased to this or that major company, smaller halls to possibly less respectable, more fly-by-night groups, the sort who were here one day, gone the next. None of the major or minor troupes had a fixed base; they moved from one location to another, wherever and whenever a suitable auditorium could be had. The more select theatres were casually referred to as "*tang*" or "*huiguan*", and in them banquets might be served as a prelude or accompaniment to the entertainment by a top-rated troupe; the noisier playhouses for the more general, less prosperous public were tagged "*xilou*", "*chayuan*" or "*chalou*"; here tea might be brought and sipped by patrons, but no wine or full meals. Added to the incessant din of the gongs, drums and flutes might be discordant outbursts of applause disparagingly likened to "the competing squawks of ten thousand crows". In all such premises, performances went on from morning to twilight, often without stop (despite local ordinances to the contrary).

Qing-style theatres, as shown by those surviving and still used by actors, were entered through doors flanked at right and left by black-painted wooden pillars; over the portal a signboard bore the enterprise's grandiose, fanciful name: "Play Garden", "Palace of Pleasures" or the like. Posters on garish, eye-catching red paper such as proliferated throughout the city to announce the day's programme would also be glaringly in evidence here.

Inside, most seats faced the thrust stage, but on either side were two tiers of boxes or "verandas", several consisting of three or four "side-rooms", and later as many as fourteen or fifteen, with seats reserved for dignitaries. The boxes nearest the stage, the most desirable, might be for the nobility and the very wealthy, and in particular for ladies, who, hidden behind screens or partitions, could observe the play without being seen; though it was frequently said that this arrangement allowed them to exchange flirtatious looks with the actor–singers, perhaps a *laosheng*, richly attired and flatteringly made up, thereby seeming even more handsome and virile. A poem of the time alludes to this: "Dazzling glances fly up to the gallery / Fixing a rendezvous for supper tonight."

In the boxes, conveniently, were small tables for teapots and cups. Here, too, the seats were well upholstered, which they might not be in the pit (*chizi*). A dozen or more rich spectators might occupy a loge such as this, and behind them would be space in it for their footmen or others in their entourage.

In many details, these theatres were like those in Shakespeare's England. Ticket-buyers in the pit occupied long benches, and some also had the use of convenient tables; a full house would mean having to sit shoulder to shoulder, but in China, a country of masses, such close proximity was not unusual or distasteful. Those who paid the least sat at the very back, at an angle, with a distorted view of the performance. A preferred location in the *chizi* was at the left, a bit removed from the ear-splitting racket of cymbals, clappers and the fanfare that signalled each new character's entrance. (Traditionally, players came in from the right and exited at the left, through curtained doorways at the rear.) This seating also put one nearer the exiting actors, again encouraging liaisons with them.

The roof over the stage might be ornately decorated, architecturally pretentious. Around the stage itself, formed by black-lacquered columns and surrounded on three sides by spectators, ran a low railing; the platform was elevated a mere three to four feet, the playing area a square measuring seventeen to twenty feet all about. At the back was a huge curtain, perhaps crimson with gold-embroidered figures or patterns. Behind it, the hidden backstage was extensive, perhaps sixty or seventy feet wide, twenty feet deep; here the actors awaited their cues, and properties and costumes were stored, alongside two small rooms, one in which posters were prepared, and one to which those in the cast might retire at intervals to refresh themselves with sips of tea.

Oil lamps were the source of light, so air in the crowded enclosure was likely to be warm, stifling, conducive to sleepiness, an effect offset by the ongoing musical uproar, the shrill singing, the actors' exclamations, the pipes, gong, whining fiddles and staccato drum-beats.

The price of admission to each theatre is known in exact detail to historians but is meaningless in terms of today's currency. In some instances the charge was not for a seat, only for the tea.

The companies, or "societies", that were organized to produce stage-works with a commercial purpose usually had to include one or two persons who possessed degrees in literature; the reason for this is not clear, but perhaps it was to make sure that some member of the troupe had educated taste and an acquaintance with the classic dramas that might be revived, and also have at least a measure of respect for the integrity of the cherished works. The authorities were on guard against the increasing "vulgarity" of the popular stage.

In the Qing era, actors having become ever more important than the plays in which they appeared, they had an even greater say in adapting and often high-handedly altering the scripts they chose, not only when reviving classic pieces but also in working with authors and introducing fresh subjects.

Perhaps for this reason, as well as for others already given – above all, a repressive climate of censor-ship instilling unusual caution – the final decades of the nineteenth century yielded few new dramas of striking merit.

The plays of the day did not, could not, sharply mirror the changing, violent times in which they were written. Added to this, a huge library of classic scripts overhung Qing writers, discouraging fur-ther efforts. Instead of those who had close ties to the stage, it was now scholars, philosophers, closeted men of letters, always held in the highest regard in tradition-loving Chinese society, who resumed the task of providing new scripts, but their output was imitative, unexciting, often stiff and archaic; too much of it was didactic and pedantic. With the poetic Kunqu no longer in vogue, the stage held far less attraction to men of genuine literary gifts; the theatre was not a place in which to gain a lustrous reputation; or, if they attempted to join it to earn a few taels, they hesitated at signing their names to their work, another way of evading the wrath of the authorities. Even so, a few new plays were above average, if not distinguished. Among them were several created early in the century by Shu Wei (1765–1816), who left his home when he was seventeen (1782). He descended on his grandfather in Peking, in the family's ancestral residence, and spent much of his time at books found in its excep-tionally well-stocked library. His studiousness was not fully rewarded: though he earned a licentiate or "second degree" (1788), each of his nine attempts to pass an examination for a doctorate met with humiliating failure. Nevertheless, he obtained minor government posts that had him journeying about China. In 1797, while he was in Kweichow Province, a serious Miao uprising occurred. In his role as adviser to the provincial governor, he composed a message to the Miao people so eloquent in respond-ing to their grievances and protests that some of the tribesmen able to read Chinese were "moved to tears by his noble and persuasive words"; shortly, the rebels laid down their arms.

Back in Peking (1809), Shu Wei was brought to the notice of Prince Zhaolian, for whose private troupe he wrote six plays more or less in *zaju* style; the prince, much pleased, paid him generously. Some believe that in preparing these scripts Shu Wei had a collaborator, a friend, who was responsible in whole or part for the music, though Shu Wei himself was professionally adept at playing the *di*, *qin* and drums, and had great skill at composing songs, his drafts so competent that actors never had to ask for changes in them. He was also an accomplished painter and calligrapher. As a playwright he was better at dialogue than plot-making; he tended to resort to well-worn themes. In 1815 the death of his mother left him so overcome with grief that he could not eat, and his own death ensued two and a half months later.

Four plays are the legacy of Ling Tignan (1796–1861), of Kwangtung Province. His scripts reached print during the 1820s and were followed five years later by a thoughtful commentary on drama. Possessed of many talents, he was employed at times as a diplomat as well as an authority on coastal defence; he was also a biographer and historian – he studied the life of countries, including Great Britain, and argued that Christianity was not a suitable faith for his fellow Chinese.

Twice as many plays were contributed by Zhou Leqing (*fl.* 1829–52), a native of Chekiang Province, who wrote all eight of them while he was *en route* from there to Peking (1829). Based on familiar subjects, in which the dominant notes are those of tragic loss, he blithely transforms them into comedies or, at very least, contrives to have them end happily, however incongruously, prompting one critic to say that Zhou Leqing trades "nobility in the face of sorrow" for too easy laughter.

Yan Tingzhong (*fl.* 1839–52), a friend of Zhou Leqing, was a son of Yunnan Province. In a preface to one of his plays, he stated: "If there is no one who will enjoy my music, I shall sing it for the cicadas and the ancient trees to hear," a resolve many other long-unheralded poets have shared.

Though he enjoyed wide popularity, Huang Xiequin (d. *c.* 1862) had a lifelong struggle with ill health, which foreclosed his holding government posts. In garden retreats, which he himself built, he devoted himself to gardening – flowers and slender bamboo trees – as a setting for convivial gatherings with friends, who drank wine and half-seriously read aloud their poetry. From 1830 to 1847 he composed seven plays. His halcyon existence was interrupted by the Taiping Rebellion (1861), during which he had to take flight. In old age he had second thoughts about his plays and destroyed the blocks from which they were printed; however, his son-in-law subsequently retrieved them and had new editions issued. Huang Xiequin's plays were on ancient subjects or else derived from tales of the Ming and Qing periods.

Over the years, from the mid-eighteenth century, several dramatizations of Cao Zhan's much-loved, celebrated novel, *Red Chamber Dream*, were ventured. In the first two decades of the nineteenth no fewer than three playwrights in Kiangsu Province found material in the book's various chapters and episodes for colourful stage-fare. The most successful of these works was one by Hongdou Cunqio, whose name – or pseudonym – has to be translated as "Love-seed Village Wood-cutter".

In the second half of the nineteenth century good new plays were even rarer. But rising above mediocrity was Chen Lang (*fl.* 1885), who, when not serving as a salt official, found time to fashion eleven scripts.

Many of the other scripts being produced came even more than before from the hands of actors, had "vulgar and yokelish lyrics", were bawdy and, in the view of the more educated, not worthy of preservation in print, or fit to watch. A critic, Jiao Xun, placed blame for this on Wei Changsheng, who had abandoned the spirit of Yuan drama, where stories were concerned with "loyalty, filiality and honour, and had a strong effect on one's emotions". Such plays were still put on in rural areas, where even old farmers and fishermen, women and little boys could understand them, because their language was plain and straightforward. But now, due to the infection spread by Wei Changsheng and his imitators, all that was heard was "lewd, bawling, smutty-humoured songs". Jiao fervently hoped for a reversion to what theatre had been in previous days.

Several collections of Pihuang plays came out late in the century. In 1862 a volume containing forty short scripts in the new genre was published by Yu Zhi (1809–74), who toured the country with his own acting company. His temperament was evangelistic, and his hope was that his plays, which preached the more sober virtues, would have a lasting edifying effect on spectators. Another anthology of forty-six Pihuang works was assembled and published (1860) by Li Shizhong, but the names of the authors are omitted.

The excerpts that today make up much of the repertory of Peking opera have been so condensed and altered that, in many instances, even scholars cannot recognize their source; it is likely, also, that the original full-length scripts are lost, and their dates, titles and the identity of their composers are long since forgotten, hence exceedingly difficult to trace.

The members of the anti-Western political group, calling themselves the Boxers, were increasingly hostile to the dowager empress. She adopted a defensive stratagem, that of diverting their enmity towards the enclaves of privileged foreigners; this led to a murderous uprising against non-Chinese citizens and their legations. The outbreak provoked another invasion by Western troops. After sacking and looting Peking, they extracted a ruinous indemnity from the nation. The old lady and her court fled to Hsianfu. In 1908 she died, after first "arranging" that the imprisoned Kuang Hsu, rightful claimant to the throne, opportunely met his death the day before.

Kuang Hsu was succeeded by his infant nephew, P'u Yi, whose brief reign ended in abdication. Manchu rule was over. The revolutionists treated him magnanimously, sparing his life, allotting him a comfortable palace and a sizeable annuity.

More turmoil followed. In 1912 China became a republic under Sun Yat-sen, and the influence of the West on its distinctive art and culture was now a tidal sweep obliterating much of what had long been vital to it.

Favourite works from which short pieces are still being derived by the Peking Opera come from every past period. (To clarify: "Peking opera" is a genre of play rather than just one acting company, though China's foremost stage, a national institution situated in the capital, is also familiarly known by that name and specializes in works in the Pihuang style, along with other kinds of musical drama, as has already been remarked.)

The Sorrows of Han, frequently presented, originated in the Ming period; it concerns the woes of an emperor who is deceived by a wicked counsellor, and whose beloved kills herself rather than marry another. At the climax, the scheming minister's head is chopped off and given as an offering to the shade of the self-slain lady whom the emperor ceaselessly mourns. The play also inveighs against the decadence brought by riches, and by irresponsible rulers who cause national disasters.

Highly esteemed is *The Sufferings of Tou-E*, recounting the vicissitudes of the Chao family. Persecuted by the evil T'Anku, the orphaned descendant of this clan chooses an odd way to take vengeance on the tormentor. Voltaire, who delighted in reading Chinese plays, came across this script by Chi Chün-hsiang and tried his hand at a free adaptation, *The Chinese Orphan* (1755), which had a Paris production. Goethe, too, was tempted by the theme but left his version of it, *Elpenor*, unfinished; he could not handle it to his own satisfaction, his aim having been to fit it into the form of a classic German tragedy.

Pathos rules in Kuan Han-ch'ing's *The Exchange of Wind and Moon*, especially in the scene where a forlorn girl has to robe her mistress for the marriage ceremony at which the fortunate lady will be claimed by the man beloved by the slave girl.

In *The Ch'ingting Pearl* (also called *Demanding the Fish-tax*) a terrible requital is sought by a poor old man, Hsiao En, who for a long while has been relentlessly exploited by his all-powerful superiors. He resists paying an unjustly large tax on his catch. At the instigation of a rich landowner, the law punishes him cruelly for his stubbornness, whereat he retaliates against not only the greedy landowner but his whole family, in a way that to most Western readers will seem to be excessive retribution. (This play sometimes bears another title: *The Right to Kill*.)

From the fourteenth-century Ming dynasty, *The Beautiful Bait* tells of a young lady who is used to lure a villainous general to his death, a tale reminiscent of Judith beguiling Holofernes in the Bible. It is adapted from an epic novel of the same period, *The Three Kingdoms*, which in turn is based on a historical incident in the latter half of the Han dynasty (206 BC–AD 220), when a weak emperor was in the toils of his ambitious prime minister, Tung Cho. (This script was enacted in the West, including New York, in the mid-twentieth century by the touring Foo Hsing Theatre of Taipan, which chose not to offer it in translation, making it unintelligible to most. This was before wearing earphones at a foreign-language play let one hear the dialogue rendered into one's own speech, and surtitles had not been introduced.)

For a long time even printed translations of classic Chinese plays were almost non-existent. Two rare exceptions were *Lady Precious Stream*, adapted for the London stage, and then New York, where it evoked much approval as an exotic, charming novelty, by S.I. Hsiung (1934), who later did the same for *Romance of the Western Pavilion* (or *West Wing*). Most notable of modern adaptations have been those in German of *The Circle of Chalk*, first by the poet A.H. Klabund (1925), given a beautiful production, and again by Bertolt Brecht. Written between 1944 and 1945, the Brechtian version had its première in English at Northfield, Minnesota (1948), followed by a début in German in Berlin at the Theater am Schiffbauerdamm (1954), with many script changes by the polemical Brecht to make his political points. (His title for the play is *The Caucasian Chalk Circle*; it has a musical score by Paul Dessau.)

Lady Precious Stream centres on a faithful young lady who is made to suffer by a wicked brother-in-law. She is married to a gardener, a young man of her own choice, who has gone away, leaving her penniless. When he returns he has become the husband of the loving but predatory Princess of the Western Regions. His neglected first bride plays various games, teasingly, before she agrees to take him back. The infatuated princess must be content to accept the role of second wife. In Hsiung's English adaptation the princess and the gardener are not wedded, though she helps him to attain the status of royalty. She remains his friend and respects his earlier, deeper bond to Lady Precious Stream. The play's tone is one of romantic high comedy, at times admixed with touches of pathos.

The original *Circle of Chalk*, a satire aimed at official corruption – which is why it attracted Brecht – has to do with a law clerk misled in an affair with a married woman. She poisons her husband and cunningly shifts the guilt to his second wife, the mother of a child who is now the heir to his parent's fortune. With further intervention and plotting by the law clerk, the bewildered second wife is convicted of the poisoning; she undergoes much fear and suffering before a higher, wiser judge probes the evidence and acquits her. But now, undeterred, the first wife lays claim to the boy, asserting that he is really her child. The judge is faced with a Solomonic task. In his courtroom he draws a circle of chalk, portentously stating that it is magical, and places the child in the centre. Only the actual mother can free him from it. This psychological ploy succeeds: the true mother regains her boy, and the guilty ones are exposed.

Other standard items in the Peking Opera repertory include *The White Snake* and *The Empty City Ruse*. In the first of these a white snake, having become immortal and dwelling in the heavens, transforms itself into a beautiful girl and returns to earth. Encountering a blue snake, a lesser immortal who has similarly metamorphosed to lovely human form, Lady White – as the snake is now known – chooses her as a maidservant. Together they take up housekeeping in Hangzhou.

Lady White meets a young man, Xu Xian, judges him handsome, weds him. The trio move to a city along the Yangtze River, where the husband, at his wife's instigation, sets up a medicine shop. With her magical powers she provides him with nostrums that work marvels, and he prospers greatly.

Xu Xian is warned by a Buddhist priest about the true nature of Lady White, her innate reptilian character. He is given a potion for her to drink, which will cause her to change back to her former self. The drink fulfils its task; when Xu Xian sees his wife as a snake he dies of fright. She goes to the heavens in pursuit of him, and with much difficulty obtains another medicinal herb that restores him to life.

He is not only without gratitude for all she has done on his behalf, but even more afraid of her than before; he takes refuge in a Buddhist monastery, whose staunch abbot vows to protect him. Lady White's pleas to the abbot are rejected; furious, she recruits a large army of underwater creatures and attacks the monastery.

The battle between the two forces is indecisive: the abbot, though also a master of magic, cannot capture Lady White, nor she seize the fugitive Xu Xian. Finally the abbot guesses what motivates Lady White: she is pregnant. He advises Xu Xian to rejoin his wife until the child is born. On the husband's arrival Blue Snake lifts her sword, but Lady White stops her. After the child's birth Xu Xian gains the assistance of the abbot-magician in having Lady White revert from her mortal shape and be imprisoned as White Snake under the Thunder Peak Pagoda by West Lake in Hangzhou. From there she is freed by her loyal maidservant Blue Snake, and the two other-worldly figures leave for heaven once more.

The Empty City Ruse borrows an episode from the famous novel *The Romance of the Three Kingdoms* about a war between the Kingdoms of Shu (221–63) and Wei (220–65). Sima Yi, heading the Wei forces, has them seize strategic places that encircle Hanzhong. In a counter-effort, his opponent, General Zhuge Liang, orders his men to hold Jieting, but his subordinate Commander Ma Su fails to do so, losing the battle and fleeing the city, which is occupied by the enemy. The Wei troops advance on Xicheng, where Zhuge Liang stays on, but without adequate support. Warned that Sima Yi's men are closing in, the wily Zhuge Liang has the city's gates thrown open and mounts the city wall. In clear view, he pretends to relax, plays his lute, quaffs wine. His few soldiers are disguised as street-cleaners.

Beholding Zhuge Liang's strange behaviour, and aware of his reputation for trickery, Sima Yi halts his troops' forward march. He suspects that Zhuge Liang has prepared an ambush into which he is luring the invaders; growing cautious, Sima Yi draws back, retreating forty li and changing his plans. He has been outwitted; the delay allows reinforcements to arrive, headed by the ever-victorious Zhao Yun; they rescue Zhuge Liang. For his failure to obey orders Ma Su is executed by Zhuge Liang, who blames himself for having misplaced his trust in him. This story provides many logical pretexts for boastful singing, acrobatic feats and martial arts.

Leaving a Son in a Mulberry Orchard depicts a father's harsh self-sacrifice for his child. In *Beauty Defies Tyranny* Zhao Yanrong, daughter of a sycophantic court minister, is sought by the emperor. To avoid being possessed by him, she feigns insanity. Her "mad scene", a dance, is a display of the utmost virtuosity. A like opportunity is granted the *dan* portraying Su San in *Lady Magnolia*, in which a wronged courtesan is brought to trial, only to discover that her long-lost lover is seated on the panel of judges. Yang Yuan, concubine of the Tang emperor Ming Huang, imbibes too much after being disappointed by a missed rendezvous in *The Drunken Beauty*. An incident in the novel *A Dream of Red Mansions* provides an extract, *Daiyu Burying Flowers*. And so on . . . the list unrolls: *The Goddess of River Luo*, *The King's Parting from His Favourite*, *Fanjiang Pass*, *Autumn River*, *Calling Off the Feast*.

(New World Press, in Beijing, has issued a booklet, *Peking Opera and Mei Lanfang* [1981], by Wu Zuguang, Huang Zuolin and Mei Shaowu, containing English synopses of twenty-five works with roles taken by the great actor, among the 100 in which he regularly appeared. The Foreign Language Press, also in Beijing, has put out a volume, *Selected Plays of Guan Hanqing* [or *Hong Sheng*, 1956], translated by Yang Xianyi and Gladys Yang. Both books have been of considerable help in the preparation of this chapter.)

Since the pieces on display are merely excerpts – highlights – from vanished full-length plays, most of their authors unknown and the works having no completely discernible plots or continuity, their quality as drama can hardly be appreciated. What are offered are samples, rather skeletonic. This may explain, along with the formidable language barrier, the opinion among Western critics that with very few exceptions even the classic Chinese plays are of scant worth. Most general historians of theatre pay them little heed. Sheldon Cheney declared, "Chinese drama has no literary value for us." Vera Roberts lists only four titles, two of them *The Lute* and *The Circle of Chalk*, with not even a sentence of description or commentary. Margot Berthold alludes to about ten famous scripts, mostly the same as those cited by the other chroniclers, but with hardly any discussion of the plays' content. (All these writers do go into a good deal of detail about Chinese stage techniques.) John Gassner remarks: "The examples with which we are familiar are exceptionally clear and forthright. It is to their lack of intense passion, to their relatively uncomplicated characterization, and to the fact that the Mandarin poets disdained so popular a medium that we must attribute a want of greatness to the Chinese drama. Even with this concession, however, the customary funeral oration on the Chinese plays is somewhat inappropriate. At least a number of them compare favorably with great stretches of European drama. The law of averages itself might make this inevitable if we remember that in the ninety years of the Yuan dynasty alone some five hundred plays of known authorship were written by eighty-five playwrights."

Also, from Gassner: "Tragedy does not figure prominently on the stage, although it is not absent in so mournful a work as *The Sorrow of Han* . . . or *Beauty*, the heroine of which is taken from her home by marauders and dies patriotically. Satire, however, is rarely absent in a nation which has had so many and such long-standing reasons for disillusionment. Love, in particular, is treated with the irony characteristic of a race that regards it as a form of childishness and banished actresses from the stage, leaving most feminine roles to highly paid masculine specialists like the famous Mei Lanfang."

Actually, Western critics have very little acquaintance with classic Chinese drama. Few of them have read the scripts or have seen productions or can interpret the symbolism inherent in how the works are presented. One reason is that for decades after the establishment of the People's Republic the country was in turmoil and largely closed to foreigners. Hopeful and sagacious as he always was, Gassner added this sentence to his few paragraphs a half-century ago: "What new developments may arise cannot be foretold at this distance, but it is possible that the reawakening of the Chinese people will provide a fresh incentive to significant dramatic composition." Indeed, this has happened, with an incursion of Western ideas.

Chinese artists have a striking sense of the dramatic, an unsurpassed flair for "theatre"; to be fully and fairly judged, their plays must be seen, and at such moments can be enthralling. "Theatre" is not experienced in a reading but only when an offering is beheld in its usual, entire, dazzling panoply. This holds for every genre of "theatre", wherever produced. With their unerring feel for what commands the stage, the Chinese create astonishing effects, imagery that remains quite hauntingly bright in the fortunate spectator's memory. There are scenes of "raw emotive power"; robust humour abounds, together with delicate, ebullient fantasy and a profusion of lyric poetry that flows on unceasingly, the compound of all this being kinetic "theatre" of a high order.

Even though the text and substance, the fun and sentiment, of thousands of Chinese plays are little known in the West, the unique means of projecting them have been widely influential and imitated. The conventions of staging evolved by Chinese performers have proved attractive everywhere. Like India, China is a subcontinent; its people, a mixture of many races, speak a babble of dialects, the majority using Cantonese or Mandarin. For centuries, political and linguistic divisions prevailed between North and South, as well as between the central regions and those remote from them. By the end of the Manchu reign, however, the country's culture had become surprisingly homogeneous. Throughout China, and among its immense population, the idiomatic facets of painting and theatre vary in only small ways. The stage shows a slight Indian influence, but it in turn has exerted a pervasive effect on near-by Asian countries, apparent in Tibet, Vietnam, Korea, Japan and Okinawa. A swarm of venturesome overseas Chinese, who settled everywhere in the Far East and Pacific archipelagos, have carried their values and art with them, and not least their long-cherished theatre.

In the second half of the twentieth century Peking opera troupes began to tour in Europe and North America, displaying their brilliant fare and inspiring further emulation. But even if these companies had stayed home, by possessing a history of over 2,000 years and an audience drawn from the largest population in the world, Chinese theatre, very different in its concept of staging, should have been accorded far more attention in Western chronicles of the drama.

Totally artificial, Chinese theatre is dedicated to *illusion* – which is why it is hailed by perceptive critics as *pure* "theatre", a rarefied aesthetic experience. The spectator's own imagination is engaged, providing whatever realistic elements are lacking, and thereby he or she becomes a participant in the creation of the work. The action takes place visibly on stage, but the setting and many material aspects of the story exist only in the spectator's mind, given only the most minimal suggestions and stimuli. The two "theatres", the actors' and the onlooker's, are combined for the full event to be realized. This has been likened, on a primary level, to a child's daydreaming and "make-believe", a reversion to and refinement of a drive instinctive in the psyche, and never outgrown. (This theory was propounded two centuries ago by the German dramatist–philosopher Friedrich Schiller.) Theatre like that of the Chinese fulfils an inherent human want, the wish and compulsion to play, an exercise of the fancy, yielding pleasure and sometimes exhilaration.

Essential to stylized productions is the Property Man, a role originating with the Chinese. On the almost bare stage, this attendant comes and goes, dressed totally in black, his dark garb implying that he is invisible. He brings each actor the properties required at a certain moment in the action: a sword, a fan, a brush and writing tablet, a message on a scroll, a magic wand, a change of costume, a flower, a chair, a table. Then, when the player no longer needs it, the Property Man relieves him or "her" of it. This leaves the stage clear of solid obstructions and allows the actor to gesture with both hands, to resort to acrobatics, to dance, to engage in combat, or otherwise move as unencumbered as possible while weighed down by heavy, full, sweeping ornamented attire.

To counter the absence of scenery, other than an elaborately embroidered or painted backdrop, verbal descriptions of the setting may suffice, but often mere acrobatic pantomime proves quite enough to indicate that an imaginary wall is being scaled, or a door is being forced open, or even a suggested lake is being paddled across in a gently rolling, bobbing skiff. A chair, brought on, is supposed to be a throne, a mountain to climb, or a tower from which an alert watch is kept on an enemy.

The actor's gift for pantomime is always under challenge, though by now most of the gestures and physical betokenings are traditional and quickly recognized by the spectator. To portray the wind, a player bearing a black flag runs across the stage; if wading in water, he carries another little flag on which fishes are painted; or flags set in a line may be the banks of a wide river. A chair set on its side is a crag to be ascended; a rug with a floral design is a large garden. A castle is represented by a blue cloth with white bricks depicted on it. A curtain hung between two chairs is a bedchamber. Two yellow flags, with wheels pictured on them, are held aloft by the actor to indicate that he is riding in a rickshaw, and by his swerves as he proceeds he conjures up the obstructing traffic through which the vehicle is weaving. A tasselled or tufted whip in his hand, while he strides vigorously, means that he is astride a cantering horse. Should the hero fall from his steed, the compassionate Property Man, with foresight, will have already supplied a cushion to ease his landing. An actor bearing an oar is clearly travelling by boat. A red flag brandished before a character's face signals that he has been decapitated; a red sack beside him represents his chopped-off head. If an actor crosses his eyes and sinks back into the clasp of a companion, he is obviously in the unhappy throes of death. A ghost signifies his ethereality by wisps of straw dangling from his ears. Spirits of long-dead ancestors return in black veils. The visage of a person who is ill is hidden by a yellow veil; a bride is singled out by a red veil. A round head-covering on an official alerts us that he is dishonest. Movements about the stage, as far as possible, are circular due to a belief that the circle represents "the perfect union of opposites", the *ying* and *yang*.

Some effects are realistic, fire and gunpowder in particular – gunpowder is a Chinese invention.

To learn such symbolic gestures and physical signings, scores of them, a painstaking apprenticeship is necessary; it follows that a goodly number of newcomers belong to families of actors, who hand on respected conventions from this generation to the next.

A few pieces of white paper thrown into the air by the Property Man suffice to convey the image of a snowstorm, while each banner held up behind a general stands for 1,000 men accompanying him into battle, so five flags providing him with an army of 5,000 men. In a struggle no actual blows are struck – the spectator is asked to take them for granted, and readily does so. An important incident of combat is underscored by even livelier tumbling. Leaps and applause-getting somersaults may illustrate how a fortress wall is surmounted. Bouncing feints, whirls and thrusts, mimed agile spear-throwing or loosening of arrows, portray a martial confrontation, but always without physical contact.

Make-up, as said before, indicates character, but not realistically; again, conventions dictate what is chosen. Cosmetics are applied with mask-like thickness. A white-powdered face identifies a man as powerful but treacherous; scarlet emphasizes his honesty and fidelity; green and black denote personal crudeness. Heroes wear light make-up and rouged shading; some are beardless. The refined features of the "flower", or heroine, are flour-white, eyebrows heavy with mascara, eyes deeply shadowed, lips very reddened – the markings extend from the nose over the soft cheeks, and even cover the eyelids. The flush is considered voluptuous and enticing. The deeper the flush, the more alluring and salacious is the effect. The mouth is painted into a tiny pout called "the small cherry". Hidden by the headdress is a painfully tight bandeau drawing up the flesh of the face and lifting the eyes into an exaggerated slant, almond-like. The smile of the "flower" is often described as lascivious, though usually her conduct is virtuous.

Other roles may call for even more grotesque make-up: accordingly, they are known as "painted faces". The designs reveal that these persons are either remarkably good or exceptionally wicked. The good characters put on oily paints, and their faces shine; but the evil ones are so thickly powdered that their features are dulled. White symbolizes ruthlessness; green and blue are worn by demons and obstinate ruffians or outlaws, purple by robbers; but red on a man's face is a sign of his virtue, and yellow of his strength and wit. The whiter the features, the wickeder the character portrayed. The length and colour of a beard – red, black, brown, blue or white – betoken the wearer's official rank, social importance and masculinity, as well as his age. The hero never has a moustache, the villain sports a lengthy one. Altogether there are some 250 cosmetic designs, each one assigned to a distinct type of person. The make-up hardly attempts to seem "natural" – artificial eyes are painted above or below the actual ones, and fangs are sometimes added to the chin. Gods use golden paint to enhance their features. Clowns are mostly bare-faced, save for a patch of white smeared around the eyes and the bridge of the nose.

As already noted, the costuming is gorgeous, though occasionally for realism's sake a beggar may appear in rags. (Because the robes are so expensive, minor companies may rent them – many are, indeed, of museum quality.) The "flower" is attired in embroidered silks and satins; her gown might also be tinselled, and she carries a scarf that she manipulates gracefully. She may also require long, full sleeves, flinging them up in a frenzied, distraught manner, as does Zhao Yanrong in the great scene in *Beauty Defies Tyranny* where she feigns madness, abruptly dropping her arms, shivering in terror, throwing off her coral diadem and loosing her hair, to let it fall before her face, while she laughs insanely. Sleeve-play may express many emotions, from joy to despair, and is a second language. Gossamer, the fluttering sleeves have been likened to butterfly wings.

The "flower's" feet are tiny, as befits the historical roles she invariably undertakes. Such feet are called, with a Chinese love for vivid simile and metaphor, "golden lilies". To achieve the effect, the female impersonator must fit his feet into wooden shoes scarcely more than an inch high and three inches long, a torturous effort. In movement, he is virtually standing on his toes, much like a Western ballerina. The tiny shoes, painted with floral designs, are laced up to the calf, a detail concealed by the slender but flowing trousers long chosen by Chinese women. Only the shoes show. The performer's gait is affected by these narrow "stilts", but they also make him ("her") look taller, over-topping the hero and even the villain. They also induce the "flower" to sway – or teeter – as though on a tight-rope, the neck and back rigidly upright, while swinging the arms for balance. The second women, in "sub-dued dress" roles, are similarly noted for the lyrical movement of their long, white sleeves.

Scholar heroes wear identifying hats: oval, with starched wings, that flutter at each shake or nod of the head. Their apparel is apt to be white, pink or light blue. The "painted faces", the more bizarrely made-up warriors and aggressively sinister counsellors, have broad, padded shoulders, heavy silk robes brocaded in patterns that suggest armour or military insignia, perhaps embroidered tiger-heads – a high-ranking general may boast four pennants on his back, and high pheasant plumes in his head-dress; and to help him look impressively tall, high, thick-soled shoes, reminiscent of the *cothurnus* of Greek and Roman tragedians. Such styles derive from the aristocratic dress of medieval times, from the eighth century to the sixteenth, with much borrowed from the Ming period.

Again, symbolic meanings are attached to various colours, a concept pervasive in Chinese thought, where each musical note is given cosmic significance. Such out-of-this-world importance ascribed to anything as mundane and frivolous as stage dress is perhaps ascribed less weight, yet does prevail. A civilian is clothed in blue, an official in red, an old man in brown, a rascal in black, an emperor in yellow.

In this thoroughly stylized theatre the highest art is that of an old man portraying a young girl. He is truly creating an illusion. Indeed, female impersonation is admired throughout much of the Far East. For a girl to act the role of a girl is too simple. The "flower" is nearly always the star part. Audiences come to see their favourite impersonator in such roles, which call for the heroine to be, in turn, graceful, vivacious, courageous, naïve, pathetic. The second woman is likely to be a mother-in-law. The male *chou* (clown) may be a comic maidservant. (The ban on women on the stage is said to be due, in part, to a Qing emperor's imprudent marriage to an actress.)

The music dictates the rhythm of every performance, especially that of the "flower" with her "language of the fan" and "language of the sleeve", as well as other prescribed gestures of hands and fingers. As has been remarked, uninitiated Westerners often find it difficult to appreciate the charm of the unnerving – to them – whining vocal and instrumental accompaniment. Both young male and female players use a falsetto voice.

A typical orchestra has eight players, seated in clear view at left on the stage, or else at the rear of it or above in a small balcony. The instruments for Pihuang are the *huqin* fiddle (or a twentieth-century replacement, the mellower two-stringed *erhu*); also, the *yueqin* (guitar), the *sanxian* (banjo), the *di* (flute), the *suona* (clarion), the *ban* (clapper), and a range of gongs, cymbals and drums. A military drama may use percussion solely. To beat time, the conductor employs a clapper; he also plays a small drum. Each musician is apt to preside over more than one instrument, so the sound may be augmented by rattles, reed organs or horns. The player may not depend on printed notes, the score likely to have been personally handed on from teachers to pupils over long stretches of time. Both performer and musician rely greatly on memory, the actor having mastered as many as 100 or, as with Mei Lan-fang, 200 parts.

The close affinity between actor and musician is an essential one; for every shading of character, broad or subtle, their coordination is necessary. The second woman, the "subdued dress" who takes old women's roles, usually has the longest, most poignant arias. The "painted faces" sing gruffly, in their natural masculine voice, in a manner appropriate to their harsher persona. Comedians also intone robustly. There are a few quiet moments, in passages in Kunqu, but otherwise the music goes on continuously at full blast, high-pitched, ear-piercing, endlessly repetitive.

Pihuang music, prevalent in Peking opera, is simpler than most previous forms; overall it is less varied, which allows both the singer and the spectator to adapt and respond to its changing moods more easily. The scripts are also likely to contain fewer arias, and the lyrics, rhymed couplets, usually but not always of equal length, seven to ten syllables, tend to be more clearly comprehended because the syllables are elongated, the singer dwelling on each one. This makes the proportion of melody seem larger than it actually is. The music is set to the words, rather than the words being chosen to match the score. Many other rules govern here, of course, of a highly technical nature. A mixture of provincial dialects, from Hupeh, Anhwei, Szechwan and Peking itself, may result in inconsistent pronunciation of words and phrases in the lyrics. The street-wise *chou*, in particular, uses much Peking slang and frequently resorts to colloquialisms, but even élite spectators are likely to be well acquainted with these.

The prominence of gymnastics in Chinese "opera" is astonishing to Occidental observers. Even the "flower" may vent feelings in this most externalized fashion, executing somersaults or springing leaps while in the tiny, cramping shoes, a striking stunt that always wins the audience's loud approbation.

Once more, what counts most in this theatre is the acting, and after that the lavishness of the costumes and properties, and the strange evocativeness of the make-up, far from any kind of realism. What might have been the literary value of the original, classic texts is difficult to judge, so many of them having vanished, with only excerpts, brief, treasured episodes now retained, and many of them greatly altered.

When Chinese methods of production were finally discovered by the West, they exerted a major influence on twentieth-century stagecraft and theatre theory, instantly capturing the interest and enthusiasm of Russian and German playwrights and directors – Evreinov, Meyerhold, Tairov, Brecht, Piscator – and scene designers, in the eruptive spread of a new movement, Presentationalism. In a slightly later phase, in North America and England, some details of the technique were adopted by Thornton Wilder and Dylan Thomas in their widely accepted plays *Our Town* and *Under Milkwood*, works that were both liberating and seminal. (Wilder, son of an American consul, had grown up in China and had frequently been exposed to its highly imaginative, poetic style of staging.)

— 3 —

DEVIL DANCES, SHADOW PLAYS

Any hasty survey of the traditional ceremonial plays and dances of other countries in the Far East reveals them to be almost as immemorially old and largely shaped by Indian and Chinese prototypes, the degree of resemblance varying with their peoples' contiguity to those huge civilizations. The theatre arts here are those of Ceylon, Burma, Thailand, Cambodia, Java, Tibet, Korea and the Philippines.

In the 1950s Faubion Bowers travelled through most of these lands and observed their sacred and popular dance and drama forms, which he described in his *Theatre in the East*, to me a helpful guide, as has been Leonard Pronko's *Theatre East and West*. I have also drawn on Margot Berthold and Oscar Brockett, who take up the subject more briefly, and on Vera Roberts, whose comments are even more glancing.

By the time I paid a second visit to some places in the Orient in the 1980s, many of the classic plays and dances and entertainments were scarcely to be seen, especially in Burma, Cambodia and Tibet – civil wars and radical changes in governance had almost made their aesthetic heritage extinct or Western influences had sadly altered them, at least for the moment; though possibly they will return, a rebirth most likely to happen in Cambodia, after the temporary reconstitution there of the monarchy (1993).

In Ceylon (now Sri Lanka) the music shows its indebtedness to that of nearby India; yet exorcism rites, preserved in its world-famed Devil Dances, are indigenous (Sinhalese), unlike those found anywhere else. Such ritual observances are meant to drive out the evil spirits besetting a sick or insane person, to aid a pregnant woman or assist a family badly in need of better luck. The ceremony is usually performed by a professional cast at night by torchlight on a road or in a garden near the dwelling of the unhappy victim. A shrine is erected, and the invalid lies on a dais. The dance of purification goes on from dusk to dawn in clouds of incense. It embodies much symbolism based on local demonology, and here again some of the men impersonate women.

More important artistically are other dances designated as Kandyan, religious in origin and brought from South India at least 2,000 years ago, losing their sacred character in some places, growing partially or purely aesthetic in such instances and performed for the amusement of kings and their guests. Essentially mimetic, presenting scenes from court life, parodies of elephants walking or birds swooping, these dances also became part of the great annual procession celebrating the country's most precious relic, the public showing of Buddha's tooth.

When the kings could no longer afford to maintain the dance troupes, the Buddhist clergy took over the obligation. The dances are held in temple courtyards as part of religious services. Sacred at the start, then secular, the Kandyan dances are sacred once more. What is primary are the spectacular costumes of beaten silver, the participants glistening from their conical and wide-brimmed headdress to their epaulettes and breastplates, cinctures and bracelets, all inset with huge sapphires. The choreography owes much to Indian idioms, with some local variations.

Though drama was less significant as an art in Ceylon, four kinds of folk plays developed. Kolam is the most ancient and enduring, albeit of a minor order. A Kolam play begins with an explanatory song and masked-dance prologue, the masks made of beautifully painted, carved wood, varying in size according to the status of the characters represented – those for the king and queen are very large, covering the entire head; they are fashioned of hollowed-out tree-trunks and consequently are so heavy and high that they must be supported by wooden swords held upright by the dancers, who must be guided by attendants, the performers in royal roles being unable to lower their gaze to note their own movements. The regal masks also have elaborately filigreed headdresses on which are stylized figures of flowers and birds.

In the prologues, the emphasis is on pantomime rather than speech. The enactments that follow are accompanied by chants, the singers keeping time to the rhythm of drums, while the masked actors offer the story with a reliance on a plenitude of tumbling and vigorous acrobatics. Each character is a stock figure, the number of them limited to how many masks already belong to the troupe; new characters can only be added if more delicately carved masks are prepared for them by the master of the troupe. Demons and gods of many kinds, in vivid costumes and maskings, take part in the unfolding narrative, which is usually an anecdote from the life of Buddha or one of his saintly disciples, and the denouement is apt to be a miracle performed by the Heavenly One. Reward for conjugal fidelity, and punishment for adulterous acts, are the frequent themes: again, a moral resolution is achieved through the supernatural aid of the Buddha.

A lesser, provincial form of Kolam is the Sokari, staged by certain hill-tribes in the Kandy and Badulla regions. The plays mostly concern the misadventures of a lovely but faithless wife named

Sokari. The plots of both Kolam and Sokari will sound familiar to some Western readers: for example, a scholar–prince weds the daughter of his master. While taking home his bride, he is waylaid by a hunter who is immediately attracted to the young wife. The two men fight to possess her, and when the sword is struck from the prince's hand the wife retrieves it, but, more impressed by the hunter than by her husband, she gives the weapon to the attacker, who slays the prince. After that, the murderer robs and abandons the young wife, declaring that if she wantonly betrayed her husband she might in time act the same way towards him. Then Buddha appears in the guise of a jackal to reprove and chastise her, with a moral allegory as an epilogue. (This would seem to be a forerunner of *Rashomon*, the famed Japanese tale.)

In another well-known Sokari, the adulterous wife has an affair with the doctor who has pronounced her husband dead, though actually her ailing mate is still alive. (Here are echoes of *In the Shadows of the Glen* by John Millington Synge, the Irish dramatist.)

A comparatively recent folk form is Nadagam, dating from the early nineteenth century. Short-lived, it consisted mostly of songs, loosely integrated, on themes drawn impartially from Christianity, Occidental fairy-tales and fanciful incidents in the life of the Buddha. The songs, rather than the play-texts, have survived, and sometimes the music from them accompanies puppet shows given in scattered villages.

Plays called Pasu, too, have links to Christianity: they are Sinhalese versions of the Passion of Christ, presented at the Easter season. But they contain elements displeasing to the Church and have twice been banned, the second time because women participated in them. The earlier ban was due to the scandalous conduct of mischievous boys who with blackened faces took on the roles of devils.

In Burma (later Myanmar), bordering on both India and China, enthusiasm for theatre and dance seemed to be a marked characteristic of its culture. In the southern regions of the country, especially, a fondness for a form of musical drama known as Zat Pwé prevailed. The inherent gaiety and charm of the Burmese was said to have found its full expression in these plays, largely devoted to accounts of kings and queens and dynastic struggles, with orchestral accompaniment, perhaps a dozen native instruments, the most prominent apt to be teakwood xylophones and oddly shaped and ornately encased drums, along with bamboo tubes, castanets, tiny cymbals and heavy gongs. The popularity of the theatre was evident in villages as well as in cities, with dramatic performances a part of every festival, especially when the moon was full. Some of these were given on temporary bamboo stages under thatched roofs in huts with enclosures surrounded by palm-leaf woven fences, the spectators seated cross-legged on the bare ground, or on mats, with a few chairs for notables. But in Rangoon (later Yangon), the capital, the audience might be very large, in the thousands.

The more ancient folk plays borrowed Indian themes: vignettes from Buddha's life, particularly about his youth and the events leading up to his Enlightenment, though no actor ever committed the impiety of appearing as the Holy One himself. Dance forms, too, had great antiquity and can be traced to the ninth and eleventh centuries.

Burma's major drama, however, was of more recent date, the close of the eighteenth century. In the early nineteenth century a Ministry of Theatre was set up to enforce rules and decorum, the latter with specific reference not only to plays on sacred themes but also to those voicing political views, which were likely to intrude. In these more modern Zat Pwé scripts scheming pretenders to the throne were depicted, along with their royal victims. There were, in all, six types of Pwé, of which Zat was the best liked. Usually, after the depositions and flights of monarchs, the dramas ended happily with blissful marriages and triumphant restorations and righting of all wrongs. Comedy alternated with tears, and there were song and dance intervals to lend weight to the mood of the scene just preceding. Exotic costumes – conical golden headdresses, bedizened satin robes and silver weapons – were a high feature. Another important aspect was the music, exceptionally harmonious and pleasing, even to Westerners, and very expressive as well as complex. Performances of these musical dramas started at nine in the evening and lasted until four in the morning, watched by rapt, tireless audiences. Plays were published in book form and sold thousands of copies.

Early ambassadors to the court at Peking are said to have introduced themselves by an "alphabet dance" in which by gestures they extended homage to their then Chinese rulers. The dance interludes in the Zat Pwé were exuberant, energetic. The dancers, heads crowned with flowers, crouched, leapt, swirled about. The performers usually used fans, which they manipulated in a number of ways. Sorrow was seldom represented (the Burmese believing that only the joyful express themselves in dance), with grave moods suggested by a more stately pace. Clowning was prominent, and mostly the good humour of this smiling people was evident in their dances, too. A condensed form of Zat Pwé, consisting only of clown and dance elements, was frequently offered and known as Anyein Pwé. This ebullient entertainment would last about two hours and has been likened to a minstrel show.

Large, lengthy religious pageants, Yein Pwé, were given on special occasions, very holy ones, as more often were puppet plays; and to both kinds of works Zat Pwé owed pantomimic and dance gestures, the movements of the actors and dancers resembling those of marionettes attached to strings. Though the puppet theatre had a fervent vogue during the eighteen and nineteenth centuries, it eventually lost favour.

Nat Pwé, or the Spirit Dance, was another Burmese theatrical form. The purpose was to exorcise thirty-seven kinds of spirits, and also to aid in divination; therefore the dance was enacted only on days (or, rather, nights) that were astrologically auspicious, in addition to the Burmese New Year, which comes in spring. The dancers sometimes became possessed, falling into rigid or quivering trances. Many changes of costume were required during a dance seance of this kind, and incense was burned, while much sprinkling of holy water on the entranced participants took place, along with propitiatory offerings of flowers, nuts and other foodstuffs. At the end, gold coins were collected in a gilt bowl from the spectators. The spirits to be appeased were mostly pre-Buddhist ones.

In the northern regions of the country, bordering on China, there was no drama and dance was predominant. Hill-tribes such as the Shan, Chin, Kachin and Naga had their own spring and harvest rituals, to simpler music provided by drums, cymbals and gongs. There were no professional performers – this was folk art. Some dances were merely processional, young couples slowly moving in circles and other graceful patterns, while singing and gesticulating. Or there might be attempts to imitate animals – a flying horse, a bird, a yak – in whimsical costumes that put one in mind of the non-human figures in Aristophanic comedies. As birds, the dancers might strut, peck, hunt for food, flirt and mate, go off with ruffled feathers – strong totemistic elements were evident here. A third category was the "fight-dance", Lai Kai, a display of virtuosity in combat, with or without weapons, to drum-beats. When swords were used a real element of danger was present, of gashing or grazing. Sometimes the combatants employed flaming torches, whirled in a "fire-dance", as they ducked and feinted, a genuinely perilous enactment, since it would have been easy to singe or burn an opponent or oneself.

Thailand (long known as Siam) shares a boundary with Burma and for periods was conquered and occupied by the Burmese; its art, therefore, shows much Indian influence. Most theatre forms in Thailand, such as the Khon, Lakon and Likay, are comparatively recent, developing in the past two centuries, but dance in that country has a longer history. The oldest, classic dance movements have been absorbed into more modern postures and gestures. Borrowed from the Indian *mudras*, the symbolic finger messages have become even more subtle and even attenuated, to the point where they merely suggest rather than clearly communicate their meaning. They have become simple expressions of general sentiments and emotions: joy, sorrow, anger, love and so on. But they are still a sign language that can convey ideas, and they derive from the "alphabet dances" that have been remarked upon as having been performed by the early Burmese. Originally, the "alphabet dance", or Maebot, consisted of sixty-four "letters" – gestures, movements and poses that signified such poetic thoughts as

"Swan in Flight", "Putting the Lady to Sleep", "Wedded Love", "The Peacock Dances", "Bee's Caress", "The Cockatoo". King Rama I (1736–1809) shortened the list to nineteen that are still mastered and enacted and, along with an exercise called "Dancing to the Fast and Slow", constitute the basis of all Thai dance, much as the five fundamental "positions" are the primary material and tools for the choreographers of Western ballet. Some of the nineteen have lost their original intent and have become quite abstract.

Besides the "alphabet", other classic Thai dances depict stylized combat, or military strategy, or embody propitiatory ritual; some call for manipulating weapons – krisses, lances, swords, shields – or sashes, exotic feathers, illuminated lanterns; and the dancers' hands may sport long, silvered fingernails. Many of these works illustrate incidents from the *Ramayana*, the sacred Indian text, and invoke disguises and metamorphoses. The *Praleng*, the most ancient composition of all, presents a pair of masked participants who respond to the sharp sound of clicking bamboo xylophones. Very often the *Praleng* serves as a prologue to programmes of Khon and Lakon. Supposedly it is modelled on the deportment of supernal beings. It is offered as a compliment to the gods, whose favour is besought. In most instances the dances are accompanied by expository chants, but not so with the stately *Praleng*.

Cambodia was even more noted for its classic dances; the sequestered troupe attached to the court at the Royal Khmer Palace in Phnom Peng was hailed as a national treasure, but it performed only for the king, his retinue, nobles and distinguished guests; rarely was it seen by the populace. The dancers' movements were much like those of the Thais, showing the same strong Indian imprint, which is explicable because for centuries Thailand (Siam) governed Cambodia, after having conquered it in the fifteenth century. Artists in the royal troupe have often been compared, in pose and dress, to the stone images of celestial dancers, *apsaras*, that by the thousands line the crumbling walls of Cambodia's world-famed ruin, Angkor Wat. The Khmer civilization reaches back to the eighth century AD, and it is believed that into the mid-twentieth the royal dancers continued to use exactly the same prescribed choreography as that represented by the carved figures. It is said that in some of the larger temples, in the ninth to twelfth centuries, there were companies of as many as 600 dancers available to take part in festivals and rituals.

The appearance of the royal Cambodian troupe at the Paris Colonial Exposition in 1908 introduced to European intellectuals the beauty and marvellous skill of hallowed forms of Far Eastern dance. One of those who was much taken with this sinuous and flexile choreography was the sculptor Auguste Rodin.

The Cambodians' costuming, bejewelled silks, satins and velvets, also closely resembled that of the Lakon performers in Thailand, except that here all the gems were genuine. The music was similar, too, though perhaps a bit more refined. Singers here, too, outlined a theme in poetic phrases.

Mimed by the dancers with symbolic gestures, once again, were stories borrowed from the *Ramayana* or the Buddhist canon. A frequent character, the sage or *kru*, voiced priestly wisdom that inspired a youth to an extraordinary deed.

Members of the troupe began their apprenticeship early: the young girls were taught by older women. The training took many years and, with long hours daily, was arduous; the consequence was the attainment of amazing suppleness. Larger girls were assigned to men's roles, while a pair of men in the troupe portrayed animals, demons and comics. Over the centuries the dances retained their sacred aura.

The girls given the male roles wore breeches and glamorous tunics. Their shoulders boasted raised epaulettes to make them look more manly. The female costumes were somewhat like saris. The glittering pagoda-shaped headdresses were called *mokots*, and all the dancers had plain anklets. The costumes were so form-fitting that the performers had to be stitched into them before each venture.

The royal troupe's last visit to the West was in 1971, just after the overthrow of the country's ruler, Prince Norodom Sihanouk. With the ascent of the ascetic, ruthless Communist Khmer Rouge, the company was disbanded and many of the members, who not only took the roles of princesses but had that rank by birth, fled abroad.

Laos has historic folk dances, as has Malaysia, which is noted for its dances of possession, but neither has developed any of formal, classical stature. In the far-flung archipelago now known as Indonesia, however, the islands of Java and Bali are celebrated for the dances and music that are very much alive and highly prized throughout the Western world. Here Indian choreography is found in its purest, most attractive flowering. What is more, dance and music are integrated into the daily life of the people; the arts are not segregated or reserved for a noble élite but at their classical best are freely shared and participated in by the lowliest field-workers and villagers.

Every hamlet in Bali has a gamelan orchestra and dancing troupe. Competitions between the artists or neighbouring villages occur frequently. These are festive occasions. Local rajahs and rulers also sponsor their own troupes.

The music is of exquisite delicacy; the dancing, again, extraordinarily subtle. Similarly, the isles of Sunda, Sumatra, Borneo, Celebes and many others – there are thousands of islands large and small in the Indonesian archipelago – have contributed local variations, some folk, some of classical Indian descent. A good many are mere excerpts from now forgotten dramas; others are masked dances, or processions of salute and welcome and deferential obeisance. Still others are marriage or funeral dances; war dances; dances of farewell; animal imitations – horses, monkeys; or just abstract, serimpe, having lost their original intent. If they have narrative content they tend to be derived from outstanding episodes in the *Ramayana* or from the epic *Panji* cycle, a historical record of Hindu–Javanese sovereigns who reigned over portions of the scattered archipelago from the seventh to the fourteenth centuries.

The palaces of sultans in Jogjakarta and Solo (both in Java) have the most admired troupes, whose repertory in some instances goes back 1,000 years. The traditional symbolic gestures are faithfully preserved. The batik costumes here are harmoniously colourful and lavish, with many gold and silver ornaments. Elongated gold and silver fingernails are a feature, most obvious because the hands and finger-work play such an important part, curling, weaving, arching, fluttering in filigrees of movement. The body sways and turns languorously and sinuously; even the toes are amazingly flexible. The rhythm is sometimes soft; sometimes, for the men, virile and fiercely energetic.

Moments of pause, immobility, repose, are equally important. They lend a meditative, sometimes melancholy cast to many performances. In static poses are hints of serene Buddhist withdrawal and Yogic concentration. This is universally characteristic of dance in the Far East and will be observed in Japanese theatre, too.

Penchak and Silat, types of fighting dances, are especially designed for lithe athletic young males. Both genres have a clear affinity to early Chinese combat dances and the jujitsu and karate forms of the Japanese. Some of these are accompanied by perilous weapon-play with long swords, curved daggers or javelins. If properly staged, they are bloodless. This is true, too, of stylized conflicts between youthful men and women. The requisites are perfect muscular control and balance as well as extra strength and dexterity.

Special costumes are worn for the Penchak – garments of "black cheesecloth bordered with silver thread", much like Chinese pyjamas; in addition "the crotch of the trousers hangs down to the knees and the wide waist is bunched together and fastened with a belt. On the long sleeves of the jacket, chevrons of silver thread denote the performer's rank. A tightly wound turban of sober blue or brown batik keeps the long hair of the performers from tumbling over their eyes, and when, in a sudden scurry of activity or during a swift locking of hands or feet, it flies off, you are sometimes surprised to see a shock of grey hair and discover that the young-looking performer is in reality an elderly gentleman. Many of the performers have fierce moustaches that curl at the ends, and on the forefinger of their right hand some of them wear a large agate set in silver as a symbol of strength." (Bowers, from whom this is taken, describes many of these fighting dances in very specific detail, especially those enacted in Central Sumatra.) Ceremonious courtesy – bowing, with hands clasped before the face; as well as sometimes kneeling, with an apologetic glance towards the audience, against the chance of a clumsy gesture – precedes and follows each combat.

As previously remarked, dance in Bali has a wholly Indian origin. Muslims conquered Java, but never this beauteous, terraced nearby island, one deemed by some to be the most paradisiacal on our planet. The charming, handsome folk who inhabit it are blessed with a natural physical grace; they attribute it to their way of life, their walking in the rice paddies, and the supple, rhythmic work there, that heightens an inherent gift for pliant movement. Since they tend to labour in teams, they have also developed a habit of moving in unison, a simultaneity of nervous impulse and gesture. Another factor cited is their native good humour; they are creative and aesthetic, qualities that pervade their unique culture, which – though in some aspects theirs is a primitive society – is inexhaustibly rich, manifesting itself in wood-carving, painting, treasured textiles, drama.

Dances are performed on every occasion and on every pretext, daily or nightly. By one calculation, the Balinese spend a third of their waking hours attending festivals. The island has about 10,000 villages, in each of which are three temples. Festivals are held at intervals of 210 days, which island-wide adds up something like 100 a day, not counting those that are part of private occasions, such as weddings, cremations and tooth-filling ceremonies. They are the community's prime source of diversion.

The dance-forms are both traditional and innovative; though the principles of Indian choreography are kept, many novel touches have been incorporated into them and wholly new dances added to the repertory, testimony to their creators' endless originality.

Fans and silken, silver-fringed sashes are essential accessories. The narrative element is slight, and the pace tends to be faster than elsewhere in these Far Eastern regions. Until recent years women's parts were danced by young boys. When girls succeeded them, they had to be virgins – in fact, not yet at the age of menstruation. Today, women do dance publicly, and often take men's roles. So the Asian audience's demand that the performer offer an illusion still rules. Besides the classic, familiar Legong, the modern and popular Kebyar, the flirtatious Gandrung, the devotional Gabor, there are many other common forms such as the trance-dances and fire-dances in which the performers seem invulnerable to kris-wounds and flames. Religious beliefs prompt many of the dances, a good number of them symbolizing the Sivaitic conflict between good and evil, god and demon, man and harmful spirit. The spiritual is opposed to the carnal. The metallic-sounding music – bells, gongs, cymbals, bamboo harps, trompons – is contrapuntal, again far more complex than anywhere else in the Far East, and requires concerted playing to a degree that is also unique in the whole Orient.

The Legong embraces many special forms and offers varied contents. An example is the *Begong Keraton*, relating a historical romance, based on an actual incident dating from the twelfth and thirteenth centuries. The noble characters are represented by three dancers. First, a court lady, Tjondong, appears on the scene and hands a fan to each of them. Then the story unfolds. The Princess Rangkesari has been abducted by the Prince of Lasem, but she refuses to yield to him. She learns that her betrothed, the Crown Prince of Kahuripan, is on his way to rescue her. Feeling pity for her infatuated captor, she warns him to release her and escape punishment, but he is fiercely determined to keep her. Hastening to meet his rival, he encounters a raven – a bad omen. He drives away the dark bird, continues on, engages the Prince of Kahuripan in mortal combat and is killed. *Baris*, a warrior dance, is usually performed by boys as part of a temple ceremony. With fierce, flashing eyes and bold grimaces, coupled with strong but graceful arm thrusts and hand gestures, the fledging actors mimic preparation for battle.

The *Oleg Tambulilingan* depicts a flirtation between a male and female bumblebee. Sucking from petals in a beautiful garden, they flit merrily from flower to flower, until they fall in love with each other.

The *Pendet* is a religious dance belonging to temple ceremonies. With offerings, silver bowls filled with blossoms, male and female priests (*pemangkus*) go from shrine to shrine with prayerful gestures, and at the end empty the bowls and toss the flowers at the audience in an act of homage and blessing.

New dances of every sort are created, faddishly sweep the island, and before long are replaced by new ones similarly short-lived, while certain revered older forms go on almost unchanged.

Some dance forms such as the Penchak, and folk plays, are preceded by the *Randai*, in which a group walks slowly in a circle, anticlockwise, "pausing at intervals, slapping the cloth between the crotch, standing on one foot like a stork for a long time", by this means preparing the sense of balance required for the subtle turns and leaps that will follow. "Sometimes the group pivoting on one foot twist and turn as if corkscrewing themselves down to the ground and then unwind and rise back up to a standing position. The leader shouts 'ap ap' to control these practice movements. They finally clap their hands three times, make an obeisance (hands together in front of the face)", directed towards the premiere dancer, and then the combat or story begins.

In the *Kuda Kepang*, described as "voodoo-like", the dancers call on self-hypnosis and believe themselves to be horses, achieving an effect that to one Western observer is "repellent, degrading and absolutely enthralling". Another famed piece, the "monkey dance", consists only of rhythmic chanting by a crouched male chorus, at an ever accelerated pace, that eerily resembles the falsetto bark and chattering of the beasts that in large numbers inhabit the hills of Bali.

Drama is a minor art in Java and Sumatra. Sandiwara is a term (borrowed from the Malay) for a stage-work with music and singing put on for special occasions – a birth, circumcision, marriage festivity – by wealthy families. A platform is improvised in the open air, perhaps in front of the family's dwelling, and neighbours, friends and relatives gather to witness the performance. The offerings are mostly historical chronicles, revolving about dynastic struggles; or else plays of domestic intrigue, in which a virtuous stepchild is made to suffer by a cruel stepmother, who at the climax discovers the errors of her wicked ways, for the adopted child is kinder to her than her own offspring; and, of course, there are farces with much slapstick and noise. The comic players may be masked. The universal themes of disguise and then exposure in "recognition scenes" abound. A popular subject is that of a stranger who visits a village and purports to be an important government official – a durable plot that reappears in Russia in Nikolai Gogol's nineteenth-century *The Inspector General* (or *The Government Inspector*) and in Germany in Carl Zuckmayer's *The Captain von Kopenick*. In the larger cities Sandiwar troupes perform nightly at theatres.

Another dramatic form is the Wayang Wong, in which actors take over the roles of puppets. This form descends from the Wayang Kulit, or shadow-play, a 1,000-year-old genre of Hindu origin popular throughout Indonesia, and especially to the present day in Bali. A white sheet is hung by the puppeteer across the platform or booth, and huge torches are lit behind it. Translucent puppets, of water-buffalo hide pounded to paper-thin dimension, are mounted on bamboo slivers and the moving parts deftly manipulated, while pressed against the white screen. They move only their arms, to which are attached clay-like hands. The plots are extracted from the *Ramayana* and *Mahābhārata*. A narrator, or *dalang*, recounts the story being enacted. Since darkness is a requisite, the performance usually begins at dusk and may last until daybreak causes the images to fade. The setting for the Wayang Kulit is often a clearing before the men's house of the village.

The audience, squatting on the ground, is likely to be vociferous in commenting on the action. Usually the story is a violent one – a battle with demons, a quarrel between princes over a royal succession, a scene of love and rejection, or a passage of bawdy humour – evoking falsetto catcalls and high nasal laughter from the rapt spectators. But there are also moments of languorous eroticism, heightened by the music, soft and swift, or harsh and clanging.

Different from the Wayang Kulit is the Wayang Golek, in which the brightly painted puppets are shown without the white screen. A banana-tree trunk provides a stage. Both these forms are cheaper to produce than a drama with a live cast, and costumes cost little or nothing, and there is no scenery. Hence, shadow plays and puppet plays are readily accessible everywhere in the scattered islands.

The works in this repertory inevitably preach a moral lesson: the virtues of courage, loyalty, elegance, propriety and respect are strongly endorsed, and before the wind-up "refined" conduct is shown as preferable to "coarse" behaviour.

The puppet theatre has had a discernible influence on classical Indonesian dance: the impression of one-dimensionality presented by the dancers, whose hips and shoulders remain always in one plane, is like that given by the thin, flat leather marionettes flitting across the luminous white sheet or dangling jerkily above the banana-tree trunk, at the *dalang*'s behest.

Bali has a more emphatic kind of drama, Arja, that deals with events in the island's history. Civil warfare and dynastic feuds are the most frequent topics, and the actors wear elaborate costumes of gold-painted cloth, the queens and princesses having flower headdresses. The lines are declaimed with a sing-song intonation that rises and falls, sometimes descending to a moan. The nobles recite in high Balinese or Javanese, while their retainers speak colloquially, so that the spectators have little difficulty following the plot – a device also employed in Sanskrit drama. Arja also goes on throughout the night, entertaining the seemingly tireless onlookers. The plays are well attended.

As the outdoor performance progresses at exhausting length, some in the crowd of watchers rise to stretch their cramped muscles, wander about to refresh themselves at the nearby stalls vending fruits, fish or pork fat on sticks like candied apples, the odours of cooking hanging over the grassy clearing on the humid night air. Along with the pulsating gamelan music – drums, gongs and a variety of xylophone-like instruments, tinkling and clashing incessantly accompanying the dramatic action – are the outcries of the delighted audience. From it comes hoots, catcalls, whistles at the appearance of evil-doers, laughter at the comic interludes, perhaps when a god over-imbibes and gets intoxicated, or another character is dallying illicitly with his inamorata and is unaware that his wife is about to arrive and catch him *in flagrante delicto*.

The lively people of the Philippines have a legacy of exceedingly varied folk-dance. The innumerable islands comprising that tropical, verdant archipelago are the dwelling places of a wide band of tribes and races, with separate religious and cultural roots: descendants of aboriginal Igorots, invading Moros (Muslim), conquering Spanish (Roman Catholic), are major parts of the mixture, and traces of Indonesian and Japanese influence are evident.

Costumes and language, as well as styles of dancing, reflect this diversity, as does the music, composed of many strains. But apart from the folk-dancing, no classical or distinctive "art" form evolved here until the mid-twentieth century.

In dance and drama the Spanish inheritance is dominant. Among such dances in Laguna are the

Pandango Malaquena, adapted from the Fandango or Malaga in southern Spain – Bowers noting that "the women dress in the puffed sleeves and the shoulder-framing wide collar of old Spain: the men wear the *barong tagalog* shirt made of diaphanous pineapple fibre, with ruffles and frills running down the front and around the cuffs. Both sexes are shod in comfortable house slippers. The couples form a square and amid much hand-clapping and kiss-throwing at their partners, they skip in and out of the dances' regular, symmetrical, four-square formations."

In Batangas Province the couples doing the Subli make use of bandanas and wide Panama hats. Kneeling and snapping their fingers rhythmically, the women are encircled by their male partners. At moments they dance with their hats on, at other moments the partners grasp hold of each other's hats; they criss-cross in ever more complex ways, "in and out, over and under", never letting go of the broad-rimmed Panamas, and then gradually extricate themselves from the entanglement. The pattern is repeated with their large bandanas, in movements that Bowers likens to a Handkerchief Dance in Sumatra.

Some wealthy, conservative families on the islands of Iloilo and Cebu were still holding formal balls when Bowers visited there. An opening dance at these was the Rigadon d'Honor, a stately quadrille performed by ladies in crinolines and their escorts in tuxedos, the gentler sex adorned with heirloom diamond tiaras, and the men boasting pearl studs. During the evening the most repeated number was a minuet, the Maria Clara, which in an earlier period had been so overwhelmingly popular that it was almost looked upon as a "national dance". Though much of its vogue was gone, it was still done in the larger villages at the homes of the "best families", those tradition-minded, as well as on stage in historical dramas. The ladies' dresses, of "light blues and starched whites", have wide collars and long frilly sleeves, and each female dancer has a fan; the men are elegant in velvet jackets and tight-fitted trousers. Much bowing and many curtsies occur, and the partners hold their hands high in gentle claspings; a few quick polka steps are introduced at intervals.

An echo of protest against colonization is preserved in the Palo-Palo. The musical accompaniment is a lone violin. Bowers: "It shows a row of Spanish soldiers, with stiff, high, military hats, blue sashes, and wearing shoes, fighting against barefoot natives, scantily clothed, and wearing bright red and orange bandanas wrapped around their head. The soldiers are armed with swords, the natives with gaily decorated wooden sticks. The two sides move in stilted, high-stepping hops and jumps, and from time to time their weapons clatter against each other in stylizations of mock combat. Neither side wins, to judge from the dance." (Bowers does not say where or by whom the Palo-Palo is performed, but presumably now only at a Fiesta Filipina arranged for special occasions.)

Traditional religious pageants and dramas, of the sort given in Spain, South America and Mexico, are mounted on appropriate holy days, such as Passion Plays during Easter Week. No pre-Spanish drama developed here. Some Moro folk plays, celebrating the triumph of Christianity over Islam, might be classed as indigenous, but these date from the comparatively recent seventeenth century and have almost vanished.

Two dances that hearken back to pre-Spanish times, and so might be called native, are the Binusan Candle Dance and the even better-known Tinikling. In the first of these, to the music of a guitar and the rhythmic clapping of the audience, the performer, male or female, rests a glass holding a lighted candle on his or her head, assumes various awkward positions in a virtuoso display of balancing, even rolling on the floor, and writhing, turning, twisting at an ever more rapid beat, always keeping the glass secure and the candle alight, and always in response to the dictates of the music and measured clapping.

The Tinikling involves four people, each with a long bamboo pole. Forming a cross with these just above the floor, they leave a small open square in its centre. Rhythmically, to music with a 4/4 beat, they shuttle the poles, closing and reopening the square; the trick is to hop into and out of it on only one foot without getting caught, at the risk of injuring an ankle or tripping and sustaining a worse hurt. Though seeming simple, the feat is exhausting; many walk away limping. The pattern of hopping in and out may be varied and grow dauntingly complicated, increasing the element of harm. Still so highly popular that Bowers tags them "national pastimes", the Tinikling and the Binusan Candle Dance require, as he says, athletic skills and a good sense of timing rather than physical grace and artistry. Dances similar to the Tinikling are found elsewhere in the Far East, though it is mostly identified with the Philippines. Its origin is elusive. One suggestion is that it was inspired by the rice bird that greedily and cleverly pecks at traps set out by farmers during the harvest season, the deft little bird extracting the kernels while evading the pincers that would cripple it.

In the mountains of northern Luzon the tribes of aboriginal Igorots have dances for frequent occasions: weddings, burials, conferring of tribal titles, planting, harvesting, setting off for war or headhunting. Since headhunting is no longer an approved custom, the nut of a tree fern substitutes for an actual trophy; except that, among the Ifugaos, a carved wooden head serves as a satisfactory replacement. This dance is now performed to observe any death from a violent cause – a fall, a lightning bolt, a clawing by a wild animal. But there is dancing for less momentous emotional reasons, to express joy or gratitude when an official or visitor presents a pig to the village, or after bouts of drinking – the name given for such dances is "general welfare", a communal celebration. There is much over-indulgence in the local rum in this region, a habit which bloats the pretexts for dancing.

The most colourful dances flourish in the Kalinga hill area. Men and women circle clockwise to the sound of chants and gongs of two sizes, the larger bronze discs called "male" and the lesser "female", the older ones having tones clarified and mellowed by alloys of gold and silver. Bowers:

> The rhythm for each type of dance varies rather more than the actual gestures do. Sometimes the arms extend out like airplane wings and the hands pat the air. The women rarely lift their feet but clutch the ground with their toes and wriggle along the circle. The men hop a good deal, and sometimes slap their feet against the ground with a loud smack for emphasis. Both men and women saw the air with their hands in regular, back and forward motions. Sometimes they hold the flat palms near the hips, sometimes they rub the back of their index fingers against their hips as if poking at the ground behind them. The dancers themselves add a kind of percussion to the throbbing of the gongs. They breathe heavily, sigh and heave or pant, and these sound effects substitute for a drum. The climax of the Vengeance Dance comes when the dancers emit several long sustained hushes, like "shh,shh,shh." This means, I am told, "Keep quiet, for we have succeeded and taken our revenge."

Most often the dancers are scantily clad: for the males a mere loincloth and a hat shaped like a basket and adorned with red hornbill feathers; for their female partners a brief, woven skirt and blouse. This was to change after the Second World War, during which the islands were fought over and occupied by Japanese and American forces.

Artistically, the best dancing was to be found among the Moros in the southern Philippines, the people Muslims, darker complexioned, less European. Exceptional dancing was seen by Bowers on the islands of Luzon, Jolo and Sitankai.

In the town of Dansalan, a small provincial capital on Luzon, he was a rare visitor and a guest of the local mayor who had a special programme staged to honour him. He was greeted by four girls, "lightly powdered and with flowers in their hair", seated before a long file of *agongs* – "round, brass pots with a knob on top" – that the girls were striking with sticks embellished with paper frills, an instrument called *kulingtan*. In addition, two handsome young males were hitting gongs with tiny hammers. Besides them, on the floor, a fifth girl was playing a cymbal, its handle also decorated with flowers. To complete the orchestra, a man was pounding a drum resembling a goblet. The melodies were "shuddering, fragmentary", with abrupt changes of rhythm. Bowers was told that the piece was dedicated to love-making: only the unmarried were allowed to perform on the *kulingtan*, lest married players be romantically and lustfully aroused and led astray, resulting in violent quarrels and divorces. A week before Bowers's visit a youth playing the large gong, while his beloved presided at the *kulingtan*, had been stabbed and seriously hurt by a jealous rival.

Next, the visitor was paid a tribute in song by a man of fifty years or so, wearing a wine-coloured velvet cap and a red-plaid sarong over a white shirt with blue collar and cuffs, the pocket embroidered with yellow flowers, and loose-hanging pants. He was introduced as an eminent singer and dancer. His unique musical instrument was a tall, silver spittoon, richly engraved, and in one hand he held a fan, opened and extending to a width of fourteen inches. To Bowers, the man's voice had the humming quality of turtle doves; his melody was dulcet, and occasionally he added trills. Of red-pine stays, the fan was covered with blue paper and enhanced with paintings of white birds. First covering his chin with it, he began waving it in a circle, while with his other hand he used a thin bamboo sliver to hit the resonant spittoon, matching the beat to his song. The fan moved incessantly, a "one-hand dance", swooping in the air, dipping down. He rose from his chair to enlarge upon the fan's archings. He tapped his bare foot on the floor to augment the song's rhythm and the fan's sweep, and intermittently spat into the spittoon, usually after the strain of a very long melismatic phrase. He betrayed signs of exhaustion, his head wobbling as his voice quivered. His face was red and his neck veins dilated from his efforts. In his song he mentioned by name some of the spectators, including Bowers and the mayor. The audience guffawed, loudly approving. With his other hand he picked up a second fan, flower-painted, and now employed the pair of them for an airy, graphic description of a curving mountain rim, a rippling lake surface, a bird in swift flight – a picture of the very scene in which the crowd was gathered.

Two young men succeeded him, one with a love song – he was beside himself with that emotion – and the second with a war song – preparation for battle, which he also mimed by dancing with two fans, spreading the spokes to peer through them, flicking them and throwing the fans down, while the spectators exhorted him to move ever more vigorously.

A pair of fans was also used by a dancing girl. Her face was framed by her dark hair tied in a knot behind one side of her brow; her attire consisted of a blouse of the fine pineapple fibre, transparent, and a skirt of white and gold. Of matching gold, all made from coins, were the necklace, buttons for her blouse, bracelets, earrings and a brooch with which she was bedecked. She had no partner; apparently all the dancers were soloists. Manipulating her fans as she sang, she walked and swayed with abandon, almost informally. Though shy in aspect, she insinuated by her manner that she could be more seductive in a private encounter.

To the south west are the Sulu Islands, a low-lying, sandy chain of which the largest occupied outcrop is Jolo, also its capital city; the chief occupations of its people are pearl-diving and collecting turtles' eggs and birds' nests, commodities much favoured by the Chinese for special-tasting soups. The population is very mixed, many of the inhabitants living in houses built on stilts over water and a good number of others, called sea gypsies, making their homes in small boats and boldly supporting themselves by piracy, a tradition handed down from their Malay ancestors. In contrast to these fierce citizens are eunuch *suwa-suwa* dancing boys, the castrated sons of prostitutes.

Trained and dedicated from childhood to be entertainers, these effeminate young males tend to be of somewhat more than average height, and to have frizzy hair (an effect, Bowers speculates, that might be due to frequent use of a curling iron), and they are prematurely inclined to plumpness. Though somewhat disdained by the respectable elements of the local society, they are often hired to dance at wedding ceremonies and on other festive occasions. Usually they combine forces with a prostitute or dancing girl (possibly their mother) on a programme likely to start with a Sangai, a quick, rhymed, metrical chant that serves to introduce the principal dancer. Reflecting Jolo city's mixed racial strains, the chant may be in Tagalog, English or the island's own dialect. It is sung to an accompaniment carried by a bamboo xylophone; a homemade violin (or *bula*, resembling a small cello); gongs and drums. The performer, male or female, shows an Indian influence on this dance by sliding the head from side to side, double-jointedly cracking the elbow, and engaging in rapid finger-work, while vibrantly moving up and down from a static position or circling energetically in a walk.

The term *joget* is applied to all four basic types of dance in Jolo. Though it means "singing", here *suwa-suwa* implies that the dancing and singing are being performed by a troupe of professional prostitutes and eunuchs, or again, here *joget* may also suggest that two boys are singing and dancing together.

In the *Kasi Kasi Joget*, a love dance, a pair of boys move in a circle, one following the other, each with his palms upraised before his face. Bending their knees, they flutter their slender curved fingers like butterfly wings.

To celebrate good times, prosperity, the dancers add pairs of castanets, held in each hand, to much the same bodily movements, in the *Joget Bula Bula*; the rapid clicking is heard above the music.

A feature of the *Joget Ivan Jangai*, a dance dedicated to long life and peace, is the silver claws attached to the performer's nails. The claws, which curve backwards, symbolize longevity and by their shiny length draw more attention to the finger-play. Again, the other movements are much like those of the *Kasi Kasi Joget* and *Joget Bula Bula*.

A mid-twentieth-century addition to the islanders' repertory is *Ma Dalin Ma Dalin*, inspired by the presence of American soldiers during the Second World War. (Spoken aloud, *Ma Dalin Ma Dalin* is recognizable as the natives' version of *My Darling My Darling*, a song popular in the United States at that time and doubtless often heard on morale-boosting broadcasts wherever the troops were posted.) Yet for this dance there is no music. Wearing open-heel sandals, the boys deftly press on them with their toes so that the leather soles slap percussively against the floor in a regular beat, as in American tap dancing. Timed to the taps, the boys exchange short couplets in song and tease or extend erotic invitations with finger-gestures. Bowers offers approximations of the words: "How nice you are; I can hardly express my love for you." And: "A bird in the tree can hardly compare with your beauty." And: "Come to my island; I will comfort you there." The hand movements are like those of a master of sleight of hand.

A variation of the *Ma Dalin Ma Dalin* is the *Kinjing Kinjing*. Throughout the dance one participant bobs his head up and down and evasively shifts it from side to side, while the other pokes his finger at his partner's nose, always missing it; yet with the two of them creating an attractive pattern of movement. Introduced by the dancing troupes, *Ma Dalin Ma Dalin* was shortly taken up by young men all over the island, becoming a hard-breathing craze. A dance hall was built for it in the centre of Jolo, where night long the boys engaged in the challenging exercise, while the girls watched and applauded. Unfortunately, the repetitive pounding *en masse* of the sandals on the floor shook the flimsy structure and soon caused it to collapse, a literal instance of a performance "bringing down the house". The dance is now done only by members of professional troupes.

Another dance, observed in smaller villages on the island, has to do with a fisherman spearing his elusive prey. Formerly there was a sword dance, but it has been banned, since the participants often became too angry, which led to fatalities. These were folk offerings, not enacted by the troupes.

Finally, there are blind singers, capable of "short" little dances, to Bowers the words of their songs lyrical and affecting, truly poignant. They gesticulate as they sing, hands illustrating the motions of sea waves, the dartings of birds, or whatever else might be their subject.

Bowers concludes: "*Joget* dances, which are the slenderest enucleations of almost passing thoughts, do not lend themselves well to description or analysis. The movements are fairly varied, the flexibility of the fingers and arms is extraordinary. The angularity of the motions, particularly in the gesture of framing the face with the hands, arms extending out at shoulder level, the elbows and wrists bent at right angles, and the finger curved upwards making a picture frame around the head, is a new and pleasing extension of the concept of dance movement. The chief joy of these dances is the wonderful sense they give of whiling away one's time amusingly and pleasantly."

The first scholars to write about "drama" in the Philippines – Spaniards in the nineteenth century – asserted that the natives of the archipelago had no indigenous "theatre". Plays telling stories were not performed anywhere until after the islands' conquest and rule by the Spanish. Bowers accepts that as true. In the view of Professor Doreen G. Fernández of Manila University those historians are mistaken. (Her book, *Palabas*, is where most of the information that follows here has been garnered.) She suggests that they were thinking of "drama" in terms of what was happening on stages in Madrid during the late Renaissance – that country's literary Golden Age, contemporary with Shakespeare's day – when Lope De Vega, Calderón and Molina were pouring out scripts to delight the king and his court and the eager public. The indigenous "theatre" of the Philippines, before the arrival of the Spaniards, was very different, hardly as developed. It was "folk", both spontaneous and traditional. If not storytelling, it was a natural expression of emotion; it was practised and seen everywhere. As Fernández insists, the Filipinos are a very histrionic people.

The dancing and miming observed by Bowers are in many instances descended from centuries-old primitive religious rites and heartfelt attempts at imitative magic, futile but psychologically helpful efforts to ward off the hostile forces of nature – the earthquakes, volcanic eruptions and tidal waves that frequently inflict the islands. As virtually everywhere else in the world, the natives believed that by propitiation, submission and imitation they could control those foes. They also held innumerable ceremonies to celebrate other happenings important to them: births, matings, menstruation, hunts, circumcision, savage war between tribes. They enacted jocular playlets to keep drowsy mourners awake night-long before a burial. They paid homage to seasonal changes, the advent of a time for sowing or harvesting rice or grain. Magellan and other explorers sent back fascinating accounts of what they saw of these well-enacted ceremonies. (Magellan witnessed the solemn sanctification of a pig, the ritual arising from totemism, a belief in mankind's kinship with the animal realm, a token of respect and gratitude to the tribe's major source of food, the gesture of thanks a seminal element of the earliest "theatre".) Some of these dances and sketches are still found in the more than 7,000 remote and scattered islands of the archipelago.

The first staged "drama", as one is now more apt to define the word, was composed by a Jesuit scholastic, Francisco Vicente Puche, while he was *en route* from Spain (1598). After the establishment of Spanish sovereignty in this new possession, the militant and very intellectual order in which Puche was enrolled, a fervent "army" in defence of the Faith, had lost no time in sending missionaries intent on teaching and converting the unblest, pagan natives awaiting them there. For the Jesuits, theatre was a proven educational tool; they were employing it all over Europe. Students, memorizing lines, learned Latin – and Spanish, too; the play itself carried and inculcated moral messages and explicated Roman Catholic doctrine. Jesuits were among the principal authors of such didactic plays.

At the request of the Governor of Cebu, the King of Spain had chartered an elementary school in that city; it was to be used mostly for the education of the children of local Spanish administrators. Puche's script came into their hands. Fernández recounts: "He had started writing it during the boat trip from Manila to Cebu 'to the measure of the oar stroke and the swing of the sailors' chanteys,' and when he was halfway through, a sudden breeze blew his manuscript into the sea. Undaunted, he wrote it all over again 'without hesitating over a single word,' and when the new bishop, who had accompanied Puche on the voyage, arrived in Cebu a month later to be installed in the cathedral, the play was rehearsed and ready for the occasion." Another Jesuit, Puche's superior, on hand, commented for posterity that the play was "most agreeable, learned, dignified, and devout, and gave extraordinary pleasure to all the citizens, who had never before seen such a thing in their city".

It was apparently a short piece. Several years passed before anything full-length was put on, but a chronicle published in 1601 mentions that young boys were depicting "in their own languages the lives of saints, with such interior feeling that the spectators, both Spaniards and Indios, are moved to many tears, to compunction and to change their lives. This was seen in the town of Sinola, where the presentation of the *Last Judgment* made such an impression on many unbelievers that almost all asked with great earnestness and humility to be baptized, and this was done." An *Annual Letter* of the Jesuits (1602) also reports a reliance on dramatization to proselytize at the Antipolo mission where a "play in Tagalog, which is the language of this island, was performed by the boys of the boarding school of this town, to the delight and satisfaction of the people. The boarding school makes progress both spiritually and temporally, the natives helping to support it with sizable donations." The Jesuits knew how to attract and hold converts, and they were effectively resorting to the Filipinos' own speech, no longer clinging steadfastly to Latin and Spanish, though those languages were ever more used by graduates of the colleges set up by the order.

Decidedly it is to the Society of Jesus that credit is due for bringing with them Westernized theatre. In their elementary schools children under eight took part in Christmas plays about incidents in the life of the Nazarene. Parents and the public attended these portrayals. Tagalog was increasingly used, but its limited vocabulary often frustrated dramatists who sought to write dialogue that was eloquent, pungent and poetic. This lack continues to handicap native playwrights to the present day.

In Manila women were excluded from the academic ceremonies. The Governor's wife interceded, asking the ecclesiastic authorities to transfer the event to a church. They tactfully assented. She and her entourage of noble ladies were impressed by the children's "wit, grace, agility, and understanding". Their inborn histrionic trait was evident.

To quote from a document (1610) in *Palabas* once more: a play about St Gregory the Great was performed with

such devotion and modesty that everyone was greatly taken by it and since the point of the play was the example of alms-giving which the saint gave, the people were greatly encouraged to do likewise.

The people derive great profit from these plays. They are an exceptionally efficacious means of teaching our religion, not only because they come in vast numbers from all parts to see them, but because they grasp more readily what is taught in them. Thus, in order to make them love the virtue of chastity and show them how in time of need, sickness, and danger they should have recourse not to their idols but God, we presented another play on the life of the glorious virgin and martyr St Cecilia, in which the first lesson was brought home by the incident of the two crowns which the angel brought to the saint and to St Tibertius, and the second by the prayer which she made to God.

A major celebration was that ignited by the beatification of Ignatius Loyola (1611), founder of the ever-aggressive Society. Word of the canonization was greeted in Manila with rounds of artillery fire, clamouring church bells, jubilant recitations, lavish processions, music and plays. The other religious orders joined the festivities. Tagalog songs and a ferocious sword dance were interspersed with those in traditional Spanish idioms. Similar observances in honour of the new saint were held in other cities around the far-flung archipelago.

In the same exuberant spirit, on an even more elaborate scale, subsequent news from the Vatican of the election of more saints and the issuance of new dogma set off longer and yet more costly holidays, one of them going on for fifteen days, with dramatizations in Spanish and Tagalog nearly always a part of them.

The first play on a local subject, not inspired by a Biblical story or describing the torturous death of a Christian martyr and the miracles that followed, was staged after the victory of Governor General Sebastián Hurtado de Corcuera over the Sultan of Mindanao whose people were viewed by the Spanish invaders as "Muslim bandits" on land and marauding pirates at sea. Returning to Manila after his lengthy, finally successful campaign, the Governor General and his warriors were accorded a "Roman triumph" (1637), his ship welcomed by "gaily decorated sampans", salvos and a parade that passed under arches. Among the marchers were survivors of those enslaved by the Muslims and now freed, prisoners of war, cannons and other weaponry seized from the enemy, his tattered flags and other booty. In the evening in the Jesuit church, after fireworks, students re-enacted Corcuera's climactic battle against the Sultan from a script hurriedly written by Fr Hierônimo Pérez. The role of Jesuits in the campaign was emphasized. Some historians designate this as the true beginning of Philippine theatre. The play was in the form of a *comedia*, standard in Renaissance Spain and consisting of three acts in a light or serious vein, perhaps with interpolated songs and dances. Of significance is that it was a formally structured work and dealt with a topical theme as well as an indigenous one. It was not only the first all-secular script, but also the first concerned with the conflict between Christians and

Muslims in these remote Pacific islands, the endless struggle over religion and territory that was to be treated in many ensuing dramas. Because its author was a Jesuit, as were many others later, for a long while the Muslims depicted in the scripts resembled the Moors of the North African littoral with whom the Spaniards were always fiercely at odds, rather than those occupying close-by, disputed sections of the archipelago. It was a war of which most of the outside world knew little. In addition, most of the Manila-based writers of Spanish birth – Jesuits, laymen – had no first-hand acquaintance with their feared, murderous neighbours.

The Jesuit dominance of theatrical activity began to diminish as the eighteenth century unfolded. Having been exposed for three prior decades to *comedias* in Spanish or in the vernacular, Spanish would-be playwrights born in the Philippines and native aspirants incrementally developed the *komedya*, also known as the *moro-moro*, their own form of play. These were exceedingly lengthy, lasting three to five hours, of an afternoon or evening, and in past times even several days or a week, though that would be an exceptional event. For content – plots, people – the writers raided the metrical romances popular in Spain and Portugal and dealing with imagined kingdoms, the majority of them Moorish, where magic potions and baffling tricks prevailed, and arabesque palaces rang with the clash of steel on steel along with the fearless exploits of valorous cavaliers, as in the cape-and-sword stage-works of dramatists in Madrid and Seville; and there were still pious tributes to the lives and sufferings of marvel-working saints. The *komedyas* were mostly in Spanish and in verse – the lines either six, seven, eight or twelve syllables – but some in Tagalog. The characters became stereotypes – the hero most likely a Christian prince, the heroine a Muslim princess. Or the premise is reversed: he is a Muslim prince, she is a Christian princess. Their mutual love is complicated by warfare between the kingdoms, Christians against the infidels. Their hoped-for match might be the cause of the hostilities. At the end the Muslim royals are converted to the true faith or else they die, or both things happen. Peace is restored. There is nearly always a clown figure for comic contrast. Songs, dances. Minor characters provide small variations. Adhering to an ever-effective formula, the *komedya* was an admixture of melodrama and fantasy, and quite simplistic. Many were composed by poets locally esteemed, their background provincial, but even so, well aware of how the plays should go, and able to conform to an unvarying pattern.

The values, implicit and explicit, that govern the characters at all points are those formerly obtaining in Renaissance Spain: preservation of honour counts above all else, and there is unfailing regard for hierarchy, respect for rank, obedience to a firm code. But love is also a paramount force, especially for Filipinos. When it cannot be reconciled with honour and duty, intense conflict ensues.

The poetry is conventional, the imagery well-worn, consisting, as Fernández puts it, of "flowers plucked from familiar gardens" and too often hyperbolic. The hero is handsome and the heroine unusually lovely.

At first the stage for these was a temporary structure of bamboo and timber. When it became a permanent fixture it was divided in two, each half showing the façade of a palace, and each a different colour, to indicate which edifice was Christian, which Moorish. Possibly one might have a balcony from which jousting and tournaments were viewed. Interior scenes might be suggested merely by strategically placed chairs and a throne, and exteriors – forest, mountains, gardens – by lowering a painted backdrop. Or by potted plants. Good and happy events – love passages – most often occurred in rustic settings, evil deeds and cruel intrigues in rooms of the palace.

The principal characters did not simply enter on stage or exit, but did so only to the accompaniment of band music. They did not proceed directly to their destination but marched in step to the music in a prescribed order from one corner of the stage to the other and then across the entire front, and finally at a diagonal to upstage centre where the sovereign was enthroned and awaited them. This was rather like the approach of a Japanese nobleman to his despotic, wary Shōgun. Also ritualized was the pace of the actors portraying royal personages and courtiers and observing a tradition: "step-pause, step-pause"; it created the illusion of distance, the sense that palace rooms were vast. It also suggested that processions were long and stately. Other characters moved briskly with a well-executed two-step.

The male dancers, twirling swords to music and posturing flamboyantly, were like toreadors but actually borrowing their arrogant stance and gestures from native martial arts performed with wooden batons. (Bullfights had been imported to the Philippines.)

The faith of the characters was easily identified by his or her costume: "bright red, orange or fuchsia" for the Moors and "navy blue, sober black or purple" for Christians. The same array of colours symbolically differentiated a wearer with good intentions from one with evil motives. Towards the end of the *komedya*'s long run the figures were less "stock", not as one-dimensional.

The Moorish garb assured that the stage made a bright display. To the extent that the characterizations allowed, the attire of all in the cast was ostentatious. Males might be in uniforms, dashing in capes, their jackets boasting gold epaulets, buttons and braid and perhaps a row of medals. The women glittered, as befitted royalty and aristocracy. Theirs was the Spanish *haute couture* of the seventeenth and eighteenth centuries. Their sheathing, flouncy gowns were adorned with "sequins, beads, embroidery, fringes, and feathers. The design, color and decoration of the royal ladies' costumes were a closely guarded secret only revealed on stage, because the women in the *komedya* were the focus of attention and of dreams. They reflected the folk understanding of beauty, wealth, and royal magnificence – splendor to aspire for and dream about." (Fernández)

Since magic (*mahiya*) was much involved, special effects might abound. To the astonishment of spectators, a princess might emanate from a flower before the gaze of an enthralled young man, healing waters might gush from a stone, or the hero take flight, soaring away astride an eagle. To stage these required technical know-how. If a committee of prominent citizens was sponsoring the production, the members relied on former professional actors versed in stagecraft. They obtained the services of a director, prompter, band leader, who helped to select a script, choose the players, build and paint the sets. Much of this work might be done by volunteers from the community, some of whom were altruistic and civic-minded – or, in the instance of a saint's play, very devoted – or most likely a bit stage-struck and anxious to take part.

The few present-day *komedya* are a binding force, encouraging communal feelings, bringing citizens together in an enjoyable joint enterprise. Performances are free. Spectators may watch rehearsals.

If the actors are amateurs, recruited from dwellers in the town, they face the difficult task of learning how to speak in a rather unnatural way. The delivery of the lilting declamatory poetry is very special, with caesuras – pauses – after six syllables at the end of each line, clause and stanza. The result, says Fernández, is that every word is clearly intelligible without a microphone even at open-air presentations where large crowds are assembled in a huge field ringed with good stalls.

The *komedya* went through several phases during the eighteenth and nineteenth centuries, becoming reinvigorated and rebounding in wide favour, flourishing until about 1982. They were sought after to provide entertainment at festivals. Such plays faded away first in Manila, where there were many other distractions, and later in the outer regions where most of the population speaks Tagalog. A few survive here and there, where they are traditionally a feature of a specific holiday, as in Rizal, Iligan City and Parañque. Those depend largely on community funding. Of course, the growing sophistication of spectators has been another factor in the near disappearance of the native *komedya*.

Cultural agencies have been attempting to shorten, revitalize and update the *komedya*, giving it new, more relevant content; it would not be just about converting the infidels. But it would no longer be folk-art.

Though less important on the scene, the Jesuits did not cease to foster religious "theatre". Their offerings took several forms, categorized as plays based on the liturgy – perhaps a dramatization of the Seven Last Words of Christ enacted in a church early on the morning of Good Friday – or Palm Sunday processions graced by singing together with the tossing of flowers; and plays without links to liturgy but with a devotional intent. Depending on their length, these non-liturgical works are designated as the *salubong* and the *panunluyan* – this pair the shortest – and the extensive *sinakulo*, stretching from Palm Sunday to Easter, a full eight days. Add to these the *tibag*: much like a *komedya* and dealing with a search for the Cross and its triumphant discovery in medieval Spain, these are staged on carts trundled through the streets at the head of processions. Two separate lines of marchers come from different starting-points and finally meet. On one cart the players mime the Mater Dolorosa, the Virgin mourning her crucified Son, and women make up the procession; the other represents the Risen Christ, with all its train male. A structure – *galilea* – has been erected at the broad place where the parades merge and a throng awaits the climax. From overhead an angel – a child in a suspended chair – is lowered by a pulley to clutch and lift off the Virgin's mourning veil. A chorus of voices rings out exultantly, *Regna Corli, Laetare*, hailing the Son's resurrection, a defeat of death. This dramatic celebration is repeated in other towns throughout the islands, though it may be with variations. A mechanical doll may replace the child. The height from which it is dangled, slight and steep, may differ. Instead of a chair, there may be merely a rope around the child's waist, or the child may be embowered in giant flowers and the chair raised rather than lowered. Again, instead of a child, doves may carry away the veil. All this is folk-art tinctured with sophistication.

The *sinakulo* noisily thrives in the towns of Luzon, and particularly in Rizal, Cavite, Pampanga and Bulacan. An institution since its beginning in the eighteenth century – the date is conjectural, but possibly 1704 – it is what is called today a Passion Play, a portrayal of Biblical incidents, moving in chronological sequence – from the creation of Adam and his rib-born Eve in their leafy Garden of Eden, paradisiacal with pomegranate trees, to a manger and the birth of Jesus, the raising of the shroud-wrapped Lazarus, and ending with the Incarnation of the Virgin Mary, all performed by amateurs, several compelling sketches put on each day during Holy Week. These, too, are greatly anticipated community projects, prominent local citizens offering financial support and others their labour to provide costumes, props and sets. Much folk-art comes into view here. Scholars believe that the *sinakulo* originated with readings aloud of Biblical glosses by Gaspar Acquino Bélen – hence the 1704 dating – or more likely of the *Payson Henesis*, an account of events from the creation of Adam and Eve to the coronation of the Blessed Virgin dating from 1814. After a time, supposedly, parishioners took up being the different characters mentioned; next, they were given costumes to look more real; and finally the episodes were fully dramatized and mostly detached from the church. Over the centuries there were embellishments from a host of later sources, culminating in the *sinakulo* being a loud, elaborate spectacle.

Throughout there is highlighting of the endless struggle between Good and Evil. The latter exemplars are the Jews and rough Roman soldiers and the insidious snake enticing Eve. The good include the Disciples. A commentator, Nicabor Tiongson, propounds that the characterizations of Jesus and the Holy Family – to quote from Fernández – as "meek, uncomplaining, all-accepting . . . with lowered gaze and clasped hands", held up as a role model in the *sinakulo*, "could well have contributed to the noncombativeness, subservience and resignation of the Filipino who was a colonial for so many years. Reynaldo Ileto, however, argues in his *Payson and Revolution*, that the *payson* gave the Filipino an inner strength belied by a meek exterior."

It is feared that at the end of the twentieth century, in a more sceptical age, the *sinakulo* is slowly dying out.

The second and third decades of the nineteenth century saw commercial theatres proliferating around the islands. They were needed to accommodate the stream of *comedias* from Spain and an increasing number of acting companies touring from there. Word had spread that both a welcome and profit were to be had in the far-off Philippines. At times, too, there was an element of safety in being at a distance from home when the political climate in Spain was uncertain. The native *komedyas* also drew large audiences; the improvised timber-and-bamboo stages were no longer adequate if these productions were to keep pace with imports from abroad. The impetus to put up playhouses like those in Europe gained momentum some time in the 1820s. For certain, the Teatro de Tondo was available in Manila in 1829. Soon afterwards the capital had more "Spanish-style" edifices for dramatic offerings, and copies of them were erected elsewhere. Fernández lists nine inaugurated before the century's end, including one that was bamboo-roofed. Amateur actors, once in the majority, gave way to professional troupes, initially from overseas but now locally organized and trained for ventures by shrewd, money-making managers.

Mexico and the Philippines had been put under joint colonial administration. Whatever of artistic interest came from Spain passed through Mexico first and was mostly conceived to please the taste of its upper-class population. Among the theatrical forms the foremost were the *zarzuelas*, the Spanish operettas named after the forested, lakeside summer palace of the royal family and developed there by Calderón for their pleasure. Some of these had long-lasting runs in Mexico, being revived well into and through the twentieth century. In the islands, as had happened to the *comedias*, these light, tuneful works caught the popular fancy and were freely adapted to become an indigenous genre. Their grasp on the public was secured in 1900 when *Ing Managpe* by Mariano Proceso Pabalan Byron had its début at the Teatro Sabina in Pacolor, Pampanga. Its lyrics and dialogue were in the dialect of that region, a novelty exciting and delighting the audience. It was an immense success. Immediately, this innovation was emulated in other regions, each having its own vernacular. Outside Manila the authors and composers were mostly non-professionals. Some of their works are full-length, many only one act.

The subject-matter offers the Filipino spectator far more identification than does the typical

European operetta that is usually about glamorous princes and dukes and their flirtations and romances with beauteous ladies of the aristocracy or, in disguise, simple milkmaids and innkeepers' daughters whom they ultimately marry and raise in rank after finding that they cannot bear to live apart. Instead, the libretto of the islands' *zarzuela* reflects ordinary domestic life, the quarrels between parents and their headstrong, rebellious children, dissolute husbands habituated to gambling and drinking, encroaching poverty, crumbling marriages. There may be discussions of politics, feuding between neighbours, unexpected legacies. The stories are not frivolous but cover the daily range of family problems.

The music consists of arias, duets, choruses, an overture. A particular song may be outstanding and become a "hit", sung or its melody hummed or whistled on every hand for a time. As operetta music differs in tone, texture and dramatic force from an opera's, so does that for a *zarzuela*. (Touring opera companies sometimes visited Manila. In Spain, Fernández says, *zarzuela* scores were considered "vulgar", though that opinion is not held today.)

Eventually, by the last two decades of the century, *sarswela* was the name applied to *zarzuelas* in the vernacular, especially the one-acters, several of which might be assembled to comprise an evening's programme. These short works, scarcely more than vignettes, usually revolved about a single situation or dilemma. They might include dancing as well as sung passages – often by having a lively party scene – and provided variety, some of the playlets being quite serious, others veering into comedy and outright farce.

The populace embraced the *sarswela*, their own and fully in a vernacular, much more entertaining and engrossing than exotic *zarzuelas*. One town, Meycauayan in Bulacan Province, had eight troupes. Other towns, not so blessed, would borrow one or another to heighten an annual festival; there is always one somewhere. Talented performers became stars and were acclaimed in Manila; the principal stage for these animated productions was the Zorilla.

These troupes were a breeding ground for future generations of directors, actors, dancers, musicians and scene designers; they were no longer dependent on the tutelage of Spanish professionals. Filipino writers and composers, too, gained experience and learned their intricate crafts. The Philippines now had its own theatre.

Non-musical plays in the vernacular, some in verse but most in prose and constructed as on European stages, made their appearance in the islands during the last quarter of the nineteenth century. Such scripts earned the name "*drama*". A breakthrough occurred with the première of Cornelio Hilado's *Ang Babai nga Huwara* (1878); the opening took place not in Manila but in Hoilo; the text was subsequently published (1889). A study, quite didactic, it observes what befalls two daughters, one whose father caters to her every wish while the other suffers under too much paternal discipline. Their successful suitors also differ, one selecting a wife wholly for her physical beauty, the other because he is assured of her steadfast virtue.

This was followed, in 1898, by Tomas Remigio's *Malaya*, written in Spain and in Spanish verse, and produced four years later. It gave voice to anti-Spanish feelings. Remigio is also the author of the oldest surviving comic *drama, Mga Santong Tao*. Three church dignitaries – a parish priest, a sexton and a financial officer – have designs on a humble peasant's lusty young wife, but she deftly tricks and embarrasses all of them.

Ensuing scripts were mostly romantic and heavily sentimental. In 1898 an event took place that strongly influenced Filipino playwrights, the Spanish-American War, ending soon after the sinking of the Spanish fleet in Manila Bay and the ascendance of American rule, the archipelago becoming a colony once more. The islanders had expected that peace would bring them total freedom. Instead, they now faced a new, obdurate colonialism. Military resistance began, mostly in the form of guerrilla warfare led by Emilio Aguinaldo. The charismatic mayor of Cavite Viejo, he had been looked upon as a suspect by the Spanish, who had arranged his exile to China, from which he now returned. (The Chinese had been paid to retain him.) To those who wrote plays in the vernacular, he was instantly a hero; they rallied to give him moral support.

The Spanish had exerted a degree of censorship, much as they did at home. Criticism of their governance, in scripts by dramatists nurturing dissent, had to be oblique, could not be outspoken. Spectators interpreted dialogue, read "between the lines", sensed that a situation had an allegorical intent, an implied, inexplicit message. For what was not actually said or written an author could not be punished. He had to exercise due caution. In a play about domestic strife, with adult children complaining about harsh treatment by their parents, the writer might really be alluding to the conduct of the Spanish authorities in their relations with their Filipino subjects, and many in the audience were aware of that. Most of the analogies to the political realm were subtle, but some closely approached the edge of what was permissible. A good number of native dramatists took the risk.

The Americans were more heavy-handed; they were unaccustomed to being a colonial power. Encountering armed resistance, they overreacted. Anxious to Anglicize the archipelago, they forbade performances of plays in Spanish; they passed the Sedition Law to halt the printing, circulation or production of any literature that called for independence or separation. The Flag Law prohibited showing the Philippine banner and singing the national anthem.

The playwrights were angry and defiant. They flouted the laws, perhaps having the whole cast abruptly gather to lift strident voices in the proscribed anthem, or having the characters' costumes an assemblage of colours matching those in the flag, or having someone deliver a fiery speech advocating rebellion. Several authors were arrested, fined and imprisoned, including Juan Abad and Aurelio Tolentino who were taken to gaol repeatedly (in Tolentino's instance, nine times). Actors and stage crews were seized, and their theatres shut down. This period of "theatre of protest" or "theatre of sedition" is considered the brightest in the history of Philippine *drama*.

Aguinaldo's campaign lasted three years. Finally he was captured and capitulated; a month later he took an oath of allegiance to the United States (1901). The Americans gradually eased their tight control; in 1934 the Senate in Washington raised the islands to the status of a Commonwealth. After the Second World War and the ordeal of Japanese occupation, the last tie was cut, the Philippines now a republic. An American military base remained to guard against the possibility of a renewed Japanese attack, and before the century ended even that last vestige of foreign intrusion was removed.

Spanish sovereignty over the islands lasted 433 years; the Americans stayed for forty-four years. Both occupiers left cultural traces, as did the Japanese who laid waste to much of old Manila (1941–5).

After 1907 the Philippine *drama* reverted to knotty romantic triangles and incessant family concerns. Very few were works of distinction and scarcely any have lived on. An exception, perhaps, is *Veronidia* (1919) by Cirio H. Panganiban. First staged in his home town, Bocaue, it reached Manila seven years later and was rapturously welcomed. It had a long run, during which the "theatre was flooded with tears" by deeply stirred audiences. Veronidia deserts her husband, Roselyo, to live with Cristino, who first wooed her when they were in childhood. The child she herself left behind brings word that Roselyo, gravely ill, is dying. Guilty and repentant, Veronidia seeks to go to him, but the jealous Cristino tries to prevent her. In their highly emotional confrontation he stabs her to death. The engagement in Manila was greatly helped by the presence in the leading roles of two of the country's favourite performers.

The *drama*, its stock plots and characters nearing exhaustion from being overworked, began to lose its audience to the new media, film, radio and television that churned much the same cliché narrative material and were more easily and less expensively accessible.

Another competitor was vaudeville (*Bodabil*), along with the circus the least cerebral of entertainments. It had been introduced in 1910 for the amusement of American troops stationed in the archipelago, but the Filipinos liked it as much or even more. Two theatres in Manila, the Empire and the Savoy, purveyed acrobats, jugglers, smiling chorus girls in jazz extravaganzas, singers and comics, in a rapid variety. In time, though, *Bodabil* degenerated to vulgar burlesque and striptease shows.

During the four decades of American occupation, college graduates no longer spoke Spanish but English, and there was a growing colony of American businessmen and government administrators sent from Washington. They became an élite, well-educated class, the islands' affluent "establishment". They attended plays spoken in English, perhaps Shakespeare or Shaw, Barrie, or imports of current productions from the West End and Broadway. The major, serious drama in the Philippines was now in English, and some of the best local playwrights chose to write in that language and continue to do so. The theatre scene there offers a wide range of languages. (In a turnabout, during the occupation, plays in English were forbidden by the Japanese.) Some of the best-known and well-regarded dramatists using it after the liberation of Manila have been Wilfrido Ma Guerro – "the authentic voice of his class and generation" – with over 100 scripts bearing his stamp; together with award-winners Alberto Florentino, Fidel Sicam, Nestor Torre, Wilfrido Noelledo, Estrella Sicam and Jesus Peralt; prizes for the best works in English were given each year in a contest since expanded to include scripts in any tongue.

On a broader roster of dramatists who elected English or remained with Spanish and Tagalog are Carlos P. Romulo, a high-ranking government official at the United Nations and in Manila; Jorge Bocobo; Jesusa Araullo; Vidal Tan; Lino Castillejo. Nick Joaquin's *Portrait of the Artist as a Filipino* is deemed a major achievement. This list is far from complete.

The islands abound with drama workshops, theatre clubs, semi-professional classes in dramatic writing and play production at the universities. Theatre is in the Filipinos' bloodstream.

The drift away from Tagalog and dialects – for a while they were looked upon as inferior speech best suited for the uneducated – was reversed with a steady rise of nationalistic pride. Increased attendance at theatrical events resulted. English and Spanish plays never drew as well. The dialects were also adopted by activist, leftist groups for agit-prop street theatre. The imposition of martial law by President Marcos in 1972 temporarily ended that movement.

The early forms of theatre – *komedyas, zarzuelas, sarswelas* – are still to be found in outlying regions, especially in non-Christian, Muslim sectors, and in faithful revivals by groups devoted to the preservation of native culture and traditions. But Filipino stages today offer plays of every sort presented elsewhere in the Western world. What is chiefly lacking is money; the budgets are small.

On the vast Asian mainland, in the Himalayan fastness, the inhabitants of Tibet nurtured religious dramas as early as the seventh century AD. The works were tinctured with Indian Buddhism, which had spread throughout Asia in that epoch. As in Burma and elsewhere in the Far East, the Buddhist legends were mixed with romantic, local tales of reincarnations and further miracles attributed to the Enlightened One. Some of the plays have literary, poetic merit. A principal author was a priest, Sixth

Tale-lama Tsongs-bdyangs-rgyam-thso (hardly a name pronounced trippingly on the tongue), of the same seventh century who is also cherished, somewhat incongruously, for his highly charged erotic lyrics. Gassner, on whom I am dependent, in turn quotes from H.I. Woolf's *Three Tibetan Mysteries* concerning the devout, high-minded and theoretically celibate writer that he was "a delicate poet, in love with the arts and with beauty in all its forms, the feminine principally". The composers of many other sanctimonious scripts are anonymous, but most are assumed to have dwelt and laboured in the high-peaked lamaseries.

The plays were staged in or near monasteries by fellow-members of the priestly orders, who took all but the female roles – for those, talented outsiders were recruited. In the scripts, passages of prose and poetry alternate, and dance and masks – frequently totemistic – were used. These dramas were presented on ceremonious occasions at fixed dates, and were staged with a considerable array of liturgical spectacle, a colourful facet of Tibetan Buddhism. Lengthy narrative sections were chanted either by a Brahman, if the material was largely Indian in origin, or by a chosen actor of native stock, if the topic was mostly Tibetan. The Tibetan narrator was called a "hunter", and a group of "hunters" might also make up a chorus. A royal protagonist, given lines, would recite them very slowly, and the last words of his sentences were signals for the auditors – at court – to repeat them fervently.

In time, conventions – similar to those that prevailed in Sanskrit drama – dictated the structure of the plays quite rigidly. Despite the strictness of the form, room was left for improvisation in performance, along with excellent opportunities for acting as well as for sung narration and dance. The content was overladen with idealistic aspiration, the story delivering spiritual lessons together with explicit, uplifting sermons. Since the action entailed a host of supernatural deeds, the plays were like the European medieval mystery plays, though somewhat leavened by a light fairy-tale quality. Some have been translated into English and offer fascinating reading.

Among the best known, rendered by H.I. Woolf, are *Nansal*, *Djoazanmo* and *Tchrimekundan*. The last of these relates the charitable works on earth of a prince, actually the Buddha, who gives to the poor not only his wealth (which includes a fabulous jewel and magical properties, which unhappily fall into the hands of a foe), but also his wife and family, and finally even his eyes to restore the sight of a blind man. For all this, of course, he is ultimately requited by the god Indra.

In 1951 the Communist government in China, which had long claimed Tibet, sent troops to reoccupy it. The Dalai Lama soon fled to India after a failed uprising; many of the lamaseries were razed, and rebellious monks were persecuted, a number of them imprisoned and executed. What has been the fate of the ancient drama remains unclear, but the conquerors make no secret of their determination to extirpate distinctive Tibetan culture.

— 4 —

JAPAN: NŌH AND KABUKI

Oft told, a legend about the founding of Japanese theatre has Amaterasu, the Sun Goddess, piqued after quarrelling with her brother, and withdrawing to sulk in a rock cave. Heaven and the whole cosmos are plunged into darkness by her self-immurement. The other gods, disturbed, whisper among themselves and invent a dance, performed by the ebullient and saucy Inari (or Ama no Uzume) atop an upended wooden tub. Though she is a virgin, her gestures are indecent, erotic, and the skies echo with the laughter of a myriad other deities. The Sun Goddess, feminine and therefore curious, peers out to see what has occasioned the rhythmic thumping and laughter, and the universe is brightened once again.

To this day, the stamping of the actor's clad feet is a feature of the Japanese stage, and there are shrines to Inari in Japanese Kabuki theatres and even in film studios. She later becomes the maidservant of the Sun Goddess and consoles her at troubled moments. Today, as patron deity of performers, she – like them – "lightens the hearts of men, comforts them in distress, and makes the sun shine anew".

The period of darkness is thought to be an allusion to the early Japanese fear of solar eclipses. When the Sun Goddess ventures from the cave, a mirror is held up that redoubles her radiance at the same time that she beholds her dazzling image in it. At the sudden return of light, a cock crows. This is memorialized by the enduring custom of presenting Kagura plays – works of this era – night-long to the break of dawn and the very first cock's crow.

An alternative version of the beginning of play-acting, set forth in the *Kojiki*, or *Record of Ancient Matters* (AD 712), tells how the primal creative deities, Izanagi and Izanami, bring life into being by dancing (as did Siva) around the pillar of Heaven, while chanting:

> Begin here life of man
> Likewise with the life of woman.

A third myth, related by Berthold, concerns a dreadful conflict between two feuding brothers. The

Sea God intervenes. "The ruler of the tides gives the younger brother Yamahiko, who at first is defeated, power over ebb and flood. The elder brother Umihiko realizes what danger this spells for him. He decides to propitiate Yamahiko. To this end he smears red earth on his face and hands and dances a pantomime of drowning: how at first the waves lap only at his feet, how the water rises higher and higher until it reaches up to his neck. With the words, 'Henceforth and until the end of time I will be your jester and servant,' Umihiko submits to his brother's rule." He is identified as the first "professional actor". And Berthold adds: "This myth, which has wide ramifications throughout the Far East, underlies the legend of the descendance of Jimmu, the first Japanese emperor, from a dragon. The dragon mask, which is a symbol of the sea divinity, still has a prominent part in the Kagura dances."

From these myths, too, arise several important stage props that characterize traditional Japanese theatre: the head ornament woven of leaves from the spindle tree donned by Inari for her dance, and the bamboo branch she bears in her hand, as well as the mirror held up to Amaterasu, and the red clay that covers the face and hands of Umihiko, precursors of the masks and thick make-up used by performers throughout East Asia. This spindle tree purportedly has its roots in Heaven, and the tied bamboo leaves supposedly come from soaring Kagu mountain.

One need not study and interpret these alluring fables, however, for unlike the vagueness that surrounds the origins of other forms of Asian drama, Japanese history furnishes scholars with a much more definite chronology and far more specific details wherewith to trace the development of its brilliant and varied kinds of stages. What is more, its very early theatre forms, introduced 1,300 years ago, are still preserved and viable, excerpted and presented nightly in Tokyo and Kyoto to attentive and devoted spectators, which is far more often than Westerners are apt to see Greek tragedies and comedies.

Doubtless, Japanese drama began as elsewhere in primitive but sacred dances and rites, at seed-time, at reaping, enacted or supervised by priests; of this the evidence is plentiful. Besides such field-dances and harvest-mimings, in which the participants were masked, there are traces of a slight Indian infusion, as well as of borrowings from China and Korea – the Japanese stage has been described as a "derivative drama", a pejorative label applied to most forms of Japanese art. The "long-nosed" masks used in later dances also suggest a measure of Greek influence: as remarked before, Alexander's conquests in India brought with them examples of Hellenic art that were copied, and these ultimately reached even remote Japan, carried there by Buddhist missionaries, laden with new ideas of every sort. This is clearly seen in AD 612, during the reign of Prince Shōtoku Taishi (572–621), when Buddhism contributed important and pervasive new subject-matter to the ritual dances: the kindly and supernal deeds of the Enlightened One and his multitude of saints. And Buddhism came not only directly from India but also by way of China, and Korea and Tibet, each of their cultures adding unique features. Finally, the miracles performed by native Shinto deities were also celebrated, especially at local shrines where the miracles were believed to have occurred. Many of these reprises were pantomimic only, though perhaps they were more fully explained by the accompaniment of public readings from the scriptures.

As has been said, the Kagura – pre-Buddhist dances – had a magical intent. Etymologically, "Kagura" has several connotations, some quite elusive; but one of its meanings is "entertainment of the gods". The dancing and miming were aimed at propitiating and seeking assistance from the appropriate deities. As Berthold puts it, too, some of the enactments were "pre-historic, shamanistic invocations of demons and animals", whereby hunters anticipated the help of a god when later shooting an arrow at a stag, or when stalking a dangerous wild boar – "imitative magic" and strands of totemism; a token of this is seen in the surviving lion dance.

Another type of Kagura had to do with court ceremonies during the Mikagura, a winter festival that came into being about AD 1002, having as its inspiration the legend of Inari's uninhibited dance. It was comprised of the spontaneous antics of court jesters, acrobats and mimes, and claimed to honour the Shinto deities.

Much later, in the seventeenth century, Sato-Kagura, a religious village festival, made its appearance. It enabled local people to ask the protection of benevolent spirits as well as the exorcism of evil ones. These rites, gradually modernized, persisted until the present century, an instance being the widespread enactment of Sato-Kagura plays during a decimating cholera plague that took its harsh toll in 1916. The communal hope and belief was that the solemn rites would avert or chase away the plague.

Prince-regent Shōtoku Taishi was a zealous advocate of Buddhism. He also had a fondness for the arts and especially for the dances and plays of foreign lands. In 612, the date cited before, he proffered the hospitality of his court at Nara to a Korean actor–dancer, Mimashi of Kudara, who was leading a band of strolling players. So pleased was the Prince-regent with the troupe's performances that he persuaded Mimashi to settle at Sakurai, near Nara, and establish a school; he should teach carefully selected young persons the technique of a new dance-play as mastered by him. The name for it, Gigaku, or "artful music", is said to have been contributed by the ruler himself. Ever more taken with this new dance-form, he had it installed as part of state ceremonials. This meant that it was staged before the temples in every part of the country on the occasion of Buddha's birthday and the equally sacred Day of the Dead, the two major religious holidays. The music, heard separately, was eventually referred to as Gagaku.

Still later, the music – "elegant and noble" – when played alone as an instrumental offering came to be known as Kangen, or "pipes and strings", and when combined with stately dance-movements was called Bugaku, its performance largely confined to the Imperial Court, inaccessible to any broader audience. It is an aristocratic art form intended to be enjoyed and appreciated only by a rarefied élite, those spectators boasting a "divine right".

The history of Bugaku is recorded in a thirteenth-century treatise, *Kyokunsho*, written by the dancer Komo no Chikazane. At first it was given on level ground, without a stage, and accompanied by drums, cymbals and flutes. It began with a procession of dancers and musicians, which was followed by plays mostly pantomimic, the actor–dancers wearing grotesque "helmet masks with long beak noses, powerful jaws, and bulging eyeballs". (Some 200 of these masks have survived, most kept in the Emperor Tenji's treasure house at Nara, a few in temples at various locations.)

By the eighth century Bugaku had attained its definitive shape, possibly with some further Chinese influence – not only earlier Korean but also Tibetan idioms are discernible in it. It reached its apex in the Heian period (ninth to eleventh centuries), a notable date in its history being 703, when it was firmly institutionalized, to be enacted without lapse ever since.

An anonymous contributor to *The Dance Encyclopedia* says:

The Bugaku style is quite different from other types of Japanese dance in that the dramatic elements are of far less importance than the pure dance form. Also, in contrast to other styles of Japanese dance, Bugaku emphasizes symmetry, not only in the frequent use of paired dancers but also in the basic movement patterns of the solo dancers. . . . [It] is actually not a theatrical performance, but a ritual or entertainment designed for the palace. Slow moving by Western measurements of time, refined into a near abstraction when the dance has a definite plot, Bugaku is probably the ultimate in artistic formulation or formal art achieved through the talents of generations of dancers and musicians, who not only follow one another in time, but are descended, one from another, in a very definite family succession.

Berthold provides a somewhat more visual picture of this ancient yet still living dance-genre in its initial phase.

Bugaku required two groups of dancers: "The Dancers of the Music on the Right" and "The Dancers of the Music on the Left." The Dancers of the Music on the Right entered the stage from the right, and their musicians were stationed on the right side of the stage. Correspondingly, the Dancers of the

Music on the Left made their entrance from the left, and their musicians were stationed on the left.

The Bugaku stage was a raised, square platform, surrounded by railings, with stairs leading up to it on the right and on the left. The musical ensemble on the left consisted predominantly of wind instruments. In the ensemble on the right percussion instruments dominated and marked the rhythmic pattern for the Dancers on the Right. The performance was preceded by the *embu*, a dance ceremony of purification of cultic origin. (The introductory scene of classical Indian drama, the *purvaranga*, begins with a rite closely related to the *embu*.) Then the left and right groups begin to dance, in part in stately and part in lively rhythms. The two groups are rigorously distinct. . . . The dancers come on stage alternately from right and left, and always in pairs; those who dance to music on the left, which is inspired by Chinese and Indian sources, wear costumes in which red predominates, while green distinguishes the Dancers of the Music on the Right. This music is of Korean and Manchurian origin and adapted to the Japanese taste. The Bugaku ends, now as it has always done, with the *chogeishi* composition by Minamoto no Hiromasa (919–980).

Faubion Bowers spent fifteen years in the Far East, part of the time in an official post on the staff of General MacArthur during the occupation of Japan after the Second World War. He had an opportunity, as a "visiting dignitary", to view a performance of Bugaku. As he recounts it, the event took place in the Music Pavilion,

one of the three or four tall, two-storied concrete buildings deep within the outer walls and past the double moat of the Imperial Palace. There the visitor will sit with a handful of other persons, either guests like himself or members of the Emperor's staff, sprinkled thinly through the large auditorium. Far outnumbering the actual total of spectators, the orchestra of perhaps twenty-five musicians perform its pieces with a concentration and finish that in the West we associate more usually with huge public concerts and recitals.

The extraordinary occasion . . . begins with a series of reverberating thuds on the orchestra's giant drum. In appearance alone this drum or *taiko* shows the antiquity and far-off connection of the dancing soon to begin. The heavily carved, wooden, oval-shaped frame represents the sacred flames which encompass the Hindu god Siva. This halo of fire is supposed to have begun with the original drum rhythms with which he created the world. The thick hide which covers the drum itself is painted in red and black with two interlocking "S" shapes, familiar in ancient Chinese religion and philosophy as the *yin* and *yang* symbols of duality. As the windows and skylights shudder with the drum's sound, the musicians and dancers, dressed in costumes whose styles of long silk sleeves, baggy pants that tie at the ankle, and soft felt-soled shoes have been traditionally repeated for the last thousand years, take their places at the far end of the hall. On their heads they wear the thin, transparent, black gauze hats with curling flaps at the sides and back which announce their official rank as Regular Musicians and Dancers of the Imperial Court, hereditary posts handed down from father to son.

Several kinds of flutes, both long and short flutes, flageolets, gongs and small drums constitute the bulk of the orchestra. But three additional instruments add their special flavor to the ensemble, and give Gagaku a unique and inimitable timbre and sonority. These are the *koto*, which is a thirteen-stringed dulcimer played with the fingers on which metal or horn plectrums are attached like finger nails, the *biwa*, or four-stringed lute, and most unusual of all and unlike any Western instrument the *sho*, a miniature hand-held pipe organ of seventeen slender bamboo pipes and reeds. These three instruments give the orchestra its harmonic substance. The *sho*, for instance, plays solid chords of ten notes and while the performer blows continuously in or out through the mouthpiece he alters the inner tones as the music requires. The various melodic passages of the "dulcimer" and the "lute" add contrapuntal background passages as well to the tonal lines. But they are so intricate and considered so refined they are omitted whenever Gagaku accompanies dancing. The theory behind this practice is that only coarser music belongs with the less subtle sister art of dance and that the athletic motions of dance destroy the gossamer-spun melodies of the strings.

Then the dances begin. As the dancers move they extend their arms stiffly and symmetrically with the fingers held taut. They bend their legs in deep *pliés*. Sometimes they wear huge frightening masks with gaping maws. Meanwhile the dissonances and weird melodies of the music collide and the pulsing beats of five and nines or fours and twelves, punctuated by the drums, vibrate delicately and uncertainly in the Westerner's ears. Somehow the antiquity of the dance and music is immediately evident. In fact, the entire performance is so remote from one's previous artistic experience either in Asia or the West that after such a program it comes as no surprise to learn that Bugaku and Gagaku first appeared in Japan thirteen hundred years ago, not long after the fall of the Roman Empire and considerably before England, for instance, was very civilized, and nearly a millennium before the violin and the piano, for another instance, were used in the West. . . . Some dances are attributed to certain emperors themselves, and their fanciful and charming titles such as *Dragons Basking in the Sun*, *The Polo Game*, were danced by them. By the twelfth and thirteenth centuries, the Japanese taste for this dance and music spread to the Shōgun's court. (These were the military rulers who actually controlled the country while the emperors lived in elegant retirement which gave them leisure to continue their protective practice of these fragile arts.) They quickly took up the imperial fashion. One of them, Minamoto no Toshie, is known to have insisted on dancing Bugaku with his sword and spear to a martial piece of music known as Bairo (from Vairocano, an Indian deity of war) before engaging in any combat with the enemy.

At moments there are deep bends, and some gestures are explicit.

Keeping the audience for Bugaku so strictly exclusive has helped to preserve it as a pure art form; it has never undergone change to attract and hold the fickle favour of a less discerning public; it is much like denying access to a fragile, illustrated medieval manuscript that might be harmed by too much light and therefore is seldom opened and displayed. As Bowers observes, "The average Japanese – even if he spends his life within walking distance of the Imperial Palace – is never likely to have seen any of its repertory enacted." On rare occasions a performance open only to those specifically invited is staged at one of the great shrines, Ise or Nara. In the Kabuki theatre, too, if the text has an emperor appear, a "reasonable facsimile" of Gagaku music may be inserted into the scene. But to behold the true Bugaku has remained the sole privilege of the imperial family and carefully chosen guests, who are most likely high-ranking foreign visitors, typically ambassadors or heads of state.

In 1958 the New York City Ballet was on tour in Japan and offered performances in honour of the marriage of Crown Prince Akahito to Michiko Shoda. To reciprocate, the imperial family consented to an engagement of the Gagaku ensemble at the City Center in Manhattan the following year (1959), so it is possible – as *The Dance Encyclopedia* suggests – that more people have seen Bugaku in the United States than have ever beheld it in Japan. The truth be told, a good many American spectators, lacking the temperament and esoteric knowledge of the Japanese, found the luxurious pace of the dances somewhat taxing, though there was unanimous praise for the rich beauty of the costumes.

The strain of eroticism that runs through many Bugaku works has led some scholars to assume they derive in some measure from the *mimus* belonging to a late Roman period, a tendency which in turn was of Grecian origin; while other experts contend that the phallic elements were passed along from fertility dances in the Central Asian highlands. George Balanchine, the famed director and choreographer of the New York City Ballet, sought to create a work on a Japanese theme but having it *sur la pointe*, using classical Russian technique. He titled it *Bugaku* (1963), and it caused a considerable stir. It depicts the nuptial night of a noble couple. With the characters in filmy costumes, it is handled with great delicacy yet is remarkable for its erotic content.

Scattered elements of Bugaku found a place in folk-dances of the day and later. Other ingredients of the earliest Japanese – pre-Nōh – drama were taken from lesser court and warrior dances, knightly and chivalric in spirit, incarnating the medieval code of the Samurai, illustrated when the aristocratic participants might posture, like Minamoto no Toshie, with their flashing, metallic weapons, to an orchestral accompaniment. Gradually choruses were added to the solo performances, and this required preparing poetic texts for them. Many of these were, in essence, adaptations of Chinese court dances. They were entertainments for the nobility who took part in them, all of whom were amateurs: high-born gentlemen and ladies sang together. By the end of the ninth century professionally trained leaders took over. This form of secular amusement was called Saibara; in it the subject-matter of the songs and dances became more and more distinctively Japanese, drawing on historical themes. Saibara flourished until the twelfth century, but afterwards vanished, only a few ninth-century texts remaining in one manuscript collection. Ernest Fenollosa, the greatest European authority on Nōh drama, quotes the charming lyrics of a Saibara verse-dance:

> O white-gemmed camelia and you jewel willow,
> Who stand together on the Cape of Takasago!
> This one, since I want her for me,
> That one, too, since I want her for mine –
> Jewel willow!

> I will make you a thing to hang my coat on,
> With its tied-up strings, with its deep-dyed strings.
> Ah! what have I done?
> There, what is this I am doing?
> O what am I to do?
> Mayhap I have lost my soul!
> But I have met
> The lily flower,
> The first flower of morning.

The practice of combining dance and song continued in the Kagura – the "god dances" – widespread at the many Shinto shrines. The chorus sat to one side, chanting. The masked dancers, silent, mimed and gave expression to each sacred theme. These pious dance dramas might be enacted on the lawns before the pine-girt shrines by virgins holding symbols of nature in their hands, the movements reverent, slow, and at times majestic. Shinto being filled with nature worship, many of the Kagura lyrics are pantheistic (as are those in primal Sanskrit drama). A resemblance to the Greek dithyrambs is marked and underlines once more the universal impulse, propitiatory, magical, from which drama springs.

An ensuing phase in the development of Japanese theatre saw a broadening of the already existent forms, the scripts alternating prose dialogue and versified choric passages. The texts reached a level of genuine literary merit. This was the Middle Ages: balladry celebrating the brave deeds of knights – the Samurai – swept Japan. The tales were fashioned into epic cycles like the Arthurian romances in England. Elements of these were echoed on the stage, which thereby gained new subject-matter, becoming more secular.

During this same period, rural folk-comedy had begun to thrive, simple farces at first called Dengaku, a word meaning "rice-field music", which suggests the native roots of these rude buffooneries that comprised mostly dancing and acrobatics. They were performed in a carnival atmosphere, often in temple precincts. Along with exuberant displays of physical skill, tumbling, stilt-walking, juggling, there would be puppet plays and vulgar, popular sketches at festive events much like at the primitive Hundred Games in China which they perhaps emulated. They might also be compared to the semi-religious *ludi* held in Rome. With the advent of the Heian period, such plebeian fare gained the appellation Saragaku, or "monkey music", since to the crude skits and balancing acts were added monkeys and other performing animals. They had become a cross between the presentations of vagabond players in medieval Europe and the present-day circus. (The inclusion of the monkey as a character in Oriental farce can be traced back to China, where he appears in a clown's role, to their antics in the Indonesian shadow plays, and finally to India, where the monkey-king Hanuman is a dynamic figure in the *Ramayana*.)

The spectacles expanded, sometimes entered into by the whole population of a city parading masked and in comic costumes, their behaviour getting out of hand, riotous, and joined by even high-ranking personages waving huge fans. The sketches were more often put on by professional troupes, some of whom were maintained by feudal lords in their manor houses. But other sponsors were Buddhist and Shinto priests anxious to keep their hold on the populace by setting up a rival form of entertainment, if of a more elegant and elevated sort. By doing so they drew larger crowds to their seasonal festivals, the worshippers happy to have lighter moments alternating with the overly solemn ritual. Over the years the various kinds of farces – the rural and urban, and the temple-sponsored – coalesced, and a few companies of actors became permanently attached to the larger shrines.

By the second half of the fourteenth century the new and more respectable kind of farces had absorbed some of the disparate qualities of Gigaku and Dengaku; while retaining a comic strain, they were also filled with more serious topics from the epic military ballads, as well as Shinto themes. They acquired a new name: Dengaku-no-no. At this point, too, actors' guilds, or *za* (word for "theatre"), were being established: they were apt to be made up of members of a single family, entrance being mostly a hereditary privilege. As in ancient Greece, actors were a fortunate class, under the protection of the Buddhist temples, exempt from taxes and granted a monopoly of all performances permitted in the district governed by a particular shrine.

At long last, some actors began to enjoy personal fame, no longer anonymous, their names and qualities recorded by theatre historians. Especially noteworthy were the Saragaku player Kwanami and his even more talented son Seami, whose future influence was to be beyond measure.

In Japan, the late fourteenth and early fifteenth centuries saw the propagation of Zen, a more contemplative and pantheistic phase of Buddhism. Its "mystic chiaroscuro" wielded a strong, almost compulsive appeal for many aristocrats and intellectuals who searched for "enlightenment". Similarly, by dedicating themselves to bouts of intense meditation each day, creative artists found their thoughts and feelings greatly deepened. The cultural climate was altered and enhanced, too, by the ascendancy of the Samurai, the fierce warrior caste, composed largely of men of noble birth and boastfully claiming heroic ancestors, who vowed selfless loyalty to their feudal lords and rode about like Arthurian knights performing chivalric deeds in defence of the weak and helpless. Their code, a rigid but romantic devotion to preserving their honour, combined with the exalted ideals of Zen, inspired the better playwrights to conceive a new kind of serious drama, Nōh (or Nō), suitable for production at the splendid courts of the day, those of the Emperor and the Shōgun – the *de facto* ruler – as well as those of the many princes and titled of lesser rank. (Arthur Waley, to whose illuminating essays and acclaimed translations I owe much, says that Nō is written with a Chinese character meaning "'to be able'. It signifies 'talent'; hence, 'an exhibition of talent', or 'performance'.")

The two who are credited with fashioning Nōh are Kwanami Kiyotsugu (1333–84) and Seami Motokiyo (or Zeami, 1363–1444), the father and son mentioned just above. Kwanami, a priest, was in charge of theatrical enterprises at a shrine near Nara. He wrote about fifteen plays, some of them original works, some adaptations, personally staging and acting in them. Some claim he merely added his own music and stage effects to scripts by other authors – his predecessors or fellow priests – but this is uncertain; in any event, he raised the standard of his dramas to an unprecedentedly high level. The new form of play caused widespread excitement. The dry riverbed of the Kamo River served as the site of a huge temporary theatre (as was the custom in China), to which were attracted the emperor and Shōgun among others. Selling tickets to the throngs at these performances allowed the priests to raise funds to build more temples.

An exemplary Saragaku actor, Kwanami did not limit his new works to its ever more serious traditions but inserted elements of Dengaku and also of Kowaka, a form of recitation heightened and punctuated by the speaker's rhythmic tapping of a fan. He also borrowed from the Kusemi, a chanted dance, which reappears at moments in passages of Nōh plays; as well as from the Ko-uta, the danced form of a popular ballad. Finally, he captured a rare distillation of the dignity and austerity of Bugaku for fearsome climaxes of unearthly beauty.

Some time around 1375 the Shōgun Yoshimitsu, while travelling in Kii Province, saw a performance by Kwanami at one of the temples of Kumano. Deeply impressed, he brought him to his court and became his long-time patron. He granted him a small estate, and the actor left the priesthood. Enjoying the ruler's favour, Kwanami was able to do much to advance the cause of his theatre, as did his highly intelligent son.

Versatile, Kwanami excelled in many parts. In a tribute, Seami later wrote: "Though he could take adult male roles, he played female ones with great delicacy. And when in *Jinen Koji* and other such plays, wearing a black wig, he took his seat on the high dais, he did not seem much more than twelve years old." The Shōgun expressed his belief that young Seami could never equal his father. Furthermore, Seami added, "My late father, even when acting in the remotest country districts or out-of-way mountain villages, was at pains to adapt his performance to local manners and prejudices. The perfect actor is he who can win praise alike in palaces, temples or villages, or even at festivals held in the shrines of the most far-off provinces." (This is from Waley.)

As a playwright, Kwanami's principal talent was for pathos, interlaced with surprising touches of humour. He was expert at showing how beautiful but heartless women are eventually punished for their haughtiness. In *Sotoba Komachi*, which is among his most prized scripts, a proud lady is courted by a lover who travels long distances to woo her, defying every sort of weather, trudging through violent storm and face-whipping snow. She has stipulated that she will entertain his suit only if he journeys to see her at least 100 times. He dies, spent from his great exertions, on the final night of his unreasonable endeavour. Afterwards she loses her looks, her wealth and admirers, until she is reduced to nothing more than an ugly, daft beggar-woman. Mad, she is "possessed" by the lover whose death she has caused: his ghost leaves her only when her own life deserts her rigid, emaciated body.

Here are passages from *Sotoba Komachi*, translated by Waley:

PRIEST: Who are you? Pray tell us the name you had, and we
will pray for you when you are dead.

KOMACHI: Shame covers me when I speak my name: but if you
will pray for me, I will try to tell you. This is my name;
write it down in your prayer-list: I am the ruins of
Komachi, daughter of Ono no Yoshizane, Governor
of the land of Dewa.

PRIESTS: O piteous, piteous! is this
Komachi that once
Was a bright flower,
Komachi the beautiful, whose dark brows
Linked like dark moons;
Whose face white-painted ever;
Whose many, many damask robes
Filled cedar-scented halls?

CHORUS: The cup she held at the feast
Like gentle moonlight dropped its glint on her sleeve,
Oh how fell she from splendour
How came the white of Winter
To crown her head?
Where are gone the lovely locks, doubly-twined,
The coils of jet?
Lank wisps, scant curls wither now
On wilted flesh;
And twin-arches, moth-brows tinge no more
With the hue of far hills.

KOMACHI: Oh cover, cover
From the creeping light of dawn
Silted seaweed locks that of a hundred years
Lack now but one.
Oh hide me from my shame.

[*Komachi hides her face.*]

As shall be seen, what is clearly set here is the pattern of the Nōh, a brief ghost play, focused on a wandering spirit, who is self-tormented, seeking redemption for a past transgression.

In *The Maiden's Grave* the remorseful heroine drowns herself – in itself a sin – and suffers post-humously for her act and for her having encouraged a rivalry among her lovers that has led them, too, to commit an offensive deed.

Jinen the Preacher tells how a priest tries by a series of provocative sermons to raise money to rebuild his temple. A little girl, an orphan, offers a garment in honour of her parents. The priest is moved to tears by her gesture, as are the townspeople. A merchant, who has bought the girl as his slave, claims her. It is revealed that the child has sold herself in order to have money enough to buy the "garment of sacrifice". The priest, who had been ready to deliver another of his sermons, decides instead to rescue the girl by returning the garment to the slave merchant. He realizes that a good deed is more important than a pious preachment. Setting out, he pursues the slaver at risk to his own safety. In a boat, on a lake, he confronts the merchant and his henchmen. Because of the priest's robes, the wicked man dare not attack him – with an oar, he strikes the bound girl instead. Jinen chides him, and the slaver and his men finally respect his courage and agree to exchange the girl for the much disputed garment. But to degrade the brave priest, they insist that he first dance for them. He does so. Says Jinen:

> . . . Buddha went through great sufferings to save all living things. I will follow him; even if my body is torn to pieces, I will help the child out of this.
>
> [Translation: Makoto Ueda]

At the demand of the slaving party he performs once again, a bamboo whisk dance; then a third time, a hand-drum dance. He prevails upon the captors at last; the stubborn priest and hapless girl are freed. Symbolically, as he phrases it, he has reached "the shore of enlightenment". He has first saved himself, by having become a priest, and is now dedicated to saving others.

Kwanami's style is extremely simple, with a strong command of appropriate metaphor. His people are sharply alive, their dress and actions depicted with the vivid precision that is characteristic of the Japanese lyric and that was later to be copied in the early twentieth-century Western school of brief Imagist poetry. Jinen describes how boats were first conceptualized:

> Once there was a man, Ch'ih Yu by name,
> Who rebelled against the Yellow Emperor.
> Yet the enemy troop was beyond a sea.

The Emperor had a soldier, Huo Ti was his name,

Who, as he looked over a pond one day,

Saw a willow leaf floating on the water.

Then an insect, called a spider, also fell

From the air down into the pond; but it crept

Up to the leaf, which, as wind was blowing,

Came nearer and nearer to the shore, till

The spider reached the land of Autumn mist.

Observing this, the soldier got a hint

And developed a boat. The Yellow Emperor

Took the boat, rowed across the sea,

And easily conquered Ch'ih Yu the traitor.

[Translation: Makoto Ueda]

Before this new formulation of Nōh, a Dengaku troupe from Nara had been requested by some parish priests to appear before the Shōgun. Kwan, head of the Nara group, enlarged his solo roles (much as Thespis is said to have done in pre-Periclean Athens). He also increased the works' musical content. The hero exchanged dialogue with a chorus, a vestigial practice left over from Kagura. Kwan, his son Zei, and then his grandson On – they were a family of noted actors – encouraged other playwrights to follow their example, and many – some say hundreds – did so. Kwanami built upon the changes introduced by his predecessors. In his plays the "god dancer" gradually became a human being, the protagonist of a profound spiritual crisis – a progression following a course much like that of Greek tragedy in its rise. At times, a woman instead of a man might be the beset leading figure.

Even more substantial were the contributions of his son, Seami, to the shaping of Nōh. This began when the bright, handsome boy was only twelve. Yoshimitsu, the Shōgun, fell in love with him and had him installed at the palace. Of their intimate relationship an angry contemporary wrote in a diary: "They share the same mat and eat from the same vessels. These Saragaku people are mere mendicants, but he treats them with as much esteem as if they were Privy Counsellors." Doubtless this liaison strengthened Kwanami's hand at court. Seami was not the Shōgun's only boy-favourite; there had been another, Michichiyo, a lad of great beauty. Yoshimitsu had a deep fondness for the arts, including forms of theatre. He painted and wrote mystical poetry, the latter talent possibly also inclining him to welcome Nōh, as would his profound immersion in Zen. He had become heir to the Shōgunate and thereby the titular ruler of Japan when he was but ten years old. For a time, when he reached manhood, he had a mistress named Takahashi of whom Seami later recorded in his *Works*: "She was skilled in ten thousand arts of love and made it her business to please him. This lady died unexpectedly. It was she who had cared for the August Health, forcing her Master to drink when he needed wine and restraining him from drinking at times when abstinence was desirable. By this devoted attention to his welfare she had raised herself to a position of importance." Speaking of himself in the third person, he adds: "After this lady's death everyone recommended Seami as one particularly qualified for such a position." (Translation: Waley)

Unfortunately, Kwanami's tenure at the Shōgun's court was cut short. He died suddenly at fifty-two while away in Suruga Province. He had no more fervent admirer than his son. In his *Works* Seami declares: "From my earliest years I had the support of my father, so that the above chapters . . . do not proceed wholly from my own imagination. In the twenty years that have passed since I became a man I have practised his style, drawing on the store of things seen and heard (during his lifetime)." (Waley)

Indeed, scholars are hesitant about how much credit to give to Kwanami and how much to Seami in the fashioning of Nōh; both father and son were possessed of genius and together created sublime works of art. Seami was to write ninety-three plays (or more) and twenty-three remarkable essays on the nature of theatre and the techniques and spiritual mission and moral obligations of the actor – he shared the Shōgun Yoshimitsu's reverent adherence to Zen Buddhism. These treatises are comparable to those by Aristotle and Bharata; they contain a host of precepts that have been endlessly studied for their insight since their discovery some centuries after his death. They are also a practical manual having to do with details of staging and programming, as well as steps to be taken in training. It was not his intention to publish these essays: they were meant to be handed down to members of his "family" – the players and pupils in his company – as "trade secrets". In sum, they attest to his serious aspiration and unusual intellectual honesty.

Seami's ninety-three plays are very short, their texts seldom filling more than six to twelve pages of print. But slowly paced and with danced episodes added, they tend to seem fairly long when presented. An evening's offering now consists of five plays, differing in mood and character, in a prescribed order. Occasionally there is a sixth, as will be explained below.

Besides composing original scripts, Seami adapted a few by his father – such as *Matsukaze* – and some by others. In most instances he provided both the words and music, and of course performed in many of the dramas, lending his inimitable presence, his informing intelligence and unique self-discipline.

The ideas set forth in the *Works* represent one of the highest peaks of aesthetics ever expounded of Japanese drama. In Nōh, according to Seami, three principles should prevail. The first has to do with "imitation", a basic requirement for an actor. To capture the essence of an emotion or an object, he should neither exaggerate nor understate it. He must reproduce it exactly, and accomplish this by what is today called "empathy" – that is, his actually becoming possessed by the feeling or thing he imitates. He avoids copying mere surface manifestations, and refrains from any projection of his own personality. He dissolves his self in the object or sentiment he is called upon to create. He does this best by first going through a phase of non-imitation: he purges himself of the wish to copy the thing, and replaces that impulse by re-creating himself as the thing itself. "In the highest stage of imitation the artist becomes unconscious of his art; the imitator is united with the imitated." At this point the essence of the object or emotion is seen through the "transparent soul of the artist". That there is much of Zen Buddhism in this attitude or approach is obvious to anyone familiar with the "out-of-self" teaching of that faith.

To give specific examples: the actor who wishes to portray a madman will not simply emulate the frenzied behaviour of a man deprived of his senses; he will, instead, learn and submit to whatever it is that obsesses and torments such a man. "The true intent of a thing is the center of its existence: it is what makes an insane person insane, a forceful thing forceful, an elegant thing elegant." (These quotations are from Makoto Ueda's essay on Nōh.)

The second principle pervading Nōh is *yūgen*, the kind of beauty that arises when an imitative act is quite perfect. (This concept is not unlike that of the *rasa* sought for in Sanskrit drama.) It is the perception that even what is outwardly ugly can be seen as beautiful, if it has been truthfully rendered. Thus the beauty of a wrinkled, aged man can be shown, and Seami's phrase for this accomplishment is "blossoms on a crag". The thought here is akin to Keats's claim that truth and beauty are one and the same.

Seami declares that in earlier times, especially the tenth and eleventh centuries, the inner truth and beauty of the world were much more apparent in Japanese art. This is most evident in works of that period, such as Lady Muraski's novel *Tale of Genji*, a masterpiece in which the patrician heroines are *yūgen* personified; these fragile ladies are sometimes celebrated in Nōh dramas. Seami's vision of ideal beauty is summed up in the image: "a white bird with a flower in its beak".

Waley says that the difficult term "*yūgen*" is also derived from Zen literature. "It means 'what lies beneath the surface'; the subtle, as opposed to the obvious; the hint, as opposed to the statement. It is applied to the natural grace of a boy's movements, to the gentle restraint of a nobleman's speech and bearing. 'When notes fall sweetly and flutter delicately to the ear,' that is the *yūgen* of music. . . . 'To watch the sun sink behind a flower-clad hill, to wander on and on in a huge forest with no thought of return, to stand upon the shore and gaze after a boat that goes hid by far-off islands, to ponder on the journey of wild geese seen and lost among the clouds' – such are the gates to *yūgen*." This would seem to describe a momentary transcendence. Still, to Western minds, the exact definition of the word is elusive, as is even now the sure meaning of Aristotle's puzzling *katharsis* as a positive requirement of great tragedy.

Implicit in *yūgen*, Seami indicates, is a note of sadness, for all that is true and beautiful is also ephemeral: everything, human and natural, withers and dies. Man longs for permanence but must face the inevitability of change. The suffering that is caused by decline and death, which is experienced by all men, also contributes to the flavour of *yūgen* and is evoked by resignation to the remorseless power that controls man and his fate. In *yūgen* there is always an overtone of melancholy, for the elegance and beauty it celebrates will perish.

The third principle in Nōh is a search for sublimity to be attained through a play's proper enactment, after which for the spectator it is in his memory like "an old cedar tree standing among annual plants". Such a work is not transient, all too soon passing and forgotten, but instead is possessed of qualities that are stately, austere, everlasting. He describes three other kinds of sublimity. The first is likened to "the snow heaped in a silver bowl . . . it is pure, chill and white. A silver bowl, a wonder of art, contains snow, a wonder of nature: the container and the contained are united in the purity of whiteness." (Once more the mystical aspect of Nōh is intrinsic in this choice of metaphor. An even higher, more metaphysical sort of sublimity is illustrated by the poetic image used in the Buddhist query: "The snow has covered thousands of mountains all in white. Why is it that one solitary peak remains unwhitened?" Here is a strong hint of the supernatural: "The black peak towering among snow-covered mountains, a seemingly discordant note which yet resolves into harmony." Seami ventures into the realm of the cosmic mystery.

Yet another kind of sublimity is captured in a line from a Chinese monk also cited by Seami: "In Korea the sun shines at midnight." This seems at first glance a manifest impossibility, yet it implies "an imaginative landscape which is beyond verbal description as it lies in the realm of the absolute". In Zen the term "the absolute" refers to a sphere beyond the limitations of time and space, where all is possible, where there is "neither good nor evil, right nor wrong, one nor all". But what appears to be illogical at first impression, in the plain world of common sense, is actually possible: for Korea is to the east of China; when darkness hangs over the Celestial Kingdom, the sun is yet bright in the Korean sky. With full knowledge and insight, many things can happen that mere half-knowledge would deem impossible. "Far beyond everyday life, far beneath the conscious level of the mind, there is another order of reality of which tangible reality is but a shadow. A great work of art can introduce us into this other world: through it, even though but momentarily, we may touch on the absolute."

These are the exalted aims of Nōh as the thoughtful and ambitious Seami propounds them. For him, the dramatist is a visionary, a seer, who should reveal the "essence of things . . . so deeply hidden that man's faculties barely reach it; its beauty is too beautiful for ordinary human senses to feel or perceive". The author and actor must transmit their vision of the truth and sublimity of the world. They must preach submission to the higher power – vast, enigmatic – that inscrutably controls man's fate, and they must teach troubled mankind how to attain finally to grace and lasting serenity.

Inherent in Nōh, too, as conceived by Seami, is a belief in man's original sin. All human beings are tainted with guilt: it is a universal condition. "To live is to sin." Most Nōh plays feature ghosts, wandering on earth in a sort of purgatory. A typical drama tells of a priest or pilgrim, setting forth on a journey, who encounters a stranger – man or woman – who seems to be a living person, but who is in fact a restless, haunted spirit still clinging to the memory and place of a former existence, and still not purged of the sinfulness that inhabited him or her in a now past life. With the priest acting as catalyst or intermediary, the ghost is finally freed of the clinging mortal taint and ends a stay in Purgatory. Thus, in Seami's *The Woman Within the Cypress Fence*, a once-sought-after but long-dead court dancer is met by a pilgrim who sees her in the guise of an old woman drawing water from the White River. Later, she reveals herself as the departed soul of a court beauty, in former days beloved of the great Lord Okinori, but now sentenced as a penance to toil endlessly and humiliatingly in the shape of a wrinkled hag.

> All was a night's dream – it is no more.
> That face, rouged, of a famed dancer,
> That face, lovely, under the shining hair,
> That flower has withered, frost has fallen
> On the eyebrows that were two crescent moons.
> Water mirrors my face, old, ugly, infirm;
> The hair, once shining, is dirty weeds in mud . . .
> All shows my change, a sad change.

She laments her present hard plight:

> The moon, floating on the water, moves upwards
> On my sleeve as I lift up the bucket.
> Under the stars of dawn I draw water

From the river in the north;

Late at night I burn the firewood

Of the forest in the south.

Ice, formed of water, is colder than water;

Indigo, derived from blue, is darker than blue.

The taint of sin in my lifetime

Still remains on me and torments me.

My grief grows deeper and deeper . . .

The water in her bucket boils, heated by the fires of Hell, and scalds her. The priest counsels her:

Sorry am I to see you suffering.

Your soul, still attached to this world,

Causes you to haunt here, to draw water,

As the law of retribution orders.

Quickly, quickly, forget your passions.

He prays for her. The woman, grateful, is finally able to tell him:

. . . you have led me

By your prayers toward the merciful Heaven.

Here is my bucket, yet fire is no more.

The priest:

Draw the water, the water of *karma*,

Leave your passions and enter Nirvana.

At the close, after a graceful court dance, reminiscent of her exquisite skill in days past, the ghostly lady recites:

Life is like a foam floating on water . . .

I have come here to learn it, priest.

Cranes whooping above, I walk, and walk,

Carrying water, with weeds floating on.

Please wash out my sins, priest,

Please wash out my sins, priest.

[Translation: Makoto Ueda]

As remarked before, a traditional programme of Nōh consists of a cycle of five (or six) short works: a "god play", a "man play", a "woman play", a "frenzy play", and fifth a "demon play". The first of these, the "god play" – or "*waki*-Nōh" – is invocatory and intended to prepare the spectator for his participation in a mystical experience. It derives from the "god plays" long an established facet of Japanese dance and drama. Essentially it presents the "world of innocence before man's fall". On a second day another opening Nōh play must be selected, one different in some way. Any first piece should have an easy-to-grasp story, be spare of details, yet be dignified. "Both the chanting and dancing should be simple and direct in style. Above all, it should contain 'words of good wish'. It does not matter if a 'first Nōh' is slightly defective in other ways, so long as it contains 'happy wishes'. For they form the proper introduction." But the two pieces that follow must be really good.

The "man play" – "Shūra" or "battle-piece" – displays the warrior as sinful; accordingly, it shows him after his "fall". Seami particularly excels in such plays, for his spirit is heroic. He borrows much of his material for them from the dynastic wars of the eleventh century, when the Taira and Minamoto factions were feuding. But always evident is a Buddhist attitude of deploring bloodshed. In *Atsumori*, the victor of a duel, Kumagi, has become a priest and visits the tomb of his slain adversary. The ghost of the dead man, Atsumori, rises, appearing first as a peasant's reaper.

PRIEST: How strange it is! The other reapers have all gone home, but you alone stay loitering here.
   How is that?
REAPER: How is it, you ask? I am seeking for a prayer in the voice of the evening waves. Perhaps
   you will pray the Ten Prayers for me?
PRIEST: I can easily pray the Ten Prayers for you, if you will tell me who you are.

The reaper does not fully reveal his identity. The prayer is recited, and he disappears; then, after an interlude, he reappears as the young Atsumori. The priest assumes it is a dream. "Why need it be a dream? It is to clear the *karma* of my waking life that I am come here in visible form before you," the apparition explains. The subsequent exchange between them leads to a reconciliation between the living man and the spirit of the dead man, but first they verbally re-enact the fatal battle in sharp detail. Left behind by his clan's fleeing ships, Atsumori, on his horse, had plunged into the surf, only to be pursued into the waves and overwhelmed by the savage Kumagi.

> So Atsumori fell and was slain, but now the Wheel of Fate
>> Has turned and brought him back.
>
> [*The Ghost rises from the ground and advances towards the Priest with uplifted sword.*]
> CHORUS: "There is my enemy," he cries, and would strike,
>> But the other is grown gentle
>>
>> And calling on Buddha's name
>>
>> Has obtained salvation for his foe;
>>
>> So that they shall be re-born together
>>
>> On one lotus-seat.
>>
>> "No, Rensei is not my enemy.
>>
>> Pray for me again, oh pray for me again."
>
> [Translation: Arthur Waley]

At one point in his graphic description of their combat Atsumori resorts to a dance. The Nōh play ends in Kumagi's repentance and an unworldly peace between the two erstwhile foes, one still alive, one dead but forgiving.

The Battle at Yashima, another "man play", brings on an old fisherman who is actually the ghost of Yoshitune, the famed Genji general, now returned to the very place where the Genji and Heiki forces had fought at great cost many years before. He is beheld by a pilgrim priest. The spirit of Yoshitune conjures up in words the fierce encounter, how he himself, clad in white and purple armour over a red silk garment, entered the fray, rising in his stirrups, shouting his name and high rank. The engagement ended after dire losses on both sides, the competing forces withdrawing. Both sides felt pity for the slain, and silence fell:

> Blossoms, once fallen, never come back to the branches;
> A looking-glass, once broken, mirrors a face no longer.
> Yet a man's soul may haunt this world after he dies;
> For human passion, if too fierce to live this life.

Out of itself creates a Hell, where the soul

Goes through torments, wraths and struggles.

Like the waves reaching the shore, the sin of this world

Reaches into the world beyond.

[Translation: Makoto Ueda]

In words, too, he brings back an incident in the famous battle. He dropped his bow into the water, at the sea's edge, and it was washed away, and despite a rain of arrows that surrounded him, he swam on horseback after his weapon and retrieved it. All admired his courage, his regard for honour. His sin is that he failed to recognize that there are other values than valour and worldly glory.

A powerful "man play" is Seami's *Kagekiyo*, which relates the downfall at the hands of his foes of a renowned and passionate Taira warrior of that name, exiled in a far land and doomed to end his days as a blind mendicant. Found by his daughter, Hitamaru, after a difficult search for him, he recalls for her – with the help of the chorus – some of his mighty feats, the deeds that created his legend:

CHORUS: Kagekiyo cried, "You are haughty." His armor caught every turn of the sun. He drove
　them four ways before him.

KAGEKIYO [*excited and crying out*]: Samoshiya! Run, cowards!

CHORUS: He thought, how easy this is, killing. He rushed with his spear-haft gripped under his
　arm. He cried out, "I am Kagekiyo of the Heike." He rushed on to take them. He pierced
　through the helmet vizard of Miyonoya. Miyonoya fled twice, and again; and Kagekiyo cried:
　"You shall not escape me!" He leaped and wrenched off his helmet. "Eya!" The vizard broke
　and remained in his hand and Miyonoya still fled afar, and he looked back crying in terror,
　"How terrible, how heavy your arm!" And Kagekiyo called at him, "How tough the shaft of
　your neck is!" And they both laughed out over the battle and went off each his own way.

[Translation: Ezra Pound]

In this Nōh play the hero is not a wandering spirit, but a flesh-and-blood figure. At the end the chorus discloses that, with Buddhist stoicism, he parts from his daughter again, bidding her goodbye, describing her – poignantly – as for him "a lamp in the darkness" of his blindness. This Japanese Lear is ready to accept old age and death.

The third category in a Nōh cycle is that of the "woman play", (or Kagura, "wig-piece"). It purveys calm following the male storm, the warrior's boasts and tearful regrets. Such is *The Woman Within the Cypress Fence* discussed above. In a work of this sort, usually, an elegant lady of the court (formerly, perhaps, a bewitching dancer) is still pursued by memories of an earlier misdeed, perhaps the hidden sin of pride. Even though outwardly faultless, yet in consequence of her simple humanity she is innately guilty. She roams the world posthumously, ceaselessly offering symbolic penitential acts, as does the bucket-lifting crone in Seami's drama. A "woman play" tends to be more lyrical than a "man play", which is likely to be fierce in tone. (The water drawn by the old woman in Seami's piece has a special connotation. An Oriental commentator expatiates on this: "Water, a nature symbol signifying the source of life, is also a Buddhist symbol of *karma*, and her salvation is typically Buddhist – she gains mental quietude through the contemplation of man's mortality. The play's mood approaches the sublime.")

A "frenzy play" belongs to the fourth category of Nōh on a traditional programme. It is sometimes replaced by a "revenge play". Kwanami's *Jinnen the Preacher* does not fit into this group as easily as does *The Woman Within the Cypress Fence* into the genre of the "woman play". But usually the hero is human; no god, ghost or demon has a role. The "frenzy play" demonstrates that Hell exists here as well as in the hereafter; people are made to suffer during their lifetime as well as after their transformation by death. A favourite "frenzy" theme is that of a mother driven mad by the abduction of a child. She searches frantically for the lost one and by miraculous chance after many vicissitudes recovers her stolen infant. "We are shown that miracles are possible . . . also that a soul can be redeemed just as a lost child can be restored – but only if one dedicates oneself to that single purpose with such ardour that people think it madness".

A "demon play", the usual concluding work, depicts man in mortal combat with an evil spirit. "In a 'frenzy play' man conquers Hell on earth; in a 'demon play' he is victorious over the inhabitants of the underworld." Such a hero may be a priest attaining wisdom like Jinnen, but in a work by an anonymous author, *The Mirror of Pine Forest*, a mere country girl, simple of mind, succeeds in warding off a threatening spirit. Left an orphan, the girl mourns her mother. Her father has quickly remarried, and the child lives alone in a house adjacent to his new dwelling. The mother has left her daughter a mirror, a keepsake, telling her to look into it whenever she feels lonely. Gazing into it, she beholds an image which she has never seen before; to a country girl, naïve, the glass is quite unfamiliar; having no idea of her own appearance, she believes the reflection to be her mother's ghost. The father has been told that his daughter is calling down curses on her stepmother. When he arrives to remonstrate with her, he learns of her belief that her dead mother lives on in the mirror. He disabuses her of the fanciful idea. Left alone, the girl falls asleep and dreams – now the mother's ghost becomes visible to the audience. A demon comes to claim this lingering ghost, but the faithful, good-hearted girl's prayers redeem the dead woman's troubled spirit. The lesson of the play? Perhaps it supports the Buddhist view that all life is "illusion", as insubstantial as a mirror-image.

As has been said, sometimes a sixth play – another Shūgen or "congratulatory piece" – is added to the cycle, to beseech Heavenly blessing on the reigning house and the nobility, as well as on the actors and the stage. Since Nōh was never a popular theatre, but aimed only at the élite, this would be a bid for a benediction on the majority of the audience, perhaps even the whole of it. The Emperor and his entourage, together with members of the very upper class, professed to adore Nōh, while disdaining more common kinds of entertainment.

Seami stipulates, as has been noted, that the plays comprising a cycle should vary from performance to performance. The colour and tone of a programme is altered considerably by the choice of works from each of the five genres that make up a single presentation: the "cycle" may be lighter or darker, depending on whether the "woman play" is a bit more lyrical or delicate than the average, or whether the "frenzy play" depicts a grotesquely insane person instead of a bereaved mother gone momentarily berserk, perhaps. The director bears much of the responsibility for the arrangement; he must assemble each new offering. He can select the plays from about 250 scripts that are still enacted. There is a library containing about eight collections, with 300 texts that probably date from before the seventeenth century; those written after the sixteenth century are generally deemed to be of lesser merit. It is believed that over 2,000 scripts were composed for Nōh in its golden heyday.

The Nōh, though it began as a court and temple entertainment, developed its own stage and roofed theatre. To the stage was later added a second, lower roof, shaped like a pagoda, borne on four pillars. The slightly sloping, eighteen-foot platform of polished cypress wood on which the action occurs is mostly bare, with an invariable setting, a back wall on which is painted a single pine tree, symbol of immortality.

The music accompanying each play begins with a slow, regular tempo, but accelerates to a climax that is rapid and uneven. The orchestra consists of a man with a big drum, two hand-drummers and a flute player who emits a piercing sound at the drama's opening and at fixed intervals and to mark the climax and the ending. Of the musicians, Seami says: "They must not go their own way. Their business is to understand the actors' intentions and follow the rhythms of the singing and dancing." As a consequence, Nōh music has no independent existence. The drum-taps may be hypnotic, affecting the spectators' nervous response. By an abrupt acceleration, they can raise a needed dramatic tension. At other moments, soft flute music can relax and quiet an audience, creating the proper mood. At the back of the stage is a recess, surrounded by a railing, and occupied by the four musicians.

The sides of the stage are open. A gallery, closed off by a curtain, leads to the green room and provides an entrance for the actor; the curtain is lifted to let him make his appearance. Behind him, in two rows, squats the chorus. The stage projects into the auditorium and is viewed on three sides by ranks of spectators.

The projection or runway (*hashigakari*) is flanked by a gravel path and shrubbery, which adds to the prevalence of the colour green – the foliage and narrow walkway also separate the actors from the close-by audience. Besides having the painted back wall, the stage is further graced by three potted pine trees, betokening the endurance of "Heaven, earth and humanity". This accounts for the Nōh theatre being known as the "Pine-tree stage". (In a way this is appropriate, since many of the plays indicate a shadowed forest or lonely, wind-swept moor as the scene, though this may be an unplanned effect.) To reach the stage, after the actor enters at right past the curtain, he must cross a "bridge" or "trestle", and at left is a "hurry door", an exit for characters who have been slain or have expired from grief, contrition or simple natural causes. Originally the stage was round; then it became square. At different periods, over the centuries, minor physical details of the theatre's architecture have changed.

In Seami's day performances of Nōh began at dawn; but he also speaks of "night-time Nōh" put on by torchlight, and recommends that the playing then be "positive" – probably more vigorous – to counter the "negative" of darkness. Depending on the perceptible mood of the audience, he says, the actors must be ready to modulate and adapt their interpretations. He adds: "When the play is written by another person, the matter is out of the hands of the actor, however talented he may be; but if he writes the play himself, both the words and action are determined by him, so that if he has knowledge and talent sufficient for the writing of the text, the performance should be easy."

He favours a script that requires no more than four or five players. "In old times, even if more actors were at their disposal, in a play which only needed one or two they did not use more than one or two. Nowadays, excusing themselves on the plea that there are some actors 'over', they set in rows a number of persons in everyday costume of *eboshi* and *suo* (hat and cloak) and let them sing in unison (*dō-on utau*). This is contrary to the principles of our art. It is an indiscriminate proceeding, and has only been seen in recent years." Waley explains that this is a reference to the chorus which was introduced late in Seami's career and was a device of which he disapproved, though he came round to making use of it. In some Nōh plays as many as nine actors are cast, though that does not happen frequently.

As if to compensate for the simplicity of the stage-setting, the costumes in Nōh plays are usually sumptuous, sometimes with many jewels and glittering headdresses. Seami writes at length on just how various characters should be dressed, which ones more simply, which more elaborately. The leading character is masked – none of the others are – and he may change masks several times during a performance. The lesser figures paint their faces in brilliant hues with striking designs. Female characters wear natural-seeming make-up, a trifle heightened and formalized; these roles are taken by men. The masks are wooden; there are fifteen standard kinds and hundreds of minor variations; all are expressive. Many are ancient but well preserved and still used.

The stage is divided into two parts, signifying past and present. The acting and dancing have static moments, dramatic poses, as is to be expected in most Oriental miming. Gestures are symbolic, often containing arcane nuances. The leading actor's posture is important, and his body movements, too, of major consequence, since his face is hidden by a mask. The mask denies him any individuality; an impersonal figure, he becomes broadly representative of mankind. His gestures, dictated by tradition, are unreal, unlike ordinary behaviour. A lift of the mask indicates a smile, a downward glance that tears are falling; and raising a hand also suggests that the character is weeping. A kimono lying on the boards is meant to be a person who is seriously ill.

The actor pounds the stage-boards with his feet; the rhythm of his stamping may betray his emotional state. Beneath the platform is a hollow space that, like an echo chamber, lends resonance to the stamping. Further reverberation comes from earthen jars set there at a forty-five degree slant; or else jars are suspended on strings to provide more amplification.

A few conventional properties, stylized or skeletonized, are allowed, a framework or outline of the thing rather than the solid object itself.

As each performer appears, in his voluminous, ornate, stiff brocaded robe, he is greeted by a special musical theme – his *motif* – and he immediately launches a treble chant and appropriate dance. To override the flute, the voice is shrill, or essays very low tones. The conclusion of each recitation is marked by a tap of the actor's foot. After this, he temporarily withdraws.

Sleeve-play is prominent. The fan, much utilized, may double as a pen, a letter-cutter, a dagger or even – when spread open – a tray.

Actors are long trained, from age seven, and most often inherit their membership in a Nōh troupe. Since nobles often participated in performances, professional actors were highly respected, enjoying esteem similar to that directed to Kwanami and his son Seami. Seami sets forth rules for instructing apprentices. Until the age of twelve they should devote themselves only to dancing and recitation, and be given a free hand, not praised or blamed. If they engage in mimicry, it should be merely for their own amusement; they should receive no advice or criticism as to its accuracy. Following twelve they should gradually be taught the art of impersonation. " 'There is a natural grace in the boy's form that will be communicated to all his gestures. His faults will be disguised by this charm and his merits enhanced beyond their real value.' . . . But this 'flower' is not the real 'flower'; it is only the 'flower' of youth." (Taken from Waley)

In later teen years, after seventeen or eighteen, the charm is gone, and the youth is apt to be ungainly. "He must not be discouraged if people point at him and laugh, but must sit at home and practise such tunes as his changing voice can compass. For if he gives up now, he gives up forever." (The Nōh actor's voice should be either treble or deep bass, so the changes to which Seami refers would differ from those experienced by an average Western youth.)

Full development of the aspirant's talents will be reached at age twenty-four or twenty-five, but now there is the risk of his being over-praised by friends and doting but mistaken admirers. They will tell him that he is a master – and that will be doing him an ill service. "Such temporary success is not the 'true flower'. Thirty-five is the actor's prime." By then, if the whole empire does not applaud him, he is destined never to attain perfection, and after forty his art will inevitably decline.

On the other hand, the true master will continue to flourish even at forty-five, thereby proving his profound superiority. At that age, however, he must deny himself certain roles, especially those for which he no longer dons a mask. "For an old man is intolerable in a maskless part, however handsome he may once have been." Past fifty he must reconcile himself to taking on "passive" characters. "An exception was the late Kwanami, who at fifty-two still gave magnificent performances and won unanimous applause, though by then he appeared only in easy roles, giving them a subdued interpretation. Despite his assigning the leads to his disciples, his 'flower' was all the more evident." (In Seami's day, to have reached fifty was to be far advanced in years.)

As he tells in his notes, young and preparing for his career, Seami himself closely watched and studied the great actors of his day, their techniques and line readings, the shading of their characterizations. Among such outstanding players were Ichu and Ziami, famous for roles in Dengaku; Keno, from the Omi-sarugaku school; Kotaro, pre-eminent in Kompar; and Otsuro, an accomplished Kuse-mai dancer. He borrowed touches and effects from each of them while forming and sharpening his own style.

The actor in a Nōh play is called the *shite* or "doer"; his companion, if he has one, the *"tomo"*. The secondary lead, who looks on and explains much of the action, is the *"waki"*. Very likely he participates as the priest or pilgrim. The minor figures, or subordinates, are the *"tsure"*. Child players – boys – are *"ko-gata"*. All have specified positions on stage. One of the four pillars is where the *shite* takes his stand when not reciting or dancing; a pillar diagonally opposite is where the *waki* stations himself when idle and silent, as he is for long spans of time; the most essential musician, the flute-player, posts himself at the third pillar, and the fourth support – the "mark pillar" – serves as a fixed point to guide the heavily encumbered *shite* to the exactly prescribed spot as he moves about the wooden platform. The chorus, seated behind them, fills in when the *shite* is dancing and therefore cannot speak and if the *waki* has not taken over.

Seami decries over-acting. Yet he rejects inclination to naturalistic portrayals. For a characterization to be memorable it should hint at an element of the "unlike", the strange. "For if imitation be pressed too far it impinges on reality and ceases to give an impression of likeness." He is seeking to avoid embodying stock characters. A slight departure from the average or familiar is best. "Youthful movements made by an old person are, indeed, delightful; they are like flowers blossoming on an old tree. . . . If, because the actor has noticed that old men walk with bent knees and back and have shrunken frames, he simply imitates these characteristics, he may achieve an appearance of decrepitude, but it will be at the expense of the 'flower'. And if the 'flower' be lacking, there will be no beauty in his impersonation."

He lays down many other precepts. "The appearance of old age will often be best given by making all movements a little late, so that they come just after the musical beat." And:

Women should be impersonated by a young actor. . . . It is very difficult to play the part of a Princess or lady-in-waiting, for little opportunity presents itself of studying their august behaviour and appearance. Great pains must be taken to see that robes and cloaks are worn in the correct way. These things do not depend on the actor's fancy but must be carefully ascertained.

The appearance of ordinary ladies is easy to imitate. . . . In acting the part of a dancing girl, madwoman or the like, whether he carry the fan or some fancy thing (a flowering branch, for instance), the actor must carry it loosely; his skirts must trail so as to hide his feet; his knees and back must not be bent, his body must be poised gracefully. As regards the way he holds himself – if he bends back, it looks bad when he faces the audience; if he stoops, it looks bad from behind. But he will not look like a woman if he holds his head too stiffly. His sleeves should be as long as possible, so that he never shows his fingers.

He offers further prescriptions for playing ghosts and children: "Since no one has ever seen a real ghost from the Nether Regions, the actor may use his fancy, aiming only at the beautiful. . . . If ghosts are terrifying, they cease to be beautiful. For the terrifying and the beautiful are as far apart as black and white. . . . The outward form is that of a ghost; but within is the heart of a man." Scenes in which lost children are found should avoid prolonged clutching and weeping, as audiences do not like to be harrowed. Also: "In representing anger the actor should yet retain some gentleness in his mood, else he will portray not anger but violence." Doubtless he was a remarkable director.

As head of a semi-official troupe, Seami refined and elevated scripts given to him by his patrons. Some of these sources were quite inferior. He found himself coping with three sorts of texts.

A play based on a story in itself beautiful, the theme subtly handled and embellished with delightful passages; such a piece, properly acted, cannot fail.

A play not so well written, but with a tolerably good plot. If well acted, it might be a success.

A bad play of which one can yet make something by taking advantage of its very defects and "breaking one's bones" in the acting of it.

Further: "There are three ways to success . . . by the eyes, by the ears, by the heart. A play appealing successfully to the eye is one to which from the beginning the audience succumbs. The style of the dancing and chanting is agreeable; the audience, high and low, bursts into applause; the theatre wears an air of gaiety. Not only connoisseurs, but even people without knowledge of Nōh, are saying to themselves with one accord, 'How enjoyable!' " Such is a work that attracts because it is comparatively light and spectacular. But it must have moments of relaxed tension lest the spectators become fatigued from overly sustained excitement.

The second type of play thrives due to the high quality of its musical score, hardly owing to its intellectual content or the skill of the actors. Finally, the third kind is one that engages the mind. Here he speaks in a language compounded of Taoism and Zen, his ideas steeped in mysticism, at times a bit unfathomable. As might be expected, it is plays in this category, emotional and cerebral, that most commend themselves to him.

He observes: "People's tastes differ; to suit the dispositions of 'ten thousand' men is a task of unrivalled difficulty. Yet one's model should be the actor who is successful wherever he appears throughout the whole Empire." Consequently actors must choose scripts that match the status of the audience. They must also keep abreast of the shifting tastes of the day. This advice, to cater to the possibly unsophisticated, is offensive to Waley (whose translations from the *Works* I have used throughout). Here he faults Seami for opportunism. "He was not a profound or systematic thinker. More of a courtier than a philosopher, he was apt in moments of cynicism to regard the applause of his audience as the sole end of his art, and even to be indifferent whence that applause came"; though Seami does grant that the approval of men "of taste and experience" was more desirable than that of the crowd.

Others view Seami's statement as merely that of a pragmatic showman, working in the most costly branch of the arts and responsible for the fiscal health and welfare of his troupe. Aeschylus, Sophocles and Euripides leavened their tragic offerings by adding to their programmes the crude and pornographic satyr plays, and Shakespeare stoops to please the groundlings with broad, vulgar buffoonery – in his most magical, blithe scripts. Such is the nature of theatre, where popularity is necessary. The box-office must be kept busy. Waley concedes: "He [Seami] writes, not as an aesthetician, but as a practical man, an actor-manager. Yet he constantly amazes by his sensitivity in approaching his art, his capacity for weighing the value of each and every detail." Once again, Waley questions how much of the content in the 300-page *Works* is Seami's thinking and to what extent he was "the suave and gifted heir, pious receptacle and transmitter of his father's teachings".

The scripts are partly in prose, partly in verse – Seami himself composed the musical scores. When it comes to judging the literary merit of the plays, however, Waley unexpectedly begs off, though his English versions of them are highly praised. He pleads that the verse is in a foreign language, a difficult and archaic speech that even today's Japanese find not easy to grasp. (One is reminded of Robert Frost's definition of poetry as "what is lost in translation".) Yet in renditions by Waley and Ueda, Seami shows a dexterity akin to that of Western metaphysical poets such as Webster and Donne in repeating certain phrases and images, playing with them, varying them, giving them new significances. He is seen doing this in *The Woman Within the Cypress Fence*, where he accomplishes this much, as does the unknown author of *The Mirror of Pine Forest*. Both of them carry this off with wit and skill. Pound calls such phrases and images "pivot words"; they close off one thought and lead to a new train of ideas.

A half-dozen years before Waley brought out his collection of Nōh plays (1922), Ernest F. Fenollosa and Ezra Pound published *"Nōh" or Accomplishment* (1916). Fenollosa, long resident in Japan and interested in its classical and popular literature, had begun collecting and translating a sheaf of the Nōh plays but died before finishing his study of them. His widow turned over the scripts to Pound, who completed Englishing them; he also made them available to W. B. Yeats, the Irish Symbolist poet, who was deeply influenced by their form and content, which he sought to emulate in a number of short dramas of his own. All four of these writers were struck by the resemblance, already commented on, between Nōh and Greek tragedy. As Waley points out, they were staged in similar fashion, with scant scenery and accoutrements, in theatres – in Japan, too, sometimes outdoors – with like architectural features, the differences minimal. The speech is poetic. Both had masked actors – though, for the Japanese, only the leading player wears one – and employed a chorus for exposition and moral preachment, its role in the Nōh more subordinate, however. In essence, both are operas, highly stylized, with music and dancing prominent aspects. More importantly, Nōh and Greek tragedy arise from sacred rites, guided by the priesthood and voicing religious (or anti-religious) convictions.

Yet they are also profoundly unlike. The Nōh hero accepts his dark fate without defiance, never voicing a protest, submissive as the Greek protagonist is not. He wishes only to attain serenity, as befits a devotee of Zen. Man lacks free will; his fate is utterly determined, hence resistance is futile. The stance here is wholly defeatist. Always man's sinfulness is stressed, and his insignificance. From recognition of his innate guilt and helplessness arises the sought-for *yūgen*, the ultimate truth of earthly matters.

Every detail of a Nōh performance is intended to lend the play an out-of-this-world connotation: the sculptural masks, the long wigs, the rich and outsized costumes, the eerie music, the shrill or guttural speech, the portentous dance. Much is conveyed solely by the player's physical movement. By accepting his fate, the hero may at last reach the sublime. The climactic dance of each playlet in a cycle confers a lively or even ecstatic emotional release: the hero or heroine, having acknowledged his or her fault, now confesses and humbly repents. The dance is a purge, a *katharsis*, for both the figures in the drama and the rapt spectator.

It has been suggested that there are echoes in Nōh, these troubling ghost plays, of ancestor worship and ritual tomb-observances, as there are in the earliest Greek stage-works. Fenollosa saw correspondences, too, between Nōh and Shakespearian drama, which also grew in part from medieval miracle plays. (If Nōh began about the time of Chaucer, it reached its peak in the Muromachi era, contemporary with the writing and first production of *Hamlet*.)

Seami's last years were sometimes troubled. With Nōh suddenly esteemed in high circles, there were soon rival companies and scripts from other authors. In this competitive environment Seami was anxious to keep his "trade secrets" confined to his troupe. He put great stress on this. His purpose was to pass them on to his son Motomasa, but suddenly in 1433 Motomasa died. Two years later Seami, having displeased the new Shōgun, was exiled to the island of Sado; the reason for this is not known. One hypothesis is that because the actor was ageing the Shōgun wished him to hand over his secret manual of instructions to Onami, his nephew, who was already heading the Kwanze troupe and gaining favour, but that Seami resisted having Onami formally named as his successor and would not give his notes to him.

During his banishment to Sado, Seami occupied himself with writing *The Book of the Golden Island* in which he extols the natural beauty of his surroundings there, along with musings on various subjects. By some accounts his punishment was lifted and he returned to the court, but this is not certain. He was in his eighties when death came, and before then he was able to transmit his artistic legacy to his son-in-law Zenchiku, with whom he spent his final days.

His notes and treatises dropped from sight for over a century, but in 1600 a book, the *Kwadensho*, was issued that contained eight chapters supposedly by him, though scholars questioned their authenticity. As late as 1908 another discovery was made, this time of a somewhat different version of the *Kwadensho* and with fifteen additional chapters, gathered as the *Hanakagami* and the *Kykui*; they are accepted as Seami's beyond doubt and comprise what Waley refers to as the *Works* and are regarded as the ultimate statement on Nōh.

Following Seami's retirement and death, his son-in-law Zenchiku flourished in his stead and is remembered as the author of twenty-two Nōh scripts. Though many other writers and actors rushed in with similar plays, the basic form of Nōh was kept intact, the demanding technique set, the sober and reverential tradition lastingly preserved, to be mostly unchanged after 500 years, still a living genre. Of its structure, Zenchiku is quoted as saying: "Everything redundant has been pruned, the beauty of the essential is wholly and fully cleansed. It is the inexpressible beauty of doing nothing. . . . It is like the music of gentle rain in the few remaining branches of the famous old cherry trees of Yoshimo, Chara, and Oshio: overgrown with moss, with a few blossoms here and there." Again, an echo of Zen is audible.

Some other fifteenth and sixteenth-century contributors to Nōh are Enami no Sayemon (*c.* 1400), author of *Ukai* (*The Cormorant-Fisher*), later revised by Seami, whose self-touted adaptation is lost; Komparu Zembō Motoyasu (1453–1532), especially admired for *Hatsuyuki* (*Early Snow*), a brief, lyric piece about the escape of a caged bird, as well as *Ikuta*, pertaining to the long, costly feud between the Taira and the Minamoto; Hiyoshi Sa-ami Yasukiyo (early fifteenth century?), whose *Benki on the Bridge* is about the fabled hero Yoshitsune; and Mikyamasu (sixteenth century), credited with *Eboshi-ori*, concerning incidents in Yoshitsune's boyhood. All these works are available in English.

Acquaintance with Nōh had an effect in *fin de siècle* Ireland and England not only on the poetic short plays of W. B. Yeats but also on the dramatic work of Thomas Sturge Moore. Laden with symbols, Nōh fitted the spirit of the Aesthetic Movement. Many decades later the composer Benjamin Britten derived the libretto of his chamber opera *Curlew River* (1964) from the "woman's play" *Sumida-gawa*, in which the pathetic ghost of a mother, blaming herself, laments as she searches vainly for her lost child. Adhering to tradition, Britten has the mother's role sung by a man, as would be done on a Japanese stage. The Britten offering, well received in England, had its American début at the Caramoor Music Festival, after which it had many hearings elsewhere. It has also been performed in Japan.

Discovering Waley's handling of Zenchiku's *Taniko*, the German playwright Bertolt Brecht turned it into a school opera, *He Who Says Yes* (1929–30), with music by Kurt Weil. It tells of a self-sacrificing boy, crippled, exhausted, who asks to be hurled into an icy crevasse to perish rather than endanger his companions by delaying them, while crossing a storm-whipped glacier. A more important Brecht play, *The Measures Taken*, is also modelled on Nōh.

Considerably after the translations by Pound and Waley appeared, Donald Keene – with assistance from Royall Tyler – published *Twenty Plays of the Nōh Theatre* (1971), following his earlier detailed account of its exotic stagecraft, *Nōh: The Classical Theatre of Japan* (1967).

A French study of mid-twentieth-century productions of the dramas is *Le Nōh* by Nöel Péri, issued in Tokyo (1944). Among those responding with interest to this *outré* static form was the poet–diplomat Paul Claudel, a foremost literary figure of his day, in whose stage-scripts, though he was a devout Catholic – *The Tidings Brought to Mary* – traces of Nōh are discernible.

A special company of Nōh players appeared at an International Drama Festival in Italy where it was greeted most enthusiastically (1954). After a lapse of a dozen years a Nōh troupe visited London (1967) and next introduced its unique art to NewYork on three evenings at Carnegie Hall. On the programme in both cities was *Aoi no ue* (*The Lady Aoi*), based on a chapter in Lady Muraski's *Tale of Genji*, about the spirit of a jealous woman that attacks Lady Aoi, the invalid wife of Genji. A holy man exorcizes the envious spirit.

With the seventeenth century came a worrisome decline in the general appeal of Nōh, and its growing restriction to ever narrower aristocratic audiences because of the rise of two stronger, more entertaining popular theatres, Bunraku – puppets – and Kabuki; playhouses for these sprang up in the largest cities, Osaka and Edo (Tokyo), for a broader public. The acting troupes were no longer largely dependent on court patronage. The overthrow of the long-dictatorial Shōgunate in 1868 threatened at first to cause Nōh to disappear, having lost its chief sponsor, but it was able to regain its place along with the restoration of the Emperor's more personal rule. In the later part of the nineteenth century some subtle alterations of Nōh's style and structure were effected, but they were minor and it remained as before, an esoteric genre of theatrical art, one of interest chiefly to the highly educated. It was long supported by private clubs of devotees. This continued to be true into and through the twentieth century. About 1950 Faubion Bowers reported knowing of eighty-eight Nōh theatres in the country, more than at any other period in its history. Tokyo had just opened its sixth, the new Kanze Kalikan. He noted that to attend performances of Nōh was considered a token of good breeding. Because its archaic language is a handicap, many earnest spectators bring a printed text to comprehend what is happening, much as non-German-speaking opera-goers might peruse an English translation of the libretto while listening to Wagner's *Parsifal*, as was often done in the days before helpful surtitles could be projected above the proscenium.

With their pervasive solemnity, and the intense concentration they demanded from spectators, a cycle of five or six Nōh plays hardly provided hoped-for diversion to less than serious theatre-goers and court attendants. To lighten a programme, and thereby hold the more restless and secular-minded segment of the audience, the troupes inserted farcical material – slight, rowdy sketches – in intervals between the relentlessly sober dramas. This practice began as early as the start of the fourteenth century to assure brief respites during the annual overlong Great Prayer meetings celebrated at the temple of Mibu-mura in Aki province; at first, the skits were in dumb-show. From them evolved the Kyōgen, borrowed by Seami and others for much the same purpose, comic relief. The addition of three Kyōgen (the term means "wild words" or "idle chatter") became and remained a fixed feature of every cycle. The Kyōgen are like the satyr plays at the Dionysian festivals of ancient Athens, offering another kind of *katharsis*, a hearty laugh, after the cumulative harrowing experience of watching three gory tragedies. But they are also strikingly similar to the folk farces on view at about the same time in various parts of medieval Europe.

Some Kyōgen parody the sober Nōh dramas, as do the satyr plays in the contest entries of Aeschylus, Sophocles and Euripides. Others poke fun at the arrogance, stupidity, hypocrisy and pomposity of people in high places. Oblique hints of social criticism and protest are implanted in the skits. A frequent theme is that of the clever servant who outwits and robs his master, though he usually ends up getting a good beating. The master's concluding words are: "You rascal! I'll not let you go." This subject is found over and over in the manuscripts of Menander and Plautus, and in the European peasant farces, further evidence of the timeless and universal nature of comedy.

Most of the authors of the Kyōgen are unknown. One early figure, though his identity is not certain, is Kitabatake Gene Honi, a fourteenth-century priest attached to the Hieizan monastery, but this is a rare attribution of authorship. About 200 scripts are extant and viable in the current repertory. (Donald Keene has gathered and Englished a very large number of them.)

They are truly good-humoured, with no tinge of bitterness, and observe the proprieties. All are in prose, and very few call for music and dance. They usually employ only two or three players; there is no chorus; the lead actor is the *omo*, the second the *ado*; they do not wear masks, save perhaps when enacting the roles of a sly fox or mischievous monkey, an instance of the latter required for a playlet titled *Utsubozaru*. The sketches contain many ingredients of much earlier farces, looking back to previous centuries. Much of the laughter they evoke comes from physical antics, slapstick. The scripts have no claim to literary merit, but each competing Nōh troupe keeps secret its valuable store of them.

There is irony in *Bird-catcher in Hell* (translated by Waley), a parody of a pair of very serious Nōh plays. Kiyoyori dies and seeks a place in Heaven but is denied entrance by Yama, the King of Hell, who condemns him as a sinner for having practised a cruel trade. Says a demon: "Bird-catcher? That's bad. Taking life from morning to night." Hell should be his destination. Kiyoyori pleads his case before Yama, who is unsympathetic. Kiyoyori argues: "The birds I caught were sold to gentlemen to feed their falcons on; so there was really no harm in it. 'Therefore the fault was not his but the falcons,' themselves birds." Yama agrees, and his appetite is aroused. He bids Kiyoyori to catch more birds to eat, which the suppliant does. The demons greedily join the feast. Instead of being admitted to Heaven, the bird-catcher is returned to Earth to go about his trade for three more years for having provided Yama and the demons a rich treat. The moral of the sketch is half-hidden if rather edged.

Berthold cites a Kyōgen interlude, *Boshibari*, in which a bit of comic business is much like that in a *commedia dell'arte* piece: two servants have their hands tied together to keep them in bounds but still contrive to gain access to a barrel of rice wine and noisily over-imbibe.

Modern Nōh companies bringing their programmes to New York and other Western cities included Kyōgen as intrinsic to the cycles. The National Theatre of Japan performing at Carnegie Hall, for one, offered *Kirokuda* (*The Half-Delivered Gift*) as a component of the presentation; however, Mel Gussow, in the *New York Times*, found "the comedy unsubtle and the play tedious, although Manzo Nomura was funny at his most staggeringly drunk".

A major figure in Japan's theatre, Manzo Nomura inherited his nine-member Kyōgen troupe with which, still performing at the age of seventy, he appeared on tour in a dozen cities in the United States. In New York, Richard F. Shepard, of the *New York Times*, observed:

The Nomura Kyōgen Company does comedy, only comedy. It has been doing it for more than two hundred years, a rehearsal period that more than adequately sufficed to ready it for Carnegie Hall.

The company did three short plays in the thousand-year-old Kyōgen tradition of situation comedy that unmasks human conceit. The playlets were simple, expertly done, with a great sense of comedy. In the first a master discovers that his servants have been breaking into the sake cellar. He ties them up but they get to it anyway. In the second, a fox disguised as a trapper's uncle persuades the hunter to desist, but almost comes a cropper. In the third, a pompous mountain priest uses his arts to try to get rid of some annoying mushrooms that grow big and proliferate alarmingly. He can't and ends up fleeing from the plants.

It's material any television comic might get a routine out of, yet the Nomuras do it differently. With graceful gait, comically stricken voices that emanate from the backs of their throats, and beautifully colored costumes and animal masks, they make each little segment into a sort of poetry of fun and thought. Language is important, but even without a knowledge of Japanese one can enjoy the action onstage.

Only a few people appear on the stage in each play and the settings are sparse, almost non-existent, so that the viewer must concentrate on the human element.

Shepard interviewed Manzo Nomura, describing him as "a happy, extraordinarily limber gentleman". He referred to the venerable actor's recent official designation as "a living art treasure". This brought him a Japanese government subsidy, "'a little' to help him continue the family troupe, now in its sixth generation. His three sons and a five-year-old granddaughter, who has a bit part, work with him."

The actor discussed the art form that is his *métier*. "In Kyōgen there is a lot to make people laugh, but not just ha-ha type of laughing. There is much more to it. There is even tragedy." He insisted that Kyōgen was harder to perform than Nōh. "In Nōh, there are certain forms. Once you learn them, you can do them. But in Kyōgen you have to bring out a character. There's nothing as difficult as that, not even Kabuki. In Kabuki there's beautiful scenery, lots of people. In Kyōgen, there are only a few people onstage and you have to give it all you have, to be strong." He liked American audiences. "It's said that you never know what a Japanese is thinking. Often a Japanese audience, brought up in the Nōh tradition, won't laugh. Americans are not brought up in that tradition. They don't understand it as well as Japanese, but they laugh earlier. That's fine."

The Nomura tour was sponsored by the Japan Society and Washington University with added support by the John D. Rockefeller 3rd Fund. Another troupe, the Theatre of Yugen, under the auspices of the Japan Society, visited New York in 1990 with a programme of three Kyōgen in English: *The Owl Mountain Priest*, *Poison* and *Sumo Wrestling with a Mosquito*.

The two kinds of commoners' theatre that arose in the seventeenth century, Bunraku and Kabuki, owed much in their development to mutual exchange, each borrowing scripts, techniques and styles from the other, a strange process. Puppet shows are immemorially old and found elsewhere in the Far East, notably in India, China and Bali, but none equals the Bunraku (Doll Theatre) of Japan for seriousness and artistry. Some of the nation's favourite playscripts were composed expressly for it. It is unique, surpassing all others of the genre.

Puppetry in Japan was probably first put on display by native showmen at Shinto shrines in remote times. Later, these entertainers were joined by Chinese string-artists who came from the mainland in the eighth century AD, the Heian era, stretching to the twelfth century. These Chinese competitors with a wooden box hanging from their neck and shoulders wandered from town to town, island to island. Openings in the back and sides of the box permitted the operator to manipulate the dolls, constructed of cloth and wood. Even today it is possible to see such elementary puppet stages and jerkily mobile figures in the country's more primitive areas. Moving through market crowds, such nomadic puppet-masters take up collections, their rewards often scanty.

Over the centuries, however, the descendants of early puppeteers, assigned to a lower social caste, settled near Osaka and Kobe. They established a stronger tradition of puppetry closely linked to nearby Shinto shrine ceremonies. The use of hand-puppets (*ningyo*) began to evolve. One legend has it that a priest at Ebisu carried a doll in the image of the shrine's founder, to propitiate local deities who were inflicting punishing tempests. When the doll "danced", the storms cleared. Learning of this, the Emperor granted the priest permission to travel throughout the islands, invoking Heaven's help by staging more magic "dances" with his dolls.

By another account, blind monks sat by the temple gates reciting passages from Samurai epics, accompanying the words with a lute, the three- to five-stringed *samisen*. Two itinerant performers, Hikita Awajino-jō, a puppeteer, and Menukiya Chōzaburo, a *samisen*-player and ballad singer, elected to join forces, adding music to the doll-play and affording the ballad a visual and animated realization. Widely hailed, they came to the Emperor's attention and were summoned to his court. Soon other pairs of balladeers and puppeteers followed their example.

An oft-sung ballad, because it was much requested, related the sad quest of Jōruri, a young woman vainly seeking a vanished lover, now found, now lost again.

In time, by the end of the sixteenth century, a wide class of puppet-ballad-plays were called *ningyo jôruri*. Their offerings were the vogue in Osaka, a wealthy trade centre, where rich merchants put up money to erect an elaborate puppet theatre, and where – in the words of Berthold – "under their influence the thematic accents shifted from the courtly world of the Samurai to the trading accents and the emotional range of the merchant class".

What is now known as Bunraku began in the latter part of the sixteenth century when both the reigning Emperor and the Shōgun, Hideyoshi Toyotomi, commanded performances at their separate courts by puppeteers from the Osaka region, as well as by entertainers from the island of Awaji. At this point the doll-plays combined with and absorbed not only the balladry of the period, but also the songs of street-singers, many of whom, blind, were said to beat time with their fans. The troubadours brought a wide variety of historical and topical subject-matter to their songs, which was now embraced by the puppets: domestic intrigue, valorous military deeds, romantic adventures. Then to what had been a simple performance was added a chanting narrator, to explain what was being dramatized. His recitations grew ever more subtle and elegant, transforming a medley of plain folk-songs into an offering of high art. The recitalist kept time not with a fan but instead a two-foot-long iron rod or cane and occasionally was so carried away by the emotions he was describing that he swung wildly and destroyed the paper scene setting and knocked off the heads of the dolls enacting the story. Today, as the chief narrator accompanying a Bunraku enactment eloquently expresses the feelings of the people in the drama, he adds to his lengthy vocal feat a seemingly endless succession of facial contortions: grimaces, frowns, laughs, wry smiles.

In the wake of St Francis Xavier's arrival in Japan (1562), other Western missionary-priests brought along European puppets; they served to portray Biblical stories, emulating the teaching practice of Shinto priests of earlier days. Japanese children, already familiar with puppetry, welcomed the religious playlets. It is thought that from the European marionettes the Japanese learned how to move the puppets' eyes and mouths, attaining the remarkable expressivity that characterizes Bunraku.

The seventeenth century, the "Golden Age" of Bunraku and Kabuki, brought the erection of a more permanent theatre in Osaka, the Takomotoza, devoted solely to puppetry. And now, too, appeared one of Japan's famous playwrights, Chikamatsu Monzaemon (1653–1724), popularly called the Japanese Shakespeare, who wrote primarily for Bunraku. Of his 150 scripts, 120 were intended for performance by the dolls, though almost all were later adapted for live actors to perform in Kabuki. A chief reason Chikamatsu preferred the puppet theatre was that his scripts were more respected there; in Kabuki his lines and scenes were often altered to suit the whims or talents of a star actor.

Chikamatsu's dramas provide a broad picture of Japanese life in his epoch, and he is regarded by some as the first of the world's major dramatists to depict in mature tragedy the fate of the common man. But the Oriental view of man and definition of "tragedy", as has been remarked, are quite different from Western concepts of them.

Second only to prolific Chikamatsu was Takemoto Gidayu (1651–1743), who greatly influenced methods of production, especially the kinds of musical accompaniment to be used. He further modified the *jōruri* ballad style, bringing Bunraku to an even higher level of refinement. The classic pattern of a "Gidayu play" is in five parts: first an episode to set a mood, then one to introduce the characters, followed by a lyrical section devoted to the laments of a distressed heroine, and next one where the plot reaches a crisis and, at the last, a resolution. It may possess subdivisions in the separate episodes. A musical score is carefully and traditionally composed to fit and enhance the action in each discrete part.

The name "Bunraku" honours a famed puppeteer, Uemura Bunrakuken, who in the nineteenth century revived the then dying art of thespian dolls. Coming from the island of Awaji, which as noted was where puppetry thrived, he established himself in Osaka and built a newer theatre (1871), which in time assumed his name. His offerings, then as now, were plays for adults, not for children alone.

At the Bunraku, human manipulators appear together with the dolls onstage and are always in full view of the audience. Assistants are dressed wholly in black, and hooded and gloved, to signify that they are invisible, a hoped-for illusion. The attire of the principal handlers, of the narrators, of the musicians, is black and white and formal. Three men are required to operate each doll. Despite the presence on stage of this often large team, the spectators are soon engrossed in the play and accept with little if any question the autonomous vitality of the carved figures. It is not unusual for an audience to be moved to tears by the dilemmas of the doll characters. That they take on a life of their own is a tribute to the lively imagination of the spectator.

The skill of the handlers is truly astonishing. The dolls are about three feet high, and when dressed may weight about forty pounds – however, the size may vary. If the role calls for it they may be gorgeously dressed. As stated, they have moving eyes and mouths. Available are forty-five different types of faces, carved of cypress wood and screwed into a shoulder board. They also have arms, legs, and under their attire a bamboo hoop to suggest hips. The limbs and hoop are connected by cords to the shoulder board. Toggles on the grip help the puppeteer control the gestures and animate the facial features. Among the standard "faces" are those of "the handsome young man", "resolute middle-aged man", "vulgar courtesan", "virtuous girl or young lady", "fierce warrior", "meditative man", "stubborn father-in-law", "comical villain". In all instances the heads are disproportionately small, for the Japanese esteem small heads as beautiful. The figures wear wigs always woven of human hair, and they have appropriate headdresses. The heads are still carved on the island of Awaji and sent to Osaka.

In action, the puppets may assume forty different gestures and postures. For expedient reasons, one arm is always longer than the other; if the spectator becomes aware of this, he apparently does not care. The female dolls are without legs or feet under their long robes but are manipulated so that they seem to walk and even run if need be. The figures can heave their shoulders and wiggle their noses, lift eyebrows or gnash their teeth, and flex their fingers. They can handle fans, weapons, food and drink. (Much of this technical detail comes from an article by A.N. Nathan.)

It is claimed that at a minimum it takes a handler ten or fifteen years to master some of these effects, and a principal puppeteer may study his craft for as long as fifty years before he is deemed a master worthy to pass on his full range of tricks to others. The procedure is to learn how to control one limb and then another.

The chanter was at first hidden behind a screen, but as the subject-matter of the plays became more everyday, dealing with domestic and topical themes, he took a post in full sight. Today the "reciter" (*tayu*) sits on a slightly raised dais to the right of the stage, the script resting before him on an ornate lacquered stand. Though he pretends to read it, he probably knows it by heart. When a drama is several acts long, he may alternate with a second *tayu*. Alongside them are the *samisen*-player and a drummer.

In the course of a scene the narrator may supply the voices for a half-dozen or more characters, masculine and feminine, and do so for an hour without pause. He too requires many years of preparation: to laugh in the prescribed Bunraku manner might take five years of practice, and eight to weep in proper fashion. A senior *tayu* may contain in his memory 100 different full-length plays, all the dialogue and description, which he declaims as though he were both the full cast and interposing author.

Over the years the physical staging became more complex, much of it innovative. Soon after 1715 movable settings were introduced. Twelve years later (1727) came the installation of elevator traps able to lift scenery through openings in the floor; in 1757 the same machinery was used to establish different levels of the stage floor; and then, in 1758, the Bunraku installed an even more important invention, a circular revolving stage to effect scene changes more rapidly and smoothly; in time these helpful and ingenious devices were adopted worldwide.

Brockett offers a picture of the present-day theatre: "The long and narrow stage is divided into three levels from front to rear, each indicated by low partitions behind which the handlers sit. . . . Numerous properties are used. The narrator and *samisen* player are placed on a small turntable downstage left. This turntable is revolved at the end of each act to bring out a new narrator and *samisen* player, whose names are announced. . . . The *samisen* has a skin-covered base and is simultaneously plucked and struck. Extremely varied in sound, it can follow the rise and fall of the voice, give special emphasis, and provide punctuation to the narration and action. Its accompaniment is considered essential."

Throughout the eighteenth and nineteenth centuries the literature of Bunraku continued to grow, together with contributions from authors writing for the rival Kabuki, their works subsequently adapted for the dolls.

After 400 years the tradition of Bunraku remains pure, with scant change. A.C. Scott explains how this rigidity is maintained.

There exists an old manual of doll handling which was prepared in rhythmic stanzas, so that beginners could assimilate the rules easily. In it are given all the various directions for stance and movement in the handling of dolls of every description. A male doll steps forward with the left foot, a female doll with the right. A general looks back when he stands up, other dolls only when they leave the stage. In fear a doll turns its face left and right; to make a request it steps forward; to refuse, it retreats; the courtesan wipes away her tears with paper, the hero with his hand. A man moves his shoulders when laughing, but a woman bends downwards and holds her sleeve before her mouth. There are many different kinds of bows, ways of holding a fan or carrying a sword, and all must be mastered and strictly adhered to. The doll handler who makes a mistake in these matters is disgraced. Whatever the season of the year the fan must not be forgotten; when the doll takes off its sword, it must also discard its fan. The fan is taken up before the sword and always carried in the right half of the *obi* or sash. Details such as these are important in preserving a correct pattern of movement on stage.

One constant purpose has been to keep Bunraku free of "realism", mere imitation. By having the narrator in plain view, unrealistic style is upheld, one long preferred in the East. At the same time, the "primacy" of the written word is assured. It was, as has been observed, this respect for the text that won Bunraku the eminent Chikamatsu's allegiance. At the beginning and close of each play, the *tayu* pays obeisance to the scroll from which he has presumably been "reading". The language is poetic (by now archaic) and even on the printed page is largely beyond the comprehension of an average person. This, too, is deliberate. What Bunraku directors and producers hope to do is establish an exact balance between reality and unreality by achieving the right aesthetic distance.

The fortunes of Bunraku have risen and fallen and risen again. It attained its highest popularity in the eighteenth century, forging far ahead of Kabuki, then fell back until the advent of Uemura Bunrakuken in the late nineteenth. Its draw was declining in the early twentieth, a loss climaxed in 1926 when its theatre, located in a suburban temple district, was razed by fire. The Shōchiku Corporation, which dominates Japan's entertainment venues, replaced the charred structure with a costly new playhouse, the Asahi-za, smaller, more intimate, of dimensions suitable to the nature of the productions and reduced number of spectators – on Shōchiku's part a gesture of loyalty to tradition, since Bunraku was no longer a profitable enterprise. This more modern theatre is in the midst of Osaka's bright, bustling entertainment area. Since then the government has granted the company an annual subsidy in appreciation of its cultural importance. Its box-office is exempt from taxation. Further enhancing the company's prestige, an imperial title was bestowed on one of its renowned singers, Yamashiro no Shojo, far advanced in age.

In the mid-1950s the troupe was disrupted by a split, dividing it into two factions. Impatient younger members felt that older singers and manipulators had retained their roles too long, blocking chances for the comparative newcomers; such a seeming immortal was the great Yamashiro, and another was Yoshida Bungoro, a famed puppeteer, who near ninety, blind and deaf, was still able to handle the dolls so that they faithfully resembled young girls and seductively attractive, more mature lady heroines. Bowers reports on a performance of *Sho-utsushi Asagao Banashi* (*The Tale of the Morning Glory*) at which Bungoro, still active, displayed his undiminished skill. An unhappy young lady has been blinded by weeping about her lost lover and spends her time wandering over the countryside looking for him (he can, of course, restore her sight), earning her keep as a blind musician. What was apparent was an almost eerie relationship between manipulator and puppet. The doll's eyes are shut in simulated blindness, her wooden hands grope nervously and Bungoro stands behind her in full view, showing a withered, sightless face. Time was not on the side of Yamashiro and Bungoro, however, though Bongoro, too, was designated a National Treasure. Since then, much recognition has been given to the art of the younger, gifted puppeteer, Monjoro.

Union troubles and strikes also beset the company; wages were shockingly low, hardly enabling many of the members to support a family – an exception was the stars, but even they could not hope to grow rich or earn what was due artists of their accomplishment and status.

One reason for Bunraku's shrinking appeal, apart from the competition of films, was the rapid Westernization of Japan. The newer generation did not identify with or have sympathy for the mindset and values of eighteenth-century characters and spectators, the rigid, outdated concepts of morality and honour, of selfless loyalty. Yet the company was adamantly against adding new or even different works. When Shōchiku officials suggested that Bunraku might expand its repertory with puppet versions of *Hamlet*, *Madame Butterfly* or *La Traviata*, the esteemed *tayu* Tsubamedaiyu told Nathan: "That's carrying things too far! We must have an audience or we go stale, and I suppose I wouldn't mind doing new plays in order to get people into the theatre so we could show them the classics, but they would at least have to be Japanese plays. How far do you think the Old Vic would get if they had to do a Kabuki play in samurai wigs?" He refused to take part in any such change. The novelist Junichiro Tanizaki, in a preface to a book on Bunraku by Donald Keene, says, "The texts, the heart of Bunraku, contain many extremely irrational or downright foolish elements which people today cannot accept." This is an aspect of the theatre of which foreign admirers are not fully aware.

Besides the language barrier (the archaisms), another problem in recapturing an audience is the rising age level of members of the troupe, a persistent trend, together with the difficulty of recruiting apprentices; the training period is too long and exacting, the wages too low. The company reaches beyond its historic base in Osaka, however, regularly going to Tokyo, where it is housed in the National Theatre; and where its welcome is warmer, perhaps because there it is more available to awestruck foreign tourists.

An educational programme was started, with ten-man units performing in high schools to acquaint students with the beauty of the puppet plays, their place in Japan's cultural history. The special conventions of these dramas are explained. It is hoped that enough students will be interested and become future spectators.

Bunraku has also made frequent trips abroad. One visit was to Canada. In the United States the troupe was first seen at the Seattle World Exposition (1962), preceding its début for thirteen days at the huge, cavernous, over-decorated City Center in New York (1966), hardly an appropriate site for a puppet show. Headphones with Donald Keene's English translations of the dramas were available, but not all the wearers were happy with them: one reviewer complained that with the earpieces on he could not hear the Japanese narrator and missed his fluency and dramatic shifts of tone and pitch, his many male and female voices; yet without the hearing aid he understood little of what was happening to the characters in the story. Another chose to do otherwise, dispensing with the headphones and contenting himself with watching intently; that critic was Norman Nadel, of the *World-Telegram and Sun*, who remarked:

It's almost impossible to take your eyes off the narrator. Speaking a language which is all but incomprehensible even to modern Japanese, he possesses an eloquence, in his facial expressions and the infinite variety of word-sounds and emotional accents, which transcends mere speech. . . . It is really a musical kind of speech, or a spoken kind of music, to which the distinctly Oriental sounds of the *samisen* are exquisitely fitted. There are times when there isn't much action by the dolls on stage, and the facial expressions are too diminutive to be fully appreciated from any distance (take binoculars or opera glasses, if you have them). But the narrator and musician always command attention.

I was especially taken with Tsudayu Takemoto, the reciter for the second act of *The General's Daughter*. You wonder if he is going to survive the strain of speaking several roles through a devastating series of emotional crises. Speaking the general himself, an indestructible blind rebel, he is fearsome and delightful.

There is a great deal to enjoy at a Bunraku performance. You need patience – because this Japanese art is not for the restless – and you must break yourself of the habit of watching just the performers – the dolls, in this case. Let your eyes and ears take in the dolls, the manipulators, the scenery, costumes, reciters and *samisen* players, and such delicate little touches as soaring sea gulls fixed to the ends of flexible wands. It adds up to an evening rich in a happy variety of enjoyments.

Even more deeply impressed was Clive Barnes, then of the *New York Times*, who joined the general chorus of adulation, finding the Bunraku an unusual and thrilling experience in total theater. . . . This three-hundred-year-old puppet ensemble is clearly one of the artistic wonders of the world, an art form in its own right, and its glories are well and truly confirmed by a repeated viewing. It is entirely misleading to think of Bunraku as a puppet theater in any conventional sense. . . .

The visual pleasures of Bunraku are enormous, and time and time again the Japanese water-colorists, with their bold, bland portraits and shivering landscapes are evoked. Yet eventually what is achieved in Bunraku is a very particular kind of poetry. It comes from the actual physical circumstances, the chanting, the resolutely plinging sound of the *samisen* or *koto*, the beautifully dressed puppets, the pale, unobtrusive backgrounds.

But more than this, behind the Bunraku there seems to be a mystery or a philosophy. You watch the skillfully manipulated puppets and their urbane, almost uninterested keepers, flitting deftly around them, and somehow the whole performance takes on the quality of a metaphor for human life and tragic destiny. The puppets are reality, and their manipulators nothing more than the impersonal slings and arrows of outrageous fortune.

A reviewer for the *Herald-Tribune*, in an exclamatory vein, had this response to what he had beheld: "They're living dolls. They really are. At least they make you believe that they are alive. But these Japanese dolls speak with miraculous eloquence in gestures common to man himself, in gestures which are, indeed, alive."

The Bunraku had brought along two programmes for its New York engagement. On the first were *Msume Kagekiyo Yashima Nikki (The General's Daughter)* by Fuemi Watake (1764), and next a farce, *Tsuri Onna (Fishing for Wives)*, adapted from a Nōh Kyōgen, and, a wind-up, *Date Msume Koi No Higanoko (The Greengrocer's Daughter)* by Sensuke Suga, Wackichi Matsuda and Fuemi Watake (1773). In the opening play, Kagekiyo, a general, is exiled and blind. To succour him, his daughter Itokaki, whom he does not actually know, sells herself to a brothel to raise enough money to travel to Hiuga Island where he now lives. The money is also to let her father buy a government post from his victorious adversary. At the encounter, the girl conceals the source of the funds, saying that she obtained them from an imaginary husband, a farmer. The father flies into a rage at the thought that his daughter has married so far beneath her and accepted money from such a lowly person. He threatens to kill her for disgracing him, and the girl sadly departs. She leaves behind the money and a note confessing that she is a prostitute and explaining why she has become one. After this is read to him, the general assents to keeping the money and resolves to use it for the purpose his daughter intended.

Barnes commented: "The ideas here are alien to us not only in the matter of time – so, for example, are those of John Webster – but also in the matter of our own Western humanist tradition. Yet, equally, this recognition of honor as an emotive force gives rise to tremendous dramatic possibilities, made all the more tempestuous by what seems to us their stylization. The performance of the old general was a wonderful piece of acting – not just puppetry, for in this context puppetry has no more meaning. The puppets are only the surprising means to a perfectly conventional end."

The Kyōgen, *Fishing for Wives*, serving as an interlude, sends a war lord, Daimyo, and his comic servant, Tarokaja, on an expedition to catch themselves proper spouses. The lord brings back a beauty, the servant a shrew. "Their mission is prompted by a dream. It was very funny, full of character and obsessions."

The Greengrocer's Daughter also concerns a point of honour. The heroine, Oshichi, is in love with a samurai, Kishisaburo, who unfortunately loses his master's ceremonial sword and feels compelled to commit *seppuku* (ritual suicide) as his lord has already done; duty demands that he follow his lord's example. After bidding farewell to the girl, the young man conceals himself under the floor of her father's house and overhears arrangements being made for her marriage to a rich merchant to whom the father is greatly indebted. Reluctantly, Oshichi consents to the match, but then finds a note left by Kishisaburo telling of his dilemma and intent to kill himself. Servants discover the lost sword in the possession of the merchant. They retrieve it, but Oshichi cannot immediately return it to Kishisaburo because all the streets to his dwelling are closed – it is after midnight. They cannot be opened before dawn unless the fire bell sounds. Though the penalty for doing so is death, the loyal Oshichi climbs the bell tower and rings the alarm. Descending, she is told by the servants that the sword has been delivered to the young samurai, whose life is saved. The task of having a puppet climb a tower is a daunting one and when accomplished invariably evokes loud applause. Of this melodramatic work, which required the talents of three writers, Clive Barnes wrote:

> Pathetic and exciting – at one moment the heroine's headlong flight through the streets of Kobe reminded me irresistibly of Ulanova's Juliet running, passion-struck, through Shakespeare's Verona – this play proved amazing as a pure technical feat, but once again such feats became quite insignificant. You admired, in an offhand way, the fact that the team of manipulators was able to make the girl climb a watch-tower, but you identified with whether she was going to get there or not. . . .
>
> That is why these puppets are like no others you have ever seen. They are drawn, or rather articulated, from life. That is why you should go to see them. They make a quite demanding evening, but it is such a refreshing change for Broadway to make demands that these puppets are more than welcome, and so much more expressive than many actors.

The second programme consisted of excerpts from *Kanadehon Chushingura* (*The Revenge of the Forty-seven Ronin*) by Izumo Takeda II with Shoraku Miyoshi and Senryu Namiki (1748), the best known of all Kabuki plays (*vide* below), and the full-length *Sho-utsushi Asagao Banashi* (*The Tale of the Morning Glory*), already mentioned. The title derives from a poem on a folding screen in an inn; the poem is a favourite of Asagoa, a blind singer who entertains there. The guest, a young samurai, Jirozaemon, recognizes that Miyuga, the heroine of the poem about a morning glory, is certainly Asagoa herself, a samurai's impoverished daughter. Departing from the inn, he leaves behind for her some money, a cure for blindness, and a fan with the design of a morning glory on it. She identifies the fan and sets out to find him. Reaching the banks of the Oi River, she is halted, unable to cross its swollen flow, which is due to the spring rains; frustrated, she tries to drown herself. The innkeeper, who has been a past recipient of Miyuga's father's kindness, arrives and tries to save her. He stabs himself, and his blood, together with the cure left by Jirozaemon, restores her sight: her blindness has been caused by her endless weeping for him. She also regains her lost beauty. This brings her back to the embrace of her former lover.

Clive Barnes did not like this selection. "The pathos of the piece seems remote and pallid, and although the drama has a certain charm, and the heroine's determination recalls Brecht's heroine in *The Caucasian Chalk Circle*, the work comes as a disappointment. It also bears all the signs of having been hastily cut; one important episode in the synopsis is omitted."

Barnes offered this summary of the impressions the troupe made on him:

The art of Bunraku is a mixture of puppetry, acting and song. Interestingly, the facial movements of these wonderfully complex puppets are comparatively slight. The emotion and power are conveyed largely by their movements and gestures. After watching them for a time, they become completely real. Any fear that they might be dolls is suspended: even the inscrutable puppet-masters, as solicitous of their charges as patient male nurses, far from destroying the illusion actually seem to add to it, seeming charmingly domestic in their care and yet weaving around the actors like giant and invisible black angels or forces of destiny.

The array of authors listed for these works is a sampling of the many who, apart from Chikamatsu, singly or collaboratively, stocked Bunraku's extensive repertory. One who is absent here but deserves to be mentioned is Ki no Kaion (1663–1742). Born in Osaka – his real name, Enami Kiemon – he was to contribute about fifty plays, largely on historical subjects, a type called *jidaimono*. He was often spoken of as Chikamatsu's leading rival in preparing scripts for the puppet theatre, though actually he matched neither that master's talent nor his popularity. But he was scholarly, with a broad interest in Chinese and Japanese prose literature and poetry, and his erudition earned him much respect from fellow intellectuals.

Though effectively constructed, his plays are considered "dry" and "didactic", and few are still performed, but he had a lasting influence by introducing themes that later writers were happy to exploit, especially for major works in the Kabuki theatre. Among these are the romance between the wooden-bowl dealer and the courtesan in the play bearing their names, *Wankyu sue no Matsuyama*, and the tragic affair between another courtesan, Hanshichi, and an umbrella vendor in *Kasaya Sankatsu nijūgonen ki*. In the opinion of Ted T. Takaya, Ki no Kaion's dramatic works prove to be more meritorious on close analysis than thought until now.

After winning the critics and public, the Bunraku returned to New York in 1973, once more at the over-large City Center; and again in 1983, under the auspices of the Japan Society, in the much smaller Lila Acheson Wallace Auditorium, where the offerings were a complete staging of *The Fortunate Flowering of the Four Seasons*, together with highlights from *The Sake Shop*, *Kumagai's Camp*, and *Summer Festival*, followed by *Sambaso*, a ritualistic dance of purification. This time the house lights were not on full, as at the City Center, but partly down – the puppeteers prefer some dim lighting, so as to be able to watch faces in the audience and sense reactions. Also, no headsets were available.

In the time between the two New York engagements a filmed version of the Bunraku's production of *The Lovers' Exile* (1711), by Chikamatsu, was given a showing at the Public Theatre (1981). The story, which Chikamatsu took from a real-life scandal of his day, is once more about an indentured prostitute. A poor clerk, Chubei, is in love with her. To save her from being married to a rich old merchant, he commits a theft and buys her for himself. His misdeed is immediately discovered, and he and the girl, Umegawa, flee. But they are doomed.

Vincent Canby, film critic of the *New York Times*, had this to say:

Though the sets are delicately stylized, the theater uses some charmingly realistic stage effects. As Chubei walks along the Yokohama canal, attempting to control the temptation to steal the money, the backdrop moves from left to right to indicate his progress. When Chubei and Umegawa take flight, we see them making their way through a fierce snowstorm of rice paper that eventually sticks to the costumes of their handlers as well as to them.

Equally remarkable is the range of emotions that the dolls are able to communicate simply through body movements. The faces of the leading characters – those that must express rarefied feelings that relate to love, loss and heroic sacrifice – are immobile, as if beyond the lesser, more vulgar emotions of laughter, spite, hurt or envy. Subsidiary characters, like servants, messengers and such, sometimes have movable eyes, eyebrows or mouths.

To the uninitiated Western observer, Bunraku is a revelation, not comparable to anything in our theater.

The film was produced, directed and adapted from Chikamatsu's play by a Canadian, Marty Gross, who said that for him it was "a labor of love". Though shot in a studio, it is a straightforward recording of a Bunraku performance, to which are added English subtitles by Donald Richie.

More controversial was an off-Broadway attempt (1990) by David Greenspan to stage Chikamatsu's puppet-drama *Gonza the Lancer* with a cast combining actors and dolls. This was again at the Public Theater, one of Joseph Papp's complex of playhouses largely devoted to off-beat or *avant-garde* ventures. As Chikamatsu tells it, Gonza, a vainglorious samurai, considers himself "the pride of the martial profession", while also aspiring to be a master of the highly valued art of the tea ceremony. Overly ambitious and without scruples, he is pledged to marry not one but two women, but at the same time the mother of one of them seeks to lure him for herself. At a crucial moment, she and Gonza are discovered in an act of apparent infidelity. The characters around them are involved in their own vicious struggles and rivalries, assuring unhappy endings for most of them. Though Gonza is portrayed as more of a scoundrel than a hero, his ultimate self-sacrifice is partly redemptive.

Greenspan had seven actors doubling and tripling in twenty roles, abetted by two narrators who introduced the characters and related the tale. Mel Gussow, of the *New York Times*, found all this both confusing and deplorable.

A tall, gawky actor plays a simpering governess, a short actress with a painted moustache pretends to be an aged grandfather, and Keenan Shimizu, who has done notable work with the Pan Asian Repertory Theatre, is hamstrung by a gallery of characters, including small children and Gonza's dewy-eyed first love.

Gussow thought that the actors tended to be self-conscious.

Further divorcing the play from its source, the scenery is sparse and the costumes a motley collection that gives the play the air of a workshop. Occasionally Mr Greenspan tries to adapt a Japanese technique. The puppetry is especially ineffective. The production would certainly have benefited from the collaboration of an imaginative puppeteer or mask maker.

The atmospheric barrenness was also a flaw.

> The director's aim may have been to put Chikamatsu to the test of modernism, to see if this story of ambition, adultery and vengeance would have a relevance in today's world and theater. The result is the deconstruction of the text. Reduced to the basic narrative (in Donald Keene's authoritative translation) and staged in campy contemporary style, *Gonza* moves dangerously close to self-parody. . . . From this production, it would be impossible to comprehend how this epic playwright could be regarded as Shakespeare's equal in Japan.

Quite the opposite view was that of Clive Barnes, now with the *New York Post*, for whom the adaptation was "fascinating! A play about love, lust, betrayal and honor. It is hypnotically engrossing. Wonderfully directed – a dazzlingly eclectic staging by David Greenspan."

To preserve Bunraku, a training school in puppetry was established at the National Theatre. The troupe's many successes abroad have greatly enhanced its prestige at home, especially as Japanese nationalist feeling has risen and more pride is taken in the country's cultural legacy.

The up-and-down contest with Bunraku during the seventeenth and eighteenth centuries ended with the more vigorous Kabuki solidly in place as Japan's most popular form of theatre. Essentially this represented a middle-class revolt against the aristocratic Nōh, the esoteric pleasures of which were beyond the comprehension of most people. The initial stride was made in 1600 by a nun, O-Kuni, who was soliciting funds for temple-building, especially to restore the one at Izumo gutted by fire. To attract attention she began to dance in a new fashion, combining a vulgarization of the ceremonial sacred Kagura (Shrine Dance) with a loose adaptation of the Nōh style, too, borrowing and boldly altering its music and stern traditions. Her innovations met a delighted response. A renegade from her holy order, she formed a troupe of fellow dancers, women, children, and finally men. Her husband served as producer. The group toured, sometimes appearing in the dry riverbed of the Kamo in Kyoto, where there was a summer amusement park crowded with tea shops, small restaurants and various stalls, all tending to be lucratively thronged. (Her association with this site led Kabuki actors to be known as "beggars of the riverbed".) To the dances and music – flutes, drums and tambourines – she gradually added speech as well as song, and then playlets. Besides Kagura and Nōh, antecedents of her offerings were the ribald Kyōgen and the Taiheiki, another kind of current public entertainment in which a single actor dramatically recited stories while accompanying himself with a three-stringed guitar and rhythmic fan-tapping. Elements of all these were improvisationally melded into one, a new genre. "Kabuki" is a term made up of three Chinese script characters that suggest "song, dance and artistic skill".

In 1607, O-Kuni's troupe left Kyoto for Edo (Tokyo) and had as much success there, which soon prompted many imitators. Tea-house owners, to gain and hold customers, added Kabuki stages in their gardens, which became in a sense outdoor cabarets. An ancient document (from some time between 1604 and 1630), quoted by Berthold, gives an account of a typical O-Kuni dance-play – with specific drawings. "O-Kuni is mourning for her love and, conjured up by the fervor of her dance, the dead man's ghost appears to her. The ghost is impersonated by a young actress and enters the stage from among the public. This device heralded a development that became a principle of Kabuki stage technique. Ghosts, gods, and heroes make their entrance through the audience along a wooden bridge called *hanamichi*, that is, the flower path. It is said that the public here laid flowers at their feet – a pretty but unsupported interpretation."

By 1624 Kabuki was so popular that a permanent theatre was erected in Edo by an actor–manager named Nakamura, founder of what was to be a long-lived, most admired dynasty of players. After a few years of prosperity the various companies were shut down by the Shōgun (1627) on complaints of scandalous behaviour by women onstage and offstage. Soon a remedy was found: female roles were impersonated by boys and the playhouses were allowed to re-open. By 1652 this expedient had run its course, a ban was reimposed, the boys proving to be as immoral as the alleged prostitutes they had replaced. Thereafter the women's dances were performed by more mature men. The Kabuki became more "dramatic", offering plays with clearly designed plots, since the young people of both sexes in it could no longer just "sell their pretty faces".

This colourful, evolving theatre was an aspect of a larger alteration of Japan's feudal structure, the society that had given birth to Nōh. The dominating position held by nobles, samurai and other warriors was being overtaken by newly wealthy merchants and energetic townsfolk who had their own aesthetic or non-aesthetic demands. Kabuki, a people's theatre, was a forum for protest against the ruling class stubbornly trying to hold on to power. Many restrictions were placed on the actors and their unruly stage – on the expensive costumes, and even more on the personal behaviour of the players – but nothing prevailed; the public, both lower and middle classes, supported the morally outspoken new drama, and at last the barriers gave way and the flamboyant Kabuki triumphed.

Beginning as dance, Kabuki was principally choreographic during its first fifty years. When young women and boys were no longer permitted to participate, the remaining actors drew attention by other means. A reliance on story content, the building of suspense, became increasingly important.

More touches of realism appeared, though mostly Kabuki was still conventionalized. Again, there were infusions from folk-dance. Traces of Nōh stylization lingered, and from Bunraku – a chief source of plots whipped up by Chikamatsu and others – came a further influence, a slow, doll-like manner of movement by the actors, who frequently give the impression of being human puppets. This is particularly true in the performance of plays borrowed directly from the doll theatre, and is even more marked in a special type of acting called *ningyo-buri*, wherein the actor assumes the role of a doll and is moved about the stage by handlers precisely as they might manipulate a puppet.

Kabuki plays deal mostly with historical themes and romantic adventures; all are wildly melodramatic, implausible, pathetic, and are much too long and diffuse; and few have literary merit. Many were put together by teams of hack writers who were attached to the theatre companies; the scripts were intended as vehicles for certain principal actors. Very often a chief writer did the first few acts, or just an outline, and his assistants the rest. So, within the same drama, tone, quality and characterizations might be uneven and psychologically inconsistent from scene to scene. In the repertory are only a few comedies, and they are mostly low farces.

A frequent subject is divided loyalty: an underling is forced to sacrifice his son or wife to spare the life of the feudal lord to whom his fealty is pledged; or a wife is torn between her love for her husband and her duty to her father; such dilemmas are imposed by the rigid seventeenth-century ethical code, one that still influences phases of Japanese behaviour. If the plots are complicated, the characters are not. They are exceedingly simple. The hero faces his problems in a mood of resignation: he is passive; humbly if sorrowfully he accepts his *inga* (fate). Like the Nōh protagonist, and unlike a Greek tragic hero, he is not defiant or over-proud, nor does he achieve self-enlightenment, and nothing like *katharsis* results for him or the audience. But neither is he morally at fault: he is without *hamartia* or *hubris*. External events victimize him. Melancholy and an excessive sentimentality flood most of the plays. They are overly romantic, indeed. Yet, despite their stock plots, one-dimensional, stereotyped characters and improbable development of incidents, one shock piled wildly on another, they are highly stageworthy. They have been compared to opera libretti that seem bad and even ridiculous in synopsis but are surprisingly effective in performance.

The seventeenth-century audience was largely composed of women, who were attracted by lavish costumes and startling turns of plot and spectacular staging rather than by coherent dramatic structure. In those days few if any women were educated. The plays – *jōruri* – are likely to be from thirteen to twenty acts in length, not progressing logically but by mere expedient accretion, as do today's daytime radio and television serials, which they resemble. The actor also felt free to amend his part, to amplify it and permit himself an exhibition of his special talents, with little regard for plain common sense.

Three actors, of diverse skills, brought lustre to the Kabuki theatre. Sakata Tōjūrō (1647–1709), whose father had been involved in Nōh, began his career in boyhood; his first task was to beat a drum backstage while ghosts walked and intoned in one of his father's productions. In his maturity, having shifted his focus to Kabuki, he gained an enthusiastic following, not only as a performer, but also as an author. He had a considerable influence on the younger Chikamatsu, who took cues from watching and studying Tōjūrō at work. Tōjūrō himself, striding the stage in Osaka and Edo, was able to live in an opulent manner, profiting from many successes; in his life and his scripts he reflected a changing world, one in which avid men of commerce prospered unduly, while the samurai and their ilk lost status and grew poor, and vice and red-light districts flourished brazenly. He was not in any way a superficial actor or writer. Asserting that the artist must learn from life, he is noted for saying this about his craft: "The art of the mime is like a beggar's sack. It has to contain everything, important and unimportant. If one finds something that does not look as though it can be used at once, the thing to do is to take it along and to keep it for some future occasion. A true actor should learn the trade of the pickpocket." He was pre-eminent in roles as an affectionate lover of unfortunate courtesans in the many melodramas devoted to that subject.

His principal competitor in Edo was Ichikawa Danjūrō (1660–1704), of whom Berthold provides a vivid, if somewhat hyperbolic, capsule biography:

> In his teens he was a member of a strolling troupe. When he appeared for the first time in Edo, in 1763, he covered his face thickly with red and white paint for the part of an *aragoto* hero. This was the birth of the Kabuki theatre's make-up mask. Danjūrō took over the declamatory style of the puppet theatre, whose rhapsodist Izumidayu, in Edo, he greatly admired and took as his model. Danjūrō was a short and stocky man of astonishing physical strength and vocal power, which, as the chroniclers relate, caused not only the stage to shake but the porcelain in nearby stores as well. When he opened all the stops of emotion in some *aragoto* part, his thundering voice could be heard miles away. Danjūrō's ideal was the hero of the Samurai world. Like Tōjūrō, he wrote at least some of his plays himself or adapted them from Nōh scripts. By an irony of history this invincible hero was killed by the sword of a rival actor during a dispute in the dressing room of the Ichimura-za Theatre in Edo.

The third of this trio of early Kabuki stars, Yoshizawa Ayame (1763–?), was a female impersonator, persuasive in the role offstage as well as on, keeping on his feminine attire in the dressing room and even on the street. He rationalized this transvestism by claiming that it was imperative for him always to remain in "character". In private life, too, he played the courtesan's role, and this fixation of his helped to make it almost a rule – or, at least, a Kabuki convention – that the *onnagata*'s part was most often that of an unhappy courtesan. Another standard character is the distressed wife.

As already stated, the best Kabuki plays by far are those from the teeming fancy and busy hand of Chikamatsu Monzaemon (1653–1725); that was his stage name. He was born Sugimori Nobumori, a samurai. As was the custom, he chose for his career in the theatre – as a tribute – the name of an older performer whom he admired and hoped to emulate. This practice was followed by a host of successors to Tōjūrō and Danjūrō, few if any of whom had any familial kinship with either of them. After Chikamatsu's death, however, no other aspiring playwright ever had the effrontery to borrow *his* name. From nineteen on, having quit studies for the priesthood, the ambitious and restless young man settled in Kyoto, where he was in service to a Lord Ogimachi, and alternatively to several other noble masters. Lord Ogimachi composed plays for the doll theatre, which is how Chikamatsu first became closely acquainted with the possibilities of puppetry as a dramatic art form. In his next phase he became a *ronin* (outlaw) and engaged in many desperate forays of the sort he was later to write about, knowing the exhilaration and danger of such activities at first hand, transferring them with great authenticity to the stage. The plots of his plays are replete with violence and his language falls little short of bombast, but even hostile Western critics – such as W.G. Aston in his *History of Japanese Literature* – grant him "a certain barbaric vigor and luxuriance", and perhaps much of the colour of his dialogue is lost in translation.

Beginning with scripts for the Kabuki theatre, he became frustrated and irate. Shifting to the rival puppet stage, for which he did his best work, he turned out, at a furious pace, about 150 plays. Some are adaptations from a variety of sources. Today fifty-one survive in print and are identified by scholars as truly his – though not all agree, setting the number at barely twenty. He is said to have written so rapidly that he started and finished a full-length play in one sleepless night. Most of his output is very long, the design epic, the incidents profuse, lasting from eight to twelve hours when performed without elisions.

His range is all-encompassing: pathos and comedy, in prose and verse. He supplies horrifying scenes of torture to ensure an unceasing flow of thrills, and he is fond of capping lovers' dilemmas with double suicides, like that of Romeo and Juliet. (He is nearly contemporary with Shakespeare, but the Japanese propensity to refer to him as the Bard's equal and rival is hardly shared by Europeans, who reject it as an over-generous evaluation.) A vein of eroticism is very pronounced.

Like Tōjūrō, he was best at domestic melodramas, a genre derived from the *ningyo jōruri*. In time, four categories of Kabuki came to be recognized, the first being the historical (*jidaimono*), glorifying the heroic exploits and values of the loyal, bold samurai; the *sewamono*, picturing husband–wife conflicts in the dwellings of merchants, traders and artisans; the *aragoto*, centring on a strong man, wearing heavy make-up and given to threatening, florid speech; and the *shosagoto*, a dancing piece, perhaps without a plot-line or accompanied by a chorus chanting the words of a ballad, performed to the music of a *samisen*, flutes, a booming big drum and rhythmically slapped hand-drums. Occasionally the *shosagoto* is comic, or it may illustrate the lyrical aspects of the story.

In Chikamatsu's works the characters' basic struggle is between their all-too-human passions and the strict moral code of the period, in many ways still feudal. Ultimately they overcome doubts and hesitations and reach the right ethical decisions, though at tragic personal cost: a samurai upholds his honour by an extreme gesture, a courtesan rejects a chance to escape her lot by an equivalent deed of self-sacrifice.

The first script attributed to him is *The Evil Spirit of Lady Wisteria*, staged in Edo in 1677. He created a vogue with his *shinju* plays, as they are known, those leading to a climax involving the double suicide of ill-fated lovers, a theme that he is supposed to have initiated. His most esteemed contribution is *Kikusenya Kassen* (*The Battles of Kikusenya*), written in 1710 or 1715, which begins with a rivalry between a Tartar king and a Ming emperor for a concubine's favour. An invasion of China follows, but the immense Tartar hosts are driven off by a handful of resourceful Chinese warriors under the command of Go Sankei, a loyal general whose feats are prodigious. In the course of this bloody tale a traitorous minister blinds himself in one eye, using his own dagger to accomplish his mutilation; the Emperor is decapitated and his murderer suffers the same dire fate at the hands of the indomitable Go Sankei. The brave general rescues the hapless concubine who has been the cause of all this trouble, but she is shot and dies. Since she is pregnant by the now headless Emperor, Go Sankei saves her unborn child by personally carrying out a Caesarean operation. The infant, torn from her body, is heir to the imperial throne and is sought by his late father's implacable foes. Go Sankei slays his own son and displays the corpse as that of the little royal scion, whom he has safely hidden. Go Sankei's wife, accompanied by an imperial princess, flees to Japan, where the two women win promises of assistance. Now the central figure is Watonai, a half-Japanese warrior of great repute, who – with his aged mother astride his back – sets out to right the wrongs that have been wrought in China. With the aid of a tiger that he has tamed, Watonai defeats the minions of the evil pretender to sovereign power. He joins forces with Go Sankei, and this possibly over-heated play ends with more battles on an exceptionally grand scale.

Lighter in spirit is Chikamatsu's *Fair Ladies at a Dance of Poem-Cards*, detailing a court intrigue prompted by the jealous infatuation of an evil minister for a charming noble lady. But even this entertaining piece contains its share of beheadings and other killings, before it reaches its happy ending, where those exiled from court are restored to their rightful places at it.

Retitled in English *The Crucified Lovers* – in Japanese, *Chikamatsu Monogatari* – a filmed version of one of the playwright's typical domestic dramas was made in 1954; somewhat belatedly, it had a showing at the New York Film Festival in 1970, after which it was exhibited commercially in the city. The story is of Mohei, assistant to a scroll-maker, who is secretly in love with his master's wife. When she finds herself financially embarrassed he endeavours to help her. Their misguided efforts compromise them, forcing them to flee, and the ensuing situation leads to an adulterous relationship. The husband, dishonoured, contrives with Mohei's father to have the guilty couple returned. For their impulsive acts the castigated pair are led off in a ritual procession to a public crucifixion. In addition, the husband is ruined; his factory, the most prosperous in Kyoto, is ordered to be confiscated.

On just one viewing, Roger Greenspun, in the *New York Times*, was quite convinced that the film had greatness.

For much of its length, it takes place within a single household, and it is given to a massive exploration of the master scrollmaker's office, workrooms, kitchen, and living quarters. The interiors at times resemble a Constructivist stage set, with its allocation of levels, spaces, and connecting stairways; and the action, at least up to the actual flight, borders on the edge of bedroom comedy.

It is only after the flight – and especially during one breath-taking scene at night in a small boat, when the couple decide against suicide and suddenly learn that they are lovers – that the film opens out, just for a few moments at a time, into that gorgeous misty countryside that we have come to expect as the metaphysical universe of the Kenji Mizoguchi film dramas, such as *Ugetsu* and *The Bailiff*, with which we are already familiar.

I think the reason is that *Chikamatsu Monogatari* is in profound ways really about the rigorous complexity of its interiors and courtyards; that it is about relationships (man–woman, brother–sister, child–parent, servant–master) and responsibilities, and about the absolute fantastic interdependency of everything upon everything else. Therefore, the film's appearance is moment-by-moment an extension of its theme, and the stultifying closeness of every life with every other above it, below it, and next to it is in fact the metaphysical universe of this particular Mizoguchi drama.

That universe is somehow incomplete without its adulterous lovers (we see one pair at the beginning of the film, and then, of course, the hero and heroine at the end) and their sacrificial murders. They stand as if for all the potential of a responsive personal life that is rigorously excluded from the social structure of public and familial worlds. They are outlaws and yet they are representative (everybody's life in *Chikamatsu Monogatari*, just below the surface is, or could be, a mess); they are dangerous and beautiful; they are necessary – and they are genuinely intolerable. The master scrollmaker Ishun, an unpleasant character, is brought to ruin because he has been cuckolded – and his punishment is not less real, or less unjust, than his wife's.

I don't want to give the impression that *Chikamatsu Monogatari* is all scheme (though it is highly schematic) and without more sensuous pleasures. The performances are graceful, gentle, individualized and lovely. The music, which is mostly Japanese, ranks with the most expressive I have ever heard in a film. And the look of the film, indoors or out, is like a tribute to the traditions of Japanese genre painting and the pictorial logic of the old almost square-shaped movie screen.

The picture was produced by Masaichi Nagata, directed by Kenji Mizoguchi, from a screen adaptation by Yoshitkata and Matsutara Kwaguchi. The musical score was by Fumio Hayasaka, Tamezo Machizuki and Eijiro Toyosawa.

Often coupled with Chikamatsu's name is that of Takeda Izumo II (1688–1756) as one who did much to advance Kabuki drama. Son of an actor–manager, he wrote mostly for the puppet stage and was chosen to take charge of the prestigious Takemoto-za in Osaka when Takemoto Gidayo, its founder, retired in 1705. As with other writers for the doll theatre, his plays were appropriated by Kabuki companies who thought it urgent to use the better-constructed Bunraku scripts in order to retrieve audiences they were losing to the puppeteers. Popular among Izumo's works is his *Sugawara Denju Tenari Kogami* (*Sugawara's Writing Lesson*), another chilling story of treachery and sacrifice. In one scene a loyal retainer cuts off the head of his own son and pretends that it belongs to the severed body of the heir of his exiled lord Sugawara Michizane, so as to keep from harm the noble's boy. The episode, of course, is similar to that of Go Sankei's forfeiture of the life of his child in *The Battles of Kikusenya*.

Far better known and cherished, however, is his *Kanadehon Chushingura* (1748, or *The Revenge of the Forty-seven Ronin*) written in collaboration with Shoraku (1696?–1771?) and Senrya Namiki (1695–1751?). Scarcely a year elapses without a revival of this epic play – or, at least, excerpts from it – by the Bunraku (it was originally intended for the puppet theatre) or by various Kabuki companies. Almost fifty works have taken up this subject, starting from an actual incident about a half-century earlier (1701). Among others, Chikamatsu offered a five-act version of it, and because the tale is so cinematic it has readily lent itself to unfolding on film.

In their version, Takeda Izumo II and his collaborators expand the drama to eleven acts. They change the names of the participants and move the time of the events to several centuries earlier. A young feudal lord, Hangan, in response to being insulted by a rude fellow noble, Kono Moronao, draws his sword against him, an act absolutely forbidden in the Shōgunate's palace. For this offence he is ordered by the Shōgun to kill himself. Hangan submits to this cruel demand, committing *hara-kiri* in a grisly scene. His castles and domains are confiscated. His loyal retainers, numbering forty-seven and left masterless, are appalled and infuriated. They vow to avenge their master, their anger directed chiefly against the Shōgun and his arrogant, if craven, minion. But the forty-seven samurai know that they must be cautious and wait if they are to succeed at their mission. Their dilemma is that not to exact a penalty for their lord's death would violate their code, but to do so will surely cost them their lives, for they will be disobeying the law. Their first step is to separate, some to assume service with other masters, others feigning to take up various trades. They pretend to have forgotten their pledge as samurai. But at the right moment they reunite and set out as outlaws – *ronin* – against their enemy's castle, which they have penetrated and spied on in the guise of tradesmen, so that they are familiar with its layout and defences. Knowing that their foe has a false sense of security, and under cover of night and a snowstorm, they force the gates, slay the guards and capture their enemy. Cowardly, he refuses to kill himself, as they insist, so at last they decapitate him. They march with his head to the temple of Sengakuji, in the grounds of which their beloved master is buried, and place the bloody head on his grave. Their honour intact, they disperse again to the castles and houses where they have recently been dwelling, and each ritualistically carries out *hara-kiri* as they had anticipated they were condemned to do. They are hailed by the populace for their remarkable fidelity to their lord and the samurai ethic.

This is a mere outline of the plot which contains many subordinate complications, passages of intense pathos, as when the lord's wife learns that her husband must die – even when enacted by puppets, the scene moistens the eyes of many spectators – and, for effective contrast and relief, snatches of high comedy. A romantic figure is Lady Kaoyo, desired by the black-hearted Kono Moronao who tries to press his lecherous intention upon her and, as his overlord, threatens to ruin her husband's career if she resists. After her husband's suicide, the faithful wife performs final rites for him and cuts off her hair to symbolize that she will enter a nunnery. A high point is when Yuranosuke, the leader of the *ronin*, weeping, lifts his dead master's stained blade and tastes the blood on it to indicate his grief and as a promise of avenging fury.

On tour in New York City (1969), a company calling itself the Grand Kabuki offered four acts of *Chushingura*, evoking this response from Clive Barnes in the *New York Times*: "These excerpts showed the stately and graceful mood of the piece, its high seriousness in the Aristotelian sense of drama, its tragic sense of human destiny, and, of course, its picture of the Japanese samurai world."

In 1749, the year after *Chushingura*, Takeda Izumo II and Senrya Namiki collaborated once again, this time composing *Yoshitune Sembonzakura* (*The Thousand Cherry Blossoms of Yoshitune*), one of the three Kabuki works still most frequently performed. Having been defeated by Yoshitune, three humili-ated Taira generals seek to equal the score. The play is a perennial favourite because, as one critic has said, "it has everything: spectacle, dance, music, rapid-fire costume changes, revolving back-drops, magic acts". One of the characters is a fox who assumes human form in a spirit of "filial piety", to revenge the death of his parents, slain by hunters.

A third important Kabuki playwright, who came later, is Kawatake Mokuami (1816–93). Breaking away from the practice of joining a team paid to crank out stage-vehicles, he mostly worked alone. Even so, he provided countless scripts – some scholars believe approximately fifty, other state over 350, counting his adaptations of Nōh plays and his dipping into other sources. His popularity endures; of today's Kabuki repertory, at least half the plays offered are by him.

At the start of his career his *forte* was domestic dramas to which he brought a heightened social realism, his scripts often thronging with thieves, murderers and other unsavoury characters from the lower strata of city life. He had considerable success with these so-called "thief plays".

After the abdication of the last Shōgun and the Meiji Restoration (1868), most vestiges of feudal-ism and the samurais' domination of society disappeared; they were no longer allowed to carry swords. The Japanese public had a new outlook, many new interests and decidedly new values. Mokuami quickly grasped the significance of these widespread changes and wrote scripts on political subjects; they are termed "living history plays", he stressed historical accuracy and strove for literary excel-lence, along with doses of moral preachments. It was soon apparent that theatre-goers were less inclined to patronize these more serious dramas.

In a third phase, Mokuami undertook a series of "cropped hair plays", given that tag because they featured Japanese men now seeking to be considered "modern", cutting off their top-knots and wear-ing their hair short. He called for a stage populated with characters in more modern dress and sets furnished with many Western objects, most of them still novelties. Rejecting the past, his characters were concerned with topical problems, such as education for girls, and even compulsory schooling for all social classes, and military conscription. But some of his characterizations verged on caricatures. In many ways a writer of distinction, Mokuami offered work that is thoughtful, and studded with power-ful lyrical passages. He was an exemplar for his contemporaries, for whom he found a direction that they rapidly accepted. He was exceptional. The precedent he set of being the sole author of a script has held.

Earlier, there is some artistry in the output of Tsuruka Namboku IV (*c.* 1755–1829), who also dealt with underworld characters in a sordid milieu of "brutality, eroticism, and macabre humor". Another Kabuki playwright of this period, Gohei I. Namiki (1747–1808), first worked in Kyoto and Osaka, then moved to Edo and brought with him a more stringent kind of social realism in domestic plays described as "bare". To this group also belongs Segawa Jokō III.

The decades bridging the first half of the nineteenth century are referred to as the Golden Age of Kabuki music and dance-oriented drama. Mostly what counts in Kabuki is not what is in the usual run of plays, but how they are staged. "Kabuki" means the "art of song and dance" – it is a form of entertainment with few if any pretensions to literary quality. The extant library of scripts comprises about 350 titles, the authors – or teams of authors – largely no longer known, and the texts so fragmented by years of hack writers making revisions and extracting episodes from here and there that often a sense of the original whole is lacking. It does not matter, for usually only cherished highlights from them are enacted, a programme regularly consisting of short scenes from a number of different works; on some occasions there may be a thematic link.

From the late seventeenth to the mid-nineteenth century, star actors competed and flourished, some becoming cult figures claiming thousands of admirers. As in Nōh, acting families or dynasties were established, lasting until today; lacking a true heir to succeed a famed father and grandfather, a talented young member of the troupe is adopted and takes his foster-parent's stage-name. To this name is attached a numeral – perhaps Tōjūrō II, Tōjūrō III – indicating his place in a historical line, as with royalty. By now the identifying number is likely to be a high one, such as Onoe Baiko VII and Uzaemon XIV, testifying to the many-generational, long-lived aspects of Kabuki.

After women and boys were excluded from stage appearances, and only adult men could perform, a government decree stipulated that male actors must shave their forelocks, so that, looking more like monks, they would seem less sexually attractive. But heavy, horrific make-up required for many traditional roles made that dictate hardly necessary. Besides, erotic scenes and dances were forbidden. The actors do have the advantage, however, of frequently being garbed in dazzling robes, the heavy silken fabrics multicoloured and richly ornamented, as elsewhere in the Orient.

The long and arduous training for membership in a troupe begins when the apprentice is about six. Since there are many children's roles in the repertory, on-stage experience comes early. Most actors prepare for making a career of undertaking specific roles: an old man, a geisha, a warrior, a merchant, a high-ranking governor. As the plays grew longer and the plots more complicated, the casts became larger and the characterizations, with a few exceptions, mostly shallow and stock, further categorized into narrower types: the good-hearted courtesan, the evil-scheming courtesan; the bold warrior, the warrior torn by conflicting loyalties and thereby weakened; the resolute heroine, the timorous heroine; and so forth. There are perhaps a half-dozen kinds of villains, depending on the degree of their wickedness. Do they inflict trouble with zest or only half-willingly, still having some decent instincts? The actors do not use masks. For some roles the make-up emphasizes the bony and muscular conformation of their facial features. Brockett: "Upon a white base red and black patterns are normally painted, although demons and evil characters may use blue or brown. The *onnagata* (female impersonator) draws in false eyebrows and adds rouging at the corner of the eye and to the mouth but otherwise leaves the face completely white. Married women blacken their teeth and obliterate their eyebrows. For some of the more athletic male roles, the arms and legs are made up in a conventional pattern. The make-up of each role is symbolic of the character."

The costume worn for each role is also traditional. If the play is based on a historical incident, a garment adapted from the style of the period is likely to be used; but the companies have large wardrobes of costly attire on hand and often mix the dress of different epochs, being little concerned with details of historical accuracy. Of heavy materials and voluminous, a costume may weigh as much as fifty pounds and bears down on the actor, who may require assistance to move about gracefully. Accordingly, he is helped by black-clothed attendants, by convention to be considered invisible, who lift or shift about his train, lend a hand as he adjusts or disrobes and robes once more to change costumes, and bring him properties, a pen, a fan, a writing tablet, a sword, which he passes back when they have briefly served his purpose, leaving him unimpeded for his next move or gesture.

The fan is employed prominently. As in Nōh, it may suggest that the actor is astride a galloping horse, or aiming an arrow in his taut-strung bow, or opening a door, or even gazing at falling rain or a risen moon. A scarf, deftly handled, may convey many different things that the spectator knows how to interpret if familiar with this wordless vocabulary. Some properties are realistic, or only partly so: a horse may be represented by a velvet-covered, equine-shaped wooden mock-up; the actor, mounted on this framework, is supported by two black-clothed attendants, their presence clearly visible – at least, their legs – through openings in the trappings of the "horse". Swords, severed heads, wild beasts – monkeys, tigers – are handled in much the same way; what is being indicated is easily recognized, though it is not actually, solidly or fully presented on stage; the Oriental preference for theatrical illusion rather than simple realism is retained.

The small, square, roofed, bare stage for Nōh was abandoned as not suited to Kabuki, which recruits much larger casts and offers stories that might call for much more physical action. The platform is wider, rectangular, with a *hanamichi* ("flower bridge") extending fully into the auditorium at one side and on which all entrances and exits take place, with the performers' feet just above the spectators' eye level as they glance in that direction to follow the players' appearances and disappearances. Occasionally the setting might be as plain as in Nōh – a back curtain with a lone pine tree painted on it – but far more often it is elaborate and offers many changes of scene. Once the revolving platform was invented, it was much used, as were elevator traps that lifted or lowered individual actors. Those mechanical devices are still employed. Later, in some of the larger playhouses, a second, smaller bridge was installed; it runs parallel to the *hanamichi* at the opposite side of the platform.

The intimacy that favoured the Nōh play was no longer a consideration, but rising costs of production – large casts, expensive scenery, stars' high salaries – were. The theatres grew larger, with balconies in tiers at either side. Much of the seating area, on the main floor and in the galleries, was divided into boxes. Tickets were bought at the outer gate, and most spectators sat on floor mats or wooden benches; there were gradations in price depending on seat location. Finally a need was felt for an "inner picture-frame stage" that boasts a draw curtain and deeper space to allow various arrangements of background hangings.

Certain properties became standard and suggest where the action is occurring. An example of this, cited by Berthold, is a setting with a profusion of gold-painted screens that identify the locale of a palace in which a *jidaimono* drama is being enacted; such offerings, as a result, have come to be known as "gold-screen plays". More colour is added by the draw curtain, which has broad, vertical stripes of black, green and orange.

Scenery changes are effected without concealment, if not by use of the revolving platform or elevator traps, then in full view by the black-garbed attendants, who are sort of exalted stage-hands. The paintings on the back-drops are flat; there is no attempt at perspective, and frequently the back curtain depicts a far-off, hazy landscape, bordered on top by a black valance. The flats do not fit together neatly but expose the cracks between them; this is another instance of a desire not to be too realistic. Brockett: "White mats represent snow, blue mats water, gray mats the ground, different kinds of trees indicate changes of locale. This mingling of the familiar with the conventional makes Kabuki, among all the Oriental traditional forms, most accessible to Westerners."

The musicians may visibly occupy different spots on stage, perhaps at the right, or at the left; or sometimes at the back. The *samisen* is the most prominent instrument; alongside it are the flutes, drums, bells, gongs and cymbals; the orchestra members have on the ceremonial garb worn by the samurai: split skirt, beneath a kimono, and stiff epaulets. When not performing, the musicians are seated upright; they stare blank-faced at the audience. In some instances, to achieve a special effect, extra musicians may be hidden behind a screen at the right of the stage. The music, though subordinate, is important because it provides impetus and rhythmic cues for the dancing, and also enforces the action and character interpretation by being descriptive and mood-setting. Each dramatic work has a traditional score.

The actors do not sing. As in Bunraku, a narrator sets the scene, explains facets of the plot and comments on the behaviour of the characters, and speaks all or some part of the dialogue, the degree of his contribution varying from script to script. In plays where the lines are largely assigned to the actors, a chorus or the narrator will still insert songs and chant and recite some significant passages. In delivering their lines the actors employ an intonation that is both traditional and unique to Kabuki. The dialogue adheres to a variety of fixed metrical patterns.

Dance is an essential component of Kabuki. Incorporated in it are traces of many earlier forms, from the sacred dances, from the folk, from the Nōh, from the burlesque Kyōgen, from the rival puppets and other popular sources. David B. Waterhouse writes:

> As with Nōh, no sharp distinction can be made between dance and other stage movements. Indeed, Kabuki theatre is above all dance. It fuses many influences into a supremely self-confident whole, stylized but immediate in its impact on the audience. In contrast to Nōh, Kabuki loves gaudy, spectacular and sensational effects, and its dances reflect this taste. Two early styles were *tanzen* and *roppo*, used from the late Seventeenth Century for boisterous male entrances. These contributed to the *aragoto* (rough business) style of Ichikawa Danjuro and his line. Simultaneously the term *shosagoto* (dance style) came to be used for the dances of female impersonators; and many types were developed, notably the *henge-mono* (quick-change pieces), in which the actor changes costume several times on stage in the course of performing a dance. *Shosagoto* became the most important kind of Kabuki dance, differentiated mainly according to the various types of music that accompany it: the lyrical *Naguata*, or the more narrative *Tokiwazu-Bushi*, *Tomimoto-Bushi*, *Kiyomoto-Bushi*, and so on. The late Eighteenth Century saw a revival of male-role (*Tachi-yaku*) dancing.

A unique characteristic of Kabuki acting-dance is the *mie*, a static pose, an "attitude", struck and held for a very conscious moment, after which the actor moves on to the next *mie*, and perhaps a slow series of them. His posture in each *mie* is meant to be closely studied and appreciated by the spectator. Noise from wooden clappers lends loud emphasis to each entrance and exit.

At first only female impersonators danced, but before the end of the eighteenth century this element was broadened, and professional choreographers were necessary staff members for every troupe: in turn, they founded their own schools, training and graduating proficient students whom they licensed; some of these dance academies, now venerable, are still active after 200 years.

On occasion, Kabuki companies offer programmes made up only of dances excerpted from the dramas; this is particularly apt to occur when the troupes are on tour in foreign cities where audiences have to contend with an especially daunting language barrier.

Invariably such a programme includes one or another variation of *Kagami-Jishi* (*The Mirror Lion Dance*), perpetually acclaimed. The scenario: at New Year, in the Shōgun's castle, it is traditional for one of the ladies-in-waiting to don a lion's mask and dance to ward off evil spirits. Yayoi, who is very shy, is chosen to do this and tries to avoid it by running away. She is brought back to the palace and locked in a room there. Alone, she begins to dance, at first tentatively, wearing the mask; gradually it takes over, until she is possessed by the lion's spirit. A pair of butterflies flutter about; the lion – Yayoi – pursues them along the *hanamichi* and the three vanish.

The butterflies, now in the guise of two maidens, return in a dance. The music grows more agitated as the lion joins them, with long white mane swirling. The setting is a grove of peonies, and the pace of the dance is increasingly more furious. This item, abstracted from the whole story, may be given in an ever more simplified form, sometimes as a duet. (Actually there are no lions in Japan, so this persistent motif in its mythology is a bit strange.)

The respect for social hierarchy that infused the feudal system is still evident in Kabuki, where an actor portraying a high-ranking personage – an emperor, a Shōgun, a noble or a distinguished guest – enters and exits and occupies the stage at right, while the lowly characters are relegated to the left.

An interesting footnote is that the Kabuki, having adopted the revolving stage, was perhaps the very first to use it for flashbacks.

Edo's theatres suffered destructive fires in 1841 and again in 1855; they were replaced with much larger ones, with enhanced technical resources. Even more radical changes came after the end of the Edo era and the beginning of the Restoration, when power finally reverted from the Shōgunate to the imperial family, the rule wielded by wise, benevolent Emperor Meiji, while Japan frantically sought to Westernize. The effort was reflected in the physical theatre as well as in the content of plays. The proscenium arch, creating a picture-frame stage, was introduced in 1907 and became standard in most other Kabuki playhouses everywhere after 1923. Electric lighting was added as soon as possible, as was "flying machinery". By decree in 1868 the length of a play's presentation was limited to eight hours, and viewing was eased for spectators when mats and wooden benches were replaced by folding seats and fauteuils. The second, lesser *hanamichi* was removed, though it is occasionally re-installed if a particular drama's action requires it.

More significant than these helpful but minor physical alterations was the advent in 1883 of another rival to Kabuki itself. Shimpa (or "New School Movement") was an idealistic attempt by zealous Westernizers to use the stage as a vehicle for social protest and reform, and to have it more closely resemble European theatre, especially what was becoming known to local intellectuals about the rise overseas of the bold critical realists Ibsen, Strindberg and Shaw. The Shimpa playwrights sought to do away with Kabuki's outworn traditions, the lengthy speeches in a classical tongue not easily understood, the hackneyed subject-matter. Also, they were of the opinion that the dramatic action ought to proceed at a more rapid pace. Writers should embrace urgent, topical concerns. As John Nathan neatly encapsulates the new movement: "The early plays featured 'a martyr a minute' and borrowed a convention from Kabuki which gave a fatally wounded man five minutes to emote before drawing his last breath. His back gashed with a samurai sword, the actor would sink slowly to his knees and then go into his death throes while he declaimed: 'Down with the aristocrats! Up with the people!'"

Alas, before very long – 1888 – the chief motivation for these diatribes against harsh authoritarianism was taken away by the establishment of a constitutional parliamentary government. The need for political rebellion was largely gone.

To fill the gap, Shimpa authors next resorted to exploiting and glorifying melodramatic events in the Sino-Japanese War (1894), a victorious if gory foray. After a decade or so these ready appeals to patriotic sentiments were exhausted, and yet newer themes were required.

Shimpa writers noticed that gushy, romantic newspaper serials had an insidious appeal to female readers, who were seemingly addicted to them. Transferred to the stage, this material proved to be irresistible to large, faithful audiences of women. Very soon Shimpa completely changed its character and purpose, becoming the equivalent to what was later known in the television realm as "soap opera". Shimpa's goal now was to evoke tears, "buckets of them". The stories, well dubbed "sudsy", were mostly about the woes of distressed wives and geishas. Submissive, as the culture demands they be, they are forced to perform thankless acts of self-sacrifice.

Of this species, *famiri doroman* or "family drama", the signal work was *The History of a Woman* (1908), by Kyoka Izuma. A teaching assistant falls deeply in love with a geisha. With sincere passion she returns his feelings. But the young man's mentor, a professor at the same university, chooses the assistant as a suitable son-in-law, assuring him of a promotion and a bright future in the academic world. The geisha nobly yields her claim, persuading the young man that he must accept this opportunity, whatever the cost to her. Lovelorn, she returns to her life as a geisha, to mourn her crucial loss forever. This set the pattern for a moist flow of Shimpa scripts, all of them essentially not unlike *La Dame aux Camélias*, as depicted by Dumas *fils*. For the next fifty-six years *The History of a Woman* continued to be the top box-office attraction in playhouses offering Shimpa, until 1964, which marked the death of Shotaro Hanayanagi, the great female impersonator long identified with the role of the forlorn geisha. The play was withdrawn, for a time at least, out of respect to the memory of a truly admired artist, and perhaps because few others cared to compete with still vivid recollections of a long haunting, moving portrayal.

John Nathan, while residing as a graduate student in Japan (1938), had an unusual and amusing experience with Shimpa. He was suddenly recruited to take the role of Townsend Harris, the first American envoy to Japan (1856–60) in a work about the irascible Harris and a young geisha, Okichi-san, less than half his age, whom ingratiating officials force to serve as his mistress. Though unwilling, and loathing the *tojin* ("barbarian"), she does everything to please him, comforting and nursing him through illness, and even putting her life in jeopardy for him. But he speaks no Japanese, and she no English, so they are never able to communicate properly. In the end the ungrateful, finicky Harris, wearying of her, abruptly turns her out. She now finds herself in much trouble; her previous lover has disappeared, and the government views her with suspicion and accuses her of having provided a foreigner with glasses of milk, a practice forbidden at that time. Returning to her native village, and homeless, she is greeted with derision by her ex-neighbours; they spit in her face with ugly cries of "Barbarian lover!" Crazed with grief and shame, she slowly wanders off, disgraced and quite alone, while a huge drum thumps ominously and the spectators, eyes wet, curse the foreigner for his mistreatment of her. Nathan was enlisted for the role of Harris because he was actually a foreigner and could speak English, thus lending the part more authenticity.

The production, though lavish, was allowed only five days for rehearsal. Nathan's previous acting experience consisted of having taken part in plays at Harvard while studying there. Since he spoke English in the role, he found that "only the ludicrous and brutish aspects of the character" were imparted to most of the audience. "Not that there was anything else to communicate." The casting of a foreigner was at the insistence of sixty-one-year-old Yaeko Mizutani (the "Empress" of Shimpa, the Helen Hayes of Japan) who felt that no native actor could be as persuasive in the role of the heartless Harris.

With Shimpa offering so many stories about betrayed wives and geishas, the supply of female impersonators began to run hopelessly short. After centuries of banishment, women were at last allowed to return to both Kabuki and Shimpa stages, where they might appear in the same cast alongside the graceful, delicate *onnagata*. The first actress to be admitted to a Shimpa troupe had been Yaeko Mizutani (1928), who thirty-five years later was the luckless young Okichi-san opposite the student Nathan. But age was not a consideration in choosing players for roles. The actor selected as the geisha's lover, the handsome carpenter Tsurumatsu, was fifty-one.

From his vantage in a Shimpa company, Nathan surveyed the repertory, the performers, the typical audience. The plays, inexhaustible variations on the simple theme of feminine victimization, were truly melodramas, in that they disregarded all dramatic laws of cause and effect.

There are no conflicts generated by individual egos, no transitions, no real development. Instead, there are isolated moments of distilled joy or grief: a romance about to flower is suddenly crushed under the boot of circumstance; lonely friends find themselves radiantly and profoundly in love. The audience, which is eighty-five per cent female, responds – hysterically.

The play, definitely, is not the thing. No one pays much attention to the in-between episodes that transport the story, but when lights, or music, or a new entrance heralds the coming of an emotional moment, the audience tenses, waiting. When the heroine is humiliated – it doesn't matter why as long as every one can see that it has happened – the ladies out front turn red with rage and shame. Let the actress weep and they will weep. . . .

The chance to indulge in emotional frenzy is, of course, one explanation of Shimpa's popularity, which has bafflingly persisted despite a radical reorienting of society that should have destroyed it long ago. For Shimpa audiences – mostly middle-aged and nostalgic for days gone by – Japanese propriety still requires a man to suppress what he feels, to push it deep down inside him where it won't show. But at the theatre anything goes. The people on the stage cry when it hurts and laugh and smile when they are happy. In doing so, they touch a secret spring in the audience. The uncontrollable surge of suppressed joy or grief produces hysteria, which is followed by soothing calm.

Nathan paid close attention to the practical side of Shimpa, how the plays were staged. His close-up look is of considerable historical value.

A production entails five or six full-length plays, presented every day, two or three at the matinée and two or three at the evening performance. Most of the seventy-odd players in the troupe appear in at least three of the plays presented each month. This means that some of the actors must be in the theatre from ten in the morning until ten at night. With the exception of the stars, a title reserved for six aging veterans whose popularity has lasted a minimum of thirty years, the Shimpa actor earns amazingly little. Most have to do television work after hours in order to make ends meet.

Since the troupe must perform twenty-five days a month to stay in the black, they have only five or six days at month's end to prepare for the next performance. This rules out rehearsals as we think of them in the West. Actors cut their own lines and cues out of the script and make little booklets of them, one for each play they appear in. No one ever knows what comes before or after his own scenes. The director's job is to supply new lines, to block in crowd scenes and to come up with interesting business to fill the gaps. Interpretation is left to the actors.

The troupe does not assemble on stage until the last day of rehearsal, the fifth day, when the plays are rehearsed from beginning to end for the first and only time. Miraculously, the pieces fall together, lights and music are somehow synchronized and, except that costumes and wigs will not arrive until the opening day, there is a semblance of a dress rehearsal. Naturally, no one knows his lines. Since five or six plays must be run through end to end, this final rehearsal usually lasts all night; traditionally, the Shimpa troupe faces its opening-day audience sleepless.

But members of the casts did not complain at these difficult circumstances. One player, eyes puffy, told Nathan: "Everything is timed so that we're in the worst possible condition when the curtain goes up on opening day. The idea is that things can only improve when you're as low as you can get. The hardest part is the first week, until you know your lines. Once you've got them down, you can start having some fun."

To Nathan it was very clear that the casts were enjoying themselves, though there was a great deal of reliance on the hooded prompters lurking around every blind corner of the Shimpa stage. He was aware, too, of much improvisation.

At one point, a whole speech was lifted from one of the evening plays and spliced into a matinée performance. And it didn't matter. The audience isn't looking for polish in a performance, or even cogency. They already know the story, or one just like it, and they require only the cues, the set expressions of joy and grief that activate their tears and laughter. The main body of the play has no dramatic value whatsoever; its only function is to connect what are called *atari*, literally "strikes." The Shimpa players move into these "emotion moments" with the sureness of a well-trained basketball team: a lightning pass from upstage right, a drive to center, the lay-up, and someone tips the ball in, bringing down the house.

The acting in Shimpa is far more realistic than in Kabuki; at times, Kabuki actors cross a line and join Shimpa casts. This proved to be good preparation for the onset of Shingeki, the Westernized theatre that was to make its appearance in Japan in 1924; also helpful was the admission of women to the ranks of players after two centuries.

Bridging the leap from traditional Japanese drama to the incursion of scripts and productions fashioned in the manner of classic and modern European and American theatre were slice-of-life plays with major changes of format such as those ventured by Seto Eiichi in *Two Paths* (1931) and Kawaguchi Matsutaro in *Song of the Elegant Fukuagawa* (1935).

The period during which Shimpa outdrew its rival forms of theatre was comparatively short-lived;

its appeal lessened as it was overtaken by films and television which outdid it in offering stories drenched in sentimentality. But if it did not long supplant Kabuki, neither has it wholly vanished. It still has a public following, smaller but faithful. At its zenith, through the early decades of the twentieth century, its actors were often influential style-setters, starting vogues in modes of dress – the proper kimono, the appropriate sash – and hair-dos.

For the most part, Kabuki actors clung to their discipline and long inculcated conventions, refusing to be swayed by the frenetic advance of Westernization. As the fad for Shimpa faded, Kabuki's audience returned, and its theatres prospered once again. This was partly due to the fortuitous cropping up of a cluster of brilliant performers in the decades making up the first half of the twentieth century, legendary illustrious figures such as Baigyoku, Koshiro VII, Sojuro, Kikugoro VI, Enjaku, Uzaemon XIV, Nakamura Kichiemon, artists of talent who dominated stages in Osaka, Tokyo, Nagoya and elsewhere. They were considered "titans", exemplars of great skill.

At seventy-three, Baigyoku was still capable of playing the role of a nineteen-year-old girl with the utmost persuasiveness, the incarnation of charming youthful femininity. Similarly, one of the last-living of the group, Kichiemon, undertook the part of Kumagi, the warrior general, when close to seventy and gravely ill; indeed, he was hardly able to walk. This was witnessed by Bowers:

> Compared with the many times I have seen his other performances of the role, it was of course the least active and unenergetic. But he suffused the stage with a glow and tension I have never seen before. His voice was all the better for the inactivity of his body. His lines, for which he had always been famous, were projected with such clarity that even someone not familiar with the text could understand their import. But most of all, each meaning was so charged with feeling that actor and interpretation, stage and real tragedy become one. In the most famous scene of the play, for instance, when Kumagi, recounting a battle, casually picks up his sword and brushes it with his fan (dusting the enemy warrior he supposedly lifts from the ground), Kichiemon demonstrated in a single gesture a whole vocabulary of stage terms – case, conviction, master, focus, and meaning in movement.

His death in 1954 was thought to be the close of an era, the end of a distinguished line of performers who possessed the "grand manner"; but an impressive new group of star actors soon arose to replicate them.

Earning the tag the "Great Five", this younger band was comprised of Baiko VII, an *onnagata* of seldom paralleled gifts; Shoroku II, an especially well-trained, highly adept dancer; Ebuzi; Utaemon; and not least, Koshiro. Though they belonged to different companies, in 1960 – and again in 1969 – several of them were united in a single *ad hoc* ensemble to travel abroad as cultural representatives and were seen in New York City and other major centres. Clive Barnes reported on this offering in the *New York Times*:

> In its gorgeous trappings – finely lacquered sets, brilliantly ornate costumes – it seems remote from the Western theater and can be matched in our experience only by Kathakali dance-drama, the Peking opera and, of course, its brother Japanese forms of Bunraku, the puppet theater and the dance theater of Gagaku.
>
> Here is ritual theater of a species hardly understood in the West. Everything is delicately stylized, so that gesture becomes virtually minimal, and the actors are all but impassive in their passions. Yet within this deliberately circumscribed range of movement and expression, which is even further restricted by the artificiality of some of the movements, the actors can express humanity with all of the richness of their Western colleagues.
>
> Kabuki is far from being a remote art – indeed it was developed as a realistic counter of the more arcane and remote classic Nōh plays of the Japanese court, and from the first it has been a popular entertainment, mixing as did Greek drama, acting, singing and dancing in an early manifestation of what we now call "total theater."
>
> Yet it is not merely the unfamiliar style – tinkling, whining music, the high pitched voices, the women's roles all taken (and this is the height of stylization) superbly by men – that makes Kabuki strange and exotic to Western audiences. Any theater reflects the society that produces it – and in many respects this society is stranger to us than the art form that mirrors it.
>
> This is a Medieval Japanese world with its own code of honor. A world of lords, samurai and sudden death. The displeasure of a high lord could lead to *hara-kiri*, and honor was more important than life. Through this world stalk its heroes like puppets, only comprehensible in their actions by understanding their alien code of courtly behavior.

Further along in his review, Barnes observed:

> That Kabuki has a lighter side is shown in the evening's second piece, *Kagamijishi*, which is one of those lion dances for which Kabuki is famous. Here the form is particularly complex, for the lion is danced by a shy little lady-in-waiting, giving the actor performing the part – the company's star

Baiko, who was the wronged husband in the first piece – the chance to play both the *onnagata* role of the young girl and the magnificent Kabuki lion with its traditionally waving mane.

It is difficult to apply anything but the most subjective standards to acting so removed from Western ideals. However, it is clear that Baiko is a wonderful performer (a graceful dancer as well as an actor of remarkably controlled power) and this is also true of the other star of the troupe, Shoroku, who played the villainous and lecherous overlord in the first play.

In 1952 Kabuki received the ultimate accolade, an imperial honour, when for the first time in history the Emperor entered a public theatre and witnessed a play there, rather than confining his viewing to Bugaku and Nōh performances at court. Seemingly enthusiastic, applauding strenuously, he awarded a high court rank to the aged Kichiemon, who was also admitted to the Art Academy and proclaimed "a human national treasure". Subsequently other Kabuki actors have won official recognition of their outstanding talent, among them Baiko, who was nominated an "Intangible Cultural Person" (1968), and Senjaku, given a prize by the Ministry of Education, two in a lengthy roster.

The Grand Kabuki has visited Hawaii and Europe (1965), and Kabuki actors participated in the Universal Pantomime Festival in West Berlin (1962) and in Montreal's Expo '67. Some of the various ensembles' productions have been filmed and distributed, and others have been broadcast on television. With the lapse of another decade, the Grand Kabuki played in New York City once more (1979), presenting Chikamatsu's adaptation of a Nōh work, *Shunkan*, about an old man who exiles himself to a desolate island where he awaits death (this version was originally intended for the Bunraku). For a change of mood, the programme included *Renjishi*, based on a Chinese legend, another variation of the lion-dance theme – here a cub is trained by its parent to cope with the rigours of survival. It was performed by a father and son, Kanzaburo XVII and Kankuro, whose signature piece it had become. Still dancing the demanding role at seventy and earning praise for his dexterity and virtuosity, Kanzaburo XVII, too, had already been designated a Living National Treasure.

In Osaka (1948) the long-established theatre was foundering after the death of its great star Baigyoku, to whom the public was fanatically loyal. To save the troupe, a wealthy young critic and Nōh scholar, Takechi Tetsuji, took charge. He personally supervised the training of several young actors; they soon rose to prominence, notably the *onnagata* Senjaku, son of the venerable Osaka star Ganjiro. An iconoclast, Takechi took steps to expand the limits of Kabuki. He encouraged his actors to portray characters with far more realism, and experimented with producing a Western play in the style of Nōh, its music rendered on Western instruments. He brought in performers from other genres – Kyōgen, Shimpa, Takarazuka – and intermingled them with his Kabuki casts, to get fresh interpretations. He allowed franker displays of eroticism, shocking to many in his audiences, yet appropriate to the spirit in which Chikamatsu wrote in a less strait-laced era. All these innovations, quite contentious, brought crowds back to his theatre.

Acknowledging that the language of Kabuki was becoming less intelligible to the average modern Japanese, and seeking to have the subject-matter less remote and the characters' behaviour more human – his actors no longer fell back and crossed their eyes to indicate that they were dying, nor often moved like marionettes – Takechi Tetsuji sponsored playwrights who would bring a different approach, promoting a movement called the New Kabuki or New Historical Plays. In these productions the narrators or side-singers are absent. The actor's make-up is enhancing but natural, rather than symbolic and often grotesque. Their speech is everyday, contemporary Japanese, freed of rhetoric and archaisms.

Two contemporary leading dramatists embodying this trend are Hojo Hideji and Funahashi Seichi. Though still using historical material or episodes from classical literature, such as *Tales of Genji*, as sources, they have their people speak simply and their actors perform in a modified Kabuki style, retaining many traditional techniques and gestures, but not all, dispensing with some they deem outdated. The actors are skilful enough to preserve the atmosphere of past times, creating a convincing ambience. Yet there has been criticism from some with conservative leanings that having characters in an ancient tale and centuries-old setting speak in modern Japanese is incongruous, a "vulgarism" in the opinion of those with exacting aesthetic taste. In general, however, the public has welcomed the changes, a development which is seen by the dissenters as a threat to the formal and hallowed purity of Kabuki.

Hojo Hideji is said to be the most successful – that is, the most highly paid – playwright ever to work in the Japanese theatre. He writes mostly for specific actors, fashioning his characters to fit each such chosen player's gifts, thus ensuring a good performance as well as helping the actor to feel comfortable in his role, one that he can more easily create. His characters are not controlled by the constraints imposed on them in ages past, the social and moral inhibitions of feudal days, but give way to strong, outspoken human impulses, voicing their doomed hopes and angers; hence they are more lifelike, suffering pain and frustration, lonely and anguished.

Somewhat less of a modernizer, though almost as successful as his rival Hojo Hideji, Funahashi Seichi retains more of the antique Kabuki conventions, but has his characters express themselves with a clashing, startling clarity. A writer of fiction, with a lengthy list of popular books, he draws on his novels for the subjects of his plays, adapting them expertly for the stage, admixing in them elements of both Shimpa and orthodox Kabuki, as witness his *The Story of the Black Ships*, the script about

Townsend Harris and his geisha Okichi in which John Nathan made a brief appearance. (The piece was given in both Shimpa and Kabuki theatres, with casts that included performers trained in one or the other acting style. Unlike Nathan, Bowers thought that the portrait of Harris was surprisingly sympathetic and even admiring, showing the American envoy as courageously determined to open Japanese minds to the many benign influences of the outside world. *The Story of the Black Ships* was an extraordinary hit.) Funahashi excels at conjuring up the past with great splashes of colour, catching the inherent vigour of its people, the swagger of its warriors, the unrepressed emotions of its women, exemplified in the boldness of their passions.

In 1972 a count of Kabuki actors came to about 350, most of whom were attached to one of the various companies. A similar survey in 1987 showed that nine important theatres in four of Japan's largest cities annually presented more than twenty-five month-long Kabuki programmes. Some of these playhouses were small and suitably intimate, as was the Misona Za in Nagoya, while in Osaka the actors still had to contend with the acoustics of a huge, cavernous auditorium. With seating for 2,900 spectators, the Kabukiza in Tokyo is one of the world's largest theatres. A gala attended by many notables (an event that took place in 1987) marked its 100th anniversary. At this celebration 100 performers assembled on stage.

The Kabukiza receives a government subsidy, as do the other companies considered to be national cultural treasures. They are also managed and supported by Shōchiku, Japan's all-encompassing commercial theatrical enterprise. The stars of the Kabukiza in the 1980s were Tamasaburo Bando V and Ennosuke Ichikawa III, both of whom also took roles in Western dramas.

As described by an anonymous observer, Tamasaburo Bando V was "adored for his peerless depiction of Japanese femininity. From the precise angle of a bowed head to the postures and actions that move a kimono with womanly grace, he is the perfect court lady." At age twenty-five, in a bold experiment, he caused a storm of controversy by portraying Lady Macbeth; he was only the second actor to undertake a woman's role in a Western play. Collaborating with the French choreographer Maurice Béjart, he helped to create a work that combined elements from Kabuki and Western classical ballet.

Ennosuke Ichikawa was the frequent recipient of both cheers and catcalls for his attempts to enliven plays by adding strange spectacular effects, some of which were deemed to be unseemly "gimmicks". He dazzled audiences by remarkably quick costume changes and by literally taking flight, soaring above the stage while he was upheld by wires. He justified his resort to such untraditional tricks, asserting the Kabuki had to adapt to modern tastes or else perish. He made frequent tours abroad, to perform and to conduct training workshops, and in Paris directed a Kabuki-style production of the Rimsky-Korsakov opera *Le Coq d'Or* (1984).

Increasingly, Kabuki actors stepped out of their limited world into the realms of film and television and stagings of classic and modern plays of Western origin, or works on topical subjects by contemporary Japanese dramatists, but only to return to careers in Kabuki. By venturing in those directions, if only shortly, they noticeably enlarged and diversified their techniques.

New Kabuki, having lost its novelty, rapidly faded. As the twentieth century neared its end, Kabuki's chief competitor was no longer Nōh or Bunraku but instead Shingeki, the strong and spreading reform movement. For the time being, however, Kabuki's place still seems secure. With its brilliant costumes and sets offering a feast to the eyes, and its sentimental and violent stories stirring the emotions, it continues to provide a pure theatrical experience and consequently has a solid following.

MASQUE PLAYS OF KOREA

In Korea most forms of ancient theatre are integrated with dance, whether the performance is in a classical idiom – owing much to Chinese court dances and Indian sacred rituals – or in folk, the latter still associated with sowing and harvest festivals. Such dances and ceremonies have an immemorial history going back at very least 3,000 years. Their tie to the seasonal cycle is clearly seen in such extant traditions as the Farmers Dance. The purpose of these rituals was to offer tribute to the gods and to appease threatening ancestral spirits. It is believed that from a very early date the celebrants sang and danced and wore appropriate masks.

Supposedly Dan-Gun, a legendary king, established the first civilization on the peninsula (2333 BC); a devotee of Hanunim, the supreme deity, he honoured his god by ordering propitiatory rites consisting of music and respectful dance. In their religious festivals his people sought benefits from *all* supernal powers – many of them nature gods – in shamanistic music, singing and dancing, their fervour often reinforced by bounteous wine-drinking.

With more certainty it is known that by the thirteenth century BC the Puya, a barbaric tribe roaming the northern and central regions of the peninsula, were enacting a festival called *young-go* (or *yonggo*) during the tenth lunar month of the calendar (our December); while another folk group, the Ye, held a similar rite, *muchon* (or *much'ōn*), at a time equivalent to our October, with songs, masked dances and invocatory and sacrificial acts. A third category of dance in this primitive era was the *ch'ōngun*.

Further south, other tribes held thanksgiving festivals twice a year, after the rice was transplanted, and then after the reaping. An ancient literary work, *Munhun Tonggo*, describes these celebrations: "They were performed by a dozen dancers, who lined up in a single file, followed the leader, raising their hands up and down and stamping on the ground to the accompaniment of music. . . .The ceremonies were presided over by a shaman priest who was, at the same time, lyricist, composer-musician, and dancer." Even today the Farmers Dance, mentioned above, is closely bound to shamanism, often being resorted to in the hope of driving out evil spirits or as a form of prayer for divine aid. Early frescoes, dating to AD 500–600, also depict scenes of dancing, the performers having "shrugged shoulders, protruded hip, side-stepping with arms raised horizontally and hands dropped". At the beginning women participated in the dances, but later men assumed the female roles, and this custom still prevails in some parts of the country. Other wall-paintings in tombs, well enough preserved from 100 BC, show dances and musical instruments of an Indian character, some of the men wearing turbans.

(Credit should be given here to Alan C. Heyman for his article in *Dance Perspectives*, a brief but truly informative chronicle. Comparatively little has been written and published in English about Korean dance and theatre. For this chapter, material has been taken from an essay by Oh-Kon Cho in *The Complete Cambridge Guide to World Theatre*; also from a survey in the Gassner and Quinn *Reader's Encyclopedia of World Drama*; and from a short piece by Sohn Jie-Ae in the *New York Times*.)

After the introduction of Buddhism, its influence is very manifest, at a time more or less concurrent with our Middle Ages. This extended period saw Chinese rituals dominate. Masked dramas or dance-plays were added, too. These enacted poems, many of them didactic, are believed to have been of Turkestani, Indian or Chinese origin. Among them is the Lion Dance, which was later passed on to Japan. (Like Japan, Korea has no lions, so a pantomime imitating that beast is obviously not indigenous.)

The next faith to sweep through Korea was Confucianism. Some of the dances of this epoch satirized Buddhism and its priesthood. "The lion – whose original purpose in the drama was to devour those who transgressed the precepts of Buddha – began devouring the decadent monks themselves."

Women dancers reappeared during this period, a carefully chosen professional troupe known as the *kisseng*, modelled on the "girl entertainers" at court and in wealthy men's ornate palaces during the Chinese Tang dynasty. They, in turn, were to be emulated in Japan by the geishas. In many ways Korea was the bridge between Indian, Chinese and Japanese cultures, if only because of its geographical location. The histories tell of many "ambassadors" of Korean art at foreign courts. If the Koreans borrowed many dance forms from others, they repaid them by exporting, with some changes, what they themselves had eagerly received. In particular, and more than is generally realized, Japan's debt to China and especially Korea, in architecture, sculpture, painting, pottery, verse drama and dance, is a weighty one. As Holland Cotter has remarked, "Positioned between two historically aggressive neighbors, Korea partook of the full radiance of Chinese art and helped transmit its influence to Japan. But Korea was also savagely invaded by both countries, with the result that its own artistic traditions were all but obliterated."

Though an amalgam of many alien concepts, adopted from its neighbours and then delicately reshaped, Korean dance has unique qualities. One, as Alan C. Heyman says, is a concern with "symmetrical beauty". In the folk works, emphasis is placed much less on technique, more on the degree of spiritual exaltation and physical exhilaration, for which the terms – loosely paraphrased – are *mut* and *heung*. The court and religious dances, by contrast, are austere and rigidly prescribed.

A special feature of Korean dance is that it is often performed on the heels, unlike Western practice, in which there is an instinctive tendency to rise on the toes. As described by Dong-wa Cho, "The Korean dancer steps forward with his or her toes up. Such steps undoubtedly run counter to the natural movement of the body, but it is an important attribute to the introverted spiritualism of the Korean dance in that it holds body movement in check."

Most accounts of Korean dance-plays start with the Silla period (57 BC–AD 935), Silla being one of the Three Kingdoms, the two others – at times contemporaneous – Goguryŏ (37 BC–AD 668) and Běgzě (18 BC–AD 660). From records kept in Silla it seems fairly certain that the masque dramas were persistently developed there. A prototype was the *kiak*, imported from China (*c.* AD 700), a simple danced pantomime enacted by a masked performer before spectators in a Buddhist temple. It is thought to be the genesis of the *sandae-togam-gŭk*, variants of it still existing after a long and sometimes arduous history.

More theatrical elements were to be seen in the *kommu*, the *muaemu* and the *ch'oyongmu*. The *kommu*, a masked warrior dance, referred to a young hero who killed a royal foe. It belongs to one of three categories of Silla masked plays, the Gŏm-Mu or Sword Dance. The others are the Hykang-Ag O-gi or Five Styles, and the Czŏyong. Besides these, another group consisted of the Gi-Ag, masked religious dances offering pious devotion to Buddha. Over time, after the Koryŏ era, the Gi-Ag became secularized, in two instances evolving into the Bongsan-T'alch'um (Bongsan Masque Dance) and Yangjoo-Sandě-Nori (Yangjoo Sande Play).

The *muaemu* was a religious dance and dispensed with masks. The *ch'ŏyongmu* enacted details of the legend of Ch'ŏyong, son of the Dragon King of the Eastern Sea, and was outstanding for grotesquerie that had a strong impact.

With the Goryŏ period (AD 918–1392) the climate for entertainment changed, becoming chilled and pressed down by the weightier imposition of Buddhism on daily life. Scarcely anything of consequence but religious festivals was sanctioned. One such event was the *p'algwanhoe*, held mostly in midwinter, to pay homage to the earthly deity. Another observance, the *yondunghoe*, was a Buddhist mass celebrated in the first lunar month. Though they had dissimilar purposes, they closely resembled each other. According to Oh-Kon Cho: "Numerous lanterns of different sizes and colors were hung and a temporary high stage adorned with bright colors was built. Included in the programs were somersaults, a tight-rope display, an acrobatic dance on the top of a bamboo pole, puppet plays, and the *sandĕ-japgŭk*, or various impure forms of masked dance-drama."

To welcome in the New Year, the *narae* was performed in the palace to exorcize evil spirits. This ritual dance soon made its way outside royal precincts to public stages, where it was performed by *kwangdae* – members of professional acting troupes – who were probably the first in Korea to support themselves solely by their mimetic gifts.

By now the court was maintaining entertainers who were available whenever an occasion called for them. But an expanding circle of actors was earning a partial living by performing at private events in the homes of merchants and other people of high status and wealth. Socially, though, the new breed of actors were outcasts, forced to reside in a despised and segregated area of the city, apart from gentlefolk and well-bred ordinary citizens, and providing for themselves by undertaking drab tasks – "butchery, hunting, wickerwork" – when they lacked engagements.

In 1392 the Yi dynasty was established and assumed hereditary governance over a region known as Chosŏn by consent of the Emperor of China. This regime was to hold sway throughout a line of twenty-six monarchs until 1910, when Japan annexed the peninsula. Buddhism having grown decadent and corrupt, the Yi rulers adopted the Confucian ethical system for guidance. Many ministers and officials conformed to the court and were Neo-Confucians, their stern outlook and behaviour pervading much of the upper-class society.

The Yi era marked a peak in the evolution and refinement of Korean dance and music. A young king, Sejong the Great, the fourth monarch, ascended to the throne. He was much interested in theatrical arts. For four decades he encouraged them. With the help of his principal musician, Pahk Yun, the king had the dances fully categorized, setting down rules to direct the performers, detailing the costumes and establishing a system of musical notation. His work was carried on by a royal successor, King Sejo, the seventh monarch, whose grandson, King Sonjong, also pursued this useful task. The result was the *Ahk-Hak-Kwoe-Bum* (*Standard of Musical Science*) which precisely lists all the music and dances extant at that time, along with descriptions of stage attire, properties, instruments, and even counsel on the arrangement of programmes. The book makes possible an exact recreation today of at least two score ancient dances, and besides is a treasure for scholars.

Beginning in the middle period of the Goryŏ dynasty, the *narae* had metamorphosed into the *sandĕ*, which during the Yi reign gradually progressed to another transformation as the *sandĕ-dogam*, combining in one all the elements of Korean masque plays known up to that day. Its impulse came from the Confucian opposition to Buddhism, though this was not wholly explicit. Opening with a religious service, a plea for the actors' protection, the *sandĕ-dogam* next deviously criticized corrupt priests and aristocrats (*yangban*), then concluded with declarations about man's fragile mortality and prayers of supplication for dead ancestors. The attack on corruption did not seem to be aimed at any particular faith, but only in general against religious leaders who betrayed their calling and caused mischief at court and elsewhere throughout the nation. Buddhists and anti-Buddhists interpreted this criticism each in their own way, believing that it was meant not for them but for their opponents. Consequently both sides approved of the *sandĕ-dogam*. That it exposed the faults of the nobility and over-privileged classes further commended it to the common people, who chiefly made up its audience and who resented the selfishness, harsh arrogance and frequent incompetence of those who were of high rank and held power not because they possessed true ability but merely by an accident of birth.

Steadfastly anti-Buddhist and ever more Confucian, the Chosŏn court celebrated only a few festivals. However, the *narae* was still performed there, as was the *sandĕ-japqŭk*, which was aggrandized to become the *sandae-togam-gŭk*. Countering the Puritanism and austerity of the court, the masses took to the popular arts – literature, painting, theatre – as a result of which they flourished, patronized mostly by merchants and craftsmen. Largely these were kinds of entertainment that did not call for masks. Scholars are of the opinion that the plays were comic pieces ridiculing detested officials who were far too authoritarian. Such works are called *chaphui*, to indicate that they are an "impure" type of drama, differing from dance plays, which were deemed a superior genre. Another term for these satiric farces is *paewŭhui*.

Two other sorts of plays taking form during this era were the O-Gwangde (Five Buffoonery Play) and its derivative, the Yayu (Outdoor Play), for which the actors wore masks. Mostly the masque dramas were given on temporary stages in the open air. These structures, in fields or on a hillside, were bare of sets and curtainless. Time-lapses and changes of scene were indicated by short breaks or intermissions in the narrative flow. If a player wished to change his costume or mask, he reached into a handy box at the left of the stage for alternative attire. He could choose from twenty-eight different masks for a range of stock portrayals. The box might also contain a puppet, if one was to be employed. An orchestra of six, skilled with harps, flutes and drums, accompanied the dancers, who responded to tunes called *semaczitaryŏng*. The presentations might go on all night, visible in the flickering shadows and inconstant light of huge bonfires.

Puppet plays had also gained popularity, as elsewhere in the Orient. This genre of entertainment, probably originating in India, had been carried to China, modified there, and then brought to Korea as early as the seventh century. Despite minor changes in each country – the technique reached its zenith in Japan and Bali – puppetry is more or less the same everywhere, with only the Japanese version of it transcending fixed and narrow limits. In Korea the playlets were presented by itinerant troupes called "the song-and-dance people", who were looked down upon – like professional actors – as far outside society, untrustworthy nomads.

These local Korean puppets, remarkably versatile, united elements of the hand puppet, the rod puppet and the marionette. Each character's body was affixed to the main stick and hand-held, the arms manipulated by strings, the movements stiff, like those controlled from below by rods. The puppets, about one to three feet high, are easily assembled. The carved and painted head is of wood or papier-mâché, into which is inserted a wedge of light wood that is pierced by the main stick. A horizontal bar, serving as the shoulders, is attached to the main stick shortly below the neck, and dangling arms are loosely affixed by bolts at the bar's ends. The looseness permits the arms' mobility. Over the rectangular frame a suitable costume is nicely fitted. The operator handles one puppet at a time, recites the prescribed or improvised lines, or sings to a musical accompaniment.

The puppet sketches were orally transmitted; as a result the same stories might exist in different versions depending on which troupe had them in its repertory. But all had the same basic themes, echoing those of the *chaphui*: they poked fun at irritating, pompous officials, stressed the absurdity in the intimate, competitive, domestic relationship of husband, wife and concubine, drew a scornful picture of faithless monks and the mischief they might do and alluded to the bald corruption prevailing among persons high in authority or thriving in the shrewd mercantile class.

Typically, a puppet play had seven to ten scenes, a semblance of unity attained by having a main character who appeared in each episode and who doubled as both its central figure and as a narrator. Each scene, however, dealt with a different subject. Even so, the plays seemed better structured than the overly diffuse masked drama. The public's fondness for the puppet sketches lasted until the beginning of the twentieth century, when they were finally deemed too unsophisticated. Besides, Japanese military occupiers were anxious to stamp out relics of Korean folk culture and forbade evidences of it, a ban that lasted from 1930 to 1945.

There are two categories of puppet play. One is the Ggog-Gagsi, which requires thirteen figures in human form and two resembling animals. The other is the Mansog-Zung, performed silently except for music, by five figures, an ensemble made up of a deer, a horned deer, a carp, a dragon, and one puppet in human shape, namely Mansog-Zung. This is a piece to be given on the eighth day of the fourth month of the lunar calendar, which is Buddha's birthday.

In a later phase of the Chosŏn period, too, the one-man operetta, *p'ansori*, made its bow. Where and how it originated daunts scholars, some of whom hazard that it began early in the eighteenth century with the short chants or songs of shamans participating in religious rites. These were lifted and adapted by the itinerant players – *kwangdae* – always hungry for new material. Gradually they dropped the brief sacred lyrics and replaced them with songs based on popular tales of the day. These were also transmitted orally until the nineteenth century, when fortunately one Sin Jae-hyo (1812–84) collected all of them he could from twelve extant repertoires and preserved them in written form.

All that is needed for a *p'ansori* is a lone singer and a mat alongside him on which is seated a drummer (*kosu*). The simplicity of this staging enables the performer to travel with it anywhere and to present it to a large or small circle of spectators. He must be competent, even masterly, at singing, recitation and pantomime. His talent for song (*sori*) is the most important requirement. The range of his acting (*ballim*) need not go beyond vivid expressions of joy, heightened by gestures (*ch'umsae*), as he intersperses dialogue and narration (*aniri*). Since he may perform at taxing length, perhaps several hours, his resort to speech between songs helps spare his voice from over-strain.

At the start, *p'ansori* singers came from the lowest class of shamans, singled out and given special training because they had strong, hoarse voices – able to be heard above the noise of the marketplace – and their preparation was harsh and lengthy. If vocally inadequate, they might learn to play a musical instrument and be relegated to be an accompanist. The last choice open to them was to be acrobats or tight-rope walkers. *P'ansori* singers are still welcomed by the populace in Korea and often heard on radio and seen on television.

Early in the Yi dynasty, novel writing was introduced from China and became a popular literary exercise. As the books became richer in substance and more polished, some lent themselves to dramatization and became a goodly source for dance-plays. The eighteenth century was a peak for both the classical novel and these danced adaptations. An outstanding instance, during the reigns of Yong-jo (1725–76) and his successor Jong-jo (1777–1800), was an anonymous work, *Chun-hyang-jun* (*The Story of Chun-hyang*), which for its day was unorthodox since it was composed in Korean rather than Chinese, the latter deemed more acceptable by the élite. Its ranking ever since has been unrivalled, and it has proved to be a deep well from which librettists have drawn ideas for stage ventures.

In King Yong-jo's days another codification was issued: *Shi-Yong-Mu-Bo* (*Scripts of Current Dances*).

A description of some of the dance forms might be helpful, without going into the details of how and when many of them descended from the early *sandě* that proliferated in such diverse and interesting ways.

The beauty of ancient Korean court dance is captured in a poem by the great Chinese writer, Li Po. The poem was meant to be recited during a performance:

Crowned in a golden hat, the dancer,

Like a white colt, turns slowly.

The wide sleeves, fluttering against the wind,

Like a bird, from the Eastern Sea.

[Translation: Dong-wha Cho]

Among the court dances that have been reconstituted is the *komaboka*, which mimes the movements of boatmen with punting poles as they glide through imagined waves. The costume is an elaborate verdant silk robe and an overdress of pale blue-green, hardly a boatman's attire but attractive when worn by the *kisseng*, the palace's female troupe.

Indeed, for the troupe, authenticity took second place to splendour in dress. In other dances they might wear a garment called a *mong-du-ri*, bright green and adorned with a floral pattern of strong colours over a base of crimson that spanned the back of the shoulders. A *dee*, a broad red sash, partly covered the breasts, and terminated in a large bow behind. The costume was drawn taut, to flatten the figure and have it as sexless and non-erotic as possible. A bright red gauze-and-silk skirt and yellow blouse complemented this apparel, and the hands were largely hidden in lengthy, prismatically coloured sleeves. A flowery headdress or crown had a host of pendants and other sparkling ornaments that glinted and trembled at each gesture. The hair was black, braided and shiny, further held in place by a huge golden pin – perhaps inset with precious stones – from which hung a pair of broad red ribbons. The face had pallor; the expression was modest.

The court dances are performed by a group gliding in unison, with "dreamy undulation", while the singers' voices rise and fall rather passionately. In past days as many as 200 performers might take part on a ceremonial occasion, their movements simple but stately, arms swaying, their small, lithe bodies swinging forward and backward.

Another courtly example is the *Chuhyong*, based on an ancient legend, the *Dance of the Son of the Dragon of the Eastern Sea*. The time is the ninth century. While King Hongkang and his party are picnicking, a fog descends on them. An astrologer explains that the Dragon of the Eastern Sea is wroth. To appease the ravaging beast, the King orders that a temple be erected at once. The fog is promptly dispelled, and the pleased Dragon and his seven offspring appear before the King to express their satisfaction in song and dance. One of the Dragon's sons is appointed to the King's court and awarded a beautiful girl to be his wife. But the God of Plague falls in love with her; the adulterous pair hold nocturnal trysts. Learning of this, the Dragon's son, Chuhyong, gets rid of his rival by performing a dance while singing:

Playing in the moonlight of the capital

Till the morning comes,

I return home

To see four legs in my bed.

Two belong to me.

Whose are the other two?

But what was my own

Has been taken from me. What now?

[Translation: Alan C. Heyman]

The Dragon withdraws, promising never to intrude again, and thereafter Chuhyong's people look upon his picture as a talisman to ward off illness. (This dance closely resembles the *Barong* of the Balinese, also intended to drive off a dragon and prevent the entrance of the evil spirit.) The *Chuhyong* engages five dancers, each clad in a different colour – blue, yellow, white, black and red – symbolizing the four quarters of the universe, and its centre. A later song provides a variation:

The old man Chuhyong it is rumored came

Out of the blue sea.

He sang of the moonlight

With his shell-like teeth and reddish lips.

And danced in the Spring breeze,

Fluttering his wide scarlet sleeves

Like an eagle's wings.

[Translation: Wong-kyung Cho]

Performers of the *Chuhyong* wear identical male masks: the jaw heavy and jutting, eyebrows bushy, a long moustache, a short tuft of beard, and large earrings of painted wood dangling from the lobes. It is believed that at one time the earrings, too, were of different colours, matching those of the many-hued costumes. The garbs consist of blouses of multiple layers of brocade over loose pants, sagging belts and embroidered slippers, all parts silken. As in most palace dances, the hands are hidden by full sleeves, which in this instance are white. On the head is a "stiff black hat of fine-lacquered horsehair material that has two horizontal appendages protruding from the rear – like 'rabbit ears' – which also represent a court official".

A classical selection, described by Heyman though it is no longer performed, is the *Sa-Son-Mu* (*The Dance of the Four Fairies*). In this, some of the participants bore water-lily branches in their hands. Another boating dance, accompanied by a fisherman's song, uses ropes and an anchor as properties, to pantomime the launching of a barque.

The *Kum-Mu* or *Kahl Choom* (*Sword Dance*) recalls the assassination of the King of Silla by a young patriot, Hwangchan. Summoned to entertain the invader, Hwangchan suddenly thrusts his weapon into the tyrant's body. His deed is at the cost of his own life, but he has courageously avenged his fellow-countrymen. Each dancer dons a mask carved to look like Hwangchan, but all the performers are women. The blades they wield, of imitation metal, have small bells attached to the handle; these jingle and rattle, adding their sound to the accompanying instruments. Here the costume is black, except for a red-and-yellow tassel that hangs from a black felt hat. The dance requires no knowledge of swordsmanship, since it is typically stylized and comprises mostly graceful whirls and dips. Folk-dancers also attempt this dance, which is a great favourite.

The Nightingale Dance is exceedingly slow-moving, much like one in the Japanese Nōh, the executant attired in yellow, again with rainbow-hued sleeves. She (or it may be he) has the performance restricted to the space of a small straw mat underfoot, deftly woven with multicoloured designs of flowers and tall cranes.

The *Mu-Go* (*Drum Dance*) has the participants circle a drum; some carry a stick, some hold flowers. Those who bear the sticks hit the drum loudly, but the flower-laden merely brush it, so that the sound alternates from strong to soft.

The repertory also contains Buddhist dances, such as the *Mu-Ae-Mu*, purportedly composed by a monk in the seventh century; and the *Hahk-Mu* (*Crane Dance*) which calls for an artful imitation of the stalking birds. The "birds" peck open lotus flowers, from which spring forth child dancers, who mount the "cranes" and finally ride away.

The *Po Gu Rak* (*Ball-Throwing Dance*) is much beloved. It belongs in the T'ang-Ahk category. Two groups compete at tossing a tasselled wooden ball through a round hole in the centre of the lintel of a portable model of a Korean gate.

To all these must be added Alphabet Dances that spell out compliments to the king.

Confucian social dances are better seen in Korea than in China, the land of their origin. Mostly they are taken up with bowing to right, left and centre. They are solemn, stately, and are held twice a year to honour the birthday of the sage, an autumn event, and also to herald the spring. Some performers grasp a flute in their right hand, and in their left a stick topped with pheasant feathers and a dragon head. They wear red robes, with stiff black-and-red hats that are a feature of classical, official

Korean dress. In a second phase of the dance (the first is known as the "Civil" and the next as the "Military"), a painted shield and a hatchet replace the flute and stick. The hat, too, is changed, the new one fez-shaped, coloured red with a superimposed pattern of a pine cone. As part of this ritual, cups of "divine wine" are offered to the "spirit" and then withdrawn at the altar. The dancers beat their hatchets on their shields, while turning from one side to the other.

Shamanistic ritual includes the *Dance of the Seven Stars* in which a sorceress is disguised as a Buddhist monk bearing a rosary. She performs both a drum dance and a cymbal dance, elements of the Buddhist ceremony. In Korea today most of the shamans are aged women. Many earn a living solely by performing these dances. As in Sri Lanka, they are summoned to the dwellings of sick persons to disperse the invasive harmful spirits. Or they may attend funerals, or take part in the blessing of a new house. They impress spectators by a display of magical controls. Sometimes they dance on the sharp edges of swords that are laid on the earth, or – dressed like ancient warriors – they twirl a pair of long spears. In all these feats there are suggestions of Burmese "spirit dances" and the acrobatic stunts in Chinese opera. When the shaman dances, she usually has on a "stovepipe" hat of light red, with feathers attached to it – one each at the right and left. On the pair of fans that she waves, black and yellow, are images of deities, vaguely Buddhist in character. Sometimes she employs a single fan, her other hand jingling a small "bell-tree" that helps to summon the sought-for demon. Other Buddhist dances betray an Indo-Chinese origin, though obviously altered by their more than 1,000-year history in Korea. They supplicate Lord Buddha's permission for departed souls to enter the bliss of Nirvana. In these dances the feet are positioned at right angles to each other, and knees are bent low.

Nahi-Choom (*Butterfly Dance*) has an ethereal quality. The egregiously wide yellow or white sleeves are meant to suggest the butterfly's delicate fluttering; the hat has a peaked hood, with flaps of extra cloth and ornaments. A *kasa*, or mantle, of bright red covers the breasts and one shoulder; beneath the mantle a long frock of hemp cloth is white or yellow. Two drums supply the music. Sinking slowly, gently swaying, the dancers simulate a fragile butterfly settling on a breeze-tossed leaf. At other moments they turn on their heels, their toes pointed upwards. Or they squat, their backs to each other, and quickly alter their position by lifting themselves from their haunches and whirling about, an accomplishment of extreme technical difficulty, hindered as they are by voluminous costumes, as well as by having throughout to hold out their arms horizontally.

A variation of the *Butterfly Dance* is the *Moquh-Choom*, performed before dining as a form of grace; the participants carry long, thin mallets to strike a white-painted wooden "log" as they rhythmically circle around it. This is a symbolic chastisement of the devil for tempting them into gluttony, prompting them to the table before having first offered Lord Buddha their portions.

The folk-dances are more improvisatory and allow much freer movement. The dancers may have the privilege of creating their own rhythm and gestures, of deciding upon the length of the pauses and moments of immobility. The most popular, the Farmers' Dance, has both religious and military elements, the latter because in the past the peasantry was enrolled in a militia during wars with Burma and other neighbouring states. Some of the miming depicts the practices of mendicant Buddhist monks, while other passages are based on battle formations: parade, charge, retreat, triumph. Of the original dozen such soldiers' manoeuvres, less than half are still retained.

Despite their rural setting, the folk-dances also hold to the tradition of female impersonation, with "flower boys" donning women's skirts, white gloves and flowery hats.

Many rustic dances serve as exorcisms, to expel malign spirits or stamp them into the earth, as in the *Jinshin-bahlgi*, a shamanistic ceremony held during the lunar New Year festivals. A group of farmers circle a house, their feet pounding as one; the householder rewards them with gifts of money, edibles and wine.

Typically, a band of folk-dancers will consist of about a half-dozen peasants and be headed by a flag-bearer, holding a long pennon fastened to a bamboo shoot crowned with pheasant feathers. The leader (*sang-soë*) boasts a hat surmounted by a plume of crane feathers or, if he is poor, one made of paper. He looks like a military officer of the Silla dynasty. The plume is held in place by a wooden pin; by a twist of his head, it can be made to swivel either way – in former times a mounted officer indicated directions by a device such as this. Even now the group leader signals to his fellow dancers by means of it. The crane plume also helps him emulate the stalking and postures of the tall, gawky bird if that is desired. He carries a mallet and small gong, striking it, setting the varied rhythm, pace and motions for his group.

Music is provided by simple instruments: a two-headed drum shaped like an hour-glass is hit on one side by a light bamboo stick, and on the other by a mallet, the latter giving off a deeper tone, the former a sharper one, alternately. (Similar drums are employed in Japan and Sri Lanka.) The rhythm is ingeniously syncopated, the second drummer dancing as he plays.

A third member of the band has a smaller drum, a *sogo*, much like a Japanese "fan drum". He, too, wears a hat with a streamer that swirls about. Bobbing his head, he creates changing visual patterns with it, to the delight of spectators. Sometimes he leaps into the air, or turns on one foot, adding to the pulsing excitement of the spectacle. Later he replaces his paper streamer with one far lengthier – as much as twenty-seven feet – and slightly weighted. Pivoting his head more slowly, in an increasing radius, he swings the new streamer in broad arcs "above and below and around either side of his body". At moments, his hands clasped behind him, he skips in and out of the encircling paper ribbon, the music becoming faster and noisier, as the hard-breathing dance reaches a climax. Others in the troupe have large gongs, resounding with a solemn tone; and rasping reed pipes, and round drums. The instrumentalists do not dance, merely lending other sounds to the music. They wear paper hats fashioned into hoods, embellished with huge white chrysanthemums also designed of paper.

In another folk number, the *Mudong-Choom*, a youth garbed as a girl stands atop a man's shoulders. The boy moves his own shoulders and arms rhythmically, as the man below him dances; and this creates the amusing effect of a performance by two persons who possess only one pair of feet. (The Balinese have a dance that resembles this.)

An exorcism dance, *Sal-Pu-Ri*, should have a joyous quality. To a wordless chant – invocatory, meaningless syllables – and with much manipulation of a silken scarf and thumping of a small hand-drum, the performer seeks to convey "an abandon that one associates with the singular thrill of religious ecstasy, an ecstasy that has here become also one of sensual delight".

Pub-Ko-Choom, a drum dance, might be added by priests as part of their special ceremonies. A folk version of it is danced elsewhere, sometimes by a woman who attires herself in a monk's cloak. The *Nine Drum Dance* (*Ku-Ko-Mu*) is the most celebrated folk variant. The dancer strikes both the centre and rim of each of nine drums, large and small, loud and soft, placed in a row, starting with a slow cadence and working up to a crescendo. It is an astonishing display of skill, some of it rhythmic, some of it acrobatic and requiring sustained back bends.

With the Sandae banished from the Chosŏn court because of the Puritanism and élitism of the Confucians, who also deplored the actors' use of Korean dialect rather than classical Chinese, it was now given only in rural regions and enacted by mere commoners. It became a vehicle for angry satire, poking harsh fun at the despised Buddhist priesthood and the hated Confucian aristocracy. (The *ch'ŏyongmu*, however, continued to enjoy royal tolerance.)

Elements of shamanism entered into the Sandae plays and the various kinds of dance-dramas that gradually derived from them. Sometimes one might be staged on a day of prayer for rain. In some provinces the dramas ended when the actors tossed masks and robes into a bonfire; they were convinced that evil spirits clung to the garments worn during the ritual. While the costumes burned, spectators chanted their anxious pleas to Heaven. The masked dances were also performed in cities to shut out epidemics, or in shore villages to appease the gods, in hope of calm seas and good fishing.

The Sandae masks, those still extant, are grotesque, almost comic. The plays were very long – originally there were ten acts, divided into thirteen scenes. Each act borrowed its title from the name of the dancer who took the lead in it, perhaps portraying a Buddhist priest disfigured by some physical defect: the "Pock-marked Priest", the "Black-faced Priest", the "Priest of the Blinking Eyes".

The music for the Sandae is monotonously repetitive. Increasingly the plays were vulgarized, sometimes to the point that they were plainly obscene. The dancing, too, began to lose the refinement it once had, some of it little more than a wild thrashing about of the long sleeves, aimed of course at a comparatively primitive audience.

Today the Sandae has almost vanished. Heyman – to whom, once again, so much credit is owed for the hard-come-by detail in this chapter – could find only one troupe devoted to it in the whole of Korea.

The more developed masked dance-plays are named to indicate the regions in which they have usually been performed. They belong to two general classes: the *purakje* (village festivals) and *sandae-togam-gŭk* (court dramas). The example of village plays include, in the Eastern Central provinces, the Hahoe *pyolsin-gut*, *pom-gut*, *kwanno* and *t'ai-gut*. In other districts, such as Yangju and Songp'a, one could see the *pyolsandae*; in Pongsan, Kangnyong and Eunyul, the *t'alch'um*; in T'ongyong, Kasan and Kosong, the *ogwandae*; in Suyong, the *yaru*; in sum, a sufficient variety.

Few of these local masked plays are as prized as the Hahoe *pyolsin-gut*, put on during a village festival once every decade, on the fifteenth day of the lunar month (much like the Passion Play at Oberammergau). Orally transmitted – there is no known script – knowledge of the characters and a synopsis of the action are preserved in the collective memory of the villagers; so there is always some improvisation. Episodic, with no central theme or plot, the loosely linked incidents deal rather trenchantly with the sinful behaviour of monks, of rapacious aristocrats and of suborned officials who pay no heed to the woes of mere lowly people. Originally, to enact the work, a dozen masks were required, but only nine are still on hand. Of carved wood, the masks are kept in the village shrine; according to legend, they were shaped by a craftsman who received divine instruction about them in a dream. His name and the date of the masks are also lost – the remaining nine are considered among the finest in Korea.

In 1993 New York theatre-goers had an exceedingly rare opportunity to see examples of *purakje*. As part of a year-long, nationwide Festival of Korea, the sponsoring Asia Society and Philip Morris Company brought over a twelve-member troupe from the Eunyul T'alch'um Preservation Center, an organization dedicated to keeping that local art form alive. The visitors offered a typical programme at Alice Tully Hall.

In advance of the two-day event, Sohn Jie-Ae, a Seoul journalist, provided the *New York Times* with an explanatory article. He wrote:

For Western dance-goers who commonly associate Asian dance with colorful but formalized court rituals, the masked dance of Korea will come as a total departure. The dance form, known as *t'alch'um* (pronounced *tal-choom*), skewers the bastions of Korea's traditional society with coarse and bawdy satire, and for centuries it has provided the uneducated and the oppressed with a way to vent their frustrations.

Each *t'alch'um* performer wears the traditional, elaborate costume and uses props befitting the status of the character being portrayed, topped by highly stylized masks. Much of the humor is mimed, slapstick is used freely, and the dances incorporate many of the movements seen on a farm – the squatting during rice planting, the waving of sickles during the harvest.

In recent years, *t'alch'um* has been enjoying renewed popularity both in Korea and overseas because of its frank insights into the Korean psyche. . . . A *t'alch'um* performance customarily opens with a dance by a figure known as the Great White Lion, intended to drive away evil spirits. Then come as many as a half-dozen playlets. The first of the Eunyal T'alch'um playlets take a jab at the holy world of Buddhist monks. Eight monks enter, singing and dancing about their travels through the world outside the Buddhist temple. In the end, they resolve to forsake religious life.

The next episode pokes fun at the pomposity of the upper class. Three noblemen are ridiculed by their servant, who manages to bed one nobleman's concubine. The final episode tells of an elderly wife who finally meets up with her wandering nobleman husband. But when she discovers him with a young concubine, a fight erupts, and the older woman is killed. The performance ends with an elaborate shaman ceremony to pray for the dead wife's soul.

T'alch'um was born three centuries ago in the village of Eunyul in the northwest province of Hwanghae, now a part of North Korea. The Eunyul T'alch'um Preservation Center is representative of the original masked-dance groups, composed of farmers who performed when and where they could. The troupe touring the United States is made up mostly of nonprofessionals; among the performers are nurses, white-collar office workers, even a farmer.

Travelling with them was the Center's ninety-year-old spiritual leader, Jang Yong-Soo, who had brought the technique and lore of *t'alch'um* with him when he took flight from the Communist North during the confused days of the country's civil strife. Now too old to perform, he sat with the musicians, wearing a tasselled paper hat and keeping the beat with the Korean large gong.

In the early 1920s, when he was young, Jang Yong-Soo worked in an Eunyul noodle shop. In his spare time he learned the rules and tricks of performing in *t'alch'um*, which would be presented on holidays and special occasions. "It was a time when the traditional class structure was crumbling and nobleman status was bought and sold. 'People bought their way in, and some of them behaved very badly,' Mr Jang explained. 'And so, in the masked dance we would do things to them we would never dream of doing in reality.' "

Once in the South, where he had taken refuge, he had energetically striven to win recognition and financial support from the government there for the Eunyul T'alch'um Preservation Center as a national cultural asset, a struggle that began in 1969 and culminated successfully in 1978. He is acknowledged to have been the person chiefly responsible for the continued life and prosperity of this art form that was beloved and native to him.

Throughout the 1980s the *t'alch'um* was considerably rejuvenated when South Korean students active in the sometimes violent pro-democratic movement seized upon it to satirize the doings of the dictatorial regimes then in power. "Dances were adapted to suit the times, with the military governments cast as the oppressors and the students the oppressed."

Cha Boo-Hoi, manager of the Center, offered Sohn Jie-Ae another reason for the *t'alch'um*'s ongoing vitality: "We find that Korean youths in their teens are showing enormous interest in learning about our cultural roots."

The first half of the programme chosen for the troupe's American tour was devoted to the "refined but not rarefied" music known as *chongak*, and the ensuing segment to the folk-dance plays. For the *New York Times* Anna Kisselgoff wrote: "With shamans still active in modern Korean society and with the accessibility that stock folk characters provide, this kind of ribald form would seem to live on naturally." The critic noted that this particular type of dance-drama was specific to the village of Eunyul in North Korea and that the Preservation Center took great care to reconstruct the plays' unique dramatic structure and distinctive regional style.

In the audience at Alice Tully Hall was South Korea's Foreign Minister. To open the evening, he assisted other notables in cutting a huge ribbon spread across the stage. But this was after members of the troupe had gone through the theatre to purify it.

The orchestra, the men in red robes, the women in green and blue, played "Long Life as Immeasurable as the Sky", led by Hwang Kyu Nam, in green, who defined the pace with a clacker.

The other musical numbers were a solo by Kim Eung Soo, a virtuoso with a large transverse bamboo flute, who "amazed with the dialogue between Kyu and Lee Jun Ah, who pleased with the intensity with which they interpreted 'Song of the Son of the Dragon of the Eastern Sea'". The music's structural frame was amplified in a serene nineteenth-century court dance for eight women that expanded and contracted around a vase of flowers. Pattern was dominant, but the bending and rising step characteristic of Korean classical dance was evident. *Dance of the Son of the Dragon of the Eastern Sea,* described as the only masked dance in the repertory, was more exuberant through its sleeve-flicking and complex patterns, but even here passion was sublimated into formality.

"The atmosphere was completely different in the raucous *Exorcism Dance of the Lion,* which introduced excerpts from the Eunyul masked troupe. Despite the fragmentary nature of the presentation, the satire of the upper classes came through in the performers' ability to convey the essence of each character. The overriding sense was that of serious ritual drama behind a comic façade. In the final excerpt, *Dance of the Old Husband, the Old Wife and the Other Actors,* a concubine killed her rival, whose soul was laid to rest in a symbolic dance, fiercely performed by Kim Nam Hee as a shaman."

In the early days of the Chosŏn court the *sandae-togam-gŭk* was performed under the supervision of a master of revels (*sandae togam*) for many state purposes: to cleanse the palace of evil spirits, to welcome newly named provincial governors, to entertain envoys from China. After the post of *sandae togam* was abolished and the royal subsidy ended (1634), in the dynasty's last phase, the actors gradually returned to public theatres, the plays adding folk elements to broaden their appeal. They also took on regional colourings as nomadic *kwangdae* travelled about the country or settled in disparate cities. however, as many or more similarities than variants are evident between today's local versions of the *sandae-togam-gŭk.*

All of them include dance, song, mime, witty exchanges, rapid prose dialogue. Dance, song, and music have priority. Since mostly they are performed on outdoor stages, no curtain or formal scene-settings are required. All-important is the visual effect produced by the grotesque masks and brilliant-hued costumes, even more prominent at night in the glare of flaming torches, sticks having tips saturated with oil.

The current dances, of which there are more than a dozen kinds, have complex patterns, and these general types are further subdivided. There are too many to be described here, but two instances – detailed by Oh-Kon Cho – might be cited: ". . . the *yodaji*-dance requires forward movements; the player places both hands on the upper front of his body and, extending them forward, pantomimes the opening of his chest while his feet kick forward. Some dances are used for humorous purpose; for example, the *horijapi*-dance, which requires the lifting of the player's leg, while resting his hands on his waist, is performed to tease the other player."

With very few exceptions, all the actors wear fantastic masks fashioned of either paper or dried gourds. Some have a dark cloth (*t'alpo*) attached at the rear to conceal the back of the head. To secure the mask, other strips of dark cloth go around the neck and are tied at the nape.

A strange tradition, or at least a paradoxical one, guides the bright costuming: the gaudiest attire is worn by servants and females of dubious moral virtue.

No single author of a *sandae-togam-gŭk* work is now known, since the plot – or situation – and much of the dialogue have been passed along orally from one generation to the next, with frequent additions and improvisations by resourceful players, much as in the Italian *commedia dell'arte*. The narratives have no firm structure. The actors work from a rough synopsis or elaborate on a somewhat vague premise, heeding the spectators' response and falling back on a range of old tricks or spontaneously creating new ones, to get a laugh.

The singing, interlaced with dancing, is accompanied by an ensemble of instrumentalists, usually numbering six, playing a pair of fifes (*p'iri*), a transverse flute (*chottae*), a two-stringed fiddle (*haegŭm*), an hour-glass-shaped drum (*changgo*) and a barrel drum (*puk*). A small gong (*kkwaengg-wari*) may be added. This sort of music is called *samhyon-yukk*. Three tunes are heard most often: the *kutkŏri*, with a flowing twelve-beat melody; the *t'aryŏng*, also twelve-beat but with an accent on the ninth; and the *yŏmbul*, with six beats. As in eighteenth-century English ballad operas, some of the songs are actually borrowed from popular folk tunes, but others from the wild shamanistic chants of the Chosŏn period, and not infrequently the words have little or no bearing on the story or whatever else is happening on stage.

Oh-Kon Cho describes a regional masked dance, a *pyolsandae*, a form of *sandae-togam-gŭk*, one that might be seen in the town of Yangju, fifteen miles north-east of Seoul, and presented there not once but several times a year on important occasions, perhaps most resplendently on Buddha's birthday, when the lanes and houses are alight with tinted lanterns. The performance goes on from pale dusk to an often grey, humid dawn. (More recently the play is given by day.) The cast is made up of local farmers and lesser town officials.

The setting is an open field. The changing room is at a side of the area, and the musicians are ranged at one end of the round playing space. The spectators stand or sit facing the instrumentalists and gazing beyond them to the actors. Two doors in the changing room serve for the characters' entrances and exits.

Act One concerns a monk, Sangjwa, but Act Two shifts to nonsensical exchanges between two other characters, their dialogue having no substance at all. In Act Five the misdeeds of a Buddhist priest are scathingly exposed. Throughout, a variety of characters are brought on, stay briefly, depart and never reappear. The language is colloquial, even earthy and embarrassingly frank, unlike that of the *t'alch'um*, which is often poetic. The figures bared to scorn are the sexually promiscuous Buddhist cleric, an apostate; the elderly husband, who bullies his young wife; the dishonest, bribe-seeking petty official; the inconsiderate aristocrat who abuses his power; all these by now "stock" and a familiar array .

Early in the nineteenth century a crown prince, Hyomyong, was reputedly a choreographer of new court dances. He is credited with no less than fifty works, some of them restorations of old numbers, some original.

The Koreans were beginning to feel the pressures that were modernizing the cultures of China and Japan and other Oriental peoples. A leader in innovation, Sin Jae-hyo (1812–84), effected many improvements in the form of the classic musical drama. He used it to retell such popular, long-lasting stories as *Chun-hyang*, *Sim-chong* and *Jogbyog*, with his music giving them more emotional strength. Deemed a genius by his fellow-countrymen, he had a broad influence and many disciples. Ever since, his songs have held a place on the programmes of O-Gwangde singers, who perform them with prominent facial expressions, dramatic gestures and moves, not in theatres but on bare temporary stages.

For the most part, however, the nineteenth century brought little that was new or significant to its theatre art. Korean spectators continued to find the established genres to be adequate. Gradually, women entered the casts and not a few dancers went on to become low-ranked functionaries. Taught their roles in childhood, they were advantageously organized into a hereditary guild. In their posts as local officials they boldly forced the townspeople to foot the costs of staging plays.

By the century's end audiences began to dwindle. One complaint was that with the plays being given outdoors, and the actors speaking behind masks, much of the dialogue was unintelligible. With growing Westernization, too, dance-dramas performed with child-like masks, along with puppet plays, were considered to be outdated and hardly satisfactory entertainment.

In 1908, in Seoul, a landmark event was the opening of the Wongag-Sa, the first national theatre. Among its initial season's offerings was a Western-style drama.

With the fall of the Yi dynasty (1910) the *kisseng* – the royal troupe of young women dancers – was no longer maintained at the palace. The former members found engagements in tea-houses and public theatres. Watching dances there, the Koreans are as noisy and busy – eating, drinking – as those in China or Japan who attend a Peking opera or Kabuki. If pleased, they shouted encouragement and praise to the performers.

That the Japanese military occupiers were determined to wipe out Korean folk arts was another factor in the decline of the masked dances. Finally, during the years of the Second World War all performances were banned. The nation was split in half, the two parts now antagonists. After the hostilities, with the restoration of Korea's independence, its old theatrical forms sprang to life again in the South. Publication of the plays, study and productions of them, did much to revitalize them. The Southern government, recognizing their cultural value, acted to promote interest in them, designating them as artistic properties of real importance to the nation. In now Communist North Korea, though, the attitude towards them was quite the opposite: they were declared to be relics of a past world, decadent, and forbidden because they lacked revolutionary zeal. Also, to stern Marxists, puppet plays were viewed as suitable to amuse only a regressive, backward populace.

— 6 —

INDIA: PLAYS AND PLAYERS

The efflorescence of theatre in India, inspired by the theories and practices of one man of genius, Bharata, began to decline about the year AD 1000. The Sanskrit stage, to which Bharata's successors contributed many works, left a legacy of about 700 scripts, though some authorities limit the library to 500. In the ensuing centuries the élite – princes, their ministers and courtiers – displayed a meagre interest in plays. Ever more their preferred entertainment was dance – ritualistic, erotic, narrative – that was eventually to be come India's major theatre art form. The Sanskrit scripts, acknowledged to be classics but rarely revived, devolved into a subject for worshipful analysis by scholars; and Sanskrit was quite unintelligible to the largely illiterate Indian masses, though, as noted earlier, debased elements of it lingered on in common speech.

The chances of attaining a serious dramatic literature were also greatly handicapped by India's size, a vast subcontinent spreading from the snowy Himalayas in the far north, past mountains, deserts, plains and green jungles to the sweltering ocean beaches of Goa and Madras, a varied terrain and a nation made up of an uneasy conglomeration of peoples of different ethnic strains and fervent religious beliefs – Hindu, Buddhist, Muslim, Parsee, Sikh, Jain, Christian – many uncongenial to one another, some often murderously hostile. Coupled with this, today more than sixty languages are in daily use; they are further fragmented into more than 544 dialects. The principal tongues, numbering sixteen, and each spoken by millions, include Hindi, Punjabi, Tamil, Bengali, Telegu, Malavali, Marathi, Kannada, Oriya, Kashmiri, Gujarati and Urdu. Each expresses a distinct culture, and each in some measure has its own kind of theatre; hence for many Indians the wordless dance and mime were bound to have and retain the widest appeal, offsetting inevitable verbal chaos with visual elements of universality; though again in each region the dance, too, has different local features and characteristics. (To resolve the linguistic confusion, English, a hangover of the lengthy British rule, serves as a *lingua franca* in official circles and among the better educated; many leading newspapers and influential magazines are published in English and read by members of the higher castes and upper classes. There has been a vigorous government effort to make Hindi the national language, so far without success.) The disappearance of Sanskrit theatre was hastened by the Muslim occupation of India in the eighth century; the new rulers were opposed to it.

Poverty has also been an obstacle to the growth of a broad sophisticated audience. Millions of Indians dwell miserably in foetid, crowded cities or widely dispersed, dusty villages: they live at a level of barest subsistence. There has been considerable progress, but a great deal more is needed to help the poorest segments of the population.

The introduction of films and television in the twentieth century has largely distracted the new middle class from taking in live drama. Globally, Indians are among the busiest and most prosperous film producers. Almost all of their output, shown throughout Asia, consists of flamboyant musicals, always with dance sequences, but art films of notable quality have been made by Satyajit Ray and his disciples that have earned worldwide applause.

Despite these many barriers and problems, the rich Indian flair for colourful theatre has never been wholly suppressed. It has thrived in the creation and preservation of strange and unique dance forms. Quite as enduringly, it still finds expression in a profusion of folk plays put on for villagers. These playlets sprang up very early, in what might be designated the medieval era, and were joined somewhat later by a more literary genre, offerings looser in structure than were the Sanskrit dramas. Ultimately they have come to be called "traditional theatre". (I am quoting or paraphrasing here from writings by Henry W. Wells, of Columbia University, in the Gassner and Quinn *Readers Encyclopedia of World Drama*, as well as from Suresh Awasthi in the *Oxford Companion to the Theatre*, Myron Maitlaw in *World Drama*, and once more from the *McGraw-Hill Encyclopedia of World Drama*, as well as from scattered articles, some unsigned, in periodicals.)

The folk plays are enacted on festive occasions in the villages; they have mostly a religious content and vary to an extent determined by the ethnic identity of the actors and where the observance takes place. Even now, traces of the classic Sanskrit dramas are discernible in them, partly because they still draw on the sacred texts, especially the legends of Rama and Krishna as related in the *Mahābhārata*, as well as episodes from the *Ramayana* and the *Gota-Govinda*. The pieces in both these categories, folk and traditional, are in the vernacular – sometimes they are inelegant translations of the original Sanskrit – and, of course, which tongue is used depends on where they happen to be performed. The "traditional" add lavish spectacle and include singing and dancing and may borrow touches from a "variety" show. Two aspects of them are not found in classic Sanskrit drama: the frequent dependence on a chorus – heretofore present sparingly, if at all – along with a solo narrator (*sutradhara*) responsible for clarifying the plot, which is apt to be quite thin. (Storytelling and street singing had long been an established occupation; now their practitioners were partly absorbed into this theatre.) The language of the folk plays is not without poetic merit and is enhanced by effective mime, and there is much improvisation. As has been emphasized, seldom are repeated performances the same, yet there is a limit on deviation from an overall narrative line. This amount of freedom lends the ancient works a renewed vitality, keeping them fresh yet largely authentic.

In the countryside both types of plays are put on by travelling companies, who may resort to a multi-level stage on a cart, or a platform that can be easily moved about. This approximates the *modus operandi* of Italian *commedia dell'arte* troupes and seems to be the immemorial practice of journeying players in every epoch and clime.

Only a few of these plays have published texts, though Indian scholars are now making an effort to capture them in print, fearing that the rivalry of universally available film and television may soon cause the old offerings to vanish. Most of their authors are unknown. Wells comments that the story-lines are actually collaborations between their anonymous creators and the generations of actors who have interpreted them over ten centuries.

In the *New York Times* (1976) Steven R. Weisman reported on a visit to Brindaban where he beheld a festival honouring Krishna's birthday during which several plays were given. His vivid account conveys the psychological and spiritual aura in which such events take place.

The first shadows of dusk seem to bring this sacred old city to life with prayer. From countless corners in its narrow, winding streets comes an eerie tinkling of cymbals, the buzz of chanting and the peal of bells.

The soft night air soon becomes fragrant with incense and sweets to be offered to Lord Krishna, one of the most popular gods of the Hindu pantheon. Thousands of years ago, Krishna's sensuous adolescent adventures are said to have taken place here on the banks of the Jumna River.

On the occasion of Krishna's birthday, on September 7, tens of thousands of pilgrims flocked here this week. There were poor farmers, teachers, professionals and hundreds of mendicant holy men, or *sadhus*, with long matted hair and staffs and begging bowls.

"I became a *sadhu* to drink of God's sweet bliss," said a bearded man in a tattered loincloth whose white hair was smeared with yellow dye as a symbol of his devotion. "Here it is special because of Krishna. Here you can find peace."

Spending a day here is like going back in time. Brindaban is a small city of forty thousand people and no fewer than five thousand Hindu temples, not far from the busy trunk road that connects New Delhi with the old Mogul capital of Agra.

But it is a universe away from the world observed by outsiders. In this holiday season, one can feel in an almost pure form the emotional range of the Hindu religion, which remains one of the essential keys to understanding India today.

In nearby Mathura, Krishna was born as the eighth incarnation of the god Vishnu. To escape the evil ruler Kamsa, he was transferred at birth across the river to Gokul to be raised by poor villagers.

Krishna's humble upbringing made him perhaps the most beloved god among the farm folk and workers of India. His rise in popularity coincided with the Bhakti movement, which placed its emphasis on intense devotion, as opposed to learning or work.

Like many religious reforms in the West, the Bhakti movement sought to bring religion back to the people and away from the obscurantism of the priestly class.

Scholars say the movement has important historical and sociological implications for the masses in India. But in religious terms, it highlights a relationship between God and man that is intensely personal and even physical.

Thus one of the favorite religious episodes here is Krishna's erotic play with the milkmaids. Wearing a crown of peacock feathers, garlands of flowers and golden robes, Krishna danced and played his flute in the forest at Brindaban, bewitching his listeners and causing their clothes to slip off.

Later the milkmaids bathed nude in the Jumna River. When Krishna stole their clothes, the maidens became embarrassed and filled with love, subsequently surrendering to him in an example of the devotion a worshiper must have with God.

Devotion permeated the air of Brindaban today. All week long, the faithful attended plays, depicting the life of Krishna. The stories unfolded on stages draped in shimmering curtains of blue, gold and crimson.

Worshippers heaped hibiscus and lotus blossoms at the altar. Others cupped their hands or raised them aloft, performing *puja*, or prayer.

Everywhere the priests distributed doughy and sugary sweets called *prasad*, to be blessed and eaten or to be offered to the poor. On Krishna's birthday itself, the very religious fast until midnight.

"Here is a place where I can come to separate myself from the material world," said Mahesh Chandravajpai, a thirty-three-year-old grade school mathematics teacher.

Not far away on the muddy bank of the Jumna River, a group of a dozen farm workers from the state of Haryana said they had traveled for hours by bus and horse cart to celebrate Krishna's birthday at his birthplace. A delay in the monsoons this year had enabled these farmers to get away before harvest time.

For these and other people, the fantastical exploits of Krishna are told and retold and have the appeal of the escapist stories and fairy tales about superheroes and visitors from outer space in the West.

Some perform the meritorious act of walking round the mountain, actually a long low-lying ridge. Others walk round a small rock from the mountain placed in the larger temples in Brindaban.

Few landscapes in the world continue to hold such religious power for the people. This week villagers and city dwellers alike sat in rapt attention at a play depicting the life of Chaitanya, a sixteenth-century saint who helped revive the Bhakti movement in Brindaban.

"How can you go and leave me alone?" his mother asked the young man after he announced he would become a priest.

"Don't worry," replied the son. "Krishna will always protect you."

In sum, and interestingly, the lively Krishna is seen as a Dionysiac figure, inspiring and infusing Indian native drama much as did the young Greek fertility god in the rise of the earliest plays of ancient Athens.

As remarked before, mostly the plays are not in print but have been passed along orally from one set of actors to another. Sometimes they are presented by non-professionals. Interesting and typical is a plea by Anil Saara in the New Delhi *Financial Express* concerning the future of these works and hopes for their retention, keeping their pure style and subtle details.

Sometimes the Indian art-world manifests blind-spots that prevent it from doing the right thing even though it stares you in the face.

One of Delhi theatre's saddest features is that there is no interaction between urban groups, who are involved in learning folk-theatre forms, and the actual folk performers who inhabit the country around the city's proscenium theatres. On the periphery of the sprawling capital, traditional folk performers move from village to village, playing atop stages improvised by putting a number of bullock carts together. Far removed from them, in the air-conditioned auditoriums, the lost generations of Indian theatre struggle and claw their way through an amorphous cloud that hangs over them, in the sense that these young urban actors have no clear traditions to work within but have to chart out their own frameworks and discover the genres best suited to them and their sensibility.

So rigid is this cleavage between the urban novitiates and the traditional folk-troupes that there has been little interaction between urban artistes and the mandali of Chattisgarhi performers that Habib Tanvir's Naya Theatre has instituted in Delhi on a permanent basis.

In the late sixties, anxious to revitalise his own work in the theatre, Habib Tanvir went back home to Chattisgarh, in the interior of Madhya Pradesh, to meet his elders and his peers of the Chattisgarhi folk-theatre mandali with which Habib had taken his first steps into the theatre. Discovering that many of his friends were living derelict lives and that the old mandali had disbanded, Habib invited the players to leave their paan-shops and the booze-dens, live with him in Delhi and resuscitate the folk troupe in an alien environment.

During the last decade, the Chattisgarhi performers were an integral part of the Naya Theatre and lent its more urbanly-conceived productions the vitality and the vigour of their folk tradition. Occasionally, under Habib Tanvir's restraining urban sensibility they also moulded folk plays for urban audiences. Despite the fact that the Chattisgarhi dialect of Hindi is very different from Hindi dialects spoken in the belt around Delhi, the folk artistes succeeded in overcoming linguistic barriers and commanding the attention of the audience through the sheer plasticity of their theatrical idiom and the complex rhythms of their histrionics. Their most popular production during the last decade was *Charandas Cher*, which Habib Tanvir later revised and gave a new script to, for a children's film by Shyam Benegal.

Naya Theatre's Chattisgarhi performers opened this decade with a new production, at which they introduced yet another Chattisgarhi style – the Chandaini. According to Habib Tanvir, the Chandaini "was a rare theatre form in Chattisgarhi till about seven years ago, when we first contacted a lone old balladeer performing the story. At that time we discovered only two or three Chandaini groups. Recently, however, they have multiplied. And now there are several groups of young artistes staging Chandaini. They, however, remain confined to the districts of Raipur and Bilaspur . . . The Chandaini balladeer takes several nights to unfold his tale . . . Usually he is supported by four to five instrumentalists and singers who play their instruments and provide the vocal refrain while the main artist sings, narrates and dances his story . . . the story being secular, oral and rarely known, audience response to it differs and this difference perhaps contributes in a major way to the difference of style in Chandaini."

This tradition prompted Habib Tanvir to re-assemble the Chandaini story of the lovers Lorik and Chanda, produced by Naya Theatre as *Sone Sagar* into a regular play in which the narrative action is interspersed with the traditional song and dance of folk-theatre. Many of the moves and the stage grouping of the actors were straight out of conventional urban practices. Conforming to these, the folk artistes created a rare sense of naïveté as the symbolic nature of cross-court movements by different actors was totally eroded and categorized to the simple ends of "entries" and "exits".

It was this geometric purity of their response to the otherwise symbolic entries and exits by urban actors that prompts one to ask why urban theatre groups in Delhi do not ever work in co-ordination with Habib Tanvir's folk company settled right here in the metropolis. The National School of Drama, which has opened its doors to diverse talents in recent years, could well take the lead in this. A folk production created out of collaboration by NSD students and the capital's

Chattisgarhi mandali could provide yet another breakthrough to theatre experiments here and elsewhere.

The first thing that distinguishes folk performers from urban Indian groups is the immense complexity of the craft of acting that the former have mastered and the absolute unpretentiousness with which they can reel off their craftsmanship in the almost uncontrollable cascade. Whereas the urban actor consciously struggles to establish his stage presence, the traditional folk artiste seems to be born with it, from the very first step he takes or the very first sound he makes onstage. A magnetic presence on the stage seems to be intrinsic to the folk artiste's very personality.

The students of the NSD who, under B.V. Karanth's stewardship, have taken on the challenge of adapting their urban sensibilities to folk-theatre forms, would gain immensely by working with genuine folk-theatre people, particularly in developing the folk artiste's nonchalant air of magic – as far as stage presence and musical rhythms and the complexity of gestures and voice modulations are concerned.

Naya Theatre's production of *Sone Sagar* provided here at Delhi the same unexpectedness that Habib Tanvir says is intrinsic to the Chandaini theatre's audience back in the Madhya Pradesh villages. *Sone Sogar* was an adaptation of the Chandaini story about the young lovers Lorik and Chanda. A story that is also part of the Bihari folk-theatre tradition. But whereas the Bihari version makes the boy Lorik the prima donna, the Chandaini emphasizes Chanda as the driving force behind the legend.

The unexpected element in the Chandaini story lays in the fact that it can warm the cockles of the militant feminist's heart. Chanda is the daughter of a local king – a *rajwada*, as he is called by the north Indians. During childhood her hand is pledged to Lorik because Lorik's family – a family of Yaday cowherds – present to the king the prize buffalo *Sone Sogar* ("a sea of gold"). Chanda and Lorik fall in love in their adolescence, confident that they shall marry each other. Chanda's father, however, changes his mind. He would rather that she married the son of another *rajwada*. Indeed, Chanda is married off ruthlessly and Lorik, too, is forced to set up his own household.

Chanda, however, refuses to accept the arrangement. She deserts her husband, forces Lorik out of his benign and staid household and the two elope. Chanda's husband pursues them to seize his wife back, as the play gives epic proportions to the love triangle.

Throughout this second half, Lorik behaves like a cowed-down, indecisive creature. Chanda, on the other hand, throws discretion to the winds, rebels against her father and decides to fight the world in order to secure her beloved; and also in order to abide by a more honourable code of conduct, since her father had given his word long ago that she would marry Lorik when she grew up.

To hew closely to the authentic mode of the folk plays, however, must be difficult. Most are almost plotless, the characters mere stereotypes, outrageously blunt. A prominent figure is a clown (*vidushaka*) whose antics are meant to delight the illiterate crowd. The body of the work may be a kind of naïve vaudeville, consisting at best of little more than vocal and instrumental music, dancing and pageantry, again resembling Italy's endlessly roving *commedia dell'arte*.

Diverse folk and individualized types of "traditional theatre" have evolved and still flourish in disparate regions: the Jatra of West Bengal ("*jatra*" means "procession" or "pilgrimage"); the Yakshagana of South India; the Bhava of Gujarat; the Nautanki of Uttar Pradesh; the Tamasha (i.e. "show") of Maharashtra. Others are the Maach of Madhya Pradesh; the Bhanda-Pather of Kashmir; the Khyal of Rajasthan; and the Swang of the Punjab. Perhaps the most ancient and once wholly operatic, the Jatra has changed into a prose drama with only song interludes. It can also be found in the adjacent states of Manipur and Assam, as well to the east in Orissa. The Yakshagana, prevalent in Karnataka, favours "choreographic acting", but also includes songs. Its players are noted for ornate and bizarre attire. The costumes, as are those worn by performers in the Krishnattam ("Krishna plays") and the Terrūkuttu ("street-theatre") of Tamil Nadu, are apt to call for huge, fantastic headdresses, crowns and masks – or else application of mask-like make-up. Indeed, make-up that to Western eyes is grotesque is used liberally in most branches of "traditional" Indian theatre. The colours painted on the actor's face are usually a clue to the character he is impersonating: red proclaims that he is evil, yellow that he is virtuous or divine. Yet other designs – "lines, semicircles and dots in various hues, including white and black" – may also mark his features.

The Bhava, Tamasha and Nautanki have secular subject-matter, some of it derived from medieval tales, mythology, heroic ballads and romances, but sometimes they address current social problems. They shun religious content. Lighter and shorter are the Nagal, Swang and Bhandaiti, treating with contemporary affairs wittily and always having the air of spontaneity. To the secular genre, too, belong the Khyal and Maach; they are predominantly operatic, their scores tinctured with local idioms. Tamasha is noteworthy for its incorporation of vigorous ballad singing, which has led it to become a vehicle for acidulous political satire. Terrūkuttu and Veethi-Nattakam exploit stories from the sacred epics and are the most stylized in performance. The Bhava is peculiar, nothing more than a string of skits and playlets borrowing long-familiar situations and characters. Yet other forms are the Kucipudi of Andhra Pradesh and the Bagwat Mela of Tamil Nadu.

Considerably more ambitious than the folk plays, stagings of the "traditional" theatre display far better craftsmanship; the actors are given more polished dialogue. Indeed, some of the scripts have substantial literary merit. Though more free in structure than the Sanskrit scripts, these plays do possess some degree of defined form. A paradigm for them was the twelfth-century lyric drama *Gita Govinda*, in Sanskrit and dealing with parts of the ubiquitous Krishna legend.

Other ways of categorizing these exuberant theatrical offerings are used. One is to fit them into two broad groups. Adopting this approach, a good number of them are referred to as "temple plays". As might be expected, their content is religious or semi-religious. Legends of Rama and Krishna provide the themes of about half of the works in this cluster. Plays in the other half are inspired by romantic tales from a spectrum of secular sources, even from beyond India's borders; they may depict historical incidents, borrow materials from medieval lore, or illustrate the self-sacrificial deeds of revered Hindu saints and heroes. Again, a goodly number may examine political and social dilemmas of the past and tumultuous present.

To accommodate the religious plays, many temple complexes have appropriate theatre halls. In temples, songs and dances have long been a part of votive offerings; in time, the priests expanded their activities to sponsor larger dramatic presentations.

The Rama and Krishna cycle plays arose in the fifteenth century under temple auspices, where they were harboured from the start. The ritualistic Krishnattam comprises eight plays about episodes in Krishna's life, and particularly his frolicsome feats. (He can hardly be looked on as always favouring sexual abstinence.) The dancer–actors, employing highly symbolic, strictly codified gestures, enact the stories sung by reciters. Even more intricate and conventionalized is the "body language" used in Kathakali, another genre that grew out of the Krishnattam, extending its subject-matter by accepting *Ramayana* and *Mahābhārata* plays. Some of the best-known and esteemed examples of Krishnattam and Kathakali may be viewed in the state of Kerala.

Vishnu, too, has his cult, evoking from devotees a series of dramas portraying him in his ever-changing incarnations. From brimming votive offerings, rites and celebrations, more ambitious dramatizations gradually took shape. These plays are highly poetic, the god's spiritual nature externalized in music and dance, as well as in brilliant paintings. All these qualities emanated at a high level in the fifteenth and sixteenth centuries, a period of cultural renaissance that, as mentioned above, also gave birth to the Krishnattam. It was in this artistically rich era that scripts of the "traditional" theatre were refined and gained evident frameworks.

The Ramalila and Rasalilia, designated familiarly as the Lila plays, are likewise dedicated to Rama and Krishna and call for resplendent processions. They originated mostly in northern India. Lord Vishnu is honoured in lyric dramas known as Ankia Nat composed by Vaishnava monks in the eastern province of Assam. These, too, are mounted with much ceremony, graced with music, poetry, symbolic gestures and dance-steps.

Here I defer to Suresh Awasthi, an obvious authority, to explicate the techniques and some nuances of the music and dances.

Borrowing elements from the classical, folk, and popular theaters, the music in "traditional" theater has an integrated and independent character. In the temple-based forms, the music is highly developed and systematized; the sung dialogue is set to various *ragas* appropriate to the situations and the sentiments of the dramatic story. In the social and simpler forms the music retains its folk and popular character but has a pronounced classical flavor. There is a great range and variety of metrical forms and of singing styles.

Brief dance sequences and dancelike movements in all forms of traditional drama performances are intended to meet the needs of stylization and a nonrealistic approach to acting. As in the case of music, the dance content is richer and more developed in the temple-based forms. In the social forms it is thin by design and intended to heighten the tempo of the performance. With dancelike movements, striking poses, and codified gestures, the performance acquires a great choreographic beauty and pictorial charm.

Both music and dance serve multiple dramatic functions and are organic to the performance. The drum is the predominant instrument, helping to accentuate the actor's gestures and movements as well as heightening the tempo of the play. Music accompanies the actor's singing, and it sets the timing and pace of his movements and deepens the mood of the situation. Orchestral pieces are often used not only for the entrances and exits of characters but also as incidental music. The orchestra plays in unison with the vocal line and repeats the melodic structure, at times giving relief to the actor to present a dance sequence. The musical and choreographic structures of the performance are interdependent and fully integrated.

As has been said, "traditional" theatre also embraces social themes, or it may choose to put on farces. This secular facet of theatre began to intrude in the seventeenth and eighteenth centuries. Such offerings are likely to be enacted on level ground, with spectators assembled on all four sides, much as in Western "theatre-in-the-round". The characters are stock. Music and dance are invariably added.

In "traditional" theatre, as is true in most staging throughout the Orient, the actors must follow rules that are fixed and constricting, far more so than obtains in the West. Nearly always the characters are stock figures, their ranks divisible into three general kinds of persons: the *rajasika*, or worldly; the *tamasika*, or villainous; the *satvika*, or godly. Some shadings allow combining these principal traits in a single character, but very often an actor specializes throughout his career in embodying only one type.

Primarily the success and perpetuation of "traditional" theatre depends on the skills and charisma of the actors, for whom it is an excellent showcase. In many instances their choice of profession is owing to a family link, as is true in China and especially in Japan, and in the West. Versatility is required; the performer must be adept at singing, dancing, female impersonation, pantomime and acrobatics. This mandates a lengthy training and apprenticeship.

Often the stage is wholly plain, requiring the actor to conjure up the illusion of a setting by his mimetic skills. His mastery of dialogue must be clear and effective. To quote further from Suresh Awasthi:

Dramatic speech is determined by a set of conventions, and multiple patterns of delivery are adopted. Repetition, superimposition, simultaneous speaking, and alternation of speech between the actor and the chorus are some of the devices employed. Speech presented as rhythmic prose, as song, and as chant extends the range and the impact of the dramatic word. There is also the alternation of prose and verse dialogue. The prose dialogue is often an impromptu elaboration of the sung dialogue, thus creating new levels of dramatic action. In addition to straight dialogue, there are soliloquies, semi-soliloquies, asides, and monologues.

In the dramatic structure the chorus, a group of singers, plays an important role. . . . The chorus sings the entire text of the play and also accompanies the actors in the sung dialogue. It performs the entry songs describing the qualities and the dramatic functions of the characters. The function of the chorus is primarily to support the musical structure of the play and relieve the actors so that they can present brief dance sequences.

. . . In *Yakshagana* and *Terrūkuttu* the performance is set to a heightened pitch, and the actors move about to the accompaniment of drum music. Intermittently they burst into song and join the chorus; when the chorus sings their dialogue they dance with great gusto.

The tradition of female impersonation has its own theatrical values and fully fits in with the nature and character of this theater. Male actors in female roles show great skill in portraying feminine attributes. The dancer-actor Vedantam Satyam has attained great heights in the portrayal of Satyabhama, Krishna's consort, in the *Kuchipudi* dance-drama *Bhama Kalapam*.

The two stock characters, namely Sutradhara and Vidushaka, of the Sanskrit theater, are also found in many forms of "traditional" theater. Sutradhara, functioning as narrator, recites and sings the narrative portions and links various dramatic episodes. Vidushaka adds to the entertainment and gaiety of the performance. Even in the plays based on the epics and mythology and having religious overtones, it is through Vidushaka that social and contemporary material is incorporated into the performance. Vidushaka makes sharp comments on social situations and attacks social injustice, malpractice, and corruption.

. . . The playing area is a neutral, unlocalized space easily manipulated by the actor and capable of serving the basic requirement of "traditional" theater – multiplicity of locales and simultaneity of action.

With stylized and symbolic make-up, gorgeous costume, and huge fantastic headdress, he stands on a bare stage and creates a vivid *mise-en-scène* with his own dynamic presence. The scenic effect is strengthened by the actor's codified gait, choreographic acting, and again symbolic hand gestures. . . .

Mostly the stagings are outdoor events; the plays are presented in streets, open spaces outside towns, market squares, gardens, temple courtyards, and fields after harvest. The performance – informal and participative – is a social event, an integral part of community activity. In many cases the audiences are fully familiar with the epics and the legendary heroes. In the plays based on the Rama and Krishna legends the audiences participate in many rituals and ceremonials which are an integral part of the performance.

"Traditional" theater continues to be a living and vital theater in entertaining mass rural audiences. It also helps preserve traditional culture and disseminate epic and legendary stories containing social ideals and life values. During the Nineteenth Century and the first half of the Twentieth Century it was pushed to the background by the modern realistic theater that emerged under the influence of the British theater and Western dramatic values. After Independence in 1947 there was a renewed interest in "traditional" and folk theater as part of the cultural resurgence. Plans and programs were initiated to preserve and promote the traditional arts. The Sangeet Natak Academi (National Academy of Music, Dance, and Drama) in New Delhi, a body established and supported by the national government, played a vital role in popularizing and encouraging folk theater as did the academies at the state level. Festivals, seminars, and exhibitions revealed the richness and vitality of the "traditional" theater and fostered contacts with the Western-oriented modern theater. Gradually the playwrights and directors were drawn to it and started seeking inspiration from the values and techniques of folk performances. As a result of personal exploration of the traditional theatrical heritage, several playwrights and directors started making creative use of the elements and techniques of "traditional" theater.

Despite the limitations imposed on the actors, chances for them to innovate did arise, far more than the Sanskrit players were ever allowed. Change is bound to happen to procedures as centuries go by; the world – the context – is also changing. A heap of new conventions, governing authors as well as performers, accreted and became permanent, a revitalizing process occurring in every medium of art. How much this affected the stagecraft was determined by the locale – which Indian region – and the type of play. But in a good many instances Sanskrit precedents have continued to be largely respected. Among them are dictates on how the dialogue is spoken or sung, patterns of entrances and exits, and the handling of how time and place are indicated, along with their passing and shifting.

A play is apt to open with a very lengthy preliminary: a musical prelude, an invocatory song, a formal identification of the characters, a statement of the theme, about which there may even be an initial philosophical discourse. In Yakshagana, where the religious element is strong, age-old rituals are practised in the dressing room; after applying their elaborate make-up, the actors chant a prayer. In Rasilia the spectators participate with the players in solemn introductory ceremonies. Perhaps tribute is paid to Lord Ganesha, the elephant deity.

In the annals of the best cultural historians, theatre resembling that of the West had its advent in the nineteenth century, coinciding with the arrival of the British and their governance first of Calcutta and then of the conglomeration of sprawling princely states that made up India. Sometimes this brought plays that combined picture-frame staging and the actors' use of the fixed techniques of classical, folk and "traditional" performances. At other times the long-cherished, highly conventionalized modes gave way to realistic portrayals. The methods of presentation might change along with the kind of play being staged, with each work put on in a manner true and appropriate to its genre, the different sorts of plays alternating – one night an Indian fantasy, the next an imported English or French masterpiece. This was a reasonable and practical compromise. But if, as too often happened, the stage-idioms were intermingled, in what might be classified as a hybrid production, incongruities resulted, some amusing to foreign-born spectators, and some lending the drama an air of implausibility.

Among the first professional troupes to add European works to their repertoires were commercial Parsee companies in Bombay who might offer a local farce or serious native play one day followed by an adaptation of a piece by Shakespeare or Molière a mere day later.

About 1870 dozens of such troupes began to tour wherever Hindi was spoken in the northern regions of India. Even in remote towns they set up tents to draw rural audiences. Later they ventured southwards into Marathi and Gujarati. By the 1890s the movement, now known as "Parsee theatre", was quite substantial, well organized and with appeal for many spectators. Most of the companies had resident playwrights. The best known was Agha Hashar Kashmiri (1879–1935), whose output was copious and includes *Safed Khoon* (*White Blood*) that rings with echoes of *King Lear*, and *Ankha Ka Nasha* (*The Witchery of Eyes*), flailing at the sinfulness of prostitution. His *Rustom O Sohrab* is based on what is to Westerners the most familiar of Persian legends after its having been used by Matthew Arnold for his famed poem. Similarly prolific was Nadayan Orasad Betab (1872–1945), among whose works are *Mahābhārata* and *Satya Harsh Chandra* (*Truthful Harsh Chandra*), the latter about a king renowned for unswerving honesty, which causes him to undergo personal ordeals. Radheshyan Kathavachak, another indefatigable provider of popular scripts, derived both his *Bhishma Pratijyan* (*Bhishma's Vow*) and *Vir Abhimanyu* (*The Brave Abhimanyu*) from stories in the endlessly rich *Mahābhārata*.

The Parsee theatre also took up *Inder Sabla*, an operatic piece by the Urdu poet Amanat. Initially produced in Lucknow (1853), it was a bounding hit and widely staged elsewhere, offering a challenge that other works in the genre had difficulty matching.

Mostly delving into mythological and historical subject-matter, the Parsee plays tended to be highly melodramatic, with strong climactic scenes; they also boasted comic sub-plots and were replete with songs. Each act ended with the characters striking a tableau, carefully envisaged in the stage instructions. The texts and staging conspicuously borrowed and slapped together elements from second-rate Western theatre and native folk drama, opera, farce and balladry. The mountings were often lavish, with painted scenery and costly curtains. As in some other forms of Indian theatre, acrobatics were inserted, as well as circus devices.

Bombay also had Gujarati and Marathi theatres for ticket-buyers who spoke either of those two languages. Still other companies ventured on to the stage for spectators with a sufficient knowledge of English. One of the first "modern" Gujarati playwrights was Vishnudas Bhave (1820–1901), credited with no fewer than fifty scripts, conceptually drawn from the sacred epics. But two successful dramatists who followed him, Dayabhai Dholshaji (1877–1902) and Kanaialal Maneklal Munshi (1877–?) chose contemporary subject-matter and advocated a number of reforms. They aimed satirical thrusts at social and political injustices. In particular, Munshi argued on behalf of women, whose lot he deplored. *Kakani Shashi* (1928) was his most admired stage piece. Also enlisted in the cause of realism was Chandravadan C. Mehta (1901–?) who earned praise with *Ag-vadi* (1932; *The Railway Train*) about an ailing locomotive fireman.

The bent in Gujarati theatre was always towards commercial success, which prompted it to devote much of its efforts to putting on popular comedies. Experimental groups did not flourish, until the appearance of Mehta's socially concerned *Ag-vadi* gave impetus to this new trend.

After Independence, Gujarati theatre became even more active, not only in Bombay but also in Ahmedabad and Baroda. Several companies with serious-minded members demonstrated that the commercial stage could thrive with more substantial fare. Such ensembles were Nat Mandal, Rang Mandal and Rang Bhumi. A flock of able directors was on hand. Of help to them was the Indian National Theatre in Bombay, an organization dedicated to Gujarati stage art.

(It is tempting to go from state to state, listing a host of authors of now faded nineteenth- and early twentieth-century Indian dramas coming forth during this profound and often confusing period of transition. But it is neither possible nor practical to do so: India is too huge, and the reader would find the attempt at such a survey numbing. As stated in my Foreword, I have limited the scope of my study. Its purpose is to describe Oriental theatre. I do not have the space to cover as fully as I would like the Westernized plays now ever more prevalent in India. Such works differ hardly at all in form and subject from what is staged on Broadway and the West End; they can be understood and appreciated without any guidance from this book. I make exceptions of those playwrights who, confronting great change, wrote plays in both Far Eastern and Western styles, either alternating between the two sorts of presentation, or attempting to blend mysticism, fantasy and realism in the same script, which frequently happened in India. I will usually discuss those authors only in part, looking at what is Indian, mentioning in passing what is European. A further exception will be a few dramatists whose works are not "Oriental" but who have achieved worldwide stature.)

Marathi theatre had an earlier origin; it is traced to an incident in 1843. That was the year in which a courtier, Vishnu Das Bhave, in the minor princely state of Maharashtra, composed *Sita Swayamvar* (*The Marriage of Sita*). He was prompted to do so when a Yakshagana folk troupe from the adjacent state of Karnataka came to perform in Maharashtra. Bhave appropriated much from the Yakshagana form, especially its loose structure and reliance on frequent songs and store of incidents. In a subsequent evolution, Marathi dramatists acquired elements from Tamasha, another regional folk genre, as well as adding components from various sorts of popular entertainment, including balladry, recitation and storytelling. Throughout the second half of the nineteenth and the early decades of the twentieth centuries, playwrights such as K.P. Khadilkar (1872–1948), G.B. Deval (1855–1916) and R.G. Gadkari (1855–1919) did much to advance the cause of the Marathi stage. Khadilkar adapted a story from the *Mahābhārata* for his *Keechak-Vadha* (*Killing of Keechak*); Deval chose to examine a failed marriage in *Sharda* (the name of the heroine); Gadkari attacked the problem of alcoholism in *Ekcha Pyala* (*Only One Glass*). From 1920 on, as the topics of these three plays indicate, Marathi dramatists followed the lead of writers in other languages and regions by turning from historical and mythological subjects to now more acceptable material. Soon, as almost everywhere in India, Ibsen and Shaw were major influences. Bhargavaram Vitthol Mama Warekar (1883–1964) was the outstanding dramatist of this phase, commanding attention with scripts like *Satte Che Gulam* (*Slaves of Power*) and *Sonya Cha Kalas* (*Pinacle of Gold*), the latter piece freighted with social significance. He created almost 200 stage works in a naturalistic vein. His example encouraged other Marathi playwrights to promote progressive change in whatever might be the distinctive subculture to which they personally adhered, a profession, a trade, a prone-to-violence ultra-nationalism or over-zealous religious community crying out for better balance or economic improvement. To be singled out here (an "exception") must be Purushottam Laksman Deshpande (1919–), a highly multi-talented actor–writer whose one-man satirical sketches, which he himself performed, are a matchless contribution to India's modern stage. He is particularly esteemed for his deft adaptations of Gogol's *The Inspector General* and Brecht's *The Threepenny Opera*, as well as his own *Tuze Ahe Tuzapashi* (*Yours as Yours*), a portrait of a liberal reformer.

From Marathi theatre has come the Sangeet, a century-old form of musical drama now popular throughout India. It has attracted some of the country's finest singers. An early practitioner of it was Annasaheb Kirloskar, who in 1880 presented a Marathi version of *Shakuntala*, Kaladasa's classic Sanskrit play.

Awasthi attributes to post-Independence Marathi theatre a "great vibrancy". He cites other prominent writers of the 1960s and 1970s who were engaged there. "In their plays scathing satire blends with deep concern for the human predicament in a society of inequalities and contradictions. Also, in form there is a most theatrical and unconventional mixture of narration, dialogue, dance, song and mime. These plays with their experimental character are forcing a change in production styles and values." Such iconoclastic works called for bold staging. Happily, young, new directors were available to surmount the problems of realizing them imaginatively.

In the Punjab – in north India – modern theatre arrived somewhat belatedly. The region had an ancient and still vital tradition of balladry and mime, roaming entertainers and story-tellers. Only in 1914 did an original play on a social subject appear: *Dulhan* (*The Bride*) by I.C. Manda. After that, theatrical activity was still intermittent.

Some Punjabi poets and novelists looked to the stage, but their efforts were mostly closet dramas, better read than seen. In one arduous and demanding phase of theatre, however, those using the local language were in advance of all others in India: modern opera. For more than three decades a group calling itself the Delhi Art Theatre, located in the capital, presented operas composed by Sheila Bhatia. One of her most-liked offerings is *Heer Ranjiha* (named after the hero and heroine), derived from a Punjabi legend. As yet, few Westerners are acquainted with Bhatia's work.

In Orissa and Assam, in the north-east, the indigenous theatre has been markedly influenced by nearby Bengal, partly because the two languages, Oriya and Assamese, have a close affinity with Bengali, and the people in all three regions share a similar "cultural ethos". They also have a lively tradition and predilection for puppetry, balladry, dance and other sorts of folk entertainment, out of which a hesitant commercial stage and a modern popular theatre slowly grew through a span of several decades. After successive waves of historical-mythological and predominantly literary dramas, an "engaged" theatre dedicated to social betterment finally gained a foothold.

The sporadic prosperity of the commercial stage in Orissa was largely due to the steady output of two playwrights: Aswini Kumar Ghose (1892–1962) and Kalicharan Panigrahi (1898–1978). In the post-Independence era, however, Orissa's theatre suddenly shrank in strength and any sort of relevance. The few scripts deemed to be above average were Western in style and up to date in content. Manoranjan Das courageously explored current social dilemmas, of which there were no lack in Orissa. He adopted experimental dramatic forms in *Katha Ghora* (*The Wooden Horse*) and *Aranya Fasal* (*The Wild Harvest*), displaying his empathy for the tragic ironies that beset some lives. His scripts were translated into other regional languages and performed outside his native state. The reputation of a like-surnamed contemporary, J.P. Das, was enhanced by his *Suryastu Purvaru* (*Before the Sunset*), his accomplishments bringing him an award from the National Academy of Letters.

Assam's theatrical history began in the fifteenth century, when a social activist and religious leader, Shankardev, saw drama as an evangelical tool. His exhortative plays, composed to spread his visions and ideas, are still enacted in local prayer halls. Nothing of his legacy is perceptible in plays by nineteenth-century Assamese writers who followed the vogue astir elsewhere in India, fashioning historical and socially progressive works, most of them not actually staged but reaching only the printed page, often ornately bound in costly, gold-stamped leather. The outstanding pre-Independence dramatist, Jyeti Prasad Agarwali (1903–51), assailed overly rigid manners and attitudes, notably in his tragic and romantic *Karengar Lagiri* (*The Maid of the Palace*); this play still merits its many revivals.

The Assamese stage regained little force in the post-Independence era. A special feature of it, however, is a commercial travelling theatre that for more than three decades has mounted works mostly translated from Bengali. Though they perform under canvas, these mobile companies, comprising about a dozen troupes, carry elaborate stage equipment with them.

Manipur, adjacent to Assam, was long celebrated for its ritual theatre, embodying an ancient tradition of plays dealing with the beloved Krishna, as well as a legion of local religious figures. In addition, secular Jatra folk performances continue to be popular and available. An incursion of modern dramas, first from Bengal, occurred at the beginning of the twentieth century. Original plays in

Manipuri – and also more Bengali works, but now in translation – soon provided impetus for a thriving native stage. Especially in the 1930s, numerous acting groups were organized, affording Manipuri dramatists the essential experience of seeing their works enacted. After Independence the pace of writing and of local productions accelerated. Some playwrights sought their material in the cherished, protean myths. Leading this school was Pukhramba (1945–80), admired for his ingenuity in testing and adapting the stories, an example of his highly individual approach *Ayekpali* (*Painting*). The more recent Manipuri theatre is deemed fortunate in having a cluster of able young directors eagerly probing the very origins of Indian drama, its root impulses. Kalakshetra, a dynamic acting group headed by Kanhai Lal, dispensed with scenery and props, encouraging the players to conjure up the illusion of settings such as soaring mountains, thick forests or bridges over tumbling streams. Two other directors, Sanak Ebotombi and Ratan Kumar Thyam (b. 1948), both of whom studied at the National School of Drama, were also advocates of innovation. Thyam, along with his troupe, the Chorus Repertory Theatre, won a country-wide reputation by producing works inspired by fugitive Manipuri folk-tales. He had many of these written out, endowing the hallowed legends with updated meaning and oversaw their staging. In *Sanarembri Chevishre* (*Two Sisters*) and *Uchek Langmeidong* (*The Chorus of the Birds*) he cunningly combined music, movement and rhythm preserved from past epochs to create a fresh amalgam in which are age-old elements of Manipuri ritual and martial arts. He was also acclaimed for his staging of Bhasa's *The Broken Thigh* where he demonstrated how to reinterpret a Sanskrit drama so as to reveal new facets of its riches.

The state of Kannada, too, clung to the long-time favourite Yakshagana and drew on a wealth of retold stories from the epics and *puranas*. Over the decades there was a gradual acceptance of a modern stage. For a time the state's writers fell under the sway of Marathi dramatists whose progress was by then more definite. The first commercial troupes put on plays translated and adapted from Sanskrit, English and Marathi, the last of these quite accessible because the two regions are neighbours. Kannada's authors initially chose to turn out historical and mythological works, usually with dazzling trappings. By the 1930s realism was embraced and dominant. Social problems were broached by T.P. Kailasam (1885–1946), Narayhan Rao and others. This period is designated as the "golden age of Kannada drama" by Awasthi, who points to D.R. Bendre (1896–1981), A. R. Krishna Rao, S. Karanth (1902–97) and Adya Rangacharya (1904–84) as exemplars of it. A sturdy amateur theatre took shape. Rangacharya, also known as Sriranga, was long active, his works holding on to their appeal and many of his later scripts experimental. His socially concerned offerings included *Haijan-war* (1933). (Rangachara's home was in Mysore, which is Kannada-speaking.)

The dramatist Girish Karnad and the director B.V. Karanth jointly helped Indian theatre and

"New Wave" films attain unprecedented heights, sharpening their skills by what they learned from a rival medium. In Bangalore, the focal point of Kannada's stages, other youthful directors won prominence, each refining his idiom or enforcing his personal stamp. The 1960s and 1970s brought a coven of young playwrights, some socially committed like Chandrasekhar Kambar who exploited an intimate knowledge of folkways in his *Jokumar Swamy* (a fertility god's name) to enliven a conflict between harassed villagers and a despotic landlord. The play, in which a fertility rite is part of a complicated plot, earned Kambar the national award for 1973. Aptly, it interweaves songs, dance, a ritualistic ceremony and oral narration in a novel fashion.

From state to state in south India, whether in Kerala, where Malayalam is spoken, in Andhra Pradesh, where the speech is Telegu, or in Tamil Nadu, where the language is Tamil, cultural interaction has gone on for centuries and affected the nature and development of the indigenous drama. Each has its own format and style, and each borrows openly or unobtrusively from those around it. As has been seen, the Parsee and Marathi stage practices and choices of subject have also beamed strong influences well beyond their borders. Andhra Pradesh's Telegu stage has drawn on a range of religious and secular kinds of entertainment – puppetry, ballad singing, recitations, temple dancing – and developed more modern sorts quite hesitantly. Its reluctance finally gave way during the last quarter of the nineteenth century, when native playwrights emulated their fellows elsewhere in India and contributed works on historical and mythological topics, along with translations of the Sanskrit classics into Telegu. In this transitional period two outstanding writers were Dharmavaram Krishnamacharya and Kolachalam Sreenivasa Rao. A work of special interest is a long verse play, *Krishna Rayabaram*; when presented, its spectacular pageantry tends to outweigh its poetic content. But it typifies how old themes are refurbished and still attract throngs. Mention should be made, too, of K. Veerasalingam Pantula (1848–1919), a much-respected forerunner in establishing theatre in Andhra Pradesh.

Through the opening years of the twentieth century, the theatrical scene here was dominated by professional troupes led by actor–managers appearing in their preferred roles. The most famous of Telegu actors, Bellary T. Raghavachari, elected Shakespearean tragedies as his vehicles in the 1920s, using his own translations of them and memorably striding the boards as Macbeth, Othello and Hamlet. The introduction of realism came with *Kanyashulkam* (*The Bridal Bargain*) by G.V. Appa (1862–1915). Still viable, this play investigates the enduring and often onerous tradition of the dowry, an Indian problem even today. In general, though, Andhra Pradesh was not noted for theatrical activity, not even offering much amateur participation.

Throughout India, it is popularly held that the Malayalam drama has the richest heritage of ritual, balladry, dance and martial arts. Kathakali and Krishnattam arose there during the sixteenth century, a time when the Portuguese arrived and shared in the creation of a new theatre form, Chavittu-natakam, not unlike the medieval European miracle plays. Translations of the Sanskrit dramas in the last decades of the nineteenth century preceded a turn to Western-mode scripts, after which a new generation of eager writers rejected most of what the "traditional" theatre might have lent them. As elsewhere, mythological and historical themes largely preoccupied them for a time, and next they imitated whatever was commercially successful in Telegu and Tamil. Here, too, Shakespeare's works were favourites, when they, along with other European classics, were rendered into Malayalam and opportunistically adapted. The influence of Ibsen and Shaw was discernible in the output of N. Krishna Pillai, who earnestly dramatized social problems. In contrast, and in an effort to capture the Shavian spirit, the stage also offered a number of socially conscious comedies.

Post-Independence, Malayalam's theatre became more weighty. C.S. Sreekantan Nair reinterpreted characters who populate the *Ramayana* in a trilogy, the most effective part of the work generally considered to be *Kanchan Sita* (*The Golden Sita*). The poet K.N. Pannikar, also delving into myth and legend, wrote a half-dozen plays employing ritual, trance and states of possession to expose depths of being. In particular, his *Daivthar* (*Godhead*) won him a following, and he was also a highly regarded stage-director. G. Shankar Pillai (b. 1933), aligned with Kerala's new theatre movement, authored more than twelve plays. Among them, *Pooja Muri* (*The Prayer Room*) and *Karutha Daivathe Thedi* (*In Search of the Black God*) are much liked. Another successful dramatist of the period was C.J. Thomas. The director S. Ramanujam, profiting from study at the National School of Drama, was often sought after for his unconventional stagings.

A group of actors, known as the Chakyr, put on somewhat modified versions of the works of Bhasa and Harsha; these Sanskrit classics, once mounted at princely courts, were now presented with modest scenery quite as though they were folk plays for the delectation of comparatively humble audiences.

The Tamil-speaking "modern stage" is rated as minor. Though theatre in this southern state has a rich past, it scarcely progressed beyond gaudily mounted legendary fare. Much of this theatre imitated Tamil films: the scripts, loosely structured, had hardly any serious content.

The 1940s and 1950s were marked by the prevalence of professional troupes such as the one led by three siblings, the T.K.S. Brothers, as well as the Seva, proudly presenting S.V. Sahasranamam (b. 1913), a leading actor. They drew full houses. Even more prosperous was the Rajamanickam Company of Madras. Many of their scripts had a strong religious impulse, emphasized pageantry and made use of sensational lighting effects. Another star of the Tamil theatre was Shivaji Ganeshan, a renowned film actor who had his own stage company with which he performed at weekends, the days when he was not busy in front of a camera.

Among Tamil playwrights, Indra Parathasarthy is singled out for two historical works: *Aurangzeb* (the name of a Mogul ruler) and *Porval Portia Utakal* (*Layers of Blankets*). These plays, also well received when given in Hindi and English, are seen as having a definite contemporary application, their characters evaluated from an updated point of view.

Urdu theatre takes pride in the output of Rajinder Singh Bedi (1915–84), his virtues displayed in *Bejan Chizan* (1941), though not all critics assent, finding it too often turgid.

The frequent references to Bengal point up its importance in the history of India's drama. An early introduction to Western-style theatre happened in Calcutta in 1795; Herasim Lebedeff, a Russian, travelling with a Bengali tutor, by name Golak Narth Das, translated Molière's *L'Amour Médicin* into Bengali and staged it at a private theatre in a garden. He did not stay in Calcutta, however, and no more Bengali plays were seen there for four decades. Eventually a few more privately owned theatres were established, among them the Jorasank Theatre, belonging to the wealthy Tagores.

An early writer of note in this nascent stage is the poet Michael Madhusadna Dutt (1824–73) whose plays did not echo the anti-colonial protests filling much of Bengali drama after the establishment of English rule.

Initially, as had occurred elsewhere in the country, the new stages were occupied by revivals of the always attractive Sanskrit classics transposed into the local language, here Bengali. Gradually, around the turn of the twentieth century, wholly original works made an appearance. Leading this ever stronger movement were the actor–director–dramatist Girish Chandra Ghosh (1844-1912) and D.L. Roy (1863–1913). They wrote on historical subjects, of which there was certainly an abundance; Ghosh's *Sirajudaulla* and *Chhatrapati Shivaji* are good examples. Well accepted, they were performed not only in Bengal but also elsewhere and in other languages.

The growth of this stage was also stimulated by a line of highly gifted actors, among them Sisir Kumar Bhaduri (1889–1959), Ahindra Chaudhury – who reached his peak in the 1930s – and later Sombhu Mitra and Utpal Dutt. The Bengali theatre became noted for a high standard of performance. Ghosh, whose sentiments were nationalistic, masked them by putting his scenes in the past or resorting to myth, as in his *Vilwamangal*. His tragedy *Sirajuddaulah* tells of the last Indian ruler of Bengal, who in 1757 was treacherously delivered to the British. Roy, at first, concentrated on farces but later undertook more serious fare. His *Chandragupta* (1911) draws a compelling image of another fabled Hindu monarch, and his *Mewar Patan* (1908; *Fall of Mewar*) and *Shah Jehan* (1909) celebrate heroic past events. They were intended to inspire Indian patriots. Somewhat earlier, Dinabandhu

Mitra (1829–73) espoused the cause of anti-colonialism with his *Neeldarpana* (1861; *Nil Durpan*), a melodrama about oppressed plantation workers and a harsh overseer, a situation which leads Maitlaw to tag it "an oriental *Uncle Tom's Cabin*". Roy's scripts were also read and esteemed for their literary quality and were taken up by amateur theatre clubs.

The great figure in Bengali literature is Rabindranath Tagore (1861–1941), granted a Nobel Prize (1913), the first Asian so honoured. In 1915 he was knighted by the British government. As yet he is the only Indian dramatist widely known outside his vast homeland. (It is generally acknowledged that the Nobel Prize was in recognition of his accomplishments as a poet rather than as a playwright.)

Born to a prominent family in Calcutta, he spent most of his youth abroad until his twenty-fourth year, residing in England to study law and travelling about Europe, the United States, China and Japan. Observing everywhere, he became fully informed about various forms of Western theatre but frequently declared his chief inspiration to be the Sanskrit classics and Bengali folk plays. He was strongly impressed by the playwrights of the Irish Renaissance, those who combined fantasy and realism, as had Synge and Yeats. He wrote in Bengali. In some instances he provided English translations of his works, though critics think this was accomplished at some cost to their fluency and impact. His bent was philosophical. Though his message was addressed primarily to fellow Asians, he had readers world-wide.

He began publishing poetry at an early age. Exceedingly versatile, he was soon turning out short stories, novels, magazine articles, metaphysical essays, children's tales. Some of these were later dramatized. In all, he is credited with over fifty plays, many available only in Bengali; he also composed lyrics and music for about 3,000 songs.

He was tall, with a magisterial bearing, a piercing gaze. His moustache was heavy, his beard full and luxuriant. When hair and beard whitened with age, he looked truly noble, yet with an unworldly air.

His first theatre venture was a musical play, *Valmiki Pratibha* (1881; *The Genius of Valmiki*), about the epic poet Valmiki, author of the *Ramayana*. Tagore produced it, assuming the title role. He acted in many of his own plays and often directed them.

He preferred works bringing together instrumental music, songs, poetry, pantomime and occasional spectacle in the native tradition. Rabindra Sangeet ("Tagore music") is a term used to describe a distinctive fusion of words and music that he developed; it proves to be artistically effective. He sometimes added Western touches. He identified with the cause of India's independence from Britain; nationalistic feeling flows through many of his scripts.

A great many of his plays were produced in the family's theatre, the Jorasank in Calcutta, which he managed with his brothers; or else at his estate in Bolpur, the Santiniken (Abode of Peace), where he established an International Institute (1901) for the study of Oriental philosophy, in which he lectured and where time was also devoted to probes of urgently needed educational and social change. His plays were also performed at Visva-Bharati University, which took over from the institute and has a cosmopolitan student body.

Along with being versatile in mastering various forms of expression, his range of subjects was inclusive, from vigorous comedy to edged satire, from naturalistic forays to lyrical offerings infused with symbolism. Some of his plays are in verse, some in prose, and in some instances all the dialogue is colloquial. Most, but not all, were intended to be given on a nearly bare stage adorned with a few properties that possibly suggest the time and place of the activity or are emblematic of an innate and informing semi-abstract idea.

In his later years he dedicated himself largely to dance-dramas, their choreography in the classical Manipuri style. The symbolic works tend to have vaguely defined characters. The mood is "singularly impersonal", and Westerners may find the mystical content elusive and even unsympathetic. The dialogue, intensely lyrical, abounds with pantheistic nature imagery. Wells comments that this follows a profound trend in Sanskrit scripts, a practice that "often draws the play away from the dramatic toward pure poetry or toward declamation, whereas in Kalidasa, whom Tagore recognized as his master, the theatrical element prevails even in the most opulent descriptive passages".

Among his better-known scripts are the intense *Visarjana* (1890; *Sacrifice*), positing that a ritual propitiation and death may crown a life triumphantly; *Chitra* (1891, published 1892), observing the roles of physical and spiritual beauty in forming the bond between the sexes – this work derives from the *Mahābhārata*; *Raja* (1910; *The King of the Dark Chamber*), about a queen who overcomes an aversion to her ugly regal mate after she perceives his spiritual grace. Much esteemed is *The Cycle of Spring* (1917). In 1936 Tagore returned to the theme of physical ugliness transformed into a kind of compelling sexual attraction often allotted those who possess unusual spiritual qualities, in a new version of *Chitra*, making it over into a dance-drama and retitling it *Chitrananda*. Another of his outstanding dance-dramas is his romantic *Shyama* (1939), based on a Buddhist legend.

Perhaps his most widely performed work, not only in Bengali but in other languages including those in the West, has been *Dakaghan* (1913; *The Post Office*), a parable replete with pathos about a dying child whose soul is set free.

Rakta-Karabi (1924; *The Red Oleander*) portrays the struggle between an individual and a tyrannical government. It was the production of this play by Sombhu Mitra, a fellow Bengali director, with his ensemble Bohurupee, that finally demonstrated the power of Tagore's stage-writing. The director's wife, one of the great actresses of the Indian theatre, appeared in the leading female role. Mitra became an advocate of Tagore, bringing back *Mukta-Dhara* (1959) and *The King of the Dark Chamber* (1964), both presented very successfully and proving that they are enduring works.

Two good examples of Tagore's thrust as an occasional realist are *Lost Cause* and *The Bachelors' Club*. *Tasher Desh* mocks the caste system.

Margot Berthold remarks:

He drew both on the old Sanskrit tradition and on the modern drama of ideas to develop a new, specifically Indian style, which may be described as a loosely woven plot heavily fraught with symbolism and garbed in lyrical, romantic language. He revived the role of rhapsodist who gives a running commentary on the action, which is presented in pantomime. Tagore's work invites comparison with the "epic theatre" of Bertolt Brecht and Thornton Wilder. Tagore's figures often remain shadowy and unreal, creatures of the borderland between fantasy and reality, made even more intangible by their melancholy songs. His plays, he once said, can be understood only if one listens to them as one would to the music of a flute.

They need no external display, hardly a prop, a minimum of décor. Like ferrymen from another world, they appeal to the imagination of the audience, both the Indian public of Tagore's native Bengal and European audiences at the International Theatre Festival in New Delhi. At the beginning of his play *The Cycle of Spring* Tagore says with poetic self-sufficiency: "We need no scenery. The only backcloth we need is the background of the imagination, upon which we shall paint a picture with the brush of music."

In the view of Bernard Sobel: "His dramatic contributions are refreshing and charming lyrics, unpretentious, fluid, gracious in style, and wise and sane in philosophy." H. W. Wells says: "Persuaded of a need for propaganda and instruction and keenly sensitive to many of the pressures of modern life and thought, Tagore was above all faithful at heart to Asian dramatic traditions and to the moral and spiritual values that he prized in Indian civilization. His plays show him convinced, with Bharata, the philosopher of the Sanskrit stage, that the theatre should utilize the collective force of all the arts, with poetry, no doubt, at their head. . . . In India Tagore's reputation has always been gathering rather than losing force since his death in 1941. Though he may have left the world no dramatic masterpiece, his drama will long provide a rich mine for inspection by all progressive and adventurous servants of dramatic art."

To mark the centenary of Tagore's birth (1961), the government decreed a festival in which many of his plays were translated into still more Indian languages and performed in diverse styles representing each director's interpretation. Several books – biographies and criticism – were issued, timed to the event. Much has since been written about him.

The Bengali theatre was where a new socially engaged school of playwrights came forth in the mid-twentieth century. Many colleges were giving courses in Western drama. As has been said before, Ibsen and Shaw were being avidly read by intellectuals. Many native plays were already coming to grips with current problems: the harassing poverty, the crippling persistence of the caste system, the cruel tradition of dowries, the harshness of landlords, the humiliating subordination of women and especially the tragic plight of those widowed. The dramatists who tackled these social ills and called for many kinds of emancipation were idealistic and zealous, but their works were mostly didactic and doctrinaire. Awasthi likens some of them to textbooks.

A reaction to these scripts and to those of little merit given in the commercial theatres was a spate of plays that were overly literary, looking as ever to the historical and mythological, yet these efforts too often were dramatically lifeless.

In the 1930s All India Radio was brought into being by the government. A demand for scripts was created, distracting authors from writing for the stage. The cinema was also making sweeping inroads; many playhouses were converted to showing films at the expense of live theatre.

A signal event was the production in Calcutta of Bijon Bhattacharya's *Nabanna* (1944; *New Harvest*) by the Anti-Fascist Writers' and Artistes' Association. Directed by the ever alert Sombhu Mitra, it dealt with the Great Famine besetting Bengal that year. Impressed by the play's success, the Communist Party of India set up the Indian Peoples' Theatre Association (or IPTA) as a propaganda vehicle. Centred in Bombay, it soon had branches in several other large cities. Its work was pervasive for a time, a part of the *Zeitgeist*, especially in Bengal. A typical stage presentation by this leftist group was *Immortal India*.

In the 1950s and 1960s, given a dynamic impetus by Independence, a number of brilliant young directors became active and broadened the scope of Bengali theatre. They reached beyond vexatious language barriers to create an Indian drama that might claim to belong not merely to this or that region but instead to the whole country, an India now swept by an excess of nationalist fervour.

Because the best plays were likely to be translated into several of the competing major languages, they became in the aggregate a national literature, a *desideratum* lacking since the Sanskrit era.

Retarding true progress, however, was the seeming ineradicable antagonism between ethnic and religious groups, especially in the days of anarchy and rioting that cost thousands of lives following the partition of the country and the loss of Pakistan, together with the inception of the endless, murderous dispute over which of the two nations should have legitimate rule of Kashmir.

Again, that plays with leftist ideas sprang up with considerable frequency at this phase reflected in part that the new government under the Congress Party, founded by the martyred Ghandi and headed by Nehru after India's severance from Britain, was nominally socialist and in general unsympathetic to the capitalist West and its elitist culture.

None the less, playwrights more and more wrote Western-style dramas, and stages were crowded with imported scripts from Europe and the United States, profitable commercial fare along with the very latest avant-garde ventures. For decades India had a marked affinity with Communist Russia. So dire was the plight of the impoverished masses that to many intellectuals a promise of a quick Marxist remedy seemed to hold out brighter hope.

All these events and currents provided subject-matter for the playwrights, some taking one side, some the other, on almost every issue. Theatrical activity increased across the subcontinent. With rue, for reasons already given, I can offer only a sketchy picture of all this healthy ferment. There are too many writers to be named, too many careers to be described, and access to the plays and their content is too difficult, if not in many instances impossible. It also remains true, as stated before, that only Tagore among Indian playwrights has enjoyed an international reputation.

A handful whose work is commendable could be mentioned in passing. The Bengali theatre, for one, was now a lively scene, reaching a high point in quantity and sometimes in quality. Even more than before, the commercial stage was taken over by translations of plays that were successes abroad, and by a good many dramatizations of short stories and novels; their authors, until now working only in such genres, were suddenly impelled to try their hand at staged adaptations of their own works. Jatra troupes, exploiting folk material, also drew huge audiences. What should be conveyed is an image of a great deal of theatre of all sorts.

Arun Mukherjee is a typical figure of this period, writing plays in which he acted – fashioning the title role to fit his talents – and then staging and producing them himself as head of Chetana, his own company of players. Also conspicuous at this time was the playwright Mohit Chatterji.

In Bombay, beginning in 1944, the actor–director Prithvi Raj (Kapoor) was remarkably adept at mounting scripts in Hindi dealing with social issues; he took them on tour. Many were of middling literary quality but were appropriate vehicles for him to appear in as a star. Exceedingly emotional, plays such as *Deewar* (*The Wall*) and *Pathan* called for better relations between Hindus and Muslims and succour for the miserably poor masses. His long reign on the stage, where his polished and thoroughly professional work was deemed matchless, ended in 1960 with his physical collapse. He also made films; perhaps a record of his otherwise ephemeral art has been preserved in them.

The best playwrights using Hindi mostly found stages in the amateur theatre which continued to expand. Mani Madhukar, a satirist, employed the folk material of his native Rajasthan to take aim at social ills. His *Khela Polampur Ka* (*The Play Polampur*) scored a special hit. A better craftsman, structuring more tightly, Surendra Verma was also skilled at sharp dialogue, as demonstrated in his *Surya Ki Pahali Kiran Se Surya Ki Antim Kiran Tak* (*From Dusk to Dawn*), portraying the woes of a sexually impotent monarch. The piece was widely popular. Dr Laxmi Narayan Lal prepared more than a dozen scripts examining middle-class dilemmas; numerous amateur groups mounted them enthusiastically. Some other meritorious writers of the day were Shankar Shesh, Ramesh Bakshi and Mudrarakshash.

Scrutinizing the 1950s once again, one observes an important new wave of bold directors, among them Sombhu Mitra (1915–97) – already mentioned several times – and Utpal Dutt (1929–93), both of whom initially staged plays in Bengali; Habib Tanvir (b. 1923), who served the Hindi stage: and E. Alkazi (b. 1925), who began in Hindi and advanced to English. These four later received awards from the National Academy of Music, Dance and Drama.

The eldest, Mitra, who might be called the discoverer of Tagore, was tirelessly engaged in Calcutta for over three decades, where his troupe, Bohurupee – profiting from the presence of his actress-wife – not only heightened the theatricality of scripts by Tagore and Bhattacharya but also stirred spectators with a striking performance as Chanakya in the Sanskrit classic *Mudra-Makshasa* and portrayed the intimidated, wavering Galileo in Brecht's iconoclastic drama about that "heretic" star-gazer set in the European Renaissance (1980). Tanvir, leading the Naya Theatre in Delhi, also revived Sanskrit classics but instilled them with a folk quality, frequently recruiting cast members from folk-play companies. His most popular offering was an unique version of the long-cherished *The Toy Cart*.

Alkazi, while in Bombay, headed a group known as Theatre Unit which produced what were considered to be exceptionally good interpretations of Greek tragedies, Molière, Strindberg and other Western masterpieces. Subsequently he was named Director of the National School of Drama, which caused him to move to New Delhi (1962–76), where he had his students act in Hindi. He was applauded for his handling of *Andha-Yug* (1954; *Blind Mice*), a verse drama by Dharmvir Bharati, derived from the *Mahābhārata*, in addition to *Tughlaq*, by Girish Karnad, about a Sultan who reigned in Delhi during the fourteenth century. Alkazi, who was also a painter, displayed this second talent through the pictorial aspects of his stagings.

Dutt vented his energies in triple roles as actor, director and playwright. His company, located in Calcutta, bore the name Little Theatre Group but was later called the People's Little Theatre (1969). He began with Shakespearean productions in English, but eventually chose to have his actors use Bengali when he presented his own scripts. A Marxist, he saw to it that his plays carried political messages. He evoked strong performances from his actors, arranging scenes of mass agitation ingeniously. Among his memorable efforts were his staging of Gorky's *The Lower Depths*, in a Bengali translation, and two works of his own authorship, *Tinner Talwar* (*The Tin Sword*), a picture of life in the theatre in Calcutta during the preceding century; and *Titu Mir*, a tribute to a peasant hero who resisted British sovereignty in the nineteenth century.

Also in the Hindi theatre, a signal feature was a series of scripts by Khwaja Ahmad Abbas (1914–87), a journalist, historian and novelist, with an undisguised leftist bias. He urged reconciliation between the peoples of India and Pakistan. He made use of the semi-documentary techniques adopted for the Living Newspaper in the United States during the Great Depression in the 1930s. His aim was to give a kindly picture of the Muslim peasantry. This was hardly the kind of theatre to which the broad swathe of the Indian public was accustomed.

The appeal of both old and new forms of play-making and staging was partly met by the ever-increasing number of dramatic clubs and societies, of which by now there were hundreds. Some had come into being merely to mark special occasions, such as religious festivals and historical events. Awasthi says, however, that there were at least a dozen or more well-established amateur and semi-professional companies busily providing serious drama.

The 1960s, filled with social and political tensions, brought a further acceleration of change. Keeping pace, the theatre developed new kinds of drama but still without wholly relinquishing ties to hallowed tradition, mainly continuing to use certain age-old techniques even now beloved. The dramatists dipped as ever into the sacred epics for their ancient and universal themes. This led to further reinterpretations of historical events and heroes to reconcile them with newer social values. But erstwhile formal rules for script structure were abandoned in favour of a surge toward flexibility and improvisation. The trend was sharply away from the realistic; the climate of the times constantly invited yet more experimentation.

The foremost dramatist embracing this tendency was generally considered to be Vijay Tendulkar (b. 1928), whose work is couched in Marathi but has been eagerly and widely translated. His *Shantata: Court Chalu Ahe* (*Silence: The Court Is in Session*) employs a mock trial and an improvisatory style to bare and flay many distortions and hypocrisies in the "establishment" and in society. Similarly powerful is his *Ghasiram Kotwal* (*Ghasiram the Kotwal*), delving into the depravity of Nana Phadnavis, who in the nineteenth century reigned over the small princely state of Maharashtra. Tendulkar remained influential in the ensuing decade, the force of his work described as "explosive". One of his plays was presented by the Pan Asian Repertory Theatre in English – off-Broadway – during the Festival of India (1986) in New York. Mel Gussow, in the *New York Times*, found it to be

an intricately woven tapestry of epic elements involving dance, music and pageantry and there is Tisa Chang's staging, which is assiduous on a grand scale.

The play is set in the late Eighteenth Century and has the lineaments of a classic folk tale. Falsely accused of being a thief, a stranger is turned into an outcast. He bribes the corrupt local ruler into appointing him police chief, or "*kotwal*," and pursues a path of vengeance against the innocent as well as the guilty. Because Ghashiram Kotwal is merciless, his enemies accrue and his own fall from power is foredoomed.

Mr Tendulkar's view of the society under scrutiny is deeply cynical. The police chief outlaws all pleasure in the interest of his own distorted concept of morality. He is both individually horrific and indicative of his times. One knows that when he is deposed, someone equally evil will rise in his place.

As translated by Eleanor Zelliot and Jayant Karve, the play is pregnant with portent and favors such melodramatic statements as "the city trembles at his name." At the same time, there is a simplicity in the style of storytelling, as a narrator leads us through the mythic journey, playing the role of sardonic tour guide.

With such a large cast (twenty actors doubling in roles), there is an inevitable unevenness in some of the performances, as well as an occasional confusion about who is supposed to represent what faction or caste. The play rewards our attention. Considering the physical requirements and the budgetary restrictions of the production at Playhouse 46, the company does remarkably well in delineating the exotically detailed environment.

The actors are accomplished in mime as well as the martial arts. With the help of Rajika Puri's choreography and Bhaskar Chandavarkar's score, Miss Chang has unified a multi-ethnic company into a performance ensemble. Several individual performers stand out – Mr Shimabaku who retains a droll detachment as the narrator; Mel Duane Gionson as the lecherous chief minister; Jeffrey Akaka as a tortured victim of the police chief's wrath. In the title role, Ismail Abou-el-Kanater has a threatening presence. There is additional merit in Atsushi Moriyasu's sculptural set design and Eiko Yamaguchi's costumes. Three musicians, sitting on stage, provide a sinuous thread of music beneath the words.

Having previously presented works with Japanese, Chinese and other Asian-American backgrounds, the Pan Asian rep now reaches out to another artistic community, one that is rarely represented on the New York stage. The result is a privileged view for the theatergoer.

Adya Kangacharya, in Kannada, was another leader in this movement with *Suno Janamejava* (1960), his purpose being to record problems and pains of a culture in profound transition. The play was translated into Hindi five years later.

Badal Sircar (b. 1925), expressing himself in Bengali and also availing himself of free forms, chose the harassing problems of the middle class as his frequent subject. His *Ebam Indrajit* depicts the drifting lives, the dull and monotonous daily routine, of people trapped in that class. Other of his works are *Shesh En* (*There Is No End*) and *Baki Ethos* (*That Other History* or *Another Story*). In a later phase of his career he quit shaping scripts by conventional means and began creating them in collaboration with the actors in his troupe, Shatabdi. He put these on in meeting halls or outdoors in parks and crowded noisy marketplaces. Two plays of this kind are his *Bhoma* (the hero's name) and *Juloos* (*Procession*).

Mohan Rakesh (1925–73), in Hindi, won approval with *A Day in the Month of Ashadha*, a biographical study of the great Sanskrit playwright Kalidasa. Myth and legend are aptly threaded into a portrait of the creative artist, exposing his psychological promptings as a poet, together with episodes from his love-life. The complex bond between the sexes is also explored in *Adhe-Adhure* (*Halfway House*), an intense social drama. Rakesh preferred the structure of the "well-made" play, the accepted three-act Western format, with cunningly placed climaxes. What is most admired in his work is the dialogue, which has qualities quite new in Hindi. His death at forty-eight eclipsed his promise, but those two plays, translated to other Indian languages, remain fresh and current.

In *Tughlaq*, Girish Karnad (b. 1938), writing for the Kannada stage, confronted the contradictions and paradoxes besetting a Sultan, whose idealism causes his defeat. Karnad projects with mastery a broad historical panorama, populated with a host of well-drawn characters. The subject has a modern relevance.

All four of these playwrights received National Academy awards.

A prominent mover in establishing and leading Punjabi dramas is Singh Khosla. He acquired stage experience while at Government College in Lahore (later belonging to Pakistan) where he volunteered to be a prompter for a production by fellow-students. The play was Capek's *Rossom's Universal Robots* (also known as *RUR*). Inspired by this initiation into stagecraft, he undertook a translation of Galsworthy's *The Silver Box*, a protest against the British judicial system. He was praised for having rendered the English script into "chaste, urban Punjabi". Won over to a life in the theatre, he became the founder Chairman of the Little Theatre Group at Lahore (1945). He took a part in its first offering, a Hindi version of Ibsen's *Pillars of Society*.

After six years at Lahore, he earned a BA in Economics (probably a sound idea for a playwright) – top of his class – and then an MA in English literature. He served with the Territorial Army during the Second World War. He was earning his living as an officer of the Indian Railways, a post he held in Delhi at the time of Partition. The Little Theatre Group to which he belonged was reorganized at this point and manifested reluctance to put on a Punjabi work. Quitting it, Khosla helped to establish a new amateur group in Delhi, the Punjabi Theatre, made up of migrants from Pakistan. The company mounted a programme of two one-acters, Balwant Garggi's *Pichchal Pairi* (*Ever Thinking in the Past*) and *Do Anne* (*Two Blind Men*); he acted in the first of these. Encouraged by the troupe's reception, Khosla staged I.C. Nanda's *Beiman* (*Dishonest*) and his own *Jutyan Da Jora* (*Pair of Shoes*). In *Pair of Shoes* he assumed the role of an intellectual who arouses the suspicion of his wife when she comes upon a pair of shoes belonging to a lady to whom he has given a "lift" in his car on his way home.

From then on, Khosla would compose a script, search for a stage on which to produce it, and gather a cast whose talents he developed until they were at least semi-professional, and by any measure were lively performers. He did not allow any of his works to be published until repeatedly stage-tested.

His group also put on plays by other writers, possibly better known, among them I.C. Nanda – the "father of Punjabi drama" – Balwant Garggi, Harcharan Singh and Kartar Singh Singh Duggai, and polished adaptations by Dr Amrik Singh. After this, he set up branches of his Punjabi Theatre in Jaipur, Calcutta and Bombay.

He visited Europe, Canada, the United States, spoke on BBC radio, addressed university audiences. He displayed humour, sensitivity and a deep concern about social ills.

A collection of his one-act works was published in 1950 under the title *Homeless*; it contains *Murd e Da Rashan* (*Dead Man's Rations*), baring the greed innate in human nature manifested during a sugar shortage. This piece, first staged in Delhi and later in Simla and Calcutta (1951), was later included in volumes of *Contemporary Theatre* and *World Theatre* issued by the International Theatre Institute.

At full length, *Buhe Baithi Dhi* poignantly depicts the woes of the daughters of middle-class families as they await marriage proposals; it had its stage début in Delhi (1951). *Be-ghare*, a one-acter, is to be found in several anthologies and has been revived in English and Hindi, as well as in its original Punjabi.

Khosla introduced one of Shaw's wittiest works to Punjabi audiences in Delhi (also in 1951) with an adaptation and production of *Pygmalion*. Before that event, Shaw's works had not been accessible to speakers of that language.

Busy in many spheres of theatre, Khosla pioneered at giving children's plays in Punjabi. In serious and more ambitious full-length offerings such as his *Mar Mitten Wale*, he paid tribute to the courageous participation of Punjabis in India's struggle for political freedom. Following that came *Paro Ton Pahile* (*Before Doomsday*), cited by the critic B.S. Bawe as "the work that brought Punjabi playwriting up-to-date".

In 1972 Khosla added a political satire, *Umidvar* (*A Candidate*), to his list of credits; and in 1974, with *Shahr Di Niland* (*Auction of the City*), he grappled with another compelling issue of the day – how could a small man survive against the crushing forces engendered by an explosive urban growth. In this drama the action is set in a *paan* shop, a club-like gathering-place for the humble.

By the 1960s the English stage in India began an abrupt decline. The ensuing decade saw only two competent troupes still performing in that language: the Madras Players of that city, and the Theatre Group of Bombay. For over a century English-speaking players had been a vital influence and had been a conduit to what was being done in Europe and the United States; now, with increasing frequency, they were apt to put on current Indian works transposed into English. Alyque Padamsee, as a director with the Theatre Group, gained notice for his presentation of Tennesee Williams's *A Streetcar Named Desire* and an Englished version of Girish Karnad's *Tughla*.

In the 1960s and 1970s collaborations between playwrights and directors became more common. Several new theatres were established. A bold woman, Vijay Mehta, heading a Marathi-speaking group called Rangayan in Bombay, was unafraid to compete with the dominant commercial stage in that city. Admired for her acting, she joined her troupe in effective presentations of Kalidasa's *Shakuntala* and Visakhadatta's *Mudrarakshasa*, decreeing that both works must be enhanced by music, conventionalized movements and stylistic references to hallowed Sanskrit methods of presentation. A like-minded company, but dedicated to using Marathi, was led by Arvind Deshpande and his wife, Sulbha Deshpande, another esteemed actress. They justly boasted of high performance standards. In Calcutta, Nandikar, a Bengali ensemble directed by Ajitesh Bannerji, tended to translate and adapt classic foreign works. For them, major successes were productions of Chekhov's *The Cherry Orchard* and Brecht's *The Threepenny Opera*. Also in Calcutta, and using Bengali, Tarun Roy continued active throughout the 1970s at his Theatre Centre, producing mostly his own compositions in Bengali. Yet another feature of the Calcutta scene was Shyamanand Jalan's Anamika company. Jalan stressed how to deliver dialogue in a highly theatrical manner. Doing Sircar's *And Indrajit*, this director employed novel patterns of speech and gesture.

At his Theatre Unit in Bombay, Satvadeva Dubey offered plays in Hindi and Marathi. Awasthi says: "His directorial work was distinguished by a sense of spontaneity. He also had a good sense of language and speech, and he beautifully balanced the verbal and visual in his productions." Awasthi selects, as examples of Dubey at his best, the Theatre Unit's interpretations of Mohan Rakesh's *Halfway House* and Bharati's *The Blind Age*.

In Delhi, Abhiyan, a Hindi group headed by Rajinder Nath, made available the best works translated from other Indian languages, as instanced by stagings of Tendulkar's *Ghasiram the Kotwal* and Sircar's *The Birds Come Flying*.

Awasthi speaks of the 1970s as a time of "excitement" in his country's theatre and offers a roster of other directors who enriched the Indian stage. Many of them showed concern for social betterment, while embracing fresh experiments; indeed, naturalism continued to be out of vogue. Narayan Kavalam Panikkar, in Malayalam, was among those endlessly seeking to revive the Sanskrit classics in novel ways, scoring a success in 1980 with his handling of *Madhyam Vyayog* (*The Play of the Middle One*), which borrowed elements of the Kerala folk-plays. He arrived at a very workable style in which to mount such pieces. B.V. Karanth, in Hindi and Kannadi, proved how music and movement, added creatively to the text, heightened the impact of Shakespeare's grim *Macbeth* (1979). He did this in a production by a repertory troupe of the National School of Drama, of which he was the director; the translation of Elizabethan blank verse into Hindi was by Raghuvir Sahai. Karanth also captured audiences with his version of Karnad's *Hayavadan* and *Andher Nagari* (*Farcical Justice*), the latter a nineteenth-century French farce rendered into Hindi by Bharatendu Harishchandra.

In the Marathi theatre, Jabber Patel was another to lend his talent to a presentation of Tendulkar's *Ghasiram*, instilling in it the conventions of his region, Maharashtra. He also put on Brecht's *Threepenny Opera* in the local argot, using P.L. Deshpande's deft adaptation.

Ratan Thiyam usually composed his own scripts, achieving an extra theatricality by incorporating in them effects long used in the rituals and martial arts of his region, Manipur.

More directors who worked in Hindi were Bansi Kaul, who undertook a folk-musical version of Gogol's eternally amusing *Inspector General* that as ever won instant favour; and B.M. Shaw, whose skills were exhibited in *Trishanku*, a script also of his own devising that set forth the problems of the younger generation, and a Hindi take on Gorky's stark, challenging *The Lower Depths*.

Bombay, Calcutta and Delhi were the principal theatre centres, each of these large cities offering productions in an almost full range of native languages, along with English. The number of performances given in Bengali, Marathi, Hindi, Gujarati, Telegu, Punjai, Kannadi, Sindhi, Tamil and Malayalam was dependent largely on the extent to which each tongue was spoken by each city's inhabitants, a tumultuous ever-shifting count. Elsewhere, amateur groups predominated, but there were professional companies, some visiting, some resident and some earnestly competitive.

William Borders, in the *New York Times* (1976), reported that between ten and fifteen original plays in Bengali were currently on view every month in Calcutta that year. The city claims to be India's cultural capital.

> Because there are not enough theaters, plays are put on in libraries, school halls or whatever open space can be found in this crowded city. One troupe performs regularly in a backyard in south Calcutta. The owner of the yard doesn't like it a bit, and he is suing to evict them, but justice is slow in India, and meanwhile the plays continue.
>
> Bengali drama tends to be very realistic, frequently retelling in one form or another the story of a struggle between rich and poor, landlord and tenant. Policemen are foolish; rich men are villainous.
>
> But increasingly, these plays are getting competition for the dollar or two that tickets cost here from productions of foreign plays, either in English or in Bengali translations, much to the disgust of some Calcuttans.
>
> Like the other arts, drama inspires strong feelings in many Bengalis, and it is not unusual for a writer to borrow way beyond his means to finance the production of his play.
>
> One man recently even sold his wife's family jewelry to hire a hall.
>
> Such passions for the arts is one of Calcutta's most attractive features. But to some people here, it also seems ironic, in a city of such appalling poverty.

Today's Indian stage, using a score or more of different languages and dialects, and often mixing ancient conventions and avant-garde experimentations, is apt to baffle a Western observer. It chooses subject-matter from the sacred epics, as well as plots and characters from a profusion of folk-plays, some fantastic and some very realistic. It is stocked with heroic figures taken from the nation's unique and convoluted history, and it also deals with the dire social problems of the present moment. Contemporary topics may be presented with the utmost fidelity to sober fact, but it is not unusual for an author to insert irrelevant spectacle and dance into his serious drama. Lively and cluttered, this theatre is one of striking contrasts, self-contradictions and extraordinary variety, and consequently is unlike any other in the world.

The Little Clay Cart (Mrichakatika) by Shadraka, in a version by Jatinder Verma and directed by Jatinder Verma for Tara Arts, London, 1986. Above: Bhasker Patel as the Courtier and Yogesh Bhatt as Sansthanaka. Left: Shaheen Khan as Vasantasena and Yogesh Bhatt as Sansthanaka. Below: Scene from *Shakuntala* by Kalidasa showing the first encounter of King Dushyanta and Shakuntala; miniature from a Hindi manuscript, 1789

A Sri Lankan magic mask worn by devil dancers to cure people of catarrh

Sri Lankan dancers from Kandy

Coloured engravings by George Newenham Wright (1790–1877) after paintings by Allom Thomas (1804–1872) from *China in a Series of Views*, 1843. Above: Theatre at Tien Sing. Below: Scene from the spectacle *The Sun and Moon*

Kuan Yu – a General. He is a leading character in the 'Huarong Path' incident in the *Battle of Red Cliff*. His make-up is typical of the type used in the depiction of older military men.

A scene from *Peony Pavilion* by Tang Xianzu (1550–1617), as performed at Lincoln Center, New York, 1998

Actor Mei Langfang (1894–1961), famous for his interpretation of female roles in the Chinese opera

Tang Seng – the master of Sun Wu in *Journey to the West*. This make-up is typical of the scholar hero who appears in many of the Chinese opera.

Top left: A performance of the Peking opera play *The Legend of the White Snake*, which tells the story of a snake that transforms itself into a beautiful woman and marries an unsuspecting mortal

Left: Chinese shadow puppets

Below: Scene from a revolutionary ballet *The White-Haired Girl* from the period of the Cultural Revolution, 1966

Top right: Chinese State Circus acrobats

Below right: The new opera house in Shanghai

Above: a Korean fan dance at the Korea House Theatre, Seoul, South Korea

Right: Korean Andong mask festival; Eunyul mask dance

Top left: A Taiwanese opera troupe performing on a traditional teahouse-style opera stage

Left: A Taiwanese marionette theatre with puppets based on Chinese opera characters

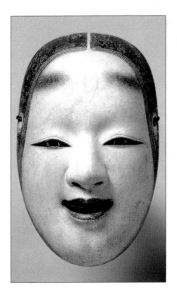  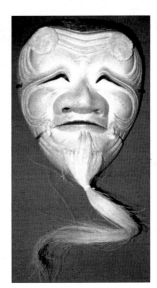 

Facing page: Bugaku dancer, Itsukushima Shrine, Miyajima, Japan. Above: Four Nōh masks; left to right, a young woman, Hannya, a female demon, Kokushiki-Jo (a version of the Okina or old man mask) and Chujo, a mask used for ghost warriors. Below: The Kanze Nōh Theatre, Tokyo

Top right: Interior of a Kabuki theatre at Edo, *c.* 1745. The woodblock print shows an actor in the play *Shibaraku* approaching the main stage by way of the *hannamichi* or aisle stage. In modern Kabuki theatres this stage is on the audience's left, and occasionally a second one is constructed on the audience's right.

Middle right: A scene from a Kabuki play showing the characters at the entrance to a house

Bottom right: A scene from a Kabuki play showing characters on a terrace

Top and bottom left: Scenes from a Bunraku Japanese puppet play

Above: Butoh dancers from the Sankai Juku Dance Company in *Jōmon Shō,* Japan, 1982.

Left: The Japanese writer and playwright Yukio Mishima

Top right: Ram Leela, Dashera Festival, Azad Maidan, Bombay

Bottom right: Ram Leela, Bombay. The actor wears the many-headed mask of Ravenna, the Demon King.

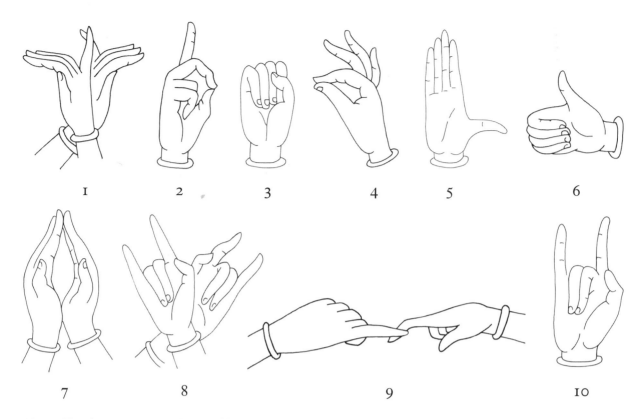

1   2   3   4   5   6

7   8   9   10

Above: Hand gestures or *mudras* used in Indian acting and dancing

1 Parting, death
2 Contemplation
3 Resolve
4 Happiness
5 Concentration
6 Denial
7 Worshipful
8 Offering
9 Annoyance
10 Adoration

Right: Indian Kathak dancers with bells around the ankles

Of significant promise, at the beginning of a new millennium, is the Prithvi Drama Festival held annually in Bombay. Leading up to this major event was the marriage of a wealthy, philanthropic Indian actor, Prithviraj Kapoor, admired for his portrayals on stage, to an English actress and company administrator, Jennifer Kendall, who was with a touring troupe playing Shakespeare. She was of a family long associated with theatre. Prithviraj Kapoor's ambition was to form a company of his own. After his death (1972), his widow and their son set out to realize his dream; they established a trust and brought together a group of performers, naming it the Prithvi in his honour (1979). Their prime interest was innovation, their taste in advance of most of their rivals. Out of this inclination evolved the yearly festival, to which the Prithvi invites companies from everywhere in India, offering plays in English or in the dialect of their native state, the speech familiar to the actors, as well as productions of outstanding presentations from abroad.

The Prithvi Festival goes on at length. Mostly it occupies the Tata Theatre, seating 1,000, and the nearby Experimental Theatre, accommodating 300. The budget is about $200,000, ambitious for India. There are forty events monthly, ranging from plays to dance recitals and concerts, and appearances by individual foreign artists. The complex houses a fine-arts library, an art gallery, a school for actors, a café. On occasions, when there is a grandiose venture, a stage in the larger National Theatre is used, but the two institutions are not linked; the purpose of the National Theatre is to preserve ancient, traditional arts and culture, of the Prithvi to encourage originality and change. Even so, a large share of the programming is perforce conventional. There are special stagings for children during the off-school season.

In good weather, in the interim between the end of a matinée and the start of an evening show, there may be open-air performances – dances, folk plays, story-tellings, music, readings – on the space in front of the Tata where spectators watch while seated on mats on the ground, much like the outdoor entertainments in the square with a splashing fountain between the two opera houses and Philharmonic Hall at Lincoln Center in New York and the modern Pompidou Centre in Paris, where spectators, made less welcome, have to stand.

The Prithvi is also a favoured place for actors mostly engaged in Bombay's tireless film and television industry to go back to when "at liberty" in an attempt to refresh their skills and recoup their zest by a return to stage interpretations that make demands far beyond those of the myopic camera. The Tata has a thrust stage bordered by tiers of seats, making for intimacy and heightening the need for poise and responsibility on the part of the performers.

From abroad have come works by Federico Lorca – in Marathi – Terence Rattigan, Tennessee Williams – also in Marathi – Arthur Miller, Neil Simon – in English – and a flood of plays in all genres and languages by contemporary Indian writers, giving them a chance of a hearing and exposing many aspects of Indian life.

The artistic director of the Prithvi is Sanjna Kapoor, a granddaughter of the founders, who took over the task from her father and her brother (1990). In preparation, she had first studied acting at the Herbert Berghof Studio in New York. She is described as a handsome woman, still in her early thirties, with dark brown hair and green eyes. Her co-director is Divya Bhatia.

7

INDIA: PUPPETS AND DANCERS

An important facet of theatre in India is puppetry. Some scholars assert that this idiosyncratic art originated about 300 BC, though later periods have been set for its inception. An early site for its birth is said to have been what is now the state of Rajasthan. By the opening centuries of the Christian era puppetry was well developed and dedicated to serving religion. It was most likely invested with an aura of the magical. Vestiges of its affiliation with worship still linger: a performance is preceded by an invocation to the elephant-headed god, Lord Ganesh, the deity of traditional theatre, and concludes with a prayer of benediction for the good fortune of the puppeteers, the community. If the figures of gods and goddesses are being fashioned or repaired, or even handled, special rites are observed. But puppetry has a secular role as well and can be a familiar part of daily social life.

With the disappearance of Sanskrit drama (about AD 1000) the little carvings became a main source of theatrical entertainment, and this was true throughout the Middle Ages. Allusions to them are come upon in the *Ramayana* and *Mahābhārata*, and later many of the puppet sketches borrow plots and characters from those sacred tales.

The puppeteers usually belong to a single family, its members numbering six or eight, who pass along their craft and performance artistry from one generation to the next. The father is in charge, and if the family is reduced for any reason he may take a second wife to bring the group back to standard size. The territory to be traversed is allotted specific villages for each family. An average tour by a company lasts about six or eight months, after which it returns to its home base and workshop – sometimes a tent – to take up other tasks and prepare for another season's journey. New material is always being added to the repertory, drawn from current events and the spectators' common life. Much of the music consists of folk-songs, but some of it is newly composed. The dialogue is often poetic. The region through which the family travels determines the kind of puppet employed, as well as the folk material that is chosen.

The figures are variously designed: some are manipulated by rods or dangled on strings; others are affixed to gloved hands and adroitly operated. Shadow plays require leather marionettes, but most widely seen are figures made of wood in differing sizes, some carved from a single block and no more than a foot and a half high, with a string attached at the waist and another at the head. At the other extreme are the richly fashioned, fully dimensional figures two or three feet high, known as the Tamil Nadu marionettes, which require the simultaneous use of both strings and rods, a difficult feat. To animate these Tamil figures, employed for the *Bomalattam*, or "dancing dolls", the puppeteer grasps and jiggles the iron rods fastened to their hands, while their other limbs are connected by the strings to an iron ring about his head, which he bobs and shakes in conformance to the music's rhythm. This certainly calls for much training and discipline.

The simpler bamboo rod puppets are found only in West Bengal and Orissa; they are growing rare. They, too, do a doll dance, called the *Putul Nautch*, in traditional Jatra dress. Large, realistic figures – they are three to four feet high – each is kept moving by two rods, one affixed to the back and the other to the head; these rods extend to the waist of an animator, who weaves and sways, as if dancing, to maintain the illusion of the figures being filled with the breath of life. The traditional Jatra skirt conceals the rod at the waist. Strings control the hands. The puppeteers are hidden behind a mat curtain, and behind them are the musicians. All the plays in which these figures are presented are taken from passages in the *Ramayana*. The Orissa rod puppets are comparatively modern, and the repertory is quite limited. Here the puppeteer works while seated.

Even more rare are the hand or glove puppets, which have survived in only three states, Orissa and Utar Pradesh in the north and Kerala in the south. In Utar Pradesh the skits are referred to as *Gulabo-Sitabo*, a name acquired from two stock characters, a pair of women wed to the same husband who engage in witty bickering with each other and much slapstick. In Orissa a similar entertainment is called *Gopi-Leela* – "the sport of the milkmaid" – because it depicts the love-making of Krishna and Radha. One manipulator handles the two figures, while a colleague sings, and both ad lib the rapid dialogue, which is in prose and often filled with jocose or mocking local allusions (much as in the European *commedia dell'arte*). In some instances a single operator tends to both figures, while at the same time singing and beating a drum. In Kerala the hand-and-glove theatre reaches an artistic peak. The figures have the same elaborate garb, headdresses, features make-up and glittering ornaments as do the local Kathakali dancers, and the playlets are similarly derived from the *Ramayana* and *Mahābhārata*. In mien the figures resemble the images adorning temple walls, in a style peculiar to each locality, and folk-paintings.

In some of the poorest areas, figures on strings are set in motion by one puppeteer, while the dialogue is supplied by singers, accompanied by instrumentalists.

The shadow shows, making use of the leather figures, are the oldest form of this quirky theatre. They are come upon in four regions: Orissa, Kerala, Karnataka and Andhra Pradesh. In size they vary, from the small, four-and-a-half-foot figures in Orissa, to some of six feet in Andhra Pradesh. Those representing divinities are made of deerskin (deemed sacred), lesser-ranked figures of the hides of goats and buffaloes. The operator may have a "cast" of as many as 200 characters obeying his behest, each perforated, brightly tinted, cut out so as to be assuming a dramatic stance. They are placed behind a white screen sixteen feet by eight, the light of a rush torch or a castor-oil lamp projecting their shadows. Awasthi tells us: "Their manipulation calls for great skill, both in animating the figures and also in adjusting their distance from the screen so as to sharpen or soften their outlines. Movement is not restricted to joints only: the whole puppet can be tilted, made to advance or recede, fall, rise, turn, hover, or descend from above. Some figures like Ravana and Hanuman are characterized by an intense shaking of the whole body and sudden leaps and dips. Recently, electric lights have been employed."

The show is enclosed in a temporary box-like structure which keeps the puppeteers from view. The screen is divided, so that gods and noble personages appear only on the right half, demons and villains on the left. Occasionally, if the action demands it, this traditional pattern may be reversed. Montage effects are achieved, and at moments of climax the equivalent of a cinematic "freeze-frame" might be used, the action halted to capture a dramatic tableau.

In Orissa and Kerala the moving images on the screen are black and white because the figures are opaque, but in Karnataka and Andhra Pradesh they are translucent and cast coloured shadows, a rather unique effect. They can be quite ambitious in conception: a hero might be shown brandishing a bow and arrow while advancing in a chariot or dashing astride a horse, perhaps even riding atop an elephant. Movement is conveyed to them ingeniously by the insertion of each puppet into a deep notch at the head of a bamboo rod, the base of which provides the animator with a handle while it also holds the figure erect. In Orissa the puppet's limbs are not jointed, but in Andhra Pradesh they are loosely knotted with thongs and can be smoothly jerked up and down, lifting or lowering their hands, arms and legs, and bending their knees.

Arrived at a village, the troupe hastily erects a box-like structure that consists merely of bamboo poles, mats, a curtain and two wooden cots. It is easily taken apart and portable, of course.

Comedy is prominent in the programmes, much of it quite earthy. A clown is frequently included, whatever the story; he is likely to contribute outright sexual jokes, puns and satirical thrusts at the expense of Brahmins, landlords, government officials and others in the ruling classes, thus vicariously venting the resentments of an impoverished peasantry. The playlets – save for those that are religious – are loosely slapped together, with some brief scenes recited and enacted from memory and others impromptu, spur-of-the-moment additions to evoke a laugh. The puppeteers are not apt to be well educated, but most are well versed in the epics, the myths and the historical legends, their main sources of lively subject-matter.

Recognizing the worth of these puppet theatres, the Indian government has taken steps to keep them alive – they are increasingly endangered by the ubiquity of films. New groups in the large cities are subsidized, and festivals are sponsored to encourage revival of the art. Experimentation has gone on, especially in combining styles to yield fresh forms. Further, there is an awareness that travelling shows can be a vehicle at modest cost for propaganda and education. The authorities have enlisted them in campaigns to urge family planning, combat alcoholism, teach hygiene, explain simple plans for economic growth at a village level. The troupes can function in places where there is no electricity and films and television are unavailable.

Puppet theatre is demonstrated, too, at the Folk Art Museum in Udaipur, a typical performance giving examples of songs, dances, comic skits and passages from the *Ramayana*. Though the programmes are supposed to be chiefly for the instruction of school children, the content of the playlets is likely to appeal more to adults, since the humour is often evoked by marital infidelity and sly thefts, a series of amusing and cunning tricks by conscienceless rascals. They go somewhat beyond the raucous, jejune antics of the European Punch and Judy.

For reasons already spelled out – the diversity and diffusion of languages and differing local customs – the more important contribution of India to the world theatre has been wordless and magnificent dance-drama, much of its mime universally grasped, its emotions conveyed by symbolic gestures, intense facial expressions and mostly plangent music.

The prompting of this dance, its origin probably prehistoric and now not fully known, seems to have been religious; it still retains a component of magic. Invocatory and propitiatory, it also became narrative and has remained emphatically so. The decline and disappearance of the ancient Sanskrit plays left the stage open for dance-drama as a principal kind of entertainment, which is what happened. Two forms gradually evolved, folk and classic, appealing at times – though not always intentionally – to different audiences, the unlearned masses and an élite, the latter the rulers, the courtiers and the intellectuals. Throughout the ages, however, the development of the classic dance took place not in princely palaces but in the Hindu temples, and its subject-matter continued to draw almost inexhaustibly on the sacred epics and thereby serve as a means of instruction and inspiration to the faithful, most of whom were humble and illiterate. It could be said that Indian classic dance fulfilled a function like that of the stained-glass windows in Chartres and other glowingly lit Gothic cathedrals during medieval times in Europe, presenting a helpful pictorial version of the scriptural stories. But the dance had a purpose and significance far beyond that, having essences that are both spiritual and mystical.

Words are a difficult medium in which to describe sinuous physical movements, which is why a verbal history of dancing is bound to be inadequate; fortunately, a visual record is come upon in the often highly erotic sculptures covering the exteriors of the multitudinous temples of India, as, too, in Cambodia and Indonesia, where bas-reliefs depict in enduring stone the otherwise ephemeral gestures and groupings of long-ago performers, their images carved delicately and in seductive detail.

Donald S. Connery remarks: "Dance formed an intrinsic part of worship in the Temples. Just as Hindus offer flowers in the Temple to God, so was He offered music and dance as being the most beautiful expressions of the human spirit. India alone has a concept of a God who dances. Siva is Nataraja, the King of dancers, who performs in the Hall of Consciousness and creates the rhythm of the Universe." (Those familiar with Hinduism know that it is by dancing that Siva brings the cosmos into being at sunrise each day. Similarly, he destroys it at each nightfall.) To quote further from Connery:

As in all Indian performing art, so in dancing the concept of *rasa*, or esthetic mood, holds the central place. *Rasa* is an impersonal sensation (different from emotion) which is shared by all. Nine *rasas* have been generally recognized: *sringara* or love in all its variations, devotion, humor, pathos, heroism, fury, terror, disgust, wonderment and peace.

In dancing, *rasa* is conveyed through *bhava* or expression. The dancer should so perform that "where the hand is, there the mind is, where the mind is, there is *bhava* and where there's *bhava*, there is *rasa*."

The technique through which *bhava* manifests itself is called *abhinaya*; it literally means "to carry forward," to convey a sentiment, a story, a situation to the audience through various means. There are four kinds of *abhinaya* which are expressed through the posture of the body and gestures; through singing; through costume and, sometimes, make-up; through facial movements to convey emotion.

According to whether there is *abhinaya* or not, dances are divided into *nritta* and *nritya*. *Nritta* is an intricate abstract dance consisting of rigid movements and poses, which are devoid of dramatic content. *Nritya* is suggestive and interpretative, with every movement and gesture invested with meaning. An ordinary dance recital would contain several items of *nritta* and *nritya*.

Wells, too, offers helpful introductory notes. "Indian dance perfected beyond any other a precise and complete language of symbolism, a parallel to the amazingly precise rules for Sanskrit rhetoric. The human figure as a whole was enlisted in this art, hands and fingers most clearly of all. The dance became a sign language, a form of silent speech. This might seem an esoteric discourse to persons foreign to the tradition, but the majority in an Indian audience at any time grasped the dancer's gesture as clearly as the poet's word. The dancer spoke. Moreover a musical symbolism of *ragas* or modes and a rigorous color symbolism added to the force and clarity of the meaning."

He points out that another circumstance helped the dance to approximate poetry and hence the spoken drama: "Indian dances as a rule narrated events related in an epic or a narrative poem known to the spectators from their childhood. In some instances, especially in folk and village presentations, a reciter actually told the story while the dancers performed it in their own medium. Thus the dancers' movements were all the closer to inducing dramatic understanding, not only because a sign gesture was known as equivalent to a known word, but because the entire story was known. The characters in drama, poem, and dance were the same. The ratio between spoken drama and dance-drama was virtually one-to-one. Moreover, the stories used in the Sanskrit plays merely passed on to the popular play festivals and village dances."

The philosophy of Indian dance differs markedly from that in Europe and America. Wells explains: "In Western dance the story does not greatly matter, though it gives the dance a firmer body and cohesion than it might otherwise possess. In Indian dance, however, the story or myth is of immense importance. The dancers are in the service of their theme, which is often religious and so much more compelling on this account. Their dance is still a form of worship and to subordinate its subject matter would be to betray its heart. Since it presents a sanctified narrative, the Indian dance can never be abstract. The plot of a play by Kalidasa matters much less than the plot of a play by Shakespeare, but the story in a dance-drama designed by Uday Shankar is much more important than the story in a ballet designed by Diaghilev."

A variety of dances are mentioned in the *Vedas*, and even more are referred to in the *Ramayana* and the *Mahābhārata*, evidence that they antedated their chief literary source and were already well established. The hero Arjuna, a leading figure in the *Mahābhārata*, is exiled; at the court of the King of Virata he spends his time and exerts his talents giving lessons in music and dance. Among his pupils are the royal princesses, which indicates that dance was an acceptable avocation for the high-born. In a fifth-century play by Kalidasa, dancing is a major ingredient, one more sign of the antiquity of the art.

An early and important treatise on dancing, perhaps the first, is the *Natya Sastra* by Bharata (*c.* 1500 BC), setting forth the aesthetic principles of music and drama. (The word *natya* means both dance and drama, an implication that the two are linked inseparably.) From then until the eighteenth century AD a host of other books were written on the subject, positing more strictures. Connery believes that at one time there must have been "a unified system of classical dancing in all of India. Each cultural area in the country acquired eventually a local idiom. Regional folk-dance themes were assimilated into classical art. Foreign influences were also at work; some isolated regions developed new characteristics."

Gradually the art of classical dance declined – much of it was lost. Its revival, early in the twentieth century, was largely owing to the vision and the efforts of a man of great talents, Uday Shankar (1902–77).

A Bengali, whose father had moved to western India, Uday Shankar was born in Udaypur, the city after which he was named. His father was tutor and private secretary to the Maharajah of Jhalawar, and in time prime minister of a princely state in Rajasthan. The boy and his younger brother, Ravi, were educated in a spectrum of Hindu arts for which they showed gifts. Ravi was later to win acclaim as a sitarist, playing that difficult instrument at recitals elsewhere in Asia, in Europe and America. Uday was entered into an art school in Bombay (1917); after two years he was sent to London to improve his painting at the Royal College of Art (1919), where his instructor was the noted Sir William Rothenstein, under whose tutelage the young man won a pair of prizes. He had already begun the study of dance in India and now sometimes performed at social functions, one a garden party (1922) for King George V. The young Uday was remarkably handsome, strong of build, with a broad, noble countenance.

In 1923 the Russian ballerina Anna Pavlova asked him to help her create two works on Indian themes. She was pleased with them and chose him to be her partner in presenting them. He rehearsed with her for three months. They were a success, and she urged him to consider dancing as a career. He toured with her company for nine months, visiting the United States, Canada and Mexico. The generous-spirited Pavlova discouraged him from continuing his training in Western-style ballet, urging him to find inspiration in the distinctive native materials proffered by his own country.

He remained in Paris for a half-decade (until 1929), performing there and in other European cities, and finally returned to India, where he quickly organized his own troupe. By the following year he deemed it ready to perform in Europe, and in 1932 invaded the United States. Subsequently, two decades having ensued, his wife, Amala, and his son, another Ravi, joined the ensemble. The brilliantly glistening costuming, the novel dance idiom, the dramatic impact of the stories, instantly brought fame to the far-travelling company, in which he was a dominant figure because of what one critic called his "magnificent sculptural presence".

Some Indian dance scholars faulted him with "tampering" with classical traditions because he theatricalized, condensed and even somewhat modernized his offerings to suit Western tastes; he was convinced that European and American audiences would not have the knowledge or patience to appreciate the works if they were presented at full length. He also imbued the decorous classical pieces with often racy folk material from Rajasthan, and even social comment. Others defended him as a great popularizer of his country's culture. Rabindranath Tagore told him: "It is because we are sure of your genius that we hope your creations will not be a mere imitation of the past nor burdened with narrow conventions of provincialism. . . . Let your dancing wake up that spirit of Spring in this cheerless land of ours." Another respected critic, Avanda Kentish Coomaraswamy, writing in America, described Shankar as "more the artist in a modern sense than is the Indian virtuoso whose art is one of fixed ends". Coomaraswamy argued that this dancer "uses an Indian technique to give expression to Indian themes. He has brought with him groups of hereditary musicians and enabled Americans to hear the instrumental music of India for the first time. . . . He has brought the Indian theatre to America as sincerely as was perhaps at all possible. He deserves all the credit for this, and all the appreciation he has received." A similar encomium came from Lincoln Kirstein, the dance historian and co-founder of the New York City Ballet: "Uday Shankar is one of the greatest dancers of his epoch, East or West, in his own idiom ranking with Nijinsky and Fred Astaire. He seems archaic Indian sculpture incarnate."

Shankar's response: "With my way, I can say in a few seconds what the Kathakali dancer says in half an hour. And there is nothing Western in this."

To deepen the study of dance, he raised funds from British and American patrons of the arts, among them the wealthy actress Beatrice Straight, to set up a short-lived research centre and arts school at Almora, a mountain village. Later, this institute was moved to Calcutta.

Uday Shankar and his dazzling company toured for three decades. His last New York appearance was in the 1960s, when he was past his physical prime and his technique was no longer as impressive, but critics and audiences still found him compelling, and his offerings as endowed with colour and drama as ever.

During his years abroad he was influenced to a degree by European and American modern dance, then being evolved by Mary Wigman, Martha Graham, Kurt Joos and Sigurd Leeder; the latter two were with him for a while at Dartington Hall, an art school in Devon (England). Fernau Hall, dance critic of the *Daily Telegraph* and a specialist in Indian dance, stated that Shankar created his own performance technique, not held back by fixed precepts; essentially he was self-taught. "The task he set himself as an Indian modern dancer with roots both in India and the West was an excruciatingly difficult one." He could not wholly break with tradition, and apparently did not wish to do so; but it is significant that his initial success occurred in Europe, where authenticity to Indian traditions was not a test because the rigid and long-revered rules were scarcely known to spectators.

He borrowed most from the religiously oriented Kathakali, turning away from the more secular Kathak that he felt tended too much towards virtuosic effects. He professed a mystical strain. "Dance is my life. When I dance I am nearer God; I am not myself."

Some of his innovations: he broadened gestures, making them more explicit than the *mudras*, the perhaps overly subtle sign language of the performers. He simplified footwork, matching it more directly, count by count, with the "curving movements of interlocked hands, arms, head, and the torso and legs".

He produced films (1945–7), among them *Kalpana* and a version of *Shakuntala*. In 1983 Ravi Shankar organized a four-day festival in New Delhi to honour his brother and mark the sixtieth anniversary of his professional career: his films were shown, his paintings were exhibited, and some of his disciples performed works that he had choreographed.

In Shankar's wake many other Indian dancers essayed professional careers as soloists or formed companies of their own, gave recitals, won followers at home and toured abroad, highly praised. Especially after Independence, the art of the classical dance was enthusiastically rediscovered and regained popularity in most parts of the country. Folk dancing, too, was encouraged, studied and classified, becoming once more a visible component of the cultural scene.

Today eight types of classical dance-drama are clearly defined and recognized, each belonging to its own geographical region, with the chief differences in styles observed between those in the north – the Kathakali, Manipur, Kathak – and the south – the Bharata Natayam – standing out as the best known.

Widely prized, the Bharata Natayam is described by an article in *The Dance Encyclopedia* – the author an American performer, La Meri (her name at birth Russell Meriwether Hughes). A distinctive characteristic of this classic form, she says, is that "the upper body is considered far more important in expression than the lower body, though it is not to be supposed that technique of the legs is lacking. There are definite positions of the feet on the ground *(boumya madala pada)* and in the air *(akasa cari)*; gaits *(gati)*, spiral movements *(bhramari)*, and leaps *(utplavana)*. Within these categories are embraced every possible movement of the legs and feet. Technique of the upper body includes movement of the waist (*kati*), shoulders (*kakes*), neck (*griva*), and arms (*vartanam*), in addition to the beautiful and complete gesture language of the hands (*hasta-mudras*). The facial expression (*mukhaja*) includes movements, with their meanings, of brows (*bhru*), eyes (*dristi*), nose (*nasa*), cheeks (*ganda*), mouth (*asya*), and chin (*cibuka*). Ground contacts, or movements of the feet on the ground (*thattadavu*), are much prized in Hindu, the mastery of contratempo, or syncopating effect in beatings, being considered a feat of great virtuosity." What are not emphasized here, by La Meri, but are most astonishing to Westerners, are the horizontal neck movements, the eyes flashing, the head seeming to slide with remarkable flexibility and rapidity from side to side across the shoulders. It is a physical accomplishment unique to Indian dance, found nowhere else.

Highly stylized, the Bharata Natayam, reigning in the south-east among the Tamils, and especially in and around the city of Madras, was favoured throughout its history by the local priesthood and royalty. For centuries its finest exponents were servers in rites at the temples. (Today temple dancing is forbidden by law; such performances, with a few exceptions, are no longer thought to have a proper role in worship.)

Scholars aver that the Bharata Natayam dates to 1500 BC and point out that the three syllables compounded in *Bharata* represent three aspects of every sort of dance; *Bha*, derived from *Bhava* or expression; *Ra*, from *Raga* or melody; *Ta*, from *Tala* or rhythm. This particular style of dancing is portrayed in bas-reliefs still to be viewed at the Natya Baha (Hall of the Dance) in the ninth-century Chidambaram Temple.

The expatriate Indian novelist and playwright, Satha Rama Rau (wife of Oriental scholar Faubion Bowers), in a brief memoir, tells of an important personal discovery: "In Madras, for the first time, I saw Bharata Natayam, an exacting and thrilling school of dance which, like so much else in India's artistic expression, originated in the temples as a form of worship. It used to be performed only by *devadasis* (God's servants) who lived in the temple environs and learned their rigidly defined choreography, both devotional and pure dance, from ancient scripture. Near Mysore, in south-central India, you can see such temples as Belur, built for the twelfth-century Queen Shantala, who was famous both for her religious devotion and her brilliance as a dancer. There, in front of the shrine of the deity, is a highly polished, circular dance floor of black marble, surrounded by pillars topped with figures demonstrating various Bharata Natayam dance poses. There the queen, and later the temple *devadasis*, performed their devotions in dance. Belur is no longer used for worship, but many other temples of south India afford views of extraordinary sculpture, in context and part of a continuing tradition which a museum can never provide."

It is possible, La Meri believes, that the shape and aura – or, better, the very ambience – of the many scattered temples in which it was performed had an influence on the choreography of the evolving Bharata Natayam. "The floor design, like the air design, is built along architectonic lines, and the whole has great strength and austerity, even in the lighter passages."

Berthold, in her *History of World Theatre*, provides a picture in detail of those temples: sometimes the religious compounds covered enormous spaces, "laid out in terraces over whole hillsides . . . there was a special assembly and dance hall (*natamandira*) and, for more general purposes, a 'celebration hall' (*mandapa*) where dancing girls, musicians, and reciters gave performances in honor of the gods. At some temples in southern India, such as the Jagannath temple at Puri, it is still the custom today for the *devadasis*, the temple's dancing girls, to dance at the ceremonial evening service."

Similar designs persist from epoch to epoch. Berthold tells us further: "Among the eighth-century rock-cut temples in the Ellora caves there stands the theatre hall of the Lailasa temple. And there are elaborate and festival halls in the eleventh-century Ghantai temple grounds near Khajuraho. Others can be found in the twelfth-century temple complex of Girnar and at the Vitthala Temple of the fourteenth-century Vijayanagar rulers."

As must also be remarked, along with the "stone history" of ancient dances found at myriad sites throughout India there are bronze portraits of long-ago performers eternally memorialized, such as the statuette of a dancing girl in the ruined lower Indus city of Mohenjo Daro. Amazing is the graphic representation in bas-relief on the columns of that Hindu shrine at Chidambaram where all 186 positions to be assumed by the classical dancer are illustrated; they accord exactly with those suggested in Bharata's *Natya Sastra*.

La Meri spells out the repertoire of the Bharata Natayam dancer; it includes *nrrta*, *nrtya* and *nautch*. "*Nrrta* is an abstract dance of pure lyricism; *nrtya* is an expressive dance, pantomimic in content; *nautch* is a combination of song and dance. The song, in *nautch*, whether sung by the *devadasi* (temple dancer) or a member of the orchestra, is illustrated with pantomimic gestures and laced with steps of pure dance. The typical Bharata Natayam program continues without interval for some three hours. Dancers and musicians never leave the platform, which is primitively lit and without curtains."

A standard Bharata Natayam recital is composed of seven sections, a sequence that has an idiomatic symmetry: three high-points are *Alarippu*, an invocation in the form of pure dance, evolving into more complex blendings of dancing and expressive pantomime; the *Varnam*, the middle and more sustained episode, in which the dancer is forced to display both emotional and physical intensity; and the *Tillana*, another passage of pure dance, that concludes the recital with a brief prayer (the *Sloka*).

"The music of Bharata Natayam is of the Carnatic style, prevalent in southern India. There are one or two singers. The chief singer usually takes on the *nattuvangam* or direction of the dance. He plays all the rhythms on cymbals of bronze. There is usually an instrumental accompaniment on a *mukhaveena* which is a small wind instrument. The most important instrument is the *mridangam*, a drum, which indicates the rhythm. The dancer wears anklets of small bells which also emphasize the rhythm."

In modern times the most renowned of Bharata Natayam performers was Tanjore Balasaraswati (1920–84), a native of Madras and a descendant of nine generations of musicians and dancers. One of her ancestors, Papammal, had fulfilled those roles at the Tanjore court in the eighteenth century. As a little girl, only four, Tanjore Balasaraswati was brought to Kandappa Pillai to be instructed in dance and acquainted with the firmly prescribed form of Bharata Natayam that had been codified in the nineteenth century by four brothers known as the Tanjore Quartet. At seven the pupil had her début, astounding her teachers with her precocious skill at mime as well as her technical control in rhythmic passages.

She grew to be tall, amply figured, moving with both grace and force. Most highly prized was her mastery of *abhinaya*, her expressiveness through mime and gesture. She performed with intense concentration and radiance, evoking in many spectators a spiritual response and a union with the Divine. Because Bharata Natayam brings spiritual release through concentration and discipline, she likened it to "artistic yoga". The effect on the spectator is akin, because at the dance he "is absorbed in watching and has his mind freed of distractions and feels a great sense of clarity".

She was adamantly conservative, arguing: "It is the orthodoxy of traditional discipline which gives the fullest freedom in the individual creativity of the dancer." She insisted that the prescribed order of the seven sections of a dance recital (referred to in a paragraph above) should be strictly preserved, so as not to lose the balance of "esthetic and psychological elements which produce complete enjoyment".

Adhering to the pure, historic style of Bharata Natayam and respectfully aware that it originated in temple rites and acts of worship, she excelled at conveying in poetic imagery the struggle of humans to attain transcendence and unite with the Sublime.

In 1962 Balasaraswati danced in Tokyo. She made frequent visits to the United States, initially on a tour sponsored by the Asia Society. She was seen at the Jacob's Pillow Dance Festival (1962). The following year she appeared at the Edinburgh Festival; her artistry called forth praise from Margot Fonteyn and Martha Graham. Other American institutions – Wesleyan University, the American Dance Festival – brought her to their stages on occasions between 1962 and 1979, and she taught at them, as well as under the auspices of the American Society for Eastern Arts, established by Samuel and Luise Scripps, two of her American benefactors.

Satyajit Ray recorded her artistry in a documentary film entitled *Bala* (as she was called familiarly).

Widow of a government official, she had a daughter and grandson, and two brothers who were musicians, T. Yiswanathan and T. Ranganathan, teaching at Wesleyan University. Her daughter, Lakshmi, is also a dancer and has performed the Bharata Natayam in New York (1986) as part of the Festival of India, at the Asia Society. She instructed at dance workshops there, as well, together with Birju Maharaj.

Among the artists invited to join in the Festival of India at Alice Tully Hall in Lincoln Center was the young soloist Malavika Sarukkai, similarly dedicated to Bharata Natayam. Interviewed by Jack Anderson for the *New York Times*, she expressed her belief that a Western spectator need not feel baffled by an Indian dance concert, explaining: "Movement impulses in Bharata Natayam arise in the center of the body and flow outward through the extremities, only to return to the center. Steps are woven together in complex patterns, and the fast footwork can make Bharata Natayam very powerful. But a good Bharata Natayam program must always evoke a sense of peace and harmony. There are moments during the solos when the dancer's ego seems to fade away and nothing is left but the ecstasy of the dance, the joy of movement and space. Such a state of being can indeed be called spiritual. You in the audience can feel a serene joy, even though you know nothing of the Hindu gods and goddesses."

Her training had begun after she reached seven. Her studies were undertaken in Bombay and Madras, the latter city now her home. In a review of the festival's opening, Anna Kisselgoff had praise for "the very pretty Malavika Sarrukkai" who lent to her offerings "an unusual mix of radiance and winsomeness".

In the south-west, around Malabar and in Kerala, Kathakali is a major art form. The name connotes "story play", and this dramatic dance with all-male casts – young men and boys – has been called "the Passion Play of Hinduism". Though its doubtless remote origin is unknown, its present format has been traced to the closing years of the sixteenth century. Its subject-matter embraces the full scope of the sacred epics: the *Ramayana*, the *Mahābhārata*, the *Gita of Jayadeva*, and other religious narratives and poems. Most distinctive are the highly stylized costumes and make-up of the actor–dancers, whose training is prolonged and vigorous to give them perfect physical control. They are also taught how to project feelings by facial expressions – *mukhaja* – and the prescribed *mudras*, symbolic hand gestures. They wear huge, gaudily painted circular wooden headdresses and below the waist, wide, white crinoline skirts. The make-up is mask-like and may represent one of five different types depending on such details as colour – *Pacha* (green), *Kari* (black) – or a beard (*Tati*), or a mark – *Kathi* (knife), suggested by a red scar. The *Pacha* character is virtuous, sturdily upright; his face is painted green. The

Kathi figure is an embodiment of villainy and heroism; his face, too, is smeared green but with the "scar", a knife-shaped pattern drawn on the cheek with red pigment; he also has a small white ball affixed to the middle of his brow and another fastened to the tip of his nose. The fifth class of make-up is the *Minukku* (polished). The application of such make-up is an art in itself requiring several hours and done by members of the troupe who have probably spent ten or twelve years of apprenticeship learning the craft. Finally, a chundapoova seed is inserted under the lower eyelid; the eyeballs are rotated until they become the proper shade of red for the character to be portrayed: "rose for amorous heroes and heroines and ruby for demons".

Singing and instrumental music are integral to the performances. They are of excellent quality; the songs must be pure south Indian *ragas* with no taint of other styles. The orchestra is ranged, seated, at the back of the stage, sometimes behind a curtain. The instruments are likely to be a *chenta*, *maddalam*, cymbals, a gong and perhaps the *edakka*. The music has been described as consisting mostly of "ear-splitting percussives". The drums, gong and cymbals predominate. The songs and dialogue are in Malayalam, the language that widely superseded Sanskrit.

In her brief memoir, Satha Rama Rau recalls:

Not until I was grown up and traveled fairly extensively in India did I discover the arts with which my South Indian grandparents were familiar.

The Kathakali dance-drama of Kerala, their performers (all men) in fantastic make-up, great billowing costumes, crowns glittering with paillettes and fragments of mirror, were all new to me. So were the thunderous drums that announced a Kathakali performance in a village, alerting everyone within earshot to start walking, children in tow or carried on a mother's hip, a father's shoulders, to the scene of an all-night show. Only the mythological stories enacted in Kathakali were a reassuring point of contact as I recognized the gods and demons, heroes and villains, fabulous animals and sorcerers from the epics.

In Madras for the first time, in a pavilion set aside for the purpose, I saw an informative demonstration of Kathakali. An intimate setting provides a valuable closeup of an art that relies on details as subtle as an eyebrow moving upward.

The new theater itself is handsome and in an innovative format; it is being used as only one site visited by the audience. In an attempt to suggest the informality of some Asian performances, the public is invited to wander around the building at intermission, eating Indian food and looking at exhibitions. The performance was preceded by a demonstration during which a Kathakali performer put on his make-up and his voluminous skirted costume.

The Kathakali itself is a hybrid form. Its subjects, drawn from Hindu epics and legends, are presented in genuine folk plays with a moral. Yet it is a nonverbal art relying on a codified dance vocabulary that is classical. At the same time, its world is filled with gods and mythical figures that have human foibles. Kathakali's very conventions are its delight – faces with colors coded to specific types, the sudden bursts of stamping solos for dancers who dance on the sides of their feet with knees bent.

The excerpts on view this time, *Daksha Yagam* (*The Sacrifice of King Daksha*), told the story of Sati, consort of the god Siva, who is driven out of a temple by her father, Daksha. Siva sends two demons to behead Daksha but then accedes to the will of the Supreme Being, Brahma, to restore Daksha to life.

As usual, the artists and musicians were excellent. T.T. Ramankutty Nair was ferocious in his arbitrariness as Daksha, and Mankombu Sivansankara Pillai was a contrasting portrait in serenity as Siva, transforming himself into a warrior on the spot. In the female role of Sati, C.M. Balasubramanian was able impressively to depict two characters at once in recalling the encounter with Daksha; M.P. Vausudeva Pisharoty and C. Gopalakrishnan roared merrily as demons.

Yet, this was an excerpt that showed none of the psychological depth of Kathakali pieces from epics such as the *Ramayana*. The intricate range of Kathakali's dances was barely evident as these artists, younger than those in the past, relied more on mime. Subtlety was played down in favor of broadness.

Nonetheless, any glimpse of Kathakali is worth a trip.

Properly, the plays are presented at night outdoors on a bare stage, lit by a pot of burning butter, lasting until daybreak. The singer gives the dancers their cues and is in effect the director. Formerly Kathakali was a feature of very lengthy temple rituals or festivals. Today, adapted to the modern stage, they are abridged to a mere two or three hours.

The technique of the Kathakali actor is composed of about 500 separate signs, a complete alphabet. The dance critic Margaret Croyden quotes from an essay by Eugenio Barba listing a few of them.

"There are nine motions of the head, eleven casting a glance, six motions of the eyebrows, and four positions of the neck. The sixty-four motions of the limbs cover the movements of the feet, toes, heels, ankles, waist, hips. . . . The gestures of the hands and feet have a narrative function and they are organized into fixed figures called *mudras* ('signs' in Sanskrit). Those *mudras* are the alphabet of the acting 'language.' . . . There are sets of facial motions to express not only feelings and emotions, but traits of character of a more permanent nature, such as generosity, pride, curiosity, anxiety in the face of death."

In short, the Kathakali actor's hands tell the story, and his face expresses his attitude and emotional reactions to the story. This dualism enables the actor to be part of the tale and comment on it simultaneously – a kind of dialectic without language.

One of the most important aspects of the Kathakali is the way in which the actors work with their eyes. "Sometimes the face is absolutely immobile and the eyes alone do the acting. . . ." In one play, Barba reports: "a butterfly burns itself in a flame. The actor portrays this with his eyes alone." Of equal importance are the movements of the various parts of the body: "[They] are completely desynchronized. For example, the legs may be moving at an incredible speed while the hands sculpt the *mudras* with a deliberate and precise slowness."

During their training the Kathakali actors work in complete silence; they endure painful exercises that result in the complete control of the actor's muscles; they follow a strict daily schedule of work, usually beginning at 4 a.m.; they are zealous, religious and live a monastic life. Particularly interesting is the Kathakali philosophy of theatre, parts of which Grotowski found meaningful. "The actor-priest offers his body to the gods," Barba writes, "like the juggler of Notre-Dame in the medieval legend offered his juggling to the Virgin Mary . . . He offers his body with humility and supplication, quite willing to make any sacrifice for his art."

When women appear in Kathakali they adopt a style known as *Mohimi Attam* which equals the male technique in expressivity but is much less emphatic. (The name is borrowed from that used by Lord Vishnu for his incarnation as a dancer, Mohimi.)

A foremost exponent of Kathakali, as well as of Bharata Natayam, was Rukmini Devi, based in Madras and a pupil of Meenakashi Sundaram Pillai.

In 1971, at the Hunter College Playhouse in New York, a seventeen-member all-male troupe from the Kerala Kalamandalam (State Academy for Theatre Arts), founded by the poet Vallathol, brought a first showing of Kathakali to North America. Two more New York visits followed (1981, 1982). Anna Kisselgoff reported on the third of these occasions, when the ensemble was on view at the Asia Society's Lila Acheson Wallace Auditorium (1982). She found fault with the setting, "a small 258-seat theatre works against the epic scale that Kathakali can offer". Nevertheless, the repeated engagements at such comparatively short intervals attested that New York's sophisticated dance-lovers were startled and appreciative at discovering this unique art form hitherto largely unknown to them – few had any inkling hitherto of Kathakali. In advance of the second event – two exhibitions on two evenings – the offering was described as "the oldest extant theatre in the world in practice". Before curtain time there was an informational lecture-demonstration, and Indian delicacies were served during intermissions. According to the *New York Times* both programmes began with a traditional benediction and ended with *Dikpalavandanam (Obeisance to the Guardians of the Directions)*, an epilogue in which an actor honours the gods who preside over the eight divisions of the world. "Tuesday's program included a short scene from *Bhagavadajjuka (The Saint and the Courtesan)*, a pastoral comedy from the seventh century AD, and *The Killing of Jatayu*, scenes selected from *The Wonderous Crest-Jewel*, which dates from the ninth and tenth centuries AD. On Wednesday, the Kerala Kalamandalam performed five scenes from the more familiar *Encounter between Ravena and Hanuman*. The public performances were presented in cooperation with the International Symposium on Theater and Ritual, sponsored by the Wenner-Gren Foundation for Anthropological Research." As part of these showings Western spectators were able to watch the actors' application of facial make-up, the ugly mask-like transformations, unmatched anywhere else in the world, carrying the grotesque to the very extreme – and beyond.

Eugenio Barba, quoted by Margaret Croyden, is a disciple of Jerzy Grotowski, the twentieth-century avant-garde Polish stage-theorist, teacher and director. Barba reveals how much Grotowski learned from the aesthetic and practice of this Indian art form. In Grotowski's production of *The Constant Prince* the player in the leading role, Cieslak, always caused much comment because his eyeballs were dilated, which is often true of the heightened expression of Kathakali actors, their eyeballs also seeming to protrude at crucial moments, emphasizing the emotion that possesses them. From this it follows that, to the extent that Grotowski's teaching and example have affected the study of acting – in some circles it has been considerable – the odd but dynamic principles of Kathakali have put a stamp on the modern Western stage, though not many European and American audiences have been aware of this.

The Kathak of northern India, as has been remarked, is the least religious of the several classic dances, though historically it was the creation of Brahmin priests – or Kathaks, hence the name – whose intention it was to narrate sacred tales in the temples and illustrate them with mime and dance. In doing so they followed the precepts of Bharata. All that changed after the Muslim invasion, when new influences were absorbed. The performers were welcome at Mogul courts, with the result that Persian elements were added to their offerings. Eventually the temple dances became mere entertainment. Women joined the troupes during the century and a half, 1526–1707, and the presentations waxed increasingly sensual. The *nautch-wali* (or nautch girls – "*nautch*" is a corruption of the Sanskrit "*Natya*") and their male partners too soon earned a reputation for loose morals.

Even so, Kathak as it took shape chiefly in Jaipur and Lucknow has a great many aesthetic virtues and demands much skill and grace. The dancers can repeat with their feet the exact beat of the drums – this entails much rhythmic stamping, and they make fine use of their anklets to which are attached a triple row of bells. The best performers are credited with being able to control the tinkle of any bell.

The technique calls for mastery of "*gaths*" and "*torahs*". The former are the mimed stretches which allow a rest between episodes of *torah*. Such pantomime might consist of *mudras* suggesting commonplace activities such as flying a kite, relating the flirtations of Krishna and his ever-present band of *gopis* (milk-maids). La Meri provides this explanation of *torahs*: "They are passages of *thatta-davu* – complicated, lively and strong – set to *bolos*, or sentences of rhythm which the dancer gives by means of spoken syllables to the *tabla-wallah* (drummer). . . . Kathak dance, traditionally executed, is spontaneously created. A complete artistic understanding between dancer and drummer makes this possible. Rhythmic passages of hands, brow, and neck are often used by women protagonists of the art."

The female dancer is apt to employ much *nrtya* (interpretive, meaningful gesturing) for which there are eleven sorts of music. Also still used are twenty-odd types of *gats*, of the 360 listed and described by a nineteenth-century priest, Prakash Kathak.

The male dancers devote more of their performance to *nrrta*, the rhythmic passages (*bolas*), of which there are a dozen kinds, all of which can be varied endlessly.

Some critics object that the arm movements and a number of body postures in Kathak are weak. This category of dance also lacks interpretive depth: the gestures are only decorative. Kathak seldom suggests the sculptural aspect of Bharata Natayam.

The usual programme opens with a dance (*amad*) that welcomes the spectators: this is followed by a display of the performers' dazzling and intricate footwork (*parans*). The third offering, *gaths*, is somewhat interpretive, with elements of *abhinaya*. The dancer is accompanied by a singer, who echoes the drum beats syllabically. He is often joined by the dancer who voices the same sounds. The instrumentalists include a *sarangi* player and two drummers.

Two outstanding representatives of Kathak have been Kalkaprasa Maharas and, at a later date, Damayanti Soshi. Others noted for their accomplishment in this genre are Birju Maharaj and Sitara Devi in male and female roles respectively; both have toured abroad. Maharaj was seen in New York in 1974. About his second appearance to that city under the auspices of the Asia Society, Jennifer Dunning wrote in the *New York Times*:

His demonstrations of Kathak technique – with its sensuous interweaving of expressive movement with abstract rhythms, sudden rhythmic changes and time beats that are extremely complex yet excitingly vigorous – were among the high points of Thursday's program. His feet are notable as they stamp, spin and skim with an attack that is both buttery soft and sharply articulated.

Mr Maharaj also offered brief and extended mime passages. A galloping horse and its impatient rider were excitingly evoked. Another highlight was his quick-changing presentation of five ways an Indian woman peeps from behind her veil. And the cherubic Mr Maharaj was hilariously convincing as a baby Krishna who comes to steal butter from a stern housewife's kitchen.

Free-wheeling and extemporizing, the program offered a glimpse of the kind of intense audience involvement that is a feature of Indian theater-dancing. And Mr Maharaj, an entertainer with a bold, flirtatious presence, immediately established a relationship with the audience that was almost as intense and familial as his rapport with his outstanding musicians. Whether singing, drumming or dancing, Mr Maharaj is a popular artist in the best sense of the term.

He has also assembled a fine group of performers, which included the delicately impassioned Saswati Sen, Mr Maharaj's lead dancer. . . . The delight of Mr Acharya, the *tabla* player, in his work and surroundings was infectious. And Prakash Parekh was the evening's gracious master of ceremonies.

The occasion of the Maharaj Troupe's return to New York was the Festival of India, during which the ensemble of twelve artists performed at Lincoln Center. (A co-sponsor was the Bharatiya Vidya Bhavan, a Manhattan-based cultural organization.) This presentation evoked an admiring response from Anna Kisselgoff, also of the *New York Times*, who did not hesitate to call him "one of the world's most distinguished dancers".

He has only to step onstage after his troupe of young male and female dancers stamped and spun in true Kathak style to immediately establish his presence and authority. With his partner, Saswait Sen, he drew from the same mythic imagery represented by the three other styles on the program.

Still young in spirit, he is a virtuoso of the finest nuance – he can make every bell on his ankle rustle through the house with a leg quiver and he can burst through a stampede with both force and refinement. The group dances (at first without him) from dazzling patterns and yet like all Indian dance, they have an inner philosophical meaning.

Nowhere is this seen better than in the link between erotic and spiritual content that colors so much of this program. A yearning for love is also a yearning for communion with the Godhead.

A feature of the program was Maharaj's challenging of his musicians to "an improvisatory duel within his specialty, the dance form known as Kathak. Freedom within structure – perhaps that is one of the special beauties of India's classical dances and every performer onstage served as a living illustration."

Sitara Devi's début in New York, at Carnegie Hall (1976), also sponsored by the Asia Society, prompted Ms Kisselgoff to say:

There is no point in comparing the two dancers beyond saying that even within its conventions, Kathak offers a rich range of dramatic and technical interpretation. Sitara has a natural ebullience that contrasted with Birju's more lilting presentation, but each is obviously an artist of the first order.

In Sitara, the combination of temperament and absolute technical control clarifies even further the frequent analogy between Kathak and Spanish flamenco. The bursts of energy that punctuated her complex footwork would emerge later as displays of passion and emotion in the dramatic sequences that alternated with the pure-dance demonstrations on the program.

In the best of such tradition, Sitara is descended from a family of artists devoted to her art – her father was Sukhdeve Maharaj, one of Kathak's gurus and a singer-scholar at the court of Nepal. This dynastic tradition is still carried on. On this program, Sitara was assisted by her young daughter, Priya Mala, as dancer, and her musician brother, Benu-Prassad Misra.

Two young and extraordinary musicians completed the ensemble. One was Satyanarayan Channu, whose impassioned singing and reading of texts not only recalled the canto flamenco itself but also reached a pitch that left at least one member of the audience transported. The other young man was Zakir Khan, a virtuoso on the *tabla*, or drums, whose father, as Sitara noted in one of her several commentaries, had accompanied her in the past.

Accompaniment is perhaps the wrong word. One of the program's most impressive aspects was the intricate interplay between Sitara and Zakir. These passages of structured improvisation always had Sitara ending on time with the musician although none of the sequences was set.

Kathak's signature style – speed, stamping footwork, pirouettes and arms flung out at chest level – hold no mysteries for Sitara. She, too, is a true virtuoso.

Yet the real depth of her artistry was revealed in the nuances of dramatic expression that she brought to a mimed passage based on the epic of the *Mahābhārata* in which she played several characters. She could suggest the unseen character through illusion marvelously. At other times, as in a dice-game scene between two opposing clans, each throw of the dice carried its own suspense. It was a total performance.

Another American visit occurred in 1986, made possible by the World Music Institute. The stage was at the Triplex Theater of Manhattan Community College; Sitara Devi availed herself of this academic setting to speak to her audience about her art, between demonstrations of it. Anna Kisselgoff was on hand.

Kathak, the classic dance of northern India, is more frequently associated with male than female performers. But Sitara Devi, India's most celebrated Kathak dancer, has proved that a true classical art form has no gender. . . . An integral aspect [of her exposition] was the repartee between herself and the brilliant young *tabla* player, Zakir Hussain, who was joined by Fazal Qureshi, also on the drums, and Ustad Sultan Khan, a master of the stringed instrument, the *sarangi*.

Kathak, whose emphasis on virtuosity was developed under the Mogul courts, involves constant interplay and rhythmic unity between the dancer and musicians. This is what Sitara Devi and Zakir Hussain demonstrated so stunningly.

Repeatedly, she would recite rhythmic syllables in advance and then she would dance while he played – both ending at the same time. Such improvisation within structure is common in India's classical dance forms. But it is especially exciting in the style.

In part this is because the pure dance passages of Kathak have a built-in bravura element. Sitara Devi, a small woman with a forceful personality, gives an added edge to the signature movements of Kathak – the arms shooting out, the stamping and the spinning.

As each rhythmic phrase became increasingly complex, the beauty of the shapes she described with her body – curved, even serpentine – became correspondingly richer.

In contrast to this vigorous "abstract" movement, Sitara Devi occasionally offered some mime passages. Her acting style is startlingly tough rather than nuanced – heightening the drama of such scenes in which the young Krishna is scolded or a mother dotes upon her child. Above all, her authority came through at every instance.

Venturing abroad, too, has been Sunayana, a Kathak dancer from Bombay, seen in a solo concert at the Alternative Center for International Art in New York (1978), where her performance ended with a standing ovation by the audience. The co-sponsor was the Indian Culture Center. Jennifer Dunning wrote in the *New York Times*:

It was an afternoon of pure magic. . . . The liveliness and pantomimic element of Kathak makes it accessible to the casual viewer although it is a style of rigorous technique and highly shaded nuance.

Kathak was originally practiced by priests who danced out stories of their faith within a temple, and it was not until the time of the sixteenth-century Mogul rule that the dance took on its present theatrical form. At Sunayana's concert there was a pervasive sense of the past as families crowded about the edge of the performance space, urging the dancer on, their excitement mirrored in the face of Hazarilal, her drummer and *guru*-husband.

Sunayana opened the concert with a customary invocation to the god Rama, then started into *Chaupalli*, a long, abstract dance piece that built from simple to increasingly intricate rhythms, stamped out at four times, the original speed to syllable patterns chanted by drummer and dancer. Although the quick rhythmic changes had an almost mathematically precise complexity, the smooth articulation of the feet, arms and hands and controlled abandon of Sunayana's whirling turns verged on trancelike ecstasy. An element of humor was injected after the dance as Sunayana demonstrated typical Kathak walks, from that of the "elderly woman who's not shy anymore" to the "man with the steady mind."

The storytelling element of Kathak took precedence in the second half of the program. Sunayana portrayed a wife intent on keeping her husband from going to war, in an untitled dance built on the interpretation of sung variations of a single line of poetry.

In the absorbingly detailed *Soorpanakha*, performed in a sitting position, Ravana, the demon temptress of Rama and his brother Lakshmana, is rejected and forced to cut off her nose. The program closed with *Dance of Spring*, a celebration of the joy of movement and its complex rhythms.

It was in the pantomimic dances that the characteristically delicate interrelationship of dance and music in Kathak was most clear and exciting. While it perfectly enhanced Sunayana's performance, the singing of young Satyanara Misra had its own great beauty.

In remote north-east India the classic dance is Manipuri, blending Hindu mythology and local folklore. It differs from the other major forms, for its prompting is wholly religious, and an entire community may take part in it. Its frequent theme is the love story of Krishna and Radha, especially the episode known as the *Ras Lila*. Another dramatic offering is the *Lai Haroba*. In both of these there are fewer *mudras*, the movements and traditional hand-signs are softer; yet there may be vigorous action when the young men enter the scene. In contrast, the young girls perform with lyrical flow and grace. The face of the performer is inexpressive; the meaning of the dance is projected through the sinuous sway of torso and arms; indeed, of the whole body. The carriage has a Far Eastern air.

The women wear small conical caps, tight jackets of trimmed velvet. Their embroidered hooped skirts are partly covered by silken petticoats. Such costuming is rich, cheerful, picturesque.

The musical instruments are the standard ones, but the melodies and the accompanying choruses have a very local flavour.

As has been remarked earlier, Tagore was largely responsible for the spread and greater popularity of this dance, which he first saw on a visit to Manipur in 1917. He was delighted to find the art of Indian dance still alive and vowed to bring it sharply to the attention of his fellow Bengalis and other compatriots. He engaged several practitioners of the dance to teach it at his institute; he also wove passages of Manipuri into his own poetic plays.

Celebrated as an interpreter of Manipuri, especially in works devoted to the legend of Krishna, has been Rashila.

Of the much-favoured Orissa, La Meri says that it is another secular dance form, similar to Bharata Natayam, "more legato in movement. It is believed to be closer to the original style of the ancient Vigayanager Empire temple dancers."

Two more dance forms, not mentioned by La Meri, are very popular among Indians, though lesser known outside the country: Odissi, of ancient origin, is distinguished by its sculptural quality while its movements are punctuated by dramatic tableaux. Some credit it with a 2,000-year history and claim that it was created by Siva himself, the god of dynamic dance. Until the fifteenth century it was enacted only by women and restricted to being a component of temple worship. The performer must possess a supple torso and be able to assume precise positions of the body's lower half. It is mostly lyrical. In fact, it is modelled on the friezes and figures on the temples at Orissa. One famed carved stone practitioner of it has said, "Odissi has gentleness and at the same time strength."

Quite the opposite is the rhythmically exuberant Kuchipudi. It dates to the thirteenth century and employs broad mime, at times lending itself to comic effects, though its content is primarily religious. It was developed by Krishna cultists as a vehicle for worship in which dance and music are paramount. At first it was undertaken only by young men of the highest priestly Brahman caste. It is a robust dance-drama requiring performers with gifts for speech, song, expressivity, intricate slapping footwork and a bouncing momentum, along with a flair for quick improvisation. Kuchipudi flourishes in Andhra Pradesh.

Many Indian artists do not limit themselves to only one of the eight classic categories but instead choose programmes in which they exhibit their versatility, perhaps offering a work each of Bharata Natayam, Orissi, Manipuri or Kuchipudi. This has become the practice among the best-known dancers, seen at home or abroad as soloists or with their own small troupes in the recent past or currently. A full roster of those who fit into this group would include Bhaska, Yamini Krishnamurti, Vedantam Satyanarayana Sarma, Ritha Devi, Shatki, Sanjukta Panagrahi and Rajani, all of whom have won plaudits from European and American critics. Naturally, the list is ever changing and is too long for more than a very few on it to be discussed as they merit. Save when caught on film, the dancer's art is woefully evanescent and never truly retrieved in words. The performers selected here have international reputations.

Prominent have been Indrani and Sukanya, mother and daughter, seen in New York (1985) and elsewhere in foreign capitals. Indrani, in turn, is the daughter of Ragini Devi (1896–1982), born Esther Sherman in Petosky, Michigan, who in her teens acquired two Sanskrit books on dance and taught herself fragments of the technique. At that time the literature on "Oriental" dance was hardly available in the West, but there was a vogue for self-conceived approximations of it. Ragini pressed on, naïvely and courageously. Marrying an Indian physicist, Ramiel Bajpai, she settled in New York City and fortunately met expatriate musicians who served as accompanists at her recitals. In 1930, after publishing a book meant to be an introduction to Indian dance, *Nritanjali* (1928), she went to India to study and round out her training. She gained celebrity there, including praise from Tagore, who voiced his gratitude to her for her efforts to revive the authentic art, then in considerable disrepute in its homeland. He stated: "Those of us belonging to northern India who have lost the memory of the pure Indian classical dance have experienced a thrill of delight at the exhibition of dancing given by Ragini Devi." She formed a company to present Kathakali in Indian cities, and was the first to present it to Westerners when she appeared in London and Paris (1938–9). Following that came recitals in New York at frequent intervals. In 1948, given a grant by the Rockefeller Foundation, she published *Dance Dialects of India*. In 1978 she returned to live in New York City. She gave her last recital in 1979 at New York University. Appearing there with Indrani, she voiced her joy at beholding "the pure tradition" passed on through three generations. She died at the age of eighty-six.

Indrani later related that, travelling to India, Ragini Devi had discovered that she was pregnant. Distressed that her career would be affected, she sought out an Indian astrologer who told her not to worry – the child, a girl, was destined to become a dancer far more successful than her mother. "My mother was then most excited and composed my name – Indrani – before I was born with a view to how it would look on posters. You might say I was born with a stage name. So I really had no choice about becoming a dancer. My mother subtly pushed me into it at such a young age that I never dreamt of doing anything else." The little girl was on stage when five, performing with her mother. A marriage at fifteen to an architect did not impede the growth of her career, nor did the birth of her two children.

Indrani's first American tour on her own took place in 1960. After 1977 she remained in the

United States to teach. She gave summer classes at Harvard University. Her choice was only three styles – Orissi, Kuchipudi, Bharata Natayam – "That's all I can master in one lifetime."

She gave joint recitals with her daughter, Sukanya, at Jacob's Pillow, the Delacorte Dance Festival and various universities. She was particularly fond of her broadly mimed, amusing portrayal of the Frog Princess in *Manduka Shabdam*, a solo in the Kuchipudi mode, in which, "batting her eyes and puffing out her cheeks", she alternated the role with one of the "ferociously glaring Demon King". When an onlooker voiced surprise that her dancing was not "cool and refined", she replied: "Oriental dance was born in the temple, but it is sensual and human and warm. Our dance is taken from mythology – but all moods and emotions are expressed in our mythology. Our gods, like the Greek gods, are made in man's image. Our dances concern every aspect of life, and that includes the romantic, the mischievous, the humorous. It's all there."

Indrani asserts that she was the first to bring Orissi to the stage. She worked to have the style granted official recognition, a matter that was debated in Parliament, with the result that the government agreed to subsidize the dance form, awarding scholarships to those who studied it.

Sukanya's first visit to the United States was to enter Martha Graham's school. Her goal was to be a modern dancer, but her exposure to this new aesthetic only strengthened her allegiance to the Indian idioms that are her heritage. Marrying, she eventually settled in Maine with her husband and two children. Jennifer Dunning, of the *New York Times*, saw her at the Theater of the Riverside Church (1985):

> In terms of sheer beauty, the highlight of the program was the delicately sensuous *Orissi Suite*, which included a prayer danced to the god Ganesh, a love song from the *Gita Govinda* and *Natangi*, a pure-dance finale. Much of the excitement of Indian classical dancing comes from the sometimes almost impossibly intricate foot-beats and the tension of their relationship to the music's equally intricate rhythms. But the emphasis here was on movement that was nearly liquid in its flow and attack, with the dancer's body softening into S-curves and sinking into the ankles, at times in squats in second position.
>
> Sukanya was also effective in two samples of Kuchipudi, where she played the arrogant Satyabhama, whom Krishna favours, in *Bahaman Kalapam*, and the imperious goddess Durga, engaged in a battle with Mahishasura, the buffalo-headed demon in *Chamundeshwari Shabdam*.
>
> Another highlight was the *Bharata Natyam Tillana*, a rhythmic pure-dance piece for Sukanya and Indrani, clad in bright pink saris and moving through fast-building rhythmic sets that ended in a finale that had the two traveling quickly in unison across the stage. The dance's fleeting, clear geometric shapes were appealing.

Besides appearing on stage with her mother, she performed in solo engagements. Jack Anderson, also of the *New York Times*, observed her at the Minor Latham Playhouse of New York's Barnard College (1987):

> On this occasion, Sukanya emphasized gentle, even playful dances. *Tarangam*, in praise of the god Krishna, was sweetly languid. *Krishna Shabdam*, another work honoring Krishna, was filled with sly glances. An *Orissi Suite* contained gracious gestures and demure poses.
>
> Three solos grew more intensely dramatic. In *Chamundeshwari Shabdam*, which depicted a battle between a goddess and a demon, Sukanya was a determined warrior. Her bearing was especially proud in *Bhama Kalapam*, which expressed the confidence of Krishna's beloved.
>
> *Mandrake Shabdam* was a little epic in movement. Flowing gestures depicted the glidings of sea creatures. Stampings and little hops indicated that Sukanya was now portraying a frog princess. And when the frog was transformed into a woman, one knew what had happened by the way Sukanya had her princess pause to admire her own beauty.

Quite different was the way in which another non-Indian, La Meri, who – as already noted – began life as Russell Meriwether Hughes in Louisville, Kentucky (1898) – arrived at classical Asian dance. After taking courses at Texas Woman's University and Columbia University, she studied ballet, Spanish and Mexican folk-idioms for a half-dozen years from teachers in San Antonio, Texas (1913–20); pursuing her mastery of other kinds of ethnic dance, she visited the Hawaiian islands for instruction there (1917); and then furthered her knowledge of Spanish dance in Barcelona (1922). Her eager quest led her next to absorb more ballet training with Aaron Tomaroff and Ivan Tarasoff as well as insights into modern dance with Michio in New York (1925). Throughout the ensuing thirteen years (1926–39) she continued her seemingly endless studies in Mexico, South America, Spain, South Africa, India, Ceylon (Sri Lanka), the Philippines and Japan. Her professional début took place in San Antonio and Dallas and on a tour of the American Southwest along the Rio Grande Valley (1918). Little known, she danced in motion picture houses (1925). She gave performances abroad, using her travels to learn ever more about her art. In New York (1940) she joined the by now famed Ruth St Denis to establish the School of Natya, which two years later became the Ethnologic Dance Center under her sole guidance (1942). The school, well attended and a source for instruction in the dances of various peoples around the world, existed until 1956. Throughout this period La Meri gave recitals of her own, lecturing widely as well as dancing. Her programmes were demonstrations of many ethnic idioms: Hindu, Burmese, American Indian, Polynesian, Moroccan, Spanish, Latin American. She choreographed original works in these genres, including some ambitious ventures: a ballet set to Manual de Falla's *El Amor Brujjo*, a Bharata Natayam adaptation of Act II of *Swan Lake*, a *Schéhérazade*. She was seen at Jacob's Pillow, where she often taught; and at the Connecticut College Dance Festivals; was on the faculty of the Juilliard School of Music Dance Department and also staged works there; and was a guest artist at many other American universities. She published a great many books and articles, including essays in the *Dance Encyclopedia* (quoted earlier in this chapter) and the *Encyclopedia Britannica*, along with six volumes of her own poetry. Having a passionate first-hand acquaintance with ethnic dances of many kinds, she was advanced in her efforts to comprehend and preserve them, making sure that their authenticity was intact. Her own preference was for Indian dance and its associated arts. The long-time presence of her active and conspicuous school in New York City, together with the frequent recitals staged there by La Meri herself and her students and disciples, did much to instil and keep alive interest among the metropolis's rather large dance-going public, so that Indian classical dance was not wholly exotic but to some degree familiar and understood.

Another American, Sharon Lowen, is particularly valued for having dedicated herself to perfection in the performance of Odissi. When she brought her group to the Uris Auditorium at New York's Metropolitan Museum of Art (1985), Jack Anderson observed in the *New York Times*:

Odissa is considered a sensuous style because of its emphasis upon rounded movements. Miss Lowen conveyed this sensuousness by her entrance in her opening solo of invocation. She stepped in a stately manner. Yet, at the same time, her upper body always swayed gently. These swayings led to undulations of the arms and poses in which the arms were curved.

Two lyrical solos began languidly, one of them with movements for the neck. Then steps accelerated and the solos concluded exuberantly.

Miss Lowen introduced three dramatic pieces by demonstrating and explaining their key gestures. Even if one forgot what some movements meant when they appeared in the solos, one still retained a sense of the dances' overall significance. Although two concerned the god Krishna, they were quite different in tone. In one, a young woman deliberately teased the god with playful, coquettish gestures. In the other, Radha, Krishna's beloved, accused him of being unfaithful. And Miss Lowen's twistings and curvings suggested both desire and sadness.

The third dramatic sketch depicted the incarnations of the god Vishnu. Miss Lowen was, gesturally, a fish, a tortoise, a boar and several other beasts and human beings. The solo's gestural profusion conjured up a vision of a universe in perpetual metamorphosis.

Miss Lowen's drummer was Padma Shri Kelucharan Mohapatra, who is also her teacher. He provided the audience with an unannounced treat by agreeing to dance a solo of his own, in which he portrayed a leper praying that the gods would either let him die or give him joy. The gathering intensity of his supplications was genuinely impressive.

Other members of the fine musical ensemble were Rakhal Mohanty, Bhubaneswar Misra and Ratikant Mohapatra.

One more American who took up and thoroughly assimilated Indian techniques is Ari Darom, who made his New York début at the Theater of the Open Eye (1979) after study with Guru Nataraj L. Rajaram in India. He presented himself in examples of Bharata Natayam, in devotional passages usually performed by women, and proved himself to be "engaging". Jennifer Dunning remarked: "The theme of much Bharata Natayam is devotional surrender to the gods. Mr Darom has immersed himself in Indian culture. He is not yet a seasoned enough performer to have developed the presence for the more abstract or lyrical dances of the eight performed. Occasionally his footbeats were a little imprecise and his upper body lacking in articulation. But Mr Darom was impressive in the more athletic, narrative dances, particularly in his use of the eyes and facial expression. His performance of *Sabdam*, a mimed song in praise of Krishna with an intriguing passage about the making of an endless *sari*, was the high point of the program."

Such crossing of the long-set lines of gender, male dancers venturing to take roles usually danced by women, and women those hitherto assigned to males, has begun to occur with increasing frequency. Notable instances have been the interpretations of Bharata Natayam by the acclaimed Ram Gopal and a younger performer Prakash Yedgudde. Another is Vedantam Satyanarayana Sarma, who excels in Kuchipudi and has been likened to "the great Kabuki specialists" and Mei Lanfang. He particularly impressed foreign reviewers by his depiction of Satyabhama, one of Krishna's two favourite wives, a highly prized part created in the fifteenth century by the revered *yogi* Siddhendra, who – legend has it – extracted from the villagers of Kuchipudi a promise that they would perform it for ever. Conforming to the saint's wish, members of eight families vowed that each would undertake the role at least once in their lifetimes.

Padmashrai Sanjukta Panigrahi, a fellow dancer, also aiming at a *tour de force*, appeared on a programme with Sharma at New York's Asia Society in an Odissi solo in which she portrayed both male and female characteristics. "Lord Siva has two different aspects," she explained. "The left half of the body is female. The right half is male. Woman is graceful. Man is forceful and vigorous. Woman creates. Man destroys. It is a whole cycle. There is no creation without destruction, no man without woman."

Ritha Devi has undertaken the same dual-sex role. Born in India to a high-ranked family, she was inspired as a child by seeing a performance by Uday Shankar, but her family would not allow her to pursue a career in dance; however, having finished college, she studied with very orthodox instructors. Some time after she became a performer and put together her own company, she was invited to participate at Jacob's Pillow, the summer dance festival in Massachusetts, as the outcome of a prolonged correspondence with Ted Shawn, its co-founder. Lacking funds for transatlantic airline passage for herself and her troupe, she could not accept Shawn's bid. Undertaking several tours of Soviet Russia, beginning in 1966, she received large sums but discovered that the surplus roubles could not be taken out of the country. On impulse, she used them to purchase Aeroflot tickets to the United States; repeating this process, she was able to manage several American tours. In 1972 she decided to reside in New York City and joined the dance faculty of New York University. From then on she gave on average four recitals annually, along with concerts at other colleges and for Indian associations elsewhere. At intervals of about two years she revisited her homeland for refreshing studies with her gurus.

In 1976 Don McDonagh of the *New York Times* wrote of her:

Rare is the artist who takes all of Indian dance as her heritage and can effectively present the correct accent of each school. Ritha Devi both can and does, and it was, no doubt, out of consideration for her audience that she confined herself to four of the eight major traditions. As it was, her program of solos at American Theater Laboratory Tuesday evening lasted nearly three hours and was a demonstration of unflagging energy and gestural expertise.

Miss Devi is a consummate story teller, even going so far as to give a precis of the entire *Ramayana* in a brief solo called *Rama's Coronation*, using the Kuchipudi style. By her own admission, her special favorite is the temple dancing of Orissa province; the sculptural Odissi style. Her telling of the suffering of Tara, widow of Vali, was particularly engrossing. In it she assumed four separate personages, including the god Rama as well as the child of Tara and Vali's union. Vali's death was replete with small stylized twitches, and when she assumed the part of Rama her small form seemed to enlarge in outline to encompass his proud bearing.

Siva's dance was given in the familiar rhythmic stamping style of Bharatha Natyam with its angular gestures and percussive subtleties. *Sutradhari Nritya* was a special novelty since the dance is ordinarily performed by young male acolytes in monasteries. As in the other dances, Miss Devi showed a great feeling for the nuances of gesture and skill in presenting them clearly.

Less receptive, though still admiring, was the *New York Times*'s senior dance critic, Anna Kisselgoff, when the artist rather boldly ventured to intermingle Indian and European–American dance idioms at a concert given in 1979.

> Trained in India, but resident for some time in New York, Ritha Devi has been a foremost exponent of the Odissi temple-dance style from the state of Orissa. She has also often included examples of the very vital and agile Kuchipudi style. Both schools were represented on this program as well, but the new element was Ritha Devi's recent attempts, by her own account, at "a blend of East and West, with shades of Odissi, Kuchipudi and modern dance."
>
> In fairness, such experiments were only a small part of the program, but their validity was open to question. The erotic metaphors that lie at the root of Hinduism's religious epics, for example, are totally remote from the Lord's Prayer. Yet this was the imagery Ritha Devi used in her mime to illustrate her own recital of the Lord's Prayer to close her program.
>
> In the same way, the curved lines of the Odissi dances have a sensuousness inherent to their content. But this sensuousness is very different from the passions expressed in the *The Song of Solomon*, to which Ritha Devi danced a solo, with the text sung excruciatingly on tape by an American purporting to be a soprano. In general, the choreography was reduced to a mime illustration of the words, too coy and too literal to provide an extra dimension.
>
> But on safer ground, Ritha Devi was very much the superb dancer-actress she has always proven herself to be. This was true in her three Odissi solos and a new solo, danced in what she called the Bharata Natayam style as it has developed in the state of Mysore.

A 1985 performance at the Cubiculo in New York elicited this notice by Jennifer Dunning:

> In the Kuchipudi section, *Chandalika* (*The Untouchable Girl*) offered Miss Devi the widest range for her considerable skills as an actress. Choreographed by Miss Devi, as were all but one of the dances in the program's seven pieces, *Chandalika* tells the story of Prakriti, a young woman of the untouchable caste who falls in love with Ananda, a gentle young monk who acknowledges her. In the end, she knowingly causes the death of her mother because of that love, and renounces Ananda and the world.
>
> Miss Devi was compelling in the lead roles and subordinate ones, and her sense of costuming hinted at both Prakriti's rather slatternly prettiness and her sweetness. Based on a play by Rabindranath Tagore, *Chandalika* suggests much about Indian society in thought-provoking, layered themes. And princesses of the non-royal type, it seems, were as much a feature of Tagore's world as our own.

Another highlight was an excerpt from *Tharangam*, notable for the impressive dexterity with which Miss Devi performed the different walks of the child Krishna and danced on a brass plate. Miss Devi can be a somewhat overbearing guide through Indian dance. Enjoyable, she seems more comfortable playing strong heroines than the familiar compliant female figure of many of the dances. In the Odissi section, for instance, Miss Devi made a unusually imperious figure out of Draupadi, who is sold off to a lecherous villain by her five husbands.

The program also included *Ardhanareeshwara Shabam*, a Kuchipudi specialty in which Miss Devi represents Siva with the right side of her body and his wife, Parvati, with her left side. Some of the Odissi pieces suffered from an occasional lack of clarity and rhythmic precision in the foot and leg work. But this was an evening of literate pleasures, and Miss Devi closed it charmingly by performing a happy birthday message to Maurice Edwards, former director of the Cubiculo, who was in the audience.

She confided that her favourite genre was Odissi, for which she felt a temperamental affinity. "With its supple torso and the precise positions of the lower half of the body, Odissi has gentleness and at the same time strength, and every woman today has to be that combination for all the battles in modern living."

Among male artists, Ananda Shankar, following the precedent of his renowned father, and paralleling Ritha Devi's experiments, freely changed traditional forms, mixing them with elements of modern dance. He failed to win approval when on stage with his ensemble in New York at Carnegie Hall (1984). Jennifer Dunning:

The problem with [their] program was that its greatest claim to artistic distinction was that it was a pleasant way to pass a hot spring evening.

The fault did not lie with the nineteen dancers, who were lively, attractive and unvaryingly cheerful, even in solemn numbers. The many different costumes were brilliantly colorful and even exotic, most notably in *From the Land of the Five Rivers*. In that dance, which reflected impressions of Punjab, the men were dressed in bright turbans and layered robes with boldly striped skirts and waved silken scarves as they danced.

There was a bow to drama in *Mother*, in which a mother and daughter part company on the eve of the daughter's wedding. *Tribal* hinted at the fierce energy of tribal dances from Northeast India. *Nrityanjali*, an homage to Uday Shankar, presented elements of classical dance, and *Night Creatures* was pure disco.

But the dances, choreographed by Tanusree Shankar, tended toward a mix of styles that was not modern, jazz or classical dance but a hybrid form as blandly all-purpose as Mr Shankar's synthesis of Western and Indian music. Only in the exuberant *Holi*, in which festival revelers mime sprinkling each other with paint, did the dance have a look of its own.

In her entry in *The Dance Encyclopedia* La Meri alludes to other more recently revived dance-dramas: Bhagawata Mela Nataka of Tanjore, religious in content, from Nataka with an affinity in style to Bharata Natayam, presented only by males of the Brahmin caste; and, in Karnataka, the rural Yakshagana, containing elements reminiscent of the early Kathakali.

A rare opportunity for Western spectators to experience Yashagana, a virile folk-dance, occurred in New York at Carnegie Hall (1979) where the Asia Society sponsored a company from India that regularly practised it. After the performance, Anna Kisselgoff commented on how the evening's offerings differed markedly in impetus from other Indian dance styles previously seen outside that country.

There is a remarkable springiness to the movements of this all-male troupe from South Kanara. With its characteristic bounce, straight-up jumps and sudden burst of vigorous footwork, Yakshagana takes on a delightful vitality. It is easy to see its appeal as genuine folk theater, albeit one with a classical base concerned primarily with moral instruction.

The excerpts on view on this occasion were drawn from the *Mahābhārata*. Kaurava, leader of the clan bearing his name, is battling the Pandava brothers and calls upon Trigartha, the demon king, for help. After the Pandava prince, Arjuna, defeats the demon, Arjuna's son, Abhimanyu, enters the fray despite his mother's entreaties. After defeating each Kaurava warrior, he is treacherously attacked by them as a group. They cut off his arms and kill him.

Considering that our sympathies should be with the Pandavas – the Kauravas are the bad ones – the emphasis on the villains in this presentation was of special interest. Essentially, they are stock characters, while the young Abhimanyu has more human traits. As played and danced excellently by Belthur Ramesha, he was the epitome of the hot-tempered reckless youth, brimming with bravado.

As are all the characters, he is first glimpsed in part behind a small curtain held by two curtain holders. His headrest – a large flattened onion-dome turban – and legs are visible. The quick steps and the way his body shoots up at a tilt informs the public of youthful energy. His first solo demonstrates the broad strokes of Yakshagana's virtuoso style. With his palm held upward or to the audience, his small sidesteps accelerate and he springs straight up or sideways, then does knee turns or jumps into a squat. Since Yakshagana is a play, he pauses to speak to his mother, played in uncannily realistic manner by Dayananda Balegara.

Typically, the music contributes and even sets the emotional tone, particularly on the tambour-like drum, the Chende, played by Brahmavara Anant Rao. The true leader of the performance was the singer Januvarukatte Gopalakrishna Kamath, with Hiriadka Gopala Rao and B.V. Achar completing the musical ensemble.

When Haradi Mahabala Ganiga as Kaurava is defeated in a duet, the young prince literally seems to jump for joy. His feet seem barely to touch the ground as he bounces up from it. Each duel is different and the nuances are suggested by the dancers playing his foes: Cherkadi Madhava Nayak, Haradi Sanjiva Ganiga, Birthi Balakrishna, Haradi Sarvottama Ganiga, and also Sakkattu Laxmi-narayana, who doubled marvelously as a yelping demon caught in the act of brushing his teeth. In all, a group of excellent actors who knew how to reach their public.

The members of this troupe were recruited from among many indigenous ensembles active at festivals in South Kanara. Yakshagana is an ancient genre, its origins, too, quite unknown: its purpose – according to Martha Ashton – is "to spread the ideals of Hinduism with entertainment depicting the adventures of the gods, heroes and demons of Indian mythology". Tradition, centuries-old, has set the sequence of song, dance, dramatic scenes and comic interruptions of the all-night performances which take place outdoors, funded in each village by a generous local patron. On such happy occasions, the spectators are seated on three sides of an earthen rectangle, ten by fifteen feet, marked by a frame of decorated bamboo poles. Throughout the night onlookers move about, come and go.

Martha Ashton adds more details: "After three preliminary sections, the story is begun in song. Themes are taken from classical Indian sacred texts including, peculiarly to Yakshagana, legends of South Kanara and stories from Lakshmisha's *Jaimini Bharata* which elaborates on the legendary wanderings of a sacrificial royal horse. Dialogue is extemporized by the fifteen actor-dancers, all male, who range from apprentices to veterans with ten years of private classes behind them. A Yakshagana performance then ends with a dance in praise of the mother goddess Durga and Lord Vishnu, as well as the deities of both the troupe and the performance's patron."

Jennifer Dunnning observed that "Yakshagana calls for the close coordination of foot movements of growing complexity with the drum rhythms to which they are performed. Rather earthbound whirls and jumps and spins are also characteristic, with differences in attack indicating the character's sex and personality. Some dances within each Yakshagana suite leave precise steps and *mudras* (symbolic hand gestures) to the discretion of the performer, and facial expressions are more natural than those of the very different classical Bharata Natayam, Kuchipudi, Odissi, Kathak, Kathakali or Manipuri styles. Costuming is exceedingly rich, some of the characters wearing huge ornate headdresses, and the make-up is intricate, with males in leading roles perhaps adorned with fierce, black mustaches, formidably darkened eyebrows, symbolic painted designs on their foreheads. An orchestra may be comprised of drums, cymbals and a harmonium."

Yet another category of highly ritualized South Indian dance-drama, Kutiyattam, traceable to as early as the ninth century, was presented at the Asia Society in cooperation with the Wenner-Gren Foundation (1982). Its sponsors referred to it as "the oldest extant theatre in the world" (a claim that would certainly be disputed by Western scholars); in any event, it is plausibly the only continuously surviving form of Sanskrit drama, one antedating the subsequently more popular Kathakali, on which it had a very obvious influence. Many of its characters are familiar from the *Ramayana*. The performers came from the Kerala Kalamandalam.

Jennifer Dunning, after the concert, wrote descriptively:

Dance and pantomime are as integral a part of the form as the recitation of text and percussion accompaniment. Elements of the drama, traditionally performed in temple theatres, are determined by ritual observances. Gestures are rigidly codified, with the hands, eyes and brows serving as important vehicles of expression. Actors may insert stories from a prescribed repertory into the narration, however, and even step aside from their characters to question or comment on the action.

That complex interplay of discipline and interpretation made for a "monologue" of stunning immediacy in *Encounter Between Ravana and Hanuman*, a scene from the *Abhishekanatakam*, a play attributed to a poet of the fourth-century BC Ravana, the mighty demon king of Lanka, recalls a conversation between the god Siva and his wife, Parvati. She is jealous of the goddess Ganga, who resides as an ornament in Siva's hair, and questions Siva about the ornament. Parvati asks: "Do I see a face in that ornament? Curls of hair? Eyebrows? Breasts? The face is a lotus flower." Siva responds. "The curls are rows of bees; the eyebrows, water ripples; the eyes, two black fish; the breasts, birds."

Seated on a stool, A.M. Siyan Nambudiri shifted from demure nag to sly but patient husband continuously, never losing the character of Ravana, which he played – an amusing and rather contemplative demon. Not at all necessary were the traditional tucks of his skirt into his belt to indicate Parvati: one look at the downcast face and the restless, delicate hands was enough. And Mr

Nambudiri's flowing, precise *mudras* told all that was needed of curls of hair and small black fish.

The relationship between Ravana and his exasperating younger brother, played by Cholayil Radhakrishnana, was as vivid, as were the antics of Hanuman, the teasing monkey chieftain, who was played by Koyappa Raman. As striking was the acting of Mr Raman as the doomed Jatayu, a beautifully costumed, mythological bird, in an excerpt from the ninth or tenth century *Ascharyachudamani* (*The Wondrous Crest-Jewel*).

Each program began with the *Nandi*, or benediction, and closed with the *Dikpalavandanam*, both traditional dances that suggested the technique and ritual importance of Kutiyattam. The group is a young one, and the immature voices of some of the actors here were slightly unsettling. The fine musicians were P.K. Narayanan Nambiar, P.V. Eswaran Unni and K.P. Achunni Poduval. Clifford R. Jones contributed the informative and colorful program notes.

Samplings of the Krishnattam, the sacred dance-drama also from south-western India and dedicated to Krishna, the beloved, frolicsome deity, were presented at the Asia Society in New York as a special event during the season of 1985. These pieces, dating from the seventeenth century, are today performed by a single troupe, originally attached to the court of Calicut and now under the aegis of the temple of Guruvayurappan. Until 1980, when the company visited Paris, few if any Westerners had seen these plays, since only Hindus are permitted to enter the shrine. This was only the group's second journey away from the temple.

The repertory consists of a mere eight works. Jack Anderson gave this account of what transpired at Asia House:

The all-male troupe of seven dancers, two singers and four drummers, directed by A.C.G. Raja, established the religious nature of their offering at the outset when attendants held a curtain in front of the audience while, behind it, the performers danced steps intended only for the eyes of the gods. At last, the curtain was dropped and what was revealed dazzled these mortal eyes.

Masked dancers were clad in elaborate costumes of almost blinding shades of red, black and gold. Their tiered headdresses rose like frosted layer cakes. Male and female characters alike wore wide and bulky bell-shaped skirts encrusted with decorations. Everything about Krishnattam looked both larger and stiffer than life. This became especially evident when the dancers posed beside the musicians and stage attendants. Whereas these simply clad figures came from our own world, the dancers inhabited the realm of myths and epics.

Given the overall heaviness of the dancing costumes, the performers' hands and feet seemed especially delicate protruding from them. Arm movements were carefully ceremonial and the feet either stamped rhythmically or shifted in measured patterns back and forth.

The program included excerpts from several dance-dramas. In the first, Krishna and his wife defeated a wicked warrior, with the aid of a magic bird. Then one of Krishna's companions tore apart another villain. This episode was followed by a plotless dance sequence, and the evening concluded with a benediction.

There were some interesting touches of characterization. Thus Krishna's wife was usually assigned demure, almost coy, poses. But when it came time to defend her husband, she boldly took up the necessary weapons.

The evening contained little of what Western audiences would consider dramatic suspense. But no such suspense was intended. What one saw was the reenactment of timeless stories. To use a Western analogy, it was as if the glowing figures of saints and biblical characters in the stained-glass windows of a great cathedral had stepped down to remind us, through dancing, of their tribulations and triumphs.

At Khajraho, in the Chhattarpur District of Madhya Pradesh, the site of many temples adorned with legions of erotic sculptures, an outdoor annual dance festival was established in 1976; it is held each March on the side of the most beautiful of the Tantric-cult edifices, the Kandaviya Mahdeva. The week-long event, initiated by the state government, draws thousands of spectators, in good part because of its unmatched setting. (The date of the festival is not fixed; it sometimes shifts slightly.) Various types of classical dance are performed, and the most celebrated artists show off their talents: at the 1980 event, for example, Sanjukta Panigrahi began the programme with a much-applauded enactment of Odissi, hailed by one Indian observer:

As she came down the steps against the grey grandeur of the temples, bowed to the Gods, her *guru* and her audience and then burst into the ecstasy of dance, one felt that she more than anyone else was all the Festival could hope for: involvement in the dance so deep and entrancing that one had no difficulty in seeing how dance and religion must have once blended together into devotion. The audience was enraptured and spell-bound, and even those who knew little of dance took away the feeling of having seen something beyond the ordinary.

After so beautiful a beginning, not all could keep up to that standard, yet Radha and Raja Reddy were also outstanding. As with the last time they danced, they had nearly completed three items, when down came the rain, welcome to the parched land of Bundelkhand. Mallika Sarabhai gave an elegant and graceful performance and concluded her dance by drawing a tiger on the board with her feet. A modern deviation but the audience loved it.

Rashmi Vajpayee, Kumkum Das, Alike Pannier were among the artists who sought, received and portrayed inspiration from Khajuraho's temples. There can be no better setting to bring out the best in those who are still to reach the pinnacle of their art: the temples provide more genuine stimulation, a more testing backdrop than the velvet stages of Bombay and Delhi.

What everyone was waiting for, however, was the last day's performance by Yamini Krishnamurthy; and in spite of the lowering clouds, lightning and a little rain, she did not disappoint. Taking time to enter into her very best, she went through displays of Odissi, Bharata Natayam and ended her performance and the festival with a beautiful and captivating Kuchipudi piece which enthralled the largest crowd of any day.

It is difficult to paint a word picture of the total impact of the festival; it is much more than any *son et lumière* show, much more than just a dance recital. Khajuraho is first and foremost the temples and they dominate the scene. To really enjoy the festival the temples should be visited for a couple of days in the mornings so that their beauty and the myriad images they offer are etched into the mind as a constant background to the dance. Only then can one see behind the delicate poses of Sanjukta Panigrahi the continuity of grace and sensuousness since dance lived in the temples seven hundred years ago.

Writing eloquently from Khajraho, Steven R. Weisman of the *New York Times* sent back a later picture of what he saw there (1986):

Under a canopy of stars, some of India's leading classical dancers performed at an outdoor dance festival this month, drawing their inspiration from the sacred stone figures that have moved artists and fascinated scholars for centuries.

The temples and sculptures in this little town in the arid and rocky plateau of central India date from the tenth and eleventh centuries and are famous for their sensuousness and explicit sexuality.

They also depict the splendors of dance, a feature of temple sculpture throughout India – the stylized dance of the gods that Hindus believe is connected to the rhythm of the universe.

Over the centuries, classical Indian dance evolved into something decadent, performed by temple prostitutes. Fifty years ago, Indian scholars and dancers began to restore the ancient, sacred tradition to dance. Indeed some critics have expressed the fear that Indian dance today has become too intellectualized and not sensuous enough.

The Khajraho Festival of Dances was begun by the state government of Madhya Pradesh to bring to life the "fusion of body and spirit" of Indian dance and to explore these many traditions in a dramatic setting.

The festival, the only one of its kind in India, draws thousands of people to see the country's finest younger and more experienced dancers in a week-long celebration of their art.

The centerpiece of classical dance is Bharata Natayam. Every series of poses, every delicate hand gesture or look of the eye is intended to express devotion, longing, fear, anger or love.

Padma Subrahamanyam, a choreographer, dancer and scholar from Madras, opened the festival with several of her own ornate compositions, based on twenty-five-hundred-year-old texts. Shimmering in incandescent silk and gold bangles, Miss Subrahamanyam performed to music of tabla, harmonium and violin that rose in the night air like smoke. Flooded with light behind her was the edifice of a temple dedicated to Siva.

"To me, dance has always been a spiritual experience," Miss Subrahamanyam said in an interview. "These temples are known for their grandeur and gigantic proportions. I felt one with the whole ethos, and you achieve that state only in such surroundings."

Even more evocative of temple sculpture was a performance of Odissi by two young women, Nandita Patnaik and Aruna Mohanty. Their sculptured movements and tableaux portrayed a love story involving the god Krishna. "I am choked with love for you," said one verse. "Why do you ignore me? Have mercy on me and remove my suffering."

Kathak, yet another dance style, featured a spinning, swirling performance of color and liquid body and arm movements by Saswati Sen, who narrated her actions in the tradition of performers at royal courts in northern India.

Inevitably, some things get lost in the majesty of the temples. Classical Indian dance is perhaps best seen in more intimate settings, where the audience can appreciate the delicacy of a raised eyebrow or arched finger.

But the overall effect of the dances in Khajraho leaves a startling impression that sheds light on the interplay between temple and sculpture. For just as the carvings blend eroticism and sacrament, so classical Indian dance draws from these two seemingly contradictory traditions.

Indeed the Khajraho Festival began as an experiment to bring temple and dance together so that the two forms could enhance each other. "The link between the two traditions of dance and sculpture was always discussed but never seen," said Ashok Vajpayi, founder of the festival and secretary of tourism and culture for Madhya Pradesh.

"Suddenly an idea that had been theoretical and abstract started making sense," he added. "In the festival, we can now see this fusion between the spiritual and the sensuous, the erotic and the divine."

According to Mr Vajpayi, dance in India always carried seductive and metaphysical dimensions.

"The dance performed here illustrates the basic mystique of these temples," he said. "We have also tried to inspire the dancers to experiment on their own. The truth is that all Indian dancers are trying to do the very same thing that Khajraho does in stone."

In the north-eastern section of the state of Tamil Nadu, in villages more or less surrounding the ancient city of Kanchipuram, the local inhabitants foster Terrūkuttu, another form of ritual folk theatre scarcely known outside that region. It is exhaustively described by Richard Armando Frasca in his book *The Theatre of the Mahābhārata* (an added source of the details in this chapter). These are dance-dramas staged by cultists in tribute to the important goddess Draupadi, whom her followers worship without the sanction or supervision of temple priests. The dramas include "rites of passage" and effect changes of social status for individuals dwelling in each community. Much mysticism and belief in supernatural forces are inherent in the participants going through this ceremony; after it they are thought to be different people. The roots of these dance-dramas are believed to extend back 2,000 years. Largely obscure today, they are ignored by scholars of Indian culture.

The Terrūkuttu enlist chant, song, and prose, along with percussion and music to dramatize significant episodes from the *Mahābhārata*. The music has a South Indian sound, an interplay of classical and folk elements. Long training is demanded of the performing troupes, whose faces and temperaments are transformed by distinctive, complex make-up, an indigenous variation of ritual mask-painting: thin lines and dots under the eyes and around the nose, thick, outsized moustaches, codified colours – red, green, rose, black – indicating the personality of each character: is he fierce? mild? honest? evil? – his qualities signalled to the audience at very first glance. The paints – or paste – applied are compounded from local materials, and the intensity of the colour is meant to be a clue. The entire face may be covered with one hue, suggesting the person's basic nature, and other traits are suggested by designs imposed over it. Warriors have red-coloured lips and black sideburns that conceal much of the chin. The gross moustache, made of hair, is artificial, held in place by strings tied at the back of the head. Even the nose is decorated with lines and dots; and the space between the eyebrows may be filled with circular and triangular patterns, which are sectarian symbols.

A leading male character may wear a crown, one of two types, and sizes and shapes denoting the degree of kingly power. He has arm ornaments that match the crown and fashioned from the same materials, mostly wood and coloured glass, covered with foil. The other characters are mostly dressed alike – "a tight-fitting, full-sleeved, usually red-colored shirt". Shoulder-pieces give him more impressive bulk and stature. "These shoulder-pieces share basically the same motifs and colorings as the crown. They, therefore, interact with the crown to form a triangular arrangement of glistening, traditional body ornamentation that surrounds and highlights the face and its make-up. The entire system encloses and dramatically enhances the effect of the performer's eyes." Scarves are draped in a complicated fashion about the neck and shoulders, and a wide skirt with horizontal bands descends from the waist – the legs are encased in black or white pyjamas. Finally, there are bells around the ankles.

The female's make-up is somewhat stylized; she is allowed to appear realistic and human, and there are contemporary touches – her sari may be of nylon; she has no crown, only flowers in her hair, little jewellery, not even a Tamil nose-ring. Her features are tinted a light rose, with a few moles added. Female roles are taken by men who sport wigs. Exceptions to those having minimum adornment are the fanged demons and fearsome goddesses, perhaps the ominous Kali.

Every dance-drama has a clown, a court jester for whom there is no prescribed make-up or costume – he freely creates his own.

Performances, open-air, begin at dusk and continue on to the humid dawn. Devotees of the cult sometimes take a ritual bath in advance, and there may be incidents of fire-walking. By the end of the ceremonies some of the dancers may lapse into trance, both they and a share of the spectators having reached a state of possession. The prime festival – the Paratam – is held annually and lasts eighteen days.

The choreography is comparatively simple and basic and has been mostly orally transmitted. Though they are not readily discernible, there are basic affinities with Bharata Natayam, suggesting that at some remote time they had the same origin, but Terrūkuttu has never had the status of a classical dance. Excerpts from it do not provide solos at recitals or concerts. Where Bharata Natayam is a fixed form that is acknowledged and respected by most professional artists, and familiar to many spectators, a considerable part of Terrūkuttu is inspirational; body movements and steps determined by the performer at any moment, prompted by his emotional state, on the spot, spontaneous. This may impart outbursts of great energy that stir the onlookers. To the male dancers, too, particularly those portraying warriors, are assigned many vigorous spins, a special feature of the Terrūkuttu. Known as the *kiriki*, they are "expressive of power, violence, heroism, and anger". Repeated rapidly they contribute to giddiness that induces trances. They are used to mark the entrances of strong characters and to heighten martial confrontations, especially if the dancer bears a sword in his hand. (Frasca himself sought training in Terrūkuttu and includes notations and drawings in his book.) Mime is little used; much of the story is told through wordless movement, the prose dialogue provided by the players themselves, the dances non-representational but summoning up the emotional colouring that envelopes each situation and action.

Connery says that the original name for classical dances in the Tamil country "was *Sadir*, meaning solo dance performances by temple dancers. . . . Though in later days the *Sadir* developed sensual characteristics (which almost brought about the extinction of this art), all *devadasis* maintained a high standard of technique and traditions. Many outstanding artists were among them, and the corruption was not of their making alone but helped by that of society in general."

Well-established academies are available to teach and preserve the traditions of the leading classical dances. Besides the Kerala Kalamandam, already mentioned, the most highly ranked are Rajarajeswari Bharata Natayam Kala Mandir, the Delhi Triveni Kala Sangam and the Calcutta Kalamandalam.

It should not be thought that since its twentieth-century revival all has been steadfastly well with classical Indian dance. On a preceding page in this chapter is a report by Steven R. Weisman for the *New York Times* on a celebratory festival by troupes engaged in this refined offering at Khajraho. That was a joyous occasion. But Weisman had filed a lengthy, very different picture of the lot of less-known performers who had been in the United States a year earlier, the group chosen as representatives of their country's arts in the Festival of India (1985).

Last Summer they were the toast of America. At the Smithsonian Institution in Washington, they enchanted audiences and mingled with Nancy Reagan and other dignitaries. Their pictures were on television and in all the magazines.

But today the acrobats, singers and artisans who starred in the Festival of India, all of them poor and many from lower castes, are back living in squalor in a New Delhi slum, looking for work and facing an uncertain future.

Coming home after performing in a distant land of affluence has been difficult. The magic tricks, glittering costumes and turbans have been put away, replaced by the familiar hard facts of poverty and discrimination.

Some made several thousand dollars from the trip, putting the money in a bank or using it to buy gold. But others drank or gambled their money away. At least one child performer was beaten by his parents for refusing to turn his money over to them, according to festival officials.

"It was my talent and my heart that mattered in America," said Ramesh Bhatt, a thirty-year-old singer, sitting on the mud floor of his home. "It didn't matter whether I was rich or poor. In India, you see that I am poor, and you don't care who I am."

"In America, the audiences listened carefully and with love," added Shish Ram, a nine-year-old singer with fond memories of meeting Mrs Reagan and others at the Smithsonian. But his father agreed that "we're not so fascinating to Indians."

About three hundred artist and street performer families live with several thousand others in the shadow of a highway overpass in a squatters shantytown of mud, straw and canvas huts. Piles of trash dot the area and water buffalo and goats meander about.

The place is a makeshift rural village, created by people who came to the city years ago to find work. The problem is that there are no schools, no sanitary facilities, no security from thieves – and few places for the artists and performers to practice their trades.

As a result, some Festival of India organizers have a new goal: persuading India to show the same support for the folk artists and craftsmen that they received in the United States.

"Sometimes I wonder if our art needs the approval of the West in order to survive," said Rajeev Sethi, director of several Festival of India exhibits. "These people represent the culture that unites us, but they're forgotten and unappreciated at home."

For years, Mr Sethi nurtured an ambitious plan to move them to a new colony on the city's fringes. There, he said, they could earn a living by entertaining tourists and others and selling their puppets, toys, pottery, paintings and other handicrafts.

"Our status has improved since we went abroad," said Bhagwan Das, a singer with dark tousled hair and a husky voice. "But living like this, how can we have a program to find work? How can we put on a show here?"

For the *Aditi* exhibit at the Smithsonian and the folklife festival on the mall in Washington last summer, Mr Sethi and his associates searched villages across India for performers and artists. About thirty of the eighty he chose came from the New Delhi slum where they had been living for several years.

Among them were puppeteers, potters, kite makers, dancers, magicians, painters and balladeers who had made their living roaming rural areas, and whose families had been doing the same thing for centuries.

"These folk artists were hurt badly by the demise of the maharajas and rajas who used to be their patrons," said Maura Moynihan, a festival coordinator and daughter of a former United States Ambassador to New Delhi, Senator Daniel Patrick Moynihan of New York.

Over the last fifteen years, they had been drifting into the big cities. In New Delhi, they make money performing at weddings, birthday parties and before tourists at the big luxury hotels.

But the work is erratic, and the performers face special problems. Their New Delhi slum has been bulldozed several times, and they are often harassed by the police because street entertainment as been outlawed as a form of begging. Attempts to change the law have been unsuccessful.

In 1979, with the help of Mr Sethi, they formed the Forgotten and Neglected Artists Society. A Ford Foundation grant established a management group that helped them find work and collect fees. Mr Sethi's idea of a separate colony on the city's outskirts seemed a natural outgrowth.

Both Miss Moynihan and Mr Sethi worry that unless something is done to help these artists, television and movies threaten to displace them even in the villages.

"Change is inevitable, but there should always be a place for these people," said Mr Sethi. "Nowadays, you're not going to call a balladeer when your camel is sick. You'll call a doctor and a balladeer because you know that a doctor can't cure your mind."

The scene is a contradictory one: poverty and a panoply of riches and glitter against a background of millions who are hungry and illiterate, a stage offering theatrical forms that are the utmost in subtlety and sophistication. Wells singles out what has been this vast country's most important contribution to the arts: "India, which once discovered the soul of drama in dramatic poetry, has sustained an insight into the mysteries of drama only in the drama of the dance, where unparalleled forms have been achieved. Solo dancers of as great genius and even as great dramatic genius as those of India have long flourished in China, Korea, and Japan, but the dramatic dance with an ensemble of characters has been most brilliantly achieved in India."

Wells summarizes: "The dance is the supreme art of India, as literature was of Shakespeare's England, music of Bach's Germany, and painting of Raphael's Italy. It is hardly too much to say that Indians are born dancers. Siva, lord of the dance, is also supreme as patron of all Indian arts, the god most commonly invoked in the prayer, or *mundi*, traditionally spoken at the commencement of each Sanskrit play. For these reasons, no consideration of Indian drama can afford to overlook the dance as drama nor regard it as materially beneath the spoken play in essentially dramatic qualities."

8

DANCE-DRAMA IN THE HIMALAYAS

India's three small Himalayan neighbours, Nepal, Bhutan and Tibet, have indigenous arts that for a variety of causes are scarcely known abroad. In part this is because for long periods these countries had closed borders, besides which their geographical location often made them difficult of access. The physical and political barriers have gradually been overcome, and tourism is even solicited.

In Kathmandu, Nepal's capital set in a valley ringed by awesome though clouded and hence not very visible icy peaks, and boasting over 2,000 temples, shrines and courtyards, a troupe of professional folk-dancers give frequent performances in an ancient palace. This is entertainment designed for foreign visitors, flocking to this picturesque city after Nepal granted permission for Westerners to enter the country in 1968.

The dances show Indian and Chinese influences, which is true of all aspects of culture in Nepal, the Indian components more evident in the lowlands, the Chinese more present along the northern border. Mongolian and Tibetan elements are clearly present, too. Yet, overall, the mixture is definably native.

A typical programme by the professional troupe in a hall of the palace begins with a "welcome dance", the performers bearing candles. The members of the company will probably be handsome and garbed ornately. In an ensuing number, a "harvest dance", the men will drink rice wine and simulate tipsiness. The third piece portrays a dramatic fight with a hideously masked demon, and the fourth – a decided high point – demonstrates how a witch doctor cures a sick peasant by using drums, bells and other noise-makers, and by swallowing fire. This is followed by a series of "animal dances" – the cast putting on striking animal disguises to depict the likely mating of yak and Yeti (he the legendary Abominable Snowman), and – a stunning contrast – a peacock dance. In the next segment, men and women compete to determine who is the most skilled and dextrous, after which there are flirtation and courtship dances. The evening concludes with an offering of thanks to the gods.

Each of the dances is drawn from one or another region of Nepal, and each represents a clan of people of a different ethnic mix. The performers are propulsively energetic, while the music is markedly melodious and rhythmic with much percussion. The instruments played are drums, horns and pipes.

In its remote, mountain fastness, Bhutan was closed to the outside world until the 1970s, but even then travellers had to seek special visas that were frequently denied. If granted, they were likely to be for short stays; accommodations for visitors were limited.

In winter heavy snow often makes the roads impassable; summers are very hot. There has never been a census, and estimates of the population vary wildly. The mountains, soaring to 15,000 feet, are spectacular.

Of great significance to the Bhutanese are their many festivals, and particularly the Tsechu, held in their lofty city of Thimphu each autumn (the exact date, determined by monks who consult a lunar calendar, shifts somewhat).

In 1980 the Royal Dancers of Bhutan performed at Carnegie Hall in New York at the start of a North American tour arranged by the Asia Society with funds provided by several institutions, and shortly afterwards (1981) a documentary film sponsored by the Asia Society and made by Richard Breyer and Brian Wood was shown on public television in the United States and elsewhere. Perhaps it was in anticipation of these two rare events that the indomitable Jennifer Dunning, staff dance critic of the *New York Times*, journeyed to rocky, remote Bhutan some months earlier to behold the Tsechu at first hand. She wrote of it in an article published shortly before the Carnegie concert.

It is October, and men, women and children dressed in long robes of intricately patterned, bright-colored silks, brocades and cottons converge on the Tashichhodzong. They file up the wide stairs into a large, open courtyard past the gently tapering white outer walls of the dzong, which looks more like a castle than the administrative and religious center of Thimphu, the capital of Bhutan. The journey on foot to attend the Tsechu, an annual religious dance festival, has taken them from the terraced rice paddies that dot the banks of the Wang Chu River, from the stone, wood and clay houses, built without nails, that cluster together to form small rural villages, or from the flower-strewn mountain passes that surround Thimphu, which lies at an altitude of seven thousand six hundred feet and from which the snow ranges of the Great Himalaya can sometimes be seen to the north.

It has begun to rain a little but only the earliest of the arrivals have managed to squeeze under the gaily painted eaves at the edges of the courtyard, and so the rest gather in the open, without umbrellas, since they are symbols of authority to be used only by the king and the head abbot of the monastery. Clowns in comically grotesque masks weave across the courtyard, clearing it with jokes and games that draw bursts of giggles from the children, for the arrivals of the lama, in his orange-and-maroon robe. Wearing the saffron-colored scarf that identifies his rank, the head abbot follows, blessing the crowd as he proceeds to the place of honor at a high window decked with ribbons.

The performance may now begin. The dancers enter the cleared circle of the arena in their knee-length, gathered scarf skirts, robes and consecrated papier-mâché and pine-wood masks. They dip and sway through the first in a repertory of stately, sometimes funny dance-dramas that will instruct and entertain the audience for the next three days, from early morning to late afternoon. The sounds of the *kongdu*, a silver trumpet once made of human thigh bone, and drums, cymbals, pipes and gongs float out across the air, mingling with the bells of revolving prayer wheels.

The audience wanders about the edges of the circle, chewing speculatively on betel nut or engaging from time to time in gamey repartee with the clowns. Families gather periodically for pic-nic meals of hot yak-butter tea and rice with pork or beef, spiced with white radish or chilies that have dried on shingled roofs, scattered amidst the anchor stones. Tatters of fog drift by, cloaking the men who have climbed up trees and roofs to get a better view. It is wise, however, to be on the ground for the visitation of the Guru Padmasambhava, the reincarnation of Gautama Buddha and the bringer of Buddhism – and dance – to Bhutan in the eighth century, impersonated here by a high lama in a wide gold mask in the festival's final, chanting processional. Blessings flow out through the crowd, which presses in on Padmasambhava, tipping the clowns to pass its babies up front.

On its ten-state tour, the all-male thirteen-member company was headed by its director, Dasho Sithe. At the end of its swing about the country, the troupe returned to New York for a final perfor-mance at the American Museum of Natural History, then went on to recitals in Europe.

The Carnegie programme was chosen to indicate the range of traditional Bhutanese dance-dramas and religious dances that might be performed by lay dancers. "Male and female characters dance on their way to heaven in *Pacham* (*The Dance of the Heroes*), a reflection of the tantric Mahayana Buddhism of Padmasambhava, which offered its followers an after-life passed in a heaven of dancing heroes and heroines dressed in shimmering scarves and crowns. In the popular and very funny *Pholay Molay* (*The Dance of a Nobleman and a Lady*), a king leaves his beautiful consort, Yidtrogma, to go to war. While he is away, a lecherous servant seduces her and she is punished, on the king's return, by having her nose cut off. A doctor is called, however – often from India or America – to put the nose back on, and love triumphs. Excerpts will be performed, too, from the five-hour *Shawo-Shachi*, a lyrical dance-drama that tells of the conversion of a fierce hunter by the tenth-century Tibetan poet-saint Milarepa. *Durdag* (*The Dance of the Lord of the Cremation Ground*) is a closing dance of exorcism for four performers wearing eerie, livid skull masks."

The performance at Carnegie Hall was reviewed by Anna Kisselgoff, the *New York Times*'s senior dance critic.

> The program got off to a spectacular start with the *Pacham*, a dance by six male dancers whose astounding knee-to-ear high jumps left many in the audience startled. The major part of the evening, however, was devoted to excerpts from dance-dramas with the accent on comic dialogue. Considering the language barrier and the consistent use of masks, it was a tribute to the vitality and clarity of the performers that their characterizations could be so communicative.
>
> Anyone who was fortunate enough to have seen the group of exiled Tibetans in Tibetan "opera" a few years ago at Hunter College would have recognized the context from which these Bhutanese dances and morality plays had been extracted. Bhutan has borrowed from the Lamaist tradition of Tibet and the stylization of its dances, even when performed by a secular group such as this one, has a strong ritual character.
>
> There are striking differences but it was not too surprising to see the Bhutanese dancers, like the Tibetans, position themselves in diagrammatic patterns – in four corners – or to hold religious symbols in their hands as they danced, knee lifted, foot flexed and usually in a hopping turn. Dramatic details were also similar. Both the Tibetan and Bhutanese groups easily identified a foreigner by giving him pointed shoes, different from those of locals.
>
> Yet because the emphasis was on accessible entertainment and because these lay dancers, as they are called, were limited to dances that do not have the mystical quality of the sacred dances performed by monks, the deeper tradition underlying this performance came across in fragmented form.
>
> Nonetheless, the Pacham, the Durdang exorcism dance and the Ging Solim, in which celestial beings drummed out serpent spirits, did have an exciting ceremonial character. The specialty of the all-male troupe is a jump with legs extended forward and seemingly touching the head, executed in a sudden spurt. The six saints in the Pacham wore yellow draped skirts, danced in bare feet and were marked by a beautiful lightness in their jumped turns with foot lifted forward and flexed.
>
> Tantric Buddhism's secrets hovered over the more sinister and accelerated exorcism dance while the third dance contrasted the whirling heavy serpent figures with the agility of the celestial beings who took their frying-pan-shaped drums into the audience as well. The manner in which they closed in on their foes built into a dramatic climax.

An extraordinary rotation of the torso, nearly a back bend, marked the performance of two dancing dogs and a dancing deer in one little play in which a holy man converted a hunter to a better life. The erotic element in Tantric Buddhism came out in ribald form in the other play about two noblemen who ordered the noses chopped off some unfaithful lady friends. Fortunately, the action was extremely stylized.

Ms Dunning had warned New York subscribers of the *New York Times* that staid Carnegie Hall might have a somewhat changed ambience.

The 57th Street concert hall may be a far cry from the *dzong*, and intermission cigarettes may take the place of butter tea, but clowns will circulate through the audience, playing tricks and coaxing the performers. And the dances themselves provide a look at a rich and well-preserved culture. While the origins of the sacred dance-dramas of Bhutan are unclear, the first recorded Buddhist dance was performed by Padmasambhava, who brought it from India to dance at the laying of the cornerstone of the Samye Monastery in Tibet. According to Padmalingpa, a fifteenth-century Bhutanese saint, the dance had been created by one of the first celestial Buddhas and passed on to Padmasambhava by his teachers. And from a vision of the *guru*, dancing with celestial attendants at his palace, the Copper Colored Mountain, Padmalingpa created many dances.

Taking on greater folk elements, the dances gradually spread and proliferated among the *dzongs* of Bhutan where, from the seventeenth century to the twentieth century, it was the custom for every family to send at least one son to learn the ritual tunes and dances and the making of *mandalas* and masks. Today, the dances are divided in three groups: religious dance performed only by monks and then ideally in private ceremony; Pawo, the dance performed by the village oracle, and the popular secular Bodcham. Several dances in the Bodcham repertory will be seen at Carnegie Hall. Masks and costumes are traditional. Individual movements and hand gestures often have religious meaning, though less specifically than those of Indian classical dance, and the dancers recite *mantras* along with the chants and comic dialogue of the dances.

Both professional and trained lay dancers perform in the festivals, which are held annually according to the lunar calendar prior to which there are day-long Tests of Dance performed without masks and costumes in the presence of senior lamas and local audiences curious to see the dancers unadorned. The dances have been recorded and codified in age-old dance manuals, but these manuals are consulted only in case of doubt. The dancers learn by the handing down of whole dances, many starting to dance in their teens. In the past, each district had its own company, but the

Department of Dance of the Royal Government of Bhutan now sends its own troupe – which will be seen on the North American and European tours – to many of the local festivals.

For the nineteenth-century British explorers and diplomatic envoys who penetrated the far-off Druk Yul, or Land of the Thunder Dragon, Bhutan was a magical land of silk-robed kings living in castles clinging to mountainsides, a land of plunging rivers and trails that wound through forests full of exotic flowers, birds and beasts, and a land of tall people who, though easygoing, seemed "victims of the most unqualified superstition."

The present ruler, young King Jigme Singye Wangchuck, is fourth in a line of hereditary monarchs established in 1907 by Ugyen Wangchuck, who unified Bhutan's regional governments and extended its foreign relations. Mountainous Bhutan remained inaccessible, however, until the early nineteen-sixties, when the closing of the Tibetan border to the north prompted the building of the first roads across the country and south to India. The hydro-electric plant and the cement factory have come now to this land of 1,200,000 people, along with model orchards and more schools and hospitals. Yet, the land of the fluttering prayer flags and hillside shrines has remained, for one recent visitor, a place of "joy and harmony." It is that reflected sense of good-humored serenity that illuminates the dances.

"We have no television station and as yet one small radio station, run by a youth association for local purposes," Dasho Om Pradhan, Ambassador to the Permanent Mission of the Kingdom of Bhutan to the United Nations, says. "There are plans to set up a radio station within the next five years to give news of Bhutan to the rest of the world. But we have kept development at the slowest possible pace so lives would not be disturbed. We would not have a cultural shock."

The Carnegie Hall exhibition was videotaped. The Breyer-Wood documentary film bears out many of the fine details of the dances noted by the *New York Times* reviewers but has the advantage of having been shot *in situ* during the actual outdoors festival in the courtyard of a monastery with the King in attendance. It shows the huge, restless crowds drawn from the whole rugged country. The film also brings other dances than those done by the company on tour: the *Deer Dance*; the *Dance of Celestial Beings and Evil Serpents*, during which the Celestial Beings bestow blessings on onlookers in the crowd by tapping them on the head; and fervent dances to exorcize demons. Incense from rooftops drifts over the courtyard, and the festival goes on for hours. In the restless crowd some eat and circle about as they watch the tireless dancers, who leap, hop, whirl, crouch. At intervals there are stately processions but more often, in contrast to them, incursions by clowns who enact rude, earthy farces. Sometimes the male dancers use delicate finger movements.

Here, too, passing mention might be made of the Bengali Chau, about which as yet too little is known abroad, and which bears a resemblance to the Tsechu. The Bengalis performed it in the hope of bringing on the monsoon early, crucially needed rains for the baked earth.

When Moana Tregaskis visited Thimphu in 1986, the Royal Dancers and Musicians were obliging picture-snapping tourists on the lawn of the Motihang Hotel with "a vigorous display of whirl and leap, skirts billowing and hands moving in the timeless gestures of Buddhist legend. . . . As heroes pierced clouds of ignorance with swords and vanquished stag-masked demons, good triumphed over evil to the accompaniment of cymbals, drums, gongs and blaring long horns."

It is a question whether Tibet should be considered in a chapter on India and its Himalayan neigh-bours, or with our earlier journey through the history of Chinese theatre. Communist China's army invaded the mountainous land in 1950, reclaiming it after long insisting on a right to it. Since 1911–12, when the Chinese had been expelled, the Tibetans had experienced a measure of independence. From 1950 to 1959 an incipient rebellion was crushed, and military rule was reimposed. The Dalai Lama, nominal ruler of Tibet, the craggy, theocratic state, fled to India. Many belonging to his loyal entourage accompanied him into exile. Others who had fought to resist the invaders crossed into adja-cent Nepal and settled there in heterogeneous colonies. Over the next two decades, which witnessed Mao's Cultural Revolution in China, Tibetan temples and monasteries were destroyed, while thou-sands of the country's Buddhist monks were imprisoned. After 1979, and Mao's death, the Chinese government, subjected to foreign criticism, made some efforts at rehabilitation of the damage, even rebuilding a few monasteries. But much of Tibet's artistic heritage was forever lost. At Beijing's direc-tion, too, Chinese immigration became an increasing flow, so that ultimately the native inhabitants were outnumbered, Tibetans reduced to a minority in what for a millennium had been their nation and an independent kingdom. The Chinese take credit for having improved roads and improved the economy by starting hydroelectric projects for a superstitious people always miserably impoverished and largely illiterate, and considered by some to have been exploited by a priestly order. In the late 1980s restlessness and dissidence among the Tibetans started up again, and anti-Chinese riots were held in check by the armed forces.

During much of the mid-twentieth century, as ordered by the Chinese occupiers, Tibet was closed to Western travellers.

In a rare report from Lhasa, a journalist observed in 1976: "Dance-drama was always dear to Tibetans, according to earlier travelers. Now, instead of monks dancing out the myths and legends of their church, richly garbed and grotesquely masked, youngsters dance out praise of activities that make their lives fuller – the entry of girls into stone masonry or, more remarkable in a country where any sort of mining was taboo, coal mining, or the introduction of new high-yield seeds. In nearly three weeks in Lhasa the writer has seen only one monk in the streets – an old man in an ocher robe, sitting, staff in hand, on the curb in the shade at a bus stop."

In the early 1980s Tibet was once more open to tourists, moderate-sized groups of whom explored Lhasa, the capital city, which had been considerably modernized by the Chinese newcomers. At the outbreak of rioting in 1987, entrance to the city was again denied to outsiders, even to newspaper correspondents.

Though not to be seen in their original and natural setting, Tibetan arts were not entirely out of view. In 1981 a troupe of sixteen exiled monks, along with the Dalai Lama, passed through New York and enacted several ritual dances for very interested spectators at the Altschul Auditorium of the Columbia University School of International Affairs. Jennifer Dunning, in the *New York Times*, remarked that the occasion could hardly be called a concert.

Choeyog Thupten Jamyang, the monastery's master of ritual, and Sharpa Rinpoche, his translator, repeatedly expressed their "deep regret that we could not bring this to a professional standard." The dances, they explained, were in the slow process of reconstruction after thirty-two of the monastery's one hundred seventy-five monks were able to flee during the Chinese takeover of Tibet in 1959. The religious center, historically the personal monastery of the Dalai Lama, is now in Dharmsala, India.

Their religious nature also removed the five dances – excerpts from ritual celebrations practiced just before the Tibetan New Year – from consideration as mere creatures of the concert stage. The proceeds from the program were to help build a monastery in India. The performers were members of the Tantric College of His Holiness the Dalai Lama. And elements of the costumes expressed, for example, such concepts as "nondualistic wisdom of bliss and emptiness" or "protection from spirits, planets and stars."

To eyes uninitiated into the subtleties of traditional Buddhist dance and music, the dance was fairly circumscribed ritual movement and gesture built on slow pivoting turns, hops and wreathing of hands and arms, performed at a stately, gracious pace to the deep roar of long horns, low-voiced drums, trumpets, cymbals and muted chants. The costumes were exotic: layers of brilliantly colored embroidered cloths and ritual implements and intricately detailed masks of gods and a very fetching deer.

But best of all was the performers' devotion to their material and audience. An assisting monk sprang center stage in the middle of a *Black Hat Dance* to rearrange a costume panel that had become twisted. The narrator explained gravely that the two performers of the *Skeleton Dance* represented emanations of the wisdom of enlightened deities and not mere bags of bones. "Please do not be afraid of them, with their fangs," he reassured the audience as he announced the *Masked Dance* of two fierce gods. "Understand that theirs is not the wrath of ordinary people but a deeper sign of their compassion for the afflicted emotions of mankind."

In a subsequent article in the *New York Times* Anna Kisselgoff added her impressions and explanatory material of consequence:

As the dance season draws to a close, it is impossible not to mention the little-publicized but greatly appreciated visit of sixteen Tibetan monks who stopped by New York to perform some ritual dances amid travels in this country with their leader, the Dalai Lama.

After the Chinese drove him out with thousands of his followers in 1959, the Dalai Lama established a Tibetan government in exile in Dharmsala, India. One of its concerns has been the preservation of Tibetan culture – apparently a much more difficult task than might be assumed, as this visit made clear. According to Choeyog Thupten Jamyang, the master of ritual at the Namgyal monastery, whose order has been transplanted to Dharmsala, many of these traditional dances are no longer performed by the monks. A concerted effort is now underway to "re-establish" them and save them from extinction.

Since the dances are religious dances inseparable from Tibetan Tantric Buddhism, their preservation is not a matter of esthetic consideration but essential to the ritual practices of a religion. Tantric Buddhism, a mystical form of Buddhism based upon texts known as Tantras has, interestingly, been one of the Eastern religions to which American artists in various fields have been drawn in recent years. The dangers of spiritual tourism are evident to anyone. But perhaps one reason for this appeal is that, along with Zen and Sufism, Tantric Buddhism offers formulas for artistic expression integrated into spiritual concerns. How these ideas are transposed to a Western culture is another matter. When Robert Rauschenberg, once the Pop Art king, became very interested in Tantrism several years ago, this interest for example, was secretly reflected in his décor and costumes for Merce Cunningham's *Travelogue*. The patchwork banners of gaily-colored fabrics and the accordion-pleated cloth fans in this dance work may have looked merely colorful. But anyone who saw the Tibetan folk opera here in 1975 or saw last month's ritual dances would have recognized his inspiration.

The real McCoy is another matter. Tantric Buddhism relies very heavily on symbols and every color, fabric and image has a symbolic value that cannot be perceived by a layman. One of the revelations of this concert by the monks at Columbia University's School of International Affairs on July 24, was its very contrast with the folk opera performances. The folk opera, known as Lhamo, was presented by another exile organization established by the Dalai Lama – the Tibetan Music and Drama Society in Dharmsala. With its wondrous crystal-clear mountain sound – in the singing and the musical instruments – Lhamo is out to entertain and instruct. Its stories tend to be morality plays about the superiority of Buddhism to prior religions and heresies. But as folk theater, its origins are secular.

The ritual dances on view this time are, by contrast, integral to religious practice. Actually, some were approximated by the Lhamo troupe. On the most superficial level, the dances were more smoothly executed by the folk-theater company, which has trained dancers if not fully professional ones in the Western sense. The ritual master, on the other hand, apologized that the monks were not able to bring their dancing "to a professional standard." Yet it was just as obvious that in their re-learning of ancient dances, the monks had a different goal. It was to enact a devotional service, where every gesture or detail was meant to be meaningful. Of course, there was an audience in the auditorium but the purpose was not exclusively public show.

Lin Lerner, an American scholar of Tibetan dance, has noted, "Dance in Tibetan culture is an enjoyable entertainment performed at social functions and a dramatic vehicle for presenting legendary stories (opera) and religious information (religious dance)." She has categorized Tibetan dance into folk, religious and opera. A crucial point made by Miss Lerner is that in contrast to folk-dance, "ritual dance has been composed by individual great teachers. It is recorded in texts and has a set pattern that must be performed accurately."

Such ritual dances were formalized in the eighth century to open Tibet's first Buddhist monastery. As Miss Lerner notes, these dances are divided into two types: "*Gar* – the more esoteric and complex form which is to be performed within the monastery and *Cham* – the dance form connected to public rituals."

The excerpts on this occasion were of the Cham type, from the Namgyal monastery, which is the Dalai Lama's own personal monastery. As explained by the ritual master, these are traditional dances performed just before the Tibetan New Year by the monks as a consecration of ritual offerings for the prosperity of all.

In Miss Lerner's words, these dances are performed at the New Year "to eliminate negativity – to cut through the ego – and to bring in auspicious circumstances." And as the ritual master's commentary for each dance explained, the general aim of the dances is a seeking of enlightenment and wisdom (hence, the monk symbolically cutting through his ego in a deer dance). The concept of impermanence in the phenomenal world was embodied in the first dance, subsequent to a magnificent if small-scale introduction by the musicians on their drums, cymbals and their astounding long horns.

Two skeleton dancers came out. The costumes looked modern, with skeleton markings, but the masks, including one skull topped by a tiara of smaller skulls, looked more traditional. The commentary warned the audience not to see the pair literally as skeletons but as "protectors of the wisdom of enlightened deities." The dance itself was a blend of lumbering grace and introduced the main motif of Tibetan dances – hops on one leg with the other raised in a flexed foot, with turns added to the hops. This dance was marked with arm swoops and torso rotating, which is not common to all the hopping dances.

The next two masked dancers with ferocious faces and ornately brocaded costumes were identified as visualizations of wrathful deities whose wrath is not external but "directed to inner delusions" such as hatred and ignorance. Carrying a ritual object in each hand (a scarf and a whisk), each dancer danced with a light spring, shifting weight, hopping in half turns. All the turns were inward. There was a set sequence to each phrase. To say the dancers looked like magical beings would not be inaccurate and we can believe the statement that "these masked dancers are manifestations of Tantric deities who appeared in a great state of bliss and ecstasy to Tantric yogis."

At his most enlightened, the dancer merges with the deity he is portraying, or becomes the deity. Such concepts are difficult to grasp. But the following *Black Hat* dance – named after its costume and here an excerpt with only three monks in place of its usual grand scale – indicated how a different level of consciousness could be reached. The dance phrases were repeated, becoming mesmerizing. Every *avant-garde* dancer should see the *Black Hat* dance.

In 1981, a few months before the new rioting in their far-off homeland, Yangla, a performing arts troupe, reached New York and the stage of the Asia Society before undertaking a nationwide tour with a programme entitled "Tibetan Opera, Music and Dance from Lhasa". An introduction by Corrine K. Hoexter to what might be expected by unknowledgeable spectators was published in the *New York Times* on the weekend preceding the event.

As recently as 1980, the remote Himalayan region of Tibet was so closed to the outside world that travel between it and the West hardly existed. Now, the first performing-arts troupe ever to visit North America from Lhasa will be performing at the Asia Society for three evenings beginning

Thursdays. Consisting of eight singers and dancers plus a musician who doubles as director, the group will present a mini-version of the traditional opera *Dowa Sammo*, as well as excerpts from several other Tibetan operatic and dance works. Bringing all these pieces to this country in their authentic state, however, required both diligence and persuasion.

Dowa Sammo has a plot that would do credit to a Verdi opera – a mix of scheming stepmothers, poison potions, mad kings, wronged wives, kidnapped children and treacherous servants. But the active intervention of demons and fairies adds a distinctive flavor; these folk operas are grounded in the Buddhism that is at the core of the Tibetan way of life.

According to Dr Lin Lerner, a dance ethnologist, the purpose of the operas was to "ask a blessing on the community and ensure a plentiful harvest."

The first folk-opera troupes were amateur groups of farmers and tradesmen who used to close up shop once a year to present plays in neighboring villages. Later, professional opera companies, supported by rich and influential patrons, were required to perform annually for the Dalai Lama in Lhasa as a form of taxation.

In general, the action of the operas unfolds in a series of set scenes – either solos or duets – with the chorus echoing the words of the principal singers. A narrator delivers the recitative, rather like a patter song from Gilbert and Sullivan, in a *parlando* style at an almost unintelligible speed. The aria-like main parts are sung in a vibrant, throaty chant punctuated by sudden glottal breaks, all endlessly sustained and ornamented with rising and falling cadences.

Despite the unusual vocal style, Tibetan folk opera tends to be realistic in movement and characterization. It differs markedly from other Asian theatrical forms that are better-known in America, such as Kabuki and Peking opera. Aimed at a sophisticated, urban audience, these latter kinds of theater have developed an elaborate, symbolic and stylized repertory of movement and gesture.

Visually riveting, Tibetan opera-theater customarily employs masks to identify supernatural beings and make-up for human characters. Men appear in richly brocaded silk robes resembling those of Manchu courtiers. The women, in gilt crowns with fanlike "wings" attached to either side, are bedecked in iridescent-hued silk blouses and skirts.

The beating of drums and striking of cymbals accompanies the action. Each type of character is personified by a musical phrase, as well as by a dance step – for example, light and delicate for the maidens, and fast and furious for the demons.

The dances are marked by intricate footwork and twirling. The men execute athletic leaps and turns; the women revolve more slowly, while their arms, encased in long sleeves that cover the hands, sway gracefully about their bodies. Mime often illuminates dramatic and humorous moments, as in a scene in which an old man, nagged by his wife to prepare for a trip to a temple festival, becomes enamored with his spruced-up appearance.

The Tibetan performers' long journey from the mountains of their homeland to the United States has been smoothed by the efforts of a woman who has made a career of bringing authentic samplings of the Asian performing arts to American audiences: Beate Gordon. As director of the performing-arts program at the Asia Society, Ms Gordon made two trips to Lhasa to assure that the program was the one she was eager to present.

Of her first visit in August 1985, she says simply, "I have never been so ill." Unaccustomed to the thin air in Lhasa, which is more than eleven thousand feet above sea level, she was barely able to leave her bed. But, told of a performance, she dragged herself to the show, carrying two bags of oxygen with her; once there, she says, she was treated to "a symphony orchestra playing *La Paloma* and a Tibetan version of the Inkspots." Fortunately, near the finale, a group performed a traditional dance.

Ms Gordon then faced a dilemma familiar to her from earlier visits to Asia: She had to convince her Tibetan hosts that American audiences would appreciate examples of authentic indigenous performing arts rather than something that had been adulterated by more modern influences.

Ms Gordon returned to Lhasa last September to double-check that the program was as originally planned. At once, she detected a taped interlude of modern Chinese music, along with a sequence from a classic Indian dance, both of which she asked to have dropped.

Ms Gordon's insistence on ensuring authenticity is rooted in her belief that Americans prefer to "go to the original source." Cultural traditions that have an unbroken history of hundreds of years, she adds, "clearly must have intrinsic value to the people who cherished them so long."

When she appraised the Yangla ensemble, Anna Kisselgoff had many reservations.

The program called *Tibetan Opera, Music and Dance from Lhasa*, presented by the Asia Society today at 2 and 8 p.m., is certainly worth a visit for anyone interested in Asian theatrical forms.

Those who saw the New York performances in 1975 by the Tibetan exile opera company that is under the Dalai Lama's patronage in India will inevitably make comparisons between that group and this one. The nine-member troupe that opened Thursday night in the Lila Acheson Wallace Auditorium at the Society has been sent by the Chinese Government, and its dancer-singers and musicians have come from Lhasa, the capital of what is now called the Tibet Autonomous Region of the People's Republic of China.

Unfortunately, the excerpts on view gave little sense of the purity and refinement that was so integral to the Tibetan Music and Drama Society, the exile group presented by Kazuko Hillyer. As folk art, Tibetan opera – which is called Lhamo – is a frankly popular form and its components need not have the codified systematization of a classical art.

Nonetheless, Lhamo is art, and the high esthetic aspect one remembered from 1975 never materialized here. The emphasis now was on comic excerpts, which can take on a crudity of their own if not balanced by the other elements inherent in folk opera of this sort. Although a secular folk theater, Lhamo has often used themes from Buddhist mythology to demonstrate the superiority of Buddhist teaching. This moral emphasis was absent on this occasion – thus omitting the thread that gives such art philosophical and artistic coherence.

Made up mainly of short excerpts, the two-hour program nonetheless offers a hint of Lhamo's mixture of dancing and dialogue with the sustained single-note vocalizing that is its trademark. The costumes were not as rich or splendid as those of other Tibetan-related performances seen in New York, and a Chinese influence was hinted at in the prevalence of Peking-Opera style gestures and the dress of some of the characters.

Through these bits and pieces – in which the public temple dances should have had more of a ritualistic character – one could still sense the mix of exuberance and discipline among the performers.

The program's first half was devoted to set pieces drawn from an opera about a wicked queen who attempts to poison her husband and whose attempts to kill his children are foiled. When she returns as a demon to duel with her stepson, good triumphs over evil but we never find out how the hero reached a state of enlightenment to do so.

None of the excerpts from the opera, *Dowa Sammo*, quite lived up to the prologue – essentially a ritual dance by masked dancers (Basang Ciren, Wang Jie, Dazhaxi Ciren, Xiaozhaxi Ciren) to the gongs and cymbals of an offstage musician. Like these dancers, some of the leading actors also danced in the prologue, with a typical dance phrase of hopping on one foot, knee raised and the opposite arm rotating a wrist.

Sangdan, as the queen, offered a persuasive emotional range both through her facial expressions and her sustained vocalizing, which often overlapped with other voices. Gesang Ciwang as the King, had a similar projection in his singing, while the queen's maid, Yangla, was certainly an expert actress. Wang Jie was the son and Baizhen the distressed daughter.

The program's second half had Yangla performing even more movingly as a bride in an arranged marriage while a masked temple dance, danced by men – including Gesang Ciwang – succeeded more in terms of virtuosity than mystery. Dacidan Duoji and Baizhen appeared in a vignette about an old farm couple.

9

BURMA AND CEYLON

About the performing arts in two of India's other close neighbours little can be learned just now. The excuse long given for excluding visitors to Burma (now Myanmar) was a lack of places to care for them, but the true reason was political. The government, a military dictatorship, was in tight control and regulated all open speech and thought. Criticism and the questioning voices of outsiders were feared. In Ceylon (now Sri Lanka) a prolonged civil war made the situation too perilous for mere tourism.

To breach Burma, visas had to be obtained far in advance, and not many were issued; a pretext for entering was an urgent or official mission. Even when foreigners were finally admitted more frequently, to boost the faltering economy in the early 1980s, the permission was for limited stays, perhaps a week or ten days.

Henry Kamm, in 1977, sent this frank dispatch to the *New York Times*:

All public expression in Burma is censored, and the press is uniform in its praise of President Ne Win's fifteen-year-old "Burmese way to socialism." But recently, press censorship has tightened to the point of not only prescribing to editors what they must not print but also what they must print. The range of optional items has become narrower than ever.

Rangoon's three newspaper editors, their deputies and their chief editorial writers must now meet daily and read for each other's benefit the editorials that each has prepared for the following morning. Together with Information Ministry officials, they subject them to criticism and agree on a mutually suitable wording. Earlier this month orders were issued for journalists not to meet with visiting foreign colleagues.

But in a country of limited literacy and no television, the popular theater takes an important place in cultural life, and Burma's popular troupes continue to enjoy a jester's freedom that dates to precolonial days. It flourished in the days of British colonialism because the ruler did not understand the language of the ruled.

"It's like walking on a roof," said Kyay Mhon, principal comic of a traveling troupe called People's Storm. "If you step carelessly, you fall off."

Stepping carefully, the twenty-nine-year-old actor-dancer explained, meant keeping remarks ambiguous enough so that when the police call on him after a performance he can offer a plausible explanation of his material that differs from the obvious political point that was made and understood.

The actor and some of his colleagues in the seventy-four-member company said that criticism about the painful inefficiencies of Burma's almost totally nationalized economy and the flourishing black market was allowed. No criticism of socialism or even implicit criticism of General Ne Win is allowable.

In fact, an author explained that in a comic historical sketch that he wrote about a Burmese king who enjoyed absolute power and a reputation for womanizing he could not fully expend his wit on those two qualities because, whether he intended it or not, audiences would read into it a caricature of Burma's present ruler.

The comedians evoked the strongest audience participation during the show in this small town in central Burma. The show began around 8 p.m. and ended at 5.30 the following morning, as is the custom. The comic interludes, which sometimes got mixed with the dancing and serious drama, were impromptu and topical and featured many pratfalls and much swordplay. Kyay Mhon showed his cut and scarred hands to prove that the swords were real.

The actor performed throughout the night, as stars are expected to do. In addition to the frequent comic routines, he played in a comic historical sketch, a modern play of romantic love, danced in classical *Ramayana* tales, played a king in a historical drama and a prince in a drama about one of the incarnations of Buddha. The program was typical of the work the People's Storm and perhaps one hundred similar troupes are expected to offer.

The People's Storm played three nights in a large, dirt-floor hall, always before packed houses. About half the audience seemed to consist of children. It is assumed that most people from Nyaungu and the surrounding villages saw all three performances. Two more shows had been scheduled but had to be canceled because the Government pre-empted the hall for a political meeting.

The spectators paid the equivalent of seventy cents for a rattan mat seating a family of five. The local élite sat on chairs – for thirty-nine cents each.

The actors' pay is correspondingly low. Kyay Mhon, as the leading comedian, earns about eight dollars a night. Above him is the author and star of the modern play and other pieces in the repertory, who earns fourteen dollars.

The star dancer of the People's Storm earns twenty dollars. But the dancer, twenty-nine-year-old Tin Tin Myint, defended herself against possible accusations of excessive earnings, explaining that she had to supply her own costumes and props, as do all stars, and that her pay was the principal income for thirteen persons, including her five children, her parents and various other relatives.

Minor actors, dancers, musicians and stagehands earn about seventy cents a night. The People's Storm performs twenty to twenty-five nights a month while on tour, which it is for about half the year. The rest of the time it plays in and around Rangoon.

On the road, the seventy-four members live communally, sleeping either in the three trucks that they hire to transport them or in the hall in which they play. They eat in a communal mess. The author writes out the plays and sketches in longhand and each actor then copies out his part.

The low pay forces some of the players to earn a little money on the side during their free afternoons. A leading actor, for instance, blows up dozens of oddly shaped balloons when he rises, hangs them on a huge rack and sells them to children in front of the theater.

"It is a hard life," said Tin Tin Myint, "but once I stand on the stage I forget that."

When I was in Rangoon and Mandalay (as they were then named, 1983), I asked to be taken to a performance of a classical drama. I was told that they were put on only by university students, and infrequently. The cities' theatres showed only films. Was this true? If so, the public's habits had changed rapidly in the six years since Kamm's report.

Before the beautiful island of Sri Lanka changed its name on gaining its independence in 1972, hosts of tourists flocked to Ambalangoda, where the art of mask-carving was inspired by devil-worship and the notorious Devil Dances were a part of exorcism ceremonies. To the hill town of Kandy, where Buddha's sacred tooth is enshrined, thousands of pilgrims made their way. The Kandean dancers were another strong attraction, and doubtless continue to be so. (These enactments are described in Chapter 3.) Since then, the long-lasting rebellion by the Tamil minority has made Sri Lanka an unlikely place to visit. For its native population, however, life goes on and religious festivals are still observed in regions beyond the likelihood of their being a scene of combat, though even the capital, Colombo, and far-off India are not spared random terrorism.

Actual travel to Sri Lanka has not always been necessary for those interested – and possibly eager – to sample and study its folk-ways. In 1978 an abbreviated version of *Thovil*, a ceremony in which a village priest and his helpers seek to drive out physical or mental illness, was demonstrated at the American Museum of Natural History in New York by a troupe whose members often practised it, brought there by the Asia Society. What the audience saw is conveyed by Anna Kisselgoff in the *New York Times*:

> The dancers and drummers provided just enough fire-eating, torch twirling and masked dancing for a layman to feel the flavor of a colorful folk ritual whose magic and purpose does not preclude entertainment.
>
> Like Western therapists, these exorcists from the southern rim of what was once Ceylon tell their patients, "Know thyself." If a dancer dresses up as a demon who is considered responsible for a particular ailment, he can be vanquished before the patient's eyes. *Thovil's* shamans are as intent about cheering up their charges as their Western counterparts, but they are certainly less pompous.
>
> Guptasena, the senior and chief exorcist who began the program with an invocation, set the tone immediately with a typical jauntiness that would carry over into his banter with the demon dancers. These dancers included Somapala, a lean, loose-jointed performer who specialized in the comic roles and the more serious job of rubbing flames against his skin and biting down onto torch after torch that he thrust nonchalantly into his mouth. Somapala was accompanied by Dharmadasa, an elderly drummer whose outward frailty belied the rhythmic vigor of his own art.
>
> A younger energetic drummer, Wimalasiri, accompanied his two brothers, Elaris and Arnolis, who performed the more acrobatic rapid dances. Significantly, although these are part of a folk ritual, they are not folk-dances. That is, not everyone can do them.
>
> Like many Asian dances in India and Sri Lanka, those performed so vibrantly in unison by the brothers had a set structure. The most typical stance found the dancers in a deep knee bend while their heads moved from side to side and their arms shot back with elbows up, only to whip forward across their chests. In the first torch dance the dancers rotated or twirled torches with crossed arms and amazing speed. The spectacular *Devol God Dance*, designed to appease a deity, contrasted this sharpness to a sudden looser posture.
>
> A member of the audience complained that in this reduced form the dances had no trancelike power. Yet the spell was there. One had only to look at a child who had marched up to the rim of the stage and who darted back when a demon came too close.

(It is said that after the museum demonstration, several persons from the audience approached the performers to ask if they could arrange for private ceremonies of the exorcism, so strong was the impact on them. They felt that *Thovil* was not just a dance.)

Folk-dances of other sorts persist in Sri Lankan villages, emanating from the routine. Some are simple, inspired by the graceful sway of young girls going to a well and carrying large clay water-pots at their hips. The gyrating masked dances are more complex and dramatic. Folk plays lack sophistication but impress and move their naïve audience by a plain truthfulness. These are popular among the Sinhalese (Buddhists), the ethnic group constituting the majority of islanders. The plays are enlivened by acrobatics, stilt-walking, fire-eating, juggling.

An unusual custom, which occurs on holidays, has the women of a village squat about a huge, circular *rabana* – that is, drum – tapping out messages to other villages, whose inhabitants respond, in a rhythmic competition resounding from hillside to hillside.

— 10 —

INDONESIA

For its art, Bali is the best known and cherished of the myriad islands making up the far-flung Indonesian archipelago.

A description of its dances and puppetry appears earlier in this book. But dances and dramas abound on most of the other islands, too, especially on Java and Sumatra. Some of them have disparate origins, the population representing a considerable ethnic mix and subscribing to rival religious faiths, Muslim, Hindu, Buddhist, Christian, their beliefs finding visible expression in ritual enactments, so that Indonesia presents a highly varied scene.

Throughout the archipelago, in the late twentieth century, the 1,000-year-old Wayang – puppet shadow play – flourishes with unabated vitality. But it has taken on a new mission, for now such shows are apt to have a political content – most unlikely to be come upon in Bali.

As always, the mounting of a Wayang, presided over and manipulated by a *dalang* – puppeteer – is sure to be a marathon event, continuing from early dusk until dawn, in village after village. Some are projected in larger towns, where they take advantage of modern sound equipment and electric lighting. They sometimes crop up on television, too. A shadow play was scheduled to be broadcast by Radio Republic Indonesia, on the last Saturday of each month in 1981, for instance. The puppet museum, near the old Stadhuis, offered a Wayang Golek – a three-dimensional piece – every morning, and a Wayang Orang was performed nightly at the hot, crowded Pantja Murta theatre near Pasar Senen. The various kinds of puppet works were also regularly exhibited at an impressive new cultural centre, Taman Ismail Maarzuki.

The Wayang Golek could also be seen that year in West Java at Bandung every Saturday morning. In other regions – Central and East Java – the Ketoprak, a variation of the Wayang Orang, was usually on display, along with the modern Ludruk, a low form of farce much liked by the masses. These gained popularity starting in the 1920s. They are realistic, have improvised dialogue and action, and add dancing and music between the scenes, though never in the body of the story. West Java has developed the Sandiwara, a modern kind of romantic musical comedy, often a feature of private celebratory events: a birth, a wedding, a tooth-filling ceremony, a coming-of-age ritual – to which virtually all the inhabitants of a village are invited to be spectators.

Tourists view the performances – some of them abbreviated – by booking attendance through their hotels. In Yogyakarta, central Java, they might be sent to the Agastya Art Institute for a programme of excerpts given every day but Saturday, or observe a play at the Yayasan Setyo Budojo, or catch a full-length production twice monthly in the southern square of the Kraton (palace square) put on by Sasono Hinggil, or perhaps even see fragments of repertory staged in the larger hotels for the benefit of guests. Foreigners are also permitted to watch *dalangs*-in-training at the Habiranda Dalang School, just off the Kraton. Jakarta's National Museum gives a play every second and last Saturday of each month in the Gedung Gaja (Elephant Building) on Jalan Merdeka Barat. They are also on view at the School of Folk Art. In Jakarta, too, is the Wayang Museum on Fatahillah Square, where a broad range of puppets is shown. Performances, some long, others shortened, take place several times weekly, mostly evenings and also Sunday mornings. (With time passing, all this information about showings may no longer be accurate.)

In 1979 David Andelman drew this picture for the *New York Times* of the role of the seemingly eternal Wayang in contemporary rural Indonesian life:

For ten hours, during the night and into the dawn, the angular black shadows flitted across the white cotton screen, dancing to the flickering light of the coconut-oil lamp – princes and queens, soldiers and knaves, farmers and clowns moving in a tapestry of life, love and war.

The puppets were acting out a story well-known to all in this tiny village deep in the jungles of Central Java. It was the *Mahābhārata*, one of the great epics of ancient Java.

But now there is more to this epic and to that of the *Ramayana*, the other major mystical tale of the *wayang kulit*, or shadow puppet show. The Government is using the *wayang* to politicize Indonesia. On May 2, the archipelago's 135 million people are expected to vote according to plan, overwhelmingly re-electing the people who have governed for twelve years.

In the home of Mayor Komari Ahadiwrijanto, where the villagers had gathered to celebrate a record harvest, puppet soldiers jerked solemnly across the screen. As the hushed crowd watched, the puppets stumbled over a barricade.

The puppet soldiers debated what to do, with the *dalang,* or puppet master, mimicking the voices. "Let's make a road out of the barricade so we can pass through," concluded the captain. "Even though it may take a long time, that's called development."

A smattering of applause and the point was made, a message that would be repeated again, subtly, delicately, by clowns, princes and heroines but without disrupting the story's ebb and flow.

On this night as on countless other nights in thousands of villages in Eastern and Central Java and now, too, on nation-wide radio, Golkar, the party of President Suharto and his military rulers, is using the characters of the *wayang* to campaign for an overwhelming electoral mandate, for birth control, for widespread use of the high-yield rice.

Even though Indonesia has a new multi-million dollar domestic satellite system, television, radio and films, "the *wayang* is still the most widespread, universal and effective mass communications medium in Indonesia," said Pandam Guritno, a leading scholar of the *wayang*.

Subtlety is part of its effectiveness, but so too is its saturation of the island of Java where the *wayang* originated more than *nine centuries* ago and where about 80 million of Indonesia's 135 million people live.

There are more than 20,000 puppet masters in Java, ranging in age from ninety down to ten. Many come from old *dalang* families, their parents and their parents' parents having been puppet masters as far back as any can remember.

Their mandate is a semimystical, semidivine gift. Reverence is paid to the mystical by Javanese from President Suharto down to the most humble village chieftain, so the puppet masters are carefully cultivated, educated and pampered by a Government that realizes their political value.

During the day before the performance at the Mayor's house here, Moro-carito, the forty-five-year-old *dalang* who produced the show, and several hundred other *dalangs* gathered in the district capital of Klaten for an education session by officials of the Minister of Culture and Education from Jakarta.

Themes are suggested during these meetings, and puppet masters are told of areas to be avoided – religious conflict, for instance, or support for a particular political party. Golkar, the Government party, does not consider itself a political party but rather a collection of "functional groups."

There are more puppet masters in the Klaten area than in any other district of Indonesia – more than 100 in an area of a few square miles. Klaten also supports the only school for *dalangs* in the entire nation, turning out about five each year.

"But it's not education that creates a great *dalang*, it's from within," said Martono Gito Supatino, Klaten's director of culture. He speaks with his hands, paces back and forth, puffs on a clove cigarette like a Hollywood producer. He pounds his chest. "If you have high culture, if you have spontaneity, you are a great *dalang*, but it must be within you."

Being a *dalang* calls for extraordinary stamina as well as artistic and musical talent and a gift for gab. For ten hours and sometimes more, the *dalang* must sit cross-legged in front of his large, white, translucent screen, a flickering lantern placed overhead to cast the shadows.

He sometimes manipulates as many as 400 different puppets that are passed to him by assistants. He directs an orchestra of drums, xylophones and gongs, using a wooden knocker grasped between his toes. He delivers a constant stream of ad-libbed repartee, chants, dialogue in the different voices of each character and at the same time threads his way through a complex story line with asides and wisecracks.

But the rewards are great. A first-class *dalang* may receive 50,000 rupiahs, or 125 dollars, for a single performance. Sixty percent of Indonesia's population earns less than that in a month. In addition, the *dalang* is respected and revered in the community.

"Our president bases much of his policy on the *wayang*," said Pandam Guritno. "This is a very religious country and the wayang is a great strength in the preservation of our moral life."

Michael Specter, writing in 1984 to the *New York Times* from Yogyakarta, pays a similar tribute to the importance and influence of this theatrical genre:

Jogjakarta has always gone its own way; its cultural primacy in Indonesia has never been challenged. It is a city of pleasant contradictions: a small town full of big ideas, a laconic village that quickens the pulse of Java, a modern place with ancient motifs.

Its *Ramayana* dancers move to a choreography that was etched into the temple stones of Borobudur 1,200 years ago. And the myths of *wayang kulit* – the shadow-puppet play that is perhaps the country's most enduring tradition – still form the core of Indonesian culture.

Populated by a world of demons, monsters, princes and clowns, *wayang* is as alive today in Jogja as it has ever been. The nightlong performances on the second Saturday of every month draw heavy crowds, and if you tell a resident you are fond of *wayang*, he is likely to ask you what your favorite puppet is.

. . . In fact, one of the quickest ways of understanding the significance of *wayang* in Jogjakarta is to visit a *wayang* workshop. At the shop of Hadi Sukirno, on Sindurejan, men carve richly detailed patterns into leather skins. When they have fashioned a character that passed muster with their watchful boss, they begin to paint the faces bright colors to protect them from evil spirits.

Wayang (the Javanese word means shadow or ghost) is the foremost dramatic vehicle in the country. Although Westerners usually regard *wayang* as a cute, if antiquated, picture show, it is more than a diversion to Indonesians. Performances in Jogjakarta are major events. . . .

The *dalang* has complete control over the play. He recites the narration and dialogue in staccato bursts of Javanese, acts as conductor of the orchestra and infuses the plot with offbeat humor, social comment or personal philosophy as he sees fit. Like Prospero, he creates a world with boundaries he can manipulate. In Indonesia's tightly controlled society, the *dalang* has unparalleled freedom of expression. Although the plots never vary, a talented *dalang* can twist them so artfully, like a jazz master improvising wildly on a well-known theme, that the most ancient of stories often seem to have been written yesterday.

Wayang is often used as propaganda. It has been used as a thinly veiled Christian parable, a call to Islamic Fundamentalism, and not so long ago, a fable meant to convey the glories of a Communist society. It is this ambiguity, coupled with the Indonesian reverence for mystical and spiritual expression, that has kept *wayang* alive through the centuries.

The persistence of a still thriving native theatre has not prevented Indonesia from developing a Westernized drama. Early to venture into this alien style was Sanusi Pané (1905–68), who used incidents and characters from Java's eleventh century for a historical play, *Airlangga* (1928). To prove his modernity, some of his prose works are in Dutch. A later script, *Manusia Baru* (1940), deals with social problems besetting contemporary Indonesia. With these pioneering works Sanusi Pané attained major literary stature in his country.

The Second World War saw Indonesia occupied by Japanese forces, and soon after the war it gained freedom from Dutch rule. These events prompted its playwrights to stage nationalistic themes. Armijn Pané (1908–70), the brother of Sanusi, turned to comedy as a vehicle for patriotic propaganda. Afterwards, in *Djinak-djinak Merpati* (1944), he portrayed a good-hearted flirt. Under that general title, his collected works were published in 1953.

Less popular, though more substantial in subject matter, is the output of Usmar Ismail (b. 1921), whose career began during the Japanese occupation. Myron Maitlaw tells us: "His domestic plays, collected as *Sedih dan Gembira* (1948), probe man's responsibility to man – as in *Api*, in which a selfish scientist is destroyed by his own military invention while his colleague is praised for finding a cure for malaria."

Most of the indigenous Javanese plays available in print are one-acters. Creative writing has been encouraged in workshops sponsored by the Indonesian Dramatic Academy and by opportunities to have the scripts produced by the Performing Arts Theatre of Jakarta. The newly opened cultural centre, Taman Ismail Marzuki, also offers a stage for modern plays.

Having worked and studied in the United States, the Balinese-born actor–director Ikranagara set up in Jakarta the avant-garde Theatre of Itself. He spoke gratefully of the diversity of sources allowing him to enrich its ventures. "We are a society coming from many tribes. Indonesians are lucky. Take just the field of drama. In Bali there are six or seven dramatic forms. Java has several varieties. Sumatra has its own kind." He defined his outlook as "post-modernist . . . drawing on old forms while rejecting folk art as an end – and a refuge – in itself". He added a mild demur: "Everyone complains about the influence of the West. I found out why: it is easier to get a grant to go abroad than to go to Sumatra." He explained that few Indonesian playwrights of an experimental bent were leftist, partly because that would expose them to the hostility of the country's anti-Communist government. Before 1965, however, a Soviet-inspired Social Realism was the vogue. Those practising it later fell victim to repressive measures, some imprisoned or finding their careers blighted.

Ikranagara himself fashioned a play for the World Wildlife Fund in which he protested against the exploitation of the nation's natural resources. Facing the anger of the authorities, he was defended by environmentalists, in particular the Green Indonesia Foundation.

The dances and puppet-plays of Indonesia are singled our as by far the most interesting of its varied performing arts. These differ somewhat from region to region, island to island, with those from Bali the most renowned.

Though the Balinese dances and shadow plays have already been discussed, it might be worthwhile to examine them more fully. There are close parallels to them in the Wayang Wong, as the Javanese dance-drama is called. In the second century Hindu traders and apostles reached Java, bringing with them their religions and culture, including their remarkable architecture. By the ninth century local idiomatic kinds of theatre and dance were implanted and well developed, as evidenced by the décor of the vast ruined temple of Borobudur, its walls covered with scenes from the *Natya Sastra*. Material for the dances and plays became over-abundant in the eleventh century after King Dharmawanga translated the *Mahābhārata*. An early borrowing from it was *The Nuptials of Arjun*, the first identifiable Lakon or derivative stage-work. About 1200 a comparatively primitive realism began to give way to stylization that was ever more intense. A century that followed, 1350 to 1439, is looked upon as a Golden Age for this ongoing process. In 1900 the many forms of dance and plays that evolved over the great stretch of time were codified by the Society of Music and Dance (Krida Beksa Wirama) at the prompting of Prince Souryadnigrat, brother of the Sultan of Djokjakarta, categorizing the distinctive characteristics of each of the ultimate and surviving dance forms and dramas.

La Meri, in the *The Dance Encyclopedia*, spells them out for us:

Historically, the *Wayang Topeng* (anciently called *Raket*) developed first, employing masked actors; it was used for magic and ancestor-worship. Then came the *Wayang Poerwa*, the shadow play (sometimes *Wayang Klitik* or *Wayang Gedog*) and after it, marionettes made of leather, *Wayang Klitik* or *Wayang Kroutjil*. From these, which could be used in profile only, grew the wooden marionettes (*Wayang Golek*) with the operator (*dalang*) speaking for his dolls. The forms of *Wayang* in which the actors were puppets, or humans with masks, are considered to be more mysterious, profound, and abstract. The next stage of development was the *Topeng Dalang*, or *Topeng Barangan*, in which the operator spoke the lines and the masked actor portrayed them. These forms – all still in existence – combined to produce the *Wayang Wong*, the most popular Javanese dance-drama.

In a play (*Ringit Tyang*), the *Wayang Wong* presents the human, unmasked actor. The appropriate actor lifts an arm to indicate that he is supposed to be speaking, while the *dalang* reads the lines. Dancing is incidental and consists of *pokok* or combat dances, and *miraga* or decorative dances. The plays last many hours, even days. The technique, depending on the suppleness of the body, is a smooth even flow of movement, somewhat as in a slow-motion film. The aim is to soothe, not arouse; a well-acted *Wayang Wong* is as sedative as a drug. . . . Choreography is arranged and altered only by members of the royal household. There are five different styles of technique: of the women; of the lyric hero (*djoged allus*); of the dramatic hero (*djoged kasar*); of the demons; and of the giants. The clown has no fixed technique; he alone may ad lib. There are three types of women dancers: the *Srimpis*, young girls of royal blood who dance in groups of four; the *Badayas*, who are attached to the court, and dance in groups of nine; the *Ronggengs*, or professional dancers. The latter are not recognized by the Krida Beksa Wirama, save that recently they have been granted the privilege of using the Badaya repertoire.

The *Wayang Wong* is the most perfectly finished theater-piece in the world. It has been protected by the most cultured people of Java since its birth. All its movements, expressions, and presentations are rigidly orthodox. The dance is an integral part of the life of the Oriental, more important to his spiritual life than anything in the Western mode of existence, save perhaps church to the very devout. The dance-drama is a composite presentation of the race history, actual and legendary. It was born as a ritual of worship, and at all times has retained this flavor. It is a spiritual exaltation in which actor and audience alike participate. The watcher is there not to be amused, but to learn and to worship. Even the foreigner feels the impact of this profound faith, as he might on entering a temple whose gods are strange to him.

Javanese dancing is far more difficult than it appears. The characteristic body-line is a rigidly straight back (doubtless, taken from the puppet play) from which the head and limbs move in steady legato spiraling movements infrequently accented with a slight staccato rhythm.

In Java, centres for preserving and teaching the techniques of these dances and plays are located in Surakarta (Solo) and Yogyakarta: their instructions differ in some details. The Yogya style is faster and more emphatic, demanding energetic gestures and fleeter movements, and men take on female roles. In Solo the opposite is the rule: women assume the masculine roles, disguising their too soft faces with painted moustaches. In both instances an explanatory text accompanies the enactment, read aloud by a *dalang*. The performers are retained by the court. The dramatic content of their offering is stressed more than its music and poetry. An exception to this occurs in Solo, where the *dalang* is allowed a degree of improvisation and more freedom in selecting the music that is used. (Even so, the score must always be classical.) The court in Solo is credited with having revived dances with masks along with many of the traits of the Wayang Wong as it is currently seen.

An instance of the ceremonial role of classic dance on this section of the island is provided by Gunilla K. Knutsson in a feature story sent to the *New York Times* (1983):

Once again, as she has for centuries, the Queen of the South Seas arrived to dance for the King of Solo. The young princes smiled and the old nobleman fretted, and a thundercloud burst, as it had to, above the Susuhunan's palace in Surakarta, central Java.

From his elevated throne in the heart of the vast pavilion, His Serene Highness Pakoe Boewan XII, appeared to be very pleased as he watched the stately and intricate movements of the wedding dance performed by nine graceful members of the royal household.

Accompanied by the rhythms of the gongs and cymbals of the gamelan – a bamboo xylophone – orchestra, the dancers repeated the steps of the *bedoyo ketawang*, as generations of princesses had before them, re-enacting the tale of the love of the Queen of the South Seas for the King.

Solo – or Surakarta, as the city is generally named now – is less than an hour's jet flight from Jakarta. Less well-known than touristic Jogjakarta, some forty miles away, Solo with its half-million inhabitants is a center for traditional Javanese dance and music, attracting scholars and students from all over the world.

The city has two Academies for the Performing Arts, where visitors may attend rehearsals and performances most days of the year. The two palaces – the Hadinigrat and Mankunegaran – also have regular dance and gamelan orchestra rehearsals. And there are dance and music events every night at the Sriwedari Amusement and Culture Center.

The most refined, and most private, dance performance in Solo takes place each May during the coronations ritual at the Susuhunan's palace. Because of the religious nature of the ceremony, only members of the court could attend until the rules were loosened ten years ago to include a few local and national dignitaries. Foreigners are rarely invited and last May only a handful of Westerners, including the Australian and Dutch Ambassadors to Indonesia, could be seen perched on raffia chairs in the heat of the tropical noon.

But while the real ceremony is closed, as many as ninety to one hundred spectators, many of them students from local dance and music academies and a dozen outsiders, attended the dress rehearsal two days before the dance this year.

The present King ascended to the throne in 1945 under the Japanese occupation. When the Dutch colonial administrators returned after World War II, they gave him some authority in return for his loyalty to them during the Indonesian struggle for independence. Although he was stripped of any power after his country gained sovereignty in 1949, he still plays a symbolic and cultural role.

His lifestyle, however, is the subject of controversy. As a Muslim, he is entitled to four wives. As a Javanese King, he has the right to keep a harem. Consequently – perhaps – he has sixty-four children, an empty treasury, and a palace that is slowly falling apart for lack of money.

In spite of these problems, the ritual has continued.

The *bedoyo ketawang* stems from the seventeenth-century reign of Sultan Agung, but some say its steps were known as early as the third century. As well as being a ceremonial dance staged for the diversion of the court, it is religious, with spiritual themes woven through its wailing verses. Above all, it is a wedding dance.

The Queen of the Spirits, so the legend goes, fled in despair to the depths of the South Seas when she discovered she had leprosy. The present King's forefather, Panembahan Senopati, visited the Queen from time to time. She fell in love with him and asked him to stay with her on the throne of the South Seas. He declined, but promised that all his descendants would marry her. When his grandson, Sultan Agung, visited her, he was charmed by the *bedoyo ketawang* dance performed at her court and invited her to teach it to his own favorite dancers. She promised the Sultan she would come each year to train new *bedoyos*. The story says that the Queen arrives as rain or a cloud.

This year, guests in formal dress – both Western and Indonesian – arrived at 11 a.m. at the pale blue and marble entrance hall crowned by the Susuhunan's coat of arms and paraded slowly through several courtyards to the tune played by a gamelan orchestra and the salute of the Palace Guard, in black stiff-collared jackets and sarongs. The soldiers carried long sabers or the gold-sheathed *kris*, a long, wavy blade.

Open on three sides – the fourth gave on to the royal quarters – the pavilion consisted of a huge painted roof supported by carved and gilded pillars. Across the hall, the main orchestra bided its time behind a cloud of incense. Under the roof, birds were building nests in the old crystal chandeliers.

The ladies of the court entered discreetly and sat on the floor behind the throne; they wore *dodots* (sarongs) in the King's colors – ocher, cream and black – and, around their shoulders, the royal sash in bright orange.

After another long moment, the Chamberlain signalled that the Susuhunan was arriving. The gamelan orchestra changed rhythm and Pakoe Boewono XII, an elegant man in his late fifties, appeared on the podium.

The second most important woman of his house (the first being his mother, absent from this year's ceremony) entered and chanted that the princes were about to arrive. The sons, with other men of equal rank in the family, entered wearing costumes similar to those of the guards, with golden *krises* in their belts. The crawling and wailing woman – some call her the Prime Minister – announced the arrival of the noblemen, who amid much polite fussing finally sat down facing the king.

It was now 1 p.m. and very hot. The guests had turned anything at hand into impromptu fans. The guard had changed, the orchestra had faded away, and the main gamelan with the sacred gong took up the melody.

Dressed as royal brides in dark blue and gold sarongs over a trail dyed red in imitation of the blood of sacrificial animals used in the past, the nine dancers took their measured steps. At each one, a sprinkle of jasmine and rose petals rose. Their hair-pieces, rolled into nets of gold and flowers, seemed too heavy for their slender necks, stretching and bowing in demure movements. Old ladies, themselves once *bedoyo* dancers, surrounded the performers with great care, crawling along to wipe a perspiring back, arrange a twisted train or adjust a slipped *dodot*.

As the beat grew louder and faster, thunder growled over the royal palace. An instant later, the skies opened. The Queen of the Spirits, the Queen of the South Seas, had arrived for her wedding.

Earlier, in 1977, Faubion Bowers had been commissioned by CBS to film such performances for a pair of television documentaries: they bore the blanket title, *A Court in Solo*. As part of the promotion for their airing, he provided newspapers with an amusing story of the obstacles he met in making the films and having them approved for release.

Part I, subtitled *The King and Queen*, is a sort of sunrise-to-sunset day in the life of His Highness Mangkunegoro VIII and his wife-sister Gusti Putri. We meet them at breakfast and follow them until nighttime ceremonials, including the solemn knee-kissing ritual with palace servants, renewing their fealty by the act of, well, knee-kissing. The climax to this first program is the *Serimpi Mondrorini*, a dance exclusive and unique in the court at Solo, danced by four princesses of the blood chosen for their extraordinary beauty, bodily perfection and identity of height, weight and slenderness.

Part II, subtitled *Sons and Others,* deals with the King's fifteen-year-old son, a star dancer at court, and with another fifteen-year-old, the son of one of the palace servants, who is circumcised in a pavilion of the east wing after something called the Horse Trance Dance, a rite wherein a woman is presumably seized by the spirit of a horse and performs all manner of astonishing feats in order to cleanse the area of any evil spirits. It was, clearly, the circumcision sequence that raised the question of getting the program on the air. But first the problem of getting into the country itself.

[He had to overcome many barriers to get official permission to record the rituals. Some articles in American magazines had offended the nation's president.] Worse, a film crew from the Netherlands – the Dutch ruled the country for 300 years and, as always with former colonies, the residue of familiarity makes for goodwill – had been permitted to film the political prisoners on Boru Island on condition the coverage would be favorable. It wasn't. The program had just been telecast in Amsterdam with devastating reactions. Further, the French film *Emanuelle II,* just released everywhere (except Indonesia), showed the innocuous Kechak *Monkey Dance,* which had been filmed in Bali but was used as a series of persistent, insistent inserts and intercuts, like a flashing strobe light, during the nude fornication scene.

Bowers finally did obtain a licence for the filming. A seemingly endless sequence of delays followed, almost exhausting the crew's budget. At long last the documentaries were completed. In America, however, they were subjected to a different kind of censorship: the sequence depicting the circumcision was excised as too graphic, too gory. Otherwise, the films were approved "as a profoundly religious experience with an artistic bow to Islam". Bowers's comment: "I can't help but feel that now what was really important about the circumcision was the mother's tenderly whispered prayers into the hair of the boy's head and the joyous feast with its cones of rice after the ceremony."

A brief account in the *New York Times* describes how the dances survive in a present-day Javanese city.

Jogja still moves to rhythms elsewhere taken for granted, and from May through October, the full moon heralds the performance of the city's most popular spectacle, the *Ramayana* ballet festival. The four episodes are carried out on successive nights at the Prambanan open stage, about ten miles east of Jogja, on the road to Surakarta. Each night the dance lasts from 7 to 9 p.m., and the festival involves more than three hundred performers. . . .

The drama depicts the struggle between the smooth rectitude of Rama and the menacing evil King Rahwana. The dancers are draped in rich and wonderful costumes that glow in the moonlight as the story unfolds through the actions of demons, gods, gnarled monkeys and lovely princesses. Although some of the original plot has been discarded, Jogja's *Ramayana* performances remain largely faithful to the Hindu epic.

If you cannot make it to Jogja during the *Ramayana* festival, you can see a two-hour version of the dance performed at various locations in the city during the week. Or drop by Pamulangan Beksa Ngayugyakarta, the city's school of traditional dance, in the evening to observe Jogja's classical technique in practice.

Art mixes with life so gracefully in Jogja that any peasant feels welcome at the home of even the most imperious *dalang*. The schools of the city, which train dancers, artists, *dalangs* and musicians, are almost all open to visitors. Watch the girls of central Java learn the studied motion of the *Ramayana*, or the oldest batik painters pass their technique along to the younger generation. Rehearsals for the state dance academy, which combines all of Indonesia's traditional dance forms, take place every evening from four to six.

Another type of popular entertainment is the Kuda Kepeng, a hobby-horse trance dance one is apt to see enacted by wandering street troupes.

Besides the outdoor theatre at Prambanan, a temple complex in Central Java, there is a similar outdoor stage for displays of traditional dances at Pandaan in East Java. A dance-lover can indulge to satiation on this island.

The Balinese performing arts, especially the music and dance, have their own characteristics. La Meri acknowledges this by discussing them under a separate heading:

Possibly in Bali, more than anywhere else in the East, the dance-drama has remained as the most important function in daily living. Birth, marriage, and death, temple festival, and village fête call for the appearance of the actor-dancers in performances which last throughout the night.

The legendary origin of the Balinese dance is attributed to Indra, the old Hindu god of the heavens. But there is little of Hinduism in the style. Scholars agree that the actual dances are the result of primitive rituals of the people themselves. Today, however, Balinese dance is essentially for exhibition and not communal.

In Java the dancers are of and in the court; in Bali the dancers are the peasants and so the dance is vigorously active. This does not imply that the dancers are untrained. On the contrary, many years of tireless effort and exercise go into the execution of the many traditional dances of Bali.

The best-known and most beautiful dance-type is the *Legong*, a pantomime-dance performed by two young girls wearing gold-encrusted gowns and flower-bedecked headdresses, each carrying a fluttering fan. Movements are lightning quick and combine at once moving brows, neck, shoulders, elbows, wrists, fingers, knees and feet. The backbone line is mercilessly cambré, i.e. bending back or to the side from the waist, and the knees are bent.

A popular and supposedly modern translation of the *Legong* is the *Djoged* in which one girl dances in the *Legong* type and boys of the audience, enticed by her, come into the ring to dance with her. The *Sang Byang* is the *Legong* dance performed by dancers while in a trance.

The *Kebiyar* is another well-known dance of the traditional repertoire. It is entirely modern, its creator, Mario, until his recent death, being its foremost teacher. It is a dance not unlike the *Legong* in movement, save that it has great virility of style and line and three-fourths of it is performed sitting down.

The shadow plays of Bali are much like those of Java whence it is supposed they came. Stories of the *Ramayana* and *Mahābhārata* are rendered by a *dalang*, while leather puppets act behind a white screen.

The dance-drama (also here called *Wayang Wong*) deals in plots taken from the two Indian epics, with *dedori* (Balinese nymphs) instead of Hindu *apsarases* dancing around the hero, Arjuna.

The *Topeng* is another form of dance-drama in which only two or three actors play all the parts, changing masks to do so. Material for the plays is drawn from Balinese political history both actual and legendary.

The romantic history of Bali is preserved in the *Ardja*, a sort of erotic opera in which princesses and princes of incredible beauty dance and sing to each other.

Not to be overlooked are the *Baris* and the *Ketjak*. Both performed by men, the former are ritualistic dances executed with weapons, while the latter are choral dances of distinct rhythmic pattern.

In Bali, unlike on the main island of Java, the dancing takes place not in theatres or folk-museums but in village temples, especially on moonlit nights; but there are also performances for tourists in hotels. Going about, after sunset, a foreign traveller is almost certain to hear the soft clang and tinkle of gamelan orchestras and catch glimpses of young, very slender figures of girls and boys carrying out the sacred rituals.

The Balinese puppetry, too, has its own style. Suzanne M. Charle, composing an article for the

New York Times in 1985, watched a typical performance put on by Wayan Wija, a revered *dalang*. He was using the Yogyakarta-type of puppet, which initially has a yellow base over-painted with black and white, and then with red and blue, depending on the traditional character it represents. As a final touch, 24-carat gold leaf is added. In Solo the puppets are all white. (To shape one of them may take as long as two months.) Before each performance, holy water is sprinkled on them. During the show the *dalang* improvises much of the dialogue and action, hearkening to the response of the eager and delighted audience. The language is Kawi, an ancient tongue largely unknown to the spectators; the brash clown-servant characters serve as translators, repeating the lines in their more modern vocabulary. As the foreign visitor listened, "the voices rose and fell, now soft and cajoling, now harsh and haughty".

The *dalang* may have 300 puppets to choose from. Here is a longer excerpt from Ms Charle's poetic account of what she witnessed.

With speed and grace the *dalang* pulled the puppets out of a wooden box, giving some to an assistant on the left – the side of evil – giving others to an assistant on the right – the side of righteousness – until both sides of the screen were filled. Such is the outcome of the *wayang* that it is not complete without the princes and queens, soldiers and competing forces, locked in an endless tug-of-war.

As he started the play, the puppets glinted in the light of the oil lamp; on this bright side of the screen, they had none of the flickering life of the cool shadows. Indeed, they were almost bit players in the sweaty urgency of the performance that heightened as the gamelan musicians furiously hammered out the theme for a red giant. Through it all, the *dalang* sat, the calm center of activity. Knocking a block of wood, held between his toes, against the puppet box, he directed the pace of the play, the tempo of the music. With seeming effortlessness, he maneuvered three, sometimes four puppets at various speeds and gaits across the screen, while dozens of other characters "stood" in the wings, their handles of buffalo horn stuck into the green trunk of a young banana palm. His voice metamorphosed from the sweet tones of a princess in love to the raging threats of a giant to the imbecilic laughter of a clown. For almost five hours, the *dalang* was producer, director, conductor, star and supporting cast, storyteller and teacher. He created a shadowy universe that hovered somewhere between the physical and spiritual worlds. Yet for all its awesome dimensions, his performance had a trancelike ease.

The next time I saw Wayan Wija, he was busy carving some new puppets. Watching, I could not help but think that the lacy, two-dimensional cowhide puppets had more substance and life for him than many three-dimensional types who walk around under their own steam.

There are perhaps 300 *dalangs* in Bali, though few of them perform regularly. Wija, at thirty-three, is one of the most respected. An attractive, lithe man with a quiet smile and dreamy look that belie a quick sense of humor, Wija appears primarily in the towns and villages near his village of Sukawati but has also performed in Japan and Vancouver. He comes from a long line of *dalangs* – at least seven generations that he can count. At twelve, he started his serious training with his father and an old, revered *dalang* in his village. Now he and some twenty members of his family are *dalangs*. Among them is one of his sisters who is one of the few women *dalangs*. Wija will tell you that anyone can be a *dalang* – he teaches his art at a local school where youths from all over Bali come to study – but it is evident that he thinks it is very hard for anyone without a clan tradition to become a first-rate *dalang*; there are so many stories to know by heart, so many mystic texts to memorize, the ancient Kawi language to learn. Above all, newcomers lack the contact with the ancestral spirit.

"Traditionally, *dalangs* were educators," said Wija. "It has always been our duty to teach moral, religious and social behavior." The *dalang* in Bali is also a priest, a sort of moral and religious bard. The *wayang* mirrors things that are happening in a community; the shadowy characters often wrestle with subjects that more substantial beings fear to touch. In one play, a young princess finds out that she is pregnant. A clown comments: "And only twelve years old. She mustn't have seen the TV shows on birth control." In densely populated Bali, where a highly publicized program of family planning is now beginning to take effect, the comment draws great laughter. But the message is clear.

Inevitably, such powerful theater is used for propaganda: During the 1945 revolution against the Dutch, *wayang Pancasila* was invented, lauding the bravery of Indonesian freedom fighters. On came the puppets, the warriors' headdresses replaced with army helmets, the traditional swords, or *kris*, exchanged for guns. Missionaries bring the stories of the Bible to the countryside, with puppets of Adam, Eve and the Devil moving through a shadowy Eden.

Even presidents invoke the power of the *wayang*: President Sukarno, a great devotee of shadow theater, constantly made references to the *wayang* in his speeches. His admirers often likened him to a *dalang*, deftly maneuvering the affairs of state. Suharto, for his part, has chosen to identify himself with the character of Semar. To outsiders, the comparison seems surprising, even crude, for Semar is a grotesque clown. And yet, *wayang kulit* audiences – which include almost the entire populations of Java and Bali, and consequently, the vast majority of Indonesians – appreciate the significance. Semar, with his bulging belly, always seems to know what to do and, by giving his master good advice in times of trouble, inevitably saves the day. More important, many believe Semar to be the incarnation of the god Ismaya – guardian of Java.

With such power attributed to theater, it is not surprising that *dalangs* on occasion make enemies. During the last election, more than a few puppet masters were reported to have run afoul of the law, thanks to their less-than-complimentary characterizations of local authorities. Even in more tranquil periods, the *dalang's* role is not an easy one. Villagers sometimes take offense at real or perceived slights; and as moral teachers, the *dalangs* can find themselves caught between two feuding groups.

For all the generations of tradition, the theater is astoundingly fresh: Recently, Wija has been creating a whole new cast of puppets from characters in the Tantri stories, tales he has researched in ancient Balinese texts that are much like the tales of the Arabian Nights. The clowns are here, as are the nobles. There is also a menagerie of animals and exotic creatures and a fourteen-piece gamelan orchestra. Wija has been working on the Tantri for three years and already has more than 100 characters.

The Tantri tales, however old, are still new to *wayang* audiences, and it was at one such play that I had my first chance to shed some light on the action for a Balinese. The hero, according to an old grandfather sitting next to me, fled the kingdom because of the treachery of his prime minister. During his flight, the king met all manner of beasts: shadowy seas swarmed with crabs, whales and an eel; the skies were crowded with great birds. Across the screen cavorted a circus of elephants and tigers, monkeys, goats and dogs. But then came a creature my friend could not recognize. It hopped across the screen in the most outrageous way; center stage, a tiny head peeked out from its stomach.

"A kangaroo," I offered. The old man was stymied. "A kangaroo," I repeated. "It lives in Australia."

"Oh, Australia," he smiled, understanding now. "A tourist." He turned to tell his friends.

A chaotic fight ensued, in which the king and evil minister came to blows, each magically changing into a succession of fierce creatures, until finally the Barong, a mystical lionlike god, put the wicked witch Rangda on the run and good, temporarily, vanquished evil – as is always the case in *wayang*. The lights came up in the pavilion and the audience filed out, fathers carrying sleeping children, old women clutching the arms of their husbands, teenagers hopping onto motorbikes to speed off into the night.

Behind the screen, the gamelan musicians stretched after their long session, some lighting up *kreteks*, clove-scented cigarettes, others gratefully accepting the dark, sweet coffee offered by their hosts. Wija, after returning his puppets to the box, assembled the band members who needed a lift and headed his van toward Sukawati. As he steered over the rough road, the gongs sounded a gentle tune all their own. At the side of road, villagers on their way home were caught in the headlights' glare; for just a moment, their long shadows played on village walls.

Troupes of Balinese dancers and musicians have toured North America and Europe fairly often. The companies are assembled by recruiting the best artists from many village groups. They do not represent a single permanent troupe established on the island. A good place to see a puppet-play is Ubud, the Balinese art colony, where there are weekly performances.

Another form of indigenous "theatre" is a martial art found in Sunda, a mountain area in western Java. An example was exhibited in New York at the Asia Society in 1977. Most of the performers – all men – were on their first journey abroad. Anna Kisselgoff reported that penca consisted of stylized movements

that could be incorporated within a definition of dance. The performers were named Did, Djadja, Holid and Abas Kohar and they frequently doubled as the musicians to create the extraordinary music that did so much to build up the tension and climaxes that made these formal duels as exciting as they were. It is easy to see elements of other Asian martial arts in penca – the chops and kicks of karate, the surprise moves of judo, the lexicon of gestures from Chinese wu-shu. Yet penca is described as an art of self-defense and, as in all such arts, the trick is not to be the aggressor, but to allow the opponent to defeat himself. "Know your enemy" is always a useful motto in such cases – and this Javanese school of self-defense is obviously rooted in character. In other words, there is a distinctly national flavor to penca – it has the same restraint, concentration and overt relationship between spirit and body that one sees, in a different way, in the Javanese court dances. Even the stance – turned out legs in a slight knee-bend – was echoed in the ensuing topeng performance.

Topeng, which was also viewed on the programme, is a masked dance-drama that is enacted in Sunda as well as in other parts of Indonesia. The sample given in New York is called Topeng Babakan. The dancers, virtuosos in emotional depth as well as technique, were named Sujana, Bulus and Sandrut. Ms Kisselgoff observed:

Topeng Babakan is theater-folk art derived from animal-worship rituals that is now refined into a sophisticated codified dance technique and a sharp distillation of character. Unlike the all-male Balinese *topeng* group presented by the Asia Society in 1973, the Sunda masked dancers stress solo work. It was the outstanding way that Sujana could create a whole world around each character that was astounding. Even more amazing was the onstage warmup he performed to "set the mood" before he donned a mask.

In each solo, the same typical double-jointed arm, with flicked out palms, acquired a different psychological tone. Bulus's comic characterizations provided their own depth, as did Sandrut's playing of a wayward knight. The musicians – a first-rate gamelan ensemble whose members' cries added to the gaiety – were an essential part of the performance.

Dance Indonesia, a troupe associated with the Jakarta Art Institute, visited the United States in 1984 and was greeted with acclaim at the American Dance Festival in Durham, North Carolina. Afterwards it performed for two evenings at the Asia Society in New York City. The company showed examples of dance and music from Sumatra, a region with its own distinct traditions. Also on the programme were two modern works that adhered to the Sumatran style.

The company, established in 1920 and directed by Wiwiek Sipala and Sardona W. Kusumo, is dedicated both to the preservation of age-old Indonesian dances and to the creation of new ones.

Jack Anderson, of the *New York Times* staff, attended the Durham Festival. Beholding the début of Dance Indonesia, he found that "the familiar and the strange were combined in a wonderful fashion". He commented:

What made the concert unusual was that unlike other Indonesia troupes that have featured Balinese and Javanese dances on their American tours, this group's dances derived entirely from Sumatra. Yet although Sumatran dance is comparatively unknown here, audiences acquainted with contemporary minimalist choreography would not have been baffled by Dance Indonesia's offerings.

Like many minimalist dances, these Sumatran dances emphasized patterns and were divided into units of activity, each of which stressed a certain type of movement that was systematically varied, developed or repeated in changing tempos. Moreover, the dancers helped make music as they moved by singing, clapping their hands and slapping themselves as if their bodies were percussion instruments.

The two-part program began with *Awan Bailu*, choreographed by Deddy Luthan and Tom Ibnur to the chanting of poetry plus traditional music for flute and percussion. The most interesting sections of this suite were dances based on movements derived from martial arts in which the performers repeatedly lunged forward and backward with outstretched arms, sometimes punctuating sequences by sudden sinkings to the ground.

In other episodes, the dancers twirled parasols, waved their arms while holding china plates in their palms and combined the martial-arts poses with the striking of tambourines. The work concluded with a processional in which dancers carried an image of Alberak, a mythological winged horse with a human face that is said to have carried Mohammed to the seventh level of heaven.

An even greater concern for rigorously patterned movement was evident in *Hhhhhuuuuu* choreographed by Nadine Dud and Marzuki Haas. This piece included dances in which the participants rhythmically hopped, stamped and slapped their sides while assembling in lines and circles.

However, the dancers were seated on their knees on the floor in the work's most amazing sequences. These contained breathtakingly intricate choreographic patterns involving swayings, clappings, finger-snappings, flingings of the arms and slapping of the floor and the dancers' knees and chests, all performed with dazzling rapidity and precision.

Because it is so little known here, it is unlikely that Sumatran dance has influenced American choreographers. Nevertheless, this work reminded many dancegoers of the use of patterned movement by such choreographers as Laura Dean and Charles Moulton. And the concert as a whole, which received a deserved ovation, suggested that choreographers the world over are fascinated by patterns.

11

VIETNAM AND CAMBODIA

The Second World War left Vietnam, the former Indo-China, divided between a Communist state in the north, with its capital in Hanoi, and a "democratic" country in the south, governed by a shrewd, anti-leftist political clique in its more sophisticated capital, Saigon. After a prolonged and surprisingly successful struggle against the French, who claimed Vietnam as a colony, the militant northerners eventually invaded the south. The ensuing jungle warfare, heightened by the involvement of American forces, ended with the latter's humiliating withdrawal, and soon afterwards a total victory for the Marxist guerrillas. Vietnam was now reunited and free, but following fourteen years of turbulence its economy was devastated and slow to recover.

Amid the destruction and impoverishment, its theatre was hardly likely to prosper. None the less, several forms of staging held the boards. Unfortunately, not much can be learned about it. It is assumed that exhortative plays were put on by both sides to support the war effort. At the end of hostilities the new Vietnam was closed to foreigners for a considerable period of time. On a Far Eastern tour on behalf of the United Nations in 1979, Secretary General Waldheim and his entourage were entertained in Hanoi. They were invited to a light variety show made up of dancers, acrobats and singers, a programme devoid of any obvious political content.

In 1985 a *New York Times* correspondent was able to pay a brief visit to Hanoi and Saigon, the latter once-lively capital by now renamed to Ho Chi Minh City and reduced to provincial status. He reported that the runaway hit of the theatrical season in both places was *Me and Us*, which he found to be "a satire on petty-minded bureaucrats who get in the way of progress. Tickets, like everything else, are for sale on the black market. There are reports that the company is looking for a bigger theatre. The play, by L. Quang Yu, got by the censors, the knowledgeable say, because it is essentially in line with criticisms made by Hanoi's economic pragmatists, who have been in the ascendancy since a party meeting in June. The play, which originated in Ho Chi Minh City (where it won an award) and has been televised nationally, ridicules the sycophancy of party officials, make-work jobs, endless political meetings and ritualistic jargon. Audiences seem to empathize with the tragic hero who is clobbered by the system for showing initiative. As a line in the play put it: he was 'wrong to be right too soon.'"

A few months later, in 1986, Barbara Crossette sent the *New York Times* a fuller picture of the capital's stage attractions:

In the cold of Winter Hanoi is often silent after sundown, with little more than the ring of bicycle bells or the clang of a streetcar to compete with the muffled conversations or coughing of unseen people in dark courtyards.

At night the old street lamps are kind to the city, powdering its aging but still beautiful face with a golden glow. Life moves indoors: to theaters, movie houses, video or dance clubs, coffee bars and small restaurants hidden from view at the tops of stairs off passageways between narrow houses.

While the Vietnamese are able to find all kinds of evening entertainment, foreigners who live here sometimes complain that the secrecy of Vietnamese life seems to extend to a reluctance to advertise its cultural joys.

One recent night at Hanoi's new culture center, a Kennedy Center-style complex built with Soviet help, people were being turned away from the season's most talked-about production because it was sold out.

The musical play tells the story of an Amerasian boy abandoned by his rich South Vietnamese mother because he is black – abandoned, that is, for thirteen years, until she finds that he, the son of an affair with "Charles Smith," could be her ticket to the United States.

The play, titled *Doi Dong Sua Me*, or, roughly translated, *Two Streams of Mother's Milk*, is a tear-jerker; a foreigner who asked to see it was warned by an interpreter that is would be "very emotional." The sniffles of the audience of 1,200 (plus five in armchairs in the aisle and some children on laps) proved him right.

The Amerasian boy, played by a Vietnamese actor in minstrel blackface and curly wig, was dropped into the cradle of a saintly village teacher and her understanding husband, whose own baby, a girl, is taken away by the influential Saigon colonel's wife. As the play gets under way, the boy is entering his teens and does not want to leave his village "mother."

"Who am I?" he cries when told he is really the son of an American soldier and a city lady in silk and jewels he does not recognize. "Where should I go now?"

For a stranger to Vietnam's long process of building trust and understanding between north and south, the play is fascinating. Its South Vietnamese setting and style allow for lavish costumes, beautifully made up women and dapper men in leisure suits, Panama hats and sunglasses.

"You must be from Saigon" is a line that brings down the house. The audience seems to enjoy not only the sights but also the southern Vietnamese songs that punctuate the drama. There is a live band in the wings.

But the play is also full of subtle messages. The southerners, if buffoons, are not entirely evil. "After re-education, I feel better about the humanitarian policy of the new regime," the former colonel says.

There are other interesting things to see and do in Hanoi – if the visitor can find them. . . . Not far away, at the French-built opera house, the curtain has just come down on a performance of *Swan Lake* by a new Russian-inspired Vietnamese ballet corps.

A ticket for a four-seat box (with its velvet rail intact) went for less than fifty cents. There was no program; a woman in a snow white *ao dai* stepped forward to read a synopsis of the plot – and the names of all the dancers and musicians – from several pieces of paper that shook in her hand.

The orchestra may have attacked the Tchaikovsky overture as if it had been written by Mahler, and the piano needed tuning. But the young dancers, faced with a house more than half empty, performed their task with enthusiasm and grace.

At a lull in the music the voice of a large man whom a visitor took to be an Eastern European talent scout rose from a front-row mezzanine seat. "I must emphasize that if we do the cultural exchange," he said in English to his Vietnamese hosts, "they must absolutely stay for two full years."

At intermission, there was a jarring note from the world outside. A couple of visitors who tried to stroll on the plaza in front of the opera house found all the doors of the building closed and padlocked.

"It's the Chinese," a guard said mysteriously. "We are afraid of Chinese mines. You know several years ago they put explosives in cinemas. We can't take chances here."

The nation's curtain seemed about to be lifted for Westerners, however. The *New York Times* announced in May 1986 that three American stage artists, the director Thomas Bird, the acclaimed mime Bill Irwin and the writer–performer Spalding Gray, had been given Vietnamese visas to explore what they hoped might be a cultural exchange between the two peoples. Their itinerary was to encompass both Hanoi and Ho Chi Minh City for about ten days. Bird, a veteran of the Vietnam War, had twice before returned to that still hostile country as a member of unofficial delegations that discussed such issues as the havoc wrought there by the deadly chemical Agent Orange and the whereabouts of still unaccounted-for American prisoners of war. The three visitors were on the look-out for troupes of music fans and actors who might be invited to appear at Joseph Papp's Public Theater in New York. For the trio to obtain their visas had taken four years. Bird predicted that Bill Irwin's non-verbal art, as displayed in his *Regard of Flight*, would be especially appreciated by the Vietnamese. "I'm told that one of the most popular things in Hanoi is the circus."

The hoped-for exchange did not occur. But a decade later, as the century neared its end, there was an official warming of relations between Vietnam and the United States, and the Asian country was once again welcoming tourists.

Cambodia (now Kampuchea) was noted chiefly in the foreign art world for its architectural master-piece, Angkor Wat, and its royal dance company, described in an earlier chapter in this book. When the nation became entangled in the Vietnam War, against its will, havoc descended on it. A Communist faction, the Khmer Rouge, carrying Marxism to a savage extreme, seized power; it was determined to wipe out all traces of capitalist and bourgeois culture. City dwellers were driven from their homes to take up agrarian pursuits, for which they were ill suited. Members of the professions and middle class were slaughtered. This dreadful regime lasted until a Vietnamese army invaded – the two countries were seldom on friendly terms – and drove the Khmer Rouge back towards the border of Thailand where its guerrilla fighters re-established themselves and continued to strike back; there were no intervals of peace.

The Royal Cambodian Ballet was an early victim. With the overthrow of Prince Norodom Sihanouk, the troupe's traditional protector, it was ousted from its breeze-swept pavilion in the sovereign's palace in 1970. Jennifer Dunning provides a vivid account of its fate over the next fifteen years:

Many of the dancers were killed. Some disappeared into the countryside, feigning illiteracy as they hid in forests or worked as farmers.

With the Vietnamese incursion of Cambodia in 1979, some survivors of the ballet company made their way to refugee camps in Thailand. There they found one another and began again. Several musicians had smuggled out instruments. Others made new ones. As they worked in the camps, refugees with training in Cambodian classical dance came to them. In six months, a group had been organized – dancers, singers, musicians and a mask-maker. Moved to a larger camp, they attracted a following among the refugees. Eventually, the group came to the attention of camp officials and was given priority status for migration.

Now settled in Wheaton, Maryland, a suburb of Washington, the group is struggling to learn English, to find jobs and to continue rehearsing and performing. Gifts from the National Endowment for the Arts, the Cafritz Foundation and the Asian Cultural Council, administered through the sponsoring National Council for the Traditional Arts, have enabled the company to buy material for costumes and masks.

The company made its New York début in 1981 at the American Museum of Natural History, which sponsored performances of many kinds of ethnic dance.

The programme opened with an invocation in which celestial nymphs are thought to descend and assume the spirits of temple carvings. Next came a candle dance based on traditional forms, choreographed and led by Nuth Rachana, one of the first male dancers to train for the hitherto all-female Royal Cambodian Ballet. The highlight was *Reamkev*, a Cambodian rendering of excerpts from the *Ramayana*, depicting "a timeless tale of love and subterfuge", in which gods and goddesses, a demon golden deer and demon monk battle monkeys and a fish queen.

Dunning wrote: "The performance is free. . . . There will be seventeen dancers, a far cry from the company of 100 that performed in their country through the 1960s. Now, the crowns worn by the god Rama and his brother Lakshmana are made of paper instead of gold, and the *kjoy*, or flute, in the musical ensemble is a converted bicycle shaft. But that the dances – and the dancers – have survived at all seems something of a miracle. The look of the dances – the one-legged stance, the fingers that curve back, the upraised arms and bent elbows – is reflected in the sculptures that adorn the temple and ruined monuments of Angkor. Like the dances, they are a product of the culture of the Khmer empire that flourished from the tenth through the fourteenth centuries. The serene faces – both carved and live – have witnessed a bloody history, from the 400-year 'tragic period' of the Cambodian arts, which followed the sacking of Angkor by the Siamese in 1431, through the 1979 invasion by the Vietnamese."

Of this occasion Anna Kisselgoff wrote in more detail:

One leaves it to the psychologists to determine why 2,000 people were turned away Sunday afternoon at the American Museum of Natural History, where the group gave a single New York performance. In 1971, when the fully professional Classical Khmer Ballet – the former Royal Cambodian Ballet – made its United States début at the Brooklyn Academy of Music, the theater was barely filled.

To say there has suddenly been an interest in a highly refined and stylized Asian dance tradition is to live outside the real world. History's recent lessons with regard to the Cambodian people have been of such epic horror that any aspect of their culture, brought into proximity with our own, cannot fail to attract attention.

It is within history's confines that one should view the musicians and dancers who offered such

a charming and well-chosen program on Sunday. They cannot be compared to the former Royal Ballet troupe, in that only about three of them studied or danced with that company. It is this core that
has trained the nonprofessionals in the troupe. Considering that it takes ten years to train such
dancers, they have done remarkably well.

It would be foolish, however, to expect to see the same delicate young women of 1971, who had
to be sewn into their costumes, so great was every detail important to their performance. Nor should
one look for the same extreme concentrations and polish in a serene fluid style that nonetheless
demands exceptional technique. Life does not offer these dancers the optimum conditions for such
perfection.

What the Khmer Classical Dancers do offer, however, is a perfectly clear outline of a distinct
and distinguished classical art. An episode from the Hindu epic, the *Ramayana*, was an especially
good illustration of how a well-known story is treated in a national style. The god Rama, here called
Ream (Yin Chamroeun) and his brother (Sek Puthyrith) rescue Rama's wife, Sita (Mom Kamel)
from the demon Ravanna (Nuth Rachna). The demon assumes a deer form, portrayed with great
beauty by a little girl, Chum Can Chivvy, and impersonates a monk (Kung Chantith). The monkey
gods (Heng Viphas, Sek Sophal) and their mermaid ally (Sin Ny) defeat the demon soldiers (Les
Vath, Van Thuon).

All these upheavals are conveyed in the most distilled of gestures, expressive movements and
sculptural poses. One has only to compare the masculine style of the Indian Kathakali dancers, who
tell the same story, to see the feminine core of the Cambodian style.

This style is epitomized in the typical pose of the dancer – fingers curving back, an elbow hyper-
extended – seen in *Apsara*, in which Sin Ny was a lovely, divine temple dancer, surrounded by
attendants. Mr Nuth Rachna's *Candle Dance*, more modern in conception, closed a program that
was always interesting and testimony to artistic concern.

The musicians were Yinn Ponn, Van Pok, Phing Sao, Sou Heurn, Prat Souzanni, U Vanna, Say
Sara and Poeuv Khatna.

The troupe gave the same programme in Philadelphia, Providence, Boston, Baltimore and Washington. They returned to New York in 1984 with a differing set of offerings at Carnegie Recital Hall.
On this occasion the emphasis was on musical numbers: there were six players of percussive and
stringed instruments, three singers and only three dancers.

In 1987 a dispatch from Thailand in the *New York Times* quoted a Prince Ranariddh saying with
"eloquent anguish": "A lot of people just talk about the war in Cambodia. But there is another

process: the Vietnamization of Cambodia. There are 700,000 Vietnamese civilians in Cambodia, and they are exploiting our soil. Even in the very small villages, there are already Vietnamese merchants. They buy rice from our people at very low prices and send it on trucks back to Vietnam. The Vietnamese have rewritten our bilateral history." He indicated that in every area of culture even more subtle changes were taking place that the foreigner did not appreciate. To illustrate this, he sketched on a notepad the evolution of classical dance students' costumes from a traditional Khmer to a Vietnamese style. "The Vietnamese have tried to Vietnamize us many times in history. But this time is more dangerous. They are supported by the very powerful Soviet Union. They also have an ideology, the Communist ideology, that is very powerful. France colonized us just economically. But now the colonization is political, physical. Maybe, and I hope not, this is the beginning of the end of the ethnic Khmer nation."

However, as the century neared its close, the Khmer Rouge finally admitted that its cause was hopeless; Pol Pot, its ruthless leader, died, and his fighters dispersed and surrendered. This led to feuding and further strife between the victors and the costly struggle for power went on. The Vietnamese army was expelled. The United Nations intervened and held elections in a half-successful attempt to restore order. For the moment, a semblance of tranquillity has been attained.

The troupe set up in exile has more or less vanished from view; there is a promise – or at least talk – of recreating a Cambodian Ballet in Phnom Penh, its new members taught by survivors of its tragically destroyed predecessor.

12

CHINA: FACING WEST

Several political events finally brought realistic prose drama to China's theatre, though traditional forms continued to dominate. In 1895 the Sino-Japanese War ended with a loss of "face" at the hands of an enemy far inferior in numbers, a defeat convincing the rulers of the Celestial Kingdom that much of crucial advantage was to be learned about Western science and technology. Long isolated and profoundly assured of their racial and cultural superiority, the Chinese were stung and shaken. The same humiliating lesson was taught them soon afterwards during the short-lived, futile Boxer Rebellion (1900) and much earlier by the Opium War (1839–40 and 1856) in which Chinese forces were routed by a far smaller British force. Obviously the Japanese borrowing of ideas from Europe and America ought to be emulated. Until now all other races were dismissed as "barbarians". Now the gates were flung open. Beginning to look outwards, China's intelligentsia quickly absorbed a range of foreign influences. Eager scholars and students travelled abroad.

The theatre not only reflected this attitudinal change but also significantly contributed to it. Peking opera and *kunqu*, another historic form of musical play, were hastily enlisted to inspire patriotism, a use to which they had often been put in the past. A number of pieces were staged that were designed to strengthen loyalty to the nation while also urging important reforms. The results were strange, quaint, often amusing. The very first attempts tended to echo worldwide events and draw locally helpful morals from them.

Such was the naïve and oblique approach of Wang Xiaonong (1858–1915) who chose Western subject-matter while adhering to the conventions of Peking opera and depicting a far-off conflict between Turkey and Poland that was intended to make a point immediately relevant to Chinese spectators. Another prolific writer who clung to traditional devices but sought to adapt them and incorporate a host of modern ideas was Huang Jilian (1836–1924).

William Dolby, in his *A History of Chinese Drama* (a principal source here), quotes extensively from *New Rome* by Liang Qichao (1850–1927) as an example of how playwrights of this period rushed to employ familiar genres to propagate what were to them new societal concepts. A disciple of Kang Yuwei (1838–1927), Liang headed this reform movement. In *New Rome*, Liang – who was also a novelist – suggested parallels between the troubles of contemporary China and those of Italy in the nineteenth century at the time of Garibaldi and Cavour and their Risorgimento. In the form of a *kunqu*, his play consists of a prologue and no fewer than forty acts, though only the prologue and a half-dozen of the acts were ever published. The action stretches from the Congress of Vienna (1814) to Garibaldi's triumphant entry into Rome. A singing Dante, astride a crane, is later joined by Shakespeare and Voltaire, all of whom appear in the prologue; the villain is Metternich, who sometimes quotes Confucius, Mencius and a number of classical Chinese poets rather than other European philosophers and authors. The principal characters resemble historic figures well known to all earnest Chinese students. In many ways this panoramic work shows the impress on Liang of Kong Shangren (1648–1718), a sixty-fourth-generation descendant of Confucius, whose forty-act musical play *Peach Blossom Fan* (1689 or 1694), dealing with extraordinarily complicated political intrigue in the declining Ming dynasty and portraying real historical figures, holds a high place in Chinese dramatic literature. In its own day *Peach Blossom Fan* had great immediacy for its imperial audience: the events it describes had occurred only five decades earlier, and Kong had gathered much of the detail from his older relatives who were involved in the incidents and knew some of the principal characters.

Liang's *New Rome* is similarly replete with music and poetry. In the prologue the author likens himself to Dante, who was not only a poet but a statesman. When the Italian announces that he is planning a trip to China "for a little recreation", a Voice Backstage is heard: "China is just a sick Oriental nation. Why do you want to go there, mighty immortal?" Dante says that while there he wants to see a play, *New Rome*, explaining, "Every word of its forty acts of lyrics and dialogue is a jewel or pearl or has literary lustre, and every syllable of its treatment of these past fifty years of political failures and successes is good medicine for human behavior." He is asked: "Why did this young man [i.e. Liang] suddenly compose such a drama out of the blue?" Dante replies: "How can one remain indifferent to things? . . . I imagine that this young man, having drifted aimlessly in strange and foreign lands, came to turn his glance upon his old homeland, and felt a burning grief for his country, which grief, since he lacked any practical means of restoring his country's might and prestige, he sought, through the trifling skills of the writer, to express in subtle and weighty words what would serve as a stimulus, a bell to call others forward. He is merely someone afflicted by the same 'malady' as I myself was of yore, a man of like mind and sympathies." Liang's choice of a medium for propaganda, however, was more often the novel.

In a new drama magazine, titled *Great Twentieth Century Stage* (1904), an article by Liu Yazi called for more plays relevant for the unhappy Chinese in the comparatively recent past of some Western countries. "What we must do now is press the blue-eyes and purple-beards [i.e. Westerners] into the garb of Jester Meng [i.e. Chinese drama], and set forth their history, so that the French Revolution, American Independence, the glorious revivals of Italy and Greece, and the cruel destruction of India and Poland may all be imprinted on the minds of our compatriots."

Dolby continues:

Other plays dealt with . . . the Russian occupation of Heilongkiang, Chinese emigrants in the United States, Napoleon in captivity . . . the Sino-Japanese War (with the Japanese as the heroes), and the loss of Annam to the French. Some plays were bitter attacks on the Quing court and regime, one of them depicting the Empress Dowager Cixi Taihou in the *chou* clown role; others advocated or attached the reformist movements, or recommended revolution. A theme of many plays was female emancipation. Many concerned heroines such as the revolutionary Qiu Jin, executed in 1907, who became a favorite subject. Some scripts condemned foot-binding, promoted women's rights and sang of female warriors. There were plays on the Boxer Uprising and Allied occupations, others con- demned Chinese traitors or extolled all manner of native heroes, recent and ancient, including military men and officials prominent in various Chinese dynasties, who had resisted the Jurcheds of the Jin, the Mongols of the Yuan, and the Manchus who founded the Qing. A topic considered of vital interest was opposition to the use of opium.

Initially most of these works stayed within the revered and accepted forms, but gradually some were – to borrow Dolby's term – "mongrel", departing in one aspect or another from age-old and long-observed conventions of stagecraft.

Plays that completely rejected the classical style and used modern themes and prose dialogue – even colloquial speech – finally came on stage in 1907. They might be translations from Japanese scripts already in Western formats, or translations from American and European successes. These were designated as *huaju* (or *hua-chü*). They found ready acceptance due to the growing interest in all aspects of Western culture, and they also had the virtue of novelty, always an attraction in theatre. The intelligentsia felt that only by borrowing from foreigners could China renew itself and regain its for- mer pre-eminence. Japan demonstrated how this could be accomplished by a people who were ready to welcome change and sponsor what was fresh and progressive.

Shanghai was where this movement finally gained impetus. The huge, thriving port city, with an enclave of foreigners, also boasted a number of colleges, some of them run by missionaries. The first step, however, was taken by a group of Chinese students of fine arts in Tokyo. Guided by Fujisawa Asajiro (1866–1917), a Japanese actor, they organized a theatre group, the Spring Willow Society.

Experimenting, they staged one act of Dumas *fils*'s scandalous Parisian hit *Camille* (*La Dame aux camélias*), which had become accessible in a Japanese translation. The performance was given by an all-male cast. Later the same year (1907), they produced a five-act offering, *Black Slave's Cry to Heaven*, their own adaptation of Harriet Beecher Stowe's *Uncle Tom's Cabin*. The Stowe novel had been translated into classical Chinese by Lin Shu (1852–1924), who had carried out the same task with the novel by Dumas *fils*. The students treated the Stowe text freely, to have it more effective on the stage. They rightly counted on its theme, oppression by whites, to appeal to an Oriental audience, which at first was largely made up of Chinese students in Japan. One member of the cast was Ouyang Yuqian (1889–1963), later to enjoy notice himself as a dramatist.

Discussing these two pioneer ventures, Edward M. Gunn enlarges on why the students chose them: "*Camille* was a Western equivalent of traditional tales about courtesans who enjoyed nurturing their young admirers but stood aside, even at sacrifice to themselves, when their lovers were ready for more responsible and respectable roles in society. *Uncle Tom's Cabin* was intended to speak more to the theme of the ethnic Han Chinese determination to overthrow the Manchu minority regime and establish a Chinese republic."

The Spring Willow Society stayed active, putting on one-act plays from France and Poland, followed – in 1909 – by *Hot Blood*, a full-length work adapted by a Japanese dramatist from Victorien Sardou's French melodrama, *La Tosca*. About this time a second amateur drama group, the Remarkable Life Society, was established in Tokyo.

Word of the success of *Black Slave's Cry to Heaven*, reaching Shanghai, prompted emulation there and in other Chinese cities. A radical politically oriented ensemble, the Evolution Troupe, consisting of professional actors, was founded by Ren Tianzi in 1910 to present works favouring an armed uprising; the company lasted only two years. (A revolution led by Sun Yat-sen did occur in 1911, though it failed to achieve its hoped-for goals.) The pace of new theatre was accelerated. A host of modern drama groups sprang up in Shanghai, Peking, Suzhou and elsewhere, though many were similarly short-lived. In 1912 several former members of the Spring Willow Society headed by Lu Jingruo relocated in Shanghai, calling their enterprise the Spring Willow Theatre. During its brief existence, a span of about three years, the reconstituted Spring Willow group offered a repertoire of eighty-one works, most of them full length. They comprised a variety of genres; some were based on Chinese tales past and current, others were adaptations or direct translations of foreign plays. Only one was a truly original, native script. A number were improvisations, merely sketched but never fully written out; they were known as *mubiaoxi*, "act-outline plays". After Lu Jingruo's death in 1915 the company fell apart. Another literary group, the Enlightenment Society, appeared in Shanghai in 1912, its name borrowed from the term applied to the new scripts of this early period, *kaimingxi* (i.e. "enlightened plays"), though such works were also referred to as *wenmingxi* ("civilized plays").

A majority of the troupes that flourished ephemerally in these years came into being at the colleges; a partial compilation lists translations of English and French classics – Shakespeare's *Merchant of Venice*, for one. Some of the groups toured Japan with their productions. A frequent source for them was Japan, where Western-style dramas were more popular and translations more available. The students found it easier to render the Japanese versions into Chinese than to go directly to European texts. Sometimes a work went through three metamorphoses, from its original language into Japanese, then into Chinese vernacular, and finally into a classical tongue; or they were performed in English or French. Eventually the ill-feeling that evolved between Japan and China discouraged this tendency and diminished the sway that Japanese theatre practices had been exerting over Chinese intellectuals.

Innovations brought about during this phase of Chinese theatre were the inclusion of women in the casts, the wearing of contemporary costumes, occasionally even for historical dramas, and the use of realistic scenery and of curtains to divide the play into acts. In historical works, too, the costuming tended to be more accurate.

By 1917 the movement began to slow. Various explanations for this are given: poor training and lack of talent among the mostly amateur performers, and stories of off-stage immorality on the part of the actors and directors. Yet another cause of the decline of the *huaju* was the advent of film, a serious competitor. This new medium drew away from the stage many of the better actors, and a considerable number of serious-minded theatre ensembles were disbanded.

A revival followed quickly, however, as the hordes of young Chinese who had gone abroad to study returned and brought a fresh perspective. Another prompting was the May the Fourth Movement (1919), a political and cultural response to the Paris Peace Treaty ending the First World War. Once again the trend was towards "colloquial, analytical, Western-modern literature" which included the *huaju*. Though films reduced the audience for the live stage, they were silent and thus of help in getting the public used to dramas that incorporated no music and were dependent wholly on printed titles. Spectators developed a liking for plain dramas, and appreciated that the spoken speech of the *huajus* had by contrast more impact.

Another change had occurred. Audiences at traditional performances were often offered only excerpts – favourite passages – from classic works, a lengthy programme of fragments. But now full-length plays with integrated stories were more often presented, as in the West.

What was lacking was good original Chinese scripts. Many of the offerings were not from written texts, and few of the scripts were ever published, so little is known about them. The best professional acting troupes also had a strongly commercial bias. Improvement began to set in, partly at the urging of the playwright Chen Dabei, who had been associated with the *wenmingxi*; new amateur dramatic societies took up the cause of a more up-to-date and literate theatre. They undertook the staging of the advanced European and American dramatists: Bjornson, Strindberg, Ibsen, Pinski, Wilde, Chekhov, Shaw. The translations were more exact than previous ones, and of better literary quality.

Increasingly the new theatre people were scornful of classic Chinese drama and its archaic conventions. They viewed it as having no more serious purpose than light entertainment, whereas they looked upon the stage as a place for the dissemination of ideas. The manifesto of the Popular Drama Society (1921), cited by Dolby, embodies this concept: "The time is past when people took theater-going as [mere] recreation. The theater occupies an important place in modern life. It is a wheel rolling society forward. It is an X-ray searching out the roots of society's maladies. It is also a just and impartial mirror, and the standards of everybody in the nation are stripped stark naked when reflected in this great mirror, that allows no slightest thing to remain invisible. . . . This kind of theater is precisely what does not exist in China at present, but is what we, feeble though we are, want to strive to create."

Brave words! But the dazzling and stylized stage was still preferred by the masses of theatre-goers and also by a majority of the wealthy and ruling classes. The *huaju* was only "quantitatively a drop in the ocean at this time", appealing largely to young intellectuals who had been exposed to Western schooling. Dolby: "They were also people self-consciously concerned with promoting bold ideas for social change. The loftiness of their mission no doubt seemed to them to contrast with the often earthy and sensual entertainments of the then current traditional drama, and with the bawdy and homosexual atmosphere of the old theater world." Reflecting their studies abroad, these progressives often sound more Western than Chinese in their writings. Shaw was particularly esteemed by this élite.

Besides Ouyang Yuqian and Chen Dabei, who gathered their own acting troupes, several authors of socially conscious *huaju* came to the fore in the 1920s: Ding Xilin (1893–1974), Guo Moruo (1892–1978), Hou Yalo. They were especially concerned with family situations, attacking basic and age-old values and customs. To present these iconoclastic plays, theatres were founded by Xiong Foxi (1900–1965), Mao Dun (1896–1981) and Zheng Zhenduo (1898–1958). In 1922 Pu Boying established the Life Art Drama Technical School, and the renowned poet Wen Yiduo (1899–1946) took charge of a drama department at the Peking Fine Arts Technical School (1925). The equally noted playwright Tian Han (1898–1968) organized the South China Society under the auspices of a film company.

At the same time an effort was now made to separate the newer forms of more realistic *huaju* from the *wenmingxi* – the earlier so-called "civilized plays" – which often included *muwaixi*, "beyond-the-curtain sketches" performed in front of the curtain to keep the audience interested and patient during scene changes. These intervals at the *wenmingxi* were also utilized to let a narrator clarify the plot by addressing the spectators directly. Replacing such works, the more recent and more integrated *huaju* were alluded to as *zhen xinju*, "truly new drama". Eventually the *wenmingxi* were banned by the Chinese Republic because they touched on too many sensitive political issues. The genre came back later as a form of vaudeville.

In 1919 the American-educated philosopher and scholar, Hu Shih (1891–1962), published an article expressing the need for a more frank and thoughtful Chinese theatre. Steeped in Ibsenism, he advocated plays that would provide critical examinations of the roots of social problems. Such scripts might be unpleasant and have unhappy endings, but that would be because they faced truth and reality, as Chinese opera seldom if ever did. He borrowed many of his critical insights from Shaw's well-known book on Ibsen. Hu Shih argued that a play should be well structured, have a logical time-span and action, explore its characters in detail and individualize them. The author should be objective, almost scientifically detached. In classical opera, only types were portrayed and then broadly. Hu Shih's essay carried weight as a statement of what the new *huaju* should be. Gradually he won an international reputation for his contributions to Chinese culture. He served for four years as his country's ambassador to the United States (1938–42), and later as President of Peking University, and afterwards as President of the Academia Sinica in Taiwan.

Though hardly aspiring to be a playwright, he illustrated some of his ideas by creating a very brief *huaju*, *The Greatest Event in Life*. Miss Tien Ya-Mei is anxious to marry Mr Ch'en, a character we never see. Her mother consults in turn an oracle at the Temple of the Goddess Kuan Yuan and a blind fortune-teller, both of whom advise against the match. Calculating by the girl's horoscope and that of her intended bridegroom, the fortune-teller warns:

If snake and tiger marry and mate,
The male will the female then dominate.
If pig and monkey you try to blend,
There's certain to be an untimely end.

Accordingly, Mrs Tien forbids the marriage. Her husband is scornful of soothsayers, however, and rebukes her for being superstitious. "This business of plaster bodhisattvas and fortune-telling is all just a swindle." The mother insists that at least this once a seer's advice is needed, since a girl's marriage is the greatest event in her life. Tien Ya-Mei claims that she has known her betrothed for many years, and clearly he and she are compatible. A tearful quarrel ensues. To the girl's astonishment, her father, too, is opposed to the marriage, though for a different reason. A rationalist in some ways, he nevertheless has a hidebound respect for social custom. He has traced back the name Ch'en and found that at one point in the past, 2,500 years ago, it was identical with Tien. Consequently, his daughter and her chosen young man are members of the same clan and cannot be joined in matrimony. The elders of the clan would severely disapprove of any such match. Tien Ya-Mien cannot believe that her father is serious, but he proves to be obdurate. What is more, Mr Ch'en comes of a wealthy family, and people might think that her father violated the laws of the clan in order to acquire a share of their riches.

With both parents arrayed against her, Tien Ya-Mei's outlook is bleak. But the ardent Mr Ch'en is impatiently waiting in his car outside the house and sends a message to Ya-Mei by a sympathetic houseservant. "This matter concerns the two of us and no one else. You should make your own decision." The girl is swayed by this challenge. While her parents are at lunch, she slips out the door and elopes with her beloved. When the elder Tiens discover her gone and read Mr Ch'en's note, they are aghast. (The English translation of this playlet is by Edward M. Gunn, who includes it in his anthology, *Twentieth-Century Chinese Drama*. The idea for Hu Shih's piece came from Ibsen's *A Doll's House*.)

Similarly schooled in the United States was Hung Shen (1894–1955). His goal as a student was to work in either ceramics or engineering, but once abroad he was attracted to the theatre and delved into Western literature and drama. He was especially impressed by the early plays of Eugene O'Neill and like that imaginative young dramatist attended Professor George Pierce Baker's Harvard workshop in playwriting, the first of its kind anywhere. Coming back to China, Hung Shen was appalled at the devastation and suffering caused by the incessant struggles between regional warlords. This led him to write *Zhao Yangwang* (or *Yama Chao*; 1922), which in some aspects resembles O'Neill's *The Emperor Jones*; it has a parallel structure and uses similar Expressionistic techniques. The title alludes to Yama, the legendary King of Hell. As in O'Neill's propulsive drama, the protagonist has a balance of admirable and repellent traits. In other ways the script differs from its model, principally in that the focal figure, Zhao Ta, is not a Jungian symbol of atavistic impulses in "civilized" mankind, compulsions lingering and universal in modern psyches. Instead, Zhao has been malevolently shaped and warped by harsh social conditions. Hung Shen is intent on pointing out the ignorance, injustice and dreadful corruption of the times. Chinese adaptations of foreign dramas tended to do this, stress the importance of social forces rather than attribute significant behaviour to innate human drives. For a good many of the foreign-educated, leftist-leaning *huaju* playwrights this was a paramount theme.

Zhao Ta is an orderly in service to a Battalion Commander stationed in a military camp in a deserted village. The time is winter in the early 1920s. It is very cold. The soldiers, who have not been paid for months, are hungry and bedraggled. The Commander lives high and gambles at mah-jong nightlong. He is admired by Zhao Ta, who has a rather shady past but is determined to straighten out his way of life. A fellow soldier, Lao Li, learns that the Commander has received funds, thousands of dollars, to pay his men and has appropriated the money for his own feckless purposes, chiefly to pay his gambling debts. Lao Li suggests that he and Zhao Ta discover its whereabouts, plunder it and desert. For a time Zhao Ta resists this proposal and tries to maintain faith in the Commander. He is finally convinced that Lao Li is telling the truth and discovers where the diverted funds are hidden. Angry and disenchanted, Zhao Ta finds them and is pocketing a share, intending to take flight, but as he is rifling the cash box the Commander suddenly returns and blocks the way. Panic-stricken, Zhao Ta shoots him. (Later it is revealed that the wound is superficial.)

In the second act, which is an extended monologue, Zhao Ta, trying to make his escape, finds himself in the freezing darkness of a forest. He hears drums beating, the sound of the Commander's men pursuing him. He loses his way. Exhausted, he staggers on, his mind unravelling. He mistakes the shapes of trees for ghosts: a wounded friend whom he betrayed and buried alive at a General's order; the bloodied Commander. He is frightened and defiant. He fires his revolver at these spectres, using up more of his remaining cartridges. Pausing, he spreads the money on the ground to count it and projects how he will spend it. Confused, he runs on, the ominous drums of his pursuers always louder. He sobs, rages, promises himself that he will give away the stolen money for charitable causes. He confronts another ghost, of a gambler who long ago misled him and whom he killed. He expends another cartridge on the fancied shape. He relives cruel scenes of looting and rape in which he had participated. Burning with fever, he strips off his clothes, then recovers and puts them on again. He wastes two more shots. Recalling other past shameful incidents, he prays for forgiveness. Certain historical scenes are symbolically enacted, among them the Boxer Rebellion; he shouts a tirade at "foreign devils". He fires his last cartridge and hurls away the revolver. The drumming grows ever closer. He holds up a tree branch as a talisman, dances and sings, prostrates himself on the ground and intones a spell, foams at the mouth. Legendary figures, in tatters and holding banners with many inscriptions, surround him.

Overtaken by soldiers at daybreak, he has travelled in a circle and is again at the edge of the woods. He flees into the trees, but is fatally shot. His body is brought out.

The hypocritical Lao Li pronounces an eloquent eulogy over the corpse of Zhao Ta and offers to stay behind alone to bury him. When this occurs, he seizes the opportunity to filch the money that Zhao Ta had concealed in a sack on his body.

(Readers familiar with *The Emperor Jones* will recognize how closely paraphrastic this is.)

Though the eulogy spoken by the cynical Lao Li is doubtless meant to be construed as ironic, the author uses it to offer explanations and excuses for his protagonist's criminal behaviour. He is likened to the downtrodden and exploited soldiers who have killed him.

Dear Yama, in the end your death didn't go unnoticed. Your comrades in orderly formations are sending you off with drums beating. Did the Commander treat you well? Of all the men in the camp, you're the only one really sincere, and really foolish. You! Your heart was too bad for you to be a good man, and too good for you to be a bad one. But good or bad, you weren't at home being either. I watched you running helter-skelter. Wherever you went, you found trouble. In your whole life, you never had a single good day. [*Tears in his eyes*] Today only Lao Li is here to bury you. [*Pause*] Lao Li is begging you to help him. Is it okay if I borrow the money around your waist for my traveling expenses? [*He cannot bear to act, stops a moment, but ends by untying the knotted handkerchief around Zhao Ta's waist, and then wraps the handkerchief around Zhao Ta's head.*] Brother Zhao Ta, if you don't turn into a ghost, then that's that. But if you do have a spirit, then protect me as I cross the forest to go home! [*Dragging the body, he turns his head and glances at the sky.*] It's getting light. [*He walks into the forest.*]

[Translation: Carolyn T. Brown]

(Spellings of names of dramatists, titles of works and places differ in available sources, and dates tend to be slightly uncertain. It is due to variations in speech from region to region and to linguistic reforms.)

Hung Shen's use of Expressionistic devices had a considerable impact. He was not the first to exploit them, but he handled them most skilfully. A number of other playwrights hurried in his train to embrace them, but the spectators' baffled and generally negative response to *Zhao Yangwang* was a warning that one could not go too far from ancient traditions or realism; the public was not ready for that much experimentation.

A feature of Hung Shen's avant-garde play that particularly displeased audiences was the lack of women characters. In his own words, the public's opinion was "unanimously that I was mentally deranged" to be against having men enact roles of the opposite sex. Overall, the author, who had read as much of Freud as of Shaw, deplored transvestitism on stage. He thought the practice decadent and unhealthy. His fellow-playwright Ouyang Yuqian suggested that he join the recently founded Shanghai Drama Association (1921). As a member of this group, which had a comparatively long life for a *huaju* company, a dozen years to 1933, he produced two works, casting the first with actresses in female roles and in the other, assigning similar roles to males, as was traditional. Dolby: "Perhaps he loaded his dice, but anyway it had the desired effect. The audience for the most part found the mincing affectations and falsettos of the actors utterly ludicrous after witnessing the actresses' display of natural femininity, and following that, the habit of impersonating females 'died a natural death' in the company."

Another of his scripts, "sympathetic to the peasant", is *Hsiang-Tao-Mi* (1933).

As a director, Hung Shen put on an exemplary performance of Oscar Wilde's *Lady Windermere's Fan*, setting high standards of production that inspired his contemporaries. (Many of the plays that were being mounted by commercial companies were far-fetched melodramas and vulgar comedies fashioned by hacks. In too many offerings, too, the actors tended to posture and declaim, and the staging lacked artistic unity.) He adapted Ibsen's *A Doll's House* and Shakespeare's *Merchant of Venice* with success.

His talents were lent to the film world as well. For two decades he was professor of literature and drama at several of Shanghai's universities.

His staging of *Wu-k'kuei ch'iao* (*Wu-k'uei Bridge*; 1930) was much praised, as were several other of his productions of Marxist-oriented plays. Increasingly, his political sympathies had moved leftwards. During the Second World War, with China once more desperately arrayed against Japan, he joined other writers and actors in using the stage to whip up self-sacrificial patriotic fervour. He elected to stay in China after it became Communist, as did many of his friends and co-workers, though his prominence was gradually diminished. He continued active in drama and film-making during the remaining 1940s. In 1953, as the Korean War raged, he and a number of well-known theatre figures were sent to the combat zone by government order to mingle with soldiers and absorb some of their feelings and thoughts as part of a "levelling process for intellectuals".

After Hung Shen's death two years later, a collection of his scripts was published.

Somewhat different was the career route taken by Ouyang Yuqian (1889–1962), Hung Shen's colleague who as a student in Japan had been a member of the original Spring Willow Society and in the casts of *Uncle Tom's Cabin* and *Camille*. Returning to China, he excelled as a female impersonator in Peking opera. He also participated in dramatic and film ventures. His aim was to meld traditional forms of opera and modern Western techniques. He joined the People's Dramatic Association, which flourished briefly in the 1920s and where he and his fellow-workers were inspired by Romain Rolland's theory of a "people's theatre", one that would be infused with "joy", "energy" and "intelligence", while it shed the long-formulated attributes of "bourgeois" and "aristocratic" theatre. Ouyang Yuqian thought that a reformed Peking opera, based on popular legends and filled with the conventional "frenzied" action, was the best medium for reaching the masses. The People's Dramatic Association did not last long enough to attain its goal, but Ouyang Yuqian persisted in his quest. As Dolby phrases it, the effort was to put new wine in old bottles, as a means of reaching and educating the peasants, to whom the traditional opera was familiar and congenial. Won over to the Communist cause, and increasingly loyal to it, Ouyang Yuqian was later appointed administrator of several government-fostered theatre enterprises and became a recognized force in the realm of entertainment and propaganda. Besides writing and acting for the stage and film, he directed some of his own plays and those of others. Like Hung Shen, he was a member of the All-China Drama-World Resist-the-Enemy Federation during the Second World War.

Typical of the hybrid genre that he espoused is his *P'an Chin-lien*, which dramatizes incidents from a classic novel set in the Northern Sōng dynasty (960–1127), and which in turn makes use of legendary characters and events of that remote era. (English translations of the novel have come from the pens of J.H. Jackson, *The Water Margin*, and Pearl Buck, *All Men Are Brothers*. Several other novels and traditional operas have borrowed the same material.) Ouyang Yuqian first wrote his version as a "spoken drama" and published it in 1928; he then decided to add operatic music to it, as well as conventional costumes and settings. He elected to play the leading feminine role, that of a "nymphomaniacal villainess". The work progresses in short scenes, in the episodic form of a traditional opera.

Chang Ta-Hu is rich, old, ugly, corrupt and politically powerful. He has several concubines, one of whom, the desirable P'an Chin-lien, resists his attentions. To punish her, he marries her off to the aged, dwarfish, physically repulsive cake-vendor Wu Ta. Soon Wu Ta dies, and gossip has it that P'an Ch'in-lien, who has taken a lover, Hsi-men Ch'ing, has been responsible for her husband's death. The nettled and lustful Chang Ta-Hu schemes to get her back and engages his resourceful servant Kao Sheng in the task. Together they begin to gather evidence by threatening and suborning witnesses, especially the late Wu Ta's landlady and the coroner who had been summoned to view the corpse.

P'an Chin-lien is bored with her lover, Hsi-men Ch'ing, but values his brute strength. She perceives in him a protector against her former master. To her landlady she complains about the lot of women, how unjustly they are treated. Her views are quite feminist and strongly expressed, and sometimes she voices a wish to die. When Kao Sheng comes with a message from Chang Ta-Hu, he is roughly treated by the two women.

P'an Chin-lien is enamored of her brother-in-law, the brave and rigidly moralistic and idealistic captain Wu Sung. Known for his feats as a "tiger-killer", he is contemptuous of the corrupt high office-holders whom he must serve. He shows no interest in her. Away at the time of his brother's death, he now hears rumours of P'an Chin-lien's infidelity. He suspects her of having murdered Wu Ta and goes about trying to gather proof of her deed. He frightens the coroner, Ho Chiu, into confessing that he was bribed by Hsi-men Ch'ing to misrepresent the facts of Wu Ta's death, which was caused not as claimed by a heart ailment but by the administration of poison. Ho Chiu was afraid to expose the truth. He shows Wu Sung the silver coins given him by Hsi-men Ch'ing and some blackened bones from Wu Ta's cremated corpse – their hue indicates poisoning. Wu Sung obtains further confirmation from Yun Ko, a young peddler, that P'an Chin-lien was a faithless wife and that her husband was aware of her affair with Hsi-men Ch'ing.

Wu Sung files a charge with the local magistrate, but the official has been bribed by Hsi-men Ch'ing and dismisses the case. Set on revenge, Wu Sung invites guests to a belated funeral ceremony for his brother. Before the assemblage he accuses P'an Chin-lien of murder. Some of the guests, nervous, beg to leave, but Wu Sung insists that they stay. P'an Chin-lien puts the blame for the crime on Chang Ta-Hu, who forced her to marry the horrible Wu Ta, and also on Wu Sung himself, who has always spurned her advances and by whom she is still obsessed. He tells them that he has already killed and decapitated Hsi-men Ch'ing and, opening a bag, lets the adulterer's head roll forth. Wu Song lifts his knife against P'an Chin-lien, who opens her robe, bares her breast and embraces him. "You love me? I . . . I . . ." His knife plunges into her, and she falls. He stares at her corpse, drops the knife. All are struck dumb.

The play is short and has an upsurging tension. Some of the dialogue carries sexual innuendo and occasionally is truly coarse. In Ouyang Yuqian's treatment of this age-old story, as Edward M. Gunn points out, the heroine is transformed from "the psychopathic, self-destructive figure of tradition into a woman who, however wanton, is an intelligent, passionate rebel against the harsh, conventional morality represented at its best and worst by the famous warrior Wu Sung, ultimately confounded as well as outraged by her. She is drawn to Wu Sung as a hero who stands above convention. Yet he does so only to reinforce convention. Once doomed to failure, she would rather meet destruction at his hands than be buried by the society she despises. Here is something approaching the full-fledged romantic transvaluation of a classic symbol of evil, now seen to transcend its conventional moral context."

Among Ouyang Yuqian's later efforts was a production of the Soviet melodrama *Roar China!* by Sergei Tretiakov.

Another of the interesting playwrights of this period, Tian Han (1898–1968) studied medicine in Japan. He found himself attracted to the new theatre movement that had its start there. He helped to establish the Creation Society. Back in China, he organized the Southern Society (Nanguo she) and began to turn out a considerable number of plays. Enrolling in the Communist Party in 1932, he fell foul of the rightist authorities along with others and was arrested that year.

After 1949, when the Party's army defeated the Nationalists and the People's Republic came into being, Tian Han, his freedom completely restored, enjoyed prominence and influence for a stretch of years, heading various cultural enterprises as a leading propagandist. In 1951, however, he was among the dramatists sent to share the soldiers' hardships at the snow-bound front during the Korean War, when China's "volunteers" opposed an American expeditionary force.

Tian Han wrote for films as well as the stage. He set a new trend in plays for adaptations of the works of Guan Hanqing, especially with his new *huaju* piece *Guan Hanqing* (1959). Like many of his other scripts, this was composed to mark an important public event, a memorial congress in Shanghai paying homage to the thirteenth-century classical Yuan dramatist on what was loosely the 700th anniversary of his death. As already mentioned, publication of Guan Hanqing's works and articles about him, a museum exhibition dedicated to him, and the début of Tian Han's fantastic play about him were features of the festivities.

In twelve scenes, *Guan Hanqing* observes the traditional structural requirements. The fierce devotion given by the playwright and his friends to just causes is vividly stressed. Historical details are incorporated into the action, but much of the detail and overall plot are Tian Han's inventions.

Guan is infuriated by the execution of an innocent young woman. A courtesan–actress, Pearl Curtain Beauty, urges him to write a stage-piece attacking the evil officials. This allows Tian Han to resort to a device familiar to twentieth-century dramatists, especially since Pirandello – though its origins are far earlier – the play-within-the play, in this instance *Injustice Done to Graceful Dou*, a work that is attributed to Guan Hanqing. Besides being an author, Guan Hanqing is a physician. He has successfully treated the mother of Akham, the Deputy Prime Minister of the harsh foreign conqueror Kublai Khan. In return for that cure he is able to gain freedom for a girl who against her will has been forced to serve in the Deputy Prime Minister's palace. Under pressure, toiling day and night, he finishes his script and stages it. It wins applause from a Chinese military leader, who orders Guan to revise it so that it may be shown before Akham and the Grand Chancellor Horikhoson, but the playwright is obdurate in his refusal to make changes. Akham, when he sees it, is displeased, halts the performance and has both Guan and Pearl Curtain imprisoned for their offence. He orders their beheading. Another actress in the company is sentenced to be blinded. Word reaches Guan in his cell that the hated Akham has been slain by the Chinese military commander. If he testifies falsely on behalf of Akham's adherents, Guan will be spared his head, but again he refuses. He contrives to have a "last" meeting with his beloved Pearl Curtain Beauty. But the political climate changes, and a petition bearing the names of 10,000 people asks leniency for the playwright and actress. Guan, unhappily exiled, bids farewell to his cherished Pearl Curtain Beauty and his close friends.

Dolby quotes a passage from scene seven in which Akham and his august visitor, the Grand Chancellor, are watching Guan's play and discussing it. Akham explains: "Deprived of their imperial Civil Service examinations under our dynasty, these Chinese with their modicum of education and book learning have no longer been able to rise to the top at one go by becoming junior or senior optimes [i.e. second-rankers] or what have you. So they've shifted their attentions to this line of activity. Actually, it's not such a bad thing, either. After all, doesn't his Imperial Majesty tell us to try and devise outlets for such people to dissipate their wits and talents? So I personally often come and listen to their baubles. For one thing, it provides a little amusement, and for another, it enables me to investigate what they are really thinking."

The Grand Chancellor concurs, and Akham adds: "But these little monkeys are devilish awkward to handle. They never rest content with their lot for a single moment. Always either saying how much better the past was than the present, or making roundabout insinuations. And even if you tell them not to do something, it only makes them all the more determined to do it. Didn't you hear just now how this play was getting in digs at us government officials."

The Grand Chancellor agrees: "Yes, indeed, I did notice it. He had some very weighty jabs at corrupt and venal officialdom. But how does that concern us, now?"

Akham exclaims: "You're too generous and fair-minded, Grand Chancellor. – If he's capable of abusing them, he's capable of abusing us, too."

The Grand Chancellor argues: "Let them have their bouts of abuse. It has certain advantages, helps to keep the administration trim."

Akham is not persuaded: "No, no, the one thing we can't do is let them talk. As soon as you loosen your grip on them, they'll be up in rebellion. Be no limit to what they might do! Terrible to imagine!" (Translator not cited)

It is easy to assume that Tian Han's comments had a contemporary relevance and that, like the hero of his play, he was daring in uttering them, however obliquely. The Communist authorities regarded the *huaju* movement with suspicion and often open hostility.

Guan Hanqing, enhanced by music, brightly evokes the Yuan era in which its story is laid. It is lightened by abundant good humour. In one of its versions the poet–hero and the singing actress are able to get together for a happy ending. The play enjoyed success and was made into a film. It encouraged other playwrights to choose ancient subjects and reincarnate the past and its values while infusing them with modern connotations.

On our shortened list of those who studied abroad and came back to introduce Western-style plays and be active in the transition from old to new is Ting Hsi-lin, who had spent time in England. Back in China, he lectured on physics at universities in Peking, Nanking and Tsingtao. He also became a member of the Academia Sinica and during the 1920s turned out a series of one-act plays lauded for their craftsmanship. Later, during the war with Japan, he completed two full-length works. His principal themes were the emancipation of women and the right of young people to choose their own marriage partner.

When the People's Republic was established, Ting Hsi-lin was appointed to several posts in political and cultural institutions and ceased his literary pursuits, which many believed to be a decided loss to the stage. His skill at construction had inspired other writers to follow his lead in preferring the "well-made" play, when that was still the most acceptable form in the Western theatre to which he had been exposed while overseas.

Typical of Ting Hsi-lin's output is his brief and trifling but neatly shaped *Oppression* (1925). A young man, an engineer, rents an apartment from the landlady's daughter, who accepts advance payment for it because he is a bachelor. When her mother learns of it she tries to return the deposit. With a young daughter, she wants only a married couple as tenants. The young man is adamant: he demands that he be allowed to move in; a shrill quarrel ensues. The mother sends for a policeman. While the would-be resident is left alone, a young lady arrives, weary, wet and bedraggled; it is raining heavily outside. She has just journeyed from Peking to take a job as a secretary with an engineering firm and urgently needs a place to stay. Having seen the landlady's advertisement, she has come to enquire about the rooms to let. The young man explains that he has already paid a deposit on them but gallantly offers to relinquish the apartment to her. He reveals that he works for the firm by which she has just been hired. When she learns of the landlady's insistence that the occupants be a wedded couple, she volunteers to pose as his wife. The deception is quite effective when the policeman appears, and the landlady relents, forced to apologize for her "error". At that point the curtain falls, leaving uncertain what is to be the future of the young man and the young lady.

The title is "mock-serious". Ting dedicated his little play to a friend whose futile search for an apartment during the previous winter had provided the subject. Unhappily, the friend died of cholera before the play was completed. Ting was moved to suggest in a dedicatory note that if his friend had shared the same good luck as the hero of this script, similarly meeting a sympathetic young lady with whom to resist " 'hand in hand' with you not only the 'oppression of the landed class' but also all sorts of bullying oppression in our society – I'm sure you wouldn't have died".

Impressed by what Ting Hsi-lin and others sought to do, fashioning realistic "well-made" plays, was Cao Yu (or Ts'ao Yu, both *noms de plume* for Wan Chai-po, b. 1910). His were to be the best-known and most applauded of all *huajus*, three of his scripts achieving an enduring popularity. Along with that, his work has been the subject of extensive criticism and seemingly endless analysis. Beyond question, he is considered to be the foremost dramatist of China's twentieth century.

His ancestral home is known to be Ch'ien-chang in Hupei province, but some details of his early life are elusive. His birthplace is thought to be the port city of Tientsin, where his father, a major general, commanded an army unit and the family dwelling was in the foreign concession. The sons were given a superior education. Even so, Cao Yu's boyhood was not happy. He was aware that his parents and elder brother lived indolently, "seldom arising before noon", while he himself was relegated to upbringing by a tutor. Later he told an interviewer, Yang Yü (1963), quoted by Christopher C. Rand: "That was a grim existence, and I hated it from the bottom of my heart. . . . Those surroundings made me a rather gloomy boy. My home and the world outside seemed so gray and hopeless that I detested them."

Happier moments came during visits to a local playhouse, which began for him at the age of three. His mother took him frequently to performances of Peking opera and local dramas, including stagings of the new *wenmingxi* (civilized drama). An avid reader of classical Chinese fiction and translations of foreign literature, he was particularly fond of the grotesque, the "macabre and diabolical".

He studied at the élite Nankai Middle School in Tientsin, where Western-style theatricals were favoured. A mere two years after the Spring Willow Society's first ventures in Japan, the Nankai School was putting on spoken dramas as an annual event. Cao Yu took roles in works by Ting Hsi-lin, Molière, Ibsen and Galsworthy – he is believed to have collaborated on a translation of the English playwright's *Strife*, though that text no longer exists.

At Tsinghua University near Peking, in addition to participation in college dramatics, he concentrated on learning foreign languages, among them English. On stage he essayed masculine and feminine characters. The custom of using men for female roles was still not entirely eradicated from Chinese versions of Western drama – above all in an all-male school. Cao Yu, with his slight physique, high voice, smooth complexion and perception of feminine grace, was chosen for roles such as Nora in Ibsen's *A Doll's House* (in which he had first played at Nankai). Moreover, since he was already experienced, he was selected while still not a graduate to tutor younger dramatic art students at Tsinghua.

During his first three years at the college he tried his hand at a translation of *Romeo and Juliet*. He discovered, pored over and absorbed in depth the works of Aeschylus, Euripides, more of Shakespeare, as well as Chekhov, Ibsen, O'Neill and other Western dramatists. He was most strongly interested in Ibsenian realism. At twenty-three, before his graduation, he wrote a family tragedy, *Thunderstorm* (1933); it was produced in Shanghai by the Fudan University Drama Society, co-directed by

Ouyang Yuqian and Hung Shen. Three years later it had a professional staging (1936) by the China Travelling Drama Troupe, which had been launched in 1933. At each showing the play was greeted with a remarkably enthusiastic reception. It is credited with having given the new genre, the *huaju*, a vital boost – a wider audience.

The many conflicts in *Thunderstorm* are exceedingly complex; some might say it is over-plotted. A prosperous mine-owner, Chou Pu-Yuan (or Zhou Puyuan), presides over a troubled household. He is cold, domineering at home, ruthless and cynical in business matters. When young and living in Wushi, he had engaged in a secret affair with a servant girl, Ma (or Shiping), by whom he fathered two sons. Grasping a chance to marry a wealthy girl, Fan-Yi (or Pan-Yi), he drives away Ma on a snowy night only shortly after the birth of their second child. Soon he is told that the despairing Ma has drowned herself along with the newborn infant. The elder son, Chou Ping, has reached the age of twenty-eight by the time the play opens.

Chou Pu-Yuan has a seventeen-year-old son, Chou Chung, by his second wife, Fan-Yi. The spoiled, idle, neurotic Fan-Yi loathes her rich, tyrannical husband, who is only too aware of her hostile feeling towards him. Attracted to her dissolute stepson Ping, who is much nearer her own age, she has seduced him. Guilt-ridden and remorseful, Ping tries to avoid her continuing advances. He transfers his affections to a very pretty girl who is a servant in the house, Feng (or Fourth Phoenix). His adolescent half-brother Chou Chung is also infatuated with her.

Actually, Ma was saved from drowning. She has married Lu Kuei, a conniver who drinks, gambles and is heavily in debt. They live in poverty. Ma, though educated, has been forced to leave her husband and take a job as a janitress in a school some distance away. One of her children, now twenty-seven, is Lu Ta-Hai, the boy presumed dead but also rescued from the river along with her. By Lu Kuei she later has a daughter, Feng, eighteen, who is the servant in the Chou household and lusted after by Ping and Chung, who are unaware of their true relationship.

Before departing for her school job, Ma has instructed Lu Kuei not to let their beautiful daughter dwell outside the protection of their roof; he himself has obtained a position as major domo with the Chous and has contrived to get work for Lu Ta-Hai in the mine and a place for Feng along with him in the house as maid to Fan-Yi, who has already grown jealous of the girl. Lu Kuei, eavesdropping and spying, knows of the illicit affair between Ping and his stepmother, and of the amorous interest both sons are taking in his daughter.

Ma, not informed as to what Lu Kuei has done, is returning to visit her family. Lu Ta-Hai, a radical, is dissatisfied with the horrible conditions in the mine where he has been toiling and is one of the leaders of an impending strike. He comes to the Chou house as a member of a workers' delegation: he has no inkling that the hated mine-owner is actually his father. Fiery in his revolt, he spouts accusations against Chou Pu-Yuan: "Your dirty tricks are nothing new to me. You'd stoop to anything so long as there is money in it. You get the police to mow down your men. . . . I know all about your record. When you contracted to repair that bridge over the river at Harbin, you deliberately breached the dike – You drowned two thousand two hundred coolies in cold blood, and for each life lost you raked in three hundred dollars! I tell you, you and your sons stand accursed for ever!"

He is dismissed from his job at the mine and later is crushed to learn that his fellow-delegates have accepted bribes and voted against having a strike. He is especially contemptuous of Ping, the boss's son, deeming him weak, feckless, dissipated, and of course neither he nor Ping, who slaps the insolent Ta-Hai's face, suspect that they are brothers.

The play abounds with endless confrontation and recognition scenes, one being when Chou Pu-Yuan and Ma come upon each other and he realizes that she is alive and Feng's mother. All these years he has regretted his cruelty towards her and has cherished souvenirs of her; the room in which they meet is filled with them. He offers her a considerable sum of money to compensate for his mistreatment of her, but she indignantly refuses it. Her attitude towards him is wholly unforgiving. She has inherent dignity and pride. Her first act is to take the reluctant Feng from the Chous' house after Ma reveals to Pu-Yuan Ta-Hai's true identity.

In tumultuous passages replete with even more conflict, Lu Kuei, too, is sent away. The action shifts to his hut in a muddy slum, where Feng is visited by the naïve, idealistic teenage Chung, who impulsively proposes marriage to her. He is unaware of her liaison with Ping. She rejects him. Chung has brought the girl a gift of cash from Fan-Yi, his mother, but Lu Kuei seizes it and goes off at once to spend it. When Ma learns of this, she insists on sending it back, even though her family is now penniless, with Lu Kuei, Ta-Hai and Feng out of work.

Ping is determined to run away with Feng, whom he now sincerely loves. He does not know that she is pregnant. He plans to assume duties at his father's mine. With Feng's help, he intends to make something of himself.

Back in the Chou house, where for various reasons all the characters are once more assembled, the story mounts to an intense climax. All the while, the weather has been hot and humid with the constant threat of a violent thunderstorm and intermittent downpours which drench almost everyone. In the final scene, when all the tangled relationships are exposed, Feng flees out into the night and rain, followed by young Chung. They are electrocuted by a loose live wire in the garden (to which there have been two earlier passing references); Ping, realizing that he has lost his beloved Feng and her unborn child and has committed incest not only with his stepmother but also his half-sister, shoots himself.

Chou Fu-Yuan is left childless, except for Ta-Hai, who hates him and everything he represents. (Translation by Wang Tao-liang and A.C. Barnes)

Here the twenty-three-year-old Cao Yu filched widely from the Greeks and Romans, Shakespeare, Ibsen and O'Neill, the result a stew of plot devices and characters from almost every past era. Fan-Yi's obsession with her stepson echoes the premise of Euripides' *Hippolytus*, and from Plautus and Terence he probably learned to rely on incidents of mistaken identity, recognition scenes, reversals of fortune and the ever-repeated changeling theme to provide surprises that grasp and hold the spectator's interest. The storm is like that in *King Lear* – "the turbulent storm within accompanied by the raging storm without". Again, much of the endless domestic intrigue is manipulated by the wily and vindictive Fan-Yi. Hers is a spirit akin to that of Hedda Gabler. (One difference: the frustrated Hedda shoots herself. Chou Pu-Yuan, perceiving his wife to be on the verge of madness, puts her under the care of a psychiatrist.) Other evidences of Cao Yu's close reading of Ibsen are clear if one recalls *Pillars of Society*, *Ghosts* and *The Wild Duck*; in these the central figure, behind a façade of respectability, is haunted by a guilty secret which is exposed bit by bit as the drama unfolds. In *Ghosts* the father has an illegitimate daughter by a servant girl, and his legitimate son, unknowing, later seeks to have an affair with her. Galsworthy's *Strife* is about a futile struggle between miners and an unyielding employer. From O'Neill the young author borrowed the insertion of lengthier and more detailed stage instructions, much like the description in a novel, enabling the reader of the published script to visualize the action and setting more easily. They are written with considerable literary distinction. There are also parallels with O'Neill's *Desire Under the Elms* in which a young second wife and her stepson are physically attracted to each other, while a hard-fisted father and son are at odds.

But after 2,000 years totally original plays are non-existent and hardly to be expected. *Thunderstorm* is a thoroughly gripping work. Despite his youth and inexperience, Cao Yu handles the many criss-crossing narrative lines deftly and plausibly, if one allows for an astonishing number of coincidences – but none more far-fetched than Oedipus' chance encounters, let us say, with his real father and mother, both hitherto unknown to him, or the many chance meetings in other classical stage works.

The pathologically jealous Fan-Yi and the cadging Lu Kuei are unsympathetic, but the other characters are portrayed with shading, even the stern Chou Pu-Yuan having his soft and sentimental moments. Cao Yu has acknowledged that some aspects of Chou Ping are autobiographical, and he had been prompted to write the play by a personal crisis. His college friends engaged in bold rhetoric and furtive deeds, young men who were outspoken and behaved courageously. In the vicarious world of the stage he projected social and moral dilemmas as he saw them and offered his own political beliefs.

Later he told Yang Yü, an interviewer, "At that time I was sincerely convinced that those who dared to revolt were masters of their fate, while I had the desire to do so but not the strength. I felt frustrated, hostile to all around me, borne off on a swirling torrent of emotion. The need to express my bottled up indignation was probably what impelled me to write *Thunderstorm*."

In a preface, he has written:

Thunderstorm is to me a temptation. The sentiment that came to me with it culminated in a sort of inexplicable vision which I saw in numerous mystic things in the cosmos. *Thunderstorm* may be said to be "the remnant of savage nature" in me. Like our primeval ancestors, I open my eyes wide with astonishment *vis-à-vis* those phenomena that cannot be explained in terms of reason. I cannot make certain whether *Thunderstorm* was motivated by "deities and spirits," fatalism, or what other apparent powers. In feeling, what it symbolizes for me is a kind of mystic magnetism, a devil that holds my psyche in its grip. What *Thunderstorm* reveals is not the law of *karma* [cause and effect], nor that of *pao-ying* [retribution for something done or given], but the cosmic cruelty [*T'ien-ti-chien-ti ts'an-jen*] that I have sensed. . . . If the reader is willing to appreciate delicately this idea of mine, this play will continuously but flickeringly betray, in spite of his attention being distracted at times by a few tenser scenes or one or two characters, this bit of mystery – the cruelty and inhumanity of all the struggles in the universe. Behind them all, perhaps, there is a ruler exercising His jurisdiction. The Hebrew prophets hailed this ruler "God;" the Greek dramatists named him "Fate;" modern men, dismissing these mystifying conceptions, straightforwardly call Him "The Law of Nature." But I can never give Him an appropriate name, nor do I possess the ability to depict His real character. For He is too great, too complex. What my emotion has forced me to give expression to is merely my vision of the cosmos. . . .

Viewed from one angle, *Thunderstorm* is an emotive vision, a sign of nameless horror. The attraction of such a vision resembles precisely that of my listening, when a child, to some elderly man, whose face was engraved with wrinkles of experience, telling enthusiastically on a bleak night the stories of will-o'-the-wisps on grave tops and walking corpses in desolate temples. My skin was studded with cold drops of fear, and the shadows of ghosts seemed to be flickering in wall corners. But strange to say, the very fear was itself a temptation. I huddled my body closer to the aged story-teller, swallowed the saliva of interest while my heart throbbed with fear, yet I grappled his wizened hand and implored, "Tell one more! Tell one more!"

Some critics see signs in *Thunderstorm* that the young Cao Yu had absorbed the Greek concepts not only of fate but also of sin and retribution. Like the avenging and harried figures in the doomed house of Atreus, Chou Pu-Yuan and Ma are punished for the heedless immorality of deeds in their youth, and suffering is visited on their children, too.

Originally *Thunderstorm* had a prologue and epilogue which took place in a Catholic hospital two years after the tragic events of the main story. Both Ma and Fan-Yi have sunk into madness. "The Furies are still at work." Ta-Hai has vanished, and Chou Pu-Yuan does penance. The play ended to the surging sound of Bach's *Mass in B Minor*.

These two scenes are omitted from subsequent versions of the over-long script, and in particular a later generation of Communist censors objected to the use of Western music and to all references to Western philosophy. They insisted on other deletions and alterations: all allusions to religion, including Chou Pu-Yuan's devotional reading of Buddhist scriptures, were cut out; Ta-Hai is no longer a foreman in the mine but a common labourer, to stress the inherent heroism and virtue of such workers. Leftist critics took exception to other aspects of the play, such as the author's surrender to fatalism and his injection of mystic touches, which – said one commentator – "only reduce the work's high degree of congruence with reality, diluting any social meaning".

According to Walter and Ruth Meserve, editors of *Modern Literature from China*, when *Thunderstorm* was restaged in 1954, "the actors were urged by a reviewer in the Drama Gazette to give prominence to the 'truth of history' in the play. By emphasizing Ta-Hai, who 'opposes the corruption of the bourgeois family,' and by playing Fan-Yi as a victim of 'the oppressors' rather than as a mentally disturbed person, the director eliminated some of the 'unhealthy elements of the script.' "

Wrote another critic, quoted by Christopher C. Rand: "If the author had concentrated his entire effort to illuminate the tragic encounters of Ma, the death of Chung and Feng, and the roots of Fan-Yi's abnormal psyche in order to induce in people a clenched hate of the feudal system, this theme and technique would obviously have been very strong and fresh. But the author, unable to do this, only uses misapprehensions of true blood relationships, deaths of characters, and insanity, thus vitiating the tragedy's effect; this cannot but emasculate its social significance. As for perceptions of the future, the play is very confused; even though the author molds the figure of Ta-hai, a mine laborer, with some success, and writes of struggle between workers and capitalists, there still seems to be weakness, a feebleness; the work is lackluster. Even after the author has whipped the black façade of society, he is unable to provide man a clear exit [from his difficulties]."

The seeming visceral appeal of *Thunderstorm* has seldom waned. It has frequently been revived on stage: there have been several film adaptations, and in 1983 – fifty years after its première – a ballet version was presented to an audience of foreign diplomats in Peking.

Cao Yu's next play, *Sunrise* (1936) shows the influence not of Ibsen but of Chekhov, though its subject – depravity in a large city – is not one explored by the Russian dramatist. Cheng Pai-lu, a country girl – her parents are intellectuals – arrives in a metropolis, possibly the bustling port of Tientsin. She quickly embraces the career of a high-class courtesan. Installed in a luxurious suite at a hotel, she receives a flow of visitors, some of them customers, others old and new-found friends and acquaintances. Among them is Fang Ta-sheng, a former suitor from her native town, who unexpectedly appears with an offer of marriage. He wants to take her back to their true home. He is appalled by the change in her. "It's horrible, horrible – it seems impossible that you can now have become so unscrupulous, so devoid of any sense of shame. Surely your realize that once one's head is turned by a lust for money, the most precious thing in life – love – will fly away like a bird."

She tells him that he is childish. Though aware that her life is superficial and that the men surrounding her are pretentious, corrupt and hypocritical, she values above all the freedom now hers, along with the attention she received from clients.

Fang Ta-sheng stays on, hoping to convert her. Others who call on Cheng Pai-lu are a raffish lot, comprising "Georgy" Chang, a drunken student just back from the United States; P'an Yueh-t'ing, a banker and persistent admirer; Chin Pa, head of a ring of extortionists; Huang Hsing-san, an old and out-of-work bank clerk; and Li Shih-ch'ing, employed by P'an as a private secretary. On hand, too, are the ambitious Fu-sheng, a wily servant who is kept busy trying to ward off bill-collectors and sycophants; Mrs Ku, a rich, fat, aged and over-painted dowager; and her cynical gigolo, Hu Ssu, who plies her with the flattery that she craves.

Just outside the hotel window a new building is being erected for the Ta Feng Bank managed by P'an Yueh-t'ing. Fu-sheng complains of the construction noise. At times the workers can be heard singing:

> The sun comes up from the East,
> The sky is a great red glow.
> If we want rice to eat
> We must bend our backs in toil.

In contrast to Fu-sheng's response to the singing, which he calls "bawling", Fang Ta-sheng finds it pleasing, and the words of it give the play its symbolic title.

Melodrama and suspense are injected when Cheng Pai-lu is alone and her suite is invaded by Hsiao-tung-hsi, an innocent sixteen-year-old girl, an orphan, who has been sold to a gang of pimps headed by Chin Pa, who also dwells in the hotel. She is resisting their attempt to force her into prostitution. Cheng Pai-lu tries to help her by enlisting the aid of P'an Yueh-t'ing, but he backs off when he learns that Chin Pa, an important creditor of the bank, is involved. The gang, suspecting where Hsiao-tung-hsi has taken refuge, force their way into the suite and search for the girl.

The Ta Feng Bank is in trouble, but P'an Yueh-t'ing assures Chin Pa, who has a large deposit there, not to be concerned. Actually, P'an is speculating heavily and the bank faces a default. He is erecting the new building to look solvent.

Li Shigh-ch'ing, his secretary, is dazzled by the rich and celebrated people he meets in the world of Manager P'an. But Li is paying no heed to his wife and family. When the unemployed clerk, Huang Hsing-san, seeks his help in regaining a bank position, he is treated with contempt. Li tells the old man that his meticulous honesty is a handicap.

The scene shifts to a brothel in a poor district of the city. Hsiao-tung-hsi, recaptured, is confined here. Despite the advice of the kindly, middle-aged Tsui-hsi, the girl resists becoming a harlot, though beaten by Black San, one of Chin Pa's henchmen. Customers, the gigolo, Hu Ssu and the servant Fu-sheng, make an entrance: they select Tsui-hsi and Hsiao-tung-hsi as bed-partners, but the girl still resists. She pours tea over Hu Ssu's expensive new suit. Black San beats her once more. When she is alone, the desperate girl finds rope enough and hangs herself.

As might be expected, nearly all these vicious, worthless characters come to a bad end. Fearing blackmail, P'an, the banker, fires his private secretary, whose neglect of his family leads to the needless death of a son. P'an himself is totally wiped out in the bank failure. Chin Pa, the mob leader, also loses his ill-gotten fortune in the financial disaster.

By now, Cheng Pai-lu, thoroughly disenchanted with her "friends", realizes that her "freedom" is an illusion. Weary of these immoral people and her sordid, aimless life, she swallows an overdose of sleeping pills, then lies on a sofa and reaches for a book that she has recently purchased. Its title, too, is *Sunrise*. Fang Ta-sheng arrives, looking for her. He does not grasp that she is dying; instead, he thinks she is merely resting. To banish the darkness of the room, he crosses to open the shutters.

TA-SHENG: . . . I can't understand your not letting the sun in. [*Going to the door of the bedroom on the left*] Listen while I tell you something, Chu-chun. If you go on living like this you'll be digging your own grave. Now listen, why not go with me after all, instead of tying yourself to these people? Now what about it? Look [*pointing out of the window*], the sun's shining, it's spring. [*The singing of the labourers is now coming nearer. They are singing: "The sun comes up from the east, the sky is a great red glow . . ."*]

[Translation: A. C. Barnes]

The general feeling among critics was that, if Cao Yu intended to match Chekhov's wry detachment, he did not succeed in doing so. His tone is often moralistic, which is hardly Chekhovian. Christopher C. Rand observes:

His intractable introspection militated against it [i.e. a large measure of objectivity]. Still, amid the naturalistic brutalities perpetrated on and by the harlots, servants, creditors, gigolos, lovers, and unseen proletarians of this play we find a wisp of the Russian master's penchant for inconclusiveness and irony, which serves to intensify the clash of expectation and sadness. On the one hand, *Sunrise* broaches the possibility of man creating a new, more favorable world for himself in spite of the fortunes that canalize him. The cries of the toiling construction workers at dawn's light seem to portend a brilliant beginning, when the chaotic cannibalism of a benighted China will yield to the red glow of social equality. And yet, the suicides of the once innocent Ch'en Pai-lu and Hsiao-tung-hsi, the family tragedy of Li Shih-ch'ing, the fatuous gamboling of Mrs Ku cast doubt on all optimism. Repeatedly we are made aware of the tragi-comic incongruities of resilient hope, naked despair, important defiance, and unqualified resignation, which are reflective of the playwright's own mental dissonances. Lacking Chekhov's stoic acceptance of an indifferent but viable world, Cao Yu plunged into existential questioning about the validity of socio-cosmic order.

Substantiating this, Rand quotes from Cao Yu's postscript to *Sunrise*:

I must confess that I am still young, and have a young man's irrepressible instincts, for as questions arise in me I cannot but immediately search out their answers. When my mind is troubled, I am confused and disquiet; I sweat, and it thrashes angrily in me like a deadly medicine swallowed by mistake. Wandering idly in this topsy-turvy society, I see so many nightmarish, frightening acts of man, which I shall not forget until I die; they turn into so many urgent problems that strike mortally upon me, that singe my emotions, that aggravate my disquiet. As though suffering from a fever, all day I sense beside me a demon of death making low persuasions in my ear, grinding at me, allowing me no peace. I envy those penetrating and perceptive people who quietly comprehend the central meaning of things, and I love those rude farm men with wide, childlike, undepraved eyes, healthy as mother cows, leading without deep reflection their simple, upright lives. I can imitate neither of these admirable people, and yet I will not continue living in ambiguity; hence, I sink like a stupid drunk into the frying firepit. This kind of distress, day after day, pierces the mark; I am locked in a room. When by accident I arrive at something, I have a spell of mad delight; I think that I have found a great

Way. But after a while, I quiet down and realize that such a great problem cannot be so dubiously solved by avoiding the difficult and relying on the easy; unconsciously I am involved in an iron web of despair, which I cannot disentangle myself from, nor rid myself of.

Besides this, the published text of the play is preceded by a number of quotations and injunctions from Lao Tzu, the New and Old Testaments – *Romans, Jeremiah, Paul, Corinthians*, the *Revelation of John* – testifying to the spiritual questions that stirred him. Effusions such as these, in an anguished, hysterical vein, accompany the published texts of his plays, expressing his fury at the degenerate world he sees about him and that he wants to destroy, though he feels his hopeless inadequacy.

I thirst to see a ray of light. I think I will not see the greater part of the sun; but during my lifetime I yearn to see a crack of great thunder come to earth and strike these squirming goblins to a pulp, though I fear the earth would sink into the sea. I am still young, yet deathless memories that make one's hair stand straight attack me from all quarters. I can think of no wise way to go, though I ponder every tack. . . . I curse injustice wherever it lies, but unless these putrid men are rid of, I cannot see much light ahead. . . . I want to write something to relieve my angry breast; I want to shout, "Your last day has arrived!" to the perverse, shameless people who have cast out the sun.

Though *Sunrise* was welcomed by enough reviewers and theatre-goers because of its bold depiction of the ugliness of bourgeois and capitalist society, orthodox Communist critics found fault with the author's show of sympathy for Cheng Pai-lu. They also objected to his clear affinity for European techniques, the way in which he shaped his characters to illustrate certain of his concepts, and his reliance on the intervention of "Fate", a supernatural force in which they had little belief, insisting rather that a drama in a time of crisis must carry an approved "socio-political" message.

In 1980, shortly after Cao Yu was permitted to visit New York, *Sunrise* was performed off-off-Broadway by the Pan Asian Repertory Theatre at La MaMa. Richard F. Shepard's notice appeared in the *New York Times*:

Under the direction of Tisa Chang, a company of talented actors is persuasively fleshing out a story that is more ironic than satiric, but does not sacrifice humanness on the altar of superficial preachiness. . . .

Mr Cao paints his picture on a broad social canvas. The plot is there, but it is not the dominant thing. Rather, he tells of wasted lives, of people whose decadent existences touch one another almost casually, but do not caress with the warmth and depth of genuine love and friendship. They kowtow to a corrupt and cruel system that is concerned only with profit, not people. Happy endings are only for the ledger's bottom line, not for the human heart.

In the lead role, Lynette Chun is beautiful and expressive. It is a difficult part that calls for a woman who is hard, yet sentimental and even wistful when the sun rises after a dissipated night. Raul Aranas is appealing, lively and stylish as the Westernized roué, spouting clichés and showing off in French. Ernest Abubba plays the pompous dry banker very convincingly, making him a despicable, greedy and yet somehow human fellow. Musapha Nor is spitefully cool as the ambitious unscrupulous clerk on the rise. Mel Duane Gionson is deliciously foppish as the gigolo. Tsering Ngudu makes credible the role of an honest, worthy but gloomy friend from out of town. Gerri Igarash as the young girl evinces the true offishness of a frightened teenager.

Sunrise tells of a specific time and place, yet Mr Cao has imbued his characters with traits that we still recognize today. The more things change, the more they are the same, and that's not even Chinese.

Cao Yu's third play, *The Wilderness* (1937), had a cold reception and in subsequent years was passed over as a lesser work. With *Thunderstorm* and *Sunrise*, it forms what is widely considered to be a trilogy, though it differs in many aspects from the two earlier works. For one thing, its setting is rural.

Chiao Yen-Wang, an avaricious Captain (his name literally means King of Hell), has an "adopted son", Ch'ou Hu (Vengeful Tiger). The Captain plots to have the young man's real father, Ch'ou Jung, murdered in order to seize his property. He sells Jung's fifteen-year-old daughter, Ch'ou Ku-Niang (Miss Ch'ou) to a gang of pimps, who force her to become a prostitute; she loses her life. On false charges, Yen-Wang has Ch'ou Hu convicted and imprisoned. The Captain chooses the beautiful Hua (Gold One), who was to marry Ch'ou Hu, to be the bride of his own son, Chiao Ta-hsing. After six years of incarceration, during which he is lamed, Ch'ou Hu escapes and returns to his former home, vowing to avenge the deaths of his father and sister, the theft of his estate and his beloved. In a prologue he is first discovered, dirty, bedraggled and limping, in a dank forest near his destination. His ankles are still bound by a chain. He is an animalistic creature, very strong, hairy and apelike.

Encountering a half-wit, Pai Sha-Tzu, nicknamed Doggie, Ch'ou Hu enlists his help to get rid of the chain – Doggie has come with an axe into the forest to cut firewood for the Chiaos for whom he works. From him, Ch'ou Hu learns that Yen-Wang, the object of his vengeance, is dead: accordingly, he determines to inflict retribution on the Chiao widow, Mu, and the son, Ta-hsing.

Hidden, he hears that Ta-hsing is leaving on a journey. This allows Ch'ou Hu to reveal his presence to Hua. She is unhappy in her marriage; her husband is kind but weak and much too closely tied to his mother's rule. With little hesitation, Hua welcomes the virile, primitive Ch'ou Hu into her bed. Her infidelity is instantly suspected by her mother-in-law, Chiao Mu, who is blind but has a quick mind and sharp instincts and has always distrusted Hua, sensing her to be a wanton.

In Act One – there are three – Ta-hsing returns after a ten-day absence. By now, Ch'ou Hu is no longer concealing his arrival. He does not identify himself as an escaped convict; instead, he says that he has come to visit Ta-hsing, his boyhood friend and "adopted brother". Hua is quite obsessed with him. The mother-in-law is ever more certain that the young woman is having an affair with Ch'ou Hu and frequently accuses her. But, blind, she cannot prove her charge. For two long, powerful and suspenseful acts the dramatic confrontation between the four characters unfolds, with the playwright wringing every sort of conflict from it. Ta-hsing is as sexually obsessed with Hua as she is with Ch'ou Hu. She begs her husband to let her go, but he cannot accept the prospect of losing her. The mother-in-law seeks to protect her son and destroy the unfaithful Hua and the brutish interloper. Ch'ou Hu, who really loves Hua, is still intent on killing the feckless Ta-hsing and punishing Chiao Mu by leaving her to fend for herself alone and sightless. Though emotionally distraught and deeply frightened, Hua is also very cunning and a match for the old woman. Her trickery leads others to call her a "fairy-fox". The combatants are forever putting on different personae, now cajoling and next threatening one another, now pitying and then hating, equivocating, wavering in their feelings and tone of speech. Dominating the room in which most of the tense action occurs is a portrait of Yen-Wang, his malevolent and watchful eyes observing the scene.

Ta-hsing is finally if unwillingly convinced that Hua has betrayed him, though he does not know with whom and desperately tries to learn the name of her lover. He grows sure that Ch'ou Hu is the one. Ta-hsing, getting drunk, promises to kill his rival; instead, he falls asleep. He is stabbed to death by Ch'ou Hu. By a former wife, Ta-hsing has an infant son. The child has been placed on Ch'ou Hu's bed not to be awakened by the quarrel and shouting. Thinking that Ch'ou is sleeping there, the blind Chiao Mu strikes the bed with her iron staff, unwittingly slaying her cherished grandson. (When writing melodrama, Cao Yu does not do things by halves.)

A posse, summoned earlier by Chiao Mu, surrounds the house. Ch'ou Hu and Hua get away by taking a hostage, the gossipy Ch'ang Wu, a friend of the Chiao family. Before leaving, Ch'ou Hu fires his revolver at the portrait of Yen-Wang; it topples to the floor.

This naturalism is abandoned in Act Three. In its place, Cao Yu makes use of an Expressionistic technique as Ch'ou Hu and Hua flee through the forest; it is night, very dark and wet. They free their hostage, the terrified Ch'ang Wu. Lost in the tangle of trees and bushes, they are pursued by the sound of a drum beating in a nearby half-deserted temple where a crazed Chiao Mu has gone to pray for the restoration to life of her grandson whom she had hoped would carry on the family name. They also hear random shots as the posse searches for them. In a rapid series of five short episodes the weary pair plunge on, lost, daunted. Their faces and hands are scratched, their clothes torn and stained with blood. Hua is near total exhaustion. Step by step, Ch'ou Hu reverts to his primitive core; he hallucinates, firing at a succession of apparitions that emanate in the mists; his murdered father and sister; Yen-Wang, the "King of Hell"; fellow-prisoners and their harsh overseer. At last, Ch'ou Hu persuades the pregnant Hua to go on by herself to attain the "golden land" he has promised her. Groping in the dark, he finds the chain that had earlier bound him. In a symbolic gesture, he casts it away. He remains behind to meet his fate, until, leaning against a tree, he sinks lifeless.

The play is grim throughout, with some flitting moments of comic relief contributed by the idiot Doggie and the garrulous Ch'ang Wu.

In a brief postscript, Cao Yu acknowledges that for the last group of scenes he borrowed two stage devices, the drum and the shots at the apparitions, from O'Neill's *Emperor Jones*. He did so unconsciously, he asserts; and only on re-reading Act Three did he become aware of what he had done. His borrowings from O'Neill, however, are far more extensive than that: the frenzied flight through the primeval forest, a futile attempt at escape that ends in the fugitive finding that he has merely been going in circles; the progressive descent of the quarry's psyche to a more primitive level, and the hallucinations, are also appropriated from *The Emperor Jones*, where the dismayed protagonist recalls haunting scenes from his prison days and evokes other images from his past. The symbolism of the brooding portrait of a father is found in both O'Neill's *Mourning Becomes Electra* and *All God's Chillun*, and a son returning to exact vengeance for a hurt done to a parent (in that instance, a mother) is also a leading theme in *Mourning Becomes Electra*, as it is in the Aeschylean tragedy that was O'Neill's source. The mother-dominated son is a favourite O'Neill character. The role of the mother who suspects that her son is being betrayed by his adulterous wife and her lover has a parallel in Zola's *Thérèse Raquin*, with which Cao Yu might well have been acquainted, and most probably he was quite familiar with Hung Shen's *Yama Chao* which draws even more overtly from *The Emperor Jones*.

From O'Neill, too, comes an ingenious employment of sound-effects to enrich the work and establish a mood: the croaking of frogs, the cries of crows and cuckoos, the baas of sheep, the rhythmic click of unseen trains rushing past – the tracks suggest a possible way of escape for Hua from her claustrophobic life on the Chiao farm – and the whine of wind through telegraph wires. Lighting effects are carefully specified by the author, and his stage instructions are once again novelistic and poetic, with lengthy essays on each character, detailing exactly his or her physical appearance and psychological traits, as well as much of his or her earlier background.

A partial explanation of the title is found in Hua's impassioned plea to be set free. "There's no use preaching to me. If you don't want to let me go, then come at me again with your knife; I can't get away. But you can't push me around with that thing all the time; I'll still be wanting to go away sooner or later. Ta-hsing, I was born in the wilderness and I grew up in the wilderness, and maybe I'll even die in the wilderness. A person only lives once, Ta-hsing. In the Chiao family I'm dead." (Translation: Christopher C. Rand and Joseph S.M. Lau)

Of considerable significance is Cao Yu's description of Ch'ou Hu in his stage instructions for Act Three:

> When, momentarily, his spirit is gripped by fear, he suddenly comes to resemble his ancestor, the primitive ape-man, trembling against the barbarity of midnight. There is an extreme disquiet in his expression; hope, pensiveness, fear and exasperation pelt steadily upon his imagination, causing in him a sudden marked rise in his hallucinations. Amid this black wilderness we can discern in him not a thread of "bruteness;" instead, we begin to discover in him something beautiful, something that is worthy of man's precious sympathy. He represents a genuine man, heavily persecuted whose injustices are being reenacted in this forest. His wiliness in the Prologue, the deceiving character, is slowly disappearing, just as Hua has reacted to this nocturnal trial by sublimating the carnal lust she has for Ch'ou Hu into a spiritual love.

The "wilderness" is allegorical in several ways. Hua cries out: "We're a couple of pitiful worms who can't be their own masters. Even the world is chaotic and without divine oversight. If we've both done wrong, Heaven must take pity on us, for we shouldn't be responsible for what we've done." Ch'ou Hu, like-minded, adds: "Heaven is partial to those in power, not to people like us." Hua: "Then is Heaven blind?" Ch'ou: "Who said it isn't." (His is not a question but a declaration.)

When Hua, affrighted, kneels and prays for a little light to show them the forest path they have lost, Ch'ou Hu explodes in anger: "Who are you begging to, who are you begging to? God, God, God, what God? [*Waving his hands in exasperation*] There isn't any, there isn't any, there isn't any! I hate this God, I hate this God. Don't beg to Him, don't beg to Him!"

He expresses a humanistic, revolutionary credo in a later heroic speech, when he urges Hua to go on and find friends of his and join them. She asks if they can be trusted. He replies: "They're all good brothers of mine, men of all talents. Tell them that Ch'ou wasn't weak, and tell that right to the end

Ch'ou Hu never begged from anybody. Tell that Ch'ou Hu doesn't believe in Heaven now; he only believes that if his brothers unite and struggle together, they'll survive. But if they separate, they'll lose. Tell them not to be afraid of authority, and not be afraid of difficulty; tell them that if we take up the struggle now, then someday our sons and grandsons will rise up."

Rand, in his study of Cao Yu's work, which he helped to translate, has assembled a number of appraisals and interpretations of *The Wilderness* by Chinese critics. One with an obvious Marxist bent is Ting I, who writes: "*The Wilderness* is the story of a peasant's revenge on a despotic landlord. The theme is good, but unfortunately the author is unfamiliar with the life of the peasants and the class struggle in the countryside. Moreover, his ideas are dominated by a belief in fatalism; as a result, the play, which could have been treated realistically, is full of mysterious, abstract, and even strange conceptions. Mysticism, symbolism and psychological analysis combine to arouse a sense of terror and create an atmosphere of dismay. The impression is of a head detached from reality."

A similar opinion is put forth by Yang Hi, who propounds that Cao Yu has lived too long in Tienstsin and Peking and consequently presents on over-intellectualized picture of Chinese life, while neglecting to tackle relevant social problems. A like complaint was voiced by Lin Mang, who felt that Cao Yu had achieved an effective degree of realism in *Thunderstorm* and *Sunrise* but failed at that in this new script: Ch'ou Hu is not a peasant but only a physical embodiment of an abstract idea. He is not a "man in society" but a phantasmal image of a human being described in his barest term. Almost to a man, the reviewers in this group applied the term "abstract" to the characters and message of the play. They are too vague, too lacking in complexity. These observers also faulted the play for celebrating "primitivism", Ch'ou Hu being the resurrected image of the nineteenth-century French idea of the "noble savage", the author implanting in his brutish hero "primitive feeling and primeval power" and implying that "a source of regeneration for an effete nation" lay in a sweeping return to simpler times and ways. It was well known that Ch'ou aspired to see drastic social change. Here he was "equating 'primitivism' " with " 'nobility,' 'beauty,' 'virtue' and 'strength' ". To those with Marxist convictions, this was unscientific thinking, mere wishful thinking, a warped vision of what should be the "new man" in modern China.

A more favourable response came from Lü Ying, who – as paraphrased by Rand – looked on *The Wilderness* "not as a realistic social play manqué, but as an abstract rendering of the conflict between Fate and man. 'Ch'ou Hu, who in his primeval setting rebels against Fate, is not depicted as a peasant. Rather, he is a symbol of primeval man in general. In *The Wilderness* the author daringly rebels against destiny, but still he does not escape the realm of conceptual thinking; in this realm the author's understanding of society's future can only take the form of pure idea: a yearning for the primeval – the reappearance of the Way of Heaven.' Thus, Lü Ying contends, the playwright advocates a rebellion against a current civilization and harbors a wish for the moral simplicity of antiquity – which is portrayed in abstract form." LüYing did not accept Ch'ou Hu as a "true representative of social rebellion, nor a psychological figure". For this view, he was taken to task and called "a reactionary follower of Hü Feng" by another observer, Ch'u Pai-ch'un.

Quite different is Rand's own reading of the play. He points out that, in this instance, Cao Yu himself provides few clues to his intention, contrary to his earlier practice – his notes on *Thunderstorm* and *Sunrise* being copious and revelatory. Here he merely apologizes for his new work's faults, saying that it is "only an uncertain rough draft which in places still has possibilities of improvement", and offers suggestions for staging it. Rand remarks: "The impression one forms of *The Wilderness* is that, like its predecessors, it is a montage of various influences, technical, literary and philosophical. It was not intended primarily as a social-political drama, though applications to Chinese society are surely one of its aims. Nor is it principally concerned with 'a yearning for the primeval,' or with 'primitivism,' though Lau's interpretation is to the point here. Instead, *The Wilderness* is a mythic, 'Taoistic' work which recasts the socio-cosmological thoughts of [Cao Yu's] first two plays in language both profane and poetic, rife with symbol and metaphor."

Rand asserts further that the play is "mythic" because, "aside from the seemingly unconscious borrowing of an Expressionistic format from O'Neill in the third act, there is an unequivocal return (with probably greater consciousness) to the themes of Greek tragic theatre. In particular, we see a number of significant conceptual extracts from Attic lore (i.e. the story of Prometheus and Io as retold in Aeschylus' *Prometheus Bound*), which imbue *The Wilderness* with the vengeance, Fate, and sympathy for human depravity that were present in *Thunderstorm*. Secondly, it is a 'Taoistic' work because it reveals a cognizance of the non-benevolent, *tzu-jan* (i.e. self-so, causeless) actions of Nature upon man, and the moral relativism and nihilism that result therefrom. . . . These two complexes of elements are drawn upon by Cao Yu to create in *The Wilderness* a remarkable blending of philosophy and sensuous, emotive energy."

In the rest of his essay, Rand spells out the close parallels that he finds between the characters and action in Cao Yu's tragedy and Aeschylus' *Prometheus Bound*, in passages too long to be pursued here. He also singles out differences between the two dramas.

The non-parallels are also important. Ch'ou is not an Olympian demi-god, but, as we increasingly learn, an imperfect mortal; indeed, with his apish physique, he seems something even less than human. Marred by an obsession for revenge, he does not merit the name Prometheus in its literal sense of "foresight," but embodies only the Titan's behemoth will to fight back in the name of human honor. As distinct from the suffering Prometheus, Ch'ou Hu is panged by moral certitude in taking his revenge, for his oppressor, unlike Zeus, is in hell; Ch'ou Hu must quench his hate and the murder of an innocent son-surrogate and the regretted destruction of a grandson as well.

... It is evident, then, that the principal characters of the ancient Greek tragedy are not retraced precisely in the chief protagonists of Cao Yu's work. But the themes of one have clear impact on those of the other: injustices suffered are compounded by the folly of the avenging victims; Fate may reign over all, but, pitiably, it is in subjects who, by their own rebellions, create ill for themselves. Still the Promethean urge is not purely negative; by it there is hope for new greatness, providing one's foreknowledge is sufficient to avoid the obstacles of Fate.

... Typically, the issue in *Prometheus Bound* results in ambivalence, in contingency, and so do the issues of *The Wilderness*.

As for the "Taoistic" strain of moral relativism and nihilism in the work, additional ideas from the first two dramas return. The notion of a non-teleological, but often "cruel," Way of Nature was mentioned in regard to *Thunderstorm* and *Sunrise*. In *The Wilderness* this idea merges with those of Fate and human revenge to heighten the mystical tone of the play and create a vision of man *vis-à-vis* the cosmos that incorporates both traditional Chinese and Western constructs. That is to say, the wilderness, this non-human, non-theomorphic force which looms threateningly in multifarious forms around the characters, has become assimilated with the spirit of oppression in the play. And yet, it remains *tzu-jan*, unheedful of human arrogance, immeasurable, and so, amoral. David Ch'en, discussing the term "cosmic cruelty" in the *Thunderstorm* preface, has discerned the "Taoistic" propensity in the trilogy as a whole.

Indeed, this "horrification" of Nature occurs in *The Wilderness* because Cao Yu has reconciled the themes of *Prometheus Bound*, the Old Testament conception of a vengeful God, and the Lao Tzu principle of *tzu-jan*. In the course of the third act, as natural terrors combine with Ch'ou Hu's hallucinations, these Heaven-man perspectives interfuse into a single mesh of obsessive vengeance and angry nihilism. Ch'ou Hu, having convinced himself that killing Ta-hsing is justified in the name of retribution, contrives also for Chiao Ta-ma to inadvertently slay her own grandson (in the hope of murdering Ch'ou Hu). Having thus overstated his thirst for revenge, he takes his lover-comrade, Hua, into the wilderness in search of that Utopia so wished for. But Ch'ou Hu gradually perceives the enormity of his act, and his growing fatigue and hopelessness exacerbates the moral pain he feels for his unprincipled rebellion. Slowly his hallucinations become more intensely real, their movement through the forest more random; Ch'ou Hu grows desperate in his vain contravention of the Way of the wilderness. He even decries Chin-tzu's suppliant call to God for mercy. . . .

Consumed by an ironic sense of justice, Ch'ou Hu must fight on, not with the help of God, but with a fateful momentum that wreaks destruction.

. . . What is crucial to our understanding of the play, however, is that in the end he is also somehow aware that, whatever the outcome, the impassive, eternal wilderness will survive everything. In other words, Ch'ou Hu's rebellion is both humanly admirable and cosmically trivial; and it is precisely the ambivalence of this combination of "Promethean" heroism and "Taoistic" nihilism that gives the play its philosophical complexity and artistic merit.

Having recognized this skillful blending of foreign and native conceptions into a single "cosmic cruelty," we cannot say that Cao Yu offered his compatriots a clear ideological basis, to say nothing of a political formula, for confronting the pressures of violent change to come. The serious seekers of "new blood, new life" found little comfort in this pessimistic synthesis of Fate and amoralism. C.T. Hsia was perhaps most scathing when, in evaluating the first three plays, he said: "They capitalize on the stock bourgeois responses to certain decadent and corrupt aspects of Chinese society and vaunt a superficial Leftist point of view, of which only the most rigorous Marxist critic could disapprove.

". . . He solemnly invokes Fate, heredity, jungle law, and the class struggle to illuminate and ennoble the melodramatic action of his plays, but syncretism only underscores his lack of a personal tragic vision."

This is probably too severe a condemnation of Cao Yu's failures. The playwright may indeed have been, at times, melodramatic and immature in his initial writings. But understood as the product of a frustrated and occasionally overwrought artist working out the disturbing contradictions of his world, this trilogy, and particularly *The Wilderness*, which combines the thematic ingredients of the first two plays, demonstrates a true tragic vision, wherein man, though he exhausts his will, cannot escape his fecklessness to resolve universal ambiguities.

The play's dialogue is "masterful", in Rand's view, the coming and going of the characters plausible and well timed, the plot logically constructed. Though many Chinese Marxist commentators found the characters too "abstract", to Western eyes they are sufficiently complex and dimensional. Rand remarks that Chiao Ta-ma (Chiao Mu) is given "multiple meanings":

She appears first to us as a virago, a witchly woman, fiercely critical and yet protective of her passive son (who represents her only source of security), and savagely belligerent toward her daughter-in-law. She thus can be identified as a remnant of the cultural past and present, an exemplar of Chinese superstition and backwardness. We see this not only in her practice of voodoo magic and "spirit-calling" throughout the work, but particularly in her metaphorical counterposition at the end of the Prologue to the "Promethean" giant tree and to the symbol of a new, Westernized future, Hua's carriage to Utopia – the train. And yet, as the play progresses, and especially so in Act Three as her haunting voice mingles with the forest gloom, Chiao Ta-ma's primitive and fearsome ways begin to take on also the unpredictability, violence, and timelessness of the wilderness with which Ch'ou Hu and Hua must contend.

On the other hand, Chiao Ta-ma arouses pity from us as a human being subject to the same "cruelties" visited on Ch'ou Hu and Hua. She has a true motherly concern for her son and grandson, for whom she will fight to the end; she will even allow Hua and Ch'ou to go away together, if only to preserve her family line. Ch'ou Hu, however, in his blind revenge, insists on isolating her in her obscurantism, a pawn to the unfeeling wilderness, "alive and alone."

Other allusions and metaphors, seen by Rand, lie in the roles of Ch'ang Wu and Doggie. The factotum, Ch'ang Wu, who gives away secrets and injects humour into the otherwise grim action, was probably the most familiar of the *dramatis personae* to Chinese audiences in the 1930s, resembling as he does the comedian of Peking opera. The innocuous, retarded Doggie's childish delight in trains – he constantly imitates their movement and the clamour they make as they hurtle past – provides a "subtle admonition". The trains symbolize, as has been said, a dream of a "passage to a new future" for Ch'ou Hu and Hua, but Doggie's adoration of them suggests that they may be nothing more than "an idiotic delusion". The struggle to attain the dreamed-of future will be far more difficult than Ch'ou Hu, Hua and their idealistic friends realize.

(One wonders if all these symbols and layers of meaning were in Cao Hu's mind and are actually in his plays, or whether they are only found there by a generous and erudite critic all too ready to make his own contributions – perhaps unwittingly – to these challenging, interesting dramas, much as a director at once and enthusiastically improves on a script entrusted to him.)

Cao Yu also participated in the All-China Drama-World Resist-the-Enemy Federation when Japan attacked his country in 1937.

Brought out during the ensuing six years of warfare, *Peking Man* (1941) is another of his major works. Once more he presents the decay of a family: here they are the aristocratic Tsengs (or Zengs), and once again the playwright acknowledges his debt to both Ibsen and O'Neill. The time is the 1920s, and mostly the events take place in the family's parlour. The members of the clan, scholarly and formal in demeanour, were once officials of the imperial dynasty and rich property-owners, but are now reduced to living on rents from the few remnants they still hold. The aged father, anticipating his end, possesses a finely lacquered coffin, and though badly in need of money he seeks desperately to avoid selling it. One of their neighbours, an anthropologist, is studying the recently discovered fossil of Peking Man – the title of the play has several implications – and discourses nostalgically on life in the old days before the onset of modern culture and morals. A shrewish daughter-in-law, Siyi, dominates the Tseng household. She feigns to be deferential, but is a scandal-monger, her mood alternating rapidly. An alcoholic son-in-law, Jiang Tai, nurtures unattainable dreams; an utter failure, he is beset by a self-destructive despair much like that of a character in a late O'Neill tragedy. A spinster niece, Su Fang, has a hopeless love for a married cousin. An old retainer, Chen Naima, shuffles about, her tongue sharp, but her heart soft. The play's three acts, crammed with melodrama, last about three and a half hours.

In 1978 a pre-eminent American dramatist, Arthur Miller, visited China and had his first meeting with Cao Yu. This acquaintance was renewed in 1980, when Miller's *Death of a Salesman* was performed at the Peking People's Art Theatre. Partly through Miller's instrumentality, this led to a staging of *Peking Man* in New York at the Horace Mann Theater at Columbia University (Teachers' College) by the Center for Theater Studies, in association with the Center for the United States–China Arts Exchange. Cao Yu, in attendance, was interviewed and fêted. (Earlier, in 1946, he had visited the United States on a year-long fellowship.) For the play's American début, Leslie Lo provided a new English translation; the director was Kent Paul, the sets by Quentin Thomas. Richard F. Shepard reported in the *New York Times*:

> The drama is at once intensely personal and extensively social in its concerns. . . . At the same time, [it] goes deeper than the breakup of an old family. It mirrors Chinese history, the decline of feudalism and the arrival of the new-rich capitalist class, neither of which, as the playwright sees it, were suitable for China trying to break out of its semicolonial status and widespread misery. . . . For modern, more restless audiences some cutting might be in order. But it tells us much about the different modes of expression of emotions that are universal. Laughter and crying, cheer and pain, know no boundaries. But here in China we see the embarrassment of personal confession. A stormy speech is followed by a quiet invitation to a cup of tea. A coffin receives an almost joyous reception. People recognizably like us but different in expression. . . . *Peking Man*, in short, or at length, is food for thought and informs us how history shaped China.

About *Peking Man* Rand notes: "Here again, an ape-like man is used as a symbol of hope that the vigor of China's earliest ancestors can be reharnessed for future spiritual greatness. As in *The Wilder-*

ness, the Faustian energies of the young and ebullient are guided toward Western Science, linking the primeval, innocent power of the ancient past with yearned-for glories to come, in order that the decrepit present may be erased."

The play also inspired a critical study by David Y. Chien pointing out numerous parallels and differences between scripts by O'Neill and Cao Yu, *The Hairy Ape and Peking Man: Two Types of Primitivism in Modern Society*.

Marxist reviewers were not pleased with *Peking Man*. They said that as always the author lacked a sound perspective.

His offerings just before, during, and directly after the Second World War show an effort to deal with concrete political and social problems; they stress an urgent need for men of goodwill and intelligence to strive for quick solutions. The reviewers took these as evidence of his growing maturity – he was still only in his thirties. Among these works are *Black Characters Twenty-eight* (1938), in collaboration with Sung Chih-ti; *Just Thinking* (1946); and *Bridge* (1947). To this period, too, belongs his film script, *Sunny Day* (1948). During the war years he applied himself to a translation of *Romeo and Juliet*, published in 1949. Most of this work is deemed by Westerners to be of lesser quality. An example is *Transformation* (1940) about a military hospital that is mismanaged by its corrupt administrators. The place is efficiently reorganized when others with the proper attitude intervene. The subject was more in line with what officials were asking of loyal playwrights. As ever, the Marxist critics were not happy with Cao Yu's dramatization of *Family* (1941) from Pa Chin's admired novel. The script exposes the flaws of the country's lingering feudal family system (but does not posit Communism as a remedy). *Bright Skies* (1954) is an anti-American script on the theme of germ warfare. This play won a prize at the First All-China Festival of Music held in Peking in 1956. Though the play is thoroughly biased, it must be seen against the feverish background of the Korean War, when Chinese "volunteers" and American forces were engaged in fierce conflict near North Korea's snow-deep, frozen border. (Chinese authorities issued a press release asserting that the Americans used biological weapons. The charge, highly suspect, has never been proved.) It may be that during these years he wrote too much.

Complying with the government's policy of having leading writers "re-educated" by spending at least a brief time mingling with soldiers, peasants and other mere workers, Cao Yu "went down" – as the saying was – during July 1950.

After the Communist takeover it had become very clear to Cao Yu that from now on his scripts must conform to the ideology espoused by the ruling party. He would be required to write plays that essentially were propaganda serving the regime's varying goals. Under rigorous scrutiny, he began to turn out historical dramas to evade the too-great risk of venturing his opinions on topical subjects. To this genre belong *The Gall and the Sword* (1962), in collaboration with Yü Shih-chih and Mei Ch'ien; and *Wang Chao-chün* (1979).

Through the initial years of the People's Republic his capability was recognized and he was given high posts in various cultural institutions. A group of prominent dramatists were similarly placed and shifted about as they were momentarily in or out of official favour. Though he sought to adhere to the Party line, he was increasingly the target of invective from higher-ups or had the unpleasant, humiliating task of public self-criticism imposed on him.

Ever more disturbed by a trend towards liberalism in the government and among the intelligentsia, Mao Tse-tung, the despotic Chairman of the Chinese Communist Party, instigated his so-called Cultural Revolution in 1966, mobilizing young people in a rag-tag force named the Red Guard and loosing them in a violent sweep against those whom he condemned as "revisionists". Progressive bureaucrats, many long-time officials of high and low rank, teachers and other academic leaders and literary figures became conspicuous as "enemies" of the state, as were those unfortunately descended from aristocratic or once-wealthy families and former landlords. Those who suffered and even perished as a consequence of this prolonged anarchic, anti-intellectual campaign numbered in the tens of thousands. (Subsequently, Chinese historians attribute this mad event to Mao Tse-tung having developed paranoia; hence he was not really to blame for what happened.)

Tian Han was among the victims, charged with having written a play, *Hsieh Yai-huan* (1961), that was a "poisonous weed" filled with heretical ideas and deeply offensive to Marxist principles. He and three of his associates, the playwrights Hsia Yen, Yang Han-sheng and Chou Yang, were denounced as "the four villains". He was arrested and removed from all his influential posts. Eleven years after his death he was officially rehabilitated, a gesture finally possible because Mao, too, was gone and his regime superseded by a more lenient ruling clique. Tian Han is also remembered as a prolific translator and for having written the words of the Chinese Communist national anthem.

Though not unscathed, Cao Yu survived this traumatic episode. Years later, when he and Arthur Miller were lecturing on "Theater in Modern China" at the School of International Affairs in New York, he recalled: "Our ears were stopped and our hands were tied, but they could not tie up our thoughts." After that, literature and the drama did not immediately get under way again. There was a remnant of fear.

Eventually he became director of Peking's People's Art Theatre, a position he still held at the time that Arthur Miller's *Death of a Salesman* was staged by it. This company, dedicated to performing *huaju*, was mostly on view in the new Shoudu (Capital) Theatre, erected in 1956 in Peking's heart. Seating over 1,000 spectators, it excited the actors by offering up-to-date technical facilities: modern lighting and acoustics; a revolving stage; wide wings for shifting sets; spacious and well-furnished dressing-rooms that could be occupied by as many as 200 cast members at the same time. In addition, it had four rehearsal halls and lounges in which the performers could take their ease.

In the prized Shoudu, however, the troupe's repertory soon came under attack. Of the plays chosen, too few had been written after 1949, the date of the Communist takeover of China, a mere three of fourteen given, though Cao Yu's own early works were included among the presentations, as well as one by Lao She. Asked several good Marxist commentators: "Where have the modern plays gone?" "Why are *huaju* troupes indifferent towards modern plays?", to which were appended statements such as: "Audiences like modern plays, and priority should be given to modern plays." The call for recent works on more topical subjects was actually a demand for scripts more freighted with exhortations and propaganda, loud praise for the ever-encroaching totalitarian state.

The company's production of *Death of a Salesman* evoked much attention, not only in China but abroad. It was considered a significant breakthrough by the somewhat more liberal post-Mao regime, a step towards restoring cultural ties with the West.

By 1983, under Cao Yu's leadership, the government-subsidized People's Art Theatre – which first got under way in 1952 – had a staff of 400, of whom ninety were actors and the rest technicians and non-theatrical employees such as cooks and plumbers.

Rand feels that, interrupted by political events, the playwright's career was never allowed to expand to its full potential, but that "even in his initial years of artistic growth, Cao Yu was able to imbue an essentially Western literary form with Chinese content and style, and to approach classical and ever cogent human issues in a newly syncretic way". In an interview, Arthur Miller, after reading Cao Yu's early plays, paid tribute to them as "grand structures" and singled out *Thunderstorm* for special praise. (Two books by Miller, *Chinese Encounters* and *Salesman in Beijing*, recount his experiences in the People's Republic. A difficulty in staging his play was that many Peking spectators had no clear grasp of what a travelling salesman's job entailed – it was not as yet a highly competitive and stressful category of employment familiar to them.)

To most Western critics, Cao Yu's wide and unabashed appropriation of plots and characters from foreign classics – whether, on his part, conscious or unconscious – could well deny him the exceptional stature recently accorded him by his fellow-countrymen. The largest share of his Chinese audience is not aware of the extent of his borrowing, which also includes novel and striking stage devices. On the other hand, only one of Shakespeare's thirty-seven scripts has a plot truly of his own invention.

One of the half-dozen leading intellectuals of the day, Guo Moruo (or Kuo Mo-Jo; 1892–1978), was more prudent and fortunate in choosing a path through these perilous times. Besides holding several lofty official positions, among them a term as Vice-Premier and similar tenure as President of the Chinese Academy of Sciences, he composed a good many historical dramas in the *huaju* genre, most of them having modern implications for the more astute members of the audience. He was noted for his classical learning that well equipped him to write plays about past figures and happenings.

Perhaps the most esteemed of his works is *Chu Yuan* (or *Ou Yuan*; 1942), portraying an ancient poet–statesman of that name. Set in 313 BC, during the sixteenth year of the reign of King Huai of Chu, the play opens in an orange grove on a morning of late spring. Chu Yuan, at forty, is a minister at the court. He has written an "Ode to the Orange" and declaims it aloud from a scroll for his own criticism; he is pleased with it, for it preaches the virtues of unshakeable integrity. He gives it to twenty-year-old Sung Yu, his pupil for whom he has written it.

The handsome young man is overwhelmed by the praise it contains. When he tells his master that he will model himself on him in every respect, even his manner, Chu Yuan replies: "Why do you want to imitate my expression and voice? Simply to imitate these things is no better than a monkey." The student should develop a wholly independent spirit and attain his own style. Chu Yuan continues with a long discourse replete with moral precepts. He also interprets historical events for the young man's edification. He makes this point: "During these troubled times, character is of paramount importance. It is easy to act like a man in peaceful times, for then a man is born in peace and dies in peace. But, during a time of great changes and upheavals, to act like a man is a very difficult thing." He cites the example of Po Yi, a philosophical administrator of an earlier day, who after a change of monarchs starved himself to death rather than compromise his principles. "He could have lived on, and nobody would have said anything; while if he had stooped a little, the Chous would probably have given him a high position. But he realized that such a high position and such a meaningless life were more to be dreaded than death."

Chu Yuan's troubles begin when the Queen, Cheng Hsui, fearful of his sway over the King, schemes to get rid of a rival. She claims that Chu Yuan is trying to force his attentions on her. The King, enraged, dismisses the minister from office and drives him from the court. Calling the disgraced minister "lunatic", Huai reverses Chu Yuan's policies. The outcast adviser warns that the kingdom, by forming the wrong alliances, faces a calamity.

The King and Queen agree that it is unwise to have writers as ministers. Literary persons should stay out of politics. But the populace consists largely of Chu Yuan's partisans. Hearing and believing that he has lost his senses, they erect a straw figure and perform a ritual dance around it and chant to summon back his spirit. He discovers them doing this and angrily interrupts them. They flee in fright.

Sung Yu, his disciple, is not the virtuous youth whom Chu Yuan had thought him to be. Behind his master's back he criticizes the "Ode to the Orange" as old-fashioned and maintains that he himself is a better poet. He and Prince Tze Lan, the Queen's lame, sixteen-year-old son, who is also a student of Chu Yuan, cynically join forces to further their careers. Tze Lan also has amorous designs on Chan Chuan, a pretty maidservant in Chu Yuan's household, but she scorns him. Sung Yu, however, disdains the girl because she is of humble origin. Convinced that Chu Yuan is a madman and out of favour, so can no longer be of help to him, the opportunistic Sung Yu takes his leave. The maidservant Chan Chuan remains loyal and refuses to believe the scandalous accusations, but most of the other servants quit the house. Learning that Chu Yuan has taken his sword and run out, the faithful Chan Chuan anxiously goes in search of him.

Outside the city gate she is told by several fishermen, who had been at court to take part in an entertainment, that they had personally observed the Queen's treachery. They assert that Cheng Hsui had laid a trap for Chu Yuan, and the hot-tempered King had not given the minister a chance to offer an explanation or to demand a proper hearing at which many witnesses could testify as to what really happened. Distraught, Chan Chuan rushes away. Soon Chu Yuan appears, bedraggled, despairing but composing a poem. The fishermen reveal that they know him to be innocent of the Queen's slanderous charge.

The royal pair and their entourage come through the city gate. With them is Chang Yi, Prime Minister of Chin, who had joined the Queen in conniving against Chu Yuan for opposing a treaty with Chin. The Queen, seeing Chu Yuan in the crowd, taunts him, keeping up the pretence that he is demented. In turn, he fiercely upbraids the visiting Prime Minister, recounting his many past lies and misdeeds; he is not to be trusted and no pact should be signed with him. Chu Yuan is taken into custody by the guards.

As the royal procession moves on, it encounters Chan Chuan. Questioned, she explains that she is looking for her master. The Queen mischievously and heartlessly tells her that Chu Yuan has jumped into the water and drowned himself. Grief-stricken, Chan Chuan vehemently blames the Queen for having driven Chu Yuan to his death. Once more the King is angered, but a fisherman comes to the girl's defence. He tells what he and the other witnesses saw happen at court. He, too, is seized by the guards. The King complains that people everywhere are mad. Prince Tze Lan and Sung Yu arrive and are introduced to Chang Yi, who exclaims at Sung Yu's good looks. At Tze Lan's request, the Queen invites Sung Yu to take up residence at the palace. She appoints him to be her steward.

Pent in a cage and dishevelled, Chan Chuan is visited by Prince Tze Lan and a now gorgeously garbed Sung Yu. She has been whipped by her guards. When she is invited to come out and relax for a while, she refuses. "I don't want to be under an obligation to anyone." She tells her two visitors to keep away from her. They offer to help her obtain a pardon if she will become Tze Lan's servant. She remains expressionless and silent. Beheading awaits her at dawn. The same dire fate impends for Chu Yuan unless she accepts Tze Lan's bid. She continues adamantly unresponsive. Finally she cries out that her master is already dead. The young men have no knowledge of it, but a sympathetic guard assures them Chu Yuan is alive. Tze Lan promises to save both of them if Chan Chuan will yield to him. Obedient to her master's teaching, the girl chooses to die honourably rather than live in shame. Irate and frustrated, the two young men leave. Darkness falls, as the moon vanishes. Suddenly the guard moves to assist Chan Chuan to escape. He tricks a watchman, steals his cloak and his key to the cage, and sets the girl free. They hasten off.

In the Temple of the Eastern Empire, Chu Yuan is in shackles. A storm rages. The Diviner presiding here is the Queen's father. A masked official comes from the Queen with a message. The Diviner is to poison Chu Yuan and set the temple ablaze. A story will be spread that it has been struck by lightning and the impious Chu Yuan has perished in the flames. This will prevent any protest arising from people at word of his death. The Diviner objects to the destruction of this beautiful edifice, but the Queen's envoy vows that she will replace it with one even more resplendent. When the messenger leaves, the Diviner engages in philosophical conversation with Chu Yuan and offers him some tainted wine. The doomed man puts off drinking it while he composes more snatches of poetry, reciting them at length. He addresses the gods, defying them. The Diviner keeps urging him to moisten his throat with the sweet wine, but Chu Yuan is not thirsty.

The storm ends; the moon shines. Chu Yuan's emotions become subdued. Chan Chuan and the guard break in to release him. Exhausted, the girl falls to her knees before her beloved master. To restore her, he gives her the wine, which she gulps down thirstily. Instantly she realizes that it is poisoned. But she is glad to sacrifice her life for Chu Yuan, who represents the future of her country, and she dies praising him. The guard kills the evil Diviner and sets fire to the temple. Chu Yuan and the guard place the girl's body on an altar and lay a garland of flowers on her body, to give her a proper funeral. They discover in her possession the scroll on which is inscribed his "Ode to the Orange". Chuan Yuan reads part of it aloud in tribute to the loyal girl. He concludes:

> Chan Chuan, my dear pupil! Chan Chuan, my benefactor!
> You have set the place on fire, you have conquered darkness;
> You are forever and ever the angel of light.

The surprisingly helpful guard, who refuses to give his name, insists that Chu Yuan shall save himself to lead the country. As the flames rise, the master spreads the scroll over Chan Chuan; the two men flee.

The first act is exceedingly slow, but thereafter the drama gains momentum and captures attention, never losing it. The characters are mostly one-dimensional, but their speech is elegant and epigrammatic. Chu Yuan is far from a perfect hero. He tends to be self-congratulatory about his moral superiority. Despite his proclivity for wise if very lengthy preachments in the opening scenes, he displays no self-control or caution when confronted by a dangerous situation, and certainly he lacks insight into the true nature of those around him. The atmosphere of the period is ably conjured up, and songs punctuate the action, and the settings and costumes should be lavish and have splashes of colour.

The play has been described at length as an example of the historical dramas written at this time. (An English translation of this script, by Yang Hsien Yi and Gladys Yang, was published in 1953.)

As remarked above, Guo Moruo was among the few prominent writers spared harassment during the traumatic Cultural Revolution; his writings continued to appear, and he was on hand at important public occasions. Perhaps he had slyly created the hot-headed Chu Yuan as a model of how *not* to behave at a moment of crisis?

Of particular interest to us is an official survey conducted by Guo Moruo of China's stages in 1950. "According to incomplete figures, in the eighteen major cities below the Great Wall there are eighty-two theatres in the North-East. There are four hundred drama groups, with forty thousand actors, musicians, singers, dancers and other members throughout the country, including those attached to the People's Liberation Army and those directed by municipal and higher governments." Twenty-five of these theatres were located in Peking. Obviously, not all of them were occupied by *huaju* troupes; most were still devoted to performances of operas and other traditional forms of entertainment – puppet plays, variety, circuses – a very considerable amount of theatrical activity, seeking to attract and please a multitude of curious but not very sophisticated spectators.

The Chinese writer best known to foreign readers was the author of a novel, *Rickshaw Boy*, a bestseller in the United States and Europe, a truly rare phenomenon. Lao She (1899–1966) also wrote a play of long-lasting merit, *Teahouse* (1957), in which a half-century of China's history is evoked. Its début took place at the Peking People's Art Theatre, where Lao She's work was much favoured. Starting at the turn of the century, the story ends in 1947, when revolutionary upheaval prevailed. During the five decades that are traversed, the playwright remarks, "empires have fallen, but nothing has essentially changed. In place of slavery to a master, there is now bondage to the state. The masses still exist in miserable poverty. Factionalism and corruption beset the government. To survive, one must be wholly pragmatic."

In 1983 *Teahouse* was brought to New York – off-Broadway – by the Pan Asian Repertory Theatre. Critics complained that the English translation by Ying Roucheng and John Howard-Gibbon was awkward, some passages of dialogue not flowing smoothly. A cast of twenty-five was needed, many of the players assuming more than fifty parts, some merely brief appearances. Mel Gussow commented in the *New York Times*:

> Detailed descriptions in the program help us keep track of the characters. There is so much quick switching of roles and of make-up that the actors' mustaches are occasionally askew. But the eagerness is infectious and Tisa Chang's staging blends the company into a uniform, understated style of performance.
>
> The Pan Asian Theatre has been transformed into a Peking teahouse, with the audience sitting close to the action. Between the acts, the house is refurbished and modernized, and tea and rice are served to a constantly shifting stream of characters. The sinister pimp of the first act is replaced by his son, a slicker version of his father, in the third act. Both roles are played with relish by Ernest Abuba.
>
> At the center of the broad historical canvas is the manager of the teahouse, played by Henry Yuk, one of the most versatile actors in the Pan Asian troupe. He begins as a patient observer of his clientele – a working-class version of Grand Hotel – and ends as an embittered old man. He and his wife, Natsuko Ohama, are as close as the play comes to having a conscience.
>
> In smaller glimpses we meet a vivid array of citizens, from peddlers to policemen who serve

whatever authority appears to be in control. There is a desperate father who sells his daughter to a court eunuch, a soothsayer who spans the centuries and two cronies who would simply like to have a quiet cup of tea together but should be on the lookout for informers.

When anything goes wrong, it is blamed on the "foreigners," people of unstated nationality who are corrupting the not-so-innocent natives. The playwright's view, finally, is cynical. For all its crowd of humanity, *Teahouse* is an elegiac epic chronicling an artist's disillusionment with his nation.

Under Miss Chang's direction, there are deft cameo performances by Tom Matsusaka, Alvin Lum, Donald Li and Christen Villamor, among others. Christine Cooper is credited with the hair and beard design, and the elaborate costumes are by Eiko Yamaguchi. As designed by Atsushi Moriyasu, the teahouse itself could open for business.

A dramatization of *Rickshaw Boy* was also chosen by the Peking People's Theatre; indeed, no other work was given as frequently there, save only for the plays of Cao Yu.

Lao She was among those who took part in the China Drama-World Resist-the-Enemy Federation between 1937 and 1945, and he, too, spent time mingling with soldiers engaged in the Korean conflict in 1953. After the establishment of the People's Republic he was appointed to high posts in organizations devoted to the arts. He turned from writing novels to preparing scripts for the stage, but often met with difficulties, finding himself at odds with officials who charged him with doctrinal errors. Nevertheless he remained a prominent literary figure until the onset of the Cultural Revolution, when his situation worsened.

One night he left home for a short walk and disappeared. The next day anxious searchers found his body floating face-down in a nearby Peking lake. Many of his friends were convinced that it was suicide, but his wife believed that he was murdered.

After his death his work was still judged harshly. Chiefly, faults were found with his early novels. In particular, his language was condemned as "vulgar".

Some years before the Maoist takeover, Communist-oriented drama had its first significant representation in the output of Hsia Yen (or Shen Tuan-hsien; 1900–1995), who had studied electrical engineering in Japan. His interests shifted to literature and leftist ideology; in 1927 he enrolled in the Communist Party and became active in the Shanghai underground. He wrote a historical drama, *Sai Chin-hua* (1936) that aroused debate, and followed it a year later with *Under Shanghai Eaves* (*Shanghai wu-yen hsia*; 1937), a piece belonging to the naturalist or "slice-of-life" school and resembling

Elmer Rice's panoramic *Street Scene* and Fujimori Seikichi's *Light and Dark*, which in turn owe a debt to Maxim Gorky, Zola and the Goncourts, in whose dramas the characters suffer baneful effects not from personal flaws but from their environment, especially crippling poverty.

In *Under Shanghai Eaves* a typical two-storey "lane house" in Shanghai is occupied by five house-holds. To show this a cross-section of the building takes up the stage, revealing details of four cluttered apartments; the attic, in which lives an old, bibulous newspaper vendor, Li Ling-pei, is not visible. A steep, angular stairway connects the flats. It is April 1937, during the rainy season. Passers-by, hurry-ing by in the intermittent drizzles and showers, can be glimpsed behind windows, a courtyard and the gateway. At moments a pale sun penetrates the overcast. Whereas in Rice's *Street Scene* the audience sees a row of houses facing a pavement, here the view is from the inside looking out of the multiple dwelling. The other tenants are a middle-aged elementary school-teacher with his wife and two chil-dren, a son and daughter, who live in what was formerly the scullery; Huang Chia-mei, twenty-eight, now ill and out of work but formerly employed by a foreign firm, who occupies the garret with his wife and his fifty-eight-year-old father, a first-time visitor from the countryside; Shih Hsiao-pao, a still youthful prostitute, who rents the front upstairs room; Lin Chih-ch'eng, the sub-lessor of the house, who is in possession of the parlour, which he shares with a wife, Yang Ts'ai-yü, and a twelve-year-old stepdaughter, Pao-chen. Other characters are K'uang Fu, Yang Ts'ai-yü's first husband by whom she bore Pao-chen; and Little Tientsin, Shih Hsiao-pao's pimp; peddlers, delivery boys and the like, mak-ing up a large cast. Street-sounds, cries of vendors, the noise of rain on gutters and tin eaves, are regularly heard.

A series of deft characterizations unfolds. Chao and his wife (who is not given a name) are forever bickering; she nags at him because he is too talkative and too satisfied with his comparatively humble lot in life and poorly paid labours. Lin, the sub-lessor, is an angry man; he works as a supervisor in a silk mill and feels exploited by his employer. He rails at the world. Huang's father, the visiting farmer, is deaf and unaware that his well-educated, only son, of whom he is proud, is actually without a job and almost destitute. Shih, the street-walker, is good-natured and easy-going, though she frequently quarrels with her pimp. A crisis occurs with the reappearance of a bedraggled, broken K'uang Fu, the former husband of Lin's wife and the father of little Pao-chen. He has been in prison for seven years. (His crime is never stated.) Earlier, he and Lin had been very close friends. While K'uang Fu was incarcerated, Lin had sought to assist his friend's bereft wife and child. He had fallen in love with Yang Ts'ai-yü and, all too ready to think K'uang Fu was no longer alive, had married her. The return of K'uang Fu overwhelms Lin with guilt, but K'uang Fu's attitude is somewhat forgiving. Word comes that there is trouble at the silk factory; Lin is needed there at once. Reluctantly he hurries off. Later, after arguing with the harsh mill-boss, he quits his job as supervisor and feels "liberated". Huang Chia-mei's father cuts short his visit and leaves behind a good sum of money, perhaps his life savings. Though not letting on, he has been aware of his son's serious plight. K'uang Fu, fearing that he cannot honestly support a wife and daughter, disappears once again; an earnest attempt to find him is futile.

The story-lines are neatly interlaced, each strand plaited ingeniously and smoothly with the next. The characters are vivid; their speech is natural and often wry. Ah-nin, the Chaos's little son, is trying to solve a problem in arithmetic; he takes his book to his mother for help.

AH-NIN: Mom, a man named Wang gets paid three hundred and fifty dollars a month, and a man named Li gets two hundred and eighty. After three years, what's –

CHAO'S WIFE [*before he can finish; as if exploding*]: I don't want to hear any more of that business! Your dad doesn't even make thirty-five dollars a month!

CHAO [*startled*]: What's that?

AH-NIN [*pleading*]: Tell me! The teacher's going to ask me tomorrow. It's something in the book. A man named Wang gets three hundred and fifty dollars a month . . .

CHAO'S WIFE [*irritably*]: Go ask somebody who's rich: I've never laid eyes on three hundred and fifty dollars in my whole life.

AH-NIN [*in resignation goes to his father*]: Dad, after three years, what's the difference between the amount of money each one had?

His father does some calculations with his pen and explains the method, then provides the answer.

CHAO'S WIFE [*still incensed*]: Three hundred and fifty dollars a month salary, saves sixty-five dollars a month, fantastic!

AH-NIN [*turns around in rebuttal*]: It's in the book!

CHAO'S WIFE: In the book, huh? This kind of book is for the rich people!

[Translation: George Hayden]

Gunn points out, however, that most of the characters do not belong to the proletariat but are "*petit-bourgeoisie*" – a teacher, a plant manager, a well-educated clerk – "whose expectations are only frustrated by the status quo". He comments: "Hsia Yen aims at . . . sociological schematization, and with a certain logic avoids creating a central protagonist and subordinates plot to concern with the situation, the oppressive atmosphere and its ingredients. . . . Critics have argued forcefully that in such panoramic works the fundamental human observations (such as the theme of man and wife versus economic necessity in *Under Shanghai Eaves*) are never developed, and there is a tendency to rely on the exposure of deprivations as being inherently dramatic when it is not. In any case, the kind of play which Hsia Yen produced was to be repeated with variations throughout the War of Resistance, Yü Ling's *Shanghai Night*, Sung Chih-ti's *Chungking Fog*, and finally an adaptation of Gorky's *The Lower Depths* by Shih T'o and K'o Ling, entitled *The Night Inn* (*Yeh tien*), which does examine the lowest rung of society, being the best known."

Throughout the struggle against the Japanese invaders, which grew into the Second World War, Hsia Yen contributed a series of plays urging resistance to the enemy. Patriotism and the extirpation of class oppression and poverty were his two major themes. His works were well regarded and popular. Subsequently, during the 1950s, he was rewarded with several prestigious posts, among them the Vice-Presidency of the Federation of Literary and Art Circles. In the 1930s, however, he had already been involved in bitter intra-party feuding, particularly in disputes with the celebrated writer Lu Hsün, who called him and some of his like-minded associates "the four villains". This label came to life again in 1966, at the time of the Cultural Revolution, when Hsia Yen and his friends were accused of fostering an anti-Maoist ideology. He was gaoled and tortured. Rehabilitated in 1978, he gained new favour and shortly was appointed chairman of the Committee to Safeguard Writers' Rights and Interests of the Chinese Writers' Association (1979).

For a span of years, until Stalin's death, China and Russia, the two Communist superpowers, had a strong political alliance. As a result the influence of Russian authors became dominant. This is seen in the output of Ch'en Pai-Ch'en (b. 1908), who in his early years studied at several universities and participated in Communist youth groups. The price he paid was three years' imprisonment (1932–5) imposed by the Nationalists' regime. Released, he penned stories of life in prison, notably *The Realm of Hsiao Wei*, which won him notice. He began to churn out a host of plays and during the War of Resistance was active in theatre and film ventures in Chengdu and Chungking. His flair was for madcap satire, broad and Jonsonian, and he soon achieved prominence in this truly difficult genre. A good example of his talent for it is *Men and Women in Wild Times* (*Luan-shih nan-nü*; 1939), in which even his stage-instructions have exuberant wit.

The opening scene is the Nanking railway station as the Japanese army is approaching the city. A clamouring mob of people are trying to leave. On stage is a cross-section of a second-class railway carriage packed almost to suffocation by those able to force their way into it. Others are pushing and shoving, climbing and elbowing, in a vain, desperate bid to board it.

Singled out are a group of intellectuals and artists who are among the fearful and aggressive passengers: Miss Violet Wave and Wang Hao-Jan, both of them writers; Miao I-ou, a translator; Wu Ch'iu-p'ing, a magazine editor; Wang Yin-feng, a female nightclub entertainer. Also in flight from Nanking on the train are Madame Bureau Chief, who brings along a portable toilet; and Hsü Shao-Ch'ing, a self-important official and businessman, and Mrs Hsü. The company also includes P'u Shih-Chin, a glib young man who prides himself on always being *au courant*, and Ch'in Fan, a redoubtable member of the Resistance. Finally, there is a mysterious woman, Li Man-shu.

In the crush, while newcomers are still trying to clamber on, the focal figures conduct themselves as though at a formal gathering, introducing themselves, exchanging chit-chat. Wu Ch'iu-p'ing, who has been publishing the defunct monthly *China Journal* which he expects to resurrect in Hankow, invites Violet Wave and Wang Hao-Jan to become contributors to it. The outwardly polite P'u is especially active in establishing a social relation with everybody. To prevent more frightened people from climbing in, the windows are shut; outside, hands pound on glass. Refugees perch on the roof of the carriage. A woman gives birth to a child in the WC, and the new-born infant's wail is heard. The locomotive's whistle sounds savagely, there is a violent jolt, the train sets off. The crowd inside the carriage cheers.

The cars bump against each other, knocking a child from the roof. A woman screams, hurls down the child in her arms, and jumps off after it. A gust of wind blows away Violet Wave's handkerchief, and Madame Bureau Chief worries about her suitcase.

In Scene Two, now midnight, the train is stalled at a rural station. The moon is bright. The people atop the carriage are cold and hungry, anxious and impatient, wondering why the train has halted. Madam Bureau Chief is still concerned about her luggage. There is talk about air-raids over Nanking; P'u relates his narrow escape from a bomb. Miao more than matches the story by recounting an experience of his own, one that sounds exceedingly far-fetched. Hsü is pessimistic about China successfully defending itself. The others speak rhetorically and sanctimoniously about the brave Resistance and the sacrifices by the fighting men at the front. Mrs Hsü is appalled by having to sit alongside Wang Yin-feng, the cabaret singer – she deems her no better than a prostitute and "unclean" – and changes her place to put at least a small distance between them. Wang Hao-Jan passes around a bottle of wine, which loosens tongues even more. P'u asks Violet Wave about her origins and how she got her strange name, a query which provokes tears and an ambiguous reply. A food vendor comes through the coach, and everyone struggles to buy something from him. He is quickly sold out, leaving many passengers angry and unsatisfied. Wang Hao-Jan asks Violet Wave to look at a manuscript and offer criticism of his poems, but she replies vaguely. People's stomachs are rumbling from growing hunger, and they become quarrelsome. Only Wang Yin-feng has brought along an adequate repast, of which she partakes while the others eye her greedily. P'u is delegated to offer to buy snacks from her, but she instantly agrees to share with everybody and accepts no payment. They wolf down her condiments. An air-raid alarm is sounded; all the passengers panic, leaping from the train. Mrs Hsü is rescued by Ch'in Fan, the Resistance fighter.

At the start of Act Two, several months have elapsed; it is summer. The little group that spontaneously took shape on the train has cohered in Hankow; most are staying at the same hotel. Afterwards they move further to the interior, far from the war. There is constant interaction between them and much, much talk. Erotic intrigues – and infidelities – spring up and are carried on.

There are grandiose plans, meetings and debates about them. This bright, talented clique – for so they view themselves – will publish a newspaper, the *Rear Area News*, to be financed by the entrepreneurial Mr Hsü, and also produce a play – they have obtained a script – that will also be funded by the affluent Hsü, the proceeds to go to charity. The editorial bias of the journal and the casting of the play lead to fervent arguments and dissents, along with neurotic backbiting and incessant gossip. Personal secrets are exposed. Basically these are shallow, always self-interested pretenders, intellectual and artistic *manqués*, whom the playwright mercilessly and progressively reduces to unedifying caricatures – with a few moments of pathos thrown in – representing a whole class that the author, a leftist, obviously dislikes. At the end, the newspaper is not published, the play is dropped. As the Japanese near the city, Mr Hsü and his unhappy wife depart abruptly to greater safety in Hong Kong and the others scurry to find new refuge from the approaching enemy.

It is impossible for Acts Two and Three to match the brilliant theatricality of Act One, the scenes on the overcrowded train. Nor is the tone of the play at all pleasant. Yet there is no doubt that the characters – even when diminished to caricatures – are instantly recognizable, all too authentic. An important aspect of the social scene is faithfully portrayed, condemned, doomed – or so Ch'en Pai-Ch'en hopes.

Most of the citizens of this chattering circle have hollow emotions. P'u, disgruntled, talks of enlisting in the army.

P'U [*standing erect*]: Ah, I've been in the rear area too long. I want to go and join the Resistance myself! I want to go to the guerrilla zone! I want to take my place out there at the front –
[*From beneath the window are heard the sound of marching feet, battle songs and shouted slogans.*]

CH'IN [*looking at P'u*]: You want to join the Resistance?

P'U [*swelling with emotion*]: Yes – I!

CH'IN [*gravely*]: If you want to join the Resistance, then practice what you preach. Empty shouting is useless. If you want to fight, you can join up anywhere. It doesn't have to be North China! Any unit will do. It doesn't have to be a guerrilla unit. Look! Aren't those recruits marching out – they are going to fight!

[*The sounds of marching, singing and shouting swell. The curtain falls.*]

[Translation: Edward M. Gunn]

It will be noted that, after the zany action, each act ends on a sober note. An orphaned child, whom Mrs Hsü has gained consent to adopt, is killed by a bomb falling in the street. Mrs Bureau Chief, who has been searching for her missing husband, discovers that he is about to shed her and marry someone else, the wedding ceremony to occur that very day. She collapses in tears.

When the participants of the group convene to read the play they are going to stage – its author is a Mr T'ang, and its title is *Men and Women in Wild Times* – they are outraged to find that they themselves are characters in it, minutely described and altogether unfavourably. They discuss whether Mr T'ang should be sued for libel.

Pai-Ch'en's scalpel is sharp and precise. Each figure in the play is archetypical of one kind of denizen in the realm of the intelligentsia, and his or her like might also be observed at a gathering in any Western capital city. The dialogue, which is acidulous, is also at times a bit coarse.

Gunn says:

Among those influenced by Gogol, the works of Ch'en Pai-ch'en during the War of Resistance include some of the liveliest social satire in modern China. Gogol's most famous play, *The Inspector General*, is known for its use of the device of a non-entity impersonating a high-level official; Ch'en Pai-ch'en's best-known work, *The Promotion Plan* (1945, *Sheng-kuan t'u*) borrows this device. More important is his readiness to use the grotesque.

. . . That so many self-appointed guardians of patriotism in the arts were appalled by Ch'en's satires could only have gratified him, since the exposure of sham is central in his work. Indeed, devotees of satire might well argue that Ch'en's positive messages in his work are too obtrusive; but the purer forms of satire were not likely to be appreciated by the Chinese Communist Party of middlebrow critics, who considered positive characters and gestures always more appropriate. This cannot detract from appreciation of Ch'en's masterful orchestration of manners and moods and his breaking away from static scenes to fluid, dynamic ones. Disorder is his trademark: be it an official's home invaded by an indignant mob, an office filled with slovenly bureaucrats, an apartment being rented to a couple just after the former tenant has deserted it, or, as in *Men and Women in Wild Times*, a train packed to overflowing with refugees and their possessions. And so this play remains among the most memorable of the war period.

Among Ch'en Pai-Ch'en's other works is *The Wedding March* (*Chieh-hun chin-hsing*). He produced a number of sketches in which he satirized United States policies. He was able to survive the Cultural Revolution and subsequently brought out *Song of the Great Wind* (*Ta feng ko*; 1977), a historical drama. In 1979 he held the posts of Vice-President of the Playwrights' Association and a lectureship at Nanjing University.

Li Chien-wu (b. 1906) studied at Tsinghua University and spent two years in Paris (1933–5). In Shanghai he became a teacher. A series of comedies, written during the 1930s, gained him a reputation in the theatre. Among these works were *To Take as a Model* (*I-shen tso-tse*) and *This Is But the Spring* (*Che pu-kuo shih ch'un-t'ien*). During the next decade he devoted himself to adapting some of the scripts of Sardou and Eugene Scribe, offered historical dramas of his own, and turned out a charming, exuberant farce, *Springtime* (*Ch'ing-ch'un*; 1944). Under the pen-name Liu Hsi-wei he wrote essays about the stage and assumed acting roles, gaining further celebrity. The Cultural Revolution was a hiatus in his theatrical and literary progress, but later he resumed his career as a respected drama critic.

Springtime is set early in the century, 1908. One of the two focal figures is a scapegrace, prank-loving youth, eighteen-year-old T'ien Hsi-erh, son of the Widow T'ien, whose life he makes miserable by his misconduct. She alternately upbraids and defends him from the chidings and beatings inflicted on him by neighbours in their North China village. He is eager to get away from his dull environment and go to the provincial capital or even Peking, where existence is more lively. He is enamoured of the mayor's elder daughter, the flirtatious Hsiang-ts'ao, and tries to persuade her to run away with him. Her father, Yang, particularly dislikes the undisciplined Hsi-erh.

The young couple's attempt to elope under the cover of night goes awkwardly astray through the unwitting intervention of her parents. This scene is in a moonlit garden which is also invaded by Rednose, a drunken watchman, as well as by two mischievous boys trying to steal pomegranates.

Taking flight, Hsi-erh has left behind a bundle which enables Mayor Yang to identify the intruder whose intention is mistakenly thought to have been robbery. The Mayor vows to have the rascal severely punished.

Half asleep and exhausted, Hsi-erh is overtaken and brought before the Mayor and Mr Cheng, the sententious local schoolmaster. The miscreant is to be strung up by his arms in the barn for three days, but Hsi-erh's mother arrives and makes up a false alibi for her son, while her sharp tongue holds Yang and his cohorts at bay. The bundle, opened, is found to contain Hsiang-ts'ao's garments and other intimate possessions, greatly angering and embarrassing the Mayor and his wife. The Widow gives her son a good hiding with a switch. He scampers off. The Widow puts the blame for Hsi-erh's errant behaviour on the forwardness of Hsiang-ts'ao. Mayor Yang and the Widow almost come to blows over this accusation. After the others have departed, Mr and Mrs Yang quarrel. He insists that his daughter shall marry an eleven-year-old husband whom he has chosen for her. Mrs Yang, who herself was wed to Yang when he was a mere boy, is stunned by her mate's wrathful edict.

A year passes. Hsi-erh, ill, pines for his beloved. Hsiang-ts'ao is now married. Accompanied by her father-in-law, Dr Luo, a respected scholar, and by her childish husband, the girl returns to visit her parents. She is being treated as a drudge by her wealthy father-in-law and has been most unhappy. The Widow T'ien objects to the meeting, and her interference infuriates Hsi-erh, which leads to further quarrelling between mother and son, culminating when he locks her behind the double door of a nearby temple, along with Mr Cheng, the schoolmaster, and Dr Luo, who were in conference inside. Then he lifts Hsiang-ts'ao and carries her off in his arms.

Rednose arrives after a delay and lets out the irate trio, long pent in the decaying temple. Mayor Yang and his wife join the excited group, demanding an explanation for what has happened. Dr Luo calls his daughter-in-law a "hussy" and vows to arrange a divorce between her and his son. He stalks off with the snivelling lad. Mayor Yang rains imprecations on Hsiang-ts'ao, who has re-appeared with her younger sister, Hsiang-chü. He threatens to kill her. His wife and the sobbing Hsiang-ts'ao plead for mercy, as do Mr Cheng and little Hsiang-chü, but the Mayor demands to be left alone with the daughter who has brought shame on him. She declares that she is ready to die. They prepare for the ceremonial rites. The Widow re-enters and adds her tears to those of Hsiang-ts'ao and Mayor Yang. Hsi-erh, also returning, pleads eloquently for Hsiang-ts'ao's hand, even though his mother protests at the match as ill suited. Her son promises to change his "wild grasshopper" ways. The Widow, suggesting that the girl be spared and sent to a convent, is told by the Mayor to mind her own business. Indignant, the Widow snatches the girl from him, embraces her and announces that she will adopt her. Hsi-erh, delighted, swears everlasting gratitude to his mother. Striding away, Mayor Yang threatens to take the matter to court. Scoffing, the Widow turns to Hsiang-ts'ao:

> WIDOW: Don't be afraid, my dear. "Trees have bark, people have face"; the last thing your dad will do will be to go to the country court and wash his dirty linen in public! [*To Hsi-erh, as if calling in the hens*] Anything else can wait until we get home. Cluck, cluck! Off you go!
> [*A low shaft of sunlight falls on their retreating figures, as the evening draws in. The farmers have finished their work in the fields and their sounds are carried from the distance – their singing, their commands to their animals; at the same time the lowing of oxen and the braying of asses, and the cawing of crows as darkness falls, weave together to make the music of the countryside.*]

[Translated by David Pollard]

The Widow is excellently characterized, resourceful and wasp-tongued. The dialogue is sprightly, if occasionally a bit earthy. The play has a brightness and breeziness that justifies its title. Those who read the text are granted a bonus, for the stage instructions – once again – are lyrical and witty.

A light work, *Springtime* hardly seems significant, but Gunn says that it is peculiarly representative of the wartime period. Composed in the mid-1940s, when audiences had become less concerned about the fighting, and in Shanghai, where the theatre was thriving and unresponsive to the local authority installed by the Japanese military, the play was not published until the war's end. *Springtime* does have a social theme and a few references to events in China around the turn of the century, the closing years of the Ch'ing dynasty. But its art is largely bent towards the creation of typical characters in a well-worn situation of frustrated courtship, freshened by Li's comic approach. Gunn says:

> At a time when the social order was breaking down, Li – much like Thornton Wilder in the West – was a sophisticated man of letters nostalgically turning back to the once comfortable features of the Chinese mental landscape. Yet – again like Thornton Wilder – Li presents real pain and pushes the action to the brink of disaster, only to arrest it with the reassertion of that which is familiar and reassuring. In such a world, authority always has its limits; anarchy is benign. If this seems an inadequately serious view of Chinese society at the time, it is nevertheless the nature of farcical comedy to rescue action from grim consequences. And if it seems out of place as the work of a French-educated admirer of Flaubert like Li, he has an authentic style, not simply pastoral imitation, loading the dialogue with the language of his native Hopei-Peking region, and spicing it with the patter of folk-style oral recitation and the derisive jingles of urchins. For readers accustomed to American English,

David Pollard's rendering of the play in colloquial British English enhances the effect of the original Chinese dialogue.

Another work choosing rural North China for its background, and bearing a title that suggests the vernal season, is *Windswept Blossoms* (*Feng-hsü*; 1945–6) by Yang Chiang (or Yang Chi-k'ang, b. 1911). A student of foreign languages in Soochow, Shanghai, and at Tsinghua University in Peking, she married Ch'en Chung-tsu, also a writer and scholar. The pair went abroad to enroll in more advanced studies in Europe. On their return in 1937 they made their home in Shanghai, where Yang Chiang taught at Aurora Women's College. Her literary output encompasses short stories, essays, and at least four plays offered between 1942 and 1947. In turn she was elected a member of the Institute of Literature and the Institute of Foreign Literature of the Academy of Social Sciences. After the Cultural Revolution she translated Chinese works and published the texts of *Don Quixote*, *Gil Blas* and *La Vida de Lazarillo de Tormes*, and brought out a volume of critical essays, *Spring Soil* (*Ch'un ni chi*; 1979) and a memoir describing existence during the Red Guard uprising, *Six Chapters from a Cadre School* (*Kan-hsiao Liu-chi*; 1981).

Windswept Blossoms belongs to the era of "Republican China". Once again a dilapidated temple in the countryside, near a railway track, is the scene. It, too, has been converted into a primary school, as was the temple in *Springtime*. Peach blossoms, blown by the wind, cover much of the stage, which is especially animated: Fang Ching-shen, the idealistic local teacher, is coming back after a year in prison, and his students and neighbours are preparing a celebration in his honour. Least happy is his young wife, Shen Hui-lien, barely more than a bride, who has found life too harsh and unrewarding in this remote area and yearns to return to her native city. She regrets having defied her parents to marry a poor man, whom she now greets coldly. She is disenchanted, no longer sharing her husband's altruistic goals of serving a backward community. He has regained his freedom largely through the efforts of a friend and lawyer, T'ang Shu-yua. (The charge against him is never specified, but presumably he has been an outspoken political dissident.) During Fang's prolonged absence an unspoken attraction has grown up between T'ang and Shen. Also interested in Shen is Yeh San, a landowner to whom belongs the erstwhile temple occupied by Fang and his wife; he now desires to repossess it, having in mind other uses for it.

Fang is anxious to resume his local projects for uplifting the life of villagers, but Shen wants no part of his crusade and soon they are quarrelling. The villagers do not respond to Fang's appeals to welcome change as he had hoped they might. He is ever more zealous, even fanatical, bordering on arrogance and self-righteousness, convinced that everybody should share his well-intentioned visions. Yeh San wants to evict the Fangs from their temple–school–handicraft centre. But setbacks do not dismay Fang; his drive and self-confidence are dynamic. He is sure that he will find some means or other of prevailing.

T'ang comes to dinner; Fang wants to express his gratitude for his friend's stalwart support. T'ang does not share Fang's social goals; he has too many family obligations and simply cannot afford to be an idealist. Extolling Shen, Fang asks why T'ang has never married. The lawyer replies that not only must he care for his mother and sister, but as yet he has not found the right woman. Fang tells him that a man in love should let no obstacle deter him from taking what he wants. Unfortunate advice. During the meal Fang gradually senses the frustrated passion that possesses both his wife and his good friend. After T'ang's departure Fang abruptly confronts Shen. His suspicions increasingly aflame, he accuses her of infidelity. She acknowledges her love for T'ang and expresses a wish to go away. She tells Fang that he selfishly requires others to subordinate their lives to him and his unrealistic projects. The argument intensifies, and at its climax Shen packs a suitcase and leaves.

After a sleepless night, Fang is exhausted. He is visited by an uncle and cousin who bring word of a job opening in the city for which he might apply, though he is not fully qualified for it. He rebukes them, saying disdainfully that he is unwilling to compromise his values, nor is he interested in making money or seeking a future high position. Hurt by his rudeness, they ruefully depart. Left alone, Fang engages in a bout of self-pity: his nobility of purpose is unappreciated.

Two men arrive and begin carrying out the furniture; they have been sent by Yeh San, who is repossessing the school. Shen reappears and drives away the men after reminding them how Fang has tried to help them at dire cost to himself. They speak scornfully of his local projects. If he teaches the children to read, they will not be good field workers. They warn that Fang is again in danger of being arrested, this time for radical proposals he has put in writing.

Fang is told that T'ang and Shen have been seen meeting and going into a hotel at the railway station. Deeply hurt and beset by jealousy, his mood is suicidal.

Actually, T'ang has been exercising remarkable self-denial. He tells Shen that he is unworthy of her: he is no more than "a cold, priggish Confucian hypocrite". She amends this to be "a warm, genuine Confucian gentleman". He considers himself to be insignificant but says that after an earlier rebellion he has reconciled himself to his mediocre role.

He escorts her back to the school. Hearing noises, Fang slips out of sight. Suddenly T'ang sees a note that Fang has left incomplete. It implies that in his misery and despair Fang is about to kill himself. They search frantically for him, even setting out for a nearby pond where he may have gone to drown himself. While they are away, Fang returns and arms himself with a pistol.

Their search futile, T'ang and Shen stumble back to the temple. She blames herself for this possible tragic outcome. T'ang, unable to restrain himself any longer, confesses his deep and gnawing love for her. Their mutual avowals are rhapsodic and overheard by Fang. He breaks in, intending to kill them both. Confronting them, he questions madly whether he shall aim at T'ang, sparing Shen, or at her, sparing her lover. Stepping forward, Shen snatches the loosely held pistol from his hand and fires it at herself. As she falls lifeless, the two men gaze at her, startled, horrified.

Much of the dialogue is philosophical, and there is much self-probing by the main characters. At times they engage in self-criticism at length, often in very literary monologues. The two men bare several facets of their personality. T'ang is modest and puritanical. Fang is alternately dedicated to helping others and contemptuous of those not sharing his charitable impulses and high purposes. He grants that he can be tough, ruthless, in attempting to serve humanity and perhaps making a name for himself. He somewhat resembles the reformers portrayed by Ibsen in *Brand* and *The Wild Duck*, especially Gregers Werle in the latter work, the confused intellectual who boasts of being an "idealist" though actually he is a psychological misfit, ever the unwelcome "thirteenth guest" at the dinner table. In his youth Ibsen had been a political activist in the cause of Norwegian independence; he quit the movement, having come to despise his fellow rebels, who called themselves "idealists" – the word was a cover for their power-hunger and self-interest, which they were in fact much too ineffectual to achieve. However, Yang Chiang may not have taken Fang from Ibsen but instead from life, where in some circles his name is legion; he is once again archetypal. Yang Chiang might well have known him at first hand.

Shen Hui-lien strikes mostly the same note throughout; hers is a litany of self-blame for past irrationality in having married the penniless and egocentric Fang.

In structure *Windswept Blossoms* does resemble an Ibsen drama, being well made, compressed in time and place. Some reviewers found fault with the melodramatic ending – a bit reminiscent of the neatly "planted" suicide of Hedda Gabler. With unusual modesty, Yang Chiang herself referred to her work as a "potboiler", but most commentators agree that it rises far above that level because of its serious and convincing psychologizing and as a picture of the misguided zeal of young Chinese intellectuals talking and dreaming of remaking their long-static society and creating a new and better nation. (One reason for Yang Chiang's deprecating remark may have been that love triangles and their resolution through suicide were clichés in the popular drama of this period.)

By 1949, prolonged civil strife brought total victory to the Mao-led Communist forces. Chiang Kai-shek's Nationalist troops were able to retreat, though hastily, to the large offshore island of Taiwan, where they still exerted rule. A Marxist regime, now established on the vast mainland, brought a heap of social changes. This was quickly manifested in the theatre, as playwrights adapted to new circumstances, most of them – as has been noted – quite readily, since their sympathies had been left-ist. The Marxists decreed that the stage should be used to indoctrinate the masses, as in adjacent Soviet Russia. Henceforth it was a tool to instruct and spread propaganda. Playwrights must be alert to each shift in the Party line; accordingly, censorship became stricter if sometimes unpredictable. Another result was that the Peking government's financial assistance to acting troupes increased, and theatres proliferated, newly established in many parts of the country.

An example of drama during this transitional political phase is *Cuckoo Sings Again* (*Pu-Ku-niao yu chiao-le*; 1957), a very popular and widely given play by Yang Lü-fang, about whom little is known. He served in the Navy; afterwards he made his home in a rural part of Kiangsu province, where he gathered the necessary material for his script. His offering was greeted with both praise and protest, and public awareness of him was surprisingly short-lived. His script seemed at first to fit what was officially desired: it deals with peasants, the hill people of central China – their speech and folk-ways authenti-cally reproduced – and it is in the preferred realistic genre. Peasant songs enliven it. The characters voice their love of hard work and they happily embrace the recently introduced farm cooperative move-ment, though not all of them are wholly altruistic. (In Hollywood the pat formula for a run-of-the-mill release was summed up as "boy meets girl, boy loses girl, boy gets girl again". Amused by the appear-ance of a somewhat similar pattern in Russian and Chinese state-sponsored pictures, the Hollywood scriptwriters said that over there it was instead "boy meets tractor, boy loses tractor, boy gets tractor again".) But Yang Lü-fang instils his comedy with more than usual charm and it is marked by a tone of gentle mockery, which is what eventually led to its inciting protests by more inflexible Party critics.

Setting his story in 1956, on a collective farm, Yang Lü-fang brings together a group of typical labourers of various ages, whose dedicated if austere leader is Fang Pao-shan, the Party Branch Secretary. A good deal of rivalry and raillery is carried on between the men and women workers; for both, the task is to gather and spread manure – an auxiliary theme is a degree of feminism, the partial liberation of women, who assume jobs and responsibilities hitherto assigned only to men. The principal role is T'ung Ya-nan, a Female Youth League member, whose nickname is "Cuckoo", a sobriquet earned because she is fond of singing folk-ballads in one of which the refrain is "*Ko-li ko-san tuo, Ko-li ko san tuo*". Vivacious and flirtatious, she is to marry Wang Pi-hau, an overly earnest Young League Branch Committee Member, her self-appointed teacher about how to conduct herself properly and carry out her duties. He finds her a difficult pupil, obedient but often too frivolous; he is jealous whenever her glance chances elsewhere, especially when it strays towards Shen Hsiao-chia, a shy young man who is learning how to drive a tractor.

For Cuckoo, one of Shen's attractions is his skill in playing a two-stringed fiddle; the music enchants her. He suggests that they rehearse together; though wishing to, she desists, because she has promised

Wang that she and Shen will not again sing together. She is the "cuckoo" who must now be silent.

Her real desire is to become a tractor-driver. When she reveals this to Shen, he helps her to prepare a formal request for instruction. He tearfully confesses to his one-armed friend Kuo Chia-lin that he is deeply and hopelessly in love with Cuckoo.

Cuckoo is accepted for the tractor-driving course. Wang is greatly alarmed at the prospect that she will be in a class with his possible rival Shen. He persuades his friend K'ung to have her name removed from the approved list of those who may attend the school.

In a sub-plot, Cuckoo's rebellious elder sister, T'ung Ya-hua, is having trouble with her domineering, "feudal-minded" husband, Lei Ta-han. He thinks a woman should stay in the kitchen and also heed her husband's every whim. In this stance he is abetted by his mother, Aunt Lei, who holds to the traditions of her own generation.

Wang, his jealousy more heated, demands that Cuckoo cease studying alongside Shen. He seeks an earlier marriage and presents a contract with five clauses he has drawn up that reduces her to a status much like her unhappy sister's. Cuckoo and Wang quarrel bitterly. She tears up the offensive contract and renounces any idea of wedding him.

Cuckoo's name is struck from the short list of those eligible to take the driver's course. Shen departs without her. Fang, the Party Branch Secretary, says that he has had reports from K'ung and others that her attitude and "behaviour style" are poor. All this while Fang is distracted by word that the collective's pure-bred pig is sick. He has no time to listen to complaints by members of the collective. When Kuo questions the Secretary's values and priorities, Fang asks: "How can people be as important as pigs?"

KUO [*doesn't believe his own ears*]: What? What? Is there something wrong with my hearing?

FANG: What happens to people is their own individual business. Pigs are the business of the whole co-op; so which is more important?

KUO: That's really outlandish!

FANG: There's nothing outlandish about it at all!

[Translated by Daniel Talmadge and Edward M. Gunn]

T'ung Ya-hua and her bullying husband Lei Ta-han continue their brawling, until she finally leaves him.

A month passes. Ya-hua misses her mate, though her younger sister tries to persuade her to forget him. His mother, an old matchmaker, and his busybody Aunt Ma try to bring about a reconciliation, but in vain. Aunt Lei, the mother-in-law, explains that with Ya-hua gone, her family's share of proceeds from the co-op is halved.

Lei Ta-han brings gifts of food and wheedles his wife into returning home. Less successful is Wang; with the help of his friend K'ung he seeks to regain Cuckoo's affections. She defies and spurns him. Wang and K'ung have stolen a diary in which Shen has confided his yearning for Cuckoo. She acknowledges a fondness for Shen. Wang vows to file a complaint and have her expelled from the Youth League.

At a meeting that is poorly attended, and that is presided over by K'ung, Cuckoo is voted out of the League. She is not even permitted to speak in her own defence.

On the pretence that an ox is sick, the one-armed Kuo and his wife get Fang to venture through a snow storm and visit their house. He hears Cuckoo's side of the story and promises to take steps to have her reinstated in the Youth League. Rebuked for being heedless to the human concerns of members of the veteran collective, Kuo acknowledges his fault.

In the closing act it is the time of the wheat harvest. Shen has finished his tractor-driving course and comes home to find T'ung Ya-nan anxiously awaiting him. She is now a youth team leader.

The old matchmaker, "Go-Between Ma", holds fast to her traditional views, but Aunt Lei has mellowed and is ready to accept the more liberal social mores of the younger generation. Wang and K'ung, angry that their schemes have gone awry, blame each other for the unwanted outcome. The members of the collective join forces with renewed vigour to increase their farm's output.

Such was the initial success of this slender little play that it was soon converted into an opera (the text was already crowded with songs) and film. The objections to it came the following year (1958) with the launching of Mao's earlier, ambitious campaign, the "Great Leap Forward", which demanded the formation of similar communes everywhere. Though *Cuckoo Sings Again* echoes with more than enough optimistic slogans, it also presents a decidedly "irreverent" view of life on a collective farm, mildly satirizing the automatic mouthing of ideological terminology and the narrow mind-set of bureaucrats such as the zealous but short-sighted Fang, the Party Branch Secretary who has a higher regard for pigs and oxen than for his fellow-workers. Nor are all the peasants as virtuous as good Marxists should be: some are manipulative and vindictive – they conspire together for their own ends and do not hesitate to abuse whatever petty authority they are given. Would life in the new Maoist era be like this? One critic, Yao Wen-yan, declared that not one character in it had a grasp of the true meaning of Socialism. The debate between critics favouring and condemning it went on for a while, but shortly Yang Lü-fang was no longer a celebrity.

Gunn observes: "There seems to have been no shortage of plays in the late 1950s and early 1960s that were straightforward panegyrics on themes of the Party and the new society." A number of periodicals and books dealing with excessively broad theories and more specific facets of what drama should be were issued, filling journals such as *Plays* (1952) and *Theatre* (1954) in which were there also suitable scripts, reviews and serious critical essays, along with a considerable amount of scholarship delving into ancient and traditional stage practices and recommendations of what were the best play formats. In addition, there were memoirs by eminent theatre figures, such as the renowned opera artist Mei Lanfang. Some of these scholarly compilations were massive, staggeringly encyclopedic, packed with anthologies of classic works, meticulously edited and annotated and perhaps a bit revised to meet current restrictions. Translations of foreign plays continued to appear, but now the range was decidedly more limited. The Russians were still the favourite source. But the German Bertolt Brecht was also looked upon with approval. From Sanskrit, Kalidasa's *Shakuntala* finally made an appearance in 1957, the first Indian work accessible in Chinese.

"Agitprop" works populated the stages during this decade and the next one. As elsewhere in totalitarian countries – under leftist or rightist regimes – playwrights here also took refuge in writing historical dramas which might or might not be allegorical with an oblique topical relevance. An instance of such a work is T'ien Han's *Kuan Han-ch'ing*, already cited. Lao She's *Teahouse*, evoking the far more recent past, was open to interpretation in the same way.

During these two decades old playhouses were renovated, among them the Guangehelou and the Tianquio – or "Heavenly Bridge" – both in Peking; while new ones were built, such as the conspicuously well-equipped Shoudu. For other kinds of entertainment – musicals, acrobatic exhibitions and spectacles – the Music Hall accommodated 3,000 spectators, and the huge Great Hall of the People held 11,000, with space on stage for more than 1,700 performers and a backstage capacity of 2,500.

Keeping pace with this expanding theatrical activity, a Chinese Dramatists' Society was founded in 1949, and a Peking Opera School in 1952. Stanislavsky's "Method" was taught by Russians in the Central Dramatic Institute, established in 1950. Various associations sponsoring local and regional kinds of drama – folk plays, *huaju*, operas, dances, puppetry – sprang up and flourished throughout the country; conferences and national festivals and competitions became ever more frequent events. This did not spell a financial easement for all the aspiring groups: many were amateur or only part-time ventures. The majority of actors continued to undergo hardships. The larger troupes, however, were apt to be state supported, which had advantages and drawbacks, since they were more likely to be subjected to political oversight. Party zealots kept up noisy debates and feuds, with opposed factions holding ever-changing views on what was the right course.

Especially risky was the task of the playwrights. In 1950 fifty-five scripts were banned, a restriction that lasted five years. During the next two years another twenty plays were suppressed by the Ministry of Culture, among them fifteen Peking operas, two *chuanju* plays, seven *pingju*; complaints against them were that either they were too "pessimistic", too "feudalistic", too "fatalistic" or "stressed super-stition". Puritanism was dominant; sexual candour, lewdness and all kinds of pornography were absolutely prohibited, as was depiction of excessive brutality on stage. Suggestions that the author still had a "class mentality" was also a fault that could lead to his work being denied a public performance or publication. For the most part, comedy was discouraged, and satire was dangerous. Comedy could easily be twisted by a sly actor and used to belittle officials of all ranks. Preferred themes were the war against Japan, the conflict in Korea, the heroic exploits of the railway builders, the selfless dedication of workers in factories and on farms, and easily solved contemporary social and domestic problems. (This brief summary is purloined from Dolby.)

A model often praised was *Test* (1954) by Xia Yan (1900–1995), set in an electrical machinery plant and containing a plethora of references to Soviet Russia and the sacrifices made by its workers. Seventeen years earlier, during the struggle against Japan, Xia Yan's *Put Down Your Whip* (1937) had borne testimony to his fiery patriotism. That script, enlarged from a one-act work written some years before, had been based on Goethe's novel *Wilhelm Meister*, with the action moved to the China of his own day. He was also a prominent film-writer. The official approval he won for *Test* was not long-lasting. Later he fell foul of the fanatical Maoists during the Cultural Revolution and was designated one of the ill-fated "four villains".

To this category of scripts calling for more effort towards reconstructing the nation belong other opportunistic pieces such as *Taming the Dragon and the Tiger* (1961), *The Young Generation* (1963), *On Guard Beneath the Neon Lights* (1965) and *Red Storm* (1965), all in an exhortative vein. (The dates are those of the publication of the scripts, not of first performance. Perhaps each of these plays had several authors, in a true collective spirit, which is why I cannot learn the writers' names.)

A few dramatists were still allowed to go abroad. As already noted, Cao Yu went to Czechoslovakia in 1949; Lao She attended a drama conference in New Delhi. Some foreign troupes visited China: for instance, a Japanese Kabuki company came in 1960 and 1966 and made a sharp impression on both occasions.

From 1956 on, a tendency to look backward to the classics of far earlier epochs grew stronger, a bout of nostalgia (and the productions were also safer undertakings). Perhaps restive or absent audiences had made plain a weariness with plays that urged them to strive harder, when their initial impulse in going to a theatre was to relax and escape from the day's tension. A great success was a revival in 1956 of *Fifteen Strings of Cash*, a dramatization by the seventeenth-century playwright Zhu Suchen (or Zhu Hao) who borrowed its plot from an even older story. It was somewhat revised. A butcher, Yow, borrows money – the fifteen strings of cash – to tide over his business. He gets drunk and returns home. His stepdaughter, Su Xujuan, asks where he has obtained so much money. Joking, he says that he has sold her. When he falls into a stupor, the frightened girl runs off to an aunt's house. A rascal, the gambler Rat Lou, happens to pass by the butcher shop and decides to rob it. Yow stirs awake and confronts Rat, who kills him with a cleaver, then hastens away with the money. A young man, Xiong Yulan, is on a journey to Suzhou with fifteen strings of cash belonging to his master, a merchant. He encounters Su Xujuan, but unfortunately just then a crowd of neighbours of the murdered butcher surround them, search Xiong Yulan and discover the very same amount of money on him. The innocent pair are dragged off to court and accused of having committed the crime. An incompetent judge presides at an inept trial; the young man and young woman are found guilty and condemned to die.

Kuang Zhong, the Prefect of Sushi, arrives to oversee the execution. Devoted to true justice, he is convinced that something here is amiss. He makes a hurried overnight journey to Governor Zhou Chen and begs permission to reopen the case. Reluctantly, the Governor consents, but sets a mere fortnight as the time limit. Kuang Zhong begins an investigation, and identifies Rat as a likely perpetrator. Aware that he is suspected, Rat flees to the countryside. He is tracked by Kuang and some constables, as well as by an elderly friend of the slain Yow. The wily Kuang, passing himself off as a fortune-teller, accosts Rat in a temple and inveigles him into betraying his guilt. After that, Kuang uses a ruse to get his quarry on board a boat that conveys Rat back to Suzhou to stand trial. But the exploit has required more time than the Governor allotted Kuang, whose own career is now at risk. The climax is the court scene in which the proof against Rat accumulates until he is forced to confess, just in time to free Su Xujuan and Xiong Yulan from imminent death.

Most famed is the ingeniously written temple scene in which Kuang Zhong, disguised as a fortune-teller, tricks the worried, fugitive Rat into acknowledging responsibility for the murder and theft by describing the gory deed to him, thereby persuading Rat that this diviner can actually read his mind. Pretending to foresee the future, Kuang Zhong also gets Rat to book passage on his southward-bound boat in order to make an assured escape, which of course he does not intend to allow.

The fervent enthusiasm with which this revival was greeted indicated the new direction of popular taste. *Fifteen Strings* was made into a highly successful film. The ticket-buying public was not eager to face the bleakness of its own day.

However, the most significant historical drama produced during these mid-century decades – an original script, not a revival – was *Hai Jui Dismissed from Office* (*Hai Jui pa-kuan*; 1961) by Wu Han (or Wu Ch'un-han, 1909–66), which is credited with having triggered – or having served as a convenient pretext for – the outbreak of the Cultural Revolution.

The author's own youth had been one of poverty. He had gone through Tsinghua University by working part-time as a librarian and schoolteacher. When hostilities with Japan began, he was at Southwest United University in Kunming. He volunteered for underground activity on behalf of the Communists. After the war, during the 1950s, he rose to chairmanship of Tsinghua's Department of History as well as becoming Deputy Mayor of Peking. He had spent time in research into the Ming dynasty and published articles on it, which provided him with material for a play about Hai Jui, meant to be a half-concealed criticism of the Maoists and particularly the harshness displayed towards those objecting to the Chairman's edicts; Wu Han belonged to a political faction that still dared to voice dissent.

Hai Jui Dismissed is not a *huaju* but instead makes use of traditional operatic techniques. At this time there was a considerable mixing of genres: operas with topical subjects, *huaju* with added music, *wuju* – "dance-dramas" – and *gewuju* – "song and dance-dramas". Dolby quotes a sophisticated theatre-goer who summed up the situation: "Some people ask me: Was it an old play or a new play you saw? Very difficult indeed to answer, because the plays I see are truly a motley. Some have old form and new theme. Some have new form and old theme. Some old forms have not absorbed many new forms, and a number of new forms have evolved from old forms. The words 'new' and 'old' are no longer adequate to circumscribe dramatic art."

In the sixteenth century peasants in the Soochow–Nanking region of central China are preyed upon by a predatory group of scholar–officials known as the Hsiang-Kuan. One of these is the evil Hsü Ying, forty-one-year-old son of a retired prime minister. He grabs the land of a local farmer, Chao Yü-shan, and kidnaps his sixteen-year-old granddaughter, Chao Hsiao-lan. Trying to prevent the abduction, the old man is badly beaten. He goes to court, but the magistrate has been bribed by Hsü Ying, whose servant, Hsü Fu, offers an alibi for his master, claiming that both of them were far away at school at the time of the purported misdeed. The magistrate orders that Chao Yü-shan be flogged to death for having brought a false charge.

Tension mounts between the Hsiang-Kuan and the abused peasantry. A new governor is appointed, Hai Jui, who is admired for his upright character and for ceaseless dedication to justice. The Hsiang-Kuan await him with some trepidation. He is not recognized when he arrives because he is not wearing his official garments, a device that enables him to learn from the peasants what has been happening here. He quickly convenes a new trial. But first he visits Hsü Chieh, the former prime minister, who is anxious to shield his errant son and vainly seeks to enlist the aid of Hai Jui.

In his resolve to see justice done, even at personal risk, Hai Jui is encouraged by his mother, a woman of high principles.

In the court, where the case has been reopened, Hai Jui cross-examines Hsü Fu, the servant who perjured himself on behalf of his master. His replies expose him as too uneducated ever to have attended any school. Obviously he was lying when providing the alibi.

Hai Jui sentences both Hsü Ying and the corrupt magistrate Wing Ming-Yü to be executed. He orders the confiscated lands to be restored to the heirs of the brutally slain Chao Yü-shan; the abducted granddaughter is to be returned to the arms of her family. Seeking to redress all other wrongs, he proclaims that without delay the Hsiang-Kuan must give back every acre of land that has been stolen. All the peasants of the region cheer when they hear this.

Hsü Chieh, the former prime minister, speeds to the Imperial Court, where he is still influential, to stay the death sentence and save his son. He succeeds in having Hai Jui impeached and removed as Governor.

From the newly named Governor sent to supersede him, Hai Jui learns of his dismissal, but the official Imperial decree has not yet reached him. Though aware that he is endangering himself, he commands that the sentences be carried out immediately; the prisoners beg to be spared, but Hai Jui is obeyed. Hsü Chieh, who in a last-minute effort to intervene has warned the resolute Hai Jui not to defy the Imperial authority, falls in a faint.

Hai Jui surrenders the seal of office. Tai Feng-hsiang, his successor, is numb with astonishment and asks if Hai Jui does not fear punishment, perhaps the death not only of himself but of his whole clan. Hai Jui responds: "A true man stands his ground and accepts the burden Heaven places upon him. To let his fear of death decide in favour of the guilty is to grovel shamelessly." Earlier, he predicts: "I have lost the silk hat of office, but not my conscience. The day will come when I hold office again, and uphold the laws of the state." (Translation: Edward M. Gunn and C.C. Huang)

This picture of baneful influence, injustice and corruption in high places, as well as the persecution and punishment of upright civil servants, was immediately read by the Maoists as criticism of the regime. Wu Han's intent was seen as subversive.

The attack against the play and its author was launched in a Shanghai newspaper in 1965 with an article by Yau Wenyuan (b. 1925). The campaign mounted as many joined in a shrill choir of vituperation against him, and other suspected dissidents were singled out. A formal proclamation of the Cultural Revolution followed early in 1966, with a list of "enemies" growing ever longer and the scope of the drive rapidly widening to comprise just about anyone holding independent ideas.

Wu Han was arrested, along with other leading playwrights. In the havoc that ensued, the theatre was denied the right to every last syllable of free speech; its sometimes eloquent voice was muted.

Other playwrights had been active in effecting change from long-lived tradition. Those who have been chosen for discussion here are representative of Westernization of the theatre during the first two-thirds of the twentieth century. That period was ended.

13

CHINA: TRADITIONS CONTINUE

Though it had sizeable audiences in the large cities, especially Peking and Shanghai, enthusiasm for Western-style drama – *huaju* – was mostly shared by intellectuals, as has been said; this was especially true among the young who had been educated abroad, and faculty and students at the universities in those cities – many with leftist leanings – and others with cosmopolitan inclinations who could boast a measure of sophistication. But given the size of China, all these were comparatively small in number, a definite minority. On the whole, the multitude – much of it illiterate – still preferred Peking opera, puppetry and dance, the traditional forms of stage entertainment. They had no appetite for ethical and political instruction or debate, which in fact was also true in American and European cities, where cerebral plays have long been rare. The populace of China was not particularly lacking in that respect. The average person did not go to the theatre for mental stimulation but for relaxation and delight, much of it mindless and merely sensuous, which the popular arts strove to provide and often did ably.

Owing to its ongoing vitality, Peking opera had been able to influence the *huaju* discernibly, and it had become the kind of Chinese theatre recognized elsewhere. The person most responsible was the world-famed actor and producer Mei Lanfang (or Mai Lang-fan, 1894–1961), to whom frequent references have been made. He was descended from a line of actors; his grandfather and father had been noted for their *dan* roles – that is, as female impersonators. At age eight he began a strenuous apprenticeship; his celebrated tutor was Wang Yaoqing (1882–1954), also hailed for his *dan* interpretations. In recent decades the principal actors had excelled in *laosheng* – middle-aged male – roles, but now Mei Lanfang was to focus attention once more on the *dan* by his supreme artistry and bold innovation. In order to satisfy the demanding Wang Yaloquing, he might repeat each passage in a song twenty or thirty times to arrive at an exact inflection. He practised the right way to walk with diminutive steps, to gesture, convey subtle meanings by his hands and fingers, manipulate his sleeves, don his slippers, open a door, raise his arms to Heaven in a plea of lamentation, stride across the stage, sink faintly into a chair. He became adept at moving about on clogs or short stilts to create the impression of his having small feet and a feminine sway; to master this difficult effect, he ventured to do it on ice in the winter. Disregarding the blisters and pain this inflicted on him, he achieved almost perfect physical control. He took instruction from other teachers in acrobatics, the art of simulated combat and other theatrical skills.

At ten, Mei Lanfang made his stage début (1904) in a *qingyi* role; that is, as a "black-clothes" *dan*, usually a graceful, refined, virtuous young lady who is much in love. He was small, delicate, and had an ageless grace. In a mere three years he joined a highly esteemed troupe, though still an apprentice. Soon he won prominence in Shanghai where he was deemed the finest of his kind of performer anywhere. He toured to all the large cities of China. In 1919 and 1925 he appeared to great applause in Japan, and in 1930 to critical acclaim in New York and other cities in the United States, though audiences there were limited and the box-office take was disappointing.

In Hollywood he was fêted by the film stars Charlie Chaplin, Douglas Fairbanks and Mary Pickford; he expressed admiration for the athletic bravura of Fairbanks and the comic mimicry of Chaplin. *En route* to the Far East he displayed his art in Hawaii. Everywhere he stirred wonder by his dramatic monologue, *A Nun Craves Worldly Vanities*. A half-decade later (1935), he visited Russia, where he was awarded honorary degrees and met Stanislavsky, and then travelled through Italy, France, Germany – a meeting with Brecht. In Russia his sword dancing and acting in *The Fisherman's Revenge* were highly praised. The avant-garde director Meyerhold and the master film-maker Sergei Eisenstein acknowledged he was a revelation to them and that they had been influenced by him. His acting style greatly impressed Brecht. He also played in London. His company did not perform in Europe as he had hoped it might; financing for his elaborate, full-scale productions could not be obtained.

The outbreak of war with Japan in 1937 found Mei Lanfang in Shanghai. The following year he transferred his company to Hong Kong. Some of the members soon went back to China, but he remained in the British colony, which was finally seized by the Japanese forces at the end of 1941. The conquerors put pressure on him to return to the stage, but he resisted their bids. He grew a thin moustache, making it difficult for him to assume a *dan* role. (He had much earlier plucked out most of the hairs with a tweezer, so that having a full mustache was no longer possible.) In 1942 he made his way to Shanghai again, where he still did not yield to Japanese efforts to enlist his talents. His funds ran low, and he sold many personal treasures including his own paintings. (Clever with his brush, he designed many of his company's sets and costumes.)

With tears of joy he heard of the Japanese capitulation and the end of fighting in 1945. He immediately shaved off the vague shadow on his upper lip and prepared to resume his career; every morning he worked to regain the requisite physical dexterity, afternoons he did vocal exercises, and every evening he perused playscripts. Within two months he was on stage before the public and winning new applause. During this post-war period, fortunately, he made several colour films, so examples of his artistry have been preserved.

A major component of Mei Lanfang's success was his long-time collaboration with the scholar Qi Rushan (or Ch'i Ju-shan, 1876–1962), the most active author of Peking opera scripts of the day. Qi Rushan, too, was descended from a theatre family; while in London and Paris (1908–13) he had observed foreign drama, leading him to feel that the Chinese stage should be made better. Starting his partnership with Mei Lanfang in 1914, and continuing it until 1931, he revised nineteen scripts and provided two-score new ones for the troupe's repertory; in addition, he wrote twenty or more books on theatre history and theory.

One of his important contributions, effected with his script *Chang E Takes Flight to the Moon*, was the introduction of historically accurate costumes and dances instead of the conventional dress and choreography adapted for stage presentation. He founded a society, a school and a museum for research into the history of Chinese theatre and for the dissemination of more knowledge about classic drama.

Mei Lanfang himself has left behind extensive writings on his career and approach to his work. Whereas most great Peking opera actors before him had specialized in a particular kind of *dan* role, he was amazingly versatile, portraying every feminine type. He had broad interests, had an open mind and ceaselessly sought to refine his natural gifts. An instance: he was a pigeon-fancier, because by constantly handling the bamboo pole that he used to train them he strengthened himself for the most physically taxing stage roles. Studying flowers in his garden, he grasped much about colour combinations of value to him for his costume designing. He had lessons in painting for the same reason, and numbered among his friends the revered artist Qi Baishi, whose striking economy of line gave Mei Lanfang points for his nuanced acting. With all his triumphs, he remained surprisingly humble. He fathered many technical innovations. His stylistic touches were widely imitated, though they also evoked protests from the more rigid preservationists.

Rosamond Gilder tells us:

Acclaimed "King of Actors" and "Foremost of the Pear Orchard" through a popularity contest, he was well-versed in the old literature of China, and this knowledge helped him to restore the long-forgotten dance to its former importance in the drama in spite of great opposition by Chinese fundamentalists. At the age of twenty-five he was engaged by the Japanese Imperial Theatre – the first time in Chinese history that a Chinese actor had appeared on a foreign stage (1919). His repertoire consisted of over four hundred plays of which about one-third were his own productions. His wardrobe and ornaments were valued at over one hundred thousand dollars.

His gestures and actions on stage were of great beauty and refinement; his every pose was a perfect picture. His dances, tied up in form and symbolism, were in no sense impeded thereby but showed remarkable adroitness and grace, and contained a clarity and persuasion which cannot be approached on the more naturalistic and cruder Western stage. He possessed a clear, penetrating singing voice and his stage presence was at once gentle and very dignified. He always took female roles (for women were long barred from the Chinese stage); in these, he was the idol of five hundred million souls. The feminine side glance, the smile, the dainty, tripping walk – all were most carefully studied. At the height of his success, he continued to study his art.

Mei Lanfang even experimented by appearing in modern dress in *Waves of the Sea of Sin* (1914) and several other plays, but after 1916 abandoned his attempt to update opera to that extent.

Other acclaimed Peking opera actors of this era were Cheng Yanqiu (1903–59), who also excelled in *dan* roles, and Ma Lianliang (1901–66) and Yu Zhenfei (1902–93), noted as *sheng* performers (serious males, with unpainted features and, frequently, bearded). Of Manchurian origin, Cheng Yanqiu had studied with both Wang Yaoqing and Mei Lanfang and had accompanied the latter to Japan. On his own, in 1932, he visited England and the European continent for exposure to Western theatre and opera. He had short stage engagements in Berlin and Nice, and gave classes in *taijiquan* boxing in Geneva. Together with Xun Huisheng and Shang Xioyun, he and Mei Lanfang were alluded to as "Four Great Famous *Dans*".

A new trend was public rejection of female impersonators on stage, though this was not directed against Mei Lanfang. One reason for this shift in attitude was that the custom of binding girls' feet no longer prevailed. The *huaju* had also introduced the custom of women playing female roles, overcoming the age-old prejudice against allowing them to participate in theatre. In 1928 actresses began to join the casts in Peking opera, too, and this soon became a regular practice. One of the most popular was Xue Yanjin, a pupil of Mei Lanfang. A drama school, the Xiju Xuexiao, was established in Peking in 1930; supposedly it was to train male and female students for both Peking opera and the *huaju*, but most of the aspirants enrolling there had the opera's boards as their goal.

Though Westerners are familiar mostly with Peking opera, other regions of China have their own traditional forms of music drama, performed in local dialect and with some unique conventions.

In Xian, to cite an instance, one can see Qin opera (*Qin-giang*), which differs from that in Peking in language, plots and situation, scenic investiture: its costumes had their origin in the ninth or tenth century, the Tang period. Qin is prevalent in Shensi Province.

Cantonese opera (*Kwantung* drama) derives from the refined, scholarly Gunchu style, an earlier South China form that faded from favour in the mid-nineteenth century. In 1982 the Guangdong Yue Opera Troupe left Canton on a tour of Canada and the United States and presented four complete works displaying settings even more detailed and fanciful and costumes more elaborate than those of the Peking company. The miming was more universally intelligible. From the Peking tradition the Guangdong Yue has borrowed a noisier, more boisterous manner, and it offers much the same make-up, acrobatics, mythical combats between gods and mortals, along with nasal singing and a cacophonous orchestra. In its repertoire on this occasion were *Searching the School* and *The Magic Lotus Lantern*. Since most Chinese who have emigrated to the United States have come from South China, this company was enthusiastically welcomed by them.

Much as there has been a blending of the vigorous Peking (North China) and more delicate Canton (South China) styles, most of the competing genres have influenced one another, exchanging characteristics, so that similarities between them abound; also some that flourished in the past and proved quite ephemeral have left traces in those that succeeded them. According to one estimate, at least 300 kinds of local and regional kinds of entertainment were being staged in various parts of China even in the mid-twentieth century. Some have long histories, going back to the Sōng dynasty (AD 960–1279) and earlier. As did Peking opera, they began in folk rituals and music and dramatic celebrations of dances, "flowery" festive events, such a "drum plays", "flowery lantern plays", "rice-seedling planting-song plays" and "tea picking plays", many of which still persist and are staged by amateur or semi-professional troupes drawn from villagers. These enactments often have a religious significance, given by the peasants to placate the gods of fertility during the growing and harvest seasons, to drive away locusts and send rain, or to plead for good fortune at the Chinese New Year; others are merely intended to yield pleasure. The actors may be illiterate and have difficulty in memorizing their lines, which are passed on from one generation to the next; the performance may take place on a makeshift stage at a temple fair, though a good number of permanent theatres have long existed. The settings and properties may be very simple, as in much of Chinese stagecraft; but the cast has make-up and costumes, and an orchestra may consist of at least a drum, clappers, gongs, a flute and a *huquin* fiddle. The spectators may have seats, or be required to stand or perch on carts. The cost of the entertainment is borne by taxing the whole village. Those refusing to pay are barred from attending; onlookers from nearby villages may come, however. Six to eight plays may be offered in a single evening, and the programmes usually go on for three or four days, many of them featuring the broadest slapstick. Other entertainments, such as processions with music and lanterns, lion dances, and boxing, acrobatics and dagger-fighting exhibitions may be put on elsewhere in the village simultaneously. Some of the secular playlets are so bawdy that an attempt was made by the government in the 1920s to ban them as immoral and dangerous, but the effort failed. These entertainments, especially, were too cherished by the farmers.

The playlets are very short, have elementary plots and structure, and in general their authors are unknown. Mostly the scripts lack literary quality. Some have undergone endless changes over the decades and centuries, during which they were revised and adapted to meet new local circumstances. The music accompanying them falls into five basic systems or categories, but that is a subject too technical for discussion here.

The more sophisticated forms of traditional theatre, the lesser rivals of Peking opera, can only be touched on sketchily. In the province of Hupeh, Hanju drama consists of four sorts, the determining factors being geographical and linguistic, just where the plays are given and which dialect the actors use. It is believed that Hanju derives from works with music that existed as long ago as the Ming dynasty (AD 1368–1644). In its own early days, Peking opera, too, owed much to it. The two genres have grown closer in recent decades, but still differ in the names given to topical roles, and slightly in the composition of their orchestras and in the rhythms and measures of their music. In 1920 Hanju drama performers established a guild that later claimed 7,000 members. In 1926 women were admitted to it and a training programme for them was set up. Soon the troupes included both sexes, with actresses outnumbering actors. In the mid-1930s Hanju companies emphasized the use of mechanical scenery, but the trend was short-lived. They also gave full-length plays – that is, plays in full rather than excepts from them – in evenings without breaks. During the Japanese war Hanju troupes took entertainment to the Chinese forces, sometimes adding patriotic works to inspire the soldiers.

In Hupeh Province another favourite form is Chuju drama, which had rustic beginnings, originally consisting of folk-singers moving about on lofty stilts. Gradually such performances evolved into comic duets between a man and a woman; next, the stilts were put aside and simple stories were developed. Such playlets, popular at festivals, were enacted on roughly improvised stages. A rhythmic accompaniment of gongs, cymbals and bells was the next new feature. The stock characters were a mere three; they borrowed folk-songs, and the action was backed by *Gao-qiang* music. A backstage chorus lent its voice at the end of the sung lines. The language was earthy and decidedly vulgar, if picturesque.

At first given by part-time actors, the Chuju grew more and more acceptable throughout the nine-teenth century; eventually they were put on by small troupes of nine or ten men. Illegal, they were usually performed very late at night, cloaked by darkness.

By 1900 the offerings had become more sophisticated, the players having assimilated much from Hanju drama. They won audiences in towns close to Hankow. Soon they are welcomed in Hankow's German enclave (1902), and next in the city's French and Japanese concessions, where the official ban against them was not as likely to be enforced.

Competing more and more with Hanju drama and Peking opera in the towns, the troupes enlarged their casts; their material acquired complex plots and the performers more elaborate cos-tumes while they acted in a style quite their own.

As the local warlords lost their grip in the regions, about 1929, a company took on the name "Chuju" and boldly occupied a large theatre in the Chinese section of Hankow. The backstage chorus was replaced by blind fiddlers. In 1929, too, Pihuang music was appropriated from Hanju drama, along with the Peking opera singers' technique of vocalizing. By now the three stock roles had increased to four. The *dans'* manner of singing, formerly soft and insinuating, was more falsetto. Song predominated, but some aspects of the prose *huaju* became evident. Folk elements were still percept-ible, as were some taken from balladry. The influence of Peking opera continued to be strong. After 1949 women appeared on the Chuju stage.

The eastern and northern regions of Fukien Province fostered Minju, presented by Fuzhou troupes. Dolby describes this as a conglomeration of several other genres having such vivid names as *pingjiang* (ordinary talk or flat talk), *Rulin-ban* ("Confucian scholar troupes") and *laolao* ("mumble-mumble"). Centuries earlier, travelling troupes appeared just after the harvest; marking off an enclosure with straw ropes, they gave performances within it. Since the playing space was not elevated, spectators and actors were on the same plane. Such offerings were the *pingjiang*, believed by scholars to have taken shape about 1800, and borrowing stories hitherto told by puppeteers. Local folk-songs and the ballads of professional singers were the sources of their music, together with some tunes from other geographical regions.

The ditties tended to be ribald with a peasant coarseness, giving offence to the more decorous. A gentleman of the day – *c.* 1800 – is quoted as saying, "Their songs are vile and vulgar, their air and manner foul and filthy, and indeed one felt most strongly that they were quite unwatchable and that it was quite impossible for one to listen to them right through to the end." But apparently he was an exception.

Five decades later, in the mid-nineteenth century, *pingjiang* enjoyed a considerable vogue. To offset it, the cultivated Pu Zishan organized a Rulin-ban, a company comprised of "handsome and intelligent young gentlemen actors" who made themselves available to entertain at birthday celebrations and religious ceremonies. At first the plays they gave were didactic, preaching moral lessons. Typical of this aim was the *Purple Jade Hairpin*, its authorship attributed to either Pu or Guo Boyin; it set a standard for the genre by being in impeccable good taste, with a plot that moved audiences, and with elegant dialogue and excellent music. Every effort was made to keep such works on a higher aesthetic level. In Rulin-ban, plots had to be well structured. The musical accompaniment, at the start simply rhythmically percussive, was later expanded to include wind and stringed instruments, to which a backstage chorus was added. Politeness was also enforced on the audience, which was not permitted to eat while the action of the play was ongoing. The companies of "gentlemanly performers" usually did not exceed more than six members, taking primary and secondary *shen*, *dan* and *chou* roles. Rulin-ban gained a considerable following, and in time a dozen troupes travelled about the province, each one enjoying financial success.

On important occasions, when generals and viceroys from other regions visited Fukien, Huizhou troupes were imported to grace their reception. The Huizhou used a different kind of music, *Kungu*, and in speech a dialect that was not fully intelligible to the hosts themselves. Hence the foreigner's singing was referred to by the folk of Fukien as *laolao* ("mumble-mumble"). Nevertheless, both the *pingjiang* and Rulin-ban players soon latched on to some of the strangers' stage techniques, blending them with their own. From 1911 on, *laolao* began to lose official support and public favour; the troupes dissolved, some of their actors joining *pingjiang* companies, a process largely completed by 1916. Rulin-ban no longer attracted spectators as it once had. *Pingjiang* troupes, now dominant in the field, absorbed more elements from their erstwhile rivals. The new form that resulted was Minju drama, with a strain of Peking opera in it indirectly transmitted by *laolao*.

The music in Minju drama is *sui generis*. The singers, even those in *dan* roles, employ a natural voice. There is a wider range of stock characters. The technical terms adopted to describe them are exceptionally vivid. Actresses were introduced into the troupes quite early, and other facets of the genre were modernized after the advent of the liberating May the Fourth Movement (1919). Aware of what was being attempted in *huaju*, the actors might lengthen the amount of speech at the expense of song, and they sometimes donned contemporary dress. With the Japanese war over, the Minju developed a fondness for putting on fantastic spectacles, in sumptuous contrast to the harsh economic conditions then being experienced by most spectators. Ancient subjects were drawn on for plots, which were now much looser and less coherent. The acting was fustian, the stage-combats excessively violent. These productions emphasized supernatural and magical effects created by stage machinery, and everything was presented on a vast scale.

Dolby allots some pages to Chanju, a term applied to various kinds of drama in Szechwan Province, amongst them *dengxi, kunqu*, Gao-*qiang*, Huqin-*qiang* and Tan-*qiang*, all save one of which had their beginnings elsewhere but were absorbed into distinctive Szechwanese genres. He gives an interesting account of the *dengxi*, the "lantern play", an indigenous form that apparently arose from rites by shamans to exorcize demons and mark a succession of festivals. Peasants and craftsmen joined the shamans in performing them, thereby creating a form of folk drama that was still being done in the mountainous regions of northern Szechwan as late as the 1930s. By lantern light, hence the name, such works were at first enacted on mats or the bare ground at night by troupes of only three actors, one of them taking the *dan* role. At the opening of the twentieth century ten of the fifty extant *dengxi* were accepted into the repertories of companies playing in cities.

The speech used in these slightly differing types of Chanju is Szechwanese dialect. The music, a variation of Yiyang-*qiang*, may include elements derived from the folk-songs of rice-planters, boatmen and waggoners. In earlier times the orchestra shared the stage; a chorus of six voices, its members not in theatrical garb, replied to the actor's lines, sometimes merely echoing them, other times varying them. The chorus also commented on the action humorously or seriously, or interrupted it. (The actor might mime some passages of peak emotion, while the chorus lent emphasis.) The orchestral accompaniment was baldly percussive. Later, around 1784, the orchestra added a fiddle and wind instruments when Tan-*quiang*, "strum music", was brought in from North China, most probably by the playwright and drama critic Li Tiaoyuan (1730–1803), or else by a touring company from Shensi Province.

Today's repertory is made up mostly of updated versions of classic works. The large cities of Szechwan possess a number of permanent theatres. Around the turn of the century a drama reform movement elicited suggestions from writers and actors. An outstanding playwright of the province was Huang Ji'an (1836–1924) who revised over a hundred ancient scripts, restoring them to availability. Early in the twentieth century women were admitted to the region's troupes. A guild to further the cause of Szechwan drama was established in 1925, not long after the founding of a special theatre company dedicated to preserving Chanju.

Elsewhere, guided by Dolby's encyclopaedic survey, one finds Guiju, also known as "Kwangsi drama"; and Dianju, also called "Yunan drama"; as well as Ganju, or "Kiangsi drama"; Qianju, or "Kweichow drama"; Xiangju, or "Hunan drama"; Yuju, or "Honan drama"; Jinju, or "Shansi drama". A very partial list. Again some of these vary only slightly from one another, though some have quite distinctive features of their own. Several are not restricted to a single province but are found widely, while others belong only to small segments of the population and are quite rare, and a good number have continued to be in flux, forever undergoing change.

Such diversity is threatened by an official edict that Mandarin is to be the sole language of China, probably ruling out this babel of dialects and along with them the many styles and techniques from which accrue the age-old, legendary richness of a multifaceted scene.

14

CHINA: MAO AND AFTER

Under Mao's regime supervision of all theatre activity was given to his third (or perhaps fourth) wife, Jiang Qing (or Chiang Ching), who had some personal stage and film experience. He was rumoured to be no longer fond of her; perhaps he assigned her the post to keep her busy and out of his way.

Born Li Jin (1914), in Zhucheng, Shandong Province, the daughter of a wheelwright, she was the youngest of a large brood. At fifteen, in 1929, she was admitted to the Shandong Provincial Experimental Art Theatre in Jinan, the regional capital. She studied drama and music, but not for more than a year. She took Lan Ping (Blue Apple) as her professional name, but had little success in her stage career. In the port city of Qingdao she met Li Dazhang, a Communist, and soon after joined the Party, which was still a clandestine organization. She was working sporadically in films in Shanghai when the city was captured by the Japanese in 1937. Fleeing to Yenan, in Shaanxi Province, she joined Mao's forces and met the leader. At the time of their marriage she was twenty-four; Mao was twenty-one years her senior. At this time, to shed links to her past as an actress, she took yet another name, Jiang Qing, a combination of Chinese characters signifying "river" and "sky blue". Assumption of Party pseudonyms was common, however. For many years she was little known, but about 1962 she suddenly became prominent and assertive and thereafter was important in policy-making, especially in all matters concerning the arts.

As Adviser on Cultural Work, her animus towards Peking opera came sharply to the fore. She voiced her objection to its subject-matter, its preoccupation with the remote past, in which dwelt lords and ladies taken up with trivial love affairs and dynastic intrigues. It was hardly a vehicle for inculcating in the masses the virtues of Communism. When the Cultural Revolution was in full, brutal sway, she forced the company to close; the actors were disbanded; many of them, like other intellectuals and artists, were sent to perform physical labour on pig farms or wheatfields or else to carry out monotonous unskilled tasks in factories. The institution's entire venerable repertory was suppressed.

In explanation, she quoted rough statistics similar to those gathered by Guo Moruo: thousands of drama troupes of every kind were active in China but they served no useful purpose.

On the traditional drama stages we get nothing but emperors and kings, generals and prime ministers, talented scholars and beautiful young ladies, and ox-headed demons and snake-gods in the bargain. Even the ninety *huaju* troupes cannot be depended upon to portray the workers, peasants and soldiers. Their principle, too, is "bigness, foreignness and antiquity," and it is fair to say the *huaju* stage, too, has been taken over by the ancients, Chinese and foreign. The theater is a place for educating the people, but nowadays all we get on the stage is a load of feudalistic stuff, all a load of bourgeois stuff. Such conditions cannot provide protection for the basis of our economy, but may on the contrary serve to destroy it.

And here is the second group of figures: there are well over six hundred million workers, peasants and soldiers in our country, whereas there is only a handful of landlords, rich peasants, counter-revolutionaries, bad elements, Rightists and bourgeois elements. Shall we serve this handful, or the six hundred million? This question calls for consideration not only by Communists but by all those literary and art workers who love their country. The grain we eat is grown by the peasants, the clothes we wear and the houses we live in are all made by the workers, and the People's Liberation Army stands guard at the fronts of national defense for us, and yet we do not portray them on the stage. May I ask which class stand do you artists take? And where is the artists' "conscience" you always talk about?

Her demand was for "operas on revolutionary contemporary themes which reflect real life in the fifteen years since the founding of the Chinese People's Republic and which create images of contemporary revolutionary heroes on our operatic stage. This is our foremost task."

Several national conferences were held in Shanghai (1963), Peking (1964) and elsewhere, at which these new criteria were proclaimed. Jiang Qing vigorously addressed the writers and producers, admonishing them to heed her strictures.

In 1967 eight models were brought forth, some of them having been created a few years before (1964). They consisted of five new Peking operas, two new ballets and a symphony, all revolutionary in form and content. Historical operas portraying the life and struggles of the people before the Party came into being were also needed. As a secondary effort, some classical works could be staged, but only after careful editing and revision.

Exact procedures for writing the new works were spelled out:

Playwrights are few and they lack experience of life. So it is only natural that no good plays are being created. The key to tackling the problem of creative writing is the formation of a three-way combination of the leadership, the playwrights and the masses. Recently I studied the way in which the play *Great Wall Along the Southern Sea* was created, and I found that they did it exactly like this. First the leadership set the theme. Then the playwrights went three times to acquire experience of life, even taking part in a military operation to round up enemy spies. When the play was written, many leading members of the Kwangchow military command took part in discussions on it, and after it had been rehearsed, opinions were widely canvassed and revisions made. In this way, as a result of constantly asking for opinions and constantly making revisions, they succeeded in turning out in fairly short time a good topical play reflecting a real-life struggle.

Her prescription was very detailed: "All localities must appoint cadres to handle this problem." This was to be done at once. The dramatists could begin with short works. Another good means of getting suitable plays was by adaptation.

In her opinion, a major fault of Peking opera was that its actors excelled at depicting negative characters, but now the performers must learn to portray robust heroes. She had a specific formula for assuring that the lead role would be that of someone positive and "exalted", brightly outshining all evil-doers.

One of the five plays to be emulated was *Taking Tiger Mountain by Strategy*, like the other four a collective effort, written and frequently altered by members of the several companies – still designated as Peking opera troupes – that presented it. It was widely seen in Peking, Shanghai and throughout the province of Shantung. Much of it was shaped, as were the other models, under the watchful eye of Jiang Qing herself, who proposed changes as the production was readied.

A historical incident provided its simplistic theme, the capture in 1946 of a bandits' hideaway by a unit of daring soldiers. The bandit chieftain was the Eagle, though in the lengthy course of rewriting he was instead named the Vulture, to make him a less glamorous figure. The play is based on a novel, *Tracks in the Forest Snow* (1962), by Chu Po. A shrewd, daring Red Army scout, Yang Tzu-jung, is on the Vulture's track and in disguise infiltrates the robber's headquarters on Tiger Mountain. He is accepted by the outlaws – actually allies of the Kuomintang (Nationalists) – because he brings with him a much-coveted contact map. He assures the Commander that the rocky fortification is absolutely safe from attack. He also impresses them by his skill as a marksman; he kills a tiger with a single shot. The bandits honour their leader's fiftieth birthday, and Yang cajoles them into drinking too much. He also suggests that they brighten the mountain slope with torches to mark the "Hundred Chickens Feast" given by the Vulture with fowls ruthlessly extorted from the loyal peasantry; the flares are a signal for a surprise and successful assault by a platoon of the People's Liberation Army.

The plot and the hero's role in it have been likened to an old-fashioned Hollywood adventure film. The script also abounds with anti-American allusions, accusing the United States of backing Chiang Kai-shek's anti-revolutionary Kuomintang, which was not wholly true – the Americans were mostly watching events in China, hesitating, "waiting for the dust to settle".

The initial version of the play had included a flirtation between Yang and the Vulture's adopted daughter, Rose, but this was cut out. Eliminated, too, was an incident in which Yang, seeking to ingratiate himself with the bandits, tells them a few ribald stories. In the view of the Shanghai troupe, "The result was that they turned Yang Tzu-jung into a filthy-mouthed desperado and a reckless muddle-headed adventurer reeking with bandit odor from top to toe. Such a character can only be a living sample advertising Liu Shao-chi's reactionary military line of putschism, adventurism and warlordism." (The Liu Shao-chi alluded to was at that time the Party Secretary; he was charged by some with having capitalist leanings.)

The Shanghai troupe that produced *Taking Tiger Mountain* later published a booklet, *To Find Men Truly Great and Noble-Hearted, We Must Look to the Present* (1971). The section discussing Yang's part is headed, "Strive to Create the Brilliant Images of the Proletarian Heroes". "While defining his ideal of the Chinese revolution, we also referred to his ideal of the world revolution. While delineating his indomitable courage and soaring spirit, we also gave expression to the steadiness and poise, the sagacity and alertness in his make-up. The description of these facts in his character rests firmly on one essential point, the soul of the hero Yang Tzu-jung, and that is 'the morning sun in his heart' – a red heart that is definitely loyal to Chairman Mao and Maoism. Thus Yang Tzu-jung appears before us as a fearless proletarian hero, with largeness of mind and a thorough-going proletarian revolutionary spirit, one who in all circumstances gives prominence to proletarian politics. It is a brilliant image of a hero who is at once lofty and mature."

According to Lois Wheeler Snow, this aim was not wholly realized. In her *China on Stage* (1972) she tells of attending a presentation of *Taking Tiger Mountain* in Peking. The actor cast as Vulture made an overwhelming impression on her: he was "superb in his role". She recalls: "His physical dexterity and grace added a supernatural quality as he literally rose in the air or bounced on his rocky throne in the throes of wily wickedness, like an Oriental Nome king. It is difficult to achieve the portrayal of complete bad or complete good on the stage. Somewhere in conveying badness an interesting contrast is bound to appear, even if it is only unintentional humor. All good is sometimes all bore."

The score for *Tiger Mountain* was contributed by Wang Chun, Liu Ju-chen and a woman composer, Sheng Li-chen; however, Jiang Qing insisted on crediting it to a favourite, Lu Huei-yung, who had been head of the Shanghai Conservatory and who was now named by her to be Minister of

Culture. Wang Chun, seeking recognition for his collaborators and himself, gave offence. He was dropped from the conservatory, and his works could no longer be played anywhere.

A second model script, the edifying *Sea Harbour,* dealt with dockworkers and how the heinous deeds of a saboteur are frustrated. Equally filled with heroics was *Raid on the White Tiger Regiment* about an attack on the command post of a detachment of South Korean troops, an actual incident a decade earlier (1953). Similarly recalling a striking military exploit was *Shajiabang,* its action occurring during the War of Resistance. Here yet another platoon, led by Guo Jianguan and Sistet Aqing, wipes out a clique of Chinese traitors and the Japanese force they are helping.

But perhaps the most effective of the five exemplary scripts is *Red Lantern* telling of the family of a railway signalman who oppose the advance of the Japanese invaders. After a production in Shanghai this opera underwent many alterations; each time the role of Li Yü-ho, the hero, was made more salient, his commitment to Communism waxing ever stronger. He lives with Granny Li, by whom he has been adopted; he, in turn, has a foster-daughter, T'ieh-mei. Each is a sole survivor, their parents and other kinfolk having been the victims of the ever-clashing warlords. They are not as yet fully aware of their true relationship but learn of it at the play's climax. All are participating in underground activities against the Japanese. Li Yü-ho is entrusted with the delivery of a secret code to Chinese guerrillas in the Cypress mountains. He is to identify himself to them by holding up the symbolic red lantern. He is captured by the enemy who try by every means to make him reveal the code, but he will not yield. They torture him, threaten him with death, but he refuses to talk. Seeming to relent, they reunite him with Granny and then T'ieh-mei in a room in which has been planted an eavesdropping device, but the three patriots are too wary and outwit them. Finally both Li Yü-ho and Granny are executed. Only T'ieh-mei escapes death. She bears the red lantern to the guerrillas, who at the last moment ambush the enemy, save her, and annihilate the Japanese leader, Captain Hatoyama, and his cruel men.

In this passage Li Yü-ho prepares to die:

> [*Sings "erh Huang erh liu"*]
> Brought up by the Party to be a man of steel
> I fight the foe and never give ground.
> I'm not afraid
> To have every bone in my body broken,
> I'm not afraid
> To be locked up until I wear through the floor of my cell.
> It makes my heart bleed to see our country ravaged,

I burn with anger for my people's suffering.

However hard the road of revolution,

We must press on in the steps of the glorious dead.

My only regret if I die today

Is the "account" I have not settled.

[*Gestures to indicate the secret code.*]

I long to soar like an eagle to the sky,

Borne on the wind above the mountain passes

Hit him when he's least expecting it.

And I guarantee we shall make his whole life collapse

in confusion and lose all sense of direction,

Just like pouring hot water on an ants' nest or setting fire

to a beehive!

A novel feature of the production of *Red Lantern* that earned it shocked comment and expostulatory debate was that it largely dispensed with the usual small string and percussive orchestra and instead was sung in many cities with a piano accompaniment, this supposedly embodying a precept of the Cultural Revolution. Yet Jiang Qing opposed all European touches, and certainly this was one; however, the innovation owed something to the teachings of Chairman Mao himself, since he had stated as a principle, "Make foreign things serve China and weed through the old to bring forth the new." His wife had been prompted to move accordingly. What is more, the production had an official imprimatur in that Mao, Jiang Qing, Premier Chou En-lai and Lin Piao, then the Vice-Chairman of the Party, were present at the début and mounted the stage to acknowledge the spectators' fervent applause. Obedient, the press rallied to defend the addition of the piano to the orchestra, and Jiang Qing was praised for having quieted those who protested against its use. Charles Mackerras, in his book on Peking opera, asserts that as rescored for the inclusion of the piano *Red Lantern* is "more exciting and the music better adapted to the theme of the drama".

This daring "experiment" did not imply that Jiang Qing had a liking for European music. She railed against any playing of it. With permission of Premier Chou En-lai, Eugene Ormandy and the Philadelphia Symphony Orchestra paid a fortnight's visit in 1974 and gave concerts that were rousingly greeted. The programmes comprised works by Mozart, Beethoven – a particular favourite of Chou – and Schubert. As soon as the orchestra departed, Jiang Qing took fierce exception to its having been invited. At her behest one obedient journalist assailed Beethoven as "a German capitalist composer". (Beethoven, on the verge of impoverishment most of his life, would surely have been surprised at having been so described.) Afterwards the only foreign music allowed was the *Internationale*, the Communist Party hymn.

Jiang Qing was aware that the cultivated, moderate Premier Chou was more popular and respected than Mao and at times intervened to subvert excesses. However, he was fatally ill, so she could be patient.

Martin Ebon's collection, *Five Communist Plays* (1975), offers the text of *Azalea Mountain* (1973), another drama written during this stressful period to conform to Jiang Qing's guidelines. (From Ebon's prefatory notes in that book comes much of the information set forth in these pages.) This work should be seen in a very special context. Lin Piao, the Party's Vice-Chairman, had not lent his support to Jiang Qing's reforms of the theatre. Suspecting that Lin Piao was planning to seize power, Mao suddenly moved against him, charging him with treason. Lin Piao and several of his supporters fled in a plane; near the border it crashed, killing all aboard. The official report said the plane's destruction was an accident, but Western commentators were sceptical. The play, *Azalea Mountain*, has echoes of this frustrated coup, if launching one was actually Lin Piao's intent.

Among the well-liked operas in the Peking repertory that had evoked Jiang Qing's displeasure was *Red Bandit*, celebrating the deeds of an authentic, living hero, a conspicuous military figure later acclaimed as Marshal Ho Lung; he had led many guerrilla operations, but had done so before the Communists' triumph. Perhaps that was now deemed a gross mistake. For whatever reason, the handsome Marshal Ho Lung was hunted down, becoming a victim of the Cultural Revolution, singled out for abuse. Seized by the Red Guards, he was made to wear humiliating placards around his neck, while being driven around Peking in the back of a truck. He was forced to attend "mass struggle" meetings, beaten, and very likely subjected to torture. After his death in a Peking hospital, no official word was issued as to what had brought it about.

Other prohibited stage-works were *Sister Chiang*, which had always won the applause of Chou En-lai; *Under the Neon Lights*, portraying the exploits of the People's Liberation Army in Shanghai, but perhaps not "correctly" enough; *The Great Wall*, or *On the South China Seas*, a Cantonese piece; and *Red Vanguard*.

Another tragic victim of the fanatical pro-Mao drive was a famous Shanghai actress, Balyan. Hounded by the ruler's followers, she committed suicide in 1966. Chu Ching-to, a leading figure in the theatre world, had the temerity to send letters to Mao protesting that his wife's policies violated concepts enunciated by Premier Chou and Mao himself. The letters never reached the Chairman; Chu Ching-to was thrown into prison and held there for several years.

In Shanghai, the Conservatory was a particular object of attack. Liu Fuan, its director, was seized and interrogated, his head forced to the floor and his arm twisted behind his back. He was ordered confined to a narrow room at the Conservatory for most of the decade, forbidden to leave it, to write music, teach or have any contact with students. The order was widened to affect much of the faculty. Many students left to pursue safer interests such as the endless, noisy political demonstrations or farm work, the best refuge.

The First of August Symphony, deemed a major composition by Liu Fuan, had been dedicated by him to the People's Liberation Army and especially to the old revolutionaries who had been with Mao on the "Long March". Jiang Qing banned it, because she sharply disapproved of Mao's former comrades – who shared his glory – and wished no work of art to honour them.

Harrison E. Salisbury, a *New York Times* correspondent, had access to China during this period and shortly afterwards and gathered first-hand accounts of events during the Cultural Revolution. He learned that the pianist Liu Shih-kun, son of Marshal Yeh Chien-ying, a long-time military colleague of Mao, was approached by members of Jiang Qing's clique. They asked him about the daily routine of his father and Premier Chou, both of whom were targeted for assassination. Liu Shih-kun refused to give the details and had his fingers broken. Salisbury adds: "He was sent to prison for a five-year term and held incommunicado. He was allowed neither paper nor pencil. He managed to tear out Chinese characters from newspapers and paste them on to bits of toilet paper with paste made from his rice gruel. When his wife finally managed to see him in prison, he slipped the bits of toilet paper to her. Ultimately Yeh's daughter and the old marshal won Liu's release."

To this dreadful picture, Salisbury contributes another detail. "A young violinist, the son of yet another of China's important leaders, became so depressed at continual attacks on his views and refusals to permit him to perform that he attempted suicide. Jumping from a window, he broke both legs and is a permanent cripple."

Both the soprano Chou Chaio-yen, China's foremost interpreter of classical European songs, and Lu Chang-ling, the country's most admired bamboo-flute player, were denied the right to appear on stage.

Jiang Qing's paranoia and xenophobia extended far beyond Peking opera and the now drastically inhibited live drama. Throughout her eleven-year tenure as adviser on all aspects of China's cultural pursuits she had absolute say about films, paintings and drawings, and literature. Her much-noticed intervention into the realm of dance will be discussed at length a few pages further on.

For a full decade, while films were under her control, no new feature pictures were produced save for a few remakes of earlier releases. She insisted that the "hero" must never die at the story's end. Later, as a concession to historical fact, she conceded that he might go to his death but always in an exalted manner. Some films created in earlier years, such as the musical and political extravaganza *The East Is Red* – brought to the public under the guidance of Chou En-lai – could no longer be shown. Also held off the screen was *Pioneers*, about the obstacles surmounted by those who had opened the Taching oilfield in north-eastern China. The *New York Times*'s Fox Butterfield recounts that when prints were awaiting Jiang Qing's nod she four times refused to look at them. Finally she did come to a screening and – in Butterfield's words – "'flew into a rage' and demanded to know whom the picture was really praising. Her concern was that the real hero of the film was Chou, the spiritual father of China's modernization plans." Eventually, Mao himself viewed *Pioneers* and passed on it. "There is no big error in this film," he commented. He added: "Don't nit-pick."

Writers of fiction bore the same burden of irrational censorship. A good many novelists gave up all hope of publication and wrote only "for the drawer". Besides, having a book issued might carry an unpredictable risk. Fairy-tales were no longer printed – they were too trivial – nor were any books imported from overseas. Scholars considered it prudent to remove copies of Shakespeare and other European masters from their shelves; such volumes on display in bookshops were either destroyed by the rampaging Red Guards or hidden by nervous shop-owners.

Jiang Qing was especially annoyed, as has already been mentioned, by dramas with love themes. Indeed, she condemned "love" as a "decadent, bourgeois notion"; while she was in charge it was no longer to be found in plays, films or fiction. In 1971 a student dictionary was published in which a blank space appeared after the word "love"; that passion was not defined. A curious result of the obliteration of "love" was a marked increase in pornography; in ever larger quantities obscene literature in manuscript form was circulated furtively by hand among the masses.

Some happenings during this phase were even more bizarre. An instance, reported by Salisbury, illustrates how historical and literary allusions became at times so closely examined and defined that no one clearly grasped what was meant by them, as well as how fearful people were. "Once all the pictures in the rooms of the Peking Hotel were taken down because someone believed they depicted people or classical Chinese scenes that could be construed as reflecting on Jiang Qing. Once the pictures were taken down at the Peking Hotel, they were taken down at all the other hotels for good measure."

An odd incident, described later in the English-language *Peking Review*, concerns the issuance of a book entitled *Unpublished Poems of Chairman Mao*. A youthful university student, Cheng Mingyan, perused the volume and, to his astonishment, discovered that many of the poems were actually from his pen. He told Premier Chou En-lai of the plagiarism. Chou praised him for speaking out and ordered the book of verse to be withdrawn and the young man to be left unharmed. Despite Chou's stipulation, the clique directed by Jiang Qing saw to it that the unfortunate Cheng was "harassed, beaten and finally gaoled".

Another account by Salisbury reveals the absurd extremes to which Jiang Qing's campaign was carried.

In 1973, a Chinese technical mission visited the United States. An American factory gave them cornucopia-shaped ashtrays as souvenirs. When the technicians returned to China, the presents were turned in to the Foreign Office and came into the hands of Jiang Qing and her supporters. In February 1974, she raised the question of the ashtrays in a formal meeting of the Communist Party Politburo. She said they were in the shape of snails and were a deliberate insult, implying that China was making only snail's progress in the world. She demanded that the Chinese Liaison Office in Washington be ordered to raise a formal protest with the US Government.

But Chou managed to win the vote in the Politburo, insisting that the ashtrays – whatever they might represent – were a trivial matter and should not be permitted to jeopardize Sino-American relations. But Jiang Qing was not satisfied. She ordered a novelette written, called *A Report Exposing Contradictions.* It revolved around a "capitalist-roader," bearing a resemblance to Prime Minister Chou, who goes abroad and brings back as a souvenir a snail ashtray. He is rebuked by a heroine reminiscent of Miss Jiang, who explodes: "You bring back a snail ashtray. You yourself have a snail on your back. You just go along at a snail's pace."

The Cultural Revolution ended with Mao's death in 1976 after some months of governmental drift during which the all-powerful Chairman was obviously losing his grip and sinking into senility. The struggle to succeed him was sudden, violent and short. Within a month Jiang Qing and three other leaders who shared her radical leftist orientations – the "Gang of Four", as their enemies called them – were arrested, tried for conspiracy against the state and sentenced to death. Her fellow prisoners, who had been Mao's most trusted followers, were Zhang Chunqiao, Yao Wen-yuan and Wang Hung-yen. All, originally from Shanghai, had been members of the Politburo. Zhang was a Deputy Premier and Chief Political Commissar of the Armed Forces. Once a literary critic, his article in 1965 attacking *Hai Ju Dismissed from Office* had signalled the abrupt initiation of the Cultural Revolution; he had since risen to be Director of Party Propaganda. Wang, a former factory worker, had climbed to prominence largely as a recipient of Jiang Qing's patronage.

At her trial, delayed until four years later, Jiang Qing was defiant. Telecasts showed her replying angrily to her accusers. Subsequently, her sentence was commuted to life imprisonment. (According to rumour, she was now suffering from Parkinson's disease.) She was incarcerated to her very last day, always unrepentant.

The new regime, much more "Centrist", was led by Deng Xiaoping, a protégé of the late Premier Chou En-lai. He had twice been "purged" by the over-zealous Maoists. Confined in a remote army barracks, he had been put to menial tasks, like so many others, at times manual labour in a tractor factory or else waiting on tables. His eldest son, hurled from a window by storming Red Guards, had been crippled for life, a paraplegic.

Deng Xiaoping stressed pragmatism. He was a moderate, not an ideologue. His much-quoted adage was, "It doesn't matter if a cat is black or white, so long as it catches mice." He felt that China had lost much by its fanatically puritanical embrace of Marxism. At the same time he had to move cautiously, as many of Mao's loyalists still held influential posts throughout the country, in the Army and in various minor ruling bodies. He advocated ending China's isolation, learning much about science and technology from the West. He set about restoring a measure of private initiative to small merchants and farmers, so-called "petty capitalism". He favoured reopening the universities and once more encouraging solid scholarship, while awarding a higher status to intellectuals. His course was zig-zag: he would venture an advance but partly retract it whenever the innovation met with too much opposition from the entrenched bureaucracy. The demythologizing of Mao was approached tactfully and very slowly.

A measure of artistic freedom was granted to writers, painters, dancers and film-makers. By Western standards the degree of free speech now allowed was hardly impressive, but to China's long-silenced authors and performers it was a cause of much excitement. Those who had survived the grim decade abruptly reappeared. (Another sign of returning "life": vendors' stalls crowded the streets, small shops opened, and a huge migration of farmers to the cities began, a forerunner of urban problems. Nor should Deng be pictured as wholly benign; he was later to prove otherwise.)

The theatre recovered gradually. From out of the shadows came the actress Chu Ching-to, ironically determined to have been "rehabilitated". She was welcomed with whole-hearted zest. The soprano Yun Hsieh-feng, though broken in health by a decade of cruel harassment, received an ovation when she sang for the Eleventh Party Congress in 1971. Once more given his due recognition, the nation's leading playwright, Cao Yu, was in place as head of his celebrated acting company. The renowned Zhao Hui-ying, a leading performer at the Peking opera, appeared again in the reconstituted troupe after five nightmare years spent planting wheat alongside a rural school where she and others had been sent for "re-education". Long-repressed plays re-occupied the stage, among them the ever-popular *The Dagger Society*. In a tribute to the late ill-fated Lao She, his *Teahouse* was revived and garnered capacity houses in 1978. Virtually all the cast, as well as the director Xia Chun, had put in ten years in the remote countryside where they waded in rice fields and fed swine. The troupe was invited to take its very successful production of the work to West Germany in the same year. If tardy and slow, the process of reinstatement was steady. Every month or two a fresh advance to the restoration of normal conditions was announced.

Attesting to the change, on the island of Hainan the long-neglected tomb of Hai Jui was once more well tended. He was the righteous sixteenth-century governor who had been sentenced to death for his compassion and honesty, a historical incident that had inspired Wu Han's allegorical play and set off the Cultural Revolution. In a nearby museum an inscription bore this eulogy to Hai Jui: "He was a good and just official. He redressed many wrong and unjust cases and was a saviour of the oppressed and downtrodden. He always kept his word." John F. Burns describes the renovated grave: "There is nothing of the magnificence associated with the greatest of the mainland tombs about this walled enclosure, but restorers have done a creditable job of replacing what the Red Guards destroyed. Up a central pathway visitors reach a marble tortoise surmounted by a stele, or marble plaque, blackened by fire and inscribed with a tribute to the mandarin's virtues. Beyond the stele lies the tomb, a domed structure in gray granite, which was smashed by Mao's young vandals. The sarcophagus disappeared at the time of the assault, but the dome has the weathered look of the original."

A new drama, *The Future Is Calling* (1979), marked the greater measure of openness on the stage. Its young author was Zhao Zi Xiong. John Wang, in a dispatch to the *New York Times*, gives us a synopsis:

[The play] deals with the current debate on "practice being the sole criterion for testing the truth," an idea first put forth by Vice Premier Deng Xiaoping in May 1978 in an effort to gain support for his modernization program. The play attacks bureaucracy and ideological rigidity in the Communist Party and the government. It ridicules the "ossified thinkers" who worship Mao blindly and unrealistically.

In a munitions factory, two secretaries of the Communist Party committee engage in a struggle not only to spur lagging production but also to "emancipate the minds" of the Party cadres. Secretary Liang of the headquarters branch is a recently rehabilitated victim of the Cultural Revolution. He is undogmatic, democratic, humane and fearless and a supporter of the "practice-as-the-sole-criterion-for-testing-the-truth" doctrine. Secretary Yu of the local branch, a survivor of the Party's many campaigns and struggles, is, however, rigid and bureaucratic; his only criterion of truth is Mao: "Say what the Chairman said, don't say what he did not." He resists any change in the *status quo* in the perhaps justifiable fear that there will be "another 1957" (a reference to an early Party purge).

The plot is hardly unfamiliar to the Chinese, many of whom must have seen it happen time and again in real life. A woman who accidentally soils a bust of Mao while dusting it is branded a "counter-revolutionary," a charge almost worse than death. A returned Overseas Chinese, an engineer, is put behind bars for his "questionable" political background; his technical skill, which is critical to the factory's production, is not utilized. A request by another engineer to reexamine the case is reviewed by no less than seventeen "responsible officials," but no one is willing to assume the responsibility of setting the innocent man free. Over Yu's objection, Secretary Liang reverses the verdicts in both cases to "defend the Party's prestige among the people." Ultimately, Secretary Yu is relieved of his post. The factory under the leadership of Liang successfully accomplishes its production goal.

The Future Is Calling, unlike *Teahouse*, rings with current political slogans; however, behind those clichés there runs an emotion that seems to touch the audience directly. The upright tone of the play offers a new moral direction, reassurance that basic human values so desperately lacking under the "Gang of Four" have not been forgotten.

What is interesting about the play is not only its message, but the fact that it was allowed to be performed without the parties concerned first seeking official permission. Previously, the Ministry of Culture had to approve any script of a play or a film before it could go into production. This practice has been stopped and theater and film producers have the right to make their own decisions.

Another interesting footnote: Because of the sensitive nature of its content, *The Future Is Calling* drew some criticism after its first performance. In several formal discussions of the play, questions were raised as to its ideological "correctness." The playwright reportedly had a few sleepless nights until Hu Chiao-mu, a member of the Central Committee of the Communist Party and its chief theoretician, gave his approval to go ahead. This paved the way for the play's current success. On July 23, the *Peking People's Daily* devoted a half page to a highly favorable review of the production, praising the play for "bravely bringing forth and answering those questions . . . which urgently need to be resolved." It should come as no surprise, then, that *The Future Is Calling* was hailed by the regime as such a model play.

Such films as *The East Is Red* and *Pioneers* were now on view, as was the previously banned *The Song of the Gardener*, a morality tale of a dedicated teacher who helps in the readjustment of a delinquent student. It had been considered unacceptable because its message ran counter to the radical concepts introduced by Mao. The film's sponsor had been Hun Kuo-feng, at that time first Party Secretary of Hunan, whom Jiang Qing had distrusted; hence her having forbidden its showing was an oblique attack on Hun, who later was to assume office as Chairman of the national Party.

Plays were still somewhat ideological, reflecting current doctrine, for the regime was still Communist and deemed it essential that art should serve the Party, but the interpretation and evaluation of scripts was less rigid and writers were allowed to picture daily life more honestly, up to a point. In addition, more dramaturgical skill was required; simply espousing the correct political doctrine was no longer enough. As before, a considerable number in the surge of new scripts were collective efforts, much as in Shakespeare's day and in twentieth-century Hollywood, but here and there a drama or farce bore a personal stamp.

An early hit was *Red Heart* (1978), which quickly outshone all other plays in the capital after getting full-page reviews in *Jih Pao* and other Peking newspapers. Its subject was the modernization of medicine, which had been a project energetically supported by the late, revered Premier Chou En-lai. A group of doctors are conducting research into heart disease but are opposed by an extremist, sinister "Gang of Four". Though the doctors are following the ideas of Chairman Mao, who advocated combining Chinese and Western therapies, and are making solid progress, they must contend with Chou's enemies who, to strike at the liberal Premier, try to disrupt the experiment. The leader of the research team propels himself into the struggle, gains the strong allegiance of his colleagues, until they finally arrive at an effective new treatment for coronary ills.

A like echo of what was happening in China's political and social realms is heard in a television play *Who Is He?* (or *If I Were Real*; 1979). Its scheduled broadcast was cancelled at the last minute. In defiance of the authorities, the managers of the Peking television station – supposedly under the control of the Central Committee of the Party – circulated a videotape of the farce to film theatres, which were soon packed with eager spectators. The script had three authors, Sha Yeh-hsin, Li Sou-ch'eng and Yao Ming-te, all of them members of the Shanghai People's Art Theatre. A stage version was fashioned and enacted for select audiences in several cities, until the Party intervened and curtailed further showings. (Even though Sha Yeh-hsin dared to protest against this official restriction, he was able to retain favour and have a speedy production of his very next work, *Mayor Ch-en*, in 1980.)

Based on a true story, *Who Is He?* revolves around a glib, handsome young man from Shanghai, Li Hsiao-chang, whose smooth talk and superior air enable him to impress, even dazzle, a circle of ordinary, gullible citizens. He passes himself off as the son of a Deputy Chief of Staff in Peking. A succession of minor officials whom he meets during his escapades seek to ingratiate themselves with this doubtless influential, youthful visitor; they fawn on him, press gifts on him – cash, train and theatre tickets, fine food and wines, a prescription for a rare medication – and mothers aggressively push forward their virginal daughters in hopes of catching his eye and fancy, leading to a match. All, in return, expect to win some benefit; a transfer to a better job, marriage, a pulling of strings in this or that important bureau. Eventually and inevitably, he over-reaches, is exposed, punished.

Though linked in part to an actual incident, *Who Is He?* obviously owes much to the classic eighteenth-century Russian farce, Nikolai Gogol's *The Inspector General* or *The Government Inspector*. (Chinese playwrights apparently had no hesitation about lifting plots and characters from foreign works. Possibly they shared the attitude of Bertolt Brecht: when accused of plagiarism, he blithely responded, "I'm a Communist, so I don't believe in private property.") But in this instance, at least, the trio of authors make no secret of their debt to Gogol. The anti-hero's inspiration to take on the guise of the son of a man of high rank comes to him when he sees a performance of *The Inspector General*. Further, this play carries a somewhat different massage from Gogol's. Gunn points to a sharply honed scene in which the farm functionaries discuss the granting to Li Hsiao-chang's much envied transfer, to be accomplished by what they recognize as a "back-door connection". Their every comment is cynical. One of them begs Li for aid in gaining a similar transfer. There is an open self-appraisal by the characters here lacking in those in *The Inspector General*. Also, as Gunn says, "In the concluding scene, the audience, far from being challenged by Gogol's line, 'Who are you laughing at but yourselves,' is not laughing but called upon to render a verdict in the trial of the youth for his impersonation. The authors' originality lies in their belief that the audience's judgment represents the ultimate in probity and wisdom . . . Other formal innovations, such as a scene played before the curtain and in the audience, exemplify the trend to experiment beyond the conventions of naturalistic realism."

The trauma of the Cultural Revolution and its aftermath resonates in a domestic tragedy, *In a Land of Silence* (1978), by Ysung Fu-hsien (b. 1947) who wrote it while working at the Shanghai Heat Treatment Plant. It was his first script to gain wide attention. The time is 1975, just before Mao's death. Ho Shih-fei, an authoritarian father of grown children, insists on arbitrarily governing their lives. At the moment he is arranging the marriage of his daughter to a man she has not met, a harshly militant Communist. Her affections lie elsewhere. A former suitor, long missing, suddenly reappears. He is accompanied by his mother who is dying and needs a liver transplant. They seek hope and help from Ho Shih-fei's son, a surgeon, Ho Wei. He tells them that the hospital to which he is attached has been forced to cease experimentation with transplants along any lines followed in the West. "Now the top level wants us to do research on a more popular kind of operation." "What kind is that?" "Mouth closure. To drill a hole in everyone's upper and lower lips, run a wire through the two holes, and then twist the wire . . ." Why has the mother waited this long to seek medical treatment? The explanation: during the Cultural Revolution she was imprisoned for six whole years, arrested and held without trial and never told with what crime she was charged. "It was all spent in a dark room, three meters square, where she ate, drank, went to the toilet, and slept. There was no window. Once she didn't see sunshine for fourteen months in a row: that was the longest time. They beat her, hung her by the hair, and kicked her with their boots. They weighed her down with bricks . . . They used what they called 'Exhaustion Tactics', not allowing her to sleep for thirteen days in a row. The moment she closed her eyes they'd whip her . . ."

Furthermore, he and his mother have no money to pay for proper hospital care. "She was in the countryside, and there was no one in the local clinic there who would dare to treat her. The first page of her hospital case history was stamped in large print: 'Stinking Reactionary'." Because of his mother's problems, he had been forced out of the Army. A flier, the only job he could find was as a waiter in a small diner in the suburbs of Peking, earning thirty-five dollars a month.

Taken to Ho Wei's hospital, the stricken woman is given tests but sent away – her condition is terminal, but there is no room for her. Her friends cannot shelter her, either: guests must have a permit from the police, who are already making enquiries about the pair. Their offence, it seems, is that they took part in a huge demonstration – a memorial tribute to the departed Premier Chou En-lai – and that the son has edited a collection of poems, *The Sword Is Drawn*, eulogizing the benign Chou, for which he is branded a counter-revolutionary. There had been an attempt to force the mother to take part in a plot against Chou; she had refused. Ho Shih-fei is anxious that they leave at once; he fears having these "wanted" suspects discovered in his house.

His wife, Liu Hsing, is given to inexplicable bouts of weeping. She has long known that he was an informant, collaborating with the Maoists. He is responsible for much of the persecution of their friends. Knowledge of this accounts for her emotional instability. She warns the fugitives that they are at grave risk and must hasten away. Affrighted, the son takes flight, but his mother is too ill to be moved and is left behind to die.

Ho Shih-fei's children suspect that he has an alliance with the most extreme Maoists, in particular through his tie with the brutal political "thug" to whom he seeks to marry his daughter. The young people's festering suspicion of him is the cause of the "spiritual malaise" that besets them. Now, in a tense confrontation, their mother openly accuses him of complicity in the harassment of innocent, well-meaning citizens, his actions spurred not by any patriotic motive but rather to advance his extensive financial interests. His children are appalled. He attempts to defend his behaviour. Everything he has done was to protect them. "I did it all for this family, all for you." To save them and himself, what else could he do? Unconvinced, they look at him with contempt and prepare to quit the house, going to their grandmother's and taking the dying woman with them. Outside, the wind and rain are howling, but this does not deter them. They go. In the brief last scene there are noble speeches. With a ringing line, the "outlaw" makes his exit, knowing that he faces death as a "dangerous subversive": "In the Revolution we shed our blood, never tears!" A poem by Lu Hs'un is quoted, including a phrase from which the play takes its title: "In a land of silence, thunder will erupt," a warning that a mistreated people will ultimately revolt.

Deserted by his family, Ho Shih-fei is alone in a suddenly empty house, while the relentless storm whips about it. Old and isolated, he shudders at a sudden clap of thunder.

Early, in an exchange with his hunted, outcast friend, the surgeon, Ho Wei, disgustedly exclaims: "The 'political line struggles' for all these years have made my head spin. Speaking the truth – that's a crime; telling lies – that's meritorious; parroting official jargon – that's safe; double-talk – earns a promotion! To hell with all that. I've vowed, I've sworn, I don't care about anything anymore, except to fill up on three meals a day and get enough sleep."

Though the play is bold, it does not go too far. The Party is not blamed for anything that is wrong, only those are at fault who are attempting to take over the Party and subvert its true, noble aims.

Though melodramatic, and not without its share of sloganeering, the drama is well constructed and contains intelligent dialogue. The characters are either all evil or all good but are interesting. The unseen villains are by implication the recently indicted "Gang of Four" who had been truly powerful and had too long dominated China. The play must have had a stirring impact on audiences who only a few months earlier had undergone experiences like those of the unhappy people on stage. Pleased with the script, the Party promoted productions in several cities.

Gunn writes concerning it: "*In a Land of Silence* looks back on Cao Yu's plays of the 1930s in particular with their stifling, gloomy corruption in a 'respectable' household and also on Cao Yu's sources, such as Ibsen. In a broader sense, [it] is a very straightforward reprise of staple themes in twentieth-century Chinese drama. The value of family solidarity is challenged by higher commitments and an authoritarian parent is overthrown: an exile returns not to the situation she expected to find but to shocking revelations that alter or ruin her vision in exile: a physician is challenged to extend his ideals of dedication and commitment to the amelioration of the sickness of society; martyrs staunchly face their demise to render their causes with unambiguous clarity and provide flawless personification of the principle of hope." However, a topical play profiting by references to very recent events runs the risk of all too soon being outdated. The operas crafted as models under the aegis of Jiang Qing were careful to prevent this from happening. In a bare three years the Party line changed – a habit of which Wo Hei passionately complains – it having been decided officially that Mao was not to be spared blame for the cruel excesses of the Cultural Revolution as he is by statements in *In the Land of Silence*. The play was no longer completely acceptable.

A "comic counterpoint" to Ysung Fu-hsien's play was *The Artillery Commander's Son* (1979) by three enterprising students at Fudan University in Shanghai, Chou Wei-po, Tung Yang-shen and Yeh Hsiao-nan. It reached both stage and television. Satires of this sort won few smiles from Party leaders; perhaps this piece got by because its ridicule is aimed not at heads of state but at minor functionaries, the "rank and file" of the bureaucracy with whom ordinary citizens had to contend daily and who are broadly lampooned. Besides, it had a strong appeal to university students who were finally regaining a measure of respect and intellectual leeway and given a larger part in the rebuilding of China through energetic modernization in all sectors of society. Humour was an excellent way to reach them and win their allegiance, by seeming to create a new political climate, one that was profoundly welcome.

A Section Bureau Chief, Sun, is impatiently desirous of advancing his fortunes by marrying his daughter Chie to the son of someone of superior rank. Nothing, he declares, is more important than making the best possible "connection". He has prepared a list of candidates for her hand. One name on the roster is that of Ch'en, whose father is a lofty Chief of Bureau, and hence influential. Chie already knows the young man and likes him, but secretly her heart belongs to Fang, a lowly worker's son. Her father is annoyed when she tells him of her feelings. He firmly rejects her choice and delivers a long speech emphasizing what a mistake it would be for her to have a husband of humble status. When Ch'en, at his parent's bidding, pays a visit, Sun is absurdly obsequious and tries in every way to promote a match.

Sun does not know that Ch'en and Fang are classmates and good friends. They join forces with Chie to deceive her overly ambitious father. Ch'en announces that he is interested in another girl and consequently is not paying suit to Chie. He introduces Fang, dressed in a military uniform, as the scion of an artillery commander stationed in Shanghai. Sun is delighted at the prospect of his daughter marrying into a General's family, bringing him a chance of climbing to an even higher position. He behaves ever more aggressively in an attempt to pair Chie and Fang. Just when everything seems to be proceeding perfectly, the supposed commander's son remarks that his social rank makes a marriage unlikely. At this unpalatable turn, Sun delivers another eloquent speech about the inherent virtues of ordinary folk and the urgent need to do away with class rankings. Fang, deceived into thinking Sun is sincere about this, happily reveals his true identity: he is the son of Sun's house-servant. Sun, astonished, self-thwarted, has to relent; Chie and Fang are united leading to a blissful ending.

The tone of this little play is sprightly; the dialogue is brisk. There are several touches of whimsy: in a prefatory episode, the house-servant, who often speaks directly to the audience, uses a magnifying glass to inspect a broken thermos jar. He proposes to resort to a like magnifying glass to study the characters who are about to appear; the curtains part further on the broader scene; it is enclosed within a huge frame suggesting a glass on a much larger scale behind which the burlesque stage action proceeds.

The serious implication of the play is that even after the overthrow of the "Gang of Four" all is not well in the state. Bureaucrats are still peddling influence and seeking to profit through private "connections"; nor has the concept of a social and political élite who enjoyed special privileges been wholly eradicated.

A two-part melodrama, *The September 13 Affair* (1981–2), by Ding Yisan, also dealt with political events fresh in the spectators' collective memory. Before reaching the boards in Peking it was serialized on television. Because of its length, the first and second halves of the stage version were put on some months apart. The story unfolds with a bundle of dramaturgical tricks, including rear projections; it is an account of Lin Piao's purported scheme to assassinate Mao and grasp power for himself. The late Chairman is the leading character and has many important scenes. He is recalling what happened at that turbulent moment and afterwards during the years of unleashed violence and vandalism. He is drawn as old and ill, weakened and confused, which explains the serious mistakes he made in his failing years, and a measure of extenuation is granted him by the playwright, whose portrait of him has obviously been officially sanctioned. Ding Yisan would not have ventured it otherwise. Many of the most atrocious deeds of the Cultural Revolution were committed without Mao's knowledge or authorization, nor had he ordered that Lin Piao's plane be shot down – it had run short of fuel over Mongolia and crashed. Mao must still be considered a great man to whose almost infallible leadership China owes much. His picture still dominates Peking's vast central square, where stands his tomb, two symbols to be reverenced. In the play, Mao objects to being the subject of a cult of personality and says he does not want the statues of his likeness in marble and stainless steel that have been erected unbidden in his honour by the devious, treacherous Lin Piao. "They make me look like a guard at the gate," the Chairman complains.

Jiang Qing is mostly seen in her boudoir in a "decadent white dressing gown". Hers is a minor role, which would not have pleased her.

The September 13 Affair was performed by a drama troupe from the Air Force's Political Department. Tickets were eagerly sought after and resold, some at a high premium.

The play's twenty-seven scenes were given pace as props were shifted to a disco beat, and much commented on was the faithful resemblance – with clever make-up – to the actual persons by the top characters, down to a mole on Mao's chin. All seemed to have been truly resurrected. They were so accurately recaptured that the first entrance by each elicited gasps from the audience. Their individual gestures, voices, and regional accents were pat.

The presentation had moments of stridency when snatches of the *Internationale* were inserted in rousing choral passages, and there were borrowings of devices from Peking opera here and there, somewhat diluting the graphic realism that otherwise marked it throughout.

In late 1981 the Party's theoretician, Hu Qiaomu, held a week-long symposium in Yenan, summoning to it eighty writers, artists and critics to discuss the current situation. He asserted that Mao had never understood creative people, though many of his theories about the arts were basically sound. Yet his guidelines were not to be looked upon as inviolate. In dramatic works "history should not be ignored nor realities evaded". This announcement apparently conferred more freedom on playwrights, film-writers and novelists, but the censorship was by no means lifted. It continued to be changeful, its rulings often seeming impulsive and unpredictable.

A really bold assault on the Communists' "by-the-numbers" idea of theatre fare were two "Existential" plays by Gao Kingjian, who was clearly familiar with the writing of Beckett and Genet. They were tricky ventures on the part of the People's Art Theatre. For *In Warning Signal*, on an almost bare stage, the cast was in street clothes. An out-of-work young man plans to rob travellers on a train, but when he boards it is surprised to find his fiancée among the passengers. A love scene between them, to the accompaniment of electronic music, was unprecedentedly explicit. In *Bus Stop*, by the same author, eight people find themselves stranded in a depot for ten years, expecting a conveyance that just never comes – an obvious parallel to *Waiting for Godot*, but here a metaphorical allusion to a decade of lost opportunities, the cost exacted from China's suffering population by the Cultural Revolution.

Bai Hua, in the forefront of those seeking to regain some freedom and freshness on the stage, had previously aroused the ire of the authorities with a film-script, *Unrequited Love*, about an artist who returns from foreign travels and is persecuted by fanatical extremists who cause his death. Though the film was completed, it was withheld from circulation, and the writer had to prepare a written acknowledgement of his faults.

He turned to crafting a piece for the stage and shielded himself to some degree by offering an allegorical work, *The Shining Spear of the King of Wu and the Sword of the King Yueh* (1982). Set 2,500 years earlier, it portrayed how power ineluctably corrupts a ruler; most spectators assumed that this was meant as a comment on the descent of Mao into a megalomaniacal self-blindness. It enjoyed a run for a season in Peking without official interference. The play evoked from Ying Ruocheng the hope that native dramatists would "move beyond this literature of conspiracy and historiography of insinuation".

An earlier sign of the liberalization of the stage was a two-week visit in 1979 by the Old Vic Theatre Company from London with its production of *Hamlet*. The first appearance in China by an English-speaking group in thirty years, it signified the removal of a long-standing barrier, a readiness to be open again to some measure of Western cultural influence. *Hamlet* might not have been the best choice to accomplish that aim: it did not represent much that was happening in the contemporary world but instead belonged to an era four centuries gone – or did that make it a relatively safe selection? And what would Chinese audiences make of it? Certainly, as the troupe's director Tony Robertson observed, Shakespeare's alienated and indecisive prince is "far from an ideal revolutionary hero"; none the less the Peking spectators responded to the tragedy enthusiastically. (A simultaneous translation into Mandarin read by local actors was available over earphones, but many followed the speeches without such aid, some perhaps not comprehending the dialogue but simply content to look at the actors' gestures and appreciate the rhythm and music of the lines. Some were familiar with the plot from having studied the text in school, or they had seen Laurence Olivier's film version, which had been brought over a few months before.) The Old Vic gave a total of nine performances in Peking and Shanghai. The title role was taken by Derek Jacobi, whose exuberant and impassioned realism – says Fox Butterfield – "alternately disconcerted and exhilarated" the audience, unaccustomed to such broad ranges of emotion openly engendered and projected.

The director and members of the cast were unprepared for the questions put to them by their hosts. "Why are your costumes so different from those in the Olivier film version?" was one enquiry. Derek Jacobi later remarked: "They seem to think there is only one *Hamlet*, only one way to do it." The Old Vic's production also dispensed with a proscenium curtain, which puzzled the Chinese. "Have you stopped using the curtain altogether in the West?" they asked. Robertson commented: "I get the impression they have been cut off so long they want extraordinary generalizations. They want to know exactly how a play is done, no questions about its content, please."

Butterfield reports: "In Peking, laughter came at an unexpected passage during the play's performance. In the gravediggers' scene, when Ophelia's body is being prepared for burial after she has drowned, there is a discussion over whether she has the right to proper Christian burial since she evidently committed suicide. 'If she were not a gentlewoman, she would not be buried on consecrated ground,' remarks one of the gravediggers. To the Chinese, that was a reminder of one of the hottest current issues here: the special privileges of high-ranking Communist Party officials."

A Shakespearian comedy, *Much Ado About Nothing*, was mounted by the Shanghai Youth Drama League at the Shanghai Arts Theatre. The text was translated into Chinese, and the players donned Elizabethan costumes; going further, they applied make-up to give themselves European facial features, in particular changing the shape of their eyes. Still prudish, the performers enacted no love scenes; when Beatrice and Benedict embraced and kissed at the end, they were surrounded by their fellow players and were out of sight of all in the audience. Harold C. Schonberg, music critic of the *New York Times*, was among the onlookers and wrote back: "The acting was broad and old-fashioned, but entirely within the Shakespeare conventions. Zhu Xijuan was the Beatrice; she is a beauty who was one of China's famous film actresses before the ban on films, and she went through the part with a great deal of temperament. Very little was cut. The translation appeared authentic, so far as one could gather. It had been made by several Chinese translators, and the directors, Zhang Ming and Zhu Yi, said that they collated the various translations for their script. There was one touch of Chinese drama. Dogberry wore a mask. Mr Zhang explained this by saying that the actor's face was so Chinese that it could not be made up to resemble a Westerner's."

Soon a good deal more Shakespeare, explored by professional actors, was on view; the esteemed Ying Ruocheng had a leading role in *Measure for Measure* (1981) and translations of *Macbeth* and *The Merchant of Venice* were to be seen. Quite ambitious was an operatic version of *Othello*, "complete with Chinese cymbals".

Modern foreign works were introduced slowly and cautiously. The People's Art Theatre, as usual in the vanguard, produced *The Visit*, by the Swiss playwright Friederich Dürrenmatt, and *The Butcher*, a West German drama about Hitlerism. The first two American stage offerings were adapted from films, *Body and Soul* and *Guess Who's Coming to Dinner*. Because both scripts presented unflattering images of life in the capitalist United States, the menace of the insidious gangsterism and perpetuation of racism, they were approved by the censors.

The much-publicized staging of Arthur Miller's *Death of a Salesman* occurred next (1983). Ying Ruocheng was the hapless Willy Loman, and Zhu Lin was Linda, his grieving wife. Their sons, Biff and Happy, were played by Li Shilong and Me Tiezeng. Miller himself was on hand to assist with presenting the tragic work; his third wife, a German-born photographer, had been teaching a course in China for some months each year, so he already had some familiarity with the local scene.

Scarcely any changes were made in the script. The actors were dressed as Americans and the setting was much like that designed for the Broadway première. Would the materialistic, "bourgeois" values enunciated by Willy sound too alien and remote to Marxist-educated spectators who had lived for decades in a world isolated from almost all others? That is the question the actors frequently asked themselves. The response was reassuring; the audience was empathetic, and the play was reported to be a major success.

Ying Ruocheng, the actor who also served as translator – the dialogue was in Peking dialect – felt that the universality of Miller's drama had been demonstrated by this production. He told Christopher Wren that, though the authorities took the play to be a depiction of the "cruelty of American capitalism", no Chinese critic agreed with that reading of it. "Instead, they sought out a lesson in family relationships, which remain strong in Chinese society. A lot of older people were dragged to the theatre by their children and told, 'You are treating us in the same way as Willy Loman treated his children.' There was no problem with identification. People who came to see something exotic soon found themselves involved. People cried unashamedly." Leaving the play, they argued about its message.

Miller's Willy Loman differs very much from the protagonists of most Chinese plays. Ying explained: "After so many years of Jiang Qing, contemporary people are programmed. When they see the main character, they expect him to be a goody goody. This man does everything wrong, everything a self-respecting revolutionary cadre would not do. He brags, lies, has affairs, raises children in the wrong way and finally kills himself. But you still end up loving him."

Another novelty, for Chinese audiences, was the playwright's use of flashbacks that "conveyed Willy Loman through time and space". Some of the early *huaju* had experimented even more freely with flashbacks, but that was before the time of many of the spectators at this staging of *Death of a Salesman*. Miller subsequently published a book about his experiences during this Peking production.

By mid-decade the nation's theatre was thriving again. In 1983, on his visit to America, Cao Yu was interviewed by Christopher Wren of the *New York Times* and provided happy statistics. China had 2,000 professional acting companies, of which 200 dealt with contemporary subjects. In the preceeding three years over 300 scripts had been published or staged. (From other sources, the number of Peking opera troupes alone was estimated to be 2,800.) In any event, the count of theatre-goers was in the tens of millions. Cao Yu was confident about the future, though he did not venture to predict what form Chinese theatre might take. Only one aspect of it seemed certain to him. "We will not allow the kind of literature that does nothing but sing praises. After ten years of the Cultural Revolution, the people's minds are really liberated. We shall never allow a writer to be condemned as a counter-revolutionary for his thoughts, whether his writing is liked or not."

Ying Ruocheng, interviewed at the same time by Wren, expressed somewhat less optimism. "In some cases, we have cast off [sloganeering]. In others, not so much. When a play has a political message not agreeable to everyone, we're in trouble because criticism in China is still political criticism. Otherwise, we're not bothered." He acknowledged: "A few years ago, we were talking about the remnant of fear in the heart of the artists. They felt afraid. I think that's mostly gone. During the Cultural Revolution, it was accepted by everyone that if you wanted to write a play, novel or work of art, you must have a message and usually a simplistic message. You must have a message before you have a play, which is nonsense, of course. The backlash to that has been strong, too. People have made a point of declaring, 'I have no message.' What they meant to say is, 'I have no message as a forerunner.' You don't write a play unless you have something to say." But he, too, did not anticipate a reversion to an "ideologically strait-laced theatre". He stated: "I feel we're in for a period of stability, with no political movements, upheavals, struggles or conflicts, which tend to make life tense no matter which side you're on. If that lasts for any appreciable time, we will have a more artistic theatre. There's never a lack of talent in China. It's whether you have the right atmosphere, the right ambiance for the talent to emerge."

15

CHINA: OPERA, PUPPETRY, DANCE

The Peking Opera – the large company in the capital – was reconstituted: as many as possible of its dispersed members were called back, and parts of its repertory gradually restored. The process was neither quick nor easy, the result not perfect. It was necessary to recruit new actors, singers, acrobats, as well. Even so, after strenuous efforts, Zhao Yan-xia (or Chao Yen-hsia, b. 1928), the troupe's female star, was able to lead a company of seventy-five through a fortnight of performances in New York at the Metropolitan Opera House (1980), prefacing appearances in nine other cities. The rebuilt ensemble had made earlier "cultural exchange" tours to Europe and Canada, but because of still troubled political relations had until now stayed away from the United States.

Though Ms Zhao's family had been poor, her father and eight aunts had been employed by the company. Her career had begun at seven. She had her first acting role at fifteen, after her eight years of rigorous induction into the opera's elaborate and exacting conventions. For a year she had the tutelage of the renowned artist Hsun Hui-sheng (Xun Hui-sheng). She finally excelled in a broad range of parts, female and male, at times arrayed in the mantle of a vivacious young lady, at other times showing the mien of a poor, virtuous maiden, or appearing as a warrior, even a clown. In 1963 she had gone with the troupe to Hong Kong and Macao, where her virtuosity had enchanted spectators. During the Cultural Revolution she had spent seven years mixing cement for construction projects. She was now fifty-two and one of four in the company ranked Grade One, which brought her a monthly salary of $250. Quite enough. Some of the younger performers earned $15 a month.

Her frequent partner, Liu Xueto (Liu Xue-tao), was also a third-generation member of the troupe. Trained since childhood, he was a pupil of Chiang Miu-hsiang (Jiang Miu-xiang) who had long acted with Mei Lanfang. Liu Xueto had made his first stage appearance at twelve. Though now near sixty, he retained a handsome youthful aspect and was still assigned roles as the leading young man.

Among the other featured performers was Yang Shao-ch'un (Yang Shao-chun) noted at thirty-eight for his impersonations of fierce warriors, some of them Robin Hood characters. He, too, was descended from a family of actors. Li Yuan-ch'un had similarly begun study at seven for his career in the theatre. He was renowned as the bold Wu Kung in *The Monkey King Fights the Eighteen Lo Hans*. Heroic warriors and scholars were also portrayed by Chang Yun-ping (Zhang Yun-bing), from boyhood a pupil of Fu Lian-chang at the Peking Opera School. In 1957, at the Seventh World Youth Festival in Moscow, as a member of a Chinese contingent, Chang Yun-ping had been awarded the gold shield. His talents had also been on view in Hong Kong, Macao and North Korea. Male roles, especially those calling for agile combat, were apt to fall to the actress Chao Hui-ying (Zhao Hui-ying), once an apprentice with the famed Kuan Su-shuang (Guan Su-shang).

In preparation for the visit to New York, the company, directed by Ms Zhao, had withdrawn to a tiny country town, Xun Yi, twenty miles north east of Peking, where day-long rehearsals in a red-brick theatre started at seven each morning. She admitted to Fox Butterfield that the cast's standards of performance had been set back by its long absence from the stage. During the horrible decade of the Cultural Revolution many students graduating from the Government Peking Opera School had acquired the wrong techniques. Jiang Yanrung, the company's stage manager, was specific about this. "Ninety per cent of them are useless to us. They were taught something that was neither fish nor fowl. They learned sports gymnastics instead of the traditional opera acrobatics and sword-play." He pointed to a team of young players engaged in a battle scene for the opera *Yen Tang Mountain*. The action called for peasant soldiers to somersault over a five-foot wall around a government-held mountain-top fortress. "You see, they hold their spears wrong." Such gaffes resulted from Jiang Qing's having ordered the acrobats to behave like twentieth-century soldiers of the People's Liberation Army rushing head-on with fixed bayonets. Jiang Yanrung complained, too, that during the Cultural Revolution young people had not been exposed to the Peking Opera's repertoire and were no longer familiar with nor had any interest in the historical epics and mythological tales from which most of the plots of classical works were drawn.

Despite technical shortcomings, imperceptible to enthusiastic Western audiences, the Peking Opera had a triumph in New York. Four alternating programmes consisted of excerpts from nine works, with spectacular acrobatics and gorgeous costuming and sets that included *The Legend of the White Snake* (*The Magic Herb*); *The Goddess of the Green Ripples*; *The Monkey King Fights the Eighteen Lo Hans*; *The Jade Bracelet*; *Yen Tang Mountain*; and *Princess Redfish* (*The Magic Pearl*).

Only a year later twenty members of a second Chinese ensemble, the Shanghai Peking Opera Troupe, offered fifteen performances at New York's Alice Tully Hall (1981). The engagement was financed by Michael Chow, who had emigrated to the United States and prospered as a restaurateur; his father, Zhou Xinfang (Chow Hsin-fang), had been a victim of the Cultural Revolution, was gaoled and died at eighty in 1975. The company's leading warrior roles were now entrusted to Zhou Shaolin

(Chow Shao-lin), another son of Zhou Xinfang. The purpose of the visit was to display to Westerners a number of innovations that Zhou Xinfang had effected in the Peking opera genre, consisting principally of less emphasis on physical dexterity and greater concern with structured plots and intensely expressive acting with a search for psychological realism, a performance in what had come to be known as the Ch'i (or Qi) style, an allusion to Zhou Xinfang's stage name.

In the 1920s Zhou Xinfang (the elder) had been the actor–manager of a theatre in Shanghai. He began to experiment, following lines somewhat like those pursued by Stanislavsky in Russia. (Michael Chow asserts that his father was not aware of Stanislavsky's theories.) Such ideas were perceived in ultra-conservative China as much more shocking than they were in Russia. Marjorie Loggie writes: "Stanislavsky worked mostly with contemporary plays in naturalistic sets. On his stage were birches, birds, beef and bread, Cleopatra's barge or the kitchen sink if necessary. Zhou Xinfang faced more formidable obstacles: few realistic props, no scenery. And what he had were plays from history, myth and legend set in rigid traditional forms. He developed a method of extracting the usable truths, and then through imagination reconstituting them into something doable on the stage within the rigid traditions of the Peking opera. Zhou Xinfang's work affected teaching all over China, in literature and film making as well as in the theatre."

His elder son and heir, Zhou Shaolin, is quoted: "The actor is very poor. He has only two eyes, a nose, a mouth, only two arms, his fingers and one leg – well, we can't use both at the same time. He must learn to be economical; never use the whole hand when a finger will do. Power in reserve is mysterious and most potent. A large gesture is often weaker than a small one executed in the proper rhythm."

Joining in, Michael Chow explained: "Ch'i is within the tradition of Peking opera. Just as a graduate of the New York City Ballet school could perform with the San Francisco Ballet, so any Peking opera-trained actor could perform the Ch'i style. . . . The actor must get into the inner motivation of the character and the play. That is the basic thing, but at one time the Peking opera forms became so strong they became stagnant."

Zhou Shaolin proffered this illustration: "The traditional Peking opera gesture for crying, for instance, is patting the cheeks. In my father's style, you can see from the feeling in the actor's face that he's going to cry before he makes that patting gesture."

The father had prescribed: "An actor should start singing with his body long before a single note passes his lips. And the music must linger, in his gestures and facial expressions, long after an orchestra has fallen silent."

Michael Chow expatiated: "The Chinese love everything very pretty. My father came along very angry. He went for the truth, and all his plays have enormous energy and roughness that becomes refined into beauty. With a painter like Van Gogh, for example, what is important is the fury with which the paint is put on, the crudeness of the brush stroke that makes up the art. There are a few basic rules in Peking opera. You must have a carpet on the floor or otherwise the actors in their high-heeled shoes might fall and hurt themselves. The floor is the earth and the stage light is the sky, so you can have no mood lighting. You must create everything yourself. The stage is bare. One soldier is one thousand. But once you catch that, you can do many things."

Michael Chow told the interviewer, Jennifer Dunning of the *New York Times*, that at Alice Tully Hall the orchestra would be placed at the back of the stage, instead, as was traditional, at the right of the spectators. "That is going back to the way it was eighty or ninety years ago. We are doing it here because we want people to see the instruments and the close relationship between the orchestra and the actors, which is comparable to the interplay in ballet. And the actors will come on to the stage from slits in a huge backdrop rather than from the wings, which is different from what we do in Shanghai but gives more of the feeling of Peking opera as it was once done in palaces and open air."

"The group is one of three Peking opera ensembles that perform in Shanghai. It has its own school in which students are enrolled at twelve for five to six years of special training. The full company numbers 250, of whom 100 are performers and forty are musicians."

Guest artists for the New York run were the actress Tong Zhiling and actors Gu Yix-yuan and Wang Zhengping, the latter highly esteemed for "painted-face" roles. These three had once worked with Zhou Hsinfang. The repertory was made up of excerpts from *Lancing the Chariots*, *The Four Scholars*, *Secret Missive/Slaying of the Mistress*, *Blocking the Horse* and *Chase under the Moonlight*.

Though the opening night went off with considerable éclat – friends of Michael Chow and a large segment of so-called "café society" filled the house – subsequent performances were poorly attended, the company often playing to rows of empty seats. One commentator, alluding to the advent of the better-known Peking Opera Troupe the previous season, compared the rival companies and offered this evaluation:

After last year's breathless excitement about rediscovering this venerable art form, this year's visit was mostly greeted by critics who confessed their ethnocultural ignorance and threw up their hands in puzzlement.

That is certainly an honest reaction; there is no way for an Occidental American without extensive study and experience to pretend any kind of expertise about this very alien artistic experience. Yet a few remarks can be ventured.

First of all, this troupe was both more and less accessible than last year's. Less, in that the repertory did not stress the spectacle and acrobatics of last year. More, because the "Ch'I" style invented and perfected by the Chow brothers' late father turned out to be considerably closer to Western psychological realism than the style practiced by the troupe from Peking.

Aided by the curious but helpful sequential photo-illustrations in the program book, which detailed the progress of the story, a Western viewer could understand quite clearly what was going on. He was aided by the literal and instantly comprehensible mime that pervades this style. This mime seems perhaps an unfortunate literalization of the refined symbolism of other forms of Chinese opera. But that refinement was apparently the true province of a still older and more obscure form, the Gunchu style, that fell from favor a century ago.

At its best, as in the verismo-like climax of *Slaying of the Mistress*, the Shanghai troupe achieved a genuine blend of ancient Oriental artifice and turn-of-the-century Western melodrama. Curious, but interesting, too, and worth more attention than New York's jaded and sated late-Summer theater and ethnic-music audience was apparently willing to give it.

Mel Gussow, in the *New York Times*, had this baffled response:

The opening of the Peking opera, Ch'i style, at Alice Tully Hall on Wednesday was a gala East–West social event, but in terms of art being communicated to a Western audience, the evening represents a severe cultural gap. Despite all the anticipation, the two-hundred-year-old performance technique, as offered for the first time in America by a Shanghai company, seems more esoteric than exotic.

While acknowledging the history and importance in China of the Peking opera – it has survived a revolution and it demands the most rigorous training – one watched this version with an awe bordering on bewilderment. In searching for the essence of Peking opera, Ch'i style, one finally must conclude that it is in the company's simplicity. As with many Western experimental theaters, a purpose of this classic troupe is to stimulate the audience's imagination. The result is the opposite; we become overly aware of a process of minimization, combined with broadness of gesture.

When the long-bearded Zhou Shaolin, the star of the company and the elder son of the legendary Zhou Xinfang, the founder of the Ch'i style, makes his hand tremble, or when the leading lady, Tong Zhiling, takes tiny mincing steps across the stage, some members of the opening night audience burst into enthusiastic applause. It was as if each actor had just performed a triple somersault or a grand jeté. Apparently these are recognizable movements, handed down through generations of actors and probably as identifiable to Peking opera followers as the tricks and winks of the D'Oyly Carte are to fans of Gilbert and Sullivan. To this viewer, the movements and mannerisms did not seem significant.

The evening is underscored with music, played by an expressionless on-stage orchestra that varies from six to eight pieces. The orchestra uses clappers, gongs, cymbals and unfamiliar stringed instruments. The music is discordant and cacophonous, and the individual singing has an alien effect on our ears. Because the music increases in intensity and volume to match the drama, one can have some understanding of the motivation behind the composition.

Similarly, one can appreciate the costumes – flamboyant cloaks and gowns and teetering head-pieces – and the elaborate makeup. The actors appear to be encased in an endless fold of flower petals. Scenery is kept to a minimum, in front of a red backdrop on a brightly lit stage, everything is emblematic; a small flag represents a chariot, two chairs become a bed chamber. The small cast mimes other aspects of the surroundings. However, the mime is of a most rudimentary nature, and often lacking in specifics. For example, when Mr Zhou turns away from the audience and places a long needle between his fingers, he is either indulging in some rite of acupuncture or pretending to unlock a door.

Perhaps the most disappointing element is the drama. The opening bill consists of three plays, two short pieces and one extended story. The first is heroic, the second bucolic, and the third domestic. At least for Western theater-goers, none appears to be archetypal or mythological. The simplistic narratives put an undue emphasis on letters, both purloined and incriminating. In the climax of one play, Mr Zhou copies one such document onto the apron of his robe, a gesture whose meaning remains obscure. However, the reactions of the characters to these missives is unflaggingly melodramatic, in the manner of early silent movies.

In two instances there is dramatic flair – the choreographic *Lancing the Chariots*, in which Gu Yixuan plays a brave warrior with a certain martial ferocity, and in the evening's main piece, *Secret Missive/Slaying of the Mistress*. This attenuated tale of a crime of passion begins with the entrance of Wang Zhengping, an actor celebrated for performing "big painted-face" roles. His make-up is as thick as a mask of villainy, his costume is voluminous and his gestures are vividly theatrical. At one point, he twitches his features from nose to chin, a feat of unusual facial dexterity.

Peking opera, Ch'i style, does not have the universal appeal of such brilliant Japanese theater as Kabuki and Bunraku. Undoubtedly its interest is largely for students of Oriental art and for those who cherish it as part of a revered tradition.

Still more Chinese opera was on display in New York in 1982 with the arrival of the fifty-five members of the Guandong Opera Troupe from Canton for a week of presentations at the Beacon Theater.

The star of the company was Hong Xiannu. The company brought lavish costumes, sequined, hand-embroidered, brighter even than those of the other groups; the musical accompaniment differed in that Western instruments were added to the orchestra.

In 1984 Professor Michael Kammen, an exchange lecturer from Cornell University, reported to the *New York Times* that Shanghai, which laid claim to being the world's most populous city and the country's cultural capital, had thirty opera houses, in each of which a performance was given almost every night, with many adding matinées on holidays.

Nevertheless, because opera is so immensely popular, reservations should be made as far ahead as possible. A week in advance is needed for the most popular productions, though popularity today has more to do with famous actors and actresses than with particular operas.

Many of the operas being performed have been written since 1949, but they are based upon traditional tales, are lavishly placed in historical settings, and feature singers wearing resplendent costumes.

The sagas are melodramatic. They endlessly reiterate moralistic points: it is difficult to be an honest official in a corrupt society, or where can I find justice in this world? Plots are often convoluted, involving long-lost relatives and separated siblings (not unlike many of Shakespeare's plots).

The audiences become deeply engrossed, and at a certain point the foreign visitor feels torn between watching the action on stage and watching the captivated audience. Many of them sit, quite literally, for three hours on the edges of their seats.

It is customary, as the opera nears its end, for those who have been seated in the rear of the house to rush forward to the stage to catch a better glimpse of the singers' faces and expressions. On one recent occasion, however, more than 100 people from the back seats became so agitated by the drama that they moved down the aisles to the front fifteen minutes before the finale. Pandemonium broke out because the people with the best seats could not see and some of the crashers even began to push and shove one another to improve their positions.

The curtain had to be closed, and the manager came out to explain that the opera would not continue until all the patrons returned to their assigned places. They did so swiftly and silently. The opera then proceeded to its heart-rending but morally uplifting dénouement.

For South China opera I recommend the People's Opera House on Qiu Jiang Road. The best orchestra seats cost forty-five cents. Those in the rear are thirty cents. Because the printed program is available only in Chinese, it is worthwhile to arrange for a guide to accompany you to explain what is happening on stage. This can be done by the China Travel Service through your hotel, and might cost ten or twelve dollars. For a group of two to four people, it is quite reasonable and sensible.

There is another reason why a guide is helpful. Often the opera is preceded by a ten- or fifteen-minute warm-up show, usually didactic in nature. It may, for example, concern the need for social order and social control. Or it may involve a feminist exhortation about the "new Chinese woman in the 1980s." The songs might tell parents to be as happy with a girl-child as with a son. They should make sure that their daughters get a good education. And, women should receive equal pay for equal work!

In 1985 a former theatre critic and film producer, Cynthia Grenier, described for the *Wall Street Journal* her impressions of a performance in Peking of *The Faithful Harlot* (*Yu Tang Chun*). One of the oldest and most cherished works in the troupe's repertoire, it had been banned by Jiang Qing. On this evening, Zhao Yan-xia had the stellar role in the restored work. Wrote Ms Grenier:

The theater proper was rather like a high-school auditorium with rows of hard plywood seats bolted to a level floor. A shallow balcony ran around the top half of the hall. The audience steadily streaming in was all Chinese except for a sprinkling of Japanese instantly distinguishable by the cut and quality of their clothes. A majority of the Chinese were male and over age forty, all in variants of the eternal Peking Drano-blue boiler suit rendered bunchy by padding and heavy undergarments.

Faces here were different, however, from the thousands we'd been seeing all around us. Many of the faces looked, well, intellectual, or as if they belonged to people in some kind of profession. They often seemed to know one another.

Despite the icy cold of the unheated theater and a pervasive odor compounded of garlic, soft-coal dust and urine, there was an undeniable mood of lively anticipation in the hall.

. . . The curtains parted. An actor in brilliant silk robes, his face painted in a comic stylization of age, walked on. A Chinese next to me in a well-cut, dark-blue uniform of good quality wool with a small stand-up white collar pulled out a sheaf of blank paper and a pencil. As the actor began speaking in what appeared to be a casually comic vein, the audience laughed and applauded. At either side of the stage were two large, lighted oblong panels displaying the ancient text of the play in modern Mandarin.

A woman walked on stage with delicate, mincing steps. Her face was wondrously made up with deep-red eye shadow fading into pink cheeks, eyes outlined in bright blue, a tiny matte carmine mouth, an elaborate, blue-silk headress with long, thick black hair gathered to one side, a bright scarlet jacket with long, white silk sleeves, red pants and an intense-yellow overskirt. She delivered an aria that ended on a kind of strangled cat twang that touched off another round of applause.

My neighbor wrote "shewhore, murder husband poisoned noodles" and gently pushed his note to me. I read, nodded. He smiled, and wrote energetically, "actress very nice." And so the evening went.

Alluding to what she knew of Zhao Yan-xia's long, unhappy exile from the stage, and now her welcome return, Ms Grenier summed up the actress's multiple talents:

Performing again for the past four or five years, singing, miming and doing the acrobatic routines in which each performer must be more than proficient, is, as it were, the Maria Callas, Marcel Marceau and Mary Lou Retton of China rolled into one.

The Peking opera that influenced Brecht, Stanislavsky and John Cage is highly stylized, yet at moments, amid their formal, ritualistic movements, the actors injected a sudden realism, which was startling yet somehow harmonious with the rest.

Interestingly, as the play unfolded, *The Faithful Harlot* even took on a contemporary resonance. Our heroine, a concubine, was falsely accused of murdering her master by his jealous wife, who had herself actually poisoned the fatal noodles and then bribed a local magistrate to imprison the young woman. The harlot sings to a new judge in the capital, telling him of her forty beatings and the ten whips her jailers broke while flogging her, and how she'd spent a year in prison without seeing a soul.

In the end, justice triumphs. The wicked wife and her lover are sent off to immediate execution.

The audience gave Zhao Yan-xia a standing, ten-minute ovation at the curtain. Were they thinking about Zhao Yan-xia's seven years of mixing cement or about Jiang Qing (Madame Mao) sentenced to life imprisonment? Or was it joy at the return of traditional plays? Nobody passed any helpful notes at this point, but eye contact was most eloquent.

Apart from being a component of the various kinds of opera and drama in China, the dance has had an independent history. As elsewhere, its origins are age-old; it arose from religious rituals and seasonal festivities that in some instances also made use of mime. Imitation, as has been frequently noted, was a way of exerting a magical persuasion over the forces of nature and the even more feared supernatural. The Chinese cosmos was filled with demons of every sort who had to be appeased or quelled.

A brief survey by You Haihai, in the official publication *China Reconstructs*, traces traditional dance forms back to the Neolithic age. "Dance is referred to in inscriptions on the shoulderblade and tortoise shell 'oracle bones,' China's first written records, which date from the Shang dynasty (sixteenth–eleventh centuries BC). (You Haihai is editor-in-chief of *Dance News*.)" References have also been found to ceremonial dances performed in the early Western Zhou dynasty (eleventh century BC) that originated at various times in six earlier eras. An instance of this is *Rose-Coloured Clouds*, believed to have been created during the reign of Huan Di, the "semi-legendary Yellow Emperor, honored as the foremost ancestor of the Chinese people. The dance is named for the clouds said to have risen in the sky when he united the various tribes and founded the Chinese nation." Among several other dances of this distant period are one that beseeches the stars for good crops, another portraying how in the eleventh century Yu the Great led his subjects in coping with a flood in the twenty-first century BC, and one depicting the battle wherein King Wu overthrew the last ruler in the Shang line and set up the Zhou dynasty.

When a slave society evolved, the aristocracy began to make use of dance for recreational as well as purely ritualistic purposes. Court entertainments developed. From 771 BC large troupes of performers appeared before the emperors of the Western Zhou dynasty and their guests. Music and dance were declared to be "uplifting and proper subjects to aid in the moral education of daughters and sons of ruling classes, and special schools were set up to train them in these areas".

Though folk-dances by peasants and others in the general populace were still a feature at festivals, court entertainments grew ever more elaborate. These reached a peak in the Han dynasty (206 BC–AD 220) and throughout the Sui and Tang epochs (seventh to tenth centuries). Also during Han days the rituals were somewhat refined. A government department, the Yuefu, was assigned the task of collecting and describing all folk-songs and dances. Under the governance of Emperor Wu Di (r. 141–87 BC) the members of this bureau gathered specific details of many hitherto, almost lost dances that had been composed during the Warring States period (475–221 BC). A considerable body of folk artists was organized, on one occasion numbering as many as 829 knowledgeable persons, of whom 142 were listed as apprentices.

Encouraged by the regime, theatricals of a popular sort were put on for the public at large. One kind was the *baixi*, or "Hundred Games", in essence a variety show. It was also known as *san yue*, or "Diverse Music", to distinguish it from the more classical entertainments at the palace. The *baixi* have also been likened to circus or fairground spectacles. Such events included martial arts, trials of strength, daring acrobatics. The lasting significance of the "Hundred Games" is that aspects of them, especially the acrobatics and exhibitions of martial prowess, were assimilated into the dance, which to the present hour strongly emphasizes such feats as flexible back-bends, rapid cartwheels, spins, dazzling leaps and somersaults.

During Wu Di's reign, too, trade routes to the "Western regions" – today's Xinjiang and territories beyond the Gansu Corridor – were opened and led to cultural contacts, so that the dances of those distant areas became known. From them Chinese performers borrowed new steps and gestures, in particular some from the "oasis kingdom of Kucha" which lay in what is now Xinjiang. The dances of Northern Zhou (sixth century AD) were soon responding to more strongly marked Kucha rhythms, an adaptation that continued in Sui and Tang years.

The music and dance idioms of India and Koro, a segment of Korea, also contributed various elements still perceptible.

The Sui and Tang dynasties, enjoying wealth and comparative stability, provided a climate in which the arts flourished. The result was great progress in choreography. At the Tang court the music and dance of preceding dynasties were codified into ten categories. The rulers, demonstrating their brilliance and power, sponsored formal and resplendent fêtes for envoys, high ministers and their entourages. The nature of such events was determined by whether they took place indoors or outdoors. If performing inside the palace, the dancers probably numbered not more than a dozen, and their delicate grace characterized them. Outdoors, the troupes tended to be far larger, with as many as 180 participants, and pageantry was salient.

Of the three most famed dances of the period, two were composed by a cultivated warrior, Li Shinin, a founder of the dynasty and eventually occupant of the imperial throne as Emperor Tai Zong. His creations were *Breaking Through the Enemy Lines* and *Jubilant Celebration*.

Popular in the Tang era, also, were performances that combined dances, music, poetry and song. Two much-liked pieces, *Rainbow Skirt* and *Feather Cape*, were purportedly conceived by Emperor Xuanzong (*c.* 712–96), though some scholars believe they were designed by his favourite concubine, Lady Yang, who performed them in a fairy costume. They reveal an Indian influence, with elements taken from the rites of Brahmin priests.

More dances, narrating intricate stories, appeared in the Sōng dynasty (960–1279). Simultaneously, folk dancing was even more widely taken up by the populace, at village festivals, trade fairs, community gatherings on any pretext. In Hangzhou the dwellers in many streets had their own troupes available to dance, sing and display acrobatic skill. Some of these dances are still current, among them *Dragon Boat* and *Hobbyhorse* – in the latter the performer dons a wide skirt, horse's head and tail.

Towards the close of the Sōng epoch, and during the ensuing Yang dynasty (1271–1368), opera began its ascent, quickly absorbing the dance, which meant the decline of dance as an autonomous art form. The rise in mid-century of neo-Confucianism, too, at the urging of the regime, had a baneful effect. The teachings of the Master were reshaped to make them a more effective instrument for controlling the masses. Accordingly, dancing was declared to be immoral, and women were said to have an obligation to stay at home; so dancing – a social activity – was largely out of bounds.

Some professional dancers still practised their art, but their numbers were few. One place where dancing remained popular was at annual festivals, especially among minority peoples who lived on the remote periphery of the vast continent. Cut off from the Chinese heartland, they preserved their indigenous traditions with scant change. Choreography in present-day China has drawn on them for substantial enrichment of modern works.

You Haihai cites 1919, the year of the "May Fourth New Culture Movement", as signalling a rebirth of widespread interest in dance. This was not quite a decade after the 1911 Revolution which had led to the fall of the last imperial dynasty. As one way to bring about change in an outmoded educational system, little children in elementary schools were taught songs and dances that inculcated in them progressive ideas and loyalty to country.

During the war with Japan (1937–45) and the War of Liberation (1946–8), which ended with the Communist takeover, songs and dances were fashioned to lift the people's spirits. Working against the odds in areas controlled by the Kuomintang, professional dancers defied Chiang Kai-shek's "reactionary" forces and put on pieces advocating resistance. In regions where the Mao-led Party had already established its rule, dance was enlisted on behalf of the Marxist cause. "The *yanggee* (*Rice Transplanting Song*), which actually dated from the Qing dynasty, became extremely popular. It was danced by everybody, workers, peasants, soldiers, and became associated with praise for the revolution and governments of liberated areas."

Even more official encouragement of dance came in 1949, after the Communist ascendancy. You Haihai recounts:

> The government made efforts to preserve and develop folk-dances. Before Liberation, most folk artists were poor hired hands, boatmen or coolies, persons of low social standing and insecure livelihood. The government sent people to seek out well-known local artists. Some had become street peddlers, others were ailing and confined to their beds, still others had been reduced to begging. The government gave them food and financial help, and employed them as teachers of the new generation of dancers.
>
> When professional song and dance ensembles were set up, their first task was to go among the

people to learn from the folk artists and salvage the heritage. These troupes and other cultural units all over the country formed groups to collect folk-songs and dances. Now, about a thousand representative dances have been sorted out. They have been published in the multi-volume *A Survey of China's Folk-Dance*, China's first history of dance. This work has been aided by a number of dance festivals.

Coupled with these endeavours, present-day choreographers have sought to create new dances that retain a "national style". You Haihai singles out as a successful example the *Lotus Dance* (1954) fashioned by Dai Ailian, who became vice-chairman of the Chinese Association of Dancers. *Lotus Dance* draws on the *yanggee* as it is still performed near Yan'an in northern Shaanxi province. Such post-Liberation dances reflect contemporary life, the impulses of a new people with new feelings.

The same year saw the first Chinese "national style" dance-drama, incorporating lingering aspects of classical dance. Such works resemble Western ballet in having a story and scenery, but are performed with a folk technique rather than in a foreign ballet style. Throughout the 1960s several excellent works in this new genre emanated, such as the *Short Sword Society* portraying a nineteenth-century revolt in Shanghai; and *The White Snake*, with a plot derived from folklore. Much admired was *The Silk Road*; and also *Princess Wen Cheng*, about a noble lady of the Tang era, a work illustrating dances of her day, including some from Tibet, where she journeys to become the ruler's bride.

Among more recent dance-dramas have been *A Dream of Red Mansions*, adapted from a celebrated eighteenth-century novel of feudal times, and *Deng Hua*, one of several based on the legends of minority ethnic groups whose special local dance forms are exploited. Thus *Deng Hua* portrays life among the Miao people. Deng Hua, the heroine, is a fairy who has come to earth and assumed the guise of a humble village girl. She falls in love with a diligent youth, Du Lin, who is leading his people in busily reclaiming wasteland. To let him know how she feels towards him, Deng Hua presents him with a silver mattock. Their wedding ceremony is a highlight of the drama, as is a Miao umbrella dance. Afterwards the pair are happy, but despite his bride's pleading Du Lin grows lazy and lets himself be led astray by an evil stone spirit. Finally, he acknowledges his errors, and he and Deng Hua are rejoined. The villagers rejoice at seeing them together once more. *Deng Hua* is a creation of the Guangxi Song and Dance Ensemble, which frequently presents it.

On the programmes of the numerous folk-dance companies that tour China are such regional selections; they are called "nationality dances". They might be a Tang dynasty *Court Dance* (Han); a *Waist Bell Dance* (Manchu); a *Making Glutinous Rice Cakes Dance* (Zhuang); a *Sword Dance* (Yao); a *Cheerful Yi Dance* (Yi); a *Husking Rice Dance* (Li); *Enjoying the Lanterns* (Han); a *Palace Dance* (Shu);

Wedding Dances (Bouyei, Uighurs – the latter are Buddhist herders of southern Gansu province); all these and scores of others assuring a colourful repertory that is often enhanced by a range of fierce or seductive Mongolian and Tibetan dances.

Of unusual interest was the discovery by archaeologists in 1978 of a set of sixty-five huge, magnificent bronze chime bells in the tomb of Marquis Yi of Zeng, a nobleman during the Warring States period (475–221 BC) in what is now the eastern part of Hubei province in central China. In the tomb's middle room were 124 instruments of eight different kinds, comprising an entire orchestra. In addition to the bronze chime bells were a set of stone and jade chimes, flutes, pan-pipes, drums, several kinds of zithers and a *sheng* (a wind instrument having pipes of varied dimensions). Despite their long interment, the bronze chimes are in perfect condition, giving off pure tones when struck and capable of emitting twelve tones and five half-tones, a scale matching that of a modern pianoforte. They reach five octaves, two fewer than a piano. The bells are so large – one and a half metres tall – that five to seven musicians are needed to play them all by striking with hammers. On the exterior walls of the tomb are inscriptions consisting of 2,800 characters that offer clues to the musical theories of not only the Warring States period but also those of the Spring and Autumn epochs that preceded it. Yehudi Menuhin, the eminent violinist, was enthralled by news of this find: "Ancient Greek instruments were of wood and bamboo and didn't survive to this day. Only in China can we hear sound as it was 2,400 years ago."

Fan Yunfang and Ding Bingchang, in *China Reconstructs*, give full details of how these instruments have been meticulously reproduced by experts from three research institutes and two universities with the help of laser holography and a scanning electron microscope. The chime bells' chemical composition, metallic content, principles of sound production, audio frequency, pitch and casting technique were analysed. The experts determined the proportion of copper, lead and tin alloy called for to yield the desired tones. Obviously the original makers of the bells had calculated precisely the relationship between the pitch of a bell and the thickness of its metallic wall. "On the inside wall of each were several cast ridges, and the geometric configuration of each part of the bell had to meet specific requirements – a great feat in casting. Thus, struck at different points it could produce two mutually independent tones. On the outside wall of each chime the name of the pitch was inscribed which would be created when struck at the marked point."

When the replicas were finished in 1979 eighty specialists in music, casting and archaeology gathered to judge the result. The cost of the project was 200,000 yuan. Only twenty-eight of the bells were made, as it was deemed that few if any theatre stages could support the weight of the full set, which would be nearly five tons.

Excited by the discovery of the Marquis Yi's chimes and orchestra, the Hubei Song and Dance Ensemble prepared a programme of music and dances characteristic of the culture of Chu, the larger state within whose sphere of influence had been the Marquis's relatively small domain. "Starting from the poems of Qu Yuan, the famous poet of Chu, composers and choreographers with the Hubei ensemble searched far and wide for historical materials and studied artifacts such as bronzes and lacquerware whose designs give some clue to the costumes and postures of dancers. They also drew on later folk-songs and dances whose roots may lie in Chu times in their efforts to portray the simplicity, boldness and splendor of Chu culture. One piece is based on the vivid descriptions in Qu Yuan's ode *For Those Fallen for Their Country*. The slow, sonorous beat of the chime-bells is followed by a mournful choral summons to the souls to come back. Then the seven-stringed zither pictures the clash of chariots, daggers gashing wide, the rain of arrows." For other works, the bells are lyrical. "*Meeting the Gods* presents dances at ceremonies of sacrifice to the spirits. Others, such as one of freemen plowing and weeding, show scenes of everyday life. Though we cannot know how close the musical pieces and dances come to authentic Chu, they are colorful and impressive in their own right."

Among the outstanding folk-dance troupes is the fifty-strong Sichuan Song and Dance Ensemble; in 1983 it was sent abroad to perform in France and elsewhere in Europe. Ye Mei – again in an issue of *China Reconstructs* – gives this account of the group's origin and aims:

Sichuan province in China's southwest is home to one-tenth of China's population. The habits and customs of Sichuan's more than ten nationalities, which include the Han (China's majority), Tibetan, Yi, Qiang, and Lisu peoples, have been a constant source of inspiration to local artists. Since 1953 when the troupe was formed, its members have learned many songs and dances from the various peoples and created numerous others based on life.

Two popular new dances, *The Cheerful Yi* and *Enjoying Lanterns* are the work of thirty-year veteran choreographer Leng Maohong. The first dance with its sprightly rhythms, exuberant shouts, and vigorous movements, portrays the feelings of joy experienced by the Yi people in the Liangshan Yi Autonomous Prefecture after they were emancipated.

In 1953 Leng traveled to the mountainous area in southwestern Sichuan where transportation was poor and the Yi people still lived under a cruel slave system. Three years later when democratic reform abolished slavery, Leng returned to witness the Yi people smashing their shackles and attempting to build a new life. Once he saw two former slaves waving their broken shackles in the air as they ran around spreading the good news. Memory of the poignant scene inspired him to create a dance. Using a Yi sacrificial dance as a base, he added lively rhythms, and created *The Cheerful Yi*, a group dance. Its première performance in Zhaojue, the prefecture capital, brought the audience to their feet cheering wildly. Word of the new dance soon spread and many ensembles, including a visiting Singapore troupe, have added it to their repertoires.

Leng choreographed another piece, *Enjoying Lanterns* (1976) when the "Gang of Four" was toppled and the ten years of turmoil ended. Once he had come across a group of children talking and laughing in front of a picture of the "Gang of Four." One mischievous boy poked a hole in Jiang Qing's glasses which amused the children even more. This naïve boy made a deep impression on Leng. Later he started observing children as he taught them how to dance. His growing understanding of children led to the creation of *Enjoying Lanterns*.

The dance starts with seven children running on stage to admire the elaborate palace lanterns. The boisterous music of wind and percussion instruments recreates the festive atmosphere of the Chengdu Flower Fair which had not been held for many years. Employing aspects of traditional Sichuan opera, the work is full of humor and character.

The simple and elegant dances of the Qiang people who live in the Jiuding Mountains of western Sichuan are also presented by the ensemble. The shoulder bells used in the dance *Lily* express the optimism the Qiang people feel about their lives and the future. The simple and bold movements in the *Armor Dance* accurately portray the boldness and fearlessness of the Qiang people.

Some of the troupe's dances are based on fairy tales. The solo *Enchanting Scene of Spring* by dancer Wang Yulan was adapted from a Sichuan opera.

It depicts the immortal white eel who envies the birth of spring in man's world and looks forward to a new life.

History has also contributed to the creation of the ensemble's dances. Chengdu, the capital of Sichuan province, used to be the capital of the Kingdom of Shu during the Five Dynasties (907–965). The relief sculptures of dancers in the tomb of Wang Jian, founder of the Kingdom of Shu, inspired the troupe. They recreated the graceful movements of palace performers and music of a thousand years ago.

In addition to dancers, the ensemble has a number of outstanding traditional instrument musicians and folk singers.

The Silk Road, to which reference was made earlier, is in the repertory of the Gansu Province Song and Dance Ensemble. Similarly, a company in Shaanxi province specializes in imaginatively recreating dances of the Tang dynasty, the decades often spoken of as China's "Golden Age". For these numbers the choreographers studied and copied multitudinous dancing postures illustrated in the murals in Buddhist grottoes at Dunhuang along the ancient thoroughfare.

The historic Silk Road was the route on which costly textiles and other merchandise were borne to and from the ancient Chinese capital of Loyang by Persian traders and others overland across Central Asia thousands of miles to Persia, Antioch, Tyre and Alexandria, and even beyond to Europe. Along the road were an endless mixture of peoples, most of them belonging to the so-called "minorities", the "six per cent of China's inhabitants who were not of the Han, or ethnic majority"; each of these had its own lifestyle and culture, crafts and arts that have persisted through the ages despite every kind of disturbance and oppression. The route dates from the end of the second century AD and was most travelled during the fifth and sixth centuries.

In 1982 the Asia Society in New York City sponsored a programme, "In Song and Dance Along the Silk Route", by a troupe representing the Chinese People's Association for Friendship with Foreign Countries. The company of seven artists, headed by Hong Daoyuan, was specially made up for this event and visited sixteen other cities in the United States and Canada; earlier, it had performed in Japan.

The first stop was Honolulu, where the tour almost came to a premature close. According to a newspaper story, the members of the company were dismayed at being given a standing ovation and decided on an immediate return home. They changed their minds when it was explained that the audience was demonstrating its exuberant approval.

On the programme were pieces typical of the Uighur, Miao and Mongol minorities, together with some numbers exemplifying the customs of the Han people. Jennifer Dunning attended a rehearsal, which she described as "an outpouring of vivid music and dance".

First there was Mr Hu (Hu Zhi-hou), his gaunt poet's face reflecting the haunting melancholy of the Han *High Mountains and Flowing Rivers*, a piece from the third century BC. It evokes the sorrow of a lute player who, having learned of the death of the friend who understood his music best, breaks his lute and throws it away.

A piece called *The Individualistic Musician* lived up to its title as Mai-malti Tulumuxi, his impassive expression barely hiding a twinkle in the eyes, stroked, plucked and slapped at the strings of his kumuzi as he whisked it through a variety of odd playing positions in a Kirghiz melody. Long braids flying, Mali-yamu Nasaier flung up her heels and flicked her hands flirtatiously in a Uighur dance of joy, accompanied by the imposing Dawuti Awuti on the stringed Uighur rewapu.

The mood became softer when He Shufeng, a Han musician, rippled through *Music at Sunset* on her delicately shaped pipa, like the kumuzi and rewapu an instrument similar to the lute. Then Ji Ya began to dance, long lithe arms rippling and feet coursing along the ground in suggestion of the eagles and horses that figure in Mongolian daily life.

Interviewing the performers, Ms Dunning learned that Ji Ya came from the Xilingele pasturelands of Inner Mongolia. Ms Ji said that her fellow Mongolians were a very lively people. Beginning her formal training as a dancer at thirteen, she had performed with a school company, one of the numerous folk-dance troupes established in minority communities. Afterwards, enrolled in the Central Institute of Nationalities in Peking, she had completed her studies and qualified as an instructor. The Central Institute conducts research into the arts such as this Mongolian dance form. Until recently the origins of the many local genres had been "lost in time"; little was known about the subject. Most delving into the history of Chinese music and art had been initiated by Europeans, few of whom had ventured into the more remote Asian regions. But that had changed. Under government auspices Chinese scholars were carrying on investigations into the sources of their minority arts.

After having professional voice training, Ms Nasaier had become proficient at "nose singing", a rare accomplishment demanding that "tones and harmony are vibrated through the nose". Her interpreter explained, "It sounds like an electric guitar." Ms Nasaier had joined the Xinjiang Song and Dance Ensemble as a singer but had closely watched the dancers and at night had practised before a large mirror that her father had purchased for her. Eventually she had become a professional folk-dancer, too, participating in regional festivals.

The mirror was the salvation of her career. During the Cultural Revolution she was not allowed to dance. The minority arts were drastically curtailed. In some villages musical instruments were hidden beneath floorboards. "But I never stopped training in front of the mirror, and everybody was surprised when I went back on stage right away." Since then she had been named vice-chairman of the Xinjiang Dance Association, a group coordinating dance presentations around the area and overseeing academic performances.

Artists such as those in this troupe are required to learn many disciplines, along with the styles of other minorities. Jin Ou had acquired his skill on the *lusheng* from his father. In his teens he had entered the Central Song and Dance Ensemble of Nationalities, located in Peking. He remained with it, rising to serve not only as a performer, but also as a director and choreographer. As part of his training he had to learn the dances of at least ten minorities, to take daily ballet classes, and become adept at "carpet training", that is, "acrobatics executed on a carpet".

He informed Ms Dunning that he spends a good part of each year travelling about in Miao communities. "The Miao people have many festivals, a lot more than the Han. And the Government gives special grant money to help people celebrate. We also go out to where the dances come from, staying a few months to learn from and perform with the local people. We perform in theatres, improvised auditoriums or even playgrounds – any flat place. Sometimes the farmers join in, and we find extra-ordinary performers to take back with us. If you separate artists or artistic workers, their art will not reflect the real life of the people. And because life is rich, dance is also very rich."

Hu Zhibou said: "During the five thousand years of our history, dance has never been separated from life: you take the tail of the ox and you dance with it. And each of China's fifty-six nationalities has many distinctive forms of dance. Dance in China is like a flower nursery, with a hundred different flowers blossoming through time."

In advance of the troupe's appearance, the Asia Society had offered a lecture-demonstration on folk-dance forms in 1981, by Xu Shuyin, a faculty member of the Peking Dance Academy. Her national tour was sponsored by the United States–China Dance Exchange Program of the University of Iowa. Mrs Xu described her travels through her country gathering details of the indigenous dances still alive among China's many tribes. She illustrated traits of the dances of the Han, Dai and Uighur peoples. In a Mongolian step variation dance, for one, the postures captured anyone riding a horse. Again, Jennifer Dunning was on hand and reported: "The sway of a load-bearing head, the angles, highly-developed arm gestures and the 'inwardness of emotions, particularly at happy times' of the Korean tribe of Yunan Province were evident in its handsome *Spinning Wheel* dance. One could see signs of the development of the Uighur dance of Xinjiang Province in a syncopated, lively salute to a mountain flower and imagine the hilly roads traveled by the tribe in the undulating *Songs Are Heard Along the Shore*, a Yunan Yi tribe tobacco-case courtship dance, in which the beat of the hand-held cases, like large castanets, accented the motions of Mrs Xu's snaking arms and crossing legs."

One number, however, disappointed the *New York Times*'s critic, a "Mongolian *Wild Geese Dance* which, with its bourrés, rippling arms and subsidings into the floor, looked suspiciously like Fokline's *Dying Swan* and very different in spirit from the other dances".

A celebrated but for a long time luckless folk-performer is Mo-te-kema, a native of Huhehot, the capital of Inner Mongolia. At fifteen, her dancing there caught the notice of Premier Chou En-lai, who saw to it that she was brought to Peking for further studies. During the Cultural Revolution, however, Jiang Qing observed her perform once and was offended by the sensuous movement of the traditional Mongol dance in which lithe arms rippled while shoulders and breasts shook vigorously. Mao's wife voiced disbelief that Mongol women ever behaved in that manner. To her, such sinuous gestures were simply obscene. In a bold retort, Mo-te-kema and two other dancers openly criticized Jiang Qing's policies. Immediately a committee was formed to condemn Mo-te-kema's interpretation of the "nationality dance". She was forbidden to make public appearances and exiled to a farming commune. Further, it suggested that she return to Mongolia. Meanwhile, she was housed in a barracks with a dirt floor. Despairing, she hung up a picture of Chou, her kind patron. Asked why she had not chosen a portrait of Chairman Mao, she explained how the generous Chou had been of help to her. She was threatened with imprisonment unless she mended her ways. The overthrow of the "Gang of Four" brought her a reprieve. Much later she told a *New York Times* reporter that when she heard that the hateful four leaders had been arrested, "I was so happy, I danced for three days." At thirty-three, a year after her release, she resumed her career, earning fervent applause as before.

In 1983 Xiong Lei in *China Daily*, a journal in English published in Peking, singled out for special notice Meng Jianhua (b. 1958), a leading performer of the Central Nationalities Song and Dance Ensemble, on the occasion of the troupe's thirtieth anniversary. Wearing a yellow turban and a red shirt, the twenty-five-year-old Meng seemed to be astride a particularly fractious steed. The animal reared, attempted to slip its leash and shake off the determined rider. With each move, the rider rose to his tiptoes, resisting the stallion's efforts to unseat him. Thrown, he rolled on the ground but still grasped the reins. As he remounted, his body drew high, graceful arcs in the air, until at last the wild creature was subdued, and the entire herd rushed forward. With further miming, he and his fellow dancers lassoed other untamed steeds and trimmed their manes. Earlier, during a national dance festival in 1981, Meng and four other members of the troupe had presented this Mongolian piece, *Song of the Horseriders*, to an audience of over 1,000, among it a group of dancers from Inner Mongolia, some of them formerly real horsemen. Backstage, removing his make-up and costume, he was summoned back to the footlights for three curtain-calls, rarely accorded a dancer in China. Then, again in his dressing room, he was unexpectedly visited by the Mongolians, who crowded in to express admiration for his remarkable projection of the "the prowess, wisdom, and optimism of the Mongolian people". The visitors were astonished to hear that Meng, a Han, had first set foot on the grassland of Inner Mongolia in 1978, three years after he joined the ensemble. They had assumed that he was a Mongolian like themselves.

Enacting the same role on a tour of Colombia, Meng had once received eight curtain-calls. His performance was later filmed for a television network in the United States.

The eldest son of an army doctor, Meng had insisted on a dance career against his parents' wishes. At an early age he began training in ballet and gymnastics. Tall, slender, energetic, adept at learning, he had the physical attributes of an outstanding ballet dancer, but at eighteen he shifted to folk-dance (1975), after finishing five years of study in a troupe attached to the Air Force. He explained to Xiong

Lei: "I was fascinated by the richness and diversity of minority dances when I first saw them during our course. I saw broad prospects for an artist in the minority dance." He did not regret the time spent at ballet, acrobatics and martial arts. "I often blend their techniques with those of the minority dance so as to enrich my expressions."

After he enlisted in the ensemble his first role was in *On the Raft*, where he had a solo in which he was a young Miao timber worker, resourceful, courageous, guiding logs along a river. Meng displayed great skill at this, but the choreographer was dissatisfied, saying that he did not depict the personality of the typical Miao worker. The young man sought out films that had logging and rafting scenes; he held discussions with Miao dancers in the company. In South China, when the troupe was there on tour, he searched for opportunities to ride perilously while standing on rafts, by gaining experience and assurance until everyone agreed that he portrayed the part authentically. This dance brought him acclaim. He continued to win great applause when he accompanied the ensemble abroad on travels to Yugoslavia, Romania and Malta in 1980.

Together with the others in the ensemble, Meng gained proficiency in the dances of the Tajik, Dai, Tibetan, Uygur, Miao, Yi, Yao and Zhuang peoples. To him, these were more than "just picturesque entertainment". He told Xiong Lei: "You have to learn the history, the environment, social customs, cultural identity and many other things about a minority before studying its dance." While in Inner Mongolia he had forced himself to overcome his distaste for mutton and to accept the Mongolian people's lifestyle. At the same time, they had treated him like a brother, teaching him to ride and lasso.

Meng somewhat shyly revealed that his aim was not just to be a good dancer. "My plan is to extend the influence of the minority dances and introduce this art world-wide."

Two other folk artists from China, Shen Pei Yi and Li Heng Da, touring the United States, were seen in a programme under the aegis of the Young People's Chinese Cultural Center at Pace University in New York City in 1985. They offered a dramatic duet, *Departure of the Newlywed*, described by Jack Anderson of the *New York Times* as "expressing the anguish of a wife whose husband must leave for battle. Movements were grandly scaled, and both performers' gestures possessed heroic intensity."

Other performers from China on view in New York were assisted by students still perfecting their skills in native works. Jack Anderson wrote:

Cui Shu-Min staged charming folk-dances. In *Bell Dance* she held two delicately chiming bells and, as she turned, her skirt swelled out in a bell-like manner. Group dances mixed students and professional performers adroitly. *Water Sprinkling Girls* was based on the custom of sprinkling water on people to bring them good luck. The women who performed the rite here took special care to do so in a sweet, decorous fashion.

The hops and skips of three women set bells on their costumes ringing in *The Dance of the Jingles*. Lines of people carried scarfs and fans in *Flower Drum Lantern Dance*. And the participants in *Red Ribbon Dance* made ribbons swirl in arcs, corkscrews and curlicues. Another dance with ribbons was Mao Jie-Meng's *Immortal's Fantasies*, in which waving ribbons resembled floating clouds.

Xue Wei-Xin contributed three works. Two men courted five women in *Give Me Your Beautiful Rose*. One knew from their graceful bearing and the way they were strikingly costumed in black jackets, gold boots and rose-red dresses that these must be the loveliest young women in their village. *Satire of a Corrupt Mandarin* was a humorous sketch that showed pranksters tricking a greedy, pompous and very drunk official.

Flight, a solo for Mr Xue, was filled with bird-like movements. But its fluidity also recalled that of ballet. Mr Xue has had extensive ballet training in China and is now studying modern dance in America.

Jiang Qi was impressive in *Golden Deer*, a balletic solo choreographed by Zhao Wan-Hua. Although the many brushing steps represented the way a deer paws the earth, they derived from classical ballet exercises. And Mr Jiang's leaps and turns simultaneously suggested the eagerness of a young animal and the skill of a talented young ballet dancer.

Critics contemplating the future of the folk arts have raised serious questions. You Haihai summarized them in his article in *China Reconstructs*: "Among those of current concern are: how to preserve the purity of traditional dance while meeting the requirement of the new times; how to enable minority dances to maintain their original style now that there is more interchange among nationalities; how to help urban youth become familiar with folk-dances which have been long done in the rural areas; how to develop our use of modern techniques to record folk-dances and thus preserve them for posterity."

Classical ballet, in the form known to Western nations, came late to China. The renowned English prima ballerina Margot Fonteyn spent part of her childhood in the foreign enclave in Shanghai – her father was in that bustling city on business – and took ballet lessons with George Goncharov, a Russian émigré teacher, in 1933. In that class, Fonteyn recalls, there were no Chinese pupils.

In 1954, however, the government decided to open a ballet school with the view of establishing an officially sponsored dance company. After five years of training and preparation, the Peking Ballet took shape. The new troupe was headed by Tai Ai-lien (or Dai Ailian) as director and Pyotr Gusev (1905–) as principal choreographer and top ballet master. It presented *Swan Lake* for Mao and other ministers in Zhongnanhai, a part of the Forbidden City where the hierarchy resided, in 1958.

Tai Ai-lien (b. *c.* 1917) was born in Trinidad, the daughter of a Chinese businessman. Her great-grandparents had settled on that distant island. Hers was a large family. At home she had her first lessons from a cousin who had appeared with Anton Dolin, then a twelve-year-old, in a musical *Blue-bells in Fairyland* in London. Years later, when Tai Ai-lien met the by now famed Anton Dolin, she asked: "Were you one of the two cats in *Bluebells in Fairyland*?" She related this story when interviewed by Anna Kisselgoff in New York City. The little girl's mother had put on a version of *Bluebells* in Trinidad, casting all the roles with relatives, among them Tai Ai-lien, merely six. To encourage the tiny dancer, her father had a gift for her after each performance.

Her next teacher in Trinidad was an Englishwoman, Nell Walton. Worshipping the ballet stars Anton Dolin and Alicia Markova from afar, the girl wrote requests for autographed photographs, which she got. In 1930 the mother resolved to take Tai Ai-lien and her sister to London for dance train-ing. The following spring, her second day in England, the girl went to Dolin's studio in Chelsea and was accepted as one of his half-dozen pupils. She was fourteen. At the sight of Dolin in tights, a garb unfamiliar to her, she began to giggle, thinking that the star was dancing in his underwear.

Her earliest stage appearance in Britain came soon after at the Albert Hall, in *Hiawatha*, a musical version of Longfellow's popular narrative poem. The arena-stage was vast. "You had to run for your life to get in on the right music," she recalled in her conversation with Ms Kisselgoff. "It was like a stampede just to get in and out."

She also entered Marie Rambert's school. Her fellow-students included such later dance lumi-naries as Vera Zorina, Frederick Ashton and Antony Tudor. But Tai Ai-lien herself was not able to get a job in a ballet company. "I was too short, and there were no Orientals in ballet. I was the wrong height and the wrong color."

She transferred her interest to modern dance, joining a troupe headed by Ernest and Lotte Berke; she also became a student of Kurt Jooss, the German choreographer then a refugee and resident in London. Thus she gained a wide acquaintance with ideas and performers influential in the dance world. She also learned methods of dance notation from Ann Hutchinson, who later founded the Dance Notation Bureau in New York.

At the outbreak of the Second World War the China Institute in London offered to pay travel expenses home for Chinese students, and Tai Ai-lien was eligible for this help. "I had never been to China, but being Chinese, I always wanted to go. My interest was to discover Chinese dance and to develop it."

She fulfilled this goal, researching many folk-dances, and performed some on stages; she joined the Communist Party and met and married Yeh Chien-yu, a celebrated painter. Together, invited by the State Department, the pair visited the United States in 1946. She had abandoned "ballet vocabulary"; she gave a recital – billed as a "Chinese Dancer" – at the Brooklyn Academy of Music.

Offered the post of director of the new Peking Ballet, Tai Ai-lien established its Western-style school and also introduced the Laban notation system to record not only ballet choreography but folk-dance and gymnastic components as well. She attached to the school an Experimental Ballet Society to give the students broader concepts and specific practical opportunities to develop them.

Her Russian collaborator, Pyotr Gusev, had completed his studies at the Maryinsky at seventeen after a mere four years (1922). He was with the Kirov Theatre troupe until 1935 and then for a year had leading roles at Leningrad's Maly Opera Theatre. Partnering Olga Mungalova, he pioneered in offering the "semi-acrobatic, semi-classical *pas de deux*" that for a time was popular at concert recitals. He also partnered the acclaimed Olga Lepeshinskaya and excelled at the supported adagio. He became an instructor at the Bolshoi in 1935, and at intervals headed its academy (in 1937 and again in 1950). For periods he led the Kirov Ballet Company (1945–51), and for a year its rival the Bolshoi (1956). At other times, for lengthy stretches, he was ballet master at the Stanislavsky and Nemirovich-Danchenko Lyric Theatre (1935–41, 1943–6, 1951–7). Apparently innately restless and always searching, he resembled Tai Ai-lien in bringing to Peking an open-mindedness and very broad experience as he taught and choreographed between 1957 and 1960. He did not linger long in China. After his return to Russia he again directed the ballet company at the Maly (1960–61). A summer's visit to Australia and New Zealand preceded his retirement in 1961. The Soviet government designated him an Honoured Artist.

It is widely assumed that because of his presence during its formative years the Peking Ballet has had a strong Russian orientation. Tai Ai-lien disputed this, suggesting that her British background was also a factor. "The Cecchetti style is the most classical style in ballet." Most English ballet dancers were trained according to the methods of the esteemed Italian dance teacher, Enrico Cecchetti.

The Ballet Rambert visited China in 1957, the first Western troupe to do so. Madame Rambert met Tai Ai-lien, her former pupil, and congratulated her. In her memoirs she wrote: "I was most impressed by that wonderful school with its perfect curriculum and felt proud of my student." In 1964 the English ballerina Beryl Grey was guest artist with the Chinese company, taking the dual roles of Odette–Odile in *Swan Lake*.

The Peking Ballet changed its name to the Central Ballet of China, probably to suggest that it had a national audience, in 1959. At the beginning of the 1960s another company was launched in populous Shanghai. But financial resources for both troupes were drastically curtailed by Mao's Great

Leap Forward, and in 1966 the Cultural Revolution had an even harsher effect. Tai Ai-lien, removed from her post, spent most of the decade between a farm and a mental institution. The companies were closed and then reorganized.

Jiang Qing had strong ideas, very much her own, concerning what a ballet company should be and do. The troupe she had reconstituted was to stage works wholly different from any in the previous repertory. Among the seven "models" already determined were two ballet scenarios decidedly feminist, that had her ardent approval, *The Red Detachment of Women* (1964) and *The White-Haired Girl* (1964–5); these dance-works were mounted under her personal supervision. This was not accomplished without controversy, a dispute that went on for several years. When the Peking company was sent to perform in Hong Kong in 1964 its programmes still consisted of French and Russian classics, *Swan Lake*, *Giselle*, *Esmeralda* and *The Corsair*, favourites from before the Second World War and doubtless representing the persistent influence of Gusev's comparatively brief tenure, but also testifying to the conservative views of Liu Shao-chi, the soon to be deposed Secretary of the Communist Party. Liu did not believe that ballet should be reformed. He said: "Changes in contemporary life cannot be forced. It is not certain that ballet and foreign opera can reflect it." This infuriated Jiang Qing, who retorted (as quoted by Martin Ebon), "Ballet has been performed in foreign countries for several hundred years. But now Western ballet is decayed and dying. It falls on us to raise and carry the red banner of revolution in the ballet." (Her manifesto was paraphrased in an unsigned article in the *Peking Review*, which observed that ballet in China had a history of less than twenty years.) It is not known whether Liu Shao-chi actually opposed Jiang Qing in this instance, or whether the statements were concocted to defame him after his mysterious death.

The two exemplary "revolutionary" ballets bear the names of no choreographers or scenarists; they are claimed to have been a collective effort by the casts and others, among them pre-eminently Mao's energetic and dictatorial wife. Her theory, which echoes her opinions about what plays should be, was that ballet should serve not an élite but the whole Chinese people together with the struggling masses of Asia, Latin America and Africa.

Another proclamation lending support to Jiang Qing's vision of a new kind of ballet was written by Wu Hsiao-ching and published in *Chinese Literature* in 1969 under the heading "A Great Victory in 'Making Foreign Things Serve China'", a reference to Mao's previous edict.

> The ballet is a classical art form foreign to China. How to deal with classical culture, particularly this
> so-called "exclusive area in art" hitherto monopolized by the bourgeoisie, involves two diametrically
> opposed policies. Should we reshape it, occupy it and conquer it, or should we bow to tradition and

allow it to go on serving the bourgeoisie? . . . The "wholesale Westernization" advocated by the big renegade Liu Shao-chi and his agents in the field of literature and art, Chou Yang and company, goes contrary to this revolutionary principle (Mao's saying, "Make foreign things serve China"). The revisionists babble that the ballet is "the acme of art, something that cannot be surpassed," and that the ballet should be "thoroughly Western," "downright Western," and "Western enough to be systematic."

. . . What they mean by "thoroughly Western" is that the characterization, theme and presentation should be all "Western:" only aristocrats, swans and immortals should be portrayed but not the workers, peasants and soldiers; only so-called "eternal themes" such as "love," "life and death," "virtue and evil" should be depicted and not the revolutionary struggle of the proletariat.

Wu Hsiao-ching warned that such reactionary Western-style works would cause ballet to "'remain forever a tool used by the bourgeoisie to enslave people mentally,' make 'history go backwards,' and thus advance 'a thoroughly counter-revolutionary line in literature and art.'"

A ferocious ideological quarrel, too, raged over an earlier original piece, "*Liang Shan po and Chu Ying-tai*", "A story of love between pampered children of the rich in ancient China", which was seen to be an attempt "to marry China's native lords and ladies to Western capitalism". The anonymous advocate in the *Peking Review* tossed fiery words of praise on the fire: "Our beloved Comrade Jiang Qing, holding high the great red banner of Mao's thought, fought against the evil wind and adverse waves to set a new course." Her efforts were on behalf of no less than three billion revolutionists in the world. In summary: "The theme of armed struggle which the ballet *Red Detachment of Women* presents is actually an extremely important subject in the international Communist movement in the twentieth century." Such a work was a start towards "the remolding of the world's theatrical stage with the thought of Mao". It would lead to "the proletariat seizing control of the situation and triumphing over the bourgeoisie in the realm of literature and art". The crucial question was, could the characters of the hero and heroine in the ballet – Hung Chang-ching and Wu Ching-hua – be depicted "with bourgeois and petty bourgeois thinking and emotions? No! Is it possible to use the dance movements of male and female roles in the old ballet without making any changes whatsoever? No! The principles on which our ballet is based are the political and artistic criteria of the proletariat. We select the best dance movements, the highlights, and the most vivid stage arrangements to portray these heroic figures, so that they appear 'On a higher plane, more intense, more concentrated, more typical, nearer to ideal, and therefore more universal than actual everyday life.'" (Martin Ebon points out that this final quotation is from Mao's own writings.)

The Red Detachment of Women rather skilfully conjoined features of Chinese drama and folk-dance with facets of classical European ballet, to arrive at a fresh amalgam. Ebon: "For instance, when the heroes appear, they all do a *liang-xiang* (take a conventional stance or pose in such a way as to let the audience gain a clear concept of the character right from the start), which has been adopted from old Chinese opera, but these are the *liang-xiang* of the ballet and no longer that of old opera."

The ballet's further new moves are detailed in Ebon's prefatory note to *The Red Detachment*, which he in turn takes from the article in the *Peking Review*:

When Wu Ching-hua appears, dashing out of a coconut grove, her pose is "fleeting but impressive, like a flash of lightning." When party leader Hung appears, disguised as an overseas merchant to get into the landlord's manor, he is "like a ray of brilliant sunshine brightening the darkest corners." The article describes these poses as "fine, expressive figures" that resemble "sculptured statues in a magnificent setting."

When the heroine is captured and flogged, her dances dramatize that she "remains unvanquished," as "her vigorous leaping movements, particularly in spinning somersaults when she is being flogged, show her fiery rebellious character." Standing "resolute and indomitable," the characterization "is a clear break from the presentation of feminine fragility characteristic of the old ballet." Further: "In the scene of Wu Ching-hua pouring out her bitterness before she joins the Red Army, she flings herself on the red flag and, full of animation, strokes it and the red armband. Then, in a lively *pas seul*, she raises her blood-stained arms and with fury condemns Nan Pa-tien's [the landlord's] cruel oppression." In the final scene, when Wu kills the landlord, the ballet creates a unique dance which utilized the "reclining fish" movement of Peking opera in a leap designed to dramatize "the heroine's political maturity and her military skill and judgment."

The polarization of characters in ballet such as *The Red Detachment of Women* is achieved, according to an article in *Chinese Literature*, through innovations that contrast "beauty and evil, in using negative characters to highlight the heroes." Specifically, "what is fine appears more beautiful, while the evil comes out more vicious this way." To bring out "the great fearless spirit of Hung Chang-ching," the party leader, "who is determined to vanquish all enemies and never to yield, the choreography generalizes his revolutionary heroism and optimism into an integrated dance of leaping, splitting, and spinning movements which portray this spirit of his thorough emphasis, varied tempo, and changes in position." The contrast is further emphasized: "On the other hand, the enemy is arranged around him in stooping movements, in contrast to his nobility. This stage pattern presents a vivid contrast of Hung Chang-ching in a series of jumps over the heads of the stooping enemy, so that he appears like an eagle spreading its wings against the storm, while the crawling enemy appears like a pack of stray dogs."

Linking the polarization within the ballet's choreography to the ideological conflict from which it emerged, the article states: "This graphic composition, brimming with revolutionary heroes as a towering Mount Tai in spirit, while the renegade Liu Shao-chi and his ilk, who trumpet about a 'philosophy of survival' in life, are in contrast but a stinking heap of rubbish at the foot of Mount Tai."

At the conclusion of the ballet, the head of Mao appeared against the backdrop, "wearing a military cap, encircled by a bright red halo." Everybody called out three times, "Long live Mao Tse-tung!" and then the curtain fell.

A Western observer, Klaus Mehnert, was led to remark that he had seen similar behaviour at ballets in Soviet Russia in the early days of the Russian revolution.

Present at the première was Norman Webster, Peking correspondent for Toronto's *Globe and Mail*, who commented – as noted by Ebon – that "the heroes were suitably heroic", "the villains – a cruel landlord and his mercenaries – were sneaky, nasty, cowardly degenerates". The first-night audience was "with the show from the start". Much applause was elicited for the dancing, "the excellent special effects (thunder and rain, exploding grenades), colorful costumes and exaggerated acting". Outstanding was the role of the landlord, "the prime creation" of the piece sometimes projected as "the perfect Western-style villain in Panama hat, gold watch-chain and black-and-white oxfords, or oozing evil Oriental tyle in magnificent colored robes. At first huge and arrogant, with cruel mustache and sideburns, he became by the end a fearful, broken creature scrabbling frantically about the stage as the Red Army moved in. The audience, which had hated him from the start, now found him a hugely amusing spectacle. Applause broke out when he was shot down."

During President Richard Nixon's epoch-making visit to China in 1972 he was taken to see the *Red Detachment*.

Harold Schonberg, senior music critic of the *New York Times*, also saw the ballet in Peking in 1972. He remarked that no composer was credited with its score which, to his ear, "sounds like Russian academicism with a touch of exoticism. Harmonically, [it] is unadventurous. It stays close to D minor and related keys. It uses a few *leit-motifs* that represent various characters. The scoring is competent but unimaginative. Largely the score is poster music, of a movie background nature, with a great climax toward the end that sings the praises of workers and peasants." One aspect that interested Schonberg was the introduction of native elements, a "full use of Chinese percussion instruments" to add "an unusual touch to an otherwise conventional example of Moscow Conservatory scoring, 1935 vintage".

In the *Peking Review* (1968) it was stated that "the composers have used a great deal of Hainan folk-song rich in local colour", by this device transforming "the ballet art which was once exclusively in the service of the foreign feudal bourgeois lords" into one for which the common people would have a more natural affinity. Once more it was pointed out that the new-style choreography "swept away the decadent, ethereal, fairy-like poses of the ballet" by blending them with "elements of the Chinese classical dance and folk-dances".

The Peking production was also seen by Faubion Bowers (1972): "Whatever the Chinese may feel toward the Russians nowadays, one debt of gratitude should be acknowledged, for having taught them how to combine toe slippers and rifles, and with splendid effect." He was reminded that some of the best Bolshoi instructors had been active in Peking, a reference to Goncharov, Gusev and Volkova. Bowers selected for particular praise Shih Ching-hua, who portrayed the indomitable heroine in the presentation he saw, as well as later in the filmed record of the piece. He described her as "the prima ballerina" of the Peking company, though the star system was supposedly proscribed. "She can do anything – a split during a leap in the air, combining a back bend in which her head nearly touches her knee, for example – and do it as well as any dancer with a Russian name." (Excerpted from Ebon)

Development of *The Red Detachment* had stirred a considerable amount of disagreement over how to characterize Wu Ching-hua, its heroine. She was "one of the labouring people who had suffered bitterly in the old society"; consequently, emphasis should be placed on "her resistance and struggles and how she matures under the Party's leadership". Those in Liu Shao-chi's camp were accused of seeking to have her depicted as a "feudal court favourite" as might have been a heroine in any number of previous ballets, imposing "on her movements of the 'spirit', sentiments of 'pity and weariness, sadness and grief', which would result in a frustration of 'the transformation of ballet'". Instead, she was shown as rash but resolute, capable of murderous anger and revenge, psychological growth, deep and single-minded loyalty.

Seeing staged excerpts from the work, and earlier the full version, Anna Kisselgoff summed up her impressions in the *New York Times* in 1978:

It would be a mistake to consider propaganda ballets such as *The Red Detachment of Women* provincial. The naïveté is deliberate and the choreography sophisticated. Unlike Soviet Socialist Realist ballet, which imbued movement with meaning and turned dancers into silent actors, the new Chinese ballet has kept the separation between dance and mime. The result is that the Chinese run less risk of reaching the esthetic dead end now acknowledged in official Soviet ballet writings – one in which the increased use of naturalistic gesture so reduced the dance element that ballets without dance became a reality.

Generally the solos are pure-dance passages in either the Bolshoi-influenced classical ballet idiom or the vocabulary of the Peking opera's dancers. In *Red Detachment* the Tyrant's henchman does a *manège* of ballet's barrel turns, the two heroes enter with *cabrioles* in beautiful soft landings and the "lackeys" swing their legs up in Peking opera's quick flexed-foot kicks. Each leading character also sums up a set dramatic passage with the opera-derived frozen pose, the *liang hsiang*. It is a pose that both symbolizes and punctuates the emotion previously expressed, serving as a kinetic exclamation point. This is not naturalistic theater. The Chinese have made their ballets as full of conventions and stylizations as Peking opera. The choreographer is thus afforded the opportunity of getting his message across and still retaining a strong dance element in separate passages. The danger at present is the poverty inherent in a continued use of the deliberately reduced vocabulary now in favor. Within the form in which Chinese choreographers are working, however, the dance idiom could be enriched. The opening is there for the asking.

The dancing itself from the dancers of the Peking Ballet was on a markedly higher level than that seen in the Shanghai Ballet. Pai Shu-hsiang, China's first Odette-Odile in 1958 and praised as such by Beryl Grey in China in 1964, returned after eight years of prohibition from dancing and hardships, to dance the heroine in this *Red Detachment*. She was, interestingly, allowed to register the nuances of emotion still missing last year in the *The White-Haired Girl*. In such "model" ballets, the characters have been designed as archetypes rather than real people. To quote a 1970 article on Chinese ballet in the magazine, *China Reconstructs*: "The dominant note of the dances of each hero is decided according to his most essential characteristic."

A caustic appraisal of the *Red Detachment* was that of Mao's successor, Deng Xiaoping, who during his "rehabilitation" was forced to attend a performance. "No more than a Gong-and-Drum show", he said, walking out. "No trace of art. Go to a theatre these days and you find yourself on a battlefield."

Quite different in origin is *The White-Haired Girl*, which is based on a "new" Peking opera (1945) by Ding Yi and He Jingzhi (or Ting Yi and Ho Ching-chei). They had heard tales about a "white-haired goddess" that some dozen years earlier were being passed around in the north-west region of Hopei Province, when that war-torn area was occupied by the Communist Eighth Route Army. Belief in ghosts, especially hungry, predatory spirits, has been immemorially prevalent among China's peasantry. The ghost might be of a murdered person, or of someone who perished with his or her fate unfulfilled, perhaps a woman losing her life while giving birth. An ancient and persistent custom is to bring food to shrines at an annual festival to appease such hungry ghosts; the ceremony is still observed in Hong Kong and other overseas Chinese communities. These many long-lived legends had led the authors to write the five-act opera libretto which, after several metamorphoses, evolved into a ballet. Some of its folkloric elements were retained in the scenario for a time, but – as Ebon informs us – were finally considered distracting in a work intended to carry a political message and so were largely excised.

The rumour is that an apparition dwelling in a temple on the outskirts of a village comes out after dark, howling and demanding that food sacrifices be brought every fortnight. When this is done, the offerings vanish by morning. If the villagers fail to comply, a strange voice emanates from the shrine: "You who neglect your goddess – beware!"

A Communist soldier hides in the temple and glimpses a white figure that comes to scoop up the food. Surprised, the ghostly phenomenon shrieks and advances on the soldier, who fires his rifle at it. The apparition falls, gets to its feet and dashes away. Two soldiers chase it through the forest and up a mountain slope, but it finally eludes capture. The soldiers, pausing indecisively, hear the distant cry of a child. At the far-off end of a mountain ravine they perceive a flickering light. Approaching it, they come upon a white-haired young woman huddled against the wall of a dark cave. In her arms is a small child. While they threaten her with their rifles, she kneels and tells her tragic story.

The daughter of an aged peasant, she had caught the eye of their avaricious landlord, who oppressed his tenants. Extorting rent-money, the landlord had driven the old man to suicide, then kidnapped and raped the sorrowing girl, who became pregnant. Sated, the landlord plotted to have her killed and replaced by a new wife. A sympathetic maidservant, overhearing the plan, aided the girl's escape under cover of night.

Taking refuge in a cave, the girl had her child. Though hungry and cold, she stayed isolated in the cave, her hair turning white from malnutrition and from her long hours in darkness. She steals food from the temple: villagers who have caught sight of her have thought her a supernatural being. At last, after the Revolution, she discovers that the world outside has greatly changed and is persuaded to abandon the cave for a life in the bright sunlight.

The tale, handed down orally, had variations, but most aspects of it were constant. He Jingzhi and Ding Yi kept the main characters and the outline of events for their opera libretto. They effected a few crucial changes, however: the work was no longer a mere ghost story but transformed into an attack on superstition, and thereby had social significance. Emphasized was the contrast between ways of life in China before and after Liberation, a change from darkness to brightness.

The opera had its première in Yenan in 1945; revisions followed in 1947 and 1949. Two years later *The White-Haired Girl* was given the Stalin Peace Prize for Literature and Art. The Cultural Revolution brought further alterations in the script. The father, Yang, no longer kills himself but is slain by the landlord's bodyguard. Suicide was now considered an attitude far too defeatist; a Chinese peasant should face disaster more resolutely. The rape and pregnancy were omitted, because such offences gave the girl personal motives to seek vengeance rather than having her inspired to act against oppression simply to serve the common good and to embrace collective instead of individual action. The heroine, now named Hsi-erh, stands out as a symbol of brave resistance, adapting herself to all the demands made of her as a loyal member of a band of militant revolutionaries.

Much the same controversy brought on by the creation of *The Red Detachment of Women* was heard again during the preparation of *The White-Haired Girl* as a ballet. Liu Shao-chi's circle – or so it was subsequently asserted – objected to changes in the story that were strongly advocated by Jiang Qing. He argued that the characters should be psychologically motivated, their actions linked to and arising from their inner struggles. He observed that the plot should be less blunt and propagandistic, the acting and direction more subtle. An essay in *Chinese Literature* covers the new debate. The author is someone attached to the Shanghai School of Dance: *The White-Haired Girl* was to be introduced by a ballet company in that city.

Liu Shao-chi, big renegade, traitor, and scab, persistently hated and opposed the proletarian revolution in literature and art. We can't compel a reflection of present day life, he babbled. Ballet and foreign-style opera are not really suitable for it. The master had only to give the word, and his slaves hurried to comply. In 1963 our school's capitalist roaders flagrantly opposed the call to write extensively about the post-Liberation period put forward by Chairman Mao's good student, Comrade Ko Ching-shih, First Secretary of the East China Bureau of the Central Committee of the Chinese Communist Party. Instead, they put on a big production of *Swan Lake* and *Red Scarfs Dance* and turned our school into a hotbed of capitalist restoration.

When, thanks to the personal attention Comrade Jiang Qing was giving us, we decided to create a revolutionary ballet *The White-Haired Girl*, the counter-revolutionary revisionist clique in our school tried to switch us into producing a sickly story of frustrated love among aristocrats in days gone by. When proletarian headquarters urged us to study the ballet *Red Detachment of Women* put on in Peking, the clique flatly refused to let us go. But they sent us to Hangchow to learn a foreign dance, *Pas de Quatre*, then being performed there.

Going on, the indignant commentator says that "the savage ambition of these counter-revolution-aries was beyond belief and that the capitalist roaders in the propaganda department of the former Shanghai municipal Party committee and their cronies in the local dance school tried to get our ballet *The White-Haired Girl* to tout Liu Shao-chi's infamous dictum: 'class struggle has ended.'" The backers of Liu also suggested a finale that would have projected "the joy of reunion and the peasants pitching into production at the expense of the ballet's powerful spirit". They also sought "to change the lyrics of a song in praise of Chairman Mao", since "those scoundrels dreaded the thought of Mao like an owl fears the sun". They declared, "What's the point of singing 'the sun is Mao, the sun is the Communist Party?' Everyone knows that. When Hung, the evil landlord, is slain at the climax, the crowd shouts exultantly 'Long live Chairman Mao!' to voice its revolutionary gratitude. Liu's fol-lowers said, 'There's no connection between the two. It spoils the effect.' Jiang Qing triumphed over them, however. As a result, old Yang furiously resists and does not feel disgraced and commit suicide but with one blow of his carrying pole knocks the landlord to the ground: nor does his daughter pas-sively submit to her captor's advances but attempts to repulse them."

Ebon, who has been largely paraphrased here, comments:

An analysis of the ballet alerts us to the symbolism of certain details. For example, during the period of the girl's bondage in the landlord's household, she picks up an incense burner, symbolic of such Chinese traditions as ancestor worship; later, when Hsi-erh has joined the Red Army, she appears in uniform and, as the Shanghai analysis put it, "shoulders a red-tasseled spear and marches down the revolutionary road" with the Eighth Route Army, thus progressing "from spontaneous resistance to conscious struggle."

Yet, moving the plot and characters of *The White-Haired Girl* further and further away from their origins prevents the mixed elements of human emotions to find expression. . . . With the girl no longer lifelike, but a heroine of almost superhuman proportions, she has moved closer to the folkloric tradition of mythology. The heroic myth of the white-haired girl who roams the wild mountainside has transformed her into a Red Goddess with white hair.

The ballet, a popular success, was eventually filmed. In the final version, as related by Clive Barnes, the girl escapes from the landlord's house where she has been held against her will. His lackeys pursue her. At the same time her lover, appalled at what he has witnessed, is converted to Marxism and joins the Red Army. The girl makes her home in the wilds. By happy chance her lover is with the detachment that liberates the village near which she secretly lingers. He finds her hiding in the shrine, and they are reunited. The landlord and his hirelings are executed, and the villagers excitedly hail the Revolution.

In 1977, after Mao's demise, the Shanghai Ballet as part of a cultural exchange programme paid a visit to Paris, followed by a month-long tour of Canada, presenting *The White-Haired Girl*. Flora Lewis, the *New York Times*'s correspondent in Paris, reported on the troupe's critical reception there and also interviewed Meng Po, assistant director of the company as well as head of the Shanghai Bureau for Cultural Affairs. In Paris, as Ms Lewis saw it, the company won more applause for its political high points than for technical dazzle in its mixture of classical ballet, Chinese dance and Socialist Realism. This had also been true in China. "The revolutionary heroine pirouettes and strikes an 'attitude' on her toes; the hero raises a clenched fist as he leaps, and one of the villains dives acrobatically to the floor, suggesting that the heroine may have plunged into the river with a movement straight from a traditional Chinese fighting dance."

Meng Po declared that this intermingling of "old and new, politics and art", was deliberate. "Chairman Mao said we must learn everything that has merit in foreign art, with analysis and criticism, of course. But transplanting pure Western ballet to China would not meet our political needs. It would be too weak, too mediocre to show the rich Chinese political life. So we have also borrowed movements from Peking opera, the martial arts, acrobatics and folk-dance to enrich the classical ballet."

Shih Chung-chin, who had the heroine's role, and Wang Ko-chun, who portrayed the villainous landlord, smilingly agreed. Both now thirty-two years old, they had enrolled at sixteen in the Shanghai Ballet School in 1960. This was their first journey away from Asia. They and Mr Meng were dressed "in Mao suits of different tones of grey and blue". The touring ensemble comprised 152 dancers, musicians and technicians. The cost of the Paris presentation was borne by the French government; it allowed each member of the troupe $5 a day for pocket money.

Meng Po stated that the *The White-Haired Girl*, as seen in Paris, would have been quite different if the "Gang of Four" had not been overthrown. "Jiang Qing wanted more fighting in the ballet, and less dancing, but that spoils the effect. And she said one girl fleeing to the mountains wasn't enough, there had to be a number of them. And she wanted things switched around so the young peasant who becomes a soldier and rescues the girl has the main part. But then it isn't the story of the White-Haired Girl any more."

French audiences noted that though the Shanghai cast danced on points, they wore – as Flora Lewis described them – "short silk tunics and loose pants that show neither the legs nor the sweep of the body's movement to advantage. They flail the air with arms and torso instead of appearing to float in the Western technique."

Meng responded: "We can float if we want to, if we want soft, light movements, but that wouldn't be in the character of the White-Haired Girl. She symbolizes tens of thousands of peasant girls, cruelly oppressed and determined to resist fiercely. Her movements must be dynamic, energetic."

Clive Barnes saw the Shanghai Ballet in performance at the O'Keefe Center in Toronto a few weeks later. Two programmes were offered, the full-length *The White-Haired Girl* and alternatively an evening of excerpts from other ballets. Barnes contributed two pieces to the *New York Times*, where he was senior dance critic. In the first, he confessed to a degree of bewilderment about *The White-Haired Girl*.

[It] is ballet, but so different, ideologically and in some ways even technically, from our own that perhaps we should find a new name for it. I am referring, almost of course, to the performances of the Shanghai Ballet, which closed its Toronto season at the O'Keefe Center tonight.

Nothing, so far as I could see, tells us who choreographed or even staged it. Curious.

In a sense the nearest we get to choreographic attribution comes in the final paragraph of the company's description of itself in its souvenir program. This reads: "Under the leadership of the Central Committee of the Chinese Communist Party headed by the wise leader, Chairman Hua Kuo-feng, the struggle to smash the 'Gang of Four,' the anti-Party conspiratorial clique of Wang Hung-wen, Chang Chun-chiao, Chiang Ching and Yao Wen-yuan, has won great victories. This excellent situation enables the Shanghai Ballet to march courageously along Chairman Mao's revolutionary road like in literature and art."

It is good to see touring cultural exchanges. We in the United States were happy to welcome the troupe of Chinese acrobats who came in return for the visit of the Philadelphia Orchestra. In some respects the acrobats were better value for Western audiences than the Shanghai Ballet – but not nearly so interesting for either students of dance or politics.

Chinese ballet owes its inspiration to Soviet ballet. After World War II, when the two regimes were on close terms, Soviet teachers worked with Chinese students in Peking and Shanghai, establishing dance academies. Some of the more promising Chinese students were sent to Russia for further study, and the Chinese, who seemed to take to the art instantly, were soon mounting productions of such works as *Swan Lake*, *Giselle*, even *Esmeralda*.

The music sounds like a mixture of Puccini (yes, *Madama Butterfly*), Prokofiev and Richard Rogers, with some local instruments added to lend color. There are singers, who appear to be contributing verbal subtitles to the action. To Western ears the score is likely to prove of more curiosity than distinction: it is naïve, and must be approached in the way one might regard a painting by Grandma Moses.

The dancing is equally simplistic, but still shows considerable Soviet influence. The women are better than the men, although all have discipline. The women seem to have a natural line, although not an unduly strong turnout. They are exceptionally graceful. The men are martial – they dance with pistols and clenched fists on occasion – with a certain facility toward the acrobatic. The acting is very stylized. The settings use a great number of back projections, painted onto slides by the original designers, and are aimed fair and square at the popular and the pretty.

It is quite impossible, and almost irrelevant, to compare this company with a Western troupe, as there is such a vast divergence in aim and aspiration. In the variety program, for example, there was a duet for a father and his daughter, who carried a pink lampshade. They were celebrating the father's success in starting a new hydro-electric power plant. This was from a ballet called *Light of Happiness*.

The variety program also brought us very enthusiastic songs about Chairman Mao and all that kind of thing. It appears absolutely sincere, without a trace of irony. Which, of course, is admirable. It would be very easy for a sophisticated observer to laugh at the Shanghai Ballet, or to see it as Western camp. But the Shanghai dancers are not laughing. They seem very serious, very dedicated, and quite extraordinarily different.

What a pity the Cultural Revolution eliminates that great art form – the Peking opera! Here – rather than the Shanghai Ballet – was something for the whole world to glory in.

Barnes's second thoughts were conveyed in a Sunday issue of the *New York Times* a few days later. He summed up his dilemma in reaching a fair appraisal of the Chinese offering:

What makes all this incredibly difficult to criticize, or even to describe for Western audiences, is simply its esthetic and political purpose. For example, both the story and the choreography have apparently been amended in the light of the prevailing political conditions. Now this could conceivably happen in Soviet Russia – no one seems to be performing Gliere's ballet *The Red Poppy* nowadays – but Western audiences are bound to find such political disputes in artistic matters puzzling. Also there is the obvious naïveté of the audience to be considered.

The variety concert was almost more revealing than the ballet itself. Most of the songs, for example, were hymns of praise to the Chinese leaders. There was a strange duet from a ballet called *Light of Happiness*. This is a *pas de deux* for a father and his daughter. He has just completed a hydro-electric power plant which will bring electricity to the region. They dance together in joy, holding a little pink lampshade that symbolizes the achievement. Odd? Perhaps – but perhaps merely different. For the Chinese might not a Prince falling in love with a Swan, even a Swan-Queen, seem even more bizarre? Yes, there is a completely different outlook here.

At the end of Balanchine's ballet *Stars and Stripes*, when the flag appears at the end of the ballet, the audience giggles appreciatively. Possibly 190 years ago, it might have been more positively moved. We are concerned here with a young society that has, indeed, been taught, almost brainwashed one presumes, to believe in the glory of its revolution and the importance of its technical progress. A peasant from Canton is going to look at ballet through very different eyes from those trained on it by a mechanic from Milwaukee.

So, possibly, the Chinese ballet is a very good thing for the Chinese – it is certainly very popular in China, and said to be among the country's most acclaimed theatrical attractions. But is there anything in it for us in the West? Personally, at present, I doubt it. By any standards, other than those of pure curiosity value, *The White-Haired Girl* is to Western sensibilities either a camp giggle or a total disaster. The choreography is banal, the music (sounding somewhere in between the more conventional Soviet composers and Broadway, with a few traditional Chinese instruments thrown in for plangent local color) is feeble. The dancers are enthusiastic, well-drilled, and the girls in particular have a certain style. But by Western levels of accomplishment they are not, generally speaking, in the first rank. The visual staging is ingenious and pretty.

Curiously enough, the now officially discredited Peking opera – with its Monkey King, its demon War Lords and astonishing acrobats – was, in fact, an art form of universal value and interest. It never appeared in the United States, but I was fortunate enough to see it many times in Europe – I loved it and never missed a chance – and this had an ethnic purity that was definitely international in its appeal. It was also enormous fun – if you recall the Chinese acrobats who came to the City Center a couple of years ago, you will get a fair idea of the physical dexterity of the Peking opera, but, of course, nothing of its dramatic flavor or its earthy and sensible humor.

Could the Shanghai Ballet, or, for that matter, Peking's apparently rather more sophisticated troupe, have a success in New York? Well, the Shanghai group wowed the O'Keefe Center in Toronto. There were people practically fighting to get in to see the last performance of *The White-Haired Girl*, and all the performances received the wholehearted support of the Chinese community, both Communist and non-Communist. This itself could be a factor in New York. But were a Chinese ballet company to come to New York, I suggest it would be better to regard it as a political gesture with special sociological interest, rather than simply as a cultural event. I learned something from my Toronto visit. But its value had more to do with the state of the Chinese spirit than the state of Chinese ballet. These people looked more politically dedicated, and essentially humorless, than any I have ever seen. They looked like inhabitants from a different, and possibly newer, world. I was fascinated and chilled.

The other Canadian cities on the company's itinerary were Hamilton, Montreal, Ottawa and Vancouver. Some 60,000 spectators rushed to buy tickets, and balletomanes from San Francisco flew north by chartered plane not to miss a rare opportunity to see what Chinese dancers were doing.

Anna Kisselgoff commented on other works more or less in the same style when the Performing Arts Company of the People's Republic of China finally reached New York in 1978. This ensemble was made up of musicians, ballet dancers, ethnic dancers and members of the Peking opera. She limited her critique to the offerings of a group within the company drawn from the 200-member Peking Dance Company, associated with the Peking Ballet; these performers specialized in folk and Chinese classical dances.

China has no classical dance tradition similar to India's traceable to a codified vocabulary compiled over 2,000 years through treatises and oral teaching. The "classical" long-silk dance and fan dance on these programs are actually in an invented contemporary idiom, drawing upon movements from court dances and Chinese classical opera – all heavily balleticized.

The balletic influence is particularly strong in the theatricalized folk-dances. This is true to the point that *Militia-women of the Grasslands*, set in Inner Mongolia, is more ballet than a folk number. It is the frank counterpart of Igor Moiseyev's *Partisans*. The difference is that the militia are not World War II Soviet partisans in the Caucasus but a women's regiment with rifles on their backs against a vibrant if poster-color background. Many of the steps and vignettes are familiar from *Partisans*. The women's high-stepping canter and wrist-flicking simulates horseback riding. During their target practice, they roll on their knees. Like two of the partisans, two militia women lag behind and strike up a comradely loiter at the end. Despite its derivative nature, this production showed the Chinese at their most successful in adopting Moiseyev's method of capturing the essence of a dramatic idea or folk-dance and theatricalizing it. By comparison, dances such as *Peacock Dance* submerged the essence of a regional motif in design and decoration.

Grasslands carries a subliminal political message: the defense of China's border against the Soviet Union. Just as *Partisans* evokes the still emotional recollection of World War II in the Soviet Union, so *Grasslands* touches upon an issue that raises strong emotions in China today. Form follows function. The virility of the form here may well be due to the conviction of the message.

Appraisal of the musical segment of the program is best left to experts on Chinese music. According to some of these specialists, the current emphasis on program music stems from a long tradition in China. We may hear sound, but a program note informs us that it depicts a chapter in the life of Mao. To re-create musical form is part of that tradition.

In the same way, the Peking opera is a theatrical form in which re-creation also plays a major role. This superb classical theater is an actor's art. It is not the retelling of a familiar tale but the actual performance that counts. When in the excerpt, *Monkey Makes Havoc in Heaven*, the entire host of celestial generals assembles for battle – the gathering recalls a board room portrait – every expression on every fiercely painted face, every raised eyebrow, glower and stance contributes to the total effect. The virtuosity of the performer is assumed. He must be a singer, actor, dancer, acrobat and martial arts expert. Yet as in any art, artistry does not stop at technique; it begins with it. It is not only Li Hsiao-chun's dexterity with sword and stick in the spectacular battle scenes we should appreciate but his superb total characterization as the deflator of the pompous.

The *Monkey King* episode no longer tells us, as in the once-standard version, that the rebellious monkey monarch is finally converted to Buddhism. But the idea of a popular hero who literally trips up the Establishment is equally traditional. When the Monkey King confronts the "giant," it is a foregone conclusion that this resplendent figure, with pheasant feathers wavering on his back and barbell type weapons in hand, is slated for a pratfall. As a warrior, he misuses his own physical strength. Like any champion in the martial arts, the Monkey King knows how to make his foe defeat himself. This may be a giant, but he has two left feet.

To relish such moments might seem to fall into an estheticism that ignores the moral and didactic import of Peking opera. The real point is that it is theater that functions on many levels at once. Its richness is its very virtue. It is this depth of both form and content that was not surpassed elsewhere on the program. . . .

China is in the midst of a dance boom. Not only are professional ballet companies and folk troupes created on the scale of the 600-member Peking Ballet, with the aim of sending out contingents of dancers on tour throughout China and the world, but amateur dance groups have been propagated through a network of regional and national festivals as well as the use of "model" productions upon which local dance presentations have been based. These productions have been didactic and propaganda tools. The very variety of the ensemble's program represents the thaw following the Cultural Revolution, when such range was banned, as were specific art forms including the Peking opera. The time and creativity lost in that period are symbolized by the heavy dependence on works created or presented in the 1950s.

In return for the Shanghai Ballet's visit, Les Grands Ballets Canadiens was on display for a fortnight in three Chinese cities in 1984 with programmes consisting of various combinations of works by George Balanchine, Antony Tudor and two native choreographers, George Macdonald and James

Kudelka. Zhang Men, Repetiteur of the Peking Central Ballet, noted resemblances between the Canadian troupe and his own, which he attributed to both companies having derived "from the great Russian tradition, and their having developed for about the same period of time". As he saw it: "Their styles are basically similar, though the Canadians in particular show a bright, vigorous, experimental spirit." Xu Yao-ping, in *China Reconstructs*, remarked that "Chinese viewers, as usual, tended to enjoy best the more traditional parts of the Canadian repertoire." In the same article he cites Zhang Men's appraisal of the dancers of the two nations. "While Chinese performers tended to be meticulous and delicate, they could learn much from the confident air of the Canadians, so important for traditional ballet. Audiences could sense this confidence, and had no other word for it but to say that the Canadians danced 'royally.'" Also, works in a modern idiom, Macdonald's *Double Quartette* and Kudelka's *In Paradisium*, "were eye-opening to the Chinese. The first, an exercise demonstrating the beauty of human bodies and physical strength, was yet emotionally resonant. The second impressed art lovers who pride themselves on their lyric refinement with its treatment of death, a daring subject usually avoided in Chinese art forms." In all three cities crowds sought out the foreign dancers; tickets were hard to get.

When the Central Ballet of China (formerly the Peking Ballet) came to the United States in 1986, its repertoire embraced neither the *Red Detachment* nor *The White-Haired Girl* nor propagandistic pieces of that ilk, but instead one act from *Swan Lake*, excerpts from works by Russian and English choreographers, a *pas de deux* from *Don Quixote* and Anton Dolin's *Variations for Four*. The only contributions by the Chinese themselves were brief scenes from *The Maid of the Sea* and *The New Year's Sacrifice*.

The tour lasted two months and covered eleven cities. The ensemble comprised fifty-seven dancers; local orchestras were employed. The Brooklyn Academy of Music was engaged for forty-seven performances, and the troupe's presence caused much excitement. The snippets of Chinese choreography hinted not at all of having been created after the models set by the opinionated Jiang Qing. To the contrary, Ms Kisselgoff found Pyotr Gusev's influence still very discernible, especially in the productions he had once directly supervised. Some paragraphs from her review are illuminating.

Ballet is an international language that is spoken in various countries with different regional accents. In the accomplished young dancers of the Central Ballet of China, who have come here to dance everything from *Swan Lake* to their own folk legends, we come across something rare in the ballet world – a determined and successful attempt to speak what is basically a foreign language.

Classical ballet is an imported art form in China, as it once was in the United States. The difference is that American ballet, as it now exists, was established in the 1930s and can trace its sporadic roots back to the nineteenth century. By contrast, the Chinese ballet tradition – and this company from Peking – was established on firm ground only in the 1950s.

Swan Lake, based on Gusev's staging (1958), is itself founded on the well-known version by Vladimir Bourmeister. There were also episodes from the Chinese fairy-tale ballet, *The Maid of the Sea*, an effort at "collective" choreography which evolved from a workshop led by Mr Gusev for Chinese choreographers in the late 1950s. The second act of *The New Year's Sacrifice*, based on a story by the Chinese novelist Lu Xun (1881–1936) and choreographed in 1980 by the Central Ballet's current artistic director, Jiang Zuhui, also draws from Soviet models that integrate folk and ballet idioms.

Yet the big surprise is that the Central Ballet is by no means an imitation of the Bolshoi. When its young dancers perform the *Don Quixote pas de deux*, they dance like young dancers anywhere today. And in Anton Dolin's *Variations for Four*, a test of the company's caliber and potential was passed with flying colors. The troupe's young male dancers look completely at home; that is, they have adapted to the streamlined silhouette and precision of the English style required by the ballet (created in 1957 for the Festival Ballet and later danced by American Ballet Theater and the Harkness Ballet).

Anyone who thinks that Soviet and English styles don't mix has been living on a desert island and has never seen Rudolf Nureyev. No dancer has given greater proof of how Soviet technique and power can be fused with the placement, line and exact finishes that Western ballet stresses in particular. Mr Nureyev, incidentally, recently supervised the staging of his full-length version of *Don Quixote* in Peking for the Central Ballet. He was invited at the recommendation of Dai Ailian, the company's co-founder who herself studied with British teachers, including Mr Dolin in London in the 1930s. These connections have borne fruit; Mr Dolin personally staged *Variations for Four* in Peking in 1983, a few months before his death.

Always a useful display piece, this divertissement shows off the Central Ballet's adaptability and versatility. The four male dancers in each cast have the kind of Soviet preparation for pirouettes that allows them to do multiple turns so well. But there is no overall Soviet style in their approach. The main point is that any good classical training can be adapted to the style required by a choreographer, especially when he stages his work directly on the dancers.

And so the Chinese dancers looked most up-to-date and modern in classical style in *Variations for Four*. They looked the most old-fashioned in *Swan Lake* not because *Swan Lake* is old-fashioned, but because this staging carries vestiges of a 1958 style that Soviet ballet today has itself modernized.

What the Central Ballet has shown us is a company in the process of finding its own style. The dancers, and especially the choreographers, need greater exposure to contemporary influences in international ballet. But this does not mean they should become confused by a variety of styles that run counter to the foundation they already have. The women have the best of the Soviet training known as the Vaganova system – the use of the shoulders and head, the strength in the leaps, the bold bent-leg arabesques and fabulous extensions.

Stylistically, the chief weakness of the company takes the form of moving from position to position without the customary flow – seen in the tendency of the corps to snap abruptly into academic poses in *Swan Lake*. This sectioning-off of movement has been seen in Western companies as well – notably the National Ballet of Canada.

But one might also ask whether this tendency to pose in classical ballet is not influenced by the way the dancers are taught to lock into the *liang hsiang*, the traditional frozen pose used in Peking opera. Such poses were integrated into the ballets on view that used elements of Chinese classical dance (not ballet) and folk-dances – the excerpts from *The New Year's Sacrifice*, with music by Liu Tingyu, and the excerpts from *The Maid of the Sea*, with music by Wu Zuquiang and Du Mingxin.

The Maid of the Sea became the season's popular, if not the critical, success. With its bright colors and precision-line choreography, the ballet could easily be dismissed as Soviet kitsch turned into Chinese kitsch that resembles Radio City Music Hall kitsch. The work is actually a nineteenth-century ballet in disguise. Mr Gusev, who supervised its original collective staging (different choreographers did different parts), seems to have based the work on the model of *The Little Humpbacked Horse*, created in 1864 in St Petersburg by Arthur Saint-Léon. The Chinese hero rescues the sea princess with the aid of magic plants, personified by dancers, just as the folk hero in the Russian ballet has the magic of the little horse to aid him. There is an underwater ballet in both.

The company presented two scenes from the *Maid* – the sea kingdom and the wedding disrupted by the demon who had abducted the maid. The work's main *pas de deux* was seen on a separate program. The choreography is bold and simple, short on combinations of varied and complex steps. The aim is to communicate and entertain. The same might be said of the excerpt from *The New Year's Sacrifice*, whose dramatic focus is on a young widow married off a second time against her will. Again the choreography is in broad strokes – with three folk-dances providing a divertissement.

Like so many ballet companies today, the Central Ballet of China is in flux. Oddly, it has the advantage of not having to look back at a recent heyday but forward toward a future that could bring it – with the development of new choreographers – into the front ranks.

As the liberalization progressed, foreign plays appeared on Chinese stages ever more frequently. Among them was Eugene O'Neill's *Anna Christie* (1985), put on by a guest director from the United States, George C. White. He found his task made difficult by cultural differences. During a rehearsal of Act Three, when Anna yields "to an impulsive moment of passion for Matt Burke", the naïve sailor, and kisses him full on the lips, the cast began to giggle uncontrollably. Kissing was never done openly in front of a Chinese audience. Above all, a girl would never kiss her lover while her father looked on. So "Anna" the tawdry prostitute, was told to embrace the enamoured Matt very closely. The play, a success, brought tears to the eyes of some spectators, with observers sitting silent as if in a trance. At the end of each performance the actors were rewarded with an ovation, people jumping to their feet to applaud explosively. What helped him, White said, was that the cast's training had been similar to his, involving the Stanislavsky method.

He was assisted by the locally noted playwright and film scenarist Huang Zongjiang, who – at White's suggestion – changed the setting to a sordid wine-shop on the Shanghai waterfront in the late 1920s or early 1930s and retitled the work *An Di*, as the heroine was now called, a common South China name. Instead of having been sent to St Paul, Minnesota, when her mother died, leaving the daughter unguarded, the prey of unscrupulous men, she has instead been consigned to Harbin, where hers was a like fate. Her father, no longer a Swedish mariner, was now a Fijian, and her Irish suitor, Matt Burke, was changed to become Ma Hai Song, a converted Catholic from Canton. White had decided on these changes so that the audience would more readily identify with the characters and their plight, but he was also anxious that their behaviour would not be taken as a typical foreign lifestyle which might be libellous.

In other cultural realms, too, the post-Mao era brought a rapprochement with the West. The Boston Symphony Orchestra was given a frenzied welcome in 1979. On the earlier visit of the Philadelphia Symphony in 1973 its members were segregated during most of their stay, permitted only a limited interchange with their Chinese counterparts. But now the Bostonians were invited to hold seminars at the Peking Conservatory for local conductors and players, to impart their interpretations of European classics.

(Here, a digression – the story is amusing. Andrew Davis, the English conductor who led the Toronto Symphony on a ten-day tour of China, met Li De-lun, director of the Peking Central

Philharmonic and was told that for ten years it was allowed to play only three pieces, one of them "the committee-written *Yellow River Concerto*". Jiang Qing had her say in the orchestra's affairs, too. One day, after a concert, she singled out the trombonists and asked what their instruments were called. When told, she exclaimed: "I don't like them. They're not to play any more." Li De-lun, apologizing, said that the fault was his but interjected that what she had heard was not trombones but tubas. Davis explained the reason for De-lun's deception: trumpets were more needed. For a decade the sound of the tuba was missing; apparently Jiang Qing was not aware of the lack. This anecdote is relayed by James Barron.)

The ban on showing avant-garde European and American sculptures and painting, and especially examples of abstract art, was lifted. An exhibition of such works in the British embassy was poorly attended in 1978, party because initially it was incomprehensible to the critics and populace alike, and because it was politely but inadequately reviewed.

In the same spirit of expanding freedom, film production was resumed in Shanghai and Canton, and Western pictures were imported, though the choices were very conservative, such as old Charles Chaplin releases and innocuous Hollywood musicals. An essential requirement was that each selection, in one way or another, must portray capitalist culture in a bad light. (Jiang Qing was fond of foreign films, particularly those featuring the Swedish-American actress, Greta Garbo, but she was opposed to letting the public see them. She had them privately screened for herself and a few high-ranked associates. A biographer, Roxane Witke, paraphrased her rationale for this: "If the people could view these pictures, they would criticize them bitterly on political grounds. Such public exposure would be most unfair to Garbo because she is not Chinese." Mao's wife explained her enthusiasm for the Swedish-born actress: "Her interpretation of nineteenth-century bourgeois democratic works is outstanding. There is a rebellious side to her character.")

With a new policy of open-mindedness so loudly proclaimed, dramatists were in a quandary. How far was too far? At literary congresses, in speeches on the subject, Deng straddled the issue. Writers could be outspoken, but they must serve the Party. The trouble was, the Party line was forever wavering, swayed by whichever faction in the divided, feuding Politburo was momentarily on top. A playscript still had to be reviewed at four different levels to get official approval before it could be staged, a process that might take years. Cao Yu's hopeful forecast that censorship would no longer beset playwrights was not wholly fulfilled; if anything, dictated by caution, a degree of censorship was self-imposed. Though they were supposedly granted more leeway, too many nervously recalled the short-lived "Hundred Flowers" period, when Mao had invited frank speech and criticism, then had abruptly clamped down on and severely punished those who dared to express dissident views.

At one large gathering of intellectuals in 1979, Bai Hua, a bold figure, declared: "Today we still cannot say that artists and writers are safe. There are still people who sign articles and books and give talks who are locked up and have [dunce's] hats put on them again." That the Party's newspaper, the *People's Daily*, printed the speech was significant. It would not have done so without assent from very high up. A year later the paper revived the topic by publishing a letter from Zhao Dan, a famous film actor, recently deceased. He was so respected that on his deathbed he had been visited by Hua Guofeng, Chairman of the Party, as well as by Prime Minister Zhao Ziyang and the Deputy Prime Minister, Deng Xiaoping, the actual leader of China – Deng cleverly avoided taking on important-sounding titles, though he wielded the utmost power. The late Zhao Dan, now beyond retribution, had written: "The Party can lead in formulating national economic plans and implementing agricultural and industrial policy, but why should the Party tell us how to farm, or to make a stool, how to cut trousers or how to fry vegetables? Why should they instruct writers how to write, or actors how to act? Literature and art is the business of writers and artists. If the Party controls literature and art too tightly, there will be no hope for literature and art. It will be finished."

In this posthumous letter, in which he could finally speak out, Zhao Dan said that he had been encouraged to learn that the *People's Daily* was "launching discussions on improving the Party's leadership over literature and art and enlivening literature and art. But I was heavy-hearted when I read in the editor's note that the Party must improve its leadership over literature and art and strengthen it by improving it. Where is the writer who writes because the Party tells him to?"

The long-popular actor – he had starred in over sixty films – had himself suffered from official wrath during the Cultural Revolution. Accused of being a "counter-revolutionary", he had endured five years of solitary confinement in a prison outside Peking.

But some members of the Politburo feared that the reforms had been too hasty and had swung too far. The prudent and pragmatic Deng was forced to retreat on numerous occasions. His opponents charged that so much "Westernization" had brought about a "spiritual pollution". Abruptly, they seemed to seize control. The reversal was pervasive. Once more, Party officials were sent to villages to tighten discipline by more fervent indoctrination of Marxist dogma. In cities, bright clothes no longer enlivened thronging pedestrian street traffic; people were again wearing dull blue and grey jackets and trousers and young men with long hair who were imitating a Western "sixties" style felt impelled to cut it short – it was safer. The Party calculated that uniform attire stifled individuality.

Private screenings of foreign films were prohibited, some of them blamed for the spread of juvenile delinquency and a breakdown of public morals. Specifically, French pictures were ruled out because too many of them were pornographic.

Tension grew after Deng Liqun, a member of the Party Secretariat and the Central Committee, took over as propaganda chief in 1982. He vigorously campaigned against the flood of unwelcome Western trends and concepts that was a consequence of China's recent open-door policy. He cited four categories of "cultural contamination": the spread of "'obscene, barbarous or reactionary things', vulgar artistic performances, gain-seeking and 'indulgences in individualism, liberalism, etc.', and writings or speeches that contradicted the Chinese Communist system" (from a *New York Times* dispatch by Christopher S. Wren). The attack was aimed chiefly at literature and the other arts, the most frequent scapegoats. Wren added: "The broad scope became more apparent when *People's Daily* published a self-criticism by Minister of Culture, Zhu Muzhi, in which he apologized for his ministry's 'slow reaction and weak attitude' in fighting the cultural contamination." As part of the campaign, several regional literary magazines were closed down, after a complaint by a prominent poet, Ai Qing, who had suffered under the Maoists, that those journals were infecting the minds of readers by printing blatantly unorthodox material.

Shortly before Deng Liqun's appointment a play by Jean-Paul Sartre was whisked off the boards in Shanghai. That was seen as an omen of further repression. Though Sartre was a Communist, he was charged with having a negative influence on the Chinese young. A performance in Canton of a musical revue was denounced in much the same tone in the newspaper *Chinese Youth*, the writer protesting that female singers wore cheongsams, traditional tight-fitting dresses with a slit along the side that bared the thighs. A senior Party official, Lin Jianqing, urged his hearers at a trade union congress to "help the workers distinguish the beautiful from the ugly so that they favour the good and oppose what is ugly, vulgar and self-centred". Ma Hong, head of the Academy of Social Sciences, warned Chinese scientists to be on guard. They should learn all they could from foreign experts but not borrow their bourgeois values. *Red Flag*, the Party's authoritative journal, railed against "frivolous and depraved drama and literature" that had become a "public hazard", poisoning the air and having a demoralizing effect.

"Alienation", a new ailment, was said to be spreading among China's young people. Its cause was laid to the ill effects of becoming acquainted with Western ideas. This was refuted by Zhou Yang, an adviser on the arts in the Party's propaganda department. In an article published in *People's Daily* he asserted that such disaffection and withdrawal was a "universal phenomenon", one not prompted by simply being exposed to foreign literature. But, in any circumstance, could it exist in a purely Marxist social order? The Party ideologues said no. Zhou Yang, quickly taking heed, admitted his error and publicly recanted. The editor and deputy editor of *People's Daily* were replaced, presumably for having printed Zhou Yang's offending essay.

Other officials of high rank explained that "cultural diversity" was definitely encouraged, but stressed that "diversification" and "liberalization" were not synonymous. On every hand rose a chorus of condemnation of the carelessness that had allowed so many harmful tendencies to flourish. As usual, voices became shrill, vituperative.

Two years later, however, Deng Liqun was suddenly dismissed from his post as propaganda chief and a different, easier atmosphere was created. And so it went. Freedom for the arts – and to a marked extent for the stage – progressed by fits and starts.

Some Western observers suspected that the repressive spell, which at first seemed to have the consent and even blessing of Deng Xiaoping, had actually been a pre-emptive move by the ever-flexible politician to let his reactionary opponents over-reach themselves, by going to extremes of strident zeal and discrediting their views.

Though the situation in the theatre improved, playwrights had another reason to be apprehensive. By now, Deng Xiaoping was in his eighties and no one could foresee what might happen after his departure. The Chinese intelligentsia had already endured too many abrupt changes of the ideological climate and paid too painfully when impetuously taking risks.

Said one non-Party writer: "They want a hundred flowers to bloom, so long as every flower is the same."

As in other Far Eastern countries, puppetry has a lengthy history in China, going back 2,000 years. Companies have mastered various kinds of diminutive animated figures operated by hand, rod, string, or casting shadows. They have also accumulated many traditions governing them.

In 1980 the American Museum of Natural History in New York was host to the Fujian Hand Puppets, a troupe of eleven artists from the southern coastal province once known as Fukien. The tour was arranged by the Asia Society, whose Beate Gordon, director of its performing arts programme, had seen the group in Changzhong, their base, where they gave presentations in a government building. She told Richard F. Shepard of the *New York Times* that the group did not look for a theatre. They were mobile, had their own lighting and all other necessary equipment, and required only two hours to set up for a performance. They disliked appearing on regular stages because the puppet stage is arranged around them and is high to start with.

Hand or glove puppets as entertainment had preceded the birth of Peking opera; as elsewhere, the tricks of manipulating the little characters had been handed on through succeeding generations. The artists constituting the Fujian company were young, in their twenties to early forties, but the troupe itself had been active through generations, carrying on a five-centuries-old style of story-telling. In the playlets, symbolism dominated, as in Peking opera; the characters were stock, hence very familiar, the plots taken from history and folklore.

Largely self-trained, the puppeteers learned by watching their elders, though recently the troupe had established a school. The operators carved their own puppets. Richly costumed in Fujian silk, the figures are about a foot or two in height, fashioned of camphor wood or brightly polished bone, with real hair affixed. Head and limbs are attached to a cotton torso slipping neatly over the puppeteer's hand. By custom, the heads are removed after a performance, so that the puppets left alone will not come to life by their own volition.

Emperors are garbed in gold; a phoenix designates an empress; scholars and maidens are dressed in pastel colours. They have pale faces, though their cheeks and eyelids are painted bright pink. Important officials are robed in blue, green and purple. Warriors boast attire of many hues. Horses, dogs, lions and tigers are often in the casts.

The puppet hands can clasp a sword or rod, a fan or book. "I tried to manipulate one," said Ms Gordon. "But I couldn't do anything with it. One of the puppet people took it and told me, 'When you hold it, the puppet is dead. When I hold it, it's alive.'"

Before arriving in New York the troupe had fared very well in Australia and Europe. Ms Gordon informed Shepard: "In Paris, people didn't believe that the puppets could have been manipulated by human hands, it was so dazzling."

Of the performance at the museum, Anna Kisselgoff wrote in the *New York Times*:

The wonder of these puppets is that they nearly "sing" and "dance" as convincingly as their human counterparts. It was the Peking opera in miniature.

Although a program provided a synopsis for the four brief plays, the action was clear enough on the small mounted stage. In *Lei Wanchun Fights the Tiger*, the tipsy hunter, Lei Wanchun, and two helpers rescue a scholar and his page from a villainous innkeeper and his servant. In *Furor in the Mandarin's Mountain*, the hero, Lo Dapeng, is swindled out of his beloved horse but finally regains him from a prime minister's son and his henchmen. *The Devil Paints a Woman* has Wang Sheng, a scholar, seduced by the devil disguised as a woman, until he is saved by his old servant. *Da Ming Fu Prefecture*, is an excerpted sequence with no dialogue, but with an acrobatic and martial arts display by rebels who pass through the city gate by pretending to be entertainers.

Yet the most striking aspect of this puppet form lies not in the stories but in its underlying multi-level esthetic. It has the moral tales and broad effects of popular theater. Yet it also has classical conventions and poetic details that reach up to another level. Its paradox consists of puppets realistically imitating a highly stylized theater, such as the Peking opera genre. Unlike Japan's Bunraku puppets, those of Fujian do not ask us to see black-clad human puppeteers and then to make believe they are not there. Nor are they two dimensional, as shadow puppets.

The Fujian hand puppets, barely two feet high, are rather the equivalent of actors who must be applauded for their virtuosity in their arias or in their swordplay.

Many moments stand out. The way the scholar in the first play opens and closes his parasol and fans himself. The dexterity of simulating spear twirling, swordplay and martial arts. The comic suppleness of a moody tiger. The touching sadness of the scene in which Lo Dapeng prepares to part with his horse. The virtuosity of a puppet thrown into the air in a fight and who lands exactly on the puppeteer's hand. The difference in gait of the characters – the spring with which Wang Sheng walks before he meets the girl-devil is an example. There is the nuanced movement of his hand, indicating tiny differences in brush strokes, as he practices calligraphy. There is a different precision as a villain aims a spear at a hero's head and misses each time.

For touring purposes, the voices and music are now on tape rather than live, as in the past. But the mastery of the puppeteers – Yang Feng, Chen Jin-tang, Zhuang Zhenhua, Zhu Yalai, Xu Lina – was never in doubt.

New York also beheld the Chinese type of shadow play: two-dimensional figures, coloured, perforated and silhouetted on a back-lighted screen. In 1958 the Yueh Lung Shadow Theatre put on *100,000 Borrowed Arrows*, adapted from a legend, in Schimmel Auditorium at Pace University.

Particularly popular throughout China, as already remarked, are exhibitions of physical dexterity. Various troupes travel throughout the country putting on what is an equivalent of the "Hundred Games". In no other nation in the world is muscular agility such an intrinsic element of theatre. Peking opera contains feats of tumbling, leaping, somersaulting at incredible speed, much of this given a symbolic aspect, or intended to illustrate the narrative – the performers suggest that they are climbing a wall, a balancing act; or are engaged in kinetic combat, or are hastily erecting a castle; or they are visually and wordlessly expressing an emotion. These moments are often the highlights of the work, and this is a graphic facet of theatre that is unique to China.

Apart from being intrinsic to many opera-stagings, there are programmes chiefly emphasizing gymnastics.

Outstanding is the Shanghai Acrobatic Theatre which is housed in its own bright, modern semi-round, domed arena in that great metropolis. What goes on there is best described as a circus, a colourful *mélange* of the talents of jugglers, magicians, the buffoonery of clowns, surrounded by heedlessly speeding rollerskaters and amazing contortionists. These acts are lavishly accoutred and brilliantly lit. Foreign spectators have been heard to say that the performances at Shanghai's Acrobatic Theatre outmatch those at Moscow's much better-known circuses.

A North American tour of a company of acrobats from Shengyang occurred in 1973 as a result of negotiations between President Richard Nixon and Premier Chou En-lai during the secret visit of the United States' delegation to Peking. The troupe of forty athletes and twelve musicians opened in Toronto for five days of shows, then moved on to Chicago for ten days. After that the group played in Indianapolis, New York City and Washington. Five tons of props accompanied them; on the stage of Chicago's Civic Opera they utilized no tightropes or trapezes. As depicted in *Time* magazine,

They did not heighten the drama of their performance with drum rolls or tense pauses. Their sleight of hand was charmingly, almost childishly transparent. The easiest of the stunts were executed with painstaking care; the most difficult were tossed off nonchalantly. Two girls juggled china vases with their feet. A man did a handstand atop a rickety pyramid of tables, chairs and bricks, then deliberately collapsed the pyramid. Two men, one on the other's shoulders, ran up and down a freestanding ladder.

One of the troupe's most extraordinary acts is the long-pole trick. One acrobat casually balances a sixteen-foot bamboo pole between his shoulders and chin. A second climbs aboard, shins up to the top, and once there slowly swings his legs out parallel to the ground. Putting one foot in a velvet loop attached to the pole, he stands, then reaches down to a third acrobat, and the two perform a series of elaborate hand-to-hand exercises.

The real hit of the show is a stunt which begins with a single girl riding onstage on a bicycle. She does a few ordinary tricks, then is joined by one girl after another until finally there are seven. When they jump off and exit, the act seems finished. But another girl appears on a bicycle. Nine others with big grins run onstage and, unbelievably, hop on the bicycle.

Most Chinese calisthenics and exercises, notably the *Tai Chi* or "shadow boxing," have their roots in martial training. Chinese acrobatics go back to prehistoric times, when the first farming settlements were begun. Then, or so many experts think, "tricksters" earned their food by performing magic and sleights of hand. Vestiges of this tradition survive in the Shenyang troupe's lion dance, which evolved from the use of animal skins to work a spell on crops, and in their twirling of plates and vases on sticks, which recalls the practice of giving gifts of food to the tricksters. Anthropologists who see a migration across the Bering Strait as the origin of the American Indian point to the similarity between the feats of these acrobats with their ancient tricks and many of the similar feats performed by American Indian tribes.

Their humble origins made Chinese acrobats social outcasts for centuries. The rarefied courts of Chinese civilization down through the Middle Ages had little taste for what they regarded as the entertainment of farmers. A few acrobats kept their craft alive into the modern era, but they were classified as social undesirables and even forced to carry the humiliating yellow cards usually reserved to identify prostitutes.

After 1949, as part of Mao Tse-tung's revival of folk arts, acrobatic troupes were newly subsidized all over China. Today almost every one of China's eighteen provinces and each big city has its company in keeping with Mao's cultural exhortations: "Let one hundred blossoms flower." By 1965 acrobats' status had risen so high that they were accused of being too bourgeois, lacking the "class character that would allow them to reflect the everyday struggles of the workers and peasants." Now they spend two months of every year in a factory or commune, working alongside the peasants by day and performing political skits and improvisations at night, adding new folk material to their acts.

The Shenyang performers, who are paid the equivalent of thirty dollars a month, lead a rigorous and spartan life, practicing three and a half hours every day and performing four or five times a week. The younger members, who are first apprenticed at seven or eight, must do their exercises in the morning and then study after lunch. For them especially, the current tour has been an eye opener. Chao Chun, twelve, the youngest member on the tour and a star of the lion dance, was asked before he left Peking if he knew where Canada was. "Not exactly," he replied, "but I do know it's very hot here this time of year."

For the next decade the Shanghai acrobats were permitted to leave China only when obliged to fulfil several brief "cultural exchanges". One such foray was in 1980, when the troupe performed in New York's huge City Center and in several concert halls in other large American cities. Touring, the troupe was intact, never part of a show with Western athletes.

Diverging from this rule, a fifteen-member team from the Shanghai Acrobatic Theatre "on loan" joined the Ringling Brothers and Barnum Bailey Circus and travelled about the United States for two six-month seasons (1986–7). Their addition to the programme was publicized as a very special attraction, and reportedly $1 million was paid for their presence, though it is to be suspected that the performers themselves were not greatly enriched by their engagement. In the words of Glenn Collins in the *New York Times*, they gave a "three-ring exhibition of precision, contortion, strength and balance that, in its stately pace and controlled grace, seems to alter the laws of the known universe as well as Western stereotypes of acrobatics".

Kenneth Feld, the president of the Ringling circus, explained: "The Shanghai acrobats start training so young that their movements are more fluid and natural than those of any performers I've ever seen. When muscle control is that exquisite, people may not realize just how hard it is." It had taken Feld nearly fourteen years and five visits to China to woo and get permission for the team to leave their homeland and journey with his circus.

The director of the Shanghai contingent was Zu Zhiiyan, "fifty-two and jolly". He told Glenn Collins that acrobatics in China was "a 2,000-year-old art that began as folk ritual and evolved into an expression of Chinese culture and philosophy". Feld said: "This special art did not seem delimited, as in the United States, by the world of the circus or desultory appearances on television sports shows." He was apprehensive that foreign audiences might not comprehend the acrobats' artistry, though spectators did seem to regard the display as an event of significance. The circus's production coordinator, Tim Holst, observed of the athletes: "When they come on, the audience senses the different pacing and seems to forget all other concerns." Collins noted:

So far, the performer most singled out by most of the crowd has been Zhang Lianhui, a five-foot-seven contortionist who manages to bend double while fitting himself within the confines of a fourteen-inch-wide, twenty-eight-inch-tall barrel.

The forty-two-year-old Mr Zhang joined the troupe at the age of ten, conceived the goal of contorting himself into a barrel at the age of fifteen, and has been perfecting his technique ever since.

Mr Zhang said he must prepare by stretching and focusing his concentration for thirty minutes before each performance. He described how he had trained himself to regulate consciously different muscle groups in sequence so he could contract his body to the diameter of the barrel as he moved through it.

"When I was learning, I used to get stuck sometimes during practice," he said. "But generally, what I do is not dangerous."

This is not true of the act performed in the center ring, *The Pagoda of Bowls*, where twenty-three-year-old Li Yueyun balances seven fragile porcelain bowls on her head and feet while being held aloft by her male partner, thirty-eight-year-old Jiang Zhengping.

The trip to America is a rare privilege for the acrobats, who are traveling with their translator, Yu

Jingshun, and their cook, Zhang Guoqing. The parent troupe has lent the Ringling circus only a handful of its more than 300 performers and staff members. Acceptance into the troupe is viewed as an honor, and 30,000 Chinese boys and girls eight to ten years old are nominated by their gymnastics teachers and screened for the sixty entry-level openings available every four or five years.

For the first year's tour Ringling spent a good deal more for the team's services, not only for their wages and travel expenses, but also for totally remodelling a circus railroad car for them.

According to Feld, in his conversation with Collins, "The customized car, part of the agreement with the Chinese authorities, had a specially designed kitchen, a recreation room complete with a video-cassette player and a built-in washer-dryer for the troupe's costumes. Including the cost of revamping the circus into a gilt-and-brocade Chinese fantasy, the actual cost was closer to $3.5 million." (In all publicity for circuses a certain amount of hyperbole is taken for granted; it is a component of the mystique of the exuberant circus realm.)

The Shanghai athletes seemed to enjoy the experience of being abroad. On the opening night in Venice, Florida, however, an American fellow performer wished them "good luck". He used the traditional stage phrase, "Break a leg." The words were taken literally by the visitors, who understood it not as supportive but threatening. A considerable amount of interpretation and apology was needed to reassure the anxious newcomers that no curse or hostility was intended.

Later Mr Zu Zhiiyan commented, "Oh yes, *you* claim it was good luck; but didn't Miss Chen twist her leg afterwards?"

Collins: "There was a moment of tentative silence, just long enough for his listeners to realize that he was teasing. Then Mr Zu and the Shanghai Acrobatic Troupe erupted in laughter."

(The origin of saying "break a leg" is obscure; it is obviously a strange phrase with which to evoke good fortune.)

Four teams from China were rotated, each group remaining in America for only half a season. To emphasize the significance attached to their visit, Han Xu, China's ambassador to the United States, twice made official appearances at the circus to watch the troupe.

This was not the last loan of the company to the West; they returned at intervals during the ensuing decades to the century's end and beyond.

Opera of the Western kind, infrequently attempted, has little following. In 1980, however, in the bloom after the Cultural Revolution, Wang Shi-guang and Cai Kexiang composed *The Hundredth Bride*, which was granted a production. John Rockwell, of the *New York Times*, reviewing a recording issued in 1986, found it sounding "cheerfully close to a late nineteenth-century European operetta, as colored only slightly by the modes and percussive accents of an older Chinese style. It's hardly great art, or likely to enter Western operatic repertories any time. But it's interesting and amusing, and the performance of the Central Opera, Peking, under a woman conductor, Zheng Xiao-ying, is nothing if not committed."

The range of professional stage entertainment typically offered in the capital could be seen in a list contained in the English-language *China Daily* on 5 May 1983. The Shanghai Acrobatic Theatre was on high-flying exhibit at the Bejiing Workers' Gymnasium; *Tale of a Golden Tortoise*, a new historical drama, revised by Chen Ben and Li Shu and directed by Liu Jingyi, was holding forth at the Guanghe Theatre; *I Want to Be a Champion* was being enacted at the Chinese Children's Art Theatre; an advance sale of tickets for *Goujian, the King of Yue*, to be given by the People's Art Theatre, was announced at the Haidian Cinema-Theatre; *Zhu Yu Assumes Command*, written by the PLA (People's Liberation Army) playwright Wang Peigong and directed by Wang Gui, was a presentation of the Drama Troupe of the Air Force at the Beijing Workers Club; *Crown Prince Mijian Visits the Palace* was being done by the Changchun Pingju Opera Troupe; a programme of vocal, dance and instrumental solos was a venture of the Central Nationalities Song and Dance Ensemble; while two foreign works could be viewed, *Death of a Salesman* at the Capital Theatre (as earlier mentioned) and Ibsen's recently translated *Peer Gynt*, the latter produced by fourth-year undergraduates in the directing department of the Central Academy of Drama, mounted in the school's new playhouse. In addition, two full-scale musical offerings were current: *Song of Spring*, enlisting the Central Nationalities Symphony Orchestra, and the May 4 Youth Festival, sponsored by *China Youth Daily* and featuring units of the Central Symphony Society, the China Broadcasting Art Ensemble, the Song and Dance Division of the PLA General Political Department, the Symphony Society Orchestra of the Beijing Film Studio and the Shanghai Ballet Troupe, together with the Song and Dance Ensemble of the Navy. All these should have assured the citizens of Beijing of enough diversion.

One reason more foreign works were not being staged was that China refused to pay royalties to the authors; it did not subscribe to the Universal Copyright Convention. Martin Levin, an American publisher who visited China in 1984 and sought to negotiate a contract there, learned that the concept of private ownership was contrary to Marxist principles. He was told, "Copyright is a device to encourage individual creativity by guaranteeing that a person will be rewarded for it, but in the People's Republic you don't have to have this additional bounty of a royalty payment. Their feeling is that literature and culture belong to everybody, and that royalties are the invention of the capitalist society." Consequently most foreign producers and playwrights were not eager to have their scripts put on in China and lent no hand to those engaged in doing it. Of course, no payment had to be made to Henrik Ibsen; hence it was desirable to reach back a century or more when electing to enact Western drama.

But another major deterrent to a culturally enriching, unimpeded exchange between China and the West was the endless lifting and reimposition of artistic censorship. Through the final decade of the twentieth century this kept on being a hit-and-miss affair, and the uncertainty it engendered could be financially costly. Western producers, performers and authors could never be sure that contracts would be honoured; too often bureaucratic interference at the last moment set up obstacles based on ideological niceties, leading to cancellations or demands for changes.

To skip ahead a few years, to the close of the 1990s, a much-publicized instance of this revolved about *The Peony Pavilion*, Tang Xianzu's classic poetic drama dating from the Ming dynasty, a work long cherished and now about to mark the 400th anniversary of its première in 1598. It contains elements that link it to the myth of Orpheus.

In the story, sixteen-year-old Du Liniang dreams of a handsome young scholar who offers love to her. Waking, she cannot find anyone like him and pines away, starving herself to death, after painting her image on the cover of her tomb. Three years pass. Liu Mengmei, the scholar, visits her burial-site in a deserted garden and beholds the likeness; he becomes enamoured of it. Her ghost comes to him, and they have a spectral romance, which culminates when the strength of his fascination and love restores her to life, but her return is accomplished partly by her command. "Dig me up," she orders. "There are only three feet of earth between us." Though strong-willed, the resurrected Du Liniang, willowy, has always been so fragile that a falling blossom threatens to destroy her. Exceedingly long, lasting nineteen hours – fifty-five scenes – and at moments quite macabre, the play has a host of lesser characters and abounds with comic relief, alternating with moments of poignancy. Usually only excerpts from it are presented.

Taking note of the impending anniversary, Chen Shi-Zeng, a Chinese-born stage director, now a naturalized American citizen working in Hollywood, seized the occasion to propose to the administration of New York's Lincoln Center that it produce the whole drama as an exotic feature of its annual Summer Festival in 1998, a daring suggestion that was courageously accepted. To make the venture more feasible, the troupe would move on to France as part of the Festival d'Autumne à Paris and perhaps to further destinations, each showing helping to reduce the considerable initial cost.

His time limited, Chen Shi-Zeng hastened, won the interest and participation of the Shanghai Kunqu Opera Company, put the chosen cast through eight months of arduous day-long and evening rehearsals and oversaw the construction of lavish, fanciful scenery, while having the ornate costumes designed and readied. The original text of the drama had to be translated, as sixteenth-century Chinese would be understood by very few players and spectators – English and French surtitles were also required. Determining precise shades of meaning was surprisingly difficult, and scholars were hired to help. All proceeded well. The sets, props and delicate attire, finished promptly, were efficiently packed. At the airport, however, there was a sudden, inexplicable delay of several days before the loading, then it was permitted – the contents of the boxes were paid for and the property of Lincoln Center. The shipment arrived on time for fitting and installation on stage but only a bare week before *Peony's* opening. In Shanghai the dress rehearsal was held. The actors, excited, prepared to depart. But, without warning, they were forbidden to leave by an edict from local authorities. Ma Bomin, director of the Municipal Bureau of Culture, declared that Chen's interpretation of the classic script was not faithful to Kunqu conventions and episodes in it were pornographic. Chen did not deny that he had freely adapted some scenes to make the story more interesting and comprehensible to Western spectators, which he felt was necessary; he rejected the claim that anything in his version was obscene. (Among other objections, in some passages he had used puppets.)

The two sponsoring festivals faced a substantial financial loss, by now having invested heavily in the scenery, costumes, rehearsal wages, travel costs, advance promotion, and looking to refunds for tickets and having their theatres empty on all the nights set aside for the cancelled run. It was too late for a replacement.

The director of the Lincoln Center festival, his letters unanswered, flew to Shanghai to plead for an easing of the ban; he was not successful. The American ambassador, interceding, was rebuffed. President Clinton, in China on a state visit, was believed to have taken up the dispute with the Politburo. If so, it was to no avail. Ma Bomin, the "czarina" of Shanghai's cultural affairs and self-appointed arbiter of Kunqu tradition, was adamant. The expensive project was abandoned. The incident was widely publicized abroad.

Chen Shi-Zeng, however, proved as resilient as the reborn heroine of *The Peony Pavilion*: he had the elaborate scenery, props and "gorgeous" costumes; he convinced the Lincoln Center administrators that he could mount the play for the next festival in 1999 and recoup the losses. He recruited actors in Shanghai and other Chinese cities – including Qian Yi, the essential Du Liniang; and a key musician, Zhou Ming – who were apparently not fearful about regaining entry to their homeland, and some with Kunqu training from Chinese colonies in New York, San Francisco and Hollywood. He had less than half the time for rehearsals, but was able to present what was greeted as a resplendent personal vision of the drama; it proved to be the highlight of both festivals, winning gratifying critical praise. In New York more tickets were sold for *Peony* than any other offering scheduled for the annual event. Over eleven days it occupied a theatre there. Each night a new and progressing sequence of scenes was given; knowledgeable spectators could choose which they wished to attend; for the less informed it was "pot-luck". On the final two days, a weekend, the full fifty-five episodes were unfolded in their exact order, from early afternoon to late night, a bit of an endurance test that none the less drew a rapt capacity audience.

From Shanghai, Sheila Melvin wrote to the *Wall Street Journal* providing background material to heighten an understanding of the play and its author. (To learn more about Tang Xianzu, see earlier pages *via* the index.) For an indiscretion – having complained to the Emperor that a number of his bureaucratic colleagues were dishonest and slovenly – he was deprived of his lucrative post as a magistrate and sent to a remote province. Miss Melvin explained:

That a seemingly innocuous co-production of a 400-year-old opera should have blown up into an international controversy surprised everyone – except those who know *Peony* well. For, since the day it was written, *Peony* has been popular, controversial and – like *Macbeth* – trailed by bad luck.

Peony took the Ming literati by storm, instantly becoming the equivalent of a bestseller and a Broadway hit rolled into one. Woodblock print editions of the book were issued by numerous presses, and countless hand-copied versions circulated. Its author, Tang Xianzu, personally supervised many productions of the opera, expanding its popularity to the illiterate. Women especially loved *Peony* – they wrote commentaries and poems about it, built altars to it, slept with it, and even asked to be buried with it. Identification with *Peony's* main character, Beautiful Du, became a craze that must have bordered on hysteria. One Chinese scholar has compared it to the popularity of Goethe's young Werther in eighteenth-century Europe; I am reminded of the cult surrounding Princess Diana. So popular was *Peony* that Tang Xianzu even had groupies – there are historical accounts of women who offered themselves up to him.

However, it is unlikely that Tang accepted any such offers. He was renowned for great integrity, and was controversial because of it. Born into an illustrious family. He was first sent to be a jail warden in Guangdong, the "pestilent south," and then transferred to a poor rural county where he founded a school, helped tenants fight landlords and defended the populace from hungry tigers. After five years of this, Tang called it quits and went back home to become a writer.

Though he gave up serving the Emperor, Tang didn't give up criticizing him. More than 2,000 of his writings are extant, many of them political. The Wan Li emperor was a troubled man who reigned for forty-eight years, most of which time he spent on strike against his bureaucracy, refusing to attend court rituals, fill vacant positions or answer petitions. Tang bemoaned the Emperor's malaise and criticized his policies. *Peony* includes several acts of political satire – which were later censored – but its politics are generally social in nature.

Indeed, much of *Peony's* popularity with women came from Tang's radical portrayal of Beautiful Du as a passionate, strong-willed woman trapped by the confines of a feudal society that insisted on arranged marriage. Beautiful Du not only pines away and dies because of a dream about sex, but returns to Earth as a ghost to seduce the man of her dreams, making love with him before marriage. When she returns to life and weds him formally, she violates custom – and the law – by doing so without parental permission.

Unfortunately, the real-life women who so identified with Beautiful Du did not have the fictional option of rising from the dead and finding the men of their dreams. Instead, they died young and became the objects of other people's dreams. History has left many accounts of young women who became immersed in *Peony* and then died. Some of these women were themselves writers and poets; Tang Xianzu wrote two poems in memory of a Miss Yu, who died at seventeen after writing a commentary on his play. The most famous of these women is Xiaoqing, a concubine sold to a man with a "jealous" wife who refused to let him visit her. Alone in a house on the shores of a lake, Xiaoqing dressed up every day, read *Peony* and wrote poems. Xiaoqing died at seventeen and a cult soon grew up around her, too. Fifteen plays were written about her by male devotees who, unsurprisingly, preferred the story of the loyal concubine to that of bold Beautiful Du.

Peony's association with untimely death gradually cloaked it in an aura of bad luck, and more than one actress is said to have died onstage while playing Beautiful Du. When the costume designer for Mr Chen's *Peony* fell ill with pneumonia and was hospitalized last May, whispers about the *Peony* curse circulated among the actors. Shortly after the dress rehearsals, two employees of the theater and a cook at a nearby restaurant are said to have died because of the bad karma created by the funeral ceremony that ends Act 20 of Mr Chen's production.

In the wake of last year's débâcle, Shanghai's Communist Party decided to remount its own version of *Peony*, a decision rumored to have been personally approved by President Jiang Zemin, and bad luck continues to trail that *Peony*. Culture officials had to cut and condense Tang's masterpiece considerably to eliminate its "feudal" aspects. It now has roughly thirty acts lasting six hours and performed over three nights. Three different pairs of actors play the lead roles, including an actress brought in from Peking opera to make up for Qian Yi's absence. Officials reportedly attend rehearsals every week to give their "ideas" to the director, and the dress rehearsal for part one was staged under lock and key. Everyone involved in the production is said to be dissatisfied with it, and many new hands have been brought in to help, including a modern dance choreographer who is perhaps most famous for the sex change she underwent in 1995. And, to top it all off, the working model for the new show is the video of the banned production – the only known template of a complete performance.

In another article in the *Journal*, Sheila Melvin itemized what is required today to present a classic Chinese drama.

When audiences enter New York's La Guardia Theater for the opening night of *The Peony Pavilion* – Lincoln Center Festival's twenty-two-hour Chinese opera – they will be stepping into a world that merges Ming Dynasty élite refinement with traditional Chinese theatergoing customs.

Mallard ducks will float on a pond that flashes gold and crimson as fish dart beneath its surface. Parakeets will sing from hand-carved wooden cages. Refracted ripples of water will shimmer on scenic backdrops that were hand-painted in China using traditional painting methods and earth pigments. A wooden pavilion will stand at stage center, its sculpted panels and hand-carved finials a silent testament to Ming esthetics. No curtain will ever block this splendid set from audience view. On the contrary, actors will be visible even as they don their hand-embroidered silk costumes. At times they will come forward on a wooden stage wing and apply their makeup in a muted spotlight. Prop men will move scenery and distribute props even as the action onstage continues. When any of the twenty actors who play more than 160 roles are not needed, they will step into the audience to toss out hot towels and fill tea cups with water poured from long-stemmed copper kettles. The musicians will be seated on-stage throughout the opera and at times will become participants in the drama.

It should all look effortless, but it took two years of gargantuan struggle and mind-boggling attention to detail to make this finally happen in New York. . . . Had the shipment not been released, the opera would have been virtually impossible to resurrect. From the start, the director Chen Shizheng and his colleagues believed that the best way to recreate this Ming opera and theater setting was to use Ming-era craftsmanship whenever possible. The 550 costumes designed by Cheng Shuyi were embroidered by 400 old women. The dragon robe worn by lead actress Qian Yi in the opera's most famous scene, "The Interrupted Dream," was stitched over a period of five months by six women belonging to three generations of the same family – the mother of the oldest woman actually embroidered for the last imperial court. The Ming-style pavilion and stage designed by Huang Haiwei was built by twelve carpenters so skilled that they had previously done repair work on the Forbidden City.

The pavilion roof alone consists of sixty hand-joined pieces and Mr Huang intended to use all wood joinery in both pavilion and stage, with no nails whatsoever. However, this plan had to be altered. Festival production manager Paul King had to consider New York City's stringent fire codes, many of which date back to a time in which theatrical lighting was provided by candles and gas lamps. The problem with Mr Huang's set design was that a considerable portion of it jutted out beyond the proscenium arch, which holds a "deluge curtain" that releases a wall of water in the event of a conflagration. So the projecting scenery had to be fireproofed with steel covered by specially treated wood.

Fire itself is a frequent part of the production. During the opera's fifty-five acts, actors brew Chinese medicine over a stove, light incense, breathe fire and burn paper people. The burning of the paper people, who accompany the deceased in the next world, concludes the funeral ceremony that ends Act 20. The ceremony – and especially the burning of the paper people – was highly controversial in Shanghai. Culture officials called it "feudal" and "superstitious" while many audience members fled in fear of the ghosts they were certain would be attracted by it. In New York, the fear is not of ghosts, but of crowd control. Worried about the "traffic pattern" that would be created by 1,000 people processing outside the theater and watching paper people burned on West 65th Street, Mr King got Mr Chen to keep the action inside the theater. Special permission to burn the dolls was needed from the fire department's battalion chief and was obtained after Mr Chen and his colleagues agreed to burn the dolls in iron braziers that will stand in the pond and be covered by wire cages to prevent any ashes from floating away.

"It's a different kind of struggle to get the piece onstage here," Mr Chen said by phone from New York. "But nobody tells you what you can do artistically – here it's the law, and protection against lawsuits." Mr Chen certainly favors artistic freedom complicated by firecodes over the situation in Shanghai – where a mid-level official can ban a production at will – but some things were definitely easier in Shanghai. To get ducks, fish and frogs for the pond, Mr Chen's colleagues simply went to the market and bought them. The animals stayed in the pond throughout the rehearsals, except for the fish which got eaten by the ducks. Canaries were borrowed from the Shanghai Zoo. When the rehearsal ended, Junju Company staffers took the ducks and frogs home and cooked them, and returned the canaries (which had been deemed too loud) to the zoo. In New York, the parakeets and mallard ducks are rented and actually have their own dressing room. Fish are rented from a company that also provides oxygenation for the pond.

The pond itself, which Mr Huang and lighting and prop designer Yi Liming constructed out of fish-pond lining purchased from China's most famous fish farmer, holds 18,000 gallons of water. It had to be pumped full with garden hoses attached to janitor's sinks. The set, costumes and props are generally none the worse for their peregrinations. Shanghai is more humid than New York and cracks have appeared in some of the furniture, but these were repaired with putty and paint. Flute player Zhou Ming was distressed to find that nearly all his thirty flutes cracked in the dry East Coast winter, but a friend in Beijing sent him several dozen made from dry northern purple bamboo. Similarly, a fresh supply of Chinese spirits was needed for the costumes; embroidered costumes are never washed, but are cleaned by spitting alcohol on the inside of the garments to neutralize sweat – so another friend brought over a case of Beijing's local firewater.

"It's been a buckle-your-seat belt ride," Mr King summed up. "But the show looks beautiful."

After Paris, the production travelled to Arts Festivals in Sydney and Hong Kong. It was also recorded on film, for later availability on television and video.

As mentioned before, Kunqu, with its soft, melodious music, originated in and near Suzhou. The works are unique in having well-preserved written scores. The actors play at a very slow pace. Only five companies are still wholly faithful to its tradition. In Shanghai the Kunqu troupe occupies an old, dilapidated, unheated but still ornate theatre in what was once the area of the French concession.

The script's political subtext lies in its setting, the Sōng era (1368–1644), just before the Mongol invasion. Tang was warning the government of his day, the Ming dynasty, against the Manchus, whose similar usurpation was impending. Portraying the Manchus as "licentious, mutton-eating buffoons", he was implying that they were not to be emulated or trusted. His criticism was so obvious that when the Manchus assumed power two acts in the script ridiculing them were later censored. The music for them has also disappeared.

Chen Shi-Zeng was not the only one feeling that the 400th anniversary of *Peony* might be celebrated by its revival. Peter Sellars, an eccentric avant-garde American stage director, devised his own idiosyncratic rendering of the revered if hitherto neglected play. From Berkeley, where the drama as Sellars conceived it was put on view at the University of California, Bernard Holland, a music critic, sent this description of it to the *New York Times*:

The *Peony Pavilion* wars have been of a civil nature up to now; traditionalists arguing among themselves about how a 400-year-old Chinese opera should be put before the public. Disputes over theatrical interpretation are often loud, but this one became an international incident a year ago, much to the consternation of the Lincoln Center Festival, which found its imported centerpiece suddenly canceled by bureaucrats in Shanghai.

Not traditional enough, said Chinese cultural politicians, although the updates of style were by all indications mild to non-existent. Other guardians of the status quo underlined the conservative view a month ago in New York with a staid if somewhat arthritic production of their own.

Now the reverent have a common enemy in the Peter Sellars *Peony Pavilion* which had its first American performances over the weekend here at Zellerbach Hall. Mr Sellars's production is also filled with reverence but for no one thing in particular. It opens its arms wide and squeezes everything within reach to its bosom.

The story, long frozen in Ming-period ritual, is not used to such freedom. In it a maiden dreams of a lover, wastes away from frustration and is resurrected, first as ghost then as reconstituted flesh and blood, when he appears.

The Peony Pavilion is a vivid example of a genre popular among the rich at the end of the sixteenth century when Chinese of all classes seemed as theater mad as their English contemporaries. Like Shakespearian drama the so-called Kunqu school of opera survives through a continually negotiated truce between preservation and rebirth. Change is simultaneously resisted and embraced among the Chinese, just as it is among modern performers of Haydn and Mozart.

Tang Xianzu's original is fifty-five scenes. The Sellars version concedes the limits of current attention spans and producers' budgets and has come up with a synopsis of about three hours. Then it lays out a series of choices: old versus new, East versus West. Having done this, it chooses not to choose among them.

So we are given multiple sets of heroine and hero: the Kunqu lovers with their delicately choreographed gestures and swooping, high-pitched song-speech; the Italian opera lovers emoting and arpeggiating like so many Rodolfos and Normas; American teenagers putting on their makeup, reading fashion magazines and dying as much of boredom as lovesickness.

There is more: a dancer (Michael Schumacher) who translates anguish into body language, and Tan Dun, a composer who revives traditional Kunqu music and adds extensive glosses of his own. One gave thanks for a Zellerbach stage big enough to bear such heavy traffic.

This *Peony Pavilion* is at heart political: a multicultural tract, a Pacific Rim jamboree. Here was Chinese theatrical tradition as interpreted by the United Nations. It is as if Mr Sellars had sat down the sixth, nineteenth and twentieth centuries along with Chinese theater, European opera and American teenage melodrama and asked, "Why can't we all just get along?"

Metaphors fly fast and furious across the stage. Chief among them may be a dreamed-of America, various yet single-minded, where many cultures tell a single story each in their own language. The narratives are not homogenized but superimposed, so that unity and individuality coexist rather than contradict.

Previous page: Kathakali dancer from Kerala, India

Above: Uday Shankar and company

Left: Rabindrinath Tagore

Top right: Shantiniken (the Abode of Peace), Bolpur, West Bengal. The theatre is part of the Tagore estate, and many of his plays were first performed here.

Right: In later years Tagore mainly dedicated himself to writing dance-dramas in the classical Manipuri style. During the performances the drummers whirl and jump as they play.

Above: The Royal Thai Dance Company

Right: Classical Thai dancer

Top left: The Royal Cambodian Dance Troupe

Left: Asparas or dancing nymphs carved during
the twelth century at Angkor Wat in Cambodia

Lekong dance, Bali

Trance dance, Bali, Indonesia

Above: Shadow puppets, Wayang
Kulit, Bali

Right: Barong, the mythical monster
who chases the dancers during the
trance dance, Bali

Top left: Kecak or monkey dance,
Bali

Left: Temple dancer, Gulah, Bali

Left and above: Shadow puppets, Wayang Kulit, Java, Indonesia

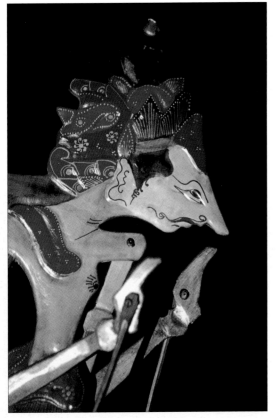

Top right: Shadow puppets, Wayang Kulit, Bali

Right: Wooden puppets, Wayang Golek, Java

Above: Barong mask, Bali

Left: Clay figure of a Cham dancer, Hoshang, a comic figure in Tibetan dance-drama

Top right: Audiences watching Cham dancers at Tashikhyil Monastery in eastern Tibet

Right: A procession of Cham dancers, Tibet

Left: Monks performing a Cham dance, Tibet

Above: Monks performing a skeleton dance, Tibet

Below: Tschechu dance, Bhutan

Right: Dancers, Thimpu Festival, Bhutan

Above: Philippine stick dance

Left: Philippine passion play showing Christ figure carrying the Cross at the annual Moriones festival

The production, shared among the Vienna Festival, the Barbican Centre in London and Cal Performances at the University of California at Berkeley, has good ingredients. As the heroine Du Liniang, Hua Wenyi is a radiant, graceful apparition; for her, passion is reticence and decorum. Reconciling her ritual restraint with the lesser levels of abstraction around her is a problem the production never solves.

For theater is not about real life, a phenomenon more accurately discovered by looking in our next-door neighbor's window. Theater is about shortened time, speeding clocks, exaggerations of speech and surreality of events. It is in short about human control over events, and the level of abstraction – the balance between natural and artificial – varies wildly at every level of this *Peony Pavilion*.

A multicultural metaphor, fusion cooking, fits Mr Tan precisely. A musician experienced in the Chinese tradition and now a freewheeling operative in the West, he is a virtual vacuum cleaner of a composer, sucking up every style, sentiment, gesture and device around him. The first half of this evening finds Mr Tan arranging and augmenting old Kunqu music. Later he uses tradition as a starting point in a great melting pot of eccentric percussion rhythms, operatic flourishes and electronic enhancements.

Mr Sellars, as always, puts on a good show. George Tsypin's design is fitted with clear plastic walls and cabinets and strewn with television screens. Mr Sellars's uninhibited pursuit of his own fancies is his truly lovable trait. Here the idea of hand-held cameras extends to players carrying their own and training them on themselves and others. A love scene of extended silence is memorably touching.

Intense in their different ways are the pairs of lovers: Lauren Tom and Joel de la Fuente as actor and actress, Ying Huang and Lin Qiang Xu as soprano and tenor. Shi Jiehua is the daintily Kunqu Spring Fragrance; Takayo Fischer is the up-to-date Madam Du. Steven Osgood conducted; Min Xiao-Fen played the mandolin-like pipa.

One entered Saturday's performance filled with admiration for such levels of ambition. One came out ultimately worn down by multiplicity, exhausted by the task of sorting out the cultural alternatives. Many elements placed together can add up to an impressive conglomerate, but there is also the danger of their adding up to nothing. It is this kind of indiscriminate generosity that undermines so much of Mr Tan's other music, and it doesn't do this production much good either.

This *Peony Pavilion* is a kind of urban, ethnic fusion, a big, teaming, multiracial Los Angeles of a production. It is heartwarming in its way, fascinating to think about, but Mr Sellars's outstretched arms simply can't hold all the things it reaches for.

From France, Alan Riding, attending for the *New York Times*, observed:

The Autumn Festival in Paris had the clever idea of offering two contrasting productions of *The Peony Pavilion* to celebrate the 400th anniversary of Tang Xianzu's classic Chinese opera. But the Shanghai Kunqu Opera company's complete twenty-hour version, originally scheduled to open this summer's Lincoln Center Festival in New York, was banned from leaving China as too "feudal" and "pornographic." So Peter Sellars's three-hour avant-garde version has had the stage to itself here.

It has left those unfamiliar with Kunqu opera (let's face it, most Westerners) with the task of evaluating the experimental without the standard of the traditional. As it is, audiences at the Bobigny cultural center outside Paris are inevitably left guessing how much of Mr Sellars's *Peony Pavilion* is original Kunqu and how much has been added to reach out to Westerners. For all that, it still looks and sounds pretty Chinese, though not exactly 400 years old.

Indeed, in a sense, Mr Sellars has brought Tang Kianzu's fifty-five-act masterpiece closer to the China of today. While Chinese opera never recovered from the censorship and dismantling of theater companies that accompanied Mao Zedong's Cultural Revolution, its survival is now threatened by the growing popularity of Western music, movies and television. So it is conceivable that Mr Sellars's Westernized homage to traditional Chinese culture would appeal more to many young Chinese than the original. This theory may even be tested if, as the forty-one year old American director hopes, the production travels to China in 2000.

Riding revealed that Sellars had been apprised of the *Peony's* anniversary at a meeting with Hua Wenyi, a Chinese actress now in her fifties and newly arrived in California (1990), who had formerly taken the role of Du and been the artistic director of the Shanghai Kunqu Opera. She served as a consultant during Sellars's staging of this "national treasure". Oddly, she approved of his shortened free-wheeling treatment of it – but deplored Chen's adaptation as not true to the original.

Entering the fray, the Kunqu Society of New York came forth with a three-hour *Peony* that it asserted was "authentic"; the cast of thirty-five filled the stage of the Kaye Playhouse in 1999, under the auspices of the China Society. Only nine of the work's fifty-five scenes were presented; thereby it steered a middle course as to length. As just noted, Bernard Holland found this production "staid" and "arthritic". James R. Oestreich, also for the *New York Times*, was not too receptive:

It was gratifying on one level finally to see such a substantial representation of the work, with much artistry and expertise lavished on it. Du Liniang was played by Hua Wenyi, famous for her portrayals of the role over the decades and now also part of Peter Sellars's touring production of the work, which turns up next week in Berkeley, California.

Because of the disruption of Chinese opera tradition caused by the Cultural Revolution, older performers have become familiar in youthful roles, and Ms Hua's artistry (if not always her voice) was often such as to encourage a suspension of disbelief. (A viewer was inevitably reminded of the older Margot Fonteyn in Prokofiev's *Romeo and Juliet*.) Sie Jiehua was fetching as Fragrance, but Wang Taiqi portrayed the dashing hero with resources grown slender and fragile.

The production offered beautiful costumes and, in the netherworld scene, skillful acrobatics. But the Blossom Fairies seemed to have wandered in from a Las Vegas stage, and the lighting was often garish. The music seemed diluted to appeal to bland Western tastes (though some lack of impact in the drums and cymbals undoubtedly resulted from the stifling acoustics of the Kaye stage).

If the attempt was, as it was made to seem, to show the one true way to draw on a venerable tradition, it left a neophyte admirer of the art form unpersuaded. Tradition, after all, is manifold, and nobody owns it.

Shanghai's Bureau of Culture was clearly challenged by these competing revivals abroad. This venerable work was being memorialized in America, Europe and Australia, but not on home ground; a local production was essential. A large sum, a quarter of million dollars, was allocated. The search for a director was frustrating; no one wanted the assignment. Those who were approached seemed to be dissuaded by what had happened to Chen. Finally one with an undistinguished résumé accepted the task; he had no background in Kunqu. As reported by Sheila Melvin to the *Wall Street Journal*, the cast – the same actors who had been chosen by Chen – got under way again. They now had to relearn their lines – this was a different translation – and interpret their roles in a new light. Ma Bonim attended some rehearsals and proffered suggestions. Recorded music, hitherto used to accompany excerpts from *Peony*, replaced the live Kunqu orchestra assembled by Chen. Outside Shanghai, criticism appeared in the *People's Daily* about the handling of the Chen venture. Lincoln Center was referred to as "the single most important arts organization in America" and praised for seeking to promote Chinese culture in the United States. The project should not have been treated so shabbily. Most other papers were silent about the issue. Interviewed by Ms Melvin, several of the actors said they had learned much from Chen and his innovations and regretted not having gone on and profited even more from his guidance. The Shanghai production of *Peony* was featured at the observance of the fiftieth anniversary of the People's Republic in 1998.

Seth Faison, in China for the *New York Times*, sent back word that afterwards the local *Peony*, having won few plaudits except in the official press, was being performed in a run-down, half-empty, moderate-sized auditorium. Many opera-goers, he said, found the production "flat and lifeless". This was not from lack of funds. "At least, there were efforts to spruce up the presentation with rhinestone-studded gowns, flowery backdrops and flashing lights, which offered an element of kitsch." Thirty scenes, totalling seven hours, were staged over three nights. Three actresses – Qian Yi not among them – alternated in the role of Du Liniang, and the three male leads also took turns. Faison was impelled to add:

> To many in the audience the seeming weakness of the Shanghai *Peony Pavilion* epitomized what is wrong with the arts here, where artistic creativity seems to be smothered by the country's vast bureaucracy, which determines what the public should be allowed to see.
>
> Communist Party officials might be expected to be on the lookout for art that is politically subversive. This often inflexible nature of Chinese officialdom can place a crushing burden on any artist who attempts to come up with anything fresh or inventive.
>
> To an outsider living here, one of China's enduring mysteries is why the world's most populous nation, brimming with talent and backed by an illustrious cultural history, should have made such a relatively meager contribution to this century's art. For instance, in the last 100 years, including the half before the Communist Party came to power, China has failed to produce its share of internationally renowned writers, composers or painters.
>
> In Chinese opera the burden of the past is heavy. A bevy of cultural officials and critics and directors jealously guard that art form, ensuring that any new interpretation that would modernize it is kept firmly at bay.
>
> It took an outsider with a special ability, Mr Chen, with both the education inside Chinese theater and the perspective of someone who had lived and worked outside China for ten years, to tackle a complex classic like *The Peony Pavilion* with success. Drawn to the work (which has stirred controversy since it was written in 1598 by Tang Xianzu), Mr Chen wanted to stage it in its original full form and he hoped to make it engaging and accessible with innovative staging.
>
> Cultural officials became deeply irritated by his refusal to act as submissive as most other directors in China.
>
> He ignored suggestions by officials about how to improve his production, but the authorities showed him who was boss by blocking the Shanghai Kunqu Opera Company altogether. Yet logic does not always work in politics. In this case not even the risk of tarnishing President Clinton's reception in China could deter the officials involved.

Apart from the adverse publicity generated by the incident, it was embarrassing to China's culture czars that it took a director from the United States to revive *The Peony Pavilion* in its full form.

Still, they immediately copied the idea and ordered the actors Mr Chen had worked with to participate. It apparently took months before officials could find a director who was willing to take on the project, and it was not hard to understand why.

"This was a rare, rare opportunity," said one of the actors who participated, expressing admiration for Mr Chen's version. "It tore my heart to lose it. But we live in China, and that's life in China."

Though scant, further cultural exchanges were negotiated at intervals, with the agile, brightly garbed acrobatic teams retaining top priority.

Both Beijing and Shanghai looked to the West, however, when they announced plans to build a Performing Arts Centre like London's Festival Hall and Barbican, Washington's Kennedy Center and New York's Lincoln Center. Beijing invited a list of distinguished European, Canadian and Japanese architects, along with some Chinese, to compete for the commission, a search taking a year and a half. Forty-four models were submitted, then revised; these were winnowed until only four remained as finalists. Chosen was a Frenchman, Paul Andreu, already working in China as designer of a new Shanghai-Pudong airport. His vision for the Centre was of a "titanium-and-glass-covered ellipsoid shell", truly at odds with traditional Chinese architecture. The argument on its behalf was that it should be ultra-modern to proclaim China's progress in the twentieth century, yet blend in at its site on vast Tiananmen Square, the historic centre of the city – and hence of the nation – also faced by the Great Hall of the People and the huge looming portrait of Mao. Stretching 400 feet long, the building's height is limited to 135 feet so that it does not overtop any other monument on the square; it will have a "cavernous lobby" leading in different directions to a 2,500-seat opera house, a 2,000-seat concert hall, a 1,200-seat theatre and a 500-seat playhouse below. The approach to the lobby is to be an underwater glass tunnel through a lake encircling the edifice like a moat. "A transparent gilt metal netting will surround the opera house to suggest something slightly ethereal, while the auditorium itself will have dark red as its dominant colour." (As of this writing, some details are not yet finally authorized or committed.) The scheduled completion date is 2003. Andreu hopes that his building will have a park-like setting. The budget is $362 million. The need for such a structure was first stated by Chou En-lai; the Cultural Revolution, and subsequent decades of bickering between political factions and the usual swarm of bureaucrats, account for the thirty-year delay in having the ambitious project finally realized. Andreu anticipated objections from conservationists and purists: "Beijing is an ancient capital, so we want coherence and unity. But it is also an international capital, so we want it to have a vibrant feel. Those demands created inconsistencies."

Meanwhile Shanghai has surged ahead, supporting its claim to be the economic and cultural capital of the People's Republic. (Together with Tokyo, it is thought to be the world's most crowded metropolis, with a citizenry larger by millions than London or New York, and far outrivalling Beijing.) Its new Grand Theatre on People's Square (finished in 1999) is diagonally across a park from the new Art Museum (completed 1996) that houses a magnificent collection, the pair lending Shanghai the cosmopolitan air to which it aspires. Another Frenchman, Jean-Marie Charpentier, is the theatre's architect. Its budget was $150 million. The exterior is mostly of glittering glass, gleaming when illumined from within after nightfall. It was faulted by some for being altogether too open. To counter that criticism, Charpentier inserted white gauze panels so that the glass seems glazed, translucent rather than transparent, achieving a shimmering effect after dark. He said that he used glass to symbolize a new cultural openness, but many thought him overly optimistic, as most of the half-closed political borders and bureaucratic obstacles to artistic freedom were still in place.

The sleek Grand Theatre has a rectangular roof that curves upwards at its narrower two ends – it might be likened to a scooped-out slice of melon – giving the building a vaguely Chinese aspect, at first glance a familiar yet surprising shape. Its location, near the Art Museum as well as the new City Hall, and overlooking a park, is considered an instance of good urban planning. Next, a concert hall is to be added to this cluster.

As a result of major civic projects in Beijing and Shanghai, a drive for more performing arts centres began sweeping through China, as other large cities tried to keep up with those metropolises. One was completed in Nanjing, and one started in Shenzen, the flourishing, dynamic new commercial hub that in fifteen years expanded from a fishing village to having a bustling population of 4 million.

But what to put in these opulent opera houses and theatre groupings? Most are too large for works of the traditional Peking and Kunqu repertoires, in which the acting is subtle, the orchestra small, and the vocalization thin and nasal so that ideally they fare best when the place is intimate. The huge houses are suitable for foreign music dramas, Donizetti, Verdi, Wagner. Having an opera house was prestigious, but did they serve a purpose? It did not seem so. Chinese spectators developed a liking for classic Western ballet. Even Jiang Qing prompted and subsidized that kind of dance. But among theatre-goers a taste for foreign opera was shared by only a few.

The first to observe it were Chinese students in Japan. Some returned from there, and later from studies in Europe, with an interest in dramas conveyed by full-throated song. Indeed, for many devotees, opera is a passion. Among music students, in particular, there was a wish for local productions of the acknowledged foreign masterworks. But only after the Second World War was a Chinese Opera Company established (1952). It was made up mostly of amateur artists – many of the better-trained musicians had left with Chiang Kai-shek and were in Taiwan. An orchestra had to be rebuilt and Western instruments acquired. Teachers came from the Tchaikovsky Institute in Moscow to help with coaching, and soon China's conservatories were turning out professional-level singers and instrumentalists. Works by Chinese composers were the first to be ventured; in 1958 *La Traviata* was the first full-length opera staged. (Nearly four decades earlier, in 1920, a *Traviata* had been performed by a visiting Russian troupe, a rare event, the very first time any such work had ever been seen and heard in pre-Communist China. The Verdi piece is adapted from Dumas *fils'* late nineteenth-century play, *The Lady of the Camellias*, which had also been made into a film *Camille* with Greta Garbo, both of which were familiar and popular among sophisticated Chinese.) For another decade, the 1960s, operas by Chinese continued to be written and enacted, along with some imported works, until the Cultural Revolution erupted and caused a complete halt. The whole nascent enterprise was eliminated. For ten years there were no opera productions. Singers and instrumentalists vanished. One of the art form's proponents, the foreign-schooled Zhou Xiaoyan, director of the Zhou Xiaoyan Opera Centre, was denounced as a "cow ghost and snake spirit" and shipped out to the countryside, where she was confined in a "cowshed for intellectuals".

After Mao, with virtually a generation of performers and appreciative listeners lost, the recovery was slow. Talented students who obtained grants to go abroad tended not to return. Many orchestras in America and Europe had Chinese players – their numbers were conspicuous – and there were a good many Chinese singers in operatic casts around the world, but few at home. One reason for their sparse ranks was the low salaries they could expect – in Shanghai about $50 a month – so low that few even bothered to audition for parts. If an aspirant was engaged, the run would be short, two or three performances. The leading roles would be given to famed singers from abroad, their voices and interpretations recognizable from recordings. They were needed to attract an audience. In the music community it was hoped that the construction of the huge performing arts centres would encourage additional opera productions, a kind of entertainment most likely to fill the empty seats at high prices. Some tickets to hear the Spanish tenor José Carreras in concert at the Grand Theatre in 1998 cost $200.

The government was steadily cutting back its financial support, each year allocating less than the year before, while persistently controlling all programming.

The boards of the Shanghai Grand Theatre were trod during its opening season by two foreign operas, Wagner's *The Flying Dutchman* and Verdi's *Aida*. Both were co-productions with European companies, the Wagner from Düsseldorf, the Verdi from Florence. Bonko Chan, manager of a state-owned freight-forwarding company and an avowed "opera fan", was the self-appointed impresario responsible for bringing over both state companies. Though critical successes, the presentations failed to pay their way. The government's subsidy is measured by the size of the audience. It is better for a small group of performers to put on a series of free diversions in a school or factory and lay claim to large numbers of spectators than to attempt a full-scale offering in a huge, half-filled theatre where the cheapest seats cost $50. Furthermore, the companies must pay rent for use of the stage, house and staff. The Shanghai Grand's general manager, Le Shengli, admitted that he had no experience with opera and scant knowledge of it. His intent was to seek co-productions with overseas organizations such as New York's Lincoln Center, but he expected that after the *Peony* fiasco the chances of arriving at such arrangements were slight. He insisted, however, that he could reach decisions without having to consult Ma Bomin and the Municipal Bureau of Culture. Instead he was subjected to the authority of Shanghai's Bureaus of Radio, Film and Television. To those aware of how matters proceed in China, this seemed a definite promise of further internecine warfare when the two local bureaux locked horns.

Though not yet in possession of its new opera house, Beijing was treated to a version of *Turandot*, Puccini's lush lyric drama set in a court in old Cathay and based on Carlo Gozzi's fable. This elaborately appointed mounting had originated at the Maggio Musicale Florentino; it was under the baton of Zubin Mehta and directed by Zhang Yimon (1998). Gaining the utmost verisimilitude, it now had as background the Forbidden City, the palace of China's ancient rulers. The production, taped, was subsequently telecast on the Public Television System in the United States.

Apparently *Aida* was admired in Shanghai. Two years later, in 2000, it was heard and seen again, but this time in the open air and with an unprecedented scope. Craig S. Smith's dispatch to the *New York Times* sounded amused and awestruck:

> Giuseppe Verdi could never have imagined the music in his famous opera *Aida* upstaged by 1,650 People's Liberation Army soldiers and a trained elephant. But that's what happened Friday when 60,000 Chinese gathered here to watch the world's biggest production ever of an opera.
>
> In an evening of not quite high culture, and a few moments of low comedy, a cast of 2,200 performed the tale of doomed love between an Egyptian general and an Ethiopian slave girl as the centerpiece of this year's China Shanghai International Festival of the Arts. And while the sound was remarkably good for such a huge venue, the theatrics stole the show.

Bad weather had threatened to spoil the production, which was scheduled for just one night (an all-Chinese cast performed to a much smaller audience tonight). But after a rainy week that interfered with rehearsals, the skies cleared Friday and the stadium was packed.

For most of the audience, the Russian soprano, Olga Roanko, as Aida and the Italian tenor, Lando Bartolini, as Radames were spotlighted figures so tiny it was difficult to tell who was singing. And few people could see the fantastic costumes by the designer, Goran Lelas.

But everyone loved the opera's famous triumphal march, which in this production featured Chinese soldiers dressed as Egyptian warriors marching in formation across the massive stage and around the stadium's oval track in a procession more befitting the opening of the Olympic Games than a three-hour opera. They were followed by an elephant, Bactrian camels, lions, tigers and racing, horse-drawn chariots.

The elephant drew the biggest applause of the evening when it stood on its hind feet and waved a forefoot to the crowd. And there was a tense few minutes when the chariots nearly locked wheels, and then two of the horses balked and had to be pulled off the stage. The audience erupted in laughter as a soldier frantically swept into a dustpan a trail of "road apples" that the horses left behind.

The crowd watched the spectacle through all shapes and sizes of binoculars while munching on tofu snacks and KFC chicken burgers. An illuminated blimp buzzed overhead.

"It's fantastic," said thirty-year-old accountant Chen Wenjun, sitting near the top of the huge stadium. As it was for most of the audience, the performance was his first opera. He was eager to hear from an American how the production compared to operas in the West. "I'll bet you haven't seen anything as grand and expansive as this," he said.

Smith does not tell who subsequently sang the leads nor under whose auspices the *Aida* was conceived and produced. By many it was probably remembered for its extravagant display rather than as a musical event. But similar *Aidas* have been staged in ruined, partly restored arenas in Verona and Rome, also with an elephant but considerably fewer "Egyptian" troops.

Fulfilling a 150-year-old treaty, the British crown colony of Hong Kong was reunited with China in 1997. Ceded to Britain in 1841 – it was actually a forcible seizure – this thriving "outpost of Empire" became the most modernized and Westernized city in Asia. Blessed with a magnificent bay and harbour, nestled beneath sloping green hills, surrounded by small, verdant islands, it soon became the most prosperous centre of Far Eastern local and foreign trade, the cynosure and envy of its neighbours. Its skyline – thrusting towers – rivalled those of New York and São Paulo; its streets were far more thronged. Into this democratic haven flowed an endless stream of defectors from the adjacent People's Republic, where turbulence and oppression reigned. Most of the refugees came from the southern provinces of China, especially from Canton, an ethnic group noted for energy and commercial acumen. Others flocked in from North Vietnam, which, too, was under harsh Communist rule. Their flights were hazardous by sea. With these influxes, Hong Kong became exceedingly crowded.

Under lenient British rule, Hong Kong's Chinese citizens paid little attention to the performing arts. Bluntly put, they were busy making money. Many had a desperate need for it, being refugees who had arrived with little or nothing. Those who could afford to seek recreation were apt to do so at the Happy Valley racetrack in the very heart of the city, and much patronized by the British as well. In the 1970s, however, the colony's Council belatedly took steps to fill what was recognized to be a long-lived cultural gap. It did so with a rush. A Music Office was set up in 1977 to assure the due training of young singers and instrumentalists. The same year the Hong Kong Philharmonic, made up of amateurs, was reorganized as a professional ensemble, and the Hong Kong Repertory Theatre and Hong Kong Chinese Orchestra were established. A bare twelve months later brought the Hong Kong Conservatory of Music. In another show of concern for the arts the Hong Kong Ballet was formed, and the Chung Ying Theatre (both troupes in 1979), and the Hong Kong Dance Company (1981). A truly sudden immersion in "the finer things in life".

To oversee and coordinate all these new activities, the Council sanctioned an ambitious Hong Kong Academy of Performing Arts, charged to "preserve and nurture the traditional arts of Asia as well as those of the West". The academy could enrol 600 trainees; scholarships were available, regardless of a student's financial need. The minimum age for entrance was seventeen, but the staff was alert for signs of talent among younger applicants, even those only eleven or twelve years old who could take classes part-time.

A place to house the academy was promptly begun, its cornerstone dedicated six months later (1982). The Duchess of Kent represented Queen Elizabeth at the ceremony. The "multilevel, mostly triangular" building, situated on the shore of Victoria Harbour, is alongside and connected to the Hong Kong Arts Centre. It cost $53 million, mostly contributed by the Hong Kong Royal Jockey Club from proceeds of races at Happy Valley and the New Territories – across the harbour – together with a grant of $10 million from the Council, as well as its pledge of $5 million annually for the academy's maintenance. Here, under one roof, are combined schools of "music, dance, drama and technical arts", with three theatres – seating 800, 400 and 250 – and rehearsal, recording and television studios, all fully equipped, along with seventy teaching rooms and classrooms, and eleven practice dance studios. The design of the building resulted from inspection of other such institutions abroad, among them New York's Lincoln Center Performing Arts complex, London's South Bank, Guildhall School of Music and Royal Academy, and Vienna's Hochschule. Basil Deane, formerly music director of Britain's Arts Council, was named the first head of the academy.

Other playhouses and acting groups sprang up. One has been the Hong Kong Stage Club, holding forth in the Shouson Theatre. A sample of its fare is described in a *Hong Kong Standard* review of a presentation of Joe Orton's anarchic *What the Butler Saw* (1983): "The play is funny and the dialogue excellent. The amateur acting is first-class and the sets are a credit to the production. It is certainly a play not be missed, especially if you like black comedy and black underwear." Another innovative group calling itself Zuni Icosahedron was equally active.

The Chung Ying Theatre's offerings are in both English and Cantonese. All these groups, appearing either in the City Hall or at the Hong Kong Arts Centre, are subsidized to some extent by the government or the Urban Council, a quasi-official agency; but they also depend on private gifts and ticket sales.

Wealthy and boasting a large foreign colony, Hong Kong was eventually regularly visited by top-flight ensembles from the mainland, Japan, America, Europe, even the Middle East. An arts festival is now held every January and February. Typically, the 1984 season brought acting and ballet companies from England and Scotland, as well as symphony orchestras from Israel and the United States (Pittsburgh); and the Wuhan Acrobatic Troupe from the People's Republic.

In return, the Hong Kong Ballet has audaciously ventured overseas. Christopher Reardon in the *New York Times*, covered one such visit in 1998:

One evening last June, So Hon Wah sat backstage at the Hong Kong Cultural Centre and pulled a pair of gold-trimmed boots off his callused feet. He was only changing costumes, he explained on the telephone from Hong Kong, but to him the gesture epitomized his title role in *The Last Emperor*, Wayne Eagling's tragic new dance for the Hong Kong Ballet. Like Bernardo Bertolucci's 1987 film of the same name, which won nine Academy Awards, the dance chronicles the epic life of Pu Yi, from his coronation at age three to his final years as a gardener during the Cultural Revolution.

With the crown colony's handover from Britain to China then four weeks away, one might have expected a ballet about political upheaval and its psychological aftermath to strike an eerie chord with both audiences and dancers. Yet, at its première last year, few dancers drew parallels between the collapse of the Qing Dynasty on the mainland and the end of British sovereignty in Hong Kong.

"I'm just a ballet artist," said Mr So, a local dancer who alternates with Michael Wang, a Shanghai native, as the adult Pu Yi. "I wasn't thinking about the political situation."

Such disregard for democracy may not be as callow as it sounds to Western ears. In some respects it was even prescient, for it turns out that the new Hong Kong functions quite like the old one, even if fewer Britons and tourists are queuing up for the ferries that ply Victoria Harbor.

The Hong Kong Ballet is now embarking on its own journey, to New York where starting Wednesday it will give six performances of *The Last Emperor* at City Center. Hong Kong's only classical ballet troupe came to the United States once before, in 1993, with narrower ambitions. This time the magisterial sets by Liu Yuan Sheng, the dean of stage design at Beijing's Central Academy of Drama, barely fit on stage.

It's a daring move for a company that began with five dancers in 1979 and just commissioned its first full-length ballet last year. With luck, ticket sales will cover half the cost of bringing thirty-nine dancers, fifteen staff members and twenty-three tons of gear halfway around the world for a one-week run. Essentially the troupe and its Hong Kong backers hope to gain enough exposure to make smaller tours feasible in the future.

Coming of age at the onset of Chinese rule presents the company with complex questions about cultural identity and the role of classical ballet in today's Hong Kong. The troupe had not even performed a dance set in China before *The Last Emperor*, which features ornate period costumes by Wang Lin Yu, the chief stage designer at Beijing's Central Opera Ballet Theatre, and a densely orchestrated new score by Su Cong, who won an Oscar for his work on the Bertolucci film.

As many of Hong Kong's cultural institutions become more Chinese, the company shows signs of moving in the other direction. In the waning months of British rule, it sent to London for a new artistic director, the former Royal Ballet star Stephen Jefferies. He, in turn, has recruited young dancers from Australia and Canada, suspended a series of workshops for aspiring local choreographers and commissioned new work almost exclusively by choreographers with ties to Covent Garden.

During a visit to New York in January, Mr Jefferies said he was trying, in part, to re-create the company in the image of the Royal Ballet, where he distinguished himself over a twenty-five-year career as a dancer of great technical and dramatic ability. It's no fluke that most of the current repertory, from Frederick Ashton's *Two Pigeons* to Peter Darrell's *Nutcracker* to Graham Lustig's new take on *Peter Pan*, can be traced to the Royal Ballet, its school or its sister company, the Sadler's Wells Royal Ballet. "We're an international ballet company," Mr Jefferies said. "That means we take the best dancers and choreographers we can find, worldwide."

Where he sees a way to build a first-rate troupe, some observers see a lingering British imperialism at work. Bruce Steivel, who preceded Mr Jefferies as artistic director, doubts postcolonial Hong Kong will support a Chinese version of the Royal Ballet. "The director needs to be someone who is Chinese," he said. "Someone who understands the Chinese mentality and understands what Hong Kong needs."

It may not be that simple. In fact, to succeed in Hong Kong, the director must walk a cultural tightrope. If the ballet becomes too British or two cosmopolitan, it may jeopardize its financial support from the powerful Urban Council, which has been earmarking more of its money for Chinese arts and culture. But unless it raises its stature abroad, it will remain dependent on the Arts Development Council, which has lately been accused of subsidizing the Hong Kong Ballet and five other performing-arts groups too heavily. The ballet draws three-quarters of its $5 million budget from the public purse.

Dancers describe Mr Jefferies as a man capable of working in two distinct modes. When rehearsing a classic ballet like *Swan Lake*, they say, he stresses precision and uniformity. But when preparing a new work like *The Last Emperor*, he gives his dancers dramatic license. Mr So described it as a kind of method acting: "He helps you pull the character out of your heart."

With fourteen of the company's forty-one dancers coming from Hong Kong, and three more from the mainland (most of the rest are Westerners), Mr Jefferies occasionally lets the troupe show its Chinese side. Recently he commissioned a dance by Yuri Ng, a local choreographer. Last year he turned to Mr Eagling, a former roommate who is now artistic director at the Dutch National Ballet, for the piece about Pu Yi.

After watching the Bertolucci film, Mr Eagling combined the autobiography of Pu Yi and the memoir by his Scottish tutor, Reginald Johnston, for insights into the Emperor's character. "For me, the most interesting thing about Pu Yi was the torment of his sexual and intellectual impotence," he said in a telephone interview from Amsterdam. "He was a prisoner all his life."

The choreographer makes no claim to authenticity. "It's not a Chinese ballet," he said. By way of example he cited a scene with two Manchurian dowagers on platform heels that were modeled from archival photographs. "I invented what I imagined it might be like to walk on those shoes," Mr Eagling said.

The production has drawn criticism in the Chinese press for using a Western choreographer. Mr Eagling, a Canadian who grew up in California, cordially dismissed the critique. "Do I have the right to tell a Chinese story?" he mused. "I guess the answer is yes. You don't have to be Russian to tell the story of Eugene Onegin.

"I was just trying to tell a story," he added. "An interesting story about a man rather than about a country and its history and its politics."

16

TAIWAN: ANOTHER CHINA

Where to put this chapter? Communist China claims absolute sovereignty over the island of Taiwan (formerly known as Formosa). The Nationalist regime, firmly installed on Taiwan, asserts that it is the legitimate government of all China. Both say that they look forward to a reunion, but there are no meetings. The Formosans, whose island it was, would like to revert to self-rule but are not consulted. The shores on both sides of the Straits separating the parties in dispute are fortified and bristle with rockets and ballistic missiles aimed at each other to prevent an invasion, which the Communists frequently threaten to undertake. It is not for the author of a book on Oriental theatre to settle the issue. Pragmatic, I shall bow to the current status quo: for now, Taiwan's drama is discussed separately here.

Having been defeated by the Communists in 1949, Chiang Kai-shek and his forces fled the mainland to a haven on this close-by island, a remarkably deft tactical feat. In power there, they perpetuated their non-Marxist policies, establishing a nominal republic, though for many years it was actually dominated by Chiang and his family: he was succeeded by his son. However, their rule became increasingly democratic, and subsequent leaders were chosen in free elections.

With American aid, Taiwan prospered, becoming the richest nation in South-east Asia, while mainland China continued to experience impoverishment and turmoil; so that the Taiwanese were not tempted to submit to Communist control; they strongly preferred their independence and a capitalist economic system. They were enjoying "the good life".

The Nationalists had brought with them most of the major treasures in China's museums, for which they built a handsome new home in their capital, Taipei. In addition, many members of the Peking opera and ballet companies had taken part in the strategic flight. As a consequence the best-trained singers, actors and dancers, who carried on their genres' purest conventions, were outside mainland China during Mao's Cultural Revolution and escaped its depredations.

By 1973 five schools for training in Peking opera techniques were thriving on the island, two of them attached to universities. That year the Chiang Kai-shek regime set up a National Chinese Opera

Theatre, as yet not a permanent institution. Less than six months later the Taiwanese government allocated $400,000 to send the seventy-three-member troupe abroad, its purpose propagandistic.

The company's brilliant productions offered an effective contrast to what was happening in the country of origin of this precious art form, a heritage which the dogmatic Jiang Qing was seeking to extirpate. The talented new ensemble was composed of descendants of former members of various mainland troupes, together with outstanding graduates of the five local academies. Some were culled from the professional companies already performing in Taipei. They travelled about the United States and Canada for three and a half months, making appearances in Honolulu, Los Angeles, San Francisco, Chicago, Boston, Washington, DC, New York City and Vancouver, BC. In most of these places Peking opera had never been seen before, or at least not by spectators too young to have even heard of the by now legendary Mei Lanfang. Some were enthralled, others bothered by the disconcerting falsetto vocalization and the symbolic make-up on the characters' faces, as well as the strange gestures. The dazzling costumes proved seductive.

The programme on tour included *The Monkey King, At the River Ford, The Cowherd and the Village Girl, The White Serpent* and *The Heavenly Angel*. Leading the troupe was Edward Chi-Hsien Yang.

After rounding North America, the journey was resumed in 1974 when Europe was visited. Six years later the company – now numbering sixty-three members – returned to New York at the Brooklyn Academy of Music. This was only two months after the début of the mainland's official Peking Opera troupe at Lincoln Center, which permitted a comparison of the two ensembles, a task few American dance critics were qualified to assume. Its new director was Chuang Pen-li, whose English was imperfect. His spokesman was Edward Chi-Hsien Yang, who had accompanied the troupe before. Interviewed by Eleanor Blau for the *New York Times*, he declared: "Traditional opera died on the mainland, while we prospered. We are the preservers of the tradition." He did not contend that the somewhat larger company from Beijing was meritless. "They are trying to bring back the tradition." But the Cultural Revolution had inflicted lasting harm. For one thing, the mainland singers and actors were not young; most of the leading performers were over fifty years old. Even the tumblers, whose feats were still fantastic, suffered from that fault. "I'm told the youngest is thirty-three." He remarked on technical differences in the singing and the staging of combat scenes.

This time the programme comprised excerpts from *The Battle on the Chang Pan Slope, The Universal Ring, The Drunken Court Lady* and *The Leopard*.

Even more popular than the Peking opera companies in Taiwan was a folk-opera troupe, Ko Tsai Hai, which regularly performed at festivals and was seen on television. Unique to Taiwan, as well, is the *qezixi* or "little song play", traced back to simple "work-songs", from which it developed, gradually adding more content and gaining a definable shape. Puppetry also draws amused crowds in villages and towns.

A troupe that won attention beyond Taiwan is the Cloud Gate Contemporary Dance Theatre, which combines stylized Peking opera movement with modern Western dance and ballet. Its founder, Lin Hwai-min, had been a student in New York. In 1973 he established his own company in Taipei. His aim was to retell ancient Chinese legends, with music by contemporary Taiwanese composers. He also borrowed Korean and Japanese idioms, blending these varied elements into a novel amalgam.

On the Cloud Gate Theatre's first visit to New York, the cast numbering twenty-four, they were hailed by Lin's former teacher, Martha Graham, as the "best dancers I have ever met outside the United States". The six-year-old company was on view at Brooklyn College's Walt Whitman Auditorium and had as a guest artist, Tina Yuan, who had been a leading dancer with the Alvin Ailey American Dance Theater. This tour encompassed forty American cities.

Lin Hwai-min, then thirty-two, talked to Ken Sandler of the *New York Times*. "We steal from everybody – and I'm proud to say that I'm a good thief – we only steal the best." Lin said that his was the island's only full-time professional dance group and its chief intent was "to speak to the young people of Taiwan".

Though the Cloud Gate dancers performed barefoot, Lin did not think his choreography should be categorized as belonging to "modern dance" as that term was currently used in the United States. "Our dancers are trained in the Martha Graham technique, in ballet and in Peking opera, but I have worked on new shadings and distortions. You will see some Graham – but distorted. I didn't study it long enough to be trapped by it. And I don't know enough Peking opera movement compared to Peking opera performers, so I cannot rely on that. I had to open my door and find something new."

He had rejected minimalism, the most recent trend, preferring to employ elaborate scenery and costuming. His first works were "abstract", which had pleased audiences but failed to move them. "They didn't understand it – there was no communication. They thought, 'You can do that at home, so why bother to go on stage.' I now think that such abstractions are phony. I'll guarantee what we do is something new that you have never seen. . . . Abstract dance is against the Chinese nature. The Chinese like to know what's going on – we're very meaning-oriented." Too frequently, in his opinion, Chinese artists had adopted Western concepts without questioning them. At the same time, he was inclined not to rely too much on traditional Chinese art forms.

Sandler quoted Lin:

"I don't give a damn what my creations are called – it's music and dance and entertaining, and it speaks to the audience, and it's valid. Martha Graham told me to forget about specific style and to do what you feel like doing – if you want to tell a story, do it. I believe that if you put on leotards and tights, people may sit there and say you're marvelous, but they won't embrace you." He hoped that Cloud Gate's offering would be "embraced by that part of the American audience that did not anticipate hitherto popular stereotypes about the Chinese and the stolid Peking opera style." [Nor was he seeking to startle with mere novelty.] "For two years [your work] could be sensational or scandalous. But you would eventually lose your track. So, you have to go out and know your past and present. And to stay in Taiwan and try to do imitations of Graham or Merce Cunningham would be wrong."

Lin had first fallen in love with dance, at the age of five or six, when he was taken to see the English ballet film *The Red Shoes*; it was in English, which he did not understand, nor could he as yet read the Chinese subtitles. "But you don't need to, for dance. I saw it seven or eight times." Next he was greatly impressed, at about twelve, by the José Limon Dance Company when it paid a visit to Taiwan.

His family had lived in Taiwan for centuries. His father, a government official, was outraged when young Lin voiced his wish for a dance career. At thirteen he had sneaked from home and, using his pocket money, enrolled for ballet classes. The schools in Taipei were conducted by Chinese who had trained abroad, but there was no local professional dance company that he could observe. The example of the *The Moor's Pavane*, as performed by the José Limon troupe, lingered in his memory. "I didn't believe that dance could be so expressive." But now his ambition was to be a writer. "I was an intellectual snob. I was a writer – I went to dance school and was always late, but, so what, I thought, dancers are all stupid."

He entered the University of Missouri to study journalism. A scholarship enabled him to extend his education at the University of Iowa. He found his interest had been diverted. Laughing, he told Sandler: "I spent more time in the dance studio than at the typewriter, and that was the end of a promising writer and the beginning of the tragic life of a dancer."

In New York he took classes with Martha Graham and Merce Cunningham. He regularly attended performances of the New York City Ballet. He was convinced that abstract dance, as Balanchine advocated, lacks heart. "To use dance as pure craft is wasting talent. It's against the Chinese nature to only move. . . . I gained a lot of discipline from writing fiction. I learned how to start a story, end it, put in texture. I choreographed on the typewriter." Several of his works of fiction were published.

At last he went back to Taiwan. Taking advantage of the burgeoning prosperity, he launched Cloud Gate. "You have to be fat to have art. I went home as a crusader, though nobody believed my goal was possible."

He found that Taiwanese composers were eager to reach an audience and persuaded that a dance company was a means of gaining one. Cloud Gate made its début in the autumn of 1973, to music by living Chinese composers.

You could hear the shadows of John Cage and Stockhausen in their work. Since then, we have commissioned about twenty scores, and the audience and the performers have grown up together. All of a sudden Chinese culture came together on the island, and Cloud Gate comes out of all this – traditional and modern, old and new.

We have a rich cultural heritage, but some of it needs to be examined with new insight. Our people and artists have to struggle for their identity.

In the 1950s, American culture dominated; people thought everything American was the best. Now we have confidence to ask the question "Who are you?" The work is part of the process of finding an answer. And maybe it will provide an answer to outsiders.

We ignored everything for economic growth; now we are the richest Chinese in history. It is time to look at our traditions. Our society is affluent enough to support culture.

He spoke gratefully of Martha Graham. Several years earlier, on a tour of Taiwan, she had visited the Cloud Gate's studio to watch a rehearsal. She issued favourable statements about his work to the local press. At the airport, as she was about to depart, "she poured out two to three hundred dollars in Chinese currency and said to me, 'Keep this for a rainy day.' She told me of having struggled during her early days; now she could help others."

In sum, that was how Lin's company reached the United States, portraying Chinese mythological characters using *grand jetés*, Graham contractions and the "orchid finger" technique of the Peking opera.

On the programmes were *Revenge of a Lonely Ghost*, based on a Peking opera in which the ghost of a murdered man seeks retribution; *Red Kerchief*, in which a girl about to wed has doubts about her husband-to-be; *Nu Wa*, in which a goddess rescues her children when the wrath of a god strikes down a pillar that holds up the sky; and *The Crossing of Black Water*, an episode from Lin's full-length *Legacy* – a dance-drama work in praise of the mainland Chinese who arrived on the island of Taiwan two centuries before in quest of a new life.

Having won enough plaudits on its initial visit, the Cloud Gate Dance Theatre undertook another visit to the United States in 1985. By now the troupe had thirty-five members. A showing at Manhattan College was viewed by Jack Anderson for the *New York Times*, but he lacked enthusiasm.

Although dreams are often misty in retrospect, they can be remarkably vivid while they are being dreamed. The Cloud Gate Taipei Contemporary Dance Theatre attempted to create a choreographic dream in *Dreamscape* on Tuesday night. But this dancing dream was much too misty.

Choreographed by Lin Hwai-min, the group's artistic director, and Lin Hsiu-wei to music by Hsu Po-yun, the work juxtaposed images of China's past with images of contemporary life. Thanks to the sets, slide projections and lighting designs of Lin Keh-hua, these images were always striking. But their significance was often blurred.

Dreamscape was also literally misty. The entire ninety-minute work occurred behind a scrim curtain. Scrims can work marvels. Slides may be projected on them as if they were walls. Then these walls can appear to melt and people behind them may create the illusion that they are merging with the projections. Or scrims can turn semitransparent, even growing so clear that audiences may temporarily ignore them.

But one can never totally forget their presence. And it was impossible to overlook the scrim in *Dreamscape*. It acted as a barrier between the audience and the dancers. Nothing ever happened in front of it. And the dancers behind it seemed so distant that their features at times were lost in the haze. The choreographers may have intended *Dreamscape* to be a vision of something long ago, far away and very mysterious. Instead, it was so remote as to be annoying.

The piece began with a young man in contemporary clothes standing before an imposing door that might have opened upon a palace or temple. Past and present were then contrasted.

In the views of the past, live dancers blended with slide projections of murals from the Tang Dynasty of the eighth century. Soloists, among them Du Bih-tau, swirled across the stage trailing scarves. Lin Hsiu-wei leaped about in a costume with long red sleeves. Statuesque figures resembling goddesses were carried in on the backs of crawling worshippers. The movements for all these scenes combined elements of traditional Chinese dance with Western modern dance.

The drabness of the present was conveyed in restless choreography for masses of people and ensemble passages for newspaper readers. Later, figures resembling mummies tried to remove their wrappings and the shadows of combatants loomed ominously on the scrim.

Many scenes were initially good to look at. But the choreographers were rarely able to sustain or develop their ideas. And some of their ideas remained vague. For instance, just what specifically was it about the past that they found so admirable? And what's so wrong about reading newspapers?

The company danced with dedication in both the murky and the lucid scenes. So, in their own way, did four live peacocks. Presumably, they were in the production to serve as reminders of ancient palace gardens. Whatever their symbolism may have been, they wandered at will across the stage.

Their parades were stately and at one point they created a pleasant diversion by pecking at loose pages left behind by the newspaper readers. Modern-dance theorists could easily call their comings and goings examples of aleatoric choreography.

To other critics, among them Eleanor Blau, the disparate images in *Dreamscape* were taken as representing modern China's struggle for identity. "A gangster in a black suit, for instance, murders a woman dressed in traditional Chinese robes. Mummylike figures try to free themselves from bandages or bind themselves more tightly. Live peacocks, traditional in Chinese dance, roam about the stage."

A different offering, at Lehman College, was covered for the *New York Times* by Jennifer Dunning. The evening featured the full-length *Legacy*, from which an excerpt had been shown during the company's previous tour.

> *The Legacy* is not quite dance, folk theater, martial arts or public spectacle. [It] merges the four forms in a work that, by its close, drew cheers from an initially hostile audience. Judging by that response, Cloud Gate may prove to be one of the most unusual cultural events of the season.
>
> Lin Hwai-min cites Merce Cunningham and Martha Graham as influences, and the contractions and seated pivots of the Graham technique are used with bold simplicity in *The Legacy*. Mr Lin created the piece early in his career, before he went to West Germany for additional dance training and came under the influence of Pina Bausch. But the groupings and stage patterns of *The Legacy* call to mind the way Kurt Jooss, an earlier German Expressionist choreographer, ordered his performers in *The Green Table*.
>
> *The Legacy* tells the story of the pioneering settlers of Taiwan, who by the eleventh century were crossing the stormy "Black Water," now the Straits of Taiwan, in flight from the wars and famines of southeastern China. The opening moments of the piece set the tone for the entire work, a series of twelve scenes performed to traditional and contemporary music, often eerie chants, and a text delivered in intermittent vocal improvisations by Chan Da. Three young people light incense sticks in the darkness and place them in a caldron in which incense will burn through the two-hour event. A long line of men and women, dressed in street pants and shirts, and skirts and blouses, moves solemnly across the stage in a stark processional that pays tribute to their ancestors who settled in Taiwan. Then suddenly, one by one, the performers planted about the stage remove and adjust their modern-day clothes to reveal the timeless robes of another age, in which they will depict the founding of Taiwan.
>
> This is stylized history, heroic poster art rendered in movement that surges monumentally across the stage, punctuated both by *tai chi* stances that suggest the drive to claim the earth, and by

taut, contracting bow-curves of the body that hint at such smaller-scaled emotions as love and loss. Slow-moving wedges and lines of flying, somersaulting dancers fill the stage. It is not at all a surprise when an eager young pioneer climbs an incline formed by the backs and shoulders of his fellows and gazes into the future.

The first twenty minutes or so of *The Legacy* went by with ponderous slowness. The audience grew restless early on. The piece does look like a sleekly staged folk ritual, more easily envisioned as unfolding in a village green or stadium than in a theater, although Lin Keh-hua's lighting placed it firmly in the realm of formal theater. Interestingly, there were sympathetic murmurs and chuckles from the audience by the scene called "Joy in the Wilderness," a charming encounter between a pregnant villager and her lover. Some phenomena transcend cultural differences. And when the stage exploded, at the end, in spectacular acrobatics and ribbon-dancing, there were cries of delight from a converted audience.

The company is a handsome-looking one, with a few faces that have the raw beauty of folk carvings. The simple but effective costumes were designed by Lin Ching-ru.

Competing with Lin Hwai-min for notice at home and abroad was Shanghai-born Chen Hsueh-tung who also fused Eastern and Western art forms in his stage-works. He studied dance in Taiwan and at New York University and the Juilliard School, before becoming a performer and choreographer in Taipei. In 1976 he started his own troupe of ten and staged productions at La MaMa in New York. Jennifer Dunning wrote of one of his programmes there in 1982:

Chen Hsueh-tung's dances work their way along with a thoughtfulness and conviction that persuade one to follow. Such was the case Friday at the La MaMa Annex, when Chen and Dancers presented Mr Chen's new *Longmen Mountain*, one in a series of modern-dance pieces on old China.

Set to wonderfully primeval clangor and chants composed by Li Tai-Shaing, *Longmen Mountain* takes its title from the name of a Chinese grotto of the fifth century, a cave-temple that served Silk Route travelers and Buddhist pilgrims. Mr Chen blends the elasticity and bold attack of Western modern dance with the flexed fingers and hands, for example, of ancient Chinese dance forms in work that is as much dance as drama.

A lone pilgrim enters the stage space, which comes to seem remarkably like a cave. He pays intent homage to religious hangings along the walls, probing the ground before him with his walking stick. Six travelers follow in a group, exploring the cave in an orderly fashion that looks, nonetheless, almost rambunctious beside his stillness.

The dance grows more frenzied as the six young men and women move in juxtaposed groups or break, one at a time, from the crowd. But by the end of *Longmen Mountain*, they are moving in unison, reverent creatures who have taken on something of the single pilgrim's gravity. Changes have occurred inside the cave, for them, at least.

Such changes seem to be a subject of interest to their choreographer. The previously reviewed *Voices of Yellow Dust*, which completed the program, took a group of the dead on their journey into the afterlife, accompanied by a guide from whom life ebbs as they awaken. That dance unfolds at as measured a pace as *Longmen Mountain*, but is a neater piece of choreography.

The likable company include Bambi Anderson, Wei Chen, Lynn Frieling-haus, Mr Chen, Dian Dong, Kristin Jackson and Long Phi Nguyen.

Subsequently, participating in the annual Riverside Dance Festival at the Theater of the Riverside Church in 1986, the Chen group offered *39 Chinese Attitudes* by Remy Charlip and *Mott Street* by the folk-singer Charlie Chin, along with two already familiar pieces by Mr Chen, *Egrets at Dawn* and *Spring Song*. (*Mott Street* was a reference to a clamorous thoroughfare in the heart of New York's Chinatown. The *39 Chinese Attitudes* was based on Chinese fortune-cookies that Remy Charlip had collected over the years. Widely recognized and serving here as a guest choreographer, Charlip was an American dancer, actor, playwright, designer and video artist.)

From Taiwan, too, came the Chinese Magic Revue to hold forth at New York's Promenade Theater in 1984. Its cast excelled in juggling, acrobatics, sword swallowing and baffling prestidigitation. Between East and West there was this unending interchange.

The scene in Taiwan included companies dedicated to *huaju* and many kinds of regional drama. Troupes were formed to perform them in the armed forces. Exemplifying the *huaju* is the verse-play *Wu Feng* by Yang Mu (one of the *noms de plume* of Wang Ching-hsien). The author, born in Taiwan in 1940 and educated at Tunghai University, later earned a doctoral degree in Comparative Literature from the University of California at Berkeley. In Taiwan he won regard as an experimental poet, using the name Yeh Shan. Interested in trying his hand at many different forms and styles, he eventually took up verse drama. In 1974 he accepted a post as Associate Professor of Chinese and Comparative Literature at the University of Washington.

Wu Feng (1979) is set in a mountainous region of Taiwan; the time is 1769 – "the eighth day of the eighth month, in the thirty-fourth year of the reign of Ch'ien" during the Ch'ing dynasty. "It has been over a century since Chinese of the previous dynasty invaded and colonized Taiwan." A group of tribesmen approach the home of Wu Feng, an aged man long since dwelling here, having been appointed by the Chinese government to act as a "liaison-interpreter" with the non-Han aborigines. The men have come to acquaint him with their plan of driving away a plague that has settled on their mountain slope, A-li-shan. Hunters are finding all the wild game dead or fled, the fish belly up in the streams and lakes, the fields of millet withered. To appease an offended local deity and save their starving people, they intend to offer a human sacrifice, a deed for which they feel a need to obtain Wu Feng's consent. The tribesmen debate among themselves how this revered old man will respond to their request. A storm overtakes and disperses them, their errand momentarily frustrated.

Wu Feng, who has been away, returns and learns from his young maidservant, Hsiu-ku, of the tribesmen's visit. He muses aloud at length on his role as adviser to these primitive folk. He is their teacher and physician, has brought many of them into the world.

> They chose me,
> The persistence and the honesty I stand for.
> Yes, the persistence and honesty that is basic to the conduct
> Of us educated in tradition, and which
> In this wilderness has become
> Supreme integrity – so what they've chosen
> Is an integrity common to all educated men in general,
> The interweaving of the values tradition has taught,
>> Something abstract, which because of me seems to have become
> something one can hold on to.
> But I am myself just a minute entity,
> Appearing by chance in the stream of history,
> Destined to grow and age at A-li-shan . . .
> They've chosen a man who rises and falls in a moment,
> And yet not me, not my name. Ah, Wu Feng,
> Love is their pretext for choosing you –
> But your name is your phantom
> – Just as you are the towering shadow identified with
> The educated of three thousand years.
>> How can you fail them and their
>> Love? Still less can you disgrace that lofty image –
>> Their belief, which is your belief.

He also meditates on how Time is his foe, for physical infirmities are overtaking him. He likens himself to "a leaf about to fall in the rain".

At evening the superstitious hunters come back to ask Wu Feng's permission to proffer a human head to the god who is inflicting this plague on them. Wu Feng tries to calm them, reassure them:

> He who loves us not is no god.
> The selfish and greedy are not god. You must know:
> When a ruler cheats and oppresses us,
> He'll be overthrown and driven to dust. That's what's meant
> When the ancients say, "Heaven's mandate is not to be slighted."
> If there is a god of A-li-shan,
> He must love you, protect you.
> He has no reason to be angry.

Some are convinced by his sage words, but not all the tribesmen are persuaded by them. They still mean to perform a bloody sacrifice. Wu Feng is determined to prevent this savage ritual killing. He enlists the aid of a youthful tribesman, Po-ti-lun. Between the young man and Hsiu-ku is a strong bond of affection.

The action shifts to a moonlit open field where the tribesmen gather to consult a shaman, who is somewhat besotted from too much wine. His fourteen-year-old apprentice, Yi-feng, sings and dances.

In the next scene, in the same place, Po-ti-lun and Hsiu-ku are alone and avow their love for each other. She also confesses her concern about Wu Feng and the fate of their plague-stricken people. The tribesmen, entering, find fault with Po-ti-lun for adhering so closely to Wu Feng instead of joining them in their search for a human sacrifice. They distrust him. Po-ti-lun is deeply torn between his two loyalties, to his master Wu Feng and to the tribe. Hsiu-ku admires his courage in defying the ruthless hunters.

Very early the next morning Wu Feng ponders his dilemma. He engages in metaphysical discourse with Hsiu-ku; though only eighteen, she apparently has a precocious intellect that enables her to express her concepts in bright poetic images. In a very long soliloquy Wu Feng recalls personal events and how his thoughts about life were gradually formed. His choice was to experience the world at first hand rather than dwell in a realm of quiet scholarly pursuits.

At noon the hunters arrive with a last plea for Wu Feng's approval. He upbraids them but then seems to yield, telling them that they should lie in ambush to await the passing of a rider in a red cap and cloak. "You can shoot him, kill him, and take his head. Offer that to the rain god of A-li-shan." Screaming excitedly, the tribesmen depart. Hsiu-ku and Po-ti-lun realize that Wu Feng is proposing to be the victim; they try to dissuade him, but to no avail. Young Po-ti-lun is ready to take his master's place and die, but Wu Feng says:

> I'm an aging mortal. My life
> Drifts like the puffs of reed catkins,
> About to fall and perish in the heavy rain.
> A spark could still set me aflame, and
> In burning I should give light to the next generation.
> The light I emit may be short-lived,
> But so am I short-lived. Po-ti-lun,
> You must live on for A-li-shan, and
> For the action Wu Feng has chosen, prove to your tribe
> That in you is my real life.

Po-ti-lun and Hsiu-ku bitterly lament Wu Feng's decision. Briefly they contemplate suicide but desist.

> HSIU-KU: Your sacrifice and mine would only prevent your regret and mine. A-li-shan will think that we're lambs led along to death by Wu Feng.
> PO-TI-LUN: Oh Wu Feng, you say that you aren't God, but mortal. Yet being mortal, how can you foretell if sacrifice is avoidable or not?

In the final scene Hsiu-ku and Po-ti-lun frenziedly try to prevent the ambush, but the tribesmen refuse to believe the couple's warning that the red-garbed rider is to be Wu Feng. They insist that no mortal man would selflessly will his own death. As arrows fly from the bows, the rider falls from his horse. His identity is announced by the boy, Yi-feng, who has been near by dancing and singing and has been a witness to the deed.

A fierce storm erupts. The tribesmen are appalled and panic-stricken; they toss away their weapons. They believe that the storm-god himself is mourning the great-spirited Wu Feng.

When the lashing wind and rain abate, the people hail Wu Feng as a god. They vow to follow a path of peace, honouring his memory. Hsiu-ku cries:

We open our arms like a half moon,
To show that we yearn for a union in love.

All join her saying:

We open our arms,
We yearn,
We love.

[Translation: Cissie Kwok and Wu Yang]

Wu Feng (Wu Yuan-hui, 1699–1769) was an actual person. From his birthplace, Fukian province, he was brought as a child to Taiwan by his father, who stayed on as a trader in the hilly region encircling A-li-shan. Wu Feng's martyrdom, a historical fact, led to his later deification as "the spirit of A-li-shan". Yang Mu's picture of the folk-ways of eighteenth-century Taiwan is credited with being highly authentic, testimony to the author's exemplary research.

Wu Feng revolves in part around the vexing question of "national identity", a problem besetting many Taiwanese, young and old: was their first loyalty owed to China, to which they laid claim, or to their tentative island "nation"? That is paralleled to the dilemma of youthful Po-ti-lun. Through forty years of occupation and rule by the Japanese, and another fifty years under the usurping Chiang Kai-shek forces, corruption had often been too prevalent. Wu Feng is a model of the consistently upright statesman, a figure to emulate, and to whom honour is certainly due. The urgent need to educate the peasantry and dispel superstition is also voiced in Wu Feng's soliloquies, and the obligation of the island's upper class to accept responsibility for doing this is another of the many "messages" implicit and sometimes explicit in the script, in which ultimate self-sacrifice and great dedication are glorified. Finally, by looking back at Taiwan's past and exploiting its folk-lore, native dance and song, Yang Mu was seeking to imbue in the Taiwanese a feeling that the island has its own, unique history and literature and is not dependent on the mainland's past and culture.

As the decades went by, the Nationalists, who had exerted some repression in governing the Formosans, slowly relaxed it and granted them a share in the island's politics, as Taiwan's much-vaunted "democracy" became ever more real.

Dolby observes: "Uncertainty has always been a prominent feature of the life of Taiwan, whether in its prodigious economic development or its often painful relationships with other nations. Yang Mu wrote *Wu Feng* after a decade of debate on the role of writers and artists in Taiwan and in the midst of complex social and political ferment. In response the play recalls a period of stress some two centuries before in the far simpler, but much starker, circumstances of a community of Taiwan aborigines inhabiting the region of Taiwan's central landmark, Mount A-li, or A-li-shan. Here the natives of Taiwan and their mentor Wu Feng, son of a Chinese trader who emigrated to the island, struggle with the question of their threatened extinction, what it signifies, whether they have any control over their fate, and how, whatever their fate may be, they should face it."

He pays tribute to Yang Mu's originality, his "ambitious use of verse in a style of his own creation. A modernist poet, he renders the past of his actions, images, and symbols, with a sense of irony and tension. . . . Yet Yang Mu's creation, for all its modernism, evokes the significance of an event distinctly rooted in the cultures of Taiwan and China and their point of mutual contact. *Wu Feng* thus may be taken as representative of the strong currents, cosmopolitan and provincial, which have exercised a complex influence on writers of Taiwan."

Semi-professional Peking and Kunqu opera companies are found wherever overseas Chinese have colonies of substantial size, as in Singapore, Malaysia, San Francisco and London. The *huaju* movement flourishes is such places, too, with playwrights keeping abreast of ever-changing times and mores. In New York City's large Chinatown a Taipei Theater provides a variety of classics and modern works. There is also a Pan-Asian Theater group whose scope is wider. In these colonies the hostility and division between Taiwanese and mainland Chinese persist.

17

KOREA: CHANGING

Western-style drama reached Korea early in the twentieth century as a consequence of the return from a ten-year political exile in Japan of the novelist and playwright Yi In-Jig (1861–1916). Preceding his arrival a new kind of entertainment had developed in his homeland, taking its place alongside the classic Sandae (Mask Drama), the traditional puppet plays, acrobatic displays, clowning, and ritualistic and folk dances. This was the Gu-gug, created in the mid-nineteenth century by Sin Chì-ho (1812–84). Combining music and dramatic action, he made use of plots from familiar Korean tales, such as the *Chunhyang*, *Simchŏng* and *Jŏg-byŏg*. According to John Kardoss, from whose *An Outline History of Korean Drama* I must freely borrow, Sin had most likely been inspired by the *pansori*, a genre of narrative song with drum accompaniment enacted "mainly by descendants of witches and sorceresses living in the southern provinces". Such series of monologue recitatives might go on for three or four hours, the lone performer assuming various roles, while frequently improvising. Sin composed new narrative songs to be delivered by Gwangde, or groups of singers, thereby creating another type of classic musical drama. The singers interpreted their roles with body language, gestures and broad facial expressions. Such performances, popular for a century, were staged outdoors on impermanent platforms and had no scenic investiture: they might be staged on a hillside or occupy the centre of a village square.

While in Japan, Yi In-Jig, a political reformer as well as a literary man, was a close observer of the Westernizing tendencies there. He attended revolutionary plays put on by Sudo Sadanori and Kawakami Otojiro, who were introducing social messages into the transitional Shimpa theatre. Back in Korea, Yi In-Jig was eager to emulate them.

In 1902, as mentioned in an earlier chapter, Seoul had its first modern playhouse: it was erected in connection with the celebration of the fortieth anniversary of the coronation of King Go-jong and resembled a small amphitheatre. Six years later, in 1908, the Wŏngag-Sa, or National Theatre, was inaugurated, and with it an era borrowing Westernized stagecraft. At first the Wŏngag-Sa presented Gwangde singers and various sorts of "Old Plays", officially sponsored dancing girls, comic storytellers. Stage props were few, and the background might be a simple white curtain. However, Yi In-Jig was named its manager, and four months after the theatre's opening he produced there *Un Sege (The Silver World)*, a dramatization of one of his novels, bringing Occidental-like dramaturgy to his country. His aim was didactic, to communicate his progressive ideas to audiences. The play is about a youth and his sister, Ok-nam and Ok-sun, who go as students to America. Sojourning for five years in a hotel, they lecture each other at length about the urgent need for economic and social innovations in their distant homeland.

The Plum in the Snow (1909), Yi In-Jig's second script, is derived from a novel by Suehiro Tetsujo (1885). In fifteen scenes, episodic in the fashion of Chinese drama that long influenced its Korean counterpart, it conveys more reformist ideas. Versatile, Yi In-Jig wrote, directed plays and managed the Wŏngag-Sa with notable competence.

At the same time the Hyŏblyul Sa, an acting group, was going about the country offering a broad variety, recitals of classical music and mask plays, and circus acts. This troupe continued its presentations and tours until 1914.

By 1911 the Wŏngag-Sa had competition in Seoul. Yim Sŏng-Gŭ (1887–1921) and fellow actors formed a company, Hyŏgsin-Dan (Reform Society), taking possession first of the Ŏsŏng-Zsa and later the Dansong-Sa theatres. They opened with *Heavenly Punishment for the Unfilial*, a translated Shimpa script. Successive programmes were made up of melodramas such as *The Law of Law*, *The Murder of the Sworn Brother* and *The Pistol Robber*. Soon a stage work of this kind, a romantic tale with a handsome hero and beautiful heroine, was tagged a Sinpa Yŏn-gŭg, or "New Style Play". Appealing to less sophisticated spectators, the company stayed in existence for nine years, breaking up early in 1920, not long before Yim Sŏng-Gŭ's death in late 1921. From the outset the troupe was greeted with standing ovations, though its offerings usually lacked seriousness and taste.

Seoul had yet another modern theatre, the Gwangmu-De, built in 1912 by Bag Sung-Pil; it offered a choice of Old Plays and New Style dramas.

After studying the burgeoning Western-style drama in Japan, the playwright Yun Beg-Nam (1888–1954) followed Yi In-Jig's example, returning to his homeland to assemble an acting troupe, the Munsu-Sŏng in 1912. The company's first venture, at the Wŏngag-Sa Theatre, was *The Cuckoo*, adapted from the Japanese. Drawing further on the Shimpa repertory, the Munsu-Sŏng put on *Buryo-gwi, Changhan Mong (Deep Sorrow Dream)*, by Ozaki Koyo, and *The Golden Demon* (1897), which went on to win great popularity. Another of its presentations was *My Sin*, a favourite on the Shimpa stage. But the Munsu-Sŏng also accepted original scripts, among them *The Youth*, by Cho Il-Chě in collaboration with Lee Ha-Mong. Eventually the Munsu-Sŏng combined with the Yuil-Dan (the Only Society), a group organized by Yi-Gi-se that performed in the Yŏhŭng-Sa Theatre. A new name was chosen after the merger, Yesŏng-Zwa (Art Star Seats). This company brought forth *Sang-Ognu* (*Double Jade Tears*), indebted to a Korean novel by an unknown author, as well as a dramatization of Tolstoy's *Resurrection*. The group also staged *The Lighthouse Keeper* and other works, but its career was short-lived.

Smaller drama groups began to proliferate, among them Yi Gi-Se's Munye-Dan (Literary Society); Kim Do San's Singŭg-Zwa (New Play Seats); and Kim So-Rang's Chuisong-Jwa (Gathered Star Seats). They did not prosper. An exception was the Chuisong-Jwa, which lasted until 1929, boasting a thirteen-year history, mostly spent on tours through the provinces.

Korean students in Japan formed the Drama Arts Association (1921) and during their school recesses took plays on travels around their country. The enterprising members of this group were Hong Hĕ-Song and Kim Su-San, who functioned as producers; Zo Po-Sŏg, Ma He-Song and Yu Czun-Sob as adapters. Their repertory included a sentimental three-act melodrama, *Kim Yong-Il*, by Cho Myong-Hi; *The Last Handshake*, by Hong Nan-Pa, which had a theme not unlike that of Ibsen's *A Doll's House*; and Lord Dunsany's pseudo-mystical *The Glittering Gate*, translated into Korean by Kim Su-San. Though the Drama Arts Association did not flourish long, Kardoss attributes to it a considerable influence on the new native theatre. Among the troupe's other accomplishments, it set standards for staging that the commercial companies soon felt obliged to match.

After graduating from the Tokyo Academy of Arts, where he studied to be an actor, Hyon Chul (1891–1965) came home and established the Academy of Arts. Three years later it evolved into the Actor's Studio which attracted notice by producing as experiments Ibsen's *A Doll's House* and two farcical one-acters by Chekhov, *The Proposal* and *The Bear*. Learned and multi-talented, Hyon Chul rendered *Hamlet* into Korean, working in turn with a Japanese version of the Shakespearian tragedy.

Not dissuaded by the failure of the Munsu-Sŏng, which he had headed, Yun Beg-Nam formed the Minzung-Gugdan (Popular Drama Society) and produced a pair of scripts from his own hand (1922), *The Eternal Wife* and *Fate*. Similarly, Yi Gi-Se, who had led the Munye-Dan, now reappeared with the Yesul-Hyophoe (Art Association) which enacted *The Tears of Hope*. But neither of these groups fared well; they toured for a while, then quickly vanished.

A considerable stir was aroused by the Twŏl-Hoe (rendered into English by some as the Earth and Moon Society, and by others as the Saturday-Monday Society), housed in the Gwangmŭ-De Theatre. In 1923 it mounted *Kilsik*, in conjunction with Kim Gi-zin, a critic; Kim Bogzin, an artist; and Yi Sŏ-Gu and Kim Ŏl-Han, a pair of journalists. This ambitious group put on works by Chekhov, Tolstoy, Shaw and other European realists. Kardoss speaks highly of the artistic standards of the Twŏl-Hoe productions, which were looked upon as remarkable for that day. Korean theatre was slowly outgrowing the New Style plays due to the intrusion and pressure of modern Western drama. Twŏl-Hoe is considered to have contributed vitally to this development. For a half-dozen years, 1925 to 1931, the troupe travelled about the country. Kardoss praises it for having "pioneered the way for Sin-Gug, or the New Drama period of the 1930s. . . . It sought to revolutionize dramatic form and technique without diminishing the play's literary values." The hope of the enterprise was to oust the Japanese Sinpa that by now had become ascendant on Seoul's stages.

An essay in the *Handbook of Korea* lends weight to Kardoss's claim:

Amateurs though its members were, the Saturday-Monday Society surpassed any other professional group with its high artistic standards and the introduction of "realistic" themes. The society's repertoire consisted mostly of original works written by its own members, but it also included translations and adaptations of world masterpieces. Popular approval was so lasting that in the ten years of its existence, it presented a total of eighty-seven works. Gradually it acquired the traits of a more commercial theater; though still led by Bag Sŭn-Hŭi, it underwent changes of membership. Popular works were revived, a signal that the company sought to play safe by offering long-time favorites. In 1932, as its repute increasingly lost lustre, it adopted a new name, Teyang (the Sun). But one could say that its day was over.

Courageously, after the demise of his Munsu-Sŏng, Yun Beg-Nam persisted in his efforts to capture a public by assembling still another group, the Manpoe-Hoe (Ten Thousand Waves Society). He signed up most of Korea's best-known players and staged two historical pieces by Victor Hugo, *Louis the Sixteenth* – his play – and from another source a dramatization of his epic novel *Les Misérables*, but the Manpoe-Hoe, too, had a brief life.

The Sanyuhwa-Hoe (Mountain Flowers Society) marked the end of the 1920s with a production of Hong No-Nag's *The Heart of One's Native Soil* (1929), and two other acting companies were launched that same year; but, like so many of other aspiring groups, it soon disappeared.

In Tokyo, Hong Ne-Song had established himself as a skilled actor with the Tsukiji Little Theatre. In 1929, home in Seoul, he gathered a company calling itself the Sinhŭng-Gŭgzang (Newly Risen Theatre); it was on stage a year later with a Korean adaptation of a Chinese drama.

As in Japan, Marxism had begun to infiltrate the performing arts. This led to the formation of the Koreana Artista Proleta Federation (Federation of Korean Proletarian Art, most often spoken of as KAPF) which got started in 1925; by 1930 it had organized an acting wing. Its members attempted to stage a radical play, *Hammer* (1930), in Fengian but were prevented by police at the behest of government censors. Undeterred, the group undertook rehearsals of a second revolutionary work, *The General Strike in Fengian*, only to be stopped again by the putative authorities (at this time, of course, Korea was under rigid Japanese control). The KAPF responded by setting up the players as an autonomous unit. Before long, similar Marxist drama groups appeared in various parts of the peninsula. Watchful officials, convinced that these "artists" were more interested in spreading Communist propaganda than encouraging theatre, arrested and gaoled all members of the KAPF in 1930. The Marxists, flexible as always, achieved another metamorphosis, establishing in the capital a professional acting company, the Seoul-Yen-Pol-Kijan (Seoul Blue Shirts) a mere year later. Seoul Blue Shirts announced forthcoming productions of left-oriented scripts such as Upton Sinclair's *The Thief* and Lou Marten's *The Miners*, as well as plays by dedicated Japanese comrades: Murayama's *All Along the Line*, Susaki's *Wheelbarrow*, Fujimori's *What Made Her Do That?*, these, too, were prohibited. (Their authors, overseas, had little fear of retaliation.)

Like their fervent counterparts in Tokyo, the Korean Marxists were not prepared to capitulate. Two more companies were set up in Seoul in 1931, the Megaphone and the New Theatrical Construction Group; the Megaphone troupe, moving quickly, was able to put on at least one play; New Construction planned several works by Korean dramatists. In time the Megaphone cut its ties with the orthodox leftists and, asserting its independence, devoted its talents to works merely espousing a socially progressive outlook. With these they toured extensively.

Proceeding apart from the aggressive Communists, and with a different purpose, an actor, Hong He-Sūng (1893–1957), and a writer, Yu Chi-Jin (1905–74), promoted Korea's first Drama-Film Exhibition in 1931. A month later they proclaimed the founding of a Society for Research in Dramatic Art; they did this in cooperation with students interested in foreign literature. To improve performance skills, the society arranged for actors to be entered and trained in an Academy of Dramatic Arts, and before the year's end the hopeful participants had established the helpful Shilbŏm-Mudĕ (Experimental Stage).

A pair of influential newspapers, the *Donga Il-bo* and *Chun Il-bo*, was also seeking to encourage native dramatists. They financed annual literary contests open to students. The prize-giving led to the discovery and presentation of several promising new plays, among them *The Country Teacher* by Yi Gwang-Nĕ, *The Clay Wall* by Han Tĕ-Dong and *The Floating People* by Kim Sŭng U. All the while, interest in drama was constantly rising in schools.

As a start, the Shilbŏm-Mudĕ proffered a series of works by European dramatists (1932). A glance at the initial list reveals that they selected Gogol's *Inspector General*, Chekhov's *Cherry Orchard* and Ibsen's *Doll's House*, along with lesser works such as Sir Henry Irving's *The Lover* and Lady Gregory's *The Prison Gate* – all worthy choices. Shakespeare was attempted, too, with a production of *The Merchant of Venice*. Of more consequence, however, the troupe immediately sought scripts by Koreans. The first to be accepted was *Tomag* (*The Earthen Hut*; 1933) by Yu Chi-Jin, co-founder of the company; it was directed by his colleague, Hong He-Sŭng .

The play, with considerable echoes of Ibsen, centres on a small, close-knit family, peasants living in an earthen hut, which one of the characters, Myong-So, refers to as a "grave". Their hopes of rescue from their lowly state revolve about a son who left for Japan seven years earlier. They are stirred from a humble but safe daily routine when word is brought to them of a package waiting at the post office. Eagerly they hasten there, but tragically the box holds not the gifts they happily expect but instead their long-absent son's ashes. A patriotic martyr, he has given his life in Japan as an activist in the struggle for Korean freedom.

Other and earlier scripts by Yu Chi-Jin include *The Clay House* and *The Scene of a Village Where the Willow Tree Stands*, both of which attack topical social injustices. A comedy with a rural setting, *The Cow*, depicts the vital role of this creature in the fortunes of poor farmers. *The Waiting Wife* is a dramatization of a historical novel.

The Experimental Stage continued until 1938, when official pressure brought its ambitious mission to a halt.

The picture of this period is exceedingly crowded, and one must depend on Kardoss for a description of it; his is virtually the only detailed historical survey as yet accessible to English readers. "Ever since the foundation of the Wongag-Sa, theatrical companies have been formed, merged, re-formed, split up, dissolved and re-established, thus enriching the nation culturally while impoverishing themselves financially."

After a run of some years, the Society for Research in Dramatic Art was disbanded, though its influence lingered. Finally it was resurrected under a fresh name, Gŭgyŏn-Zwa (Drama Research Seats). Joining it were writers who afterwards were to be recognized as Korea's literary and theatre élite. They embraced Western stagecraft. Two other major groups, Nangman-Zwa (Romantic Seats) and Chung-ang Mide (Central Stage) arrived.

A number of eminent novelists lent their gifts to the stage, some of them displaying an innate sense of drama. Among them were Yi Mu-Yong, who provided the satirical *The Daydreamers* and *Recuperation Without Payment*; Che Man-Sig, who created *The Feast Day* and *I Wish I Were a Christian*; Kim Yong-Su, who fashioned *The Fault*; and Song Yong, who composed *The Mountain People* and *The New Chairman of the Board*.

Kardoss estimated that by the mid-1930s, just preceding the Second World War, Korea boasted about 100 commercial and avant-garde troupes, assuring a broad variety of programmes: New Style Plays, New Dramas, and works that mingled elements of Sinpa and Singŭg. He designated this decade as the "golden period in Korean theatre history". By contrast, the next phase – the 1940s, which saw the outbreak of the world conflict – was "the dark age of the nation's cultural life".

Launching their invasion of China, the Japanese militarists tightened their control of Korea and its rebellious populace. One means for doing this was by indirectly fostering the Chosun Theatre Association (1940). Two years later it became the Chosun Cultural Theatre Association, which brought together sixteen acting troupes, all of which had governmental approval. (Chosun is another name for Korea.) Annual contests were held among these sixteen officially sanctioned companies, enabling the censors to supervise them more closely. Eleven musical groups were organized in much the same way.

The Gŭgyŏn-Zwa was succeeded by a new troupe, the Hyŏnde Gŭzgang (Modern Theatre), whose manager was the writer–producer Yu Chi Hub. He was associated in the enterprise with Ham De-Hun, a novelist and critic, and Zu Yŏng-Sob, also a producer. Other groups entered the field: Gŭgdan Gŏhyob (Gohyob Dramatic Society), and the Gŭgdan Arang (Arang Dramatic Society), which enlisted the talents of such playwrights as Bag Yŏng-Ho, Yim Sŏn-Gyu, Kim Tĕ-zin and Sŏng Yong. The director–producer An Yong-Il, too, was involved in these productions.

In Seoul the Cultural Theatre Association's contests took place at the Bumin-Gwan (Citizens' Hall). Regular productions were given in the capital's playhouses, chiefly the Myŏngczi-Zwa, the Hwang-gŭm-Zwa and Yagczo-Gŭgzang, the best choices for musical presentations; while dramas were staged at the smaller Dong-yang-Gŭgzang or at the Oriental Theatre, the latter dependent on assistance from the Youth Seats and the Dramatic Party Star Group.

Despite repression by the government, anxious to discourage sentiment for Korean independence, several outstanding plays were written and produced: Yu-Chi-Jin's *The Amur River*, Yim Sŏn-Gyu's *The Village of Camellia* and Kim Te-Jin's *Genghis Khan*. This took courage, as the government was determined to eliminate a native culture.

Traversing the peninsula, some companies instilled a love of theatre-going among people in outlying regions. But apart from the few exceptions mentioned, Korean drama was at a standstill, with scarcely any signs of forward development.

At the war's end the political situation in Korea was chaotic; the disorder was reflected in the theatre. As Kardoss puts it, "After forty years of repressing of every form of Korean national art, the enthusiasm of its theatre artists was boundless. But, instead of joining forces to solve the problems and improve the standards of the Korean stage, Leftists and Rightists wasted their time and energy indulging in ideological discussions."

Korea was finally liberated from forty years of oppressive Japanese rule but unhappily divided, the larger, southern part nominally democratic, the smaller, northern area taken over by a totalitarian Communist regime, the two confronting each other with fierce hostility and nervous suspicion. In the south, now known as the Republic of Korea, there was also a plethora of conflicting ideologies. The noise of the arguments between left and right could be heard in the theatre. This led to such plays as Yu Chi-Jin's *The Fatherland* and *The Self-Beating Drum*; O Yŏng-Jin's *His Excellency Yi Chung Sĕng* and *The Wedding Day*; Chin U-Chon's *Brain Surgery*; Kim Yong-Su's *The Artery*; Kim Chin-Su's *The Cosmos* and *The Playground*; in sum representing a variety of perspectives on political and social affairs. Most of the scripts expressed hope that Korea, at last emancipated from colonial domination, could now look to a much brighter future.

In 1950 the newly constituted southern Korean government named a committee to set up and oversee a National Theatre. The Bumin-Gwam (formerly the Citizens' Hall), now Seoul's largest play-house, was chosen as its site, and Yu Chi-Jin and his long-time colleague So Hang-Sŏg gathered together a troupe to work in it. *Won Sul-Lang*, by Yu Chi-Jin himself, was the first presentation. The second was a production of *The Thunderstorm*, by the famed Chinese dramatist Cao Yu. The two presentations won enthusiastic applause. Korea was the first Asian country to have a national theatre.

In addition, another organization, the Sin-gŭg Hyŏphoe (Council of New Drama), was established by the Nationalists (1950), and led to the formation of the Shinhyop Theatrical Group, affiliated with the National Theatre and intended to serve young playwrights.

Unfortunately, a few months later the Communists of North Korea invaded the Republic seeking to unite the two sections of the country, and a destructive conflict erupted. President Harry Truman sent a large American force, together with troops contributed by several other members of the United Nations, in what was called a "police action" but was in dire fact a full-scale war that raged up and down the peninsula for three years, spreading great misery and devastation. Douglas MacArthur finally scored an amazing strike by landing his men at Inchon behind the North Korean lines, but soon afterwards suffered a costly setback when the Chinese Communists, fearing the advance of American troops to their border, entered the conflict with a surprise incursion near the icy Chosin Reservoir. Finally, a truce was signed in 1953, and prisoners exchanged, leaving the border at the 38th Parallel between North and South exactly where it had been before but now guarded on either side of a demilitarized zone by permanent contingents of Korean and American soldiers. The tension between the two Korean nations remained high.

The North Korean sweep towards Seoul had caused the National Theatre to flee to Taegu, its activities interrupted. The Shinhyop Theatrical Group, under the sponsorship of the Ministry of Defence and the Air Force, took on the task of entertaining South Korean soldiers. The Shinhyop also performed for the public in Taegu and Pusan. Since there were no films, the theatre provided some in the harassed populace with their only respite from the initial news of defeat and loss of lives.

Throughout these years of turmoil a few Korean playwrights continued to turn out scripts. The ever-resourceful Yu Chi-Jin wrote *I Will Be a Human, Too*, both a plea for humanitarianism and a diatribe against the "anthill-like existence" that the victorious Communists would certainly impose on the subjugated Southerners. Similar dramas were provided by Kim Chin-su, Kim Yong-Su and Han No-dan, respectively *Out of the Waste*, *Seoul Under the Reds* and *War and Flowers*.

I Will Be a Human, Too is about a North Korean composer. War has not yet broken out. He is plagued with questions about the Communist society in which he is trapped. Frustrated, he goes to Seoul to test a new way of life. Kardoss: "The well-constructed play's theme is the revolt of an individual against forced regimentation of man's body and soul by the Marxists."

After the war, while still in Taegu, the Shinhyop troupe staged Yun Bĕg-Nam's *A Field of Flowers* (1953).

In 1957 the National Theatre returned to Seoul, as did the Shinhyop, which was now considered to be the only acting ensemble whose techniques came close to matching those on Western stages.

The Korean Research Institute for Dramatic Arts took the lead again, helping to organize the Drama Centre as a headquarters and rallying point of major theatre activities. Yu Chi-Jin, now recognized as his country's foremost playwright, was appointed its director. The Centre's initial venture was a production of *Hamlet*, followed by Eugene O'Neill's *Long Day's Journey Into Night*, the Heyward–Gershwin folk-opera *Porgy and Bess*, and the indefatigable Yu Chi-Jin's *The Han Flows*.

Post-war Seoul, entering upon a prolonged period of prosperity, was very soon enlivened by a broad range of dramas, ballets, operas and concerts. New playwrights appeared, among them Choe Pŏm-Sug, author of *The Dream City*; Im Hi-Jě, creator of *The Engine Which Lives on Flower Petals*; as well as O Sang-Wŏn, admired for *The Ignored Ones*. Others of note were Ha Yu-Sang, for *Free Marriage*; Gim Hong-Gon, for *The Well*; and Yi Yŏng-Chan, for *The Family*. Gang Mun-Sun excelled with his *The Eclipse of Life*.

Students in various places were recovering their interest in drama. This was particularly true on the campuses of Seoul National, Korea and Yonsei universities. One result was the founding in 1959 of the Experimental Theatre Group, which had a considerable impact on other troupes.

Seoul was treated to such classic foreign fare as Shakespeare's *Macbeth* and *Othello*, Schiller's *William Tell*, Georg Büchner's *Wozzeck*, Rostand's *Cyrano de Bergerac* and Chekov's *The Anniversary*, along with contemporary works encompassing George Bernard Shaw's *Arms and the Man*, Maxwell Anderson's *Winterset*, Eugene O'Neill's *Desire Under the Elms*, Sidney Kingsley's *Men in White*, Tennessee Williams's *A Streetcar Named Desire*, Jean-Paul Sartre's *Red Gloves*, Arthur Laurents's *Home of the Brave*, Frederick Knott's *Dial "M" for Murder*, and even a dramatization of Margaret Mitchell's novel *Gone with the Wind*.

That does not exhaust the roster of playwrights from abroad with whose dramas Koreans became familiar; one could add Thornton Wilder, William Inge, Edward Albee, John Osborne, Samuel Beckett, Jean Anouilh, Federico Garcia Lorca. All influenced local stage-writers in larger or lesser measure. The Korean National Centre of International Theatre assisted in cultural exchange programmes.

Kardoss: "The dramas were presented in Korean from texts translated by Korean scholars. Décor and general approach to the productions were determined by the origin of the play rather than by conventional staging. There were a number of professional stage designers in Korea, the best known of whom was Pak Sock In, whose costume designs were tasteful and imaginative."

The Drama Centre resounded with controversy over ideas about the art of theatre, what approaches to writing and staging were best, especially between the older and more youthful members. In 1963 several of the more Western-minded and younger playwrights and actors split off to form the Minjung (or Populace) Theatrical Group. They launched themselves with Felician Marceau's *The Egg*, garnering success by the use of an unfamiliar stage technique. Turning away from traditional Korean dramas, they continued to offer Western-style scripts. With help from the Asia Foundation they mounted Ionesco's *The Bald Soprano* and Guitry's *Villa for Sale*.

The same year brought another entrant, the Sanha Theatrical Group, which put on Im Hi-Jĕ's *Unwanted Men* and Bŏu-Sŏg's *A House with a Blue Roof*. Also setting out to offer serious works, according to the *Handbook of Korea*, were the Yo In (or Women) Group, the Cha Yu (or Freedom) Group, the Ka Kyo (or Bridge) Group, and the Kwan Chang (or Plaza) Group, which assured that stages in Seoul and the provinces were as crowded as ever. What hindered them, however, was the growing popularity of films, which diverted talent to the more lucrative medium and limited the size of audiences.

As a consequence, the country's little theatre movements were of prime importance. The plays there tended to be of higher quality than when commercial producers had to worry about meeting the expenses of large houses and emphasized offerings of instant broad appeal. The energetic members of the Minjung, Sanha and Experimental Groups were largely college-graduated and quite literate. The theatre-goers, too, were more knowledgeable. Kardoss: "Cheap though effective melodramas were no longer popular on Korean stages. Trite and slipshod productions were no longer put on, for 'trained' audiences demonstrated their dislike by being conspicuously absent."

An instance of how Korea now felt itself a part of world theatre was the celebration in 1964 of Shakespeare's 400th birthday. In cooperation with the National Theatre, now headed by Yoon Kil-Koo and Lee Hae-Rang, several of the small theatre groups joined in a month-long festival of producing six of the Bard's plays, *As You Like It*, *Antony and Cleopatra*, *King Lear*, *The Merchant of Venice*, *Othello* and *The Taming of the Shrew*.

Two interesting plays of this period were Han Ro-Dan's *Interchange* and Cha Bŏm-Sŏg's *Tropical Fish*. Conventionally structured, like a work by Yu Chi-Jin, *Interchange* portrays a family dwelling in a seaside villa. The characters, doomed by fate, are delineated in Freudian terms, their lives affected "by the interchange of Oedipus and Electra complexes". *Tropical Fish* treats of a widespread social problem, racial prejudice. The eldest son, who has been studying in the United States, comes home to his family with a black girl. In the face of opposition he insists that he will have her for his wife; his demands lead to a tragic climax.

Singled out for his fine scripts was Oh Yŏng-Jin, though his output was comparatively small. *A Woman Diver Goes Ashore* is about a quarrel over the distribution of an estate worth millions. The feuding, confusion and scheming among the heirs drive a woman to the edge of madness. Oh Yŏng-Jin flays his people's mercenary impulses, along with the materialistic value of a contemporary society in which, as he saw it, the "purity of human nature" was violated.

Few Korean playwrights have shone by evoking laughter, which makes the accomplishments of Lee Gun-Sam quite rare. What is more, his work belongs in the category of thoughtful comedy. In *Lion's Share, Sir* a hitherto naïve clerk recognizes that behaving and speaking sensibly have got him nowhere. He alters his pattern of conduct and succeeds beyond his dreams, only to realize that he is still unhappy.

A representative of the avant-garde, Kim Eui-Kyung, provoked a considerable debate in literary and theatrical circles with *Deeper Are the Roots*, originally called *Song of Reeds*, a grim picture of the pathetic youth of a prostitute. Kardoss quotes the critic Lim Young-Woong: "The play is unique in that it expresses the writer's own protests against reality by means of bringing forth persons whom he conceives into the society which he conceives without fixing any specific society and time."

Kim Ki-Pal proved himself to be especially deft at adapting novels to the stage. An example is *The Martyred*, taken from a best-selling book of the same title by Richard E. Kim. It raises the question of how, amid the horrors of war, God's purpose is to be understood. In his dramatization, Kim Ki-Pal resorts to a magic lantern, captions and films. Another successful adaptation, *Kiwi*, by Kim Eui-Kyung, drawn from a short story by Lee On-Yong, projects the Job-like tribulations of a former air force pilot. From his earliest days the hero's life has been filled with defeats and unhappiness. He is put forward as "the tragic image of modern man".

A look at the Drama Centre's work was afforded Manhattan theatre-goers in 1977 when the off-Broadway La MaMa Annex was host to a seventeen-member troupe from Seoul enacting a very unusual *Hamlet*. The visit was funded by the *Joong-Ang Daily News* and the Tong-Yang Radio. Possibly because it anticipated a language barrier, the *New York Times* sent Jennifer Dunning, a dance critic, rather than a drama reviewer. Her account: "This is a *Hamlet* with a difference. It may be the first version, for instance, to replace swordplay with the martial arts and the flourish of trumpets with the murmur of a bamboo flute called the *pili*. And the words of Prince Hamyul's venerable soliloquies will be unintelligible to Western audiences. That is because the lines are delivered in Korean."

One of the company's directors, Min-soo Ahn, who accompanied the acting troupe, was interviewed by Ms Dunning. He said that it was the first time any drama ensemble had appeared outside his homeland in the seventy-year history of Korean modern theatre. He explained that Shakespearian drama was a staple there and that *Hamlet* was often staged by his fellow-countrymen, as well as *King Lear* and *Macbeth*. "But this production would probably seem novel to most Koreans, too. Though the troupe does not consider itself avant-garde, it has something of a reputation in Seoul for experimentation." When formed in 1968 as a repertory company, its core was young Korean artists who had been exposed to theatrical training in the United States. "They wanted to find a new theatre form, blending traditional elements in Korean arts and what they had learned of Western experimental theatre into a universal art form." This *Hamlet* sought to add Korean folk-theatre components to Shakespeare, using Oriental concepts of time and space. "This adaptation of *Hamlet* is a composite. We've kept a quarter of the dialogue, including all the major speeches. All the passion remains, but it often comes out in dance and pantomime."

Ellen Stewart, founder and head of La MaMa, remarked: "Language here is used almost as a ritual. This production is a kaleidoscope of color and movement. Lighting is used in ingenious ways – unlike in our theater. Colors complement what is on stage, and the actors' bodies are lit in novel ways. They communicate with light. And the costumes are sumptuous."

Duk Hyoung Yoo, the company's director, felt that this *Hamlet* took on "mythic proportions. By integrating the traditions of East and West, we're able to give birth to a 'drama of truth.'"

On the same programme with *Hamlet* was an original play, *Cycle*, based on a Korean legend and similarly concerned with "the misuse of power and its personal consequences".

The musicality of Koreans has long been demonstrated and acknowledged. It has been attested by the great success of their singers and instrumentalists who have made solid and even brilliant careers abroad.

As soon as they heard it, people in Seoul grew fond of the European classical repertoire. A National Symphony and National Opera Company were organized and performed in a new National Theatre on Namsam, the South Mountain, in the centre of the capital. The Symphony made its first foreign tour in the autumn of 1976. Traditional native music and dance became regularly accessible at Korea House, a cultural centre down the hill from the theatre.

European-style opera made its bow in Seoul in 1948 when a physician, Yi In-Sun, proud of his tenor voice, overcame a series of obstacles to stage Verdi's *La Traviata*. He directed while participating in the leading role, Alfredo. Two prominent sopranos of the day, Ma Gŭm-Hi and Kim Cha-Gyong, alternated as the fickle, pathetic heroine, Violetta. The piece drew crowds to the Seoul Municipal Theatre.

A favourite native opera, *Chun-hyang-jun* (*The Tale of Chunhyang*; 1950) has music by Hyeon Jae-Myeong. It makes use of an ancient romantic story of unknown authorship. In the sixteenth century Lie Kiuhiung dramatized the tale, in Korean rather than the more traditional Chinese. Bernard Sobel has paid tribute to the play's "ornate yet delicately beautiful song style, filled with the most exquisite love poetry".

A handsome young scholar, Toh Ryong, scion of a Minister, is about to take his examinations to earn a government post. Inopportunely, he attends a banquet and becomes infatuated with Chunhiang, a dancing girl. Knowing that his father would not permit him to marry her, Toh Ryong goes through a secret ceremony. While the young husband is absent for several months on a scholarly mission, Chunhiang finds herself resisting the lecherous advances of a new City Magistrate; staying inviolate, she is imprisoned and tortured but remains true to Toh Ryong. Promoted to be a Government Inspector, Toh Ryong returns and discovers what has befallen Chunhiang. To find out what has truly been afoot, he puts on beggar's garments and finally contrives to set free his wife as well as bring the evil Magistrate to justice. After her deliverance, Chunhiang is hailed by all for her obdurate fidelity. The tale was adapted for the stage during the eighteenth and nineteenth centuries by several other writers and composers. Hyeon Jae-Myeong's operatic version enjoyed huge popularity, but had its initial run halted by the onset of hostilities with North Korea.

An opera composer who appeared during the war years is Kim Te-Hyong. His *Kongji Patchi*, the story of a Korean Cinderella, was staged in Pusan in 1952.

Broadway and West End musicals were imported or locally staged and greatly prospered in Seoul. *The Korea Herald* (published in English) for 1 May 1983 lists productions of *Oliver* and *Guys and Dolls*, the latter put on by students of the Seoul Foreign School. By the next decade the capital's theatre producers and artists were confident enough to ship a Korean-wrought operetta to New York's Lincoln Center, the elaborately accoutred *The Last Empress*.

Queen Min, wed to the legitimate heir to the throne, intrigues on his behalf. Assuming power, she urges modernization of the "Hermit Kingdom" and meets violent opposition from conservative isolationists. Having established trade relations with the neighbouring Japanese, she finds them predatory. Fearful of their intentions, she seeks alliances with Russia, France and Germany. An army coup is launched against her, compelling her to flee in disguise. With Chinese help she regains her place in the palace and rules again. But a treacherous Japanese envoy at her court plots her death. The code name for the conspiracy is "fox hunt". She is slain by a samurai. Recognized as a woman of royal spirit and high quality, she is posthumously given the title of "Empress".

The adaptation and libretto were by Kwang Lim Kim and Mun Yol Yi, the music and lyrics by Hee Gab Kim and In Ja Yang. The direction was entrusted to the capable Hojin Yun, the choreography to Byung Koo Seo. Many on the staff had studied and worked in the United States or Britain. Mun Yol Yi's book was based on his novel of the same title. The lead role of Queen Min was sung alternately by Taewon Yi Yi Kim and Wonjung Kim.

The work had its première in Seoul in 1995 and reached Lincoln Center in 1997. It was obviously designed to appeal to the patriotic sentiment of New York City's large Korean colony. The work was well attended during its limited engagement, and the critics were impressed by the professionalism of the score, *mise-en-scène* and enactment. After New York, it was revived in Seoul.

World-famed opera companies from Europe paid visits to Seoul, among them Britain's Royal Opera in 1986 *en route* to Japan and pausing to present *Turandot, Carmen, Samson et Dalilia* and *Così Fan Tutte*.

The pace of theatrical activity was much slower outside Seoul. With a benign attitude towards the arts, the government intervened, setting up a generous programme of grants to support music, drama and dance in other large cities and scattered regions. Lee Jin-hie, Minister of Culture and Information, announced plans to accomplish that end. Addressing the Fourteenth Annual Symposium of the

Korean Literary Writers Association, he specified new measures to be adopted. Folk-art festivals would be expanded throughout the provinces in a search for unknown material. A grand prize winner would receive an award from the President of the Republic, along with 1 million won. Additional large sums would be handed out for achievements in other cultural categories. A drama competition would be held in all twelve sectors of the country, but contestants from Seoul would be excluded. Along with the first prize – a presidential award – would come a chance to enter a similar drama festival in the capital. The competitions would be open to students and adults, male and female. Altogether 750 million won was allocated for the prizes in 1983, an increase of 230 million over the previous year.

Other subjects discussed at the Symposium were how to "internationalize" Korean writing and also how to make it more affirmative. Minister Lee said: "Literature in Western countries is now undergoing a process of dissolution passing the climax. However, literature in Korea and other Third World countries is in the process of integration heading for the climax."

In the arts Korea is best known abroad for its dancers, either as exponents of classical or folk forms, or as innovators of modern choreography.

European kinds of dance were first seen in Seoul when Pae Ku-ja, who had been a member of a Japanese revue troupe, opened a studio there in 1929. She is remembered as the earliest Korean to dance publicly displaying a Western style. Her *Airang* and *The Queen of Gold and Silver* possessed many freely developed elements of native folk dances. After that the Sakharov Dance Team, advocates of what they chose to call "abstract mime", performed in Seoul in 1931 and made a sharp impression. Next the Russian star Anna Pavlova visited the capital on a Far Eastern tour.

Alexandre Sakharov (1886–1963), Russian-born, had travelled to Paris to study painting. He fell under the spell of Sarah Bernhardt while watching her in Edmond Rostand's *L'Aiglon* and put aside his brush and palette to capture the "magic of movement". After training in Munich, he made his début there as a soloist in 1911, then gave a recital in Berlin, where he met and married Clothilde von Derp, who had been a dancer in some of Max Reinhardt's epic stagings. Working together, the pair developed a highly distinctive choreographic vocabulary. Contrary to what the term "abstract mime" connoted, most of their offerings had "definite themes often charged with strong emotions"; some were likened to Renaissance dance-pieces. Sakharov, gifted as a painter, designed his wife's and his own very effective costumes. The performances opened startling new vistas to Korean dancers.

The great Pavlova afforded critics, students and spectators an opportunity to see a pure example of classical ballet, an admixture of traditions descending from Italy, France and Russia, and now glimpsed in Seoul and rousing an enthusiastic response. Other foreign ballet troupes on tour further instilled in Korean audiences a liking for this kind of dance.

Coming from abroad, too, and stronger than the lasting inspiration of these three predecessors, was the temporary presence in Seoul of Ishii Baku, the outstanding forerunner in the radical new field of modern dance in Japan. He gave a concert in the capital in 1926, prompting many Korean performers to emulate him, adopting this fresh *esthétique*. The *Handbook of Korea* says that "practically all Korean dancers of modern times who later won fame had at one time or another studied under him". His approach and practices dominated Korea's modern dance circles until the mid-1940s. Cho Taek-won, the first Korean male dancer to espouse this avant-garde genre, had also been trained in Japan.

Korean "modern dancers", however, did little more than modify past forms; their interpretations were considered rather timid and superficial. Beginning in 1947, during the post-Liberation period, the theories of Mary Wigman, the German co-founder and high priestess of the modern and Expressionist movement, became known also by some in Japan. This led to a quest for a deepened psychological insight and emotional intensity in the offerings of modern dance disciples.

In the same post-war decade, however, argument and confusion prevailed among the various dance ensembles. Eventually two modern companies stood out, headed respectively by Kim Yun-sok and Song Bom.

Song Bom accrued wider popularity in 1954 at an ambitious dance festival marking the ninth anniversary of Liberation Day. On the same occasion, the artistic skill and vision of another performer, Lim Song-nam, also won special notice.

Since then a lively interest in all forms of dance – those demonstrating Korean traditional choreography, or accepting the conventions as well of European-style ballet, or adopting the dynamic range of modern genres – has expanded steadily. A number of universities with departments for training young aspirants give degrees to over 150 graduates yearly. Among the most respected professional ensembles have been the National Dance Group, the National Ballet, the Korea Folk Dance Group and the Little Angels.

A constant stream of the country's performers have toured abroad as soloists or as members of groups.

An unusual presentation was one staged by the Asian New Dance Coalition at the Theatre of the Riverside Church, the site of recitals by many small companies. Established the previous year in Korea, the Coalition was comprised of Korean, Chinese, Japanese, Filipinos and Americans, "with the aim, in part, of experimenting in the fusion of modern and traditional dance styles". On the inaugural programme in New York was Eleanor S. Yung's *Passages*, described by Jennifer Dunning in the *New*

York Times as "extraordinary . . . a hypnotic minimalist ritual set to Korean shamanistic music. . . . The dance builds from simple diagonal stage crosses to a rich but highly formal interweaving by accretion of gesture and increasingly charged dynamics, with slightly asymmetrical stage patterns. A good deal of the work's power is due to its performance by Lauren Dong, Evelina Deocares, Audrey Jung, Jean Lee and, particularly, Junko Kikuchi, all dressed in Kwok-yee Tai's simple ceremonial robes and performing with impassive intensity." *Passages*, in the opinion of Ms Dunning, came closest to the "fusion" sought by the experimental Coalition.

In 1979, too, the Asia Society and the Carnegie Hall Corporation presented twenty-five members of the National Classical Music Institute of Seoul in two evenings of Aak, a sampling of Korean court dance and music. This explanation was provided: "The term Aak refers in its strictest sense to the ancient rituals of the sun, moon and ancestors and came, in Korea, to encompass a wide variety of musical forms, all associated with the elaborate court rituals and entertainments of the Lee Dynasty, which began in 1392 and formally ended with the Japanese annexation of Korea in 1910. The Korean National Music Institute is the descendant of the Lee household, and its rich costumes and early instruments will be a feature of this performance of Aak."

Anna Kisselgoff wrote in the *New York Times*:

The program could offer only a glimpse of an ancient tradition. But every fragment seemed to contain the essence of its form. It was no accident that the overall tone of the program was consistent in both music and dance. As classical forms, each presentation was governed by a strict formal code.

Yet if the mood was formalized, it was softened by the special gracefulness that wafted through the dances and the meditative, occasionally lyric and expressive, character that penetrated the music. This was true especially of the instrumental and vocal solos. In this respect, one should immediately mention the soloists whose performances were rendered with unusually intense concentration.

They were Kyu-nam Hwang, who sat with eyes closed and sang boldly but hauntingly what was called a *Long Lyric Song*; Kyu-nam Hwang, who played the *p'iri* or Korean oboe with a richness of tone, and Sang-kyu Lee, whose solo on the *taegum* or bamboo flute had so startling a range that it suggested a dialogue between two voices.

Aak, we are told, is the generic name used today for all Korean court music and dance, although the term was originally applied to ritual music of Chinese origin. The orchestral component, which played pieces with poetic titles such as *Long Life as Immeasurable as the Sky*, opened the evening with a bright fanfare.

Although some of the dances and music date their origins from as early as the tenth century, many are openly nineteenth-century versions. In the dances, nonetheless, the formal patterns come to life; the multicolored silken costumes look beautiful. The constant movement motif of women bobbing slowly and flicking a long sleeve into the air acquires a mesmerizing quality.

Only an expert could explain the condensed symbolism behind these gestures. The story behind each dance was found in the program notes. Obviously, we are now seeing extreme distillations, whether they are called *Offering of the Heavenly Flowers* or *Nightingale Dance*. A sword dance with rotating handles on toy swords still has elements of ritual, as does the shamanistic *Dance of the Son of the Dragon and Eastern Seas*, performed in masks and by men.

All the other dances were performed by women and the most charming was the *Ball Dance* in which two teams threw something through a hole in a hanging fabric. Those who missed were marked with a black crayon on the cheek, while those on target received a flower. The score was 2–0.

A subsequent and somewhat different program by the Institute was given at Asia House in 1982. Bernard Holland, again for the *New York Times*, offered this account:

Westerners have become uncomfortable with any synthesis of the arts, preferring instead to segregate their music, art and dance in relatively private worlds. Korea's performing tradition, as seen and heard at the Asia Society, was quite another story – the sense of sound, of gesture and of color all interlocked into a single experience.

The twenty-five performers of the National Classical Music Institute of Korea showed two personalities during the delightful union of ear and eye. First there was Aak, Korea's reticent and inward court music and dance dating from the fourteenth century. And then there were the unbuttoned, often raucous entertainments of the country's folk life.

In *Long Life as Immeasurable as the Sky*, the courtly wooden flutes and oboes seemed oddly indistinguishable from the players' red silk costumes. In *Beautiful Persons Picking Peonies*, flowers plucked gracefully by each dancer balanced exquisitely against the yellow of their clothes. In *Dance of the Son of the Dragon of the Eastern Sea*, the languorous thrusting movements of scarves seemed made of blue, white, red, black and yellow. The Buddhist Ritual Dances flowed in yellow, green and pink.

There were also solos – one on the *taegum*, a transverse bamboo flute with legendary powers to soothe the waves, and then an improvisation on the *kayagum*, a twelve-string zither, played to an hour-glass drum's accompaniment.

The court music was patiently insistent, as if it had an eternity to run its course. The folk music shed itself of such weighty spiritual values and enjoyed a lightness of foot and of heart, these peasant entertainments – danced with remarkable relaxed precision – ranged from broad humor and story-telling in *Dance of the Old Monk* to the *Farmer's Festival Music and Dance*, an uproarious processional of marching and dancing to a din of drums, cymbals and brass.

Further information about the programmes was forthcoming in unsigned newspaper articles. Each evening the opening number was a fanfare of traditional military music. "It is the music that once charted the progress through their realm of Korean kings – among them, royalty of the Yi dynasty, which lasted 500 years and began exactly a century before the discovery of America." The instruments employed were equally ancient in origin: "one-tone trumpets, oboes, conch shells, drums, gongs and cymbals".

Scroll paintings, centuries old, depict processions of hundreds and hundreds of musicians playing such music on foot and on horseback, in bright yellow robes and stovepipe hats with pheasant feathers stuck jauntily on each side. Though the number of musicians has been reduced here, the scintillating yellow robes remain.

If there appears to be a great emphasis on the past, it is deliberate. All twenty-five dancers and musicians in tonight's concert are graduates of the National Classical Music Institute of Korea. The school was founded in Seoul in 1950 and is now under the directorship of Bang-song Song, who received a doctorate in ethnomusicology from Wesleyan University in Connecticut.

The Institute considers itself the successor of the Yi Dynasty's Royal Conservatory of Changak-won, which for five centuries cultivated and furthered court music in Korea until their country was occupied by the Japanese in 1910. Under the Japanese, the number of court musicians and dancers declined precipitously. So did interest in the art of Aak, as the Koreans call the wide variety of musical forms associated with court rituals and entertainments, some going back 1,000 years.

The Institute was founded to restore interest and standards of performance in the old art and to train musicians and dancers. A great deal of study has gone into the interpretation of Korean music and the techniques of performance. As a result, the Institute has found itself making instruments and costumes, and has established an archive and a library of recorded sound.

The programs reflect the color, tone and grace of a vanished life. Some historical records indicate that as early as the sixth and seventh centuries, Korean musicians and dancers were present in the courts of China and Japan. *The Ball-Throwing Dance* combines an actual court game with dance movement. Another dance, *Long Life as Immeasurable as the Sky*, described as the finest of court orchestral pieces, was written sometime between the tenth and fourteenth centuries and originated in the lament of a wife for her lost husband. Though the words have been lost, the music expresses the grief of the widow as two wind instruments play antiphonally, over the sound of a two-string fiddle and a bowed zither.

Two instruments of unusual charm, chimes made of bronze bells and stone jade, are considered national treasures and not allowed outside the country. But other instruments, at once familiar and strange, make up for the lack: bamboo oboes with reeds longer and wider than the Western variety; a graceful Korean lute, with beautifully turned pegs; an hourglass-shape drum, played by striking one side with the palm and other with a bamboo stick, and six-string and twelve-string zithers. There is also a series of wooden clappers, each twelve inches or so long, tied together with a cord of deerskin, which are used to signal the start and end of the music.

The dances, reflecting their courtly origins, are stately, graceful and full of repose. Whatever passion they picture is rigidly under control. It is dance that is almost without motion, yet its attraction lies precisely in these qualities. In *Sword Dance*, the performers at one point move forward on their heels, keeping the movement of their bodies under firm control. In *Nightingale Dance* the obvious sign of the movement is so well hidden that the dancers seem to float around the stage.

The stateliness is enhanced by sumptuous costumes of silks and satins of brilliant hue, embroidered with gold and silver thread. No nylon would ever be used. In *Sword Dance*, which commemorates the death of a thirteen-year-old boy who sacrificed himself for his king, the dancers are robed in white, red and black, wearing black festive hats with strings of beads as pendants. In *Ball Dance* costumes of purple and Prussian blue are ornamented by jeweled headdresses.

Another exotic occasion for New York theatre-goers in 1979 took place at Riverside Church, three evenings of performances by Won-Kyung Cho, whose initial programme garnered this notice from Anna Kisselgoff:

The classical dances of Korea have rightly been described as "stillness in motion" and Won-Kyung Cho proved the point very pleasantly in his solo dance concert Thursday night. Mr Cho offered longer excerpts from some Korean dance-dramas in another program last night and will do the same tonight.

The opening bill, however, was fascinating in its variety, ranging in genre from court and ritual dances to folk numbers whose lively activity differed from the solemn grace of the classical dances. These were models of distillation, relying upon a reduced number of arm gestures.

Yet these are not static dances. Rather, they are governed by phrasing that makes the dancer pause in the significant pose, always reached at an unhurried pace. Mr Cho's *tour de force* was to perform both male and female roles, adjusting his hair and makeup appropriately. His technique is not immune to physical tiredness at the close of a taxing one-man recital. But his commitment was never in doubt, and his demonstration of contrasting styles, scarves and swords in Korean, Chinese and Japanese dances was very interesting.

The typical image in the program was struck in the first *Nightingale Dance*, with the dancer in a woman's high-waisted, full-skirted costume with long sleeves flung outward from the wrist. Characteristically, the lower body created a shape under the skirt, with only a bobbing motion distracting attention from the movement of the arms brought up to the face.

This extremely formal manner was modified in *Snowy Night*, where a woman gently cried in stylized fashion, seeking a lover who never returned until she ended in a dejected posture. *Impromptu Dance*, identified as a folk dance, played on a similar theme with the woman seemingly frozen in recollection. To this viewer, such passages appeared highly modern, and how much Mr Cho himself contributed to the choreography was not clear.

The sword dance with two rotating small swords and the hour-glass-drum dance were familiar traditional items, as were two types of mask dances, in which improvisation has been considered acceptable. By contrast, the best-performed dance on the program, the Confucian *Il Mu*, was totally formal, a move from one restricted position to another.

Jennifer Dunning reviewed dance and music of a different sort brought to the Korean Cultural Service in New York in 1980, a collection of six pieces choreographed by Kim Paik-Bong, the director of dance at Kyung-Hee University.

Miss Kim based her dances on traditional Korean folk elements. The dance was at its best where those elements could most clearly be seen, as in the dipping of the body, the soft extensions of rounded arms and the slow turns of *Hwa Kwan Mu* (*Flower Crown Dance*). Less appealing were Miss Kim's infusions of Western-style modern dance, seen in the runs and chains of fast turns, the swoons and flounces of such dances as *Buchae-Chum* (*Fan Dance*) and *Sanjo* (*Virtuoso Solo Dance*), though they were performed with unfailing graciousness. The pieces tended to look alike, as well, and it was a jolt to see the endless, sudden changes of direction and small, staccato jumps of the bumble bee solo in *Sup* (*Forest Scene*) reappear in a solo – performed, like the first, by Chi Hwi Young – in *Mudang-Chum* (*Shaman Sorceress Dance*).

The three musical offerings provided the evening's high points. One was by Kim So-Hee, honored by the Korean Government as "Preserver of Intangible Cultural Property No. 5" and one of the country's most notable performers of Pansori, a style of musical theater rooted in the Korean folk culture. What a wonderful performer she is, with a down-to-earth manner and a voice that signals changes of emotions and character in seamless song. Then there was the attractive depth and raw articulation of the singer Park Kwi-Hee, "Preserver of Intangible Cultural Property No. 23," who accompanied herself on the *Kayagum*, a twelve-stringed zither, in *Kayagum Pyongchang (Song with Kayagum)*. But best of all was a clowning Pansori duet about two lovers on their wedding night, performed by the two women and Chang Duk-Hwa, their imperturbable drummer and murmurer of encouragement. A true meeting of East and West, their humor was universal.

Jack Anderson, of the *New York Times*, had praise for a mixed offering in 1982:

The Land of Morning Calm was a fine title for Sunday night's program of Korean classical dance and music at the Ohio Theater. The dances were as fresh as a Spring morning, and they all progressed at an unruffled pace.

Many involved repetitions of simple patterns, and their placidity was emphasized by flowing costumes. Wearing a long-sleeved rainbow-hued gown, Iris Park waved her sleeves decorously and stepped ceremoniously forward in a court dance. Du-Yee Chang also wore a long-sleeved costume in a solo. But his incantatory waving of the sleeves indicated that this was a dance for a shaman. Impersonating a sorceress, Miss Park held a bell and a fan in another shamanistic solo. Here, broad gestures gradually quickened, and Miss Park appeared to be conjuring up spirits.

In a purification duet, Miss Park, as a supplicant, bent low from side to side, then whirled steadily with a white scarf, her bell-shaped skirt opening outward as she turned. Again portraying a shaman, Mr Chang marched imposingly with a scarf that, according to the program note, was possessed by the evil spirits he presumably had conquered.

A masked solo for Mr Chang interrupted careful pacings with sudden jumps to suggest that this dance concerned a man torn between spiritual and carnal desires. These contrasts between varying types of movement also added touches of humor to the poor sinner's plight.

Anderson was on hand again for a second event in 1982.

Kui-in Chung led her audience from the Korean countryside to the streets of New York at Saturday night's performance by Kui-In Chung and Dancers at the Merce Cunningham Studio. The rural scenes proved more pleasant than the urban.

Arirang takes its title from a Korean mountain, and Miss Chung, a Korean-born modern dancer, made its slopes enchanted places. The dream-like work began with slow high steps. Then arms grew winglike, and the dancers rushed like a flock of birds. Much of the piece involved alternations of slow and fast movement, and among the attractive moments were a hovering solo for Miss Chung and a scene in which the cast held colored streamers and danced in a circle as if doing a Maypole dance. At last, shadows fell on this magic mountain, and *Arirang* faded away.

The dance unfolded like a landscape painting on a scroll. Because it built to no climax and its compositional structure involved little more than following adagios with allegros and allegros with adagios, *Arirang* was a placid landscape. But at least it was pretty.

In contrast, *Manhattan* was not pretty at all. The action occurred on a stage littered with shopping bags, and it was clear from the start that they would be fussed with. There were a few clever touches: for instance, when silhouetted figures appeared against slide projections of fruit stands and garbage cans. But, for the most part, *Manhattan* consisted of clichés about how the Big Apple is rotten to the core.

The accompaniments for the dances were skillfully assembled collages that included recorded scores and live percussion music by Yukio Tsuji.

The Ministry of Culture and Information dispatched a forty-member troupe of dancers and instrumentalists to Europe in August 1983 to celebrate the centennial of Korean–German and Korean–British relations. The group toured in eleven countries, among them Italy, Great Britain, France and Finland. In London, where seven performances were given, one took place at Queen Elizabeth Hall; the ensemble also visited six West German cities.

Koreans were conspicuous on the New York dance calendar in 1984. Won Kyung Cho was seen once more in a programme that featured his androgynous technique. Anderson reported:

[His] feet often skimmed the ground. Yet he seldom seemed rushed at his solo concert of Korean dances on Wednesday night at the Theater of the Riverside Church. The program included both traditional dances and works choreographed by Myung Kyun Pae. All were unhurried, and the choreography featured gentle glides, smooth runs and dignified swaying of the arms. These were dances to calm, rather than to excite, the viewer.

They fell into two basic categories. First, there were dramatic works, and the conventions of

Korean dance permitted Mr Cho to play both male and female roles. The gentleness and reticence of Korean dancing became a sign of resignation in a solo about a young prince unjustly condemned by his father. In another solo, by keeping his back to the audience at the start and focusing upon something invisible in the distance, Mr Cho created the illusion that he was a woman waiting for her husband to cross a dangerous frontier. And by going from tiny running steps to little hops and simpers, Mr Cho was able to be, first, a tightrope walker and, then, a coquette in a suite of gypsy sketches.

The other type of dance that he presented involved the manipulation of costumes, props and musical instruments. A court dance found him stepping elegantly from side to side in robes with long, dangling rainbow-hued sleeves. He rang little bells and jumped while holding a fan in a dance for a fortune teller in search of clients. And he wore a grotesque mask in a dance for a wildly hopping supernatural creature that was the evening's one totally robust solo.

On two occasions, he played a drum as he moved. Skipping through a farmer's dance, he beat a small drum and bent from side to side so that the colored streamers on his hat would swirl around him. He carried a much larger drum in the program's finale and struck it vigorously. Yet his footwork remained light. In Mr Cho's dances, energy was always tempered by grace.

Sin Cha Hong's concert was observed by Jennifer Dunning.

Korean folk dance seems to be just about all that's missing from the theater- and dance-training credits of Sin Cha Hong, who performed with her company, Laughing Stone, Wednesday in the Theater of the Riverside Church. But Miss Hong's new *Spiral Stance* has the simplicity and power of such folk dance.

Miss Hong is a minimalist with an extraordinary gift for the distillation of emotion through clear, bold body shapes and through stillness itself. In *Spiral Stance*, a solo set to a score by Michael Vetter that sounds like some distant primeval chant, Miss Hong stands in place in a pool of soft white light. Her hips circle slightly, and from time to time one foot flexes slightly and an arm winds slowly, half-circling up or across her body. She seems both motionless and a traveler, then suddenly, at the dance's end, she becomes obliterated by lighting that darkens her body within a dimming pool of light.

Her *Two-in-One*, presented recently at La MaMa, has the same pictorial and emotional force, and was once more strongly performed by Phyllis Jacobs and Karen Cahoon. But *Tripterous*, the ritualistic dance for four women that completed the Riverside program, needs a deeper self-contained space, like that of the La MaMa stage, for maximum effect.

Miss Hong makes dances for bodies and light, and the lighting designs of Blu played an important part in this powerful evening of theater.

Earlier in the year, *Aga*, a composition by Cho Kyoo Hyun, had been a segment of the Third World Theater Arts Festival held at La MaMa Annex, where it was enacted by the Empty Hands Dance Theater. The score by Pauline Oliveros combined percussion and electronic sounds. To Anderson, *Aga* resembled a gentle ritual. "Much of it consisted of slow processions while a woman who could have been a priestess placed offerings in a cooking vessel. Occasionally, the pace quickened. At one point, two women even washed their hair in the cooking vessel. However, too much of the time the choreography was nothing but stately paradings. The ritual of *Aga* may have been deeply meaningful for the participants, but it was less for the observer."

Also in the summer of 1984, a fine reception was given to the Hyun Ja Kim Dance Company, a group specializing in rural folk-works along with court and ritual numbers. Ms Dunning thought the diverse programme delightful.

One of the funniest events of the dance season took place on Thursday at Asia Society's Lila Acheson Wallace Auditorium, when the Hyun Ja Kim Dance Company presented a sample of *sundae-dogam* or masked dance drama from Kyung Sang Province in South Korea. It isn't surprising to learn that the theater form was banned from the Korean court during the seventeenth century. There can seldom have been such raucous goings-on at Asia Society.

The satire is a typical lovers' triangle involving an old man, his wife and his concubine. Dressed in robes topped by expressive, boldly detailed masks, the characters have a cartoon flavor. But the performing made them seem very real. The theater-dance piece begins with the entry of a chorus of seven drummers and cymbalists, their heads capped with helmets made of big, brightly colored paper pompoms. The six women wiggle their hips and smile and chant fetchingly as they watch the proceedings, and part of the fun was watching much of the audience collapse in giggles. And you didn't have to be Korean to succumb to the broad humor of this age-old story.

Halmi, or the old wife, played by Yung Hee Lee, was the ultimate in querulous lovers. Je Man Jung's Yonggam, the husband, was the epitome of the doddering philanderer. And has there ever been such a dimwitted dolly as Gaksi, played by Hyun Sook Kim, whose every wave of the hand depicted wily helplessness? Almost funniest of all was the "so where's the money?" gesture of Hee Soo Kim, as Pan Soo, a blind fortune-teller, as the husband commissions her to bring his wife back from death.

This was an excitingly varied program of eight traditional Korean dances that ranged from graceful and serene court dances, the performers waving long sleeves that looked like colored lanterns, to a shaman ceremony and exorcism that had striking theatrical effects but little ritual intensity. The *Popkochum*, or Buddhist ritual drum dance duet, performed by Hyun Ja Kim and Mr Jung, had a stark beauty notable for the vivid space between the two bodies as they moved through soft, flowing lines. And *Love Song*, a duet for two seasoned lovers, was performed with extraordinary delicacy by Miss Kim and Mr Jung.

The program concluded with *Changgo-Choom*, or a farmers' dance, accompanied by hourglass-shaped drums. Ordered anarchy reigned as lines of dancing musicians crossed and circled the stage, accompanied by other musicians creating wild and joyous sound of the sort that ought to accompany one to heaven.

The following season (1985) brought New York audiences the sixty-strong cast and staff of the Korean National Dance Company; the troupe took over the stage at the Beacon Theater. The engagement boasted the patronage of the Ministry of Culture and Information. Jennifer Dunning was present:

The glimpse of Korean culture was an enjoyable one presented by a company of attractive dancers and musicians. There were musical numbers that gave a sense of how traditional instruments sounded and were used. The dance was pretty and lively, and maintained a pleasant balance between popular art and traditional culture. And the dance-drama that completed the program had a great many moments of poignant story-telling.

Tomi's Story told the tale of the head of a travelling dance troupe, his wife, and the king who destroys their lives and their love for each other. The dance-drama sometimes unfolded a little slowly but its scenic effects – including two gawky ostriches and fluffy, descending clouds – were ingenious. And Kook Soo-ho and Miss Yang, playing Tomi and his wife respectively, led the strong cast most touchingly.

Song Beom was the choreographer of *Tomi's Wife*, which had a libretto by Cha Beom-suk and music by Park Beum-hoon. The work was directed by Hoe Kyu.

This exotic and sometimes quaint parade of troupes from Korea to America and Europe went on through the 1980s and 1990s. It was augmented by the thirteen-member Korean Contemporary Dance Company, founded by Wansoon Yook, and eliciting praise for "blending traditional and modern dance with an unusual smoothness". The Seoul-based Chang Mu Dance Company leaned to works in which "stormy emotions were channeled into a ritualized form". The Chang Mu recruited several of its participants from Korean dancers resident in New York. It was directed by Kim Maeja, a professor of dance at Ewha Women's University in the capital.

The Samul-Nori Ensemble brought four virtuoso dancing percussionists who, as noted by John Pareles of the *New York Times*, "created a spectacular din at the Asia Society, using two kinds of drums, and small and large gongs, pieces that clanged and thundered in carefully orchestrated crescendos. . . . The group's showpiece was *P'an-Kut*, an exorcism rite with acrobatic dancing." Before its concert at Asia House in New York the company carried out a "shaman road procession" in front of the museum on Park Avenue. A second performance was given at Irving Plaza the next evening. Anna Kisselgoff, the *New York Times*'s senior critic, contributed a second and fuller article about the Samul-Nori:

Like many ceremonial dances rooted in Asia's rural traditions, *P'an-Kut*, centers upon the power of shaman figures. The program note defines the dance as a "rite of exorcism" originally performed in an open field. "The dancers with swirling ribbons on their hats act as shamans to chase away evil spirits."

Certainly the mystical patterns in *P'an-Kut* are evident – namely, the circle and four-point form that shrinks from a square into a cluster. Not so oddly – if the cosmic concerns of such dances are kept in mind – this ancient Korean dance suggests the magic dances of Tibet. The performers' broad-rimmed, melon-shaped hats recall those worn in Tibetan dances. The four male dancers also focus on a hopping step with one knee raised, or a turn with raised knee, common to Tibet public rituals. The key difference is in rhythm, more prone here to acceleration.

Samul-Nori specializes in the ancient form of Korean music and dance called *Nong-ak* or "farmers' band music." It is interesting to note that while the musicians usually remained seated, and in the first part of the program did not dance as they played their instruments, this music, too, was originally performed while dancing.

Thus, when it is played and danced simultaneously, both the ritual origins and the esthetic dimensions of the form become more visible. The most dazzling aspect of *P'an-Kut* derives from the designs created in the air by ribbons attached to flexible stems on the hats. As three of the dancers rotate their heads, the streamers snake through the air – the equivalent of Chinese ribbon dances, albeit executed in a much more difficult way. Occasionally the dancers squat and twist their torsos so that the ribbons circle their entire bodies. One dancer eschews a ribbon for what looks like a huge plumed feather duster which, as he, too, moves his head, opens up and blooms with sudden intensity.

There is also the kind of bravura that is only too clearly the source of inspiration to certain

American dance experimentalists. The four dancers suddenly spin ferociously while moving in a circle, and their rhythms change in distinctly modular structures.

Highly praised by musicians after its 1983 début, Samul-Nori is a complete theatrical experience as well.

Jennifer Dunning reviewed another group of distinguished visitors in 1986.

There were three "Living National Treasures" on hand for Korean Traditional Music and Dance to insure the solemnity of the program, performed on Wednesday at Asia Society. But this touring company of nine musicians, singers and dancers proved that ancient folk culture can also be delightfully low fun.

The indisputable stars of the evening were Kim So Hee and Park Dong Jin, both practitioners of *pansori*, the dominant genre of traditional vocal music in the country. Accompanied by the drummer, the *pansori* singer tells an epic tale by means of song, narration and the merest suggestion of dramatic gesture.

Miss Kim barely moved at all, for the most part confining herself to shifting at times from foot to foot, shaking her fan open and closed, and pointing one foot, the fan and her finger in an amusingly forthright manner. The ancient style did not enable her to make clear the details of the excerpt she performed from *Hung-boga*, the story of a wicked older brother, a virtuous younger brother and an injured swallow. But her air of pragmatism – together with the quality of mixed speech and song of *pansori* – made this an engrossing theatrical experience.

Mr Park had the audience roaring with laughter in an excerpt from *Choonhyangga*. Oddly enough, the story involves the suicidal daughter of a geisha, a greedy and lecherous magistrate, and a virtuous young Secret Royal Inspector. But the excerpt included a bit about needing a toilet while travelling on the road. And Mr Park's bantam job, wandering hands and immense, sly gusto were hilarious. The style is companionable as well as down to earth, drawing in the listeners and playing off the drummer's beats and murmured comments. Chung Chul Ho was the sensitive and comically responsive *pansori* drummer throughout the evening.

Other highpoints of the evening were Kim Moon Sook's beautifully concentrated and inwardly focused *Salpuri*, a shamanistic folk dance in which her scarf seemed to have a delicate life of its own. *Kayagum Byungchang* was a delightful trio for Park Kwi-Hee, a third Living National Treasure, and Kang Chung Sook and Cho Nam Hee, playing and singing to the zither-like *kayagum*. But Miss Kim's heart didn't quite seem to be in her harvest dance solo, *Dupbaeggi Choom*, and Lee Mae Bang's rather busy-looking *Seung-moo* or monk's dance, with drum solo, lacked the precise balance of distance and total involvement that makes the more stylized arts of the East so exciting.

Lee Saeng Kang completed the company, which included members of the Korean National Academy for Traditional Music and Arts, and was presented by Asia Society and the Korean-American Performing Arts Society.

New York's La MaMa conducted a workshop on "Korean Dance Based on Zen Buddhism and Taoist Calligraphy" and the Asia Society sponsored a Korean Martial Arts Performance Demonstration. At the latter event, Master So-san Park, winner of numerous awards for his achievements in both the martial and visual arts, illustrated the traditional Korean techniques of formal combat, drawing and calligraphy. According to the announcement: "Swords, spears, sticks are used as weapons in Korean *Tae Kwon Do*. Master So-san will demonstrate various skills, including one in which a brush is used to defend oneself if attacked while studying calligraphy."

New York's Town Hall was where another facet of Korean art was displayed the very next year (1986). Jennifer Dunning greeted it warmly.

What promises to be one of the most charming programs of the season took place on Friday, when Pungmul Nori Ma-dang presented an evening of Korean folk music and dance. Neither the music nor the dance was entirely unfamiliar, but the program stood out for the amiable high spirits that matched the performers' impressive technique.

Presented by an ensemble of six young men now on tour in the United States, the program began with a traditional prayer and donations of money from some audience members who knelt on the stage before a small table stacked with rice cakes, which were later distributed to the audience, and drank from bowls of peasant wine. A musical segment followed, with pieces that displayed the drumming styles of four provinces of South Korea. The music, played by seated musicians on a variety of drums and gongs, was tremendously exciting, with quick-changing rhythms and shifting dynamics that built to shimmering, gut-crunching loudness and subsided to a deep, almost breathing sonority.

The six young male musicians were affecting, too, by their obvious delight in playing. Their bobbing heads, silky hair and swaying torsos offered a kind of human counterpoint, as did the small flourishes of their drumsticks. The heads were covered, in the dance segment, by hats from which long ribbons flowed. As the men beat their drums and danced, sometimes with unnerving acrobatic daring, they moved their heads sharply to form circling, snaking ribbon-writing in the air.

The bodies under the ribbons sidled, sped and flung themselves around each other on the stage

– circles within circles within circles. The group leader, wearing a hat with a frond of white feathers, cut through the stage space in a remarkable knee dance. And the segment ended with the men jumping through the two largest, whipping ribbon circles.

In the traditional manner, the performers invited audience members onto the stage to dance with them at the end. One by one, men and women of all ages joined the fray, some grabbing and playing gongs as they moved. Only a tiny, bundled child, clutching her program, stood steadfastly still.

The members of the group come from musical families in villages in Chung Chong Province. Gul Gi Jung, the puckish group leader, was an artist with that look of being a little mysteriously an order unto himself. The program was presented in New York by the South Korean newspaper *Chŏsun Ilbo*.

New Yorkers' exposure to other aspects of Korea's unique stage-art occurred with the arrival of Han Young Suk and her small troupe who had been participating by invitation in the American Dance Festival sponsored by Duke University in Durham, North Carolina. The added appearance was arranged by the Consulate Cultural Service in Manhattan. By now sixty-five, Ms Han had been awarded the title of "Living National Human Cultural Treasure" by her grateful government. This meant that she belonged to the select circle of those able to convey traditional poses and gestures in their purity, yielding the spectator a rare insight into the movement's original inspiration along with a grasp of a somewhat lost symbolism. She was accompanied by two younger partners. Anna Kisselgoff, in Durham for the festival, observed:

Han Young Suk, a woman of quiet intensity on stage and a performer of wider range than one might suppose, is very obviously a dancer's dancer.

The seven solos on view are splendid testimony to the very special nature of Korean classical dance. And that is its ultra-refinement, the extreme distillation it can bring to every movement and even every emotion.

We need not know the dramatic significance of every flick of a long sleeve by Miss Han or Lee Ae Ju, or the exact meaning of every gesture by Lee Mae Bang, the sole male dancer on the program. But we can certainly admit that when Miss Han glides about in a voluminous skirt and then suddenly raises a foot, that movement evokes a quality of wonder, so formalized is this act of simplicity.

If some of the dances have folk origins and are not classical in inspiration, they have obviously been put into a codified framework where they have a classical "look" despite any improvisation.

Thus, the dances of religious origin, even if they are not court dances, have been distinctly classicized. The surprises on the program are the liveliness and boisterousness of the music, which can offer a compelling contrast to the austerity of the dancing.

Miss Han performed three of the solos and there was a startling difference between the elegant veiled courtier who floated about in the first dance and the impassioned figure in a white hood who attacked a hanging drum with rhythms of complexity and vigor.

In this style of Buddhist dance – called *seung-mu* – and which passed down specifically in her family, Miss Han exhibits the dramatic changes that can pour out of dances that seem so deceptively contained. Both Buddhism and the use of the long sleeve in dance came to Korea from China, but interestingly, some of the old Chinese dance traditions have been best preserved in Korean dance.

In *Sal Pu Ri*, a dance said to be shamanistic in origin, Miss Han defined the clear formal outlines of her style. A tape with high pitched voices accompanied a measured dance with moments of stillness punctuated by quick scurrying steps. A pink scarf held by one or two hands, thrown over a shoulder, added a ceremonial element.

Although court dances were usually performed by a corps of dancers, the *Nightingale Dance* is a well-known solo. Miss Lee, flinging out rainbow-striped long sleeves or bobbing in place, spread her wings as only an abstraction of a butterfly could, and won our hearts.

Mr Lee had the difficult task of suggesting a youthful spirit in an aged body and succeeded admirably in *Shinnosimbullo* through sheer quality of movement, aided by the symbolic use of his fan. Miss Lee returned with a jaunty and angular masked dance from the Bonsan masked-drama plays that teach and entertain at the same time.

A surprisingly jazzy sound came from the music that accompanied *Tae Pyoung*, a dance of peace and happiness performed with exquisite authority by Miss Han. Stepping on her heel or extending one arm up and the other out, Miss Han offered a study in minimal movement but maximum internalized concentration. Mr Lee's vibrant *Shaman* dance, also performed with brilliant use of detail, provided a wonderful contrast in color. The *Seung-mu* ritual, beginning deceptively with Miss Han moving in formal elegant floor patterns and then ending in the astounding drumming, completed a program of special variety.

This is an incomplete survey of Korean dance-art as seen by its admirers abroad.

Dating back to antiquity, puppetry survives in Korea in much the same form it has had through the centuries. Probably originating in India, it was carried to China, where it was somewhat modified.

From China it was borne to Korea and next to Japan. The changes that took place *en route* did not affect its essential technique, style or purpose.

Korean puppet plays are of two kinds, the *Ggogdu-Gagsi* (or *Bag Czŏm-Zi*) and the *Mansŏg-Zung*. Most of the dolls are wooden, one to three feet in length, painted, traditionally garbed and operated with strings. Kardoss supplies further details:

> In the *Ggogdu-Gagsi*, there are thirteen puppets in human form and three in animal form. The play is interlaced with Buddhist sentiments and the main plot is humorous. Like the masque play, it criticizes the nobility, government officials, and corrupt priests and has a domestic drama woven into the story.
>
> The birthday of Buddha on the eighth day of the fourth month by the lunar calendar served as an occasion for the second type of puppet play, the *Mansog-Zung*. As in the *Ggogdu-Gagsi*, the puppeteers pulled the strings from a hidden position to the accompaniment of music, but unlike the *Ggogdu-Gagsi*, this was a silent play. The *Mansog-Zung* was performed by five puppets – a human-like puppet called the *Mansog-Zung*, a deer, a horned deer, a carp, and a dragon.

Currently little is known about happenings in North Korea. Communist and totalitarian, unremittingly controlled for over five decades by self-promoted cult figures, the dictator Kim Il Sung and his son and heir, it has been a closed society, seldom accessible to observers from the non-Marxist West. Only a few glimpses have been allowed, and these suggest that its theatre serves to extol the regime and the omnipotent President. Visiting Pyongyang, the capital, in 1981, Bruce Cumings, a scholar from the University of Washington, remarked that even the television serial he turned on was recounting episodes from the early life of Kim Il Sung. On his first night in the city Cumings was taken to a play, *Song of Paradise*, "whose theme was that all are happy 'in the bosom of the Fatherly Leader,' with nothing to envy in the world". Also, "In downtown Pyongyang, a neon sign blinks: 'Thank you, Kim Il Sung.'"

Two years earlier (1979), Kurt Waldheim, the United Nations Secretary General, made a formal visit to Pyongyang. Malcolm W. Browne, Far Eastern correspondent for the *New York Times*, was permitted to accompany the delegation to be at the ceremonies. He cabled to his newspaper:

> Virtually every event consisted of praise for President Kim and his "people's paradise," in a display of personal adulation that has long disappeared in other Communist countries.
>
> A high point was a command performance last night of the Mansudae Art Troupe, whose cast outnumbered the 500 people in the hall of the People's Palace of Culture. The show, a kind of poli-

tical musical comedy in which a reporter whose father was killed in the Korean war is the heroine, was staged with sets and special effects that would have beggared the most elaborate spectacles at Radio City Music Hall in its heyday.

It included the backlighted projection of moving scenes beyond the deep stage, elaborate props and costumes, artificial fog, spectacular lighting and fountains, and simultaneous English translation on a screen next to the stage.

A vivid battle scene depicted a heroic victory "over the US aggressors who tried to take away our happiness" during the Korean war, in which American forces fought under the United Nations flag. Secretary Waldheim applauded enthusiastically and at the end of the performance stepped on stage to present a bouquet to the *prima donna*.

Children tied the red kerchiefs of Communist youth groups around the necks of Mr Waldheim and his party before another show today, which was performed entirely by children. Accompanied by the startlingly competent orchestra of thirteen-year-olds, the children's troupe regaled the visitors with Russian-sounding music and lyrics like the following:

"Marshal Kim Il Sung is our father, the party is the bosom of our mother. Sisters and brothers are we coveting nothing the world can offer."

Another *New York Times* reporter, Nicholas D. Kristof, was able to cross the border and capture much of the scene in 1989. Some excerpts:

Here the portly forty-seven-year-old Kim Jong Il is not a terrorist, as he is labeled in the West, but the "Dear Leader," and a beacon for all humanity. Here, the holy trinity is not a Catholic teaching, but the substance of Korean worship: the father, "Great Leader" Kim Il Sung; the son, Dear Leader Kim Jong Il; and the holy spirit of *Juche*, the national ideology of self-reliance.

A Westerner visiting North Korea inevitably feels like an atheist at a convention of evangelists. The faith expressed in the Great Leader and the Dear Leader seems so excessive that it cannot possibly be genuine, and yet everyone insists that it is – even the children, girls like Han Sun Sil and Li Yong Sil. Both bright-eyed fourteen-year-olds, neatly dressed in blue school uniforms with red scarves that mark them as Young Pioneers, Miss Han and Miss Li were skipping down the street in the city of Nampo, hurrying toward a noodle stand to buy lunch, when they encountered something downright scary: an American. They knew about Americans – how the American imperialists forcibly occupy South Korea and terrorize the population – but they had never actually seen one until a reporter leaped out of his car to interview them.

"We call the Great Leader and Dear Leader our true fathers," Miss Han explained. "They give everything to children, and the Great Leader calls children the kings of the country. So we feel that they are our real fathers.

"The Great Leader is the ever-victorious commander who defeated two enemies in one generation," they continued, referring to Japan and the United States – only now they were speaking in unison, and behaving as if it was the most normal thing in the world for two teenage girls to share an identical thought and spontaneously express it in one voice.

In North Korea, the entire population seems to live on a stage – people rehearse their lines so well that it is often impossible to tell when they are speaking from the heart and when from memory. From nursery school on, the regimentation and indoctrination are inescapable. In the living room of every North Korean home, near the framed photographs of the Great Leader and the Dear Leader that hang in virtually every room in the country, a small box juts out from the wall. These loudspeakers might be seen as umbilical cords linking North Koreans to their mother-Government, by piping propaganda into every home. Even when peasants are working in the fields, they are bombarded with propaganda from outdoor speakers.

Just in case anyone should miss the point of all this propaganda, the authorities have named one suburb of Pyongyang, the capital city – Paradise.

Probably no society is so tightly monitored and controlled in all the world, and anyone who expressed "mental illness," as one Korean official described dissent, is promptly banished from the capital with his entire family. Any dissident would have to be breathtakingly brave, or stunningly foolish; disloyalty threatens not only one's own future, but that of the entire family. Entrance into university, admission to the party, access to jobs and housing – all these depend on loyalty. As a foreign resident of Pyongyang put it, "If in England people are classified by accent, and in America by their wealth, here they are classified by their loyalty to the Kims."

The North Koreans' avowals of faith in the Great Leader and Dear Leader are so worshipful that Westerners tend to think that they protest too much, that the faith must be forced. But it may be that in the majority of cases people really do love the Great Leader and Dear Leader.

Perhaps the best metaphor for North Korea is the medieval church. Much of the population consists of genuine believers, and no one pays enormous attention to the minority of heretics who are tortured and killed, the way witches or Christians of a dissident sect were killed during the Middle Ages. The state devotes vast resources to unproductive but stylish investments – such as the enormous army and the countless grand monuments to the Great Leader – just as medieval England and France spent lavishly on the crusades and on soaring cathedrals to glorify God. Maybe some ordinary North Koreans think in their hearts that it is a waste for Pyongyang to build marble-lined sub-way stations, but a good many probably accept it with piety or resignation, just as penniless congregations accepted the grand construction projects of old.

. . . From abroad, North Korea is generally viewed as an impoverished land whose people are ter-rified of foreigners and of one another, a nation as devoid of human spontaneity as of foreign exchange. The reality is more complicated. Pyongyang, for example is a beautiful, well-planned capital in a conti-nent where capitals tend to be polluted and crowded. Impressive construction projects are everywhere: enormous museums, an Arch of Triumph bigger than the one in Paris, and the ubiquitous, elegant statues of Kim Il Sung. Some factories are modern and boast imported high-technology equipment. North Korea has defaulted on its five-billion-dollar foreign debt, but not because it has no foreign exchange – it simply could not resist the temptation to spend the money on its own purposes.

. . . In North Korea, however, villagers are not allowed to move to the city to improve their lot. And in its fervor to make Pyongyang a beautiful, orderly city, the Government appears to have moved out all the handicapped and mentally retarded people. Nobody rides a bicycle in the center of the city, appar-ently because the Government frowns on them; they are regarded as old-fashioned and unnecessary now that Pyongyang has a subway that is one of the most beautiful in the world. Its trains rush along every few minutes, and the marble-lined stations are spotless; there is, needless to say, no graffiti.

North Korean officials maintain there has never been a rape or murder in the country. Li Chol Sin, the official in charge of cultural relations with the West, concedes that very occasionally there are thefts, mainly by "young pranksters," but he contends that North Korea has no prisons. Instead, he said, there are "re-education centers" for those who have made mistakes, such as drivers who run down pedestrians.

"You foreigners will never understand Korea," officials say again and again. And perhaps they are right – quasi-religious feelings for a political leader seem incomprehensible to most Americans. But a Chinese who lived for many years in North Korea said that the reverence for the Kim family reminded him of the emotions many Chinese once felt for Chairman Mao Zedong. It was a cult of personality, and unmerited, the Chinese said, but at one time it was overwhelmingly sincere. He noted that life in North Korea had improved over the years, but not quite so quickly as in South Korea, China or some other countries.

In 1999 outsiders had another chance to sample North Korean theatrical fare when a company from Pyongyang paid a visit to China. From Shanghai the well-versed Sheila Melvin wrote to the *Wall Street Journal*:

The lot of a North Korean opera troupe that specializes in a single revolutionary opera cannot be an easy one. Not only is the People's Republic of Korea one of the most isolated and economically depressed nations on earth, but the market for revolutionary operas is not exactly booming in the post-Cold War world.

So the sold-out venues, standing ovations and media blitz that heralded the Wan Shou Performing Arts Company's seven-city Chinese tour of *The Flower Girl* must have come as a welcome surprise to the beleaguered North Korean players.

But for all the hoopla, the return of *The Flower Girl* to China was tinged with a curious mix of nostalgia and regret. The popularity of the opera dates back to 1973 – the bleak days of the Cultural Revolution – when the film version took the country by storm. Back then, the censors were far more strict, and propaganda-filled North Korean features were among the few foreign films permitted.

The Flower Girl tells the story of Hua Ni and her family, servants for a rich landlord in Japanese-occupied Korea. In the eight-act opera the landlord and his wife eat, drink and generally live it up. They also constantly abuse their servants, who do little more than sell flowers, suffer beatings and sob hysterically. Two ten-member choruses – one all male, the other all female – comment on the action from the pit. The opera is filled with such stirring lines as "Who will rescue Hua Ni from this sea of bitterness?" The answer, of course, is the revolutionary army. In the final act, the army hacks the landlord and his wife to death before singing triumphantly, "Everybody rise up and make revolution with the revolutionary army!"

The opera's music is about as subtle as its plot, all soaring violins and sobbing sopranos, with a few horns mixed in whenever revolution is mentioned. Nonetheless, virtually everyone in China over the age of thirty-five has seen it at least once, and many can still sing all the songs.

Shanghai's *Shenjiang Evening News* devoted two entire pages to articles on the movie's popularity and the impact of its return as an opera. It even reprinted articles from 1973 that compared the lives of servants in pre-Communist China to the life of the character Hua Ni, and declared that "we have the same bitter experience as the millions of Korean workers, and we share the same destiny."

But China has changed a great deal since the 1970s and so has its press. Alongside the old articles, the newspaper ran new stories by writers who recalled the anguish of being forcibly separated from their families during the Cultural Revolution and of seeing their mothers sob uncontrollably during the movie. Back then, *The Flower Girl* offered hope by bitter comparison – "Hua Ni's life is even worse than mine and it has a happy ending," they thought. In a vastly different modern China, however, the harshness of Hua Ni's life is viewed as a thing of the past, and seeing the opera again is a stroll down memory lane.

For me, the opera was also a stroll down memory lane, albeit a much shorter and less traumatic one. In the spring of 1995, I was granted a visa to attend the Pyongyang International Sports and Cultural Festival for Peace. Every minute of my week in the North Korean capital was programmed, and theatrical and sports performances were an important part of the schedule.

At first I dreaded the propaganda-filled performances we had to attend. But over time I began to appreciate the moments we spent in stadiums and theaters. Even if the shows were disturbing – schoolgirls dancing around with red flowers singing, "I will always endeavor to plant for Kim Il Sungia and Kim Jongilia with vigor" or boys smashing to pieces a snowman that had a nuclear bomb in its arm – at least they were obviously performances.

Outside the theaters and stadiums, however, I spent most of my time wondering what was real and what was staged. I could be certain that the nine-course breakfast with beer served to me by my home-stay family each morning was not normal fare. And when I toured the Great People's Study Hall, I could safely assume that the scores of people perusing the works of deceased President Kim Il Sung were doing so for our benefit. But what about the women and children in flowing traditional dress playing the accordion and dancing in the woods near the spot where we stopped for lunch? It seemed far too idyllic. But would the government actually plant "extras" in the hills?

On one very bad day, I concluded that everything was "real" and that the entire population had been successfully brainwashed. North Korea, I mused, was more cult than country. We had been to a school and a "children's palace" where we saw kids learning *tae kwan do* so they could "engage in hand-to-hand combat with the imperialist American aggressors." They were also writing "reunify the motherland" in calligraphy, programming maps of a united Korea onto computers and singing their love for their "father," Kim Il Sung. The beatific grins and starry eyes of the heavily made-up kids were haunting.

When I got back to Beijing and told Chinese friends of my experiences, they laughed aloud. "Accordions in the woods! You fell for that?" one giggled. Another reminisced about the months she spent practicing "real" life before President Nixon's visit to China. "Of course they don't think Kim Il Sung is their father – they have to say those things, just like we did about Mao," I was told again and again.

It is disconcerting to think that everything I saw was staged – a drama that is a real life tragedy for those who live it – but it is also encouraging. Performances, after all, have an end. Twenty-five years ago the very same Chinese who flocked to see *The Flower Girl* in Shanghai were forced to live and act much like North Koreans do today. Now, they pay forty dollars to see a revolutionary opera, turn their cell phones on when it is over, and walk out of a theater that is more brightly lit at night than all of Pyongyang.

Perhaps as the North Korean performers watched the Chinese audience leave – the musicians actually stood and waved from the pit until the auditorium was empty – they found a little hope in the changes wrought so far in China, the same sort of hope that the Chinese once got from watching *The Flower Girl*. The hope for a better life.

For a number of years sealed-off North Korea seemed to prosper, but in the closing phase of the 1990s prolonged drought wasted its fields and the economy sagged, perhaps because of errors in policy, among them the diversion of funds to support a huge military force and to build aggrandizing monuments. Persistent rumours of severe famine and many deaths began to spread abroad. At last the regime was compelled to seek help from Japan and the United States – they responded – and to welcome a state visit by the newly elected President of South Korea in 2000, which promised a betterment of relations. Also some members of families in South Korea long without word of kinsfolk in the North were finally allowed brief reunions. To boost the economy a very limited amount of tourism was permitted – to largely unpopulated mountainous areas renowned for scenic splendour. Travel to them is by ship, so that the tourists see little of the land elsewhere. They are given no chance to meet or speak to anyone except the guides and guards. At the end of these four-day journeys, however, for an added fee they are taken to "a riveting performance of the Pyongyang Moranbong Circus". This was by a splinter unit, detached from the 500-member parent company based in the capital and founded in the early 1960s. Rigorously trained, the participants featured great dexterity in dizzying, daunting balancing acts. They dangled perilously in ever higher and more complicated configurations from poles mounted on one another's shoulders, to form fleeting human geometrical patterns with utter disregard of gravity.

Doubtless there are other public entertainments in North Korea, but their nature and quality are not ascertainable.

18

JAPAN IN THE TWENTIETH CENTURY

The energizing impulse of the new century, the twentieth, was felt in Japan's theatre about 1906, when the Shingeki (Modern Drama) movement got under way. Several earlier trends in the Meija era (1868–1909) had led to it. In 1888 a young actor, Sandonari Sudō (1867–1909), caused a furore at Osaka, making his début in a play containing overt political comment. He was one of those, along with the noted playwright Kawatake Mokuami (1816–93), who were instrumental in shaping the Shimpa (New School) movement, seeking to update Kabuki by borrowing from European models. (A fuller description of Shimpa is given in Chapter 4, together with an account of Mokuami's innovations.)

Another initiator of the Shimpa school was Otojiro Kawakami (1864–1911), an activist in many fields. Born in Hakata (in present-day Fukuoka prefecture), he was taken by his family to Tokyo. Growing up, he became by turns a novice Buddhist priest, an indifferent college student, a house-servant and finally a tramp. He next attached himself to the Freedom and People's Rights Movement, a drifting agitator in its behalf. His subversive speech-making led to many arrests and periods of imprisonment. He was viewed as a political martyr. Ever changing, he apprenticed himself briefly to a public storyteller, a traditional Japanese art, and then tried being a vaudeville entertainer, a humorous balladeer. Here he suddenly won national attention with a "talking song", *Oppekepi bushi*, satirizing the new political and social élite.

Taking a leaf from Sandonori Sudō, with whom he sometimes joined forces to write, direct and act in rather crude political dramas, Kawakami and some like-minded fellow performers barnstormed about the island with their dramatized preachments. He collaborated with Sudō to compose and present *Itagaki-Kun Sōnan Jikki* (1891), about a revered radical leader. In 1891 he had married a geisha, Sadayakko (1872–1946), then known to be a lover of Ito Hirobuni, a high political functionary. Two years later Kawakami voyaged to Europe to observe Western theatre. On his return he altered his choice of themes, dropping the political. Instead he offered a highly successful murder-mystery, *Igai* (*Surprise*; 1894). Several sequels, also popular, assured his position as the dominant figure on the stage of the day, further strengthened during the span of the Sino-Japanese War by his production of a series of patriotic and military spectacles, followed by even more hit plays.

But politics beckoned the restless Kawakami again; he campaigned for a seat in the Diet and was defeated. To ease his chagrin, he set out with his wife and a small ensemble of players on three lengthy tours of Europe and America (1899–1903), staging mostly Kabuki adaptations. While in Boston in 1899 Sadayakko was forced to assume the leading women's roles owing to the death of the company's two female impersonators. Though inexperienced and lacking formal training, she made an excellent impression. The troupe appeared at the Paris World's Fair in 1900, causing a stir among the French intelligentsia, ever attracted by the exotic. Though some Japanese critics found fault with Kawakami's interpretations, he and the members of his company won applause from celebrated foreign professionals, among them Sir Henry Irving, Eleanora Duse, Hugo von Hofmannsthal and Vsevolod Meyerhold. Parisians compared Sadayakko to Sarah Bernhardt. Back in Japan, Kawakami put on European scripts in translation, and in Western style. He produced and took title roles in Japan's first mountings of Shakespearian works. (Among his bolder approaches, he eventually staged a *Hamlet* in which the melancholy prince made his entrance on a bicycle along a flower-strewn *hanamichi*, or runway.) Gradually he gave up performing and devoted most of his efforts to altering how works were produced and local theatres were managed. Sadayakko reigned as one of the first stars of the new Japanese stage, seen by some as the peer of Sumako Matsu, also recalled as one of her country's earliest truly modern players. Kawakami and his wife took an interest in arranging for the by now necessary formal training of women for the theatre, besides which she established the children's theatre movement in her native country.

Shimpa's was a short life, however. After five years (1904–1909) it began to lose its audience, which was mostly drawn from the undemanding middle-class citizenry of Osaka and Tokyo. The plays, overly romantic and sentimental, simplistic, excessively melodramatic, are frequently likened to Western "soap-operas". As has been mentioned, a much-worked source of plots was events of the war with China. The trauma of adapting to domestic social change was another much-repeated topic. The titles of the scripts indicate their content: *The Student of Patience and the Maiden of Virtue* and *The Sublime, Exhilarating Sino-Japanese War.* Elaborate visual effects employed by Kawakami were a feature, extending to putting on stage galloping horses in battle-scenes with the din of live ammunition. Sometimes the performances were so convincing that the spectators over-reacted. In one instance a player portraying a villain was killed by outraged members of the audience. The introduction of women in feminine roles was also initially confusing and evoked protest. Mixed with the realistic acting, traces of Kabuki were quite visible; the acting might still be highly stylized.

Shimpa did not vanish altogether; it lingered on with a diminished appeal, mostly to women and elderly men, but sometimes regaining broader approval briefly. Historically the movement is important because in breaking from the fixed and long-dominant conventions of Nōh and Kabuki, and by accepting contemporary subject-matter, modern dress and Western music, it prepared the way for the ever more free-ranging Shingeki.

The major figure in the transition to Westernized drama is Shōyō Tsubouchi (1859–1935), born Yūzō Tsubouchi. A native of the village of Ōta (later known as Mino Kamo) near Nagoya, he was taken at seven to Tokyo where he was enrolled in preparatory school. In 1883, graduating from Tokyo University, he obtained a teaching post at Wasada University, also in Tokyo. Three years later he became the editor of *Waseda Bugaku*, the school's literary journal (1891). As a student he had delved assiduously into Western books. He began to translate some of them, proving himself a meticulous scholar who set a high standard for later Japanese transcribers to emulate. Between 1883 and 1928 he translated all of Shakespeare's plays, in versions that are still much admired.

He wrote many critical essays. His study of Western works persuaded him that his country's literature was in an appalling state. Japanese authors were held in diminishing respect by their fellow-countrymen. They scarcely enjoyed or merited the esteem generally accorded to writers in the West. He embarked on a campaign to lift the quality of Japanese fiction and scripts for the stage, a struggle he persisted in tirelessly. In essays he explained and analysed the principles and techniques of Western literature and demanded similar attainments for Japanese novels and plays; they should seek realism, objectivity, unity and manifest earnestness. What is more, literature must be seen as an independent art, of value solely for itself. As Thomas E. Swann paraphrases Shōyō's argument, in the *Japanese Encyclopedia*: "The political novel should be abandoned because it restricts art to utilitarian and political purposes and was too obviously a foreign, imported form. This left the tradition of the Edo period (1600–1868) popular literature (*Gesaku*) as the primary material from which to mould a new, modern fiction. Once divested of its frivolous aspects and Confucian ethics, it could be transformed and elevated by imbuing it with contemporary settings, modern manners and customs, exact description, philosophical depth and psychological truth."

To illustrate his vision he wrote and published a succession of fictional works, nine in all (1885–90). Though daring experiments for their day, they fall somewhat short of his aim, not truly going far beyond the *Gesaku* that he hoped to transcend. He lacked skill at characterization, tended to sound didactic, plotted ineptly, artificially. But they were an impetus to further innovation by others more talented in the genre.

About 1888 Shōyō shifted his attention to the stage. Here he had more success, as both playwright and critic. In a stream of essays he insisted that the drama, too, should be an art to be weighed only for its own sake. He urged more realism in plays, and advocated that the theatre be devoted to serious ends, though the scripts should avoid "moral and political preachments". The popular stage should be raised from "a vulgar entertainment for the uncultured". He saw skills of actors and dancers in need of improvement. Again, Swann paraphrases Shōyō's call: "Scripts should resonate with artistry and beauty; they should contain rational development, authentic circumstances, and genuine emotions." The new drama should carefully combine selected elements of Western and traditional drama and music, "transmuting these into a sophisticated form".

As was his wont, Shōyō promptly sought to demonstrate by example what he advocated in his essays. Over the next quarter of a century he turned out scores of plays in a remarkable range of styles, length and shape. Some of his intentions were startling, but once more his shortcomings as a creative artist are all too clear. His characters are too often stereotypes, their emotions sounding hollow; the structure of his plots is too episodic, the content often shallow. Three exceptions, perhaps, are his *Kirihitoha (Paulownia Leaf* ; 1894–5), *Maki no kata (The Lady Maki*; 1896) and *Shinkyoku Urashim* (1904), the last singled out by Swann as a "masterpiece".

Shōyō began his assault on the traditional Japanese stage by inserting just the trial scene from *The Merchant of Venice* between two Kabuki excerpts at Tokyo's Kabuki-za. Emboldened, he next put on complete Shakespearian dramas and comedies, then moved on to scripts by Ibsen, Strindberg, Hauptmann and other European Naturalists. Ibsen's characters, trapped by and rebelling against a petrified social code, sharply appealed to a segment of the Japanese public. The earliest play by the Norwegian that was seen by them was *John Gabriel Borkman* (1911). Such works imparted to his fellow-artists an impetus to explore what was being done elsewhere. Soon Chekhov, Gorky and Shaw were also on view for Tokyo theatre-goers, as were Symbolists such as Maurice Maeterlinck and Hugo von Hofmannsthal. After a while the indefatigable Shōyō was persuaded that a good means of reforming the stage and achieving progress on it might be by a resort to dance-dramas. Accordingly, he wrote and produced several of them.

Further, he helped to establish the Bungei Kyokai, a society sponsoring the arts, and set up a theatre museum attached to Tokyo's Waseda University, the school where he taught. Both institutions have carried on valuable research into many aspects of Japan's stage.

Swann places Shōyō at the apex of Japanese literary history.

He was unquestionably a powerful catalyst in modernizing Japan's literature. Much of the criticism of his deficiencies in practical application overlooks the magnitude of the forces Shōyō confronted, the impossibility of total brilliance in every area of his radical experiments, and the sincerity of his intentions and efforts. Shōyō always desired the best and was modest enough to pass the banners of artistic regeneration and refinement to more creative talents when they appeared. His supreme contribution was perhaps the absolute conviction that slavish adoption of alien forms was sterile; that the traditional literary arts could not be jettisoned wholesale but must be selectively refashioned and reanimated. Every great Japanese writer since Shōyō has rediscovered that profound insight.

In many instances the leading roles in Shōyō's plays were taken by Sumako Matsui (1886–1919, real name Masako Kobayashi), whose family in Nagano prefecture claimed descent from samurais. Her first marriage had a short life. Going to Tokyo, she married again, this time to a teacher. Frustration and boredom led her to attach herself to Shōyō's acting troupe. After a year her second husband, Seisuke Maezawa, left her; this happened just when she was assuming her first important stage part, Ophelia in *Hamlet*. She is most vividly remembered as Nora in *A Doll's House*, which helped to ignite the feminist movement in Japan, as it had earlier in Ibsen's Norway.

Hōgetsu Shimamura (1871–1918), a protégé of Shōyō, was particularly effective in directing Matsui. A liaison grew up between them; to be with her he left his wife and children, and a scandal ensued. The pair, quitting the Bung Kyokai, formed their own company, the Geijutsuza, with which they travelled widely in Japan and Manchuria. She appeared in many roles in versions of Western dramas, among them Tolstoy's *Resurrection* (a recording of her rendering of "Katusha's Song" from it was exceedingly popular), Wilde's *Salome*, and dramatizations of Tolstoy's *Anna Karenina* and Mérimée's *Carmen*. Her emotional dependence on Shimamura was so great that, a bare two months after the director's death, she killed herself.

Several other late nineteenth- and twentieth-century writers sought newness. After a stay in Germany, Ōgai Morai (1862–1922) came back to Japan in 1888 and asserted that reform in the theatre was needed but should begin not with changes in production styles but instead with a different kind of script; the text should have a more recognizable literary quality. He debated with Shōyō on the extent to which the demands of idealism should be expressed in drama, with *Macbeth* used as a starting point for the discussion. The exchange of ideas between them was broadly influential.

It was Morai who introduced the Symbolist works of Maeterlinck and von Hofmannsthal. He himself wrote a romantic tragedy, *Ikutagawa* (*River Kkuta*; 1910). Working in contrasting veins, Mokotarō Kinoshita (1885–1945) offered *Nambanji monzen* (*Before the Gates of the Namban Temple*; 1909), a "mood piece", and a somewhat more realistic script, *Izumiya somemonomise* (*Izumiya Dyers*; 1911), in which a conflict arises between "old conventions and new ideals".

Following Shōyō's lead in emphasizing characterization rather than plot and situation, as most had not done before, his converts initially chose historical subjects, which is how he had begun his change-over. They were particularly inspired by his translation of *Hamlet* and other Shakespearian works. But many elements of Kabuki were still in evidence in their scripts. An instance of this is *Horaikyoku* (*The Ballad of Mount Horai*; 1891), a verse drama by the romantic poet Tokoku Kitamura who had hardly expected to see it staged. Most of the writers in Kitamura's category were called "outsiders" because they had freelance careers; they were not retained on staff by a commercial manager. Reform did not penetrate into that world. The entertainment business was thriving, and the frenzied producers had no time or money for risky experiments.

Beside its debt to Shōyō, Shingeki owed much to the poet and novelist Osani Kaoru (1881–1928). Though his own writing for the stage was not exceptional, he had a salient part in the rise of realism: he was a co-founder with the Kabuki actor Sadjani Ichikawa II of the Jiyū Gekijō (Free Theatre) which for a decade (1909–19) offered a home to productions of modern European scripts. The company consisted of Kabuki players, including actresses, eager to acquire the latest techniques. Osani Kaoru spent several months in Russia and Western Europe to familiarize himself with the advances there. Sadjani Ichikawa II's eventual defection – he was distracted by other ventures – led to the troupe's break-up. Again, from 1924 for the four years until his untimely death, he served with great skill as director of the Tsūkiji Shōgekijō (Tsukiji Little Theatre), another group attracted to Westernization and linked to Osani Kaoru.

Another of Osani Kaoru's collaborators in these brave enterprises was the left-leaning Yoshi Hijikata (1898–1959), who had also observed theatre in Berlin and Moscow. They had what they considered to be well-founded hopes, for their playhouse was new and handsomely equipped. It accommodated five hundred ticket-buyers. ("Tsūkiji" connotes "Little Theatre"; the playhouse was located in Tokyo's Tsūkiji district.) Forty-four productions were mounted, including Shakespeare's *Julius Caesar*, Ibsen's *Ghosts* and *Enemy of the People*, Strindberg's *Miss Julie*, Chekhov's *The Cherry Orchard*, Luigi Pirandello's *Six Characters in Search of an Author*, Romain Rolland's *Les Loups* and Eugene O'Neill's *Beyond the Horizon*. Before the theatre opened, Osani had asserted in a lecture at Keio University that he would stage only foreign works because good native scripts did not exist. But in 1926 he finally chose *The Hermit* by Shōyō, a drama borrowing its subject from Japanese mythology and presenting a conflict of one man against evil forces, in which Shōyō portrays the hero memorably. After this the Tsūkiji Shōgekijō did produce other scripts by local authors who could meet the challenge of writing in accord with the best Western models. Tsūkiji Shōgekijō's demise followed two years later, shortly after Osani Kaoru's own premature death. One cause of its dissolution was quarrelsome political dissension among its members.

In 1911 another promising stage experiment was the Teigeki (Imperial Theatre Society). But before long it was taken over by the Shōchikū Corporation, a group something like the Shuberts in America seeking a monopoly of Japan's entertainment outlets and increasingly gaining control over opera, film, dance and musical revues.

Still active in the Westward move was Kichizō Nakamura (1877–1949), whose *Kamisori* (*The Razor*; 1914) was perceived as yet another "peak of Naturalist achievement".

(I have gathered much of this material from books and scattered articles by Faubion Bowers, Brian Powell, Peter Arnott, Thomas E. Swann, Kokubo Takeshi, Donald Keene, Frank Lombard, Samuel Leiter, T.T. Takaya and Leonard Pronko, and have gone often to the *Japanese Encyclopedia*.)

Some of the Japanese venturesome authors of this period, the 1920s and 1930s and a bit earlier, had local successes, though most remained unknown abroad. A biographical play laid in the thirteenth century, depicting the career of the saintly Buddhist sage Shinran, *Shukke to sono Deshi* (*The Priest and His Disciple*; 1916) won twenty-five-year-old Kyakuzō Kurata (1891–1943) the extravagant admiration of Romain Rolland, who pronounced it "one of the world's greatest religious dramas". (It is available in an English translation by G.W. Shaw.) Kurata was also a noted essayist.

A realist, Hideo Nagata (1885–1949) wrote *Kikatso* (*Starvation*; 1915). His contemporary, Saneatsu Mushanokōji (1885–1976) contributed *Aru Seinen no Yuma* (*One Youth's Dream*; 1916), bearing an anti-war message. An earlier work, *Sono Imoto* (*The Sister*; 1915), portrays the ordeal of an artist left sightless by the war, seeking to fashion a new life for himself as a novelist. Mushanokōji was the head of a group of fellow authors known as the Shirakaba School, all of whom were firmly dedicated to Naturalism. He combined his playwriting with a crowded career in politics; it was said of him, "He opened the literary windows and let in some fresh air."

Two dramatists who abandoned the romantic genre for the realistic were Ujaku Akita (1883–1962) and Homei Iwano. As Brian Powell says, few of these writers achieved distinctions as craftsmen in this new medium. They were content to have their scripts enacted by amateurs or printed and read; it was much easier to achieve publication than to gain performance by professional casts, an experience from which a young author might learn first-hand what the stage required. The Shingeki theatre continued to be mostly occupied by translations of Western classics. At the same time, modern Japanese plays were frequently dismissed as "lifeless dramatic essays" – a borrowed German term, *Lesedrama*, was used for them – and a mistaken idea prevailed that turning out a playscript was considerably less onerous than novel writing.

At first, presentation of these plays tended to be inadequate; however, as has been remarked, several directors had viewed and absorbed the methods of Stanislavsky and Meyerhold and other European masters and steadily improved their treatment of the scripts. Scene design, too, grew better.

Among the aspiring dramatists there were, as always, a few exceptions, those having an innate flair. Seto Eiichi (1892–1934) prospered by composing romantic tragedies such as *Futusuji-miji* (1931) about the involvement of a geisha and her lover, who is harassed because his business affairs are in disarray.

Yūzō Yamamoto (1887–1974), also a recognized novelist, authored a stage trilogy made up of *Sakazaki Deewa no Kami* (*Lord Deewa*; 1921), *Nyoninaishi, Toji Okichi nomogatara* (*The Story of Chink Okichi*; 1930) and *Seimei no kammur* (*The Crown of Life*; 1920). These linked works revolved about Townsend Harris, the nineteenth-century American envoy who brought Western values and manners to the long self-isolated island. (These plays, too, have been rendered into English by G.W. Shaw.) Other scripts by Yamamoto are *Eijigoroshi* (*A Case of Child Murder*; 1920) and *Doshi no hitobito* (1923). After 1928 he concentrated on publishing serial novels in which the leading characters are idealists who are indifferent to personal glory and dedicate themselves to serving what they believe to be the social good. Following the Second World War he spent much of his time and talent trying to simplify the Japanese language. Elected to the House of Councillors, he was further rewarded with the Order of Culture in 1965.

His erstwhile classmate and fellow-editor, Kan Kikuchi (1888–1948, real name Hiroshi Kikuchi), is the author of *Okujo no kyojin* (*The Madman on the Roof*; 1916), made accessible in English by Y. Iwaski and Glenn Hughes. Born to a family that was impoverished but boasted "samurai-scholar ancestry", Kikuchi showed his literary gifts before he was twenty by winning two contests in essay writing, one of them a national competition. He gained admission to the Tokyo Higher Normal School (since known as the Tokyo University of Education), which charged no tuition, but his stay was cut short when he was found guilty of a misdeed. Next he enrolled in the National First Higher Normal School (1892–7, now a branch of Tokyo University). Here he established friendships with not only Yamamoto and Ryunosuke Akutagawa but also Masao Kume; all three of them were later to win fame as authors. Akutagawa is celebrated for his short stories, especially the immortal *Rashomon*. Once more Kikuchi was forced to leave a school, this time when he was falsely charged with a theft in the college dormitory. He was able to enter Kyoto University, from which he graduated in 1916 after completing studies in English literature, with a special emphasis on modern Irish drama. While at Kyoto in 1914 he was asked by his former fellow-students to join in putting out the literary journal *Shinshicho* – the third series; some of his earliest one-act plays were printed in it. When the magazine was reorganized and issued – the so-called fourth series – more of his short plays appeared in it. As has been noted, Shingeki authors had their scripts printed rather than enacted, since the commercial theatre expressed little interest in them. One of these early scripts was *Chichi kaeru* (*The Father Returns*; 1917), which had been suggested to Kikuchi by the English dramatist St John Hankin's *Return of the Prodigal*. Kikuchi's treatment of the subject attracted no attention for a while, but later won immense respect and is now considered one of the best Shingeki works. Powell tells us, "The play, which displays considerable technical mastery in construction and characterization, depicts the superior power of family affection over rationally conceived hatred and proved to Japanese audiences of the time that new plays could affect them as deeply as their best-loved classics."

Kikuchi became a journalist, on the staff of the newspaper *Jiji shimpo*. The literary magazine had been abandoned, and his plays that had appeared in it were almost forgotten. Only Akutagawa had won a reputation. Kikuchi, too, gained notice with his *Mumei sakka no nikki* (*The Diary of an Unknown Writer*; 1918), a thinly fictionalized depiction of the envy he felt at the better fortune of his ex-classmate Akutagawa. Another of his stories, *Tadanao Kyo gyojo ki* (*On the Conduct of Lord Tadanao*; 1918), a historical piece, provided a modern interpretation of the ruthless behaviour of Matsudaira Tadanao, a seventeenth-century despot. A monumental novel, *Shinji fuji* (*Madame Pearl*; 1920), was serialized in important newspapers in both Osaka and Tokyo and finally brought Kikuchi the popularity and acclaim which he so much desired. This breakthrough was capped by the production of *The Father Returns* on the boards of a major Tokyo theatre, where it was highly applauded for its "originality".

Three years later he started his own magazine, *Bungei shunju* (1923), which reflected his disapproval of a growing Marxist trend in Japanese literature. He wanted to counteract that leftward tendency. The magazine project almost came to an end because of damage inflicted by the Tokyo earthquake, but it soon got under way again and achieved an astonishingly large readership. Throughout two decades, the 1920s and 1930s, he exemplified "moderate" journalism and was looked upon, as Takeshi Kokubo puts it, as the "*ogosho*" – "grand Shōgun" – of Japan's cultural scene.

In the aftermath of the Second World War the Occupation authorities considered him to have been one of those who had too strongly supported the chauvinistic military government that had carried out Japan's foreign aggressions. He was not allowed to seek public office or hold any sort of official post.

In 1927, at age thirty-five, his friend Akutagawa killed himself. Long ill, he feared losing "his grasp on reality" – his mother had been insane. Kikuchi established the Akutagawa Literary Prize in his memory (1935), and a similar prize in honour of another intimate friend, Sanjūgo Naoki. These two awards, which soon inspired many others, have long carried much prestige; they are perhaps the top recognition given to writers in Japan. He also brought new concepts to journalism in his magazine, and used the journal to encourage many younger authors. He is credited, too, with having been instrumental in founding what later became the Professional Writers' Guild of Japan.

A number of his scripts have been published in English in a volume titled *Tojuro's Love and Four Other Plays*, edited by Glenn Hughes. He has been the subject of several critical studies.

Masao Kume, who as a youth belonged to the same literary coterie as Akutagawa and Kikuchi, especially in putting out the memorable journal *Shinhichō*, won his lasting niche as a dramatist when his *Gyūnyūya no kyodai* was produced at the Yurakuza Theatre in 1914. Later he wrote novels and in the 1930s enjoyed much success with his books. He also issued a volume of poetry – *Haiku* – employing a pen name, Santei.

Sentimentality is a mark of the dramas of Kawaguchi Matsutaro (1899–?), best remembered for his *Furyu Fukagawa-uta* (1936), which traces the altered fortunes of a family who preside over a public eating-place.

Steadily, Shingeki took on a leftist political tone. Among its new offerings the most prominent were proletarian dramas with settings both domestic and foreign. In particular, the Tsūkiji Shōgekijō succumbed to the growing Marxist trend. A leader among leftist playwrights was Tokuago Sunao (1900–1958), who dramatized his own "worker's novel", an autobiographical account of a mass strike against publishers in which he had played a prominent role; the book had been published not only at home but also in France, Germany and the Soviet Union.

The Shingeki movement now gave birth to earnest and aggressive ensembles such as the Proletarian Theatre and the Japan Labour Theatre, presenting agit-prop stage works with titles like *Slaves After All* and *Who Fires the Worker?*

Playwrights in this group included Seikichi Fujimori (1892–1977), who hitherto had written romantic fiction distinctive for its sensitivity. Aspiring to a place in the theatre, he gave it scripts laden to some extent with Marxist ideology. He scored greatly with his *Nani ga Kanojo o sō saseta ka* (*What Made Her Do It?*; 1927), which was accepted by a commercial management. His heroine, unable to withstand the pressures of a malign social system, is driven to suicide.

Tomoyoshi Murayama (1901–77) was drawn to Expressionism but now made a leftist commitment. His *Boryokuda ki* (*Record of a Gang of Thugs*; 1929) was about a strike by labourers on the Peking–Hankow Railway in 1923. The strike failed, but *Boryokuda ki* was acclaimed as the best Proletarian drama by a Japanese.

By 1938 all the Shingeki performing groups were Marxist-oriented except for the Bungakuza (Literary Theatre), led by Kunio Kishida, which was formed that year with the aim of maintaining an apolitical stance. The others suffered regular harassment by the police. The audience for Shingeki was largely made up of sympathetic trade-union members and a segment of the intelligentsia.

Some Shingeki playwrights did withstand the strong left-wing climate. Mantaro Kubota (1889–1963), in his *Ōdera gakkô* (*Ōdera School*; 1927), adapted from his earlier novel, portrays the headmaster of a small school who faces the failure of his school and tries to prevent it. He relies on the emotional appeal of traditions but learns that his sentimental love for them is not shared by others. The work is exceedingly well structured and has striking truthfulness. Also resistant to the claims of the Proletarian movement was Kunio Kishida (1890–1954). He placed high value on language. In *Ushiyama hoteru* (*Hotel Ushiyama*; 1929) he depicts with sharp skill details of the setting and lifestyles of Japanese dwelling as expatriates in French Indochina. Kishida subsequently headed a circle of dramatists associated with the periodical *Gekisaku* (*Play-writing*).

When Japan's militarists invaded China and later joined Nazi Germany and Fascist Italy in the all-out hostilities of the Second World War, Shingeki performances were banned; the left-leaning playhouses were closed, including the Tsūkiji Shōgekijō. Hijikata Yoshi, its head, was arrested and imprisoned, as were many other "subversive" playwrights, directors and actors, bringing the movement to a full stop. Some members of it were exiled. The government, in the grip of jingoists, sponsored the New Tsūkiji Theatre (1940, National Theatre), designed to give the modernized stage a more acceptable orientation.

Since Proletarian Theatre was interdicted, erstwhile members of that school shifted to what they called "Social Realism", offering plays that avoided outright political advocacy but did treat with serious contemporary topics. This resort is seen in such scripts as *Hokuto no kaze* (*North-east Wind*; 1937) by Eijiro Hisaita (1898–1976) and *Kazan baichi* (*Ashes from the Volcano*; 1937–8) by Sakae Kubo (1901–58), both of which display more persuasive characterizations than previously found in plays by Japanese leftist playwrights. In addition, both avail themselves of broad canvases, without the authors losing control of their material. They are faulted, however, for being excessively wordy, which results in their having a platform of static moments.

Other leftist writers solved their dilemma by changing their coats, shedding their former political convictions and embracing more conventional subject matter. *Bui* (*Buoy*; 1940) by Juro Miyoshi (1902–58) is a very personal examination of the author's emotions during the final stages of his wife's mortal illness. The play is a moving revelation and affirmation of the courage a man sometimes summons up when undergoing intense stress.

This period is also marked by the reinvigorated appeal of comedy, though the humour was now of a more thoughtful kind. Similarly, melodrama was more welcome, but playwrights had to meet a demand that the plot and action be handled with more logic and a more proficient technique.

The war years necessitated stage-works that would boost public morale. Such chauvinistic plays were taken on tour.

Historical dramas found favour. A major contributor to this genre was Seika Mayama (1878–1948), who shaped a fresh and lengthy version of the legendary *Forty-seven Ronin Incident – Genroku chushingura* – which appeared serially from 1934 to 1941 and has since had revivals. Mayama had learned his craft through long experience writing scripts for the Shimpa theatre, and as an early Naturalist.

The work of Uhei Ima (or Harube; 1908–) was exceptional, being lyrical with a tinge of satire, qualities not generally characteristic at that time. Satirical notes are also present in the output of the indiscreet Tadasu Iziwa (1909–), who was chastened by the authorities for his *Choju kassen* (*Battle of the Birds and Beasts*; 1944).

Near the fighting's end, in 1944, the Haiyuza (Actor's Theatre) was organized. The post-war years, however, were difficult ones for Shingeki: playhouses were scarce, the amusement tax very high. Several reconstituted groups fused to put on *The Cherry Orchard* in 1945, a sign that a fondness for Western-style plays was still alive in part of the theatre-going community. Chekhov, Gorky and other Russian writers have been constant favourites of Japanese performers and theatre-goers.

Nor did the post-war stage abandon Marxism, as was soon evidenced by the advent of the Mingei (People's Art Theatre), a group that began to gather in 1947 and took definite form in 1950. Except for a surge of anti-Communism in 1950, leftists and other Shingeki playwrights were given unprecedented freedom and took full advantage of it. Social and political subjects of wide scope were debated in the scripts. The times were desperate, the war damage great, evoking provocative drama. Throughout this period the Mingei, Haiyuza and Bungakuza were the leading Shingeki companies; many lesser and more transient groups emulated them. In 1963, because the hitherto apolitical Bungakuza had gradually accepted plays with more controversial social content, some of its members prompted by Tusumeari Fukuda seceded to constitute a new group, Kuma (Cloud), that avoided partisan social commitment. Fukuda (1912–), noted as a translator of all of Shakespeare's plays, contributed a number of pieces of his own, some of them satirical. Among them were *Kitty Taifu* (*Typhoon Kitty*; 1950); *Ryu wo Nadeta Otoko* (*The Man Who Stroked the Dragon*; 1952); *Yurei Yashikiru* (1953), a tale of the supernatural; and *Arima no Miko* (*Prince Arima*; 1961).

Still another stage promising to promote modern works was the Gekidan Shiki (Four Seasons Troupe). So there were opportunities for Shingeki to thrive and expand.

From Kaoru Morimoto (1912–46) came *Onna no issho* (*A Woman's Life*; 1945). Matsuyi Akimoto (1912–) stirred arguments with *Reifuki* (*Dressed for the Occasion*; 1949), about the harm caused by the age-old family system, a code of conduct cherished but often so repressive that it may lead to violent emotional outbursts.

Though many pre-war dramatists remained active – Kishida, Hisaita, Kubo, Miyoshi – and lent a sense of continuity, the post-war theatre diverged considerably from what it had been before. Japan was experiencing rapid cultural change, and this was to be seen in the work of the newer, younger playwrights, many of whom could scarcely recall what conditions had been like before the cataclysmic events of the Second World War. Indeed, as a glance at their birthdates reveals, some of them been mere children then. They not only could not remember the past world but they also renounced much of what they learned about its values.

A play in an Existentialist vein depicting with striking emotional force the homecoming of a war veteran, *Kumo Hateta* (*Edge of the Clouds*; 1947) by Chikao Tanaka (1905–95), a native of Nagasaki, gave the Bungakuza its first major success. Tanaka had formerly been associated with Kishida's Gekisaku. Like other members of that group, he sought to combine in his work distinctive speech and intense thought and action. In his *Kyoiku* (*Education*; 1954) he externalized the "self-delusion and mutual distrust of his characters" by having three extended passages of dialogue alternate between prose and verse, the language at times abstract, at other moments very specific. Tanaka commanded notice with several other works, among them *Maria no Kubi* (*The Head of St Mary*; 1959) and *Tsuke Akirakani* (*A Bright Moon and Rare Stars*; 1962).

A graduate of Keio University, Tanaka had established himself as a playwright with his first effort, a one-acter, *Ofukuru* (1933). Two decades later he won the Yomuri Prize with his script *Kyōku* (1953). He became a Catholic convert. In 1981 he was elected to membership in the Japan Art Society. His wife, Sumi Tanaka, also had a solid career as a playwright and novelist.

Hideji Hōjō (1902–77) grandly exploited spectacle in his *Kakka* (*Honoured Sir*; 1940), while sentimentalizing its hero. It was a work hailed as portending "a new richness" in modern Japanese theatre.

Kiyomi Hotta (b. 1922) drew a broad audience with *Shima* (1957), the first drama to treat with the physical and psychological consequences of the dropping of an atom bomb on Hiroshima. An antiatomic-bomb protest is also sounded by Yushi Koyama (1906-82) in *Tsisamboku no ki no shita de* (*Under the Taisan Tree*; 1962), which conjures up with adeptness the quality of life on the shores of Japan's Inland Sea.

Stamped as "promising" was Ken Miyamoto (b. 1926) when his *Mechanism Sakusen* (*Mechanical Tactics*) was produced in 1962. He placed himself in the Marxist camp with his *Meiji no Hitsugi* (*A Meiji Coffin*; 1963).

The Bungakuza was floundering under debts piled high after the war years, capped by the failure of its first poster production, *Kawa* (*River*) by Katsuichi Wada (1900–), but solvency was regained the next season by a hit revival of *Onna no issho* (*A Woman's Life*; 1945) by Kaoru Morimoto. In this tragic work, started shortly before the author's death at thirty-four, a woman endlessly makes sacrifices to aid her family. The unhappy picture it gives no doubt reflects an experience familiar to many in the audience who were suffering from the hardships and chaos ensuing in the months that followed the nation's military defeat and humiliation. The play's success was due in part, too, to a moving portrayal by Haruko Sugimura in the leading part. During the earlier run of the play, air-raid alerts often interrupted performances, driving spectators from the theatre to shelters.

Another joining the ranks of the Bungakuza in 1949 was Michio Kato (1918–53). In 1945 he had written *Nayotake*, derived from a classic tenth-century legend, *The Tale of a Bamboo Cutter*. It relates how a lovely child is discovered living within a bamboo tree. She grows to beautiful young womanhood and at last returns to her celestial home. Kato's sensitive and imaginative treatment captures the lyricism of the original story, its delicate mood, and the play has become a modern staple in the repertories of Kabuki troupes.

A native of Tokyo, Seiichi Yashiro (b. 1927) studied French literature at Waseda University. After graduation he spent some years as a translator from the French and also as a stage director, absorbing theatre. He, too, associated himself with the Bungakuza in 1949 after the company accepted his version of Molière's *Les Femmes savantes*.

His first original script, *Shiro* (*Castle*; 1954), is a study of characters whose differing pasts affect their behaviour in post-war Japan, and also explores the emotion of love, in an effort to define it. A young woman is married to a man many years her senior and for whom she feels no attraction at all; she is obsessively drawn to a young clarinet player, though he is a hoodlum and is having an affair with an actress much older than he is. A theatre is the locale, with a castle set up on the stage awaiting the production of a Western drama. During rehearsals a number of personal confrontations occur, until the wife and the others realize how complex and ambiguous are their relationships, which have none of the clarity they previously attributed to them. Perceiving the young musician's unwillingness to reciprocate her passion, the frustrated wife kills herself.

T. T. Takaya comments:

On one level, Yashiro describes accurately the young people of the immediate post-war period who had lost all idealism and joy of life. For them, death was a perfectly reasonable alternative to the dream, their perception now of a monotonous future without hope. The abrupt ending to the play poignantly underscores this philosophy. The perplexing problems of love, egoism, self-sacrifice, sin and redemption – those issues that the young wife in *Castle* refused to face – become the recurring themes of his later works.

. . . Yashiro is not simply an entertaining playwright. He is a deeply moral writer who always reveals his own personal concern with the basic problems that have troubled Western man and particularly Christians.

Plays about religious conversion are scarce in the modern Japanese repertory. Yashiro takes up this subject in his autobiographical *Yoake ni Kieta* (*They Vanished at Dawn*; 1968), in which he expounds openly on the impulses that led to his acceptance of Catholicism.

He borrows from a folk-tale once more in *Esugata Nyobo* (*Portrait of a Wife*; 1957), and again examines the confused post-war scene in his *Kuro no Higeki* (*Tragedy in Black*; 1962).

Yashiro is most admired, however, for his series of three plays about the so-called *ukiyo-e* artists of the late Tokugawa era (1600–1867). They deal, respectively, with Sharaku Kō, in *Sharaku* (1971); Katushika Hokusai, in *Hokusai Manga* (*Hokusai Sketchbooks*; 1973); and Inransai Eisen, in *Eisen* (1975).

One of these, *Hokusai Sketchbooks*, was produced in Hollywood in 1981; an English version is available in Takaya's anthology, *Modern Japanese Drama*. Episodic, it chronicles the great artist's life through a span of fifty-five years, from when he is thirty-five until he is ninety, allowing the actor to exhibit much virtuosity. When first met, Hokusai is in "the prime of life", tall and robust, with a dashing presence and an air of arrogance. He is obscure and penniless, unable to sell his pictures. He is still seeking his own style, a personal idiom. Moody, his feelings shift rapidly, the changes preceded by what he calls an "inner thundershower": a sudden deluge of mixed emotions. He is stubborn, uncertain, selfish, with a sharp cynical sense of humour, especially in his vigorous pursuit of women, each to serve as model and mistress for a time. Married, he has abandoned his wife and daughter. Throughout the script, flashbacks depict his earlier years, his miserable childhood – he was brought up in the poorest section of Edo in the Honjo area. His father cleaned sewers. After his parents die of starvation, he is adopted by a well-to-do mirror polisher, who later becomes his rival for the favours of a mysterious young woman, who has saucy eyes but a strange air of detachment. Sent to art school, Hokusai quarrels with his teachers and mentors. He is born to go his own way. Much of the play is taken up with Hokusai's and his lecherous foster-father's attempts to bed this elusive and enticing but icy-cold creature, but they are for ever frustrated. In middle age Hokusai is joined by O'ei, the daughter he has abandoned. She is now sixteen, deeply fond of her errant father, and patiently bears with his drinking, whoring and especially his rowdy arguments with his landlady, with whose husband – in a subplot – O'ei is in love. The husband is a shoemaker, five years younger than his wealthy wife, and aspires to be a novelist.

Hokusai draws erotic pictures of the girl for whom he lusts. He refuses to sell them, keeping them for himself. She invites him and his foster-father to meet her in a field under a tree; there they find her in the arms of a naked youth. Hokusai is baffled by her conduct. He vainly tries to explain it to himself. He realizes that her world is wholly different from his and beyond his understanding. For him this is a lesson in humility.

Several of the characters die. From "Heaven" they look down and comment on the still living characters and provide exposition, constituting a chorus filling in the events transpiring between episodes. In his forties, Hokusai has established his name and is selling his paintings, mostly to foreigners, particularly the French. But he is so capricious and difficult that he drives away customers and is still poor. Secretly he designs kites to make money, but to save his pride he signs his daughter's name on them. She remains with him because she feels that he is "childlike". At eighty-nine, after an unceasingly dissolute life – he has been married and divorced three times – he lives as ever in squalor. A visitor is the former shoemaker who did achieve his ambition to become a popular novelist; over the years he has grown blind. Hokusai, aware of his daughter's unfulfilled love for the aged, sightless man, persuades her to go with him, since she is more needed there. Hokusai himself has found a new model who closely resembles the tantalizing young woman who long ago escaped his clutches. (She has been murdered by a ruffian whom she has betrayed in an affair.) His new model resists his senile physical advances but stays on, her motives clearly mercenary.

Gutsy and fanciful, the script is laden with historical details that create the period and the man, and it is enriched by discourses on art that relate Hokusai to the French Impressionists to whom he was an inspiration. At moments these passages do seem a bit didactic, and the shifting time-scheme is now and then erratic and confusing. (Yashiro has invented some of the characters and their actions – the play is not true to life: to cite just one instance, Hokusai had not one but three daughters.) One possible defect is that the enigmatic first model is the most interesting character in the play. Hokusai fits the stereotype of the raffish artist, the François Villon, Christopher Marlowe, Arthur Rimbaud, Amedeo Modigliani, the determined bohemian who embraces poverty and drinks too much, wasting his opportunities. Some spectators with middle-class values find it hard to sympathize with one of his feckless sort. Others will greatly envy and admire him for his rebellious spirit.

About the three plays that depict the *ukiyo-e* illustrators Takaya writes: "In these works Yashiro demonstrates his mastery over an uninhibited ribaldry drawn straight from Edo culture caught by his lively language and quick humor." At the same time he seriously probes the basic motivations that guided their fascinating careers.

In *Hokusai Sketchbooks*, he lays out the individualistic philosophy of a famous craftsman who stubbornly defends his lifestyle and artistic freedom within a closed feudal society. The play presents an assortment of colorful characters whose diversity is not dimmed even in a regimented social system. The triumphant open expression by a man whose zest for life overcomes seemingly insurmountable adversities has universal meaning.

As a professional dramatist, Yashiro employs styles ranging from the realistic to the Theater of the Absurd. He also incorporates elements from traditional Japanese theater. His urbane approach to playwriting represents a middle position with which to enlarge the repertory of the modern Japanese theater. His special talent lies in fresh, sparkling dialogue, skilful stagecraft, warm humor. His is a consummate gift for capturing the nuances and flavor of the Tokyo dialect, which has direct links to the common people of Edo. *Hokusai Sketchbooks* is typical of that easy, balanced mood, which accounts for his wide popularity.

A post-war dramatist of consequence is Junji Kinoshita (b. 1914), a son of Tokyo, who at seven was taken by his parents to western Japan; there he had his initial schooling. In 1936 he entered Tokyo University, where his major study was Elizabethan drama. While at the university he saw productions of Shakespearian and Shingeki plays by left-wing groups. Powell observes that "simply to attend performances by these groups was regarded by students and intellectuals as a form of symbolic protest against the increasingly militarist character of the Japanese government". The Social Realist scripts of Sakae Kubo especially impressed young Kinoshita. He hoped to obtain a post as a lecturer on Elizabethan theatre after his graduation, but incidents in 1938, when the rulers purged many academic leaders, changed his plans. He felt that if he remained in academe expediency would force him to compromise many of his principles. Encouraged by Yasue Yamamoto (b. 1906), a professional actress who had been associated with the Tsūkiji Shōgekijō, he chose to be a playwright, to serve the causes in which he believed.

He had already written *Furo* (*Wind and Waves*; 1935), a piece that had to wait two decades to be produced (1954). A historical drama in a realistic style, it follows the fortunes of a young samurai who eagerly searches for new values and ideals during the first years of the Meiji era (1868–1912). Some years afterwards the dramatist's former teacher, Yoshio Nakano, urged him to peruse Kunio Yanagita's *Zenkoku mukashibanashi kiroku* (*Complete Compendium of Japanese Legends*), which he found inspiring. He saw the possibility of creating a new type of Shingeki, eventually called *mingwegeki* (folk-tale play). He set himself to fashioning three of them (1943), among them *Tsuru nyobo* (*The Crane Wife*), which a half-dozen years later in a revised version became his acknowledged masterpiece, *Yuzuru* (*The Twilight*

Crane; 1949). Meanwhile he published several more of his *minwageki*, as well as a translation of *Othello*, and a trio of short plays for radio broadcast. In 1948 he joined a small, new acting group, Budo no Kai (Grape Society), headed by his sponsor Yasue Yamamoto. It was this company that staged his *Yuzuru*, with Yamamoto herself as the ill-fated crane. Her interpretation of the role was credited with contributing substantially to the play's enormous success. The play established *minwageki* as a very popular genre and led to the formation of the Minwa no Kai (Folk-tale Society) in 1952, with Kinoshita a charter member.

Couched in "exquisite poetry", the story has a motif found in myth everywhere; elements of it are also seen in the opera *Lohengrin* and the ballet *Swan Lake*. In the snow country the simple hunter, Yohyo, dwells happily in a cottage with his beautiful wife, Tsu. He does not know that in her previous incarnation she was a bird; wounded by a hunter, she had been rescued by the kind-hearted Yohyo. Falling in love with him because of his directness and honesty, she had transformed herself into a woman by an act of will, to marry and live with him.

Tsu weaves a splendid cloth called "One Thousand Herons"; it is made of her own heron feathers. A pair of evil men see it, buy it from Yohyo, and ask how they can obtain more like it. Greed awakes in Yohyo. He begins imperiously to demand that Tsu weave more and more cloth, and she tries to serve him by yielding to his wish. In order to do so she conceals herself behind a screen and reverts to her bird origin, so as to provide more feathers.

Eager to please him, she imperils her very life by plucking so many feathers from her skin. His impatient greed mounting, Yohyo peeks behind the screen and learns her bravely kept secret. Exhausted, heartbroken, she can continue as a woman no longer. She prepares to leave him: "Do not forget my love. Keep my cloth for ever, and do not forget me. I shall never forget you." Then, as a heron, she takes flight, soaring heavenwards as the twilight darkens.

Yasue Yamamoto alone appeared in almost 1,000 performances of the play, and it has been translated into more than ten languages. It holds a perennial appeal to amateur drama groups. Eventually it served as the libretto of an opera with a score by Ikuma Dan, a work that was twice heard in New York, first in Japanese at Hunter College Playhouse (*c.* 1961) and then in an English translation performed by the Harmonia Opera Company (1981) at the Martin Luther King Auditorium near Lincoln Center. In the latter instance the work was directed by Kenya Oda. The cast was composed of Japanese and Western singers; the conductor on the first night was Anthony Morss, and James Demster wielded the baton for the second. The English version of the four performances had Anthony Morss and Tomoko Shibata taking the title role on alternate nights.

Preceding the staging of *Yuzuru*, the Grape Society had put on *Hikoichi-banashi* (*Tales of Hikoichi*;

1948), in a comic vein, recounting the cunning deceptions of a smooth-tongued, lying young man.

Kinoshita finally took a teaching post at a private university in 1949, and during the next decade became a spokesman for Japan's new drama, discussing problems and possibilities. He wrote more *minwageki*, such as his *Akai Jimbaori* (*The Red Tunic*; 1947), but began experiments with other stage-forms, especially approaches to contemporary subjects. Three plays – *Yamanami* (*Mountain Range*; 1949), *Kurai hibana* (*Dark Sparks*; 1950) and *Kaeru shoten* (*Ascension of a Frog*; 1951) – enhanced his stature even more and are now considered to have been a transition from his scripts dealing with the remote past to what came to be called *gendaigeki* (modern plays).

In 1955 Kinoshita travelled very widely, visiting India, the Middle East, Russia and other European countries, China. A Chinese play gave him the idea for his *Onnyoro seisuiki* (*The Rise and Fall of Onnyoro*; 1957), about a bully who routs two afflictions that plague a village, but then is humiliated when he realizes that he, too, is looked upon as undesirable.

Political events, such as the riots set off by the United States–Japan Security Treaty (1960), concerned Kinoshita ever more strongly. He externalized his own uncertainty by writing about those who must decide how to resist the powerfully onward current of history. This brought forth *Okinawa* (1961), *Otto to yobareru nihonjin* (*A Japanese Called Otto*; 1962) and *Fuyu no jidai* (*The Winter Season*; 1964). *Okinawa* covers the struggle of the people on that island during occupation by American troops. The second of these plays is based on a scandal reported worldwide, the Victor Sorge Incident (1941), which involved spying by a double-agent. "Otto", the Soviet Russian designation for Ozaki Hotsumi, betrays his country in an effort to halt Japan's impending participation in the Second World War, and ultimately kills himself. Another weighting of responsibility for the war is to be found in *Shimpan* (*The Judgement*; 1970).

Kinoshita has composed a novel, *Mugen kido* (*Track Without End*; 1966), depicting twenty-four hours in the lives of three train engineers and how each is subjected to "dehumanizing" technology. Throughout the 1970s Kinoshita also brought to completion his translation of all of Shakespeare's plays, a task that seems to have attracted and challenged Japanese writers.

He published a considerable number of essays on drama, some of them theoretical. He was particularly interested in the problem of dialogue, trying to discover how Japanese could best be employed as a speech on stage. While simultaneously searching for a legendary figure who might serve as a dramatic hero, he came upon *Heike Monogatari* (*The Tale of the Heike*), a twelfth-century romance, originally transmitted orally by minstrels. He discerned that its language was more dramatic than later versions of Japanese and, as an experiment, arranged for group and solo recitations of this classic story. These have been recorded (1969) and are available under the title *Heike monogatari ni yoru gundoku: Tomomori* (*Group Readings from Heike Monogatari: Tomomori*). He also felt that Tomomori, a character in the romance, was precisely the dramatic hero whom he had envisaged as the result of several decades of pondering what traits and predicament such a perfectly chosen figure should embody. This led to a full-length script, *Shigosen no matsuri* (*The Dirge of the Meridian*; 1977), in which Tomomori is the focal character. In it are included the *Heike Monogatarai*, those he had previously adapted for recitation, and his own account of how the struggle between two major clans ends with the decline of the Taira. In it are also echoes of the Shakespearian.

Kasmi to hito to no aida (*Between Man and God*) is yet another examination of war guilt, the trial of "Class A" criminals before the Tokyo International Military Tribunal, and of the lesser "Class B" and "Class C" offenders in courts elsewhere, some outside Japan. Kinoshita the moralist was obsessed by this highly relevant subject.

He has translated many Japanese classics, drawn from the eighth through the nineteenth centuries, into modern Japanese. His essays and scripts, especially the more experimental ones, reveal his intense study of Western drama, extending from Greek tragedy to John Millington Synge. He has also carefully examined all technical aspects of stagecraft, from writing to production. He is most admired for his concept of the dramatic hero. Facing overwhelming forces, the hero resists them, an attitude – as we have seen earlier – that is not characteristic of the central figure of a classic Japanese drama. He derives the consistent images of the hero from Greek drama. It is hardly present in Nōh or the folktales from which he has drawn much of his material. What is more, he has embodied the principle of resistance, having taken part in the violent 1960s' demonstrations. (He also announced his conversion to Marxism.) With ten full-length plays to his credit, as well as dozens of shorter works, including scripts for radio and television, and his theoretical writings, he has exerted a major influence on the post-war Shingeki movement. Prolific, versatile, boldly and imaginatively experimental, he has been untiring in his quest for a new Japanese drama, one that is both poetic and realistic, and one that is steadfastly earnest. His works have attained translation into English by A.C. Scott, and into other languages, especially Italian.

By the mid-1980s, despite all this activity on stages, only two Japanese playwrights had acquired great reputations not only at home but also in the Western world. Both boast idiosyncratic personalities that quickly made legends of them, always helpful in building a career. The first and perhaps more eccentric was Yukio Mishima (1925–70, pseudonym for Kimitake Hiraoka). Tokyo-born, he was the son of a senior bureaucrat in the Ministry of Agriculture and Fisheries. His paternal grandfather, though governor of a province, was of peasant ancestry, a fact seldom acknowledged by the boy. His father's mother was descended from an upper samurai family, however.

The grandfather had left his post following an electoral scandal. The distinguished novelist Margaret Yourcenar, in her study of Mishima, emphasizes the firm and perpetual influence over him exerted by his grandmother, whose marriage to the philandering governor was an unhappy one. She was the great-granddaughter of a *daimyou* (prince), and herself was "a sickly creature, somewhat hysterical, subject to attacks of rheumatism and cranial neuralgia". By some reports – quite reliable since they come from Mishima and his father – she also suffered from a venereal infection transmitted by her "merry" husband. The child was forced to spend most of his early years with her.

In her quarters, where she kept the young boy, this disturbing and touching grandmother seems to have lived a life of luxury, sickness and revery far removed from that bourgeois existence in which the next generation sought refuge. The imprisoned child slept in his grandmother's room, was witness to her nervous breakdowns, learned very young how to dress her sores, accompanied her to the lavatory, wore the girl's dresses which on a whim she sometimes had him put on and was sent by her to the ritual spectacle of Nōh as well as the melodramatic and blood-thirsty Kabuki, which he was later to emulate. . . . To this precocious contact with a sickly body and soul he owed, perhaps, an essential lesson: his first knowledge on the *strangeness* of things. Above all, it allowed him the experience of being jealously and madly loved and of responding to that great love himself. "At the age of eight I had a sixty-year-old lover," he says somewhere. Much time is saved by such a start.

No one would deny that the child who was to become Mishima was more or less traumatized by the bizarre atmosphere, as biographers oriented toward modern psychology will stress. Perhaps he was even more bruised and hurt by the financial problems of the family, the result of his grandfather's follies, by the undeniable mediocrity of his father and by the "insipid family quarrels" which he himself describes, that daily bread of so many children.

. . . It is not true that his other paternal ancestors belonged, as he chose to imagine, to the military clan of the samurai, whose heroic ethics he adopted toward the end. . . . In fact, the world of officials and educators from which Mishima came seems to have adopted the ideals of fidelity and austerity of the ancient samurai without always feeling obliged to follow them in practice – as the grandfather proved.

. . . In Mishima's case, it is the almost carnal link between a grandchild and his grandmother which puts him in touch with a Japan of days gone by.

The behaviour of the boy's father was oddly ambivalent. Yourcenar gives this brief profile of him:

[He] appears to have been a sullen and correct bureaucrat, compensating with his circumspect life for the grandfather's improprieties. Only on three occasions is his behavior startling: three times, while taking his son for a walk in the fields along a railroad track, he held the child in his arms – Mishima tells us – barely two feet away from the furiously charging express train, allowing him to be blown by the whirlwinds of speed; the child, already a stoic – or more likely petrified by fear – was incapable of crying out. Curiously, this unloving parent, who would have had his son follow a bureaucratic rather than a literary career, forced the child to undergo a test of endurance like those which Mishima would later impose upon himself.

The mother, who belatedly reclaimed her son from her despotic mother-in-law, belonged to "one those families of Confucian tutors who represent the very backbone of Japanese logic and morality". She was to take a sympathetic interest in "the writings of this adolescent intoxicated with literature".

In childhood he was drawn to the morbid, pictures and tales of knights slain in battle, samurai warriors bowed over in the act of ritualistic suicide. It is significant that a painting of the martyrdom of St Sebastian, painted by Guido Reni, evoked a sexual response from him.

Delicate, bookish, precocious, the youth attended Gakushuin, the Peers' School, where he stood out as highly intelligent and talented, qualities attended by a "citation for excellence" from the Emperor.

He began writing fiction while a schoolboy and at sixteen was already having stories published in a well-regarded magazine, *Bungei Bunka* (*Literary Culture*). Even this very early work is marked by an "aestheticism" and an "aristocratic style" and betrays what he himself later described as "my heart's leaning toward Death and Night and Blood". Apprehensive that his parents might not like the boy's stories, his teachers chose for him the pen name that he used ever after.

He had a very large, erudite vocabulary and nurtured a predilection for metaphor. He was particularly fond of and influenced by the essays and aesthetic theories of Oscar Wilde and evolved and consistently employed a similar artificial style. He could write in the argot and sometimes did, but he preferred verbal elegance.

At the Peers' School, where the regimen was Spartan and the emphasis was on sports and other rough, manly pursuits, he was somewhat of an outsider. That he was "literary" often caused him to be looked at askance, and besides he was not truly an aristocrat by birth.

While he was at school, during the Second World War, he began a lifelong friendship with an older writer, Yasunari Kawabata, later Japan's first recipient of a Nobel Prize for Literature. A tie between the two was a liking for beautiful Japanese prose and a broad knowledge of their nation's classics, an accomplishment not common among young intellectuals of this time, and also an amazingly wide acquaintance with European literature, both ancient and contemporary.

He entered Tokyo University to study law in 1944 but after his first year was drafted into military service. He saw no combat, which disappointed him. He was physically weak, with a frail constitution. By his own account the war stirred him deeply, leaving an active residue in his psyche. He declared that he had expected to die, a sacrifice to the Emperor. But not all his biographers accept this self-projected image of him. They say that he was actually frightened at the prospect of being killed in battle and sought to avoid being conscripted by lying to medical examiners, and was greatly relieved by being spared any mortal risk.

In 1947, after Japan's humiliating capitulation, he returned to the university and resumed his law studies, but soon left. He followed his father's example by entering the bureaucracy, getting employment in the all-powerful Ministry of Finance. Before the year was out he quit to pursue his fortunes as an author.

His first novel, *Tozoku* (*The Thieves*; 1946–8), portrays two young aristocrats who are compulsively attracted by the idea of suicide; the story is not highly regarded, one reason being that it deals with people who are too exceptional and perhaps implausible, though his years at the Peers' School had given him an intimate knowledge of the character and behaviour of the members of an élite class.

The same year, 1948, Mishima was invited to associate himself with a group that edited and issued the periodical *Kindai Bungaku* (*Modern Literature*). Most of its members had Marxist leanings, and he did not fit in very well. Though later in his career he was considered a rightist, since he openly advocated nationalism, militarism and a kind of Emperor-worship, he was basically apolitical and in his writing often flayed the overly aggressive rightists. He was equally opposed to the excessive materialism of the politicians, powerbrokers and business magnates who dominated post-war Japan; he felt they were only interested in wealth and had cast aside most samurai traditions. He said repeatedly, "Modern Japan is ugly."

His second novel, *Kamen no Kokuhaku* (*Confessions of a Mask*; 1949), won him early fame at twenty-four. It is transparently autobiographical, describing how a troubled, sensitive youth tries to cope with the bisexual and sado-masochistic impulses he harbours. The book was shocking at that time, but surprisingly many critics did not grasp its true significance, some taking it to be merely a parody. They attributed the hero's homosexuality as just a phase in his passage to maturity, or as meant to be a symbol of "the aridity of the post-war world". At times Mishima himself insisted that the character had no reference to his own nature, but to his friend Donald Keene, a literary historian, he conceded that the book's title was an allusion to "the uninhibited and arrogant public mask that he deliberately assumed to conceal his gentleness and vulnerability". Gradually, the mask became "a living part of his flesh".

He was devoting himself strenuously to physical culture, building up his body, until he was exceedingly muscular, with impressive arms, chest and torso. He eventually excelled in weightlifting, boxing, Karate and Kendo (Japanese sword-play). He frequently let himself be photographed semi-nude, and the pictures were widely distributed. They, too, became part of his public persona. In his writings he emphasized the virtues of *masuraoburi*, "the masculine traditions of the warrior".

In translations, *Confessions of a Mask* was avidly read in Europe and the United States. He followed it with over thirty more books, some of them of scant literary merit – but others works of recognized distinction. His routine was to spend a third of each month turning out essays and popular fiction, and then dedicating the remainder of his time to his more serious art, such as his *Ai no kawaki* (*Thirst for Love*; 1950), which again treats with sexual fantasies that lead to violence and death. Mishima told confidantes that the heroine of the novel, Etsuko, a widow who has become the mistress of her father-in-law but is obsessed by a strong, healthy young farmer, was actually in his imagination a man. She – or he – kills the farmer, Saburō, when he responds to her (or his) forbidden passion. She – or he – has always wanted him to reject her illicit love.

In 1952 Mishima made the first of several trips abroad. He was particularly excited by a visit to Greece, which had been of marked interest to him since his boyhood. It inspired his novel *Shiosai* (*The Sound of Waves*; 1954), which borrows from the legend of Daphnis and Chloe but transfers the setting to an islet off the coast of Ise and changes the characters from a shepherd and shepherdess to a Japanese fisherboy and fishergirl. It is a work in a brighter mood than that of his previous fiction and enjoyed immense popularity.

Choosing sensational themes, he also published during this phase *Sei no Jidai* (*The Age of Youth*; 1950), *Kinjiki* (*Forbidden Colours*; 1951) and *Higyo* (*Secret Pleasure*; 1952), all of which "explore an underworld of sodomy, destruction, and despair in a spirit of defiantly heretical aestheticism that brought comparisons to the early Gide".

His most highly esteemed novel, *Kinkakaji* (*The Temple of the Golden Pavilion*; 1956), is about a young, badly educated, ugly Zen acolyte isolated from his fellows by a paralysing stutter. His loneliness is compounded by the enigmatic complexity of his Zen master, and an example of corruption posed by a friend. What most attracts and compels his adoration is the beauty of the golden temple, an unattainable object. He feels that he can only emancipate himself from its spell by destroying it, which he finally does. (This is Mishima's interpretation of an actual historical incident, the burning of a treasured temple in Kyoto.) Anthony West is among others who praised the story for its "psychological penetration and its vivid evocation of the life of Kyoto in Japan's cruelly testing years of defeat".

By now Mishima was a cult figure, enthusiastically admired by the rebellious young, the so-called "wounded generation". In public he was flamboyant and incessantly in the news, appearing on television and even acting in films, in one instance in the role of a gangster. He recorded songs and contributed articles to the popular press in which he set forth his iconoclastic views on politics and contemporary culture. He was successful in his efforts to court and hold on to his ever-growing status as a celebrity. He won several major literary prizes. His wife, Yoko, was noted for her beauty; they had two daughters. He was looked upon as a model husband. He lived in an "opulent Italianate villa" that he had built to his order in Tokyo, the house stocked with precious *objets d'art*. A gourmet, he had his wife take classes for the preparation of Western cuisine.

His entrance to the realm of theatre came about through the persuasion of Seiichi Yashiro, and he soon demonstrated an innate dramatic flair, taking naturally to writing for the stage. He was prolific. In most of his plays he adapts the form and often the themes of Nōh dramas but modernizes them. Many of them, like the Nōh plays, are quite brief. He sought to preserve and continue a classic tradition, while ingeniously updating a good many aspects of it. This was his steadfast aim in much of his prose fiction as well. He had always taken intense pleasure in reading Nōh plays and seeing enactments of them, and he frequently borrowed situations from them not only for his stage-works but also for his novels and numerous short stories. The young Japanese were indifferent to the Nōh and other classics and believed a sharp break from the past and its literary forms was desirable and even essential, but Mishima fervently strove to keep those genres alive by reinvigorating them and giving them new relevance.

He later oversaw the productions of some of his works. (He also wrote a short film based on *The Golden Pavilion*, directed it and took a role in it.)

His first effective stage venture was the one-act *Kataku* (*House Fire*; 1949), put on by the Actors' Theatre, the same group that subsequently presented his *The Damask Drum* (1952), labelling it "a modern Nōh play". He also had two works presented at much the same time by the Art Theatre, *Kantan* (1950) – his first real success with a drama – followed by another piece in the same Nōh-like mode, *Sotoba Komachi* (1952). Mishima was closely associated with the Literary Theatre through most of a decade and a half, until the end of 1963, when he joined Yashiro and some others in founding the Neo Literature Theatre (usually called the NLT). In 1969, however, he and some of his friends quit the

NLT to set up the Roman Gekijo (Romance Theatre) where his last scripts were presented – this was, of course, during the final year of his life.

By far his best-known full-length play is *Sado Koshakufujin* (*Madame de Sade*; 1965), written in a completely Western style.

Condemned for his aberrant sexual offences with whores, the Marquis de Sade has taken flight, his present whereabouts unknown. His mother-in-law, Madame de Montreuil, tries various stratagems to win him a royal pardon. His virtuous wife, Renée, defends him: "Mother, in the end everything in Nature is appropriate." The equally dissolute Comtesse de Saint-Fond warns that Alphonse will never change: "How can you persuade a patient that he must be cured – against his will – of an ailment that gives him such pleasure? The most striking characteristic of the Marquis's illness is how pleasant it is. No matter how loathsome it may seem to an outsider, this sickness has roses under its surface." When Madame de Montreuil learns, to her horror, that her son-in-law has seduced and run off with her other daughter, Anne, she abruptly ends her efforts on his behalf and betrays his hiding place to his pursuers.

Six years pass. The Marquis, who has been incarcerated, is granted a new trial. He is fined, set free and exiled from Marseilles. Renée and her mother, who have stayed apart, are reconciled. Renée has endured hardship in cold poverty. For this reason her mother has once more intervened on her son-in-law's behalf. But another motive for Madame de Montreuil's aid is that her daughter has plotted and taken part in de Sade's several escapes from prison, all of which too soon ended in his recapture. This show of resolve by the quiet, hitherto meek Renée has favourably impressed the elder woman. They are visited by the Comtesse de Saint-Fond who tells them that she has reached a full understanding of de Sade's unusual sexual tastes, since she herself shares an aspect of them, having lain naked to serve as a table on which was rested the chalice at a black mass; then the symbolic "blood" had been poured over her. She describes this rite in titillating detail. She also informs Renée, who is eager to depart to be reunited with her long-absent husband, that the Marquis is again confined to a dungeon, one that is dark and damp. This, too, has been the doing of Madame de Montreuil, who had hoped to win back her daughter's affection by a generous gesture but at the same time is determined to free Renée and her equally susceptible sister Anne from the psychological hold over them by the evil de Sade.

During the second act Renée speaks of her miserable state: "I have learned that happiness is something like gold dust in the mud, glittering in the pit of Hell." "People dread sin and unhappiness as if they were contagious diseases you might catch by getting too close." "How to describe happiness? It is a piece of tedious work, performed by a woman, something like embroidery. She painstakingly weaves in, eye by eye, solitude, boredom, anxiety, loneliness, terrible nights, frightening sunrises, and makes of them a little tapestry with the usual roses. Then she breathes a sigh of relief." Of de Sade: "His desires flare up with desecration, the way it arouses a horse to trample pure crystals of frost beneath his hoof." And: "He is a worker bee of pleasure." The masochistic Comtesse de Saint-Fond explains: "When you gradually come to demand more and more spice in your pleasures you remember how much as a child you enjoyed being punished, and you even come to feel cheated unless somebody is punishing you." She adds: "Yes, I knew that the Marquis de Sade was the bloodstained abortion of God, who could become himself only by escaping from himself, and that whoever was there besides Alphonse – the women he tormented and the women who lashed him – were Alphonse, too. The man you call Alphonse is only a shadow." Madame de Montreuil, to Renée, who voices loyalty to her husband: "When you mention the word 'devotion', it sounds strangely indecent. . . . When the purest word in the world is used in relation to Alphonse, it turns black as Chinese lacquer." She accuses Renée of being secretly pleased that de Sade is in gaol: "As long as he is shut up in prison you have nothing to worry about. When he is alone, deprived of his freedom, utterly dependent on you and you only, you are liberated from jealousy. Now it is his turn to be jealous. Didn't he send you some horrible letters under the delusion you were being unfaithful?" Renée charges her parents with hypocrisy, that her mother had "brass breasts". "Father delighted in those breasts because the two of you liked conventions better than love." And: "You came and went as you pleased among the rooms, talking about honour, character, reputation and the like. You never attempted, even in you wildest dreams, to imagine what it would be like to unlock the strange door that opens on a sky full of stars." Her mother retorts: "That's right. We never tried to open the gates of Hell!" Renée: "The world is filled with people who despise what they cannot imagine." Also: "You have divided people into compartments, the way you put handkerchiefs into one drawer and gloves into another, or the way you decide that sweetness belongs to rabbits and vileness to toads. You have put Madame de Montreuil into the drawer marked 'propriety', and Alphonse into the drawer for revolting immorality." Her mother: "Things are put into different drawers because they have different natures. There's no arguing that." The two women part after Madame de Montreuil exclaims that at moments her daughter's face bears a look like that of de Sade himself.

A dozen years elapse. It is nine months after the outbreak of the French Revolution. Renée's hair is streaked with white. The revocation of all Royal Warrants of Arrest means that de Sade will soon be freed again. She is being visited by her mother. Anne comes to announce that she and her husband are leaving France for Venice, while there is still time. She believes that the King should flee, too. Madame de Montreuil declares that she will remain in Paris. Anne relates that the Comtesse de Saint-Fond, perversely amusing herself in Marseilles by playing the role of a prostitute, has been trampled to death in a riot. "Her mourners were astonished to discover that the corpse they had been carrying was no longer a girl's but an old woman's. This detracted not in the least from her glory. Her dead body, feathers plucked and wrinkled thighs bared, was borne in triumph through the streets to the sea. . . . That, as you know, marked the beginning of the Revolution."

Another reason Madame de Montreuil is not alarmed is that her son-in-law should be able to protect her. He will be in favour with the new leaders, having been persecuted by the former regime. "He's made friends of all kinds among the revolutionaries while he's been in prison, and he promised that if ever I had any difficulties he would speak to them on my behalf." Indeed, she comments, all moral values have been upset, and what was viewed with opprobrium before is now likely to meet approval. "Alphonse might just as well be set free. He can brandish his whip, pass around sweets. When the whole world is free to run riot, who will blame Alphonse for his licence? I confess it, I am still convinced that he is an unmitigated scoundrel. But criminals, lunatics and paupers rule the roost now, and Alphonse qualifies on all three counts."

A long-time intimate of the family, the pious Baronesse de Simiane, has finally joined a religious order. Renée has summoned her, saying that she, too, wishes to enter a convent. Why, having struggled eighteen years to liberate her husband, has she decided to leave before his homecoming? Renée, like the Baronesse de Simiane, remembers what a blond, handsome young man Alphonse had been. The sentimental Baronesse is convinced that he has recovered his purity. "The Marquis de Sade loves his enemies and wishes to forgive them everything. I am sure he fully admits his sins. The night smeared with blood has given way to the dawn, and its holy light shines into his heart." She believes that Alphonse will follow his wife's example and be led "step by step into the light". But Renée does not share that hope. For Alphonse, she declares, "The light was holy, I am sure, but it seemed to be shining from a different place." "What are you saying? There is only one source for the holy light." "Yes, that's true. The source was the same, I suppose. But the light was deflected somewhere and shining from a different direction." Then she speaks of the book, *Justine*, written by her husband during the time he was pent in prison. She has read the manuscript and recognized that the two focal characters in it, Justine and Juliette, resemble herself and Anne. The author visits every conceivable torture, humiliation and misfortune on the virtuous Justine, who finally perishes. "Madame de Simiane, don't you think that writing such a horrible story is a sin of the mind?" "Unquestionably it is a sin. Polluting your own mind and poisoning other people's is a sin, beyond a doubt." So Renée is convinced that Alphonse is unrepentant. As she now perceives it, "He was trying to create not the emptiness of acts of the flesh that vanish the instant after satisfaction, but an imperishable cathedral of vice. He was trying to evolve in this world not sporadic acts of evil, but a code of evil, not deeds so much as principles, not nights of pleasure so much as one long night to last through eternity, not slaves of the whip so much as a kingdom."

She asserts that the revolutionary world in which they are now living is one created by the Marquis de Sade. "He no longer has a heart. The mind that could write such things is not a human mind. It belongs to some different order." Again, she says, "Alphonse has built a back stairway to Heaven." To this, she adds a lengthy, metaphor-filled coda in which she pictures what he is really like.

The servant, Charlotte, announces that the Marquis has arrived and wishes to enter. Renée asks how he looks. He is so changed, the servant can hardly recognize him: he is dressed like a beggar, his clothes dirty and patched; his face is puffy and pale, and he is grown so fat that he can hardly get through the door. His eyes dart about, his jaw shakes a little, and he has only a few yellowish teeth left in his mouth. After a moment's silence, Renée instructs Charlotte: "Please ask him to leave. And tell him this: 'The Marquise will never see him again.'" Throughout, de Sade never appears on stage.

In a postscript, Mishima explains:

Reading *The Life of the Marquis de Sade* by Tatsuhiko Shibusawa I was most intrigued, as a writer, by the riddle of why the Marquise de Sade, after having demonstrated such absolute fidelity to her husband during his long years in prison, should have left him the moment that he was at last free. This riddle served as the point of departure for my play, which is an attempt to provide a logical solution. I was sure that something highly incomprehensible, yet highly truthful, about human nature lay behind this riddle, and I wanted to examine Sade, keeping everything within this frame of reference.

This play might be described as "Sade seen through women's eyes." I was obliged therefore to place Madame de Sade at the center, and to consolidate the theme by assigning all the other parts to women. Madame de Sade stands for wifely devotion; her mother, Madame de Montreuil, for law, society, and morality; Madame de Saint-Fond for carnal desires; Anne, the younger sister of Madame de Sade, for feminine guilelessness and lack of principles; and the servant Charlotte for the common people. I had to involve these characters with Madame de Sade and make them revolve around her, with something like the motions of the planets. I felt obliged to dispense entirely with the usual, trivial stage effects, and to control the action exclusively by the dialogue; collisions of ideas had to create the shape of the drama, and sentiments had to be paraded throughout in the garb of reason. I thought that the necessary visual appeal would probably be provided by the beautiful rococo costumes. Everything had to form a precise, mathematical system around Madame de Sade.

I began to write the play with such thoughts in mind, though I cannot be sure it has gone quite according to my plans. One thing I am certain of, however, is that this play represents a pushing to their logical conclusions of views I have long entertained about the theatre.

It is strange, when I stop to think of it, that a Japanese should have written a play about France, but I was anxious to make a reverse use of the skills Japanese actors have acquired through performing works translated from foreign languages.

I have in several instances deliberately altered facts in the lives of the historical characters of the play. These changes were dictated by theatrical necessity. I trust they will be forgiven, for this is not, after all, intended to be a historical play. Of the six characters, Madame de Sade, Madame de Montreuil, and Madame de Sade's sister, Anne, are historical; the other three were created by myself.

[Translation by Donald Keene]

Frederick Luley says: "With this play Mishima had crossed into a foreign culture; the bridge between East and West proved too much in everyday life. His loss was one neither culture could afford."

Madame de Sade is also praised for its persuasive evocation of a sophisticated drawing room in the era before and during the French Revolution. As the quotations evidence, the dialogue is seldom natural. The characters are given to lengthy narratives that serve as exposition, often an inept device which points up a lack of physical action. This results in many static episodes, and dramatic suspense is rarely created. It is the subject matter articulated so frankly that holds the attention. The people are psychologically complex, and the Marquis, though never seen, is convincingly realized.

Some have found a good many autobiographical hints in the play, with the author likening de Sade to himself. This possibility has been explored by his biographers, especially by those with a Freudian approach. It is easy to do this.

The strange play, in which sexual depravity is aphoristically described and discussed in the incongruously elegant and decorous setting of an eighteenth-century French drawing room, has had stagings abroad, a notable instance being a production in Stockholm in 2000, directed by the much-admired Ingmar Bergman.

The same year (1965) brought forth his short *Yoroboshi* (*The Blind Young Man*) staged by NLT at Shinjuki Hall in Tokyo, and revived a dozen years later at the National Theatre (1976). Westerners find it enigmatic, but it is meaningful to sensitive Japanese spectators for whom it is filled with significant allusions to topical concerns, among them the holocaust that levelled Tokyo and irradiated the citizens of Hiroshima and Nagasaki. And personal revelations, too, in extravagant language.

The place is a simply furnished room in a domestic relations court. Left sightless and "abandoned" by his parents during an air-raid, five-year-old Toshinori was rescued and exploited by a beggar, who used the boy as a decoy to solicit alms. A couple, the Kawashimas, were anxious to adopt a son. As they later testify: "We wanted to personally save a child who was at the utmost depth of misfortune and to give him all earthly pleasures. . . . We saw a helpless, blind child in rags, begging. He was sitting on a dirty straw mat, next to his grimy boss. . . . After one glance, I knew this child had to be ours." To them, the little boy had a special glow. "He looked like a prince." Paying the beggar, they bought the child.

Fifteen years have gone by. Toshinori's real parents, Mr and Mrs Takayusu, have traced their lost son and filed a claim to recover possession of him. The difficult and delicate case is being heard by a woman member of the Board of Arbitration, Sakurama Shinako.

The Kawashimas describe Toshinori, now twenty, as very strange: he is aloof, shows no emotion; he has a hard shell which they cannot penetrate. Coming to the court to confront his newly found birth-parents, he seemed extremely bored. At other moments he grew excited over trivial details and became unruly.

The Takayusus cannot believe this, because as a small child he had been amiable, gentle. They are certain that, hearing their voices, the shell will melt. They had thought him dead and had mourned for him, but had always hoped that he had survived the air-raid on Tokyo. "When we saw a cloud at the seashore, we thought it looked just like our child. And when we heard the voice of the neighbour's child coming from across the fence, we were startled, thinking it was our own Toshinori's."

The Kawashimas assert that their legally adopted son has no wish to leave them, and Mr Kawashima warns that in fact Toshinori is a "dangerous maniac", very hard to control.

The blind Toshinori is led in, carrying a cane, wearing dark glasses and attired in a well-tailored suit. He treats both pairs of parents with contempt. He alludes rudely to the obsequious Kawashimas as "stupid" and rebukes the Takayusus for having sought to save their own lives during the air-raid, rather than trying to rescue him. When they try to embrace him, he brushes their hands away.

Even stranger than the sightless young man's behaviour is that of Miss Shinako, the mediator. "You mustn't get emotional," she tells them. "In any event, this is a place of peace where disputes should end with smiles." She holds an "invisible balance" in her hand and will deal impartially with both parties. "To me, most disputes are mere illusions – just deliberate tricks played by a strange, evil spirit. All complicated situations are also illusions. The world is actually simple and eternally silent. At least, I believe that. So, I have the courage of a white dove that descends on the sand of a bull ring during a savage fight and waddles about awkwardly. Why should I mind if my white wings are spattered with blood? Blood and fighting are both illusions. And I can walk calmly among you. . . . Just like a dove strolling on a beautiful temple roof next to the sea."

Toshinori's speeches are both vivid and cryptic. He is told: "Your mother's crying." He replies: "So what? I can't see anyway." "But surely you can hear her voice." He says: "It's a dear voice." His father exclaims: "Toshinori! You're beginning to recognize us!" The son says, spitefully: "Recognize what? I only meant that I missed the sound of someone crying. I hadn't heard that for a long time. It's a typically human sound. When this world comes to an end, man will lose his power of speech and only cry out. I'm sure I've heard that crying once before." A moment later, as Mr Takayusu continues talking, Toshinori cuts him off: "There you go chattering again. You ruin everything through words. The humanness of the sound has faded away again . . . It's terribly hot. Like being in a furnace. The flames are blazing furiously on all sides. The flames are dancing around me in a circle. Isn't that so, Miss Sakurama?"

The young lady arbitrator compliments him on his proper attire, but he disparages his suit and indexes the trivial debris in his pockets: "matches, loose change, transfers, safety pins, losing lottery tickets, dead flies, and pieces of an eraser . . . lint".

Mrs Takayusu protests: "He's grown up all twisted!"

Toshinori objects to "this feeling of being strangled and this feeling of the sweat-soaked underwear sticking to my skin. I've been forced to wear a silk collar and a cotton straitjacket. Isn't that so? I'm a naked prisoner."

When Mrs Kawashima agrees with him, placatingly, he snarls: "Mother is always so understanding."

To quiet him, both the Takayusus and Kawashimas assent to his being called "a naked prisoner", but their attempt to please him evokes his scornful laughter.

A few minutes later he proclaims: "A light shines in all directions from the centre of my body. Can you see it?" They assured him that they do. He informs them: "Good. You've got eyes solely for that purpose. To see this light. Otherwise, it's better you should lose your eyes somewhere."

They remark to one another about his sensitivity on the subject of eyesight. He shouts: "Shut up!" He commands that they see only what he wants them to see. He spouts a list of absurd, fantastic images – a white, winged horse crouching inside a refrigerator late at night; a cuneiform typewriter; a dark, green, deserted island inside an incense burner. "You must all instantly see that kind of miracle – any kind of miracle. You're better off blind if you can't . . ." (Here, possibly, Mishima is depicting the task of the poet and the reader, the writer whose creative imagination conjures up miracles, the listener who is captured by the poem and submits to it?)

Now Toshinori insists that he is bodiless, without shape or substance. "I don't have a form, but I'm light. I'm a light inside a transparent body."

The four elders, daunted, accept his self-description.

As if carrying further an ethereal portrait of the artist, he opens his jacket: "Look carefully. The light is my spirit . . . Unlike the rest of you, my spirit wanders naked around this world . . . My light can burn another body, but it also produces burns on my spirit. Ahh, it's such a struggle to live naked – like this. It's such a struggle . . . Since I'm a hundred million times more naked than the rest of you . . ." (Again Mishima seems to be referring to the artist who, at whatever cost and however painfully, bares his most intimate feelings and thoughts.)

Toshinori declares the world to be already gone. "Can you understand? If you're not a ghost, then this world must be. And if this isn't a ghost . . . [*He points directly at Mrs Takayusu*] You are!"

Though still in a mood to appease the young man, Mr Kawashima cannot stop himself from exclaiming: "Didn't I say he was a maniac?"

Reverting to a normal state, Toshinori asks for a cigarette, then speaks once more of the world having come to an end. "We're all living in terror." He adds: "Even so, the rest of you don't recognize that terror. You're living like corpses. What's more, you're all cowards. You're insects." He deluges them with insults, but they refuse to pay heed to them.

Miss Shinako declares the contest between the two couples to be a draw. She asks both the Takayusus and Kawashimas to withdraw while she talks privately to Toshinori. She is warned by his foster-mother: "Though I think you already know, the child is dangerous. Very dangerous. And you must be careful of the venom he carries." (This is thought by some to be an ironic comment on Mishima himself, his reputation.)

Toshinori smiles coldly, pleased at having driven away those quarrelling over him. The Kawashimas are his slaves, he observes, and the Takayusus are "unredeemable fools".

He speaks seductively to Miss Shinako. He has been told of her beauty. "Since the seeing eyes see only form," he – blind – has a surer, deeper perception.

Over and over he speaks of "flame", recalling the night of the fiery air-raid that seared his eyeballs. When Miss Shinako comments on the sunset, which is like a furnace, he goes into a long and eloquent "aria" about the cataclysmic night when his world was consumed in a huge blaze, one that still burns furiously in his mind. It is a picture, for ever alive for him, that he prophesies will soon be repeated. He hears a dreadful sound in a vast quiet, "the agonized cry of humanity". Everywhere are the dead. His words create his dreadful vision for her.

He collapses. She kneels beside him, until he regains consciousness. Had she, too, seen the end of the world? Her answer: "No, I saw only the sunset." He pushes her away: "You're disgusting." She refuses to leave him, a fondness for him born in her.

> TOSHINORI: You're trying to take the scene of the end of the world away from me.
>
> SHINAKO: That's right. And that's my job.
>
> TOSHINORI: I can't live without it. And you're going to take it away from me though you realize it?
>
> SHINAKO: Yes.
>
> TOSHINORI: You don't care if I die!
>
> SHINAKO [*smiling*]: You're already dead.

Soon they are clasping hands; she promises to stay with him. He says, "I don't know why but everyone loves me." (Translation by Ted T. Takaya)

Some details of *Yoroboshi* are based on a well-known Nōh play, and its form parallels that of works in the centuries-old genre. It is brief, moralistic, has a simple setting, revolves about an initially baffling encounter with a ghostly figure from the past: some part of Toshinori has died. The language is heightened. Similarly, an earlier, evil incident is revealed at a present meeting and determines its tone and outcome. Some of the symbolism that resonates with abounding metaphors in the poetic script is likely to elude a Westerner who lacks an intimate knowledge of Japanese history, mysticism and philosophy, and who is not fully aware of how Mishima introduces variations on the drama that is the source of *Yoroboshi*. Takaya, in his prefatory essay, comments:

> The elegance and economy of this traditional theatre is brilliantly evoked on the contemporary stage in a context of fire-storms and universal guilt. Although his modern Nōh play has no dancing, classical music, or chorus, and the performers appear without masks and are dressed in modern clothes, nevertheless Mishima is able to effectively produce the mysterious mood unique to the Nōh theatre.
>
> Among the classical theatres of Japan, whether Nōh, Kabuki, or Bunraku, realism *per se* was never an issue: the elements of drama, dance, and music were integral parts of the total theatrical experience. Thus a renewed appreciation of the richness and diversity of Japanese classical tradition heralded by playwrights like Mishima provided an impetus for redirecting the modern Japanese theatre to its own cultural past as a source for creative activity.

Yorobushi, together with *Sotoba Komachi*, translated by T. T. Takaya and Donald Keene, respectively, were staged off-Broadway for a limited run in 1980. The cast was Asian-American.

After a visit to New York in 1957 which had a depressing effect on him, he articulated a metaphysic which he designated as "active nihilism".

Mishima's neo-classicism, his attachment to the past, also prompted him to write new Kabuki plays, borrowing familiar themes from that more recent stage and handling them in a fresh, very personal manner. He experimented; he adopted the styles of dialogue of Kabuki authors in successive periods of the history of the genre. Drawing on Western mythology and subject-matter, as he did with his *Madame de Sade*, he offered his own version of Racine's *Phèdre*.

His displeasure with political and social affairs in Japan in his own times sharpened. He spoke of his fellow countrymen as "drunk" with prosperity. In a Quixotic effort to counteract vulgarity, materialism and corruption, in 1968 he organized the Shield Society, a paramilitary unit of zealous young men dedicated to defending the Emperor – though not specifically Hirohito, then reigning as nominal ruler. Under pressure during the American occupation, Hirohito had renounced his hereditary claim to divinity, earning Mishima's disdain. His concept of "Emperor" was somewhat abstract. The Shield Society was ultra-nationalistic, and it was made up of only 100 aristocrats, with an aim of recapturing "a high ideal or grace lacking in the contemporary world". As a political force it was popularly looked upon as laughable.

In 1970 Mishima reached forty-five. Two years before, for the third time, he had been nominated for a Nobel Prize, an honour that was to go instead to his friend and mentor Yasunari Kawabata. For several years Mishima himself had been working on a quartet of novels bearing the general title, *The Sea of Fertility*, an allusion to a barren plain on the moon which he likened to the contemporary moral landscape. In a letter accompanying the final volume sent to his editor in New York, he stated: "In it I have put everything I felt and thought about life and the world." He confessed to feeling "utterly drained and exhausted".

Gathering four dapperly uniformed students who belonged to his Shield Society, he drove with them in a new automobile to the headquarters of the nation's Eastern Ground Self-Defence Forces, seized and occupied it, binding and holding prisoner the garrison commander, General Kanetoshi Machete. The invaders were armed with swords and daggers, much like ancient samurais. When guards rushed to the rescue, Mishima's little band drove them back, slashing a number of them and locking them out. In an attaché case the playwright had brought a cherished antique sharp-bladed weapon and a shorter knife.

He demanded that the garrison troops assemble on the parade-ground below the balcony on which he appeared. His audience of 1,200 soldiers saw him wearing in "kamikaze style" a fluttering headband.

In a ten-minute speech that was hardly heard over the din, he exhorted them: "Listen to me! I have waited four years for an uprising. Are you warriors? If so, why do you guard a constitution that denies the very reason for your existence? Why can't you realize that while this constitution is in force, you cannot be saved? Is there none among you willing to hurl his body against the constitution that has rendered Japan spineless? Let's stand up and fight and die together for a cause that is far more important than our lives. That's not freedom or democracy, but the most important thing for us all, Japan."

His facial expression was described as "frozen in a frantic vice".

His words were greeted with derisive shouts by the throng of soldiers below. Cries of "Fool!" and "You idiot!" drowned out many of his words, his voice growing hoarse as he tried to make himself heard, his gestures for emphasis – his hands were in white gloves – futile. Recognizing his plea to be in vain, he finally announced: "We're going to enter our protest against the constitution with our deaths." His last cry to the crowd was "*Tenno Heika Banzai!*" (Long Live the Emperor!)

Returning to the commander's office, Mishima bared himself to the waist and knelt in front of the bound General, who gazed on in horror and beseeched, "Don't be a fool, stop it!" Heedless, Mishima carried out *seppuku*, the ritual samurai suicide also called *hara-kiri*. With a ceremonial dagger he stabbed himself in his left abdomen, disembowelled himself, then ordered one of his young disciples, Masakatsu Morita, to behead him. With one stroke of the seventeenth-century sword Morita decapitated his leader, then thrust a knife into himself and was killed by another assenting student. The others in Mishima's little band, weeping, saluted the dead pair and gave themselves up. They were sentenced to four-year prison terms.

Fastidious to the very last, Mishima had bound his loins with a white cloth to catch and contain any excrement that his disembowelment might let loose from his entrails.

Hearing on a radio broadcast of his son's attack, his father complained: "What troubles he causes me! We'll have to make apologies to the authorities . . ."

Later Mishima's wife declared that she was not surprised by his grandiose gesture of self-destruction, but had thought it would not happen for another year or two. Her husband had once said of her, "Yoko has no imagination."

He had visited his parents on the preceding day. His mother subsequently remarked, "He looked very tired." On his desk he had left a piece of paper on which he had written: "Human life is limited, but I would like to live for ever." These signs are interpreted by Yourcenar as indications that he had not acted impulsively but had meticulously prepared himself for the mortal deed.

When callers came with condolences, his mother told them: "Don't grieve for him. For the first time in his life, he did what he wanted to do."

Japan's Prime Minister, at the initial report, burst out: "He was mad."

The author's death, with such anachronistic theatrical trappings, was a global sensation, featured on the front pages of newspapers far from Japan. A good many attempts were made to interpret it. It was not considered to have been an act of pure patriotism by Mishima. His life-long infatuation with thoughts of violence and death was recalled.

In a short story, which he later made into a film (1965) with himself in the leading role as a young army lieutenant, he had enacted and glorified the rite of *seppuku*. Such a death, he declared afterwards, was "the ultimate dream of my life".

Some of his friends and critics believed that he felt himself at the end of his literary career, depleted of inspiration; some propounded that he feared growing old, no longer strong and virile. They argued that he wanted to perish while he was still "beautiful" enough to ennoble the deed by self-destruction.

Kenkichi Yamamoto proclaimed that Mishima's existence had "reached its apex in one pyro-technic explosion beyond time and space – one flash in the darkness and nothing else". He had died at forty-five, which was just the appropriate age, asserted Yamamoto – fifty would have been too late.

These theories were plausible. Shortly before his final move he had accepted a Japanese book-seller's suggestion that he pose for a series of photographic illustrations – fifteen – of a male's body after drowning, a hatchet buried in his brain, death by duel, *hara-kiri*; and three weeks before his aborted attempt to lead a national uprising he had consented to having a set of pictures of himself in the nude exhibited at a Tokyo department store.

It was universally agreed that the double suicide had cost the nation a great talent and a young life.

The headless body was cremated. He left as a personal statement two farewell poems – in the form of the thirty-one-syllable *waka* – one of which read:

> The sheaths of swords rattle
>
> As after years of endurance
>
> Brave men set out
>
> To tread upon the first frost of the year.

Harold Clurman, the American director and critic who had twice met and interviewed the play-wright in Tokyo, ventured this partial analysis in reviewing two biographies (by John Nathan and Henry Scott-Stokes) published soon after Mishima's final gesture.

He was above all a romantic esthete. Elegance, refinement of manners, courtliness of behavior held him spellbound. He compensated for his shyness by becoming something of a poseur, a show-off. He disguised his inner frailty by bravado; he aimed to shock. The chivalric prowess and grandeur of the samurai (lordly warrior) tradition fired his imagination like some epic spectacle which was not only to be admired but emulated. A fascination with blood was not so much a trait bespeaking cruelty as the visible symbol for him of human vitality. He could fancy nothing more marvelous than death on behalf of a great cause. Quintessentially Japanese, he ascribed this configuration of attitudes to the persona of a god-like emperor. But it was not, it must be stressed, the real emperor (Hirohito) he idealized but the emperor of ancestral memory.

A Freudian might deduce from this complexity symptoms of a homosexual disposition unconsciously prompted to punish itself. Both Nathan and Scott-Stokes alternate between finding the key to Mishima's personality in its erotic core or in his esthetic nature. What for me is most significant is a matter which extends beyond the individual case of Mishima himself.

"All I desire is beauty," Mishima wrote in his diary. He wanted to make himself beautiful as well as strong. Beauty for him was purity, a purity which might realize itself in noble action. But his love of beauty was not simply personal. Partly on its account he hated post-war Japan.

. . . As Nathan points out, "Having established the crucial necessity of defending the person of the emperor, Mishima defined His Majesty's principal enemy as 'any totalitarian system on the left or right.'" What Mishima invoked was a "cultural emperor" – a figment of a poet's mind. Like many artists, Mishima arrived at what he supposed to be a political position through his esthetic sensibility. "The whole of Japan," Scott-Stokes repeats Mishima as having told him, "was under a curse. Everyone ran after money. The old spiritual tradition had vanished."

The unquenchable thirst for beauty in him developed into a destructive force. The thirst turned against itself. For just as a drive toward absolute purity may lead to a self-imposed martyrdom, so extreme estheticism may prove self-depleting, a humiliation. The same is true of a mythmaking romanticism.

. . . Mishima was forever seeking a faith, a religion, a God he could not find. Man cannot live by beauty alone: the esthetic and the romantic idea, when divorced from the whole context of existence, contains the seeds of extinction. They are death bearers, and the Mishima formula, as John Nathan makes clear, was one "in which Beauty, Ecstasy and Death were equivalent and together stood for his personal holy grail." The equation is suicidal. Mishima's life was the enactment of a fiction. Every aspect of his final solution: the frenzied harangue from the high point of a public monument to the assemblage below, the preconceived order to have his head struck off by a sword in the hand of his closest friend in the company of his other companions, were all part of an elaborate ritual.

Yet, as a Japanese professor at Kyoto said to Clurman, Mishima was a man of a "frightening talent". Yasunari Kawabata, who knew him so very well, declared: "[His] was the kind of genius that comes along perhaps once every three hundred years." In the *Times Literary Supplement*, the unsigned author of an obituary notice granted: "His vitality, his capacity to tell a story and to evoke atmosphere, his insight into the seamier or less rational sides of human character, and his architectonic style make him a writer of great importance not only in Japan but also in the literature of the modern world."

Though he died in mid-life, Mishima left a vast output (depending on the source): forty-seven novels; eighteen plays – some speak of as many as thirty-three, though another list credits him with twenty-one full-length dramas and thirty-one one-acters; twenty volumes of short stories; as well as numerous collections of poems, articles and essays on a very broad range of topics.

Eight years after his death a six-day display of Mishima's dog-eared manuscripts, some published and others hitherto unknown, proved to be a magnet for more than 20,000 young persons, silent and attentive, who filed three-deep through the exhibition in the Isetan department store. The event reawakened debate on the significance of the playwright's life and career. His wife, Yoko, said: "I really want him to be understood as a literary man, leaving out exaggerated aspects and bringing back the pendulum of opinion, which swung too far to one side." But many concurred with Momo Iida, a hostile leftist critic, who asserted: "The political significance of that *hara-kiri* at Ichigaya has not faded away. . . . The actor named Mishima is dead, but his ghost can well replay that drama in the hearts of the people. In fact, this ghost today is more alive and vivid than ever before."

The display included a mock-up of the Mishimas' "once-celebrated" drawing room in his Tokyo home, with its French and English antiques. Alongside a chair stood a "life-sized bronze nude statue" of him. Echoing through the exhibition was a recording of Mishima reading from his *Icarus*, a piece in which he likened himself to the mythical Greek whose wings melted and plunged him to death when boldly he flew too near the sun.

Shinchosha, his publisher, reported that sales of Mishima's books had been steadily mounting. Discussing the duration of his cult some critics suggested it was due to his dynamic personality and compared his attraction to that of Byron and Hemingway. Iida found a more sinister reason for the writer's lasting appeal. "As long as political corruption, economic exploitation and other modern ills prevail, the ghost of Mishima remains immortal."

The next year (1980), the tenth anniversary of Mishima's suicide evoked a memorial service at his tomb in Tama Cemetery attended by a score of former members of the now defunct Shield Society and representatives from other rightist groups. Another thousand admirers of his literary works gathered in a Tokyo hall to hear speeches lauding his contributions. In all, six observances were held in the capital. The occasion was also marked by a television programme: on it survivors of the Shield Society voiced lasting devotion to their lost leader. (By some accounts, the writer spent $200,000 of his own to train the group. He designed the uniforms with the assistance of a tailor who had cut a suit for General de Gaulle.)

In 1984 the playwright once again became the focus of a controversy when a very ambitious film, *Mishima*: *A Life in Four Chapters*, was shown at the Cannes Film Festival. The rights to his personal story had been obtained by Leonard Schrader, an American living in Tokyo, from the widow, who set as a condition that the film should contain no references to his bisexuality – a trait which she denied had been his – or to the violent circumstance of his death. Schrader, a teacher-missionary, wrote the scenario in English, and had it translated into Japanese by his wife Chieko, after which he turned the project over to his brother, Paul Schrader, an established Hollywood director, who further revised the script.

Schrader told Aljean Harmetz that the work was structured as two grids, one atop the other. "'The stylistic grid is the last day of Mishima's life which is shot in color in pseudo-documentary style like a Costa Gavras film. Everything in his life prior to November 25, 1970 was shot in black-and-white and static in composition. Then there are excepts from his novels *The Temple of the Golden Pavilion*, *Kyoko's House*, and *Runaway Horses*. The stories from the novels use stylized sets designed by Eiko, who didn't design anything else in the picture. That's to make reality seem synthetic.'" Also, the narrative flow "is interrupted for black-and-white flashbacks and for glimpses of Mishima's fantasy life through an excerpt from the appropriate novel. 'At the moment of Mishima's death, you see how each of novels – his fantasies – ends.'"

The film pleased many of the critics and was widely regarded as a high point of the festival and deemed certain to win the top honour, but it did not. Instead it was awarded a special prize for its avant-garde score by Philip Glass, stylized sets by Eiko Ishioka and cinematography by John Bailey.

Released shortly afterwards in Paris, *Mishima* was well received and ran in nine theatres concurrently. In the United States, however, it was less enthusiastically noticed. Vincent Canby, in the *New York Times*, said: "[It] is as crazy and doomed an endeavor as Mishima's attempt to save modern Japan – to cleanse it of corrupting Western influences. Here is an American film, in Japanese with English subtitles, written, directed and photographed by Americans, made in Japan with a Japanese cast, which attempts to reveal the spiritual mysteries of an essentially Japanese phenomenon. That it doesn't succeed is almost a foregone conclusion. What is surprising, however, is that *Mishima* is as tolerable as it is, given all the strikes against it." Canby thought that the picture would puzzle those who had not read some of the playwright's novels. "It is a splintered portrait of the man, composed, in part, of fairly conventional biographical data – about his unhappy childhood and his eccentricities as a literary lion, but including nothing about his wife and children or his relations with his parents in later life. These sequences are supplemented by highly stylized excerpts from the novels, which attempt to dramatize his love of Beauty (with a capital 'B'), his increasing dissatisfaction with Art ('Art is a shadow'); and the question that came to haunt him as he approached middle age, 'Can Art and Action still be united?'"

The picture was banned from the Tokyo Film Festival on the pretext that it might provoke hostile demonstrations by right-wing organizations. Many Japanese theatres refused to show it, expressing the same fear. Gossip had it that the government exerted pressure to keep the film from being made because its portrait of Mishima as a right-wing martyr might embarrass the party in power.

The task of raising money for the film was prolonged – five years – and difficult, complicated by the threat of a lawsuit, pursued by Henry Scott-Stokes, a *New York Times* correspondent in Tokyo, who objected that a substantial amount of dialogue was taken from his published biography of Mishima. (Scott-Stokes's book is a source of some details in this chapter. He admitted to having invented stretches of dialogue ascribed to Mishima in his account of him.) After many setbacks and delays, during which Francis Coppola, George Lucas and Thomas Luddy – all major Hollywood figures – took over as co-producers, the film was ready for entry at Cannes. The Japanese dialogue was retained, with subtitles in French, English and other languages. The title role was played by Ken Ogata, famed in his homeland.

Both his widow and his literary executor threatened to sue because the terms of the original contract had been breached: some scenes were too gory, and there were intimations of an early homosexual inclination; besides, some of the material used was derived from a book to which the producers had not obtained rights. The possibility of legal action was another excuse put forward for excluding the film from the Tokyo Festival. An open letter, signed and sent to the festival's ruling committee by eighty prominent European and American film-makers, was refuted by its recipients. They claimed that the producers of *Mishima*, who had not submitted a proper and timely application for a possible showing, were merely seeking to gain helpful publicity by stirring up the controversy.

(Though Mishima was notorious for celebrating homosexuality and sexual deviance, he had married at the insistence of his mother, who feared that the aristocratic line descending from her side of the family might disappear. After his death she and their children fiercely defended his reputation – and copyrights – objecting to unflattering verbal depictions of him.)

Well-known abroad, too, Kobo Abé owes much of his international stature to a widely distributed film made from his novel, *The Woman in the Dunes* (1963), which won him a cult following. Gradually his reputation as a dramatist has also grown.

Born in Tokyo in 1924, a doctor's son, he was given Kimifusa as a first name – Kobo is its Chinese equivalent. His father, engaged in research at the Manchurian School of Medicine in Mukden (now Shenyang), had been visiting the Japanese capital. The child, not yet a year old, was taken back with the family to Mukden, where he stayed and was schooled until he was sixteen. He admits to having no "roots" in Manchuria, or special fondness for it, however. In later years he recorded his place of origin as Hokkaido, where he also spent several years. Characteristically, he has described himself as "a man without a home town".

In an article in *World Authors* he recounts: "The first writer to influence me must have been Edgar Allan Poe. At junior high school, I made myself popular with my classmates by assembling them during the lunch hour and telling Poe stories. When I ran out of Poe, I had to make up similar stories of my own. In those days, I liked to paint pictures in imitation of the Constructivists, and to collect insects, and to solve mathematical problems, especially geometry. I was a wretched linguist. As for sports, I was required to practice kendo, Japanese fencing, and to run the 2,000-meter race."

He fell ill with tuberculosis. During his recuperation, which lasted a year, he – as he puts it – "devoured Dostoevsky". Then Japan joined on the side of Germany and Italy in the Second World War. As a medical student he was exempt from military service.

His autobiographical summary continues:

Fascism was gradually intensified, and though I was opposed to it emotionally, at the same time my sense of isolation led me to desire assimilation, and I read as much as I could get of Nietzsche, and Heidegger, and Jaspers. . . . My teachers urged me to major in mathematics at the University, but my father was determined that I should become a doctor, and in 1943 I re-entered the University of Tokyo as a medical student.

Emotionally I was very disturbed and my state of mind grew steadily worse until I was cutting classes often. I recall this period in my life very indistinctly, though I do remember being taken once to a mental hospital by a friend. Possibly I was the more normal of the two, for shortly afterwards my friend went mad. At any rate, for that two-year period I did almost nothing but read Rilke's poems on form and structure, which were an obsession with me.

Late in 1944 I heard a rumor that Japan would soon be defeated. Suddenly, a passionate desire for action revived itself in me and, conspiring with a friend, I forged a certificate of ill health and crossed the ocean to Manchuria without a word to the University. At that time, the government had to be convinced that your reasons for wanting to travel abroad were sufficient before you could leave the country. Happily, my father had opened his own hospital in Manchuria, while my friend's father was a high-ranking official in the Manchurian government. We had heard that his official duties brought him into contact with the bandits in the Manchurian backlands, and we planned to join up with them, and why not, since Japan was soon to be defeated anyway?

As it turned out, though, my life, until that day in August when the surrender came, was spent in peaceful idleness with my family in Mukden. Then, suddenly, the war was over, and a vicious anarchy reigned. The state of anarchy made me anxious and afraid, but at the same time I suspect it thrilled me too, aroused my hopes. At least that terrific wall of authority had disappeared. There was a typhus epidemic that winter and my father, who had been treating victims all over the settlement, contracted the disease and died. In this way, I was released from my obligations, first to the state, and then to my father.

But survival itself did not become a real agony until the end of 1946, after I had shipped back to Japan. I was extremely poor and undernourished; just staying alive from day to day took all my energies. I lived in a shack. By peddling charcoal and bean curd in the streets and taking whatever odd jobs I could get while I went to school, I managed somehow to graduate, but I lacked the funds to pursue a medical career further. Sometime during this period I began jotting stories down in my school notebooks, and the year after I graduated an editor happened to see one and it was published in a magazine. For the first time in my life, my own ability had earned me some money. And so I became a writer. In 1951, I received the Akutagawa Prize for Literature, and knew that I would never retrace my steps.

I will never forget that my adolescence began amidst death and ruins.

While still at university he married a nineteen-year-old art student. His wife, Machi, has gifts matching his: an artist and stage-designer, she has won high praise with her illustrations for many of his works.

For a time the newly-wed pair shared a hut in a scorched field. Afterwards they found lodging with a friendly artist and then moved into a tiny "cupboard-like" room of their own.

He had chosen gynaecology as his specialty. By one account, he failed his examination and got a passing grade only after assuring his professor that he would never practise.

He began his literary journey by bringing out, at his own expense, a book of verse, *Mumei Shishu*

(*Poems by an Unknown*; 1948). The poems reveal the influence of Jaspers and Heidegger, who were then the most prominent exponents of Existentialism. He was also interested in Marxism.

His short stories, of which he turned out many during the 1940s and 1950s, had a style and subject-matter that were likened to those of Franz Kafka; they are studies of people pervaded by moods of alienation and a loss of identity. E. Dale Saunders says of these pieces: "[They] apply not only to Japan, though that is invariably the setting of his works, but also to modern industrial society in general. In this sense, Abé is less specifically Japanese in his approach to modern social problems than such other giants of modern Japanese fiction as Jun'ichiro Tanizaki, Yasunari Kawabata or Yukio Mishima. Yet in another sense Abé is very Japanese; he is not fluent in any foreign language, and his contact with foreign literature has always been through Japanese translations."

Abé denies, however, having been affected by Kafka or anyone else. Typical is his tale of a homeless derelict whose body unravels into a cocoon. Another fable, *Dendrocalia*, tells of a man who is transformed into a strange, ugly plant. In the Botanical Garden this plant-man is tended by a mysterious person called K, who has promised: "I should like to offer you a room for yourself. There every precaution is taken to make the climate that of *hahashima* [mother island]. It's a paradise in a way, you'll see. As well as being under special government protection, care is taken that no harm can possibly come to you."

Secured in the Botanical Garden, the plant-man – Mr Everyman – feels a thick nail penetrate his stem as K affixes a card to it, labelling him *Dendrocalia Crepidifolia*. Thereupon K breaks into triumphant laughter. Henry Scott-Stokes and others interpret this as "a criticism of Socialism, but also of Japan's legacy of Fascism – or of *any* oppressive state".

His reputation gathered momentum: he was singled out as radical, anti-Establishment. But this did not hinder him from gaining awards. He was given one for his story *Akai Mayu* (*Red Cocoon*; 1950), and the next year for his novel *Kahe-S*. Another, the prestigious Akutagawa Prize, came in 1951 for *Karuma-shi no Hanzai* (*The Wall – The Crime of S. Karuma*). By now he had fashioned distinctive devices that enabled him to shape uniquely fantastic works that served his allegorical purpose. For example, in *The Woman in the Dunes*, a schoolteacher, an amateur entomologist, is exploring a distant shoreline for rare specimens of beetles. In this remote place he comes upon a colony of people dwelling in shacks deep in the sand pits. Their time is chiefly spent struggling against the fear of being buried in the shifting heaps of sand. Tumbling into one of the treacherous pits, he cannot climb out of it. He becomes the captive of a young widow, who is also trapped in the pit and with whom he must share the unending fight to resist the sand and survive. An anonymous critic remarks:

Out of this bizarre situation, Abé constructs a story of great narrative fascination in its account of survival techniques in an immensely specialized environment, and of the young man's ingenious escape attempts. And it is no less absorbing and convincing as a study of a developing emotional relationship which is full of universal implications – about the fragility of identity, about freedom and responsibility, fear and compassion, and about the whole nature of human societies. What so impressed the many critics who admired the book was the texture of its writing. Action is slowed almost to a standstill to permit the microscopically detailed description of physical particulars. Above all, in a way which reminded many readers of the French New Novelists, the sand itself is scrutinized with such intensity that it becomes a protagonist in the novel – sometimes a creeping, suffocating enemy, sometimes a golden film that lends beauty to the human body.

The film made Abé famous. He wrote the script for it, elaborating on his novel. Among those reviewing the picture, a dissenter has been the film and drama critic Stanley Kauffman, who gives most of the credit for its success to the director, Hiroshi Teshigahara.

Teshigahara is a better artist than Abé. All through the novel we are conscious of the plot device: a trick situation set up to demonstrate points, like a laboratory experiment. The film shifts our attention from device to drama because the two chief characters and the environment are not only much more convincingly created here but more poetically employed. Even allowing for the fact that it is easier to take a picture of a sand dune than to describe it, Abé's prose (at least in the English provided) does not equal Teshigahara's eye, and the novelist's structural sense – of sentence, paragraph, chapter – is inferior to the director's visual structures, his feeling for rhythm and montage.

The film makes clear that the teacher did not stumble but was pushed into the pit. He has been tricked into sharing it with the overweight woman, only to have the ladder removed in the morning, preventing his escape. The widow is made a captive in the same way. The village is short of manpower, and the pair are kept as working prisoners. They are ant-like. The idea is also that they should beget children to enlarge the inadequate labour force. This makes the reference to the policies of a totalitarian state even more edged.

Finally achieving a sexual liberation through his relationship with the woman who holds him a prisoner, the trapped teacher experiences a sense of freedom that he had never known before.

Saunders points to Abé's inspired use of irony:

The hunter becomes the hunted; the aggressor the victim. In *Woman in the Dunes*, the insect collector who catches beetles and pins them to a board for classification is himself caught by the villagers, incarcerated in a hole in the sand, and observed in much the same fashion as he had observed his specimens. The inversion of roles is strikingly demonstrated in the way a beetle sought by the collector habitually eludes its predators. The insect lures a pursuer farther and farther into the desert until the chaser is overcome by fatigue and thirst. Then the beetle takes over the role of predator, devouring its prey. The analogy with the insect collector's fate is obvious.

Another recurrent element in Abé's writing is the city, the modern urban agglomeration – impersonal, stifling, and ugly. Modern man is lost there, in a labyrinth – Abé uses this word frequently – the key to which he is eternally seeking but never finds. The frustration of life under such conditions is overwhelming and emasculating. Man is reduced to mere object; he becomes lost in the maze of the city and ceases to exist because he cannot be seen. For Abé contemporary life is isolated and lonely. Dangerous as well as destructive, urban living is something to flee from, for it crushes man and renders him impotent. In *The Woman in the Dunes*, the hero physically withdraws from the city; in *The Ruined Map*, by losing his identity he turns away from the city; in *The Box Man*, he rejects the city by secluding himself in a box.

Abé's novels – by 1979 he had published eleven – give clues to his often *outré* plays that too often baffle unprepared spectators. Most of his book-length fiction has been translated into English by either Saunders or Donald Keene, and some also into Czech by Vlasta Winkelhöferová; his work is said to be popular throughout Eastern Europe and is available in Russian. By the same year his stories and novellas numbered fifty-three, evidence of his energy and teeming imagination.

A brief glance: *Tanin no Kanin* (*The Face of Another*; 1964) is about a scientist whose features are horribly scarred in a laboratory mishap. Painfully he constructs a new face, but is now unrecognizable. Behind this "mask", which conceals his "real" self, he undertakes the seduction of his own wife. Here the search for identity is the problem once more. Another repeated theme is that of loneliness, especially that felt by man in an urban society. It reappears in *Moetsukita chizu* (*The Ruined Map*; 1967). A detective is tracing a missing husband. He never finds him; instead, he empathizes with the vanished man so strongly that in the end he blurs his own identity. He gradually becomes the man who is his quarry. Here is another turnabout, a psychological revelatory reversal of roles, like that of the insect collector in *The Woman in the Dunes*. The setting is Tokyo's corrupt, nightmarish underworld. *Inter Ice Age 4* (1970) enters the realm of science fiction to tell of the creation of a computer able to predict the future: at the end, a climatic shift submerges the whole earth beneath surging waters – the story has been categorized as a "philosophical thriller". *Hako Tako* (*The Box Man*; 1973) is "a chilling, hypnotic vision of a man who puts a box over his head and sheds the trappings of identity, hoping for anonymity and freedom, but discovering instead a world of collusion and deception". *Secret Rendezvous* (1979) veers into "wild comedy", following the desperate search by a man for his wife who has disappeared into a vast, bizarre underground hospital – it "brilliantly" satirizes the modern world of medical care, of which Abé had been a first-hand observer. A critic in the *Chicago Tribune* found the book "gorgeously entertaining".

All these attitudes and devices are found in Abé's plays; by 1979 he had written fourteen stage-works and fifteen television and radio dramas. From the start he chose socio-political subjects, as in *Doreigaru* (*Slave Hunt*; 1952), *Yurei wo Kokoni Iru* (*Here Is a Ghost*; 1958), *Kyojin Densetsu* (*The Legend of the Giants*; 1960) and *Josai* (*The Fortress*; 1962). A typical script, his *Omae Nimo Tsumi ga aru* (*You, Too, Are Guilty*; 1965), was put on by the Actor's Theatre and directed by Koreya Senda. The loneliness imposed on city-dwellers is the theme of *Tomadachi* (*Friends*; 1967). A young man lives by himself, until his home is invaded by a large family who insist that their well-intentioned aim is to relieve his solitude. Elements of the Theatre of the Absurd are clearly here. Despite the young man's protests, the interlopers assert that the wishes of the majority must prevail; they take away every vestige of his previous liberty. This piece was thoroughly revised by Abé in 1971, just before Donald Keene undertook its English translation. An Equity showcase production of it was presented at Shelter West in New York in 1976 under the direction of Michael Kolba and Atsumi Sakato. At Abé's request it was given a non-Asian setting and cast.

In Tokyo the intervention of producers, directors and actors was not to Abé's liking. He declared: "Modern theatre is in a terrible state in Japan. Plays are performed one after another in rapid succession after very short runs, and acting styles are hopelessly outmoded." He was determined to overcome that. He felt that he must either do so or abandon writing for the stage. Accordingly he established his own company, the Abé Studio, to assure himself sole control. He gathered a band of young actors in their mid-twenties and offered productions of acknowledged high quality. His wife designed the settings and costumes, while he himself handled lighting and sound effects. Besides his own plays he put on dramas by Harold Pinter – *The Dumbwaiter* (1973) – and other modern writers. (He had met Pinter and was on friendly terms with him.)

The troupe's rehearsal room – "tiny and dingy" – was located in the basement of a Tokyo church, the Yamate in the Shibuya section, that was hospitable to avant-garde artists and their projects. It was a centre for radicals during the turbulent 1960s.

Abé remained the company's only financial backer. He was no longer poverty-stricken. In 1972 a fifteen-volume collection of his works had rapidly sold 750,000 sets. Foreign rights, from massive distributions of his books in Russia and considerably more modest ones in the United States, had also enriched him. He paid taxes in 1977 on an income of $94,000. He visited Moscow in the mid-1950s. Though still a professed Marxist, he now drove a costly imported Mercedes-Benz automobile and indulged a growing fancy for various kinds of electronic gadgetry, including Moog synthesizers. Scott-Stokes stresses that other popular authors in Japan are likely to earn far more.

With his own acting company Abé became even bolder in conceiving his work for the stage. He moved far from conventional theatre. In a trilogy of short plays, gathered under the title *The Man Who Turned into a Stick* (1969), based on three of his own odd tales, he attempted to externalize matters that could not be adequately written about but needed to be made visual in acting, shown in order to be shared and emotionally experienced. When the scripts were translated into English and published, Donald Richie reviewed them in the *Japan Times*:

> In these three short plays the subject can be written about but its experience is necessary to make it emotionally comprehensible. Words, particularly written words, have a way of limiting any feeling of actuality and rendering the ambiguous as unequivocal.
>
> Therefore, to say that these three plays are about contemporary alienation, that they stress the hopeless plight of the modern individual, that they reflect the shattered contemporary psyche through the devices of psychological and literary allegory – to say all this is to say nothing at all pertinent about the effect of the plays when they are witnessed or even read.
>
> The first of these small dramas, *Suitcase*, is about two women, one of whom has a suitcase, this object being played by a man. It belongs to the husband of one of the women and is presumed to contain his ancestors. The women suspect a parable but the suitcase refuses to help elucidate its purpose. Curious, they fiddle with the lock. Yet, when the have unlocked it they cannot bring themselves to open it. The wife understands that, given her life with the suitcase, "nothing is going to happen, providing I don't pay it any attention."
>
> Various interpretations clamor for attention, many possible meanings intrude themselves, even after such a short *précis* of the play as this. But Abé is not going to settle for any single one, particularly when his reason for casting these ideas in play form was to create as many alternatives as possible.
>
> The second play, *The Cliff of Time*, is about a boxer who loses a championship bout during the dialogue which comprises the play. It is understood that "you can't go on if you lose this one," you cannot continue – in life, presumably – without winning whatever it is you have set out to win. Yet the failure of the fight opens up new alternatives for the boxer, things he could not do (eat chocolate

bars, smoke) while still boxing. The message is opaque and the meaning is properly multifarious.

The last play, which gives the collection its title, is about a man who turns into a stick and is examined by several supervisors from hell. The stick is played by a man again and the "plot" is complicated in that two hippies with standards quite different from the infernal envoys get hold of the stick first. At the end the audience is indicted. "Look – there's a whole forest of sticks around you. All those innocent people, each one determined to turn into a stick slightly different from everybody else, but nobody once thinking of turning into anything besides a stick. . . . You may never be judged, but at least you don't have to worry about being punished."

Again, possible interpretations occur. The theme of the play seems to share much with those of the novels *The Face of Another* and *The Box Man* – modern man's abject willingness to turn himself into an object in order to survive. Or is it, rather, a necessity rather than willingness? Or is it, perhaps, not rather something in man's nature? And so on, each conclusion drawing forth another, until the proper degree of confusion is reached.

This stimulating kind of confusion is necessary because Abé – one of whose favorite metaphors is the maze – is bringing up important matters of which nothing is known. Since nothing is known about them, we cloak the fact by naming them – we call them alienation, etc. Abé's refusal to so limit these ideas is contained within the ambiguities of his plays and, indeed, his decision to present them only in a situation – the drama itself – where he can show without explanations. His aim is to make you see without the blinders of terminology, to make you feel without the clothing of rationality.

This being so, he might be a bit more austere than he sometimes is. To tell you, as he does, that the subtitles of the plays are to be *Birth*, *Process*, and *Death*, is to lend a somewhat ineffectual hand in pulling you out of the morass into which he has, with excellent reason, plunged you. To give in to easy whimsy and fancy as he does in the ending of *Green Stockings*, and most of the second version of *Slave Hunt*, is to beg the very questions he is asking.

The richness of ambiguity demands that the creator be also ambiguous. More to be trusted is Abé's trust in his own ambiguity, as when he speaks of the creation of this trilogy. "Suddenly, from the midst of a thick fog, a large shape loomed up and by the time I became aware of it, the three existed before me as a single work. I accepted this combination just as it was, without hesitation, as an absolutely inevitable reality." That this reality is also plainly arbitrary is beside the point. The point is that, once he has written it, it becomes real. One works with what one has. To paraphrase Sartre: what is important is not what life has done to you but what you do with what life has done to you.

In these three plays, then, Abé is continuing a search, one both methodical and haphazard, for the way to communicate through demonstration something about us and our time. His efforts are largely successful. If I could have shown you these plays rather than merely written about them, none of these words would have been necessary: they would indeed have gotten in the way, as indeed they have. They will, however, perhaps indicate the nature of the most interesting drama now being written in Japan.

Columbia University awarded Abé an honorary degree of Doctor of Laws in 1975. Travelling to New York to accept the honour, the playwright and his wife Machi had difficulty gaining admittance to the United States, since both had formally joined the Communist Party in 1950. Their active participation in the movement had lasted only until 1956, just before the Hungarian uprising, however. Visiting that country, he had sent back to Tokyo headquarters a report predicting the likelihood of a popular revolt. Until then he had been organizing literary groups among workers in slum areas. The Abés' official expulsion from the Party occurred in 1962. The United States Immigration Service granted the pair a visa of only two weeks' duration and restricted them to New York and its environs during their stay.

Abé has withdrawn from politics, except on an occasion when he and fellow-writer Yukio Mishima together denounced Mao's Cultural Revolution in 1966 for its inhibition of artists' freedom of expression. He told Scott-Stokes: "I believe that the state should interfere with people's lives to the absolute minimum necessary for government. The great danger is that governments, nation states, continue to get more powerful to the point where man's very existence is imperiled." Though he did not agree with Mishima's rightist political views, Abé counted him a close friend. He had no similar tie with any other Japanese author.

Abé brought forth his revised version of *You, Too, Are Guilty* in 1978. Though having much of the spirit that infuses a work in the Theatre of the Absurd, the script borrows more directly from aspects of the medieval morality play, its characters identified only as the Man, the Woman, the Man Next Door, the Woman Next Door; these four comprise the principals, along with a Dead Body and a Policeman. Besides these, there are five walk-on roles: a Woman Shopper, a Newspaper Boy and three more policemen. The couple living next door to the Man break into his flat and deposit the body of a dead man; he has a bloody forehead, is shoeless. Moments later they return with the shoes, which in their haste they had overlooked and left behind in their own apartment. The Man enters, discovers the body, panics. How can he explain its presence? He is further under pressure because he is expecting the Woman, with whom he has a rendezvous, to arrive at any moment. As he hears her approach he pushes the corpse under the bed, then notices a bloodstain on the rug and tries to cover with a book. As the harassed Man carries out this manoeuvre, the Dead Man emanates in another part of the room and begins to converse with him, offering both criticism and advice. At times the Dead Man serves as a chorus, commenting ironically on the Man's frantic expedients; in these passages, however, he might be merely voicing aloud the Man's disturbed thoughts. Though the Dead Man is visible in the room and speaks clearly, he is seen and heard by no other character. The Man's seemingly irrational behaviour puzzles the Woman, who is nervous about her first assignation here. The Man Next Door knocks and persistently seeks to enter, but does not succeed – obviously he is trying to learn how the Man has disposed of the corpse. The Man suspects that his neighbour, having committed a crime, is seeking to shift the responsibility for it.

The Man finds ridiculous pretexts for getting down on his knees "like a turtle" and cleaning the spotted rug, while the Woman stares at him – she has anticipated that he would be a more aggressive seducer. Disappointed in him, she considers breaking off their budding relationship. She compares him to a previous suitor who was inadequate and finds them too similar in some ways. Then she recounts a strange dream about a maltreated child that had haunted her ex-lover. To her, the Man looks like the boy who, in the dream, had finally starved to death. She leaves. After a few minutes the Man also goes out. The stage darkens.

Carrying torches and wheeling a baby carriage, the couple from next door force an entrance into the flat again, retrieve the Dead Body, stuff it into the perambulator, depart. The Woman returns, lets herself in, undresses and slips into the Man's bed to await him. At last he appears, accompanied by several policemen. He has been to the police station to report the presence of the unidentified corpse. The officers search in vain for the murder victim. The Dead Body manifests itself, crosses the stage to the other side and addresses the audience: "Testing one-two-three . . . [*Dropping his voice*] Can you hear me? No, how can you? That's impossible. Testing one-two-three, testing one-two-three . . . [*Looking over the audience, Dead Body shakes his head* vigorously.] I know you can't hear me . . ." [*Quick curtain*] (Translation by Ted T. Takaya)

Some of the dialogue is cryptic. It is not explained, for instance, how the woman could know about the facial resemblance between the Man and the starving boy in her former lover's dream. The play, however, seems to be concerned with the fading processes of memory. When the Man is wiping off the incriminating bloodstains on the *tatami* (straw rug), Dead Body protests at their being removed: "Damn it! Thanks to you, I'm about to get killed for the second time . . . First it was my physical death, and now – within the hearts of living men . . . How can the law be so lopsided? It only punishes killers who are charged with physical death and winks at the second kind of murder . . . Since judges have never died before, I guess it can't be helped . . . But, in fact, the second kind is far more terrifying . . . For the victim, his having been alive becomes a total waste. It's as though he had never lived at all!" Again, he proposes that there should be "Memory Insurance". While still alive, he had made payments on it. "Indeed, social living itself is the premium for this kind of insurance to assure the proper distribution of your memory after you are dead . . . Does not this tacit understanding account for the utmost mutual respect shown to nationality, status, date of birth, name, etc. – all signs meant for others to recognize? Therefore, the preservation of Memory Insurance should be the collective responsibility of every individual as long as he is alive and the task of redeeming the payments on behalf of the dead is a sacred duty that no living person can evade." This idea, introduced suddenly into the script near the end, and then as quickly dropped, is probably not one that the audience is likely to grasp as the play moves swiftly to its climax.

Takaya interprets *You, Too, Are Guilty* as a work that "treats with sardonic humor the possible bond between the living and the dead. The strangeness of the 'social contract' that Abé uses as an arresting theatrical device is reminiscent of his best-known novels." In all the novels and plays, Takaya says,

Abé addresses himself directly to the problems confronting modern man. The enigmatic, Kafkaesque quality of these works suggests the nagging perplexities of the existential situation. In his effort to find new approaches for presenting these issues, Abé constantly experiments. To force his audience into a deeper awareness of the basic intention behind his plays, he offers stage pyrotechnics deliberately calculated to expose the ironies and paradoxes of man's existence. *Friends* and *The Man Who Turned into a Stick* reveal vigorous playwriting that demands an alert perceptive audience. Although as a dramatist Abé appears, at times, to be unconventional, incomprehensible, and even unJapanese, his basic aim is nothing less than a constant dissection of his society, which is forsaking many of its traditional assumptions and values and becoming part of "one world."

But Takaya does not clarify how *You, Too, Are Guilty* fulfils any of those goals. Since the Man does not know who the anonymous victim is, how can he be expected to remember much about him? What recollections does he owe him? Nor is the fading of memory a "modern" phenomenon. It is, however, a universal one – and the search for the "universal" is one of Abé's often stated intentions.

The same year (1978) Abé startled Tokyo spectators by an ingenious production of his *The Rules of Lifesaving*. Having only a diminutive stage, he concealed his players in numbered boxes that were plastered with old newspapers. The actors, when they had lines to utter, popped out of their boxes, now and then climbed out to wend a path between them, and then jumped back in again, slamming down the lids over their heads. Abé explained: "It saves space."

The next year the fourteen-member Abé Studio and its leader peformed in New York at La MaMa Experimental Theater. This was arranged by the Japan Society, which was funding a $2 million,

450-event programme of art exhibitions, films, lectures, concerts and dramas. The company was also seen in Los Angeles, Denver, St Louis, Chicago, Washington, ten cities in all. It was on this occasion that a lengthy article by Scott-Stokes appeared in the *New York Times Magazine*, better acquainting the American public with Abé and his unusual works. As an example, the company offered *The Little Elephant Is Dead*, a piece earlier staged in Japan. Of his feeling about its New York première, the playwright told Scott-Stokes: "It's the theatrical challenge of a lifetime. A chance to compete with the best directors, the Peter Brooks and Grotowskis of this world, on their own territory." The work is so strange and elusive that it is best to quote the description of it by Mel Gussow, the *New York Times*'s off-Broadway drama critic:

Kobo Abé, the celebrated Japanese novelist and playwright, believes in a theater of action and imagery. As he says, "Within the words themselves there must be action." An Abé play, such as *The Little Elephant Is Dead*, which begins a week's run Monday at La MaMa Annex, has a script – one that is poetically descriptive, but not fully suggestive of the sweep of the experience. In the case of Mr Abé, the play is the performance.

That play, written, directed and scored by the author, and designed by his wife, Machi Abé, is a sequence of impressions, both visual and aural. The world is illusory; watching it, we enter Mr Abé's fantasy. In a sense, the author is like an action painter, drawing from a palette of light, sound, film, props, and actors. He is equally connected to experimental theater and dance. We can feel sparks of, among others, Robert Wilson, the Open Theater and Alwin Nikolais.

The essence of *The Little Elephant* is a large white drop cloth – a stage-filling parachute silk that acts as a magic carpet. It lies flat, or snakes into ripples, or rises into the air. Depending on the light, the cloth can be translucent or opaque. When they are behind the cloth, dancing in silhouette, the actors look like primitive cave drawings. Inside the cloth, they also animate it into strange, ballooning shapes. Scurrying outside the cloth, actors wearing costumes and enameled masks look like startlingly contemporary versions of Kabuki.

Consider the opening pictures. An Abé-ian box of light is sharply focused in the center of the stage. Then the cloth, manipulated by actors, begins to float – in tune with an electronic score, identifiably Oriental in tone, played by the author on a Moog synthesizer. The light changes from green to pink to blue. Blackout. When the light returns, the cloth is broadly striped. The actors, still hidden underneath, stand tall. With bright signal lights held high in outstretched arms, they are a landscape of white stalagmites. Then they begin to move and to bend, becoming an anthropomorphic chorus of long-nosed anteaters.

The moment is hypnotic and also highly comic. As we immediately realize, this is experimental theater with a sense of humor. *The Little Elephant* is not a nightmare, but a dream such as might be recognized by Lewis Carroll.

The evening is a journey, led by an actor carrying a suitcase, marked with an arrow. There is not much dialogue, but as points of reference, English subtitles are projected on the performers' costumes. Some of those costumes resemble oversize origami. They look like one thing until they are unfolded; then they become something totally different. It is as if they are going through an instant metamorphosis. Actresses spread their arms and turn into colorful cloth envelopes. The costumes, in common with the ground cloth and, seemingly, with the cast itself, seem to have an elasticity. They stretch, and so does our perspective.

The images tumble quickly and freely; the show lasts barely more than one hour. To the sound of breaking waves, the journey proceeds underwater. Actors carrying film projectors flash pictures of fish on the undulating sheet. Later they superimpose enlarged sculptural faces, turning the stage into a Brobdingnagian environment.

Occasionally, we see characters: the devil tosses Eve an apple. Is *An Exhibition of Images* the story of evolution? Meanings are caught on the wind. One should relax and enjoy the imagery.

The actors have the mobility of dancers, the agility of acrobats and the eyesight of owls. Can they see under the cloth in the dark? Tumbling and twisting, they merge into a bulky gray elephant. One man climbs aboard for a ride. Just when we think that we have been confined in an unearthly zoo, confirmation is delivered by a subtitle: *"Don't feed the animal."*

Finally, the cloth is inflated. It billows into a gigantic cumulus cloud. Then it settles down to rest, resembling nothing so much as a large, inviting pillow. Mr Abé's dream of a play continues in our imagination.

The Little Elephant Is Dead does not overtly possess the social commentary of *Dead Class*, Tadeusz Kantor's Polish theater piece that played a short engagement at La MaMa earlier this season. However, in common Mr Kantor and Mr Abé have original and transforming visions and a company that behaves as an extension of their own sensibility. As action artist, Mr Abé is a grand performer and designer in the theater.

About the company and its production, Abé had this to say to Scott-Stokes:

My actors have to be young, because the work is hard physically, and they are all fully trained gymnasts and dancers still at the peak. I think I have mastered the synthesizer sound now and we've also been working with the big cloth for three years. These are "givens" in *The Little Elephant*. . . . They create the "environment." My intention is that the play's dream images – like the image of the little elephant itself in the play – remain mysterious and unexplained.

To go to America, I had to solve one problem: how to get across the text. None of us speaks English, apart from a couple of guidebook phrases. I hit on the device of having the cast beam onto each other's bodies sections of the translated text cut up to fit an eight-millimeter projector frame. As the text is short, we had no basic problem. The other choice was to give the audience headphones, but then they lose the music or just sit there with their heads stuck inside a box. The actors wear big cloths and all they do to make screens is to stretch out their arms and legs. Those who are not bound by conventional theater will have no problem, I hope. The lines at the end of the play – "In the love for the weak there is always an intent to kill" – provide a headstone for the whole edifice. I use the same lines at the start of my new novel, *Secret Rendezvous*.

He responded to a query by Scott-Stokes with a tentative summary of both the novel and play and other works:

One interpretation could be my disenchantment with Socialism at home, with the welfare state and the encroachment of the state on people's lives. But I would have to add that this is not first and foremost a political play. *Secret Rendezvous* describes a vast hospital which the patients will never leave. The doctors are eye-rapers, they eye patients and nurses alike – and are unable to consummate any relationship. The doctors – the government – bug the patients, they tape their rooms and they are voyeurs. This is a parable of city life.

In my play, I try to convey similar truths. All I can say is that governments are getting stronger, that nation states threaten our existence. This is, to be crude, the "message." I want to scare people a little. We say government should look after the weak in society. In your country, Britain, that means paying the hospital bills. In the United States, it means "welfare," so-called. I protest. You see, government has an unconscious propensity to kill. Look at people on welfare. They are deprived of volition, they lose their existence in the name of virtuous government.

Yes, there's a hint of nihilism in my work, more than a hint, I trust. My plays and novels tend to fly apart into a thousand pieces and it's hard work to put the bits together again. But anyway, I want to succeed in America. It's the first time I take my theater to a place where there's competition. . . . I want to be a big success!"

Before each day's rehearsal at the Studio the actors did gymnastics and practised relaxation through breathing exercises for two hours. The white cloth spread across the stage is one that he had been using for three years. His wife often asked him to replace it with a fresh one, but he settled for having it washed now and then. She declared, "It's a bore to keep on laundering the same damned sheet, but he's mean, he won't get another one."

Abé himself provided the score for *Little Elephant*. The synthesizer fascinated him. His friend, the distinguished composer Toru Takemitsu, has stated: "His results with previous plays are not good as music. But I expect that in the future he will feed into the tape sounds of musical instruments, voices and so on – he's obsessed."

The use of the synthesizer began with his *The Ghost Is Here*, the score for which was by Toshiro Mayuzumi. Among Abé's other works are *Midori-iro no Sutokkingu* (*Green Stocking*; 1974); *Wē: Shin-Doreigari* (*Wē: New Slave Hunting*; 1975); *Annainin* (*Guide*; 1976); *Suichu Toshi* (*Underwater City*; 1977); *Imeji no Tenrankai* (*Image Exhibition*; 1978); *S. Karuma-shi no Hanzai* (*The Crime of Mr S. Karuma*; 1978). All these were presented by his troupe.

Abé acknowledged to Scott-Stokes that he worked rapidly, emulating Pinter. He alternated between plays and novels. "Theater and the novel appeal to different parts of me. If I can write something in a novel, then I never try to make it into a play. The writers I appreciate are those who emphasize the gap between theater and novels. I like Beckett. His novels and plays are totally different, aren't they? I like Ionesco, but his plays are a bit too close to novels for my taste. The novelist who interests me most is [Gabriel García] Márquez, who is in line for the Nobel Prize this year, I hear. I also admire the Irish writer Edna O'Brien."

Another of his friends is the New Wave French author Alain Robbe-Grillet, with whom Abé was planning to collaborate on a book of photographs shot by him of Tokyo street-scenes.

The literary scene in America was not to Abé's liking. "Established and older writers in the United States do not interest me," he said to Scott-Stokes. "The vital people are Latin Americans like Márquez, but a new generation is coming along in America – and this may be where the future lies."

He visited New York again in 1986 to attend an international gathering of Pen, the organization dedicated to preserving freedom of speech for authors everywhere. Interviewed on American television, Abé repeated that he sought to convey his ideas by non-verbal devices as much as possible. *The Little Elephant Is Dead* invokes "dream-images. But when I say 'dreams', I mean 'reality'." He was always in search of something new and wholly his own. His wife contributed that it was very hard for her to work with him; he never explained what his plays were about: she found them difficult to grasp.

Abé added that he chose actors who were not only agile but had "creativity and imagination". He started rehearsing his plays before he had a written text and steadily evolved one.

In Japan Abé was not much in public view. He granted few interviews, shunned panel discussions on television; his novels were issued after long intervals, sometimes as much as five years apart. In his *New York Times* article Scott-Stokes gave this physical description of his subject at fifty-five: "[He] is a bushy-haired, black-browed man of middle height with thick arms and a disarming smile. He has a broad face and wears heavy, black-framed eyeglasses. He wears nondescript clothes – polo shirts and tan pants – over a frame which, during the eleven years in which I have known him, has grown slightly fat." Addicted to cigarettes, Abé smoked two or three packs of them a day. Machi Abé, "constantly at her husband's side, offering and seeking advice, was a tall, attractive woman in black boots and skirt with a fat yellow stone on her finger".

Abé commented on his work over the years in letters to his American publisher, as well as in an essay, "Moscow and New York", and in his conversations with Scott-Stokes: "Anyone can see that I am making deliberate and laborious progress downward into Hell on Earth. The novels get darker and more depressing, I agree, but you also ask: 'Do I have an escape route?' All that matters is to ask that question. Naturally, I don't have an answer." Also: "We have lost our myths – the good full earth, the secure home – gone." He is gripped by modern man's alienation. "But is that loneliness really a patho-logical phenomenon? It seems that from *The Woman in the Dunes* on, through *The Face of Another* . . . I have unintentionally explored the problem of loneliness. And as a practical conclusion, I feel that this loneliness is not at all pathological but the normal approach to human relations. . . . What is necessary is not a recovery from loneliness but rather a spirit that regards loneliness as to be expected and goes further, searching for an unknown, new path."

His audience in Japan tended to be largely the open-minded young, especially university students who had little enthusiasm for the by now ever more conventional Shingeki. After the troupe's return from its 1979 tour it reoccupied the glittering Parco Theatre, built by a wealthy businessman, Seiji Tsutsumi – a department store owner – to make available a stage for concerts by Toru Takemitsu, plays by Abé, and other independent and avant-garde art projects. Such ventures, Tsutsumi said, seldom drew enough ticket-buyers to be self-sustaining; he was one of the few men of business ready to help experimental artists. "What I do is provide them with a place where they are assured of an audience – mostly youngsters, people whose taste is being formed. Older and middle-aged people just aren't interested."

Attending a performance of *Little Elephant* at the Parco, Scott-Stokes observed that the spectators were "young girls and students in spotless blouses and shirts, an almost silent audience. . . . There was an occasional giggle but no animation." Machi Abé commented, "It was quite different in New York. There was cheering and interruption – a huge, vital audience at La MaMa Annex."

Scott-Stokes's own conclusion to his *New York Times* report on this visit: "Tokyo is the liveliest center of the arts in Asia, with several symphony orchestras, national, municipal and private art galleries, and powerful companies such as Suntory, the whiskey company, and Fuji Television, that sponsor the arts. But it has not been an easy place for artists to work, at least since the early 1970s." One explanation for this was the rising costs of all such offerings, the traditional as well as innovative.

The playscripts of Masakazu Yamazaki (b. 1934), though less well represented abroad, have earned him a high degree of recognition in Japan. Exceedingly versatile, he is also a distinguished theatre historian, critic and aesthetician. Born in Kyoto, he was taken when only six to Manchuria, where he lived until his impressionable twelfth year. By his own account, this had a lasting influence on him, much as similar stays there had on Mishima and Abé. The years were those of catastrophic events at the end of the Second World War. J. Thomas Rimer, who has published an extensive interview with Yamazaki, quoted him as saying:

> The experiences I underwent when Manchuria collapsed were fundamental in my development. My whole view of life was profoundly changed. In terms of providing material for my own writing I became interested not, say, in portraying delicate psychological burdens within a family; rather, I was captivated by the idea of a theater in which a man's fate could be thrust directly onto the stage of history.
>
> My first clear memory of my involvement with the theater remains that of the winter when I was twelve years old. My father was ill, on the verge of death. I sat at his pillow and read to him the works of Shakespeare in the Shōyō Tsubouchi translation. Manchuria had fallen. It was the period when both Nationalist and Communist troops were occupying the country. The streets were full of those dead from cold and starvation. Even in our home only the stove in my father's sick room could be kept burning. . . . This volume of Shakespeare was the only remaining item on our bookshelves. With the sound of cannons in the distance, I watched my father's face, from which consciousness slowly faded as I read to him. *Coriolanus, Henry IV, The Tempest* . . . I didn't understand every word of the text. Yet reading those plays aloud seemed somehow a suitable way to counter-attack our misery through the strength Shakespeare's strong words and imagination lent me.

Following his father's death, the boy returned to Kyoto, enrolled there in high school and afterwards in Kyoto University. He told Rimer:

> It seems that I consciously avoided having much to do with literature. I suppose my attitude was one common to young people: while I had a strong fascination with the movements of human personality, I was easily fatigued by its complexities, and I found an awareness of emotional turbulence rather distasteful. I felt the emotional element in our nature could be abandoned and reason might suffice to solve our personal problems. At first I was interested in the social sciences, then I studied philosophy with an emphasis on phenomenology. I saw that nothing could free us from being dominated by our emotions and that the only possibility of deliverance was to find a means by which our emotions might be expressed in art forms, as R.G. Collingwood suggested. About the time I graduated from Kyoto University, I was attracted to literature once more. And again it was to the drama that I turned.

Inspired by his new concern, he went abroad and entered the Yale Drama School with an enabling Fulbright Scholarship (1964–5).

> I felt convinced at the time that, unlike the novel, the drama can portray men's outward aspects; the undulations of subjective emotions are not immediately revealed. I found myself altogether satisfied with a form of literature that can capture in outline an emotion exposed through action. My first play was *Ite cho* [*Frozen Butterfly*; c. 1956]: it had one act, four characters. The dialogue went on unabated over two hours! It was performed both in Kyoto and Kobe, but I suspect that actors and audience alike felt as much fatigue as pleasure in their participation. If nothing else, I learned from this experience to allow enough time for the audience (to say nothing of the actors) to have a smoke or use the restroom! But I was only twenty-two and knew almost nothing of the demands of the theater.

Among Yamazaki's major successes have been historical plays, such as his *Zeami* (1963), which brought him the Kishida Prize for the best modern drama of the year, and *Sanetomo shuppan* (1972), which won him an award at the National Arts Festival. Asked by Rimer why he elected such subjects, Yamazaki replied (his statements seeming to have been thought out and written in advance):

> For me, the plot and *mythos* of a drama must always be separated. The plot serves to provide the framework of the play and in its construction must show originality, but the *mythos*, which provides

the thematic material that the plot merely serves to explicate, must remain universal, transcending any merely personal level of understanding. The theater must create a dialogue between stage and spectator. In order for that conversation to develop in a rich and active way the topic, the "space" in which that conversation begins must represent something shared. The *mythos* provides precisely that communality. For that reason, too, myth, legend, history, or even some well-known contemporary incident can serve those purposes most effectively. That is why I often look to incidents from either European or Japanese history. I wrestle with an image "shared in common;" then, taking that image as my ground, my own personal vision can begin to manifest itself.

Then again, using history as the basis for drama permits the author to keep a necessary psychological distance from the world of his play while also helping him to create that world with a proper density, in neither too precise nor too abstract a fashion. To put it another way, if one writes without recourse to history, in an attempt to portray the contemporary world directly, one risks losing oneself in the creation of endless detail concerning psychological reactions and attitudes, or he runs the danger of creating merely an allegory based on a lifeless and abstract idea.

He ruefully acknowledged to Rimer that Japanese theatre-goers were no longer well prepared to grasp the full substance of historical dramas, since the post-war generation was taught about the past with a stress on the "so-called 'scientific approach'", an emphasis put on economic and social analysis. "The force of the individual act in history has been slighted. Most younger members of the audience have little knowledge of the more factual facets a playwright might choose as a background for his story." He had appreciated the truth of this when his *Zeami* was first presented in Tokyo. In the decades since the 1960s that situation had somewhat improved. He took care, however, to make the historical background of his plays as clear as possible. As a result, he now hoped that foreign audiences, too, could easily comprehend them.

Zeami, staged by the Haiyuza troupe in Tokyo, portrays the great fifteenth-century playwright who was the founder of Nōh; indeed, the first scene takes place in a garden outside the palace of Yoshimitsu, the powerful Shōgun (Prime Minister), on the day that the Emperor, paying a visit, is for the first time a spectator at a Nōh play.

Decades earlier, the Shōgun, attracted to Zeami – the handsome, talented son of a travelling actor – had become the boy's lover and patron. But now, with Yoshimitsu's health seriously failing, Zeami foresees that the light which for so long has created the Shadow which he has been, will soon be gone. He faces a real and metaphorical extinction. He recognizes that as an actor, living mostly in the characters whom he depicts, he remains insubstantial, with barely any personality of his own. He is always dependent on a light cast by others; a patron, a playwright, an audience. Lord Ōe, a young nobleman, puts it this way, alluding to the actor's versatility: "[Zeami] is the Shadow of us all – old man, young girl, courtier alike. And who gives life to the Shadow? The eyes of us, who look on." He discourses: "Mankind arrives in those spectators' seats with a grudge against the world. And there, on the stage, the Shadows of that world are on display before us. So we take our revenge by attributing to them more life than they possess. In the end, from those same seats, we can triumph over all the vicissitudes of the world . . ." He adds that, though Zeami is a mere Shadow, he is a brilliant one.

In four acts and an epilogue the drama covers the player's career from his fortieth to his seventieth year.

In the background, providing the play's minimal dramatic surface, is an intrigue between the sons of the dying Yoshimitsu as to which will be his successor. Zeami's help is solicited by Yoshitsugu, the younger son, but the actor refuses it. He remains aloof and distant throughout, even though his own future is imperilled. Similarly, though he is now married and has children, Zeami is still promiscuously in pursuit of other women; they are greatly drawn to him. At risk to his life, he is strongly infatuated with Lady Kuzuno, the fascinating mistress of the fatally ill Yoshimitsu; at first she teases and taunts him, but before long yields to his advances, partly because the mocking Shōgun permits it, but after a single night with her Zeami behaves with cold indifference towards the affection she openly displays for him.

A secondary figure, the youthful courtier Lord Ōe, is drawn to a street girl whom he cannot marry because of her humble birth. He has a mask fashioned in her image. "At first the mask only served to divert me when I could not have her with me. Later, I began to love the mask, even when the girl was at my side. The mask seemed neither bright nor dim yet somehow it was so much more beautiful than the living girl herself. . . . A curious rivalry developed between the real girl and the mask. Finally, the mask triumphed over the girl. I embraced the mask and forgot her. The Shadow murdered the living reality." For years Ōe carries the treasured mask so that he can fondly gaze upon it. A day of intense disenchantment arrives, however, when he discovers that a hideously wrinkled, aged woman – the Old Sorceress, who has been seen in episodes throughout the play – is the original of his precious, beautiful work of art. It is Zeami who devises this shattering moment of revelation.

Lord Ōe offers this description of the gifted, chameleon Zeami as an actor: "A likeness capable of reflecting all the myriad wonders of the world. A living counterfeit."

In another incident, Zeami contrives the theft of an extraordinarily well-carved statue of the Buddha and, heedless of all warnings of supernatural vengeance, commands his son to cut off its head: its face will make a superb mask for him to wear in a Nōh contest. After the son hesitantly obeys, the father says: "Was it painful for you, Motoyoshi? Those who watch our art demand this of us. You may well detest the audience that watches you. A great performance may require that."

At the end he acknowledges: "I wanted to see how far I could go on living my life without a crutch of any kind." He has accomplished this at the expense of his family, who felt that he was never a person to whom they could turn. His wife, Tsubaki, perceives that he has only been able to communicate with them through his stage-scripts.

Motomasa, the eldest son, rebukes his father: "The theater has made a plaything of you. It has stolen from you your own humanity." Zeami defends himself: for him, the theater has been a stronghold from which to attack his enemies. His son says: "A stronghold? Rather a shackle and chains. . . . Your enemy is the theater, the theater that occupies your very soul." He accuses his father of having driven Lady Kuzuno to madness and death because he was afraid to help her lest he might harm his theater. Planning to enter a monastery, Motomasa tells his father: "You, who thought to defy the Light, became in the end only the Shadow of a Shadow. How lacking in any human dignity. How miserable. Behind a screen of elegance and beauty, your theater harbors all the malice, all the envy of the world." Motomasa offers to stay if Zeami will abandon his theatre. For a brief while his father considers making this sacrifice.

Zeami's nephew, On'ami, hoping to supersede him in the Shōgun's favour, endeavours deviously to obtain his uncle's secret notes – guidelines – to good traditional acting. But the wary actor outwits him. Without the closely guarded notes, On'ami does eventually replace Zeami.

Yet Zeami is forever expressing aloud what he feels an actor should be and do, his valuable insights and beliefs couched in aphorisms, some gnomic, others very pointed.

For the most part, Yamazaki's Zeami is enigmatic, betraying a minimal degree of inner change and then only when he is near death.

Lacking a conventional plot, the script has a measure of unity because the same characters appear in the successive episodes: they age; those who die, like a dancing girl, Hagi, are replaced by their offspring – Hagi's daughter, and even later her granddaughter; or, as in the instance of Yoshitsugu and Motomasa, by their ghosts. This enables more actors to play several roles.

Zeami adheres to his austere concept of the player's craft: "The performance should earn the respect and esteem of all. The art. But not the actor." He tells Hagi's daughter, Kikyo, whom he has adopted, "Art is a Hell." He has no intention of letting her undertake a career on the stage.

The play is cerebral and lacks vitality. Only at the very end, when he is outcast from the court, his career descending from eminence to obscurity, does Zeami betray a slight degree of doubt or inner change. In the final scene he voices a mild regret that his relationship with his loyal wife and rebellious sons has not been warmer. Throughout, his sons dislike him and disobey his dictates, paying little heed to his warning that the theatre is not a good profession.

In his interview with Rimer, Yamazaki said that he had borrowed several episodes from Zeami's own plays, "but nothing whatsoever from his dramatic style, for this style is closely allied to the style in which such drama is performed. To separate the two and to try to give life to such traditional forms of drama would be difficult indeed." He foresaw, however, that in the future such experiments might be worthwhile.

Sanetomo was produced in Tokyo by the Te no Kai troupe. Three years later (1976), through the efforts of Professor Rimer, it was staged in English at Washington University, St Louis, Missouri, where Rimer had a faculty post. It was on this occasion that the lengthy, searching interview took place.

The epilogue to *Zeami* brings on a chorus and dancers. Zeami, white-haired, walking unsteadily, has learned of the heroic death in battle of his eldest son Motomasa. The younger son, Motoyoshi, repulses his father, who is then pushed about by the unruly dancers until he falls in a faint and is trampled upon. In the darkness that ensues, a bell tolls. Motomasa's ghost appears to the dying Zeami. The ghost, complaining, has not been able to sleep; Zeami tells him: "You had no long life to suffer through as a Shadow. You became Light. And like Light you have faded." Zeami continues: "I shall take the image of your melancholy figure and put it on the stage. You shall serve as a model for the apparition of a defeated warrior."

The sound of a drum is heard; the ghost of Yoshitsugu replaces that of Motomasa. Yoshitsugu, too, begs for quiet and oblivion. Zeami denies him any surcease. This ghost beseeches: "As long as you, the Shadow, live on, as long as you reflect what we have been, those of us who represent the Light can have no rest. Give it up! I am tired. So tired."

The gloomy laughter of the ghost of Yoshimitsu pours out from below the earth. He, like his son Yoshitsugu, begs for pity. Zeami, having made manifest his patron's every act, has deprived him of sleep.

Also in ethereal guise, an apparition of Lady Kuzuno seeks Zeami's forgiveness for her disdainful pride when he had first beheld her. Zeami replies that her beauty is eternal. She protests that she is wretched and ugly, her guilt revealed in every aspect of her face. She, too, is eager for rest.

The epilogue bears many resemblances to a Nōh play.

Motoyoshi, kneeling, lifts his stricken father. An official messenger informs Zeami that he has been banished to the distant island of Sado.

Zeami collapses again. As he is borne off, he glimpses a young girl, Kaede, who looks much like both Hagi and her daughter Kikyo. It is Kaede who unwittingly trod on his recumbent body. He bids her to sing, and she reluctantly does so. The song "I'm Glad the Nightingale Is Dead. I'm Glad the Flowers Fall" is one that Hagi and Kikyo often sang. The stage is filled with dancers. (Translation: J. Thomas Rimer)

Rimer points out that in this play, and in its successor *Sanetomo*, Yamazaki chose two of the most conspicuous figures in Japanese art and literature. The two are, essentially, what is popularly known as "culture heroes" or, as Rimer terms them, "'modal personalities,' that is, personalities who serve as models, positive or negative, for later generations. Such figures seem to exemplify crucial, basic attitudes and so continue to fascinate at other times, assuming occasionally metahistorical status." He quotes Philip Rieff, who has written that such personalities "in effect define the nature of their culture and, indeed, seem to change as their culture changes, since successive generations redefine such modal personalities in terms of their own preoccupations and concerns. Rieff has chosen Freud as the modal type of personality for the twentieth century in the Western world and has gone on to suggest that, in any culture, it is the perceived personality, not the abstract idea, that remains the crucial element. . . . Sanetomo and Zeami stand as forceful personalities about whom each generation has found it necessary to take a stand." What Yamazaki has done, in Rimer's view, is to recreate "in modern psychological and poetic terms" the lives of these two all-important men.

Rimer adds: "In the case of Zeami, Yamazaki seems intent on using his chief character as a trenchant example of the tension between a total dedication to art and the human pressures of society, family, and the familiar world. Zeami stands as a kind of secular priest, ready to abandon every human compromise, even those that seem in his best interest, for what he takes to be the dictates of his art. The play is thus not merely 'about' Zeami himself but about larger, philosophical issues, and it succeeds where other plays about dramatists (dramas about Shakespeare, for example) often fail."

While Yamazaki was studying at the Yale Drama School, an off-Broadway production of *Zeami* in English had a brief run (1965). This earlier translation is by Kenneth Butler. Rimer's subsequent text contains some revisions by the playwright and is described as a reading version rather than an actors' script. The play has also been staged in Italy (1971).

Not all critics fully share Rimer's enthusiasm for the play. As an artist, the self-controlled, detached Zeami is quite the opposite of the wild, roistering hero of Yoshiro's *Hokusai Sketchbooks*; and as theatre *per se* the piece is perhaps too cerebral.

Yamazaki shares with Pirandello a fondness for having a play within a play, as in the Italian writer's *Tonight We Improvise, Six Characters in Search of an Author, Henry IV*. In *Sanetomo* a troupe of actors are rehearsing a play about a young elusive twelfth-century poet–statesman, the Third Kamakura Shōgun, a hereditary title.

The setting consists mostly of platforms of different heights, and boxes that are moved about to serve as chairs or ramparts, granting the spectator's imagination full licence to visualize the many scene-changes. Light-effects indicate the time of day, dawn or sunset, and enhance moods to match the dramatic action. The actors wear modern-day rehearsal clothes with a few touches to suggest medieval Japanese attire.

This device is similar to that used by Maxwell Anderson in *Joan of Lorraine* a quarter of a century earlier, the presentation of a play along with the actors' preliminary discussion about it; but here there is a difference – Anderson's actors, doubtless influenced by "Stanislavsky's Method", are alive in the twentieth century, whereas Yamazaki's are supposed to be gathered in the twelfth century and talking about a contemporary. As far as it is possible to do so, the line is blurred between past and present. The actors must seek to abandon their modern identities and convince themselves that they are living 800 years ago and probing for the truth about someone recently in their midst. If he is to be portrayed faithfully, they must know his traits, his motivations. They debate this earnestly, at moments passionately.

Sanetomo is an enduring puzzle to his family, his court, his subjects. After hearing their arguments, Chen, one of the actors, exclaims, "You are all wrong. He is a saint in my country of China and greatly honored." Another rejects that kindly estimate of Sanetomo: "Why, he killed his own brother! He stole the title of Shōgun." The debate progresses; a third performer, Miura, teasingly sums up: "There was no 'who' for him to be. He was clever enough never to truly reveal himself. Then again, it seems to me that we ourselves may have been taken in, seduced by shadows."

Later, the actor who is assigned the role of Yoshitoki, Sanetomo's uncle, says, "I was terribly fond of him. But for me, too, he was like some lovely nimble bird. Seduced by the glitter of those beautiful wings, and notwithstanding my own shrewdness, I allowed myself to be taken in by his whole bearing, his manner that was so hard for me to grasp. And I began to meddle in things. I ran around, trying to put a rope on him, to pull him into my hand, so that I could observe him at leisure. It was all for nothing."

To enhance their striving to be twelfth-century actors, the players no longer use their actual names but instead respond only to those of the characters they are to portray – each one, fully abandoning his former identity, is wholly immersed in another life and persona. They stay with him in his existence outside the theatre. Before the end an actor may also be transformed to become the ancient ghost of the performer or the person he was impersonating. Ghosts have a prominent role in Japanese dramas.

The era in which the play takes place was one of great turbulence. A civil war beset the Heian court in Kyoto. In its train, a military government under the Shōgun was installed in Kamakura, a northern port city. The historical details are very familiar to Japanese students. Audiences would most likely bring enough knowledge of the background.

In 1185 a victory established the power of Yoritomo Minamoto, father of Sanetomo. To lessen the influence of the Kyoto court, Yoritomo set up a regime in Kamakura. He married Masako, of the powerful Hōjō family, to further strengthen his hold. His title went next to his eldest son, Yoriie, though Masako and her brother Yoshitoki Hōjō actually grasped the reins of government. Finally, Yoriie was deposed, banished, slain, presumably by order of his heartless mother and uncle. Sanetomo, younger brother of Yoriie, was named to succeed him, though a boy of eleven. Two strains warred in him and laid conflicting claims to his loyalty: his father was a Minamoto, a vanishing clan; his mother a Hōjō. Sanetomo had considerable literary talent. He studied under some of the most accomplished writers of the day. Yamazaki incorporates some of Sanetomo's *waka* – thirty-one-syllable poems – in the play, which hews closely to historical facts to the extent that they are known.

Yoshitoki, the rapacious uncle, doubles as narrator, supplying much of the exposition, specifying the progression of dates and momentary situations. He is Masako's younger brother; he has joined her in the murder of her elder son, Yoriie; and they have battled, defeated and exiled their own father, Hōjō Tokimasa, maternal grandfather of Sanetomo. They have committed these deeds to preserve the Shōgunate for the Minamoto family.

Ten years have elapsed. Sanetomo is twenty-two. It is spring 1213. He is handsome, his features impassive, giving scant hint of his thoughts and feelings. Hamlet-like, indecisive, often idle, he occupies himself with writing poetry while overseeing the construction of a Chinese-style boat. Though he meticulously performs his ceremonious duties, he is the apparently willing puppet of his power-hungry mother and devious uncle, who view him warily, unable to penetrate his bland reserve. Endlessly they scheme how best to manipulate him. His wife, Azusa, rebukes him for his show of weakness; she had expected to marry someone of more force.

Through two acts, cut up into twenty very short scenes, intrigues and broader struggles for dominance swirl about the easygoing young man. Tanenaga, a nobleman whom Sanetomo has long cherished, is imprisoned for sedition and awaits sentencing. His uncle, the warrior Yoshimori, begs that mercy be shown to his nephew, and Sanetomo is visibly moved to tears by this plea. But then, to the astonishment of Yoshitoki, who has counselled that the formidable Yoshimori's petition for leniency be granted, Sanetomo banishes Tanenaga and confiscates his lands and possessions. The harsh ruling precipitates ferocious civil strife, in which the Shōgun's party eventually triumphs. In the battle on stage, the warriors ride wooden horses.

At court, rumours abound that Sanetomo holds converse with a ghost; his mother and uncle vainly spy on him to learn the truth about this.

Chief among Sanetomo's enemies is his teenage nephew Kugyō, son of the murdered Yoriie, who has an equal claim to the Shōgunate and burns to occupy it. In a long sequence, while Sanetomo is asleep, his crafty, ruthless mother Masako, his conspiring uncle Yoshitoki and his resentful nephew Kugyō unburden their inmost thoughts to him. Presumably he dreams this. He awakes and finds the real Yoshitoki standing over him and engages in a discussion of policy with him. Elsewhere, in passage after passage, Masako and Yoshitoki seek to analyse the young man on whom their fates may depend; his mother instinctively distrusts him, but his clever uncle Yoshitoki has conflicting emotions, unwittingly fond of him, fascinated by his calm youth and comeliness.

Over the months Sanetomo's public behaviour undergoes a change. He becomes more active in fulfilling his obligations as governor. He wins the allegiance of his people by a number of theatrical gestures: during a period of storms and heavy downpours, threatening floods, he lashes himself to a mast in the pelting rain and prays to the Buddha. When the perilous gales end he is hailed for his piety and courage. His foes watch him uneasily. He pushes on to complete the huge ship and voices his intention to sail off and dwell two years in China. Is it possible or wise for him to be away that long? He orders that a memorial service be held for his murdered brother. Yet his manner is still whimsical, playful. His wife, Azusa, complains to Yoshitoki that her husband conducts himself as though life is a joke.

In a token of reconciliation, Sanetomo appoints Yoriie's son Kugyō steward of the sacred shrine at Hachiman; unappeased, Kugyō, now in his twenties, plots to overthrow Sanetomo. He joins forces with the warlord Miura, hostile to the Minamoto clan. They suspect that the shipbuilding enterprise is a subterfuge: the dedicated workers Sanetomo has gathered are really being trained as a secret army. Masako opposes her son's plan to sail to China, a perilous voyage; Yoshitoki is ready to sanction the journey, viewing it as evidence of Sanetomo's growing independence. He is no longer a mere puppet, always submissive to the will of his elders. Yoshitoki welcomes this sign. At the launching, however, a disaster occurs: at first the ship is too heavy to be budged, and when more pressure is added the keel splits and the vessel falls sideways and sinks. To everyone's amazement Sanetomo beholds the spectacle lightly. Yoshitoki offers to have the vessel replaced but Sanetomo dismisses the prospect. With a buoyant smile, he says, "To do the same thing again. There would be nothing interesting in that. And I have a great new undertaking that I must hurry to begin." He has in mind winning higher rank at the Imperial Court in Kyoto, rising there from office to office. Azusa is delighted to hear him propose this but a nobleman, Lord Ōe, warns that pursuing such bureaucratic advancement is a "dangerous amusement". Sanetomo replies: "I wonder. Remember, my ship was no mere toy. Do you think seeking high court rank is any more dangerous than building a ship." Lord Ōe: "Your Lordship increased the size of the ship beyond its proper due. That's why it eventually broke to pieces." Sanetomo concedes: "You may be right. But the point is I saw the whole thing through. That's why I can feel at peace about it now. Then, there remains the question of my poetry collection." He will have his verses copied on splendid imported Chinese paper, and send a bound volume to the Emperor.

Yoshitoki murmurs to himself, quoting one of Sanetomo's poems:

> The world itself
> Is but a reflection in a mirror:
> If it seems to be there it is,
> If not, then there is nothing . . .

In an epilogue Yoshitoki recounts how a year after the wrecked ship was left rotting on the beach Sanetomo – now twenty-seven – had climbed from rank to rank in the imperial hierarchy and attained the topmost post, Great Minister of the Right. Twelve months later on a snowy morning, while on a pilgrimage to the great shrine at Hachiman to offer thanks for his ascension to his exalted position, Sanetomo was ambushed and slain by Kugyō, partly through the contrivance of Yoshitoki, who had foreknowledge of the assassination and took no steps to prevent it. The death of Sanetomo helped Yoshitoki win Miura's support in a conflict with the Emperor. Miura slays Kugyō, severs his head and brings it to Yoshitoki to seal their new alliance. Though he subtly cherished his nephew, Sanetomo, Yoshitoki finally found him too much of a puzzle and too heavy a burden. He simply could not understand why the young man was always serene and cheerful.

The actors continue their dispute over the characters. What motivated the actual historical figures? The player who is Sanetomo insists: "I am just an ordinary man. I'm not trying to tell you any lies. I'm not acting out a play. When Yoshimori Wada died, I was truly grieved, from the bottom of my heart. But my uncle's concept of politics excited me. And I was fascinated to the same degree by the role of Shōgun bequeathed to me by my uncle." Masako says that her son did rise to the rank of Great Minister of the Right and was of considerable help to her at times. "Why bother to understand what he was thinking?"

Yoshitoki murmurs absentmindedly:

> If not, there is nothing . . .
> If it seems to be there is . . .
> If not, then there is nothing . . .

Azusa assumes responsibility for Sanetomo's death. She should have led her weak husband, rather than have always been submissive to him. Displeased with the play's mournful ending, she impulsively demands that the episode of the ship's launching be restaged. "Please do this for me. Anyway, it's only a foolish dream of mine. After all, you wouldn't make him any more a hero, just by doing this."

Yoshitoki concurs with her request, to satisfy some prompting of his own. With considerable enthusiasm the scene is re-enacted, this time with the sails lifted and billowing in the wind, as all cheer and shout: "Ho! Ho!" The stage darkens; music is heard; voices cry, "Sanetomo, Sanetomo, Sanetomo. . . ." (Translation by J. Thomas Rimer)

To the very end, a Pirandellian ambiguity about the hero prevails. Perhaps an even more complex and enigmatic portrait is that of the wily Yoshitoki, whose feelings are mixed, and who frequently wavers. He has affection for Sanetomo but wearily destroys him.

Yamazaki has revealed that this work was partly inspired by his study of Shakespeare's *Hamlet*. Similarities, though not exact parallels, are quite discernible. Sanetomo has a worldly, treacherous mother, a manipulative, unscrupulous uncle, and it is hinted that his father's death, caused by a fall from a horse, was in fact not an accident. He seeks counsel (though futilely) with ghosts. He is indecisive (but is he truly so?); and is intellectual, sensitive, fanciful. The loose, episodic structure of the drama could be called Elizabethan.

Rimer remarks:

Yamazaki does not imitate Shakespeare, but he does make a number of ironic and poetic references to *Hamlet* that, for a Japanese audience, are both astute and audacious. For a Western reader, such references may work in a reverse fashion, making a familiar story serve as a lens through which to look at the complex political world the playwright has put on stage in *Sanetomo*. The helpful metaphor works both ways.

The text of *Sanetomo*, in comparison with that of *Zeami*, is more restrained, darker, and, in the original, surprisingly witty. Much of this wit springs from the ironic juxtaposition, for a Japanese audience, of the popular modern notion of the character of Sanetomo against the image created by the playwright. To a certain degree, this level of comprehension must remain missing for foreign readers who cannot savor the full flavor of certain scenes for which they lack background. There are examples of similar plays in our own tradition: the same kind of ironic juxtaposition can be seen in Ionesco's *MacBett* (1972), in which Shakespeare's *Macbeth* is recast along the lines of the modern playwright's concerns.

Sanetomo exemplifies Yamazaki's belief that the "self" – he prefers to speak of it as the "ego" – is never a constant. It is always in flux. "It is rare that others can correctly grasp the real motives of an individual. And it is rarer still for most human beings to possess a consistent understanding of what such an essential personality might be." Hamlet is a universally accepted character because he is indecisive and resolute, cautious and bold, infused with ironic existential humour and deep despair. He is believable as is no other stage figure. The wayward Zeami, given to irrational caprice, embodies – to borrow from Aristotle – a "consistent inconsistency"; a major artist, he is "childlike". Sanetomo weeps over young Tanenaga's plight, then punishes him with unexpected severity. Not only are people unknowable to others, they are basically unknowable to themselves.

Rimer asked why Yamazaki chose a drama to illustrate his concept of the unceasing mutability of human nature, its paradoxical quality, that leads to many surprises. Yamazaki's explanation:

> Looking back over my past work it now seems clear to me that, without purposely setting out to do so, I have somehow reflected through the themes of my plays, from *Zeami* onwards, my lack of trust in this modern conception of the "ego." Most of the major characters I have created do not believe in their own ideas or in their own social positions, nor do they hold any firm convictions concerning their own future hopes. Nevertheless, I worked hard, both in *Sanetomo* and in *Zeami*, to indicate my belief that such men are neither nihilistic nor cynical in their attitudes. For me, such men are by no means unique or exceptional.

This inconstancy also applies to a person's self-perception. Sanetomo's "self" is never fully and finally formed. The souls of such people are vacuums. This was particularly true of post-war Japan, as Yamazaki saw it:

> Of course such a human personality can be portrayed in any form of literature, but I think drama remains the most effective vehicle. First of all, because a drama is built on conversations, and secondly because the role of the actor also enters in. In a drama, dialogue replaces the words of a narrator in fiction; the speeches of no character can be taken as absolute. Whatever one character may say can be either contradicted, corrected, or sustained by the words of another. The impression is therefore easy to create: any real truth that exists must be relative. Again, one character may view the world in a particular fashion, but it will be viewed by others quite differently: thus the self-image or "ego" of that character may be controlled by means of such other views. During the course of a drama we can watch as a man tries, in front of the others, to construct his own self-image, and we can witness as well the difficulties, indeed the vanity, of such an effort.

The actor, for his contribution, helps heighten the sensibilities of the audience so that they, too, can come to understand that the "ego" of the character represented on the stage is not merely flat, not merely an "essence." Certainly if a man who really resembled Hamlet saw even John Gielgud in the part, he would feel that he was merely watching a performance on the stage and that this theatrical Hamlet could not represent the character in totality. Inside any man there exists the "he" he plays himself and the "he" actually played; in the drama, because of its very nature as an art form, this profound fact of human existence is rendered comprehensible.

Here Yamazaki spoke of Pirandello as the playwright who had remained most highly conscious of this function of the theatre and had made the best use of it.

Another question was submitted by Rimer: "In writing plays that involve historical characters, men such as Zeami and Sanetomo, men whose lives and artistic works are well known, do you attempt to stay close to the historical facts? Or, to put it another way, do you use these characters as pretexts for speculations on the meaning of the present as we understand it? To what extent is historical validity of interest to you? What kind of 'aesthetic distance' from the present can the use of such characters provide?" Yamazaki's answer:

In writing plays that involve historical subjects, I always try to interpret the facts. But I have never ventured to forge one! In both *Zeami* and *Sanetomo*, for instance, all the dates, the names of the characters portrayed, the episodes shown, and the artistic works quoted, are correct historically or, at least, as faithfully rendered as they can be in terms of our own present knowledge of the past. I create particular episodes in these plays within the limits imposed by the main lines of the established biography of the personality concerned. The views on aesthetics revealed by Zeami in the course of the play reflect quite precisely what he himself wrote concerning his theories on art and the role of the artist. For me, the use of such historical material has a particular benefit. It is not that I wish merely to take advantage of the freedom they permit my imagination. On the contrary, such materials provide me with a resistant framework to challenge my imagination. In other words, I do not use the past as a means to speculate on the present. I try to use my contemporary sensibility to search out the meanings, the implications of the past.

Another point raised by Rimer: "Both *Zeami* and *Sanetomo* use artists as main characters. Are there not peculiar problems involved in creating art about art?" From Yamazaki:

The most fundamental problem, of course, lies in the impossibility of actually showing on the stage the scenes in which these artists demonstrate their creativity. It would take Zeami himself to permit my audience to witness a performance by "Zeami" on stage. And it would make a farce out of my tragedy should I try to depict Sanetomo composing his poem while shaking his head and walking back and forth in his garden. In view of such difficulties, I am careful to avoid using artistic works as materials for my plays. Rather I try to take from such works the aesthetic and philosophic view of the world they provide. Such becomes my subject.

After *Sanetomo* was staged in the Edison Theater at Washington University the company travelled to New York for a one-night presentation of the drama at Japan House. The cost of the playwright's journey from his homeland was borne by the Japan Foundation, which also helped to fund the translation and publication of the script in English.

The Boat Is a Sailboat, an ingenious comedy-drama, is another of Yamazaki's plays rendered into English. Its première took place at Kinokuniya Hall, Tokyo, in 1973 under the guidance of Tshifumi Sueki, the same year as *Sanetomo*'s first performance. The presentation was by the Te no Kai (Hands Group), a small ensemble established by Yamazaki together with the avant-garde playwright Minoru Betsuyaku. A topical work, *Sailboat* has a realistic setting, a cramped apartment just taken by thirty-eight-year-old Hiroshi Tatsuno. He is moving in as the curtain rises on the scene.

The place, having been abandoned by its former occupant, is still in disorder. The new occupant is accompanied by a friend, Satomi, section chief of the office where Tatsuno works; and by Yumi Amano, the eighteen-year-old daughter of the apartment-house manager, who opens a window, gives him the door-keys, and remarks that Tatsuno is an unusual tenant, inasmuch as he has rented the flat without having previously inspected it. Tatsuno explains that he is used to doing that, because of frequent job transfers to various regions of the country. He has never been disappointed with his choice of premises. He learns from Yumi that Mr Murai was also a bachelor who never stayed long in any city and had left very abruptly without giving a forwarding address, though without owing money. "He suddenly packed his things into a Rent-A-Car early in the morning and left with a friend. He said he'd drop by soon. We waited, but that was the last time we saw him." She is somewhat nervous, fearing that Mr Murai might have fallen into some sort of trouble. She is also concerned, after the movers arrive, to note that Tatsuno has no furniture, except for a very old rocking chair, and little personal baggage. He explains, "Since I was a child, I've moved around dozens of times, and it's become a habit with me. As soon as I settled down in one place, I started thinking about the next move. After a long while I found out this was the easiest method to follow."

YUMI: And aren't you lonely? Without your own furniture and things?

TATSUNO [*slowly shaking his head*]: When you take good care of something, you miss it when you
lose it. I was still small when I lost some furniture for the first time. The whole town was
burned out in an air-raid, and only this chair survived out of our whole house. Since then I've
bought furniture, but every time I moved something would turn up missing. And that would
make me feel miserable. Finally, I began to think it was best not to have things of my own.
That way I'd never lose anything again.

YUMI: Is this chair really old?

TATSUNO: It was Grandfather's. He was a sailor and came home just four or five times a year. He
felt really at home only after he sat in this chair. I can't quite understand that feeling today.

He promises Yumi that when *he* moves again he will leave his next address.

Beginning to clean the flat, Tatsuno and Satomi find clues to the personality and habits of its most recent mysterious occupant. Apparently an amateur artist, Murai has left behind a fairly well-executed drawing of a nude woman, who is winking and sticking out her tongue. A note informs his successor that "high-quality canned salmon" can be found in the refrigerator. *"Bought on special but the content is guaranteed safe. Please help yourself. April 10. From the previous tenant."* Tatsuno admires the vanished Murai's quirky sense of humour.

This provokes an outburst from Satomi, who has known Tatsuno since they lived together in New York. Why does not Tatsuno marry and settle down? Satomi speaks highly of wedded life and dispraises bachelorhood, its aimlessness. He says that if Tatsuno wants to rise in their company, he should get a wife and present an image of greater stability. In earlier days Tatsuno had gone steady with a girl for a year, then without explanation had taken off, leaving her heartbroken. Satomi had not understood Tatsuno's behaviour then or since. "It was a perfect match. You were so enthusiastic. But you suddenly broke it off with a single phone call and ran off to our Kyushu branch office on a new assignment. Why?" It is a pattern that Tatsuno has followed repeatedly.

Tatsuno explains: "I got this terribly strange feeling at the last moment. It's always the same. I start asking myself, must my life's partner be this woman and no other? Out of the tens of thousands of women to choose from, does it have to be this one standing before me?"

The telephone rings. Mr Murai, in his haste, had not had it disconnected. A woman's voice asks for him; distraught, she apologizes for her conduct when she last saw him. Tatsuno tells her that Murai has moved out. The woman, embarrassed, hangs up. But a few minutes later she calls again to ask for Murai's forwarding address. When Tatsuno tells her that no one has it, she begs for his aid in obtaining it and says that she'll call again in a week. "Please help me . . . I'll never forget it for the rest of my life."

Other bits of the jigsaw puzzle of Murai's identity are filled in: his picture in a booklet, "*Membership List of the Keisei Senior High School Alumni Association. Class of 1950*". That makes him the same age as Tatsuno himself. Details of his daily routine are suggested by other objects found in the rooms. Tatsuno amuses himself by piecing together a circumstantial portrait.

Satomi feels that the flat is depressing, a bit run down, almost haunted. He urges Tatsuno to find other rooms, but the advice is rejected. Satomi leaves, saying, "Goodbye. I'll see you at the office."

A knock. Tatsuno opens the door and is greeted by a man carrying a suit. He is from the Makita Cleaners. The shop is moving out of Tokyo. Murai had been told about it, but at every attempt to deliver the garment he has not been home. The manager of the apartment-house will not take it. Tatsuno hesitates, but finally agrees, though he refuses to accept responsibility if the suit is damaged or lost.

The delivery man tells Tatsuno that Murai spoke of himself as the eldest son of a landowner living in a fine house in the San'in area. "Oh? Did he tell you that?" "Yes, sir. He was a pleasant and cheerful customer. And he often mentioned his birthplace." In addition to providing a description of the country house, Murai has spoken of returning there to take over the estate. "He said a man shouldn't be a rootless plant. You won't be young for ever. That's so true. Today, Tokyo is no place for humans . . ."

Another visitor arrives, an elderly man named Heigo Nishiki, who identifies himself as a guard at the small museum. He, too, wishes to get in touch with Murai. His reason is unusual. A valuable statue, a golden bronze Buddha, was lent by the museum to a prominent man who returned it two weeks late. Nishiki is convinced that this is not the original figurine but a copy, not true gold and bronze but an alloy. Since he is not an expert, he cannot be certain of the deception.

"I've been working at that art museum for eighteen years now. I've no special education and began working there at middle age. But I'm more familiar with that museum collection than anyone else. Or rather, I can safely say that my whole life was totally dedicated to gazing at those pieces on display. I've spent my life looking at that statue in the morning, in the afternoon, and even at night – under the beam of a flashlight. And these eyes tell me there's something strange about that statue."

He is afraid to speak to the museum director about it. If a scientific investigation bears out a substitution the director would find himself in a serious predicament, for an important patron of the museum would stand accused of theft. Nishiki fears that he might lose his job, and he still has a child in primary school to support.

Nishiki had confided his doubts about the golden bronze Buddha to Mr Murai, who had some knowledge of art and sensed that something about the statue was amiss.

Emotionally wrought, Nishiki begins to weep. He needs help.

A woman appears in the doorway. Tatsuno guesses at once who she is, Shima Sawada, who had phoned. Actually, he had anticipated her intrusion. Once more she apologizes for her nervous behaviour. She catches sight of Murai's suit, back from the cleaners, and utters a short cry. Tatsuno says: "He apparently forgot and left it. Won't you take it with you?" The woman: "He didn't forget. He left it behind." "He did?" "Rather, he thrust the suit back at me. It was my only gift to him. He simply hated getting anything. He finally took it, after I almost begged him. There's no reason why he should forget . . . If he left it behind, he'll never come back."

Nishiki exclaims: "How could he be so heartless!"

A loud telephone ring. The three persons in the room are startled by it. They instinctively approach it, then look at one another: who shall answer it? By the time Tatsuno reaches for it, it stops ringing.

Act Two takes up the story three weeks later; Tatsuno has tidied and furnished the room modestly but comfortably. Murai's suit still hangs conspicuously on the wall of the *tatami* room or alcove. Tatsuno, Satomi and Yumi are poring over the cost and wording of a "personal ad" about the suit that Tatsuno contemplates inserting in a Tokyo newspaper. Would the notice bring any result? But why is Tatsuno bothering to consider paying for one?

TATSUNO: At least two people desperately need his presence.

SATOMI: You mean a poor girlfriend he dumped and a crazy museum watchman.

TATSUNO: He's not crazy.

In any event, it is not Tatsuno's problem. Satomi observes, sharply: "You're a kind person, all right. You treat everyone kindly but you seem to be mocking them." Is all this a practical joke? "Tell me, what are you planning to do with your own life? This is the most important period in your career. You should be concentrating your entire attention now on your own affairs."

Yumi senses that Tatsuno is not looking for Murai for the sake of anyone else; he has some unique interest in the missing man. She guesses that they have an affinity, a resemblance. "Weren't they born in the same year, and don't they like to move a lot? Besides, they're cheerful, sociable, a bit talkative, and have no strong attachments to their personal possessions."

Tatsuno concedes that he and Murai are somewhat alike . . . but apparently the other man does have one clear attachment . . . to his birthplace, the fine house and property in the country that he had often mentioned.

Tatsuno himself has no such link – his first home was wiped out by the war. The whole town was effaced – the temple, the school, the town office had been wrecked, even his birth certificate was destroyed. Afterwards a modern-minded mayor had built an entirely different town in the ruins. Even street names and house numbers were changed. As for schoolmates? An alumni club? No. "After the primary school was hit by a bomb, the student body was absorbed into another school. As for the junior high school, they said the educational system was being revamped. And it was dissolved while I was still going there. We moved a lot during my senior high school days. I just don't know which is my *alma mater*."

Yumi asks: "Doesn't that make you feel lonely at times?"

Tatsuno: "The trouble is, I don't feel lonely at all." The loss never bothers him. "Of course, my section chief often takes me to task. He says that explains my strange personality."

Tatsuno has parents, but no family business or estate to take over. Members of the family are content not to be mutually tied down, "so no news means good news".

At moments, he acknowledges, he has a feeling that "the ground beneath me seems to give way, and I can't get enough brute strength to keep on living. I can, at least, notice that, as I grow older." He ends with a sudden, lonely laugh.

Yumi perceives that Tatsuno's absorption in the enigma of Mr Murai has a peculiar origin: "Finding someone who is only slightly different from yourself is like discovering a new facet within yourself. Perhaps a potentiality you haven't noticed before . . ."

Satomi, still trying to make a match for his friend, is frustrated. He bursts out: "You give me the creeps. When it comes to the important things in life, you can't get interested at all. On the other hand, if it's something trivial, you develop a mad curiosity . . ."

Tatsuno admits that he would very much like to meet and talk to Murai. He is experiencing a loss of excitement over living. "I don't have a clear notion of things I really want to do, or conversely things I want to avoid. Especially, when it comes to what's five or six years ahead. I realize I don't get a strong urge to try becoming a success at it." He no longer works conscientiously and is never totally involved in anything.

Satomi complains that Tatsuno is always playing a game, though he carries out his daily tasks perfectly, both in the flat – which he keeps neatly – and at the office. Indeed, Tatsuno fixes up and improves each new apartment whenever he moves. "Somehow, I can't settle down unless I do that," Tatsuno says. But hardly anyone ever comes to see where he lives. "No matter. A new apartment is like a total stranger. And this is the best way to become good friends in the shortest possible time." Soon after, always restless, he will go elsewhere.

Satomi emphasizes that Tatsuno really is isolated. "It's not only the apartment. Even people are all total strangers to you. You treat everyone kindly, but you've no close friends . . . No one treats you informally, or sets about seeking your company."

Tatsuno accepts this. "I was born this way, so I really can't say . . ."

An overwrought Nishiki pushes in, his entrance prompting Satomi to go.

Nishiki is still worried about the possibly fake golden bronze Buddha. The director, whose judgement would be challenged, is presumably an expert in such matters, and Nishiki's job would be endangered. Murai, having nothing to fear, had offered to speak to the director so as to spare Nishiki from the risk of dismissal. Tatsuno suggests a number of tactful approaches to the director, but Nishiki rejects them. Why not simply do nothing? Nishiki utters a painful cry: "Mr Tatsuno! Are you suggesting that I should always remain in this emotional state? Are you telling me to keep silent when a terrible crime is being committed right in front of my eyes?" He proposes that Tatsuno speak to the director, as Murai had promised to do.

"That's crazy! Absolutely crazy! I couldn't do it. Besides, I've never seen the statue."

"As a matter of fact, Mr Murai hadn't looked at it carefully, either. But he trusts me as a man . . ."

"What an irresponsible person! . . . Absolutely irresponsible! That's impossible! I couldn't do that!"

His voice lowered to a whisper, Nishiki explains why learning the truth about the statue is so important to him. Though an officer in the Second World War, he could not find a decent job afterwards. He had finally taken a position as museum guard as a last resort. "At first I liked the place because I didn't have to talk to anyone. But, Mr Tatsuno, can you understand the feelings of a man who has gazed silently for eighteen years in the same room? No matter how often I look, nothing changes. And it's my job to make sure it doesn't. If you're a carpenter for eighteen years, you become a professional. You need only plane a single piece of wood to prove your qualifications. But what have I to show for my time spent? . . . Can you understand? Why does a person like me exist in this world? . . . Well, to make sure that the display in the museum stays the same as the day before." So he cannot allow the deception to succeed. "I simply cannot tolerate a rascal who tries to rob someone like me – who has so little to begin with. That statue being stolen makes me as angry as the entire Japanese army being totally destroyed."

Tatsuno is touched by this.

In a quaking voice, Nishiki shouts: "My close friend committed *seppuku* on the evening of August 16, twenty-five years ago." (The reference is probably to the day of Japan's surrender.) "I couldn't go through with it. I was a coward. Since then, I've lived on idly . . . I'm still a coward." He weeps.

Tatsuno asks for time to think over Nishiki's request.

Sawada Shima, former lover of Murai, comes by. She and Tatsuno have been meeting at intervals.

From here on, much of the play is taken up with a convoluted discussion of their relationships, which becomes intimately and minutely probed. They talk often about Murai, Tatsuno behaving in each new situation as he believes he might have done.

Shima is "modern": she has shed the constraints that in the past were imposed by tradition on every Japanese girl. She finds her emancipated role a difficult one. It would be much easier if her parents had selected a husband for her. Instead, she must make her own decisions and is daunted by having to do so. "You know how an ordinary girl talks about free, romantic love and all the rest. About how she wants to really talk things over, get to understand the other person, and then choose the right partner . . . That's impossible for me. I don't know what that means. Is there anyone you can't understand if you really talk frankly? I can understand all men, no matter how repulsive or wonderful they may be. I get to know them individually as they really are. But since that always happens, how can I ever settle for a particular person? I find it impossible to choose one rather than another."

Like Tatsuno, she is adrift. "I'm not complaining. If I could have someone, it wouldn't matter who. And I wouldn't mind living with him, either. But I can't get all excited thinking he might be the only one for me."

She discusses her past: her childhood, the death of her father, the irresolution of her mother, who shifted many responsibilities on to her very young daughter. "No one had any authority over me, and I had no chance to rebel. And since there was no need to, I never developed a tendency to assert myself."

Finally, she had met Murai. Tatsuno speculates: "He was the sort of man who didn't expect you to love him and took you against your will."

She laughs. "And then, I was neatly abandoned against my will."

Tatsuno describes himself as the complete opposite of Murai.

Soon after, having become his lover, Shima moves in with Tatsuno.

Five months later, which brings the story to Act Three, Tatsuno and Shima contemplate marriage. He favours it. She is hesitant. For her the apartment is still inhabited by her recollections of Murai. He is here, with them. Tatsuno and Shima have never stopped referring to him. She likens the invisible Murai to a person at the other end of a telephone wire. "Have you ever imagined that if you follow the telephone line far enough, maybe it suddenly ends without going any farther?"

She muses: "Come to think of it, from the very beginning my relationship was like a telephone conversation. Murai was definitely right before my eyes, but we had no witnesses. We had no mutual friends, and I never mentioned him to anyone. And now I'm not quite sure that he ever existed."

With a sardonic smile, Tatsuno adds: "Like with me, for the last five months."

Their conversation about marriage goes on: the advantages and drawbacks. Would she go on at her job? Would they have children? He finds her evasive and complains that she avoids talking seriously with him. He recalls her having once told him that when she discusses anything intimately with a man, she becomes confused about her own identity and feelings. As he now sees it, all they do is meet at the flat, eat out, come back, and sleep together.

They bicker on and on. She charges that he, too, seldom talks seriously, and then does so only because he is certain that she will change the subject.

He retorts that she has always treated him as though he were Murai's *alter ego* . . . One moment she says that he is just like Murai, and the next that he is quite the opposite.

He has decided to quit his job and go into business for himself. She is strongly against his doing this. He insists that he has good connections and there will be little risk. She is still adamantly opposed. He feels a need to be doing something different. The argument trails off.

Nishiki, breathing heavily, breaks in without announcing himself. He is very excited, his eyes strangely set. He accuses Tatsuno of not having kept his promise to intervene on behalf of the golden bronze Buddha. So Nishiki himself has acted. "Thanks to you, I met the director by myself. I may be old, but I'm not a coward like you. I looked at him straight in the eyes and yelled at him. And as a result, beginning tomorrow I am magnificently unemployed."

Is Nishiki drunk? He claims no, though he had imbibed a sip. But the question of authenticity of the figurine has been cleverly put off: "Listen to this. That statue was sent off to America yesterday and won't be back for six months . . . It seems that there's a travelling exhibit on over there. And only that piece was selected from our museum. Ha, ha, ha. What a neat trick. If in six months they find something peculiar about that statue, it would be impossible to determine when or where it happened."

Though very frightened, Nishiki had confronted the director, who had turned pale at hearing the guard's suspicion. "You'll never know how scared I was. I was so scared that I was shaking like a leaf . . . But I couldn't wait any longer . . . Thanks to your cowardly behavior, this Heigo Nishiki won't have to feel ashamed anymore. Now I've fully redeemed myself before my old comrade who committed suicide so gallantly – long ago."

Nishiki shouts that Murai, too, was craven. He had disappeared the very day that he was to confront the museum director. Nishiki is now of the opinion that Murai and Tatsuno might be the same person. "He said he envied me because I had something which I could really get involved in. He said he was sorry he was of the post-war generation and had nothing like that at all."

Half-drunk, half-crazed, Nishiki collapses, groaning, on a table top. "Please let me stay. Let me remain as I am . . . Where do you want me to go? I've no job anymore. How do you expect me to face my family?"

They carry him to the bed.

Shima announces that she intends to break off with Tatsuno. He asks her not to go. At last they must speak openly to each other.

Two strangers arrive: a young man, Hajime Takai, a member of the Mountaineering Club of the Agricultural College; and Genzo Iwakami, much older, a retired junior-high-school teacher. Takai, who once accompanied Murai on a climbing expedition and had deemed him an interesting companion, has come to share reminiscences with him. Iwakami is going about Japan visiting former pupils, of whom Murai had been one. What has happened to those boys? The teacher has held on to the fifty most promising essays written by them. He is somewhat disillusioned by what he has now learned; those who showed a fondness for him have since fared least well. Murai has been the most difficult to locate; Iwakami has been to several places in search of him, but in vain. Everywhere people spoke well of him, but apparently he had told many falsehoods about his past. He lied about his family owning a large house and estate in the country. Actually he was an evacuee from Manchuria, where he had lost his father. (The details here accord with facts of the playwright's own life.) Tatsuno is eager to hear Murai's schoolboy composition, which is a brief account of his early years, and the passing of his father, an official who met a "useless, dog's death". Young Murai wrote: "My friends ask me if I miss my home and school in Manchuria. This question does not mean much to me. While I was being raised in that remote region, my parents told me I should never miss my home in Japan. And now my teachers say I must forget the past and live for the future. So, wherever I go from here on I will probably never long for the past or feel lonely. Maybe I will become the most cheerful and liveliest person in Japan. Still, I sometimes wonder. Is someone like that really happy?"

Unfortunately the rest of the essay is torn off. Iwakami says: "Since I gave him a grade of ninety, he must have written about it further in an interesting way."

Tatsuno is excited by this discovery. "I think Mr Murai is quite talented."

Iwakami wonders why Murai has never settled down or found a suitable marriage partner.

Takai reports that while Murai and he were hiking he had asked the same question. "He said he has a strange habit. As soon as he gets good at anything, he wants to run away from it." Murai claimed to have been a professional photographer for magazines and advertising agencies. "But he didn't want his entire life decided so soon. He majored in law at college and quickly passed the bar examination." But he did not stay in the law for long; he took up painting. His work impressed an American art critic, who invited him to New York for three years of study. That career, too, had palled. "He finally had to get away from himself," an impulse that had led to several other kinds of jobs since. Murai had been a racing-car driver, then had attempted very difficult climbs on his own as a mountaineer. "As soon as everything began to go his way, he always wanted to run away. He's terribly afraid that he would be cast into a particular role."

Takai, the student, is baffled by this. Tatsuno tells him that he is naïve.

"I beg your pardon?"

"Of course you are. Mr Murai has a habit of lying. You were being teased."

"That's not true. And I've checked on his mountaineering." Shima, who has given a different picture of Murai, suddenly testifies that he was not lying. "He was exactly as Mr Takai described him! *I lied.*"

Tatsuno, overwhelmed by all these contradictories, closes his eyes. Shima sinks limply in a nearby chair.

A deft bit of "business" occurs here. Tatsuno reaches into his pockets and frantically searches for something to smoke. He brings out two packages that are empty, and finally a third containing a single, bent cigarette. "*The packs, which have been roughly thrown on the table, are all different makes.*" Takai remarks: "Oh, you mix your brands, too, like Murai . . . He never settled on a favorite brand . . . He couldn't make up his mind because he was quite able to distinguish the unique flavor of each one. When he was still young, different brands were introduced and taken off the market in rapid succession. He laughed and said his generation might be characterized by its lack of a favorite brand."

Shima relates that Murai behaved towards her exactly as he had about his cigarettes. "It was impossible for him to love anyone, including me. No one . . . Yes, like his cigarettes."

She wants to be loved but fears that Tatsuno resembles Murai too closely.

He tells her: "Shima, you've turned out to be a very ordinary, gentle girl. And you need someone with whom you can share a mutual understanding and a man who can express his love for you with conviction . . . Then why didn't you tell me that, from the beginning? I'm not Murai. If you had been honest with me, everything might have worked out fine."

They agree that the complicated game they have been playing is farcical. They have been making the wrong demands on each other. They see that a future together is hopeless.

Nishiki, awaking from his drunken stupor, shouts: "Don't be fooled, everyone. That fellow may call himself Tatsuno, but he's lying through his teeth. He's actually Toyojiro Murai, using an alias. Of course, Murai may be an alias, too. And beginning tomorrow, Tatsuno may use another name." His last words for Tatsuno are: "You pandering coward!"

In the epilogue Tatsuno is packing to move out and bids farewell to his faithful friend Satomi.

Having quit his job, he is ready to start his own business. Satomi wonders whether his friend's intentions towards Shima had not been serious.

"Yes – at first. In any case, we were meeting in that rather bizarre fashion . . . Now, I think that girl still loves Murai."

But hadn't Tatsuno himself been in love with her?

"That's what I'm not sure of. It might be several years before I can see that clearly."

Satomi sighs and shakes his head. "And when you finally find out, it'll be too late. Isn't it always that way?"

Tatsuno quotes a poem:

> Did you come to me
> Or have I gone to you?
> I do not remember.
> Was it dream or reality?
> Was I sleeping or awake?

That is a verse written in the tenth century. Tatsuno adds: "I feel kind of strange when I realize that lovers like Shima and me were living, even in those days."

The movers come. Soon nothing remains in the room but the solitary rocking chair, which is left behind.

Yumi stops by to say goodbye. She informs Tatsuno that her father has spotted Murai. In Tokyo. "He's apparently a taxi driver. Father was waiting for the signal to change at an intersection. He was sure that the cab which stopped in front of him was being driven by Mr Murai. It pulled away quickly, so he couldn't call out to him. But he says there's no mistake about it."

After Satomi departs, Tatsuno picks up the telephone and tells the operator the line is to be disconnected.

Nishiki enters. Tatsuno bids him adieu and wishes him good luck. "Please take a long rest and get well. Your museum director says he won't fire you."

It is obvious from Nishiki's behaviour that he is mentally confused.

The phone rings. Nishiki grabs the receiver. A woman's voice, pleading, asks for "Kawahara", a former tenant. She begs to see him again. The museum guard does not respond but slowly hangs up.

A strange man enters, introduces himself. He intends to lease the flat but first would like to look at it.

Nishiki: "No, it's not for rent. Mr Murai lives here."

"That's strange. I was told it would be vacant this month."

"There's no mistake. Mr Murai will always be living here."

The prospective occupant goes downstairs to ask the manager whether the flat is or is not available. The movers return for the rocking chair, but Nishiki has seated himself in it. He refuses to stir from it. After exchanging glances among themselves, the moving men begin striking the stage set until only the blank-faced Nishiki in the chair, Murai's suit hanging on a post, and the telephone are visible. Though the dangling line is severed, the phone rings again. The museum guard does not respond to it. From offstage, children at play are heard singing a primary school ditty:

> The boat is a sailboat with three masts
>
> What is a mere thousand leagues of sea . . .

It has been heard as an intermittent refrain throughout the play. (Translation by Ted T. Takaya)

A cascade of paradoxes – some critics have said perhaps too many – the play is by turns a challenging social allegory, a witty fantasy, an intellectual farce that is at moments poignant, especially in the portraits of the distrait Sawada Shima and the pathetically trapped and unbalanced Heigo Nishiki. Yamazaki has paid grateful homage to Chekhov, a writer whose example is sensed in these two characterizations, as well in the final tableau, similar to the ending of *The Cherry Orchard* where the senile, befuddled house-servant Firs, overlooked, is left behind to perish in a boarded-up room on the Ranevsky estate. Though *The Boat Is a Sailboat* is highly verbal, it employs well-conceived stage "business" and advances rapidly. Overall, as theatre it is compelling and brilliant.

Takaya summarizes:

In this drama, Yamazaki skilfully develops themes of alienation and confused identity in likable, ordinary protagonists in the setting of modern Tokyo. The erosion of old, universally accepted values and the emergence of ambiguous new values is expressed by indirection, and personal happiness seems less accessible than ever. For example, Tatsuno, the principal character, has no genuine passion or zeal for life. He compulsively moves from job to job and constantly forms new human ties, desperately trying to acquire a temporary respite from gnawing anxiety and a sense of isolation. Some readers may be reminded of Pirandello or the Theatre of the Absurd, but Yamazaki is not bound by any narrow dramaturgy, as was often the case among the pre-war modern playwrights.

In his summary picture of a generation that is rootless, cynical, nihilistic – and, as Oswald Spengler predicted, restless and nomadic – Yamazaki suggests that in turning their backs on age-old traditions the young survivors of Japan's catastrophic defeat are at loose ends. He is greatly resourceful in introducing the multiplying intrusions into Tatsuno's life by the unseen Murai – most of them quite plausible – and is suggesting that Tatsuno is losing his identity to Murai, as implication that Tatsuno really has little of his own identity and even less to share with anyone else. A minor character finally catches a brief glimpse of the iconic Murai. After many mutations, he is driving a taxi, and not likely ever to be sighted again, lost in the scurrying, horn-blowing traffic of a Tokyo rush-hour. No better way to vanish with anonymity, uncounted in the city's millions.

Another of Yamazaki's plays – a self-confessed favourite of his – is *O, Eroizu!* (*Oh, Héloise!*; 1972), exploring the familiar tragic history of Abélard, the twelfth-century cleric and scholar, and his student and secret *innamorata*, the nun Héloise. He had hopes for a foreign production of it: "It seems to me, that since I dealt there with a Western legend, that of Abélard and Héloise, whatever might represent my 'Japanese' style or sensibility would be more conspicuous to a Western audience, separated from any 'Japaneseness' in the subject matter itself."

A more recent work is *Hideroshi and Rikyu* (1978). He has also proved his versatility by having provided the book of a musical comedy.

By 1980, when he was forty-six, Yamazaki's output for the stage – apart from his many other publications – comprised eight volumes of full-length plays and two of short scripts. He was now at Osaka University, teaching, heading a new programme concerned with the whole panorama of world drama. Rimer observed: "His interests are wide-ranging and his knowledge of Japanese and Western theatrical history profound."

To Rimer he specified the earlier writers who had most impressed him and consequently affected his work.

The playwright who, both in his conception of man and in his theatrical manifestation of that conception has influenced me most is Shakespeare. Among Japanese dramatists, surely Zeami: yet what I learned from him concerns the basic principles of the drama, particularly as regards his view of mankind that one finds concentrated there. In terms of particular techniques from their works, Pirandello taught me to hold the artistic point of view that "a play is a play, not a reflection of reality." Chekhov gave me an image of theatrical figures who, during the course of a drama, continue to search for themselves while all the while wearying of that same search.

Kabuki and Bunraku have contributed nothing to his stage practices or thinking. He has derived little from Nōh, but did perceive a likelihood that the Nōh formula of attributing to the leading character a double identity, two contrasting personalities in the man or woman, could be applied to modern theatre with powerful effectiveness. Such disguises are found in Western theatre as well; for example, in *Oedipus Rex*, where the hero is both a "great king" and a doomed patricide, and in Shakespeare's comedies, where girls pass themselves off as young men.

> The pattern is surely one of universal application. . . . In the case of the Japanese theater, however, this piling up of multiple personalities does not exist merely for the purposes of dramatic conflict; indeed, this piling up does not accompany such conflict but actually *forms* the central element in the drama. It seems to me that, theatrically speaking, such a mode of viewing the structure of character remains a unique feature of traditional Japanese drama, and one that might well be made use of in our contemporary theater.

On average, his plays had from seven to fifteen performances in Tokyo, though they and other modern dramas might also be produced in other large cities. About 10,000 copies of his published scripts were sold, though several times as many people had read his works than had ever seen them performed. It was ironic, Yamazaki said, that the short runs created a demand for more and more new plays to keep the troupes busy and their stages occupied.

In the interview with Rimer, he gave a helpful picture of the Tokyo theatre scene as it existed in 1980 and the years immediately leading up to it. It resembled that provided by Kobo Abé. Entertainment of a lighter quality was relegated to the commercial playhouses that were mostly devoted to local adaptations of Broadway musicals. This limited the likely number of ticket-buyers for serious Western-style dramas. Reflecting the earnestness of the coterie seeking such works, the plays put on in the smaller venues broached political subjects, with a predominant leftist tendency, which for some decades was "fraught with danger" and further discouraged less politically committed persons from attending with any regularity. For many years theatre in Japan had been widely considered as too often frivolous and even flagrantly immoral. To counter and improve that image, the New Theatre groups over-stressed their concern with more worthy topics, leading to a degree of heaviness that was off-putting. To the general public many of the Shingeki plays were boring. The intelligentsia preferred reading instead of theatre-going. On the printed page a theme could be far more carefully examined, the book perused in a more congenial setting, at the reader's self-chosen pace. The stage was mostly devoted to tragedies, many in the mode of drab realism, and usually overly didactic, loaded with sharp attacks on the current society. Nor was the writing, with a few exceptions, of a high order. At the time of the interviews with Yamizaki, very few modern Japanese plays were ever brought back; the overwhelming majority had proved to be ephemeral. Revivals of Western classics had a stronger attraction, and there was a growing curiosity about recent successes in New York, London and Paris; foreign works were apt to be more sophisticated, better structured, altogether more stageworthy.

Young Japanese playwrights found that having their scripts published was a good way of gaining early recognition. Three magazines accepted play-texts, and the best of these were likely to draw the notice of the New Theatre troupes eagerly on the look-out for them. The Kunio Kishida Prize, awarded yearly, singled out the one deemed by the periodicals' judges to have been the best new piece of the season, an honour that usually assured the author's future.

A large publishing house, Shinchosa, brought out play-texts in book form, independent of their history on stage. Many works were available for reading though they had not as yet been performed. This virtually never happened in England or the United States, where a drama had to have been a pronounced success in the West End or on Broadway before it had a chance of reaching print.

The New Theatre, beginning with small professional and semi-professional acting groups, continued to exist quite apart from the commercial stage, something equivalent to off-Broadway and London's fringe theatre. The audience consisted largely of intellectuals. The actors themselves put up much of the money to fund these enterprises. Players lucky enough to get roles in films and television contributed a share of their earnings to support their less fortunate colleagues, who often got no salary. Sometimes the performers went through the audience selling tickets for subsequent offerings. The New Theatre had leeway to cut corners, too, because the actors had no union, though Yamazaki doubted that would last much longer.

"The theater (and here I include the purely commercial theater as well) has a relatively small part in the conception of entertainment held by the public. Japan has no Broadway, nothing like American musicals, with their tremendously broad appeal. Ordinarily, the Japanese are not accustomed to taking the family out in the evening. 'Entertainment' happens at home – reading a book or looking at television. This habit is reinforced by the new urban building pattern. City workers now live farther and farther from the center of downtown. Once home, they are reluctant to return to the city in the evening."

A new happening in Tokyo, however, was the irruption of "Underground Theatre", or Angura, a movement that Abé had anticipated at least a decade earlier. Most of the writers participating in it were Absurdists, among whom Minoru Betsuyaku (b. 1937) was the recognized leader.

As with Abé and Yamazaki, Betsuyaku spent his childhood in Manchuria; he was brought to Japan only after the Second World War. In 1960, having reached twenty-three, he was at Tokyo's Waseda University, in the Department of Political Science and Economics. Practical and personal interests led him to withdraw to take a staff job with a trade union. His writing career began during the early years of that decade.

He first gained notice as a playwright with *Zō* (*The Elephants*; 1962), put on by a group of Waseda students, Jiyū Butai – the Free Stage – who presented it at the Actors' Theatre. Ordinarily, the Free Stage offered its productions on the second floor of a coffee shop near the Waseda campus.

The Theatre of the Absurd had been flourishing in the West for ten years or more – Abé had seized upon it, but for a span was its sole Japanese practitioner; now the Waseda group was catching up. To present works by adherents to this new kind of mocking and fantastic stage-work, Betsuyaku and his fellow enthusiasts established the Waseda Little Theatre (1966), which was active in the city for nine years, at the end of which it was reorganized (1975) and chose to take over a converted farmhouse on a foothill of snowy Mount Fuji and continued to perform. The original Waseda Little Theatre could seat only about eighty spectators, but the company owned the space outright and hence had complete independence in the choice of subject in scripts and other aspects of artistic policy.

"A strange play", Takaya says of Betsuyaku's *The Elephants* (1961). In one act, it is about an uncle and nephew who are hospitalized, victims of radiation sickness after the explosion of an atomic bomb. For a time the old man has made a fetish of publicly showing off his frightful scars. The characters are nameless. The uncle dies; the young man survives him but only to confront a similar death before long. The ending is ironic. The plot is wispy; there is scant physical action. The only dramatic tension arises from the verbal exchanges.

> Betsuyaku successfully achieves this effect in the dialogue by the constant repetition of key words and phrases found within the play. These are often delivered like a chant – that is intended to hypnotically influence the audience. Much of this technique, so effective in Japanese, is lost in an English translation, where a faithful rendition of the original passages would sound monotonous and even distracting. The playwright builds up the play to a high emotional pitch through the skillful alteration of the ordinary language pattern, subtly modifying and rearranging its rhythm and tempo. He boldly challenges his performers to invent new ways to deliver the lines and convey precisely the emotion and meaning behind the spoken word.

Takaya points to Ionesco's *Rhinoceros* (1959) as a possible precursor. Both plays ominously imply that sooner or later a nuclear war or blighting disease will end mankind's unhappy history.

Also from Betsuyaku's busy pen (or typewriter) came *Matchiuri no Shojo* (*A Little Girl Who Sells Matches*; 1966) and *Fushigi no Kuni no Alisu* (*Alice in Wonderland*; 1970), displaying his "unique stage language" and forbidding outlook on a future to him conceivable only in terms of catastrophe. "He often presents a modern allegory whose simple language and seemingly ordinary actions veil the bittersweet ironies and inescapable absurdities of the human predicament."

Typical of the "Underground Theatre" offerings is Betsuyaku's *Ido* (*The Move*; 1971), seen at Kinokuniya Hall in 1975, directed by Toshiro Hayano, and presented by the Hands Group. Once again the characters are nameless, as they often are in Absurdist plays – and Medieval Moralities – in an attempt to lend them universality. Here they are identified only as Woman, Man's Wife, Man's Father, Man's Mother, Young Man, Second Man, Second Woman, *et al* . . . The action is covered in six scenes and a very brief epilogue. The initial episode has for its setting a brightly lit, single telephone pole. "*Pasted around its base are various posters such as: 'Cats to Give Away.' 'No Urinating,' and 'For Rent: A Cut-Rate Six-Mat Room. Please Telephone.' Farther up and girding the pole – a sign: 'Yamagami People's Finance Company.'*" But apparently this is a desert. A family appears – Man, his Wife, their infant, their elderly parents – pushing a cart piled high with furniture, household implements and ample provisions of food. They stop to partake of afternoon tea. They chatter incessantly, quoting remarks that people have made in the past. The conversation is much like that in an Ionesco play, compounded of clichés and banalities. A dispute rises over whether or not someone should climb the telephone pole: the Wife thinks it should be done, the Man refuses to undertake it, the Grandfather is willing to do it but is clearly not agile enough. An ill-dressed Young Man enters. He is invited to share their tea but declines because it would spoil his appetite for supper. On his own initiative he climbs the pole, peers about with a telescope which he carries, indicates that he sees nothing but a further line of telephone poles. He descends and suddenly departs.

Scene Two finds the family encamped by another telephone pole. The Young Man returns; the child, in its carriage, is crying and no one is in sight. He tries to quiet the distressed infant, shaking a rattle and picking up and patting the little one. The Wife appears, bearing a pail of laundry. Where are the others? The baby's nappy needs changing. She asks the Young Man to assist her. While he obligingly does so, she continues her often irritating rambling prattle. The Grandmother runs in – the old man has collapsed. She and the Wife frantically search for a flask of brandy in the heaped-up cart. They request that the always agreeable Young Man watch over the baby; the women hurry off with the stimulant. Left alone, he inspects the jumbled contents of the wagon and remarks to the infant that these people are quite disorganized and have brought all their possessions with them. The Man comes, accompanied by the two Women and half carrying the Old Man, who is promptly stretched out on chairs to rest. Seemingly he has suffered a touch of sunstroke. Grandfather soon claims that he has recovered, but his daughter-in-law insists that he cannot resume the long journey afoot; she will carry her child, and the Old Man will be placed in the baby carriage. Though he protests, this expedient is accomplished. The Young Man is recruited to join the family; his task will be to push the carriage with the Old Man in it. The party sets out once more.

Scene Three introduces a new couple – bill-posters, husband and wife. They are examining still another telephone pole; it is bare and made of concrete – they discuss the comparative merits of a concrete pole versus one of wood. The Husband argues that a wooden pole can have individuality, lacking in concrete; and, though it is more difficult to paste a poster to a wooden pole – a concrete one is smoother – tearing the poster from the wooden one is not as easy. Here, too, the extended conversation between them is dull, repetitive, almost pointless. While the pair work, the Husband complains of hating his job, which he has had for thirty years. He was happy when all poles were made of wood. Isn't it time for him to make a change? But what other work is he qualified to do? They apply the advertisements for the cat, the six-mat room for rent, and determine that there are still fifty-five more poles for them to cover before the day's end.

Enter the Young Man, pushing the carriage with the Old Man asleep in it. He engages the bill-posters in conversation while waiting for the rest of the family to catch up with him. He exchanges commonplaces with the couple about their duties and asks where they will go when they finish here. They plan to turn back. He urges them to push on, go further in the opposite direction – that is always his goal. He requests that they take care of the Old Man, and he himself suddenly leaves. The bill-posters are vexed by having this responsibility abruptly thrust on them. They debate whether they can start back, as they intended to do, abandoning the aged man. What if some further ill befalls him? Would they be held to blame? Approaching the carriage, they discover that the "sleeping" Old Man has expired. Horrified, they are concerned that they will be considered at fault in his death. Had the Young Man been aware that he was transporting a lifeless body? Should they take off at once, leaving behind the corpse, as he had just done? But the family arrives. The bill-poster couple apprise them of what has happened, and the members of the family stand petrified.

Scene Four discloses a grave marker where the Old Man has been buried. The bill-poster couple have assisted in the funeral, garnering the family's gratitude. The question now is whether the journey should be continued. The bill-posters' opinion is sought: they advise a retreat, but the Man insists that dangers, even the possibility of a death *en route*, had been anticipated; all this had been talked over previously and the matter decided; like the Young Man, he declares that they must push on – "To climb over the dead and advance", heedless of any cost. But the women's resolution is wavering. The

Grandmother says: "Frankly, I've had this terrible craving to go back, from a while ago. I want to see the Kimuras and the Yamadas and Kobayashis. And Dr Kawata, too. I've got to tell them. About Father, I mean. Then I'm sure they'll all mourn for him. I know he'd want it that way." A quiet argument ensues. The Man's resolution is unshaken; he will go on, even if he must make the journey alone. His wife finally shares his feeling: "I suddenly want to go on, running all the way. I want to run and run, as far as we can go. And get there as soon as we can." The next morning the bill-poster couple bid farewell to the family, who resume their exhausting onward march.

And so on, for two more episodes and an epilogue, all much the same.

Vaguely allegorical – the characters do not precisely reflect consistent and simplified human traits – the script may be read in a number of ways. Takaya provides clues to the author's intention: "In this strangely haunting play, Betsuyaku offers an abstract treatment of human existence and destiny, focusing on a single family as it embarks on a journey to nowhere in a futile and pathetic quest for a better life. The agonizing trip reduces the original party of grandparents, a couple, and their baby to only the husband and wife. Yet, despite the mounting terror and anxiety, they desperately press onward as though eagerly anticipating their ultimate doom."

A co-founder of Angura, Jaro Kara (b. 1941), has been categorized "as one of Japan's most formidable dramatic visionaries", and has declared that he looked to the movement as a way of searching for his personal identity and the collective identity of his post-war generation. His play, *A Cry from the City of Virgins* (1967), is described as "metaphorically knotty", but none the less has exerted enough appeal to a segment of his country's young and venturesome to account for repeated revivals, while he has continued to revise it again and again. It has been open to endless interpretations, having aspects that are both surreal and hallucinatory. In 1999, three decades later, it was produced by the Japan Society in New York, a sign that it was now deemed a minor classic of its kind. The avant-garde director was Sujin Kim, who told Penelope Renner of the *Village Voice* that he expected it to be subjected to a great many "misinterpretations" by American theatre-goers. At its centre is a soldier, Tabuchi, who while undergoing surgery has revealed to him the "possible" existence of a twin sister being held in the grip of a scientist attempting to transmute her body into glass – and only he, Tabuchi, can rescue her, which he impulsively sets forth to do. The bewildering substance, "glass", is a *leitmotif* throughout the script, where are frequent allusions to it, not too successfully. Kim explained: "Glass is transparent, it's neutral and cold, but it has a sparkle and a life of its own. It's a delicate balance. A large influence on the visual style of the play is the search for permanence. Things that are mineral, nonorganic, hold interest – these, at least in an illusory sense, don't fade away. Within that palate, glass is the most attractive element." Another object featured in the play is an ice castle, symbolizing the West as first viewed by the Japanese as "pure and pristine", a social order for which they yearned as they sought to free themselves of their contaminated history.

Wishing to break away from tradition, Kara had his plays put on in a tent, shunning any permanent enclosure. "The circus was a huge inspiration. The circus to me was not just a fun and beautiful place, but also a place where you can run away, that's scary and threatening as well."

He also abolished the rankings of the dramatist and the director, stipulating that actors are more important than either and should have the final decisions about the productions.

Concerning his script: "The play is ultimately a joining of that which exists with that which doesn't – reality and unreality. A large part of the play's vocabulary is universal. What I'd like to share are my dreams and my terror."

Besides Absurdists, the Angura was originally made up of many leftists, mostly college students and intellectuals who dissented from the current political situation. One cause of their discontent was the US–Japan Mutual Defense Treaty of 1960, to which a Marxist faction was strongly opposed. They chose the stage as one way to voice their protest but failed to evoke much popular support. This added to their frustration and alienation, emotions also expressed in their plays. They were equally convinced that the response of the modern theatre movement to the social and governmental crisis was quite inadequate. What was also called for was a revolt against the New Theatre's conventional realism, which by now had been accepted by much of the Establishment. The left wing of the "Underground" manifested its rebellion in even more extreme and daring experimentation. Small companies sprang up, as had the Waseda Little Theatre a few years earlier, in coffee shops, private apartments, basements, tents, outdoors in squares and fields, or on trucks that toured the streets in cities everywhere in the nation. Most of these fervent ventures were short-lived, however, because the troupes lacked funds or were too amateurish. Only a few remained active after the 1960s.

But they had a lasting impact, for they were a training ground that let a whole generation gain practical experience in all aspects of stagecraft, as playwrights, directors, designers, technicians. They also sought to distance themselves for ever from Western influences, though perhaps they succeeded at this less than they supposed, because they were not really well enough acquainted with the progress of the drama abroad. At least, they no longer considered themselves inferior to European and American stage-artists and craftspeople. In combining native forms, drawn from Kabuki and Nōh, with foreign ones, they were boldly eclectic. They felt free to adopt or reject all traditions, to alter audience seating arrangements and to do away with the proscenium arch, two patterns imported from the West. The structure of plays was greatly varied, no longer following models handed down from Japan's past or more recently "well made" and borrowed from Sophocles, Eugene Scribe, Ibsen, Pirandello and other European masters.

Fifty years and more had elapsed since the Tsukiji Little Theatre was launched, and what was once avant-garde was now somewhat dated.

Among other innovative new dramatists thereafter have been Takayuki Kan (b. 1939) and Makato Sato (b. 1943), who challenged their predecessors by selecting fresh subject-matter and novel methods of examining it. Leonard Pronko comments that Shuji Terayama (b. 1936) blends "melodrama with irony, exaggeration with flatness, and originality with the clichés of Pop Art". His themes are largely personal, unlike those of Kara that are at least indirectly political. Terayama's have an affinity with the shocking, far-out concoctions of Genet and Arrabal, the one French, the other Spanish. (Available in English is Terayama's *La Marie Vison* [*Mink Mari;* 1967], about the fancies of a homosexual who dwells in a world of his imagination and who, seeking a personal and very bizarre revenge, focuses his mothering attention on a little boy.)

Another singled out in this younger group is Tadashi Suzuki (b. 1939), about whom Pronko writes: "[He], in a sense more traditional, is known particularly for his adaptations of older works – for example, his *Trojan Women* – which blend avant-gardism with a solid understanding of traditional Japanese theatrical techniques. All avant-garde theatres in Japan seem to look back to the prewar years with a certain nostalgia and to the future with a certain perplexity. Their inventiveness in blending the traditional with the contemporary points in a hopeful direction, for many critics feel that a truly Japanese modern theatre cannot evolve without taking into account the rich heritage of the past."

Heading a troupe from the Waseda Little Theatre, Suzuki visited the United States with his versions of Euripides' *Trojan Women* and *The Bacchae*; the first was staged at Brooklyn College in 1979, and was seen again when the company returned after three years for two appearances at the Japan Society in 1982. During the same stay, *The Bacchae* was offered by a bilingual cast of Americans and Japanese at La MaMa Annex. The American actors had been trained in the very special Suzuki methods.

The Trojan Women evoked this appraisal from a reviewer in the *New York Times*:

For his production, Mr Suzuki has crossbred Greek tragedy with the classical Japanese forms of Kabuki and Nōh and transmogrified Euripides into a contemporary Japanese author. Mr Suzuki's *Trojan Women* is an outburst of anguish about the ravaging of the human soul.

Performed in Japanese, the work may be difficult for American audiences to follow. Retaining only the skeleton of the original, this version takes place in Japan after World War II and centers on a nomadic woman (Miss Shiraishi) alone with a bundle of her belongings. She is soon possessed by the demon of Hecuba, and, later, Cassandra, as the story sweeps between ancient Troy and modern Japan.

Warriors, as wild-eyed as a Toshiro Mifune samurai, run berserk through the land, raping Andromache and dismembering her son (represented by a stuffed doll). The invented character of Jizo, the Guardian Deity of Children, stands as immobile as porcelain, a totemic figure unresponsive to a holocaust.

On the other hand, violent emotion is conveyed in the acting of Miss Shiraishi. With Medusa-like hair and a voice that can surge from a zephyr to a cyclone, she is a bonding of natural elements. One does not have to understand Japanese to appreciate her expressive acting or to feel the psychic wounds that she suffers as her homeland is devastated.

The actors emphasize quickness of movement as well as dexterity. A chorus of old men, skitter-ing across the stage in knee-bent position, becomes a keening tribe of chattering water birds; the warriors are scavengers screeching a reign of terror, in the background there is a throbbing musical score, which eventually is supplanted by a rock song with barely perceptible English lyrics, ending the evening on a plangent contemporary note. Mr Suzuki's free adaptation of Euripides impales our attention and Miss Shiraishi is, as intended, a fierce mystical presence.

A third American viewing of the production occurred at the Chicago International Theater Festi-val in 1986. William Henry III, in the magazine *Time*, was moved by what he saw.

The troupe, which mingles ancient and modern art in a melodramatic spectacle, has influenced a number of young American directors, notably Peter Sellars of the American National Theater at Washington's Kennedy Center. *Trojan Women*, in the repertory for a decade, has become the company's signature piece. Not much of Euripides' tragedy is recognizable to non-Japanese-speaking audiences, except a particularly vicious dismemberment of a doll representing Astyanax, the last male member of the ruling house of Troy. Most of the piece is a sung-spoken graveyard lament by an old and penniless woman who imagines herself to be Hecuba, the bereft and enslaved queen of Troy. Menace and suffering pervade the foot-stamping movement by the supporting cast of sixteen, and in the lead part, Kayoko Shiraishi is an embodiment of timeless agony.

The Bacchae was staged at the School of Fine Arts at the University of Wisconsin before coming to the La MaMa Annex. Mel Gussow, for the *New York Times*, gave this summary of the occasion which marked Ellen Stewart's twentieth anniversary as Director of La MaMa:

Tadashi Suzuki's Japanese versions of Greek tragedy are interpretive rearrangements rather than adaptations. Filtering classics through his very contemporary vision, he presents rituals in performance.

His productions are, first of all, physical. By his own design, the director leads his actors in exercising body language – strange, spasmodic movements that often seem to defy traditional use of muscles. Actors wheel rather than walk on stage, as if propelled by interior motors. They drop to the floor with the suddenness of a rifle shot. Even in repose, their faces have the iconographic expressiveness of Kabuki.

Because *The Trojan Women* was performed entirely in Japanese, it was somewhat screened from American audiences. *The Bacchae* has the benefit of several talented American actors in key roles. They speak their lines in English even though the response is in Japanese; in effect, they become our translators. The work achieves verbal was well as visual texture.

The evening acts as both a departure from, and a distillation of, the original. Excising much of the text, including the character of Tiresias, Mr Suzuki retains the essence of the conflict: King Pentheus' war against Dionysus, his seduction and his death at the hands of the bacchantes, led by his mother, Agave.

The director has solved one of the play's problems – the overlong anticipation of the entrance of Agave – by having his leading actress, Kayoko Shiraishi, play both Dionysus and Agave. As one realized in *The Trojan Women*, when Miss Shiraishi is on stage it is difficult to notice anyone else. She is like a Fury that has assumed human form. Her Dionysus is, naturally, extremely feminine and sensual; her Agave is a vengeful and, later, a grieving mother.

Equally basic to the performance is the stage design: setting, costume, sound and color. The chorus is dressed in stark black and white; the bacchantes in a blaze of red, Pentheus (Thomas Hewitt) in a tapestried robe. A humming background of music and electronic sounds alternates with silence just as the impulsive movements alternate with stillness.

Having seen Mr Suzuki's *Trojan Women*, one is prepared for the final, tone-switching turnabout that suddenly brings the play up-to-date and acts as a kind of Suzuki signature. At the end of the opening-night performance, the actors demonstrated a few of their demanding physical exercises, a regimen that would tax a contortionist. Uniting the classical – Japanese as well as Greek – with modern performance techniques, Mr Suzuki is a pioneer in creating his own kinetic theatrical idiom.

Perhaps inspired by Suzuki's experiment was a somewhat similar presentation of Euripides' *Medea* put on by the Toho Company, a twenty-five member, all-male Japanese ensemble brought to New York in 1986. The engagement was co-sponsored by Joseph Papp's New York Shakespeare Festival and Japan's Agency of Cultural Affairs, with financial help from Hitachi America Ltd. The performance was held in the open-air Delacorte Theater, a feature of Central Park. The actors combined traditional Kabuki and Nōh techniques, and their interpretations were embellished by original Japanese music and excerpts from the works of George Frideric Handel. Bonfires and dragons lent colour to the stage-business. As described by Dena Kleiman, Mikijiro Hira portrayed the vengeful Medea, wearing a "kimono-like cape made of many strands of *obi*, the traditional Japanese sash. His face painted white, he had gold beads dripping from his black-lined eyes. He wore false breasts – exposed – a multicolored veil, an intricate headdress of fuchsia hair. His lips were painted green." The costume weighed forty-four pounds, and – according to Tadao Nakane, the troupe's leader – was fashioned with only the reverse side of the obi, "so that it is not obviously Japanese but gives 'only the color of being Japanese'". Alluding to the protruding breasts, Papp reminded Ms Kleiman that Dame Judith Anderson had once essayed the role with one breast bared.

The production, mounted at a cost of $300,000, was directed by Yukio Ninagawa. He placed the story in a Japanese temple "somewhere in time". The leading actors were surrounded by a black-clad chorus. Papp observed to Ms Kleiman: "The formality is the thing. The movement is not totally contemporary. Audiences will be exposed to the highly ritualistic flow." He ventured: "It is appropriate that this should take place in the home of Shakespeare. I think Euripides could be a close associate."

The première of the production had occurred in Greece in 1983, and after its New York engagement the troupe was to travel to Expo '86 in Vancouver, British Columbia. This *Medea* evoked comments such as, "the message is understandable even in Japanese. The issues are so close to the heart, they are understandable in any language."

Shakespeare was given even more "revisionist" treatments by Japanese avant-gardists. In a Tokyo suburb, Mitaka, the director Yoshiyuki Fukuda staged a much-applauded *Hamlet* which was seen in 1986 by Suna Chira, who interviewed Fukuda and reported to the *New York Times* on his interpretation of the play. Here is some of her account:

> The stage is set in 1945 Japan, and the lights dimly illuminate a scene of destruction and desolation. Enter Hamlet, clad in khakis, a rising sun emblazoned on his sleeve. The melancholy Dane is lost in post-war Japan, a world reduced to rubble and despair.
>
> This *Hamlet* weaves the themes of Shakespeare's great tragedy – the chaos and moral break-

down of ancient Denmark – and the confusion in Japan following its defeat in World War II. Hamlet's individual quest for identity and purpose mirrors that of an entire society.

Hamlet asks the question, "To be or not to be?" said Yoshiyuki Fukuda. "And I thought; to be what? Is what we have now – the entire post-war period – good?"

Hamlet is a very popular play in Japan. Mr Fukuda continued: "When I examined the themes of chaos and destruction of moral values, I felt that the time that kind of thing was happening in Japan was after World War II. I was asked if I was denying the wonderful results of post-war history. But I think we achieved only material wealth – I don't think we achieved anything spiritual."

In order to link the action of *Hamlet* and the events of post-War Japan, Mr Fukuda chose the device of a play within a play. On one level, the audience watches a production of *Hamlet*, being played, intact and in its entirety, by human actors and marionettes. But the play also follows the puppeteers over the forty years since the war, and their lives reflect the post-war changes in Japanese society.

To Shakespeare's drama, Mr Fukuda adds his own beginning and end. When the curtain rises, the audience gazes at the stricken landscape of 1945 Japan. The stage is bare save for some débris and a sheet of corrugated metal. A soldier in uniform enters, returning from defeat to rejoin his family, who operates a marionette troupe. The troupe is about to embark on a production of *Hamlet*, and they cast the soldier in the leading role. Following this introduction, the play as Shakespeare wrote it begins.

While the action of *Hamlet* continues uninterrupted, the passage of years is indicated by the costumes worn by the members of the marionette troupe. At first they appear in tattered kimonos, then they change into bouffant skirts, and two-tone shoes, and finally into bell-bottom jeans and beads.

As the troupe grows more prosperous, it buys a small television set, which is placed on the balcony that separates the troupe's living quarters from the stage on which *Hamlet* is performed.

As the action of *Hamlet* continues, images flash by on the screen – of the 1964 Tokyo Olympics, the student demonstrations of the late 1960s, the suicide of the writer Yukio Mishima, and the Lockheed bribery scandal that brought down Prime Minister Kakuei Tanaka. The images serve as a commentary and also connect the themes of *Hamlet* with the events of post-war Japan.

The director changes sets and adds touches of his own to emphasize parallels to Japanese history. The character of the Ghost appears dressed in military uniform, a powerful symbol of the military past that haunts Japan just as he haunts Hamlet's conscience. At another point, an actor dressed as an American soldier appears with two Japanese prostitutes on his arms, then briefly tugs at the strings of one of the marionettes acting onstage – an allusion to the years of American military occupation following Japan's defeat.

The issues Shakespeare raises – of inaction, resolve, morality, corruption and duty – are those Mr Fukada applies to Japan today. What is post-war Japan, the production seemed to ask, and where is it headed? The director does not supply any handy answers, but he asks the questions in a pointed way. Hamlet's famous soliloquy, "To be or not to be," is often translated in Japanese as "To live or die." In the translation prepared for this production, the phrase becomes, "Should we go on as we are?"

To hammer home the themes of identity and introspection, Mr Fukuda adds a scene after the traditional ending of *Hamlet*. From the back of the theater the curtain rustles, and the actors cry out "Who's there?" Hamlet strides onstage and repeats the phrase, "Should we go on as we are?" and answers, "It is I, prince of Denmark," as the curtain falls.

Mr Fukuda said he added this resurrection as a way of pointing out that the questions the play raises – and the uncertainty and chaos of Hamlet's world – do not die with Hamlet. The ending aims, he said, at contemporary Japanese who have been too complacent about the world they have made. The production suggests that they might do well, like Hamlet, to search their souls anew.

Kato Keinichi, a popular young performer, took on the title part in *Richard III*, a very free "rearrangement" of another Shakespearian drama, during the preceding season (1985) at Kinokuniya Hall in Shinjuku. His director contributed Kabuki touches, calling on the cast for much leaping, tumbling and stylized combat. Despite Richard's traditional limp, the star was continually jumping on and off a mid-stage flight of steps. This production had considerable appeal to younger ticket-buyers.

The idea of presenting Euripides and Shakespeare in a hallowed Japanese manner was shortly emulated in the United States. The Kabuki master Shozo Sato, while lecturing on art and design at the University of Illinois, put on successively a *Kabuki Medea*, a *Kabuki Macbeth* and a *Kabuki Othello*, making use of an "unusual fusion of Eastern and Western classical theater forms". The first two were beheld by "enthusiastic audiences" at Chicago's Wisdom Bridge Theater and Washington's Kennedy Center. The *Kabuki Othello* was staged by the People's Light and Theater Company, a non-profit professional troupe in a renovated eighteenth-century grist mill in the small community of Malvern, Pennsylvania, twenty-five miles north west of Philadelphia. The theatre seated 400. After the play's opening it was moved to the Annenberg Center at the University of Pennsylvania and finally to Chicago.

As adapted by Karen Sunde, the setting was no longer Venice but sixteenth-century Japan; Othello was not a Moor but an Ainu, regarded as a native Caucasian but also an outsider since he had come from a remote, northern island. The adapter explained: "I tried to approach *Othello* as a story or myth rather than, say, a very famous play." Dance, music and stylized movement were added, along with special voice intonations characteristic of Kabuki speech requiring an emphasis on certain words and phrases, by adjusting the tone, pitch and volume. The cast was comprised of Western actors and dancers wearing period Japanese costumes, some of them of intricate silk. Desdemona's kimono was made from a two-century-old brocade. A film company in Tokyo provided the armour donned by Othello and Iago.

Danny S. Fruchter, the producing director of People's Light, said that this Japanese version of *Othello*, by a shift of perspective, afforded new insights into that masterpiece. It had proved to be an economic way for a non-profit, professional troupe like his to undertake a classic work. The venture was financed jointly by the Annenberg Theater, the Wisdom Bridge Theater and the Krannert Center for the Performing Arts at the University of Illinois.

The Noho Theatre Group, an "international performance company" founded in Kyoto in 1981 by Jonah Salz and Akira Shigeyama, was also dedicated to blending Western and Eastern cultural idioms. In particular, it has adapted Nōh dance-drama techniques to stage poetic plays by William Butler Yeats, who much earlier was drawn to and influenced by the Nōh drama, introduced to him by Ezra Pound. Examples of the company's work were demonstrated at the New York City Center in 1986, when the solo dance, *Hawk Dance*, an excerpt from the group's version of Yeats's *At the Hawk's Well*, was performed by Akira Matsui, to music composed by Richard Emmert. Jennifer Dunning, in the *New York Times*, characterized it as

a dance of quiet power and beauty. . . . Matsui has the carriage of a traditional Nōh dancer here. But there is more than a hint of a strong, soaring bird in the way his arms reach out, to the sides and upward, fingers flattened together like wing-tips. His concentration is fierce as he stands, almost motionless, or crosses the performing space in a gait between a walk and a slow run. Best of all, however, are his pivot-spins to increasingly frenetic music, which pleasingly call to mind Yeats's pernes and gyres.

Mr Matsui hefts and manipulates a long ceremonial sword with a lethal-looking blade in a ritual dance from *Funabenkei*, a Nōh play about an old warrior. Again, his control and concentration are striking, as he spins and glides with the sword, moving forward in a wonderful wiggle-footed surge then suddenly sitting on his feet. Mr Matsui's *Rojin No Mai* (*Old Man's Dance*) from the Yeats production was close in spirit and style to pure traditional Nōh dance.

Also in 1986, the Noho Group exhibited its unique interpretation of two pieces by Samuel

Beckett, *Act Without Words* and *Quad I and II* at the American Folk Theater in New York. In the *New York Times* Mel Gussow published this notice of the event:

> *Quad* is a ghostly sonata – a brief wordless exercise in movement and geometry. Four performers, armless in sack-like gowns, their faces hooded in cowls, move in swift triangular patterns within a large square marked by light. To the sound of insistent drums, the four rush through predetermined steps, singly and in groups. Looking like spectral monks scurrying to prayer, they studiously avoid contact with one another, just as they avoid the center of the quadrant. The author labels that spot "the danger zone."
>
> A feeling of peril permeates this intricate "piece for four players, light and percussion." In his text, Beckett describes the scenario in choreographic detail. The movements themselves become, for the players, a means of survival.

Beckett had written this work for television; it was first presented in Germany in 1982.

In a *New York Times* article surveying Tokyo's stage in 1986, Michael Shapiro depicted the activities of the independent and "Underground" theatres, after a discussion with two participants in them. One was Hideki Noda (b. 1937?), the youthful author of *Kaito Ranma* (*Cutting the Gordian Knot*), a play comprising "a jumble of images, including a giant spider, a palm reader, Agatha Christie, two men living on a manhole cover with the dancer Isadora Duncan and a pair of Japanese folk heroes". Shapiro commented: "Non-traditional theater has been an element of Japanese culture for 100 years, but in its most dynamic forms – particularly today – it is consigned to out-of-the-way theaters where actors sometimes work without pay."

His report bears out Yamazaki's account of the state of the non-commercial stage at that time, and the answer to it already provided by such dramatists as the self-reliant Mishima, Abé and Betsuyaku, who had effectively launched their own stage ventures. Shapiro continued:

> What may best typify this theater is the length of a play's run; it is seldom more than a week, because there is not enough business to warrant longer engagements. When a play closes, the theater company returns to its studio to begin work on something else.
>
> What is new is often exemplified by the vision of one individual, because the heart of the non-traditional theater company in Japan has customarily been a single person, such as Mr Noda, who is his company's writer, director and star. Mr Noda writes and produces two or three plays a year, as if he were trying to squeeze in as much as possible before his time ends.

This theater has not produced a body of work that stands clearly apart as Japan's modern drama – not because Japan lacks fine playwrights but because the country's nontraditional theater is essentially composed of period pieces. It is an amalgam of themes and styles that reflect the thinking of a succession of generations when they were young. When these generations grew into adulthood, their theater disappeared, or rather became yet another in a series of statements locked in time. Because this theater speaks so consciously and passionately to a particular group and era, its ideas and language seldom say something to subsequent generations.

"The principle is a reaction against," says Donald Richie, a cultural historian who has written extensively on the arts in Japan. "You can equate what the new forms are by finding out what the previous form wasn't."

Shapiro put this assessment to Noda and Eriko Watanabe (b. 1937?) both of whom concurred with it.

"We are called the generation with the Peter Pan complex," added Miss Watanabe, a playwright and director who headed a Tokyo theater group. "We are uncertain. We are light and empty inside, like a magazine you read once and throw out. We have everything and yet we have nothing – those are the expressions used. The war ended a long time ago. There's no key issue for us. People in theater used to have something to throw stones at. But today people know nothing about poverty. Everybody is obedient.

"Today we have a yearning for the past, so that's why I have to put something that appears unrealistic on the stage," Miss Watanabe adds. "It's like an illusion, and every piece reflects an illusion that people have in 1985."

The illusions Miss Watanabe speaks of are reactions to a society that, in its rush to rebuild after World War II and the intense pace of the rebuilding, has consigned its citizens to lives with limited choices; the emphasis is on meeting society's expectations. Rather than lash out at the limitations, she says, her plays look for happiness in a different realm. For example, she says, if a woman has no option but a housewife's existence, nothing prevents her from dreaming that her life is very different. In her most recent play, Miss Watanabe focuses on the death of an eighty-year-old who began believing that she was a young mother again.

. . . While Miss Watanabe writes about dreaming, Mr Noda probes ever deeper into the question of identity, a widely discussed issue in Japan today, especially among the young. Identity is a curious matter in Japan, a homogeneous society where everyone knows who he or she is but is not.

Shapiro traces the ever-changing movements, the steady advance from Kabuki to Shimpa, which was succeeded by Shingeki in which one faction was the Proletarian Theatre, and which has been giving way to the "Underground" stage.

After each movement took its turn probing and often attacking society, its passions ebbed and it moved toward less politically charged entertainment. Shimpa companies, for instance, shifted from commenting on the impact of rapid social changes to presenting adaptations of such nineteenth-century Japanese romantic novels as *My Own Sin* and *No Blood Relation.*

Because Japan retains an affection for nostalgia and sentimental drama, these period plays continue to find an audience here. Theater companies still present Shimpa romances and tragedies – the unhappy ending is almost always the more popular – in theaters filled mostly with middle-aged and elderly women. Still other companies succeed commercially by offering Shingeki adaptations of Western drama. Ibsen is still popular in Japan, as are Neil Simon and *Fiddler on the Roof.*

Shapiro quotes from Donald Richie:

The style and content of today's nontraditional theater is very different. Today's new theater, Mr Richie explains, is the product of a generation weaned on television and comic books. It often makes use of the surge of quicksilver images that characterizes Japanese television and the word-play and fantasy that fill the comic books – thick as telephone directories – that are seen everywhere in Japan. "It is a reaction against excessive realism. It seems to be fast theater. It's very high-speed froth."

"Froth" was certainly not what Hideki Noda intended to offer. Some of his contemporaries seemed not always sure what being Japanese meant; especially as the nation saw more and more of the world beyond its borders and struggled to determine just where it fit in.

Mr Noda has taken his search beyond Japan. "My interest has shifted from the identity of a person," he says, "to the identity of all of mankind."

His most recent play is a fanciful look at evolution – the story of a moment three billion years ago, in the course of the development of a single fetus. Mr Noda sets his play on the fetus's fortieth day, the point, he says, at which the fetus can either begin the process of reasoning or sprout wings. The playwright makes use of such disparate elements as the astronomer Galileo, Tom Sawyer, Halley's Comet, schoolboys on vacation and music from the movie *Starman*, as well as the issues of brain death and organ transplants. The play ends before the climactic moment, and the audience is left unsure whether the fetus will think or fly.

"I wanted to write a play about why man can't fly," says Mr Noda. "I look at things as they are in a very odd way. In my fantasy, of course, man is better off flying. Everybody knows that man cannot fly. But I want to offer a dream to the audience on a summer night, a dream that man can fly."

Mr Noda sees his generation as being overwhelmed with choices born of affluence and not knowing what to choose. "The younger people cannot be sure of what they're doing," he says. Ironically, it is his often bewildering plays – like those of Miss Watanabe – that offer his generation a moment of clarity. Mr Noda purposely uses images and forms that are the currency of today's Japanese youth, and, like Miss Watanabe, incorporates elements from the drama of previous generations that have become part of the Japanese stage vocabulary.

Mr Noda's characters speak in the monotone chanting of Nōh plays. He sets his stages with the physical spareness of Kabuki. Because his works contain familiar images, he says, his audiences – primarily young but also including some older members – can respond to his plays together. And that is especially comforting for a society whose social order and notion of harmony is built upon cohesion within the group.

Mr Noda says that he likes to think that he writes plays unique to his era, but concedes that, though form and theme may differ, certain ideas and questions endure.

"I like to create plays that only those living in 1985 can create," he says. "But I'm sure people living 100 years ago had the same interest in their own identities."

Masakazu Yamazaki, when interviewed by Thomas J. Rimer, was asked whether these iconoclastic groups had not "taken away the creative energy of the New Theater", the trend to which he himself belonged. He replied:

The greatest service performed by the so-called "Underground" theater has been in undermining the narrow concept of realism maintained until now by the New Theater movement. These performers, rather than creating a monotonous copy of the gestures of everyday life or merely acting out explanations of the current social situation, appeal directly to the spectators' sense of theatrical possibility through physical dynamism. Until now, realistic techniques have had the strongest influence on our acting style; though the techniques of non-realistic bodily expression available in contemporary art forms such as modern dance are as yet not well-established in Japan. Therefore the emergence of this new and extravagant impromptu style has been quite a shock to the New Theater.

As a result, some insist the "Underground" theater has brought revolution. But I do not believe the vital destiny of our modern theater has been truly changed.

Why do I feel this way? In the first place, the obvious results suggested by impromptu acting are easy to observe – a disregard for the dramatic text and a tendency to create an "anti-literary theater." Yet ironically, this improvisional art without a text slips easily into conventions of its own. Since the actor's body and brain cannot take the time on the stage to respond deeply to a given situation, the performer is compelled to respond with habitual clichés. At first glance, the results may seem expressive, fresh and accidental; yet actually such expressiveness tends merely to repeat itself, since the actor only uses himself as a model.

He found fault, too, with the "Underground" theatre's growing reliance on improvisation, its rejection of the text, in search for spontaneity.

I once had the opportunity to see the splendid New York production of Richard Shechner's *Dionysus 66*. I found it the very best of its kind. And yet, the experience taught me an important lesson. In the play, there are many occasions when the various actors are called on to create improvised conversations. They exchange trivialities about their everyday affairs and so create a free and lively impression. By accident, however, I happened to see the play on the day of the funeral of Robert Kennedy. One of the actors suddenly remembered the assassination. "Hey," he said, "what did you do yesterday at Bob's coffin?" Suddenly the actors lost all their suppleness. They stiffened. An awkward silence followed for several seconds. I suddenly realized that all of that self-generated "ordinary" conversation that seemed so fresh and natural was only possible as long as the actors were merely reacting to situations familiar to them, repeating their reactions by reflex. Faced with an unusual event – the murder of Robert Kennedy – the flow of their actions, codified by force of habit, was suddenly broken. The fact that they were really in a kind of stupor was suddenly clear.

A situation such as the death of Robert Kennedy is momentous; no ordinary words or gestures can convey the emotional confusion that everyone feels. In order to absorb the situation, then manifest it in words that carry fresh power, a certain time is required for the very choice of these words. A playwright can create such words quietly, in his study, choosing phrases and gestures appropriate to the situation. There are no doubt many reasons why the text is important in the theater, but surely the most vital of them involves the ability to remove the real action of the play from mere stimulation and response. Unlike the animals, man has the special ability to respond to a given stimulus with a deliberated reaction. The drama functions to compress this reflex-like process of deliberation. To put it another way, the drama does not merely serve to add "poetry" to the physical movements of the actors but rather acts so as to concentrate the genuine human meaning of those actions.

Rimer had noted that the custom of the Japanese theatrical troupes seemed quite different from the American director–producer arrangement. "Indeed, it seems rather difficult to imagine all the advantages and disadvantages of a system so different from our own." Yamazaki answered:

> The greatest advantage of the company system lies in the fidelity and devotion of the actors: through their efforts, plays that are not merely commercial in nature get produced. By the same token, the greatest danger of such a system lies in the possibility that the maintenance of the troupe may eventually represent its only purpose, transforming it with just another commercial group after all.
>
> I believe that the present situation in the theater – and its future problems – remain about the same both in Japan and in the West. Since the end of the Second World War the theater has shown an intense concern for problems of methodology and technique, ranging from the "Theater of the Absurd" to the "anti-literary theater" of the 1960s. By the early 1970s this fever had passed and there seemed to be a general sense of a loss of direction.

Throughout this period Japan's commercial theatre, in large measure made up of Broadway and West End works, was thriving. In the same two years covered by the two cited surveys (1985–6) Andrew Lloyd Webber's *Cats*, playing in a tent next to the Osaka railway station, was sold out weeks ahead, while the American *A Chorus Line* was still prospering in Tokyo. A glance at theatre listings in a Tokyo newspaper in 1983 also mentions local productions of Tennessee Williams's *The Glass Menagerie* enacted by the Milwaukee Repertory Theater and Peter Shaffer's *Amadeus*, along with offerings by the historic Bunraku and a programme of Kabuki plays, and the Nichigeki Music Hall (the striptease theatre, featuring at the moment *Hello Music Hall – Oiran*). In all, nine theatres were advertising their presentations.

Prominent in the commercial theatre was Kazuo Kikuta (1908–73), who commanded many talents. Starting as the author of short farces for small playhouses in the Asakusa entertainment section of Tokyo, he had his first hit with *Ako gishi meimei den*, a parody of the Kabuki classic *Kanadehon Chushingura*, which he fashioned as a vehicle for a popular comedian, Enoken (real name Ken'ichi Enomoto).

Kikuta obtained a post as resident playwright (1933) for the Warai no Okoku (Kingdom of Laughter) company, led by Roppa Furukawa. Skilled at plot construction, working with a firm hand, he became the foremost writer of what was called the "pre-war 'script-first' school of comedy", suggesting a lesser emphasis on improvisation by the cast. During the Second World War he had a major success with his *Hana Saku Minato* (*The Port Where Flowers Bloom*; 1943), featuring a pair of confidence men who seek to deceive some simple fishermen. In post-war years it was a script against which other comedies were ranked.

The Occupation era saw Kikuta shifting from the theatre to radio broadcasting, for which he wrote a trio of exceptionally popular, long-running series, not comedies but dramas: *Kane no Naru Oka* (*The Hill Where the Bell Resounds*; 1947–50); *Yama Kara Kita Otoko* (*The Man from the Mountain;* 1945); and *Kimi no na wa* (*What's Your Name?*; 1952–4).

Ending this phase of his career, he was chosen as head of the stage division of the Tōhō Company in 1955, which he managed in an innovative spirit. He set up Tōhō Kabuki, directed by Kazuo Hasegawa, a troupe that integrated classical and contemporary popular elements in its productions. He also introduced the unlimited run, breaking from the custom of booking an attraction for a fixed showing of a month or less. This change proved of special advantage to him, when his comedy *Gametusi Yatsu* (*Crafty Rascal*; 1959) established a record by occupying a Tokyo stage for an unprecedented ten months.

He influenced the style of Tōhō stage musicals, adding cosmopolitan touches to presentations such as *Morugan Oyuki* (*Oyuki Morgan*), about a geisha who weds a member of the fabulously wealthy American J.P. Morgan family, a piece that starred Fubuki Koshiji. J.L. Anderson, in a biographical sketch, says, "Having revolutionized the indigenous musical theatre, Kikuta began to produce Japanese versions of Broadway musical comedies such as *My Fair Lady* after 1960 as yet another step toward his lifetime goal of providing Tokyo with the world's widest range of theatrical experiences."

Plays for special audiences had become a feature of the Japanese stage. Kaze-No-Ko, or Children of the Wind, was one such enterprise. Seen in New York at Asia House in 1985, it evoked a happy reaction in Anna Kisselgoff, writing in the *New York Times*. She described it as a "troupe for children that aims delightfully to reach the child in all of us", a group of performers that is "apt to proclaim its faith in youthful innocence".

Tuesday night, this company of adult actors and agile mimes made sure that goodness won over stupidity and that expressions of universal emotions needed no subtitles. Kaze-No-Ko was founded in 1950 by Yukio Sekiya. Under his direction, Kaze-No-Ko uses simple props with high sophistication.

In many ways, it resembles American children's groups, such as the Paper Bag Players. At the same time, its specifically Japanese nature is evident on several levels. There is a strong recourse to symbolism in the props, and the symbols themselves are likely to consist of hand fans, origami animals made of folded paper, makeshift blossoming cherry trees created by bamboo poles. At other times, ingenious pictorial imagery emerges from sticks and ropes held and moved by the nimble performers. For all its play with form, this imagery is never abstract. It is always concrete.

Using the techniques of its own classical theater, Kaze-No-Ko also establishes its distance from them. When the actors move the sticks and ropes into figures, they might resemble the black-clad Bunraku puppeteers who manipulate lifelike figures. Yet unlike the Bunraku puppeteers, Mr Sekiya's do not pretend to be invisible. The startling aspect is how their own expressions and acting correspond exactly to the emotions expressed by the figures they hold together. When a lost pony made of sticks cries "mama" and the word is created above him by other sticks, the actor at the head of the group cries, too.

It is a theater, then, that operates on several levels. Followers of the dance avant-garde will be startled to recognize how many of the Japanese children's games in the first section have found their way into the work of Kei Takei, an experimental choreographer from Japan based in New York.

In *The Green Field*, a green rope became a horizon for flowers, butterflies and caterpillars – all made of rope themselves. A wide variety of fowl, including a magnificent peacock, emerged out of origami forms in a retelling of *The Ugly Duckling*. The final scene was nothing short of a poetic pageant.

A bright student, Yutaka Higashi, dropped out of Waseda University (*c.* 1969), obsessed with the idea of forming a company of young players who could produce popular musicals that he felt a compulsion to write. He recruited a troupe that he named the Tokyo Kid Brothers (perhaps an unfortunate choice, because it sounded too much like a mere cabaret revue) and mounted *The Golden Bat* (1970) which had surprising success, emboldening Higashi to take it to New York for a run at the receptive La MaMa, the off-off-Broadway house where experimental foreign works were welcomed, especially if they were emphatically *outré* as well as exotic. The success was repeated there. A second Higashi musical, *The Moon Is East, The Sun Is West* did well enough to earn a European tour. The troupe had less luck with *The City* (1974) which was met with considerable indifference in New York. Indeed, in the decade following *The Golden Bat* the Tokyo Kid Brothers underwent many changes and vicissitudes. All but one of its original members drifted away, requiring that Higashi constantly replace them. He was exclusive: on average, three out of every 100 applicants were accepted at an audition. An associate said of the troupe's initial good fortune in New York with *The Golden Bat*, "It was really an accident; we didn't know what we were doing." Writing about the group, Scott-Stokes suggested that the generous reception meted to the performers while they were abroad was "perhaps thanks to sheer energy, rather than skill. They were a travelling commune that seemed to have great emotional appeal, but no organization." Higashi himself agreed: "That was a time when we were all poor, really poor." *The City* had probably failed largely because it had no storyline. Again, a company member recalled: "Higashi-san was desperate. How he hated that show!"

The setbacks did not stop the ambitious producer. For seven years he worked in films and television commercials for funds to sustain his troupe. At the end of that time he had a new work ready, *Shiro* (1981), lavishly mounted and once again intended for export. It was unusual for a Japanese musical of this scope to invade Western commercial theatres.

Scott-Stokes was present at the dress rehearsal in Tokyo, at which everything seemed to be amiss. A nervous Higashi shouted at his leading man, Kyheo Shibata, a television star, who was reciting his lines with no intonation, the flatness rendering his English mostly unintelligible. Heavy objects were crashing behind the scenes. A tiny actress, encased in armour and riding astride the shoulders of a sturdy male actor impersonating a horse, toppled from her perch and lay quite stunned for moments. The outlook was one of despair, but eventually order evolved out of chaos. A good sign: the chorus was reduced to weeping by one of the songs.

Studying the new work, Scott-Stokes defines Higashi's idiom as "the right mixture of blatant sentimentality and deliberate *kitsch*. It's an echo of the old Kabuki tradition. There is lots of colour, noise, action – and tears, with elaborate tableaux and gorgeous costumes adjusted on stage by kuroko (black-clad stage-hands)." This time Higashi provided his offering with a "storyline", though one that he claimed was simple as was demanded by a Kabuki-style musical. "A group of wasted youth of 1982, the robot generation, tumble through a time warp into the seventeenth century, 1623, just before the great Shimabara Revolt – and at the end slip back through the warp to the present." Scott-Stokes elucidates:

The Shimabara Revolt, the greatest uprising in Japanese history, was led by a sixteen-year-old messiah, Shiro Amakusa. The agrarian revolt, inspired by a crude Christianity that the Shōgun wished to exterminate, was put down with the killing of 20,000 men, women and children.

Mr Higashi's story – not so simple as he maintains, but then that's Kabuki's tortuous way – requires the robotic youths of 1982 to pass through their time machine to the year in which Shiro was born. They meet the baby, they see beatific visions of him as a child on a horse, they slaughter and are slaughtered. They return to the modern age with a taste of Zen philosophy and the samurai spirit. So this musical is a magical mystery tour of ancient Japan.

It's all done tongue in cheek. In the finale, the leader of the 1982 gang – also named Shiro, confusingly, and played by Mr Shibata – stands far backstage in a gorgeous white kimono, an incarnation of his messianic namesake. He strips off the kimono to reveal a rock star's shiny, spangled garb. Back to our age.

Scott-Stokes asked the composer: "Why the Shimabara Revolt?"

" 'I was born there,' Mr Higashi replied. 'I stayed at Shimabara until I was eight. That story always fascinated me. And then there's much mystery about the historical Shiro. We are left guessing from the records as to who or what he really was.' "

A history of the Shimabara Revolt by the late Professor Ivan Morris of Columbia University says that "almost everything told about Shiro, the obscure youth from Kyushu who is said to have commanded 40,000 country people, 'is bizarre and incongruous' ". Scott-Stokes adds, "Mr Higashi's aim in this joyous samurai musical is to build a fragile castle on that old life. . . . Like Mr Higashi's previous work, the musical is studded with Americana. It closes with a last shout of 'Shiro' from the cast, an affectionate echo of the child's cry that ends the old movie *Shane*, the director said. If all this sounds risky, the entire show is a gamble befitting the theatre, a great throw of the dice. No one else in Japan but Mr Higashi would risk the spectacle of fully armored samurai trundling about the stage in horned hats to music from a tiny rock combo, reinforced by the magical *shakuhachi*, or bamboo flute."

Mel Gussow, of the *New York Times*, was not overwhelmed:

The confrontation between contemporary street kids and medieval warriors is a promising idea, but the issue is confused in the telling. The dialogue is in long bursts of Japanese, followed by an often indecipherable bullet of English. Only a few of the actors are intelligible to American ears. The dialogue, when we hear it, is excessively platitudinous, as in the statement "People say life is illusion."

Mr Higashi should have forgotten the illusion of a plot and perhaps even the attempt at English – and occasionally that is what happens. At such moments we can sit back and enjoy the floating images and visual splendor. In the hands of the designer, Shigeru Uchida, the La MaMa Annex stage has never looked more opulent, with a carpeted stage backed by frescolike curtains that change pictures from savage samurai to peaceful cherry blossoms.

Masae Yoshida's costumes are a gorgeous arboretum, and some seem to bloom as we look at them. At one point, kuroko, or shrouded stagehands, shadow two of the actors and silently pull strings behind their backs, causing the outer garments to drop away and to reveal even more colorful clothes underneath.

Takashi Yoshimatsu's score, though evidently influenced by *Hair*, has an exotic Japanese flavor and is played on instruments that include a *shakuhachi*, *wadaiko* and *parchasion*. One of the three is a large, booming kettle drum.

Shiro seems to be in perpetual motion, with choreographed samurai swinging swords and slashing the air with a limb-threatening deftness. The Tokyo Kid Brothers have an eagerness and an infectious enthusiasm for their performing that often override questions of verbal communications.

The grandiose scene-and-lighting effects won praise from other critics. Leah Frank, in *Other Stages*, wrote: "*Shiro* is a visual orgy of drifting, mood setting fogs, muted reds, shining golds, burnished oranges, and splashes of brilliant grass green." Jennifer W. Graham, in *Horizon* magazine, was much impressed by the spectacular staging and performances:

Shiro actors clash swords and dance with parasols on intricately painted floors in front of exquisitely painted, moving backdrops. The production uses almost 200 mechanisms for lighting effects, such as those used for hurtling back through time. Abundant smoke and fog add a mystical, time-past quality, especially effective during the samurai sword fights.

... Musically, *Shiro* has been compared to *Hair*; *Shiro* is a rock musical, but it is much more than that. Instruments associated with rock music – guitars, bass, percussion – are used by the seven-piece band, but the same band members also play the bamboo flute, the *koto*, and other traditional Japanese instruments. The effect is a blending of time and space.

After its New York engagement *Shiro* was presented at the Kennedy Center in Washington, DC, and then went on an extended tour that began in San Antonio, Texas, and took in twelve other cities in various parts of the United States and Canada, including Montreal. A videotape was made of it for subsequent showing on cable television.

An intrepid group venturing abroad to exhibit its art outdoors at the Lincoln Center Fountain Plaza in New York in 1986 was the Yass Hakoshima Mime Theatre, whose members emulated the classical mime style of Marcel Marceau with added elements drawn from the traditions of their own country. A performer and choreographer, Hakoshima also created stage movements for plays by Jean Cocteau and Thornton Wilder. Films illustrating his work are in the collection of New York's Museum of Modern Art. At his American appearance he enacted six pieces with a musical accompaniment that ranged from the Japanese folk drum to the art-rock of Tangerine Dream.

In Tokyo, Osaka, Kyoto and other large cities, troupes devoted to the classic drama still held forth. In 1983 a National Nōh Theatre was completed in Tokyo's Sendagaya district. William Weaver, an opera historian, observed in a *New York Times* article in 1985, "Tokyo does not seem to me a theater city, the way London is, or New York. It has no West End, no Broadway; theaters are scattered all over the place, and even the National Nōh Theatre is in an out-of-the-way, suburban area – the taxi ride costs almost as much as the not-cheap ticket." Yet he was much impressed with the new playhouse and pronounced it much worth a visit. "Nōh was originally performed on outdoor stages; here the modern architect has created an airy pavilion-like theater inside a simple auditorium. All is pale wood, imparting a sense of natural grace. The building encloses a delicate, green garden and an elegant, quiet restaurant. The performance began at one p.m., and several people were ahead of time to enjoy a substantial bowl of *soba* to tide them over." He saw two short offerings, a fifteen-minute Kyōgen, about a wily peasant and an arrogant lord and some knockabout action, and then an hour-long Nōh drama, "the story of a deranged mother searching the banks of the Sumida River for her lost son. From his grave he appears to her and comforts her." (This is the Nōh play *Sumidagawa* that Benjamin Britten adapted for his ninety-minute opera *Curlew River*.)

Weaver noted that many Japanese in the audience closely followed a printed libretto. "The occasional rustle of pages turned in unison reminded me of concert performances of unfamiliar operas in Carnegie Hall. The actor playing the mother, masked, relied on stately gesture, subtle inflection of voice, and sheer, charged presence, to convey the beauty of the words and the depth of emotion. It seemed strange to me, to be moved by something so deliberately unrealistic: no set, a few props, stage-hands visible, no illusion; the actor playing the madwoman was the tallest member of the company, and his voice, though artificial, was definitely male, not the haunting falsetto employed in other forms of Japanese theater."

An anonymous reporter gave *Horizon* magazine a fuller description of the new structure, the first national theatre ever built specifically for performances of Nōh. "In contrast to the centuries-old art form it houses, the exterior has a contemporary look. Once inside, however, traditional style prevails. The stage and bridgeway (used by performers to make their rather extravagant entrances and exits), as in every Nōh theater, are the centerpieces. The 400-year-old cypress used to construct the stage – which looks something like a stripped-down pagoda – is almost as old as Nōh itself."

Minoru Kita, president of the Japan Nōh Theatre Association, expressed a hope that the just-completed facility would attract larger audiences to this traditional art form, which until now had been the choice mostly of the upper class, "the *daimyo* lords of the feudal eras and the turn-of-the-century aristocracy."

In addition to its stage and auditorium, the theatre complex included a 50,000-volume library for Nōh scholars, a rehearsal studio, and classrooms for training successive generations of Nōh artists.

In the United States a half-hour English-language film about the Nōh, produced in Japan in 1978, was broadcast by the Bravo television network in 1986. The film offered excerpts from plays, along with illustrations of Nōh props and stages, and explanations of themes and the discipline required of the performers.

Osaka's long-famed troupe of puppeteers continued to journey abroad; nine members were at Japan House in New York in 1983 with a programme that comprised *Natu Matsuri* (*Summer Festival*); *Osono's Lament* (an excerpt from *Sakaya*, or *The Sake Shop*); highlights from *Sambaso*, "a ritualistic dance of purification"; *Kumagai's Monologue* (from *Kumagai Jimya*, or *Kumagai's Camp*); *Manakurabe Shiki No Kotobuki* (*The Fortunate Flowering of the Four Seasons*). A previous visit had occurred in 1973, when – according to Scott-Stokes – the company had mistakenly booked into the City Center, a hall far too large for this intimately scaled entertainment. On that occasion, too, performances had been staged with the house-lights off, though the puppeteers always wanted them on in order to catch the audience's reactions and temper and pace the performance accordingly. Another error: many spectators wore headsets that provided a simultaneous English translation of the dialogue. This had deafened them to the recitative by the *taiyu*, or storyteller, and the musical accompaniment – on the three-stringed *samisen* – traditionally integral to a Bunraku enactment.

Mel Gussow greeted the company with this review:

The hooded puppeteers resemble bishops in chess, a game with which Bunraku can be compared in complexity. This is a multidimensional theater combining dance, mime and original musical and vocal techniques.

The puppets draw their energy from the puppeteers who surround them like a cloud – a triple shadow. The impassivity of the puppeteers is in direct contrast to the expressiveness of the figures under their domination. The expressiveness does not derive primarily from the puppets' facial features but from the manipulation of their bodies. Emotion comes through movement. Bunraku puppeteers are choreographers in motion, articulating actor-dancers through their steps.

Sound comes from a box-like side stage shared by narrators and *samisen* players. They sit formally as if preparing for a ceremony. The narrators tell the story while playing all the rules. They weep, they wail and, when called upon, they laugh uproariously. The emotion transcends the language barrier. Plucking *samisens*, the musicians supply punctuation and a rhythmic underpinning.

In *Osono's Lament*, a brief extract from a three-act play entitled *The Courtesan's Gorgeous Dancing Robe*, an abandoned but still faithful wife announces her grief. At one point, Osono places her hands over her eyes as if shielding them from a burning memory. The gesture is simple and graceful. Simultaneously the narrator cries out in anguish. The counterpoint is a kind of Bunraku equivalent of cinematic crosscutting. The lament is performed by the three principal actors of the youthful Osaka ensemble: Toyhotake Rodayu 5th as narrator, Tsuruzawa Seiji on the *samisen* and Yoshida Minosuke 3rd as puppeteer.

The puppets are beautiful sculptural objects – dewy maidens, courtesans, heroes and fierce warriors. One of the most colorful is a sword-brandishing street fighter, described in the program as a "Japanese Robin Hood," who battles injustice even when it occurs in his own family. In the climax of the piece, he strips off his costume – itself a feat of puppet dexterity – and in a flamboyant dance reveals that his body is tattooed from wrist to ankle.

The first half of the program is devoted to solo excerpts from long plays, the second half to a richly populated dance-theater work, *The Fortunate Flowering of the Four Seasons*. The vista changes from a pavilion background to a seascape of gently cresting waves, a setting that is inhabited by a wistful "fishing girl," a chirping bird and a dancing octopus. The evening is filled with such charm and ingenuity.

Last seen in New York ten years ago on the larger City Center stage, Bunraku benefits from the intimacy of the Lila Acheson Wallace Auditorium in Japan House. . . . In Japan, Bunraku goes back three centuries. It continues to be a living art form.

The Classical Performing Arts Mission of Japan appeared at Asia House in New York in 1981 for three evenings of classical theatre encompassing Kabuki music and dance and examples of Nōh and Kyōgen. The farce players were led by Mansaku Nomura, and the Nōh actors by Nagayo Kita, master of the Kita school of Nōh, together with members of his company. Anna Kisselgoff was there:

Neither Nōh nor Kyōgen constitute a naturalistic theater. Both have strong conventions and although Nōh is more formal, the Kyōgen actors are heavily stylized. This was immediately apparent in *The Owl Mountain Priest*, in which Mr Nomura played a distressed man who seeks out a mountain priest of self-styled authority to cure his younger brother of owl-like symptoms. It was a tribute to all the actors, with Ishida Yukio as a pompous, cheerful charlatan and Ogawa Shichisaku as the dazed brother, that the situation was so merrily comprehensible to all. Not only was the victim not cured but Mr Nomura and Mr Ishida also began to hoot and flap their arms.

The gift for subtle expressiveness through limited means was made even clearer in *Tied to a Pole*. Here, Mr Ogawa was the master who tied up his two servants to keep them from drinking his *sake*. How Mr Nomura managed to drink it anyway – with wrists tied to a pole in yokelike fashion – and how he allowed Mr Ishida, hands tied behind his back, to drink as well, was all part of the witty denouement.

The Kita group presented three brief Nōh dances known as Shimai. The most brilliant in effect was *The Ground Spider*, performed with proper formality by Uchida Anshin and Umezu Tadahiro. This duel between a samurai and a spider was distilled breathtakingly when the spider threw out a "web" of paper streamers that shot out spectacularly like fireworks in the sky.

Two more extreme examples of this distillation were seen in Sasaki Muneo's impressively intense journey as a princess – here with no makeup – from *The Blind Prince* and in Mr Kita's solo in the title role as a bandit chief in *Kumasaka*. Much of the mood in these dances was garnered from the singing and chanting of the chorus, with the reciting highly agitated during Mr Kita's duel with an unseen opponent. The way he made us sense his foe's moves was amazingly rendered through his own "reactions" – ranging from an unwavering tight-lipped gaze to an accelerated pursuit on the knees.

The kind of masterful control Mr Kita exerts over his every movement was seen very differently in his bold contemporary experiment, *The Mask*. Using four masks to denote laughter, weeping, anger and resignation, Mr Kita not only summed up the essence of each emotion but did so by contrasting the subtleties of Nōh-based movement with Ishii Maki's electronic score, which included overt laughing, weeping, and roaring in the contrasting Gidiayu acting style. The nearly imperceptible turns of Mr Kita's head as he "wept" suggested the depth that Nōh provides, and one wondered if it were matched in the score.

A troupe offering only farces, the Kyōgen Theater, again headed by Mansaku Nomura, visited New York in 1984. Faubion Bowers discussed this robust stage-genre in an illuminating essay in the *New York Times*:

The lady is grieving, weeping at the announcement that her husband must leave on a business trip. Her tears look real, but she has been furtively dipping her fingers in a tiny cup of water and dampening her cheeks. The household manservant suspects the deception and slips ink in the cup, with obvious results. Furious at being found out, the wife pursues her husband and his servant, and inks their faces, too.

The master of the house is tired of his two servants stealing his finest wine every time he goes on a journey. He ties them up in seemingly foolproof fashion and goes on his way. Once he is out of sight, the pair work out a solution and by the time their master returns, the wine is gone and the servants are drunk.

No, this is not *commedia dell'arte*, stock as the situations seem with their crafty servants, pompous masters, rotten priests and virago wives. Nor are these Shakespearian rustics, or characters from ancient Greek satyr plays or Roman comedies. Yet they are certainly akin to them, because of the universal, basic humor common to all mankind. These are some of the playlets that make up Kyōgen, a very Japanese form of classical theater, which dates back as far as the fourteenth century and which still plays full tilt as part of Japanese life.

Kyōgen, making one of its occasional visits abroad, comes to New York City this week, but this time with added flair. In as close an approximation as possible to old Japan, the visiting Nomura Kyōgen Theater troupe is giving four performances of two plays and an opening ceremonial dance, *Sambaso*, at Lincoln Center Tuesday through Friday, pretty much as they are presented during Summertime festivals in their native shrines and temples – open-air, free to the public, and illuminated by huge flaming torches. For the outdoor event, a stage platform of resonant cypress wood will cover the reflecting pool between the Vivian Beaumont Theater and Avery Fisher Hall. Passers-by may view the proceedings from any of three sides, and the Henry Moore sculpture that rises from the pool will substitute for the traditional pine tree backdrop.

. . . Kyōgen has been somewhat neglected by foreign audiences, overshadowed as it is by the other three great, historical theaters of Nōh, Kabuki and Bunraku. Nōh's intensity and Buddhist overtones were first introduced to us in translations and variants by W.B. Yeats, Ezra Pound and Arthur Waley. (Yeats once tried his hand at a Kyōgen, *The Cat and the Moon*, but not many people remember it.) Nōh adaptations and derivatives by Jerome Robbins in his ballet *Watermill* and by Benjamin Britten in the opera *Curlew River*, for example, have further spread Nōh's good word. Over the past twenty-five years Kabuki, with its resplendent makeup, costumes, scenery and array of star actor-dancers, has steadily built a following here. The Bunraku puppet theater, as well, like Kabuki dating from the seventeenth and eighteenth centuries and almost as gorgeous though on a smaller scale, stands supreme in its ability to infuse life and heart into the inanimate.

Kyōgen, more modest in scope, still yields to none in artistry or perfection of detail. It has no masks, uses no makeup and little music, and its costumes are colorful but charmingly simple. Its repertory consists of perhaps 300 playlets, each lasting around half an hour. The plots always establish an absurd situation from which two or three characters must extricate themselves. The variety is as endless as man's failings are inexhaustible, for nothing escapes Kyōgen's eagle eye of mockery. The denouement of each skit is invariably to the disadvantage of the powerful, and inevitably at the expense of the fraudulent.

Like everything in Japan, Kyōgen's origins are lost in the mists and myths of time, but by the fifteenth century the form was well established as "comic interludes" sandwiched between rigorously somber acts of Nōh dramas. The name literally means 'crazy' (*kyō*) 'words' (*gen*), and derives from a ninth-century Chinese poem to the effect that even a fool's utterances constitute worship of Lord Buddha. In the 1400s Zeami, the theater esthetician, spoke of Kyōgen's popularity as "rustic scenes from real life" so much "admired for their impression of rarity and truth." Originally, the plays were written by the actors themselves, and Zeami had commented that "an actor is like a brave warrior on the battlefield without arms."

It is interesting to note that the audience for Kyōgen was the same as for Nōh, consisting of aristocrats, even though the upper classes are roundly ridiculed in these playlets. Once in 1424 a Kyōgen master was punished for depicting a destitute lord at the Imperial Court, but still, Kyōgen was unquenchable. Moreover, it thrived even in the face of the Confucian edict forbidding educated gentlefolk from laughing in public. Only "the delicate smile" was permitted. Zeami got around that one by saying that "Kyōgen should kindle the mind to laughter, a laughter that delights the laugher."

At first Kyōgen was thought unworthy of being written down, and only transmitted orally. Fortunately this meant that its language (but little else about it) changed with the times. While Nōh grew more stultified and remote from ordinary man, Kyōgen kept pace. Not until the seventeenth century was Kyōgen finally recorded and fixed in the form of texts for posterity. In Japan today it is appreciated by the learned elderly and, surprisingly, has become something of a cult among youth. In it the young find at once a hallowed tradition and a highly accessible one.

To a large extent the present widespread recognition of Kyōgen owes to the Nomura family, an acting dynasty whose roots trace back to the sixteenth century and whose performers continue to dominate the field. As in all traditional Japanese theaters Kyōgen, too, is a father-to-son business.

The Nomura Kyōgen Theater, twelve of whose top artists are appearing here, has been designated as an Important Cultural Property by the Japanese Government. Mansaku, who specializes in female roles, and his older brother, Manojo, are already honored with the rank of Intangible Cultural Property, despite their relative youth. They are fifty-three and fifty-four years old, respectively. Their father, the legendary Manes Nomura, who died in 1978 at age eighty, was the recipient of the Government's highest title, Living National Treasure.

Among the novelties of this Kyōgen tour will be the first appearance abroad of Mansaku's thirteen-year-old daughter, Yoko. She will be seen as a stage attendant, supposedly invisible to the audience but necessary to keep the stage tidy in case of a dropped fan or a mussed costume, and will also appear as a mushroom in one of the plays.

Young Kyōgen actors generally start their careers by age five or six and continue on stage all their lives. Zeami suggested seven as the ideal age for beginners, but added "in every child there is a natural bent." Mansaku Nomura made his debut at age three.

A glimpse of the programme seen in New York is provided by Jon Pareles of the *New York Times*:

Every gesture and every sound are timed to the split second in the Kyōgen style of Japanese theater. In that, Kyōgen (literally, "crazed words") is not so different from other kinds of stage comedy. But in Kyōgen plays, which were first performed in the fourteenth century as a light interlude between Nōh dramas, actions and dialogue have been analyzed and stylized, their sense of time made elastic. Centuries before videotape, Kyōgen exploited slow-motion and something like instant replay, so that ordinary events become ceremonial and, with repetition, comical.

The Nomura Kyōgen Theater from Japan completed the New York portion of its American tour Wednesday with a program of two plays at the Japan Society; because of schedule conflicts, this reviewer could see only the first one, *The Bridegroom on the Boat*.

The bridegroom (Yukio Ishida) faces in-law problems before he knows it. He is taking a jug of *sake* to his bride's parents as a gift, but on his boat trip to their home, the ferryman (Mannojo Nomura) demands one, then two, then three swigs from the jug. The bridegroom reaches the home of his bride (Matsamuro Nomura) to find, luckily and embarrassingly, that the tipsy ferryman is also the father of the bride. Drinks are shared, disgruntled bridegroom and cowering ferryman are reconciled, and with a song and dance, the bridegroom joins his new family.

The play uses such archetypal comic situations as mistaken identity and intoxication, and the bridegroom's incipient seasickness, in carefully elaborated crescendos. It takes place on an almost bare stage and uses a minimum of props – fans, a bamboo cane for the ferryman's oar, a jug, a carrying pole and an exaggeratedly large *sake* dipper. The actors are not masked, but their faces stay virtually impassive at all but climactic moments.

There are a few bits of near-slapstick. In one, the ferryman vigorously rocks the boat and the bridegroom; later, the antagonists lunge at each other before realizing they're too drunk to fight. For most of the play, however, the actors are almost still, kneeling and facing the audience. Yet the tone of the dialogue – accelerating from a slow, formal singsong to gruff, percussive squabbles – and the actors' poses and calibrated gestures carry the action forward so clearly that no translations are necessary.

More significant were the repeated American engagements at close intervals of the Grand Kabuki in 1977, 1979, 1982 and 1985. Earlier visits had occurred in 1960 and 1969. In 1979, under the auspices of the Concert Arts Society, the troupe appeared at New York's Beacon Theater and was headed by the revered Kanzaburo Nakamura XVII, who was accompanied by his son Kankuro V as well as the highly talented Tomijuro Nakamura V. The company also performed at the Terrace Theater, opening that fourth auditorium in the Kennedy Center in Washington, DC, and completed its tour with five evenings in Los Angeles. In the *New York Times* Richard Eder wrote:

The Grand Kabuki is back in town, though for those who saw it in its last visit in 1977 there is a word of advice. It is still a marvel but it is not the same marvel.

Grand Kabuki is not a company in the sense, say, that the New York City Ballet is a company. It is the name given to an enterprise that has been bringing across eminent performers in the classical traditions of the Japanese theater. The artists that have come this year are different from those who came last time. What we see is a different stretch of the same river.

For the first and major part of the program it is a stretch that has the excitement of genuine exploration. Things in unfamiliar guises reveal themselves suddenly as missing pieces of our own consciousness. The results are delight and a startled gratitude.

The first part of the program is one act from a five-act Kabuki play, written in 1719. This act is called *Shunkan*, which is not the name of the play itself but of an older Nōh play upon which it is based. The program's second part is briefer; a combination dance number and skit entitled *Renjishi*, or as translated by Faubion Bowers – who provides, via earphones, a model of discreet and useful translation – *A Continuity of Lions*.

Shunkan, which Mr Bowers tells us is one of the gravest and most poignant of the Kabuki dramas, is about the priest Shunkan, exiled on a barren island with two companions. A message, conveyed in two parts by a cruel and a kindly messenger, respectively, announces the end of their exile. But one of Shunkan's companions has fallen in love with the daughter of a fisherman. The cruel messenger refuses to allow her to come along; Shunkan protests, kills the messenger, and is left alone when the others leave, in an exile that is now eternal.

The themes – exile, protest against injustice, charity – are centered on the character of Shunkan. And the art that gives a piercing voice to these themes is that of the seventy-year-old Kanzaburo Nakamura 7th, who plays the role. Kanzaburo has the official title of National Living Treasure and it is easy to see why.

Shunkan is staged with a single set: a collection of stylized cardboard boulders, a bamboo hut, a single tree and a backdrop of waves and the sea. It is simple, but deceptively so. The boulders are moved and combined so that a ship, tiny on the horizon, can then appear downstage and big enough to carry people onboard. At the end, when Shunkan is left alone, the boulders are assembled to construct a promontory.

The actors are stylized, in gestures, costumes and makeup, but to different degrees. The evil messenger is painted red and carries enough in the way of swords and apparel to make him resemble the heavily laden White Knight in *Alice*; the good messenger's face is whited and his costume is an innocent mint-green. The young lovers' faces are also thickly whited and their gestures are stiff and impersonal.

Shunkan, by contrast, wears a simple robe, and his face is made up gray but not so thickly as to disguise expression. His desolate old age abandoned by life is the focus of the play. The variety of his expression and the relative still formality of the others' faces operate this focus; he is the ground and they are the shadows passing over it.

To a beautifully sung commentary by the equally aged Hinatayu Takemoto – also a Living Treasure – Kanzaburo's Shunkan makes each emotion into a virtual history. At the beginning, head bowed, he registers the sadness of exile not with a simple expression of grief but with grief set in dialogue with diffidence, as if man and his fate were equal partners in some larger enterprise. His joy when told that one of his companions has fallen in love touches on timidity; Kanzaburo's aged smile is almost a giggle but it is so fragile that tragedy shows beneath it.

The sword fight between two feeble men – Kanzaburo is old and starving and the evil messenger has been disabled by a sword cut – is a fierce and frightening affair in its nightmare slowness. And the final scene, after some rather awkward shifting about of boulders, with Kanzaburo staring out to sea and his face immobile and moving at the same time, is overwhelming in its grief.

After this powerful work, the *Renjishi* seems disjointed and relatively trivial. The first part, in which Kanzaburo plays an old actor and Kankuro plays his son – he is his son, in fact – is a graceful dance in which the two represent two lions. It is interrupted by a comic skit showing a dispute between a priest and a nun of different sects. Then the two actors return, this time wearing full lion manes, and do a more agitated dance, consisting most spectacularly of the frenzied and rhythmical tossing of these manes.

It is a pretty sight but it does not convey, at least at this cultural distance, much more than a sense of dexterity. *Renjishi's* main strength, in fact, is the beautiful and varied music, sung by several singers and accompanied by a band that includes *samisens*, flutes and drums.

On this occasion David Oyama published an article with comments by a number of leading New York directors and stage figures whom he had asked, "What influence can such a totally different form of theater have on American theater? What, if anything, had they learned from it." The summary:

For Harold Prince, currently directing the new Stephen Sondheim version of *Sweeney Todd*, the great lesson of Kabuki was that "with all its rules and traditions, anything theatrical is acceptable, and that to be naïve and child-like in the theater is to be desired." It is an attitude which Mr Prince has tried to emulate since his production of Mr Sondheim's previous musical, *Pacific Overtures*, three years ago, in which he adapted numerous Kabuki techniques from an American standpoint in order to find a metaphor for the Westernization of Japan.

"It would be arrogant and stupid for me to suggest that what we did was Kabuki, but what fascinated me most – and what I did try to infuse into *Pacific Overtures* – was the peculiar energy of Japanese theater and their unabashed enthusiasm for theater itself."

The avant-garde East European emigré, Andrei Serban, had recently directed *The Cherry Orchard* in Japan and had observed the work of the classic ensembles there. He told Oyama that he saw Nōh and Kabuki as "the single living example of what the Elizabethan theater must have been like. It is living proof of what theater was like hundreds of years ago, when it was something much, much stronger than it is today. By seeing the Kabuki, we must question why we work in theater and why our theater is so much less complete than the Kabuki and Nōh. And our actors must ask again, when they see a Kabuki actor, who does everything, 'What does it mean to be an actor?'"

Lee Strasberg, the noted founder of New York's Actors' Studio, fountainhead of the Stanislavsky Method in the United States, accepted Serban's appraisal. "The Kabuki is a reaffirmation of what can be done on the stage. It is all there – the excitement, color, dynamics, everything that thrills theater people. Here is an unusual opportunity to see the equivalents of our classical theater because the early forms of Western theater are the same as these forms of Japanese theater. And that in itself is extraordinary." Oyama continues:

Mr Strasberg, however, believes that, in acting technique, the Kabuki actor confronts basically the same problems as the American actor – problems of concentration and motivations. "How can the actor commit himself? The discussions which one reads in the Kabuki *Actors Analects* sound like the discussions about the Method today," he suggests. He believes that "dramaturgically, Kabuki and Oriental theater have had a great influence – Brecht and Thornton Wilder's *Our Town* are the outstanding examples – but in the study of acting, it may now be the other way around. But, of course, as I said, the Kabuki is a great stimulus to us to see what can be done on a stage."

Faubion Bowers, the pre-eminent American authority on the Kabuki and Japanese theater, is credited by the Japanese as having saved the Kabuki from clumsy censorship and destruction after the war when he served as an aide to General MacArthur and later as a censor of the Japanese theater. He believes that American theater can borrow "broad concepts" from Japanese theater, but paraphrasing the actor Koshiro VIII, Mr Bowers noted that "when foreigners try to play Kabuki, it loses its scent. However gifted we are, we can't learn Kabuki. There is nothing to be learned, only enjoyment."

Kabuki as a private discipline to add certain techniques to the American actor's handbook, he feels, is all right "but it can never be applied. Kabuki is totally unrelated and worlds apart from American theater, and if Americans try to apply it, it always ends as a spoof, as *The Mikado*, as *Japanaiserie*." Nevertheless, Mr Bowers said, he believes American directors such as Elia Kazan and Arthur Penn have used certain Japanese techniques to imaginative effect in stage productions such as *Cat on a Hot Tin Roof* and *All the Way Home* (based on James Agee's *A Death in the Family*).

At the end of *Cat on a Hot Tin Roof*, Maggie reaches up to turn out a light, and she turns off an invisible light. Well, that is from Kabuki. Arthur Penn was inspired by *Chushingura*, the Japanese classic play, and completely changed his concept of *All the Way Home* to use stylized tableaux. Mr Bowers is currently editing a television film of the Kabuki *Terakoya* which he recently shot in Japan with the renowned *onnagata* (actor of female roles) Utaemon Nakamura VI. He is also doing the simultaneous translation for the performances of the Grand Kabuki troupe on the current tour, and it is to be recommended highly for maximum understanding of these plays.

A former Kabuki actor, Onoe Kuroemon, the son of the great Kikugoro VI, now teaches Kabuki movement at the Loeb Drama Center at Harvard University. Mr Kuroemon believes that American actors can learn a great deal from the discipline and spirit of Kabuki. "Many people think that Kabuki is stylized and fixed, but this is not true. The Kabuki actor has complete freedom to create his own style based on tradition and experience. It is not unlimited freedom, but he is free at any time to create."

Comparing the training of young Kabuki actors under the tutelage of master actors to our theater training, Mr Kuroemon remarked that it is equivalent to our actors being trained to do Shakespeare only by the likes of Laurence Olivier and Richard Burton.

And that is something to consider.

During its 1982 engagement in New York, the Grand Kabuki occupied the stage of the Metropolitan Opera for twelve performances. The company, on a month-long tour of the United States, was made up of seventy-seven actors, musicians and technical crew members; it was led by Nakamura Utaemon 6th, Nakamura Kanzaburo 17th and the singer Kiyomoto Shizuatayo, all three of whom had also been designated Living National Treasures by the Japanese government. Besides a stay at the Kennedy Center in Washington, the troupe participated in the World's Fair in Knoxville, Tennessee. Funds for the tour came from the Japan Society, the Matsushita Electric Company and the Government of Japan.

Jennifer Dunning, in the *New York Times*, reviewed the various programmes. She noted that curtains were used to lower the top proscenium at the Metropolitan's arch and that a *hanamichi* was constructed to extend the action into the auditorium, thereby replicating the traditional Kabuki stage. Of the performances, she said:

The superb Kabuki actors brought here by the Japan Society have offered many revelations in their regrettably short season. There is the noble elegance of Fukusuke, for instance, and the virility of Ebizo. Utaemon stands out among the players of female roles, a larger-than-life Kabuki Bernhardt, and who will forget Tamasaburo, with hands like long translucent carvings? Best of all, there has been the great Kanzaburo, so poignantly believable whether playing the Lear-like General Kumagai, the companionable boatman or *Sumidagawa* or the hen-pecked philanderer in *Migawari-Zazen*.

Tomijuro came close to that high standard of versatility Tuesday, when he moved from the quaking old stone-cutter in *Kumagai Jinya* to the tough and canny retainer Benkei in the season's first performance of *Kanjincho* (*The Subscription List*). Like the mid-nineteenth-century, Nōh-derived play, the role of Benkei is one of the most famed in the Kabuki repertory. It demands a big voice and presence, skill as a dancer, and an ability to invest a typical anti-hero with mobility and earthiness. Tomijuro had all of these.

Moments go by as small eternities in Kabuki, while hours pass with surprising quickness. *Kanjincho* is a prime example of that skewed sense of time, as it focuses on an incident at a barrier when a guard, Togashi, tries to turn back a group of priests who he suspects are the fleeing overlord,

Yoshitsune, and his servants. In a complex mesh of feudal obligations, Benkei takes the extreme act of striking his lord to convince the guard that Yoshitsune is the lowly porter he pretends to be. Togashi lets them through, knowing that his treacherous act must end in suicide. Their mutual admiration for one another's bravery creates a strong bond between the two enemies, but Benkei must be on his jubilant way.

Intent and full of amusing pieties, Benkei's reading of an imaginary list of the would-be priests' charitable subscribers is a signature moment in Kabuki drama. But as exciting for the Western viewer were Tomijuro's flashing eyes, the flowing hands of his rascally call to prayer and the deft implacability of Benkei's small bulky frame. His fierce final dance, all swaggering lunges and weighty, fluttering bourrées, was a wonder, as were the subtle comic touches of the drinking scene that builds up to it.

Kanjincho is also full of formal beauty. A brief skirmish between opposing retainers is accomplished in two stark lines of men, their feet trembling with rage against the ground. The soft-colored, boxy trousers of Yoshitsune and his followers tantalizingly recall Oskar Schlemmer's Bauhaus costume constructions. As Togashi, Fukusuke's stylized walk in his long functionary's trousers and his last, still pose added much to the play, as did the exciting singing and playing of the Nagauta and Narimono Ensembles ranged in full panoply at the back of the simple set.

But best of all was the scene in which the agonized Tomijuro begs for forgiveness for slapping his lord, a perfect foil as played by Kankuro. He approaches the serene figure falteringly on his knees, hands raised in supplication, his voice a piteous low wail to rather querulous reassurances. The stage picture is as striking visually as it is touching. And Tomijuro's stirring departure along the *hanamichi* had the audience cheering.

Once again at the Metropolitan, in 1985, the Grand Kabuki brought five plays new to New York. There were two programmes on alternate evenings. *Shibaraku* (*Just a Moment*) has been "a bravura vehicle" since its advent in 1697. In this, the full company joined Danjuro XII, featured as the heroic Kagemasa, "wielding his six-foot sword with magnificent bravado to rescue innocent victims of a band of scheming villains". The role of his arch-enemy was played by Shoroku. *Tachi Nusu-Bito* (*The Sword Thief*) gave the young star Tatsunosuke a chance to portray a wily thief who dupes a tipsy country samurai and filches his weapon. *Kojo* (*Name-taking Ceremony*) presented one of Kabuki's most solemn events, the award of a new name to a great actor, "equivalent to a promotion in the centuries-old hierarchy of acting lineages". In this instance, Ichikawa Ebizo X became Danjuro XII, "the most illustrious name for an actor in Kabuki's long history". The longer *Sakura-Hime Azuma Bunsho* (*The Scarlet Princess of Edo*), a masterwork of the nineteenth century, is packed with such dramatic elements as love, mystery, rape, murder, satire and comedy. Tamasaburo was cast as an acolyte and later as the resplendent Princess Sakurahime, brought from a high position to utter degradation. Opposite her was Takao, in quick role-changes from a virtuous priest seeking to save the girl's soul to a rough scoundrel who is causing her ruin. In *Tsuchigumo* (*The Earth Spider*), adapted from a classic Nōh piece, a handsome young nobleman is afflicted by a strange illness. His retainers discover that he is under the spell of an evil magician. They pursue their lord's enemy. To elude them, their sly foe metamorphoses into a huge spider and tries to ensnare them. The dual part of the magician–spider was assumed by Shoroku.

Excerpts from the Grand Kabuki's repertory were filmed and later broadcast (1986) on New York's Channel 31. The showing was preceded by a half-hour documentary setting forth the traditional techniques of this unfamiliar art form. The film included an interview with Tamasaburo, the rising young actor who essayed female roles. Faubion Bowers also participated in the programme.

William Weaver, in Tokyo, saw and admired the work of another Kabuki interpreter, Ennosuke III, whose versatility and deftness at quick changes enabled him to undertake several roles in a play. Thus, in *Futago Sumidagawa*, he depicted a noble lord, a faithful retainer and a decayed samurai reduced to carrying on as a slave-trader. Weaver attested: "A rather portly man in early middle age, Ennosuke 3rd is capable of breathtaking acrobatics, brilliant mime and inspired dancing. Usually at least one of the parts will be a ghost or a goblin; and he also plays animals – for example, an endearing fox." He served as a director, too, and was fond of dazzling stage effects. In his own version of *Futago Sumidagawa* he had the last act end victoriously with a conflict between the loyal retainer and a huge carp under a cataract of tons of actual water. The ensemble at the Kubukiza theatre struck Weaver as altogether "magnificent". Kataro, the actor portraying the aristocratic Lady Yoshida, was "a miracle of harmonious movement and touching vulnerability. And the other *onnagata* are on the same high level." Weaver singled out for applause Sojuro, who "specializes in devoted old nurses and wise ladies-in-waiting", and an assured child actor, Kamejiro, a nephew of Ennosuke and son of Danshiro ("awesome interpreter of black-hearted villainy"). In another Kabuki play Kikugoro was the faithful governess Lady Masaoka, bound to protect her charge, an imperilled child-lord. Her son, of the same age as the young noble, is killed. She must hide her grief while in the presence of others. But when at last she is alone with her son's corpse she is able to voice her profound despair. Weaver recalls, "Kikugoro gave a bravura performance – one that ranks with Callas's mad scene in *Lucia* as one of my great theater-going experiences. Kikugoro also played the demented mother in the *Futago Sumidagawa*, a less spectacular role, but equally demanding. A spectator with no Japanese could yet derive enormous pleasure from these performances, as a listener with no Italian could enjoy the Callas Lucia."

Opera as composed and performed in the Occident was slow in reaching Japan. The first opportunity for the natives of the island to hear any sort of European music came with the advent of Portuguese and Spanish missionaries in the sixteenth century, but a ban on Christianity in 1588 put a stop to the importation of all foreign scores. Almost 300 years later, during the Meiji Restoration, the prohibition was lifted (1868), and interest in foreign musical forms gained rapidly. Military band marches and Protestant hymns won popularity, while the Meiji government sponsored wide acceptance of European methods of singing in the education curriculum. A Music Study Committee was set up by the government in 1887, and teachers of music were brought from abroad. The Tokyo Music School was established, and by 1890 a music journal began publication. In 1894 an act from Gounod's *Faust* was staged, and in 1900 recitals of various kinds – piano, violin, singing – were frequent. At about this time Japanese composers of Western-style music made an appearance.

The most distinguished forerunner was Kōsaku Yamada (1886–1965). Born in Tokyo, he studied at the city's Music School, composing for the voice and seeking mastery of the cello and theory. At twenty-two (1908) he undertook further instruction in Germany at the Berlin Hochschule für Musik; among his teachers were Bruch and Karl Leopold Wolf. He displayed outstanding talent there, turning out chamber music and symphonies. In 1912, at twenty-six, he completed his first opera, *Ochitaru tennyo* (*The Depraved Heavenly Maiden*); it was scheduled for performance two years later, and he went back to Tokyo to make ready for the première, but the onset of the First World War led to the production being cancelled. A second opera, *Alladine et Palomides* (1913), also went unstaged.

He could not return to Berlin, so he occupied himself with organizing the Tokyo Philharmonic Orchestra and conducted its initial concert, the first of its kind by a Japanese ensemble. His skill as a conductor was rapidly acknowledged, and at the same time he was composing prolifically. In 1915 he wrote a *Prelude* for chorus and orchestra, based on the Japanese national anthem, to mark the coronation of Emperor Taishō. The next year he collaborated effectively with the dancer Bac Ishii on three "dance poems" (1916).

Yamada visited the United States in 1917, and in 1918 an evening's programme devoted solely to his works took place at Carnegie Hall with the New York Philharmonic under his baton. A number of his songs and piano pieces were published by such prestigious houses as Fischer and G. Schirmer. He lingered in the United States to serve as guest conductor of several other orchestras, including on his programmes scores by Richard Wagner, who as an arch German nationalist was then out of favour with patriotic American audiences.

Home in Japan once more, Yamada encouraged the staging of dramatic music. He established the Nihon Gakugeki Kyokai (Japan Association for Music Drama), and soon after (1920) put on the third act of *Tannhäuser* and Debussy's *L'Enfant prodigue* in Tokyo and Osaka. In September 1922 he joined with a friend, the poet Hakushu Kithara, to launch a journal, *Shi to ongaku* (*Verse and Music*), that sought to arrive at a perfect union of the separate art forms.

An anonymous biographer in *Grove's* says of Yamada: "He was now well recognized for his orchestral works, such as the symphonic poem *Meiji shoka* (*Ode to the Meiji*; 1921) which demonstrated his mastery of orchestral technique in a style drawing on Wagner, Strauss and Scriabin. At the same time he began to compose numerous vocal pieces with piano, trying to combine the tradition of the *lied* from Schubert to Wolf with subtle Japanese melodic features. Indeed, throughout his career he was concerned to find a musical style which would relate closely to the melodic and rhythmic elements in Japanese speech intonation."

The hostilities now over, Yamada returned to Europe to learn about post-war musical trends. Having updated himself on the subject, he took up his tasks in Japan again, seeking to gather a new orchestra. In 1925 he finally brought into being the Japanese Philharmonic Society. This made possible a five-day festival to which, on his initiative, forty-seven Russian musicians came from Manchuria to play Russian and Japanese orchestral works. He dissolved his own instrumental group, however, when Hidemaro Konoe formed the New Symphony Orchestra (later called the NHK Symphony Orchestra). Henceforth Yamada directed all his energies to composition.

In 1929, after a fifteen-year delay, *The Depraved Heavenly Maiden* was finally staged at the Tokyo Kabuki Theatre. He received a commission two years later to visit Paris and provide a new work for the Théâtre Pigalle. He astonished nearly everybody by delivering an opera, his third, *Ayame* (*The Sweet Flag*; 1931), in less than two years.

His route back to Japan lay across Russia. He led several acclaimed concerts while in that country and included his own scores on the programmes. He was invited back to the USSR in 1933 for further engagements as a composer–conductor. In 1937 the Japanese government sponsored a European tour enabling him to lead foreign orchestras playing his works. He was designated a chevalier of the *Légion d'honneur* and elected an honorary member of the Debussy and Saint-Saëns societies in France.

In 1939 Yamada completed his most successful opera, *Kurofune* (*The Black Ships*); it and another piece, *Yoake* (*The Dawn*), were produced in Tokyo in 1940.

His last opera, *Hsiang Fei* (1946–7), was less well received when belatedly presented in Tokyo after the Second World War (1954).

Yamada was constantly given recognition: the Asahi Cultural Prize (1941); election to the Japan Academy of Arts (1942); the NHK Broadcasting Cultural Prize (1950); the Medal of Honour with Blue Ribbons (1954); the Japanese government's Cultural Order (1956).

He was prolific to an almost incredible degree. He is credited with at least 1,500 compositions. No full catalogue of them exists or ever will, if only because many of his manuscripts were lost during an air raid on Tokyo in 1945. The Toyama Music Library in Tokyo contains much of what is left. More than 750 of his scores were published in fifteen volumes entitled *Yamada Kosaku Zenshu* (*The Complete Works of Kosaku Yamada*; 1931); a subsequent venture to round out the list was left unfinished after ten volumes were issued (1963–6).

Once again borrowing from the unsigned article in *Grove's*: "Yamada's works show, in their thematic materials and orchestration, the clear influence of Wagner and, still more strongly, Strauss, with occasional characteristic features of French impressionism; yet he never lost his identity as a Japanese composer. Though Straussian elements are particularly dominant in the large-scale works, his solo vocal pieces are in a much lighter style, imbued with emotional sentiments and a lyricism that brought them to popularity. He was the foremost Japanese advocate of German Romanticism and as such laid the foundations for modern Japanese music in the European tradition."

The outbreak of the First World War and the Russian Revolution had brought European musicians as refugees to Japan, among them Sergei Prokofiev. Their presence further encouraged the growth of Western-inspired musical activity. Besides German Romanticism, elements of French Impressionism entered the works of other Japanese composers, while they sought to retain idiomatic strains in their scores.

During the Second World War all musical activities fell under strict control by the military government. The rule was relaxed after 1945, and musicians eagerly sought to catch up with modern movements abroad. Orchestras and opera groups sprang up, and new music schools and colleges proliferated. Many music festivals were established, and cliques of composers who adopted various contemporary modes – including the avant-garde – issued manifestos. Among these were those advocating dodecaphony and *musique concrete*. At the same time some composers held to nineteenth-century styles. After 1960 virtually all Western movements had Japanese counterparts, and some local composers like Yamada gradually acquired reputations abroad and had their works played by foreign orchestras.

Virtuosos from every region of the world now found hearers in Japan and discovered it was profitable to visit there. In addition, tours by such major ensembles as the Metropolitan Opera Company of New York and La Scala of Milan, as well as Russian troupes, attracted large audiences. The general preference of Japanese opera-goers is still for internationally renowned artists in the standard European and American repertoire.

For a while, local companies had difficulty in gaining a footing. The Tokyo University of Fine Arts and Music added an opera department, headed by Jan Popper, a Californian, and before long a good supply of young talent was available. Works by Verdi, Puccini and even Britten given by indigenous casts were soon heard, and eventually Tokyo had two opera companies, the Fujiwara and the Nikikai, both emphasizing foreign works with librettos translated into Japanese. The Nihon Toshi Center Hall, in a hotel complex, housed their presentations: it seated 1,000 patrons, though frequently it was not filled to capacity.

A considerable number of ambitious Japanese composers became interested in fashioning operas. So far, the best known has been Ikuma Dan (1924–2001), whose one-act version of a modern classic, Junji Kinoshita's folk-drama *Yuzuru* (*The Twilight Crane*), was mentioned earlier in this chapter. Dan, a noted conductor, is the grandson of a prominent businessman. Descended from a family of scholars, he was exposed to Western music in his boyhood and demonstrated his talent while still quite young. He graduated from the Tokyo University of Fine Arts and Music in 1945. In barely five years he gained recognition with his *Symphony No. 1 in A* (1950). His first and still most popular stage-work, *Yuzuru*, followed shortly (1952). It illustrates and overcomes what is said to be the chief problem of a Japanese composer who elects to write in a Western style. In this piece, as Iwatake Toru says, Dan "attempted to synthesize the essence of traditional Japanese theatrical arts such as Nōh, Bunraku and Kabuki with Western opera". It has had more than 200 performances at home and other countries.

Twice staged in New York – in Japanese around 1961, in an English version in 1981 – *Yuzuru* elicited critical approval there. Edward Rothstein, of the *New York Times*, hearing the English offering, had a few reservations:

> The opera, modeled on a Japanese folk-tale, retains a powerful mythic core, when it is not ornamented with sentimental children's chanting and two overly crude villains. The orchestral score, with its Oriental shadings of Puccinian and Menottian lyricism, supports and drives the tale toward its end.

> On Saturday night, with Anthony Morss's able conducting, harp pluckings and drum taps gave Tsu's loom fateful accents. As Tsu, the soprano Tomoko Shibata acted with such finely controlled sensitivity that her sometimes tight and light voice added to Tsu's fragility. Charles Abruzzo was an

engaging and touching simpleton as Yohyo; Jerome Mann and Dennis Raley were his greedy tempters.

Weakened and saddened, Tsu's origins revealed, she finally departs, transformed back into a heron.

In the *New York Daily News* William Zakariasen wrote:

Ikuma Dan is a distinguished composer whose symphonies have on occasion been heard in the US, usually via Japan's Toshiba record label. His style is basically late-Romantic, with predictable influences of Richard Strauss, Italian Verismo and the French impressionists.

Yuzuru is permeated with the flavor of Puccini (believe it or not, *Madam Butterfly is* quite popular in Japan), but there also is quite a bit of seasoning from Sibelius. The two composers' styles, at least as homogenized by Dan, actually work together very well, and happily Dan doesn't handle them in a merely imitative fashion.

Yuzuru's vocal lines are grateful, musical themes are strong and identifiable, and the orchestration is most atmospheric. An occasional lack of musical propulsion to underline the drama is its only fault.

The libretto of *Yuzuru* – translated on the Japanese recording of it as *The Twilight Crane* – is a fantasy regarding a wife's eventual reincarnation into her former life as a heron.

The plot isn't as exportable as the prevailingly beautiful music, but the work was quite excellently performed (in an uncredited but good English translation) by Aemiko Iinuma (a superb Japanese soprano of great emotional communication), tenor Philip Salter, baritone Paul Mastrangelo, bass Eugene Green, the Metropolitan Opera Children's Chorus and a well-drilled (if string-weak) orchestra under Anthony Morss's direction.

Kenya Oda's inventive staging showed his credentials as director of Tokyo's famous Fujiwara Opera Company. *Yuzuru*'s presentation was a most worthy venture on all accounts.

Anthony Coggi, on New York's WFUV-FM, had only praise.

Dan's score is not at all forbidding; it is firmly grounded in Western musical techniques and esthetics. It is facile; it's lyric, it's tuneful; it's quite dramatic; and not surprisingly, it contains melodies based on pentatonic scales. In fact the overall effect is not unlike Puccini's *Madama Butterfly*. It also contains a number of particularly felicitous touches associated with the Bird's plucking and weaving.

The performance was an extremely fine one, and if I give first mention to conductor Anthony Morss and his orchestra, it's not intended to slight the excellent soloists. I've had occasion to compliment Mr Morss's conducting in connection with his performances with the Verismo Opera and Sacred Music Societies in recent years, and he certainly did not disappoint on this occasion.

The cast, as I said, was quite good, especially Philip Salter who displayed a free-ringing tenor as the husband, and Aemiko Iinuma, Tsu, the lady who can turn herself into a bird. She has a fine lyric soprano, and her quick, bird-like movements were theatrically effective. Paul Mastrangelo and Joseph Eubanks as two rogues were well in the picture; and the cast was completed by eight of the most beautiful children I've ever seen on stage.

Billed as a one-act opera, and running about as long as Strauss' *Elektra*, it was performed on this occasion in two acts. I'm ambivalent on this point. The intermission frankly interrupted the work's momentum. On the other hand, I'm not sure that interest in the somewhat limited premise of the work could have been sustained through an entire evening without one. At any rate, the company is off to a good start.

Yuzuru brought Dan a heap of honours and awards, too many to list here. He gathered more with later operas, including *Kimimimi zukin* (*The Listening Cap*; 1955), produced in Takarazoka, near Osaka; *Yo Kihi* (*Yang Kwei-Fei*), presented in Tokyo in 1958; *Hikarigoke* (*Luminous* Moss; 1958), given in Osaka in 1972; and *Chanchiki* (1975); though none matched the lasting success of his first effort.

He wrote music for children and scores for films, at times under contract to submit four a year.

Iwatake Tōru says about Dan's varied contributions: "Each manifests a mastery of compositional techniques, a keen sense of structural balance, and above all, melodies that are dramatic yet highly intimate."

His versatility was further proved by his getting the Yomiuri Literature Award in 1967; for fifteen years he wrote a weekly column for an important magazine. He also served as director of planning for a widely broadcast television programme bringing information about the people, customs, geography and music of many countries outside Japan. Always searching for unknown folk music and collecting ancient instruments, he paid ten visits to China to examine musical artefacts dug up when a fifth-century tomb was found and excavated there.

Kanazawa Masakata remarks that Dan's later works tend to be more dissonant, but that his output remains "tonal, basically romantic, and inclined to the exotic". Six volumes of his essays, entitled *Pipe Smoke* (1965–72), have been published; his gifts as a literary humorist further account for his popularity.

Minoru Miki (b. 1930) was born in Tokushima, Shikoku. His family was musical, several members performing ably on various Japanese instruments. In high school the youth had his earliest encounter with European-style music when he participated in a choral group. At twenty he took up study of the piano and harmony, having decided on a professional career in that realm. Entering the National University of Fine Arts and Music, he delved into the technical aspects of composition (1951–5). Though only twenty-three and still a student, he won second prize with an orchestral work in a radio contest in 1953. After graduation he continued to write large-scale works in a Western mode, earning his living by composing film scores, mostly for documentaries. In 1960 he became chiefly interested in choral music; the following year he associated himself with a group known as the Tokyo Liedertafel and provided it with original pieces. By 1963 the Liedertafel presented a whole programme of just his works. But now he was also trying his hand at compositions for traditional Japanese instruments. Gathering select and expert players he formed the Ensemble Nipponia in 1964, dedicated to indigenous music, and added to its repertoire some of his own pieces. The ensemble having given seven recitals under official auspices, and having established Miki as an outstanding composer, won an Art Festival Prize in 1967.

He was still affiliated with the Tokyo Liedertafel; in 1968 he led it on a concert tour of West Germany. The year 1970 saw the recording and issuance of an anthology of his work, including a specially commissioned piece, which garnered for him a *grand prix* at that year's Art Festival.

He moved from East to West and back again physically and artistically so often that he was referred to as the "pendulum man".

Kanazawa Masakata, in *Grove's*:

Miki mastered the techniques of European art music with astonishing rapidity. . . . His early instrumental works and a large number of choral pieces of 1960–63 demonstrate his attempts to combine European and Oriental features in his own style. However, the formation of the Ensemble Nipponia marked a turning point; from then on he gradually departed from the European tradition and began to explore original techniques appropriate to Japanese instruments. In doing so he depended a great deal on effective combinations of timbre and a strong sense of rhythm; his rhythms may be determinedly violent, irregular in beat or completely free and improvisatory, while he has benefited from his close contact with performers in developing music requiring a high degree of virtuosity.

For the stage Miki contributed an operetta, *Mendori teishu* (*Husband the Hen*; 1963), put on in Tokyo; and a musical play for children, *Kikimimi*; and an opera, also seen in Tokyo, *Shunkin sho* (*Spring*

Harp; 1975). Another opera, *An Actor's Revenge,* was given its world première by the English Music Theatre in 1979, and later was offered by the Opera Theater of Saint Louis (Missouri) in 1981, with the composer holding the baton. A reviewer in *Opera News* had this to say:

> Under Colin Graham's razor-sharp direction it proved to be a remarkable series of poetic images in sixteen flash-back scenes, prologue and epilogue. One came away from the Kabuki-inspired opera with more a sense of its theatricality and visual impact than of its music *per se.* Timothy Jozwick designed a simple set of Japanese screens on a polished wooden floor with ramp, enhanced by Miller's lighting, which produced stunning effects, especially in the back-lighting of the screens, the use of shadows and a brilliant fire sequence.
>
> Peter Docherly's costumes were just right, as were Paul Alba's authentic wigs and makeup. Together with Graham's sophisticated direction, slow and ritualistic in the Japanese tradition, one became immersed as the emotional climax was reached: the death of Lady Namiji. The libretto by James Kirkup concerns itself with love, greed, revenge and a spiritual union that ultimately transcends such worldly preoccupations, all played out in a measured, formal manner. This Eastern pacing, plus the Japanese instruments (string and percussion), is blended with a kind of Western lyricism (a soaring Act I love duet, for instance) and Western orchestra. This is a bold hybrid, its Eastern effects providing punctuation for emotional underscoring, at the same time helping to paint specific pictures as well. The Brittenesque vocal setting is effectively lean, often in chant style, often taking off in a difficult, sustained tessitura. Miki led his work with incisiveness and balance.
>
> Mallory Walker earned honors in the long, demanding tenor role of Yukinojo (the *onnagata,* the idolized Kabuki actor specializing in female roles), while dancer Manuel Alum brought grace and variety to the dancing/acting half of the role, the concentration of his eyes and gestures riveting as he wrought vengeance on those who drove his parents to death. Cynthia Clarey sang sweetly and acted with fragility as Lady Namiji, ultimately undone by the plot, while Scott Reeve (Kikunojo), David Evitts (Heima), William Dansby (Lord Dobe), Richard Croft (Kawaguchiya) and others made the most of their roles. Keiko Nosaka, to stage right with her koto and samisen, provided constant interest with ravishing playing.

On a six-week tour of the Far East in 1986, Britain's Royal Opera visited Tokyo, Osaka and Yokohama. One work offered was Puccini's *Turandot,* and the troupe's managers were concerned about how Japanese audiences would respond to the pseudo-Orientalism of the music, choreography, costuming and setting; the production had originally been mounted under the direction of Andrei

Serban, who employed a tiered stage of "Eastern design" with the leading singers, masked chorus and dancers occupying the foreground. The performers adopted ritualized gestures and movement. The venture was acclaimed, however.

Various troupes are preserving classic dance forms, notably solemn Bugaku, an eighteenth-century dance-play originally enacted by Japanese samurai; Shudun, a very abstract women's court dance about the pangs of rejected love, derived from a Kabuki offering and adapted to add an Okinawan gestural style; and Chijuya, a lively folk-based work often featured at village festivals; it belongs to a genre that evolved when court dances were too stately for the populace whose likings had to be met after the Japanese ended the sway of feudalism in Okinawa. An eighteen-member ensemble, the Court Dance Theatre and Music troupe from Okinawa, was founded in 1969 by Minoru Miyagi, a leading performer. The group was presented at Asia House in New York in 1977 with a programme built around *Revenge of the Two Sons*, a Nōh-influenced work.

The journeys overseas of this and other companies are subsidized by the Japanese government, or by foundations in New York, repeatedly by the Asia Society, the American Museum of Natural History, the Japan Society or multinational corporations seeking to burnish their public image by supporting cultural activities. For domestic political reasons the government is particularly interested in pleasing the Okinawans, who are not ethnically Japanese and at times grow restive.

Gagaku was heard in the United States when Lincoln Kirstein, general director of the New York City Ballet, arranged a guest season by a Tokyo troupe in 1959. It was an unprecedented event: few people outside the Imperial Music Pavilion or one of the major shrines at Ise or Nara had ever witnessed Bugaku danced to Gagaku, and it had never before been performed abroad. Most likely the consequence is that more Americans than Japanese have been permitted to watch this rite. The foreign visit was a part of the celebration of Crown Prince Akahito's marriage to Michiko Shoda that year; it was also a gesture of reciprocity for a previous visit by the New York City Ballet to the island-nation. Many in the audience in New York found the enactment colourful and sculptural, but to a Westerner stultifyingly slow.

Some groups, both at home and when going abroad, mix classical works with more recent ones on their programmes. In addition, regional folk-dancers are featured; they may be theatricalized, not wholly authentic.

In 1978 the John D. Rockefeller III Fund provided a $48,000 grant to install and maintain an Asian Dance Archive in the New York Public Library of Performing Arts at Lincoln Center in New

York. The core of the collection was made up of 3,418 books and periodicals, more than 5,000 photographs and 500 slides, 125 volumes of manuscripts and 160 films and videotapes of Asian dances. Two and a half years were spent assembling the materials. The library's own dance collection had already produced nineteen hours of performance films and thirty-three hours of taped interviews, some of which captured the dancers in action while they recalled details of past productions and costumes. Of particular note are microfilms of Bugaku manuscripts dating from the thirteenth, sixteenth and seventeenth centuries that have long been housed in the Library of the Imperial Household in Japan, and Indonesian materials that were gathered by Claire Holt, an anthropologist and art historian. Other films were donated by the NHK–Japan Television Broadcasting System.

Classical ballet as performed *sur les pointes* in Europe and North and South America seemed to be an art very alien to the Japanese; foreign critics said that women of this branch of the Oriental race, unlike the slight, graceful Chinese, tend to have stubby legs, bowed inwards, ill-suiting them for a leaping, spinning form of dance. Their unique Japanese tradition calls for the almost static pose and reliance on manipulation of the hands in symbolic gestures. But that explanation by outsiders has proved to be somewhat in error. The delay in taking up Western-style ballet was due more to social factors, such as the usual Japanese resistance to deep cultural change and a clinging to revered conventions (as opposed to an undesirable susceptibility to superficial fads); the Nōh and Kabuki genres have a lengthy history and arise from psychological traits special to these long-isolated, homogeneous people, who characteristically are intensely nationalistic, an aspect reflected in all their arts.

Notwithstanding all this, the Occidental form of ballet slowly gained acceptance in Japan. After all, this art form, too, is highly stylized and so has an innate appeal. Like Nōh, it is aimed at an élite, spectators with an inclination to aristocratic fantasies; and it contains elements of universal myths and age-old fairy-tales.

Giovanni Vittorio Rossi, an Italian ballet-master, introduced this type of dance to Japan as early as 1912. He was hired by the newly inaugurated Imperial Theatre of Tokyo to give instruction in the European classical repertoire as well as in the basic techniques used in performing them. In 1916 Ishii Baku, Rossi's most accomplished disciple, gave an influential recital in which he offered a "dance poem" based on verses by Yeats.

Better known abroad was another of Rossi's pupils, Michio Ito (1892–1961), who also created "dance poems" of unprecedented sensuousness. Ito took lessons in Germany, settled in the United States during the First World War and married an American dancer, Hazel Wright. While in New York he had a role in *Bushido*, a Japanese drama put on by the Theater Guild, and for some years, beginning in 1920, worked with John Murray Anderson to present a series of revues, the *Greenwich Village Follies*.

He offered recitals and also taught. During the 1930s he produced a number of Japanese dramas at the Booth Theater. He had a lasting grasp on his American pupils and is still well remembered and highly regarded. Returning to Japan in 1948, he staged Gilbert and Sullivan's ebullient *Mikado* in Tokyo. He managed a television studio and handled tours by Oriental dancers to the United States, to which he himself paid his final visit in 1959.

Among the most important American dancers who are said to be much in his debt were Ruth St Denis, Martha Graham, Lester Horton and Pauline Koner. His style, a fusion of East and West, featured energetic upper body–arm activity and employed symbolic gestures to transmit dramatic meanings, while the face remained immobile, to exclude the dancer's personality and heighten the idea being conveyed. Saturu Shimazaki, later a choreographer who also took up residence in New York, said in 1979: "When I first saw the works of Ito presented in Japan, I cried. It was so beautiful. Even though I was twenty-one years old, I decided to become a dancer, and immediately knew I had to come to New York. In Japan, the Ito school no longer exists – only the old Graham and Germany's Mary Wigman schools exist. That's why we have to come to New York, to study different schools of movement."

Throughout the 1920s and 1930s other dancers who boldly adopted a Western style – ballet and modern – won notice. Quite a few emulated Ito and went to Germany to train, some of them enrolling in Mary Wigman's Institute; others studied in the Denishawn School in Los Angelos or like Saturu Shimazaki chose New York. Among these venturesome young artists were Seiko Takada (1900–1977), Takaya Eguchi (1900–1977) and Misako Miya (1900–).

The superb Anna Pavlova arrived in Japan, danced her *Dying Swan* and other typical items on her programme at the Imperial Theatre (1920, 1922), having a great impact, winning new converts to Western classical ballet. Her success also prompted other foreign ballerinas and their troupes to include Tokyo, Osaka and a few more of the larger Japanese cities on their globe-circling itineraries.

Gradually it became popular among upper-class Japanese families to send their daughters to ballet classes, so that many girls and even a few boys became proficient in the demanding techniques. This fad was also testimony to Japan's expanding prosperity.

The reign of the militarists during the 1930s and anti-foreign emotions aroused throughout the years of the Second World War were an impediment to the growth of interest in any Western art form. After 1946, with hostilities over, a production of the full *Swan Lake* by an all-Japanese cast provided a new impetus. Visits by prestigious European and American companies were responsible in good measure for renewed interest in this dance. In succession came Moscow's Bolshoi, London's Royal Ballet, the Paris Opéra Ballet and – as already mentioned – the New York City Ballet. They attracted sell-out crowds. In 1976, for instance, Leningrad's Kirov Ballet appeared in twenty-one Japanese cities for fifty performances, its busiest schedule in its two-century history.

Japan's first aspiring professional group, the Maki Asami Ballet Company, made its bow in 1962. Within little more than a decade some fifteen Japanese ballet troupes were active. By consensus, the foremost ensemble was the Tchaikovsky Memorial Tokyo Ballet Company, which garnered a good measure of approval on several European tours.

The principal influence on Japanese ballet students was exerted by Russian dancers and choreographers. Appreciation of technical details at each performer's command was increasingly sophisticated. The public saw ballet on television, and Japanese travelled abroad and had more opportunities to attend professional offerings of it. Andrew H. Malcolm gives this picture of the situation in 1976: "Thousands of Japanese, mostly young women, study ballet in hundreds of studios throughout this ancient island nation. . . . Experts estimate that in Japan there are more than 600 ballet schools or studios, some of course of questionable quality, with total enrollments numbering more than 60,000, probably 15,000 of whom are adults. No one has yet decided to keep track of attendance at ballet performances here, but an official of the Japan Ballet Association puts last year's figure at perhaps 72,000, the great majority concentrated in the Tokyo area. The opera, meanwhile, attracts about 150,000 people, while symphonies (Tokyo has seven) draw around 200,000." A prominent dance critic, Hiroshi Eguchi, told Malcolm: "The ballet audiences are thin still, but they are double what they were ten years ago."

Two pupils of Akiko Tachibana, a leading teacher, gained a definite celebrity during this period. Yoko Morishita (b. 1948) was broadly acknowledged to be the first internationally acclaimed Japanese *prima ballerina*; she was a guest artist with American Ballet Theater as well as with British and Italian companies. Diminutive, enchantingly skilled, she was described by Eguchi, an observer of the scene for almost five decades, "as the best dancer I've seen over all these many years". When abroad, Morishita was partnered on occasion by Rudolf Nureyev and Mikhail Baryshnikov; when at home, her cavalier was usually her husband, Tesutaro Shimizu, to whom was attributed "a noble line and an impressive technique . . . a lyrical style". Some critics objected that, though proficient, he lacked an ability "to astonish or dazzle an audience". He was the son of Mikiko Masuyama, another of Ms Morishita's instructors. Her interpretation of the Odette–Odile roles in *Swan Lake* was said to be almost without peer worldwide. She assumed principal *virtuosa* assignments in the full classical repertory.

Another Japanese star was Norika Ohara (b. *c.* 1943), at one time a fellow-student and room-mate of Yoko Morishita. She won applause in Great Britain as guest artist with the Scottish and Festival Ballets.

Malcolm noted, however, that generally ballet performed "by Japanese for Japanese" was not yet of first-class calibre. Eguchi agreed with his interviewer's somewhat harsher assessment: "Certain Japanese dancers have remarkably improved their technique and have won international recognition. But on the whole, Japan is still a developing country in the world of ballet. To be an art, you must have tradition, like the three or four hundred years of dance history in Europe. Japan has no ballet tradition yet. We have only sixty years."

Chieko Hattori, then president of the Japan Ballet Association, agreed with this appraisal. "The present situation of Japanese ballet is chaos. There is no community ballet company, no national or public ballet company. Most performances are done in studios for the students themselves. A couple of times a year, a private ballet company will rent a hall for two or three performances attended by relatives and friends. But it is a great financial sacrifice." She saw a promising sign, the emergence of ever better qualified performers. "Japanese ballet dancers simply mimicked good foreign dancers. There was no deep understanding of ballet's true art. But that is changing."

Malcolm reported, too, that three of the many troupes received financial assistance from the government, but added that it was impossible for the professional ballet dancers to make a living merely by performing. They added to their incomes by teaching for many hours a week.

By 1981 a further measure of improvement was perceptible. But Professor David Raher wrote with some asperity from Kyoto, where he had been a visiting lecturer on drama at Doshisha University:

> The question repeatedly asked is why do we rarely, if ever, see Japanese ballet in the West? The answer to that question was sought by this observer for over a period of two years. Direct enquiry from the assortment of ballet entrepreneurs in major centers for performance there have invariably produced the kind of inscrutable response that is manifest in a slight shrug of the shoulders and a discreet, enigmatic smile.
>
> There is little question about the powerful arsenal of ballet dancers in top professional condition, in Japan, patiently awaiting world-wide recognition. For the past fifty years or so, the Japanese have been stockpiling an army of well trained dancers (products of a Japanese-cum-Russian school), graduates of the dozens of ballet academies proliferating throughout the main arteries of contemporary Tokyo, Osaka, Kyoto, Kobe, Nagoya and cities in the southernmost as well as northernmost regions of the country.
>
> True, the majority of the outstanding dancers are – as elsewhere in the world – women. Among these are impeccably trained corps-de-ballet girls, impressive soloists and several ranking ballerinas.

He paid tribute to Yoko Morishita in particular. Then he sought to find what was at fault in the general situation.

In a city that nurtures a dozen or so ballet groups (we cannot label them companies as they perform only sporadically) under the supervision of the Japan Ballet Association, it is a rare occasion when one can attend a so-called "season of ballet," as it is known in the West. At best one can anticipate a schedule of three or four performances, though not necessarily given consecutively. Is it possible that after fifty years or so of inductive training and performing, the Japanese have not yet grasped the concept of a season of ballet?

Perhaps at the root of this kind of provincialism is the attitude of conservatism exercised by the ballet groups in question. Almost without exception the administrative heads are women – either managers of large, commercial ballet schools or former dancers (i.e. soloists) with local groups, who promote their private interests through periodic public performances, utilizing long-paying students enrolled in their schools while occasionally importing principal dancers from abroad to lend a touch of glitter to the event.

The end result is the perpetuation of programs given throughout the year very much resembling the "galas" often given in Paris and less frequently in New York or London. Everyone gets a chance to show what he or she can do, but no one cares very much about who or what is responsible for what is being done. In other words, the artistic direction tends to be rather loose. It can be, and often is, great fun. But is it "art?"

More problematical than fragmented programs, however, is the unrelenting perpetuation of the standard, classical works in the ballet repertory, of which *Swan Lake* is the standard bearer.

. . . I believe it is safe to say that Japanese ballet has a firm, comprehensive grasp of this nineteenth-century gem. And, given their unswerving devotion to the music of Tchaikovsky, the Japanese would no doubt be contented to go on performing his ballet works until the end of time. . . . A Freudian would undoubtedly describe the condition as a "case of arrested development."

The degree of consistency with which this "arrested development" is emphasized is demonstrated by the number of performances one may witness of a hackneyed repertory which includes, among other perennial favorites, *The Sleeping Beauty*, *The Nutcracker*, *Giselle*, *La Bayadère*, *Le Corsaire*, *Coppélia*, and *Cinderella*. The above-mentioned ballets, moreover, are being presented in a variety of stagings, owing to no one particular authority, no single individual of discerning taste and imagination whose guidance in these matters could conceivably result in a more stimulating evening in the theater.

. . . And what more convincing argument can one supply than a visit to the Tokyo Bunka Kaikan (Tokyo's Metropolitan Opera House), or the Festival Hall in Osaka, when local ballet is being presented. Capacity audiences are comprised chiefly of ballet students, their mothers, grandmothers and, on rare occasions, a senior male member of the family recruited to film or photograph the proceedings on stage. Here and there, with careful scrutiny, one may discover a genuine balletomane, or even that rarest of homo sapiens, the ballet critic.

Much can be said for the family concept in Japan as applied to business organization. It appears to work admirably, as anyone observing Japan's economy can tell you. But the same concept when applied to art clearly becomes a case of euthanasia. When applied to the medium of ballet, it is administering last rites to a form whose vitality and life depends on frequent transfusions of new ideas, often in such cases supplied by foreign sources.

It is not the intention of this observer to demean that segment of native choreographers, designers and composers whose creative gifts, as applied to the ballet, surface from time to time. It is simply that there is an urgent need to point up the necessity for leadership of a critical, discerning nature. There is need for an imaginative ballet administration willing to take risks, whose efforts will burst the seams of strangulating conservatism and thereby bring life and excitement to the ballet.

He cited a provocative new work by choreographer Giro Arima entitled *Orashoi*, a ballet based on the libretto of Takino Endo, concerning the sixteenth-century persecution of the Christian missionaries in Japan and their Japanese converts to Christianity.

In a recent program in Tokyo, Star Dancers, a group with a reputation for being more innovative than the others, presented a program inspired by the designs of three of Tokyo's most prominent commercial artists. It was an evening vaguely reminiscent of the début of Roland Petit's Ballet des Champs Elysées in Paris in the Fifties when the décor and costumes designed by Christian Berard were as much an occasion for critical acclaim as the ballets themselves.

A lesser-known Tokyo group, the Ballet de Chambre de Hirofumi Inoue, stirred the imaginations of balletomanes by presenting a darkly, but boldly conceived work based on a fourteenth-century Nōh play entitled *Tomonaga*. In it, choreographer Inoue treats the saga of a Samurai too gentle in disposition "to uphold the tradition of courage and brutality," in the abstract fashion of *Yugen*, or "the remote and unfathomable world of the Nōh drama."

In August of this year, Norboru Miyagi, a brilliant dancer and recent émigré from Les Ballets de Roland Petit, in Paris, created a ballet entitled *Basketball*, which was as contemporary and fresh in spirit as was Jerome Robbins's *Interplay*, when first given in New York in 1945. The young Japanese choreographer has been commissioned to provide a new work for the Kansai Ballet Association, entitled *Millie the Maypole*, a fantasy based on a scenario by this writer. It will be given its première in Kyoto in February.

Though the notion of a national ballet has not escaped the reflections of the warlords among the competing groups in the Kanto area of Tokyo, the initiative to bring about such a development for Japanese ballet does not appear imminent.

Professor Raher, ending on this pessimistic note, called for a Japanese Diaghilev.

A surprising acceptance by the Japanese has been given to modern dance, a field in which some of the troupes have made original and distinctive contributions. The genre would seem to be the antithesis of much that is traditional in Japanese culture. Upon their return from Germany, Takaya Eguchi and Misako Miya brought the ideas of Mary Wigman and of Harald Kreuzberg, the Expressionistic *neuer Tanz* (new dance), with its wholly different vocabulary of movement – angular gestures, foot-stamping – and startlingly fresh subject-matter, a frequent reliance upon improvisation, sometimes performed to no musical accompaniment or with a nerve-shattering dependence on percussive instruments. In such works, psychological realism and stark emotionalism have priority. Throughout the late 1920s and into the 1930s twice-monthly programmes by modern dance groups held the stage at Tokyo's Hibiya Hall to large audiences, who also flocked to festivals of Expressionistic compositions given in the autumn and spring.

In the next decade Western-style was the preferred dance entertainment, but that changed after Martha Graham and her company arrived in Tokyo in 1955; the Graham idiom descended from Denishawn and bore an affinity to Wigman's objectives. Her example stimulated anew the modern dance movement in Japan. Young people flocked to New York to apply to her school, and not a few remained there. Much of this foreign study was made possible by government grants beginning in 1964. A procession of other touring modern dance troupes in Graham's wake acquainted the public with up-to-date avant-garde techniques. Modern dance studios proliferated. By the mid-1970s a survey indicated that 30,000 pupils were enrolled in the modern-dance schools, a figure hardly comparable to those dedicated to ballet, yet a substantial number.

Graham's most prominent local disciple was Akiko Kanda, who during the 1960s and 1970s was applauded for her versatility. According to T.R.H. Havens, her works "dealt with the transformation of woman, past and present, and the music, settings, and costumes meticulously fitted the movement". Havens, tracing this period, names Suzushi Hanayagi (b. 1927) and Bonjin Atsugi (b. 1936) as two other "major choreographers of great range and satiric wit". Four Japanese companies were invited to display examples of their work at the American Dance Festival, Duke University, in Durham, North Carolina, in 1982, among them the Bonjin Atsugi group. Later three of these troupes lengthened their tour and were seen at the Jacob's Pillow Dance Festival, and all four were on view at the Pepsico Summerfare Festival, in Purchase, New York State. Anna Kisselgoff, reviewing three of the companies – that led by Atsugi, a second headed by Miyako Kato and a third calling itself the Waka Dance Company – expressed disappointment at what she saw.

What they had in common was a middle-level respectability, lacking a true creative spark but earnest in their attempt to keep up with an all-purpose modern-dance formalist approach. The fact that there were no surprises is in itself no surprise.

Japanese modern dancers resident and active in New York have familiarized local audiences with the idea of marrying postmodern American sensibilities with a time sense inspired by Japanese classical theatrical conventions.

In general, however, Japanese modern dancers have been influenced by Americans. Several have become leading members of Martha Graham's company. John Cage's influence on *avant-garde* Japanese composers has forged a link between Merce Cunningham's company and the Cage disciples from Japan who are among Mr Cunningham's composers. It should be noted, of course, that the Cage–Cunningham esthetic was itself deeply touched by Zen teaching.

The Cunningham–Cage connection and its aftermath in postmodern dance is apparently the crucial one for all these troupes.

The second program was seen here Wednesday and Thursday. Mr Atsugi, who studied at Juilliard, choreographed a minimalist and repetitive trio to a tape of repetitive modular music. In *Tearing Sign 8*, one woman (Yukiko Tanegashima) and two men (Mr Atsugi and Gen Watanabe) in yellow leotards began with a core movement phrase. Rising on tiptoe as if on the edge of a precipice, arms held up with limp wrists, the trio performed a series of minute shifts in weight. One foot turned inward, the other knee turned in, the pelvis was rotated. This unison dancing gradually moved into a stronger dynamic. The phrases not only recurred but also would look different because they were either performed by the three dancers separately or facing different directions or in a new part of the stage.

In a way, the same movement thus acquired a new meaning. The main interest lay in the extremes of the piece. From the small articulations of the beginning, the dancers eventually moved into a violent type of breast beating, which itself was then performed slowly and more lightly. One could call these extremes typical of a society that accepts both flower arranging and *hara-kiri*. And this would also be, possibly, a misleading comparison.

For these are choreographers who strike one more as modern-dance choreographers than especially Japanese ones. Miss Kato, who also studied in New York, offered the best work, *Point, Distant View and Cantata*. Two seated women rang bells and vocalized over a tape of Javanese music as eight women in white dresses with black disks danced very fluidly into different, often whirling, patterns. Again the movement was minimal, with a shoulder rotation as a motif and with few conventional dance steps. In the end, the dancers clustered together, the very opposite of a Japanese paper flower opening up in the water.

Snow Don't Be Stopping by Shigeka Hanayagi was an overt attempt to juxtapose two positions. Omote Hanayagi, a woman in a kimono, encounters a man, Isao Gokita, who wears tights. Snow falls on the stage. The hidden story is too hidden and suggests the risk in combining highly symbolic and straightforward art forms.

To this period belongs Hyo Takahashi, considered by some to be an outstanding modern-ballet choreographer. His *Foreign Affairs* was performed by Eri Najima in New York at the Larry Richardson Gallery in 1981. Set to a score by Brian Eno, it blended discernible elements of traditional Japanese dance with some borrowed from the martial arts.

Havens named Yukiko Tanegashima (b. 1937) and Gen Watanabe (b. 1939) as two other pioneers of the modern style. "[They] composed works of dissonant abandon, in which the dancer set aside existing conventions of movement and danced seemingly at random, without apparent value or meaning."

He discourses on why such innovations had a mesmeric appeal:

Modern dance was especially well-suited to the artistic realism of post-war Japan, with a social system in which communication without words had long been favored. It offered clusters of visual images, not the simpler clarity of ballet, yielding complex and often elliptical glimpses of daily existence in an urban world. Art as an imitation of life had its outlet in movement mainly through modern dance, which took all of society and nature as its themes, not just religious or aristocratic subjects.

Ballet and modern dance both thrived in the 1970s for several reasons. One was the esthetic merit of the compositions and the skill of the artists themselves. Another was that many Japanese enjoyed more leisure time and greater economic prosperity. Physical education in elementary schools since 1947 gave greater emphasis to the elements of Western-style dance. A high-technology media system spread the arts to nearly every village in the country, intensifying the post-war Japanese fascination with American culture, including its dance forms. Finally, the striking visual imagery of modern prints, films, and television helped to heighten the appreciation of dance as "music made visible." The result was a level of public interest that was capable of sustaining innovations in creative movement scarcely surpassed in any other country.

A radically different kind of modern dance took form in the 1960s. Given the name Butoh, its origin is credited to Kazuo Ono (b. *c.* 1906). Born in Hokkaido, he grew up and excelled as an athlete. At the Japan Athletic School in Tokyo he sought a degree in physical education, intending to teach it. One night in 1929, seated in the third balcony of Tokyo's Imperial Theatre, he saw the great Spanish dancer La Argentina. He was so moved by her art that he determined to become a dancer. He studied with Baku Ishii and, even more zealously, with Takaya Eguchi, absorbing from both of them the concepts of Mary Wigman and German Expressionism. He gave his first full recital in 1949, when he was in his mid-forties, two decades after the start of his training. In 1954 he met Tatsumi Hijikata (b. 1928), who became a disciple. The two developed a kind of dance that, as Havens puts it, "extended Suzushi's concentration on the body, producing works that made movement an absolute of its own, beyond Graham's and Kanda's fusion of mental and physical activity". Ono acknowledges that Hijikata was chiefly responsible for this new genre. The pair gave their first joint recital in 1960. Ono's son, Yosito, later collaborated with his father and Hijikata in their studio.

Ono made his American début at New York's Joyce Theater in 1985, at the age of seventy-nine. His main offering was a curious one: *Admiring La Argentina*, fashioned from reminiscences of his fateful beholding of the Spanish dancer almost fifty-six years earlier. He told Jennifer Dunning that for him it had been the moment at which he first understood the creative process. He had long been fascinated with human birth and life in the womb. "'I had read about the creation of the world in the Bible. I'd always accepted it as legend, but in La Argentina's work I saw it realized in front of my eyes.' He recalled thinking at the time, 'If this is creation, I would like to lift one corner of it.'" He illustrated this for Ms Dunning by carefully turning up the edge of a sheet of paper. "'I could not be in the midst of creation, trying to help. When you stand before God and the face of truth, you must be modest.'" Forty-seven years later, in 1976, he had happened upon an abstract painting by Natsuyuki Naknanishi in which he had perceived La Argentina. Arriving home later that day, he found a poster of the Spanish dancer awaiting him: it was a gift from two of his pupils, Eiko and Koma, who are to some degree adherents of Butoh. The face on the poster seemed to speak to him: "'Please, Mr Ono, dance with me.'" This had inspired the work of homage to her that he had long "'wanted in his heart'".

On the evening-long programme was another shorter work, *The Dead Sea*, that – in his words – had arisen from his sense of "'an infinity of memories of past human lives'".

In the *New York Times* Jack Anderson reviewed the presentation:

Kazuo Ono summoned up ghosts on Friday night. . . . The spirit he tried hardest to reach was that of La Argentina, who at her death in 1936 was considered the leading Spanish dancer of her day.

Mr Ono saw her in Tokyo in 1929 and her concert inspired him to be a dancer. . . . He never forgot her. And in *Admiring La Argentina*, a solo lasting about an hour and ten minutes, Mr Ono, now seventy-nine, paid eloquent tribute to her.

At no time did he reconstruct her dances in a scholarly fashion. And even though he always wore articles of women's apparel, he never seemed to be trying to imitate La Argentina literally. Rather, he evoked her energy and, in so doing, appeared both venerable and childlike. And he was accompanied by recordings of La Argentina's castanets, recorded tangos and selections by Bach and Puccini, and a Bach prelude played on the piano by Martin Goldray.

Mr Ono was first seen as a member of the audience. Wearing an enormous hat and a black gown and wrap, he rose from a seat, looking a bit like both the Madwoman of Chaillot and the faded star Gloria Swanson played in *Sunset Boulevard*. After tottering to the stage, Mr Ono dropped the wrap and became a girl in the springtime of life.

Later, still in a woman's wig and high-heeled shoes but now wearing a male athlete's trunks, Mr Ono moved diagonally downstage, reaching imploringly toward the sky. Simultaneously a man and a woman, he transcended sexual distinctions.

Returning in a Spanish costume, he gestured to remind one of the flamboyance of some Spanish dances and the coquetishness of others. Then, wearing an ashen robe, he could have been paying tribute to the emotionally candid solos of such pioneers of modern dance as Isadora Duncan and Mary Wigman. This sequence emphasized that all performances are, in some sense, farewells, for they can never be repeated. Yet, because they may leave indelible impressions, performances can also be said to occur in eternity.

Of her meeting with the artist, Jennifer Dunning wrote further:

Kazuo Ono totters, flounces and slashes through stage space, a primeval specter that is half death, half lingering sweet perfume. Offstage, however, the seventy-nine-year-old "father of Butoh" is a remarkably cheerful and practical man, given the dark quality of that Japanese experimentalist theater-dance form.

By now, New Yorkers have seen several styles of Butoh, most notably that practiced by Sankai Juku, whose eerie depictions of creation and cataclysm were seen here last season. But for Mr Ono and his student Tatsumi Hijikata, who helped shape the style, Butoh seeks simply to turn away from the techniques of traditional Japanese and Western modern dance and look inward. Butoh is grounded in the life of the mind and memory and in the personal "biographies" as Mr Ono puts it, that exist within a universal history.

But there is a gentle, humane flamboyance about Mr Ono and his work that is distinctive. The passion of a lifetime is summed up, most typically in *Admiring La Argentina*, one of the two pieces performed here. The evening-long solo is, like all his work, improvised on stage after long periods of research, reflection and, in some cases, rehearsal. "Every day you live," Mr Ono said, speaking in Japanese translated by Ruby Shang. "You do not have to rehearse for that." Performed in stark makeup and exotic dresses, *Admiring La Argentina* alludes both to himself and to the famed Spanish dancer who was a major influence on his career.

. . . His store of memories is available to all, from his pupils to the audiences who watch him perform Butoh and participate spiritually in the performance. Mr Ono rises to imitate his own spiritual participation in the performing of others. He is wearing shiny penny loafers with his stylish clothes. "If you take a new step," he said of his American visit, "you should have new shoes."

Butoh got most of its primary characteristics from probings by Tatsumi Hijikata, himself a dancer and – as has been said – a former pupil of Ono and for a time his co-worker. His Asbestokan Modern Dance Theatre, active through the 1950s and 1960s, inspired many of Japan's Underground groups who followed his lead in staging "complex theatre pieces blending elements of traditional theatre and dance with contemporary obsessions and shock techniques. . . . The irrationality and disjointedness of these lengthy, slow-moving, intense wordless dramas seemed to reflect the absurdity of the post-war world."

Hijikata called his creations Ankoko Butoh – "dark, black, gloomy dance". Others translate the term "Butoh" to connote "obsessional dance" and depict a typical composition in this vein as one in which "larval creatures move to excruciatingly slow rhythms and suggest through startlingly visual images, performed with incredible intensity, the cruelty, inhumanity and senselessness of contemporary life". In an article discussing Hijikata's contribution, Terry Trucco has written: "Using movements seldom associated with dance, he evoked images once considered shameful, hidden and ugly – harsh, often raw moves that could none the less tap those lost energies and unleash strong expressive forces. A product of its time, Mr Hijikata's Butoh was filled with protest, anger and brutality, all designed to shock. He used nudity. He performed in crematoriums. In his most famous piece, *Revolt of the Flesh* in 1968, he slaughtered live chickens on stage and danced in their blood."

One of Hijikata's protégés, Akaji Maro, a well-known avant-garde actor, founded in 1972 the Dai Rakuda Kan, a troupe that put fully as much emphasis on the grotesquerie of Butoh. Affirming this, one member of the company had all his teeth extracted to aid him in contorting his face. The Dai Rakuda Kan company had visited Paris, as had Kazuo Ono, both of them winning enthusiastic followings. In 1982, the Dai Rakuda Kan made its first appearance in the United States; it was one of the companies performing at the American Dance Festival in Durham, North Carolina, mentioned earlier. The troupe impressed both critics and spectators by its power. Anna Kisselgoff was in Durham and sent back this account:

> Mothers fled out of the theater with their children. Wide-eyed adults sat – occasionally – on the edge of their seats. Imagine a Japanese version of the Living Theater with a touch of Hieronymus Bosch, and you can almost pin a label on the Dai Rakuda Kan company or envisage its exuberantly received American debut at the American Dance Festival here.
>
> Founded in Tokyo in 1972 by Akaji Maro, an actor who became a dancer, the troupe is not a dance company in the conventional sense. Adherents of the performance-art trend in the United States, however, will have no trouble feeling at home with it. Mr Maro, who has as shrewd a finger on the pulse of Western sensibilities as he does on his own Japanese roots, must now be counted a leader in the international nonverbal-theater movement.
>
> In fact, the imagery dreamed up by Robert Wilson and other Americans in this area of experimental theater and dance activity now looks quite tame by Dai Rakuda Kan's standards. A chance to see the Japanese group's production, *Sea-Dappled Horse*, in the New York area will come next weekend at the Pepsico Summerfare Festival at Purchase.
>
> Dai Rakuda Kan, whose name means "Great Camel Battleship," is deliberately grotesque – anti-establishment in its stance and in its play upon Kabuki's traditional spectacular effects. The twenty performers are said to have a communal lifestyle. It was not surprising to see both male and female members of the troupe make their first appearance in G-strings and gray or white body make-up.
>
> Mr Maro's theater is a protest theater – exemplifying a love–hate relationship with current

Japanese values, or with the West's corruption of those values. It is also a visionary theater, sometimes quite wonderful, often incomprehensible and occasionally pretentious.

Sea-Dappled Horse, which was performed at the festival Friday night in Duke University's Page auditorium, is a dream and a nightmare, totally visual and yet largely influenced by Kazuo Ohaku's sound score – either gentle as a breeze or as terrifying as a tornado with a rock beat. It was in fact, the combination of roaring sound and the menacing entry of Mr Maro, towering on stilts in a kimono and a gleaming white bald pate, that drove the mothers up the aisle.

Sea-Dappled Horse, however, has no overt violence. It has rather a story-book aura, and its truly poetic passage occurs midway in the piece. Suddenly a group of gray men enters, torsos bare and with wavering gold antennas on their crowns. They "ride" their horses, figures doubled over in children's print quilts, some of whom have snouts. The riding, however, consists of the knights standing by the "horses" while both sets of figures just bob up and down.

The gray men then sit and offer a ritual of twisted torsos and even more twisted faces, the grimaces becoming stranger and funnier, the eyes of the men, ringed in red, glowing like embers. The knights "ride" off. Suddenly the fantastic horses turn into horrible little girls.

The quilts are thrown off, a recording of the *Songs of the Auvergne* blasts on, and the girls, in red bows, pink dresses and ratted hair, bounce around until Mr Maro, similarly dressed, comes in as the belle of St Trinian's.

It might be surprising then to suggest that *Sea-Dappled Horse* is actually concerned with Creation and ends with an image of Hell. The first scene is primal. Near-nude figures, biting on a single rope that joins them, strain against a series of door panels. A doubled-over inarticulate figure appears, a foil to Mr Maro as, reportedly, the god who created Japan.

In the end, three gray men run down the aisle onto the stage, red bloody capes behind them. White, the mourning color of the East, envelops the stage in cloth panels. Black figures with lanterns suggest a funeral. For all its collectivity, the group is always centered upon Mr Maro in several guises. Often artificial, this focus upon a strong figure is the weakness of *Sea-Dappled Horse*.

Three years after Maro formed his company, designated as a representative of the second generation of Butoh, one of his pupils, Ushio Amagatsu, gathered together another – a third generation, so to speak – titling it Sankai Juku. This company, too, gained international prominence. Encouraged by the welcome given to Ono and the Dai Rakuda Kan in Europe, the Sankai Juku company went to Paris in 1980 and settled there; they mastered the language, and Amagatsu chose a French wife, by whom he has a daughter. Incessantly touring the Continent and the British Isles, the troupe performed in small towns and even on farms. They accepted invitations to prestigious arts festivals, as farflung as Warsaw, Madrid, Avignon and Edinburgh. In four years they exhibited their skills in over twelve countries.

In 1982 they returned to Japan for a single performance in Tokyo; the theatre was sold out weeks in advance; unhappy latecomers waited outside in a downpour, hoping to get tickets at the last moment. Further appearances were arranged. A local critic, Marie Myerscough, commented: "The Japanese seem a bit embarrassed that everyone else is looking at this phenomenon they themselves have ignored in the past." Terry Trucco observed:

> Mr Amagatsu has taken a lot of his ideas for Sankai Juku's choreography from books on prehistoric man. He also enjoys observing people. "When I'm walking down the street, I try to make mental notes of the impressions that linger in my mind," he says.
>
> Butoh training can be brutal, particularly because it is so different from that of conventional Western dance. The object, the troupe explains, is to remove all strain from the body, making it malleable while maintaining strict control. In one exercise the dancer walks briskly. At the sound of a handclap, he instantly goes slack. If he's holding something, he drops it.
>
> To hone their own Butoh vocabulary Sankai Juku's members lived and trained together during the troupe's early days. Such times are long gone. They now maintain that intense training is no longer necessary, and all live what they term ordinary lives. They eat what they want, smoke cigarettes and drink alcohol. When not performing they even let their hair grow out a bit. . . .
>
> They [i.e. the Japanese public] still may not like it, but now they will at least deal with it. Butoh is still looked upon as a faintly distasteful Underground art, well outside the mainstream. Performances are given in small theaters and jazz clubs, and nearly all of Japan's forty-odd performance troupes and individual dancers support themselves with outside jobs.

That was a prime reason the Sankai Juku members – Goro Namerikawn, Keiji Morita, Yoshiyuki Takada, Atsushi Ogata, and their leader, Ushio Amagatsu – had elected to go abroad.

In 1984 the troupe reached Toronto, where the *New York Times*'s ever-alert critic Anna Kisselgoff reported on it.

> The sight of four near-naked men, their chalk-covered bodies as white as alabaster as they dangled upside-down along the glass surface of a Toronto office building, might make even a blasé New Yorker take notice.

For this was hardly a variant of the "human flies" who scale the towers of the World Trade Center. It was, in fact, Sankai Juku – a Japanese avant-garde dance group that is part of a controversial anti-Establishment movement called Butoh. Typically, Butoh remains an underground phenomenon in Japan while in Paris, where Sankai Juku has now moved, it is all the rage.

The initial impact can certainly explain why. Friday's outdoor event was sensational. As the four men, with shaven heads, were slowly lowered from the top of the building by ropes at their ankles, a fifth in a skirt-like robe rose up on the roof to blow a huge conch shell.

Like a distant colossus glimpsed from afar, this archaic living statue appeared like a god in the sky. Myth and megalopolis converged into one striking but daring image. Modern technology – a glass building whose elevators were visibly moving up and down in their transparent shafts – counterpointed the slow descent of bodies involved in equally visible human risk. The ordinary below met with the extraordinary above – the image of unfamiliar Japanese gods descending from the heavens to create the world we know only too well.

The effect, on a brilliant sunny day as hundreds gathered at the foot of the Bell Building in Toronto's Trinity Square, was spectacular. And Sankai Juku has a shrewd sense of spectacle.

The public relations aspects of such street events, including one a week ago at the Royal Ontario Museum as part of the group's North American début in the Toronto International Festival, are obvious.

Sachio Ichimura, the company's manager, explained that Butoh had sprung up because its adherents looked on language, traditional theatre and other modes of expression as having grown weak. Butoh was a new way of recovering their elemental energies lost over the years. It also rejected both the dominance of Western dance and the bonds of traditional Japanese dance. As a representative of third-generation Butoh, the Sankai Juku shaped work that was "highly refined, having rid itself of the art's rawest edges".

A Japanese critic, Miyabi Ichikawa, objected that the troupe's creations were "sleek and sophisticated, bloodless and commercially packaged". As others saw it, Sankai Juku had lost its Butoh roots, but its progression was a logical one. Concerning this, Trucco held that, clearly, "Sankai Juku has replaced Butoh's old sense of rage and protest with what seems a desire to touch the energy of the cosmos. Some see it as intellectual Butoh."

In one of several manifestos Sankai Juku declared: "Our choreography shows transformation and metamorphoses as natural processes of existence." Trucco appends: "Sankai Juku's use of prehistoric imagery is a way of tapping what they see as energy lost to man with civilization, energy that has been suppressed, as the troupe puts it. 'That's why in our work we try to get back to the Jōmon Era (8,000–300 BC).' 'It was a time of great freedom,' says a member. This suppression has occurred in the West as well as the East, they add."

Jennifer Dunning summarized the reception at Durham:

Sankai Juku, which is said to mean "school of mountain and sea," seems to focus on nature imagery. The preverbal and the prehistoric appear to be its concerns, and these can take the form of themes that deal with the creation of the world, of evolution and by implication, apocalypse.

For Butoh is a post-Hiroshima phenomenon, stemming from the work of several male Japanese dancers familiar with German and American modern dance as well as ballet and other European dance idioms.

Jōmon Shō (*Homage to Pre-History*) on Saturday featured Yasukazu Sato on the drums à la Gene Krupa. Such juxtapositions of the contemporary, including jazz, with imagery that aims to elicit memories of the primordial, is typical of Butoh. Unlike Buyo, a word for dance used by conventional dancers, Butoh favors the lower body. For all its protest against tradition, from East and West, it uses the concentrated stillness and distillation common to Japanese classical theater dance.

It is this extraordinary physical control and concentration that is obvious in the street event *Sholiba*, as the dancers are first lowered in jackknifed position and then slowly stretch down, moving parts of their body in isolation.

The same technique lies behind the imagery of *Homage to Pre-History*. Sankai Juku is not as grotesque here as Dai Rakuda Kan. But its members are expert at suggesting the nonhuman, lumps of clay that evolve into fish in sacklike robes, repeatedly flailing on the ground. If two abstract forms – two huge metal rings – suggest a sun and moon, the prevalent imagery is of constant identification with natural forms. It is not what Sankai Juku says that is profound. It is how it reaches us through sensation, how we "feel" matter forming organically.

In a ritual of seven episodes, every facial muscle and minute flicker of every clawing red finger seemed to play a role in filling out the shape that evolved. Hieronymus Bosch's unhappy souls seemed not too remote from the foreshortened figures, tubes hanging from an ear or bloodlike arrow at a cheek. Mr Amagatsu's solos, all torso distended and rib cage protruding, struck the jarring note, representing sickness. Four hunters appeared to exercise a healing power in a ritual stick dance.

Somewhere, Sankai Juku strikes a nerve. It appeals to the senses. The predominantly young audience roared its approval at the end.

In the Sunday edition of the *New York Times* before their engagement at Purchase, Anna Kisselgoff had another piece on this startling company.

Something dark and definite has stirred in the Japanese dance world and we are just beginning to feel the effect. Granted, there is nothing totally "new" in the arts nowadays. Nonetheless, the rise of the dance esthetic in Japan that calls itself Butoh signals a phenomenon unto itself. A compound of the grotesque and the beautiful, the nightmarish and the poetic, the erotic and the austere, the streetwise and the spiritual, Butoh is a highly theatrical form.

. . . What is Butoh? Even the word has different connotations for many Japanese, whether they are concerned with dance or not. Certainly it means dance but it is used in opposition to another Japanese word for dance, Buyo. Butoh, significantly, derives from a word having to do with ancient ritualistic dance. And certainly the prehistoric and the ritualistic are among the prime concerns of Butoh's choreographers.

Japanese dancers have been familiar with German dance Expressionism for three generations, and those who would care to see Butoh's imagery as related to images close to Mary Wigman's or Harald Kreutzberg's hearts would not be remiss. In fact, both Butoh and Pina Bausch's dance theater in West Germany are the leading examples of the new and current Expressionism in dance.

Each group uses images that include pain and suffering, that are often violent and that shock. Both are clearly part of a theater in revolt. There are European critics who have drawn a connection between these trends and the countries in which they have grown – that is, the Germany that emerged from the Nazi camps of World War II and the Japan that emerged from Hiroshima. Apocalypse casts its shadow.

Butoh's primary theme seems, indeed, to be the creation and destruction of the universe. As different as Butoh groups are among themselves, they seem inexorably drawn to the depiction of life forming on earth, seen as a painful process. Moreover this emergence from the primordial begins with an image that suggests that an unnamed cataclysm has preceded it.

The cyclical nature of things is strongly felt. In this sense, Butoh – sometimes called dance of the dark soul – has a nihilist strain. It deals with annihilation as well as rebirth. Death seems to come before life. There is little room for free will here and it might be misleading to see any existentialist framework.

Although the roots of Butoh can be traced to the 1960s and earlier, it is a trend that surfaced in the 1970s. Butoh dance groups have performed in Europe since 1978. Ostensibly, Americans did not see any Butoh troupes until 1982, when the American Dance Festival in Durham, NC, invited

Akaji Maro's Dai Rakuda Kan company to make its United States début.

Yet perhaps we have been seeing Butoh in the United States without being aware of it – just as Molière's *bourgeois gentilhomme* found he had been speaking prose without knowing it. I refer here to the fact that certain Japanese dancers resident in New York have also studied with the teachers who spawned the Butoh movement and whose work – as is now evident – draws from the same esthetic. The connection was very clearly made recently when Eiko and Koma, who have presented their pieces in New York since 1976, performed at the American Dance Festival shortly after Sankai Juku appeared in Toronto.

Philosophically, Butoh concentrates on metamorphosis and transcendence. The distinguishing mark of Butoh style – the physical fact before us – is a body slowly changing shape. With extraordinary flow, the human form is remolded by each dancer to the point that mutation becomes more normal here than the normal. Eiko and Koma's hour-long *Grain* is especially startling in this respect. Eiko's ability to make her body assume an unexpected form – so that it no longer looks like a body – is striking, even disturbing because it looks aberrational, nonhuman. Nude and bent with her head to the floor so that her posterior is raised upward, Eiko offers an unidentifiable abstract shape. Similarly, when four of Sankai Juku's men are suspended from the ankles, first in a folded clump, they suggest unformed matter. This reminder of the material in man dominates Butoh. The spiritual struggles to emerge with obvious difficulty.

Mr Amagatsu's statement of belief is pertinent. "Butoh belongs to life and death. It is a realization of the distance between a human being and the unknown. It also represents man's struggle to overcome the distance between himself and the material world. Butoh dancers are like a cup filled to overflowing, one which cannot take one more drop of liquid – the body enters a state of perfect balance."

The last sentence is apt in view of the dancers' exceptional physical control as their bodies change shape with excruciating slowness. Nudity is common to Butoh and is used not only for occasional brutal, nonsensual eroticism, but also to exhibit this control.

Homage to Pre-History (Jōmon Shō), which Sankai Juku presented in Toronto, has seven scenes with nature images in their subtitles. Plastic panes stand in four corners, a rainbow is projected on a blue background. Yasukuzo Sato's music – light percussion to jazz drumming – and the sound of a conch introduce the lowering of four men by their ankles from the proscenium. Lumps assuming human form, they suggest mythical gods coming to earth.

The theme is evolution and creation – in process – and the male dancers' ability to suggest matter forming organically runs through the stage action. Two huge rings symbolize the sun and moon.

They lie on the ground and are raised upright until they intersect. Mr Amagatsu moves through a sculptural grotesque solo, mouth open, torso distended. In the next episode, the men are fish, in sacks with fins, flailing repeatedly and propelling themselves across the stage. Mr Amagatsu returns, a foreshortened mutant, a blur behind a pane in the section, "Sickness is incurable." Nonetheless there appears a healing power to the ritual stick dance then performed by the men, who suddenly become individualized. They perform sequences of accumulated gestures. The four men then lie in fetal position around Mr Amagatsu and rise, magnetically exerting a force upon him. Suddenly all stand frozen, like fossils.

Homage to Pre-History is dreamlike, even poetic at times in its organic unity. Its imagery seeps in through our epidermis. Yet it is also remote. The feeling is that of watching fish, albeit exotic and fascinating ones, in an aquarium.

By contrast, Eiko and Koma use nature imagery in allegories calculated to stir an audience. In their new *Elegy*, each stands nude by a puddle, from which they have seemingly emerged and into which they sink hopelessly again. Butoh's belief in the primitive as a source of theatrical vitality is even more striking in *Grain* precisely because its characters are so primitive. A man and woman have a brutal sexual encounter. Their mating rite is paralleled by images of sowing and reaping of grain.

A blackout separates the episodes, implying the passage of time as the man and woman appear in different clothes, becoming more "civilized" but still prone to primal urges. Nude and only a form at first, Eiko is next seen clothed, grain dripping down from her hands. Koma, first infantlike, discovers grain under the mat where he lies. Jumping on the mat, he sends this grain – his own seed – flying into the air. The ritual planting (Eiko throws the grain up in a rainbow arc) is shattered when Koma, having been raised to life, returns dressed as a pilgrim and assaults Eiko with bull-like force. The harvest is symbolic. The grain is now rice brought in on a ceremonial tray by Koma who forces Eiko to eat it. Connoisseurs of Japanese erotic films will be at home here. Oddly, there is a delicacy about Eiko's and Koma's performance that makes the other Butoh groups seem coarse. With their chiaroscuro lighting (by the designer, Blu), they view the elemental from a refined perspective.

With its entrance prepared by extensive publicity, the company reached the environs of Manhattan. Jennifer Dunning was once more among the critics on hand for the event but did not agree with Kisselgoff's previous judgement:

The eagerly awaited first New York performance of Sankai Juku, a leading Japanese experimentalist dance troupe, was greeted with cheers and a standing ovation on Saturday at the Pepsico Summerfare '84 festival at the State University of New York at Purchase. Clearly, the company created the same impact here as it had in recent performances in Toronto and at the Olympic Arts Festival in Los Angeles.

In *Kinkan Shonen*, the group takes on the origins of life in seven scenes. The work opens with a boy standing, it seems, on some shore or at the edge of an empty place. Dressed in short pants, a jacket, and a schoolboy's cap and boots, he seems to gaze out into eternity. His body is dusted white, in Butoh fashion. He falls, he shivers, he sleeps, he wanders and runs. He seems to pluck food from the air and eat it, mouth quivering open like a fish. He rolls in what looks like a hill of flour, gobbling some and spitting it out.

The fish image is carried through in the following six scenes, performed by men in varying stages of primitive white-coated dress, who move before a textured wooden wall fashioned of hanging panels. They pulse and purse their open mouths like fish, wiggling gill-like fingers in the air. There is a fetal look, too, to their activity, which is clearest in the shape and wavering of their bodies curled upon the floor.

The overall look is of a processional, broken by several bold stage effects. In one scene, a man walking in a crouch, his shortened body covered by a tiny, course-textured purple robe, seems to be a dwarf laughing eerily as he stalks about the stage watched by a still, seated figure. In another, four men are spread about the stage, wrestling and writhing slowly and posing like living statues created by George Segal, strange vacant grins wandering across their faces from time to time. And in the final scene, described in program notes as "the shore – toward eternity," one of the performers hangs upside down by his legs, a feature of the Sankai Juku style of Butoh.

There is a jolting naïveté about this scene, however, and the work in general, possibly because it is early vintage Sankai Juku. The hanging man has the look of the apocalyptic revelation of the monolith in the film *2001*, and dangles to Muzak-style jazz based on the popular theme from Dvorak's *New World* Symphony.

The vanity of nature is the earnest subtitle of a scene in which a man clutches a live peacock, who lurks fetchingly in the shadows at the back of the stage throughout the rest of the piece, like an actor uncertain of his cues.

Kinkan Shonen is, in the end, a surprisingly tame and unevocative work, despite strong ensemble playing by Mr Amagatsu, Yoshiyuki Takada, Keiji Morita, Goro Namerikawa and Atsushi Ogata.

Having evoked acclaim and controversy, with style and content possessing shock value – and especially helped by having been depicted as "darkly erotic" – Sankai Juku was brought to the City

Center later in 1984. The engagement was prefaced in the usual spectacular fashion by an outdoor exhibition of the dancers' prowess. A brief newspaper account was headlined "Terpischore on 55th Street" and read:

Wearing an eggshell white robe and a thin red feather from his ear down the side of his neck, Ushio Amagatsu cuddled a large pink conch shell. He caressed its folds and raised it to his lips. Haunting sounds that might have come from the depths of the sea echoed along West 55th Street.

Four members of the Japanese dance troupe Sankai Juku appeared on the roof of the City Center yesterday. Virtually nude and painted from head to toe with white makeup, they stood on a ledge and swayed. Arms outstretched and hands flexed like talons, they resembled giant white birds.

Several hundred people gathered to watch their descent of ninety feet. They curled into fetal positions and were slowly lowered on ropes, swaying like human pendulums. Halfway down, they stopped, uncurled and danced – wiggling fingers, arching backs, crossing arms, writhing in midair. They were lowered to the ground, where they danced some more.

The crowd burst into applause.

After the display yesterday, the group repaired to the nearby Carnegie Delicatessen – for dill pickles and pastrami on rye.

Amagatsu was interviewed by Ms Dunning, who sought further insight into his work. Her report begins:

A midget laughs mysteriously. A peacock wanders about the stage. Fish-men slither, stalk, parade and throw themselves on the ground, then stand stock still. Heads are shaved and nearly nude bodies are coated with flour. Raw rice is gobbled from the floor. The scene is unlikely, but New York audiences haven't been at all fazed by the peculiarities of Sankai Juku, the Japanese experimentalist theater-dance company that's playing at City Center through Sunday.

Sankai Juku bills its work as an "eternal voyage" and "dance on the universe." Is it dance? Or theater? Or bizarre dreamscapes? Ushio Amagatsu, the thirty-five-year-old founder of the Tokyo- and Paris-based company, isn't saying. He wants audiences to watch without preconception as his men engage in their strange encounters.

"I hope everybody who looks at us makes his own trip into his interior," Mr Amagatsu said the other day, speaking through an interpreter, who is also a performer in the company. "That's the most important thing."

Mr Amagatsu has done research in the legends and myths of the world. "The roots of everything are common essentially," he said. "They are universal." He admits to having read the theory of Carl Jung, whose writing on archetype and dream has stirred many a creative impulse. And Mr Amagatsu has been affected by Surrealist art and theater. But at its heart, his work aims to reach back into a common consciousness of the prehistory that many of his pieces touch upon.

The primordial fish-men sway through *Kinken Shonen* (*The Kumquat Seed*), which will be performed afternoons and evenings tomorrow and Sunday. Subtitled *A Young Boy's Dream of the Origins of Life and Death*, the full evening piece moves slowly through seven scenes filled with mystic images.

Jomon Shō (*Homage to Pre-History*), a full-evening work to be performed tonight, is subtitled *Ceremony for Rainbow and Two Grand Circles* and was inspired by primitive cave paintings.

He began his training in Western classical ballet and modern dance. In 1970, he encountered a form of Japanese avant-garde dance called Butoh, which he describes as "a realization of the distance between a human being and the unknown."

"It also represents man's struggle to overcome the distance between himself and the material world," Mr Amagatsu has written. "Butoh dancers' bodies are like a cup filled to overflowing, one that cannot take one more drop of liquid – the body enters a state of perfect balance."

Sankai Juku has no school, but conducts sporadic workshops in which it teaches the students to work against tension and toward a natural body. "It is getting to certain states," he explains, "rather than learning some technique or form." The five members of Sankai Juku prepare for each performance by entering "a quiet, calm state."

The performers have come to be known as the men who hang upside down by their ankles. Was there some symbolism there? The action, Mr Amagatsu says, has the elements of both death and birth in it. But could it be healthy? "When you think of it as something dangerous, *that's* dangerous," he says.

In September 1985, after appearances in London, Ontario, Washington, DC, and Boston, the troupe was in Seattle. To proclaim their impending engagement, the four dancers were hanging upside down from the top of the six-storey Mutual Life Building, while the fifth member stood on the roof sounding the conch shell. Two thousand people had gathered to watch them from below. After about ten minutes a rope broke, dropping Yoshiyuki Takada to the pavement; he was rushed to a hospital, where he died. He was thirty-one and had been with the company for ten years, during which the feat had been carried out around the world more than 100 times.

Jedediah Wheeler, a witness, recounted: "There wasn't panic or confusion at all. There was utter silence and then an overwhelming rush of tears and people hugging each other and comforting each other that went on for at least an hour afterward. The outpouring of emotion is very strong here. There was a candlelight vigil at the death site by members of the Seattle community, and people are leaving flowers, wreaths and poems."

Only one of the ropes had been tested beforehand; it was one of the three untested ropes that had come apart. A spokesman for the dancers said: "They do not carry their own rope, because building heights vary and so forth. They ask the local promoter to provide three-quarter-inch used hemp, and the key element is that it be used, because a new line twirls and spins. What that would do on the descent is that the body would spin, which is not the effect they're looking for. This is a slow thirty-minute descent, and there's a lot of stillness involved."

Sankai Juku immediately cancelled the rest of its ten-city American tour. The company, mourning, stopped practising during the next four months. After recruiting a new member, they started rehearsing again in February 1986. Jennifer Dunning spoke to Ushio Amagatsu in May when the troupe was in New York once more to perform at the City Center. He told her that it had been a difficult phase to traverse for the survivors. Gradually the troupe had reaffirmed its identity. "We felt that time stopped in Seattle. To start up again takes a little while. But we came slowly out of how we felt and started to create another piece. Different members had different feelings. We talked about when we were ready as a whole to come back." An agreement had not yet been reached about when to resume hanging upside down from a high building. "In about a year we may. Right now we are trying to decide peacefully."

He revealed that the imagery in *Jōmon Shō* and *Kinkan Shonen,* which once more were being presented at the City Center, had grown out of visual symbols used in previous works. "It is a continuous flow, a process of development. Like everyday life."

Amagatsu explained to Ms Dunning how the creation of a Sankai Juku piece happened. It began with an idea, "culled often from poetry, painting or music", that he has been exposed to. Cave paintings in the south of France and in Spain inspired *Jōmon Shō,* and his childhood dreaming by the sea, in Yokosuka, yielded the central imagery for *Kinkan Shonen.*

The motivating imagery comes from "parts we left undone" in previous pieces, Mr Amagatsu said. "It is something I have seen from the top but not the bottom. I haven't seen all the angles. Something has been left out, on purpose or not." The basic idea for the dance is pretty much set before he begins work with the other performers. "When we move our bodies, we decide what feels right. And that develops into the movement that works well for the piece."

The company's name may be translated to "mountain-ocean private-lesson." In Japan, college students go to a "juku" for intense, concentrated preparatory lessons. Given the closeness of the Sankai Juku experience, how did the troupe go about finding a new member? The company only briefly had a school, in 1975, although it would conduct two days of workshops in late June at City Center. Thoru Iwashita, the new performer, had worked two years with the company, seven years ago, while studying philosophy in college, then went on to explore his own dance-movement style.

"The backgrounds of all the dancers are all very different. They are not people interested in this or that. Body type is not important. Personality is most important, and not trying to change shape or image. What is important is what is developed within, and how it is expressed in the body."

Jack Anderson, on behalf of the *New York Times*, was at City Center to judge the reconstituted company. Like Ms Dunning the previous year, he was not in accord with Anna Kisselgoff's high regard for the offering.

The most spectacular performer in *Kinkan Shonen* was not a dancer but a peacock. Making its entrance in the third scene of Ushio Amagatsu's ninety-minute choreographic work, the bird stayed motionless while Mr Amagatsu held it as if it were a piece of cloth. Then it flapped about and perched on his back. Later, it strutted this way and that. Finally, it rose in a stately flight up to the balcony. No doubt about it, the peacock was just fine.

The rest of the production was more controversial. Intended as a symbolic depiction of a boy's coming to terms with life and death, *Kinkan Shonen* was an example of the Japanese Expressionist style known as Butoh – a style that prompts strong reactions of both approval and scorn.

Mr Amagatsu was the protagonist, appearing first in a schoolboy's uniform and the chalky makeup for which this troupe is noted. Presumably in an attempt to acquaint himself with nature, he rolled in a sand pile. Other members of the all-male cast wore long women's gowns and made ominous clawing gestures. The violence of nature was again suggested in a nude wrestling match. Hunched up to resemble a midget, Mr Amagatsu danced a grotesque comic solo, after which he stretched out into his full height. At last, in an apotheosis that may have symbolized enlightenment, he dangled upside down from a triangular red pennant. And, of course, the peacock did its own routines.

One had to admire the muscular control of these performers and their ability to stretch out actions over long periods of time. The production's ceremoniousness clearly impressed many of those who beheld it. Nevertheless, I must confess that I found this example of Butoh boring.

Mr Amagatsu appeared to believe that solemnity of manner guaranteed profundity of content and that ritualism was eloquent for its own sake. His symbolism was opaque and, by having dancers constantly grimace and open their mouths in silent screams, he belabored his serious intentions.

Equally unsatisfactory was his treatment of time. By slowing time down, some choreographers manage to transport viewers into a whole new dimension. Mr Amagatsu, in contrast, merely reminded one that slow motion was slow and it was hard to understand why so many actions had to be taken at such a ponderous pace.

No wonder the peacock made an impression. By suddenly taking wing in all its glory, it did more than any choreographic sequence to remind one of the mysteries of creation. Indeed, through its flight, it magically transcended the production's pretentious histrionics.

By the early 1980s Japan had more than forty groups fitting into the category of Butoh. Another dancer who visited the United States was Kuniko Kisanuki; in 1985 her first appearance in Manhattan was evaluated by Anna Kisselgoff.

Japanese modern dancers have often performed in New York – and some are leading members of American troupes, such as the Martha Graham Dance Company. Yet it is only with the recent performances here of Japan's innovative Butoh dance theater that light has been shed on a current experimental dance that seems specifically Japanese.

Kuniko Kisanuki, a twenty-six-year-old deceptively delicate-looking dancer, does not belong strictly in the Butoh genre. At her New York début last night at the Joyce Theater, she came across as a dancer first – impressively trained by any standard. Her ability to hold the stage for just over an hour in a solo work testified to the fascination she exerts by merely moving her lean flexible body into the most unexpected of shapes and images.

But in the end, it does seem that Miss Kisanuki is very much on the Butoh wave-length. She has the same extraordinary body control and by extension the same strange ability of Butoh performers to project organic growth of one form into another. Like some Butoh dancers, she can make her body suggest non-human form.

In the New York première of her solo, *Tefu Tefu*, nature imagery seemed dominant. To see a dancer suddenly transformed into a piece of driftwood, with all the beauty of nature's own abstract forms, is to see a highly gifted dancer.

The program note says that *Tefu Tefu* means butterfly and includes a poem Miss Kisanuki wrote about catching butterflies as a child. The last lines are translated: "That night in my dream appeared countless angels, / and a fine powder fell to my lips. / Around that time I began to dance."

The solo on view is said to be Part VI of an ongoing series called *Tefu Tefu*. Butterflies are not at issue in this chapter. Instead, one feels that Miss Kisanuki shows herself on a cyclical journey – coming down the aisle in the theater onto a darkened stage and eventually leaving it by the opposite aisle.

Butoh's general themes of metamorphosis and transcendence, of death or nothingness preceding birth or rebirth are implied by the dancer-choreographer's fetal position near the end – toes locked like an infant. Lighting (by Yoshiaki Kubo) and décor (by Seigo Yatagai) are crucial to completing the images. A light beamed at the audience is also beamed straight at the dancer when she first enters to a distant percussive beat. Wearing a fringed simple dress (by Riyoko Shinohara), she is seen initially in silhouette until she is bathed in a golden glow against four tattered cloths that suggest both sails and slopes.

Miss Kisanuki often plays with contrast. Stillness finds her tilted forward like a piece of wood in sand. An intermediate phase takes her into various flexed-footed double-jointed movement. Seemingly free of adult joints, she also springs up and down in a squat. Early on she does a neck-stand, her feet rising up into an image of a tree.

Foreshortened or stretched out beyond expectation, she can also, as she does a bit jarringly in the last third of the piece, insert a conventional dance step – a Graham jump to the ground or an arabesque. These moments coincide with the strange singing chorus that bursts out sentimentally over the basic rhythmic beat on the tape (music composition credited to Bun Itakura, "sound design" to Kazutaka Fujii).

Since the birth sequence has just preceded these passages, perhaps the figure onstage is maturing into more identifiable human activity. If *Tefu Tefu* has a weakness, it is the obscure relationship of some of the images to the piece as a thematic whole. The piece is possibly more introspective than expected.

Miss Kisanuki projects a sense of discovery toward the end. Nonetheless, it is her extraordinary movement quality that always comes to the fore. When she finally mounts the steps of the aisle, she seems to float up.

Whatever one thinks of her choreography, Miss Kisanuki, as representative of a new generation of Japanese dancers, simply does not look like dancers we usually see. She is different and she is worth a trip to the Joyce.

Affiliated with Butoh, but not wholly accepting its premises, were Eiko (b. *c.* 1952) and her male partner Koma (b. *c.* 1949) who settled in New York in 1976. As noted earlier, they had been friends and pupils of Kazuo Ono; they had presented him with the unusually inspiring poster of La Argentina that seemed to speak to him. The pair – they are known only by single names – had met while students and from then on danced only with each other. Another of their instructors was Manja Chmiel, a disciple of Wigman and an exponent of German Expressionism. Eiko and Koma developed their own idiom, however, creating "postmodern work that they hope will be universal". Eiko told an interviewer: "We are Butoh-influenced, but we are not Butoh performers. We are minimalists. It's quite a clear concept – less is more."

A reviewer in the *New York Times* cited Eiko's self-description as truly accurate. "Followers of Underground dance were stunned by an extraordinary performance of intense stillness, of stark minimalism. . . . Rooted in Butoh, the pair combine the Japanese classical movements of slowing time and consciousness of the universality of nature. Eiko and Koma's physical control is so intense that their often nude bodies change shape, assuming unexpected, almost nonhuman forms."

Their frequent recitals have been highly esteemed by New York critics. A fuller discussion of their repertoire belongs to a survey of the New York world of dance rather than that of Tokyo and Osaka.

Conveying the spirit of Butoh, also, was the Muteki-sha group, invited to be part of a series of dance programmes at Asia House in 1985. One reviewer was moved to depict the event as "a production from which one staggered, stunned by a performance of incredible intensity".

The visit of Martha Graham and her troupe to Tokyo in 1955 prompted not only a revival of interest in modern dance but also a flow of dancers and their students to Europe and especially the United States. The enthusiasm she aroused was partly a reaction to and escape from the rigid conventions governing the arts in Japan. As Faubion Bowers saw it, a nerve was touched. While ballet was voguish among intellectuals, for those more purely devoted to dance itself, long dictated, the alternative offered by Graham suggested that there were new opportunities for a native creativity that did not call for imitation of what the West was doing. There could be complete freedom, they could do what they liked. What ensued was almost an angry reaction to long-cherished traditions that had ossified. Besides that, local dancers thought Graham the greatest thing they had seen. They understood her technique totally. She was not only an emancipator, but someone from whom they could learn much.

Beate Gordon, director of the Performing Arts Program of the Japan Society, noted: "After 1955, a great many students came to study at the Graham school – some were on Fulbright scholarships, but most were financially hard pressed." Ms Gordon started the Performing Arts Program at the Japan Society in 1956 to assist those students – musicians and dancers struggling in New York. A project called "Japan: Old and New" was founded to afford them a chance to perform for audiences in and around New York. The dancers were paid a small amount, $25 for each engagement. "Hirabayashi, Ichinohe, Hanayagi were some of the earlier modern-dance performers in the group." (They, of course, were not exemplars of Butoh.) These expatriates, and those who followed over the next two decades, were in flight from the heavy weight of conformity at home. Bowers: "Japanese society was so restrictive that the new generation could not stand it. There was no room for originality and wildness, so the young artists came to America and thought they could do anything. And the Americans are so gullible, they supposed it's all Zen. Some of the Japanese *avant-garde* – or 'Angura' – choreographers got away with it here." Also the Japanese were very dependent on Western recognition. "Unless you had a reputation in the West, the Japanese public didn't pay much attention to you. So the troops flocked to New York."

Michimiko Oka, of the New York-based Alvin Ailey troupe, supported this: "There are a lot of dancers in Japan, but they want to learn new things. So they all seek New York. It's true that a dancer-choreographer will come to New York and put on two or three recitals and then return to Japan and become accepted immediately."

Several Japanese dancers were members of the Ailey company, which was ethnically mixed yet predominately composed of blacks. One of the Oriental members was Mari Kajiwara, born in the United States, who joined Ailey in 1970 when she was eighteen. Eventually she functioned as his assistant for five years and also staged several of his works for other troupes. "I think it's due to a natural affinity that the Japanese dominate the modern-dance world. Martha Graham always said that the Oriental body was perfect for her technique – it's more rounded, the back is flexible and long. So, I've always accepted it. But I'm not sure if the style is different because I'm Oriental or whether it's my being more reticent than others." She suggests that not only Graham but several more Western modern-dance choreographers had looked on the physiques of Orientals as having a fascinating potential, particularly the deft, petite women. At the same time, as has been noted – Japanese aspiring to be classic ballet dancers have met with rejection by European and American choreographers who cite the Western young with slender, long-limbed bodies as the ideal; consequently, Japanese dancers have turned to the modern field.

In the Ailey troupe, too, was Masazumi Chaya, singled out for his comic roles. "At the beginning, I was imitating, because the Ailey repertory is very American. But I have my own spiritual way of expressing movements, and Alvin allows this difference in his dancers. I never feel uncomfortable, and as long as I am doing the steps, I don't have to be black or white as long as the choreography can be felt in my body."

Ailey acknowledged that by including Orientals in his long-successful company he had learned much. He felt that his own "roots" were partly Asian. "My teacher was Lester Horton. I learned the theatrical tricks from Lester by way of Ito – the use of few props to suggest a big space, the use of long blue-silk sheets to represent the water in *Revelations*. You see, I'm especially attuned to the Japanese sensitivity. When Chaya and Oka auditioned for me in 1972, they were marvelous. They couldn't speak English, but they could already do all the funk, all the soul naturally and organically. They already had everything from the beginning – blues, jazz, spiritual, ballet. And they bring to us what is traditional about themselves – the tradition of Nōh, Kabuki – but also they reflect twentieth-century ideas."

A shrewd and eminent authority in Japanese culture insists that it is an error to consider its people only "imitative", a view owing much to China, Korea and the Occident. Instead, he says, they "have long had a very clear self-identification". The consequence is a tendency among them to be self-conscious about what they have appropriated from others. "Although they started learning from the West ahead of anyone else, and did so more successfully than anyone, Japanese culture remains very Japanese – in personal and social relationships – but it also has a remarkable capacity for taking in things from the West."

Japanese performers in New York, the crowded centre of the modern-dance world, appeared as solo recitalists, members of groups largely comprised of Caucasians, or as heads of their own all-Japanese troupes. One of them was Kenji Hinoki (?–1983), who after studying with Ruth St Denis from 1936 to 1939 returned to Japan and established himself as a major figure in the modern dance field. One of his prominent pupils, Kei Takei, became director of a troupe called Moving Earth, whom New York dance-lovers had an opportunity to see in 1982, when the company appeared at the Performing Garage in Soho. Jennifer Dunning, after a conversation with her, reported sympathetically:

> The notion of the avant-garde may bring to mind fur-lined teacups and dancers standing to the sound of telephone time signals. In the case of Kei Takei, a leading avant-garde choreographer, such frivolous images are far from the mark.
>
> Taken as simple stage pictures – and her theater-dance pieces often look like tableaux staged by an architect with a painter's imagination – Miss Takei's dances might pass for the latest experimentation. Her dancers, dressed in loose, white clothes, crouch, collide and spill out over the stage. Props have the look of totems – strange and yet oddly familiar.
>
> Miss Takei is interested in the natural world and ritualistic behavior. What is important is the "something inside, a spiritual thing, the light of religion," as she puts it, that animates her work and draws dancers and audiences to her. Everything springs from intuition seriously considered. Stones

sing, radishes resemble humans, and dances grow out of enduring impulses like these.

Miss Takei has choreographed for companies around the world, from the Netherlands Dance Theatre to the Yemenite Inbal Dance Theatre of Israel, but she is probably best known for *Light*, a suite of dances she began in 1969 and which was given a seven-hour performance in 1975 at the Brooklyn Academy of Music. The pieces to be seen this weekend are excerpts or whole dances from Parts 15, 16 and 17 of *Light*, dances whose intense, private images are suggested by such subtitles as *Vegetable Fields* and *Dreamcatcher's Diary*.

"Kei's spirituality is a cosmic kind," said Laz Brezer, a member of Moving Earth. "She feels the community of all living things, a belief that is close to the old-time Shinto doctrine of Buddhism."

The name Moving Earth was chosen for its simplicity, though the company often gets calls asking for its out-of-town trucking rates. *Light*, too, seemed to her an important and far-reaching symbol – "I didn't know many words in English."

A student of classical ballet, modern dance and Japanese classical dance in Tokyo where she was born, Miss Takei was spotted by the choreographer Anna Sokolow, who suggested that she come to New York and study dance at the Juilliard School. Three months after she came to the United States on a Fulbright Scholarship she was invited by Louise Roberts, head of the Clark Center for the Performing Arts, to submit a dance for the center's New Choreographers series.

Miss Takei stayed at Juilliard for a year, but her problems with English were severe enough for her to leave to study dance with a wide variety of teachers, from the experimentalist Trisha Brown to Russians that everybody called "Madame" at the American Ballet Theater school.

Little of this shows in her dances, however, and her greatest artistic influences have been the modern dance teacher Kenji Hinoki and Kiyoe Fujima, who teaches Japanese classical dance. She served with both of them as a devoted live-in apprentice.

Miss Takei comes to rehearsals with her dances set in her head and takes little from watching the performers improvise, as many choreographers do. But the performers, who are both trained and untrained as dancers, serve as a strong family unit.

"I like them to be physically strong," Miss Takei said. "Physical people with good spirits, and willing to work. They like my pieces. And there's something interesting about them as human beings."

"There are times when the movement and the accompanying chants seem draining to perform. Kei tries to keep it as pure and simple as possible," said Mr Brezer, a Canadian who has performed with her for three years. "She doesn't want it emotional."

It does not bother Miss Takei that audiences often misinterpret or see only certain themes in her dances. "People take a few of the meanings, like layers in a dream," she said. "Just not all."

It is not necessary, for instance, to grasp the foreboding sense of war and malevolent influences that inspired the emblems of disease in *Light, Part 15*, or the feeling of the dark acquisitiveness of the world about her that led to the belligerent and funny exchanges of clothes in *Light, Part 17*.

Asked about the white radishes that come pelting down in *Daikon Field*, a solo from *Light, Part 16*, she said: "I've wanted to dance with Daikons, or radishes, for a long time. I admire them. I appreciate them as I eat them."

A solo dancer with Moving Earth was Chizuko Kuramochi, another of Hinoki's former pupils, whose offering preserved the choreography of his highly respected teacher.

Some other performers and troupes passing through New York or permanently engaged there during the 1970s and 1980s have been the Kazuko Hirabayashi Dance Theatre, Saeko Ichinohe and Company, Mariko Sanjo, Izumi Tanaka, Suzushi Hanayagi, Satoru Shimizaki and Dancers, Tokunaga Dance Ko, the Hiroshima Dancers, Min Tanaka and Tomoko Ehara. Many of their works, commingling traits and gestures of East and West, were eclectic, and some groups were not all-Japanese but included Western members.

Michiyo and Dancers, a troupe of nine with Michiyo Tanaka as its artistic director, was presented by the Japan Society in 1987, offering a range of five original works; the programme was highlighted by *Bird's Eye View*, choreographed by Ms Tanaka, who sought to interpret the woodblock print series *Fifty-three Stations on the Tokaido* by the celebrated Edo-period artist Ando Hiroshige; this dance composition had music by the techno-pop composer Ryuichi Sakamoto.

Among those who made a significant impact, Junko Kikuchi (b. *c.* 1948) was designated by Jennifer Dunning in the *New York Times* in 1980 as "one of the most gifted performers on the modern-dance concert circuit today". Bonnie Sue Stein, of the Asia Society, which sponsored a presentation by Ms Kikuchi, said of her in 1984: "She has the dynamism of Western dance, the elegance of Japanese dance." Kikuchi, daughter of a Tokyo merchant, began her study of dance at the age of seven, because of parental concern about her health. "I wasn't ill," Kikuchi told Philip Shenon, also of the *New York Times*, "just a weakling." At nineteen she made her formal début. She received several important dance awards. "What had started as a tonic had become a career."

In 1976 she was drawn to New York by the offer of a scholarship from the Joffrey Ballet, in its school. She accepted: "I felt the need for ballet training. In Japan, there're very few places where we can get that type of preparation." After a year she left classical ballet for modern dance once more, performing with the Nikolais Dance Theater and next the Merce Cunningham Dance Studio. Ending a seven-year absence from Tokyo, she returned home. In 1984, when New York saw her again; her pro-gramme featured *Passages*, which among its other intentions sought to trace "the path of a dancer's career". The choreography was her own and, in the words of Shenon, "it shows Miss Kikuchi at her best, exploiting the mix of international styles that had become her trademark".

Ms Kikuchi told Shenon that what concerned her was not the attention and acclaim she had received, but rather the doing. "Doing, doing, doing. I know that dance is what I need to do. I need to follow it." Her attempt has been to balance the best of both nations: "precision with energy, humility with freedom, restraint with daring". Shenon describes episodes in *Passages*:

> The curtains, the backdrop, the floor, all are gray. And from the audience's right, she bounds on stage without warning. She is clothed in a costume of layered, off white cotton. Her feet kick wildly, hap-pily against imaginary sand until, suddenly, she stops, her limbs stiff as a startled fawn. Her right leg rises slowly, until it is parallel to the ground, and she holds it there for several seconds.
>
> Kikuchi at one moment is spinning her arms like a baseball pitcher, her feet making a mechani-cal patter that would seem to match the roar of the crowd. The next moment she is frozen, her hands raised in a perfect alignment with the slight tilt of her head.
>
> She explained: "Rather than choosing one certain style, I know my influences come from many places." Her hope was that her dancing had left behind the "incessant 'tenseness' of much of tra-ditional dance without losing its delicacy". Her lengthy stay in New York had been critical to her later development; it had given her work an independence that it needed.

Yasuko Nagamine (b. *c.* 1936) was another who blended dance styles in rebellion against her country's inbred formality. Scott-Stokes wrote from Tokyo in 1982:

> One of the great moments in Japanese theater is the start of a Nōh play. A multi-colored curtain at the side of the stage is suddenly whisked up. The actors glide into sight, their feet in white *tabi* socks. They make no sound beyond the rustle of rich silk kimonos. With solemnity, the actors take up pos-itions on stage. The restraint, the formality and the subtlety attached to gesture – the angle of a mask, the shade of a kimono sleeve – all these things are quintessential Japan.
>
> Nothing is hurried. The action is so slow that members of the audience become drowsy. Heads nod in brief snatches of sleep. About two-thirds of the way through the play, a performer may lift a heel in a padded *tabi* sock and bring it down gently on the floor. After the slow buildup, the soft thud comes like a thunderclap. The climax of the dance approaches.

But imagine the antithesis. A performer, instead of slowly building up to a peak, launches into a furious stride across stage at the outset. This person has no *tabi* on her feet. Her bare heels, hardened by karatelike exercise, beat a tattoo on the wooden floor, setting off what sound like multiple explosions. Amid all the racket, set against the chanting of a chorus, the kimonoed figure, with her dress seemingly about to burst, continues to crisscross the stage, to squat, to leap, to yowl, to hammer on the floor – for eighty minutes. Despite the fast pace she set at the start, Yasuko Nagamine has the stamina to maintain it to the end.

Miss Nagamine, who will perform her dance *Dojoji* on Friday at Avery Fisher Hall in New York, is one of the most remarkable dancers to appear in Japan in decades – a maverick with enormous energy. The opening steps of *Dojoji*, choreographed by her as a solo, and set to a Kabuki score with sixteen musicians and chorus people, are a deliberate attack on the Nōh tradition.

"The Nōh's boring," she said in an interview here, shortly before she left for New York. Yet she is much more than an iconoclast.

Miss Nagamine is steeped in the Nōh and loves it, despite her disavowal. Her dance starts with a pastiche of the Nōh, as a prelude to evocation of a still deeper tradition in Japan – that of the shaman. In *Dojoji*, a tale of a maddened, evil serpent-woman who hunts an inoffensive monk to death, she explores the roots of Japanese civilization, a shaman tradition that predates the Nōh and may be felt to underlie much in modern Japan still. Whereas the shamans go back to prehistoric times, long before Buddhism came to Japan from China in the seventh century, the Nōh is only 700 years old.

The clue to Miss Nagamine's performance as a modern-day sorceress of Japan lies in her use of her hands, less in her body, whose movements are obscured by the kimono. She uses her hands, with knuckles pounded into peeling flesh – "They are just as hard as those of any man who does karate – I don't feel a thing" – to beat repeatedly on the stage, then make arabesques in the air, as if climbing a silk rope or stroking leaves. She weaves spells with those blunt, clumsy-looking fingers. That is the root of her erotic magic.

At forty-six, Miss Nagamine is at her peak as a dancer. She won three major awards in the late seventies. She obtained the Japanese Arts Festival Grand Prix twice for *Dojoji* and for a dance based on a Lorca poem, *Elegy for Ignacia Sanchez Mejias*. She also won a prize for her dance version of the *Salome* tale dramatized by Oscar Wilde.

Earlier, she trained as a flamenco dancer in Spain in the sixties. A decade abroad appears to have given her the chance to work off an outer husk of Japaneseness. The dances she creates have a primitive vigor that recalls the *Many Oshu* (*A Collection of 10,000 Leaves*), an eighth-century anthology of poetry that epitomizes the early vitality of Japan that later became overcivilized and self-conscious.

Meanwhile her performance in New York may be a first and last Nagamine *Dojoji* abroad, for financial reasons. She said that it cost her personally close to $150,000 to get her thirty-six-member company plus a special stage – a hollow wooden floor to go over the Fisher Hall stage – to New York. Miss Nagamine gets no state or foundation subsidies like those given the Grand Kabuki, which will perform in New York next month. "But it's been my dream," she said, "to perform in New York."

In 1984, however, she was back with an enlarged company to present a dance-drama, *Mandara*. For this,

The stage will be filled with fifty-eight Japanese Buddhist monks intoning traditional chants. In addition, the production will embrace the ritual solemnity of Japanese Nōh theater and the emotional fervor of Western modern dance, as well as elements of Spanish flamenco, Miss Nagamine's specialty.

Two years ago at Avery Fisher Hall, Miss Nagamine combined Kabuki and flamenco. She has toured with Peter Orwa, a dancer from Kenya, in programs of what she terms African-flamenco and she has united flamenco with modern dance and rock-and-roll.

In a recent interview she said that *Mandara* was born out of a desire "to reflect the wisdom of Buddhism in dance form." The work is based on a Japanese legend about a demon-possessed woman who murders an innocent man and is led to repentance when she hears the chanting of monks.

When she declared that she wished to include monks in the production, everyone she spoke to was appalled, Miss Nagamine said. Japanese monks never appear in theaters and even when they chant during public ceremonies in temples they turn their backs to any spectators present. Instead of finding monks, Miss Nagamine was told she ought to hire actors. Nevertheless, she was determined to use real monks because she valued the genuine spirituality of their presence.

Then a friend who was a student of Buddhism introduced her to monks of the Shingon sect. Believing that wisdom can be gained through sense perception, they proved willing to chant for the dance. Even so, Miss Nagamine said, since chanting is a form of meditation, during the course of the work they must always gaze downward and avoid following her actions on stage.

The monks will be led in the chants by Kenyo Komatsubara, chief abbot of the Buzan subsect of Shingon Buddhism, and their Carnegie Hall appearance will be the first time these monks have traveled outside Japan. For the monks, the performance is part of a year of celebrations marking the 1,150th anniversary of the death of Kukai, their sect's founder. Upon her return to Japan in

November, Miss Nagamine will perform *Mandara* with the monks at the dedication of a new statue of Kukai at a monks' school. It will be the first time that a woman has been allowed to participate in such a ceremony, she said.

But her discovery of flamenco as a child changed her life. This occurred near the end of World War II when, she says, the Government, in an attempt to encourage Japanese patriotism, forbade foreign music. Yet one of her friends owned a recording of flamenco music and when she heard it, Miss Nagamine was overwhelmed.

. . . Although she once thought of gaining a university degree in economics, dancing triumphed over academic studies, and in 1960 she went to Spain. There she met José Miguel, who has been her partner in many productions and who will again dance with her in *Mandara*.

Although she is a dancer with a very personal style, the actual choreography of her works since 1975 has been by Mizuomi Ikeda, a modern dance choreographer she has known since they were students together in Tokyo. Miss Nagamine explained that they collaborate "in workshop fashion." Instead of imposing ideas upon her, Mr Ikeda suggests, arranges and edits Miss Nagamine's steps. And, Miss Nagamine said with a smile, should she reject his suggestions, "He is very patient."

Miss Nagamine has not hesitated to combine flamenco with other art forms. "If I like a piece of music or a dramatic idea, then I dance to it," she said. "And my basic training as a dancer is flamenco."

Pointing out that flamenco dancing emphasizes originality, she said that after studying in Spain she realized that, although she could do Spanish flamenco, she could never be Spanish. "So," she concluded, "my originality as a flamenco dancer lies in the fact that I am Japanese."

Mandara is translated as *Reincarnation*. Jennifer Dunning provides us with the story:

In the first section, Miss Nagamine battles energetically with two ruffians and finds herself falling under the spell of an evil spirit, played by José Miguel. In the second section, she twists and tumbles from one pair of restraining arms to another, whirls through the fog and is raised triumphant, dressed in white, in a moment that presumably signifies she has found that purity.

All this took almost two hours to accomplish. There were one or two fairly striking pictorial effects and the hint of an interesting idea in a duet for Miss Nagamine and Mr Miguel as separated partners. But for the most part, *Mandara* served to provide Miss Nagamine, who specializes in mixing dance forms, with a chance to display her talents. Whatever they may be, they were poorly served by the piece, which was directed and choreographed by Mizuomi Ikeda.

The fifty-eight monks, from the Shingon School Buzan Sect, were wonderful, particularly when they built at the end to boisterous shouts. They were unable, however, to bring a saving air of ritual to *Mandara*, given the busyness of the production and Miss Nagamine's utter lack of theatrical presence in it. *Mandara* made for a remarkably unrevelatory evening in the theater.

It was, none the less, a spectacle somewhat unusual for the engagement of a dance company, since the outside of Carnegie Hall was bathed in klieg lights for the occasion, while inside the stage was filled with tinted fog.

Quite as odd as the matching of Japanese and Spanish gesture and movement was the hybrid style formulated by a performer known as Shakti who mingled elements of the traditional dances of two Oriental lands, both of them having for her an inherent affinity. With a company of thirty dancers and musicians from Kyoto she presented a three-act offering entitled *Himiko* (*Sun Goddess*) at New York's large Avery Fisher Hall in 1984, under the auspices of Kazuko Hiller and the Concert Arts Society.

Anna Kisselgoff was not persuaded that *Himiko* was an artistic success.

You can see anything you wish in New York – even a dancer who dances out Japanese legends in an idiom derived from Indian classical dance and who sometimes wears a bikini while doing it.

Shakti, the exasperating but talented young woman in question, is also a Barnard College graduate and holds a master's degree in Indian philosophy from Columbia University. On Friday night, she and her company of dancers and musicians from her native Japan made their United States début.

Who are these headstrong women from Japan who invade Lincoln Center with a full panoply of traditional musicians and then proceed to act in a manner most untraditional by any standard? Like the fiery female performer who stamped her way through a blend of flamenco and Kabuki at Fisher Hall a couple of years ago, Shakti offers a brand of eclecticism that becomes a highly personalized approach to performing.

And while Shakti is obviously a very good dancer, supple and nuanced, seductive in her self-aware stage presence, she is also what used to be called self-indulgent.

The daughter of a university professor from India and a Japanese dancer who teaches classical Indian dance, Shakti heads, in effect, an Indian classical dance company in Japan – and one with a contemporary twist. As seen in the solos in the first part of Friday's program, she is a charming, vibrant performer of Indian classical dance.

The major portion was a two-hour dance drama, *Himiko*, named after what the program note

identified as a Japanese sun-goddess. Shakti herself has taken the name of the Hindu principle identified with creative energy of the universe. Her Himiko is really the original Shakti in disguise.

We see her first in a white gown and diamond choker. A destructive force as well as a creative
one, she embroils the Sun God, danced with a strange finesse by a highly muscular performer named
Chuck Wilson, with the Earth deity – portrayed as a lusty pilgrim by Katsuumi Niwa, a tenor with a
Juilliard degree and a voice to prove it.

At this point the traditional big drums on stage gave way to what sounded like a New York
experimental concert. Mr Niwa uttered a variety of high-pitched sounds and Shakti, in purple bikini
and a fishnet, did a Salomé-like dance straight into the Earth deity's embrace.

Many of Shakti's ideas make sense. Her best idea was to abstract the essence of her story. The
initial repetitive patterns of her female chorus as she hopped in turns are close to Tibetan dance
inspiration and relevant to a Buddhist inspiration. Similarly, the goddess in her destructive aspect is
an essential part of the theme. But to portray this demonic side merely through an exercise in hair-
flinging – and Shakti's hair is very long – is not enough. Suddenly, free form becomes only free.

When Shakti reappeared two years later with another ambitious piece, Jennifer Dunning was
somewhat kinder, though not fully won over:

Shakti has a lush presence and way of moving. And her *Salomé*, performed on Wednesday at the
Triplex Theater as part of the Fools Company's International OFFestival, serves primarily to focus
on that lushness. Choreographed by Vasantamala and Shakti to an uncredited score of mostly tra-
ditional-sounding Indian music, *Salomé* aimed to explore "the energy of life and death that must be
released in order to live and in order to die." The symbol of that energy is Salomé, and she is never far
from center stage. Shakti, a young performer of classical Indian dance, is lovely to watch, and the
scenes are compelling where she flirts like a baby tigress with the impassive Jokanaan, played by
Tetsuro Yamasaki.

There is some impressively dramatic staging at the start, as Shakti establishes Salomé's strength
and her intensity of desire. The space between Shakti and Jokanaan, for instance, is highly charged,
and the chorus of four impassive women is often used, interestingly, almost as an element in the stage
design.

Only Salomé lives as a fully fledged character. It is a valid approach. But nothing in the relationship tenuously depicted here between Salomé and Jokanaan supports Salomé's overextended throes
of passion as she dances before Jokanaan's severed head. And the head and basket in which it rests

are not crafted with the sophistication of Shakti's pretty costumes, designed by Vasantamala.

At half its length, *Salomé* would have provided a good showcase for this Indian–Japanese dancer and the way she has chosen to use Indian dance styles and motifs in contemporary forms. The program was completed by three dances in the Odissi style of Indian dance.

Shakti's endeavours had considerable financial support from the Kyoto Chamber of Commerce and Industry, and several large corporations also contributed to the funding. Koichi Tsukamoto, president of the Chamber, explained their aim and why Shakti had been chosen to embody it.

I believe that promoting international exchange in the fields of art and culture is a very important concern in the modern age. Achieving this goal will no doubt further the development of friendly political and economic relations between nations and lead to mutual prosperity.

Born in the city of Kyoto, the home of Japan's oldest culture and a place that has evolved its own unique culture, Shakti has adopted the best aspects of the culture and arts of the United States, India and Japan, and created a new dance form, which has been described as "sculpture in motion" and "like a dancing phoenix." I believe she is one of the promising artists of the twenty-first century.

At present, the Kyoto Chamber of Commerce and Industry is carrying out an aggressive international exchange program. To this end, the dancer Shakti, who is of Japanese and Indian parentage, is an elegant cultural emissary for Kyoto. She will be a bridge of mutual understanding between the United States, India and Japan. On behalf of the people of Kyoto, I would like to convey to Shakti our heartfelt best wishes for a successful New York première.

To this gracious message was added another from Soshitsu Sen XV, Grand Master of the Urasenke School of Tea:

It has been my belief that peace is attainable in our present world. My goal for over thirty years has been to bring together people from all over the world to quietly share a simple bowl of whisked green tea. In this way they might understand that people only appear to be different, but are the same in their hearts.

A truly "international" person finds the essence of the human heart in his or her practice – whether it is studying the Way of Tea, painting, architecture, Zen or dance.

Shakti is one of the rare people. Her Japanese and Indian ancestry, combined with her education in America, give her a unique perspective of human nature that we can all appreciate through her dance. Her intention in the dance piece *Himiko* is to reveal the union with nature as experienced by one of Japan's earliest queens.

Union with nature. Peace of mind. It can be reached through the Way of Tea, or through dance, with its great moments of significance and beauty. I am grateful for the chance Shakti has given us to share her vision, for through such sharing I believe we can have greater peace in the world.

Yet another visitor from Japan, in 1987, was Yoshiko Chuma and her company, fancifully named the School of Hard Knocks. The troupe's offering, *The Big Picture*, left Jack Anderson somewhat bemused.

Ever turn on your television set and find yourself bewitched by a movie that is absolutely incomprehensible – because you missed its beginning – and yet compelling? Yoshiko Chuma offered a dance like that Friday night at the Bessie Schönberg Theater. *The Big Picture* was simultaneously a musical, a dance extravaganza and a melodrama.

The music was by Nona Hendryx, who sang impassioned songs about geographical and emotional distance. Additional music was provided by Dan Froot and Gayle Tufts.

Against backdrops of maps and cityscapes by Yvonne Jacquette, dancers rushed, jumped and swung one another about at the choreographic equivalent of supersonic speed. There were also moments when they could have been members of rival gangs slugging it out or spies spying on other spies.

They also talked. They talked about movies and airplane disasters. But, most often, they talked as if they were involved in a plot. Although viewers had to decide for themselves whether that plot was a movie scenario or an actual conspiracy, the dancers did seem to be acting out a story about a woman asked by a stranger to take a package onto an airplane. One never learned whether that package contained drugs, a bomb or only a gift for a friend.

By keeping her audience guessing, Ms Chuma helped generate dramatic suspense. Yet because she also implied that everything in *The Big Picture* was ultimately part of a movie script, she made the work less compelling than it could have been. Its incidents seemed to cancel one another out. Yet if Ms Chuma had somehow managed to hint that her most extravagant fancies could also become terrifyingly real, she would have had a production that was heavy drama as well as light entertainment.

Nevertheless, as entertainment, *The Big Picture* made one so curious about its dramatic twists and turns that one had to keep watching.

Manuel Alum, a Puerto Rican-born modern dancer, founder of a troupe (1970), went to Tokyo by himself to learn what he could about art forms there. Given a six months' study grant by the United States–Japan Friendship Commission, he took lessons briefly – just one week – with Daisuke Fujima, a member of one of the two main *iemoto*, or "families", of classical Japanese dancers. Alum told Henry Scott-Stokes: "He liked me because I picked up quickly. I could see just what he was doing – and he suggested that we do an evening together, ending with a duet." This led to a joint recital in 1980 at Toranomon Hall, for an invited audience, at which each performer had solos and finally a joint number. Such a concert was unprecedented, a rare event. Scott-Stokes relates, in a dispatch in the *New York Times*:

Mr Alum is small, with long legs, a phenomenal leaper in his early years, who came to learn about Japanese culture and – quickly – discarded everything modern here. "All that is 'new' is imitation in Japan," he said, "only the old – the Nōh, and a classical dancer like Takahara Han – is really new."

He traveled around the country, visited Beppu, where he was immured to his neck in hot mud, a Japanese-style sauna, went to see Nōh plays in Kyoto and at Hiroshima, where a stage is set above the ocean at night, and saw the elderly Takahara, probably Japan's finest dancer, perform her classical repertory. "It was Nōh or nothing," he said. "I found Kabuki gaudy and superficial, however colorful."

But he tired of tourism: "I wanted to dance. I've got nothing to hang on a wall and I don't enjoy talking or explaining my work, so when I communicate I have to dance. That was the first of my troubles. There was nowhere to go. For some reason, Tokyo is virtually without a wooden floor where a modern dancer can go." Mr Alum did his "stretches" in the water in a metropolitan swimming pool, and he stretched around the garden of International House, where he stayed, and in its corridors – to the surprise of visiting academics from the United States.

Mr Fujima is twenty years older than Mr Alum and has a large stomach for a dancer. But age and weight are not crucial in the case of a Japanese classical dancer, who is expected to improve as the decades pass and to perform no acrobatics. The dance is slow and performed in enveloping silk trousers, kimono and trapezoidal hats to the slow beat of drum and to recitative. It has a melancholy and introspective esthetic created here 1,000 years ago.

The Fujima *iemoto* raised the money for the performance, $5,000 to pay for the hall, programs, sets – however bare – and accompanying musicians and technicians. A brother insisted that in return for financial backing, Fujima incorporate in the program a "dance" by three martial artists, experts in karate, that struck Japanese in the audience as incongruous – but funds are never easy to raise for the arts.

The karate men sucked in their chests, spat and raged like cats.

Mr Alum drew on his repertory for the evening: *On the Double*, in black tails and tights, to music by Rossini with a double bass thwacking away; *The Cellar*, an evocation of prison that impressed the British sculptor Henry Moore when performed at Spoleto, Italy, a decade ago, performed by Mr Alum in wool hat and with bared shoulders – and a signature piece, *Dream REM #1117*, to music by John Cage and inspired by a dream Mr Alum had when he was learning the Yaqui Indian deer dance, and *East – to Nijinsky*.

The Japanese audience responded to *Dream*, in which Mr Alum lies, balances and rotates on a heavy wooden chair placed on its side, raises his fingers above his head in a Pan-like movement and comes close to apotheosis. There is an otherworldliness about *Dream* that perhaps reminded them of the Nōh and its ghosts, spirits and shamans.

Mr Fujima started with *Shojo*, the tale of an angel who gets drunk. The dance is performed in a floor-length orange wig and pale green split trousers three feet wide, and is a solo, accompanied by flute, drum and recitation. Mr Fujima dipped a fan into a turquoise vase, dropped sake into his mouth with a brief flutter of the fan and subsided in a rustle of green onto the stage at the end of the piece. His second dance was *Semimaru*, a blind man's lament, again performed at a slow pace – not *On the Double* with Mr Alum.

How would these two dance together? Anticlimax followed. Mr Fujima decided against the duet on the advice of his entourage. Like many figures in the arts in Japan, he is surrounded by acolytes – relatives, fellow performers and musicians – who counsel against risk, and they considered a duet with Mr Alum a gamble in which the Japanese might show to disadvantage or be a foil to Mr Alum.

"It was madness," Mr Alum said. "All of a sudden we were competitors. What started out as an evening by friends became a clash of cultures. Who was best? Which was the finer tradition? Fujima saw me dance for the first time, doing my own work, and said something about 'disco-dancing' – I had to put him right. The original idea of the duet collapsed."

Three gold screens were set center-stage for the finale. Mr Alum appeared alone in a white puffy costume by Issey Miyake, Japan's top resident fashion designer. He fluffed the garment, and withdrew from it to show a skin-taut tattoo shirt with the kind of design favored by Japanese *yakuza*, or gangsters, dark purples and a flash of orange. On his lower body he wore a white fundoshi, or loincloth.

The function of the gold screens became apparent when Mr Fujima followed in kimono, dancing to music that resembled a composition by Pink Floyd, the British rock group, set to Mantovani's strings. Mr Fuijma surged forward, fluttering silver rods and a gold-colored toy, a carousel, while the thousand violins swept overhead. Sweat fell on his silks.

Mr Alum tried for Japan and Mr Fujima tried for the West. And if only they had danced together! But Japan is not a place for artistic risk-taking since the nineteen-fifties or early sixties, at the latest.

"I leave Japan a bit frustrated," Mr Alum said after the performance and before his return to New York last week. "There's so much that could be done here, and then you run into this inflexibility – that's the arts in Japan right now."

Upon his return to New York, Alum gave a recital, *Made in Japan*, and was asked by Jennifer Dunning about his experiences abroad.

"I've been a foreigner all my life, but in Japan I was *really* a foreigner. The biggest problem was space to work in. There is no space in Japan. So I knocked on doors and said: 'I want to perform here.' I guess my modern dance training helped with that! They have a different way of doing things in Japan. Here you make contacts on the telephone. There you meet for breakfast, lunch and dinner to get acquainted. But they are so organized. The people I'd eat with knew everything about me."

His performances were received with everything from polite disbelief to enthusiasm. "Modern dance is dated in Japan. It's very Graham, very Cunningham. The Japanese dancers were wonderful technicians but you'd see them running around with scarves to Ravel, dressed in the latest style of leotards, or dancing very intellectualized stuff. It isn't a country of concepts but esthetics. They spend their time refining."

And, although several venerable classical dancers welcomed his interest and worked very generously with him, Mr Alum was uncomfortable with the restrictions of tradition. "The Japanese are wonderful people, but I'm so glad I'm an American," he said. "Where else can you just lock yourself in a studio and work very hard? Over there it takes more than that – things like family, and money. Tradition protects you, but it also makes it difficult to grow."

Mr Alum traveled across the country, using Tokyo as his home base. There he stayed at International House. "It was a little stuffy, but they had the most beautiful garden. Every breakfast I'd look out at it and knew I'd have to dance there. But people didn't dance there, though I found out it was where the first emperor ever saw a Kabuki play." Finally he was given permission to perform privately in the garden. "And now I hear they are having Summer festivals there!"

In 1984 there was a major incursion into Japan by foreign performers when the American Dance Festival marked its fiftieth anniversary by sending six noted teachers to spend a month leading instructional workshops in Tokyo and elsewhere. Among those participating were the choreographers Bella Lewitzsky, Ralf Haze, Kei Takei, Betty Jones and Ruby Shang and a dance therapist, Martha Myers, dean of the festival, who lectured on anatomy and how to prevent physical injuries. Two dance troupes, Laura Dean Dancers and musicians and Crowsnest, also had a role. Yoko Ondo and Sakumi Hagiwara joined the faculty to teach Japanese folk dance and video photography. This was the second part of a formal cultural exchange begun in 1982, when four Japanese companies had been invited to Durham, as noted earlier. Funding, an always essential aspect of any such programme, came from the Japan-United States Friendship Commission, the Japanese Dance Critics Association, the Contemporary Dance Association of Japan and the Yu Modern Dance Company of Shikoku, representing a range of interests.

Terry Trucco, writing from Tokyo, had these impressions of the ambitious project and summed up the state of modern dance in Japan:

Unlike the American original, which now spends six weeks at Duke University in North Carolina, the exported festival has traveled – a week of classes in both Shikoku and Osaka, and two weeks in Tokyo.

The festival has attracted 550 students, including 250 here in Tokyo, and its organizers are pleasantly surprised. "It takes three years for something like this to get going, but we're very pleased," said the festival's director, Charles Reinhart, who began planning the festival abroad in 1978.

Miyabi Ichikawa, a Tokyo dance critic and lecturer who organized the Japanese effort, said he hoped to make the program an annual event. Attendance at the performances was not too good, he admitted. And there was the problem of financing for next year – the Japan–US Friendship League underwrote a large part that year. But the festival did attract considerably more students than expected. And modern dance in Japan was gradually getting more popular, he said.

Indeed, most students, who came from all over Japan as well as from Korea and Taiwan, gave the festival high marks, praising the teachers. Top-notch American instructors regularly visit Japan these days, but rarely in a group where students can compare a wide range of styles and ideas.

. . . A visit by Martha Graham in the mid-1950s established American dance as a major influence, but modern dance's popularity has always been eclipsed by ballet. While traditional Japanese dance and even ballet attract general Japanese audiences, modern dance relies on its own special following – and to an alarming extent on the friends and relatives of the dancers themselves. These days modern dance is experiencing a scrappy but energetic phase.

"The situation here is reminiscent of what modern dance was like in the United States in the

1940s," Miss Lewitzky said during a break between her two afternoon classes. "It's very popular and there's tremendous energy, but it's also struggling to stay alive."

The typical company director generally does everything – teach, choreograph, rent the performance hall and sell tickets. In spite of all the work, much that is performed is still derivative.

Yet many believe the potential exists for the Japanese to have a strong influence on contemporary dance. The *avant-garde* movement in Japan is very different from that in the United States and in some ways better, Miss Lewitzky said, referring to the Japanese postwar dance strain known as Butoh. "Our postmoderns tend to be very abstract, but Butoh is postmodern expressionism."

According to Mrs Myers, "What Japanese dancers have going for them is tremendous dedication and a capacity for practice and hard work. They also graciously take correction. My dancers here are enormously eager. Their concentration is amazing."

The tone of a recent afternoon festival class held in the shiny new gym of International Christian University, in suburban Tokyo, was distinctly Japanese. Students, mostly young women in a rainbow of practice clothes, were wordless and watchful during Miss Lewitzky's advanced modern-technique class. With an interpreter at her side, Miss Lewitzky, in black leotards and footless tights, demonstrated a complex combination, then tapped the rhythm on a hand-held drum as her students performed.

When a tall young woman with a ponytail got a jump wrong, Miss Lewitzky took her by the hand and walked her through it. Blushing, the dancer apologized for her error and bowed deeply. Another performed an elegant string of leaps, which Miss Lewitzky complimented and asked to see again. The young woman leapt, and the class vigorously applauded.

The biggest difficulty for the instructors has been language. Both Miss Shang and Miss Takei speak Japanese. Others muddled through with interpreters, which seems to bother the instructors more than it does the students.

But by the third week, everyone had picked up tidbits of survival Japanese, which they used as liberally as possible: "A five, six, seven, eight, moichido (again)!" yelled Ralf Haze, taking his jazz dance class through an elaborate hip swivel.

Broadway-style jazz dance is probably the most popular contemporary strain in Japan right now, Mr Ichikawa said, and if the festival returns to Japan next summer, it will be offered again.

"We had too many modern instructors this year," he added. "I'd like more variety. Next time I'd like to add ballet and Butoh . . ."

Though modern dance seemed to have only a limited audience at home, its extreme and most serious incarnation in Butoh is the art form for which Japan has recently been best known abroad.

GENERAL INDEX

Notes: Titles of plays and other works which receive frequent mention or detailed analysis have independent main headings; works receiving only passing reference appear as subheadings under the author's name. Detailed analysis is indicated by **bold** type.

INDEX OF PRODUCING COMPANIES/VENUES

INDEX OF CITED AUTHORS

Notes: Books are indexed under the author's name, followed by the title where this is mentioned in the text. Reviews are indexed by the title of the periodical, followed by the reviewer's name where given. This index lists only modern authors; ancient commentators such as Bharata are to be found in the General Index.